Praise for *My Struggle*

"Questions about precisely what fiction is and how it relates to reality, and the extent to which traditional narrative can be a delivery vehicle for saying something true about life . . . lie at the intellectual and aesthetic heart of Knausgaard's huge undertaking."
—DANIEL MENDELSOHN, *The New York Times Book Review*

"Knausgaard succeeds in producing prose that is 'alive' . . . Such transgressive blurring of the borders between the public and private, sayable and unsayable, can be both life-affirming and riveting." —*The Economist*

"The book's confrontation with taboo subjects exerts an extraordinary pull on the reader, who is unable to look away and must see how far he will go. Nevertheless, what is perhaps most radical about reading the novel is the feeling of intimacy it creates . . . What helps give the unwieldy tome some pacing and lightness is the narrator's charisma and self-deprecating sense of humor. Knausgaard's virtuoso exposition of awkward everyday social interactions is unmatched in contemporary literature."

"At last, the highly anticipated conclusion to Knausgaard's six-part masterwork arrives in English . . . Perhaps most notable about Book Six is a four-hundred-page examination of Hitler, Nazism, and the nature of evil, which draws parallels between *Mein Kampf* and *My Struggle* . . . This uncomfortable comparison simultaneously explodes the purview of what fiction can do while zeroing in on the unique concerns of [Knausgaard's] narrator. Perhaps the most compelling of this epic's installments, and an undeniably impressive literary accomplishment."

—DIEGO BÁEZ, *Booklist* (starred review)

"Knausgaard explores the various ways language can be leveraged for honest disclosure and tragic nationalism . . . and whether confessional style can be a force against propagandistic writing . . . [*Book Six*] caps a remarkable achievement. For nearly 3,500 pages, Knausgaard has confessed, complained, reminisced, spouted off, made himself look ridiculous, and considered what it means to be candid, giving his life artistic shape while fighting against artifice. The book's very existence has prompted eye-rolls; many of its pages do as well. But his all-in temperament richly rewards anybody who takes first-person writing seriously. A fittingly bulky end to a radical feat of oversharing."

—*Kirkus Reviews* (starred review)

"The final book of Knausgaard's six-volume masterpiece goes maximalist and metatextual, examining the impact that the autobiographical series has had on the author's life and the lives of those around him . . . The rationale for his project comes into brilliant focus. This volume is a thrilling conclusion to Knausgaard's epic series." —*Publishers Weekly* (starred review)

My Struggle

My Struggle

BOOK SIX

Karl Ove Knausgaard

TRANSLATED FROM

THE NORWEGIAN BY DON BARTLETT AND MARTIN AITKEN

Farrar, Straus and Giroux ◆ *New York*

Farrar, Straus and Giroux
120 Broadway, New York 10271

Copyright © 2011 by Karl Ove Knausgaard
English translation Part 1 copyright © 2018 by Martin Aitken
English translation Part 2 copyright © 2018 by Don Bartlett
All rights reserved
Printed in the United States of America
Originally published in Norwegian in 2011 by Forlaget Oktober,
Norway, as Min kamp 6
English translation originally published in 2018 by Harvill Secker,
an imprint of Random House, Great Britain
First published in the United States in 2018 by Archipelago Books, New York
First Farrar, Straus and Giroux edition, 2019

Library of Congress Cataloging-in-Publication Data
Names: Knausgård, Karl Ove, 1968– author. | Bartlett, Don, translator. | Aitken,
Martin, translator.
Title: My struggle. Book six / Karl Ove Knausgård ; translated from the Norwegian
by Don Bartlett and Martin Aitken.
Other titles: Min kamp. 6. English
Description: New York : Farrar, Straus and Giroux, 2019. | Includes bibliographical
references.
Identifiers: LCCN 2018060825 | ISBN 9780374534196 (pbk.)
Classification: LCC PT8951.21.N38 M5713 2019 | DDC 839.823/74—dc23
LC record available at https://lccn.loc.gov/2018060825

Designed by Abby Kagan

Our books may be purchased in bulk for promotional, educational,
or business use. Please contact your local bookseller or the Macmillan
Corporate and Premium Sales Department at 1-800-221-7945, extension 5442,
or by e-mail at MacmillanSpecialMarkets@macmillan.com.

www.fsgbooks.com
www.twitter.com/fsgbooks • www.facebook.com/fsgbooks

1   3   5   7   9   10   8   6   4   2

PART ONE

In mid-September of 2009 I went up to Thomas and Marie's little retreat between Höganäs and Mölle, he was going to take some photos of me for the forthcoming books. I had rented a car, a black Audi, and headed north along the four-lane motorway in late morning with an intense feeling of happiness in my chest. The sky was clear blue, the sun shone like it was still summer. To my left the Öresund lay glittering, to my right yellow fields of stubble and meadows stretched inland, separated by stone walls, streams lined by leafy trees, sudden woodland. I was struck by a feeling that such a day wasn't supposed to happen, and yet there it was, an oasis of summer in the midst of autumn's paling landscape, and the fact that it wasn't meant to be like that, that the sun wasn't meant to shine so brightly, the sky wasn't supposed to be so saturated with light, tinged my joy with a sense of unease, so I tried not to think about it in the hope that it would pass of its own accord, sang along to the chorus of "Cat People" as it came through the speakers at the same moment, and took pleasure at the sight of the town appearing on my left, the harbor cranes, factory chimneys, warehouses. These were the outskirts of Landskrona, gliding by as Barsebäck had glided by only a few minutes earlier, the nuclear power station's characteristic and ever-ominous silhouette rising in the distance. Next up was Helsingborg, and from there it was another twenty kilometers or so to Thomas and Marie's place.

I was running late. First I had sat for a long time in the parking garage, in the roomy Audi's temperate interior, wondering how to start the ignition, unable to bring myself to go back to the rental office and ask in case they took the vehicle away from me once I had revealed such towering ignorance, and so I sat and pored through the handbook, flipping backward and forward through the pages, finding nothing at all about how to start the engine. I studied the dashboard, then the key, which wasn't a key at all but a card made of black plastic. I had unlocked the doors by pressing on it and wondered now if the ignition worked by some similar system. I searched the steering column in vain for a diagram. But there, wasn't that a slot of some sort? Maybe that was it?

I inserted the card and the engine purred. The next half hour I spent driving around the center of Malmö looking for the right road out of the city. By the time I eventually drove down the entrance ramp and onto the motorway I was nearly an hour behind schedule.

As Landskrona disappeared behind the low fold of the glacial ridge, I fumbled for my mobile on the seat next to me, found it, and pressed Geir's number. It was Geir who had originally introduced me to Thomas, they had met in a boxing club where Thomas had been working on a photo book about the sport, while Geir had been writing a dissertation on the same subject. They made an odd couple, to put it cautiously, but held each other in the highest regard.

"Hi there," said Geir.

"Hi," I said. "Can you do me a favor?"

"Sure."

"Could you give Thomas a call and tell him I'll be an hour late."

"Will do. Are you on the road?"

"Yes."

"Sounds good."

"It's fantastic, for a change. But listen, I've got to pass a truck now."

"And?"

"I can't talk on the phone at the same time."

"Someone ought to investigate your multitasking skills sometime. Catch you later, then."

I hung up, changed gears, and passed the long white semitrailer truck, which swayed gently in the turbulent air. Earlier in the summer I had driven the whole family up to Koster and nearly had two accidents on the way, one due to hydroplaning at high speed, which could have ended very badly indeed, the other not quite as drastic, but frightening nonetheless; I had changed lanes in a traffic jam outside Gothenburg without seeing a car coming from behind, and we only avoided a crash because the other guy was so quick on the brakes. The angry blast of his horn cut straight into my soul. After that I took a break from driving, and felt a little fear every time I thought about it, which was probably a good thing, but still, even passing a truck had become an ordeal, I had to force myself to do it, and any long drive filled me with anxiety for days afterward, like a hangover. The fact that I had passed my test and was actually allowed to drive a car was something my soul cared little about, it lagged behind and was still living in the days when it had been a great recurring nightmare of mine that I got behind the wheel of a car and drove off without knowing how. Ridden with angst, negotiating the bends of Norway's roads with the overhanging threat of the police catching up with me any minute, I would be sound asleep in bed somewhere with the pillow and the upper half of the duvet soaked in sweat.

I left the motorway and joined the narrower main road to Höganäs. The warmth outside was visible in the air, something about the substance of light and sky, they seemed veiled in a way, and the glitter the sunshine sprinkled over everything. The world was wide open, that was the feeling of it, and everything shimmered.

Ten minutes later I swung into the parking lot outside a supermarket and got out. Oh, such a rush of well-being in the air, it seemed pervaded by the blue of the sea, though without being hot in the way the air is hot in summer, there was a hint of coolness and sedateness about it. As I crossed the asphalt toward the supermarket, whose flags hung flaccidly from their poles, the feeling the air gave me reminded me of smoothing one's hand over marble on a sweltering hot day in some Italian town, that coolness, as subtle as it was surprising.

I bought a box of raspberries to give them, and a packet of cigarettes and some chewing gum for myself, put the raspberries on the passenger seat, and started the ignition again. The narrow road, lined by the hedges of small whitewashed cottages, led down toward the sea only a few hundred meters from the supermarket. Thomas and Marie's place was right at the bottom, with the sea to the west and a vast green field to the east.

Thomas came across the lawn in shorts to greet me as I got out and shut the car door. He gave me a hug, one of the few people who could do so without it feeling too intimate. I wasn't sure why. Maybe it was down to the simple fact that he was fifteen years older and, although we didn't actually know each other that well, had always been sympathetic toward me.

"Hi, Karl Ove," he said.

"Long time, no see," I said. "What a gorgeous day!"

We crossed the lawn. The air was completely still, the trees stood completely still, the sun hung suspended above the sea, sending its scorching rays out over the landscape. And yet all the time the same coolness in the air. It had been ages since I had felt such calm.

"How about some coffee?" said Thomas as we paused at the rear of the house where the previous summer he had made a timber deck that stretched like the deck of a ship from its outer wall to the thick, impenetrable hedge that cast its motionless shadow a couple of meters back toward the house.

"Yes, please," I said.

"Great, have a seat and I'll get you some."

I sat down, put my sunglasses on again, and leaned my head back to soak up as much sun as possible while I lit a cigarette and Thomas filled a receptacle with water from the tap in the little kitchen.

Marie came out. Her sunglasses were pushed up onto her forehead, and she squinted at the sun. I told her I had read about her in *Dagens Nyheter* that morning, there was a piece about an art controversy she was involved in. I had forgotten what it was exactly they had written about her, despite racking my brains, but fortunately she didn't ask, saying only that she would check it out at the library, she was on her way there anyway.

"Has your book come out yet?" she asked.

"No, not yet. It'll be out on Saturday, though."

"How exciting!" she said.

"Yes," I replied.

"See you later, then," she said. "I take it you're staying for lunch?"

"Yes, that'd be nice!" I said back, and smiled. "By the way, I brought Linda's manuscript with me. I'll give it to you later."

Marie had been a supervisor at the writers' school in Biskops-Arnö and had agreed to read the manuscript of a novel Linda had just completed.

"Fine," she said, and went inside again. Shortly after, a car started at the front of the house. Thomas came out with two cups of coffee and a plate of muffins. He sat down and we chatted for a bit before he went and got his camera and took a few photos as we continued talking. The last time I had been to see him he had been reading Proust; he still was, he said, just before I came he had been sitting there reading the part about the grandmother's death. That's one of the finest passages, I said. Yes, he said, getting up to photograph me from a different angle. I thought about what little I remembered about the grandmother's death. The way it came out of nothing. One minute she had been getting into a carriage to take her through the Jardin du Luxembourg and the

7

next she was struck by a brain hemorrhage from which she died only hours later. Or was it days? The house milling with physicians, the all-consuming anguish that bears down during the first phase of grief, apathy continually interrupted by the unrest that comes with hope. All out of the blue, the shock of that.

"Great," said Thomas. "How about if you move your chair over to the hedge there?"

I did as he suggested. When he was done he went inside to study the images away from the light. I went and got more coffee in the kitchen, glancing at the photos he was clicking through on the camera screen as I stepped past.

"These are quite good," he said. "As long as you don't mind having a long nose."

I smiled and went outside again. Thomas wasn't out to make me look good, nor to capture some particular expression, rather the opposite, so I understood, he wanted me the way I looked when I was relaxed, without posing.

He came back out with the camera and sat down in the sun.

"Are we done?" I asked.

"Yes," he replied. "They've come out nicely, I think. I might take a couple of full-lengths, though, a bit later on."

"Great," I said.

A low murmur of voices came from the other side of the hedge. I crossed my legs and looked up at the sky. There wasn't a cloud in sight.

"I was at the hospital visiting one of my best friends before we came down here," he said. "He's broken his neck."

"How terrible," I said.

"Yes. They found him in Gullmarsplan. No one knows what happened, he was just lying there on the square."

"Is he conscious?"

"Yes. He can talk and is quite lucid. But he can't remember a thing about what happened. He doesn't even know what he was doing in Gullmarsplan."

"Was there alcohol involved?"

"Not at all. No, it's an illness he has. Similar things have happened to him before, he can pass out in his apartment and wake up again without knowing where he is. But this time the consequences were more serious. I'm worried he might not pull through."

I didn't know what to say and nodded. We sat there in silence for a while. Thomas looked at me.

"Like to go for a walk?"

"Yeah, why not," I said.

A couple of minutes later he closed the gate behind us and we tramped off across the grazed pastures that sloped gently down toward the stony beach, where waves rolled lazily in from the sea. Some longhorn cattle stood and stared at us from the top of a small hill. We were only about fifty meters away from some houses and the busy road that ran behind them, but it felt as if we were walking on a deserted heath. Maybe it was the sea, and the way the pasture ran all the way down to the beach. Normally in these parts land like this was the most valuable of all and rarely given over to grazing.

"There are some old bunkers from the war up there," said Thomas, pointing toward some low concrete structures a bit farther ahead. "We're very close to Denmark here, of course."

"We had some where I grew up," I said. "But they were German."

"Really?" he said, lifting his camera to take a photo of me in profile against the sea.

"We used to play there when I was a boy," I said. "The bunkers in the woods were especially fascinating. Just the fact that they were there! This was the late seventies. The war had only been over for thirty years or so."

It was windier here in the open, but the waves that lapped the shore were low and lethargic. The cattle had begun to graze again. There were cowpats deposited everywhere they had been, some soft and mushy, others dry and shriveled.

"We've got something of a rarity over there," said Thomas. He gestured toward a small pond in a boggy area of reeds and moss, sheltered from the sea behind a rise in the landscape.

"And what's that?" I asked.

"You see the pond there?"

I nodded.

"There's a species of toad in it not found anywhere else in Sweden. It lives right here. In that little pond."

"Really?"

"Yes. They've got a few in Finland too, apparently. The European fire-bellied toad, it's called. If we're lucky we might be able to hear them. Their call sounds like little bells. I heard a program on the radio once where they recorded the ones here and compared them to the Finnish ones. Let's go see if we can hear them."

We trudged over to the edge of the pond. There wasn't a sound to be heard apart from the wind buffeting our ears and the gentle rush of the sea.

"No," he said. "Sometimes they're just quiet. They're in decline, too. In the old days, not so long ago actually, this whole area was underwater. Then the houses got built, and the water has retreated since then."

"How come they only live here?"

"No idea. It seems they used to be found in a number of other spots as well, then they started to die out, apart from here. I suppose the conditions here must have suited them particularly well."

"How strange."

"Yes. A shame you didn't get to hear them! The sound they make really is rather special."

We walked on to what had once been a little fishing village, now a summer retreat. All the old cottages had been done up, the gardens meticulously kept, shiny new cars in the driveways. We followed the road that ran between them, and after a short while we were sitting once more in the little back garden we had left an hour before. Thomas got some more coffee going, Marie was preparing lunch.

Shortly after, as we enjoyed our omelettes with fried potatoes, bread, and beer, we talked about Jon Fosse. Marie translated his plays into Swedish and had just finished one that was to run at Stockholm's Royal Dramatic Theatre that autumn. Fosse is a writer who has gone from describing the world the way it appears, the social-realist nightmares of small, unapproachable states-of-affairs in his early novels, brimming with neuroses and panic, to describing the world the way it is in essence, dark and open. From the world the way it can be inside the individual, to the world as it is between us, this is the line of development in Fosse's work. The turning toward God and the divine follows on from that. Anyone investigating the conditions of our existence must sooner or later investigate that too. The human domain has both outer and inner boundaries, in the space between them lies our culture, which is what makes us visible to ourselves. In Fosse's work it is subdued and almost indefinite, open to outside forces, the wind and darkness, which seem to rise and fall in the people he writes about. In that respect there is something premodern about them, in that all the things with which we fill our time, newspapers and TV programs, the vortex of politics, news, gossip, and celebrities that make up the world we live in, or mine at least, are something Fosse's characters stand outside. The simplicity of his later work prompts some to speak of minimalism, its darkness eliciting comparisons with Beckett, but there is nothing minimalistic about Fosse's work, rather it is essentialistic, and not in any way Beckett-like, Beckett being hard, ironic, without hope, his darkness is cold and filled out by laughter, whereas Fosse's darkness is warm, comforting, without laughter. Perhaps because he has come to that point from within, rather than going the other way like Beckett?

I could express nothing of this to Thomas and Marie because, as with most of the books I read and the art I look at, I relate to such things through something other than thoughts. Fosse is like this, Beckett like that, I know that, but then it stops there.

"How's it going with your uncle?" Thomas asked. "Is he still angry? Last time we talked you said he was taking you to court."

"Nothing's happened yet," I answered. "The book's at the printers, so if there's going to be a court case it'll be after it comes out. He's threatened to go to the papers as well. That's what I'm most afraid of, in a way. That they get hold of a story."

"But if he doesn't want anyone to read what you've written, then that wouldn't be the best way of going about it. It wouldn't be rational," said Marie, lifting her fork to her mouth.

"True, but rational doesn't come into it."

I pushed my plate away and leaned back.

"Thanks," I said. "That was delicious!"

I needed a cigarette but held off until they had finished eating.

Thomas looked up at me.

"Smoke, if you want," he said.

"Thanks," I said. I lit up and gazed out at the dark blue ribbon of sea above the green hedge, the way it glittered on the horizon, where the sunlight erased everything like a bomb, and the sky, lighter in color because of the haze, rose up.

It was such a fine day.

They started to clear the table, I left my cigarette in the ashtray and gave them a hand, putting the plates on the counter next to Marie, who began to rinse them in the sink. She was pushing sixty but came across a lot younger, the way so many writers do; only now and then, in the briefest of glimpses, did her true age become visible in her face. The impression of the face and the face itself are two different things, interwoven, a bit like those drawings that look like one thing if you look at the shading and another if you look at the other parts, perhaps, apart from the fact that a face is so much more complex. Not only does it change from hour to hour depending on the moods that ebb and flow behind and all around it, but also from year to year depending on the kind of relationship you have to it. My mother's face, for instance, appears mostly unchanged to me, what I see is "Mom," the way she has always been, but then she can turn her head slightly in a certain way and all of a sudden, like a shock, I see that she has become elderly now, a woman approaching seventy with perhaps no more than ten years left to live. Then she can turn again and say something, and once more all I see is "Mom."

I sat down again outside. The cigarette was still burning, I put it between my lips and sucked so hard it made the filter hot. I looked up at the sky, then at Thomas as he came out with the box of raspberries in his hand.

"We used to hear nightingales here," he said, sitting down at the other side of the table. "Not that many years ago either."

"What happened?" I asked.

He shrugged.

"They just vanished."

Driving home an hour later, the sun hanging low over Denmark on the other side of the strait, I thought about those vanished nightingales. It was the perfect beginning for the novel I was going to write when *My Struggle* was finished. An elderly man, full of years, potters about in his garden on the Swedish island of Gotland, reads in the shade, goes for long walks in the woods or along the endless beaches, retires early to bed in the evenings. It's summer, the sun beats down in the day, the vegetation is dry and scorched, and he is all alone with not a living soul for company. He thinks about a conversation he had more than thirty years before, sitting in the sun at a cottage on the Öresund coast, during which his friend Thomas, long since dead like so many of his friends are, told him the nightingales had vanished. It was the first he'd heard of it. Not long after, he saw a TV documentary about bees vanishing in the United States. From one day to the next they were gone, no one knew where, whether they had found some new place to go or simply died out. One Sunday, out with his family in the great beech woods outside the town where he lived at the time, they had seen hundreds of dead bats scattered everywhere on the ground. The newspapers carried reports of similar occurrences, flocks of birds falling from the skies, huge shoals of fish floating dead in the sea. Something was happening in the world and no one knew what. The fish, could it have been a volcanic eruption under the sea, gases rising and killing them off? Or was it caused by man? The birds, was some sickness running rampant among them? But then why would they fall down at the same time? Was it some kind of stress? The wild salmon disappeared, some suggested farmed salmon were to blame. Certain species of butterfly vanished – had there been a change in the environment so rapid that they had been unable to adapt? And then, in the space of a couple of summers, the great bird colonies stopped coming to their nesting grounds along the coast to the north. This time no one could even hazard a guess as to the reason why.

Every night before he goes to bed he writes a few pages in a notebook, mostly for his own sake, his days out there on the island being so alike that without his notes everything would merge seamlessly into one. He notes down the things he does, the way he feels, what he sees, and now and then events from his past life, which in that way emerges unsystematically.

That was the idea I had, and I elaborated on it in my mind as I headed south. In order to have the afternoon to myself I had taken the morning shift with the children, fed and dressed them and got them off to the nursery, and it was with that thought in mind that I had driven up to Thomas and Marie's when I did, it would give me some time left over to spend sitting at a café in Helsingborg. I took a left, passing at first through a semi-industrial area that gradually transformed into detached residences followed by long rows of linked houses on both sides of the road, eventually going down a steep hill, at the bottom of which was the town center, the harbor glittering in the light of the low-hanging sun.

I had been there once before with Linda and the children, it had been our first trip after I passed my driving test. Being a registered bad debtor, I was unable to borrow money or even rent a car in Sweden, so Linda had made the reservation in her name, it was a bulky, unmanageable vehicle which looked like a minibus. We came crawling into the town, my heart thumping in my chest, it was all I could do to steer properly, but at the same time

I felt buoyant, driving gave me an immense feeling of freedom, as though being motorized solved all my many problems. Now I knew there were parking spaces at the far end of the expansive quayside area and I drove slowly in that direction.

An enormous cruise liner lay at anchor off the pier. It looked like it could carry several thousand passengers. I locked the car and ambled off. On the other side of the strait, surprisingly close, was what I realized must be the castle at Elsinore. The thought that I was looking at Hamlet's home made my spine tingle. I tried to eliminate everything that had since appeared in the world in the way of cars, boats, and buildings, to see only the castle in the landscape, to think of how enormous the distances were at that time, how little space people occupied within the world, how vast the gaps between them, and gazed across at the place where the young prince, broken with despair at the death of his father, seemingly at the hands of his uncle, had perhaps lain on his back in bed, staring up at the ceiling, tortured by the colossal meaninglessness that had come between himself and all things, his friends Rosencrantz and Guildenstern, seated on a bench in the courtyard, casting their long shadows across the cobbles, drunk on light and boredom.

I stood there staring toward the castle for a moment before turning and walking along the quayside toward the town. Here and there, tourists were leaning over the railing, peering down at the cool blue of the water. Maybe there were fish swimming around, or maybe it was the deep itself that fascinated them.

The town center was situated at the foot of a steep ridge; this was the only town in Skåne I had seen with hills and rises like this. It gave a completely different sense of space. I entered the pedestrian street, at the bottom of which was a park; there, beneath tall, shady deciduous trees, I spotted a pavilion, and a few minutes later I was able to sit down and order a coffee. The other people at the tables were speaking English with American accents, they must have come from the cruise liner.

I looked up at the treetops. The leaves were not yellow, but their green was not quite as fat and pastose as it had been in summer, it was drier now, and paler. All around me the sounds of the town swirled in the air. Tires rolling against asphalt, a rumble of car engines, footsteps, voices, laughter.

Hamlet was written at the close of the sixteenth century. The earliest edition still in existence is from 1603. A few years ago I would have thought of that as being a long time ago. I didn't any longer. The seventeenth century was only a few generations away. Goethe, for instance, must have run into people who had been born in the seventeenth century. To Hamsun, Goethe would have been someone who died a generation before he was born. And to me, Hamsun was someone who died a generation before I was born.

No, the seventeenth century wasn't long ago at all.

A waitress in a black apron crossed the road carrying a tray. The café itself was housed in a building on the other side. She skipped up the two steps to the pavilion, halted, and placed a cup of coffee, a small jug of milk, and a thin paper sachet of sugar on the table in front of me. I handed her thirty kronor and told her to keep the change, *det var greit*. She didn't understand and began to rummage in her apron for coins. I held up my hand and said it didn't matter. *Tack*, she said, and wheeled away.

The coffee tasted bitter, it must have been standing for ages. It wasn't what people were drinking in the hot weather.

I lit a smoke and looked out at the rooftops across the way, a zinc-clad chimney reflecting the glare of the sun, though without its movement, making the light seem like it was emitted by the zinc itself, an inexhaustible source. The gray-black slating that surrounded it, the fire escapes disappearing down into the backyards on the other side.

Everyone's life contained a horizon, the horizon of death, and it lay somewhere between the second and third generations before us, and the second and third generations after us. We, and those we lived with and loved, existed between those two lines. Outside were the others, the dead and the unborn. There, life was a chasm without us. That was why a figure like Hamlet could be so important. He was a work of fiction, someone had made him up, given him thoughts and actions and a space in which to act, but the point was that fiction was no longer a valid dividing line, a valid distinction, the moment one stepped beyond the horizon of death. Hamlet was neither more nor less living than the historical figures who had once occupied the earth; in a certain sense anyone from then was fictional. Or, since Hamlet was made of words and ideas, the others of flesh and bone, was it only he and his life form that could overcome time and mortality?

Does he rise now in his chilly chamber? Does he climb the narrow steps out onto the roof, to the parapets? What then does he see? The blue waters of the Öresund, the green land on the other side, the low-lying expanses stretching away and beyond. What thoughts does he have? Shakespeare told us. The earth appears to Hamlet as a sterile promontory. The air, this most excellent canopy, this brave o'erhanging firmament, this majestical roof fretted with golden fire, as he describes it to his two friends Rosencrantz and Guildenstern, is to him but a foul and pestilent congregation of vapors, man but a quintessence of dust. This was what he saw over there at the castle. The English word *vapor* is the same one as was used of the darkened mind, and the space that opens out there, between the mind's and the world's darkening, appears like an abyss.

I took my mobile out of my jacket and pressed Linda's number. She answered right away.

"Everything all right?" I asked.

"Fine," she said. "We're in the park. The weather's gorgeous! Heidi refused to walk, but we worked it out. When will you be home?"

"Soon. I'm in Helsingborg. It'll take less than an hour from here, I suppose. There's the car to take back, though, and then I'll have to walk. Do you want me to get some things on the way?"

"No, I think we've got everything."

"Okay," I said. "See you. Take care."

17

"Bye," she said, and we hung up.

I sat for a while with the phone in my hand and gazed up the road. Two women wearing skirts and sandals and carrying bags made of some lightweight material came walking along the sidewalk. Behind them a man on a bike, a child squeezed into the kid's seat against his back. Both had helmets on, the man wore glasses and a suit. I thought about Heidi and smiled. She invariably wanted to be carried. If it was up to her she would never walk a single step. She had always been like that, right from the start. I was so close to her then, after she was born. Vanja was jealous and claimed Linda's attention as much as she could, while I carried Heidi around until she was eighteen months and John came along. It stopped then, our closeness to each other. Every now and again I felt a twinge of sadness about it. But that was how kids were, everything came in phases, and phases came to an end. Before long they would be grown up, and the children they used to be, whom I had loved, would be gone. Even seeing photos of them from as recently as a year before could make me feel sadness at the fact that the children they were then no longer existed. But mostly they took up so much of our lives now and whirled up our days with such intensity there was no room left for such feelings. It was all here and now with them.

Not without relief, I dropped the car key through the mailbox of Europcar an hour later; that both I and the car were still in one piece after a long day on the roads was by no means to be taken for granted. The sun shone against the tall black spire of Saint Peter's church above me, while the street beneath my feet was shadowy and cold as I walked along. I went as fast as I could, feeling guilty as always about being away from the family, or rather about leaving Linda to deal with the children on her own. I couldn't help it. I strode on, past the Hansa arcade, past Hi-Fi Klubben and Orvars Korvar, the hot-dog joint, before crossing over to the canal that ran through the little park, past Granit and Designtorget, across the bridge and onto the pedestrian street at the end of which towered the yellow-white Hilton hotel. The streets were busy, the tables outside both cafés were full, young girls chatting in pairs or small groups, some teenagers being boisterous, and a couple of men my own age, rather more subdued in body language and dress. All sat soaking up this unexpected summer's day. I felt calm and excitement at the same time; it felt good, but underneath was anxiety.

Our apartment was on the little square across the road from the Hilton. A steady flow of people from early morning to late evening passed our entrance door, which was tucked in between a Søstrene Grene store and a Chinese takeaway. On the square itself there was a fountain, the trickling sounds of which went on through the night, and a big octagonal fast-food stand that blared out soulful pop and eighties hits to its customers, mostly people from outside town, who sat at the tables stuffing themselves with grilled sausages and hamburgers, with bulging carrier bags at their feet. The benches a bit farther away were occupied by homeless people. Ours was the top apartment, on the sixth floor, with a balcony running its whole width at the front. Once, Vanja threw a lighter over the railing, and it had hit the ground and exploded, just missing a couple of passersby who leaped into the air and glared up at us while I waved my hands in apology, trying to tell them it was an accident and hoping they weren't going to get angry.

I glanced up at the railing, so high above the sidewalk, and got my keys out of my pocket. This involved another memory, for tucked in behind the plastic window tag attached to the key ring was a photo of Vanja and me, the two of us together on a boat, we were on our way to look at dolphins on the Canary Islands, she no more than three years old, holding my hand and wearing a white hat and a look of anticipation. I tapped the orange key card against the panel next to the door, there was a click, I pushed the door open and went inside, pressed the button for the elevator, and checked my phone while I waited. No calls, but I knew that already. The only people who would call my cell were Yngve,

Mom, Tore, Espen, and Geir Angell. Each followed their own pattern, and none of them was due to call just yet. I spoke to Yngve and Mom about once a week, Mom on a Sunday evening usually. Espen I spoke to about once every couple of weeks, Tore maybe once a month. With Geir it was about twice a day. That was pretty much my social life outside the family. But it was enough, and it was how I wanted it.

The elevator arrived, I stepped inside and pushed the top button, studying myself in the mirror as I slid slowly upward through the dark and narrow shaft that ran through the middle of the building. My hair had grown long over the summer and I now had a beard of sorts. My beard growth had never been impressive, the cheeks always seemed to remain bare, so every time I looked at myself in the mirror I kept wondering if it looked stupid or not. It was hard, if not impossible, to decide, there being no obvious criteria to apply. If I asked Linda she would just say it looked fine. Did she mean it? Impossible to tell. And obviously I couldn't ask anyone else about so intimate and vain a matter. So a couple of weeks earlier I'd shaved it off. When I showed up at the nursery the next day, Ola, the only other person there of my age, father of Benjamin, Vanja's current best friend, and a head of faculty at Malmö's university, had stared at me and asked if there was something different. Hadn't I had some facial hair or something? He was being funny, not referring to it as a beard, and it made me think shaving it off had been the right decision. But then, on the Friday, I picked up some of the photos we'd taken that summer. I sat with Vanja, Heidi, and John at the café at Triangeln where we went every Friday after nursery, they had ice cream while I sat with a coffee, and we looked through the photos together. One was of me standing on a beach over in Österlen with John on my arm. I looked unusually good, I thought to myself, there was something about the beard and the sunglasses that made me seem . . . well, so *masculine*. And with John on my arm to complete the picture, I looked like . . . well, dammit, yes, like a *dad*.

There and then I had decided to grow the beard back. Only

now, on my way up between floors, I wasn't so sure. I was going to Oslo the next day to do interviews for the launch of the first book. This forced me into considerations about shirts, jackets, trousers, shoes, hair, and now beard. For the past few years I hadn't been bothered about that sort of thing, hardly giving a thought to the clothes I wore, simply grabbing something to put on if I happened to be going out, which was basically only when I was taking the children to nursery or picking them up again, or if we went out somewhere with them on the weekend. I was living in a city where I knew only a handful of people and didn't care much about what they might think. This gave me a sense of freedom and allowed me to run around in baggy old pants and big grubby coats, awful woolly hats, and sneakers, but now, from the end of summer on, with publication approaching and my first interviews in five years having all been arranged, it was a different situation altogether.

I turned automatically as the elevator approached the sixth floor, after three years I knew exactly how long it took to ascend, stepped out onto the landing with its clutter of kids' stuff – two strollers, toddler roller, Vanja's scooter, and Heidi's bike with training wheels – and opened the door of the apartment.

Coats and shoes dumped on the floor, toys strewn all over, TV sounds from the living room.

I took my jacket and shoes off and went inside. Heidi and Vanja were snuggled up close in one chair, staring at the TV. John, standing in the middle of the floor in his diaper with a toy car in his hands, looked up at me. Linda was sitting on the sofa reading the newspaper.

The rug was bunched up, cuddly toys lay thrown about the entire room, as well as a number of books and plastic toys, felt pens and sheets of paper they had been drawing on.

"How did it go, all right?" Linda asked.

"Yes, fine," I said. "Nearly bashed the car when I was getting gas. You know, that cramped underground place. Apart from that, fine. Thomas and Marie say hello."

"Did you give her my mansucript?"

I nodded.

"How are we doing, girls?" I asked.

No reaction. Their little blond heads were motionless as they stared at the TV. In the same chair: apparently they were getting along today.

I smiled, they were even holding hands.

"Daddy basement?" said John.

"No," I replied. "Daddy's been driving a car today."

"Daddy go to basement!" he said.

"Are you hungry?" Linda asked. "There's some leftovers out there."

"Okay," I said, and went out into the kitchen. The dishes were still on the table, the girls' plates almost untouched, they hardly ever ate at dinner, never had. To begin with, Linda and I had argued about it, I wanted discipline when it came to meals and felt they should sit at the table until they had eaten up, whereas Linda held the opposite opinion, that when it came to food everything should be as free as possible, with no compulsion. What she said had seemed right to me, it sounded awful to talk about forcing them to eat, so ever since then we had let them do as they wanted. Whenever we came home from the nursery and they started going on about being hungry they had a slice of bread, an apple, some meatballs, or whatever was left over, and when dinner was ready and on the table they could sit there for as long as they felt like. Usually, that was no more than a few minutes during which they prodded a bit and took a few small mouthfuls before sliding off their chairs and toddling off into the living room or their own rooms, leaving Linda and me to eat at opposite sides of the table.

I piled up a plate with macaroni and meatballs, Sweden's national dish, cut a tomato into bite-sized wedges, squirted some ketchup over it all, and sat down. The first year we lived in Malmö I talked about it with one of the other dads from the nursery. How did they cope at mealtimes? They never had any trouble at all, he said. She always sat nicely at the table and cleaned her plate. How on earth did they manage that, I wanted to know, biking up alongside him on our way out to Limhamnsfältet to play football as we did every Sunday morning. She knows she has no choice, he said. How does she know that? I asked. We broke her will, he said. She sits there until she's finished, it doesn't matter how long it takes. One time she sat there until late. Sobbing, and shouting all sorts of things at us. Wouldn't touch a thing. But after a long while it sank in, she ate up and could leave the table. Three hours, I think it took! Since then there's hardly been an issue. He looked at me and beamed. Did he realize what he was telling me about himself, I wondered, but said nothing. It's the same whenever she throws a tantrum, he went on. I've noticed Vanja gives you a bit of trouble every now and again. Yes, she does, I said. How do you tackle that? I hold her still in a firm grip, he said. No drama, just hold her still until it passes. It doesn't matter how long it takes. You should try it, it works like a dream. Yes, I said, I certainly need to think of something.

The odd thing about that conversation, I thought to myself as I spooned the barely warm food into my mouth, was that I had gauged him – or rather both parents – to be alternative, meaning soft. He carried the youngest around in a sling, the way dads like him were supposed to, and on a trip we were on with the nursery I had overheard him talking about the advantages of it as opposed to a BabyBjörn baby carrier. They were more than ordinarily concerned that food should be healthy and additive-free, their kids' clothes were as far as possible made of natural fiber, and they were among the most active at parent meetings. So the fact that such uncompromisingly Victorian parenting methods should suddenly be revealed in their case came as a surprise to me. Or maybe it completed my understanding. I had always wondered how come their eldest daughter, who often played with Vanja, was always so reasonable and cooperative. She never spent a second in her stroller and walked everywhere they went, as opposed to Vanja, who could start pestering me to get in behind Heidi as soon as we were more than a few meters away from the nursery gate.

There had been occasions every now and then when I'd seen no alternative but to break her will, and of course eventually I had succeeded, but never without feeling awful afterward. It couldn't be right, surely. On the other hand it was *good* for her to sit and eat with us, *good* for her to walk, *good* for her to get dressed herself, *good* for her to brush her teeth and go to bed at a resonable hour.

Once, Vanja had been at their place, it was her first ever sleepover. I went to pick her up the next day, they said everything had gone fine, but I could tell from Vanja, who kept wanting to be as close to me as possible, that it hadn't been quite without problems. There had been a minor episode, he said, but we sorted it out no trouble, didn't we, Vanja? What happened, I asked. Well, she asked for more dinner, but then after we'd given her some she wouldn't eat it. So she had to sit there until she until she did.

I stared at him.

Was he mad?

No, he was already rummaging around to find her socks for me and I said nothing, even though I was furious. Who did he think he was, assuming he had the right to force *my* child to adhere to *his* ideas? I took the socks he handed me, helping Vanja put them on as she stretched out first one foot then the other, before giving her her coat, hoping and praying she was going to put it on herself so I wouldn't have to do it for her under his critical gaze.

Linda was enraged when I told her what had happened. By then I had changed my mind about it, it wasn't that bad, besides it was probably good for her to see that different people had different rules.

"That's not the point," Linda said. "They're criticizing us, aren't they? How dare they. Who do they think they are? You should hear how smug she is. You wouldn't believe it."

"They invited Vanja to do a fun run with them in the woods,

24

I forgot to mention it," I said. "It's next weekend, in the Pildammsparken."

It was the sort of activity we never would have got involved in on our own. Vanja was excited at the prospect. She'd get to stand behind a starting line with a number pinned to her chest, and to run with a lot of other kids along a path through the woods, and when she crossed the finish line she would get a medal and an ice cream.

It fell to me to take her to the start, along with her friend from the nursery and her friend's mother, while Linda looked after Heidi around the finish line. Vanja was proud of her number, and as soon as the starter shouted *Go!* she took off as fast as her little legs could carry her. I trotted along beside her under the trees, with all the other moms and dads. But after a hundred meters or so she slowed down, then came to a complete standstill. I can't, she said. Her friend and her friend's mother were of course well ahead of us by then. They stopped, turned around, and waited. Come on, Vanja, I said. They're waiting for us! Let's run! And so we ran, Vanja in that wobbling way of hers, me loping along like an elk; we caught up with them and we all ran side by side, until her friend and her friend's mother once more began to edge ahead of us and we again fell behind. She ran like the wind, that girl. Vanja panted heavily at my side and came to a halt. Can't we walk a bit, Daddy, she asked. Yes, of course we can, I said. Just for a little bit though. They waited patiently for us until we caught up with them again, and we forged on together for another hundred meters perhaps, before the gap between us opened up again. Come on, Vanja, I said. Not far to go now. You can do it! And Vanja gritted her teeth and ran on, maybe it was the finish line that lay ahead and the ice cream she knew would be waiting for her that gave her renewed energy. Her friend was about twenty meters in front of us, she was a good runner with a light and effortless step, and if it hadn't been for us she would have been over the finish line well before. She turned and waved to Vanja, but then as she turned again she stumbled and fell headlong onto the path, where she sat clutching her knee and sobbing. Her mother stopped and bent over her. We were approaching now, and as we came up to them, Vanja was about to stop too. Come on, Vanja! I said. You're almost at the finish! Run as fast as you can! And Vanja heard me and ran as fast as she could, past her friend, whose knee was grazed and bleeding, with me alongside her, past child after child she ran, as fast as the wind and over the finish line!

Behind us her friend got to her feet and limped on. An official hung a medal around Vanja's neck, another handed her an ice cream. I won, Mommy! she shouted out to Linda, who came smiling toward us pushing the pram, with Heidi at her side. Only then did I realize what I had done, and blushed like I'd never blushed before. We ran past her! So we could be first! While she, the little girl who had stopped and waited for us along the way, sat bleeding on the ground!

Back at the finish, it was now her turn to receive her medal and ice cream. Fortunately, it seemed there were no hard feelings on her part. Her father came toward us.

"Looked like you really wanted the win there!" he said with a laugh.

I blushed again, understanding that he didn't realize it was true. That he would never in his wildest fantasy think that a full-grown adult could behave in such a way. He was making a joke out of it precisely because it was unthinkable that I should have urged my daughter on so she could win over his daughter, and to have done so in such an unsportsmanlike way. They weren't even four years old yet.

The girl's mother came over and said the same thing. Both of them took it for granted that it was Vanja who had pressed on and that I hadn't been able to stop her. They could understand a four-year-old not being able to show empathy with a friend her own age. But the idea of a nearly forty-year-old man being equally incapable was naturally beyond their imagination.

I burned with shame as I laughed politely.

On the way home I told Linda what had happened. She laughed like she hadn't laughed for months.

"We won, that's the main thing!" I said.

Two years had passed since then. John had been only a month old, Heidi nearly two, Vanja three and a half. I remembered it so well because we had taken so many photos that day. John with his big baby head and narrow, wrinkly baby eyes, kicking his slender bare legs, waving his slender bare arms in the stroller. Heidi with her wide eyes, short little body, and fair hair. Vanja with her delicate features and her character's singular blend of sensitivity and fervor. Then as now I was unable to fully grasp the connection between us, mostly I looked upon them as three little people with whom I shared my home and life.

What they had, and what I had lost, was a great and shiningly obvious place in their own lives. I often thought about it, the way they woke up every morning to themselves and their world, which they would inhabit all through the day, taking everything as it came with no questions asked. When we were expecting Vanja, I had been worried my gloominess might rub off on her, I had even mentioned it to Yngve once, who had said that children are basically happy, it was their point of departure, and so it had turned out, always they strove toward gladness, and as long as no complications arose, they were forever happy and buoyant. Even when that wasn't the case and for some reason they were feeling sad, despairing, or upset, they never removed themselves from who they were, but accepted everything completely. One day they would look back and ask the same questions as me, why had things been the way they were then, why are they like this now, what exactly is the meaning of my life?

Oh, my children, my beloved children, may you never think such thoughts! May you always understand that you are sufficient to yourselves!

But most likely that won't happen. All generations live their lives as if they were the first, gathering experiences, progressing onward through the years, and as insights accumulate, meaning diminishes, or if it doesn't diminish, it at least becomes less self-evident. That's the way it is. The question is whether it has always been that way. In the Old Testament, where everything is expressed through action and the narratives are closely bound up with physical reality, and in the ancient Greek epics, where lives unfold in similarly concrete fashion, doubt never comes from within, as a condition of the individual's existence, but always from without, by some external occurrence, for instance a sudden death, and is thus bound up with the conditions of external, earthly life. The New Testament, however, is different. How might we otherwise explain the darkness in Jesus's soul that eventually drove him to Jerusalem, there to close door upon door until only the last and simplest remained? His final days can be interpreted as a way of eliminating all choices, so that responsibility for what was to happen, his slow death on the cross, would not be his, since he would be directed there, so to speak, by the will of others. The same thing occurs in Hamlet, his soul too is darkened, he too approaches his demise with open eyes, in such a way that it appears governed by fate and thereby inevitable. In the case of King Oedipus it *is* fate, he is genuinely oblivious, but for both Hamlet and Jesus it is a choice they make and a direction in which they choose to go. Oedipus is blind, Hamlet and Jesus see with open eyes into the darkness.

I got up, rinsed the plate, and put it in the dishwasher. We had been given the plate by the same couple when they were moving house and didn't need it anymore. They had actually helped us a lot. What had we done for them in return?

Not much. I always listened patiently to whatever they talked about, asking questions and making an effort to seem interested. I had introduced him to our Sunday football. And I had given him a signed copy of my previous novel inscribed with a dedication. Two days later he told me he had given it to an uncle "who was interested in books." But it was for you personally, for goodness' sake! I thought to myself, though I said nothing; if he hadn't grasped the fact on his own I wouldn't be able to explain it to him.

This was how it was having children, you found yourself thrown together with complete strangers, people who were sometimes impossible to understand. Once he told me he and his wife liked to talk in the evenings in such a way that I understood that their talking to each other was something out of the ordinary, impressive even. After that I would often make a point of suggesting to Linda that we should talk. It became a joke of ours. Most likely they had similar ones about us. Nevertheless we kept on seeing each other right up to the time they moved, me especially in fact; I spent countless afternoons with him at different playgrounds, listening to all his ideas about how the world and everything in it hung together while our kids were playing.

On one such occasion he had a book with him by someone called Wolfram, which he would leaf through. It seemed to be about certain recurring patterns, in everything from leaves to river deltas, and contained a lot of line graphs. My first association was to Thomas Browne and his seventeenth-century treatise on the quincunx figure, the pattern on the five side of a die and its occurrence in nature, then to something I had only just read, in the book Geir Angell was writing, about how all complicated systems – society, share markets, weather phenomena, traffic – sooner or later break down because of instabilities brought about by the systems themselves. I found this idea striking, since the patterns these breakdowns form are the same in artificial systems as they are in nature. The sky was blue, and as wide as it is only at the sea, and although the sun hung low the air was still warm. The play area with its sand and its meticulously designed play structure, so typical of Sweden, was surrounded by an area of trampled-down gravel with a broad though shallow paddling pond in the middle that some of the children kept throwing armfuls of leaves into. Beyond the gravel there was a lawn, and beyond that an area of houses. The green grass took on a sheen in the sunlight. I said it looked interesting, that patterns occurring in different fields could be so fundamentally alike. He nodded and started talking about evolution. He said the complicated organisms and complex systems all around us are in actual fact quite simple, and that this had to be understood in the light of the huge period of time in which they have developed. A million years, he said, is so much time we're incapable of grasping it. So try thinking of twenty million years. Or sixty million. But time in itself is simple. The principle of evolution is simple, too. It's all about optimization, the best way of going about a matter. In other words, the most efficient. Everything in nature strives for efficiency. When the ice opens up, the crack travels by following the points of weakness. When glass breaks it's the same thing. The cracks follow the weakest points.

"But there's no will in it," I said. "It's pure mechanics. A law of nature."

"Law?" he replied. "Forget laws for a minute, they'll only distract you. What's important is what happens. A glass breaks at the point where it breaks most easily. A branch snaps at the point where it snaps most easily. It's the optimization that's the thing. Leaves need sunlight, yes, so they seek the most efficient way of getting some. If the branches have to lift them higher, then the branches will lift them higher. If you place obstacles in the path of ants, what happens at first is confusion, but the confusion is only temporary, because if you go back after a while you'll see that the ants are now following a new path which is the shortest route around the obstacles. They optimize. The ants don't know it's the shortest route, in the same way as ice is oblivious to the fact that it cracks along the path of least resistance."

He leaned forward, placing his hands on his knees, shaking his head slightly until his hair was the way he wanted it. His daughter was sitting on her haunches in front of the twenty-centimeter-high wooden fence that penned in the play area, lining up little stones along the top of it. The sun shimmered against her waterproof yellow trousers. Vanja was climbing on the red play train. On her knees, she turned and looked at me. The wind blew her hair in front of her face, she pushed it back, the wind blew it forward again. I waved to her and glanced around to see what Heidi was up to. There she was, sitting on the little bench inside the train. Her posture was exactly the same as his, bent forward with a hand on each knee. *Little person*, I thought to myself, something Linda would say so often about her. Then she got up and stuck her head out the window, and watched the other children as they carried their bundles of leaves to the pond from under the tree on the lawn.

I leaned back on the bench. Under the trees that lined the park some fifty meters away, a chunky woman came along pushing a bike at her side. The trees above her head swayed gently in the wind, filling the street below with shifting nuances of light and shade. On a balcony no bigger than a box or a cage, a few meters up on the front of one of the apartment buildings behind the trees, a man and a woman stood looking out, each with a glass in their hand. From the gateway below, two men appeared lugging a table between them. A third man, who had been waiting on the sidewalk, flicked a cigarette onto the ground, climbed into the back of the van that was parked there, then emerged again with a gray blanket bundled in his arms. In the blue sky above them a plane angled steeply upward, impossible to separate from the white trail it left behind.

The world is old, yet simple, I thought to myself, and everything in it stands open.

It was as if my soul lifted as the thought occurred to me. But then a yell went up from Heidi and my eyes darted in the direction of the play train. She was lying on her stomach in front of it with her face in the sand. I dashed across and picked her up, scanning her face for blood, but she had been lucky, it didn't look like she had been hurt at all. Three times that month she had fallen badly, twice banging her mouth hard, once on the edge of the table and once on the tabletop, there had been blood everywhere and we had had to take her first to accident and emergency then the dentist. For some time following these accidents she would put her hand to her mouth whenever she fell, it didn't matter where the hurt was coming from. This time, though, nothing had happened. I hugged her tight, she put her face to my chest and sobbed, but soon she lifted her head and began to look around her and I was able to put her down again. When I returned to the bench and sat down next to him he was immersed in his book. A sudden movement in the upper corner of my eye caused me to look up. It was a leaf falling to the ground. Or rather, not falling at all. It was twirling, round and round, like the rotor blades of a helicopter, descending gently through the air.

Thinking about this made me remember something I had read some months before, it was a passage in a Swedish book called *Linjen* that brought together a dialogue between Heidegger and Jünger in which the latter had written something about patterns that had made a deep impression on me at the time and melded into some other thoughts I had with such intensity and fervor that I had jotted it all down on one of the blank pages under the heading "The Third Realm" with the idea of it forming the basis of a new novel.

I couldn't remember what exactly I had written and so I went into the living room to look for the book again. Linda put her newspaper down as I came in.

"What time are you leaving tomorrow?" she asked.

"The flight's at seven," I said. "So about five-ish."

"Are you nervous?"

"A bit. It'll be worse tomorrow, though."

My eyes passed over the spines of the books on the shelves. The ones on the bottom shelf had all been shoved in, some so far they had vanished into the depths. It was John's doing, and I had long since stopped bothering to pull them out again after his ravages, he was only going to shove them back again, probably within a matter of hours. Let's have a look . . . H, H, H . . . there! Jünger/Heidegger, *Linjen*.

"Bath!" said Vanja.

32

"Speak in full sentences when you speak," I told her.

"Bath!" she said again, and looked at Linda.

"*Can I*," I insisted.

"Can I have a bath?" she said.

"Are you up to it?" Linda asked me.

"Yes, of course," I said. "But then will you put them to bed?" She nodded.

"Wait just five minutes," I told Vanja, beginning to leaf through the pages of the book that was now in my hand. The passage in question wasn't from Jünger's text as I had thought, but from an entry in his diary quoted by Anders Olsson in his afterword.

On our way back along the shore we discovered a bank of shells. None of the mussels and clams that had been washed up there was bigger than a bean, many were smaller than a pea – but what we saw was the universe itself, with its ovals, circles and spirals, in the space of perhaps a foot. Obelisks, Gothic and Roman arches, serrations, lances, tacks, crowns of thorns, olive trees, turkey wings, tooth marks, rakes, spiral staircases, kneecaps . . . And all shaped by waves.

"Bath now!" said Vanja.

"Are you a little baby tonight, or what?" I said.

"Bath!" said Vanja.

"Bath!" said John.

"Let me just look at this book, then we'll go and have a bath," I said. "Five minutes."

I leafed forward to the final, blank pages and read what I had written.

Lucretius – On the Nature of Things
Nazism
Africa
The atom bomb
A man alone on Gotland
Eugenics

Atoms
natural science
biology
species
materialism

Title: The Third Realm
Aristocrat
Mass
Hölderlin
Heidegger
Jünger
Mishima
Patterns in the universe, the great and the small
Faust

The body, the blood
the biological
the clear, open
the sacred
the obscure

Animals that can be controlled
Albertus Seba
America, discovered, but left in peace

That was all.

The way I remembered this, it had been a detailed noting down of concrete ideas, a universe in which the novel would be set, but it was nothing other than the usual affinities I felt to certain words and the associations they awoke in me. "The body, the blood," "biology," "the atom bomb." And Lucretius's *On the Nature of Things* had been appearing in my notes ever since the midnineties.

But it *was* a novel. It *was*. A world described through the material and the mechanical, sand, stone, shells, atoms, planets. No psychology, no feelings. A story that was different from ours, though similar. It was to be a dystopia, a novel about the final days, told by a man alone in a house, in the midst of a dry, warm landscape in late summer. And I had an ending ready, I had told it to Linda, who had lit up, it was sublime, amazing. It *was*!

"Okay, do you want your baths now?" I said, returning the book to the shelf.

The girls slid down from their chairs and skipped off to the bathroom.

"Yes!" cried John, and toddled after them.

Even before I caught up with them, the girls had pulled off their clothes and were standing naked in front of the bath. I took the yellow Jif bottle from the shelf under the mirror, unscrewed the green top, and squirted the bottom of the bath with detergent.

"A shark!" said Heidi, peering over the edge. It was the shape made by the dribbles of detergent that fascinated her.

"Is that what you think it looks like?" I said.

She nodded.

"If a shark comes you have to hit it on the nose," said Vanja. "To scare it away."

She demonstrated what she meant, batting the air with her little fist. I wet a sponge under the tap in the sink and wiped the bath clean, then rinsed it with the showerhead, watching the water as it took with it the yellow detergent, which here and there dissolved in tiny clouds, pressed the rubber-edged metal plug into the drain, turned the mixer tap on, put my hand into the thick gush of water to gauge the temperature, and straightened up.

"Okay," I said. "Everybody in!"

As Vanja and Heidi climbed into the bath I helped John off with his clothes. He stretched out an arm, his other hand was clutching a rubber duck. I took his arm out of the sleeve and he changed hands.

"That's right, John!" I said, and pulled the sweater over his head, tossing it in the direction of the laundry bin, from which

35

our dirty clothes seemed to be advancing like a plant, unbuttoned his trousers, took them off, tore open the tape of his diaper and lifted him into the bath, where he immediately began splashing with both hands.

"I saw a witch today on the street, Daddy," said Heidi.

"It wasn't a witch," said Vanja. "It was an old lady."

"But what if she *was* a witch?" I said, crouching next to the tub.

"There's no such thing as witches," said Vanja.

"Are you sure about that?" I said.

She looked at me and smiled.

"Yes," she said. I could see part of her was going to say no.

"Imagine if I were a wizard," I said.

"You're just an ordinary daddy!" said Heidi.

I laughed and got to my feet. The water reached their tummies now. They loved bathtime, all three of them, and always had. I wondered why. Maybe it was the sudden switch from one element to another? Heidi gripped the side of the bath with both hands, then put her feet up on the other side to make a bridge. *Look, Daddy!* she cried, and let herself go with a splash, showering me with bathwater in the process.

"Stop that!" I said firmly. "You can hurt yourself! And look at me, I'm soaked!"

She laughed. John laughed too. Vanja made to repeat the stunt.

"No, you don't," I said.

"Just once!" she pleaded.

"Okay, then," I said, and stepped back out of range. The splash was even bigger this time; the floor was awash.

They howled with laughter. When John decided to try I took his arm and held him back. No, no, I said. Yes, I want to, he said. No, I said. Yes, he said. Yes, I said. No, he said. And with that the danger was averted.

"C'mon, let's get your hair washed," I said.

"John first," said Vanja.

"Okay," I said. "Did you hear that, John?"

"I won't," he said.

"Yes, you will," I replied, putting my hands on his shoulders and pressing him gently back into the water. At first he resisted, then when I kept pressing he wailed and started to squirm. I let go.

"All right," I said.

He shrieked. I took the shampoo bottle with the pictures from the Pixar film *Cars* on it that he had chosen himself in the supermarket and squirted the thick red liquid into my palm. When I'd finished washing their hair I ordered them to stand up, took three cloths off the pile on the shelf, put soap on them and washed all three of them between their legs. It felt like an assault, that was the thought that came to me every time. Imagine if someone came in and saw what I was doing, what would they think? A perverted father rubbing the crotches of his daughters? It was a thought only a man who had witnessed the incest hysteria of the eighties was capable of thinking, I knew that, but all the same it didn't help, the feeling was there and couldn't be ignored, and when they sat down again and I rinsed the cloths, wrung them and hung them over the radiator to dry, I was as relieved as ever that no one had come in and seen me.

"Pull the plug out, Vanja," I said.

"A bit longer, Daddy!" she pleaded.

I shook my head.

"It's way past bedtime already."

"*Snälla, pappa,*" said Vanja. Please, Daddy.

"*Snälla, pappa,*" said John.

"Not tonight," I told them. "Come on. If you won't, I'll do it myself."

Vanja sighed and pulled the plug out. The water began to subside around them. When she was younger, Vanja had been afraid of the little whirlpool at the drain, I understood she thought it was alive, and no sooner had I pulled the plug than she would clamber out of the tub as fast as she could, as if pursued by some terrible peril. Neither Heidi nor John had ever liked it much either.

I held my hand out to Vanja. She took it and climbed out. I dried her with a big bath towel, draping it over her shoulders before she ran off. I did the same with Heidi, relishing the feeling of drying them, the way they stood still and waited for me to finish, a bit like the way a horse will stand still to be groomed, I imagined. John sat down in the bath again, amusing himself with the plug, putting it back in the drain and pulling it out over and over again. He protested as I lifted him up, kicking his legs like a reluctant cat, only then to stand still like his sisters when I put him down and toweled him dry.

I wiped the floor with his towel, hung it up on the rack above the bath and followed them into the living room, where Linda had got Heidi and Vanja into their pajamas. The big bath towels were two heaps on the floor.

"I'm just going to pop out to check my e-mail," I said. "Okay?"

Earlier that summer our Internet had stopped working, maybe it was because we hadn't paid for it, or maybe there was some technical problem. Whatever the reason, I had solved the issue by conducting all my e-mail correspondence from an Internet café close to the square.

"Fine," she said. "I was thinking we might need something for breakfast in the morning. Maybe you could get something while you're out? Milk, perhaps. And some bread."

"I wasn't thinking of shopping," I said.

"Okay. Don't, then," she said.

"No, it's all right," I said. "It's not a problem. Milk and bread."

The air outside on the square had a nip about it and I zipped up my jacket before going over toward the Internet café a bit farther up the street on the other side of the road. I went there at least twice a day, there was a lot going on at the moment, with manuscripts flying backward and forward between me and the publishers, and furthermore I had sent a copy to all the people I had written about, and responses were coming in all the time. The first book was all finished and would be back from the printers in two days. The second book was in its final stages, now it was to be edited, then proofed, and everyone I had written about would be given a chance to read it. The mere thought made me feel like I was burning up inside. Despair, guilt, and anxiety were the emotions that flared, and the only way I could keep them at bay was by the thought that as yet no one knew, nothing had happened, but it helped less and less, the day was approaching when I would have to give up the manuscript to Linda and she would begin to read what I had written about our life together. The only thing she knew was that I had written about us. She had no idea what or in what way. She had said that I had to include all the fluctuations and not keep anything back, that the worst thing that could happen was for me to portray her as dull, dreary, weak, what in Swedish she called a *mes*, and every time I said I was dreading her reading it she would reassure me and tell me everything was bound to be fine. There's nothing to be afraid of, she said. I can handle whatever, as long as it's true. But Linda was a romantic at heart, she accepted the despondencies and conflicts of day-to-day life as long as the idea prevailed of there always being something else to fall back on, our love for each other, our lives together. In the space of only a few minutes she could go from shouting her head off at me to declaring that she had never loved anyone the way she loved me, whereas I was completely the opposite, storing up and accumulating grievances and frustrations, which then lay like a sediment inside me, fossils of emotions, darkening my mind increasingly until eventually I became as hard as stone, unreceptive to reconciliation and tenderness. I had written about this and had no way of knowing if she could forgive me for it, since it was from that perspective she was being seen.

Why had I written such things?

I had been so despairing. It was as if I had been shut away inside myself, alone with my frustration, a dark and monstrous demon, which at some point had grown enormous, as if there was no way out. Ever-decreasing circles. Greater and greater darkness. Not the existential kind of darkness that was all about life and death, overarching happiness or overarching grief, but the smaller kind, the shadow on the soul, the ordinary man's private little hell, so inconsequential as to barely deserve mention, while at the same time engulfing everything.

If I was going to write about it I would have to tell the truth. Linda agreed with me on that. But she didn't know the nature of that truth. It was one thing having an idea what her husband was thinking in his darkest moods, but quite another to read about it in a novel. And our life together was what the novel was all about. Her life, Linda's, and mine, Karl Ove's. It was what we had – in fact, it was all we had.

Oh, I was so completely in the shit. To have to hand her the manuscript and say, here, read this, it's being published in a month.

I stopped at the crossing and waited for green. The big shopping mall next to the hotel had just closed; at this time of day there were fewer people about, apart from at McDonald's and Burger King, where groups of young people, mostly immigrants, hung around outside. Many of the city's immigrants hailed from Iran, thereby belonging to the people once known as Persian, an army of whom under Xerxes had invaded Greece almost exactly twenty-five hundred years before.

Only a few weeks previously I had read a novel by Eyvind Johnson, *Molnen över Metapontion – The Clouds over Metapontion –* published in 1957. It was one of the purest works of modernism I had read, certainly from that part of modernism that had been interested in the classical age, such as Ezra Pound's *The Cantos*, Hermann Broch's *The Death of Virgil*, and James Joyce's *Ulysses*, or, for that matter, Paal Brekke's *Roerne fra Itaka – The Oarsmen of Ithaca*. Like all these works, Johnson's opened up a space between the *then* of the ancient classics and the *now* of the moderns, though it was perhaps even more concerned than they were with the time that lay in between. The novel began in southern

Italy just after the war, and what went on in it there at that time, which to a large extent revolved around a Swedish writer's journey in the footsteps of a French archaeologist he had encountered in a German concentration camp, alternated with events that had taken place in the same landscape four hundred years before Christ. A landed estate, an estate owner, his slaves, one of whom escapes and gets caught up in a military invasion cutting deep into Asia, all described in the minutest detail. Particularly lucid and exciting were the author's portrayals of the passage of such huge numbers of men through increasingly foreign land, from the coasts of the Mediterranean to as far as Babylon. But the most foreign thing about the book for me wasn't the history of the ancient military campaign or the slave quarters, which were so far away in time that the reader couldn't help but sense the author's efforts to make them come alive, but rather the Italian village of 1947. The landscape is barren and without event, such occurrences as take place being small and almost indiscernible, and while I knew that another kind of writer, a Latin, say, like García Márquez, Vargas Llosa, Cela or, why not, Cervantes, would have been able to bring forth the exact same landscape with a patent and natural intensity, the people who populated it quivering with love and longing in such a way that we would not have doubted that the place in which we found ourselves was the center of the world, Johnson's very distance to what he describes, his remoteness to his characters, their work and their emotional lives, is crucial in respect to what perhaps was the focus of his efforts, the chasm of time that separates us from ancient history and the sense of meaninglessness that arises on that account. Nothing happens here, people are mere guests in a landscape that is like the seabed in an ocean of time. Occasionally, a tension occurs, for instance the war two years previously, whose truth, however, is no different, a fact that becomes apparent in the passages depicting the ancient military campaign, devoid of any suggestion of greatness, heroism, or historical momentousness, continually deconstructed into its individual parts, a creaking wheel of oak, dust kicked up by horses' hooves, the individual's dreams of riches, the individual's denigration of defeat and flight. But this is a novel, a program. What isn't a program is the depiction of postwar Italy, since it is affected to such a great extent by a mood that is already alien to us but to which the novel is proximate and conversant with, unlike Antiquity. When I read the book, the Italy of 1947 in fact felt more foreign to me than the Italy of the centuries before Christ, presumably because the latter was based on literature I knew, whereas the former was based on nothing other than life as it occurred at that time and which is barely to be found anywhere else than here. We are so endlessly far away from it, and yet our parents and grandparents were alive then. No era can surely have undergone such radical transformation as our own, the second half of the twentieth century has so little in common with the first, it seems as if they occurred in different worlds entirely.

My eyes found the steps leading down to the Internet café. A new rush of anxiety surged inside me. For a month now I had been receiving the most abhorrent e-mails because of the novel I had written, and I knew there would be more, though not where they would be coming from. It was the same with the phone; every time it rang I froze. True, it had been that way ever since the night I had been called by a person demanding to speak to the rapist Karl Ove Knausgaard, but that was seven years ago and the alarm I had felt at the time had paled together with the recollection; with the book it all came back with renewed force, what I had written had to do with other people, their reactions were beyond my control, and what I had done to them, they could do to me, I knew that; everything I had ever done could be used against me. As long as it was private, as long as it stayed between them and me, I could handle it. But it was terrible, I was crippled with fear every time I checked my e-mail, every time the phone rang, so much so that I could hardly move, would sit paralyzed in a chair or lie paralyzed in bed for hours at a time, and yet I knew it would pass, sooner or later I would have battled my way through it and would be able to see things in their true proportions. But if it got out . . . If someone went to the papers . . . I knew I wouldn't be able to cope.

The light changed from red to green, I crossed over, and the wind blew my hair into my eyes; I swept it back, folding it behind my ear, a motion of the hand that I knew looked feminine but nevertheless had to be done, hurried over the road, descended the three steps that led down to the Internet café, pushed the door open, and went in. The place was almost completely dark inside apart from the glow of computer screens in a row along the walls, most of them taken up by youths absorbed in games. They shouted out to each other as they played, presumably it was the same game, nearly always soldiers on a mission into some hostile world, whether it was a city, a deserted factory area, a desert landscape, or a forest.

The guy at the first station turned his head.

"*Tjena!*" he said. "Where have you been all day, writer? We've been waiting for you!"

"Hello," I said. "Have you got a computer for me?"

"Nineteen's for you."

"Thanks," I said, then went and found number nineteen, pulled out the chair, and sat down.

I opened the browser and typed in my WebMail address. During the few seconds it took for the page to open, I held my breath. Then the column of names appeared before my eyes, the unopened messages in bolder script, and I took them in at a single glance.

Nothing bad.

An inquiry from a TV program, one from a bookshop in a shopping center in Sørland, one from a bookshop in Oslo, and one from a folk high school in mid-Norway. I wrote to Silje at the publishers, who had passed the messages on to me, asking her to decline the invitations politely. She had also sent me a change in my itinerary for the following day, *Aftenposten* had pulled out, and *Bergens Tidende* was sending a different journalist than originally announced, so my schedule now looked like this:

43

9:00–9:45: NTB
Gitte Johannesen
At the publishing house

9:45–10:20: Bergens Tidende
Finn Bjørn Tønder, phone interview
At the publishing house

10:30–11:15: Fædrelandsvennen
Tone Sandberg
Etoile

11:15–12:15: Morgenbladet
Håkon Gundersen
Etoile

12:15–12:45: lunch

12:45–13:30: Dagsavisen
Gerd Elin Stava Sandve
Etoile

14:30–15:15: Sondagsavisen
Gry Veiby
Recording at NRK

15:15–15:45: NRK Radiofront
Siss Vik
Recording at NRK

The schedule was much the same as when my previous novel *A Time for Everything* had come out five years before. Lumping everything together meant I didn't have to spend more than a single day on the media. *Dagbladet* and *Dagens Næringsliv* had interviewed me in Malmö a few days previously, *Aftenposten* had pulled out, *VG* wasn't interested, so everything was covered.

Originally, *Bergens Tidende* had been sending Siri Økland, and it was a shame she wouldn't be coming, we had been literature students together in Bergen twenty years ago, and although we hadn't known each other then we always said hello, and that, together with the fact that we were of the same generation, made me feel secure. If I felt insecure in an interview situation I hardly ever said anything at all, they had to drag the words out of me, it was never any good. Prior to my previous book coming out, *Dagbladet* interviewed me in Stockholm. I hadn't talked to anyone about the book and felt uncertain as to what it was actually about and how good or bad it was, and added to that the photographer had been present during the entire interview, it had taken place at Saturnus, he said he knew Tore Renberg well and sat there staring at me with a half smile on his face that had me on edge the whole time, making me hear everything I said the way I thought it sounded to him, pure lunacy, Noah's Ark and Cain and Abel, angels and the divine, so after a few minutes I shut up, muttering a simple yes or no in reply to her questions, my cheeks blushing madly if I did make some attempt at a reasoned response. All I could think about was whether I could ask her to send the photographer away so I could talk more freely, but I didn't have the nerve, and there was not much else I could do.

Before the interview got under way I'd leafed through Gombrowicz's diaries; it was the fifth time I'd tried to get into them, the fifth time I'd read the first ten pages without getting any further, and that same afternoon I put the book away. But the woman interviewing me had noticed I had it with me and made a little aside of it. "Knausgaard reads Gombrowicz," a caption said. It haunted me for years after. I was contacted several times by newspapers and journals wanting me to write something about the Polish author for their pages. I, who had read only the first ten pages of his diary, and none of his novels or plays, was now thought to be a Gombrowicz expert. The horror of this was compounded whenever I happened to run into Dag Solstad, since Solstad held Gombrowicz very much in esteem, he was one of his favorite writers, and because I hadn't confessed to not having read him the first time he mentioned him to me I had to keep pretending to him that I was a Gombrowicz aficionado. Once, he came over and told me he had just attended a Gombrowicz seminar in Stockholm and had been expecting to see me there. Oh, but I'd had so much going on at the time, though obviously I would have loved to have gone. Had it been interesting? And so on.

I closed the browser, got to my feet, and left a ten-kronor coin on the counter as I passed, pulled open the door, and went up the steps, out into the swell of twilight, which was pierced only by the headlights of dark, sleek cars and the gentle hum of their engines.

The children were all still awake when I got back. *Pappa*, *Pappa*, they shouted out as soon as they heard the door open. I took off my shoes, hung up my jacket, went to their room, and stood in the doorway.

"Go to sleep," I said.

"But we can't," said Vanja, their spokesman in such cases.

"It's boring! Can't we stay up just a little bit longer? Just a teeny-weeny bit?"

"No," I said. "It's way past your bedtime."

Heidi, who had the top bunk, drew herself up onto her knees. "*Kram*," she said. Cuddle.

I went up to her and she wrapped her arms around me and pressed her cheek as hard as she could against mine.

"*Också kram!*" said John. Me cuddle too.

He was lying on his back in his crib, clutching his pillow in his hands. He dragged it around with him wherever he went and it was the first thing he asked for when he came home from the nursery. Pillow, want pillow!

"You'll have to stand up if you want a cuddle," I said.

He did as he was told. I kissed him on the ear and he giggled. He was the only one of them who was ticklish.

"Vanja?" I said.

"Only if we can stay up!" she said.

"But it's not for my sake!" I said. "It's for yours!"

"Okay then," she said, and leaned forward. I cuddled her, rubbing my hand up and down her delicate spine.

"Little treasure," I said. "Sleep time now, okay?"

"Okay. But don't close the door!"

"I won't," I said.

She was slightly afraid of the dark, not much but enough for her to want some light when she went to sleep. Once, when we had been at Linda's mother's in the country, Vanja must have been about eighteen months old at the time, she had a nightmare. She cried, and when Linda asked what the matter was she said she had dreamed about the swimming pond. We were puzzled, but the explanation came a few months later. On a visit to a zoo we paused at a glass-fronted enclosure and looked in at a splendid monitor lizard. When Vanja laid eyes on it she recoiled and cried out in fright, *Swimming pond! Swimming pond!*

Now she lay in bed gazing up at me.

"Night night," I said.

"Night night," she replied. "Daddy?"

"What?"

"Who's tucking me in tomorrow?"

"Don't think about that now. Go to sleep."

Vanja preferred Linda to do everything, and for me to do as little as possible. For her, the height of joy was Linda tucking her in two nights in a row. That was just the way it was, I ranked second and always would, unless someone else came and took my place. But I didn't mind, Linda was closer to them and it was as simple as that.

I went into the living room where Linda, who was watching television, turned her head and looked up at me.

"I forgot to pick up milk and bread," I said.

"Doesn't matter," she said. "Aren't they asleep yet?"

"No."

"What are you going to do tonight?"

"Pack a few things. Decide what to wear tomorrow. How about you?"

"I don't know really. I'm a bit tired. I think I might have an early night. In fact, that might not be such a bad idea, with you not being here tomorrow."

"No," I said. "It's only two days though. And your mother's coming."

"I know, I didn't mean it like that. It's no bother."

I went into the bedroom and picked out two shirts, a couple of sweaters, some T-shirts, two pairs of pants and two suits, took the whole pile with me to the mirror in the hall and began trying things on. The children were giggling in their room, I started to get annoyed, went in, and turned the ceiling light on. They were all piled up together in Vanja's bed. I took hold of John by a foot and an arm, snatched him up, and lifted him back into his bed, turned around and repeated the procedure with Heidi, all without a word and so firmly it verged on the unreasonable.

"That's it," I said. "Now go to sleep. Do you hear me?"

"Yes, Daddy," said Vanja. "But they all crept up to me. I couldn't stop them."

"All right," I said, and turned off the light.

"Mean Daddy!" said John.

I said nothing, closed the door, and went back to trying on clothes. A pair of black Lindeberg jeans, a blue Ted Baker shirt, and the gray Ted Baker jacket. Then there were the shoes, a pair of Fiorentini+Baker, bought in Edinburgh a few weeks before like the rest of the gear. I'd been taking part in a literary festival there, Yngve and Asbjørn and a couple of their friends had traveled over to see me, but when it came down to it, just before I left the hotel to walk up to the venue, I asked if they'd mind not coming after all. They must have thought it a bit off, the festival was the whole excuse for their trip, but they didn't seem to mind that much and traipsed off to get something to eat instead. Most likely they were just as afraid as me that I was going to make a fool of myself. At least, I'm sure Yngve was, he identified with me. Onstage I was interviewed together with a Dutch author about fifty years old, who dressed eccentrically, spoke perfect-sounding English, and had written a novel based on Dante's *The Divine Comedy*. His name was Marcel Möring. He looked after me the whole time we were onstage, noticing how nervous and uneasy I was about the situation, and afterward as we sat down ready to sign books, each with a glass of wine in front of us, and he had a queue of people lined up at his table, all praising him for his perfect English and telling him how fascinating his book sounded, whereas my own table was completely ignored, he whispered politely that he had started out in exactly the same way and that as a rule nothing ever took off abroad, but it didn't matter, the important thing was this, the chance to gallivant around the world and meet new people. He gave me his card and vanished into the night with his young wife, while I sloped off to a pub to meet up with the other Norwegians. The next day Yngve did me the favor of going shopping with me, unlike me he always had a good eye when it came to clothes. If he gave the nod, I bought it; if he shook his head, I put it back.

I turned and twisted uncomfortably this way and that in front of the mirror, the trousers didn't quite go with the jacket, and wasn't it a God-awful cliché anyway, authors in suits? How boring was that?

I went back to the closet and stared at my other jackets.

There was an anorak-like thing, which I thought was nice, but it probably wasn't right for a book-launch interview.

Suddenly there was a commotion going on in the children's bedroom, one of them was crying, another screamed. I stormed in and turned the light on.

"That's enough! Back to bed, all of you!"

It was John doing the crying, Heidi the screaming. Vanja was in the middle with her hands covering her ears. I snatched John from the huddle, this time more firmly than before, and plonked him down in his crib, where he sat clutching the bars like a prisoner in jail, howling and sobbing. John hit me! Heidi yelled. I picked her up and put her back in her own bed.

"John's still little. Besides, I'm sure there was a reason. Now go to sleep. You too, John," I said, turning toward him.

"Mean!" he replied between sobs. I went up and crouched down at his crib.

"I'm not mean at all," I said. "But you're going to sleep. I won't have you wandering around anymore. You can see what it leads to, you end up hurting yourself. Now lie down."

Oddly enough he did as he was told. I turned off the light, closed the door again, and went back to trying on clothes, item by item, in every conceivable combination. Linda could get annoyed with me about it, I knew that, she disliked anything that resembled vanity. I could spend more time figuring out what to wear than what I was going to say to an audience. But once I knew I was going to be on view, I became obsessive about it. It didn't matter if the clothes were cheap or expensive, new or old, it was the ceremony of it, shirt on, shirt off, the stubborn self-appraisal, good, not good, awful, better, or maybe this one instead?

After half an hour, constantly aware of what Linda might be thinking, I went back into the living room.

"Can I wear this?" I asked.

"Absolutely," she answered. "*Du ser jättefin ut.*" You look good. It was what she always said, but I needed to hear it nonetheless.

A hefty thud came from the children's room, a thump against the wall.

"What's the matter with them tonight?" said Linda.

This time it sufficed to open the door. John scuttled immediately back across the floor and Heidi scurried up the ladder to her bunk.

"I mean it this time," I said. "Once more and I'll be really angry with you."

They lay quite still and peered out with wide eyes. I went into the bathroom, found the scissors, and began to trim my beard.

There was a little patter of feet in the hall. It had to be either John or Heidi.

"Back to bed, this minute!" I shouted.

"I can't sleep!" said Heidi, appearing in the doorway.

"Come on," I said, lifting her up and carrying her back to bed. I stood for a minute behind the door, before opening it again to see Heidi on her way down the ladder.

"Back to bed!" I said firmly. "It's sleep time!"

"But I can't sleep," she said. "I'm awake!"

"I know what we can do," said Vanja. "We can hold hands and close our eyes and fly away to ketchup land!"

"Okay," I said. "As long as you go to sleep, then."

And they did, they held hands, closed their eyes, and were quite still. Ketchup land was something they had heard about at the nursery, so I assumed, not really wanting to know since it filled me with such a sense of unpleasantness, ketchup being red, red being blood, blood being dead. And there they lay with eyes closed . . .

I went back to the bathroom and picked up where I'd left off with my beard. Again there was a patter of feet in the hall, whoever it was scurried past into our bedroom. I flung the door open to see Heidi climbing onto the bed. She turned toward me.

"Back to bed!" I shouted. "At once! I've just about had enough. Come on. Off to bed with you! You're NOT staying up. DO YOU HEAR ME?"

She took one look at me and burst into tears.

Oh, Heidi!

"I was only getting a book!" She sobbed. "Grown-ups can't get mad at children!"

I felt so sorry for her I almost started crying myself. Fortunately she didn't react with rage, as so often before – in such cases it was impossible to comfort her. No, she simply wept, and I lifted her up, held her little body close to mine and carried her back to her room, switched on the light and told them I would read them all another story. Heidi snuggled into my arms, Vanja sat up and buttoned up the coat of one of her many cuddly dogs, listening with one ear, while John messed around on the floor playing with whatever toys he happened to find. I read them a story about the Moomin who wakes up in winter while his parents are still hibernating, he can't wake them up and so he goes off on his own. Heidi twisted about, wanting to know this and that – Why are they laughing at him? It's not nice to laugh at other people. What's he saying there, Daddy? – while Vanja snorted at such childish questions and John immersed himself with his own projects on the floor, which now involved something he could press to make a loud noise like a siren.

By the time we reached the end of the story and I turned the light off again, they had finally settled down. I went in to Linda, who was watching the news, and said I wondered why they were so difficult tonight. She said Heidi had slept two hours after nursery school, and John had slept until late, too. I sat down, put my feet up on the table, and stared at the television.

We went to bed an hour later. Kissed each other good night, turned off the light. I was nervous and realized right away it would be a while before I could fall asleep. I was nervous about the next day, the round of interviews that lay ahead, but not for the old reason, the way it normally was, the horror of having to talk and take up space, and be quoted on everything I said, the horror of making a fool of myself; this time I was scared about what I had written. The novel, which would be out in two days, and which had been given the title *My Struggle 1*, had been written in solitude. Apart from Geir Gulliksen and Geir Angell, no one had read any of it along the way. A select few had been aware of what I was writing about, among them Yngve, but they knew none of the detail. After a year like that, where the only perspective that existed was my own, the manuscript was ready to be published.

Four hundred and fifty pages, a story about my life centered around two events, the first being my mother and father splitting up, the second being my father's death. The first three days after he was found. Names, places, events were all authentic. It wasn't until I was about to send the manuscript to the people mentioned in it that I began to understand the consequences of what I had done. I sent it out in late June. Yngve had to be first. There were things I had written about him that I had thought and felt but never articulated. As I sat down at the computer and attached the document to the e-mail I had written to him, I felt like dropping the whole thing, calling the publishers and telling them there would be no novel this year either.

I sat there for half an hour. Then eventually I clicked send and it was done.

The next day we went to the beach at Ribersborg, it was Sunday and there were lots of people there, we found ourselves a spot by the pier leading out to the open-air baths of the *Kallbadhus*. The structure dated back to the first decade of the twentieth century and was built on poles a hundred meters from the shore. John was asleep in his stroller. Vanja and Heidi paddled for a while at the water's edge and collected shells, Linda and I sat farther up the beach watching. After about half an hour John woke up and we took them to the bathhouse café, finding a table outside next to the railings at the end, the water glinting and glittering all around us as we sat with our ice cream. It was almost like being on a boat. We had the bridge to Denmark on one side of us, the Turning Torso skyscraper on the other, and the Barsebäck nuclear power plant visible in the haze to the northwest.

I saw all of this: people swarming on the long city beach and on the wide footpath behind it, cyclists and roller skaters whizzing by, the row of concrete blocks from the fifties or perhaps the sixties, the city's final bastion against the sea, that great light-catcher, calm and in no way dramatic here in the strait facing Denmark. The couples and the families sitting all around us, summer-clad and tanned, the big sky above us whose blue had no end until evening, when it would fade to gray and the first stars would seem to emerge from the space beyond, making visible its enormous distances. My own children sitting on their chairs with their short legs sticking out in front, absorbed in their own little worlds; ice-cream wrappers, dripping lollipops, and ice-cream cones. Linda, now and then wiping their mouths with tissues, her eyes almost hidden behind her sunglasses. I saw all of this, though as a film, something of which I myself was not a part, my thoughts and feelings being somewhere else. It was Yngve I was thinking about, though not actively, it was more like he just kept appearing in my mind. He was my brother, we had grown up together and I had leaned on him nearly all my life. We had been so close that instead of accepting his weaknesses or short-comings the way I accepted my own, I identified myself with them and took on responsibility for them, however indirectly, in the feelings that ran through me whenever he did or said something I wouldn't have done or said myself. No one knew this, not even Yngve himself, because how could I ever express such a thing? Sometimes you're not good enough for me?

What was to be gained by telling things the way they were, representing my own feelings toward him? Compared to what I could lose? He could say fuck you, I want nothing more to do with you.

What would I do then? Remove it all? Or keep it and lose a brother?

I would keep it and lose a brother.

There was no doubt about it.

Why?

Was I mad?

Both Vanja and Heidi had bitten off the bottoms of their cones and were having a job licking up the ice cream that was now melting and dripping from two different places. John had chosen a popsicle, in principle it was easier, but he was so little he was having problems too. His fingers and chin were red and sticky from all the juice. But they were all immersed in what they were doing, which was good.

"What are you thinking about?" asked Linda.

"Yngve," I answered.

"It'll be all right, I'm sure it will," she said.

"That's easy for you to say," I said.

What I had written about Linda was much worse. But all I could do was take things one at a time.

A new wave of horror and shame washed over me.

Home again, I was checking my e-mail about twice every hour. It was Sunday, so my in-box stayed empty all day. Yngve was at Mom's in Jølster, which I was glad about, it would give him the chance to talk to her about it, which might soften his reactions, so I thought. We put the children to bed and sat for a bit on the balcony, and I checked my e-mail one last time before going to bed: nothing.

The next morning his reply was in my in-box.

Your fucking struggle, said the subject line.

I stood up without reading it and went out onto the balcony, sat there smoking and looking out over the city, cold and despairing.

But I had to read it.

His words were there, whether I read them or not.

I could put it off until evening, but that would only prolong my suffering, and the result would still be the same.

I stubbed my cigarette out and got to my feet, went inside into the living room, walked past the kitchen, where John was sitting in his chair with a spoon in his hand while Linda was reading the newspaper, into the bedroom, sat down on the chair, moved the cursor to the text line, two clicks and there it was.

Just wanted to scare the hell out of you, but the last few days have been rather intense, seeing my life pass backward and forward in front of my eyes on account of your book and me going through old papers and letters here, yours and mine.

I don't quite know whether to go into the book or our lives and the relationship we have to each other, the latter definitely needs to be treated differently than it has been until now, or maybe not? As far as the book goes, there are passages that are extremely unpleasant for me to see down on paper, even if I can see why you've included them.

The part with you, me, Ingar, and Hans really made everything go black for me. Obviously, I've seen you feel ashamed of me in certain situations, and still do see that. It's hard, because it touches on aspects of myself that I'm painfully aware of — the way I can sometimes not be there inside myself; the way I can criticize things that I haven't thought of myself; preferring the role of someone who reads Adorno rather than actually reading Adorno. Mediocrity combined with poor self-awareness and big ambitions doesn't come out very well. But reading it again it doesn't seem as bad . . . it's about you, not me. Which I suppose doesn't leave much room for the times I've been ashamed about you!

"We rarely looked each other in the eye." Is it as bad as it's made out to be here? Do we look at each other any less than other people?

And Yngve and Espen not getting along? That's simply not true from what I can see . . . I thought it was Tore and Espen who didn't like each other?

I'll read the rest over the next few days. Maybe you can give me a call?

Yngve

I went out into the hall and called him up. There was a slight feeling of uncertainty between us. He told me again about how he'd felt reading what I had written, but he wasn't angry, it was more like he was accepting some personal criticism, and that created a buildup of pressure in the situation that I found almost excruciating, because he had no reason to. Not looking each other in the eye, the fact that we never shook each other's hand, or physically touched at all, were things we were unable to talk about, it was out of the question, but when, a few weeks after this phone conversation, he came to see us in Malmö with his two kids, Ylva and Torje, he looked me straight in the eye and put out his hand as soon as I opened the door. No irony, no subtleties, he wanted to make amends. My eyes grew moist and I had to look down.

After Yngve had read it, I put off sending it to the others I had written about. I was dreading it all summer, until eventually at the beginning of August, only a month before publication, I mustered up the courage. I sent an e-mail to Jan Vidar asking how he was and received a reply within a few hours, he and his family were doing fine, he was going off on a fishing trip with some friends of his the next day, it was a thing they did together, Finnmarksvidda in the summer. I hadn't been in touch with him for years, the last time I saw him was when I had been in Kristiansand beginning a new novel after my debut, *Out of the World*. It was nearly ten years ago. In the book that was coming out now he was one of the most important characters. We had been best friends from when we were thirteen until we were seventeen, or thereabouts, after which we drifted apart. They had been significant years. We'd moved from Tveit, I was new at the school, he came up to me and we made friends, spent all our time together, not least with the band we went on to form. When I started writing about that time I found it all to be so much closer to me than I had imagined. The atmosphere of our house, the woods at the back, the river below, all the things we did together, which basically wasn't much at all, and yet it had been everything. The person Jan Vidar had essentially emerged for the first time when I sat writing about it all in Malmö more than twenty years later.

I had Googled him, and besides a number of hits to do with angling competitions where his name appeared, a band came up in which he clearly played. Several of their songs were online. I listened to them. They were a blues band. He was the guitarist, and his solos were really good. What had happened? We had been awful back when we played together. Since then my playing had not developed in the slightest, it was still exactly the same as when I was fifteen. But he had turned into a virtuoso. Because I hadn't seen him in all those years it seemed baffling to me. In my mind he was still seventeen.

I sent him the manuscript and hoped for the best.

I sent it to another old friend too, Bassen, he appeared only fleetingly but had been an important figure for me then and we had kept in touch for some time, I still had his number. He read through it right away and had no objections to the use of his character and name, and yet the conversation I had with him was unsettling, he said there would be trouble and that I shouldn't rule out the possibility of proceedings. That hadn't occurred to me, and we talked about it for quite a while. He was a criminologist with Statistics Norway and knew what he was talking about. My first thought was that he was exaggerating, but something about the gravity in his voice told me otherwise. Sued? Action for damages? For writing about my own life? If anyone reacted negatively I would alter their names, it wasn't that big a deal.

Another important character was Hanne, my first real love, once the light of my life, my everything. It had not worked out for us back then, and apart from a brief encounter in Bergen, we hadn't seen each other since. She too was viewed from my immature perspective, which moreover was suffused with infatuation and conceit.

I tried to get hold of her address, but couldn't find it on the Internet, and she wasn't in the phone book either. I called Bassen again, the three of us had been in the same class together, he dug out a number he thought might be hers, I called it, no one answered. I tried again, several times, but there was never anyone in.

Tonje, to whom I had been married, hardly appeared in the book, only fleetingly in the parts concerning my father's death, but I sent it to her too, explaining that there would be five more books coming out and that I anticipated her playing a more significant role in one of them than was the case here.

Finally, I sent the manuscript to my uncle Gunnar. He was

ten years younger than my father, which meant he had been little more than a boy when his elder brother had married and his first child came along. From growing up I remember him as a young man in his twenties, very different from Dad. Gunnar had long hair, he could play the guitar, and he had a boat fitted with a twenty-horsepower Mercury motor. Once, he managed to get Yngve the autograph of IK Start soccer player Svein Mathiesen, it was a big thing and it wouldn't surprise me if Yngve still has it. Gunnar was a person Yngve and I looked up to, someone we always hoped would be there whenever we went to visit Grandma and Grandad in Kristiansand, or be with them when they came to visit us. By the time I was in my teens, he was married and had his own family, lived in a neat row house, and spent his free time in summer out at the cabin Grandma and Grandad had bought in the fifties and which he gradually took on. He was a joker with a line in puns, in that way he was like Yngve, and he was responsible, the last ten years of our grandparents' lives it was he and his wife who were on hand to help them with whatever they needed. As Dad began to let go of me and everything else, Gunnar's role in my life changed. Presumably he remained the same, but my attitude toward him changed. In my mind he had sussed me out. At that point I'd started writing for local papers and had become visible in a way I sensed he disliked, and at the same time I'd become wayward, ditching school, drinking, occasionally smoking pot, an outrageous transgression I for some reason believed Gunnar to be aware of, unlike everyone else around me, and this rubbed off on the way I related to him. In the years after I left home, at the age of eighteen, I didn't have much contact with him, but the few times I visited him it was obvious to me that his children had complete trust in him, there was no sign of terror in their eyes when they looked at him, and I respected him for that. When I came into my twenties, with Dad becoming increasingly alcoholic, Gunnar became the representative of all that was orderly and proper, to which I, unlike my father, aspired, and as such I made Gunnar a kind of father figure, as well as a kind of superego. If the kitchen was littered with empties, I would think, What would Gunnar say if he came in now and saw this? If I had been absent from lectures for a few months, I would think, What would Gunnar have to say about this? Every time I did something excessive, Gunnar would appear in my thoughts. It had nothing to do with the person he was, it was something I had constructed, and yet it was by no means completely without foundation: during the summer when I was writing what would be my first novel I stayed for a while at Mom's in Jølster, I was twenty-eight years old, and one afternoon when I was visiting my maternal grandmother's sister Borghild and chatting with her about what life on the farm there had been like in the old days, since I was thinking of using it in my novel, Gunnar had been to see Mom and taken her to task for me being such a slacker and a layabout who was never going to make anything of himself. Because my father was no longer able to take responsibility for me, my mother needed to step up, he said, and at the very least stop encouraging me in my starry-eyed dream of becoming a writer. But there was a solicitude in that, too, I thought, and my feelings were divided: on the one hand I wanted to write and was willing to make any sacrifice in order to do so, and moreover I was drawn toward the avant-garde, ever since my teenage years I had despised all that was conservative and staid; on the other hand, the avant-garde filled me with anxiety, and the pull toward the conservative, the staid, and the secure was at least as strong; it was a big part of why I got married and went to university at all. My father couldn't care less about me, so when Gunnar came and condemned the life I was leading, I felt there was something good in that, too: at least he cared about what became of me.

Perhaps he felt divided, too. When Dad died in Grandma's house and I went down to Kristiansand and cleaned up and took care of the funeral arrangements, he invited me out to the cabin one day for a break, and we went for a walk together across the meadows and among the trees, he told me what Dad had meant to him, and it felt like he wanted to get closer and share it with me. Later that summer he had gone to see Mom again, they spent a holiday every year at a place only a couple of hours from where she lived, and on that occasion he had been full of praise for Yngve and me, how well we had handled the situation when our father died. Only a few weeks later my first novel came out, and when it did everything went back to as it had been before. My father appeared in the book, and my father's brothers too, not ostensibly, but clearly enough for those close to the family to realize who the characters were modeled on. When I sent a copy to Gunnar I included a letter in which I put down a few words about my relationship to Dad and my respect for Gunnar as a father, sensing I suppose how he was going to take it and hoping it would soften his reaction. He was furious about the book, but instead of calling me on the phone or writing me a letter, he phoned my mother and let her have it. She refused to take responsibility for what I did or wrote, telling him I was a grown man and that she wasn't going to interfere. Six months later, however, he called me, the book had won the Critics Prize, I was staying at a hotel in Oslo and had just accepted the award when a man called, introducing himself by a name I didn't recognize. The voice, though, was familiar, and after a few seconds I realized it was Gunnar, he had introduced himself using the name I had given to one of the father's brothers in the novel. He wanted to congratulate me, and apart from him asking if we were having a drink to celebrate, it was a pleasant enough conversation. After that we met at Grandma's funeral and at the division of her estate, and then one summer when I was at Mom's together with Linda, Vanja, and Heidi he was suddenly standing there at the door, he just thought he would say hello, he said, would you like some coffee, I said, no, thanks all the same, he said, we're on our way south, just passing through, but come in at least, I said, but no, really, it was quite all right, so we stood there in the garden, exchanging pleasantries for perhaps three or four minutes before he got back in the car and drove off. Linda and the children were upstairs asleep, I said I could wake them so he at least could see my children, but he didn't want that either, it was too much trouble, then after they'd gone Linda and I laughed about the whole thing, since he had obviously only stopped by out of a sense of obligation and nothing else.

So that was the situation when I had to send him the new novel. I knew he wasn't going to like it, and the thought of him reading it scared me. But there was no way round it. So on the last day of July 2009, a month and a half before the novel was due to be published, I sat down in front of the computer and wrote him a note.

Dear Gunnar,
It's been a long time. Hope everything's good with you and the family. I was in Kristiansand this spring at a playwriting seminar and was intending to stop in and see you, only then there was a funeral in Ålesund I had to fly up to – Sissel's sister Ingunn had died – and my schedule was just too tight. Sissel's brother-in-law Magne, who was married to Kjellaug, died too in the spring, so it's been a rough year for Mom. Here in Malmö, though, things are well, all three children are in nursery school now, and Vanja will be starting school in the autumn, so the worst of our toddler years will soon be over.
The reason I'm writing to you now though is a different one. The fact is I've written six autobiographical novels – three coming out this autumn, three in the spring – all dealing with different parts of my life, and basically all names and events included in them are authentic, meaning they describe actual occurrences, though not in any great detail. The first of the books will be published at the end of September – the first part takes place in Tveit in the winter and spring of 1985, which is to say the time Mom and Dad split up and Dad began his new life with Unni, and the second deals with the days in Kristiansand following his death. You appear briefly in the first part, giving me a lift down to a friend's house on New Year's Eve, and briefly in the second, when you and Tove come to the house and lend a hand cleaning the place up. As such, it's a positive por-

trayal, obviously, because that's the way I think of you, so that's not the difficult or painful part of it — this lies in the fact that I am laying bare the private life of our family, something neither you nor anyone else in the book has asked for. On the other hand, this is a book about me and my dad, that's what it deals with, my endeavor to understand him and what happened to him. To do that I have to go to the core, the inferno he made right at the end, in which he destroyed not only himself and the house but also Grandma's final years, besides harming everyone else close to him. Why did he do that? What made him do it? Was it something he had inside him all the time when we were growing up? I don't know if you realize this, but my father has had me gripped in a vise all my life, even after he died, and if I am to tell my story, that's where I have to delve. The fact that this story also involves other people, among them — and perhaps especially — you, torments me severely, but at the same time I've been unable to see any way around it. The rot and repugnance the book describes all comes down to Dad, no one else was to blame, but I can't describe any of it without reference to the context in which it took place. That's the way it is. Right now I'm sending the manuscript to everyone who plays a part in it. Yngve has read it, and Mom as well. Now I'm sending it to you, attached to this e-mail. If you would like your name to be changed, and your background made anonymous, I am of course willing to do that. It wouldn't be difficult, but the real problem lies elsewhere: that something you would prefer left alone, out of sight, is now going to be held up on display. Again, I'm sorry about that, but he was my father, the story I tell is my own, and unfortunately it looks like this.

    All the best,
    Karl Ove

During the next couple of days I checked my e-mail several times an hour. Whenever the phone rang I felt stabs of anxiety. But nothing was forthcoming. I took this to be a good sign, he was reading the novel and thinking about what to say and how to react. Either that or he was away at the cabin.

It wasn't until the fifth day that I heard from him. As soon as I saw his name in my in-box I stood up and and went out onto the balcony, sat there for a while, smoking and gathering courage. The children were at the nursery, the sounds of the city rose toward me. The worst that could happen, I thought to myself, was that he would be angry with me for writing about the things I'd written about. But that would pass. All I had to do was take it, and it would pass.

I couldn't undo what I'd already done. Not only had I made the decision that it was what I wanted, but I'd also worked under the banner of that decision for more than a year. The will of one person couldn't change that.

That was what I thought. But it wasn't what I felt. I felt like I did when I was a little boy and had done something wrong. I was afraid Dad was going to come and be angry with me. There was nothing worse in all the world. After I left home and became an adult, the fear remained, it was with me all the time, and I did everything I could to keep it from breaking out. Dad was no longer around, and my fear of his rage had been transferred onto others: I was twenty years old and scared stiff of other people being angry with me. It never went away. When I left everything behind and moved to Stockholm at thirty-three, the fear was still inside me. Linda, whom I met soon after, was temperamental and often unreasonable in her outbursts, and yet I allowed myself to be intimidated completely, even the slightest raising of her voice was enough to fill me with anxiety, and the only thing I could think about would be to make it go away. Even as a forty-year-old, sitting on the balcony on a morning in August 2009, I was scared of someone being angry with me. Whenever I gave anyone reason to be, I became so terrified and despairing and so full of anguish, I never knew how I would ever get over it.

This fear of people being angry with me was the child's fear, it didn't belong in the adult world, where it was unprecedented, yet something inside me had never made that transition, never become adult and hardened in that way, so the child's emotions lived on in the adult. The adult, which is to say I, was completely at the mercy of the child's emotions, sometimes it hurt so much I could hardly bear it, knowing as I did that I was an adult and acutely aware that the feeling and everything to do with it was deeply shameful. Why was this? If my sense of self had been strong and whole, if I'd been more assured, I would have been able to say to myself that I did this and I'm accountable for it, and if anyone has another opinion that's their business, not mine. If they wanted argument, I'd give them an argument. But my sense of self wasn't at all strong or whole, I wasn't at all assured, and my self-confidence was completely built around what other people might think of me. My own thoughts and opinions didn't matter in that respect. I was still living in the world Dad had set up for me, where everything I did basically came down to not doing anything wrong. What was wrong was not defined by any set of rules, but was instead a matter of what he at any given time decided was wrong. These circumstances I transferred to my adult life, in which they no longer existed apart from inside me. But Dad was dead, he'd been dead for eleven years. I knew all this, but knowing didn't help, the feeling wormed its way through and did as it pleased. The only thing I could do was to meet it head-on and stick it out.

I stood up and went into the bedroom where the computer with the Internet connection was. I opened the e-mail. It was short, and nothing to be concerned about.

Hi Karl Ove.
Would you please send me an e-mail address for your contact(s)
at your publishing house.
Gunnar

I read it through a few times, trying to make out what lay behind the words. He hadn't started with "Dear," as I had done, but if he

was fuming about something then surely he wouldn't have written, "Hi Karl Ove." The fact there was a period after my name
indicated a lack of enthusiasm, otherwise there would have been
either an exclamation mark – which I didn't think was in his
nature – or a comma, or else nothing. A comma or nothing would
have been neutral and objective, a period was making a point,
stern and unpermissive. His use of "please" pointed in the same
direction. "Please" was formal, more formal than the uncle–nephew
relationship warranted, so my understanding was that he didn't
care for the manuscript. At the same time, it was a marker of
politeness, which might indicate that he wasn't fuming at all, I
thought, otherwise wouldn't he just have dispensed with courtesy
altogether? The fact that he hadn't put anything before his name,
either "Best regards" or "Yours" or something equally friendly,
indicated the same thing as the opening, that this was a formal,
matter-of-fact kind of inquiry on the computer screen in front
of me. I knew he'd never cared for me, that he saw me as an
attention-seeker, someone who wanted to be different for the
sake of being different, who believed himself to be more than he
was, and moreover without any sense of responsibility or order,
and I took the content of his brief e-mail to be more indicative of
that than of what he thought about the novel. Wanting the addresses of my contacts at the publisher was a good thing, too, it
seemed to say he would be putting any objections to them rather
than to me personally. More than anything else, I was afraid of
any direct contact with him. If he was going to be writing to the
publisher, it would hardly be to rip into them.

   I typed the e-mail addresses and phone numbers of the director of publishing Geir Berdahl and commissioning editor Geir
Gulliksen, and sent them off to him. I went back into the study.
The volume of work I had to get through was enormous and I had
no idea how I was going to manage it all. In April I had sent
twelve hundred pages off to the publisher, the idea all along having been for a single novel, to be published in the autumn, but
then it had grown, it was too long, and the way I was thinking

now was it was going to be another three hundred pages or longer still, which begged the question of how actually to publish the book. I'd discussed the matter with Geir Gulliksen over the phone. Was publishing a novel that ran to fifteen hundred pages at all feasible? Everything was feasible, he said. It could also be put out in two volumes, either at the same time or with a few months in between. Although this was more rational and would moreover have the advantage of giving me a double payout of two basic fees, a matter that was far from insignificant in view of our, to put it mildly, frail finances of the past few years, I nevertheless still preferred the book to come out as a single volume. It would be a statement, something there would be no getting away from, Norway's longest novel. Geir said he would run it past some other people at the publishing house and call me back. He did so a few hours later. He said that the proposal he wanted me to listen to, as suggested by Geir Berdahl, was probably unrealistic, and that I might not like it at all, but it was definitely worth considering.

"Let's hear it, then!" I said.

"We put it out as a series of twelve. A book a month for a year. We could set up some kind of deal so people can subscribe and get the whole lot. What do you reckon?"

"It's a fantastic idea!" I said. "Absolutely brilliant!"

"Yeah, I liked it too. It'd be a bit of a challenge, though. We'd need to find the funding somewhere. I'll go ahead and look into it, then we'll see."

"It'll be like Dickens or Dostoyevsky," I said. "A serial novel! I really like the serial aspect of it. Like when the Wedding Present released a single once a month for a year, then put them all together to make an album when the year was up. It's a gimmick, but why not?"

"It's not an ordinary novel. It's fitting we do something special with it. Think of how it'll affect the way it's received. How would they review it? Each book as it comes out? Or the whole work as one at the end of the year?"

"It's fucking genius, Geir! Say hello to Berdahl and thank him for me."

"I think it's good too, and I'll do what I can to make it work. It'll take time. But let's say for now I go ahead and look into it, then I'll give you a call in a couple of weeks, okay?"

As soon as we hung up I went straight into the study and set about dividing the novel into twelve. If it was going to come to fifteen hundred pages in all, then each book would have to be roughly a hundred and twenty-five pages. I searched for places where one book could end and another begin. It was the first time during the year I'd been working on the novel that I'd felt anything remotely like joy and enthusiasm. I imagined the paperback with just the title printed on it, as they used to do in the nineteenth century. Subscription coupons in the newspapers and magazines that could be cut out and sent in to the publishers, the way people did in my childhood.

Nearly three weeks went by before Geir phoned back. When he did it was to tell me they couldn't make it work with twelve separate publications, there were too many practical problems and the figures wouldn't add up. He suggested six instead. Three in the autumn, three the following spring. I hesitated, not wanting to let go of the idea of twelve and once a month, almost pleading with him to think again, he could see what I was saying, he said, but it had turned out to be impractical, we ran the risk of ruining the publishing house, as far as I could understand him. Six had been difficult too, but eventually he had managed to get them all covered by the State Purchasing Program, thereby minimizing the financial risk.

"That's unbelievable," I said. "How did you manage that? Isn't there a strict rule they only purchase one work of fiction a year per author?"

"Yes. I had to present my case. It's a very unusual project. They listened and agreed."

That decided, I had to split the novel once more. In principle, I could just put two and two together of the twelve, making each book about two hundred and fifty pages. But that would be the same length as any average Norwegian novel, and with the subscription and serial idea abandoned it would be odd to simply break the narrative in one book to pick it up again in the next. Six books that weren't independent of each other, that didn't seem good to me. I needed to divide them differently so that each became a stand-alone book in its own right, which was to say I had to end up with six novels that could also be read as a single, continuous narrative. Doing it that way, the first book came to four hundred pages, the second to five hundred and fifty, and the third to three hundred. After that I ran out of material. If I was going to do it that way, I would have to write three new books in ten months. Which wasn't implausible, I'd been doing about ten pages a day for the past six months as it was, in the region of fifty pages a week given the fact that I wasn't allowed to work weekends. Subtracting ten pages for unforeseen difficulties, I could do around a hundred and sixty pages a month. If I rounded that down to a hundred and fifty, I could spend two or three months on each book and still easily do three, even having a month in hand.

I was almost burning with impatience and expectation as I sat down at the computer and scrolled through the manuscript. It was obvious I couldn't just divide it up into stand-alone books as it was, I would have to write beginnings and endings, bridges and transitions, move and delete sections, but that wouldn't be hard, the various parts differed from each other already because of how I'd tried to write my way into the period in which each narrative took place, not least by matching my reflections as closely as possible to the age of the first-person narrator in each book. The ten-year-old reflected on sweets, the twenty-nine-year-old on pop music, the thirty-five-year-old on parenting. Oh, it was going to be brilliant! Six books! Fuck, I was going to wipe the floor with them!

This afternoon in August, as I sat down to work after having read Gunnar's short e-mail, the first book was ready for typesetting; the last thing I'd done, after receiving two reader's reports, was to turn the mainly fragmentary and disconnected account of the year I'd spent living with Dad when I was sixteen into a cohesively told story, and the only thing left to do, as far as I could see, was to alter names if any of the people I had written about so wished. The second book was largely finished, all that remained was some minor work at the end, after which Geir Gulliksen was going to read it one last time, and once I'd gone through his suggestions and criticisms, that too would be ready for typesetting. The third book still needed a good deal of work. It wasn't where I wanted it to be, it was far too anecdotal, lacking in epic sweep, and had no clear thread besides the chronology.

This was perhaps the greatest difficulty in writing autobiographically, finding out how material was relevant. In real life, of course, everything was relevant and in principle equal, since it was all there in existence at the same time – the great oil tankers at anchor in the Galtesund in the seventies, the plum tree outside my window, Mom's job at Kokkeplassen, Dad's face when he drove by in the car and I was out somewhere and saw him, the pond where we skated in winter, the smells inside the neighbors' house, Dag Lothar's mom that time she made milkshakes for us, the strange car that was parked one night down at Ubekilen, all the fish we had for dinner, the way the pine trees in next door's garden swayed back and forth in the strong autumn winds, Dad's rage if I happened to dig my knee into the back of his seat in the car, the waffles we made every Tuesday, my great infatuation with Anne Lisbeth, the soccer balls Mom and Dad brought back for us from a trip to Germany, mine green with red hexagons, Yngve's yellow with red hexagons, the way we stood one day and kicked them as high into the air as we could to see if they could reach the military helicopter that happened to come sweeping low over the playground. The last of these recollections alone brought with it a host of other recollections, because while they were in Germany I had stayed with Grandma and Grandad on Dad's side, and Yngve with Grandma and Grandpa on Mom's side, a week I remembered so much from, and so very clearly, in particular the days we spent at the cabin. And that was what my entire child-hood was like inside me – a thick garland of memories, one on top of another. To write was simultaneously to retrieve them from my mind and put them into words, and as long as this retrieval went from the inside to semioutside, by which I mean the words as they came to me in the process of writing, there was no problem, but what the novel as a form required was that my recollections be moved one place further still, to the unfamiliar reader. Rele-vance was a matter of communication, establishing community out of what was one's own, and the novel was one of the forms of relevance. The poem was another, less obvious, since it was shared by fewer people. Quality was bound together with exclu-siveness, and everything to do with high and low literature, pop-ular and elitist, was all about that. The wider the reach of the novel, the greater the community it strove toward, the easier it was to grasp, and the less challenging it became, in the sense that the reader's own efforts and participation diminished. In this there was a simplification, too. A novel that was meant to say some-thing true about reality could not be made too simple, it had to contain an element of exclusiveness in its communication, some-thing not common to or shared by all, in other words something of its own, and there, at some point between the madman's own particular and therefore uncommunicated ramblings, meaning-less to everyone but the madman himself, who found them fasci-natingly relevant, and the genre novel's fixed formulations and clichés, which had become clichés by being familiar to everyone, was the domain of literature. The highest ideal for any writer was to write a text that worked on all levels at the same time. The only writers I could think of who had done that were the authors of the first two Books of Moses – Genesis and Exodus – and Shake-speare. The *Odyssey* and the *Iliad* had achieved that once, but what at the time had been broad in reach, the epic poem, was now foreign in the sense that its relevance had radically declined. Not that I thought about any of this as I wrote, the problem there being real and tangible, how to turn all these recollections, which were almost inexhaustible, into a coherent narrative? And how to do so in such a way as to remain faithful to what was mine about them?

I went back and forth through the text without being able to collect my thoughts, or even to read what I'd written, my concentration was nonexistent, the only thing I could think about was Gunnar and his reaction. After a quarter of an hour like that, I got to my feet and went out of the study. As I went through the hall I heard the elevator on its way up. Most likely it was Linda; at this time of day there was hardly any activity in the building. I stood still and waited, heard the elevator doors open, and the next moment she stepped into the hall. She was wearing her blue and white sailor dress, she had eye shadow on, and her lips were painted red. In each hand was a carrier bag, and she had her little black backpack on her back. There was a busy air of eagerness about her; she'd hardly put her bags down on the floor before she came up to kiss me, then bent down and took off her red shoes while telling me about all the things she'd bought.

"They had these filing boxes or whatever down at Granit, the ones I was saying we could use for our mail, one for you and one for me. So now we don't need to leave all those letters and bills lying around all over the place. Do you want to see?"

I nodded and she produced the two boxes, which were like little sets of drawers.

"Nice, don't you think?"

"Yes," I said. "What's in the other bag?"

"A dress from Myrorna, a shawl, and a skirt. Dirt cheap, they hardly cost anything at all."

She took the three items out and held them up against herself one by one.

"Nice, don't you think?" she said again.

"Yes," I said.

"They hardly cost anything at all," she said.

"It would have been all right even if they had," I said. "It's not that."

"What, then?"

"It doesn't matter."

"Yes, it does! Tell me. Have you had lunch, by the way?"

I shook my head.

"There's some bolognese left over from yesterday, is that okay?"

"Yes."

"Go on, tell me, then. What is it? Something wrong?"

"No, not at all."

She went over to the mirror and held the dress up against herself again.

"It is nice, isn't it?" she said. "We can heat it up in the microwave, no?"

"I'll do it."

I went into the kitchen, took the plastic container with the meat sauce out of the fridge, then the spaghetti, divided it between two plates, and started heating the first one in the microwave as I stared out the window, all the roofs in their various shades of red which seemed so close, the light blue sky above them. I've felt a twinge of guilty conscience from boyhood at being inside on such a fine day. It was one of the things Dad would never tolerate. If the weather was fine, you had to be outside, no excuses. Stupid as I was, I could wander around the neighborhood finding no one to hang out with and nothing to do, it was the holidays, people had gone away, either for the day in their boats or their cars, or else farther afield, enjoying bigger adventures. All I wanted was to be inside with my books, and as I walked aimlessly about I could make myself cry with self-pity.

"How's your day been?" asked Linda, sitting down at the table and opening the newspaper that was folded in front of her.

"I got an e-mail from Gunnar," I said.

"Oh? What did he say?"

"Nothing. He just wanted the address of the publisher. But it was enough to stop me working."

"You needn't be so worried," she said.

I took a deep breath. She looked up at me.

73

"What's wrong?"

"I thought you didn't like shopping," I said. "I thought you loathed it."

She stuck her tongue out at me.

"You're so stingy sometimes," she said.

"Stingy?"

"You're not begrudging me, are you? I'm feeling happy, that's all. I thought I'd get myself something for when I go away, and I've been thinking about what to do about our mail for months. Aren't you glad I've figured it out? So we can keep things neat?"

"Of course."

"Good."

She returned to the newspaper.

Then she looked up at me again.

"Anyway, you buy all your clothes from Spirit, fifteen hundred kronor for a pair of trousers. I've never said a thing about that."

"That's because it's my money."

"That we could have spent on something else. The clothes I buy cost a third of the ones you buy, if not a quarter."

"All right, yes, but that's not the point. Forget it. The last thing I want to do is argue."

"Who wants to argue? Not me."

The microwave pinged. I took the plate out and put it down in front of her. She got up and turned the radio on.

"We're friends, then," I said, and put the second plate in the microwave, set the timer to four minutes, shut the door, and pressed the start button.

"Karl Ove, I love you. Of course we're friends."

"Okay," I said.

She carried on reading the paper. The news came on the radio. The microwave hummed, the green plate and its mound of spaghetti bolognese rotated sedately in its chamber. I got the knives and forks out, and two glasses, and filled a jug with water.

"Can you pick them up today?" she asked.

I didn't answer until she looked up at me.

"Yes," I said, charging the word with as much reluctance as I could. "If you can't, then I suppose I'll have to."

"Of course I can. But it was my turn this morning. So it's your turn this afternoon."

I looked down without saying anything. The microwave pinged again, I took the plate out, put it down on the table, and began to eat. Linda watched me for a moment, then put the newspaper aside before she too started eating. I was finished in a couple of minutes, the food was barely warm and offered nothing in the way of resistance, the only thing to do was shovel it in. Although Linda was still eating, I left the table and went out onto the balcony, where I sat down, put my feet up on the rail, poured myself a cup of coffee from the vacuum jug, and lit a cigarette. The basic rule of our relationship was that we shared everything. From that point of view it was only fair and reasonable that I picked the children up if she had dropped them off. But the thing was I worked in between, while she didn't. On this particular day I'd got up at four thirty to get some work done before the children woke up, after which I helped her get them dressed and ready to go, and then I'd gone back to work, during which time she had sat in a café, shopped for clothes, and bought a couple of filing boxes. If the kids took up 50 percent of the day, and work another 50 percent, then I was doing 75 percent of the total job and Linda 25 percent. Whenever we argued, I would tell her. But I didn't want to argue now, so I left it at that.

I looked out over the city. I could see what looked like the small shadow of a Mercedes logo on a wall across the street below, perhaps cast by the sun shining on a parked car somewhere, I wasn't sure, but I'd seen it before and it seemed to indicate a habit, someone who always parked in the same place. Far, far away, a crane rose above the rooftops. Since all I could see basically were rooftops, any deviation would always stick out; if a person happened to be up there for whatever reason, I would see them, even if they were several kilometers away, the dark figure of the body against the brightness of the sky.

I stubbed my cigarette out in the upturned flowerpot I used for an ashtray, swallowed the last mouthful of coffee, and went inside. Passing the kitchen I saw Linda was on the phone. I paused to hear who she was talking to. Helena, I realized after only a few seconds. She looked up at me and lifted her hand as if in acknowledgment, I smiled and carried on into the bedroom to check my e-mails. It was already a quarter to two by the clock on the computer. Half an hour and I'd have to get going.

No e-mails.

Relieved, I lay down on the bed and stared up at the ceiling. It was too late to start on anything now anyway. A faint, rather nauseating smell of food filled the air. When we first moved here I thought it came from our nearest neighbor, but after a while it struck me the smell might be coming through the ventilation system, in which case it was most likely from the Chinese takeaway down on the ground floor. I got up and opened the door onto the balcony, then stretched out on the bed again. The sounds of the city trickled into the room. I heard footsteps in the hallway. They stopped and the bathroom door was opened and then closed. The old saxophone player whose spot was by a pillar only a few meters from the entrance to our building, where the flow of people crossing the square was greatest, began to play. He always played the same thing, a minute-long fragment of some tune, presumably on the assumption that his audience was always new. That a man seven floors up had to listen to every note, not just day after day, but month after month, was something that almost certainly didn't occur to him.

Diii di daaa da dididi daaaa.

Diii di daaa da dididi daaaa.

Diii di daaa da dididi daaaa.

I closed my eyes. There was a rush of water from the toilet, the door was opened and the footsteps stopped in front of the mirror in the hall. Was she looking at herself or sifting through the letters that lay strewn over the little table against the wall?

Ba daaaa! The sound the telephone made when returned to the charger.

Had she taken the phone with her to the toilet? Or just put it down on the table as she went past, only now putting it back in its place?

She came toward me.

I opened my eyes and saw her pause in the doorway.

"I'll pick them up," she said. "After all, you're going to be on your own with them for a few days."

"No, I'll do it," I said. "I can't get any more work done today anyway. You can pack or something."

"You sure?"

"Do you want me to say it again?"

"Okay, okay. You pick them up, I'll drop them off in the morning before I go."

"What time was your train again?"

"About half past eight," she said, and sat down at the computer. She was going off to visit Helena and Helena's new boyfriend Fredrik at an old farmhouse somwhere in mid-Sweden and would be gone until the weekend, when Geir and Christina were coming to stay with us. I hadn't met Fredrik, but from what I'd heard he was the complete opposite of Helena's previous partner, the charming and rather dodgy Anders. Fredrik was a fireman, an incident commander working in Stockholm, and had bought a house in the Dalarna region, taken it apart, transported it to Uppsala and rebuilt it plank by plank, and done it so well there had been articles about it in lifestyle magazines. That was all I knew. Apart from that, Heidi, who had met him once, was a little scared of him. He had let her comb his hair on that occasion, and Helena had said it meant she couldn't be that scared of him, but Heidi said she'd been scared of him the whole time, even when she was combing his hair. Helena laughed about that. Heidi loved her and would always sit as close to her as possible to be sure of her attention, and chatter on about all the things she'd been up to since the last time they saw each other. She talked to her on the phone too, and often made drawings of her. Heidi was attracted by all that glittered and shone, she loved dressing up more than anyone, five outfits a day was by no means unusual, and in Helena she had found her only truly glamorous role model.

"Are you looking forward to some time on your own?" I said.

Linda nodded without turning around.

"But I'm going to start missing you after a couple of hours on the train. Are you sure you don't want to come?"

"Positive. I've got to work. Besides, it'll do you good, not having the children around."

"I suppose so. And Helena does always look after me."

"Good, then," I said, getting to my feet. "I'd better get going."

"Are you bringing them straight home or going to the playground first?"

I gave a shrug.

"Can you give me a call if you're going somewhere? So I can come too?"

"Will do. See you later."

"See you."

We went to Magistratsparken, the place the children called the "normal park." Other parks we frequented were the "spider park" in the Pildammsparken, the "shark park" in the Möllevangen neighborhood, and Lugnet, a few streets behind where we lived. Besides these there was another playground we went to in the Pildammsparken, and one in the Slottsparken that we called the "troll's forest," as well as another one some distance away by the fire station, where we hardly ever went but which they liked because it had some very unusual apparatuses. Almost all their time outdoors was spent in these parks. The rest of the time they were inside, either at the nursery or at home. I didn't like it, it was so remote from the upbringing I wanted to give them. But there were no alternatives, we couldn't afford a house, and being registered bad debtors we couldn't get a mortgage. On the other hand, they didn't seem to be suffering in the slightest as their heads poked out from among the leaves of the tree they called the "climbing tree." I sat on one of the three benches at the other end and skimmed through a newspaper I'd bought to keep myself occupied, glancing up at regular intervals and scanning the various children at play until locating my own. Vanja could be trusted completely, and I didn't think Heidi would get it into her head to go off on her own anymore either, but John was still unpredictable, all of a sudden he'd be on his way across the grass toward the road that ran next to the park, and if I didn't keep a watchful eye out and immersed myself in my reading instead he could be gone when I looked up, and I might only discover him when I extended my field of vision and noticed his little figure in the distance toddling off toward the road.

Now, though, he was standing tugging on the swing, calling for me at the top of his voice. I got to my feet and went over to him, lifted him up and put him in the seat, drew it back, and looked him in the eye. Are you ready? I said. Yes, he said in a serious voice. I pulled him back into the air and let go, and he immediately started to laugh. Ten swings, I said, and began to count. After ten I stopped him, he protested, and once he realized I was going to lift him up he gripped the swing tight with a look of panic in his eyes. No, no, no! I put him down on the ground, where he lay on his belly, pressing his face into the sand, shouting and screaming. By the time I sat down on the bench again his tantrum had turned to tears. He cried and sobbed heartrendingly, as if he'd been orphaned and hadn't eaten for a week, and someone had smacked his bottom for good measure. I located Heidi and Vanja, lit a cigarette, and picked up the paper again. Subconsciously I must have registered the situation that would soon arise, and only a few seconds later I lowered the paper and the dad who'd been on his way toward the swing with his son held tightly to his chest now put him down in the seat. A big person launching a little person, the way a big boat launches a little boat, I thought to myself. But John was still lying underneath the swing, and he wasn't thinking of moving for a while yet. I got up and went over to him. Up you go, out of the way, I said. Other people want to use the swing. He didn't say anything, just kept on sobbing, his little shoulders shaking. I picked him up like a tortoise, lifted him a few meters to the side and put him down again. There we are, I said. You can go and play again now. I turned and went back to my bench. I felt guilty, I ought to have comforted him until he stopped crying, but for one thing the reason for his disappointment was completely disproportional to his reaction and I didn't want him to start thinking this was the right way to deal with adversity, and for another, my strategy was to intervene as little as possible when I was out with them, I wanted them to be able to look after themselves.

But it wasn't only children who had difficulty keeping things in proportion. When I thought about the way I'd dealt with Vanja and saw from the photos how little she'd been then, it was as if the bottom dropped out from under me. Had I stood yelling with rage at that little creature there? Had I snatched her up out of her stroller and put her down hard on the floor, dizzy with frustration and anger, she eighteen months old and utterly innocent of anything? It was the most painful thought I knew. How could I have done such things? What had I been thinking? How was it possible to so totally lose one's sense of reality? I didn't see how little she was, my objective view was completely absent, both she and Linda and everyone else around me were sucked inside that inner vortex where the most unreasonable things became reasonable and justified. And I didn't have anything else to compare with, that was all there was.

John had stopped crying but was still lying with his face in the sand. I reasoned I had to give him a way out. The big swing was free now, I noticed, so I put down the paper and went over to him.

"Do you want to try the big swing? Would you like that?"

"Ye-es," he said.

"Come on, then," I said. He got up and followed me, wiping

his tears away with his hand and leaving dark streaks on his cheeks. The big swing was in the shape of a cradle, there was room enough for several children inside, and mine at least loved to lie there and look up at the sky as they swung back and forth at speed. As I lifted John inside, Heidi and Vanja came running across the playground toward us.

"Us, too!" they cried.

"Yes, but John's with you now," I said. "So I can't swing very high, okay?"

"Okay," said Vanja.

"Okay," said Heidi.

I lifted them up and pulled the cradle as far back as I could.

"Are you ready?"

"Yes."

"Are you sure?"

"Yes, Daddy. Swing us now!" said Vanja.

I did as she said.

John cried out in protest.

"I don't want to!"

I stopped the swing, lifted him out, and put him down. He stretched his arms toward me. I ignored him and pulled back the cradle, and he began to wail.

"Okay, if you're going to be stubborn," I said, lifting him up then holding him with one arm while I swung the girls with the other. His little body against mine felt warm and good. He put his head on my shoulder. The cradle came toward me, I sent it back. The girls were lying on their stomachs with their heads poking over the edge, staring toward the road. Their dresses and their hair flapped in the wind. All around there were children, crawling, waddling, running, and climbing, the figures of their parents poking up, some with sunglasses on and cell phones in their hands, others absorbed in their children's activities. Beyond the playground there were lawns where tall trees stood, sedate and bathed in sun, offering circles of shade to all those who had come to the park that afternoon. Most were young, nearly all were white. Many lay on their own in the grass next to a bike; the way they had rolled their trousers up and removed their T-shirts suggested improvisation, a sudden impulse followed on the way home from work. Others sat around in groups, mostly students from the *gymnas* or university students. Here and there a couple lay tightly entwined, completely immersed in each other. The Pildammsparken on the other side of the old football stadium attracted mainly immigrants, whole families out picnicking into the evenings, occasionally the thud of drums could be heard rising up through the sunlight, as if from the depths of a dream. The way the shadows grew with evening, and the way the sun sank down, not into the sea or the forest, but into the city, had a dreamlike quality about it, I always found myself thinking when we were there. The world dissolved when filled with sunlight, that was the feeling I had, the relationships between all things vanished, everything seemed suddenly to exist on the same level. It was the job of culture to define those relationships, establish hierarchies of connections and draw together what lay dispersed into particular, meaningful patterns. That was why we had novels, films, TV series, poems, and plays, but also newspapers, television news, and gossip magazines. That a culture originating in a sun-scorched landscape, underneath a burning sky, along the fertile banks of a river, would draw the world together in a different way and create other meaningful patterns was obvious. I had no idea what the difference consisted of, for it was so big that their language to me sounded like so much coughing and spitting, and the letters of their alphabet looked more like bushes in the desert than writing, but I had an idea that everything surely had to be impenetrable to begin with, and while it might gradually open up as the language became understood, it could never be as self-explanatory as it was to us, and presumably never become possible, nor therefore desirable, to embrace. For culture's greatest role comprised the way it worked between people, its tissue of collocations, accentuations, and self-imposed constraints was so fine and complex that most within the culture were familiar only with the particular shadings that concerned his or her own layer of society, and possessed only superficial knowledge of the others. But everything had its own significance, that was what culture was. The fabric of a pair of trousers was significant, the width of a trouser leg was significant, the pattern in the curtain hung in front of a window was significant, the sudden lowering of a gaze was significant. The particular way a word was pronounced was significant. What a person knew about one thing or another was also significant. Culture charged the world with meaning by establishing differences within it, and those differences, in which everything of value existed, varied from culture to culture. That the units were becoming increasingly bigger, and cultures increasingly similar, was a discouraging thought, at least for someone like me who was fascinated by differences and attracted by impenetrability. The wonder of Japan, a country that had been isolated for so many hundreds of years and had developed what seemed to us in every way to be such a peculiar culture, almost completely closed to us, and yet existing before our eyes. The thought of that culture dissolving into that of the West and being lost forever, to exist as a mere variation of our own, was as great a loss as the extinction of any species of animal. But the Western world was so strong, and so expansive in its nature, that it would soon have the rest of the world subsumed within it, not by violence, as in the days of colonialism, but by promise. In this wide perspective, I was against immigration, against multiculturalism, against notions of sameness of nearly every kind. In the narrower perspective, that which related to the tangible, day-to-day reality of where I lived, in Malmö, it was hard not to look on immigration as an enormous resource all the while I could see how explosively vibrant and full of energy the city was compared to, say, Stockholm, where all the immigrants lived in the urban outskirts and the faces you saw in the city center were practically all white. Malmö, it's true, was run-down and poverty common to see, but at the same time the city vibrated in its contrasts, which all had to be brought together in synthesis and most surely were a gift to anyone who grew up there, with so many different experiences and backgrounds existing together side by side, and where a lot of what came about for that same reason came about as if for the first time, with all the freshness and vigor of the new.

"I envy them that," Linda had said one evening not so long ago after we'd picnicked in a corner of the big park and were heading home again with the kids in tow.

"Envy them what?" I said.

"The whole family out together. Parents, grandparents, children and grandchildren, uncles and cousins."

She nodded toward a congregation of people gathered around a barbecue, perhaps twenty in all, the elderly seated on chairs, the youngest running around playing. There were more like them, scattered across the lawns. The air all around smelled of smoke and grilled meat.

"It used to be like that here, too," I said. "Three generations ago, maybe. In rural areas at least. My maternal grandmother grew up with it. Well, not barbecuing in the parks, exactly. But they lived together in big families."

"It all looks so *himla mysigt*. They all seem to be having such a fine time," she said. "And here we come with our tiny little nuclear family. There's only us! Imagine if there'd been more of us, think of how different it would have been!"

"Yes, but our life's not that miserable, is it?"

"No, no, I don't mean that. It's just that – "

"You're a romantic. You see the aura of it, and you want it too." She shook her head.

"It's not that I want it. It just seems so . . . well, as if there's so much more life around them."

"Your mother's stayed with us. And my mom's been here quite a lot. You're always glad to see the back of them."

"I know, but that's exactly it. It's all so centered around us, you, me, and the kids. Think what it'd be like if there were lots of others we could be with, we could forget all about ourselves!"

The sun behind us had been red and hung like a bauble above the rooftops, I remembered, and then I looked at John to see if he'd fallen asleep on my shoulder for once, but I found myself looking straight into his open eyes and stepped a few paces back.

"All right, that's your lot," I told the girls.

"But Daddy!" Vanja said. "We've only just started!"

"Just a bit more?" said Heidi. "Please!"

"No," I said, putting John down so I could go back to my bench, and then I saw Linda crossing the circular gravel-covered area with the wall around it in the middle of the park.

"Look, Mommy's here," I said. The girls crawled from the cradle to meet her, John toddled off toward her, and her face broke into a wide and joyful smile as she crouched down to receive them. A stark contrast to the times I came home and she would be lying in bed oblivious to their expectant calls of *Hello?* and *Mama?* as they came in.

I went over to the bench and folded the newspaper and was about to drop it into the basket under the stroller when a sudden unease came over me.

Where had it come from?

I looked over at Linda, she was on her way toward me with the children all around her. It wasn't that.

The book.

Of course. That was it.

"Hi," said Linda.

"Hi," I said. "You haven't got any cash on you, have you?"

"No, I don't think I have. What for?"

"So we could get some ice cream at the kiosk over there. I've only got twenty kronor and I don't think they take cards."

"Yes, they do now."

"Do you want ice cream?" I asked them, looking down at their little faces.

As we walked beneath the trees a few moments later on our way toward the pedestrian crossing, I argued against my unease, telling myself I hadn't written anything bad about the people now reading it, reminding myself that I'd been afraid of how Yngve would react and yet how well that had turned out.

"Were they all right at nursery today?" Linda asked.

"Yes, I think so," I said. "I didn't ask. They were happy enough when I picked them up."

We stopped at the crossing, and Linda and Heidi scrabbled to press the button first, but Vanja got in before them and pressed it triumphantly. Heidi started to cry.

"You can press it next time," I told her.

"Vanja pushed," she said.

"You shouldn't push, Vanja," said Linda. "But look, we can go over there now and then you can have your ice cream."

Heidi stayed put with her head lowered as we began to cross the road. I went back and lifted her up, and carried her the rest of the way to the kiosk.

"Why does Heidi get carried and not me?" said Vanja.

"Because she was crying," I said. "I can carry you a little on the way back."

I poked my head through the hatch and seeing no one there I rang the small shiny bell on the counter.

Jan Vidar was perhaps the person whose reaction I was most nervous about. He was and always would be fifteen to me, and I hadn't exactly depicted the world we had together back then as anything fantastic. Maybe it was fantastic to him? Maybe he gilded the past?

A woman, Romanian-looking, appeared from a small back-room and came up to the counter in front of me.

"Okay," I said, looking down at the children. "Just point to the one you want, but don't be too long about it." I looked up at the woman. "Two coffees to start with. Milk in one."

"I want a . . . Calippo," said Vanja.

"Cola flavor, or the green one?" I asked her.

"The green one," she said.

"And a Calippo fruity," I said to the dark-haired woman.

86

"I want one, too," said Heidi.

"We'll make that two," I said. "What about you, John? Can you point?"

He pointed to an ice-cream sandwich. Whether he knew what he was doing or not was a different matter.

"And a sandwich."

She entered the amounts, I held out my card, she shoved a little card reader across the counter and pressed some keys. I inserted the card and she stepped over to the freezer. Behind the few chairs and tables, a fat young man came walking along the path with a little dog. I saw how Vanja followed it with her eyes. He was so fat I thought he must be on disability benefits. Cheap, khaki-colored shorts, air-force-gray baseball cap, black T-shirt. His entire body quivered as he went, he seemed almost to roll at the joints. I entered my PIN. The woman straightened up.

"What sort of dog was it, Vanja?" I said, pressing okay.

"A terrier, I think," she said.

Heidi sat on Linda's lap, in the shade of the parasol. John had climbed onto the chair and was trying to press a straw, now flattened at the end, into a crack in the table.

"Sorry, we're out of Calippo fruity," the woman said. "Will cola do instead?"

"Yes, that's fine."

The little card reader came abruptly to life and ejected a slow ribbon of paper from its innards. The woman handed me the two popsicles and the ice-cream sandwich, then tore off the receipt, I took them over to the children, and when I came back she gave me the coffee in two paper cups with the receipt. I handed one of the cups to Linda, who was opening the wrappers, sat down at the table, and took a sip from the other.

Gunnar had been angry when *Out of the World* came out. But that was the first time I'd got anything published, it was completely new, and I guessed it must have been a shock for him to recognize himself in one of the characters, but more than ten years had passed since then, and the fact that my previous novel had been nominated for the Nordic Council Literature Prize must have altered things a lot; I wasn't just someone idling away his time with dreams of being a writer, I was an acclaimed author, not only nationally but internationally too, if only moderately so, but what little had been written about my books in the foreign newspapers had almost certainly been mentioned in *Fædrelands-vennen*: the review in *Frankfurter Allgemeine* that called the novel a masterpiece, and perhaps the one in *The Guardian* too, even if that had been more ambivalent. He almost certainly wouldn't be pleased about me writing about Dad and Grandma, but what I'd written about him could hardly give rise to displeasure, he came out well, was treated respectfully.

"I think I'm starting to get in a tizzy about going away," said Linda. "I feel a bit worked up."

An elderly man biked past with something flapping against the spokes and a pedal that scraped the chain guard.

"You mean about the train journey?" I said.

"Yes. I always get excited about traveling, I have done ever since I was little."

"What did you say, Mommy?" said Vanja.

"I said I'm feeling nervous about going away tomorrow."

"Why?" Vanja asked.

"Yes, why?" I said. "It's nice to have butterflies."

"Just think, I went on my own to Hydra when I was seven," she said. "It's not worth thinking about, is it?"

"No, it isn't."

"What isn't what?" said Vanja.

"I went all on my own to an island in Greece when I was only two years older than you are now. Well, not completely on my own, I went with a family, but my mommy and daddy weren't with me."

"That was in the seventies," I said. "They had different ideas about raising children then."

"It was extreme, even for the seventies," she said.

"Have I ever told you about the first time I traveled alone?" I said.

Linda shook her head.

"That was in the seventies too. Only I wasn't as tough as you. I was in the first grade and missed the bus home from school. I stood there crying and the caretaker came over. We had a fantastic caretaker, we used to go and see him sometimes in his workshop. Anyway, he said I could take the next bus that came along. It'd be going in the other direction, but we lived on an island, so it was bound to go past our house sooner or later. I got on and didn't recognize a soul. Then when we turned left instead of right I got scared and forgot all about what the caretaker had said, or maybe I just didn't believe him anymore. Eventually, I panicked and pulled the bell cord. The bus stopped, and there I was standing by the side of a road I'd never seen before, most likely miles from home.

"What did you do?" said Linda.

"There was another boy who got off at the same place. I told him I was lost, he said I could come home to his place, so I did. It was a dark house right next to the road. His dad called mine, and he came and picked me up."

I looked at Vanja.

"That was your grandfather," I said.

"And yours, and yours, too," said Linda to Heidi and John.

"I know," said Vanja. "He's dead."

I nodded.

"He died before I was born," she said.

"Mommy's daddy died too," said Heidi.

"He died on New Year's Eve," said Vanja.

"Yes, he did," I said, and looked at Linda. She smiled.

"But you met him, Vanja," she said.

Vanja nodded gravely.

"Two times," she said. "In Stockholm."

"I was born in Stockholm," said Heidi.

"Yes, you were," said Linda, and held her tight.

The next morning I woke up at four thirty, switched off the beeping alarm, picked up my pile of clothes, and took them with me from the bedroom into the hall so I wouldn't wake Linda, picked up the two newspapers that had been dumped on the floor outside the door, put the coffeemaker on, scanned the arts and sports sections, and munched on an apple while waiting for the coffee to be ready. When it was, I drank a cup and smoked a cigarette on the balcony. The sky was a haze, the gray half-light of dawn still lingered between the buildings below, and there was something raw about it; it was mid-August and autumn would soon be here.

I lit another cigarette to put off starting work for as long as possible, but stubbed it out half-smoked and went inside to the study, switched on the computer, sat down, turned on the lamp attached to the bookshelf with a clamp, and flicked through the stack of CDs on the floor next to me, deciding on *Giant Steps* by the Boo Radleys, which instantly transported me back to the mood of Bergen in the early '90s. I'd barely played the album since, and for that same reason, not wanting to revive the feelings. I sat for a while debating with myself as to whether to put something else on instead, at the same time opening the manuscript of the second book and scrolling through the document. No, it wouldn't do. I picked out Josh Rouse's *1972* instead, it was soft and pleasant, verging on Muzak, and would be a good start to the day.

An hour later I heard a door open. I turned the music down and listened. Feet padding through the hall. It had to be John or Heidi. Not that it mattered much; if one of them was up, the other would soon follow.

I opened the door and went out into the kitchen. John stood with his pillow in his hand and looked up at me. It was twenty to six.

"It's still night," I said. "Go back to bed."

"I'm not tired," he said with a twinge of resentment in his voice, as if I'd accused him of something.

"Do you want some breakfast then?" I said.

He nodded. I lifted him up into his chair, got the muesli out of the cupboard and blueberry yogurt from the fridge, poured some into his bowl, and put it on the table in front of him, then handed him a spoon, which fortunately he accepted.

More padding feet. I turned, and Heidi was standing in the doorway.

"Morning, Heidi," I said.

She didn't answer, just peered at me with narrow eyes and messed-up hair.

"I want some too," she said.

"Of course," I said.

"Hi, John," she said.

"Hi," said John.

I put a plate and spoon out for her.

"Are you all right here on your own for a few minutes?" I said.

Heidi nodded and started eating. I went into the study again, leaving the door ajar so I could hear them, and tried to get back into it again. It was harder without music, but only a few minutes later I was writing again, about a trip Geir Angell and I had made to Søgne just after his mother's funeral, when I'd been doing a reading at a rural high school. I had no idea exactly why I was writing about it, apart from the feeling the room had given me then, in the darkness under the glittering stars of winter.

"Daddy?" said Heidi all of a sudden behind me, and nearly gave me a heart attack.

"What's the matter?" I said, swiveling around.

"John wants out of his chair."

I got up and went back into the kitchen, lifted him into the air, and put him down again on the floor. His diaper was so heavy it hung between his legs. I tore open the tapes at the sides and dumped it in the bin under the sink, told him to stay put, which

91

he did, went and got a clean one from the bathroom, then put it on him under Heidi's watchful eye.

"We want a bath," said Heidi.

"Well you can't have one," I said.

"What?" she said.

"You can't have one," I said.

"What?" she said again. It was a habit she'd got into, saying what to everything, sometimes it made her sound like she was slow-witted. I didn't care for it.

"No," I said. "You're not taking a bath."

She twisted her face angrily at me, then turned to her brother, who was down on all fours immersed in something over by the base of the wall.

"Come on, John," she said. "We'll go and play in the living room!"

It was five past six. The buses had started running outside. Their dull, heavy sounds were like groans. I went into the bedroom to wake Linda up. Vanja was asleep beside her. She usually came in from their room in the night, sometimes she was already asleep in our bed when we turned in for the night. We'd only just managed to get her to sleep in her own bed when Heidi was born, but Linda felt so sorry for her then that she let her sleep with us instead, and from then on she'd insisted we stay with her until she fell asleep. Only that wasn't enough, so if she woke up on her own she'd come into our room.

"It's ten past six," I said. "Heidi and John are already up. Can you get up now, do you think, so I can get a bit of work done?"

"Mm," she said.

I switched on the computer on the desk, logged on to my e-mail, and without expecting anything checked to see if any new messages had come in during the night. Fortunately, the only thing in the in-box was the *Agderposten's* daily news update which I'd been receiving every morning ever since the time I tried to access their archive to see if I could find anything in it about Dad. There'd been some technical glitch that meant I never got in, but they'd got my address and I'd never quite managed to remove my name from their mailing list. Still, it could be quite nice, too, scanning its small-town news stories in the mornings. I deleted it and Googled myself, finding nothing new, surfed around a bit, and then, without Linda having stirred in the slightest, went back into the study again, closed the door behind me, put some music on, and tried to get back into it again. But the little break had been enough to put me off. When I got started in the mornings, my mind was as yet undisturbed by anything else, and the transition from sleep to text was smooth and fluid. As the day progressed I had to expend more energy to surmount an increasing resistance, and by the time the afternoon came around, the only thing I could do to eliminate it was sleep and start again.

It took nearly an hour to get into the swing of things again. Not long afterward, Linda knocked on the door wanting to know if there were any clean socks anywhere or if they could just have bare feet in their sandals. I swiveled around and gave her my coldest look. She closed the door hard again. I was seething. Their voices came from the hall, Vanja and Heidi shouting at each other. I sensed she was having problems getting them to cooperate and felt guilty enough to go out and see if I could help, though not guilty enough to look her in the eye. I stood behind Vanja, gripped her foot, and thrust it into her sandal.

"*Ai!*" she cried. Ow!

Always, always a Swedish *ai!*, never a Norwegian *au!*

I pushed the little straps through, bent them back, and pressed them tight against the Velcro or whatever it was.

"Have they got sunscreen on?" I asked.

"I don't think they'll need any today," Linda replied.

"Are their teeth brushed?"

"John's are. Heidi's and Vanja's aren't. We haven't got that far yet."

I tore open the bathroom door, stuck the two toothbrushes under the running tap, squeezed the toothpaste on, and went out again, handed one to Linda, and stood in front of Heidi with the other.

"Open your mouth," I said.

She pressed her lips together.

Sometimes it was for fun, but not this time; the look she gave me was narrow and rebellious.

"Is it because I've been in a bad mood?" I asked.

She nodded.

"Well, I'm not anymore," I said. "Do you think you could open your mouth now?"

She didn't.

"You don't want me to use force, do you?"

"What?"

"Use force. To make you brush your teeth, even though you don't want to."

"What?"

"I'm finished!" said Vanja, and flashed her sister a cheeky smile. John stood trying to open the front door, he was on tiptoes and had managed to get his fingers on the handle, but couldn't quite get the grip to pull it down.

"Mommy has to do it," said Heidi.

"Okay," I said, handing the toothbrush to Linda, for whom Heidi immediately opened her mouth and bared her teeth.

"Have a nice time," I said.

No one answered.

"You could at least say goodbye," I said, looking at Linda.

"Bye then," she said. "But I'm coming back before I go."

"Okay," I said, and returned to the study. I sat there motionless in the chair and waited until I heard them get into the elevator, then the elevator as it began its descent through the building, before clicking on the minimized document that within a second unfolded on the screen in front of me.

Linda came back half an hour later. I went out to say hello, she wanted us to sit with a coffee on the balcony, and we sat there for ten minutes each smoking a cigarette and hardly exchanging a word.

"Have a nice time all of you while I'm gone," she said when eventually she stood with her suitcase in front of her in the hall.

"I'm sure we will," I said.

"I'll give you a call before their bedtime tonight, is that okay?"

"Of course. Take it easy up there. And say hello to Helena and . . ."

"Fredrik. I will."

We kissed each other, she closed the door behind her and I went and checked my e-mails, one from Play.com, otherwise nothing, before going back into the study, where I sat down and started writing again. I spent half an hour talking to Geir Angell on the phone, ate a packet of cold fish cakes for lunch, made a fresh pot of coffee, and then when I came back in from the balcony there was an e-mail from Gunnar.

The subject line said "Verbal rape."

Opening it was out of the question.

I stood up and went through the apartment, grabbing the phone on the way, sat down on the balcony, and called Geir Angell again.

"That wouldn't be you again, would it?" he said.

"I just got an e-mail," I said.

"From your uncle?"

"Yeah."

"And he doesn't like you?"

"Don't know, I haven't read it. I'm too scared."

"How bad can it be? Get in the game. Stop being an ostrich."

"The subject line says 'Verbal rape.'"

"Like I said."

"I'll have to read it," I said. "Might as well get it over with. Listen, I'll send it on to you, you can read it as well, and I'll call you back right after. Okay?"

"Sure."

We hung up and I lit a cigarette and stared out across the rooftops. My heart was beating so fast it felt like it was trying to get out.

Verbal rape.

I swallowed a mouthful of coffee. I thought about going for a walk somewhere and leaving it for a bit, sitting in a park maybe, or looking in the shops. But I knew the thought of what the e-mail might contain wouldn't let go of me, that I wouldn't be able to relax whatever I did.

I got to my feet and went into the bedroom, clicked on his message even before sitting down, and read it through as fast as I could, as if the dread consisted in the encounter between my eyes and his words on the screen, rather than in what they said.

I'd imagined all kinds of things, but not this.

It was as if he were standing there screaming. It was my mother who was behind the novel, he wrote. She hated the Knausgaards, and always had. For all those years, she had indoctrinated me with her hatred, brainwashed me, until eventually I had lost contact with the real world completely and written this despicable, immoral, and self-centered shambles of a book so I could get back at the family and line my pockets. It was an act far worse than anything I believed my father had ever done to me when I was growing up. The source of all my books was my mother, all of them carried the mark of her hidden revenge motives. They were riddled with untruths, mean-spirited depictions, and an outlook on human nature he found completely alien to the family. I needed therapy.

He wrote that he was holding the publishing director personally responsible and would be taking action for damages if the manuscript came out. He left his e-mail unsigned.

Having read the e-mail, I barely managed to get to my feet again. I couldn't think straight. All I knew, as I typed Geir Angell's address and forwarded the e-mail to him, was that I had to talk to someone. I went through the apartment again. I stood in front of the window in the living room and glanced down at the square below, went into the kitchen and stared out at the roof-tops, went into the children's room, glanced around, Heidi and Vanja's bunk beds, John's crib, turned and went out again, into the bathroom, turned on the tap and washed my hands, went into the living room, opened the door of the long balcony, the sun was shining and it was hot, I gripped the railing and leaned forward to look down on all the people below as they passed along the sidewalk, let go and went back inside, paced the floor, and then I made a decision, there was a document attached to the e-mail, I might as well read that too, it certainly couldn't get any worse.

It was a letter addressed to Sissel Norunn Hatløy, my mother. In it, he informed her that he had now read "the author's" latest manuscript. It was such that he had no words to describe what he thought of me. But he did so anyway. A concentration of the most negative characteristics imaginable. I glorified myself, I was a helpless wretch, a base individual. The strange thing, Gunnar wrote, was that the people I was attacking were the Knausgaards, whereas she, my mother, was completely untarnished. Not a single word against her had the author written. Why? His own picture of her was rather different, he wrote: she had neglected Yngve and me entirely when we were growing up, all she had been interested in was herself and what he called her quasi-philosophical ego, which I was now perpetuating. Not a thought for other people, only herself. No empathy, no feelings of solicitude, only self-infatuation. She ought to have been a pillar for my father when we needed her most, but she hadn't. He called it neglect. That was the essence, the important thing. I had never understood that because she had brainwashed me. I believed everything she said, and because she hated the Knausgaards I hated them too. Then he went on to describe the way he remembered her when she first came into their family.

He'd been only a young man at the time, and Mom's presence had clearly made an impression on him, because he used the strongest words to describe the way she came across, so cold and inhospitable anyone would think it was a glacier he

97

was describing. There was no warmth in her, and no personality, she took no part in the family's life together, but would sit on her own in a corner, reading a magazine, occasionally scowling at them as she puffed on her cigarette. She communicated with no one and never had a kind word for any child in her vicinity, which I took to be referring to himself. It went on: she never once invited him to their home after he grew up, and never paid a visit to see his children, and in the company of his own sociable and loving mother she seemed positively miserable. In his words, he had felt sorry for his elder brother having to live with Mom and had always wondered why she turned out the way she had, what could have made her come across so unpleasantly, and he recalled a trip to Vestland to visit her and her family when he was twelve years old. He described her mother, my grandmother, as autistic, racked with all manner of neuroses and feelings of inferiority. He referred to the farm where they lived as wretched and called it a peasant smallholding. When he met my grandmother at the time, when he was twelve, he realized how such an abnormal desire to be someone could arise in her daughter, and how her son, my uncle Kjartan, could end up writing poetry about crows, something he apparently considered as ridiculous as it was inane and shameful. My mother lacked upbringing, had never developed any ability to show empathy or solicitude, to create a loving, caring environment, and this she had passed on to me, who suffered from exactly the same deficiencies.

He was writing to her to underline the fact that she remained responsible for me, who he referred to as "your friendless son," now that I was so completely far gone as was the case. He likened me to Dad, stating that I was just as unreliable as he had been and suffered from the same personality disorder. Then he compared me to Mom and declared that I was just as cynical and lacking in empathy as her. But was that anywhere in the book? No, that perspective, which apparently was the true perspective, was totally absent. Mom's culpability in Dad's demise was obvious to anyone who cared to see, he believed. Dad never got what he needed from her, which was to say love, intimacy, companionship, warmth. Gunnar had realized this even at the age of twelve, but to his brother, Dad, such an insight had come all too late.

By way of conclusion he asked her to get me to stop the project and to find me a place in a psychiatric ward somewhere instead. Otherwise, if we went ahead and the book got published, he would take action for damages. He was going to put a stop to this hateful attack on the Knausgaard family, which she was behind, by whatever means might be necessary.

The letter was signed not in his name, but as my father's brother.

I lay down on the bed and remained there motionless. Suddenly, this moment was all there was. I can't recall its exact nature or how it felt, eighteen months having passed since, and I am no longer in the grip of its explosive alarm. I can comprehend it, and even comprehend it well, but I can't resurrect it. Reading those messages again now, I am filled with the most unpleasant emotions, and they confirm to me something I've always known, always felt, but compared to the force by which it became apparent to me at the time, this is merely a shadow. During those days in August 2009 it paralyzed me totally. If I'd had even the slightest inkling that such anger lay in store for me I might have been able to prepare myself for it and thereby have softened the impact, or, and even more probable, simply not written the novel in the first place. But in all the time I'd been working on it I had never, not once, anticipated a reaction remotely like it.

The phone rang in the hall.

It had to be Gunnar.

There was no way I could speak to him. It would be the same as when I'd done something wrong as a boy and heard Dad's door open downstairs. He's coming. He's coming.

But it could have been Geir Gulliksen or Geir Berdahl, too, seeing as how the e-mail had been sent to them as well.

I jumped to my feet and dashed into the hall. Just as I got there it stopped ringing. I lifted it from the charger and pressed to see incoming calls.

10, said the display.

It meant the call was from a hidden number. Geir Angell's was always a hidden number, so it was probably him. I usually joked about it being only the police and Geir whose numbers couldn't be seen. But it wasn't only a joke, because somewhere deep down I was still expecting a call from the police.

I took the phone with me out onto the balcony and called Geir.

"Hello, Gunnar speaking," he said. "Is that my despicable, friendless nephew? How dare you call this number?"

"Did you just call?" I said.

"Well, if you're going to be like that about it, yes," he said. "What's up, are you in a bad mood now?"

"Bad isn't the word. Have you read his e-mail?"

"Of course I have. He has a fine turn of phrase, your uncle, hasn't he?"

"He has, yes."

"I couldn't stop laughing."

"I bet you couldn't."

"Forget about him. He's angry with you. It's not hard to understand. But that's all it is. It's not like you've done anything wrong."

"Obviously I have. And he's going to take me to court. I don't doubt him for a second."

"But that'll be excellent! You should hope he does, it'd be the stupidest thing he could do. You'll be rolling in money! Everyone'll be wanting your books if it comes to a court case! This is literary history in the making. And you'll be a millionaire. There's no better scenario."

"I can think of a couple."

"Come on! What have you done exactly? You've written a book about your life, from where you stand. It's all about liberty. Liberty's something you take. If it's given, then you're a slave.

100

You wanted to write about your life the way it is. There's a price for that. That price is what you're looking at now. You didn't think about your uncle, which means you've been thoughtless. That's what it costs. Yes, he's angry with you. Yes, I can understand that. He's entitled to be angry with you, from where he stands. But that's where it ends. Do you get what I'm saying? You haven't written anything bad about him. You've written about your own father. That's your prerogative, your fucking inheritance, that's what he left you. No one can deny you that. They can be angry with you, they can be seething mad, they can make life difficult for you and your family, but that's it. You didn't do anything wrong. You have my complete forgiveness. It's only a pity I wasn't a Catholic priest."

"Yeah."

"What do you mean *yeah*? Get a grip, man. You'll be rich. You should be laughing."

"It's no laughing matter."

"Of course it is! And reading that e-mail made me realize where all this is coming from. You're not the only lunatic in the family. You're all like that. Your dad, your uncle, you."

I said nothing. Predictably, his attempts at cheering me up weren't helping in the slightest, but I was glad he was trying nevertheless. We talked for an hour or so, about the same thing the whole time, the letters and the new situation they had presented us with. Geir thought I should just go with the flow. Moralizing had never created anything of its own, all it did was reject the created. And the created was the same as life itself. Why reject life?

Geir was a Nietzschean through and through. He could see things from the outside, that was his strength, but at the same time it meant that outside was where he was. I was in the middle of it all, and if there was anything in which I could find no comfort it was vitalism, because vitalism was the same as transgression, and if this was about anything, it was basically about fear of trangression.

As we talked, the phone beeped for an incoming call. I ignored it the first time, but when it came again I said to Geir I'd have to hang up and see who it was.

At first the display said simply there was an incoming call. I didn't take it, it could have been anybody. But then the number appeared. It was from Oslo. For all I knew, Gunnar could have been in Oslo, but the chances were slender, and besides I thought I recognized the first three digits, they belonged to the publisher Oktober.

I pressed the green key and put the receiver to my ear at the same time as I opened the door and went into the living room.

"Hello?" I said, going over to the window.

"Hi, it's Geir Berdahl."

"Hi."

"I got the e-mail from your uncle."

"Yes," I said.

He laughed uneasily. I stood at the window and put my forehead against the cool glass.

"Strong stuff."

"Yes."

"We need to tackle this properly."

"Yes."

I went over to the bookshelf and stared at the titles.

"We need to accommodate your uncle as far as possible. And we need to give ourselves some room to maneuver. We certainly can't allow him to make this a matter for the courts. I'm assuming it's not a problem for you to change the names of everyone on your father's side of the family?"

"No, not at all," I said, and went over to the opposite wall, turned and went back. "No, no problem. I offered to do that in the letter I sent him."

"Good. Then I can tell him we're changing the names. And anonymizing what needs to be anonymized, as far as we can."

"Yes."

"I'll get in touch with a law firm we use. Just so that you know.

We need to be sure that whatever we do is current and aboveboard, you realize that, of course."

"Yes."

"You've certainly got his back up, though, haven't you?"

"I'll say."

I went into the kitchen and stood there looking at the row of cupboards above the sink. I went into the kitchen and stood there looking at the row of cupboards above the sink, one of them was open, one of the shelves, the one where we kept the glasses, was nearly empty. They must have been in the dishwasher.

"He might just want to put the wind up you a bit," he said.

"He has."

"All right, Karl Ove. Keep working at this as best you can. I'll call back once I've spoken to the lawyers."

"Okay."

"Bye for now."

"Bye," I said, and hung up. I went back into the living room, then through the hall to the bathroom, where I turned on a tap and rinsed my hands in hot water. I went outside onto the balcony, but realized I couldn't sit there and smoke on my own, it would be too empty and still, so I went and got the phone I'd put down on the kitchen counter and called Linda.

"Hi!" she said.

"You sound happy," I said, going back into the living room and stepping up to the window. "Have you arrived?"

"No, I'm still on the train. I slept for a bit. Now I'm reading. What about you?"

"Not so good, I'm afraid. I got an e-mail from Gunnar. He's seething. Out of his mind with rage, pretty much."

"Oh no," she said. "What does he say?"

"You can read it when you get back. He wants to stop the book getting published, and if he can't he says he'll take us to court."

"You're joking?"

"I'm afraid not. It's about as bad as you can imagine."

"I can tell from your voice. Do you want me to come home again? I will if you want."

"No, no. No. Definitely not. Don't even think about it. You deserve this little break on your own. Everything's fine here. It's just the shock, that's all. It'll pass. I spoke to Geir Berdahl from Oktober, they're getting the lawyers in and trying to patch things up as best they can. I'm in good hands. Everything's fine."

"Are you sure?"

"Yes."

"Okay."

"I just wanted you to know, that's all. Apart from that, every-thing's fine. I'll give you a call tonight, we can talk about it some more then if you want. Is that okay?"

It was okay. Linda had never met Gunnar, but she'd heard a lot about him. And it had left an impression on her that he'd stood there in the garden at Mom's without wanting to come in and meet the children or Linda herself. He was also the only one of those invited who hadn't come to Vanja's christening. Neither of these occurrences had seemed odd to me at the time; in the garden he was in a hurry, and as for the christening he simply hadn't been able to come. Now I saw things in a different light, the light of hatred in which he had written his letter. That hatred couldn't have arisen only now, suddenly, merely as a result of the book I had written, it must have been there long before, latent through all those years. I had felt it, had always felt it, and yet always thought it was my own paranoid unease. I didn't think anyone liked me, but that couldn't have been true, not really, he was my father's brother, why wouldn't he like me? If I did some-thing he didn't approve of, wouldn't he give me the benefit of the doubt? That was how I looked at it, to combat what I told myself was all in my head, but now, in the tone of his letter, all sem-blance of such thinking vanished. That was how it was, and it had been like that for a long time, perhaps always. In his view, my writing the book confirmed to him what he had always thought about me. I had a small, though in my own view excessively large ego. I was unreliable and deceitful. I'd always felt it whenever I was with them, that I was deceitful. How did it come to that? If ever there was a thing I disliked and didn't want in my life it was deceit. Deceit could only make others, and thereby myself, look upon me as deceitful.

Why?

There was a simple answer. I had something to hide from them. A part of me I couldn't show or use in their company. And this fact, that there was something I had to avoid at all cost, made my behavior seem furtive in some way, thereby damaging my entire person and character. I tried to be like them when we were together, to talk like them, to be among them in their way, but in recognizing that I wasn't like that at all, like them, among them in their way, he saw through me. The betrayal started there.

I stood for a moment with the phone in my hand, staring through the living-room window at the buildings outside. I couldn't work, I couldn't read, I couldn't watch a film. I couldn't go out and meet someone either, not knowing anyone in Malmö well enough. All I could do was talk to someone on the phone. It wouldn't help, but it would make the moment tolerable, the mere fact of there being someone outside all this who would talk to me about it. So in the two hours that remained of the day, before I had to pick up the children from the nursery, I was on the phone. I talked to Geir Gulliksen about what to do, I talked to Espen, who told me I mustn't change a word of the manuscript, not to give in to pressure, but to dig in and endure, I talked to Tore, who knew what it was like writing about things in a way that approached actual biography and how that could be taken by family, and I talked to Yngve. He was distraught, he'd always got on well with Gunnar and there was no way he wanted to get caught in the crossfire. I told him it was my novel, I was the one who had written it, and that he had nothing at all to do with it, which Gunnar would surely understand. The way I saw it, Gunnar had always liked Yngve, always gone out of his way to keep in touch with him. Finally, I called Mom, she was on her way home from work and hadn't seen his e-mail, but would open it as soon as she got in. By then it was ten to three. I put my white sneakers on, got the keys from the cupboard, took the trash bag with me, and went down into the basement, where I tossed it in one of the big garbage containers, went out through the back door, and followed one of the streets that ran behind the building in the direction of the nursery, the way I always did when I was feeling down and didn't want to be seen by anyone. I recognized the feeling I got when I emerged under the warm, deep-blue sky of August and walked along the exhaust-filled Föreningsgatan, past the cluster of figures who always stood smoking on the corner by the traffic lights, crossed over, went down the little stump of cobbled street up to the next junction with its row of young deciduous trees, dark green and shaded by the tall line of buildings, it was the same feeling I'd had the days after Dad had died, and the days after getting the phone call with its accusation of rape, the way the surroundings seemed almost to be erased, as if I'd wandered inside a zone so charged with force it extinguished everything else in its vicinity. I saw everything, I saw the cars, I saw the Lidl supermarket, I saw the pedestrians and the cyclists, registered what they were wearing, mostly shorts and T-shirts, skirts and dresses, but here and there a nice shirt and trousers, I saw the Montessori school on the other side of the crossing, the African hair salon, the Polish food store, and the row of little antique shops as I walked past, I saw the owner of one sitting on a chair on the sidewalk, as so often before, his old golden retriever dozing next to him, but none of it mattered, it was without substance and possessed no weight. And in this way I saw my own children, too, as they came to greet me in the nursery's backyard. I bent down, I held them tight, because it was what I had to do, but not even that had substance enough for me to extract myself from my mood.

Two of the staff were sitting on a bench chatting while kids ran about playing all around them. The yard was asphalt with at one end a windowless wall maybe six stories high that looked mostly like the wall of a fortress and blocked out the sun for the better part of the day. Up against the wall was the sandpit and next to it a three-meter-tall playhouse. The storeroom on the other side was full of tricycles, bikes with training wheels, buckets and spades, balls and hockey sticks, as well as a miscellany of plastic toys that at the end of the day lay strewn across the entire area. The parents took turns putting in a week's work every six months, besides taking care of administrative duties and the day-to-day cleaning. I had done my best to avoid any position of responsibility, had never involved myself in the committee, for instance, never been in charge of human resources, recruitment, or finance, always making sure to take on the most practical and least prestigious job of all, as part of the cleaning group. It was wholly manual work and it meant cleaning the entire nursery maybe five or six weekends spread over six months. Besides that, I cleaned on the days when the daily cleaning roster said it was my turn. Still, it suited me okay, requiring nothing more than the time it took, so when I was finished that was it. The only drawback was that every time I let myself in to clean on a Sunday evening I felt the strong urge to do a good job, which meant I always ended up spending a lot more time on it than was necessary. Most likely that was the reason I was asked to take charge of the cleaning group after my first six-month stint. I said yes, and from then on was charged with organizing the spring clean as well as drawing up rosters and keeping supplies of everything we needed, which didn't bother me that much, but when the year came to an end and jobs were to be redelegated at the annual meeting, I asked to go back to being an ordinary cleaner again. There was something about the prominence of being in charge that I didn't care for, as well as the fact that it also involved having to pass on any complaints about the cleaning from the staff to the parents who had been sloppy, which happened on occasion, and I could stand there wanting the floor to swallow me up, full of shame at having to inform them, because they were adults, and who was I to tell them they hadn't done their job properly and would have to do it again? I could do it once, twice in a pinch, but that was it.

I went up to the staff. Nadje, who grew up in Iraq and always kept the children under strict control, and Karin, one of the regular supply staff, formerly full-time, who had always felt very affectionate toward my children.

"How did it go today?" I asked.

"Fine," said Nadje. "No problems. John got his cheek scratched, not much, but he had a little cry about it and he's fine now."

"Who scratched him?"

"Heidi did. She said she was sorry," said Karin. "She was just as upset as John."

"Okay," I said. "We'll be off, then."

I turned and called their names. John came right away, but Heidi, pedaling away at top speed over the asphalt with Malou in the trailer behind her, gave no indication of having heard me. Vanja was lying in the sandpit having her legs covered in sand, with Katinka doing the shoveling. I went over to them.

"Come on, it's time to go home," I said.

"*Lite till, pappa, var så snäll,*" said Vanja with a grin. Please, Daddy, just a bit longer.

"Five minutes, that's all," I said, and sat down on the big stone opposite the bench. My body ached, and after having let go of Gunnar for a few seconds my thoughts seemed to return to him with renewed force. I'd been hoping that being with the kids would help and give me a new perspective, but it was just the opposite, I found myself feeling sorry for them having me for a father, for the person they saw and related to wasn't the same as who I was inside, and this would gradually dawn on them when they were old enough to be able to judge the people around them in terms of personal qualities and character traits, rather than just how they appeared to them in ordinary interaction. I wasn't good enough for them, but that wasn't the sad part of it, the sad part was that they didn't know.

"How's Linda?" Karin asked.

"She's fine," I said. "She's away at a friend's in the country at the moment, enjoying a break. Just for a few days."

"That's brave of you, having all the kids on your own."

"No, not at all," I said. "They're no bother."

That they never gave me any trouble was because I was strict with them, far stricter than when Linda was around. I wouldn't put up with things and gave them no leeway. They found this out soon enough and acted accordingly, but it wasn't good. The nursery staff didn't notice, seeing me only at drop-off and pickup times, and in those situations, with so many eyes upon me, my behavior was no different.

For crying out loud.

What a fucking mess.

How the hell could I ever have put myself in such a spot? What was I trying to do? Why couldn't I keep all the badness to myself like other people did? But no, I had to go and shove it in everyone's face, and drag others down with me in the fall.

Gunnar had done nothing apart from living his life as best he could, and now this.

I felt like shaking my fists at the sky and yelling at the top of my lungs. Instead I sat and stared at Heidi as she bombed around on her bike, John, who had climbed up next to Karin and now sat gazing up at the roof, Vanja, whose legs were now almost buried in sand, a stiff smile on my face to indicate how great I thought it was having children.

I stood up and went over to Vanja.

"Time to go home," I said. "No buts."

"But I've got no legs!" she said. "Look!"

"Is there a shark in this sand?" I said.

"No," she said. "I was born like this."

"All right, but it's still time to go."

"Why?"

"*Because.*"

"Okay," she said, getting to her feet again and brushing away the sand that didn't fall off on its own. I went over to John and lifted him into the air, he giggled until he realized he was going in the stroller, but after protesting a bit he gave in. Now only Heidi was left. I wasn't in the mood to look for her and shouted for her to come right away. When she didn't, I pressed the button for the gate, walked the stroller over toward it with Vanja holding tight and then opened it. "We're going home, Heidi," I shouted, and with that she came running.

"*Vänta!*" she called out. "*Vänta!*"

"Yes, we're waiting," I said. "But you didn't come when you were called!"

In a sulk, she gripped the stroller without speaking. Sometimes all I had to do was look at her and wink, or make a face as if I was angry with her, for her sulk to dissolve into a smile, often a devilish one at that, and then came the annoyance at having been fooled, at which point she would hit me, but with a gleam in her eyes. Other times her resentment lay deeper. This was one of those times.

We walked along the sidewalk, the street was full of cyclists, people on their way home from work. Vanja couldn't stop talking. I listened with half an ear in case she looked up at me expecting a reaction of some sort, and noted that she was weighing up the pros and cons of the two breeds of dog she'd been interested in that week. Heidi walked along on the other side of the stroller, silent and in her mood, while John had descended into his usual stroller coma.

"Where's John? Did we leave him behind at the nursery?" I said, thinking he needed some attention too, in case he felt left out.

"Here! I'm here, Papa!" he cried, turning his face to look at me.

"There he is, our little John-boy!" I said, glancing ahead toward the pizza restaurant on the corner, where a few customers were sitting out eating under the green parasols. Some afternoons when I'd come past with the kids the place looked like there was a mafia convention going on inside. Elderly Italian guys in brown suits, short and stocky, with shifty eyes.

I looked back over my shoulder. Behind us, a woman in a black dress came hurrying along, almost dragging a boy by the arm, he was maybe nine years old, they overtook us and about ten meters farther on she shoved him up against the wall, where he pulled his pants down and started pissing while she glanced up and down the street. I couldn't believe my eyes. His piss flowed across the sidewalk.

"What's he doing?" said Vanja, looking from them to me.

"It looks like he's having a pee," I said.

The boy shook himself and zipped up his fly, and then they hurried over the road and continued on along the other sidewalk, whereas we turned left at the bike shop and made our way toward Södra Förstadsgatan. Just before the 7-Eleven we came to a halt. Heidi refused to go a step farther.

"I'm tired," she said.

"Oh, Heidi," I said. "Come on, it's not far, we'll be home in a minute."

She shook her head.

"I want in the stroller," she said.

"But it's not big enough for two, it'll break. Remember when the wheel came off?"

"I want some fruit," she said.

"You can have some fruit, but not here. You can have a banana when we get to the shop."

"I want it from that shop," she said, pointing back from where we came.

"You want to go back?" I said. "All that way?"

"Yes."

Vanja, who was still standing on the other side holding on to the stroller, laughed.

"Vanja," I said. "That's enough, don't interfere."

"She laughed at me," said Heidi. Heidi hated more than anything the feeling that people were laughing at her.

"No, she didn't," I said. "We'll walk on to the shop and you can get some fruit there."

Heidi looked at me. Then she turned and ran off as fast as she could along the sidewalk. She stopped halfway and glared at me in defiance.

"Stay right here, Vanja," I said. "Promise?"

Vanja nodded and I ran after Heidi. As soon as she saw me coming she set off again. As I caught up with her she stopped and wrapped her arms around a lamppost as tightly as she could.

"That's enough from you," I said, wrenching her away and carrying her back to the stroller. She screamed at the top of her lungs. People stopped and stared. It was what she wanted. But they couldn't see that. They thought I was hitting her or something. I thought the same thing myself whenever I saw mothers or fathers stooped over their children like that, their aggressive body language always made me think they had to be bad parents, people of the worst possible kind, even though I knew what it was like.

I put her down.

She yelled and said she wasn't going anywhere.

"Do you want me to carry you?"

She shook her head.

"What do you suggest then?"

"*Jag vill ha en frukt! Från* den *affären!*" she yelled. I want fruit! From that shop!

I lost control immediately. I grabbed her hard by the arm, pushed my face into hers, and hissed at her.

"That's enough from you! Do you understand? Come here!"

Tears streamed down her cheeks.

"Do you hear me?"

"I won't!" she screamed. "*Du är dum! Du är en skitpappa!*" You're stupid! You're a horrible daddy!

"What did you say?" I spat, trying to keep my voice down so as to not give anyone watching ammunition.

"*Du är en skitpappa!*" she said.

Vanja grinned.

"It's nothing to smile about!" I said, and right away her face changed to serious. But then, for some incomprehensible reason, I smiled too, and Vanja started to laugh.

"You're all laughing at me!" Heidi yelled. And then she ran off again. This time she only made it a couple of meters before I caught her and hauled her back over my shoulder, then held her out in front of me.

"Are you going to walk with us?"

She shook her head.

"Put me down!" she shouted.

"Do you want me to ask John if he'll walk? So you can sit in the stroller?"

She nodded.

John, realizing what was happening, was already gripping the stroller tightly with both hands.

The thought occurred to me that Heidi might have a bruise on her arm in the morning. It made me think of a case I'd read about, in Norway, a registered nanny who had broken a child's leg forcing him into his stroller.

"Come on, John," I said. "I'll carry you, and Heidi can sit in the stroller."

"My stroller," said John.

"I'll carry him," said Vanja.

He went for it! I lifted him onto her back, he put his arms around her and held tight while Heidi got into the stroller, and our little circus procession finally set off again. Vanja could only manage as far as the 7-Eleven, but being out of the stroller already, John didn't mind at all being carried on my arm instead.

Heidi had fallen asleep even before we got to the supermarket. So that was why, she really had been tired. I bought some falukorv sausage, a recipe mix for beef stroganoff, a packet of rice, ingredients for a salad, milk and yogurt, a large Pepsi Max. I was angry with myself for taking my frustrations out on the children. And yet it didn't stop me being strict with Vanja as we passed through the supermarket. No, I said. No, you're not having one of those. Come here, now. Come here, I said! Oh no, you don't! It was like somehow existing on different levels, all of which had suddenly become active at the same time. One that was absorbed in the letter from Gunnar and an almost savage feeling of despair. One that was thinking about what to have for dinner, and that steered the shopping cart around the store accordingly. One that regretted having treated Heidi the way I had before. One that was annoyed by Vanja's behavior. One that was sad to see her obey, because maybe it meant I was strangling her spirit. One that was pleased she did as she was told.

The arm I was using to carry John was aching from his weight by the time it got to be our turn at the checkout. I put him down so I could place the groceries on the conveyor and he ambled off to the end and tried to climb up, it was one of those things he liked to do, to kneel on the shelf underneath and watch the groceries come gliding along. I lifted him up, then took the last items from the cart, inserted my card into the card reader, keyed in my PIN number, confirmed the amount when it appeared on the display, removed the card, and slid it back in my pocket.

I bagged the groceries, lifted John onto my arm, and then we set off home.

"Who did you play with at *dagis* today?" I said, and looked at Vanja, mostly to see if she was feeling affected by my harshness. "Benjamin or Katinka? Or Lovisa?"

"*Inte Lovisa*," she said. Not Lovisa. "*Og liiite Benjamin.*" And Benjamin a teeny bit.

A beggar, one of the most active, had stationed himself outside the bank. He was on his knees with his hands folded in front of him, rocking backward and forward as he glared at the passersby. In front of him was a cap with some coins in it.

"Why's he sitting like that?" said Vanja.

"He's begging," I said. "He wants money."

"Why hasn't he got any money?"

"I don't know," I said. "He probably doesn't have a job. So he begs to get money for food."

"Why didn't you give him any?"

"Because he's not doing anything. If he'd been playing an instrument or something I'd have given him some. That's what I usually do, anyway. But sometimes I might give something to beggars anyway. If I feel sorry for them. Never much, though."

"Why didn't you give him any then?"

"What a lot of questions," I said, and smiled.

She smiled back.

"He's most probably from Eastern Europe. That's a group of countries a long way away. They come here to beg for money. They're a kind of gang."

"A gang of thieves? Are they thieves?"

"Not exactly. But they've basically made it their job. Which means there's no point begging anymore. Begging's not a job."

I laughed at my reasoning and Vanja smiled at me. I picked up speed so we could cross while the light was still green. On the other side of the road, the old saxophonist sat playing his amputated little tune. Now I'd have to give him something. I dipped into my pocket and fished out what was there, stared at the coins that lay in my palm, and handed Vanja five kronor.

"Do you want to give him this?" I asked.

She looked up at me with fright in her eyes. Then she nodded, a grave little nod, and stepped forward almost on tiptoe, slow, measured paces, and tossed the coin into his open instrument case. He winked at her, and she scurried back to my side.

We needed to get some fruit as well. The stall didn't take cards, so I put John down on the ground and waited my turn at the ATM, glancing at the faces of those standing around or passing the long curve of the building that occupied one corner of the square and on whose top floor we lived. I was keeping an eye out for Gunnar. I knew the chances of him turning up here were minimal, but there was little that was rational about this, it was basically all feelings, and the depths of those feelings were unfathomable.

The woman in front of me, with short sandy hair and glasses and an almost cone-shaped body, snatched her receipt from the machine and stuck her card back in her pocket, casting a quick wary glance at me. I inserted my card and tapped in my PIN, withdrew three hundred kronor, and checked to see what John was doing while I waited for the transaction to complete, he was already on his way over to the fruit stall, hugging the wall of the building, small as a tree stump.

"Do you want to hold the money, Vanja?" I said.

"Can I keep it?"

"No, but you can pay for the fruit."

"I don't want to."

"Okay," I said. "Give it to me then, I'll do it. Look at John, have you seen him? Do you think he's forgotten all about us?"

She laughed when she realized he'd gone over to the shoe shop. I wheeled the stroller over to the stall, then trotted off to bring him back, picked out a bunch of bananas, put some apples and oranges in a couple of bags, filled another with green grapes, and handed the whole lot to the stallholder, who I supposed was from Turkey, or perhaps Macedonia or Albania. He weighed the fruit and put it all in a big white carrier bag, I handed him some money, and when he gave me the change I saw he'd knocked eight kronor off the price, I thanked him and crossed the square with Heidi still asleep in the stroller, handed the key card to Vanja, who held it up to the panel and pushed the door open. I wheeled the stroller inside and turned it around so I could drag it up the two steps. Heidi's head bumped this way and that, but without her waking up. John was already at the elevator, trying to reach up and press the button.

"You're too little," I said. "Try again next year."

"Lift me up!" he said.

I did, and held him up so he could see the elevator through the small rectangular window in the door when it came gliding down to find us.

When we got upstairs I pushed the stroller into the hall. If I woke Heidi up now she'd cry and whine for an hour at least, and I wasn't in the mood. The price for leaving her be was that she wouldn't be able to sleep when she went to bed tonight.

I put a film on for them so I could make the dinner in peace.

Then I gave them each an apple, got the groceries out of the bags and sorted them, fruit in the fruit bowl in the cupboard, milk in the fridge, vegetables on the counter, falukorv on the chopping board. I'd thought about boiling some rice but changed my mind, there was still some macaroni left, we could have that instead. I went and got the phone in the hall, called Geir Angell, measured out some water and milk, put it in a saucepan, added the recipe mix, and started stirring all before he answered.

"What are you up to?" I asked. "You normally answer right away."

"I was in the bath, my book got wet and I had to dry it with the hair dryer."

"The hair dryer?"

"That's right, the hair dryer."

I made an incision in the tight dark red sheath of plastic around the sausage, tore it away, and began chopping the meat into little chunks.

"How's it going?" Geir asked. "Still as bad?"

"Still as bad."

I filled another saucepan with water and put it on the heat.

"He's got me in his power. Him turning against me is the worst that could happen. But being scared stiff of him is only part of it. There's the issue itself. I've offended him. He didn't do anything, he didn't ask for this. And once it gets published he won't be able to defend himself against it either. It's his mother, after all. They're real people."

"Have you ever been in doubt about it?" Geir asked.

"No, but you know what it's like when you're writing."

"I know what it's like to be written about."

"You didn't call for two days. You were pissed off with me."

"At first, yes. But then I thought about it. I think Ernst Billgren got it right when he was asked to comment on having appeared in *Den högsta kasten*. He said he was aware there was a character in the book with the same name as him. In my case, I can't see it that way, what you've written about is too close to home for that, but the point is that he indicates an escape route that's open to any person in a novel. There's a character in that book who's got the same name as me."

"But you're a literary person. I've never seen a book in Gunnar's house. I don't think he reads. That makes it a different thing altogether."

"You talk about him like he was defenseless! For God's sake, didn't you read what he wrote? He's making you out to be half-baked! And sending it off to your publisher! He's out to destroy you, Karl Ove. He's not defenseless. You can't just sit there and let him get on with it. I bet you've even thought about not publishing the book at all?"

"That goes without saying."

"In which case you'd be letting an accountant in Kristiansand decide the path of Norwegian literature. You can't do that, can you?"

"I will publish it."

I went to the cupboard and got the box of macaroni out, shook some into the boiling water, stirred a bit with a fork, and turned the heat down.

"The question is by what right. The right of literature? That means I'm saying literature is more important than the life of the individual. And not only that, I'm saying my literature is more important than his life."

"But it's not his life! It's your father's life. He's the brother, you're the son. The son's closer."

I angled the chopping board over the saucepan and scraped the chunks of sausage into the sauce, took four plates out of the cupboard and put them on the table, opened the drawer, and got the knives and forks out.

"And then there's the law," I said.

"The law can't preside over literature."

"Of course it can."

"Of course it *does*, would be more accurate. Mykle was taken to court, but his book still gets read."

"There's a big difference between offending the sexual morals of the day and offending an individual. Besides, there was another aspect to the Mykle case. Maybe it was what broke him in the end. The people he wrote about recognized themselves. And not just in any old context. All the women he slept with recognized themselves in his descriptions. That was what the scandal was really all about. Tarjei Vesaas spoke about it, as far as I remember, once he realized. 'Rather unfortunate,' he said. Something like that, anyway."

"Ha ha ha!"

"You can laugh, but Vesaas was a decent man. Maybe the most decent Norwegian ever. If he says something isn't good, you can be damn sure of it."

"Didn't you say they found an envelope full of Marilyn Monroe cuttings among his things after he died?"

"I did, yes. Even in sin he was decent."

"Sounds like it."

I got four glasses out of the cupboard, turned off the two rings on the cooker, and filled a jug with water.

"Anyway, I've got to go," I said. "I've got the dinner ready."

"Are you going to be okay?" he said.

"Yes, yes. I just have to get through it, that's all."

"What exactly are you scared of anyway?"

"What, do you think the papers aren't going to write about it? That they're just going to let it pass without mention? It's going to be a storm. I'm going to be all over every newspaper in the land."

"Lie back and think about how rich you're going to be instead."

I didn't bother answering, and went into the hall.

"Cheer up. It'll be fun!"

"Speak to you later," I said.

"Hope so."

"All right."

I hung up and put the phone back in the charger.

119

"Dinner's ready," I called into the living room. Vanja said something I didn't catch. I went in.

"John's asleep," she said.

He was lying there like a little cushion in a corner of the sofa.

"We're the only two awake, then," I said.

"Mm," she replied, immersed in a film, *Totoro*.

"Dinner's ready," I said.

"Can I have mine in front of the television? Please?"

"Seeing as it's only you," I said. "And if you promise not to make a mess."

She nodded. I went back into the kitchen and transferred the macaroni into a colander, then spooned some onto the plate, dished some of the sausage stroganoff onto it, cut a tomato into wedges that I placed next to the sauce for the sake of presentation, and took the whole thing into the living room and put it in front of her. I wasn't hungry in the slightest and made do with chomping a tomato on my way into the bedroom to check my e-mail. There was nothing more from Gunnar, and nothing from anyone else involved. Still, just seeing his name, and the subject he'd given his e-mail, "Verbal rape," was enough to petrify me. I stretched out on the bed and stared up at the ceiling. The fear and dread came back in full. I couldn't use the children to keep me going, that wasn't good, they were supposed to need me, not the other way around.

I got to my feet and went to the bathroom, found the blue IKEA bags, and spent a couple of minutes sorting through the pile of dirty clothes, telling myself I'd have to go down in the morning after I'd dropped the children off and see if there was a slot so I could do the washing, then all of a sudden I couldn't be bothered and went back through the hall, stopping in the doorway to check on Vanja, she had a forkful of food paused in front of her mouth, completely spellbound by what she was watching.

Totoro roared. It was a terrifying roar, but he was good at heart, that much was obvious, and there was something reassuring about it.

The phone rang.

I looked at the display.

Linda.

I answered.

"Hello?" I said.

"Hi, it's me," she said. "How're things?"

"Good," I said.

"Did you get home all right?"

"Yes, everything went fine."

"Can I have a word with them?"

"Heidi and John are asleep. I'll see if Vanja wants to."

I held the receiver against my chest as I went into the living room.

"Do you want to say hello to Mommy?" I asked.

"Can you pause it?" she said.

I nodded and she reached her hand out for the phone.

"Hi," she said, and went out of the room. I looked around for the remote, finding it on the bookshelf, pressed pause, and went out after her. She'd gone into their room. When she saw me she closed the door.

She'd grown up so much she wanted to be left alone when she was on the phone!

I checked on Heidi, she was still asleep in the stroller. Then John, he was asleep too. I opened the door onto the balcony, lit a cigarette, took a few drags, stubbed it out, and went in again. I didn't know what to do with myself, too much on edge to sit down.

I went into the kitchen and filled a glass with water from the tap, downing it in one gulp. I got some coffee going, and the sound it made as it began to trickle through the machine was soothing, I'd been hearing it all my life and had always connected it with something good.

All I wanted was to lie down next to someone who could run their fingers through my hair and tell me everything was going to be all right.

I hadn't wanted that since I was a little boy.

No one had ever done that then. Now there was someone who could, if only I let her. I never had. There was something shameful about it, degrading almost.

Nevertheless, it was what I wanted.

I went into the hall and opened the door of the children's room. Vanja had climbed onto the desk and stood there chatting away.

"Can you give me the phone back when you've finished talking?" I said.

"I'm finished now," she said. "Bye."

She handed me the phone.

"It's me again," I said, and went down the hall. "What did she tell you?"

Linda laughed.

"All about what she did today."

"She didn't tell me anything," I said. "And as soon as I gave her the phone she went into her own room, as if she didn't want me to listen."

"It was so nice talking to her. She's such a big girl all of a sudden."

"She is, yes."

"How are you feeling?" Linda asked.

"Not so good. It'll get better, I suppose. I miss you."

"I miss you, too. Do you think you could call back later?"

"Yes, of course," I said.

"I think we're having a barbecue. Maybe if you phone about ten-ish?"

"Fine. Speak to you then."

"Bye."

I hung up. Vanja had resumed the film herself. She'd barely touched her dinner.

"Can't you eat something?" I said. She sighed, took two mouthfuls, then pushed the plate away.

"Is that all?"

"I'm not hungry."

"But you'll be pestering me for a sandwich soon. It's better to eat your dinner."

"I'm not hungry, I said."

Now it was my turn to sigh. I picked up the plate and took it into the kitchen, leaving it on the table for her to eat later, went out onto the balcony, looked down at the square, went inside again, looked at the clock on the kitchen wall, half past five, then went into the bedroom and checked my e-mail. Nothing. I opened a couple of online newspapers, *Aftenposten* and *Dagbladet*, then *NRK*, and after that a couple of book blogs I half kept up with. One of them had come to my attention after I'd been invited to contribute an article. I declined, but would sometimes read what others were posting there, mostly one-book authors, occasionally someone better known. Those who commented all seemed to be people who were writing and wanted to get published, they were especially interested in the process and anything that had to do with the way publishers worked. The way they looked at literature and the things they wrote about authors were for the most part childish, they got steamed up about the slightest thing and seemed to view themselves as important people with important opinions.

It struck me that was exactly how Gunnar saw me.

It was almost word for word. I had a small though in my own view excessively large ego, he had written.

In other words I was a small person, yet blind to the fact, considering myself important, and what I did to be equally important.

It was a rather accurate description, I was indeed a small person. But the high thoughts I had were not about myself, but about what I did, or was capable of doing. In more positive frames of mind I believed I could achieve something big one day. But could a small person create something big? Didn't external greatness have to be founded on internal greatness?

How could I dismiss the people who posted comments on the blog as inconsequential? I was elevating myself above them, and so I was the same as them, important in my own eyes.

In my own eyes I was a better writer than most. Only seldom did I read the work of another novelist and think, I could never do this. But after my first novel came out that was how I looked at it, what I had written was so close to my own person I told myself anyone could do the same thing, all they had to do was write. Yet with the second book I had not only written in the third person, but also told a story as far removed from myself and my own reality as I could. That extended my radius. The unattainable for me was closely bound up with the person who had written it. Thomas Bernhard, for instance, what he wrote and achieved was completely out of my reach. Jon Fosse the same. But not a writer like Jonathan Franzen. Him I could match, and probably even surpass. The same was true of Coetzee, he also was a writer who lacked the distinctive aspect of personality that could take his writing that final stretch of the way; what he wrote didn't seem out of reach to me, and he'd been given the Nobel Prize. The issue was whether or not excellence was bound up with the personal. If that was what made the excellent excellent. And what point could there be in attaining the level below excellence, that which was good, perhaps even recognized internationally as high standard, if the excellent still remained? Clearly, it was because the value lay in the work, not in the appraisal of it. It didn't matter what kind of work you did, you were obliged to do your best. A joiner's work had to be as good and precise as possible. There was satisfaction in that. Should an ordinary joiner, whose work was run-of-the-mill, without panache, who went to work every morning and was there for his family in the afternoons and evenings, be troubled by the existence of a master joiner somewhere in Austria, a joiner who produced the most magnificent work, and ask himself what point there could possibly be in all his own solid yet unspectacular work? Should he lay down his hammer and nails because of that master joiner in Austria?

Of course not. He should carry on with his work, to the best of his abilities. Perhaps even be glad to at least be a better joiner than the one the newspaper had written about only recently, people knew about him, he wasn't as good a joiner as everyone said. His work might seem good, but on closer inspection it was shoddy. Thank goodness one's own work was solid!

The value lay in the work itself, not in the appraisal of it.

But to Gunnar I was nonetheless still a status seeker with ideas above his station, a bigheaded nephew willing to trample on the dead in order to make himself superior.

To him what I did was entirely without value.

And writing was such a fragile thing. It wasn't hard to write well, but it was hard to make writing that was alive, writing that could pry open the world and draw it together in one and the same movement. When it didn't work, which it never really did, not really, I would sit there like a conceited idiot and wonder who I thought I was, supposing I could write for others. Did I know any better than everyone else? Did I possess some secret no one else possessed? Were my experiences particularly valuable? My thoughts about the world especially valid?

Gunnar had pointed his finger at me. He had said, I know you. You think you're someone, but you're just a little shit. And you've meddled in something that's none of your business, something you don't even understand. If you go through with this, I'll take you to court. I'll make you bleed. I'll destroy you. You little shit of a nephew.

That was what he was saying.

He had warned me of it back when I was seventeen and had written disparagingly about Sissel Kyrkjebø in the local newspaper *Fædrelandsvennen*. Who do you think you are, he'd said, seventeen years old and writing so unfavorably about an artist who can sell two hundred thousand records? He was embarrassed by me, presumably also because we shared the same name and he would be associated with what I'd done. Kristiansand was a small town, and everyone read *Fædrelandsvennen*.

I was proud my name was in the paper. But when he said those words to me I squirmed on my chair and blushed, what he said hurt. I measured the world by my indie yardstick, it was how

I judged the quality of everything in the field of culture. He knew nothing about that world at all, to him it was nonsense, and that was what I felt, that he was measuring me by the real world. The adult world, the world of responsible people. I opposed that world, but that was when I was on my own, because no sooner was I confronted by it than what did I do? I bowed my head in deep and heartfelt shame.

I shoved the chair back, my face burning, and went in to check on Vanja.

"Do you want to watch the film or *Bolibompa*?" I asked.

"*Bolibompa*," she said. "Is it on now?"

I nodded, turned the DVD off with the remote, and switched the kids' channel on. She'd been sitting on her own in front of the TV for a long time, it was a lousy last resort, and though I was distraught and restless I sat down on the sofa beside her. Because she seldom climbed onto my lap of her own accord but was often glad when I picked her up, I put my arms around her and lifted her onto my knee. She wrenched my arms away, but stayed put.

John lay motionless at the other end, his breathing a murmur, his hair damp with sweat. The sun was a barrage against the window, but the blinds kept most of its rays out and transformed those that came in into a white, hallucinatory shimmer, apart from the window of the balcony door, which was unprotected and allowed a cylinder of light into the room, full of floating specks of dust that whirled like electrons in the air.

"I'm hungry," said Vanja. "I want a sandwich."

I took a deep breath.

"Vanja," I said. "What did I tell you! I said you'd be wanting a sandwich soon. You haven't eaten your dinner yet. You can eat your dinner instead. You can see that, surely?"

She didn't answer.

"Do you want me to bring over your plate again?"

"No. Can I have an apple?"

"If you eat some more of your dinner."

"I don't want any."

"Okay, then," I said. "You can have an apple, if that's what you want. But you can go and get it yourself."

She slid off my knee, scurried out into the kitchen, and when she came back, already munching on an apple, she climbed up next to me.

I got up and went to find some clean pajamas. The air in their room was warm and close, I opened the two small vents above the window and the sounds of the city seeped inside.

There were toys all over the floor. I made a mental note about having to clean up tomorrow, opened a drawer, and found a nightgown. Heidi could sleep in the dress she had on, John in his shorts; if I was lucky they wouldn't wake up when I carried them to bed.

"Here, put this on," I said, tossing the nightgown into Vanja's face. She picked it up and gave me a fleeting smile, then started to get undressed with her eyes glued to the TV. I went and fetched her toothbrush and once she'd got changed I brushed her teeth.

"Do you want to read here or in bed?" I said.

"*Bolibompa*'s not finished yet!"

"It'll be finished in a minute," I said. "Bed or sofa?"

"Bed."

I went in and scanned their bookshelf, picking out three books so there was a choice. *Rapunzel* by the Brothers Grimm, *Gittan och fårskallarna*, and one of the Petra books, the one where she starts nursery school.

"What about John and Heidi?" she said after I turned the TV off. "Don't they have to go to bed?"

"I'll carry them in after I've read you a story."

"I want to be carried in too."

"All right," I said. "And are you going to pretend to be asleep?"

"No. Just carry me."

I lifted her up and carried her to the bed, sat down next to her, and said she could choose a book. She picked *Rapunzel*. A good choice, I liked it too. Earlier that summer I'd spent two days

127

in Germany, I'd done a reading at a castle in the same area the Brothers Grimm had collected many of their folktales, so I was told.

"Rapunzel, Rapunzel, let down your golden hair!" I said to Vanja as she sat there beside me on the bottom bunk, looking at the pictures as I read out loud. I had no idea why she'd got attached to this particular tale when there were so many of the others she didn't care about. It started with a man and a woman having to give their child away to a witch, and to a child that surely had to be the most primeval of all fears, perhaps that was what appealed to her, or perhaps it was the strangeness of a woman letting her hair down from a tower and a man climbing up it to set her free. For me the fairy tale was a kind of literary archetype, or rather a primordial force of literature itself, since on the surface everything was about transformation, including the world's own transformation into fairy tale, and at the same time this transformation involved a kind of simplification, reality contracting into a small number of figures that were so precise and so perfectly honed after having been through so many differently shaped experiences that their truth surpassed any individual experience of the circumstances, this was the same for everyone, and when these different figures were set into motion, the depths in each and every listener opened, and those depths were bottomless. For many years I'd thought of having a novel take place in that domain, in the forests, where there were trolls and ghosts, workhouses and kings, talking bears and foxes, and in the nineteenth-century reality of the Norway through which Asbjørnsen and Moe had traveled when they collected their folktales. Kristiania, Telemark, the valleys of inner Østland. But it would take years of work, and time was something I didn't have at the moment. Nevertheless, whenever I read folktales to the children, the thought came back to me that the potential was there. One of the Grimms' tales was especially compelling, the woman who falls into the well and comes out into another world. Sadly, the version we had was a dreadful translation, which was a shame. Vanja didn't know that though, and it was for her sake we were reading.

"The end," I said when we finished the last page. "Sleep time now."

"Will you tickle me and sing a good-night song?"

"Of course," I said. She lay down on her tummy, I drew up her nightgown and ran my nails lightly up and down her back. That was what she meant by "tickle," and we had to do it every night while we sang.

> *Vem kan segla förutan vind?*
> *Vem kan ro utan åror?*
> *Vem kan skiljas från vännen sin*
> *utan att fälla tårar?*
>
> *Jag kan segla förutan vind,*
> *Jag kan ro utan åror.*
> *Men ej skiljas från vännen min*
> *utan att fälla tårar.*
>
> *Who can sail without the wind?*
> *Who can row without an oar?*
> *Who can leave a friend so dear*
> *without shedding tears?*
>
> *I can sail without the wind.*
> *I can sail without an oar.*
> *Yet not leave a friend so dear*
> *without shedding tears.*

After I'd sung I tucked her in under the duvet, took off her glasses, and put them on top of the little set of drawers next to her bed.

"Daddy?" she said.

"Yes?"

"Can I ask you something?"

"Yes, what is it?"

"Why can't he leave his friend without shedding tears?"

"Why do you think it's a he?"

"Because it's you singing."

"You're right, I hadn't thought of that. I suppose it's because he's very fond of his friend, don't you think?"

"Yes," she said, and put her head down on the pillow, apparently content with the answer. "Night night."

"I'll be back again in a minute," I said. "I've got to put John and Heidi to bed as well."

"Oh yes, I forgot."

I fetched John first and put him down carefully in his crib, then Heidi, which was more of a problem, I had to get her out of the stroller, and my efforts woke her up. No! she wailed, squirming as I clutched her tight to my chest and scuttled into the bedroom, depositing her inelegantly on her bunk above Vanja's, hoping that reality's intrusion into sleep would be so brief as not to get the better of it, and luckily, after drawing herself up onto her knees and staring at me for a few short seconds, she lay down on her side and closed her eyes, and before long her breathing grew heavy again.

"Night night, little one," I said to Vanja, and switched off the ceiling light.

"Can you leave the door open?" she said.

"Yes, of course," I said. "Sleep tight."

"Sleep tight."

I went in and checked my e-mail. There were no new messages. It was a relief in one way, but disturbing in another, since Tonje and Jan Vidar had both been sent copies of the manuscript some time ago, and that neither had got back to me about it could only mean one thing.

To allay their worries a bit, or assume some kind of control over them, I decided to send both a new e-mail. To Tonje I wrote:

Dear Tonje,

Not having heard back from you, I'm assuming maybe you're upset and shocked at having been dragged into a novel just like that without having asked for it. The way I see it, I'm not holding you up in any bad light, on the contrary, as Tore said when he read it, "Tonje's a princess, her entry makes you glad," but at the same time I understand that just being included in a novel is to be held up in some way. If you want, and I'm sure you do, I'm quite willing to change your name and those of everyone in your circle so that you can't be associated with the novel (in any other way than having been married to its author, but of course that's unavoidable).

All the best,
Karl Ove

To Jan Vidar I wrote pretty much the same. Once I'd done that I looked in on the children, they were all asleep now, picked up the phone, went out onto the balcony, sat down, poured myself a coffee, lit a cigarette, and called Mom.

She answered right away.

"Hello? Sissel speaking," she said.

"Hi, it's Karl Ove," I said. "Have you read the e-mail now?"

"Yes, I have."

"What do you think?"

"I'm incensed, I must say," she said. "And upset. I've been sitting here trying to work out what to say to him. But I suppose it's best to wait a while."

"You shouldn't reply to him," I said. "If you do, you'll be meeting him on his own terms, you'll be descending to his level."

"That's true," she said. "Your grandfather once said folly isn't worth an answer. It's a good piece of advice. But I'm so angry I'd like to give him a piece of my mind. He signs himself your father's brother. Well, your father would never have done anything like this, I want you to know that."

131

"I don't know what to believe," I said, and laughed uneasily. "You're my only source as far as all this is concerned."

"What do you mean?"

"That's what he says, isn't it? That I got it all from you."

"Oh, that. It's sort of an odd opinion, that I should be responsible for you when you're forty years old. How long can a person be held responsible for what their children do?"

"He watched me grow up. I think to him I'm still a teenager."

"You might be right there. But the idea of me hating the Knausgaards like that is just ludicrous. I've no doubt I was shy and reserved when I came into the family as a twenty-year-old, he's right about that, and your grandmother on your father's side was certainly a very warm and sociable person, especially to you children. So there is a grain of truth to what he says. In a way he's describing a caricature of me. I can see I could be perceived like that."

"A cold wind from Vestland?"

"Yes. Visiting us that time obviously left an impression on him. A peasant smallholding, he calls it. Funny to see that word again, but compared to what he was used to, we were poor. It was a totally different culture. Maybe it frightened him. Grandmother was quiet, she never said much, that must have been different for him too."

There was a brief silence. I lit another cigarette and put my feet up on the railing as I stared at the gray-blue summer sky with all its planes on their way in and out of the two airports, Kastrup and Sturup.

"There was something he wrote that touched me in a way," I said after a moment. "That bit about him having known us when we were little. You know, where he talks about "the boys"? He says you neglected us by not putting Dad right and intervening when we most needed it. I had no idea anyone else could see that Dad maybe wasn't good for us. But he saw that. He must have, for him to put it like that. His conclusion is different from mine, because I was there and I know you were the one who rescued me, but just the fact someone else could see what was happening, or there was some knowledge of it, touches me, strangely enough."

"Everything's about being seen. I understand if you feel that way. Especially if you put him in your father's place, as you say."

"Yes, there is something there. I feel that. Some deeper structures."

"But your father saw you, I want you to know that. He knew you for who you were."

"I'm not sure about that, to be honest."

"Well, it's true. He did."

I cried when she said those words, though quietly and without it affecting my voice, so she wasn't aware of it. We talked for another half hour or so about Gunnar and what he had written, not so much about the book that had provoked him as about the family, both Dad's and hers. She told me more about what it had been like for her coming into his family back at the beginning of the sixties, and some more about the person he'd been then. She had done the same when Dad died, I'd called her several times a day, and what she did was to raise him up for me, reminding me over and over that while he may have been tormented he had also been a person who made an impression on people: intelligent, insightful, knowledgeable, inquisitive, farsighted. She knew I needed another image of my father and gave me the man she had known, showing me the way he had appeared in the eyes of an adult when I had still been a child.

She was doing the same thing now.

I was being drawn further and further into something whose deeper nature was as yet unknown to me. Gunnar's letter gave a picture of the family I'd grown up a part of that was completely different from my own, and the picture Mom gave of Dad was different too, impossible to reconcile with my own experience of him. It was as if everything was suddenly turning in on me.

The first thing I did once I'd finished talking to Mom was call Linda.

"Hi," she said.

"Are you on your own?" I asked.

"Yes. I'm sitting in my room here. It's such a lovely place they've got. And Helena's taking such good care of me."

"Did you barbecue?"

"Yes, it was really nice," she said. *Jättemysigt*, in her Swedish. "But how are you doing? And how are the kids?"

I told her about our day. We discussed Gunnar's e-mail and the letter he'd sent to Mom, but it wasn't the right time for it. She told me a bit more about what she'd been up to, what they'd been doing, what the place was like. While she was talking I remembered another conversation we'd had once, early in the summer the year we first got together as a couple. She had gone to her mother's place outside Gnesta, it was the first time we'd been away from each other. I missed her so much my whole body hurt. That time, too, I had tried to imagine what the place where she was staying looked like, picturing a house, a garden, a forest. Later, in the first weeks of autumn, I saw it with my own eyes, and of course it was quite different, much more forceful in its impression, and the first, almost dreamlike images that had come to me vanished without a trace, displaced by reality's chunky solidity. She told me she'd been at the beach that day, that she'd been lying on the jetty with her mother, reading out loud three texts that I'd written that had just been published in a book I'd given her. Her mother thought they were fantastic, she said, and laughed with joy. Later in the evening she had told them all about me, and she said they liked me already. I sat in my apartment, her dark voice in my ear, and imagined the room in which she sat, the person I loved and wanted more than anything else.

In the photos we took at the time we looked almost frighteningly young. Linda was twenty-nine, I was thirty-three. Linda still looked young, whereas I looked like I'd spent the intervening years living on the street, there was something ravaged about my face now, the deep, almost parodic furrows in my brow, my nose longer and more pointed, and my eyes made me look like I was glaring even when I felt most at ease.

How I'd loved her then. She was the only thing I cared for. I didn't give a damn about anything else. It couldn't have gone on like that, of course not, I would have burned out, but was this really where we were meant to go? Was this what we were together for?

But it wasn't too late. Nothing had been lost. Everything was still within reach.

"I wish you were here now," I said.

"I'm so glad to hear it, Karl Ove," she said.

"I'm not just saying that."

"I know. I miss you, too."

"That's what I mean. Being away from each other's a good thing."

"Ha ha."

We said good night, I hung up and went in to check my e-mail again. Not a word from anyone. I surfed the Web for half an hour before getting undressed and going to bed. It was only ten to nine, but if I was going to get through the next morning without irritation I had to wake up rested. And Heidi had fallen asleep so early she'd probably be up and about at five, if not before.

I woke briefly at about half past ten when Vanja came in dragging her duvet behind her, but fell asleep again right away. The next time I woke, John was standing at the bed staring at me holding his pillow.

"Is it morning yet?" he said.

I glanced at the time. Five fifteen.

"Nearly. Do you want some breakfast?"

He nodded.

"Go into the kitchen then, I'll come in a minute."

He did as I said.

I got up, and Gunnar's e-mail came back to me. I went through the hallway and picked the papers up off the mat before going into the kitchen. It faced directly east, where the sun already reddened the horizon. I lifted John up into his chair, put a plate of muesli and yogurt in front of him, filled the coffeemaker with water, put a filter in the filter holder, spooned in the coffee, and switched it on. As it ticked and gurgled, I skimmed the culture and sports sections in the two newspapers.

"Hi, Daddy!" said Heidi, appearing wide awake in the doorway.

"Heidi-Hi," I said. "Muesli or cornflakes?"

"Cornflakes. But I want to pour the milk."

"Okay," I said.

She went off and I heard her come dragging her little chair from the bedroom through the hall, she used it to stand on when she was rummaging for clothes among the big piles in the IKEA cabinet on wheels that we'd put by the cupboards. A few minutes later she came in dressed in a rose-colored top with strawberries on it and a blue Hello Kitty denim skirt. The top was her absolute favorite; if it was up to her, she'd be wearing it round the clock.

"You look nice," I said.

She smiled, but said nothing.

"I look nice too," said John.

"But you're not even changed yet," I said. "Heidi is. That's why I said she looked nice. You've still got your clothes from yesterday on!"

I filled a bowl with cornflakes and put it in front of Heidi along with a carton of milk, went out onto the balcony to get the vacuum jug, filled it with coffee, took a cup from the cupboard, poured myself the few mouthfuls that wouldn't fit in the jug, and went out onto the balcony again. The only handle the door had was on the inside, it was a nuisance, all of a sudden the kids could push the door shut, and if they did I'd be locked out. They were too small to open it themselves. Vanja could, but she was asleep. So I turned the handle into the locked position and left the door ajar before sitting down and lighting a cigarette.

There was a chill in the air, but the sky was clear and the red sun was on its way up over the horizon. My stomach muscles ached, it felt like I'd been working out the day before. Most probably it was from all the tension.

A movement at the window caught my eye and instinctively

I jumped for the door to make sure it didn't get locked, then re-alized there was no danger and sat down again.

Heidi pushed the door open.

"I spilled, Daddy," she said.

"It doesn't matter," I said.

"Can you come?"

"Let me drink my coffee first, then I'll come. Go back in."

Instead of doing as she was told, she opened the door wider and stepped out onto the balcony.

"Heidi," I said. "Go inside! You're not supposed to be out here."

"I only wanted to see," she said with a sulk.

"Go inside, I'll be there in a minute. Okay?"

"Okay."

Why couldn't she have waited, so I could have this little mo-ment to myself with my coffee and my first cigarette of the day? Five minutes in peace, that was all I asked for.

I took a last drag and drew the smoke down into my lungs, swallowed what was left of my coffee, and went inside. It wasn't just a little she'd spilled, it had run over the edge of the table and onto the floor. I tore off some paper towels and began to wipe it up.

"Was it on purpose?" I said as I cleaned up the mess, looking up at her as she sat on her chair watching what I was doing.

She shook her head.

"All right," I said. "But eat what you've got in your bowl, at least!"

"But it's too full," she said.

I said nothing, but took it over to the sink, poured off some of the milk and the cornflakes, wiped the bottom and the edge of the bowl, and set it down in front of her again.

"There you go," I said. "Now you can have your breakfast."

"You're angry," she said. Coming from her, it was an accusation.

"I'm not angry, Heidi, not at all. I just don't want to spend the morning cleaning up after you, that's all. But it wasn't your fault. It's all right."

"Is it morning?" said John.

"It is now," I said. "When the sun comes up, it's morning. When it goes down, it's evening."

"Not in the winter," said Heidi.

"No, that's right. But in the summer it's true. And whose birthday is it in the summer?"

"Me!" said John.

"Next week, already!" I said.

"What am I getting?" said Heidi.

"You? It's not your birthday, is it?"

"But Daddy," she said.

"I don't know what you're getting," I said. "How about a bag of *gulrøtter*?"

"What?"

"*Morötter* in Swedish. A bag of carrots, how does that sound?" I said.

"What?"

"Just pulling your leg, Heidi."

"What?"

"*Jag skojade*," I said.

"*Du får inte skoja*," she said. Don't make fun.

"Not even a little bit?"

She shook her head.

"So I'm not allowed to be angry, or make fun?"

"No."

She bent forward and started slurping her cornflakes and milk. John had finished, there was yogurt all around his mouth and the table in front of him was spattered with soggy muesli.

"Do you want some more, John?" I said.

He shook his head. I went around the table and lifted him up, snatched off a sheet of paper towel and wiped his mouth, took off his diaper, and dropped it in the bin underneath the sink along with the used paper towel.

"John's a bare-bottomed boy," said Heidi.

"I am NOT!" said John, immediately incensed, and stomped off.

Heidi laughed, a bubbly little giggle. I gave her a smile, grabbed a clean diaper from the bathroom, and went after him. He ran as soon as he saw me.

"Stop!" I said, and ran after him. I lifted him up, he kicked his legs, but not in any protest, and lay still when I put him down on the sofa and put the diaper on him.

"There you go," I said, and went into the bedroom to switch the computer on and check my e-mails. Vanja had pulled the duvet up over her head, a wisp of hair on the pillow was all there was to indicate someone was underneath. I left her alone and logged on to my e-mail, nothing, apart from the news update from the *Agderposten* and a message from Amazon. I skimmed the headlines of the online newspapers, first *Klassekampen*, then *Aftenposten*, *Dagbladet*, *Dagsavisen*, *VG*, *The New York Times*, *The Guardian*, *Expressen*, and finally *Aftonbladet*.

With Vanja on the left side of the stroller, John inside, and Heidi on the right, I stepped outside some half an hour later, walked to the crossing, went over, and carried on up Södra Förstadsgatan all the way to the 7-Eleven, where we first made a left, then a right, and ten minutes later we were outside the nursery entrance, where Vanja keyed in the code and Heidi swung open the gate. The others who had arrived were all out in the yard, so I just lifted John out of the stroller and parked it by the wall, made eye contact with Nadje so she knew the children were there, and headed home again. On the way, I stopped off at the 7-Eleven to buy cigarettes and a box of matches. I stood outside and lit up with a big green garbage truck making a racket in the street behind me. The noise echoed off all the walls, its own little cacophony.

They probably weren't called garbage trucks anymore. I wondered what they might be called instead. Environmental service vehicles, perhaps?

I walked along the street smoking my cigarette. There was a steady stream of buses now that the morning was under way, they made the ground shake as they rumbled past. The air was crisp and cool in the shade, warm and gentle in the sun; it looked like it was going to be a fine day. Not that it mattered. I was going back to bed, and hopefully I'd get some work done later.

The building we lived in came into view. I flicked my cigarette into the road as I walked the last stretch, past the huddle of pale, empty faces at the bus stop as a bus pulled up with that sound they made of something being ripped apart, a sound it had taken me more than a year to realize came from the contact between the iron grids of the gutter and the big wheels of the buses, crossed the road, and walked up to the entrance door, where I tapped the panel with my key card. I took the stairs, put the cigarettes down on the hat rack, unplugged the phone, pulled the blinds in the bedroom, and lay down to sleep.

I woke up an hour and a half later having dreamed. My T-shirt was damp and the pillow I'd been lying on soaking wet. A craving for sugar drove me into the kitchen, where I pulled some grapes from the bunch and crammed them into my mouth to restore my blood sugar. After that I went back into the bedroom and checked my e-mails.

There was a new message from Gunnar in the in-box.

I got to my feet again and opened the door of the balcony, walked along the dark planks of the decking to where the sun was, and looked across at the Hilton, the three elevators that slid up and down in their glass tubes.

I had to stand up and take it.

I had to meet it head-on, I couldn't hide.

So he was angry with me. So I'd done something terrible. I would have to answer for it. Take everything as it came. It was as straightforward as that.

But first I needed a cigarette.

I went in and took the packet from the hat rack, then went out onto the balcony on the other side, which was already boiling hot in the sun. I didn't feel like sitting down, just lit up and gripped the metal railing, staring six floors down at the felted roof below, then sat down anyway, took three drags of the cigarette, stubbed it out, went back into the bedroom, opened the e-mail, and read it as quickly as I could.

He began with a couple of formal comments about having made his objections to the book clear to the publisher over the phone, but given the importance of attaching a date to his objections in the event of any proceedings, he felt obliged to write to me again by e-mail. He made the following absolute demands. He and his wife were to be removed completely from the book. The description of his mother and her life before and after Dad's death was to be removed from the book. The description of the final phase of his brother's life, which was painful to his next of kin, was to be completely removed from the book. The description of his father's brothers, and the fictitious and untruthful stories about their relationships to each other, were to be completely removed from the book. There had never been the slightest conflict between them, they'd been the best of friends all their lives. All mention of the Knausgaard name was to be removed from the book. All remaining names were to be made anonymous. All mention or description of identifiable residences having belonged to his family were to be removed from the book. All errors of documentary fact had to go. He had noted more than fifty of them, he wrote, which were either downright lies or the result of ignorance. Nothing pertaining to these lies would he require to be rectified now, this would follow in the event of proceedings being taken. He found it telling that the dominant role played by the author's mother regarding his brother's tragedy received no mention in the book, though he would not insist on it being included. There was much more still to be said on the matter, the issues mentioned simply being a few of many, and he sincerely hoped he would not be compelled to make them public at some later date. That such a respectable publishing house as Oktober would even consider publishing a novel of this nature without contacting those involved was something he found scandalous. That he had indeed been contacted, and that his letter was in reply to that contact, didn't seem to have occurred to him. He was too angry. He characterized my manuscript as a documentary portrait, which presumably was why he thought the family ought to have been contacted by the publisher, so that they could have been alerted to all the lies, all the distortions, all the glaring omissions. How could such a respectable publishing house fail to check the sources and their credibility? This was all the more serious in view of the manuscript having been written with one thing only in mind, which was to make money. That was the only reason I was exposing members of my family to the public eye, so I could get rich. Publishing such a book was utterly unacceptable, for not only was it untruthful, it was also an invasion of privacy. In the event of his failing to receive an immediate reply to his letter, the book, together with the e-mails in his possession, would be passed on to a lawyer, as well as to the newspapers, at the earliest opportunity. He named *VG* and *Dagbladet*. If this book, which distorted the truth and lied about the facts, was to be published, then the rest of the story, mark his words, would have to be told too, and in the language of the tabloid press. All the money I, the author, together with the publisher, envisaged earning would be lost in damages.

So he was going to take it to the papers. And the courts.

I lay down on the bed and curled up in a ball, clutching a pillow. A moment later I got up again and went into the hall, picked up the phone, and dialed Geir Angell's number.

"Another e-mail," I said as soon as he answered.

"What's he saying, anything new?"

"He's going to the papers with it if I don't do as he says. And he's going to claim for damages as well."

"Relax. Can you send me a copy?"

"Yeah. I'll do it right away."

"I'll call you back once I've read it. Okay?"

"Okay."

I hung up, went back into the bedroom, and forwarded the e-mail on to Geir, then went into the bathroom with the phone still in my hand. I stared at the three blue IKEA bags, went into the kitchen, filled a glass with water from the tap and drank it. I put the glass down on the counter, went into the living room and opened the door of the balcony, only to close it again the same instant, went into the bedroom, lay down on the bed, sat up and stared at the display on the phone. I called Geir Angell again.

"Are you that fazed?" he said.

"Yes," I said.

"Let me finish reading it through. Hang on a minute."

I got to my feet and went over to the balcony door, pulled on the cord that lifted the blinds, fastened it tight, and went out into the hall.

"He's not saying anything new here, Karl Ove. He's making threats. He's saying he'll sue for damages if the novel comes out in its present form and that he'll go to the tabloids and give them his side of the story. But the book hasn't been published yet. The only story at the moment is there's an uncle who wants to stop a novel about his family. No one can pass judgment before it's out. And if he goes ahead like he says, it'll be fantastic publicity. Everyone wants to read that kind of thing. Relax. He's angry, that's all. He can't do anything."

"He can go to the papers, and he can go to the courts. It's no wonder I'm scared, is it?"

"No, I understand that. But there's no need to be. He's huffing and puffing now because he wants the book stopped. He's trying to frighten you into doing what he wants."

"He's doing a good job."

"But you've no idea if he's actually willing to do what he says."

"Oh, what a mess!"

"Relax. Everything's going to be fine!"

"This is hell. It's just hell."

"What, someone being angry with you?"

"It's not some trivial little thing, like you're making it out to be."

"I'm not saying it's trivial. I'm saying it's not as bad as you think."

I said nothing, just stared out the window in the living room, the sunlight glittering in the windows of the Hilton.

"How about I come down?" said Geir. "We're coming on Friday anyway, and I'm on my own here with Njaal, so it makes no difference whether I'm here or there. What do you say?"

"Are you sure?"

"Of course. I'm not getting any work done anyway, with Njaal under my feet."

"Isn't he in day care?"

"Do you want me to come or not?"

"I'd never have asked under normal circumstances. You know that. Besides, it was your idea."

"Is that a yes?"

"Sounds like it."

"Great! We'll leave first thing in the morning, so we should be there about . . . well, twenty-four hours from now, or thereabouts."

We chatted for another half hour or so. When we were finished, I called Geir Gulliksen. He answered right away.

"Did you get the e-mail?" I asked.

"I did, yes," he said. "He's hopping mad, this uncle of yours, isn't he?"

"What I'm scared of is him going to the newspapers. They'd jump at the chance of making a story out of this."

"You don't think he's just trying to put pressure on?"

"I think he's angry enough to do anything at all."

"He says he'd give them the manuscript. That'd be against the law. The novel hasn't been published yet, and the rights to the manuscript are yours. But I'll ask Geir Berdahl to get in touch with him. The important thing is to make sure we handle things properly."

"What about his list of demands?"

"No more than expected. What he's after really is for the book not to come out at all."

"Changing the names of everyone in the family, anonymizing people and places, that's all fine by me. But removing my father and my grandmother is out of the question. There'd be no novel left if we did. And I can't take Dad's name out either. He's what the novel's about. He was my father. I *can't*."

"We'll deal with all that as we go along. But the novel doesn't stand or fall with the names."

"Not those on the periphery, no. But I draw the line at my dad's name. I won't give that up."

"The important thing now is to make sure he doesn't go public. We need to accommodate him as far as we can."

As soon as we hung up I called Espen. After I'd talked to him, I called Tore. Then Linda. Then Geir Angell again. I was on the phone all day, and when I wasn't pacing about with the phone to my ear, I was lying stretched out on the bed with the blinds down, wishing it would all go away. As I lay there the phone was in my hand the whole time. I was aware of the risk of trying people's patience; if I called Espen or Tore again, for instance, I'd be approaching the limits of what I could reasonably expect from them. I was sure they didn't see it that way themselves, but I did, they had work to do, families to attend to, lives to live. Linda was different, but she was on holiday, I couldn't heap all this on her now. I had no such qualms with Mom, she would always put herself aside when it came to Yngve's and my problems, but she was at work in the daytime, and I couldn't just barge in there with my troubles. I could do that with Yngve, but with him it was more complicated, he was involved, not on the outside like everyone else, but caught between a rock and a hard place. That left Geir Angell, I wasn't worried about pestering him, I could quite easily ask him to put everything else aside and listen to me going on about the mess I was in, but even with Geir there had to be a limit somewhere, I'd spoken to him three times already today, so a fourth would surely be pushing it.

As I lay there quite motionless, staring at the desk under the window, only half an hour from having to pick up the kids, the phone lit up. I looked at the display. It was a 0047 number. A mobile. But Gunnar couldn't get to me unless I answered, I told myself, then felt an immediate wave of relief as the number was superseded by Yngve's name and it began to ring.

"Hello?" I said.

"What a terrible drama this is with Gunnar," he said.

"I know," I said. "I'm really sorry. But at least he's not dragging you into it."

"She's my mother too, you know."

"Of course."

"Did you know he thought about her like that?"

"No. I had no idea."

"Me neither. We'll just have to hope he doesn't go to the papers. What is the publisher saying about it?"

"They want to accommodate him as far as possible. They've got some lawyers looking into it."

"What are they saying?"

"I don't know. They're still looking at it."

I could hear he was upset. Why couldn't I just have left well enought alone, why did I have to go and poke around in such a sewer of old resentment?

I dropped the phone into the charger and went into the kitchen, ate two slices of bread with liver paste and pickled beetroot while standing by the counter, well aware that on an empty stomach it would be virtually impossible to get the kids home without taking my annoyance out on them at some point. I washed the bread down with a glass of water, wondered if I had time for a cigarette on the balcony before I went, then decided to have one on the way instead, lifted the trash bag out of the bin under the sink, tied a knot in the top, and sat down on the mat in front of the door while I put my shoes on. After that I took the keys from the cupboard, picked up the trash bag, and took the elevator down into the basement. The door that led to the storage rooms belonging to each apartment was open, a man came toward me, it was our neighbor on the other side of the landing, a huge brick house of a man, he was in his sixties and naturally I ran into him now and again on my way up or down, he always filled in the uncomfortable little pauses with some comment about the weather, often padded out with a supplementary inquiry about the climate in Norway. I said hello, he said there'd been a break-in during the night and that I should check our storage. I told him we had nothing valuable in it, and they'd be doing us a favor if they'd made off with what there was. He didn't appreciate the comment, burglary was a serious matter, or maybe he just didn't understand what I said. Probably that, I thought to myself, and went out through the other door and down the passage to the refuse room.

I slung the bag into the big garbage container, which was completely empty, and went back out of the dingy, grubby space and along the passage again, where I noted that the pane in the outer door at the top of the stairs had been smashed. It often happened. The first bike I owned in Malmö disappeared after three days, I'd been stupid enough to leave it outside after locking it. The next one I made sure to always leave locked in the basement, only one time I forgot to lock it, and surprise, surprise, the next day it was gone. They'd had so much time they'd unscrewed the child seat and left it neatly on the floor before making off. Another neighbor, an elderly woman who got stuck between floors in the elevator one morning, thumping her fists against the door, her shaky voice calling for help, had said when we moved in that the place was like Chicago. I loved that expression for the fact that while Chicago had been the very epitome of crime and violence in the fifties, the image had lived on, into the new millenium, in the minds of the old. It was like Chicago here, they stole bikes from the basement and broke into the storage rooms, where would it all end?

The light outside was bright and I put my sunglasses on. The air was warm, though not still in any way, a breeze came from across the street and the leaves of the tree in front of me rustled. The cars were tailing back at the traffic lights. Pedestrians were crossing, their hair blowing about in the gusts. People on the sidewalk passed me like shadows, I saw nothing, registering only their movements, regulating my own automatically according to theirs. Past Åhléns, Hemköp, Maria Marushka or whatever the hell it was called, the shop Mom always went into whenever she came to stay, Myrorna, 7-Eleven, and then, on the corner of Norra Skolgatan, the Hojen bike shop. The street lay sheltered from the wind, and heat rose from the asphalt. Cars rolled gently, almost unnoticeable in the swarms of bicycles on their way from Möll-evangen to the city center. The owner of the little immigrant store stood on the step and looked around. I stopped at the nursery entrance and tapped in the entry code. They were out playing in the yard. There was a water sprinkler in the middle, surrounded by children, some of them naked. They shrieked and giggled. A bike with a trailer attached stood parked a bit farther away. It belonged to one of the parent couples who'd been there when we started coming. Many others had come along since then, we were already veterans. The problem was I'd written about this particular couple in the second book.

But for the time being I felt safe. None of the people I could see in front of me here in the yard knew anything of what I'd done. Book 2 wasn't out for another two months yet, and the way things were going it was more than doubtful it would ever get to be published in Swedish.

"Daddy!" shouted John, and came running across the asphalt.

I lifted him up and tossed him in the air.

Vanja was sitting on a swing together with Katinka, they'd seen me and were yelling as loud as they could. Heidi was standing, her face visible in the open window of the little playhouse next to the sandpit. She noticed me and came running out. I lifted her up too. Then I went over to the staff to hear if everything had been all right. All fine, they said, the children had been cheerful and full of beans.

Half an hour later, I finally managed to get them together and accept the fact that it was time to go home. John was in the stroller, Vanja and Heidi walked along on either side, holding the handle tight. Vanja chattered all the way. Heidi said something now and then, completely unrelated to what her sister was talking about, while John sat quietly, staring out at whatever appeared in front of him. When we got to roughly the same place as the day before, Heidi again refused to continue, and it took ten minutes before we got going again. Outside Hemköp it was Vanja's turn, no way was she going to let me do the shopping before we got home. Couldn't I take them home first and then do the shopping? I tried to explain to her that we couldn't do that while Mommy wasn't at home, but she was having none of it. Five minutes later, after I said they could each have a bun, we walked through the automatic doors into the chill of the busy supermarket. John wanted out of his stroller, he said, I tried for as long as I could to hold him off, he wasn't nearly as disciplined as his sisters, to put it mildly; he could stop in front of something he decided he wanted and not budge before I put it in the basket, or he could suddenly take off on his own, but eventually I gave in and lifted him out of the stroller. Over by the milk I realized he'd disappeared. I told Vanja and Heidi to stay put and went down the aisles looking to both sides. I found him by the dog food, lying on his back looking up at the ceiling. He chuckled when he saw me. I grabbed the collar of his T-shirt and lifted him up, carrying him like a sack over my shoulder back to the stroller, and he screeched and giggled all the way until he realized he was going back in the stroller and went sulky. I bought a pack of yogurts, which settled him a bit, and then we walked back down the aisle to the checkout, where I paid, bagged what we'd bought, and went out into the sunshine again. Vanja and Heidi munched on their buns. We crossed over and went into the shopping precinct, not to buy anything, but because it was a shortcut. It wasn't far from the back entrance to the playground. I carried Heidi for a bit so as to get on, she sat on my arm, and with the other I carried the bags and pushed the stroller. After a while I put her down and picked Vanja up instead, anything else was out of the question, everything had to be in equal shares. When we got to the playground, which was teeming with children, I sat down on a bench and smoked a cigarette while they darted around from one piece of equipment to the next. After only a few minutes John came toddling up to me, he flopped forward onto the bench and said he wanted to go home. I tousled his hair and said we'd be going soon. No, now, he said. No, soon, I said. And then my phone rang. I was quite unfazed, the only people who knew my mobile number were people I trusted. Private number, said the display.

"Hello?" I said.

"Hello," said Geir. "Are you out and about?"

"Yeah, I'm at the playground."

"How are you feeling?"

"I haven't jumped off the balcony yet. I take it all out on the kids instead."

"You're not the type to commit suicide," he said. "Your method's to stick your head in the sand."

"True," I said. "But the most fascinating thing about the ostrich isn't that at all. I saw this documentary about them once. They're huge and really strong, and with the claws they have they can be lethal, so do you know what the farmers do to get close to them?"

"Put a sack over the ostrich's head?"

"Well, once they get that far, yeah, they go completely still. But before that. Before they go up to them and put the sack on."

"No, what?"

"They hold a stick up above their own heads. A broom handle, whatever. As soon as the ostrich sees something taller than itself it won't attack. Its brain is that tiny. Ha ha ha!"

"Ha ha ha!"

"It's got three rules it lives by. If a broom handle comes along that's taller than me, I stand still. If I'm threatened, I stick my head in the sand. If someone puts a sack over my head, the world disappears and I no longer exist."

"Those are your rules you're talking about."

"Why do you think I mention it? Still fascinating, though, don't you think? The ostrich is such an ancient creature. It doesn't

150

need a bigger brain, it's looked after itself perfectly well all this time."

"You can keep your fascinations to yourself."

"It's the same with crocodiles and sharks. They're so ancient. They behave quite mechanically, there's no improvisation, no element of choice for them, they're not able to assess anything. If something falls in the water where they happen to be, they open their mouths and try to swallow it. Whether it's a plastic container, a mine, or whatever, it all goes in, down the hatch. I love it, the thought of everything once having been so primitive and simple, a kind of biological-mechanical world, and the fact that a few creatures descend from that and are with us here now."

"I hear primitive, simple, biological-mechanical, and guess what, crocodiles and ostriches aren't the first things that occur to me."

"You're the last Freudian."

"Everyone is. They just don't know. I'm telling you, Eros and Thanatos, that's all you need. But in your case, the ostrich maneuver isn't going to do you much good now. You're going to be visible everywhere when your book comes out. You're going to be an ostrich without sand."

"Hang on a minute. I feel an inspiration. There's a poem coming on . . . I am John Lackland, ostrich without sand, dim and witless, you understand."

"That's the spirit! Well done, Karl Ove! There comes a point where you've got to laugh. It's the only thing you can do. Life's a comedy. Everything's stupid when you come to think about it."

"That wasn't me talking. It was someone else, talking through me. I'm just an instrument. The truth is I'm at my wits' end."

"That's why I prefer Cervantes to Shakespeare. Comedy is truer than tragedy. You've got to laugh at it all."

"That's because you're from Hisøya. You people never take life seriously. You're all nihilists and cynics. But I'm from Tromøya. The very focus of gravity and tragedy."

"I thought that was Athens?"

"Well, you thought wrong. People often get Arendal and Athens mixed up. Aristotle was from Froland, and Plato came from Evje, they say. The Cynics originated on Hisøya. Aristophanes lived in Kolbjørnsvik. And Sophocles hung out in Kongshavn."

"Yeah, if you say so. Anyway, I was only calling to ask if we needed to bring some bedding with us, duvets and whatever else."

"Don't bother. We've got everything here."

"Okay, good."

"Speak to you later then."

"Not much choice, I'm afraid."

As soon as we got home, Vanja, Heidi, and John disappeared off into various corners of the apartment while I dumped the shopping bags on the table and put the things away in the cupboards and the fridge, slashed open two packets of fish cakes, and fried them while I got the potatoes and some cabbage on the boil and grated some carrot. I'd only cleaned the kitchen the day before, now it was a mess again, and I decided to try to tidy up a bit while the dinner was getting ready, but managed only to empty the dishwasher before having to change John, he'd dirtied his diaper, and what usually took just a few minutes now turned into a performance, we'd run out of wet wipes again and I had to wash him down with the hand shower in the bath. He cried at the top of his voice as soon as I put him in the tub and kept trying to climb out again, I gripped his arm with one hand and showered him with the other while he howled.

"All finished," I said once he was clean, and turned the water off. "It wasn't really that bad, was it?"

He carried on howling. I lifted him onto the floor and rubbed him dry with a big bath towel. I realized I could forget all about getting him into a clean diaper and a clean pair of shorts, he'd just have to go around with no clothes on until dinner. Then Vanja yelled, and Heidi began to cry. I left John and went to their room to see what was going on. Heidi cried even more.

"What's happened?" I said.

"Heidi hit me!" said Vanja.

"Vanja hit me!" said Heidi.

Vanja had been teasing, as she did from time to time, and Heidi, who wasn't as verbal or as quick yet as her eighteen-months-older sister, had hit out at her in desperation.

"You're not to tease, Vanja," I said.

"I wasn't teasing," said Vanja. "And she hit me!"

"I know, that wasn't nice of her. You shouldn't hit, Heidi."

I looked at them in turn.

"There, are you friends now?"

They both shook their heads.

"In that case, I can't leave you on your own together. Heidi, you can come with me into the kitchen."

"No," she said.

John padded into the hall, barefoot and naked.

"Vanja, then?"

"I want to stay here," she said.

"Can I leave you here together, then?" I said. "With no fighting?"

Vanja nodded. Heidi shook her head.

"Okay," I said. "I'll leave you here. But any fighting or crying and you'll have to work it out yourselves, do you hear? I have dinner to make."

I went back into the kitchen, where John was trying to climb into his chair. The children eating undressed was one of the things I wouldn't allow. I went to the bathroom and got a clean diaper, then dug out a pair of faded gray shorts both Vanja and Heidi had worn when they were little, and a green T-shirt with a blue dolphin print on it, which I got him into before lifting him up into the battered old high chair. The fish cakes were almost black on one side, I flipped them over, turned the heat down, poked a testing skewer or whatever it was into the biggest of the potatoes, which was still hard in the middle, put the plates out on the table, filled the jug with water, got some drinking glasses and put them out, and the knives and forks, took a serving dish from the cupboard on the opposite side, and handed John one of Vanja's little plastic dogs, only for him to throw it disdainfully on the floor, announcing that he was hungry and didn't want fish cakes.

I took the last of the clean items out of the dishwasher, and put them away in the cupboard and the drawers. Heidi started wailing again. A moment later she came into the kitchen and clutched me tight, then stepped back and told me between sobs what Vanja had done. I didn't quite understand what she was saying, and told her dinner was ready and that she could sit down at the table. The potatoes weren't done yet, but the smallest of them were probably okay, and I needed to get some food into them now.

I strained the water from the potatoes, put them one by one into the dish with a spoon, slid the fish cakes from the pan onto the same dish, cut the cabbage up and arranged it around the edge, and put the grated carrot in a little glass bowl on its own.

"Vanja!" I called. "Dinner's ready!"

I put two fish cakes on each of their plates, along with a potato I skinned for them, got up again and went to get Vanja, she was sulking on the floor with her back against the wall and wouldn't look at me when I crouched down in front of her.

"Food's on the table, Supergirl," I said. "Come on, come and get your dinner."

"You only listen to Heidi," she said.

"That's not true. I didn't even hear what she said, if you really want to know. Come on. You need some dinner in your tummy. That's why you're fighting."

"Why?"

"Because you haven't eaten."

"I'm not hungry."

"Okay, just come when you're ready."

I sat down at the kitchen table again, cut their fish cakes up for them, placed a small portion of cabbage and a bit of carrot on their plates, even if I knew they wouldn't touch it. I spooned a pile of vegetables onto my own plate, followed by five fish cakes, and had devoured the lot in minutes. It was ten to six. I got up and started loading the dishwasher. Heidi slipped down from her chair.

"*Bolibompa*'s on in a minute," I said. "Do you want me to switch it on for you?"

She nodded. Behind me, John shouted that he wanted to watch it too. I lifted him down, switched the TV on with the remote, went in to tell Vanja that *Bolibompa* was starting, then went back to loading the dishwasher; Vanja came in and picked up a fish cake with her fingers, she knew I didn't like them doing that, but I didn't say anything, put some detergent in the little compartment, slammed the door shut, and pressed on. I washed the frying pan and the pots quickly in the sink, dried them and put them away. I left the food on the table, hoping they might be hungry later on and eat what was left, then went to the bedroom to check my e-mail. Making sure to avoid seeing the two e-mails from Gunnar, I went through my new messages, none of which was particularly important. Once I'd done that I phoned Linda and asked if she wanted to speak to the children, not so much for her sake or theirs, more for something to happen. John said hi and sat nodding to what she said at the other end, then handed the phone back to me. Heidi talked about what was on the TV without saying it was something she was watching, so it sounded like she was in Flowerland herself, whereas Vanja did the same as the day before, went off on her own with the phone in her hand.

"Me again now," I said when Vanja came back five minutes later and handed it back to me. "Are you having a nice time up there?"

"Yes. It just feels a bit funny being here without all of you, that's all."

"I'm sure it does," I said. "But that was partly the idea, wasn't it?"

"We've been at the beach today. All we've done is lie about all day. We're having a barbecue again tonight."

"It must be reassuring having a fireman around the place, then," I said, opening the door onto the balcony and stepping out.

155

The wooden decking was warm, and the metal railing I leaned my arms against was positively hot.

"He's an incident commander," she said.

"Even better."

"You'll have to meet him. He's from way up north, from Norrland. Completely down to earth and unflappable, it doesn't matter what happens. Just like my family up there, you know. Like all Norrlanders."

"What are you doing now?"

"Lying down, reading. All that sun's made me tired, I think."

"I've hardly been out of the apartment," I said.

"What have you been doing? Working?"

"No, nothing like that. Just been on the phone."

Behind me, John squirmed around the door. He looked up at me, his eyes asking if it was all right, and when I didn't say anything he set off toward the far end, twenty meters from where I was sitting.

"About those e-mails?" she asked.

"About those e-mails, yes."

"I feel sorry for you having to spend so much energy on all that."

"I don't have much choice really."

"I know. But I still feel sorry for you."

"It can't be helped. Listen, do you think we could talk later instead? I'll have to be getting them off to bed soon. The place could use a bit of cleaning up as well."

"Yes, all right. Will you call me?"

"I will. Speak to you later."

"*Hej då.*"

At the other end of the balcony John was climbing onto a chair. I hurried over. Standing on the chair, he'd be high enough to fall over the railing. It had been our worst fear ever since moving in.

I put my arm around his midriff and lifted him down just as he was leaning forward to get a look at all the people down below.

"You can run back instead," I said. "I'll chase you."

"Okay," he said, and pattered off. I lumbered along after him, he turned and shrieked when he saw how close behind I was, I let him run on a bit, then snatched him up into the air.

"Again!" he said.

"No, we're going in now. It's bedtime soon."

"No!" he said.

"Yes!" I said, leading him into a trap, our old yes-no routine, where I suddenly said the opposite, confusing him into doing the same, before he realized and switched back, and by then he'd forgotten all about wanting to be out on the balcony.

I went and got their pajamas from their room, and they got changed in front of the TV, complaining when I switched it off, they wanted to see what was on next, and then, when they couldn't get their way, they were hungry all of a sudden. The fish cakes wouldn't do.

"No," I said, sensing my patience about to run out. If I gave them a slice of bread each, they would sit still and eat it while I read them a story. If I didn't, they would twist and moan, and most likely steer the situation off into a dead end where the only way out would be to impose my will on them, meaning there'd be tears and sulks all evening, or else give in, which was the same as losing face.

Knowing what was most advantageous didn't mean I was going to end up doing it. With my patience ebbing, the urge to put my foot down became all the stronger.

"Fish cakes or nothing," I said.

"But we're hungry," said Vanja.

"Eat your fish cakes, then," I said.

"We don't want fish cakes."

I gave a shrug.

"You'll have to go to bed hungry, then, won't you?"

"But Daddy," said Vanja.

"End of discussion," I said. "Off to bed with you and I'll read you a story."

I found *Out for a Walk* for John, and *The Three Little Pigs* for Vanja and Heidi.

Vanja sat up against the wall under the window with her arms folded in front of her chest.

"I'm not listening," she said.

"Me neither," said Heidi.

"Then I'll read for John," I said, and lifted him onto my lap. I'd been reading *Out for a Walk* ever since Vanja was ten months old, both she and I knew it by heart. Now I raced through it as fast as I could without any thought for John wanting to show me he knew what all the things were called. When I'd finished, I carried him over to his crib and pulled the blind down.

"Night night," I said, and left the room, went into the living room, and out onto the balcony, where I sat down and lit a cigarette. A few seconds passed before Vanja appeared in the door.

"I'm hungry," she said. "And you haven't read to us."

"Go to bed," I said, and stared out at the rooftops and walls, which were blushed by the sun.

"Waaaaarh!" she wailed.

"What's the matter with you tonight? It's late, time for bed."

"You're stupid!" she yelled.

"That may be so," I said. "But I'm still your daddy. And if your daddy's stupid, then it's a shame for you."

She turned and went back in, her shoulders shaking a bit too exaggeratedly, I thought. I poured myself half a cup of coffee, it was tepid now and I gulped it down in a couple of mouthfuls. I went inside again, the place sounded like a zoo. Both Vanja and Heidi were yelling and carrying on.

"What's the problem here?" I said firmly, standing in the doorway of their room.

"You're stupid!" Vanja shouted.

"I'm hungry," Heidi wailed.

The tears were streaming down their cheeks.

"I want Mommy," said John in his crib.

"Mommy's not here," I said. "And if you're hungry you can eat the fish cakes from dinner. If you don't want them you can lie down and go to sleep."

I closed the door and stood there quietly in the hall. A moment went by before it opened again. It was Vanja.

"Back to bed, do you hear me?" I said. "I've just about had enough of this."

I took her by the arms and pressed her back into her bed. Then I gripped Heidi by the waist and lifted her up onto her bunk, closed the door again, went into the living room, and turned the TV on, it was the news, images of vast fires in what I took to be Greece. There was a banging on the wall, I went and opened the door of their room. Vanja was lying kicking her feet against the wall. Heidi lay crying in the bunk above.

"Listen," I said. "I don't want any more nonsense. You can have an apple each. Will that do?"

"Yes," said Vanja, and stopped kicking.

I went out to the kitchen and got three apples, filled two drinking bottles and a sippy cup with water, and took it all with me into their room.

"Do you want me to read?" I asked.

They nodded. I lifted John up, Heidi climbed down by herself, and soon all three were gathered around me, each wanting to be one of the pigs in the story, as if nothing had happened. I sang the same song for each of them while stroking their backs, and they were quiet and agreeable and ready for sleep after all their crying.

"Will you leave the door open?" said Vanja.

"Of course," I said, and went to the kitchen to get some more coffee going. When it was ready I poured a cup, went out onto the balcony, and phoned Mom.

"Hello? Sissel speaking."

She sounded tired.

"Hi, it's Karl Ove," I said. "You weren't asleep, were you? You sound a bit tired."

"Do I? No, I wasn't asleep. I lay awake last night, though, so perhaps I am a bit, now that you mention it."

"Was it Gunnar's letter keeping you awake?"

"Yes. And thinking about what to say in reply."

"I thought you weren't going to?"

"I'm not. I was just thinking about it, that's all. I was livid, you understand."

"Did you read the one I sent you today?"

"Yes."

"What do you think?"

"I think the consequences for you are going to be quite far-reaching. If he goes to the papers or takes you to court. It'll be a huge strain. You're going to get a lot of negative publicity. The pressure will be enormous. People can crack in that situation."

"Are you worried about me?"

"Yes, I am."

"Well, you shouldn't be. I've always taken care of myself."

"But you've got a family to think about as well."

"Are you saying I shouldn't publish the novel?"

"That's for you to decide. All I'm saying is you should think very hard about it. Whether it's worth it."

"That's just what Gunnar wants."

She sighed.

"Yes," she said. "It is. I mentioned it to some people at work today. Some of them thought it was your book that was outrageous, not your uncle's reaction. That's what the public is going to think. Gunnar's going to come across as the ordinary man in the street, decent and law-abiding, whereas you risk being made out to be some kind of criminal. That's one thing. The other is they can easily set you up as representing some kind of elite, with Gunnar as the everyman. You can imagine the field day VG will have."

"So what? I can't let what people might think determine my every move, surely."

"I'm just thinking about the consequences, that's all. You mustn't let this destroy you, Karl Ove."

"I'm not going to have a breakdown just because someone writes something negative about me in the papers, Mom."

"No, that's not what I meant. You're strong, I know that. But think of Mykle, how it broke him. The comparison's a relevant one in my opinion. The pressure it put him under. It destroyed him."

"You're not really asking me to backpedal on this, are you?"

"No, I'm not saying that at all. I'm asking you to think very carefully about it, that's all."

"I'm already thinking about it. In fact, I'm doing nothing else. But withdrawing the novel isn't an option. I'm not going to do it, not in any circumstances. I can't just give up at the first little sign of resistance."

"It's hardly a little sign, is it? You mustn't underestimate it."

"No, of course not. I appreciate what you're thinking, and I'm glad you're telling me."

I went inside, dropped the phone in the charger, then put my head around the door of the children's room. They were all well away, their breathing heavy with sleep. I went into the living room, the floor was littered with clothes, towels, and toys dumped all over; the mat was bunched up, the armchairs shoved up close to the TV, the white woolen throws we used to hide the stains on them tossed on the floor, as was the one from the sofa, whose cushions were even grubbier, if that was possible. I left it all as it was, went to the bathroom and filled the IKEA bags with dirty clothes; I'd have to remember to do the laundry tomorrow or else they'd soon have no clean clothes to put on. I left the bags up against the laundry baskets and went to the bedroom to check my e-mails. Neither Tonje nor Jan Vidar had answered. I logged off and went through the hall, picking the phone up as I went, then, with the phone in one hand, I switched off the dishwasher and opened it, and a cloud of steam tumbled out into the air. I went into the study, there was a note on the desk with what I thought might be Hanne's phone number on it, I picked it up and took it with me onto the balcony. The number belonged to a person named Hanne, but the surname was a common one, so I was by no means sure the number was actually hers.

I put the phone on the table, sat down, poured myself some coffee, lit a cigarette, and looked out over the rooftops with a feeling of unease.

All day the light and warmth had been infused with a kind of density, something listless that had latched unnoticeably on to the ethereal quality of June and July, for summer was now drawing to its close, the world receding into the shadows, darkness encroaching. I longed for it. I wanted the darkness. I wanted to disappear, to be visible no more, neither to myself nor anyone else. I wanted my feelings to sink down inside me, like the sap sinks through the tree in autumn, and for my thoughts to flutter to the ground, like leaves from the multitude of branches on which they had unfolded in spring.

I hadn't spoken to Hanne in almost twenty years. I'd often thought about her, though more and more infrequently, until I'd started work on the novel and found her occupying my mind increasingly as I sat in the study and wrote. If I opened my door and went into one of the other rooms, where Linda was perhaps, those thoughts would disappear again, bound up as they were with a time in my life that had been lost, whereas the time that surrounded me was alive and existed in all things, and by virtue of its being concrete and near made the past into what it was, spectral and vague. Nevertheless, I felt guilty. To ease my conscience, I occasionally told Linda what I was writing about, trying to make light of it, and she seemed to approve, until one morning she told me what one of her girlfriends had said when she'd mentioned what I was writing about. "You mean he's writing about his old flames?" her friend had said. "And you're putting up with it?"

Now there was another step I had to take. I couldn't possibly publish the novel without Hanne reading it first and approving.

I called the number.

No answer.

Like the other times I'd tried, and I was just about to hang up when a voice came on the other end.

"Hanne speaking."

"Hello, Karl Ove here," I said. "Is this the Hanne I used to go to school with?"

There was a silence.

And then that wonderful, effervescent laughter I hadn't heard for twenty years.

"Karl Ove!" she exclaimed. "Is this the Karl Ove who used to send me notes during class?"

"It is," I said. "How are you?"

She laughed again, that same laugh. She'd always been the cheerful kind, never far from gladness, and it was something she clearly hadn't lost.

"I've always imagined you were going to phone someday," she said. "Or else we'd bump into each other in an airport or somewhere. Isn't it strange? I felt sure we'd meet again. How are you? I see you live in Malmö now? I've read about you in the papers, of course. A good thing you didn't follow my advice and become a teacher!"

"I suppose so," I said. "I have a wife and three children here. How about you? I'm assuming you've got kids?"

We exchanged information about our lives for a while. She lived in the Mandal area, with the same man as before, had been in charge of a nursery, and was now working at a school.

"Anyway, it's not just for old times' sake I'm calling," I said after a bit. "It's more specific than that."

"I thought it might be," she said.

"The thing is, I'm writing a novel about my life," I said. "Parts of it are about when I was sixteen. And seeing as how you were so important to me then, I've written about you, too. All names and places are authentic. I realize that might cause some difficulties. So I'd like you to read it before it comes out."

She was completely silent.

"If it's not okay with you, which I would totally understand, because it's a lot to ask, then of course I'll change your name and make you less recognizable."

"You mean you've really written about me?"

"Yes."

"I don't know what to say."

She fell silent again.

"But it's not so much about you as about me," I said. "I was in love with you, to put it bluntly. I've written about that. If you don't want to be in the novel in that way, with your name, I mean, I'll just change it. It's not a problem. Are you surprised?"

"Yes."

She laughed.

"Do you remember much about that time?" she asked.

"Sort of," I said. "Not so much exact details, but moods, that kind of thing. The feeling of it all is still very much there for me."

"I remember a lot. I think about it sometimes. I've always thought we'd meet up again and talk about it. About back then."

"We still can," I said. "As long as I haven't ruined it all by writing about it."

"I doubt that," she said, and laughed.

"Can I send you the manuscript today, then, and let you get back to me once you've read it, so I know if it's okay or not?"

"Yes, of course. I can't wait. I'm a bit nervous now, though!"

A silence ensued.

"It was so nice hearing your voice again," she said.

"Same here," I said. "Your laugh's exactly the same, do you realize that?"

"No," she said, and laughed again.

"I'll send you the manuscript, then maybe we can talk again?"

"Fine."

"Speak to you soon, then."

"Yes. Take care."

"You, too."

I hung up and lit a cigarette. The conversation had gone much better than I had feared. And yet I was thrown off-balance. I had gone into something I couldn't control. She had said she remembered that time very well. I didn't. Or rather, I remembered a few episodes very well. Others I recalled only faintly, shaping them in my writing, inventing dialogues, for example, which, no matter how likely they might have been, certainly weren't accurate. How was she going to feel when she read them? After all, she had been there herself.

I stubbed the cigarette out and went inside, into the children's room, and paused for a moment. John lay curled up on his belly, and had kicked off his duvet as usual. Vanja was lying on her back, spread-eagled, her arms above her head in a V, like a snow angel. Heidi was on her side, her head resting on her upper arm. There was something dark on her cheek and under her nose. I put the light on.

Her face was covered in blood, smeared across her lower cheeks and chin, the pillow was dark red. My heart began to pound, as if suddenly I had found myself on the edge of a precipice. I went to the bathroom and quickly wet a facecloth with hot water, then went back and began to wipe her face. She opened her eyes and looked at me.

"You've had a nosebleed," I said softly. "It's all right. Just lie still and let me wash it clean."

When I had finished, I took the soiled pillow and gave her one from our room instead. She laid her head on it and closed her eyes, and I smoothed my hand up and down her back a couple of times before turning the light off and leaving the room, first to rinse the facecloth in the bathroom, wringing it out and draping it over the radiator, then going back out onto the balcony, where I pressed Linda's number on my phone. It rang for a while at the other end, and when eventually she answered, she sounded like she had been asleep.

"Hi, it's Karl Ove," I said. "Did I wake you up?"

"Yes, I must have dropped off."

"Oh, sorry. I didn't mean to."

"That's all right. How are things at home?"

"Fine. They're all fast asleep. Nothing much happening here otherwise. We were at the park after nursery, then they watched the children's programs before bedtime. The place is a mess, that's the only thing. I can deal with that tomorrow, though."

"You're so good."

"I don't think good is the word," I said. "Anyway, how are things at your end?"

"Fine," she said, and yawned.

"Have you been at the beach?"

"Yes, it was gorgeous."

"Geir's coming tomorrow," I said.

"Already? I thought that wasn't until Friday?"

"He's on his own with Njaal. I suppose he thought he might as well come here."

"You and Geir on your own with four kids. Who'd have thought?"

"I know. It must be a sign. The end is nigh."

"It'll be good for you, though."

"Yes, I'm sure it will. I was thinking we could get some prawns in when Christina comes on Friday. What do you think?"

"Sounds good," she said, and yawned again.

"I'll let you get back to sleep, then," I said. "I think I'll be off myself. I better, if John's going to wake up at half past four again."

"Kiss them from me. I miss you all."

"I miss you. Good night."

"Good night."

I went back in, dropped the phone into the charger, looked in on Heidi to make sure her nose wasn't bleeding again, checked my e-mails, no new messages, surfed the Net for a bit, then sent a copy of the manuscript off to Hanne, made myself a glass of squash in the kitchen and took it with me out onto the balcony, smoked one last cigarette, brushed my teeth, and went to bed.

It was just after five when I woke up and saw John standing beside my bed with his pillow in his hand. I sat up. His nose had bled too. What was going on? A dribble of coagulated blood streaked his lip under each nostril, and there was some on his cheek as well. Worried, I went to the bathroom and wet another facecloth. Nosebleeds weren't dangerous, they happened all the time, but two kids during the same night, could that be a coincidence? Wouldn't it have to be the same cause? It was scary enough as it was, them bleeding, but to think it might be a symptom of something else was worse. A dryness in the air, perhaps, I thought to myself, giving his face a couple of wipes with the cloth while he tried to squirm free.

"There we are," I said. "Should we have some breakfast?"

"Yes," he said, and went off toward the kitchen in that totally placid way of his. His diaper drooped between his legs, I took it off, got a clean one, and put it on him while he stood waiting, like a racing car during a pit stop, it occurred to me. Then I lifted him into his chair, got the muesli out of the cupboard, and went to the fridge to get the blueberry yogurt, only to realize we'd run out.

"There's no more yogurt," I said. "Do you want milk instead?"

"No."

"What, then?"

"I don't know."

A door opened in the hall, it was Heidi. She came in and sat down on her chair.

"Hi, Heidi," I said.

She didn't answer, but from the little smile she tried to conceal by lowering her chin I could tell she was in a good mood just the same. We had breakfast, the sun streamed in, I woke Vanja up, brushed their hair and teeth, got them dressed, grabbed the trash bag from the kitchen, and then we all got in the elevator and went down together.

When I came home again I threw a load of laundry into one of the machines in the basement, then phoned Geir Angell to see if they were on their way. They were, he reckoned they would be arriving around one or so.

I checked my e-mails again. There was a new message from Gunnar. It was addressed to the publisher, with me copied in. The heading was "Libelous author and publisher." He began by stating that he had already established that the events and descriptions he wanted removed from the book consisted of lies and half-truths, gross distortions and outrageous assertions, and were moreover of such nature as to unquestionably be in breach of Chapter 23 of the criminal code, concerning defamation. He had witnesses, he wrote. His wife had kept a diary that could be presented as evidence in court. Their children could take the stand. Furthermore, there were any number of people who, in a professional capacity, had been in regular contact with his mother during the time laid out in the novel. There were health visitors, there were home helpers, and neighbors and friends as well. All would be able to testify that what I had written in my book was false. He gave an example. The novel said that Dad had moved back home to Grandma's two years before he died, and I had described in detail the wretched conditions in which they had lived. None of what I had written was true. It was pure fabrication. Dad had not been living in Kristiansand. He had been living in Moss at the time. According to Gunnar's version, his life there had been nothing but normal. He had an apartment, he had a car, he had his job teaching at the *gymnas*, he had even been in a relationship. He had only stayed with his mother in Kristiansand the last three months, that spring and summer. And there he had died of a heart attack, Gunnar wrote, making it sound like it had happened under quite ordinary, unexceptional circumstances. My account was therefore incorrect, and twisted to meet my own ends. I was making myself out to be a hero who came and cleared up the miserable mess my father had made. Only there was no mess, Gunnar claimed. He had gone to the house shortly after the ambulance had been there and his brother's body had been removed from the chair in which he had died. All that day, and the one after that, he had stayed there in order to help and be with his mother. During that time he had quite naturally cleaned the place up where it was most urgent. What I had written, that the house had been littered with bottles from the front door all the way up the staircase, was utter nonsense. It simply was not true. By the time Yngve and I turned up a couple of days later, he had already taken care of most of what needed doing, all that remained for us to do was to help with a few items that were too heavy for him to lift on his own. The only room he hadn't touched was our father's bedroom, where his clothes and personal items were, having naturally considered it right not to interfere with them, since he was our father.

After that Yngve and I had been over to their house for dinner with Grandma, he wrote, and it was strange because I couldn't remember that at all. The work I had put in at Grandma's he reduced to nothing. It was his wife who had done the bulk of the cleaning up, changed the curtains, helped Grandma in the bath. I, the writer with his head in the clouds, had merely swanned about, bucket in hand, incapable of making a difference, such were the abilities I lacked, something that was attributed to my mother, who had never had a clue about even the basics of keeping a house clean. Yngve had hardly been there at all, having made himself scarce after a single day. And then I had the audacity not only to present things as if I had straightened the place up on my own, but also to portray his and my own father's mother as a geriatric alcoholic. But Gunnar knew why: once, when I was still at the *gymnas* in Kristiansand, she had caught me stealing red-handed. I had stolen money from her, he wrote, had been caught, and had resented her ever since for that reason. Grandma had also expressed concern to my mother over my wayward behavior, I spent too much money, and took drugs, so her worries were hardly without foundation, but how had my mother reacted? Rightly, she had been angry. But with whom? My father, for having left us.

Then he turned to other faults in the manuscript. I had never had a great-grandmother on my father's side who lived to be over a hundred and died falling down a staircase, it was pure invention. My father had never had a cousin who won a beauty competition. I wrote that we used to hire a certain function hall for family occasions, the Elevine Rooms, but that was nonsense, and had never been the case. As for my grandfather and his brothers, they had been the best of friends all their lives, and had never, as I had written, fallen out and stopped speaking to each other. Grandma had never stolen money from her employer, the true story was different altogether, and in fact rather funny. Gunnar himself was another victim of my mendacity; he had never said we could take the money in the envelope under the bed and not declare it to the tax authorities, as I was claiming.

At the end of his lengthy exposition he turned to the love and care he and his wife had given his parents in the autumn of their years, making it possible for them to stay on in their own home and enjoy a relatively large degree of comfort. This was a fact completely subverted in my novel, inasmuch as anyone reading my account on its own would think he had not been fond of his mother at all and had neglected her entirely. Nothing could be further from the truth. To anyone who knew how much they had put into that home, how cozy and pleasant their times together there had been, my description of the situation was immediately fallacious. But then that was me through and through, so I understood, because in the next sentence he was warning the publisher against me and my deceitful nature, manifested in the way I sat, hunched forward, and the way I held my head, always with my face turned away from whomever I was talking to, with a cheerless, scowling expression, eyes full of guilt and brooding speculation. They should not allow themselves to be fooled. What I stood for was not goodness and truth, despite the impression I tried to give, what I stood for was in fact the opposite. I was a notorious liar, I was a quisling, I was selling my grandparents and my father for blood money in a quest for fame, to which end I would shun no means, however shabby. If the publisher did not halt this project he would take legal action. In order to avoid such a step, he wished to put forward a proposal. I had written so lavishly about angels in my previous novel, as my uncle Kjartan had about crows. The publisher ought therefore to suggest to me that I write a book about devils. They were on a level with which I was familiar. And in that I could make use of the literary talent I had inherited from my father.

In Gunnar's eyes everything was different. Together with his wife and children he had infused the final years of my grandparents' lives with meaning. They had helped them out in practical matters, but also been on hand socially, visiting them one or more times a week, taking them out to the cabin, taking them to visit Grandad's brother, spending Christmas with them, Gunnar and Grandma laughing and joking as always. A totally normal, well-functioning family, no big secrets, no skeletons in the closet, no dark clouds on the horizon. Apart from one, the fact that his brother was an alcoholic. Yet it didn't affect his life too adversely, he still taught at the *gymnas*, had his girlfriend in Moss, and was an altogether excellent and well-liked teacher. He'd had his problems in life, notably with his first marriage, which had been cold and without love, as Gunnar saw it, and that coldness had left its mark on his children, who, once they grew up, gradually distanced themselves from their father, but also from their father's family. The youngest, Karl Ove, was the worst, though Yngve, too, had drifted away. They lived in Bergen, in Vestland, where their mother's family were from and still lived. But in Kristiansand things had been fine until Gunnar's brother moved in with their mother. However, that was only for a very short time, eight weeks, and then he died in the living room, of a heart attack. Grandma had her home help and her nurse, Gunnar and his wife had been there for her too, always on hand, and although Dad drank a bit, it hadn't stopped him being able to drive Grandma over to his other brother at Hvaler the summer before he died, and at the same time he had even been busy selling his place in Moss. He was fine, and she was fine too, they both were, but of course it had been a shock to her when her son had died. The place had been a bit untidy, there were a few bottles lying around, but that was only to be expected when a person had a drinking problem, it was nothing alarming, not in the slightest, nothing that couldn't be cleared away in a morning or two.

Gunnar was the only son who had stayed behind in Kristiansand, he was the one who had looked after the family, made sure Grandma got her home help, and her nurse, no one else had been around. Gunnar had never hurt anyone, there wasn't a blot on him or his behavior; on the contrary, he was cheerful, helpful, stable, a pillar of the community as well as of his own family. A good son, a good brother, a good father, a good citizen.

His brother's sons come down for the funeral. He leaves things to them. They clean up a bit, take care of the service, then clear off again. Ten years pass. Then he gets sent a novel the youngest has written. He can't believe his eyes. Everything that was so fine and decent has been turned into an inferno. He writes that the father had been living there for two years, that he sent the home help and the caregiver away and turned the respectable home into something more like a squat, making his mother out to be a drunken, senile old woman. Nothing of what Gunnar has spent so much of his adult life upholding is represented, everything is made out to be misery and squalor. How will it look to his friends and neighbors? How could Gunnar allow all this to happen to his mother and brother? The truth is it never happened. But how can he get that across? It says so in the novel. Is the author a liar? Apparently, yes. So then he's faced with two issues: why is the author lying, and how can Gunnar stop his lies from getting out? The author is lying because his mother, that ice-cold, egotistical woman, has brainwashed him, made him look negatively on everything to do with his father's family, and because when he was young and took drugs his grandmother had rejected him, something he had never forgotten. When his father and grandmother died he decided to seek revenge, with all the means at his disposal. He hated his grandmother, he hated his father, and at the same time he was intelligent enough to express his hatred in the form of a book and make money from it. Moreover, he had the audacity to play the hero, making out that he had cleaned up after his father, whereas the true story was that there had been hardly any cleaning up to do, and what little there was had been taken care of by Gunnar himself. He had then tricked the publisher into taking on this series of lies, this hateful project, which they had done only because they had no way of knowing the truth. They had trusted the author and bought his story without reservation. In order to stop the book, the publisher therefore had to be made aware of the truth. So he wrote to them, and to the author's mother and brother, but not to the author himself, his deceit being of such proportions he no longer wished to have anything to do with him, he never wanted to see him again for having deliberately twisted the truth in order to destroy his family. But there was another reason too: along with the manuscript the author had sent a letter explaining why he had written what he had written, and from that letter it was obvious he had no idea what he was doing. And since this was the case, Gunnar was compelled to target the person who knew better, the person who throughout all those years had distorted the author's outlook on reality to such an extent that he no longer knew what was real and what was a figment of his imagination. He was a Judas, a quisling, but he was steered by his own mother. Gunnar had seen the origins of her coldness himself, her mother, the author's maternal grandmother, had appeared almost autistic that summer he had visited them when he was twelve years old, she had clearly been ridden with inferiority complexes there in that peasant plot beneath the fells. The woman's son, the brother of the author's mother, had lost his senses and been committed to the madhouse on more than one occasion. He wrote poetry, his last collection had been about crows. This environment, of raving lunacy and insensitivity, with all its failing mental health, autism, crows, and emotional dispassion, was what the author had inherited and made his own, it was from this premise that he had written about his father, a good man at heart who perhaps in frustration at the life into which he had been tricked, with the cold woman from Vestland, had not always treated his sons the way a father ought, as Gunnar had treated his own sons, but never improperly and certainly not in any way that could warrant the picture the author had drawn of his father. He saw things through his mother's eyes, but didn't realize it.

So it wasn't my writing the truth about my father and what had happened to him in the later years of his life that was Gunnar's main issue with the novel, it was my lying about him and that period, and the fact that it made Gunnar seem guilty in the eyes of others, which was grossly inaccurate and, not least, unwarranted.

There was no doubt he meant what he was saying, that his perception of the events in question was quite different. That made me scared. If there was one thing I feared in myself, it was not being reliable. I had written that Dad had lived with Grandma during the last two years of his life, spiraling them both into decline. I had written that he had sent the nurse and the home help away. Gunnar denied both these things, and said he had witnesses to the contrary.

Where did my version come from?

How did I know it had been two years?

I had no idea. It was something I had written, and it had to have come from somewhere, but where?

I had been in Kristiansand at the time I started writing *Out of the World*, in January 1996, when Dad's drinking had been severe and he was living with Grandma. True, he still had his apartment in Moss, but as I understood it he spent most of his time at her house, and for some reason my perception was that he had moved in with her for good that summer, two years before he died. But how I had arrived at that understanding, I didn't know.

Could I simply have assumed as much, and then allowed that unconfirmed assumption to morph into certainty, subsequently elevating it to absolute truth when I started writing about it ten years later? It was not only possible, it was likely. If Gunnar said he'd only been living with Grandma for three months, and he had witnesses to confirm it, then surely it was true. I had also written that he had sent the home help and the health visitor away. Where did that come from? I didn't know that either. Somewhere in my mind I had a very vague idea it had come from Gunnar himself, perhaps he had told Yngve over the phone that Dad had sent the home help away and was out of reach, wasn't that what that phone call had been about? That Dad had barricaded himself in at Grandma's and that Gunnar felt there was nothing left he could do, having already tried to step in and appeal to Dad's reason, but to no avail? It was from that phone call, too, that I knew Dad had broken his leg and had been lying there helpless on the floor for some considerable time at Grandma's before Gunnar found him and got him to the hospital. That event had etched itself into my mind, since it told me things must have been bad, but the exact circumstances of what had happened were unclear, I couldn't put a date on either the event itself or my being told about it. But it was also possible the information about the home help being sent away had come when we were there, after Dad had died, when Gunnar was describing to us what had happened. I didn't know. He might have been exaggerating, it might have been his way of saying Dad had made it impossible for him to intervene, or maybe the home help didn't come that often. Maybe it was only the home help, the person who came to do the cleaning up, he'd been talking about, and not the nurse? But as far as I remembered I hadn't written anything about the nurse. A third possibility was that no one had said anything of the kind and it was just something I'd assumed on the basis of the dreadful state of the house; it was hard to imagine anyone had done any cleaning for a very long time, therefore the home help must have been sent away, and the person who had sent them away must have been Dad. Maybe that was what I'd got into my head in 1998, and what to begin with had been little more than a vague theory had now become a solid truth ten years later.

I didn't know.

But I felt certain Gunnar knew, and if he was so absolutely

positive that was what had happened, then surely it had to be right.

In which case I was unreliable. In itself this was a crushing admission. But had I been unreliable in everything I had written? Did it in any way alter the fundamental truth of the novel if Dad hadn't lived with Grandma for two years but for three months, and the home help hadn't been sent away but had kept up the normal routine?

Yes, it did. It would mean I'd be talking about a few days of misfortune and consternation in a world of peace and tranquillity, not about a catastrophe that had been going on for a couple of years. The only thing I knew was that the sight that met Yngve and me when we entered the house back then had been dreadful. Gunnar was saying it was untrue that the place had been littered with bottles from the front door and all the way up the staircase, that in the two days before we arrived he'd cleaned and neatened the place up, and that only Dad's room and some of the heavier items had been left.

Hadn't there been bottles? The way I remembered it, there had been empties all the way up the staircase from the living room to the top floor, there were shopping bags of them dumped underneath and on top of the piano, and the kitchen had been crammed too. But what about the staircase leading up to the living room? I had no recollection at all. I must have exaggerated. Unreliable, again. The way Gunnar was looking at it, this was about maintaining that it was he who had cleaned up the mess, not us. I vividly remembered Yngve and I spending that day and the next clearing up and scrubbing the place down, whereas what he described was a distracted author swanning about with a bucket without even the most elementary idea about what to do. I had no recollection either of our having had dinner at their place, in fact I felt sure it had never happened. But still I couldn't rule it out entirely, there were a lot of things in my life I couldn't remember. What he wrote about our going out to the cabin with Grandma, and me diving off the jetty, was true, but that had taken place outside the novel's time frame, after its conclusion. Giving Grandma a bath, washing the curtains, Gunnar and Tove's efforts when it came to cleaning the place, all that had happened after the two and a half days I'd described. The way I saw the business of cleaning the house up was the exact opposite of Gunnar's: the way I recalled it, I had found it decent of him to step back for a couple of days as he did and let Yngve and me assume responsibility, it was a way of saying to us that Dad had been our father, a way of returning him to us. Gunnar had been back and forth, helping us out with good advice, taking the furniture we lugged out of the house together away to the dump on a trailer he hired. He had not neglected anything, in fact he had behaved impeccably, but hadn't I written about all of that?

If he was right about what he was implying, that the sight that confronted us in the house had been quite normal, and that my depiction was grotesquely exaggerated, then everything fell apart. It bore down on something fundamental, first and foremost of course the very premise of the novel, that it was describing reality, but also its motive, the reason I had written about my father's death and the dreadful days that followed. When Yngve, in a car full of empty bottles, had turned to look at me and said that if I ever wrote about this no one would believe me, it was for that very reason, that everything we had seen had been like something out of a novel or a film, and not reality.

In the years that followed, I willingly told anyone who cared to listen about Dad and his demise, it made me special and perhaps interesting, too, it made me into someone who had seen a few things, gave me a certain air of casual disregard and depth, something I'm sure I was trying to attain, I'd always carried that inside me, the desire to be someone, and that notion of elevation had always been a part of my motivation for writing. Holding forth in that way about my father and what became of him always left me with a bad taste in my mouth, because I was exploiting him and the tragedy of his life for my own ends. But that was small scale. The novel blew it all up and made a big thing out of it. I was exploiting him, yes, I was climbing on his corpse. And I was doing that simply by writing about it. At the same time it was the most important story in my life. If it wasn't true, it meant I'd exaggerated things in order for Dad's fate to make the greatest possible impact, thereby lending me some of the recklessness and destructive force I thought I needed for me to become a real writer instead of someone pretending. In that case I wouldn't just be letting him down, but myself as well. It was this that Gunnar's letter addressed, as forcefully as if he'd punched me: I had lied. There had been no bottles on the staircase up to the living room. Dad had not been living there for two years. The home help had not been sent away.

If I accepted that perspective, on the other hand, I would be obliterating myself. Not once had I considered myself to be exaggerating when writing about what had gone on in the house, not once had I considered myself to be exploiting Dad and Grandma, the events I was describing were too overwhelming for that, and what I was delving into was too important.

I'd written about Dad. I'd written about my fear of him, my dependence on him, and the enormous grief his death had filled me with. It was a novel about him and me. It was a novel about a father and a son. It didn't matter that the very sight of the words "legal action" terrified me, and that my insides turned cold when he wrote that he had witnesses to the effect that I was lying, I couldn't give up the story of my father.

Not even if it was a lie?

Without realizing, I had touched on something dangerous, more dangerous than almost anything else.

But why was it dangerous?

He had to attack Mom because he felt that was what I'd done in writing the novel, attacked Grandma and Dad. It was retaliation. An eye for en eye. He was only doing what I myself had done, the difference being his retaliation lacked symmetry: my novel would be published for anyone to read, it would be available in all bookshops and all libraries. His e-mails would be read only by those he sent them to, which was to say the publisher, Mom, Yngve, and me. Because our strengths were so unevenly distributed, he was rectifying matters by hitting us even harder.

I sat down and switched the computer on, opened the document containing the novel, and started to read. In the light of what had happened in the past few days, nearly every page had me feeling uncomfortable, all the old friends and classmates I'd written about could react in exactly the same way as Gunnar.

I called Geir Gulliksen so we could discuss the purely practical implications of Gunnar's e-mail, the fact that I was going to have to alter some specifics as to time, the two years Dad had lived with Grandma in the novel, maybe by just not being specific at all, as well as correcting the errors that had occurred. I asked him what we should do about all the other names. Geir considered that anyone from my childhood or youth who was described in a relatively neutral way could stay as they were without any problem, this was quite without risk, whereas I would have to anonymize the ones I'd written about in a way that could be perceived as compromising, for instance if I'd gone into their family relations, a father who drank or was violent or who in any other way had done something that might be considered questionable. Geir's views calmed me down, he was talking of the basis of the novel, it was the novel we had to focus on, the editing of the manuscript.

After I'd spoken to Geir I called Yngve. We talked back and forth about what we remembered from the days surrounding Dad's death, he couldn't recall that many details, but hadn't balked at anything he'd read in my description. In the event of our being taken to court, he would be my only witness, though I didn't mention this at all. A court case was the worst thing that could happen, and the publishers were doing everything in their power to prevent it, I knew that. The second-worst thing that could happen was something leaking to the papers.

All of this was about Gunnar and the way he saw the novel. What we were talking about was basic human consideration. But there was another, more literary, critical issue about the novel that I'd been thinking a lot about in the interim between completing the manuscript and being made aware of Gunnar's objections. It, too, concerned truth, though more from a formal perspective, and what set me off was that I'd read a short novel by Peter Handke called *A Sorrow Beyond Dreams*, it was about his mother's suicide and thereby autobiographical. In contrast to my own prose, which constantly leaned toward the emotional and evocative, Handke's prose was dry and unsentimental. When I started writing I'd been trying to achieve a similar style, if not dry, then raw, in the sense of unrefined, direct, without metaphors or other linguistic decoration. The latter would give beauty to the language, and in a description of reality, especially the reality I was trying to describe, that would be deceitful. Beauty is a problem in that it imparts a kind of hope. As a stylistic device in literature, a particular filter through which the world is viewed, beauty lends hope to the hopeless, worth to the worthless, meaning to the meaningless. This is inevitably so. Loneliness beautifully described raises the soul to great heights. But then the writing is no longer true because there is no beauty in loneliness, not even in yearning is there beauty. But while it may not be true, it is good. It is a comfort, a solace, and perhaps that is where some of literature's justification lies? But if that's the case, then we are talking about literature as something else, something unto itself and autonomous, valuable in its own right rather than as a depiction of reality. Peter Handke tried to get away from this in his novel. It was written a few weeks after the funeral, and in it he endeavored to approach his mother and her life in as truthful a way as possible. Not truthful in the sense of things actually having occurred, her having been a real person in the real world, but truthful in its insight and the way that insight is conveyed. He refrained from representing his mother in the text, to have done so, I felt in reading the book, would have been a violation of her as a human being. She was her own person, living her own life, and instead of representing that life, Handke referred to it as something existing outside the text, never inside the text. This meant that he wrote in very general terms about the connections of which she was a part, about the roles she assumed or did not assume, but this general aspect could also potentially be a problem, he stated at one point, in that there was a risk of it becoming independent of her and taking on its own life in the text by virtue of the author's poetic formulations – a betrayal of her, this too. As he wrote, "Consequently, I first took the facts as my starting point and looked for ways of formulating them. But I soon noticed that in looking for formulations I was moving away from the facts. I then adopted a new approach – starting not with the facts but with the already available formulations, the linguistic deposit of man's social experience." In these formulations he searched, as it were, for his mother's life. And he did so, as far as I could understand, in order to protect her dignity and integrity, but something else was going on in the text too; when a person is portrayed from a social viewpoint, through the contemporary eyes of society's culture and self-understanding, with all its various roles and limits, that person's inner being, her singular, individual existence, what used to be called the soul, vanishes, and, I considered, Handke's book was perhaps a story about just that, the suppression of the individual by the social world, the strangulation of the soul. After all, in the end she took her life. Handke steered away from all affect, all feelings, anything anecdotal, anything that might inject life into the text, always insisting that he was writing a text, that the life he was describing exists, or existed, elsewhere, and when, after some seventy pages or so, he arrives at the moment of death and the funeral, which takes place on the fringe of a forest, he writes, "The people left the grave quickly. Standing beside it, I looked up at the motionless trees: for the first time it seemed to me that nature really was merciless. So these were the facts! The forest spoke for itself. Apart from these countless treetops, nothing counted; in the foreground an episodic jumble of shapes, which gradually receded from the picture. I felt mocked and helpless. All at once, in my impotent rage, I felt the need to write something about my mother." This sudden insight into the nature of death is the novel's true starting point. I recognized that insight, it was mine too. However, the book I had written was the direct antithesis of Handke's, its antipode.

I wrote that I had the same insight as Handke when he stood there at the graveside and looked toward the trees and realized that nature was merciless and that the forest spoke for itself. But was that true? How could it be true when that insight had prompted Handke to write a book about his mother and his mother's death in which she was not represented but merely referred to? Given shape only by way of the time in which she lived and the formulations and insights of that time, viewed as an individual who had a certain number of types to choose between, socially and historically determined, albeit of course not without her own personality, though this was not given shape, because then it would have become "typical" of her, and paradoxically a deceit, for the reason that she was always, and invariably, something else. Death in Handke's universe was merciless, and the life he described was merciless too, and given that this is true, his book could not be about mercy. From a literary perspective, mercy lay in beauty, which is to say in the beautiful sentence, and in the creative manifestation, the fictionalization, the secret alliance of events that crisscrossed any novel, because this crisscrossing in itself was an affirmation of meaning and cohesion. So how could Handke's insight be the same as mine when I had written a book about my father's death in which I allowed the text to represent him as if it were in the text that he existed, which is to say making him an object of the reader's own feelings, in prose that sought to form and shape, to creatively make manifest throughout, since it, or its author, was aware that shaping a character into life, making him manifest in that way, rouses or manipulates feelings in a world that was not merciless, because meanings and cohesion would continually be established by their different routes, regardless of what the text otherwise had to say about the matter?

Handke wrote, "The people left the grave quickly. Standing beside it, I looked up at the motionless trees: for the first time it seemed to me that nature really was merciless. So these were the facts! The forest spoke for itself." I wrote, "And death, which I have always regarded as the greatest dimension of life, dark, compelling, was no more than a pipe that springs a leak, a branch that cracks in the wind, a jacket that slips off a clothes hanger and falls to the floor." That was beautiful, it was something, whereas what it described was nothing, empty, neutral, as hopeless as it was merciless. Handke did not lie, or at least he made the greatest efforts not to. I was lying. Why?

When I looked at a tree, I saw that it was blind and arbitrary, an entity that had come into being and would die, and which in the meantime was growing. When I looked at a net full of flapping, silvery fish, I saw the same thing, something blind and arbitrary that came into being, flourished, and would die. When I looked at photos from the Nazi extermination camps, I saw people in the same way. Limbs, heads, bellies, hair, genitals. It had nothing to do with the way I considered them, what I saw was the way these people were viewed at that time, which made it possible for so many to have known about those atrocities and even to have taken part in them without raising a finger. That it was possible to see things in that way was frightening but did not make what was seen any less true. It could be taken as nothing, and all thoughts that sought meaning in the world would have to relate to that zero point. I looked at a tree and I saw meaninglessness. But I saw life, too, in its pure, blind form, something that simply existed and was growing. The energy and the beauty of that. Death was indeed nothing, a mere absence. But just as blind life on the one hand could be viewed as a force, something sacred and – well, why not – divine, and on the other hand as something meaningless and empty, death too could be seen in that same way, its song too could be sung, it too could be infused with meaning and beauty. This was what made German National Socialism so infinitely significant to us, a mere two generations having passed since the Nazis were in power, and under their reign of terror, modern in every respect, all three of these perspectives prevailed at once: life as a divine force, death as beautiful and meaningful, human beings as blind, arbitrary, worthless. This aspect, which prior to Nazism belonged to art and to the sublime, became a part of the social order. Handke's mother was a young woman when all that took place, and after describing her childhood years, in Austria between the wars in relative poverty and ignorance, when her wish to learn something, anything, was considered utterly unrealistic and undesirable, Handke sketches out the new mood arising in and around National Socialism, with demonstrations, torchlight parades, buildings festooned with new emblems of nationhood, and writes, "The historic events were represented to the rural population as a drama of nature." Of his mother he states that she continued to have no interest in politics, since "what was happening before her eyes was something entirely different from politics. 'Politics' was something colorless and abstract, not a carnival, not a dance, not a band in local costume, in short, nothing *visible*."

Nazism was the last major utopian political movement, and it showed itself in nearly every way to be destructive, it has made all subsequent utopian thinking problematic if not impossible, not only in politics but also in art, and since art by its very nature is utopian, it has languished ever since, self-examining and suspicious, something of which Handke's novel and nearly all novels by authors of his generation are an expression. How can reality be represented without adding something it doesn't have? What does it "have" and what does it not "have"? What is authentic and what is not authentic? Where is the line between what is put on and what is not put on? Does a line even exist? Is the world anything more than our conceptions about it? Language has no life of its own, is not itself alive, but invokes life, and the primal mise-en-scène of this, the very source of creative literature, is found in the *Odyssey*, when Odysseus and his crew moor on the Oceanus River after visiting Circe, and Odysseus offers a sacrifice to the dead on the shore. The dark blood drains darkly away into the pit, and the dead souls flock around it. He sees young girls in bridal dress, young warriors in bloodstained armor, and old men, their screams are terrifying, and the fear runs through him. The first person he recognizes is Elpenor, who died during their stay with Circe and was left unburied. He speaks to Tiresias the soothsayer, who tells of the future, and then Odysseus's own mother drinks of the blood, she recognizes him and tells him how she died. Odysseus wishes to embrace her and approaches three times, yet three times she escapes him, like a dream or a shadow. She tells him her sinews no longer keep flesh and bone together, the funeral pyre having turned her body into ash, and all that is left is her soul, which wanders about. Literature invokes the world as Odysseus invokes the dead, and regardless of whatever way it does this, the distance is always unbridgeable, the stories always the same. A son loses his mother three thousand years ago, a son loses his mother forty years ago. That one of these stories is fiction, the other fact, does nothing to alter their fundamental likeness, both are made manifest in language, and in that perspective all of Handke's efforts to avoid the literary become futile, there is nothing in his depiction of reality that is more real than Homer's. Nor is that what he seeks to do.

Handke endeavors to write about a human being, his mother, without invoking her, without giving her blood in such a way as to make her manifest as something reminiscent of her previous, living form, in other words denying her the fictional life that might connect up what is dead, her existence in the past, with what is living, the mind of the reader. What the language invokes instead is what surrounded her, the shapes in her life, and although her identity, that which was particular to her, becomes visible in this way, it does not speak to us. Moreover, what is invoked by the language is not something found on the other side of some unbridgeable abyss, for these shapes are in themselves of the language in a certain respect, though not in a wholly literal sense. In this way Handke manages to achieve what he presumably set out to, which was to represent reality in a truthful manner. Another way of doing the same thing might be to remove the narrator entirely and simply present the reader with the documents in which the mother was mentioned or which concerned circumstances of which she was a part; in that case the relationship between reality and its representation would be as good as congruent. The "as if" of art, the abyss that separates it from reality, would then be removed completely. Or, more correctly, would merely be sensed as the will that tracked down the documents, gathered them together, and arranged them in a certain order. Of course, the reader might regard that order as manipulative, since in reality the documents were arranged horizontally, in various archives, in different locations, and even a chronological principle would represent an intrusion and create effect: the last entry in the medical journal is followed by the postmortem report, and the reader wipes away a tear.

The important thing for Handke was to describe his mother without traducing her, which is to say without intervening in what was singular to her, out of respect for her integrity. To me this was not a good thought at all, since I had written about a similar set of events in my own life and had done so in a way that was almost diametrically opposed to Handke's, reaching continually toward affect, feeling, the sentimental in contrast to the rational, and dramatizing my father, allowing him to be a character in a story, representing him in the same way as fictional characters are represented, by concealing the "as if" on which all literature depends, and thereby traducing him and his integrity in the most basic of ways, by saying that this was him. I had said the same thing about all the novel's characters, but only in the case of my father had I done so in a way that failed to show consideration to him and the person he was. He had been dead for more than ten years, but that only made it possible, it didn't justify it.

I had thought about none of this while I had been writing, neither the manufacture of reality, representation, nor my father's integrity, everything took place intuitively, I began with a blank page and a will to write, and ended up with the novel as it was.

In that there lies a belief in the intuitive that is as good as blind, and from that basis a poetics might be derived, and an ontology too, I suppose, since for me the novel provides a means of thinking radically different from that of the essay, the article, or the thesis, because reflection in the novel is not hierarchically superior as a pathway to understanding, but coordinate with all the other elements in it. The room in which it is conceived is as important as the thought itself. The snow falling through the darkness outside, the headlights of the cars gliding past on the other side of the river. This was perhaps the most important thing I learned at university, that practically anything at all can be said about a novel or a poem, and what is said may be as likely as it is plausible, but never exhaustive, perhaps not even important, since the novel and the poem are always entities in their own right, singular and existing as they are, and the fact that what the novel or the poem says cannot be said in any other way makes them essentially mysterious. The world is mysterious in exactly the same way, and yet we tend to forget this all the time, always giving precedence to reflection whenever we look at it. What does it mean to "walk"? Is it putting one foot in front of the other? Yes, it is. But describing the motor function, the putting of one foot in front of the other, says nothing about what it feels like to walk, of the difference between walking uphill and down, walking along a stone jetty or up a flight of stairs, across a lawn or on the mossy earth of the forest, barefoot or in boots, and even less about the feeling of watching others walk – the pedestrians bustling across the square on a Saturday morning, the lone man striding through snow-covered fields or a person you've known for a very long time, the way their entire character seems to be contained in the way they walk when they come toward you. You see it at once, here "he" or "she" comes. In that unique pattern of movements is all that you know and have experienced about that person, though not as separate, clearly divided parts, what you see is in a way the sum of that person, what they "are" to you. They come walking, you see them, and that's it. One could delve deeper into this, for example scientifically, in which case it's all about muscles and sinews being deployed in a particular way so as to make it possible to put one foot in front of the other, the way the blood runs through the arteries and veins, the gases it transports, the cells and cell walls, the mitochondria and the strings of DNA, not to mention the impulses that race through the nervous system, sent on their way by a will or a wish for movement in the form of chemistry and electrical discharges in the brain, which then begs a whole series of questions. What is will? What is a wish? What is a motor impulse? What form does it have? If it is chemistry, then what is the connection between the various chemical reactions and what we know as will, or the urge to do something? These impulses do not belong to the conscious mind, but to deeper-lying and considerably older parts of the brain, unchanged through millions of years right back to the time our first and most distant ancestors emerged into the world, like the apes in almost every respect apart from their hip sockets and the length of their arms, as well as a few more physiological peculiarities that made it possible for them to do what no other animal until then had been able to do, and which none other is able to do to this day, which was to walk upright on two legs. Walking upright on two legs is what above all distinguishes us as a species. This property characterizes not only our physical but also our mental reality, since we orient ourselves in the world of thought as if it were topographical, a landscape through which we walk, from the depths of the subconscious to the sky of the superego, one political utopia farthest to our left, the other farthest to our right; some thoughts are nearby, either easy to grasp or hard to see because we are right up close, some thoughts we need to reach for, others are higher up and can only be made our own by the greatest, most alpine of efforts, while others are low and grubby, close to the ground and to the earthly.

As a writer you can go that step further or, as Lawrence Durrell describes the process of writing novels, set oneself a goal and walk there in your sleep. The act of "walking" is inexhaustible;

however, literature's job is not to be exhaustive but to construct the inexhaustible, at least it is for the kind of literature that aims to represent reality and our ever-changing, fluctuating reactions to it. The trees that are, to put it in the manner of Rilke, and we who pass by it all, like changing breaths of wind. The forest speaks for itself, Handke writes, there is an abyss between us and it, but if nature's mercilessness appears threatening, it is not because it is turned away from us, as it can appear when we look at it, in its almost dreamlike remoteness, but because its muteness and blindness exist in us all. Merciless is the beating heart. Odysseus tried to build a bridge across the abyss, between what was culture and what was nature in his being when he spoke to his heart and beseeched it not to beat so hard. The abyss is inside us. I saw it the first time I stood in front of a dead body. I didn't understand it, but I saw it and knew. Death is not the abyss, but exists in the living, in the space between our thoughts and the flesh through which they pass. In the flesh, thoughts are a kind of intruder, conquerers of a foreign land, who leave it just as quickly again the moment it becomes inhospitable, which is to say when all movements cease and all warmth seeps away, as it does in death.

But it wasn't simply a dead body I saw back then. The dead body was my father. My vague notion of what death was constituted only an infinitely small element in the barrage of thoughts and feelings that consumed me. In front of me lay the person who had created me, his body had made mine, and I had grown up under his supervision, he was the single most important and influential person in my life. The fact that he was dead did nothing to alter that. Nothing was concluded that afternoon in the chapel in Kristiansand.

After speaking to Yngve I took the elevator down to the basement and walked through the damp bunker-like passages in which the ceiling lights futuristically came on by themselves one by one as I proceeded, and reached the laundry room at the exact moment the display on the last of the machines changed from one minute left to zero. I transferred the wet clothes into the tumble dryers, and stuffed the last of the dirty ones into the washing machines, sprinkled washing powder into the little trays, and switched them on, and a second later the machines rumbled and spluttered into life. I stood for a moment, watching their drums revolve, the way the clothes inside became more and more saturated and were slung against the glass, wrenched from sight, slung against the glass, my thoughts wandering to the worst possible scenario, a court case. I saw myself in my mind's eye arriving in a taxi, the blitz of photographers as I left the building, the headlines in the newspapers, Knausgaard the Liar, Shambles, Should Never Have Been Published, Admits Lying, Knausgaard Raped Me, because I understood all too well that proceedings of that kind would kick up all sorts of other accusations, and that an autobiographical project in which I also wrote about others opened the floodgates for just about anything to be said about me by anyone at all. On its own terms, I wasn't anticipating the novel making any major impact, and neither were the publishers, ten thousand copies were being printed to start with, that was a lot, though no more than my previous novel, but if there was going to be a court case, sales no doubt would rocket. It would be a scandal then, dirty and sensational, and all kinds of shit would be dug up about me. In my thoughts, I sat in the witness box, which for some reason I imagined to be a kind of desk not unlike the ones we'd had at school, on a low platform in the middle of a packed room, answering the most provocative and insinuating questions imaginable. The first was why had I written the novel in the first place. Why had I used people's real names instead of concealing their identities, as was the practice in novels running close to real events, and had been for as long as the genre had existed. Why real life? What was the point? At first I found myself unable to answer and shifted uneasily in the chair, stuttering and stammering much as I sometimes had onstage, most recently in Munich, where many

190

of the small audience that had found its way there had got up and left, something that consumed me with shame whenever I thought about it. But what was the point of wallowing in thoughts of weakness and wretchedness, I thought to myself, and looked up at the ground-level window just below the ceiling, through the cracked pane of which I glimpsed the asphalt outside.

Why not fight back? I straightened my shoulders, and there, in the midst of all the journalists and inquisitive onlookers, perhaps a hundred in total, I began to speak, vividly and full of insight, about the relationship between truth and the subjective, literature's relationship to reality, delving into the nature of social structures, the way a novel of this kind exposed the boundaries to which society adhered but which remained unwritten and were thus invisible insofar as they were melded into us and our self-understanding, and how they for this reason had to be breached before they could be seen. But why did they have to be seen, my defense lawyer asked. There is something all of us experience, which is the same for all human beings, I replied, but which nonetheless is seldom conveyed apart from in the private sphere. All of us encounter difficulties at some point in our lives, all of us know someone with a drinking problem, mental issues, or some other kind of life-threatening affliction, at least this is the case in my experience; every time I meet a new person and get to know them, some narrative like this will eventually come to the surface, a tale of sickness, decline, or sudden death. These things are not represented and thereby seem not to exist, or else to exist only as a burden each of us must bear on our own. But what about the newspapers and the media, the defense lawyer then asked. Surely there's enough death and sickness there? Of course, I said, but there it is presented as facts, described from a distance as a kind of objective phenomenon. The ripple effect of such cases, the impact on the individual and the next of kin, is ignored or briefly referred to as something external. Moreover, it has to be something spectacular to be written about. What I'm talking about is day-to-day life. The metaphor for that is death. Death is present in all our lives, firstly in the shape of something that happens to someone we know, then, eventually, to ourselves. People die in droves every single day. It's something we don't see, it's kept from us. We don't like to talk about it either. Why not? It touches the very depths of everyone's existence. Why do we suppress that? It's the same with aging and human deterioration. If you get too old to look after yourself you're put in an institution, hidden away from everyone. What kind of a society are we living in, where everything that is sick, deviant, or dead is kept from sight? Two generations ago, sickness and death were both very much closer to us, if not a natural part of life then at least unavoidable. I could have written an article about all this, but it wouldn't have said much because arguments have got to be rational, and this is about the opposite, the irrational, all the feelings we have about what it means to confront what has withered away into death, and what that actually is. I remember the first time I saw real sickness, my maternal grandmother was in the final throes of Parkinson's disease, and the sheer physical frailty and human suffering was an enormous shock to me because I had no idea it existed in that way. I knew there was sickness, but I didn't know it was like that. I had a similar experience the first time I worked in an institution for the mentally deficient, I was stunned by what I saw, all those deformed bodies and crippled minds, why had I not known that this, too, was part of the human experience? It had been kept out of the way, but why? It made me think about what physicality actually is, what it means, the animal or biological, material nature of the human body and its absolute closeness to the world, in contrast to the world picture and self-understanding that comes out of our reflections as to who we are and what kind of terms we exist under, not just in the limitless amounts of scientific research we produce, but also in the limitless amounts of news stories and programs we read and watch, in which this perspective is absent. What I was trying to do was to reintroduce a closeness, trying to get the text to penetrate that whole series of conceptions and ideas and images that hang like a sky above reality, or cling to it like a membrane enclosing the eye, to reach into the reality of the human body and the frailty of the flesh, but not in any general way because generality is a relative of the ideal, it doesn't exist, only the particular exists, and since the particular in this case happens to be me, that was what I wrote about. That's how it is. It was the only goal I had, and that's the reality of the matter. Some people are of the opinion I had no right to do what I was doing because in doing so I was involving other people besides myself. And this is true. My question is why we conceal the things we do. Where is the shame in human decline? The complete human catastrophe? To live the complete human catastrophe is terrible indeed, but to write about it? Why shame and concealment when what we are dealing with here is basically the most human thing of all? What's so dangerous about it that we cannot speak of it out loud?

Gunnar's lawyer, who had stood pensively listening to all this, looked at me in a way I took to indicate sarcasm.

"All well and good, Knausgaard," he said. "But the truth is that your father's demise did not occur in the manner in which you have described. We have witnesses. He drank and had his problems, certainly, but his demise was quiet and uneventful. Moreover, the fact of the matter is that your grandmother did not drink at all. The two years you, in your colorful depiction, would have them living and drinking together exist only in your imagination. He lived with her for three months. The house was not littered with empty bottles. Nor did you wash the house down, as you have written, because your uncle did that. And therefore my question to you is this: Why are you lying about these matters? You, who wish to write about the world the way it is, why should you, of all people, depict a world that never existed? That is the issue facing us today. You can try to hide behind as much existential intellectualism as you like, to my mind it's pretentious gibberish, so pompous it makes me feel sick just standing here listening to it. However, that is not the matter at hand, at least not today, but from what I can deduce from your self-exalting and conceited claptrap, you consider what you have written to be the truth, this to your mind being the whole point of your despicable and duplicitous novel. Only then it turns out not to be the truth at all. Can you explain that to me?"

I stared at him stiffly, unable to move.

"It's how I remember it," I said after a while.

"Not good enough!" the lawyer barked. "You have offended these people, desecrated the memories of two deceased members of your own family. You sold your father and grandmother for blood money. And all you can say is it's how you remember it? Violating the privacy of your family is a serious enough matter on its own, a criminal offense, but to have lied about your uncle's mother and his brother exacerbates that offense tenfold. We're talking about defamation of character, carrying a sentence of up to three years' imprisonment."

He wiped the perspiration from his brow and swept his blond hair from his face in one and the same movement, then looked at me, waiting.

"But I did wash the house down," I said. "It's not true that I can't manage things like that. I may have exaggerated the chaos inside the house, but it was dreadful. And as for what I've written about my father, it's my own story I'm telling. That can't be against the law, surely? Can it?"

I consciously avoided glancing at Gunnar, who sat proudly in the first row, having refused to acknowledge my gesture of reconciliation in the minutes prior to proceedings commencing, when, heroically and forgivingly, I had extended my hand toward him, and crossed the floor back to my seat to await the testimony of the first witness, the Swedish essayist, professor, and member of the Swedish Academy Horace Engdahl, the man who for many years had announced the winner of the Nobel Prize, known for his literary elegance and incomparable style, classmate of suspected Palme assassin Christer Pettersson, and friend of the wild and fearlessly gifted writer Stig Larsson. I had seen Engdahl at a seminar in Bergen many years before; he had veered off the theme and talked about Carina Rydberg and her novel *Den högsta kasten*, *The Highest Caste*, it was at the time when the controversy surrounding that book had been at its peak in Sweden – she had written about actual people, using their full names – and Engdahl had said that, quite apart from the bickering to which it had given rise, the book was first and foremost a brilliant work of literature. I suppose I was hoping he would say the same about my own book. On the other hand, I found myself thinking as I stood there, staring emptily at the washing machine and the soapy water that sloshed against the glass, there was something essentially elitist and superior about the man, he was a literary aristocrat, and how was that going to look in court, with Gunnar coming across as the man in the street, the everyman who quite unwittingly found his life destroyed by his writer nephew? People would think it could happen to them, too, and shudder at the thought. I would be made out to be the basest of human beings, a kind of literary vampire, brutal and without consideration, self-seeking and egoistic. Perhaps an aristocrat wouldn't be the right person to argue in favor of such a practice?

A door opened in the passage, perhaps it was someone who had booked the washing machines I was now using, and I turned my head to look, but the faint footsteps came to a halt at another door, which whoever it was then opened. I waited a few seconds for them to go inside, then went out. The sounds of the laundry room were cut off abruptly by the heavy slam of the steel door closing behind me. It felt like I was in the depths of some great factory, I thought to myself. I went up the stairs, through the door, and out onto the square, I needed to get some cigarettes. The fruit merchant waved at me, I was probably his best customer. I smiled and waved back, twirling my key strap around my index finger and crossing to the other side of the square, glancing as always at the shoes in the window of the Nilson store as I went by. Lars Norén had written about a Nilson shop in his expansive diaries, which I'd read halfway through the previous summer, he'd expressed astonishment at the fact that a woman – I couldn't quite remember if it was his daughter or his new girlfriend – could buy her shoes there, apparently Nilson wasn't good enough for him, he bought his own shoes in a different class of shop altogether, so I understood, though until then I'd always thought of the place as having a certain status. Now it was impossible for me to go past the store without thinking about it, Norén's cosmopolitan consternation at the provincial footwear habits of others. I glanced at another shop on the other side of the street, as was my habit, since it sold underwear and often displayed posters of scantily clad women in its windows, before pushing open the door of Thomas Tobak and stepping inside, where Thomas himself looked up amiably, before looking down again at a receipt he seemed to be checking.

"Hello there," he said.

"Hello," I said. "Three packs of Lucky, please."

He picked them off the shelf behind him.

"No papers today?" he asked.

I shook my head.

"A hundred and forty-seven, then," he said.

I took my card out of my back pocket.

"You can use this one," he said, nodding at a new card reader he'd got, one that read the chip rather than the magnetic stripe, which was good for both of us, since the stripe on my card was rather the worse for wear and he'd had to key in the number manually on more than one occasion. Not that he minded, he always had plenty of time for his customers, no matter how busy he was.

"Well, that's something," I said. "Thanks a lot!"

"No problem," he said.

With the three packs in my hand I went out again, into the pedestrian street that ran down to the first of the canals, then on to Gustav Adolfs torg, teeming with people on Saturday mornings but now almost deserted.

The children.

Where were they?

I stopped.

They were at the nursery. I'd dropped them off there.

Or had I?

What had I done that morning?

Flustered, I tried to recall some definite occurrence that would confirm to me that I had taken them to the nursery and delivered them there, and then, in the same instant, I remembered we'd gone back for Vanja's glasses, and everything was all right.

I started walking again and went around the corner, past the flower stall first, then the fruit stall, still with a vague sense of unease; I hadn't given the children a thought all morning, and if they'd been anywhere else but at the nursery I would have been grossly neglecting them. The previous summer I'd read about a Danish father who forgot to stop off at the nursery one morning, his child had been asleep in the back when he parked the car, he explained, and he had gone into work oblivious. The child had died in the heat. Something similar could easily happen to me, I'd often thought, and if I happened to be out with only two of them, I could find myself suddenly stricken with terror. Where's John? Have I forgotten him somewhere? Where is he? Where the hell is he? And then I would realize he was at home with Linda and everything was all right. But even though I'd been through it before, the fear could come back at any time, where is he, with Linda, how can you be sure that wasn't yesterday, think back!

I passed the key card over the panel and pushed the door open. A postman was delivering the mail, putting it in the various mailboxes. I nodded and stopped. He dropped a small pile into ours, I waited until he stepped out of the way, then retrieved it, opened the elevator door and flicked through the bundle on my way up. There was a letter from Svea Inkasso, the debt collection company, three bills, a *Bamse* magazine, and an advertising brochure from Spirit. I opened the door and went inside, dumping it all on top of the pile on the table under the mirror before taking my shoes off and putting them away in the cupboard. I put two of the cigarette packs in the drawer of my desk, took the third out with me onto the balcony and sat down, poured myself a cup of coffee from the vacuum jug, opened the packet, took out a cigarette, and lit up.

Above me a pigeon cooed, the sound came suddenly and was very close. I looked up, it sounded like it came from inside the roof.

Uuhh-huu-huuu, it said.

Uuhh-huu-huuu.

The bird scratched about up there, presumably it was the sound of its claws against the zinc I could hear, it had tried to change position and now couldn't get purchase. Oh, its claws, they were so prehistoric, what were they doing on modern metal?

I poured myself some more coffee.

The pigeon sailed into the air above me, gliding toward the rooftop on the other side, perhaps two floors down, where it settled on a TV aerial.

Faintly, as if from the depths of the apartment below, came the sound of a door buzzer. A few seconds passed before I connected it to Geir being due. I got to my feet and went back inside, down the hall, as it buzzed again.

I picked up the entry phone.

"Yes?" I said.

"It's Gunnar. Is that you, you bastard? I'm here to get you!"

"Come in," I said, and pressed the button until I heard the door open downstairs, then hung up, opened the door, and stood waiting at the elevator.

Geir emerged shoving a big black suitcase in front of him. Njaal came out behind him, hugging his leg; the look he gave me was partly suspicious, partly curious. Geir put his hand out without smiling, then looked up at me.

"Hi," he said hurriedly, as if he'd lost his breath, already leaving the greeting behind.

"So you found it all right?" I said.

"I have been here before, in case you'd forgotten," he said, bundling past me into the hall, where he put the suitcase down and bent down to help Njaal off with his shoes.

"How could I forget?" I said.

He looked up and smiled.

"Relax, it's going to be all right."

"What is?"

"Whatever's worrying you."

He bent down again and took his sandals off.

"Where are Heidi and Vanja?" said Njaal.

"At the *dagis*," I said. "They'll be home again soon. You can play with their toys while you're waiting."

He stepped cautiously toward their room.

"Good to see you," I said as Geir straightened up.

"I'm sure," he said. "You'll be saving a fortune on your phone bill now."

"You think I call too often, is that it?"

"Often?" he said. "It's all I do! Get up, brush my teeth, talk to you, have some lunch, talk to you, have some dinner, talk to you, brush my teeth, go to bed. I wonder what's going to happen tomorrow, I think to myself. Who knows, maybe Karl Ove might call?"

"Do you want some coffee or something?" I said.

"You bet I do."

He followed me into the kitchen, angling his head slightly upward, the way he often did when we hadn't seen each other for a long time, a wide, sardonic smile on his face, as if to say, I know you.

And in a way, he did.

When we moved to Malmö I had been afraid Geir and I would lose touch. That's what distance does; when the time between conversations gets longer, intimacy diminishes, the little things connected to one's daily life lose their place, it seems odd to talk about a shirt you just bought or to mention you're thinking of leaving the dishes until morning when you haven't spoken to a person for two weeks or a month, that absence would seem instead to call for more important topics, and once they begin to determine the conversation there's no turning back, because then it's two diplomats exchanging information about their respective realms in a conversation that needs to be started up from scratch, in a sense, every time, which gradually becomes tedious, and eventually it's easier not to bother phoning at all, in which case it's even harder the next time, and then suddenly it's been half a year of silence. But that didn't happen. Far from it, we were in touch even more after I moved away, we talked more often on the phone, and for a lot longer, to the extent that sometimes I found myself wondering if it was normal, which filled me with a vague sense of unease because I didn't want not to be normal. A typical day would be me phoning him first at nine in the morning, when we would talk for anything from twenty minutes to an hour and a half, then I'd call him again in the afternoon, when I'd read him what I'd written during the day, and he would comment on it. He never criticized but would discuss what I'd written in such a way as to open it up, presenting other perspectives and possibilities, which I would often make use of in what I wrote the day after. Occasionally, we spoke in the evenings too, though I tried to keep it to a minimum, sensing that Linda perhaps found all this talking to Geir rather excessive. But I had no friends in Malmö, no other writers I saw, and the only space I had in which to talk about the things that interested and occupied me was this, and since it had been going on for several years I saw no need to be any different to what I was, no need to pretend I was any smarter than I was or say anything else other than what I actually thought. Many of the ideas and conceptions I discussed either directly or indirectly in the book had come from Geir, just as we also talked about the directions in which they took me. He was an influence, my thoughts were increasingly similar to his, and the only redeeming aspect of this, because that was the way I looked at it, was that I allowed the thoughts I so shamelessly appropriated from him to find resonance in what belonged to me, my own story and biography, as well as the fact that I likewise played a part in his work and development, though not as significantly and in a quite different way that was less threatening to his own integrity. Six years previously he had traveled to Baghdad and stayed there before, during, and after the American invasion of Iraq. His intention was to write a book about war, and he had entered the country as a human shield, a cover that gave him enormous freedom and allowed him to interview all kinds of people who in one way or another were affected by the war. He had spent the six years since his return writing that book, a process that slowly but surely was approaching its conclusion.

His working title was *Against Better Judgment*. It could have been his motto. I poured the coffee into the mugs and handed him his. Outside the window the rooftops and their ridges, red against the sky's blue, seemed to slant inward, it was something to do with perspective, I was looking at them diagonally from above, and it created an illusion. It had struck me the very first time I had stood here looking out. We were being shown the apartment, and that faint feeling of dizziness it had given me made me certain I wanted to live here. Now I was used to it, but Geir being here made me notice again.

"Anything more from him?" he said.

"From Gunnar?" I said.

He nodded, and flashed me a grin I might have taken to be malicious if I hadn't known him better.

"No. Enough's enough, don't you think?"

"Absolutely," he said, still grinning.

"You can wipe that smile off your face, then," I said.

"I'm in a good mood, that's all. Oh, but you wouldn't have noticed, would you? Ha ha."

"My problem's a bit bigger than that."

"I know. Your problem is that you're a bad person."

"Exactly."

"And, I should add, one of the few true narcissists."

"If you say so."

"There's no doubt about it. The only reason I point it out is because I'm one too."

"I'm not sure I follow. You put up with me and all my morbid self-absorption, because you're just the same, morbidly self-absorbed? Wouldn't it be more logical for you to hate me for taking up time better spent on yourself?"

"My ego's big enough for it not to bother me."

He looked up at me and grinned again as he lifted the mug to his lips.

There was a crash from the living room.

"Njaal, what are you up to in there?" he called.

Njaal's little voice said something back.

"Do you want to come outside while I have a smoke?" I said. He nodded and we went out onto the balcony. On our way we saw Njaal sitting on the floor surrounded by toys he'd taken out of the round ottoman, it was the lid that had dropped on the floor. We sat down on either side of the little camping table. I lit a cigarette and put my feet up on the railing.

"Do you want something else to think about?" he said.

"That wouldn't be bad," I replied.

"I was in town the other day and bought a pair of clogs."

"I don't think this is going to be enough to lift me up into the light," I said.

"The reason I bought them was to annoy my neighbor," he said. "If it doesn't work, I'm going to buy some for Christina and Njaal as well."

"You mean you're wearing clogs indoors now?" I asked, and looked at him inquiringly.

He nodded.

"It's a war. As soon as I get home I put them on and jump up and down on the floor for an hour or so."

"Like Donald Duck, you mean?"

"No, Donald Duck gets mad, that's all. He's totally irrational. This is rational. I'm exploiting the advantages of the terrain. I'm higher up than him. My floor is his ceiling."

"Haven't you thought about beating him up? Dragging him out into the woods and giving him a good hiding?"

"That would be too brutal, even if it is touch and go. And we could lose the tenancy. I don't want to risk that. There's no rule against clogs, though. No one can deny me clogs. If he laid a finger on Christina or Njaal, that'd be different. You've got to measure your violence. It's all about violence against over-violence. I could have shot him, but that would have been excessive. The same goes for beating him up. You've got to wait and see how the conflict develops and tailor your violence according to how much is reasonable. That's Clausewitz. Violence is a means of removing a problem. A practical measure."

"So you've thought about beating him up, then?"

"Of course I have. But this is the best solution. I'm going to be wearing clogs until he gives in. If it takes a year, I'll wear clogs for a year. If it takes ten, I'll wear them for ten."

"You're out of your mind."

"Not in the slightest! I'm involved in a conflict with my downstairs neighbor. He attacked me. I tried to be reasonable, but it didn't work. So I'm retaliating. I'm not doing anything against the rules, and he'll discover that soon enough. And then the only way he'll be able to stop it will be to give in. He knows that. There are three ways he can get out of this. One, he moves out. Two, his wife apologizes to Christina. Three, he never speaks to us again and never so much as looks at us when we meet, i.e., stays well and truly away. If you ask me, my guess is he'll go with the latter. But we'll see. For the moment, he's sticking it out."

"You make it sound like a normal way of dealing with things," I said. "But it's not, is it? No one resolves a conflict by buying themselves a pair of clogs and tramping around in them indoors. And the way you talk about it as well. Exploiting the advantages of the terrain. Anyone would think you were an army unit taking a hill in Vietnam or something. But it's an apartment in Stockholm we're talking about."

"A conflict is a conflict," he said. "I know this is going to end

203

it. There's no way he can win. No one can withstand the sound of clogs on a floor. He'll last a month, maybe two. Then he'll come creeping and ask what he can do to make me stop. You'll see. It'll be problem solved."

"Not his."

"No, but his is unsolvable. Mine, on the other hand, isn't.'"

A few months earlier Geir and Christina had moved out of their two-room apartment in Västertorp to a four-room in the same neighborhood. Even as they were moving in, their downstairs neighbor had complained about the disturbance as they lugged their furniture and boxes up the stairs. He complained about their hammering when they were hanging their pictures on the wall. They told him they would try to move in as quietly as they could, but that it was impossible for them not to make some noise. A few weeks after, he complained about doors being slammed and Njaal running across the floor. Geir fitted rubber strips around the doors and cupboard doors, and put more mats down on the floors. The neighbor wrote a formal complaint to the landlord. Besides the noise from the apartment, there was the noise in the stairwell whenever they went in and out, and the stroller inside the street door. Geir responded in a letter to the effect that they were as considerate as they could be. They never played music, never held parties, and went to bed every night at ten. The noise their neighbor was complaining about was the same as that made by any normal family with children, and there was nothing to be done about it. His letter, as I understood it, only made the neighbor even more furious, he had even confronted Geir one time in the basement. The situation reminded me of when Linda and I lived in Stockholm and had a neighbor who likewise complained about everything we did and behaved threateningly toward us. We too had tried to accommodate her demands, but they had been too unreasonable for it to work. We solved the issue by moving out. I still felt the panic grab hold of me if one of the children was noisy, if they happened to kick a radiator, for instance, or thump around on the floor. A chill of anxiety would run through me, and I'd be there like a shot to make them stop. Our neighbors here had never complained, it was the fear of our Stockholm neighbor that still lived inside me, three years after we moved away. I'd spoken to Christina about it, and her reaction was the same as mine, to try to eliminate the cause and tiptoe around. Geir was made of sterner stuff. He didn't internalize, he retaliated. He had resorted to buying the clogs now, he told me, because of something that had only just happened. Christina had been out on the balcony with Njaal and had gone in again for a moment when she heard shouting from the balcony below. What's going on up there? It turned out Njaal had opened the lid of the parasol stand, which had been full of water, and some of the water had dripped down onto the neighbors below. Christina had no idea what had happened, and said they hadn't been doing anything. Whereupon the wife had shouted to her husband that the bitch was being cheeky. As soon as Geir heard about this he got in the car, drove into town, and bought the clogs he'd been tramping about in ever since, from when he got up in the morning until he went to bed at night.

"It sounds like you're enjoying yourself while you're at it," I said.

"Not the actual going around in clogs. They're a bit clunky for my liking. But the thought of it driving him mad down there without him being able to do a thing about it, that's different. That gives me pleasure, yes."

"I'd prefer if it didn't," I said.

He laughed.

"A few weeks and I can take them off again."

"You're not solving anything. He's just going to find something else to rile you with."

"If he does, I'll step things up. It's a war. The point being that the enemy has to be made to understand you're always going to be ready to go a step further than him. And when he does, that's when you've won."

"But there's a difference between major and minor conflicts, isn't there?"

"That's where you're wrong. The principle's exactly the same. As soon as he realizes he's not going to get anywhere with me, and that I'm willing to take it further than he is, no matter what he decides to do, then he'll surrender. Wait and see."

"I will," I said.

"Your strategy, putting up with everything and hoping it'll all go away, doesn't work with that kind of person."

"That's what you say," I said. "But I'm still not sure you know what you're doing."

Njaal opened the door and stepped outside.

"It's high," he said.

"Yes, very high up," said Geir.

Njaal got down on his knees and peered through the gap between the concrete floor and the railing.

"There's something there!" he exclaimed.

"Is it that paintbrush?" I said. "Vanja dropped that. There are some lighters down there too, I think. Ones I've dropped."

"Can I throw something down?" he asked, and looked up at his father.

"I don't think that's such a good idea, Njaal," Geir said.

"How about we go out to the garden?" I said. "Let him run around a bit? I don't need to pick the kids up for another couple of hours yet. We could go in your car."

An hour and a half later we sat chatting on a couple of chairs by the hedge, in a hum of wasps and bumblebees as we watched Njaal run around on the grass. We had a paddling pool, but he didn't want to go in. Now and again he came up to guzzle some fruit juice, in that unrestrained, greedy way in which children drink, and then he'd be gone again, on his way across the grass in the direction of something else that had caught his attention. When we bought the place it had been one of the neatest of all the cabins. Two years on, and everything about it had fallen into decline. But in the frenzied flourish of summer it wasn't hard to call the garden lush instead of neglected. And anyway, this wasn't a day to worry about it.

There was a sound of lawn mowers, and two gardens from ours two families stood nattering away in their Skåne dialects, but apart from that the place was quiet. I tried to explain to Geir how I felt, to define the emotion so he could understand, and ended up calling it terror. I could easily see how superficial it all seemed to anyone on the outside. It wasn't in the least bit likely that Gunnar was going to call or turn up; he had severed all contact with me, any correspondence went between him and the publisher, with me copied in. Maybe he was afraid of me and hadn't the guts for a direct confrontation? Judging from what he'd said about me, this was wholly unlikely. In his eyes I was a sixteen-year-old lay-about with no self-knowledge, a money-grubber inflamed with hatred. It was far more likely he was avoiding me because I was a disgrace. A third and final possibility was because he didn't think I was responsible for my own actions, I was a Knausgaard, after all, and this was his way of going easy on me. At one point this had been what I'd thought, and it still made me feel strangely warm, but I had long since realized it was a kind of wishful thinking.

We talked about it. Which is to say, Geir talked and I listened. I'd heard everything before and was convinced I'd thought every thought that could possibly be conceived on the matter, when all of a sudden Geir asked:

"How old is he, anyway?"

"About fifty-five, I think."

"And here you are. Gray hair. Gray beard. Forty years old. You're about the same age. You shouldn't put up with someone your own age treating you like that."

"That never occurred to me."

"What?"

"That we're the same age."

How odd that this should be such a liberating thought. Most

of what Geir had said had already occurred to me and I'd thought about it myself, but not that. Gunnar and I were the same age. He wasn't above me. One thing was recognizing this, another was understanding it.

"He saw you when you were in diapers, that's the problem here. You're always going to be a kid to him. But it doesn't mean you have to be a kid in your own eyes when you're dealing with him."

"He's my dad, isn't he?"

"I know that. But you're more than just feelings and irrationality. You're thoughts as well, and rationality. Let them take over. It'll all sort itself out then."

"You make it sound like I've got a choice."

"And?"

I raised my hand in the air.

"Enough for now. How are things, anyway?"

He laughed. "Oh no, you don't."

"All right, so it was an abrupt change of subject. But only so you'd take the hint. Isn't that how it's supposed to work?"

"What?"

"Social interaction. The conversation has to move on at some point. It's the normal procedure, so I'm told."

"I think we've gone beyond polite convention, don't you?"

"Certainly not. How are things, anyway?"

"Let me see," he said. "I sit in my room and write . . ."

He looked up at me.

"Same as usual in other words. There you go. Should we talk about Gunnar again?"

An hour later, as I carried the two chairs into the open shed at the side of the little cabin, I felt a sense of relief. Maybe things weren't that bad after all. Maybe it wasn't the end of the world. I put the glasses and cups on the counter in the kitchen, heard Njaal running on the gravel outside the gate, locked the door and went out through the garden, breaking into a trot so as to catch up with them. We'd left the car in the parking area a hundred meters away. Every garden I passed was immaculate, with little ponds and sculptures, hedges straight and trimmed to perfection, lawns like billiard tables. The people who owned them moved out here in May and stayed until September, most were retired, and to them gardening was a lifestyle. I found it all so ghastly. I hated the place, really hated it. Being here was like being on display, viewed not as the person you were, whoever that was, but as the person you looked like you were. The fact that I knew the rules of such places from my own childhood did nothing to improve matters, for how on earth had I got myself into buying a property, however small, in the midst of this inferno? How could I have been so oblivious to myself?

I caught up with Geir and Njaal just before the barrier where the parking area began.

"The next novel I write starts here," I said. "Have I told you that? The last world war never happened and Nazism spread peacefully through Europe. The main character grows up here. All through his childhood and youth he's been thinking about Africa. That's the first sentence: 'In all the time I was growing up I read about Africa. It filled me with a yearning so great it was almost unbearable.' Something like that. I read this article once in *Dagens Nyheter* about the Nazis' plans for the world. They mapped out this gigantic port on the coast of North Africa. The rest of the continent was just darkness, nothing there. That would be a good framework for a novel. A world planned and ordered down to the minutest detail, everything in it utterly controlled in all its aesthetics, and then this other world in which everything is unknown, unpredictable and improvised, where things happen and are then just gone again. Do you see what I'm getting at?"

He nodded.

"I see you needing a hideaway from what you've got going. It's an escape attempt, pure and simple."

"You're probably right. But I mean it, seriously. Africa is something else entirely. I saw that when I went there, and I've seen it in lots of documentaries, too. What we haven't understood yet is that Africa is our utopia, not this."

Geir opened the car door, and Njaal climbed onto the backseat. I waited until Geir got him strapped in, then got in the passenger side. A couple of other car doors were opened and closed a bit farther away, it reminded me of a parking lot next to a marina or a landing stage, people lugging cooler bags back and forth, and camping chairs, people in shorts and skirts, their tanned skins, their lazy movements, the extravagance of the great blue sky and the serene surroundings, broken by such trivial occurrences, objects lifted and carried, doors slamming shut, the mutter of voices.

"We should stop all development aid to Africa. Stop all trade and pull out completely, let them get on with it. The way it is now all we're doing is carrying on the colonial relationship, which says we're better than them, look at the way they do things, they can't govern themselves, can't keep anything in order, they can't even manage to organize schools. It's a mess. They've got wars, child soldiers. All that shit. No, cut them off, leave them all to it. Close the continent. I hate that underlying thought that runs through everything we do in the world, the idea that everyone's got to be like us. That's the real hell. The bigger the differences, the better, as far as I'm concerned. African cultures are so glaringly different from our own. They're the utopia, not us."

"You like that wording, don't you?" said Geir. He put on his awkward-looking aviator sunglasses and pulled slowly away across the dusty parking area toward the shady asphalt of the road at the top end.

"What, the utopia part, you mean?"

"That part, yes."

"But it's what I think."

"I know you do. It's that yearning of yours for the seventeenth century, only in another bottle."

"Maybe. But anyway, a dystopian novel with a main character who grew up here and who longs for Africa, and probably goes there at some point. When the narrative takes place he's an old man living on an island in the Baltic."

"Let me guess. You went there on holiday? Slite, on Gotland, was that it?"

"Thereabouts. It's not much of a plot, but it's a start."

"What are you going to call it?"

"*The Third Realm*."

"Another Nazi title."

"I suppose, but it's a good title."

"I'm sure it is. Didn't I think of it?"

"I don't know. Did you?"

"I'm pretty sure. But you can't remember, can you?"

We left the cabins, Geir halted at the roundabout until there was a gap, then drew slowly away, accelerating out of the curve. There was a bus pulled in at the bus stop, apart from that the road ahead was empty. It was half past three, still a while before the rush hour got going.

"You've got a funny kind of memory. Someone will say something to you, or else you'll read something, then you forget all about it until all of a sudden it pops up again while you're writing, completely removed from its orginal context, as if you'd thought of it yourself."

"Isn't that what they call plagiarism?" I said, feeling a warmth rise to my cheeks.

He looked at me for a second.

"No, it's what's called freedom. It's because you're made in such a way that you're writing a novel, whereas I'm writing nonfiction. I've been destroyed by academia. It makes me check and double-check everything I do. I can't write a sentence without adding a footnote with a reference. I'm tied down. You're without bonds entirely."

"You're reliable, I'm not."

"All right, no need to be harsh on yourself. What you're doing works!"

"I suppose you're going to tell me it was you who came up with the *My Struggle* title as well?"

"Well, now that you mention it."

"Seriously?"

"It was in a sentence you said, my struggle, and I said there you go, there's your title. That's how it was."

"Shit."

"It's how you work. Your head's this simmering pot, everything goes into the soup."

We drove along Bellevuevägen, lined with low detached homes in light-colored brick. It looked like Denmark, the way a lot of things did in Malmö and Skåne. Geir stopped at a light by the Statoil station, Njaal kept shuffling back and forth in his seat like he was trying to take in as much as possible of what was going on outside. The light changed and Geir accelerated quickly, soon we were stuck behind a bus. There was a big advertising banner running under the rear window. It was for a local firm of real estate agents and showed four smiling women in dark suits that made them look a bit like airline hostesses. I'd seen the image lots of times before, it was all over the buses in the city, and the bus shelters too, so I'd already had time to consider it before it turned up again in front of us now.

"See that photo there?" I said.

"Yes, what about it?" said Geir.

"I bet I know which one of those women you'd fancy," I said. "And don't deny it just to spite me if I'm right, okay?"

"Okay," he said.

"You'd go for the one on the right."

He laughed.

"Correct," he said. "But the only reason you got it right is because you like her too."

"No, mine's second from the left. I've stared at that picture so many times."

"Straight up?"

He laughed again.

"It's not often you surprise me. How did you know which one was mine?"

"I know you. It was a no-brainer."

"Can't say the same for you. I'd never have thought you'd pick her. For me there's only one in it, the one on the right. It's inconceivable anyone could think differently!"

"Make a right here," I said. Geir indicated and changed lanes, the bus heading straight on.

"It's like with those clogs," he said. "Before you told me I was mad, the thought never even occurred to me it was anything but normal. To me it's a completely logical, reasonable thing to do."

"You mean jumping up and down on the floor wearing clogs to get back at a downstairs neighbor?"

"Not to get back at him. To resolve the conflict. To break his will. But apart from that, yes, to me that's perfectly natural. I had no idea anyone could think otherwise."

"I thought you were a sociologist."

"I am. But I'm a human being, too."

We passed the Kronprinsen, a high-rise housing project built in the sixties, which until the Hilton went up had been Malmö's tallest building. The road was edged by the trees of the Slottsparken on our right, and we followed the increasing flow of cars, which glittered in the sunlight.

Geir laughed.

"You got me there. You mean you actually *knew*?"

"Nothing odd about that, surely?"

"Yes, there is. I didn't know myself."

After we'd parked the car, I rode up in the elevator with them and let them in, then went out again to get the children. John got off his trike as soon as he saw me and came running. The girls were in the sandpit next to the little playhouse, they had seen me but weren't letting on. With John on my arm I went over to Karin and asked her how things had gone. Fine, she said, the older ones had been in the park before lunch, John had stayed behind. They were all in good cheer and it had been a lovely day.

"John still hasn't got any diapers, Karl Ove," said Nadje, who was sitting on the bench just behind us.

Oh fuck, I knew there was something I'd forgotten!

"Sorry," I said. "It slipped my mind completely. I can run over and get some now, if you want."

"No need. As long as he's got some tomorrow, that'll be fine."

"I'll make sure of it. Sorry. Were you able to work around it?"

"We borrowed a couple."

"Okay, thanks, much appreciated. I completely forgot."

She smiled wearily, I smiled back and carried John over to the stroller so Vanja and Heidi could see it was time to go instead of just hearing me say so.

"Time to go, girls!" I called out.

There weren't that many children there, a lot of them were still on holiday. Of all the parents, we used the nursery the most, at least so it seemed to me, but perhaps it was just because I felt so guilty about all the times ours were on their own here while I was writing. I pulled the stroller over to a chair in the sun and sat down.

"Five minutes!" I called. "That's all, okay?"

Vanja looked across at me and nodded. I leaned back and gazed up at the sky, it was bright blue, the wispy elongated clouds that were so typical of summer floating like vaporous sheets in the distance. I felt the air on my face, a cool breeze sweeping over the rooftops, whirling through the yard, brushing all things, my body too, my sticky skin which shivered with pleasure at the unexpected, delicate chill. I felt the urge for a cigarette, sat up straight in the chair, and looked at John in his blue sun hat, the grime around his mouth, his unworried radiance as he sat there staring at two children who came biking past. Either he wanted something and would be tormented if he couldn't get it, or else he wanted nothing and was simply himself, at ease with the world as it was.

"Vanja and Heidi!" I called out. "Come on, time to go!"

"A bit longer!" Vanja shouted back.

"We have visitors," I said. "Njaal and Geir have come. We can't keep them waiting much longer. Njaal's looking forward to seeing you."

"Are they here now?" she asked, and looked at me inquisitively. I nodded.

"They came a bit early. Come on, let's go. You can get a banana on the way, if you want."

"An ice cream," she said.

"You and your ice cream," I said, and gave her a stern look.

"Can we?" she asked again with a cheeky smile.

"Well, okay," I said.

"Heidi, we can have an ice cream!" she shouted out.

I looked down at the ground, embarrassed that the other children should hear that mine were having ice cream. Or rather, embarrassed that the staff should hear me say so out loud for anyone to hear.

"We're getting an ice cream, Karin!" said Heidi, her hand already gripping the stroller.

"How nice," said Karin with a smile.

"While the summer's still here," I said.

"Enjoy it!" she replied.

"Will do," I said, pressing the door opener. "Vanja, do you want to run on and open the gate?"

Like a wind she swept past me, pulled the handle down and heaved open the gate, three big steps back, her little body bent almost double as she pulled.

"Well done!" I said. "Say goodbye to all your friends."

Vanja and Heidi ignored me completely, while John, who no one could see in his stroller, waved and shouted, "*Hej då!*"

"We have visitors at home, Heidi and John," I said as we strolled along the shady sidewalk. A gust of wind pressed Heidi's skirt against her legs and held it there for a moment.

"Do we?" she said. "Who?"

"Njaal and Geir. Can you remember Njaal?"

"A little."

215

"He's one day younger than you."

"What?"

"His birthday's the day after yours."

We stopped at the crossing, then went over. John protested, he wanted to go on the other side. He twisted around in the stroller and glared at me full of rage and despair.

"Do you want an ice cream too, John?"

"Yes," he said, and turned round again.

When we got to the two yellow mailboxes outside Hemköp, I said:

"Right, I want you to listen now. You can have your ice creams when we've paid for the shopping and not before. Okay?"

All three nodded and we went inside into the supermarket's icy environment. Vanja and Heidi ran off, presumably to the ice creams, while John wriggled to get out of his stroller as fast as he could. I stopped and lifted him out, his feet hardly touched the ground before he was off after the girls. I snatched two packets of red sausages, the ones with the highest meat content, something I had suddenly and rather neurotically become obsessed with after someone at the nursery made me realize there were big differences from brand to brand, then dropped a bag of hot-dog buns into the basket along with a regular loaf, a bag of coffee, the dark-roast French blend I'd settled for after six months of experimentation and had since stuck to, a liter of milk, a liter of yogurt, a six-pack of beer, toilet paper, and a packet of four bars of soap, seeing as how we had visitors and they probably washed their hands more than we did, and finally three ice creams.

John wanted to walk the rest of the way home, which meant I could put the shopping in the stroller.

Had it got colder now?

Yes, the temperature had dropped in the short time since I left the apartment.

"I can see Malmö!" John shouted. Somehow he'd got it into his head it was our apartment that was called Malmö.

Vanja looked at me and giggled.

216

I smiled back at her.

"Is there anyone on the balcony, John?" I asked him.

"No-o-o," he said.

"There's a young *gutt* waiting for us at home, did you know?" He looked up at me, perplexed.

"Daddy means a *pojke*!" said Heidi. A boy!

"*Just det*," I said. "*Jag måste tala svenska nu.*" That's right. I'll have to speak Swedish now.

"*Pappa, inte*," said Vanja. Don't, Daddy!

"Are you ashamed of me?"

"No, you're just stupid."

"That's true."

The light changed from red to green just as we got to the crossing. I reached my hand out, John took it, while the girls held on to either side of the stroller. On the opposite sidewalk I gave the keys to Vanja, who ran ahead and opened the door, holding it open for us so I could maneuver the stroller inside and pull it up the three steps after me, while Heidi and John stood heaving at the elevator door without it budging in the slightest.

The laundry. I'd forgotten the laundry.

I opened the elevator and pushed the stroller inside, tipping it onto two wheels to make room for us all. Vanja pressed the button for the sixth floor. Heidi, who had also wanted to press the button, started crying. Vanja mimicked her, Heidi lashed out. Vanja hit her back, so by the time I opened the door of the apartment I had two screaming kids on my hands, both howling for their mother. But as soon as Geir and Njaal came out of the living room they fell silent. The children stood and took stock of each other for a few seconds, the same way dogs do – what kind of children are you, they seemed to be thinking – before accepting the new situation and sliding off into their room, apart from John, who had plonked himself down on the floor in his blue hat and was trying to take his shoes off.

"Sausages for dinner," I said.

"Great!" said Geir.

I went past him into the kitchen, where I put the shopping down on the table and started putting it away.

"I forgot the laundry downstairs," I said. "Can you get the sausages going while I go down and get it?"

"I'm good at sausages," he said. "We ran a sausage business once in Uppsala, did I ever tell you? The Svea Sausage Company. Two bikes with a frying pan and a grill mounted on the front. We went all over town. They were painted the colors of ketchup and mustard, red and yellow. And there was a big metal sausage on the back. It's the only decent job I've ever had, now that I think about it."

"Here are the sausages, then," I said. "There's a pan in the cupboard over there."

"Ossie-Pete, did I ever mention him? He gave free sausages to any girl who showed him her tits. Lots did."

He laughed.

"I think that was probably the first thing you told me when I arrived in Stockholm," I said.

"Good times. We used to sit there drinking until the bars closed and all the students came out, about one in the morning, then we'd light the paraffin lamp and start selling. Huge lines there'd be. It was all about grabbing the best spots before anyone else got there on Saturday nights. Like the square outside the Celsius House, you know, the guy with all the degrees. It's at an angle to the street, because Uppsala burned down and nearly the whole town had to be rebuilt, but Celsius's house wasn't touched. I studied aesthetics there. It's where I met Christina. She was taking photos of our sausage bikes. I'll have to show you some time. Delicious sausages, they were."

"You never told me how much money you made out of that," I said on my way into the hall.

"Oh, you know, up and down, it depended," he said from behind. "I can't remember exactly. No, hang on a minute, there was a first of May when we made twenty thousand kronor. We're talking back in the early nineties here. Twenty-four hours nonstop grilling sausages. We were so exhausted we couldn't be bothered dividing all the takings up properly, it was like here's a pile for you and here's a pile for me."

"That's a lot of money," I said, stopping in front of John, who was still in a struggle with his shoes on the floor.

"The most I earned at one go was at a Danish longball tournament for political economists. They wanted a sausage stand. None of them actually bought any sausages, but they'd guaranteed me a minimum, two thousand an hour. And, of course, I still had all the sausages left to sell afterward. I tell you, though, we were the bottom of the barrel. I mean, this was Uppsala, with all its academic traditions, all the stiff-necked snobbery. A sausage vendor wasn't exactly well respected."

"Do you want to come down into the basement with me, John?" He nodded.

I put the shoe back on him that he'd managed to take off, then stepped into my own, while Geir stood leaning against the wall reminiscing about his sausage days.

"We put the boiled sausages in the freezer, then heated them up again. Sometimes we could only sell them after it got dark, they were almost green. The students never knew whether they were puking from the alcohol or the sausages. Do you remember Cuba Cola?"

"I do, yes," I said, my hand on the door handle.

"We used to have that. Everyone used to comment on it, I haven't seen it since the seventies, but we hardly sold a bottle. Then we tried Pommac for a while. But who drinks Pommac with hot dogs? It was a disaster, of course. French mustard, we had that. No one wanted it. Too sophisticated, I suppose. Do you know the Swedish slang for a hot dog?"

"No, tell me," I said, pressing down on the handle and opening the door.

"*Raggarballe med svängdörr*. Dick in a swingdoor. Ha ha ha. You wouldn't believe it, would you? Arf, arf."

"If we're not back in half an hour it'll mean someone's done us in for breaking the laundry-room rules," I said.

"We had our own little sausage logo on the front of the bikes as well," he said. "Made of metal, too."

"Anyone would think you hadn't seen another human being in years, the way you're going on," I said.

"Someone has to say something," he said. "Seeing as you're not, I mean. Can't you take your phone with you?"

I closed the door behind me, lifted John up, and rode the elevator down with him sitting on my arm. As soon as we reached the basement he bombed off along the passage on his little legs. In the laundry room itself he immediately started playing with the sweeping brushes. Someone had put our clean clothes nicely in the bags for us. Although this was a kind gesture, with no hint of annoyance in the form of a note about sticking to our times or reporting the matter to the caretaker, I still hurried back out again in case I ran into whoever was responsible, John in one hand, the two IKEA bags in the other. There had been feces on the sofa, I remembered all of a sudden, perhaps prompted by the two beer crates and the carrier bag that someone had left up against the wall, which we passed again on our way back through the basement. And there had been empties all the way up the staircase to the upper floor. The place had been littered with them. Plastic bags full of empty bottles under the piano. But maybe not on the staircase from the ground floor to the first floor? I couldn't remember. Yet Gunnar seemed certain. He said he had proof, if it came to a court case.

What was I going to do if it went to court?

Oh, hell! Hell, hell, hell.

I lifted John up so he could press the button for the elevator, then put him down, only for him to reach out for me again, his arms in the air, perhaps because he wanted to see the elevator arrive, the light of its interior appearing in the rectangular window of the door. I lifted him up again. My body was weak with dread. He was so angry with me. He was so terribly angry with me.

"There!" said John.

And, sure enough, a light descended!

I opened the door, holding John up so he could press the top button, then putting him down again and studying my reflection in the mirror.

There wasn't a trace of my inner turmoil to be seen. Just a serious-looking face with sad eyes, that was all.

John crouched and examined a little strip of red plastic on the floor that had caught his attention. It looked like one of those plastic binder things.

After some trouble he managed to pick it up between his little fingers.

"Look, Daddy!" he said, holding it up.

"Oh yes, that's good," I said.

Inside I was trembling, and nothing outside could help, it was as if everything was trembling there, too.

The elevator stopped, I opened the door, John toddled out with his head down, absorbed in his bit of plastic. I cast one last glance at the mirror, stepped the few paces across the landing to the door of the apartment, which John was already trying to open, though without succes, and with ill-concealed annoyance prized his hands from the handle and opened the door.

Inside, the children were watching TV while Geir stood at the stove stirring the contents of the big saucepan he'd found, from which a thin, almost invisible veil of steam rose.

"How's it going?" I asked.

"Fine," he said. "I put the TV on. Is that all right with you?"

"Yes," I said. "I'm not a fan though."

"You might not be, but the kids love it."

I was sticky with sweat, not because I'd exerted myself in any way, but because the air was so humid. Through the window I noticed the sky to the east had gone cloudy and was now gray-white rather than the clear blue of only an hour before.

"If it were up to them, they'd watch TV from the minute they got up till they went to bed," I said. "That's why we've got rules."

"Are we going to debate morals now? I'm not sure sausage is all that good for them either, but it tastes great and they like it."

"There's more than seventy percent meat in those sausages," I said with a smile. "Morally, they're beyond reproach. And now I'm going to have a smoke. Do you want to come with me?"

He nodded and followed.

"Actually, I have one principle when it comes to what Njaal watches," he said from behind. "I try to slip something useful in every now and then, something educational. It's not easy, though. All he wants is entertainment. It's like pornography."

I sat down, held up the thermos, and caught his eye, raising my eyebrows in inquiry. He shook his head, then leaned back against the railing. I poured myself a cup and lit a cigarette.

Here and there the gray-white cover of cloud slashed open, and gashes of dark drifted across the sky.

"Looks like there's a storm on its way," I said with a nod in its general direction.

"Is there?" he said, turning to see, then looking back at me. "But you play with your kids, don't you? You might not like it all the time, but you do play with them. I do nothing. I rely more on warmth and humor."

"So I'm cold and humorless when I play with them, is that it?"

He laughed.

"I don't play with them much at all, to be honest," I said. "I spend a lot of time with them, but I never exactly get down on the floor with the Lego or the farm animals."

"Don't give me that. You take them to the swimming pools on weekends. You take them to the park. You play football with them."

"Sometimes, yes. But that's not playing, is it?"

"True, if you want to be nitpicky, that's up to you. But what I mean is you spend a lot more time and energy on your kids than I do on mine. That's not to say Njaal doesn't give me any joy. I believe the Chinese. They say a man doesn't realize he's a dad until his child's five years old. There's a lot of truth in that, if you ask me."

"You won't be a dad before next autumn, then."

"Exactly."

"You've only got one child, though. That makes it different. Once you've got three, you no longer have any choice in the matter."

"I do tell Njaal I love him. In those words."

"I can't say the same. I don't think I've ever said that. There's a limit."

"Draw not nigh hither. Ha ha ha!"

"Tread not upon the grass, my boy. Skjæraasen, wasn't it?"

"Leave tender shoots to sprout! No, I can't remember. But I think it has to do with the way we are, not just the roles we choose. Some people love to play. My dad's got a way with children, they love him. The neighbor's little boy still invites him to his birthday every year. He's knocking on eighty now. The same outlook on life as Goethe. 'For nothing brings us closer to madness than distinguishing ourselves from others, and nothing maintains common sense more than living in a normal way with many people.' *Wilhelm Meister's Apprenticeship.*"

"Only someone on the outside, who doesn't live in a normal way, could say something like that."

"That's the big difference between you and me, I think. Nearly everyone I know has a father who failed them in some way. And everyone tries to compensate for that failure in the way they relate to their own children."

"It keeps the world going round, doesn't it?"

"Even if you succeed, like my dad did – and I'd say he was an ideal father – the ideal doesn't necessarily get passed down. What happens then is that the sons haven't got anything to make up for. So you're a better dad than your own father, while I'll be a worse one than mine, and when it gets to Njaal's turn he'll be compensating for that in the way he relates to his own kids, who for their part are going to be just as hopeless as me, their grand-dad. The ideal doesn't get inherited, that's the point."

"A kind of dialectics of hopelessness, is that it?"

"Exactly. Having a decent dad doesn't help in the slightest."

"Of course it does. It's a good thing in itself. Having a stable and harmonious life, I mean."

"But what do we get out of a harmonious childhood? I know loads of people whose childhood was fantastic, but where did it get them? What have they done?"

"But that's like an industrial viewpoint on life. As if it's got to have a product. If that's the idea, then you're right. Nothing comes of a harmonious childhood. But what if it's the harmony itself that's the point? What if the meaning of everything is just a well-balanced life?"

"Oh, come on, you don't really mean that! I'm much more in line with Ayn Rand, who writes that only a few individuals, a very small number of us, keep the world going. They're the ones who make something of life, who achieve something in the world rather than just using or enjoying it."

"But even in those people there's a sense of restlessness. That's why they create or act the way they do, because there's a restlessness inside them, something incomplete. But what they're aiming for, all the time, is harmony. All through their twenties and thirties and forties. The aim is to be able to sit in a garden and watch the sprinkler watering the lawn, with their children all around them, and to be able to think, right, that's it, I'm happy now. All human urges are about the urge for harmony."

"Listen, Aristotle, didn't you just write that you weren't interested in happiness?"

"Yes, but not that I'm not interested in harmony."

"Same difference. But you're right in what you say about restlessness and feeling incomplete, that it's the strongest force of all. What's happened in our time is that restlessness is no longer translated into action. Restlessness doesn't produce anymore. We live in the age of therapy. Restlessness isn't wanted, we try to remove it by talking about it. We've got one Vision Zero after another, trying to live immaculate lives in immaculately happy families, and our explicit aim in life is to eliminate road traffic deaths. But it's a chimera, a great big lie. It's ridiculous that we even believe it. But we do. Harmony, happiness, and no more deaths in traffic. Give me a useless dad who doesn't give a shit! Give me a godforsaken awful childhood! Because something comes of that. Something gets created there. In the disharmony and the dissonance."

"I can agree to that in theory, but not in practice. I look at my kids and the only thing I want is for them to be happy. To have as good a life as possible."

"Well, all I can say is I hope you fail!"

"Actually, it's something I think about a lot. What kind of impressions they'll be left with from their childhoods when they get older. What all this is to them. I've no idea myself. And what they'll have from me. No idea."

"They're very different as well, in character, I mean. What you give to Vanja and Heidi might be exactly the same, but you can bet your life their experiences of it are going to be different, and they'll understand it all differently too, in later life."

"Yeah, I suppose so."

"The truth is we don't know what we're doing. We don't know where it's going to lead. It's a known fact that children of divorce are overrepresented in the crime figures, and the younger they were when the parents divorced, the greater the risk of them getting into trouble. But we won't give up the right to divorce, so instead we say it's best for the kids. In any system it's impossible to foresee all the effects. To get back to the automobile: if anyone had said the invention of the automobile was going to kill thousands of people every year, would we have put it into production and centered our lives around it the way we have? No. So we don't talk about that, we say the automobile brings us freedom and opportunity instead. And when capitalism increased its hold and we needed more labor, did anyone say women have got to leave the home now and start producing goods, so we can double the labor force? Not to mention double the number of consumers? No, they didn't. That was women wanting the same rights as men. The right to work, what kind of a right is that? How's that supposed to be liberating? It's just the opposite, a prison. The consequence of that is that our kids are farmed out to an institution from the age of two, and what happens then? Mom and Dad are almost driven insane, aren't they? They're riddled with guilt, so they spend all the time they can on their kids when they're not at work, trying to be as close to them as possible. Compensation, compensation, compensation."

"The road from sociology to paranoia is shorter than one might think," I said.

"What, don't you agree?"

"Actually, yes. Especially the part about the chimera, as you called it. If you read Marx, *Das Kapital*, much of it's about exploitation of the workers. They slogged away for sixteen hours a day under the most degrading conditions. So one of the most important goals of the workers' movement was to limit the amount of work. Work was seen as something the employers – the capitalists, if you like – forced on the workers. It was slavelike. Nowadays, though, people work themselves into the ground of their own accord. Why? Because the idea has arisen that they realize themselves through their jobs. So work has become the opposite of alienating. Now it's self-realization. Everyone works like mad now, because it's good for them. The same with consumption. We find our identities in the purchase of goods that are mass-produced. You'd think it was a joke. But the worst thing is you're not allowed to say that, it means you're paranoid. And what's more, that criticism has turned into a cliché, it's become invalid by virtue of being repeated too many times. I remember when I was a student and read all that criticism and was totally in agreement with it at the same time as I was living my life in exactly the same way as what I was criticizing. It didn't even occur to me then. And even if it had, I wouldn't have done anything about it. The two spheres are separate. What you know, and what you do. They never join up. They're like east and west. Or, at best, like the tie and the vest."

"You couldn't stop yourself there, could you?"

"No, but the point is it's no longer possible to live in any other way. There are no alternatives. It's seeped into everything."

"Do you remember what you said once about Nazism being like amateur night? Well, it's true. We, on the other hand, lead professional lives. And how can we not? I can't ignore thinking about safety when it comes to Njaal, for instance. I can't let him ride his bike without wearing a helmet, or run around at will in the neighborhood, even though it's what I did when I was a kid."

"Why, because you'd feel guilty if he fell and hit his head?"

"No, it's not as simple as that. Once the thought's there, that they have to wear a helmet and you've got to go with them everywhere they go, it's no use trying to escape it anymore. It becomes my thought too. We can't do anything other than wish the best for our children. Now, this is what happens to be best. But what governs that is the thought of what's best. Because whether it really is best is something we've no way of knowing. When Njaal started nursery school, I wanted him to go to the nearest one, because that was the most practical, but Christina went all over, checking out all these different nurseries, because she wanted the best. But how could she know what was best for Njaal? Who knows what's going to happen in a place, who he's going to meet and what it's going to mean to him? We can't control life, only our thoughts about life. So everything that has to do with our kids is actually all about us. It's the tyranny of good intent. All we can do is try for the best, it's impossible to imagine any other way, but the consequences are beyond our control."

"We're starting to get old, that's what it is," I said.

"We are. How old was Voltaire when he wrote that all you need in life is a garden and a library? Certainly not twenty, that's for sure."

"Wasn't it Cicero who said that?"

"Was it?"

I shrugged.

"Anyway," I said. "I got a letter about six months ago with that quote in it. Only I read it wrong. I saw *hagle* instead of *hage*: 'He who has a shotgun and a library wants for nothing,' I thought it said."

"Ha ha ha! A lot more credible, too, if you ask me."

"Completely in your spirit."

"Yeah, but why do you think men went to war? Why do you think men would put everything, even their own children, aside in order to fight and kill? The answer, of course, is love. The love they felt was no less than the love women felt, just different. Now we connect intimacy and closeness with the truest of feelings. I've lost count of how many times I've read people ridiculing men's ways of dealing with emotions. Slapping each other on the back, that sort of thing. But a woman doesn't know what it means to get a slap on the back when you're down in the dumps. Men's emotions are worth no less, if anyone believes that, just because they're not expressed the way women's are. What I'm saying is there are many different kinds of solicitude, and intimacy isn't necessarily going to be right in itself. There's no monopoly on feelings or caring. What happens if you're all over your kids all the time, what does that get you? Nothing."

"Harmony."

"Nowhere near. I've yet to meet anyone less harmonious than you when you weren't writing and all you had was your family. And when all these men start making amends for their own childhoods, they overcompensate, and in overcompensating they create the opposite problem. We go to the opposite extreme, wrapping them up in cotton wool and giving them whatever they want, in that way making sure they're not going to feel any sense of gratitude or meaning, all they get out of it is an extreme childhood, only in a different way. So compensation doesn't get you harmony or equilibrium. That said, however, I do know I'm a shitty dad. I had to face that when Njaal came along. It wasn't nice. All the bad sides of me suddenly became significant. I try to be good for him, but most likely that's not good enough. When he grows up he'll be able to judge me for it. That's his prerogative. But I can never judge him. Never. That's a right I don't have. And that's where your uncle is wrong. He can't take your father's side and judge you. He hasn't the right. No human being has. The children can judge the parents, but never the other way round."

"Did you have to bring that up?"

"What?"

"Gunnar. I'd just managed not to think about it for five minutes."

"It's not worth worrying about."

"Of course it is," I said.

Next to us the door opened and Heidi put her head out.

"When's Mommy coming home?" she wanted to know.

"Tomorrow," I said.

"I want Mommy," she said.

"I know," I said. "Do you want to speak to her on the phone?"

She nodded. I stubbed out my cigarette and got up, went inside with Heidi following on my heels, picked up the phone, and pressed Linda's number.

"Hi, it's Karl Ove," I said when she answered. "The children are missing you. Want to say hello?"

"Yes, of course," she said.

"Here's Heidi, then," I said, and handed her the phone.

"When are you coming home, Mommy?" she said.

I went into the living room.

"Do you want to speak to Mommy on the phone, Vanja?" I said.

She nodded and got to her feet.

"Me too," said John.

"Not just yet," I said. "Heidi's talking to her now, it's your turn when she's finished."

Vanja sat down again and stared at the television. I recognized aloofness in her body language and could tell she was holding back her feelings, it always happened sooner or later whenever I was on my own with them, but meant nothing other than that she was missing Linda. If Linda had walked in through the door

229

now she would have run toward her and hugged her and told her about all the things she'd done while she'd been away, and not moved an inch from her side the rest of the evening. She accepted the distance I kept as a necessity, not consciously of course, but still for her there was always an element of enduring when we were on our own together, of holding out, the opposite of letting go and living.

I went back out to Heidi again, she was looking at herself in the mirror while listening to what Linda was saying at the other end.

"Can you say *hej då* to Mommy now," I said, "so Vanja and John can talk to her too?"

"*Hej då!*" she said, and handed me the phone.

"Are you ready for the other two?" I said.

"Yes, put them on."

I stood in the doorway.

"Vanja?" I said. "Do you want to speak to Mommy now?"

Vanja shook her head.

"She doesn't want to," I said. "But here's John for you."

John took the phone and pressed it to his ear. His entire little self lit up in a smile as soon as he heard her voice.

"Yes," he said with a nod. "Yes."

"Bit of a disaster with the sausages, I'm afraid," Geir called out from the kitchen.

I went to see what was the matter.

"They've split. There are two things that matter when it comes to heating up sausages. One is to put a laurel leaf in with them. The other is they're not supposed to boil."

"You're trying to teach your grandmother to suck eggs," I said, and peered into the pan. The pink meat peeped out from the red skins of all the sausages.

"I'd never be so presumptuous."

"It doesn't matter," I said. "They still taste the same."

I took five hot-dog buns from the packet, put a sausage in each, placed them all on a dish, squirted ketchup on, and took it all into the living room.

The phone was dumped on the sofa. I picked it up.

"Hello?" I said, but it was dead and I dropped it back in the charger under the mirror in the hall. When I came back into the living room they'd each taken a hot dog.

"There's more if you want," I said. "Just say the word. We'll be in the kitchen."

I went in and got the mustard out, a coarse local variety from Skåne I'd been putting on everything for a while, fished out a red sausage with its split skin, put it in the bun, and sat down at the table, where Geir was already demolishing a hot dog.

"They're good, the Danish ones," he said.

"Mm," I said. "You should taste the mustard, it's good too."

"I'll have some on the next one. It reminds me, do you remember that advertising campaign a while back for Gilde sausages?"

"No."

"You must. Gilde sausages have a slight curve to them. They made this slogan about them putting a smile on your face. Some feminists reacted, claimed it was sexist. They even confronted Gilde's managing director about it. But he had no idea what they were talking about. They're sausages! he said. Ha ha ha!"

The sky was completely dark in the east now, and where it was lighter, above the outskirts of the city, it was streaked by what had to be rain. I felt a headache coming on.

"It was good, what you said about Marx," Geir said after a while. "The way we work just as much, only now it's because we're realizing ourselves. The fact is, people made fortunes from other people's work then, and people make fortunes from other people's work now. There's no difference, it's all the same, apart from the way we look at it."

"Mm," I said. "I think it has to do with having to learn to live with something. It's an adequate response to a real issue. As long as we can't stop working, we have to change our reasons for doing it. The motivation, I mean."

"It's funny," said Geir, and got to his feet. "A job was a job to my dad, something that had value on its own. The job in itself was what it was all about. He went to work because he had to. Did his best and kept his head down at the same time. The idea of him realizing himself would have been completely alien, I'm sure."

He lifted a sausage out of the saucepan, placed it in a hot-dog bun, and sat down again. I shoved the jar of mustard across the table toward him.

"But your argument about us doing everything in order to compensate isn't right," I said. "Normally, we've always reproduced the pattern, repeated what we ourselves experienced as children. My dad's dad used to hit him, so Dad hit us. Not often, only occasionally, but the fact that it existed as a possibility meant it was something he could resort to every now and then. He never made any effort to compensate for anything at all. It wasn't a part of the role. You were brought up in a certain way, and that's what you did with your own children. We're the ones trying to compensate all of a sudden. Do you remember what I said about Rudbeck that time? From his biography? His father hit him and humiliated him, but he didn't internalize that, never saw it as part of his psychological makeup, but as something objective, an action belonging entirely to the external world. That was in the seventeenth century."

"I remember. It was my university lecturer who wrote that book."

"So the question is, on the one hand, why we give such weight to the traumatic, or construe things as traumatic at all, and on the other, why we bring up our own children differently, in a new way."

"You think that's something we choose, then?"

"No, just the opposite. Things have changed, beyond doubt. And all of us are a part of that change. I think it's a response to something. I think the very fact our kids are in nurseries from the age of one, and that we surround ourselves with all sorts of crap that just alienates us, TV, computer games, all that kind of stuff, on its own means we just have to get close to our children. Kids used to be at home all day, a place they felt was theirs, and there were grown-ups around, maybe not close in that sense, but they were there. When that place no longer exists there has to be some compensation. That has to be compensated for. No one planned it that way or probably even thought about it. It just gets like that, and becomes an imperative. That's what I think, anyway."

John came into the kitchen and stared at Geir.

"Do you want another sausage?" I asked.

He shook his head.

"*Korv*," he said.

"Ah, a *korv*," I said, and smiled. "Yes, you can have a hot dog, of course you can."

I made him another, taking the mild mustard from the fridge and squirting a long ochre-colored dribble along the length of the sausage before handing it to him. He started munching at the same time as he turned and went back in.

"There's no alternative either," I said. "The only alternative to capitalism in our time has been Nazism. The Nazis attempted to change society from the bottom up and start something radically different. And we know how that turned out."

"It's a shame the Germans lost the war, but a good thing the Nazis didn't win it, as I usually say," Geir said. He had a red streak of ketchup across his cheek.

"Daddy?" Heidi called out from the living room.

"Yes?" I called back.

"I want another hot dog!"

"Come and get one then!"

"No, you have to come!"

"No!"

"What?"

"No!"

Silence.

"And what does all this thinking about safety actually do?" said Geir. "What happens when we're in this state of high alert as to what can go wrong and what we can do about it? All it does is increase anxiety and heighten our fears. We used to walk to school. None of us got killed. Now they're all taken in cars. None of them gets killed either."

"Daddy!" Heidi called out.

"Yes?" I called back.

"Come here!"

"No, you come here!"

"Okay," I heard her say, and I got up to fix another hot dog. It was ready for her when she came in.

"Do you want a glass of water, too?"

She nodded.

"Does Njaal want another hot dog, do you think?"

She gave a shrug and went off again. I filled four glasses with water from the tap and took them in, handing one to each.

"Do you want another hot dog, Njaal?" I said.

He nodded without taking his eyes off the TV.

"How about you, Vanja?"

She shook her head.

"When's Mommy coming home?" Heidi asked.

"Tomorrow," I said. "Do you miss her?"

Heidi nodded. Vanja stared. John looked up at me and smiled. "*Mama!*" he said.

How I ever could have produced such a happy little boy was a mystery.

"Want a beer?" Geir said when I returned to the kitchen.

"Yeah, why not?"

"So we structure the social space," he said, opening the fridge. I sat down, and he handed me a beer. "We redesign the physical environment. We're on high alert as to everything. We know who designed the fork we use to eat with. We eliminate every peril and take precautions against everything. Spontaneity goes out the door. Why do we want to get rid of our spontaneity? Where does that get us? Spontaneity can't be predicted, it can't be repeated, and repetition is the key to all control. That's where we are."

"In a way the circle's complete," I said.

"How do you mean?"

"The Neanderthals," I said.

"Ah, your favorite subject. And what insight have you gleaned from their sad life today, I wonder?"

"Do you think they were spontaneous?"

"If you put it like that, the answer's probably no."

"In the two hundred thousand years they lived in Europe they didn't develop in any way whatsoever. They were still doing exactly the same things, in exactly the same way, when they disappeared as when they came. They even inhabited the exact same places. There was a tribe in France that lived in the same cave for forty thousand years. They only moved on when it started to collapse. Imagine one and the same family living on the same farm for forty thousand years. It's completely unthinkable. But not to them. They were making the same tools, hunting by the same methods, eating the same food. Nothing about them changed. Fascinating, don't you think? The fact that our closest relatives were incapable of change. The fact that progress was a completely unknown concept to them. No improvisation, no spontaneity, it just didn't exist. The first humans were an inconceivable revolution when they turned up. What set us apart from the Neanderthals was exactly what we're now trying to get rid of."

"Is this where you say it's not that long since the first humans arrived?"

"Yes, but it really isn't that long! And at that time there were many different kinds of humans living side by side. It's got to happen again. Think, say, three hundred thousand years in the future. By then there should be other kinds of humans here too. Maybe even in sixty thousand years."

"Well, give them my best."

"Ha ha. But you know how many Neanderthals there actually were, don't you?"

"No, tell me."

"At most around twenty thousand. Perhaps as few as ten thousand. Somewhere in between. And that was the lot! So imagine what Europe looked like then. Completely devoid of humans, only animals and birds, and forests and plains, and these fifteen thousand inflexible Neanderthals dotted about a few caves around the continent. That's it."

"Your utopia."

"Not far off. But do you know what the biggest difference was between the first humans and the Neanderthals?"

"No hot dogs?"

"The humans had jewelry. They wore the teeth of the dead around their necks. Meaning they were thinking in symbols. There's something more than this. And to the Neanderthals that was a completely impossible thought."

"I wonder what the idea was," said Geir. "The teeth around their necks."

"What it says is there's something more."

"Yeah, that's what makes me wonder. Teeth are just teeth. The way the Neanderthals existed in the world seems more reasonable to me."

"There's a decent chance we've still got Neanderthal genes in our DNA somewhere. Not in Africans, because there weren't any humans when the Neanderthals left Africa. But in Europeans, certainly. I don't think the Neanderthals died out. I think they mixed with humans and merged into them."

"You do, huh?"

"Yes, why not? It's not unlikely, is it? And so far the Neanderthals were here longer than us. They didn't know that, of course."

"I don't suppose they did."

"So we've gone from a world without mystery to one that's full of mysteries, then back to one without again."

"It's amazing the state actually gives money to people like you to sit around and ruminate, and write books about what you've been ruminating on."

"There was a small subspecies of humans on an island called Flores in Indonesia. They lived in a cave there. By all accounts no more than fifty to a hundred individuals. They were only about a meter tall."

"Midgets?"

"No, a completely distinct species of human. They lived there well after humans came along. The people who live there now tell strange stories about small people coming and stealing their vegetables. I've actually heard one of those stories. This man said the women slung their breasts over their shoulders when they ran. Where the hell would a detail like that come from? The way he described them they were like little trolls of some kind, creatures of mythology. Goblins, or something. But then they found the skeletons in the cave. Tiny little people."

"Where do you get all this?"

"Late-night TV documentaries. I watch them a lot. I've no idea how much is true and how much is nonsense. But it fascinates me all the same."

"Obviously."

"It's got to do with the utopian as well, I think. Things actually were different once. Not just the environment, but being human itself was different too. I want alternatives, that's all. Anything would do, really."

"So you'd like to be a Neanderthal, is that what you're saying?"

"No! But the fact that history is over, that there's no future anymore other than the repetition of what we've got now, makes me feel insanely claustrophobic. I don't necessarily have to do anything different, or be anything different, that's not what I mean, but I do want the possibility of a completely different life to exist."

"We live in the age of Vision Zero. It means we have zero visions."

"That was neat."

"I know."

I stood up and went into the living room. Geir came after me. *Bolibompa* was finished, they were watching something for older kids now. I switched it off and glanced at Geir.

"Should we get them bathed and off to bed?"

"Why not."

"Who's for a bath?" I said.

"Come on, Njaal," said Vanja, slipping down off the sofa. Njaal followed her, then Heidi, too. I picked John up and carried him to the bathroom after the others. I put him down on the floor, got the detergent from on top of the cupboard and sprinkled the white Ajax powder into the bottom of the bath, got the scouring pad from under the sink, moistened it, and began scrubbing the enamel. As it dissolved in the water, the white powder not only became liquid, it turned yellow, too. I was fond of yellow. Yellow on white, yellow on green, yellow on blue. I liked lemons, their shape as well as their color, and I liked the great fields of rape that spread their intense yellow out across the Skåne landscape in the spring and summer, beneath the tall blue sky, amid the green. And I liked the white Ajax powder that turned yellow when it dissolved in water.

As I scrubbed, the children undressed, and I sensed how the room behind me was all arms in the air and little bodies bent double. I turned the shower on and rinsed away the detergent and the hairs that were left behind from the last time they were in the bath, put the plug in, flicked the diverter valve, and stuck a finger into the thick spout of water that came plunging like a little waterfall from the tap.

"In you go!" I said.

Vanja and Heidi climbed in, Njaal was a bit uncertain and looked up at his father, who had been standing silently the whole time watching them, while John put his arms in the air in front of me. I pulled off his T-shirt, his shorts and his socks, and once I'd got his diaper off and dropped it into the bin under the sink I lifted him up and into the bath, his legs dangling like a little monkey's.

"In you go, then, Njaal," said Geir.

"You can sit here!" said Vanja, indicating the space between herself and Heidi.

Njaal hesitated. But after a moment he gripped the side of the bath, lifting first one leg then the other over the edge and into the water. His limbs were as delicate as his features, his brown eyes and fair hair, the slight blush of his skin. He was a sensitive boy, his eyes were attentive, but he was full of energy as well, and the two sides of him seemed to collide. There was a lot of Christina in him, not quite as much of Geir, at least not in any way that was immediately apparent.

Geir had turned away from a lot of stuff, but that wasn't to say it wasn't still there inside him, only that it was concealed. Now and then I wondered if it was concealed from him as well, and in what way it then existed. Geir's mother had always tried to keep him as close as possible, making him feel guilty when he wasn't there, a possessive, dominating woman. She had been ridden with anxiety, as far as I could gather, and it seemed to me that freeing himself from her had required quite a vast effort. He had scant respect for feelings and the emotional, he hated anything that wasn't rational, everything that said one thing and meant another, he was rational almost to the very extreme, and since he was always on his guard, always examining the reasons behind any emotion, he was a total cynic. He didn't care what other people made of him. More than one of his friends had broken off contact with him for not making any bones about what he thought. On one occasion I'd come close to doing the same. Somehow or other I'd managed to offend him without realizing, and the next time we spoke he launched into me, going straight for my weakest point, the children, in this case Vanja. At first I didn't realize what was happening, he was laughing and joking about her sensitivity and the problems she was going to have later in life with me and Linda being her parents. He was specific and very pointed about it, but I didn't understand what was going on, not even after we'd hung up, apart from finding myself thinking that I didn't want to talk to him anymore. A few minutes later he called back to apologize. He said he'd been offended and that he hadn't meant what he said. I accepted his apology but still didn't call him for a few days because what he said had been so cruel. He must have considered it and meant what he said in order to say it, I thought to myself, regardless of how irrational his behavior had been. But it all blew over, we stayed friends, and I'd learned something. The odd thing was that he'd said exactly that during the first few days after we met each other in Stockholm. If you offend me, you'll never know about it, he said. He was proud and self-respecting, it might even have been his foremost characteristic. And true enough, I'd offended him without realizing, or rather I knew, but had no idea how. Then, toward the end of my first year in Stockholm, he simply left one day. Christina called a few days later to say he'd gone to Turkey. It was only half true, the fact was he'd gone on from there to Iraq, so I discovered by chance a few weeks after.

Geir in Iraq?

A human shield?

Without a word to me?

It didn't stop me exploiting the fact to make myself interesting in social gatherings. The imminent invasion of Iraq was a matter everyone was talking about, and now I could say I actually knew someone who was in Baghdad at that very moment, and not only that, he was there to be a human shield.

A little more than three months later, he called me. He was in Stockholm, did I want to meet up? He was buzzing with vigor when we met at a restaurant in Gamle Stan, beamingly happy, a completely different person from the disillusioned man who, sunk into despair, had left the city a few short months earlier. It felt like he'd been off in outer space and gained a completely different perspective on life as it was led on Earth; what had tormented him earlier, tormented him no more. From the war he had brought back endless amounts of data, raw material he would spend the next six years working from, and which now, as we stood here in the bathroom of a Malmö apartment this evening in August 2009, had become a finished documentary book. Not one day had he taken off from that work, as far as I knew. Every weekend, every holiday, he had worked. When I began writing my autobiographical novel, our lives had become almost parodically similar, everything was suddenly about what we were doing in our little rooms, practically cut off from the rest of the world apart from our families. I read what he wrote, he listened to me reading out loud what I wrote, but the relationship was not symmetrical, for whereas I had lived my life with the flock, reading the same books as everyone else, thinking the same thoughts, he had headed off on his own even at the age of twenty, and the knowledge he had thus acquired independently was what I drew on, to such an extent that what I was writing now would have been unthinkable without him. Even though it was an autobiographical novel I was writing. It was uncomfortable in that I had turned out to be so weak and amenable to influence, and the fact that I had been compelled to borrow from him in order to become stronger and better effectively undermined my sense of self even more. At the same time I didn't feel inferior to him when we were together or spoke on the phone, if that had been the case we couldn't ever have been friends. It was actually the exact reverse, it was the very fact that I didn't need to adjust myself according to him, didn't need to take into consideration what he might believe or think about what I said, that was the important thing. I felt ashamed with everyone I met, and by that I mean pretty much everyone, there was always something there that made me feel I wasn't good enough, something I couldn't live up to, or some mark I overstepped, if only in thought. The fact that I'd started to write about this, the way I actually saw myself, was madness, sheer madness, since it meant exposing myself to the only thing I was really afraid of: the disapproval of others. Without our regular phone calls I would never have managed, during them I built up a kind of defense, and my transgressions seemed almost to lose their force accordingly. So yes, his influence being as great as it was gave me freedom and independence, which were strangely and despairingly closely bound up with the opposite, constraint and dependence.

But what is influence exactly? Parents showing the world to their child and explaining how it is ordered? An Iago whispering in Othello's ear? And when does influence go from good to bad? Or, put differently, what is independence?

The most shameful thing that can happen to a writer is to be caught plagiarizing the work of another writer. The second most shameful thing is for one's work to imitate that of another writer. Being unoriginal is not shameful in quite the same way, but it is equally degrading – to call a novel unoriginal is one of the worst things a reviewer can say about it. That it is shameful for one's work to imitate that of another writer, and not shameful, merely degrading, to write something that is deemed unoriginal, is a crucial distinction that speaks volumes of the importance we attach in our day and age to the cult of personality, how imperative it is that something may be traced back to a single, wholly independent individual, who in many respects is considered sacrosanct insofar as the distinctive characteristics he or she has developed are not permitted to occur anywhere else. The important thing is not what such a voice says, but that it says so in a way that is peculiar to itself.

The reader, however, is unconstrained by such insistence on independence or individuality, on the contrary, literature's entire system is based on the reader submitting to the work and vanishing within it. Admiration of, and submission to, the individual was by no means a dominant characteristic of our culture prior to the Romantic era and may be understood only as a result of a fundamental shift within the social world whereby the I took on a whole new aspect compared to just a few generations earlier. Yet the Romantic I, swelling above its banks, whose foremost feature is to be unique, is no unambiguous marker of this alteration of the I, for the very reason that it presupposed that every other I, which is to say the readers, or, as our own language would have it, the consumers, subordinated themselves and accepted their status as nonunique. The Romantic or political genius, Goethe or Napoleon, functioned in much the same way as kings always have, representing sovereign power, excess, pleasure, and pomp, living their life on everyone's behalf, and the celebrities of our time are one extension of that. This is a mechanism of social security in that we are brought up to believe we are unique and genuinely assert our own selves whenever we utter or do something, whereas in actual fact we are as good as identical, and in order not to be crushed by that truth, which naturally would pulverize any conception of who we might be, we elevate to a superior level all those individuals who in some way stand out and excel, who go beyond what is normal, whether by running exceptionally fast, jumping exceptionally far, writing exceptionally well, singing exceptionally beautifully, or simply possessing exceptionally good looks.

Should we wish to remove someone from such a pinnacle and return them to earth, the most effective regulatory mechanism is parody: he is not unique, someone else exists who talks like him, looks like him, behaves like him. And we laugh. Should we not only wish to remove someone from such heights, but furthermore destroy him or her, we need only to demonstrate that whatever he or she has done or said is a copy of something someone else has done or said. Identity is thus a kind of taboo because it is found all around us, though cannot obviously be named, since it refers to something else that is greater and more dangerous. In a number of primitive cultures shared identity was indeed taboo, as is shown by prohibitions on imitating another person's gestures or voice, and through the ritual killing of twins. The frequent occurrence of the doppelgänger motif in literature during the second half of the nineteenth century, and the great horror that was attached to it, is an expression of the same thing, though almost with renewed intensity, as if the threat of the identical had come closer with the advent of the urban masses of the cities. In the century that followed this was the one great issue, the relationship between the one and the *all*, between authenticity and identity. It is impossible to comprehend World War I without this background, or indeed World War II, which was a direct repercussion of the first. The consequence of that enormous disaster was that the unique and the local were irretrievably lost. Or rather, they exist still, but are hidden from us and may no longer be invoked, existing no more as a value, a goal, or a utopia, which is to say as something superordinate, but only as something subordinate, in the life of the individual and in the form of a paradox: each individual I is unique and inalienable, though in exactly the same way as every other. We elevate some individuals among us but are unable to acknowledge the fact, and we are permeated by others, unknowing that this is so, or unwilling to recognize it. Yet it is in terms of influence that this becomes tangible and visible to us in its entirety, in the striking difference between acceptable influence, that which the culture deems desirable to reproduce, and unacceptable influence, that which cannot or must not be reproduced. The harmless form of influence concerns that which belongs to us all and which runs through the social and intellectual domains – if I read Foucault and am enthused by what I read to such an extent that I absorb it entirely and make it my own, beginning to think and write in the manner of Foucault, I have made no transgression, nor have I lost anything, for Foucault is of such status now that his thoughts belong to everyone, in the same way as Kant's or Hegel's, or for that matter Plato's or Aristotle's, comprising a kind of intellectual foundation, a place from which our thinking might issue, by now quite impersonal, albeit attached to certain names. Our entire world of ideas is made up of similar such places, this is what our culture is. We vanish within that culture, though without losing our identity in so doing, since our identity is formed by the culture, for instance through general conceptions of what comprises a subject, an atom, the air, or a home, expressed in every dimension of the language and the culture. The fundamental principle of that identity of which our we is comprised, and which is also the locus of what we call morality, is unoriginality, receptiveness to influence and subordination. Identity is synchronistic, which is to say complete at any given time, and yet changeable. Its borders are temporal; what was generally seen to be true two generations ago – for instance that it is acceptable to punish a child physically or that homosexuality is shameful – is no longer so, and if we were to put those assumptions forward today we would either be ignored or condemned. What applies in the area of morality applies also to science; the structuralist model of understanding that was ubiquitous in the arts during the sixties, for instance, is now invalid and no longer applicable. This we-identity is nonindividual, which reveals itself not least in the fact that the same people who in the sixties believed it was acceptable to punish a child physically, or who found homosexuality shameful, or considered the structuralist model of analysis to be an adequate tool by which to understand the various expressions of culture, no longer hold the same views, or, if they do, no longer make them public. The fact that we nevertheless think all our opinions and beliefs to be personal and individual, reached by way of our own mature consideration, completely ignoring the role played by time, is one of the most important social mechanisms of all, since without it the apparent relativity of morality and science would dissolve all imperative and we would be destroyed in a chaos of independence. This is why we cultivate independent expression in art, that which is unique and particular, and only there do we apply such a powerful mechanism of sanction as the concept of plagiarism, whereby we are able to sustain the idea of our individuality. If this had not been the case, there would have been no difference in meaning between socialization and plagiarism. All learning takes place through imitation; as children we imitate the language and behavior of our parents, as we grow up we imitate the language and behavior of our friends and teachers, and once we reach adulthood we imitate the language and behavior of those around us at that time.

Nearly every instance of language uttered in the public sphere is nonindependent and unoriginal, which is to say devoid of any personal mark of the sender. The most widespread form of public language is journalism, which stands out by its very anonymity, and it is impossible to trace back the language used in any newspaper article to the individual journalist who wrote it, all is written in the same way, in the same style, and moreover they write about the same events and source information from each other without the notion of plagiarism ever occurring to anyone. They imitate each other, one article is copied from another, and this is so because it is *we* who are writing. The same is true of manuals and instructions for use, and dissertations, and textbooks. Only in fiction is there any expectation of a unique "I," whose greatest and most important constraint is not to imitate, not to copy anyone else or say what they've said, at least not in the same way. The more distinctive a writer is, the greater he or she is perceived to be. Many people seem to think that literature has to do with the creation of knowledge, or the generation of insight, but such things are merely a by-product, something that may accompany literature or not; the most important aspect is its individuality, which lies in the inimitable tone of the particular. But this individuality is not without limit, it can occur only within the boundaries of the we; when it transgresses those boundaries, stepping outside and expressing something utterly unreasonable, it will be condemned or ignored. A writer who for instance advocates the physical punishment of children or who condemns homosexuality in our day, fifty years after these were generally accepted viewpoints, needs to be extraordinarily inventive if he or she is to be accepted, which is to say forgiven, whereas a writer who for instance denies the extermination of the Jews in the Holocaust would never be accepted or considered to be great, regardless of how exceptional a level of literature he or she might otherwise achieve. These two premises of literature, that on the one hand it should be as individual as possible, meaning it should express the inimitability of the singular I, and on the other hand that it should exist within the boundaries of the general, meaning it should express the we, are at odds with each other, since the more unique I am, the further I am from the we. The fact that Knut Hamsun could pen Adolf Hitler's obituary and include in it the most outrageous sentence in all of Norwegian literature, we bow our heads, and the fact that Peter Handke, perhaps one of the world's three best living authors, if not the best, could speak at the funeral of Slobodan Milošević, thereby disqualifying himself completely from anything that might be called the cultural majority, are two obvious expressions of the inherent opposition between the unique I and the social we, otherwise known as morality, that literature embraces. Only a writer could have penned the Law of Jante. The fact that the Law of Jante found such widespread resonance is ironic, since what Sandemose's rules express is the very tyranny of the majority, but it is no more ironic than readers cultivating the value of the individual while collectively submitting to one. But precisely by being so closely joined to a particular individual, the voice of the best literature concerns not only the collective, as an example of an I-possibility all I's consume, but also in fact the one, which is to say the actual person in that actual place and in that actual time, and that identity in itself bears with it an insight not found anywhere else. For this reason, literature is inalienable. Because regardless of how consumed we are by each other, regardless of how collectivist our I's happen to be, they are in fact alone, experiencing everything alone, and that experience, that of being human, of existing in the world, cannot be expressed generally, within the horizon of the we, since in that case no we exists. A newspaper article or a TV report is always about one or more people in some other place, an experience none of us knows. A novel or a poem is also always about one or more people in some other place, but is presented in a language that renders its experience unique, and that unique experience intervenes in a completely different way in our unique existence. It is not about recognition or validation, but about truth.

But what is the truth of our social existence? Writing about socialization and plagiarism is one thing, quite another is to witness someone mimic you in a parody, imitating your voice, your gestures, your pose and bearing, the sheer unpleasantness of that, or to sit writing in the knowledge, deep down, that what you are writing is not something you have thought of yourself, not something you have drawn from your own chest, but something you have taken from someone else, and not just anyone else, someone belonging to the great we, but someone close to you, someone you need to be able to look in the eye. The full force of the social world resides in this. Not in the superordinate structures, the great community, the we that is all of us, for these are abstractions, but in the direct encounter, one person face-to-face with another. The force is in our gaze. This is the truth of our social existence. The social world is local, it belongs to the individual, in any given situation. Indeed, every gaze is unique, it belongs to the individual, and for this, and nothing else, we are responsible. This is the truth of our social existence, and therefore it is also the truth of our morality. A morality that proceeds from the community of an all, that proceeds from we, is dangerous, perhaps more dangerous than anything else, because committing to an all is to commit to an abstraction, something existing in the language or world of ideas, but not in reality, where people exist only as separate individuals. In this sense, Knut Hamsun and Peter Handke's morality is utterly superior to that of their critics.

The I of literature resembles the I of reality in the way the uniqueness of the individual may be expressed only through what is common to all, which in the case of literature is the language. All I's of literature make use of the same words, the only difference, that which separates one literary I from another, is the way in which those words are ordered, and the fact that it is possible, in that nonuniform distribution, so very marginal when seen from afar, for an I as vital and significant as Emily Dickinson's to emerge, is remarkable indeed. And it becomes no less remarkable when we consider that practically no one read her poems while she was alive. The overwhelming loneliness and longing she apparently felt is long since dead and buried as we read them now, all that remains is their articulation, which we awaken the very moment we allow our gaze to fall upon the words she wrote such a long time ago, and succumb to them. From that moment she sings within us. But what did she get from it, one might wonder, given that she never could have predicted that her poems would find readers throughout the world, be considered among the very best of the period to which she belonged, and be read long after people would normally have forgotten all about her and her life, though presumably they were written without thought of any reader at all? Why articulate what it feels like to be alive, rather than simply feel and think?

Why write?

I am alone as I write this. It's the twelfth of June, 2011, the time is 6:17 a.m., in the room above me the children are asleep, at the other end of the house Linda is asleep, outside the window, some meters into the garden, the early sun of dawn is slanting down on an apple tree. The leaves are mottled with light and shade. A short while ago a small bird sat in the fork of the tree, in its beak was something that looked like a worm or a grub, it paused there for a moment, throwing its head back as it tried to swallow. It's gone now. Behind that same fork in the tree where it sat the girls' bathing suits have been hung out to dry; all day yesterday they were in the wading pool a bit farther down the garden, half hidden by a willow. The grass outside, which is mostly in shade, is still wet with dew. The air is filled with the twitter and song of birds. Six months ago I sat in exactly the same place, in the early mornings, the children sleeping above me, Linda at the other end of the house. There was a fire in the stove then, and outside it was pitch-dark, the air filled with whirling snow. For more than three years I have spent my mornings in the same way, sitting here or at home in the apartment in Malmö, bent over the keyboard, writing this novel, which is now drawing to a close. I have done so alone, in empty rooms, and as I have worked, my publishers have published what I have written, five volumes so far, about which I know there has been a lot of talk, much written and said in newspapers and blogs, on the radio, in journals and magazines. I've had no interest in that discourse and have kept out of it as much as possible, there's nothing there for me. Everything is here, in what I am doing now. But what is that, exactly?

What does it mean to write?

First of all it is to lose oneself, or one's self. In that it resembles reading, but while the loss of the self in reading is to the alien I, which, by virtue of being so obviously apart from the reader's own singular I, does not seriously threaten its integrity, the loss of the self in writing is in a different way complete, as when snow vanishes into snow, one might think, or like any other monochromism with no privileged point, no foreground or background, no top or bottom, only sameness everywhere. Such is the nature of the written self. But what is this sameness of which it is comprised and within which it exists? It is the singular language of the self. The I comes into being in the language, and is the language. But the language is not the property of the I, it belongs to all. The identity of the literary I resides in the choice of one word rather than another, but how poorly held together and centered that identity is. In a way it resembles the one we have in dreams, where the conscious self distinguishes just as little between us and what constitutes our surroundings and experiences, and our I is in effect deposited inside a room in which the green bench to our left is quite as central to who we are as the wriggling fish to our right, or the Neptune-like figure rising out of the water that at that same moment floods the floor beneath the sky across which a red bi-plane passes. The difference between dreaming and writing must surely be that the former occurs without our control, in one of the body's unconscious modes, and is without purpose, whereas the latter is controlled and goal-oriented. This is true and yet not, for the crux of the similarity has to do with the absence of any localization of the I, the fact of it being dislocated and no longer centered, and the question that is thereby raised, for is it not the property of being centered that in actual fact makes up the I? The very act of holding together? Yes. But the truth of the I is not the truth of one's own particular being. What rises between all the various fragments, far out in the realm of all that is not held together, is also the hum of the own, the peculiar timbre of the self that resonates throughout our lives, that part of us to which we wake up in the mornings, beyond any thought we might happen to think, any feeling that situation might give rise to within us, and which is the last part of us we release before succumbing to sleep. And is it not this hum of the own, this distant reverberation of the self, that pervades all music, all art, all literature, and moreover all that is alive and able to sense? It has nothing to do with the I, even less with the we, only with our very being in the world. When I look at the little sparrow outside, the way it perches on the branch in the sun and throws back its head to swallow the worm or the grub, I cannot imagine that it should be completely without awareness of its own being. Perhaps that awareness is even stronger than ours, since it cannot possibly be overshadowed by any thought. The thoughts that hold together the I can be dissolved in the acts of reading and writing, though in two different ways, in the first instance by entering that which is alien and comes from without, and in the second instance by entering that which is alien and within us, which is the language at our own disposal, in other words the language in which we say I. In writing we lose control of that I, it becomes incalculable, and the question is whether the uncontrollable and incalculable properties of the singular I in actual fact are a representation of its true state, or at least the closest we can get to any representation of the actual self.

What do we say when we say I?

A famous diary from 1953 begins as follows:

Monday
Me.

Tuesday
Me.

Wednesday
Me.

Thursday
Me.

To me, this is a lesson in literature. The I behind this "me," on its own and uncommented upon, may refer to anyone at all, such an I is without identity and open. The issue of who the writer is, when the reader has nothing more to relate to, cannot be resolved. It may be your downstairs neighbor, the man from the kiosk on the square, your child, August Strindberg, Sølvi Wang, or Niki Lauda, to mention just a few of the names that for some reason spring to mind at this moment. The I is absolutely anonymous, in the sense of being nameless. But a nameless I may nevertheless, by virtue of the words surrounding it, convey a clear sense of a certain character, a kind of I-mood that prompts us to relate to it as if to a real person of flesh and blood, even in fact allowing us to come closer to it than to any real person, because the language of the literary I is explicitly tied to inner thoughts and feelings, the I when the I is alone, a dimension that vanishes in the physical encounter, where the body's frame is a barrier, not hostile or protective, but simply as it is, possessing its own language, besides the encounter between I and you also establishing a we, with its own particular rules and regulations, a social world, which only the intense infatuation of love can dissolve, though never completely, the social attaching also to that connection; no couple in love behaves uniquely. Against this can be said that the literary I, no matter how naked or how intimately it presents itself, is social, too, by virtue of the expectation of a you that any I contains, and therefore is always already a we. Indeed, this lies in the very nature of the I, which is an appeal – we have no need to utter I in the presence only of ourselves – and in that appeal there is always another, and thereby a we. This applies too to the I of this diary. An I, or me, on its own is anonymous, neutral, and without character, but precisely by playing on the you, in this case the expectations we have of any I in a text, this particular I is able to infuse itself with meaning and say something about what an I is, without stating anything beyond "me." What happens when it is repeated four times? In a sentence, together with all sorts of other words, we wouldn't notice, but unencumbered, naked and accorded a line all to itself, the utterance becomes preposterous. Me, me, me, me: I, I, I, I. It expresses narcissism. But at the same time, by its nakedness it is as if that narcissism is being exhibited, and in this lies a conscious mind, someone saying, I know what I'm doing. What is the nature of that knowledge? I know it's narcissistic, but I'm doing it anyway. That is, I am not hiding myself. I'm telling it like it is. I am at root narcissistic. But who am I? As of yet, the I is all of us. That is, every me is narcissistic, but this it admits, and in this admission lies a duality: narcissism is a weakness, something unwanted; if it were not, then we would not attempt to hide it, so the fact that narcissism is being exhibited here is an admission of weakness, at the same time that admission also lifts up the I and distinguishes it, because it is candid, and candid narcissism stands in opposition to hidden narcissism in that the former aspires to truth, whereas the latter seeks to conceal the truth.

There is also something aggressive and hostile in the repetition of this "me." Fuck you, it says. You can believe what you want. Here, I, and only I, prevail.

"Me" completely on its own is anonymous, neutral, and without character. Repeated four times it becomes a literary and social program, since after having read the first four diary entries, one understands that this is a me in opposition to the social world, which it considers to be hypocritical and insincere, unlike its writing, which aspires toward that which is true and sincere by sticking to its own, which is to say the me that opens out toward us by putting itself on display, at first anonymous, neutral and without character, and which by virtue of the repetition then sheds the neutral and the characterless, and in its fourth instance stands trembling, truth-thirsty, reality-craving, superior.

And then it is literature.

But if I had begun this novel in exactly the same way it would not have been literature. Although the pronoun "me" does not in any way belong to Witold Gombrowicz, the author of that diary, and he likewise has no right of property to the repetition of that pronoun four times, meaning that legally or morally there would not have been anything in the way of my making use of that exact same opening, this would not have been the case with regard to literature, since the entire value of that opening lies in its uniqueness and its expression of uniqueness. If I had used the same words, Witold Gombrowicz's me would have superimposed itself onto my own, and my "me" would thereby have become a parody, expressing lack of originality where Gombrowicz expresses the opposite, originality, and thereby I would have undermined what the utterance is saying, that truth lies in the unique I, and only there, since the I that would have been saying this would not have been unique and primary, but Gombrowiczized, socialized, plagiarized.

My literary I was most likely Gombrowiczized, because his diaries had such a great influence on the way I thought about identity, sociality, and literature, but it was also Larssonized, Proustized, and Célinized, if not to say quite Sandemosial and thoroughly Hamsunified, and if I were to attach an image to those influences it would perhaps involve a boy, let's say he's fourteen years old, living next to a river, with a section of rapids about three kilometers down from the house, and the rock over which the water rushes, swollen and shiny as steel, is smoothly eroded and covered with algae, meaning that a person can swim out above the rapids and allow themselves to be swept along by the current, something he often does, this boy, together with his best friend and all the others who congregate there in the summer evenings, there being hardly a better feeling in life than this, to sense the might of the river, the increasing velocity, the surge of descent as he is swept away and slung into the depths downstream, plunged into the turmoil of tiny bubbles, allowing himself, if he wishes, to be carried into more gentle waters, there to clamber up onto the land again, or else swim back upstream as far as he is able, until the current becomes too strong and he is brought to a stand-still, unable to progress any farther no matter how hard he struggles, eventually to be swept away downstream again. To sail down those rapids is like writing, carried from one point to an-other by forces beyond your control, but what you experience on your way is experienced by you alone, since I cannot imagine the other kids could have seen or felt the same as he, and if those evenings, with their setting suns and as yet warm rocks through swiftly cooling air, where great swarms of insects hung sus-pended in pockets of light, the resounding rush of the river and the joyful shrieks of boys and girls, the almost electrically illu-minated trees, behind which an old-fashioned gravel track led to a manor farm presumably built in the nineteenth century in con-nection with the sawmill at the falls, and beyond the manor farm the sunlit, tree-covered slopes above which the sky slowly dimmed, eventually, toward midnight, opening to the light of the few stars bright enough to pierce the pale night of summer – if those evenings, with the slant of farther slopes on the other side of the river, dark and shadowy at the bottom, shimmering orange at the top as if ablaze, and an asphalt road with a bit more traffic along whose straights and bends the kids who lived there would cycle or race their mopeds to call on each other – if all this remained in their memories it would be in ways completely dif-ferent to the way it did in his, this fourteen- or fifteen-year-old boy with no greater joy in life than this, to be within this space that resounded with the clamor of its thunderous waters and the exuberant voices of young humans, lit by the sun or dimmed by its absence, so strangely desirable that the very thought of it fills him with joy even now, twenty-eight years later. The feelings that come to him on this reflection may be no less intense than those of the others who were there, this is certainly possible, since different things will attach themselves to us, and his experience is by no means more significant to him than to the others, it is simply different. It is unique. And a starting point for a hundred novels at least. Boy at river below sawmill one evening in summer. A writer of Sandemose's ilk would most probably have zoomed in on the girl in the red bikini both he and his friend desire, then followed the three of them through life, since here we have a very fundamental psychological as well as social structure, two on one, and archaic in nature, the taboos surrounding it are basic. A Proustian writer would probably have ignored the physical-concrete aspect of the situation and emphasized its reminiscence in memory, which by virtue of being a representation is connected with all other representations, which is to say that it shares the characteristics of the work of art, the reproduction of something no longer here but which nevertheless remains within us, in the almost dreamlike haze that is such an important element of our reality, where the girl in the red bikini, dipping her toe in the river in the shade of the trees, perhaps resembles one of Rembrandt's young Dutch women of the seventeenth century, Susanna, for instance, or that of one of the figures seated or standing on the smooth rocks, dressing or undressing, are fleetingly reminiscent of Pierre Puvis de Chavannes's paintings from the latter half of the nineteenth century in which the human has a near-sculptural quality, certainly not psychological, and where the various poses, which lead the mind back to the high classical phase of Greek Antiquity, four and three hundred years before Christ, when the self did not turn inward to seek harmony there, but outward, might claim this to be a constant quality of the human, rather than something cultural or relative, which would also be the case here with these youthful Scandinavian figures on the rocks by the river. A Hamsunite, where would he or she have gone with this? To the drone of the moped as it rounds the bend beneath the fell? To the rush of the river, the sudden bashfulness in the eye of a girl as she glances down? Or to the house of the fat mini-mart owner on the new estate from the sixties and his efforts to make a living independently of the supermarket chains? The tattered remnants of aristocracy in the family who perhaps own, perhaps no longer own, the manor farm by the river? Or perhaps to the self, the self observing itself, suspiciously monitoring, cracking down at the slightest hint of pretense, in that impossible desire for authenticity that once led Nagel to suicide in a town thirty kilometers from this place in distance, ninety years in time. Oh, here were already priests and the daughters of priests, *lensmenn* and their sons, blood that rushed in the veins, hearts that pounded in the chest, here were the most refined and the coarsest of emotions, all a writer would have to do would be to start.

I first read *Pan* when I was fifteen years old, in the house that lay three kilometers from those rapids, and the forceful feelings it described found resonance in my own. Maybe that was why my love life proceeded so miserably in the years that followed, my understanding of girls, falling in love, and having relationships being too rooted in the late nineteenth century. But the novel that made the deepest impression on me in those years was Bram Stoker's *Dracula*. Reading it was a feverish experience. I had no idea why, and still don't. I never identified myself with the Count, he who drained the blood of others, but with his victims, who after having been bitten by him lost not only their blood but also their independence. Knowing me, I most likely read *Dracula* as a novel about submission and liberation from submission. Not that I ever thought that explicitly, I never thought at all when I was reading, but it was what I felt. The sheer sense of triumph and joy that gathered in my chest when finally they drove the stake through the vampire's heart would seem to indicate that was the case. And rather than seeing the writer as a vampire sucking the blood of those around him, which is a tantalizing trope for the business of writing about other people, at least as this is perceived by the public, I saw the writer as someone in danger of losing his independence, a person held captive and paralyzed by the power of another, who fawningly acts like him, pale, bloodless, and ghostlike. Perhaps because I have always had such a weak ego, always felt myself inferior to all others, in every situation. Not only the brilliant individuals I have met, who with their charisma, intelligence, and talent have outshone all others, but also taxi drivers, waiters, train conductors, in fact every kind of person one can possibly meet out there. I am inferior to the man who washes down the stairs and the corridors in the building in which we live, he possesses an authority greater than mine in that situation, so if he says something about the stroller, for instance, and the bikes left outside our door, in a voice that carries even the slightest hint of annoyance, I tremble. I am inferior to the female assistant in the shoe store when I go in to buy shoes, she has me in her hands, so to speak, full of an authority to which I yield. But the worst for me are waiters, since their role is so obviously to serve and be there to please, it is their job to submit to the wishes of their customers, and the fact that I feel inferior to them, at their mercy even, the fact that they can see that I'm not a good diner, for instance, and don't quite know how to taste a wine, or what it's supposed to taste like, matters in which they are expert, is a humiliation every time. And it goes on. All the journalists I meet, even those twenty years younger than me, are my betters, and I always do what I can not to bore them, I often say things I don't even mean simply in order to present them with something. When I moved to Stockholm at the age of thirty-three, outwardly a man, inwardly still a sixteen-year-old, and met Geir Angell there, who I hadn't seen since the spring we went out drinking together a few times in Bergen twelve years before, it was one of the first things he said to me. You've got the most warped self-image of anyone I've ever met, he told me. You've got absolutely no insight into yourself. Hasn't it ever occurred to you that it's the others who are boring? That it's the others who are unoriginal and haven't a thought, that they're the ones who are imitative and full of platitudes? No, I said, because it's not like that at all. Listen, he went on. I saw you when you were twenty. You were totally different from anyone else I knew at that time. You were out on your own.

It didn't surprise me in the slightest when I saw you were getting a novel published. Who else back then did anything like that? No one. There was an intentness about you that . . . well, no one else had. Those sad eyes of yours. If only you could have seen yourself! Ha ha ha! And now you've written an amazing novel. You'll write another, and another one after that. You've got to stop measuring yourself against people who are only bureaucrats in their own lives and in those of others. And you've definitely got to stop thinking they're the ones who are interesting while you're the nonentity. They're the nonentities, and it's glaringly obvious to anyone.

I continued to deny it but felt flattered nonetheless, who wouldn't?

I resisted. What he said felt like a poison spreading through my veins.

Not only did he listen to what I told him about my life, he also found it interesting and wanted to talk about it on our endless wanderings around Stockholm. How everything had centered around my father when I was growing up, my attempts to please him, the terror that was always there, the circumstances of his death. My relationship with my brother, which had been complicated when he got together with a girl I was in love with, and which was close and distant at the same time. The confidence I shared with my mother, her analytic approach to reality. My various romantic relationships, though these were not numerous. The way I was in awe of women, to such an extent that I was unable to approach them. How twice I had slashed my face in fits of despair. My vanity. My fear of coming across as feminine. My joy at being drunk, my infidelities, my constant feelings of inferiority in every respect. My triumphs, which could not outweigh my failures, neither in number nor in their sheer intensity. He took all of this and composed a picture of my psychological and social character he then analyzed and discussed. He construed me as a kind of baroque entity, abnormal and warped, whose inner being was utterly out of sync with its outward expression – completely the opposite of how I saw myself, which was ordinary to the point of self-erasure, this very ordinariness being my problem as a writer. I enjoyed football, both playing and watching; I enjoyed light-weight American films and could still read comics now and again; I watched the weather forecast on TV, or the news, because of the gorgeous women who sometimes appeared on the screen, and could develop small crushes on them; I enjoyed much the same music as when I was twelve, and if I liked a book or a painting I would never know why and would have to resort to words and thoughts I had picked up from others and which thereby were wholly lacking in authenticity. I had nothing special to say about anything, because I was a nobody, with nothing distinctive about me. Yet by simply talking about myself to someone who was not only genuinely interested but also analyzed everything, identifying or establishing connections between all the various parts, that ordinariness was turned into something extraordinary and unique, even to my own mind. It was as if my self had been kept frozen and had now begun to thaw. It creaked as it stirred, so long had it lain stiff and immovable. I soon got the feeling my inner being was inexhaustible. It was a good feeling. The idea that things I said could be interesting was a new experience. I'd always found myself dull. What was interesting was connected with the feeling of inexhaustibility, because there were no limits to the inexhaustible, and limits were what had kept everything out of reach and frozen. I almost never confided in anyone, thinking nothing I had to say could be of interest to anyone, and from that perspective, which was the social perspective, the expectations of the you as constructed by the I, confidence was a non-starter for me, and this was basically how I was with everything. I was mute in the social world, and since the social world exists nowhere else but in each individual, I was also mute toward myself, in my inner being. Only once before had I felt such inexhaustibility, and the situation had been almost the same: another person had seemed to be genuinely interested in what I saw and in what I had to say about myself. That person was Arve, he was ten years older than me and had acquired such insight into the world it meant he could laugh at everything. He was on a completely different level to anyone I had met until that point. Arve was supreme, in a way, independent in the true sense of the word. He was also demonic, or at least played the demon with me, forever tantalizing. What did he tantalize me with? Freedom. What was freedom? To be free was to transgress. To identify everything as being subject to constraints, stuck, ossified, and to remove oneself from that. Not necessarily the social world as a set of rules for behavior, which then Bohemian-like could be ignored, but the mind-set those rules entailed. What Roland Barthes referred to as *doxa*. But Arve hitched up with wife Linda, who I had very quickly fallen in love with, and I closed the door on everything that had happened, including what I had learned from him in his capacity as freedom's demon. None of it mattered anymore. I returned to my own life, that's how it felt, as if for some days I had been living another life entirely, only then to find it wasn't for me, it simply wasn't mine. I had no business encroaching on the wild. I was pleasant, thoughtful, and responsible, apart from the times I was drunk, when a strong urge always rose in me to let people down. Eventually I did, and when that came to light, a year later, I ran away to an island and lived there completely on my own for several months, during which I felt I needed to make a decision and stick to it for the rest of my life. I needed to become a good person. It was in the winter and spring of 2001. In the spring of 2002 I left everything behind and uprooted to Stockholm. There I met Geir and eventually Linda. While meeting Geir gave me a viewpoint on myself and a space in which it could be articulated, in other words remoteness, which was invaluable, meeting Linda gave me the opposite, in that encounter all remoteness was dissolved, I became closer to her than I had ever been to any other person in my life, and in that closeness there was no use for words, no use for analysis, no use for thoughts, because when all is said and done, which is another way of saying in life, when it presents itself in all its intensity, when you're there, at the center of it all, with your entire being, the only thing that matters is feeling. Geir gave me the chance to look at life and understand it, Linda gave me the chance to live it. In the first instance I became visible to myself, in the second I vanished. That's the difference between friendship and love. That the two things came into my life simultaneously meant for a while everything was turned upside down, all of a sudden, almost from one day to the next, I found myself plunged into something completely new. Everything was wide open, nothing was impossible anymore. And in the sky, in that fantastic summer of 2002, the sun shone, sinking red into the Mälardalen every night, as if shrouded by a veil of blood, its last rays glittering gold on all the city's towers and spires, and I was immortal. Seven years later, toward the end of the not-quite-so-fantastic summer of 2009, here I was with Geir again, in the bathroom of our apartment in Malmö, watching the four kids splashing about in the bath as the sky outside, which I couldn't see but whose light I could sense through the rectangular windows, gradually darkened.

"Looks like we've got the hang of it," he said.

I turned my head to look at him. He was smiling.

"How do you mean?" I said.

"Kids."

"What are you talking about, Daddy?" said Vanja.

"We're talking about being *fedre*," I said.

"What's that?" she replied.

"It's what Geir and I are," I said, leaning forward and turning off the tap. "Fathers."

I wondered if his pleasure came from seeing Njaal with other children, a relatively rare occurrence with Njaal being an only child, and the fact that he seemed to be handling it so well, or whether it was down to Geir himself having organized the trip, since normally it was Christina who took care of everything to do with Njaal, while Geir mostly sat in his study writing. He had never immersed himself in the daily routines I dealt with, the clothes and the laundry, food and cooking, children's play and bedtimes, it was his choice and he had always been quite clear on the matter, that he didn't want anything to do with any of that, and yet I often thought he must feel he was missing out on something occasionally, not the practical things but what came with them in terms of involvement. I didn't think that was the case, but the sudden pleasure I saw in him as they sat there playing in the bath perhaps suggested it. I wasn't going to ask him, it was one of those things I was reluctant to bring up, sensing it would be touching on something I didn't want to touch on. It would be an infringement.

What was so dangerous about closeness?

Getting close to someone meant seeing things the other person didn't, whether it was because they didn't want to, or because they couldn't. Geir had an explanation for everything, but that didn't mean that everything about him was explained. He controlled every situation in which he was involved, with the exception of those that included children; the intimacy they afforded, so unaccountable in nature, was something he was unfamiliar with, and this unfamiliarity was plain to see. I had always thought he wanted it that way, but when I saw the smile on his face as he watched Njaal with the others, the sudden sense of pleasure that came over him, it struck me that perhaps he felt the lack of complete familiarity that Christina for instance enjoyed to be something lacking in his life.

What would he say if I told him this?

That it wasn't true?

That it was true, but it was the price he paid for being able to do what he wanted?

That it was his problem, not Njaal's, and therefore unimportant?

That it was no price at all?

After writing this yesterday morning, I took Heidi and John to the nursery, where I was putting in a shift. The staff told me I could get off early to go to Vanja's last-day-of-school event if I wanted, so I took Heidi and John with me and went to the church a few blocks away where it was taking place. Compared to the last-day assemblies of my own school days, which had taken place in a chapel with hymns and a priest in full garb in an atmosphere that was starched and solemn, the last thing we had to endure before the summer, which seemed to us to be ready and waiting outside, Vanja's last day was like something from a different world. A choir of nine- or ten-year-olds sang pop songs by the likes of Christina Aguilera and Mariah Carey; two kids of the same age played piano; some others, slightly older, perhaps twelve or thirteen, performed a rap. After each performance the church erupted into exuberant applause. It was like an audition for *American Idol*. The priest spoke about how important it was to be joyful, he told them fame and fortune didn't matter and that everyone was equal. There was no mention at all of God, Jesus, or the Bible. After the sermon, which lasted all of five minutes, the pupils who had stood out most during the year were called forward. They received diplomas. Some for their fantastic grades, some for their fantastic personal qualities, which, judging by what was said, consisted of taking responsibility for others and caring. The whole hour-long event concluded with the graduates from the ninth grade being called forward in turn to receive a flower. As I walked back with Heidi and John holding my hands, we came up behind a group of kids, maybe thirteen or fourteen years old. All were crew-cut, dressed in jacket-and-trouser combinations, boisterously back-slapping, laughing, and shouting exaggeratedly, as many had done in the church. They had clasped hands when greeting each other, applauded and whooped when one of their own, or someone they respected, took the stage to perform. This macho behavior, which seemed so out of place in their ungrown bodies, several sizes too big as it were, and which for that reason came across as rather comical, was nevertheless genuine in that this was their ideal, and nothing else. These boys wanted to be hard, strong, and tough, and they were in the majority. The others, pale and spindly youngsters with glasses and smidgens of gel in their hair, hadn't a chance against the swagger of the immigrant-community kids. After we got back to the nursery and I was busy filling the dishwasher and wiping the kitchen counter, the nursery head asked me how the event had gone. I said it was like being in the United States. That I'd never seen anything as Americanized before. The best students singing and performing for the others, diplomas awarded to those who had stood out. And the absurd sermon given by the priest, who said everyone was equal, while everything that was going on around him said the opposite, with some students singled out as being more valuable than others and put on display in all their glory. Yes, said the director. When I was a kid, the last day of school was a solemn occasion. We sang the national anthem. But that was banned. They said it was racist to sing the national anthem. Can you imagine?

I could indeed. Equality was the supreme principle, and one of the consequences was that expressions of the singularly Swedish were seen as exclusive and discriminatory, for which reason they were shunned. When it came to religion, one had to tread carefully, church had long since been separated from state, and now things had got to the stage where priests no longer mentioned God or Jesus or the Bible when addressing schoolchildren, since this could cause offense to the many who came from Muslim homes. It was this same ideology, hostile to all difference, that could not accept categories of male and female, he and she. Since *han* and *hun* are denotative of gender, it was suggested a new pronoun, *hen*, be used to cover both. The ideal human being was a gender-neutral *hen* whose foremost task in life was to avoid oppressing any religion or culture by preferring their own. Such total self-obliteration, aggressive in its insistence on leveling out, though in its own view tolerant, was a phenomenon of the cultural middle class, that segment of the population which controlled the media, the schools, and other major institutions of society, and it existed, as far as I could tell, only in northern Europe. But what did this ideology of equality actually entail? A recent study said that differences between pupils in Swedish schools had never been greater than they are now. The gap between the ablest children, for whom the future is bright, and the least able, whose futures lie outside the zones of influence and wealth, is widening year by year. The trend in the study is clear indeed: the strongest pupils are those from Swedish backgrounds, the weakest are from immigrant backgrounds. While we might be concerned not to offend people from other nations and other cultures, and go so far as to eliminate everything Swedish, this happens only in the symbolic world, the world of flags and anthems, whereas in the real world everyone who does not belong to the Swedish middle class, which is hostile to all difference, is kept down and excluded: most immigrants in Malmö, welcome as they are, live in ghetto-like public housing projects outside the center, in miserable apartments, areas where unemployment is massive and prospects are dim. It is also the case that the middle class, hostile to all difference, prefers not to send its children to schools attended by children from immigrant communities, thereby further reinforcing the segregation, with a knock-on effect on the next generation. Many immigrant children have parents with no education, and what the Swedish school system formerly considered to be a priority, lessening differences by providing equal opportunties to able and less able students alike, has now been completely invalidated as a guiding principle, the result being that the haves receive more, the have-nots less. Equality in Sweden is confined to the middle class, they alone are becoming more equal; elsewhere the only equality is in the language, managed by the same middle class. In Sweden something happening in language is much worse than something happening in reality. An instance of one moral code applying in language and another in reality used to be called a double standard. This was what was going on at Vanja's last-day-of-school event; the ideal of everyone being equal, and fame and wealth being unimportant, applied in the language of the priest, whereas the reality surrounding that ideology said the opposite: the most important thing is to be rich and famous. Every child there harbored that dream, it was in the air. And the more I see of it, this self-blind and self-satisfied ideology of equality, believing as it does that the conclusion it has reached is universal and true and must therefore govern us all – although in fact it is valid only to a small class of the privileged few, as if they comprised some little island of decency in an ocean of commercialism and social inequality – the more the significance of my life's struggle diminishes, for what difference does it then make if I spend more or less time with my children, if I change their diapers or don't change their diapers, if I do the dishes or don't do the dishes, if I spend time on my work or don't spend time on my work? Oh, how then, for crying out loud, can we make the lives we live an expression of life, rather than the expression of an ideology? All the thou-shalt-nots by which our small middle-class lives were constrained, all the things we weren't supposed to say or do, or else were obliged to say or do, how I longed not to give a damn and do as I pleased.

But that wasn't possible. I become panic-stricken at the thought of anyone feeling annoyed, I want everyone to feel comfortable and am willing to give up everything that is mine in order for that to happen. If someone does not feel comfortable, I close my eyes to it or withdraw, since the only way I can deal with people not feeling comfortable is if they do so somewhere other than right in front of me. Out of sight, out of mind. It can even get to the point where for long periods I won't open letters I receive for fear they might be unpleasant, since what other letters are there but letters from reality? Something's burning in the Rosengård District, but the papers aren't reporting on it because reporting on it might lead to other problems, might put racist ideas in people's heads, so they close their eyes, shut their mouths, turn away. As such, I am the very epitome of Swedishness, but to be Swedish is also to possess something else, something alien to me, which is social adroitness. The ability to talk about matters great and small in a personal way without ever getting personal, which Swedes master to perfection, is something at which I am utterly inept; either I blurt out something so private that people look down or become ill at ease, or else I go on about something so remote from myself that everyone else quite naturally is bored to death. There is a colloquial elegance about Sweden that is collective and very much a part of the social world, something sophisticated and impressive, quite absent in Norway, where such casual refinement is always individual, attaching to those who have been fortunate, either in something they've just said or in their lives altogether.

A siren suddenly screamed out of nowhere, rising sharply, then stopping abruptly outside the building. I leaned forward and looked out; most likely it was over the road at the hotel, which with its many guests sometimes had to call for an ambulance. Businessman with a heart attack, I usually thought to myself; what else could happen to a person staying at a hotel?

This time it was a police car.

"What's going on?" Geir wanted to know.

"A police car outside the hotel. Maybe they caught that dyslexic thief, the one with the misspelled youth."

"Ha ha."

"Should we get them dried now?" I asked, and looked at him inquiringly.

Geir shrugged and threw up his hands.

"Looks like they're still having fun, if you ask me," he said.

"Can you keep an eye on them for a minute then? I just need to check my e-mails."

"Gunnar haunting you?"

"Not only."

I went past him and into the bedroom, sat down on the chair, and clicked into my in-box.

There was a new message, from Jan Vidar.

Hi Karl Ove
Sorry to get back to you so late on this, came home Sunday and have been a bit busy since, a lot going on at work. I'm not

shocked, and not angry either. Why should I be? Past is past, and writing about it isn't going to change anything. Besides, there's nothing there that can't see the light of day as far as I'm concerned. I think I've got a fairly good idea of who I am and the way I was, and I really don't care too much about what other people might think anymore. So if it benefits your story you can do what you like, it's all fine by me.

Apart from that I must say the book knocked me out. Maybe because it's all so close to home – or maybe it's the way you write that does it, I don't know, but others besides me are bound to get off on it. Fantastic and gut-wrenching at the same time. So incredibly exact about what it was like. Lots of stuff I'd forgotten – suppressed, maybe . . . but it all came rushing back full power. Fantastic, the way it set off so many thoughts about how and why.

Anyway, there I was, in the wilds of Finnmark, reading more than I was fishing. Came across an old peat hut and spent a lot of hours inside with your book. Incredible place, Bilbo Baggins could have lived there . . .

Hope it works out with your uncle and the rest of the family. And that they get the point.

If you're up for a coffee or a beer next time you're around, just give me a call. It'd be nice.

All the best to you and yours too.

Jan Vidar

It had been a long time since I'd felt as glad as I did after reading something. But there was also a tinge of what felt like grief in that joy, because with him coming across as generously as he did here, it became clear to me that I hadn't done him justice. I was indebted to him. I had no problem with that; the sliver of despair I felt had to do with the time that had gone, it was there, in the past, *back then*, and I wished I could make up for that imbalance. Another thing which occurred when he said the novel had knocked him out was that I then assessed the forthcoming ook in that light, and it was so radically different, having so little of the narrative thrust of the first book that no one would ever be able to say the same about it. In other words, it was less of a book, and that thought deflated my spirits.

I sat there for a minute in front of the computer in the bedroom, staring out the window, first at the railing of the balcony, then at the front of the hotel on the other side of the road, the three elevators that slid up and down in their unpredictable patterns, as the gleeful sounds of the children in the bath swelled and diminished in the background. I felt a sudden and very strong sense of closeness to Jan Vidar. The emotions of that time welled inside me, I saw the faces of his parents and his sister, recalled the smells of their home, and the landscape that had been ours, with all of its little places, glowed with the intensity of the most compelling memories. At the time it was just a landscape, almost insignificant, certainly when compared to the landscape in which I had grown up, which even then had been saturated with emotion, but now it, too, had become the Landscape, laden with significance and meaning. The same thing occurred with respect to those who had lived there. The number of people we come close to during our lives is small, and we fail to realize how infinitely important each and every one of them is to us until we grow older and can see things from afar. When I was sixteen, I thought life was without end, the number of people in it inexhaustible. This was by no means strange, since right from starting school at the age of seven I'd been surrounded by hundreds of children and adults; people were a renewable resource, found in abundance, but what I didn't know, or rather had absolutely no conception of, was that every step I took was defining me, every person I encountered leaving their mark on me, and that the life I was living at that particular time, boundlessly arbitrary as it seemed, was in fact my life. That one day I would look back on my life, and *this* would be what I looked back on. What then had been insignificant, as weightless as air, a series of events dissolving in exactly the same way as the darkness dissolved in the mornings, would twenty years on seem laden with destiny and fate. The people who had been there then would become even more important, infinitely significant in as much as they had not only been shaping my perception of who I was, had not only been the people through which my own face emerged and became visible, but embodied the very understanding of how this particular life turned out the way it did.

I thought about all of this. And then I thought about how I had always considered time to be vertical. Time was to me a kind of ladder one climbed, whose rungs were ages – at the bottom one's time at preschool, then school, *gymnas*, university, and so on. That thought had never been explicit to me, and I had never pictured it as such in that way, but somewhere in the depths of my conceptions some idea of that nature must have existed, subconsciously shaping the way I perceived things, and perhaps the most surprising thing I discovered while writing this novel was that everyone who had appeared in my life, even my friends at nursery, my mother's co-workers at Kokkeplassen, the neighborhood kids in Tybakken, the cleaning lady we had there, my old teachers, and everyone else who had been there in my vicinity from when I was six months old to when I was thirteen, existed simultaneously with me now, and had always done so. Moreover, everyone I had known from my time in Tveit and in Kristiansand, at school and at the *gymnas*, existed on exactly the same level, in that same horizontality. Not one had sunk into the depths of history! All had lived their own lives, lived through exactly the same things as I myself, and had been contactable throughout this time, through all these years. They were a phone call away.

It had never occurred to me before. I had thought my life to be lived only in my immediate and most intimate surroundings, and that every place I ever left had gone from my life at that same moment.

Naturally, I didn't really think that to be true, had never even entertained the thought, but something inside me had certainly experienced things in that way, that the places I left, and the people who populated them, died away after I was gone. For that reason it had not been them I had written about, but my recollections of them. The fact that they still existed in their own right, at the same time as my writing about them, had not occurred to me.

At the time they took place, the events of my life had possessed a weight of which I had been wholly unaware. Now that I could sense that weight, paradoxically it was gone, as if my life and the person I had been were now fixed, and that nothing of what had taken place then could change the fact. It was only a feeling I had, but it was strong. I was somewhere else. Now it was my children who were living through days heavy with destiny and fate. Although I knew this was so, I had difficulty putting myself in their place, seeing things through their eyes, not the way they saw them now, but the way they would later realize they had been seeing them. To me, the life we lived together was a long series of everyday events, and all I could do was behave accordingly, as if caught in their trap. The idea that this time, too, would one day be gone often filled me with consternation. Now was the time I could be close to them, my children, now was the time I could give them all my love and attention. In only a few years – and a year in the life of a forty-year-old passed with the hurtling speed of a locomotive compared with how to them it crept along – they would be beyond it all, adults in whose past, the time and events by which they were formed, I had never quite been present. This and nothing else would be what they judged me by. But even when they judged me I would still be the person I was, with the knowledge of what everything had been like and why, something to which they would not, and perhaps never would, have access. So what I hoped for was for them to grow up in a world that received them well, and in that way to gain independence from me and us.

I got up and went back to the bathroom. The sky rumbled abruptly over the city.

"Did you hear that?" I asked.

"It's thundering," said Vanja.

"Time to get dried," I said. "Come on, out you come."

One by one I lifted my three children out of the bath, draped a big towel over each of them, and quickly rubbed their tummies and backs before sending them out to make room for Geir and Njaal. I got some underwear out of the drawer in the bedroom for Vanja and Heidi, and a fresh diaper for John from the little bathroom, then handed nightgowns to the girls, who had already climbed into bed, before helping John with his pajamas.

"When's Mommy coming home?" said Vanja.

"Tomorrow."

"I want Mommy now!" said Heidi.

"It won't be long before she's home," I said. "First you go to sleep, then you go to *dagis* tomorrow, and then when you come home she'll be back."

"Mommy," said John.

"You'll see," I said. "She'll be back before you know it. Vanja, do you want to choose a book?"

I sat down on the bed. Heidi and John sat down next to me. The sky rumbled again. Vanja and Heidi both looked at me, Vanja from the bookshelf over by the wall.

"It's nothing to be frightened of," I said. "It's a nice sound, don't you think?"

Heidi shook her head. Vanja took a book and brought it over to us, then sat down slightly behind me.

The air in their bedroom felt dense and clammy, my head was still thumping slightly.

The book was about a little girl who was very timid and un-adventurous, she was in nursery school, and one day they were on a trip, she got separated from all the others and met a pack of wolves, who at first were scary, yellow eyes among the trees, but then when they came up to her it turned out all they wanted was to play. The game they liked best was one where they were patients in a hospital, they could lie there on their backs without moving while she went around and tickled them. The next morning they took her back to the nursery, and on the last page she

273

could finally do what she hadn't had the courage to do before, which was to jump down from the roof of the little playhouse.

Their little breathing bodies cuddled up to me, absorbed by the story. The thunder rumbling closer in the sky. The drumming of the rain on the balcony and on the square below. The innocence, all that was pure and fine in them.

I got up. They wanted more, but I told them one book was enough, it was late and time to sleep, they had to be up in the morning. I lifted John up and carried him over to his crib, pretending to drop him from on high, catching him again as he fell. He laughed and said, again, Daddy. I said no, turned to Heidi and told her to climb up into her bed and Vanja to get into hers, and then I would come and tickle them.

I sang Heidi a song about a mommy troll putting her children to bed, and another for Vanja about a little songbird, and the one about sailing without a wind for John. They seemed ready to sleep, but a bit overtired, too.

"Can the door stay open like that?" Vanja asked.

"Of course," I said.

"What if the lightning strikes here?" she wanted to know.

"It can't," I said.

"Will we die?"

"No, no, no. The first thing is it can't happen, because lightning always strikes the highest point. What's the tallest building here?"

"The hotel?"

"Exactly. So if lightning strikes here it'll strike the hotel instead. And the hotel's got lightning conductors, so nothing will happen there either."

"But if," she said. "Will we die?"

"No, we won't. We're safe here. And now it's sleep time for little tots. We've got to be up early in the morning."

"Night night," said Vanja.

"Night night, Vanja," I said. "Night night, Heidi."

She didn't answer. I went over to her bunk and peeped in. She was fast asleep. Sometimes she could just fall asleep from one moment to the next.

I smoothed my hand over her head. She was snoring slightly.

"Night night, John," I said.

"Night, Daddy," he said.

"Heidi's snoring," said Vanja.

"Yes, she is," I said. "She's fast asleep. And in a minute you'll be asleep too."

"But she's snoring!"

"Just ignore it, you won't hear her then," I said, stepped out and closed the door behind me.

"DADDY!" Vanja shouted.

The door.

I opened it again.

"I forgot, that's all. Go to sleep," I said, left the door ajar, and went into the living room. I heard Geir's voice in the other room, opened the balcony door, stepped out, and sat down in the chair.

Oh, the air was so cool and delightful.

A diagonal bolt of lightning cracked out of the heavy gray cloud and vanished again. I lit a cigarette. Another lightning bolt, to the south this time, sliced through the sky. The thunder came rolling in. Raindrops splattered white against the black roofing and were felt six floors below, and on the roof of the building opposite it looked like they were rebounding. Another peal of thunder, this time accompanied by a crackling fracture, so loud that no other sound compared, it seemed almost to make the entire city shudder.

It was fantastic.

I inhaled, put my feet up on the railing and stared out. Lightning lit up the sky in different places, now to the south, now to the north.

Fantastic.

Next to me the door opened. Geir put his head around.

"How about a beer?"

"That wouldn't be bad," I said. "Just the one, though."

"If I meant two, I'd have said so," he replied, closing the door again. I got up and went inside after him.

"Just need to call Linda first," I said.

He nodded as he opened the fridge door. I went out to the mirror in the hall, picked up the phone from its charger on the table underneath, pressed her number, and stepped over to look in on the children. Vanja was lying on her side and looked up at me.

"Who are you calling?" she asked.

"Aren't you asleep yet?" I said.

"I can't," she said.

"Is it the thunder?" I said, and at the same time Linda's voice came on the other end.

"Hi!" she said.

"Hi," I said. "How's it going?"

"Fine. How's everything at home?"

"Fine," I said, going into the bedroom. "The kids are, anyway. Heidi and Vanja have been playing with Njaal."

"That's good," she said.

"It's thundering like crazy here," I said. "The whole sky's lit up with lightning."

"How exciting," she said. "Are you and Geir all right?"

"Yes, I think so. We were out at the cabin. Now we've just been in all evening. Gave the kids a bath. Heidi and John are asleep. Vanja's awake. They're missing you."

"I'm missing them, too!"

"You'll be home tomorrow, though," I said.

"Yes," she said.

There was a silence. I bunched the duvet up against the wall, then lay down with it under my back for support. Thunder cracked again, closer now.

"Did you hear that?" I asked.

"No," she said. "What was it?"

"Thunder. *Åska*, as the kids say. When I first came to Sweden I thought it meant ash, like from a volcano erupting. Which is a whole lot more dramatic, I suppose."

She laughed.

"I miss you," I said.

"Honestly?"

"Yes. But you're coming home tomorrow."

"Yes," she said. "How's it going with Geir, anyway? What are you doing? Sitting around talking?"

"Basically."

"What about?"

"All sorts. My uncle, mostly."

"Any more e-mails?"

"Yes. A long one. He's threatening to take me to court. He says he can prove I'm lying. I don't really know what to do about it. I have no idea whether he's right or not. If I've exaggerated things, I mean."

"But it's a novel, Karl Ove."

"Yes, but the whole point is it's meant to be true."

"Who says you have to have seen things the same way?"

"That's not the issue. It's the facts that matter. But it goes a lot deeper than that. It doesn't make sense otherwise. It feels like I've gone to hell. I can't explain it. It's just hell. And then I start getting scared about all the other people I've written about. You, for instance."

"There's no need to worry about me. You've nothing to fear there."

"You don't know that."

"Yes, I do. At least, I think I know pretty much what you think about me, and about us. Not everything, of course, and not in detail, but more or less."

"What if it's worse?"

"I can deal with it. As long as it's true."

"I hope you're right. But there's your mother as well."

"She'll be fine."

"Are you sure?"

"Yes. She'll cope. I know she will."

I got up and opened the balcony door, leaving it slightly ajar.

Fresh, cool air tumbled into the room. The rain was beating down, pelting against the wooden decking.

"Are you outside now?"

"No, just at the door in the bedroom. How's the weather where you are?"

"Nice. Blue skies. We've been swimming all day. I've been lying in the shade reading."

"Sounds great."

"But I miss you all."

"It's funny," I said, "but when you're not here they always seem to behave a bit better. I mean, they don't pester in the same way, or fight like they usually do. At the same time, they're not quite as much at ease. I'm sure of it. They stick it out with me, in a way, they know what rules apply and abide by them, but what you have is what they miss. It doesn't matter how nice and amenable I am, or how strict and distant. It's not the same kind of intimacy."

"Is it so bad?"

"No. It's strange, that's all. They hold something back. Not John, of course, but the girls do. It's my role, and I think it has to be like that, but I get something different back from them than what you do. Something less."

"Sometimes I wish they were like that with me. They're all over me when we're together. It's like they have to be right up close all the time. Pestering and going on. You can actually sit and read the paper when you're with them. I can't do that. They crawl all over me if I try."

"You need to set a limit."

"When I'm on a high, it's fine. When I'm down, it can be unbearable."

"I know. I live here too."

"Anyway, let's not talk about it. Are they asleep now?"

"Yes. I said before. Apart from Vanja."

"That's right, you did."

"Do you want a word with her?"

"No, not when she needs to go to sleep."

"What time will you be back tomorrow, anyway?"

"Sometime in the afternoon. Three or four-ish, I think."

"Christina will be here by then. I was thinking prawns. Is that all right? And white wine?"

"Yes, fine."

"See you tomorrow, then."

"Yes, see you tomorrow. I love you."

"Love you," I said, then hung up, closed the balcony door, and sank back onto the bed with the phone still in my hand.

All I wanted now was to be in the midst of my family, to live my life there, and so strong was that desire that it filled me with impatience, as if it would soon be too late.

I got up again, dropped the phone back in the charger in the hall, went to the bathroom and took a leak, washed my hands, discovered there was no towel on the hook next to the sink, went back into the bedroom and found one in the knee-high pile of clean washing beside the bed, dried my hands on it, and hung it up, before going back out onto the balcony, where Geir had sat down in my chair, and for a few seconds I stood there staring at him, nonplussed.

"Anything the matter?" he asked. "Your beer's on the table."

"No, nothing's the matter," I said, and sat down on the other chair. I was so attached to habit that everything seemed wrong from there. Only by an effort of will was I able to remain seated. It was no big thing, and yet something inside me had to be held down in order for me to stay put.

Lightning flashed in the sky. I counted the seconds until the thunder followed. It wasn't far off.

The sound that came was like a rockfall, an irregular, tumultuous crash that made me look up into the sky as if it could be seen – it was impossible for the instincts to comprehend that such a noise wasn't from something material, but arose on its own.

"Cheerful as ever," said Geir.

"Are you criticizing me too now?" I responded.

He laughed.

279

"No, that's right, I forgot. I came all this way to comfort you and cheer you up, didn't I?"

"You make me sound like a seven-year-old."

"It wouldn't be far off. I've never seen you so out of yourself. You're in shreds, man. And all because your uncle's angry at you. It's beyond me. I've never cared one way or another if anyone wanted to be angry at me. That's up to them. You're taking it pretty badly, I must say."

"It's not just that long nose of yours that makes you look like an elephant. It's the thick hide you've got as well."

He laughed. I lit a smoke. It helped, him being there.

"In the nineties there was some trouble with elephants in South Africa," I said. "Whether there were too many of them or whatever, I don't know, but anyway the authorities set up this program. They shot all the adult elephants, captured the young ones, and moved them to a different part of the country. Those elephants are adult now. And they're deeply traumatized. They're aggressive, hostile to humans, and antisocial. They've got all the symptoms of post-traumatic stress disorder. The point is they're sensitive. They saw their parents killed, and elephants always react when one of the herd dies, they become beside themselves with grief, circling the place where the dead elephant lies or lay for days on end. They're very social animals. So with seeing what happened and then being moved to a different area, the young elephants freaked out. They're not well. They're angry and destructive."

"So what are you trying to say? That I'm sensitive even though I'm thick-skinned, or that a traumatic childhood will always leave its mark, whether you're an elephant or a Tromøy goat?"

"Neither. It just came to mind, that's all. It made an impression on me. And I thought it might interest you, having written about PTSD and all."

"It's a bit gushy for my taste. And I'm not that sure whether elephants suffering from it too adds or subtracts."

"Adds. It becomes universal."

"It limits our scope as well though, doesn't it? If elephants can be traumatized, then trees can, too. There they are, all depressed in the forest after that nice little fellow alongside got chopped down on Christmas Eve. On the other hand, what's to say we can't just care less? As Nietzsche says, empathy merely increases the amount of suffering in the world. Instead of just one, there's two."

"He was a hard case. But all told probably the nineteenth century's most sensitive man."

I took a swig of the watery beer. The can was cold against the skin of my fingers. Its metal yielded with a snap when I tightened my grip. I put it down on the table, lit another cigarette with the stub of the first, leaned back in the chair, and let out a sigh.

"Another one of your East European sighs," said Geir.

"I got an e-mail from Jan Vidar," I said.

"Yeah?"

"He had no issues about being in the book."

"I never thought he would."

"No. It made me feel happy."

"But it doesn't help?"

"Of course it helps. It doesn't change anything for Gunnar, not by a long shot. But at least he didn't say anything about being unreliable. Neither did Yngve actually, come to think of it."

"That's not what it's about, you can see that, surely? He just doesn't want you writing about your dad, period. He must have had it in for you for years. You and your mom. The way he made out in that one e-mail that it was like a sociological demonstration of the sum conflicts between town and country, urban and agrarian, bourgeoisie and peasantry, rich and poor. The Hatløys unworthy of the Knausgaards. Ha ha ha! Who ever heard of Hatløy and Knausgaard? Who knew there was any difference? It's Olsen and Fredriksen. Only not for Olsen, because Olsen's Olsen, and Fredriksen's something else altogether!"

"That's just it. Every family has its own story, and even if everyone else has, too, it's still theirs. What I've done is make ours public. Now everyone's going to be able to read about it, and it won't be just the family's anymore then. I'm giving it all away. And it's not mine to give. That's the crux, I suppose."

"It is. But it's hardly against the law, is it?"

"Legally, you mean?"

"What else?"

"I don't know. Libel is, but then they've got to prove that what's written is incorrect. That's what Gunnar says he can do. If he can, and the court upholds that, I'll be found guilty. Otherwise it's all down to invasion of privacy, as far as I understand it. But privacy can be invaded even if what's written is true. Then it would have to be weighed up against freedom of speech and so-called artistic expression. Dad and Grandma are dead too. That's probably a part of it as well. In which case he's offended on behalf of the dead."

"Think of it. You're calling witnesses. He's calling witnesses. The whole damn book's going to have to be read out loud. The proceedings are going to take weeks. The papers will be writing about it every day. You'll become a millionaire out of this, Karl Ove. The book's going to be selling like hotcakes."

"How come what I see as absolute hell on earth, the worst thing imaginable, can sound so appealing when you talk about it?"

"I wouldn't know. Maybe it's my healthy, unsentimental outlook on life?"

"But what if he really can demonstrate that what I've written isn't true? What if I really am found guilty?"

"All the better! Everyone wants to read a book full of lies about real people!"

"Come on, be serious for a minute. It is actually serious."

"Certainly! But okay. What do you want me to say? Bad boy! Boo-hoo! Bad man! Come on. We've got the legal aspect. That's a gray zone. You might be found guilty, you might not. It's all relative. Then we've got the human side. That's where you're suffering. Your uncle's taken your father's place, and you're scared of him. It's all to do with you, your childhood, and your psychological makeup, not the novel. You've got to keep the two things apart. I'd say your anxiety here is verging on the pathological. In a way, you're a wreck. No offense! But that's how I see it. You write about all this, and it's got to come from somewhere. You look at your mom's family. You look at your dad's family. You try to understand. There's nothing wrong with that. You shouldn't believe there is. It's not wrong. It may feel like hell now, but that's a different matter. That's basically how I look at it."

"You can look at it like that. But as soon as doing what you have a right to do starts to affect others, it all changes."

"You are going to publish this book, aren't you?"

"Yes."

"Then there's nothing more to be said. You've made up your mind. Made your decision. It's going to affect others. So what? Did you kill someone? Did you assault someone? Did you steal from someone? Did you write anything bad about them? No. You've written very kindly about Gunnar. You've got to try to see things in their actual proportions. Gunnar's not your dad. You're not a child."

"No."

"End of story. Comfort and support enough for one day. How about another beer?"

"All right."

He got up and went past me, his face pale in the dim light of the storm. The raindrops were smaller now, they fell in curtains outside the balcony and over the city. To incur the wrath of another person was bad enough in itself, but nothing compared to my no longer knowing what had actually occurred. What was actually true. I couldn't rely on myself and my own recollections, they were infected by the writing. I knew that from earlier, that writing about a recollection changed it, all of a sudden you no longer knew what belonged to the recollection and what belonged to the writing. I didn't know what was true. In order to find out what was, I had to rely on external factors. Which was to say what others had seen and could recall.

There was a tremendous crash as the sky cracked above my head.

What the hell was that?

I jumped to my feet and went inside, my heart beating like a frightened animal's. I'd never heard thunder that loud in my life. The lightning must have struck right where we were.

Geir was at the window looking out. Njaal lay fast asleep on the bed by the wall.

"Did you see that?" Geir said, astonished. "The hotel took a direct hit."

"No, I didn't. But I heard it."

"Thunder and lightning at exactly the same moment."

"Daddy!" cried a voice from the children's room. I went in. Vanja and Heidi were sitting up in their beds. Heidi was crying. John was asleep on his side, his mouth pressed open against his arm. His hair was damp with sweat.

"I'm scared," said Vanja.

"Me, too," said Heidi.

"It's all right, nothing's going to happen, little loves."

"I don't want to sleep on my own," said Vanja.

"But Heidi and John are here," I said.

"It's not the same," she said. "I want to sleep with you."

"Me, too," said Heidi.

I looked at them for a moment.

"All right, then," I said. "Come on."

Heidi held her arms out and I lifted her down from the bunk bed. They scuttled out into the hall. By the time I came after them into the bedroom they were already tucked under the duvet.

"We don't want to be on our own," said Vanja.

"Is it going to thunder again?" said Heidi.

"It might," I said. "But it's not dangerous. And I'll be coming to bed as well soon. Okay? Do you think you'll be all right on your own for a few minutes?"

They nodded.

"But the door has to be open!" said Vanja.

"Of course," I said. "Night night."

I went back out into the living room. It was empty. But the door onto the balcony was open, so I stepped outside.

"Everything all right?" he asked from my chair.

"I think so," I said, sitting down in the other one. "But I think I'll be off to bed in a minute. John's probably going to be up at five. And if I don't get my sleep, everything's bound to go off the rails. But stay up and have a drink, by all means."

"Very generous of you," he said.

"The Elephant Man sat on his own a lot," I said.

"Didn't he wear a paper bag over his head?"

"No, no. A paper hat. He had a whistle as well. Here comes the Elephant Man! he'd shout, and blow his whistle when he was out for a walk. It was never a dull moment with him."

"You'd better get off to bed. You clearly need a rest."

"You're right," I said, getting to my feet. "Have you got everything you need? Sheets, bedding?"

"All sorted."

"Good night, then. Sleep as long as you want in the morning, no need to get up with us."

"Will do. Good night."

I went inside, paused in the doorway of the kitchen for a second, decided to leave the dishes until the morning, disconnected the phone, and went into the dim light of the bedroom, where Vanja and Heidi lay with eyes closed, their breathing regular and heavy, like two little animals. Vanja was lying crosswise. I lifted her up and laid her down straight, side by side with Heidi. She didn't stir. I got undressed and lay down next to them. How small they are, I thought to myself, staring at them for a moment before closing my eyes and drifting into sleep, the night inside us that seems so vast and boundless when we are within it yet can never be greater than ourselves.

A few minutes after five thirty John was standing by the side of the bed shouting at me to wake up. I put on my clothes from the day before and took him into the kitchen. Outside, the sun was coming up over the horizon. Its rays were sharp and penetrated the room. Everything became visible in its light, the bits of food on the floor, the trail of coffee stains that ran from the counter on the right to the sink on the other side, the globules of fat that specked the surface of the sausage water in the saucepan, the two bloated sausages that lay at the bottom, split open, the two empty milk cartons next to it, the open packet of margarine, so soft it was almost a fluid, its yellow color much deeper now than when it had been taken from the fridge. The Wetex cloth, stiff as a shell when dry, draped over the lip of metal that separated the twin bowls of the sink, like some odd fitting that was a part of it, originally white, now a grimy gray. The glasses and cups, plates, and bowls that were piled up in the sink, spilling out over the stainless-steel draining board like some encroaching plant of glass and crockery. The two empty jars of pasta sauce left unrinsed behind the tap, insides red with what remained of their contents. The transparent plastic cheese wrapper, which to a distracted eye made it look like the label with the logo on it hung in midair above the chopping board that had been pushed back against the wall. The beetroot juice the wood had absorbed. The withered plants in the window, dead for months, so much a fixture now that no one thought of throwing them out anymore. The table, with its glasses and plates, the jug of water with its tiny bubbles, the dried-up crumbs and other detritus that pointed to where the children sat, the empty bags of fruit that lay dumped, like little hangars of plastic among the drawings and drawing pads, crayons and felt pens, not to mention the two shelves on the wall next to the window, swelling like some coral reef with objects the children had collected and kept over the past couple of years, from sweet dispensers in the shape of princesses or Disney figures, little boxes full of beads, bead boards, sticks of glue, toy cars, and watercolors, to oddments of jigsaw puzzles, bits of Playmobil, letters and bills, dolls, and some marbles with little dolphins inside that Vanja had wanted when we were in Venice the previous summer. The shelves were a kind of station; once something was put there it was out of circulation and stayed there. We had a number of such places where the lives of objects came to a sudden end, most notably the long counter in the hall, presumably once used as a kind of sideboard for serving food before it was taken into the dining room, since it had those kinds of cupboards above and below, which were now crammed with all manner of stuff we must once have thought we needed but no longer knew we had, some three cubic meters of discarded lamps, used and unused lightbulbs, candles, piles of printer paper, rolls of undeveloped film, heaps of photographs, loose as well as collected in the little yellow folders in which they had been delivered, cookery books, assorted children's clothing, woolen tights from winter, odd socks, odd gloves, a pink Hello Kitty rain hat, a number of T-shirts, most likely outgrown, a hoodie, a thick sweater, napkins bought in abundance from IKEA, flowerpots, cables from old computers, extension cords, ballpoints and lighters, old paperbacks, washed but unironed tablecloths, invitations and advertising brochures, glossy weeklies, unused sparklers, a collapsed rice-paper lamp shade, the children's birthday train with wagons with numbers on them in which you could put little candles, balloons and whistles, bits of their wooden train set, including a station building and a locomotive, drawing pads, DVDs, CDs, tea towels – all in all a mountain of stuff that from time to time sent Linda into panic mode, the sudden feeling of utter chaos it could bring about would be too much for her. Not infrequently she came home with organizers and storage boxes to help her get on top of things; different boxes for different objects, a shelf for my mail, another for hers, with our names on them, like other people had, people who were tidier than us, but these systems would collapse after only a few days and everything would be chaotic again. It could get on my nerves, too, and about once every six months or so I went through the lot, sorting and tossing, whittling down these bulging piles, only for them to swell again within weeks. It was as if they were alive, drawing objects toward them and consuming them, growing bigger and stronger all the time.

Happily, the children didn't seem to be bothered. Conceptions of inner and outer chaos were not yet relevant to them, they approached the world as an unproblematic place most of the time, which was probably right, I thought to myself now. The material world was neutral, we wove our inner psychological landscapes into it, coloring it with our conceptions until it couldn't help but be messy. But it was a practical issue, nothing to do with morals. We weren't bad people for being messy. Our messiness was not a sign of poor moral fabric. I could tell myself this, but it didn't help, the feelings it stirred in me were too strong; as I moved around in all our mess it was as if it were accusing me, accusing us, we were bad people, unfit to be parents.

"What do you say, John, do you think I should clean things up a bit while you're having your breakfast?"

He looked up at me and nodded. I let the blinds down, lifted him into his chair, gave him his cornflakes and milk, which he seemed happy with, and began emptying the dishwasher.

"Coffee, Daddy," said John.

"Yes, in a minute," I said.

"No, now!" he said, jabbing his spoon in the direction of the coffeemaker.

"All right, then," I said, and switched it on. The shadows from the blinds were slats of darkness on the table, between them the light shone with particular intensity, almost scintillating, so strongly that the shadows had no definite boundaries but were as if diluted by the light at their edges.

John kept looking at the coffeemaker then back at me as I finished emptying the dishwasher and began rinsing the plates and glasses, cups and saucepans, before loading it again and switching it on.

There was a patter of bare feet against the linoleum in the hall. Heidi appeared in the doorway and blinked at us with bleary eyes.

"Hi, Heidi," I said. "Did you sleep well?"

She shook her head as she came in and sat down on her chair. Her hair was sticking up, her face streaked, as if it had yet to regain its elasticity after the inactivity of night.

I put a bowl and spoon out in front of her, the box of cornflakes, and the carton of milk. I got myself a cup, poured the now brewed coffee into a thermos and took it out with me onto the balcony, where I sat down with a smoke, leaving the door half open so I'd know if anything happened inside. Gazing out over the kilometers of rooftops I remembered I'd had a dream. I'd been sitting in the same place. The sky had been black and crisscrossed by planes. Some had been very close, great jumbo jets with every detail of their fuselages plain to see, others merely lights passing beneath the stars. The feeling it had given me had been intense and fantastic. Fantastic, fantastic it had been, and then I'd woken up.

I leaned back and put my feet up on the railing. The sun, bright and blazing, had warmed up the air around me considerably, and its rays burned against my face, sparkling in the window, the tabletop, and the shiny metal of the thermos.

Low-flying planes sweeping between tall buildings, sometimes skyscrapers, sometimes ordinary towers, were something I dreamed about recurringly, perhaps two or three times a year. Sometimes I was on board myself, other times I looked at them from a distance. Even in the dream I found myself marveling at how beautiful and unreal they were. Occasionally, I saw great plane disasters too, entire scenes in which they came hurtling from the skies to crash into a building or a street, exploding into flame. For that reason, the attack on the World Trade Center in 2001 was like watching a dream to me. All the elements were there. The skyscrapers, the great shining airplanes, the impact, the flames. But while these dreams were oddly concentrated, always centered on some single point around which all my feelings in some way seemed to be gathered, the true-life event was quite differently open and expansive, and I felt I could both remove myself from it and connect with it.

The job of the terrorists was to penetrate into our subconscious. This had always been the aim of writers, but the terrorists took it a step further. They were the writers of our age. Don DeLillo said this many years before 9/11. The images they created spread around the globe, colonizing our subconscious minds. The tangible outcome of the attack, the numbers of dead and injured, the material destruction, meant nothing. It was the images that were important. The more iconic the images they managed to create, the more successful their actions. The attack on the World Trade Center was the most successful of all time. There weren't that many dead, only a couple of thousand, as against the six hundred thousand who died in the first two days of the Battle of Flanders in the autumn of 1914, yet the images were so iconic and powerful that the effect on us was just as devastating, perhaps more so, since we lived in a culture of images.

Planes and skyscrapers. Icarus and Babel.

They wanted into our dreams. Everyone did. Our inner beings were the final market. Once they were conquered, we would be sold.

I took another slurp of coffee, wiped my mouth with the back of my hand, stood up, pressed an index finger against one nostril, and with a swift, forceful exhalation expelled a glob of mucus from the other out over the balcony.

"You do your morning ablutions al fresco, I see," said Geir. He was standing in the open doorway watching me. "Lovely!"

"I'm glad you appreciate it," I said, and sat down again. "I did that on a beach in Greece once when I was nineteen. There was an American girl lying there sunbathing, she turned to her friend and said, Did you see that? How disgusting!"

"She wasn't far off the mark, if you ask me," he said. "Is there any coffee around?" His voice was rusty, it had been idle all night.

"Sure," I said. "Cups are in the cupboard in the kitchen. Coffee in the thermos here."

I was about to go in and check on Heidi and John, and I would have to get Vanja up at some point as well, but I stayed put, thinking it would be rude to leave him on his own just as he'd come out to chat. I shoved the thermos across the table, stubbed my cigarette out on the side of the upturned flowerpot, whose terra-cotta red was almost obliterated by a blackness of soot and ash, like the wall of a fire-ravaged house, then dropped the end into the little hole in the top. But I hadn't done it properly, smoke began to curl up into the air. I reckoned it would burn out on its own, and lit another as Geir came out and sat down.

"Are they all right in there?" I said.

"Think so," he replied. Blinking up at the bright sun, he unscrewed the lid of the thermos, removed it, and poured himself a cup of coffee.

"You don't need to take the lid off every time," I said. "All you have to do is unscrew it a bit."

"Engineer all of a sudden, are we?" he said, leaning back and putting the cup to his lips.

"I'm an engineer of the soul," I said.

"That's the smuggest thing I've heard anyone say in ages," he said, and closed his eyes completely after taking a slurp. He opened them again and looked at me as he put his cup down on the table. "I'd say garbageman of the soul would be more accurate."

"Refuse disposal officer, if you don't mind," I said. "You know they call the garbage room in the basement here the Milieu Room, don't you? That makes 'milieu manager of the soul' the most correct title."

"Milieu consultant of the soul."

"That's it."

"Your ashtray's on fire, in case you hadn't noticed," he said.

"So I see," I said. "I was hoping it was going to put itself out. Doesn't look like it though."

I lifted the flowerpot up, and all the cigarette butts that had been crammed inside its thick earthenware walls tumbled out into the saucer. A couple of them were still burning and I stubbed them hard before trying to put the pot back on top. The sheer number of cigarette butts meant I couldn't get it to stand level, even when I tried grinding it into place. Eventually, I lifted it up again, swept the cigarette butts into a pile with my hand, and put one edge of the pot down on the saucer, flicked the cigarette butts that had already fallen down again back into place, and was finally able to put it back like it had been before.

"Looks like it's going to be a nice day," said Geir. "What should we do? Any suggestions?"

"We could go somewhere, I suppose," I said. "After I've taken the kids to the nursery."

"Sounds good. Not to a beach, though. I hate that."

"A town, then? Lund? Trelleborg?"

"Lund. I've always wanted to go to Lund."

"Lund it is, then."

I got to my feet and stubbed the half-smoked cigarette against the side of the ashtray.

"Let me get them dressed and ready."

When I went inside and into the hall, Heidi was standing on the little kids' chair in front of the cupboard, rummaging through the top shelves. She was the only one of the three who chose what she wanted to wear. Now it was the blue top with the white flowers that she was after, and a denim skirt, apparently, with a pair of pink Hello Kitty tights.

"That'll look nice," I told her as she climbed down and put her arms through the holes of the sleeveless top.

"Take the chair back into your room when you're finished," I said, and cast a glance into the kitchen, where Njaal was sitting without a shirt on, his legs dangling in the air as he ate his corn-flakes, Geir leaned against the counter watching him, arms folded against his chest. I went into the living room, where John was sitting on the sofa dropping a buzzing locomotive onto the cushion next to him, picking it up, dropping it again.

"Time to get dressed," I said. "Stay there and I'll get you some clothes."

I found a yellow T-shirt with a red ladybug on it in the cupboard, and a pair of green pirate-style trousers with a drawstring at the waist, took a clean diaper from the bathroom, where I also wet a facecloth with warm water and rubbed some soap into it, washing him as he stood with legs apart on the floor in front of me to get rid of the faint, yet pungent, salty odor of urine left by his diaper. It was a smell that stigmatized, belonging to children whose parents were less than rigorous with hygiene. Once it was done, I went out and dropped the used diaper into the bin under the sink, took a towel back in with me, dried him, put his clean diaper on, and his clothes, and straightened his hair with my hand.

"There you go!"

"Socks!" he said.

"You can put your sandals on today, the weather's nice. You don't need socks."

"I want socks!"

I went into their room and rummaged around for two matching socks in the drawer. There must have been forty socks or more, and amazingly no two seemed to be alike. I took them all out and dumped them on Heidi's bunk, laying them out as if on a shop counter to be sold, and began sorting through them systematically. Yellow, green, blue, red, pink, purple, turqoise, brown, white, black, gray, orange, and every shade in between. Striped, spotty, patterned. Some with cars on them, others with rabbits or dogs or cats. But all were different. I had to go into the bedroom and rummage through the pile of laundry on the floor. Socks were always at the bottom, they percolated down through the layers, as if consciously seeking the ground, and after finding five I took them back into the children's room to see if they matched up with any of those I'd laid out. Luck was on my side. I now had a single pair of purple socks. While they were slightly on the feminine side for John in my view, I took them into the living room with me and put them on his outstretched feet.

I found a dark red sweatshirt with long sleeves and a unicorn with long hair and big eyes on the front, and a pair of thin, mint-green cotton pants, and took them into the bedroom, where Vanja was still asleep, the duvet kicked aside. Her spine was visible, a faint rise under the skin of her slightly hunched back, from whose upper part the shoulder blades curved away on each side of the fair hair that veiled her head and neck so finely and was such a radically different material to the skin. The hair was to the body rather like the petals were to the stalk of a flower.

I lifted her onto my lap. Her skin was so warm, the way it is only after a night's sleep. I held her tight with my arms, opened the neck of the sweatshirt with my hands and put her head through. She put her hands into the sleeves herself and wriggled them into place, then pulled the bunched-up garment down over her belly. I put her feet into the trouser legs, first one, then the other, and inched the trousers up to her hips, then she arched her back, I gripped the waistband and pulled them up over her bottom.

"There we are," I said. "Do you want a *macka* to take with you and eat on the way?"

She shook her head.

"A nectarine," she said.

"But we haven't got any," I said. "An apple."

"Okay," she said.

I followed her through the hallway. The whole of one wall was built-in cupboards, whose light-brown color and fittings harked back to the fifties. Some were so full that clothes and shoes fell out if you opened them. Baggy coveralls, ankle-length boots, thick sweaters, everything from winter was here, as well as all the other stuff we didn't need on a daily basis. Behind the jackets and coats on their hangers under the hat shelf there were hooks in the wall where we hung all the backpacks and tote bags that over the years had accumulated to such an extent that they no longer really hung there at all, but were more like a growth. In the children's smooth backpacks were sandwich boxes whose contents, when we forgot to empty them, molded away, and the thought of their organic matter following the laws of the organic while buried among layers of synthetic materials, independently, without being in contact with any like matter, was something that fascinated me, at least after the box had been discovered, its contents thrown out and its plastic surfaces scrupulously cleaned. All over the floor, though mainly up against the wall, under the row of cupboards on the one side, the mirror and a long white bench on the other, were toys and dolls, scattered like debris from a plane crash. Normally I tidied up and did the cleaning if we were having visitors, but this time it was only Geir and I hadn't bothered. Besides, I'd been too worried. But today Linda would be back, and Christina was coming too, so there were no two ways about it. It would have to be done after I took the kids to the nursery, I told myself, following Vanja into the kitchen. The sun had moved upward and across the room in the short time we'd been awake, and its light no longer shone horizontally into the kitchen, but slanted down onto the wall where the counter and the dishwasher were. Vanja went to the cupboard and opened it, took one of the big red apples from the plastic bowl we kept our fruit in, and handed it to me.

It was a Red Delicious, most likely genetically modified, for the white flesh never went brown in the air the way the apples of my childhood always did, and they never seemed to rot, either. It was scary and went radically against all my conceptions of right and wrong. The fact that I still bought them was because Red Delicious had been such a luxurious apple when I was growing up, something special that we normally only ever had at Christmas, when they nestled, shiny and red and magical, in the fruit bowl, simultaneously hard, crisp, and succulent, the way no other apples were.

"What are you giving it to me for?" I said.

"The label," she said, putting her finger on the little sticker with the fruit company's logo on it, a little red-and-black ladybug on a white background.

I took the apple in my hand and scratched at the label with my fingernail, but it was so short it wouldn't catch, and I had to press through the skin of the apple in order to remove it.

"You ruined it!" Vanja said as I handed it back to her. "I want a new one!"

"Well, you can't have one!"

My reaction was so firm she gave up at once, put the apple down on the table, and marched off. I followed her. When she went into their own room, I went into the living room, where Heidi was sitting on the sofa drawing, John was sprawled on his back with his feet up, gazing at the ceiling, and Njaal was crouched on the floor putting Brio train tracks together. I sensed Geir was in the other room and went over to the sliding door and looked in. He was standing in front of the bookshelf with a book open in his hands.

"What have you got there?" I said.

"A book about Joyce," he said, holding it up so I could see the cover.

"Oh, that," I said. "Someone who knew Joyce in Trieste. A ship's captain, I think. Not literary at all, as far as I remember. They became friends and he wrote a book about him years after."

I turned toward Heidi.

"Time we were off," I said. "Go and put your sandals on."

"Is Njaal coming?" she asked.

I shook my head.

"Njaal's on holiday. Aren't you, Njaal?"

He didn't answer, his brown eyes looked at me nonplussed.

Heidi got down. I followed her out into the hall, brushed her teeth, then Vanja's and John's, said goodbye to Njaal and Geir, and went out onto the landing, not unnoticed by the neighbors, I imagined, for the children's noise levels were always in the upper reaches whenever we were on our way in or out, and the sound they made ricocheted off the walls and down through the floors. I had often heard them on the sixth floor while standing waiting for the elevator at street level.

That'll be the Norwegian's family setting off, I imagined them thinking. They're running late today. Or else, That damned Norwegian and his kids again.

Arriving at the nursery, Vanja keyed in the code, I opened the gate. The children already there were out on their trikes, the staff were sittting about on the benches. Heidi clung to me, her arms around my legs.

"I've got to go now. Mommy's picking you up today."

"Is Mommy coming home?" said Heidi.

I nodded.

"And it's Friday today. You can all have ice cream."

I lifted my hand and gave the staff a wave, pressed the door opener, opened the gate, and went back the same way we came.

It was hot in the sun, but in the patches of shade I passed through the air was cool and had a dampness about it, as if the autumn had come too early and decided to wait there so as not to disturb the grandness of summer, master of all seasons.

I veered right into Hemköp and went in through the doors that automatically slid aside, grabbed a basket before going through the two barriers that likewise opened automatically, glanced up at the monitor above the fruit display, and saw my image looking up and to the right, something Heidi and Vanja had yet to understand, for how could they be looking to the side when they were staring straight at the screen? Vanja and Heidi would sometimes do a little dance there on the supermarket floor, while John waved to himself from the trolley, we were like a traveling circus with dwarfs. I put some tomatoes in one of the plastic bags that weren't entirely transparent but grayly translucent as if they were full of smoke. The tomatoes were from the Netherlands and still attached to their little green vine stems, in contrast to the Swedish ones next to them, which lay packed together, red and shining, with neither vine nor stalks, presumably the reason why they cost five kronor more per kilo. After putting the bag of tomatoes in the basket, I picked up a shrink-wrapped cucumber and placed it next to them, then went over to the cheese display and tried to decide between a Danish Gouda, which was cheap, a Swedish Grevé, which Linda preferred, and a Norwegian Norvegia, which tasted much the same as the Grevé but cost almost twice as much. We had guests, I told myself, we could save money another day. Besides, the advance on the novel would be paid soon. What difference did forty kronor make?

With the Norvegia cheese in the basket, I went on to the bread. The bakery was one of the supermarket's biggest sections, I guessed they had somewhere between fifty and seventy different kinds of bread, maybe more, all arranged on displays that stood like islands in the middle of the floor. In Sweden bread came sliced and wrapped in plastic. That way it had a long life, but was always soft and lacking both crispness and the very particular good taste of fresh bread. Here, though, they also had a shelf of fresh-baked loaves, mostly with names evoking a simpler, more natural life, words like *rustic, country,* or *farmer's* were splashed all over them, and they emphasized the grain varieties too, unlike the sliced breads wrapped in plastic, which were more inclined to words such as *sport, energy,* and *health*. When I was growing up, in an age that to my children would one day appear as remote as the 1950s of my own parents had to me, bread came in paper bags, and its consistency and taste changed from day to day, from the delicious freshness of the first evening, when the crust was still crisp and the crumbs soft and moist, until the last hard crust was devoured two or three days later, with all possible degrees of taste and consistency in between. I remember many other families put their bread in a plastic bag as soon as they brought it home, which kept it moist a lot longer, but the crust would lose its crispness. We kept ours in a paper bag, meaning the crust stayed crisp, whereas the moisture disappeared. There weren't nearly as many different kinds of bread back then, I could think of only five off the top of my head: *kneippbrød, grovbrød, wittenberg, loff,* and one that was introduced when I was maybe eight or nine, *grahambrød*. That was it.

I had become a man of yesteryear, and it had happened fast, I thought to myself, and turned to the shelves of fresh-baked bread.

They had seven rolls for ten kronor, so I took one of the paper bags meant for loaves and put seven rolls inside, scrunched the top end together and dropped it in the basket, then moved on to the milk and dairy, grabbing a packet of coffee and a one-and-a-half-liter Pepsi Max on the way.

I also remembered the supermarket where we used to buy our bread. I remembered what it looked like outside, and what it looked like inside. I remembered when it was built, the enormous flat expanse of concrete they laid next to the road only a few hundred meters from our house, and the shop that rose up bit by bit on top of it, with its name proudly displayed on the side, like on a boat: B-MAX. To us it was Bemaks, a place on the same footing as other places in the vicinity, like *"ubekilen,"* "the fell," "the main road," "Gjerstadholmen," "the floating jetties," "the bridge." Even after the supermarket changed its name, it was still referred to as Bemaks. It was my first supermarket; before that there was nothing. Not a single recollection of a single shop. I was about five when they built it. God knows where my parents did their shopping before.

Besides Bemaks, we soon had Stoa, the cash-and-carry where we went maybe twice a year to buy in bulk. Ten-kilo sacks of sugar for preserving fruit or making fruit syrup in the autumn, a crate of lemonade for Christmas or the summer holiday, economy bags of flour, that kind of thing. Dad was fond of it, I think, he liked shopping for food, not in the local shop, where people would recognize him and where it was only ever the day-to-day items we tended to buy, he left that to me or Yngve or Mom, but in the bigger supermarkets outside the center, where you bought in bulk, he liked that. I think he liked the idea of throwing his money around on those occasions, the big man about town, that must have been it. Or maybe it was the opposite he was looking for, the security of gathering provisions, keeping a stock.

I stopped at the dairy section and took a carton of milk; it was for the children, so I chose the one with the highest fat content, 3.5

percent, then moved on and picked up half a dozen eggs the box said came from "cage-free hens indoors," prompting me to scan the other kinds to see if there were any from "mistreated hens crammed together in cages," which didn't seem to be the case, and so I carried on toward the checkout, along the deserted aisles, between the refrigerated counters and the shelves of shampoo, through a small section of "organic sweets," then the glitzy inferno of normal sweets, which took up about the same amount of space as the bread.

But from all the numerous times I'd been to Bemaks, and it was from Bemaks I caught the bus to school, to Bemaks I came running with a shopping list in my hand from Dad at least twice a week through all those years, I had retained only one real memory. It was one time when I was there with Mom. I'd seen a special-offer sign saying the yellow boxes of Nesquik, the chocolate milk powder, were down to only one krone. It was so cheap I felt sure Mom could be talked into buying some. Only one krone, only one krone, I kept saying as I dragged her over to where the cardboard sign was. But it says minus one krone, she said. They cost one krone! I insisted. No, she said, it means one krone off. There's a difference. And so I had to do without Nesquik that day. But the memory has stayed with me.

Why would that be? There were myriad things I'd seen and done there, a whole galaxy of events.

I stood in line at the checkout to the left. There were only two people in front of me, both with so few items they held them in their hands, as was often the case at this time of day. In the afternoons the place came alive with customers dragging the new wheelie baskets along behind them. It was one of the saddest sights I knew, all semblance of human dignity evaporated the moment a person went with that of all options. The feeble, characterless action of trundling instead of carrying. The fussy little wheels, the long black handle, the basket that followed on behind like a small dog. The clatter of the wheels was earsplitting from the moment one became aware of it.

The very thought deflated me.

Life was there to be felt, that was what we strove for, but why? For our headstones to say, "Here lies a person who liked to sleep"?

When I opened the front door I found the apartment completely silent. For a moment I wondered if they'd gone out, but then I heard a noise from the children's room and guessed it to be Njaal playing while Geir sat reading somewhere.

"Anyone home?" I called out.

"Ah, there you are," said Geir from the living room.

"I bought some bread rolls if anyone wants some," I said, took my shoes off and put them in the cupboard, picked up the bag, and went into the kitchen. The dishwasher was finished, so I dumped the shopping on the table, switched it off, and opened the door, the steam billowing out into my face, making me step back instinctively.

I took the cutting board out and put it on the table, found a bread basket in the cupboard, and tipped the rolls into it. Fresh rolls with lots of butter and yellow cheese, I could hardly think of anything better. But my tastes were simple. The salt of the cheese and the butter against the mild wheat flavor of the bread, and the thin, yet hard, crisp crust that broke into pieces the moment you bit into it was something I'd never grown tired of. So my mouth was watering as I cut into one of the rolls and covered its surface with butter and three thick slices of cheese.

"Njaal wants one too," said Geir, coming to the table.

"Help yourself," I said.

"Don't speak with your mouth full," he replied.

"Have I told you what Vanja's excuse is whenever she does something wrong?" I said.

He shook his head.

"She says it's our fault for not bringing her up properly. And not only that, she says it's too late now."

"She may have a point there," Geir said, angling the knife and scraping it across the surface of the butter, causing it to collect at the blade like a lateral moraine.

301

"Of course she has. I just hadn't thought it would be so obvious to her, that's all."

Geir spread the butter over his bread, picked up the cheese
slicer, and cut off a slice.

"No fingers on the cheese!" I said.

"Seriously?" he said. "You mean there's a rule against it?"

"Isn't there?" I answered. "You're the sociologist."

"Amazing how much I get to be the sociologist here, isn't it?"

"I only mentioned it once yesterday, and once now."

"Well, it's twice too often," he said, taking the two halves of
the roll into the living room. I went after him, cramming the last
bite into my mouth.

"I was thinking of cleaning up a bit before we go out. If
it's okay."

"I'll give you a hand, if you want."

"Great."

Njaal sat with his elbows on the table, bread in hand, looking
at me while he ate.

"When will Vanja and Heidi be coming back?" he asked.

"This afternoon. About three o'clock, I imagine."

"And what are we going to do today?" he said, and looked
across at his father.

"We're going to Lund," Geir said.

I started picking up all the towels, trousers, tops, and socks
that were lying around the living room.

"Can I take my bike?" said Njaal.

"Of course you can," said Geir. He gathered some apple cores
together on a plate and stacked some plastic cups. I went into the
bathroom and pressed the clothes down into the laundry baskets,
which were already full. I straightened up again. Maybe I should
check and see if the laundry room was available in the basement?

No, it would only complicate things.

I left the bathroom and picked up the dolls that were scattered
around and put them in the dolls' bed in the children's room. One
of them had blue marks drawn on its face, they looked like a tribal

tattoo, a rather unnerving contrast to its innocent baby features, which made me turn it facedown. I gathered up all the soft toys and dumped them on the end of Heidi's bed; she was so small she only took up a third of its length. Mostly, they were dogs, cats, and rabbits, but there was a lynx too, as well as a panda, a lion, a tiger, a parrot, a crow, a lamb, a cow, an elephant, and a crocodile. I positioned them so they were all looking out into the room, above and below each other, and that was unnerving too, perhaps because there was something accusatory about the combination of staring eyes and silence, or else it was because they looked like dead creatures with faces and eyes that seemed to be watching us from the other side. I picked up the toys strewn about the living-room floor and put them away in the round brown ottoman and the three mesh baskets we used for the purpose, while Geir picked up all the children's books and magazines he could find.

"I want to help," said Njaal.

"You can pick up the toys in the hall and put them . . . I don't know, where should he put them?" Geir said, looking up at me.

"I'll get you a basket," I said, went and got it and put it down on the floor in the hall. But after putting a few odd toys in it, Njaal decided he would rather play with them instead. Geir tousled his hair as he went past with a pair of purple plastic shoes in one hand, I noticed, and I stepped aside to let him through, then emptied the dishwasher in the kitchen; the heat had nearly left the dishes now, but remained in the cutlery.

"It always looks a lot worse than it is," I said to Geir. He was standing in the doorway now, looking like he was about to ask for another job.

"I find the impression of mess and the mess itself to be quite congruent," he said. "But maybe that's because our place is always tidy. I put everything back right away. It never gets a chance to get out of hand."

"I'd like it to be like that here, too," I told him. "Only there's always something that prevents it. It just isn't possible, apparently."

"I like it here," he said. "There's something relaxing about messiness."

"As long as it's not your own," I said.

"Exactly," he said. "Christina always says I need some chaos around me in order to get things done. Like the war in Iraq. It doesn't get more chaotic than that. Then I can get to work cleaning it all up."

"That's not a bad theory," I said, closing the cupboard where we kept the glasses and cups, then opening the one next to it where the plates were. "You've got no chaos inside you at all, so you need some outside instead. I'm the opposite, chaos on the inside and a need for tidiness on the outside. Only I fall short on the last part."

"You re-create your chaos, I re-create order. We're as much geometry as we are psychology."

"I know," I said. "Does that mean the living room and hall are okay now?"

"Not quite. I don't know where things go."

"Wherever you think's suitable. As long as it's out of the way."

With all the dishes put away, I filled the dishwasher again with what was left, sprinkled some powder in the little compartment, snapped the cover shut, closed the door, and put it on the sixty-degree program. After that I went into the living room, got the vacuum cleaner from behind the door, pulled out the cord, plugged it into the socket, and switched it on. The bag was full, so there was practically no suction at all, I had to put the nozzle on top of everything that was heavier than dust and hair for it to be sucked up. Beads, crumbs, scraps of paper, the odd fruit pastille, little unidentifiable bits of whatever. A small insect scuttled along the baseboard; in Swedish they were called *silverfisk*, what the Norwegian was I had no idea and had no recollection of ever having seen one before I moved here, though I couldn't be sure, it sounded wrong that there should be an insect that was only found here. They looked like a little tail with feet, tiny in size, and they lived wherever they could keep themselves hidden: in piles of clothes, underneath mattresses, in the folds of blankets, and in laundry baskets. If I went to the bathroom at night they could be in the middle of the floor, dark against the light-colored linoleum, immediately darting for cover in the nearest place they could find, like behind the baseboard. I squashed the ones I could, but their resources were clearly inexhaustible, since they never at any time seemed to be fewer in number.

Silverfiskarna. A novel by Vilhelm Moberg.

I reached under the sofa with the head of the cleaner, sweeping it back and forth a couple of times, then moved on to underneath the table, which was the area I really wanted to get at, the children had at least one meal a day there. When that was done, I sucked up the dust that had accumulated around the doorsills and behind the doors before switching it off, pulling the plug out, and finally, the highlight of any vacuuming session, pushing the button that made the cord come swishing back at high speed into the belly of the device.

"All done," I called out, returning it to its place.

Geir came out from the children's room.

"Are we finished?"

"It'll have to do. We can always do a bit more when we get home."

"No need. It looks fine as it is. Shall we get going?"

I nodded.

"Just need to check my e-mails first."

Njaal came sneaking up on Geir from behind and walloped him on the backside as hard as he could.

"You little terror," Geir exclaimed. Njaal shrieked with laughter. "I'll get you for that," said Geir, reaching out and grabbing him as I squeezed by into the other hall, past all our beach things, which had been dumped against the wall, a green parasol, two folding chairs, a kind of sunbed, baskets full of beach toys, as well as our two big suitcases, one a hard plastic shell, the other soft and made of some kind of fabric, gray and black respectively, and the two drying frames, folded and leaned up against the wall, with yellow and green towels draped on them from when we were at the beach the previous weekend, and the children's beachwear. The light was dim in the bedroom, the air dense, so I opened the door onto the balcony and left it ajar before sitting down and switching on the computer. I heard them laughing and carrying on while I waited for the computer to start up, stared at the blinds without seeing them, it was Gunnar I was thinking about, and the fact that Linda was coming home and that I had to remember to buy white wine somewhere before we came back.

Right.

I opened my e-mail account.

Gunnar.

Should I wait? I could wait, surely? Wouldn't the day be ruined otherwise?

If I waited, though, I wouldn't be able to think about anything else.

I opened the message and started to read.

He had signed himself as my father's brother.

I sat for a moment without moving.

"Are you coming or what?" Geir called from the hallway.

"Just a minute," I said back, hardly managing to raise my voice so he could hear me. "I've got a new message here."

I heard him approach.

"Didn't hear you," he said.

"Another e-mail," I said.

"Gunnar?"

I nodded.

"Mind if I have a look?"

"Be my guest," I said.

He stood behind me while he read.

"So shall we go now, then?" he said after a while. "You can't let this throw you. There's nothing new in it."

"True. But now he says he's got a lawyer. And he's using the word 'vendetta.'"

I got to my feet.

"It's really getting to you, isn't it?" said Geir.

"Yes, it is," I said.

"Come on," he said. "Let's go to Lund."

"I need to speak to Yngve first," I said.

"Okay," said Geir, and followed me back out of the bedroom. Njaal had been standing with both hands on the door handle looking in at us. I took the phone out of the charger and pressed Yngve's number as I crossed the floor, opening the door of the balcony before it even started ringing.

"Hello," said Yngve.

"Did you get that e-mail?" I asked.

"Yes," he said. "I'm writing a reply right now."

"A reply?"

"That's right."

"Are you sure that's a good idea?"

"Listen. He's putting forward a whole load of accusations against me. It's completely unreasonable what he's doing. I'm going to tell him so."

"What do you think you're going to achieve by that?"

"I don't know. But I need to tell him now that he's gone too far and it's not going to be without consequences. He can't say whatever he likes just because he's angry. Besides, I'm not you. And nor is Mom."

"I'm really sorry I got you into this mess," I said.

"What you did is the reason he's reacting, but it's not your fault he's taking it out on us. And you can hardly be to blame for his reaction being so completely out of proportion either."

"I'm sorry all the same."

"We lose an uncle, that's all."

I went in and dropped the phone back in the charger, then looked at Geir, who had sat down on the chest, or whatever it was called, that we had in the hallway.

"I just need to read it again," I said.

"No, you don't," he said. "Come on, I don't want to be sitting here all day. You've already read it, for Christ's sake!"

I didn't say anything, but went back in and sat down in front of the screen again.

"Right, we're off!" Geir called out.

"I'm ready now," I called back, switched off the computer, got up, and went into the hall. They were outside on the landing, waiting at the elevator. I put my shoes on, got my sunglasses from the study, then remembered we needed to go out the back way, and went into the kitchen again.

"Now what?" Geir shouted after me. I didn't answer him, lifted the trash bag out of the bin under the sink, tied a knot in the top, picked up the other full bag I'd left up against the wall on top of some newspaper, and went out to the elevator. Njaal, who was wearing a pair of khaki shorts and a white sleeveless top, held his nose as we went down.

The elevator came to a gentle halt in the basement, I held the two trash bags in one hand and opened the door with the other. I rummaged in my pocket for the key, then realized I'd forgotten to lock the door upstairs. But then again, what did we have of any value? Three computers, that was it. The TV was from the eighties, only a very nostalgic thief would want to run off with it.

"Yes?" said Geir.

"Won't be a minute," I said. "Just wait here."

My fingers finally got hold of a key, allowing me to retrieve the bunch from my pocket. I tapped the key card against the panel until the green lamp flashed and there was a click as the door unlocked. My energy was almost gone as I walked the fifteen meters down the passage to the door, after which came the stairs, then another door into the refuse room.

I stopped and placed my palm against the cold wall, wanting to put my face against it as well, and if I'd been on my own I might have. Instead I put my hand, which had already absorbed some of the coldness of the wall, to my forehead. Geir and Njaal stopped in front of the door and stared at me just as I was about to go on.

"Is this it?" Geir asked.

"Yes," I said. "It took me weeks to find my way around down here with all these doors."

"There are four," he said. "How difficult can that be?"

I didn't answer him, opened the door, and went up the stairs. "You can wait here," I said. "I'm only tossing the garbage out."

The stairs on the other side of the heavy steel door were black and slippery, presumably from the liquid that forms in the bottom of garbage bags, deposited by months, perhaps years, of minor leakages. The smell was pungent and mellow at the same time. Ventilation ducts were suspended from the ceiling, the rest was bare wall. I opened the lid of the nearest garbage container, which was big enough to conceal an entire dismembered family, and slung the bags over the side. I felt sick, my whole body was aching. I couldn't trace it back to anything specific – something in particular that I'd done wrong – it had to do with everything, me in my entirety, and for that reason it couldn't be helped. Even if I did retract the damn book it wouldn't make any difference. Apart from pleasing Gunnar and making him think he'd put me in my place, perhaps even crushed me, and that justice had been done. His demands were justified, his rage was justified, and it was the sheer force of it all I was unable to withstand, it pinned me to the ground, took me apart, rendering me and everything about me worthless. Worthless. Even my own children vanished in his rage, even they lost their worth, for I was the only father they had, a person unable to keep himself in check, whose outline was blurred, so fundamentally lacking in empathy, he could destroy the lives of others without even knowing.

When I came out of the refuse room they were waiting in the light of the open door. Which is to say that Geir was standing there, holding the door open, while Njaal had gone outside into the yard that lay in the deep shadow of the tall building at whose foot he stood. He stared at a small white van that was reversing. Probably deliveries to the back door of the Chinese takeaway; the delivery man would knock on the door as hard as he could with a length of piping left there for the purpose, and if he was lucky one of the people who worked there would come out after a minute or two. Boxes containing canned soft drinks, canned goods, and noodles.

Njaal ran across the yard and out onto the sidewalk, where the light was bright and warm.

"Mind the road!" Geir shouted. "Stay on the sidewalk!"

Njaal sent us a look as if to say he was being underestimated.

"I know!" he shouted back.

"All right," said Geir. "It looked like you didn't, that's all."

He twirled his key strap around his finger.

"Are you going to start whistling now?" I asked.

"What do you mean?" he said.

"Your body language is so cheerful."

"It's a nice day. The sun's out and I'm on my holidays. Of course I'm cheerful! Not even a misery guts like you can alter that."

He started whistling.

Fifteen meters ahead of us, Njaal had stopped next to their car, a red Saab from some time in the nineties, which meant it was anything from ten to twenty years old. I hadn't a clue about cars, and the nineties were like yesterday to me. That twenty years had gone since they started was incomprehensible.

"Ouch!" said Njaal, putting his hand against the bodywork.

"You didn't think of parking in the shade?" I said.

"Like you would have done, you mean?" said Geir.

"If I were as anal as you, yes."

He laughed and unlocked the car, strapping Njaal into the child seat while I got in the front of the boiling-hot vehicle. In front of the three cars in the parking area at the bottom of the cul-de-sac was a tree, its leaves glittering in the sunlight, and on the other side of it lay Föreningsgatan, along which I'd walked a couple of hours earlier with Vanja, Heidi, and John.

Geir got in, shut the door, and put the key in the ignition. I fastened my seat belt, discovering the sunglasses I'd slipped into my pocket. I put them on. They were Polaroids and I'd bought them on the Lido in Venice the previous summer. I liked them, there was something of the seventies about them. Vanja had said I looked like a thief. I liked that, too.

Geir pulled his seat belt across his chest and clicked it into place, released the hand brake, threw the car into gear, and pulled slowly away down the road. There was something rash about his driving; not that he drove too fast or took chances, it was more his movements when he was behind the wheel, the abrupt way he looked over his shoulder when changing lanes, the sudden- ness with which he flicked the indicator, as if only just remem- bering at the last minute, or the way he kept glancing to all sides on straight stretches of road. Most people I knew drove as if they were at one with the vehicle, as if the instruments and controls were an extension of their own bodies, but Geir drove like he was operating some unfamiliar machine.

"Which way?" he said.

"I'm not sure," I said. "I usually just go straight on until there's a sign out of Malmö. It tends to work okay; the motor- ways take you out of town, and they all connect up in one way or another."

"You don't say," he said. "Well, I like to know which way I'm going. Still, render unto Caesar the things which be Caesar's."

"I'll render you in a minute," I said.

"I refuse to laugh. Not even a smile for that."

We passed the Konserthuset, following the wide, avenue-like road in the direction of Värnhemstorget, a ribbon of glittering cars reflecting the sunlight from their various parts, a wing here, a windshield there, a bumper or a door handle.

Geir pressed a button on the inside of his door and my win- dow slid down. The wind rushed in as if through a funnel.

"You've got the technology, I see," I said. "What year's this thing from, anyway?"

"It's a 2001."

"Really, 2001? I reckoned it was from the nineties. You mean it's only eight years old?"

He nodded. I looked up at the signs above the roadway.

"The highways are that way," I said. "Any will do, it doesn't matter."

"Gothenburg or Stockholm or Ystad or Copenhagen or Trelleborg?"

"Take your pick. The worst that can happen is we end up having to go back."

He sighed.

"Go with Gothenburg, then, if it means that much," I said.

"I will, then."

We approached the big junction where four different roads converged, all multilane. I glanced at the faces in the cars alongside, the way they were all in their own worlds, as if unaware that they were barely half a meter away from other people, separated from them only by a transparent sheet of glass.

The lights changed, the first cars pulled away, and a few seconds later the movement was transmitted to us. Our line of vehicles snaked onto the on-ramp, its members accelerating onto the motorway according to individual preference, soon drawn out over several hundred meters of road. Geir kept to the inside lane, observing the speed limit, meaning that we were continually overtaken as meter upon meter vanished beneath us and the landscape outside changed from the built-up topography of the city, almost devoid of vegetation, to the more open lots of industrial sites and car dealers, fenced off from each other by tall wire mesh.

"What did I tell you?" I said with a nod toward the sign telling us the Lund exit was a kilometer up ahead.

"I never said you couldn't get lucky," said Geir. "How are you doing, Njaal? All right?"

"Yes."

"Shall we have an ice cream when we get to Lund?"

"Yes."

We passed from rural landscape to industrial sites, then residential areas, and eventually found ourselves in the city center, which was markedly smaller than Malmö's; the buildings were lower, the streets narrower, the pace slower. Geir's head was go-

312

ing back and forth between the side windows and the windshield as he scouted around for a place to park, hopefully still keeping an eye on the traffic around us.

"There's a big parking lot in the center, I seem to remember," I said. "If you keep going straight, I'm sure we'll find it."

Instead of doing as I said, he signaled right.

"But it's down there!" I said. "Look, just around that corner!"

"It's no entry. You see that big round sign there?"

"Oh, is that what it means?"

He looked at me.

"You are joking, I take it?"

I shook my head and he burst out laughing.

"I was pretty impressed that you could pass your written exam after only reading up the night before. Now I understand things a bit better."

"I keep telling myself I should brush up a bit on road signs. Only I can't bring myself to do it. I have my license now, don't I?"

"Here we are," he said, and signaled left, turning onto a short ramp that led into a parking area.

After the rush of wind from the road, the air into which we stepped seemed oddly still. It shimmered in the heat above the asphalt, but was otherwise as calm as the waters of a small inlet, and we were beneath the surface, if that was what it was.

One day in the middle of the nineteenth century in one of the villages that line the Vestland fjords, during the hay harvest, the sun shining as it was now, when all the villagers were hard at work in the fields, a disaster occurred. Everyone died, and no one was spared to tell what happened. They were found the next day. A young man who was meant to be working for his uncle that day discovered them. The house was silent when he got there, he went in, his uncle's wife lay dead on the floor of the kitchen, her face twisted almost beyond recognition, her eyes bulging, the blood had run from her ears and nose. He rushed out, up the steep hill, whose grass was only half mown, and there he came upon a group

313

of men who looked like they were resting, only they turned out to be dead too, presumably struck down on the spot, with exactly the same appearance as the wife in the house. Bulging eyes, blood seeping from their orifices.

It was the beginning of a novel. Something had happened, no one knew what, and after a few generations it became just a tale, eventually, in our day, all but forgotten.

But then it happened again. And someone, the novel's protagonist perhaps, stumbled upon the tale and uncovered the connection.

Yes. The unfathomable depths of the fjord beneath its blue-green surface, the green sides of the valley, so exceptionally intense in color, the white-clad tops of the fells under blue, cloudless sky. The grass tickling against moist skin, the steady hum of insects. The scythe that sang as it mowed, the clatter of its metal against the sharpening stone, the feeling of vast silence beneath it all, evoked by the fells and the fjord and the sky together. And then, disaster.

I stood there, staring down the street as Geir opened the trunk, took out Njaal's yellow balance bike and assembled it. The black jeans I was wearing stuck to my skin, and my feet, encased in tight black man-made fiber and the black leather of my shoes, were so hot and slippery with sweat it was like they hardly belonged to my body at all, but were creatures in their own right. Two blotchy red brothers, perspiring stokers of coal.

Njaal got on his bike and gripped the handlebars tightly, feet planted on the ground. The bike was made to look like a lion, with a face painted on at the front and a little tail at the back.

"That's a cool bike you've got there, Njaal," I said.

He was so proud he didn't know where to look.

"Yes," he said eventually.

Then he set off, paddling along, scooting faster and faster across the parking lot. Geir checked to make sure the car door was locked, put his keys in his pocket, and went after him.

"Not too far ahead, Njaal!" he shouted. "And keep to the sidewalk!"

As he reached the curb he stopped abruptly by putting his feet down hard on the ground.

"Impressive technique," I said.

"Yeah, he's really good," said Geir.

"What do you want to do? Are we hungry?"

"Let's see the cathedral first, eh? Then grab some lunch afterward."

"Sounds good."

It was the air that had gone. Sucked up from the earth by some thunderous implosion, first a rumbling in the distance, then louder and louder, the wind picking up as the noise increased, until suddenly, as they stood bewildered and anxious, everything went totally silent. Not a sound was heard. They looked at each other, all was still and they found themselves unable to breathe. They dropped to their knees. Clutched their throats. The blood thumped in their veins. Their stomachs turned. Eyes wide and staring. They fell to the ground, twisting and writhing like worms. And all in silence. The life vanished from them, one by one, and there they lay, motionelsss one and all. Everyone in the fields, everyone in the houses. All the birds, and all the animals. And then, perhaps seven or eight, maybe ten minutes later, the air returned in an ear-splitting tumult, as when a dam is opened and the water comes crashing down on the dry riverbed.

But what then?

What would happen then, and why?

Njaal scooted along, now behind us, now in front, as we walked toward the cathedral that rose up so serenely over the rooftops as if it were the most natural thing in the world. All around us people strolled with their shopping bags, and on a square we crossed they were sitting on benches and at café tables, some with bikes parked in front of them, students most probably, while cars rolled sedately by, their tires rumbling gently over the cobbles. There was an ambience of peace and tranquillity about the town, bordering on the slumberous. It was hard to imagine that Malmö was only minutes away by train, life there was so very different. Malmö was a working-class city, built not for the eye or the mind, but for the body, with its long rows of identical brick buildings, its streets a busy turmoil of life and contrasts. Lund was complete, and probably nearly always had been, built up around a small number of more or less permanent structures established by the church and the university, institutions concerned with preservation, whereas Malmö had been built up around production. In Lund it was the town that shaped the people, in Malmö the people that shaped the town. The fact that Bergman's main character in what was perhaps the best of all his films, *Wild Strawberries*, journeyed to Lund, was surely by no means incidental, for the journey is the journey toward death, and while life may be fluid, death is stable and immutable, and of all places in Sweden Lund would have to be closest to such a state. The people of Lund were of course just as alive as the people of Malmö, and their town just as alive; the difference was between the expected, that which is already established and which people merely populate, and that which is created in the moment. It was a matter of forms and roles.

"The people in your subdivided community have fled from exactly that in Malmö," said Geir as we crossed the area in front of the church. "They've built themselves a little Lund out there. You're right to call it death."

"The average age must be seventy," I said.

"Ugh!" he said. "How the hell you could ever be so stupid as to buy that little dolls' house out there, I'll never know. It's exactly what I've spent my whole life trying to get away from."

"And with so little success," I said.

We stopped and looked up at the church exterior, whose Romanesque weightiness appeared not to strive toward the heavens in the way of the great Gothic churches, appeared not to want anything but this, endeavoring instead to make the best of its own place. The distinction here was not between down and up, but between in and out.

"Fantastic church," said Geir.

"Do you want to go in?"

"Yes. Where's the entrance? This way or that?"

"We went in the other side when we were here," I said.

We walked around the side of the church. Geir turned and called out to Njaal, who was perhaps forty meters behind, scampering along on his yellow lion bike. On the other side was a park. Green trees rose from green grass and stood motionless with their swells of foliage, through which not a breath of wind passed. Njaal came biking past.

Where were the children? Had I forgotten them? Were they at home in the apartment?

No. I'd dropped them off at the nursery.

Or was that yesterday?

No. I was certain of it. We tidied up after I got home. They weren't there then, they were at the nursery.

"There's a door over there," said Geir. "It can't be the main entrance though."

"No, they usually put the main entrance at the front in the olden days," I said.

"Your irony only reflects poorly on yourself," said Geir. "You're the one who's been here before." And then, abruptly: "Njaal!"

"Yes," Njaal shouted back, by now some way farther down the path that led through the park.

"Come here!" Geir called. "We're going inside!"

"Okay," said Njaal, and came paddling back toward us. I gazed at the enormous blocks of stone, which had once been light in color, but which now in places were almost black. At the base they were green.

"Leave your bike here, we're going inside the church now," said Geir.

"I want to take it with me," said Njaal.

"It's not allowed, you little terror. No bikes in God's house."

"No balance bikes, anyway. Pedals would have been different."

"What?" Njaal looked up at me.

"Karl Ove's only joking," said Geir. "Leave your bike and come here!"

He did as he was told and we went into the church, which seemed so much bigger and vaster than it looked from outside. Here there was any amount of striving to the heavens.

I wasn't in the mood for churches and wandered around halfheartedly, sitting down on a pew after a short while, not even trying to identify myself with what the surrounding imagery expressed. Geir and Njaal disappeared from sight, when they appeared again they came up to tell me they'd been down in the crypt. I went outside for a cigarette, Geir wanted to look around a bit more, so I sat down on the steps and stared out into the park, the smoke of my cigarette a wispy cloud about my head while I thought about the new idea I had for a novel, how it might connect up with what little I already had. The dystopia. The world that never was. The man who grew up in a place where Nazism constituted the social order. Why Nazism? I'd seen a picture not long before, from a Nazi propaganda poster, depicting a bridge in a mountainous landscape, and it was so stirring and filled me with such an odd sense of longing that I wanted to investigate it. To create just such a world. I knew instantly that the lower-middle-class horror of the subdivision gardens in some way joined up with that image. I'd read another article, in *Dagens Nyheter*, about the biological manipulation of animals, dealing partly with an experiment in the sixties when a team of scientists had implanted electrodes in the brain of an ox and succeeded in making it walk and stop – a picture showed how the ox, which had come running toward the scientist, had halted abruptly in front of him when he flicked a switch on the box he held in his hand; and partly with an ongoing experiment with a fly in which they had implanted a light-sensitive gene from an eel which allowed them to steer it, albeit not minutely or with any exactness;

every time someone directed a light at the fly it took off. What these experiments stood for was horrendous and shook me to my very foundation. The problem was that it belonged to our time, structurally, politically, socially, the whole mentality of it, and that its myriad meanings would evaporate as soon as I tried to insert it into another, counterhistorical reality. Perhaps what I had were two different novels. That would become apparent to me as I went along, I thought to myself. The world was so big and diverse that opposite forces were always at work somewhere, no particular outcome was ever guaranteed, the future was wide open and uncertain, and if the sun went down in that future, it would go down on us, not on those who were to come; for them it would rise.

"There he is, all on his own, the friendless wretch," said Geir behind me.

I turned.

"Are we ready for some lunch now?" I said.

He nodded and I got to my feet. My legs felt like they were shaking, but it was only a sensation. I tossed my cigarette onto the gravel as Njaal got back on his bike and we walked off, me with my inner being in turmoil, Geir in good cheer, I assumed, since he was twirling his key strap again and trying to tell me how marvelous the church had been inside. Friendless, he'd said, and the situation I was in returned to me. Gunnar's awful e-mails. The lawyers poring through my manuscript. The court case that lay ahead. The newspaper headlines.

"You seem a bit miserable," he said.

"Yes," I said. "Sorry. I'm not the best of company."

"Are you going to start apologizing for that now as well? As far as I'm concerned, you can be as miserable as you like. Everything has its value."

"No, the moods of others can hardly be said to seep in and affect you," I said. "You're always yourself, regardless."

"What you're saying is I'm thick-skinned. You said that yesterday, too."

"But you are."

"If you say so. How about that place?" he said, indicating a restaurant maybe twenty meters up a side street we were passing.

"Can't we sit outside?" I said. "So I can smoke?"

"Sure. On the square, then? There were some outdoor cafés there."

We went over and sat down at a table inside a roped-off serving area. A girl in her early twenties was sitting at a neighboring table with a woman I supposed was her mother, about fifty years old. Apart from them the place was deserted. The girl was typing on her phone, the mother smoking and staring out over the square.

"Do you want pizza or spaghetti?" Geir asked Njaal, who had produced a toy car from somewhere and was now playing with it on the edge of the table, his chin supported by his hand, elbow on the table.

"Spaghetti," he said.

"Good," said Geir. "How about you?"

"I don't know really. Carbonara, I think."

"Nice choice. I'll go with the carbonara as well."

He put the menu down on the table. The waitress came over and we ordered. While we waited for the food, Geir expounded on the concepts of sensitivity and insensitivity. He pointed out how odd it seemed that I, with my wish to write about all that was authentic, and who had written so freely about death and the body, had not written about sex. I was too sensitive, he considered.

"I'm discreet, that's all," I said. "Besides, as I see it sex is over-amplified in our culture."

"Overamplified?"

"Yes. Do you remember what you told me once, about the guy who vanished in a huge avalanche and was buried alive under meters of snow?"

"I do. You often come back to that, don't you?"

"Yes, because he disappeared to go jerk off. It's a superb illustration of our sexual urge."

"The way it exerts itself on every situation?"

"No, the minuteness of it. It's so incredibly small. A tiny little ejaculation in a huge mass of snow. Sex is completely out of proportion, we give it so much space and attach so much meaning to it, but in actual fact it's nothing. Totally verging on zero."

"I may be a fool, but I'm not an idiot!" he said in English. "We're talking about the way it is. Not the way we want it to be. You want life to be big and meaningful. Noble, even. Sorry. It is small and lonely. It's never going to be better than that orgasm in the snow. Sex and death, that's all there is."

"Then why do you even bother talking to me, if that's the case? Shouldn't you be at home jerking off? Or sticking your head in a bucket and putting a gun in your mouth?"

"What do you know? I often jerk off when I'm talking to you."

"So that's where those funny noises come from. I thought it was the dog slobbering over its dinner."

"We haven't got a dog."

"No, exactly. The truth's always something else."

"Good point," he said, and smiled the way a person who is basically rather pleased with themselves may sometimes smile, as if they can hardly contain their pleasure.

The waitress came over from the counter with a plate of pasta in each hand. I looked at the table, there was a basket of bread on it, and a small bottle of olive oil; had she put them there without my noticing?

"Two carbonaras," she said, putting two plates down in front of us. "Yours is on its way," she said to Njaal.

"Have some bread while you're waiting," said Geir, handing him a piece. He took a bite as he watched a pigeon wander about between the tables, then glanced up at me.

"It's all about the difference between is and ought to be," I said.

"Do you remember what Pessoa says? 'How can I face Leopardi's atheism with gravity and pain when I know this atheism may be cured by sexual intercourse?'"

"Yes, but that's just it. I can accept reducing things down in order to get to some form of truth, but what I don't understand is why that reduction always has to end in sex."

"The reason you don't understand it is because you're an aesthete. You shun what is base. You shy away from the body. You know what Luther wrote?"

"No."

"Dreams are untruthful. Shitting the bed, that's the only truth."

After we'd eaten, we strolled toward the botanical gardens. In the middle of the park there was a small pond full of water lilies, and next to it a little café where we sat down and had coffee in the flickering shade beneath a tree. There were some ducks whose young – which last time I was here, with Linda in the early summer, had been small and fluffy – had grown considerably while they had retained their youngness, the offspring of both animals and humans had awkwardness in common, as if, because of their sudden size, something monstrous had come over them. Of course, Njaal wasn't bothered about such things, he chased them around for a while, trying to get close enough to pet them, but every time he got near they scuttled away, their heads held still on relatively slender necks, and eventually he lost interest and began tossing stones into the pond instead, until Geir told him to stop, and he sat down in the gravel by the table to play with his car again.

I thought about something Vanja often asked, about why grown-ups never played. She couldn't grasp that we found it tedious, and the conclusion she drew was that in that case she never wanted to grow up. Life was running around and laughing, playing with long-maned plastic ponies and little Japanese figures with big eyes, swinging on swings, spinning on carousels, climbing in trees, splashing in wading pools and pretending to be a whale, a shark, a fish. Not sitting in a chair reading a newspaper, looking serious. Or, like now, sitting still at a table and talking, with long pauses in between where nothing was said and no one did anything.

The people at the other tables, mostly elderly, conversed in low voices, now and then there was a chink of cutlery, a fork against a plate, a spoon against a cup, which then died away in the still air under the treetops.

It felt like we were in the depths of summer. As if we were a part of some Impressionist painting, for no one had captured that feeling better than the Impressionists, and the question was whether it had actually been they who created it. Whether such a feeling had even existed in the world before they came upon it, with all their conceptions of color, light, and shade, their endeavors to reproduce the exact moment. Before that, painting had always been geometric, had always been concerned with the solidity of objects and people, and with the borders between them. That which is here, the ways in which entities that are here are connected, and that which is there, which is to say beyond here, is what such paintings investigate. But in a world sunk into shadow, specked with flickering light, where one thing merges into another, the questions are different. What is visible and what is invisible, what is clear and what is obscure, what can we see and what can't we see, and, not least, what is this feeling that so compellingly pervades what we see? A writer such as Marcel Proust would be unthinkable without Impressionism, since his entire work is built around the relationship between recollection and oblivion, light and shade, visible and invisible, and the compelling feeling the world, especially the sunken world, yet also the prevailing world of the present, awakens in him, is shaped, if not brought into being, by the eye of the Impressionist. With Cézanne, the question is: what does it mean to see? With the Impressionists, the question is: what does it mean to experience seeing? Regrettably, their radicalism has completely disappeared from our cultural consciousness, now all that remains are the fine colors and the flowers, a fate Proust avoided, his own fine colors and flowers existing in words, and he could certainly never be suspected of appropriating beauty by copying an appealing motif, which incidentally would be one possible definition of *kitsch*.

The fact that art has become so cerebral that everything to do with feelings is left to the simpleminded, is perhaps the best argument there is against progress, for the very reason that such a standpoint, which it seems must take precedence over our human experience, is so stupid and unintelligent as to be truly simpleminded itself. When the imperative of craftsmanship in art was abolished, it was because the idea that art should be about reproducing the world as exactly as possible was deemed old-fashioned and therefore no longer necessary. So it was abolished. But one doesn't have to think too hard in order to understand that this wasn't the reason that painters and sculptors spent all their time during their crucial formative years of youth copying others or mechanically reproducing models or objects. They weren't doing it so they could learn to copy reality, because the reproduction of reality has a cutoff point any reasonably talented student would achieve fairly quickly. They were doing it so as to learn how not to think. This is the most important thing of all in art and literature, and hardly anyone can do it, or even realizes it is the case, because it is no longer taught or conveyed. Now everyone thinks art is to do with reason and criticism, that it's all about ideas, and the art schools teach theory. Which is decay, not progress.

Geir drew his chair back in the gravel and stood up.

"Do you want some water?" he said.

"Yeah, I think I will," I said. "Can you get me a top-off as well?"

I picked up my coffee cup and handed it to him. It had stains all over it, mostly spots but streaks too, the way my coffee cups always did for some reason, I had no idea why. Other people's coffee cups tended to be shiny and untarnished on the outside. I supposed it was because I held my lips in a certain way that allowed coffee to dribble between them and the cup, but while I didn't understand how this could be the case, I was unable to do anything about it; no matter how hard I pressed the cup to my lower lip, there were stains all over it by the time I was finished.

"Where are you going, Daddy?" said Njaal, looking up.

"Just getting some water."

Njaal got to his feet and went after him, wriggling his hand into Geir's. I got my phone out of my pocket and called Linda. She answered right away.

"Hi, it's Karl Ove," I said. "Are you home?"

"Yes. I just got in the door. Where are you?"

"We're in Lund. Sitting in the botanical gardens."

"How nice."

"Yes, it's pleasant. But you're picking the kids up, right?"

"Yes. I'll go over in a bit."

"Okay, I just needed to make sure. Anyway, we'll be getting back soon, so I'll see you later."

"Did you buy the wine and the prawns?"

"I'll get them when we get back."

"I can get them if it's easier."

"No, it's okay. I'll do it. See you soon."

"Okay. Bye."

"Bye," I said, then pressed the red key and put the phone back in my pocket just as Njaal and Geir emerged again from the little pavilion-like structure that housed the actual café. Njaal was holding a glass in both hands, taking small, cautious steps, it was an important job he'd been entrusted with, while Geir walked behind him with a cup of coffee in one hand and a glass of water in the other.

"Thanks," I said. "I'll pay for the water, seeing as you got lunch."

"Ha ha."

He sat down, took the glass Njaal had been carrying, and downed its contents in one. His face glistened slightly with perspiration.

"Is it time we were heading off soon?" he asked.

"Yes," I said. "I called Linda. She just got in."

He checked the time on his phone.

"Christina should be arriving soon as well. Drink your coffee and we'll get going."

"One more smoke," I said. "Then we'll go."

Njaal picked up his bike and got on. I took the last cigarette out of the pack and lit up, crumpled the empty pack in my hand and looked to see if there was a garbage can close by. There wasn't.

"You're not to bike in the park here," said Geir. "Wait until we leave."

"Why?" he said.

"People are eating! You wouldn't want people biking around in your lunch either, would you?"

"No," he said with a chuckle.

Geir looked at me.

"You've gone quiet," he said.

"That's what Arvid always used to say, I remember. In Bergen. You've gone quiet, have you shit your pants or something?"

"Here we go again."

"I know. I'm sorry."

"I was thinking about what we were talking about yesterday. About being a dad."

"Yeah?"

"My principle is whoever wants something the most should do it. And whoever that is decides everything. When Njaal was born, Christina could hardly sleep at nights in case she missed something. She had a superb job at the opera, but she quit that to spend as much time with Njaal as possible. Her doing all the practical stuff isn't because she's a woman, it's because it actually means something to her. If she'd been eager to do something else it all would have been different."

"Yes," I said.

"Not only does she put more into it than me, she also gets a lot more out of it. It's highly meaningful to her."

"I remember running through the streets to send off a roll of film for developing when Vanja was born, and then running all the way back. I didn't want to miss anything either."

"But you wouldn't want to stay home full-time for three years, would you?"

"No."

"It's so easy to get swallowed up in all the softness and warmth, so easy to think that's all there is. But we don't create anything in that space other than more softness and warmth. I see it as a weakness. That's why I have no respect for men who just wander into all that. Everyone hails them for doing it, but all they're actually doing is shirking a responsibility. A major responsibility, at that. I agree with Karen Blixen when she says you can't go chasing the Holy Grail with a baby carriage. You can't have both. There's only one kind of masculinity. You're either more of a man or less. That's fucking it. There's no such thing as masculinities in the plural. Oh, how I despise that word. It makes me want to throw up. There are certain words that absorb everything about an age that you don't like. That's one of them. I can't take it. The same goes for women, too, of course. There's only one femininity. Mind you, if this were the sixties, when men went to work and women stayed at home, I could well imagine me staying at home with Njaal. It's the thought of a prevailing ideology, a consensus idea governing my life, that I can't stand."

"But if that's true, it's just a protest. I mean, if the point is just to do the opposite of everyone else, then you're just as trapped as all the others."

"You're right. I take it back. The point is just that it's totally absurd for other people to be telling me what I'm supposed to be like with my own son. You know, when I was in Iraq, during the war there, while the bombs were coming down, I was interviewed by a journalist from *Aftonbladet*. Do you know what he asked me?"

I shook my head.

"Who does the dishes at home? Can you believe that?"

"What did you tell him?"

"I refused to give him an answer. Anyway, we've got a dishwasher."

"You call that little tin can a dishwasher?"

"Don't underestimate it. We never argued over anything as

much as we did over whose turn it was to do the dishes. As soon as we got a machine to do it, it was problem solved."

"Small machines for small problems."

"Why do you think he asked me that? I'll tell you. He wanted to know if I was a good person or a bad person. If I did the housework, I was a good person. If I didn't, I was a bad person."

"Mm," I said. "Shall we get going? I'm done now."

We got up and left the café area and walked back through the park. I stopped where a tree had been cut down and stood for a moment reading the sign that had been put up next to it. It said the tree had died from a disease that had hit almost every tree of its kind in Skåne.

Bloody hell.

I walked on and caught up with them at the entrance gate. We followed the fence for a bit before crossing the road and entering a picturesque little street of small, low houses with flowers growing up their walls. As we got closer to the car, and thereby the apartment in Malmö, I felt a rising sense of unease, back to the apartment meant back to the book. I smoked a cigarette, it was something to do, and doing something took attention away from my thoughts, if not much then a little bit at least, and that was better than not at all. I smoked, I stared at the things around me, trying to think about them instead, and checked my phone that no one ever called.

"When was Linda picking the children up?" Geir asked, the parking lot maybe fifty meters ahead of us.

"About now, I should think," I said. "Why?"

"So someone will be home when Christina gets there."

"She has a cell phone, doesn't she?"

"Yes, that's true."

"Is she getting the train from Båstad?"

"No, the way I understood it she was getting a lift with someone who was coming this way."

Christina had taken a course for school photographers and was going to be taking photos of school classes in the Stockholm area all autumn. She had done the same thing the year before, and the money she had earned during that period had kept them going all year. Geir no longer had his job at the university, and the unemployment benefit he had been getting for a while had stopped. The book he had sacrificed everything for, which wasn't yet finished, and which on my advice he had submitted to first one publisher, then another, so that they might be involved at the earliest possible stage of the process, had been turned down by both. I had no idea how they managed to get by, but he said it was just a matter of discipline. They did all their shopping at Willys, where they bulk-bought discount goods, and with anything else, such as books, CDs, and DVDs, he would spend hours looking for the cheapest price online. I had no idea what they did about clothes, but Christina was a trained designer, and my guess was that they bought secondhand and that she mended and adjusted.

Geir pressed the key, the car lights flashed with a beep. I opened the door and got in while he opened the trunk for Njaal's bike. I tipped my head back and closed my eyes. Outside, the sound of Geir rummaging in the trunk was neutral, a noise like any other, rising and spreading out into the air, but inside it was different, it was the sound of something going on in the car, in some way belonging to it. The difference was immense. What was going on outside seemed safe and unthreatening, whereas what was going on inside was something one was defenseless against.

Outside the car windows, Malmö began to materialize. The big housing blocks on the edge of the city, which in Malmö were of yellow brick, loomed up. Rows of windows, rows of balconies, and between them parking lots and lawns. The quiet residential areas of detached homes where the well-off lived were on the other side of the city, by the sea. That's what money bought, lots of space and distance from others. But not too much space and not too much distance. In the forests you could have as much space as you wanted and there could be miles to the nearest neighbor, but no one with money would ever dream of living there. Space and distance were valuable only if there were other people nearby who had a lot less space and lived a lot closer to each other.

We drove past supermarkets, car dealers, shopping centers, gas stations, rows of buildings gradually appearing on each side, the shops to begin with selling cheap and simple commodities, becoming increasingly expensive and more exclusive the closer we got to the city center. Here were people, milling along the sidewalks, striding past the windows, cars passing in the streets with windows of their own, traffic lights and pedestrian crossings, squares and sidewalk cafés, little parks, big parks, a canal, a railway station. Hotels with flags flapping at their entrances, sports shops, clothes shops, shoe shops, electrical dealers, furniture shops, lamp shops, carpet shops, eyewear shops, bookshops, computer shops, auction houses, kitchenware dealers. Picture-framing shops. Chinese restaurants, Thai restaurants, Vietnamese restaurants, Mexican, Iraqi, and Iranian restaurants, Turkish and Greek restaurants, French and Italian restaurants. McDonald's, Burger King, pizza joints. Cafés, cinemas, a concert hall. Theaters, an opera house, nursery schools, record shops, bus stations. Unemployment offices, linen shops, a hospital, an old people's home, doctors' offices. Opticians, ear specialists, heart and lung specialists. Dentists, orthopedists, psychologists, psychiatrists, pipe-fitting firms. Funeral parlors, DIY shops, home interior shops, photo shops, banks, yoga studios, pubs, flower shops, health shops, amusement arcades, tobacconists, camping and outdoor stores, children's clothes shops, baby shops, massage institutes, car rental firms, pet suppliers, toy shops, churches, mosques, schools, information points. Hair transplant institutes, law firms, advertising agencies. Hair salons, nail studios, pharmacists, clothes shops for fat people, surgical appliance shops, workwear dealers, garden stores, exchange bureaus. Musical instrument shops, computer game shops, bus card kiosks, radio, TV, and hi-fi dealers, sausage stands, falafel bars, suitcase and bag shops. The whole of this enormous world, teeming with detail, was divided into intricate, finely meshed systems that kept everything apart, at first by its very division into sectors, which meant that rubber tap washers, for instance, were to be found in a different place than nylon guitar strings, and a novel by Danielle Steel in a different place than a novel by Daniel Sjölin, which was a kind of rough, initial sorting, then by infusing the various goods or services with value, thereby grading them in ways no school could ever teach, and which therefore had to be learned ad hoc, outside any school or institution, and which furthermore were forever in a state of flux. This was the difference between a pair of McGordon jeans from Dressmann and a pair of Acne jeans, or a pair of Tommy Hilfiger jeans and a pair of Cheap Monday jeans, Ben Sherman or Levi's, Lee or J. Lindeberg, Tiger or Boss, Sand or Peak Performance, Pour or Fcuk. It was what sort of signals a novel by Anne Karin Elstad sent out compared to a novel by Kerstin Ekman, and how both of these related to a collection of poetry by Lars Mikael Raattamaa, for instance. The reason why reading Peter Englund was a bit more exclusive than reading Bill Bryson, albeit not by much. The reasons why one could no longer express fascination and enthusiasm about Salman Rushdie without seeming culturally adrift, left behind in the late eighties, while V. S. Naipaul was still accepted. The knowledge that meant I could go into a clothes shop and buy the jeans or suits that were now held to be superior, though not by all, select the books in the bookshop that gave me the greatest degree of cultural credibility, purchase the music in the record store that was deemed more than averagely sophisticated, even when it came to traditions and genres I didn't know much about, like jazz and classical, I'd picked up enough to get by, perhaps even in some lucky circumstance to pass for a true connoisseur. This was the way with almost everything. I knew perfectly well what kind of sofa sent out what kind of signals, and the same was true of electric kettles and toasters, running shoes and schoolbags. Even tents were something I would be able to appraise, at least to a certain extent, in terms of what kind of signals they sent out. This knowledge was not written down anywhere, and it was hardly accepted as knowledge at all, it was more an assurance regarding the way things stood, and it fluctuated according to the social strata in such a way that someone from the upper classes would be able to frown on my sofa preferences and the sofa knowledge I was thereby demonstrating, just as I in turn would be able to frown on the taste in sofas of people belonging to a lower status group than myself, not in any way denigrating them as human beings, because I wouldn't dream of doing such a thing, but their sofas. I might not say so out loud, for fear of seeming judgmental, but I would think, God, what an awful sofa. Such knowledge, which applied to nearly all brands and their practical and social significance, was immense, and, I occasionally thought to myself, not that different from the knowledge so-called primitive peoples once possessed, where they not only knew the name of every plant, tree, and bush in their surroundings but also what kind of properties they had and what use could be made of them, or the knowledge people of our own cultures possessed only a few generations ago, for instance in the eighteenth century, when most people also knew the names of all the plants and trees in their vicinity, and the names of all those who lived in the villages they lived in, both the living and several generations of the dead, just as they were familiar with and able to identify by name all localities, great and small, in their surrounding area. Naturally, they knew the names of the tools they used and the work they were appropriate to, and of all the animals, their various parts and organs. This knowledge wasn't something they considered, nor was it ever made a show of in any way, since basically they were unaware of its existence as such, so closely was it bound up with their own being. Such is the case, too, with the immense knowledge we ourselves possess, of the difference between strong and mild mustard, for instance, a grilled or a fried sausage, a sausage with cheese in it or one with bacon wrapped around it, a bread roll or the kind of potato pancakes we Norwegians call *lomper*, raw or roasted onions at the gas station's grill stand, or of the difference between the various kinds of mustard in our supermarkets, like the French

Dijon mustard, or English Colman's, or the particular variety that belongs to Skåne, not to mention wines, which are so culturally expressive and so extremely saturated with social meanings. Like the people who went before us, we don't give a thought to the knowledge required for us to get through the day, we don't see it, it's a part of us, it's who we are. Our world is this: Blaupunkt over bluebell, Rammstein over rowan, Fiat over foxglove.

One of the three parking spaces at the top end of Brogatan, by the back entrance to our building, happened to be free as we drew up, this was hardly ever the case and I said to Geir we were in luck.

The sun, which when we left had been above the building housing the job center, was now above the bank, and its rays, slanting down toward us, were filtered through the foliage of the tree that grew in the nameless square meters of space between Brogatan and Föreningsgatan, causing the car roof and bodywork to flicker in the play of light and shade that manifested itself in iridescent nuances of red, from very bright and intensely lustrous to a darker dullness.

I got the key out of my pocket and crossed the area behind the building, which was in shadow most of the day, for which reason the temperature there was markedly lower than it was only a few meters away, tapped the orange key card against the panel, pulled the door toward me, and held it open until Geir and Njaal had gone in. I followed them down the stairs, they stopped at the door that led into the basement passage, which I opened in the same way. The air was cool and smelled of brick, fusty in the way of everything that was under the ground. Through the door at the other end, just as we entered, came the Polish woman who lived two floors below us, a blue IKEA bag in one hand, her grandchild in the other. I sent her a nod but she didn't see us, or pretended not to, and we went through to the stairs, where I pressed the button for the elevator, which was at the floor above us and came gliding down after only a few seconds.

"Now we'll see if Mommy's arrived," said Geir.

"And Vanja and Heidi," said Njaal.

John's stroller was parked outside the door, and as I went in I saw the little pile of shoes on the mat in the hall.

"Hello!" I called out.

"Hello," Linda called back from the kitchen. I stepped a bit farther inside so Geir and Njaal could come in. As I bent down to take off my shoes, first Linda then Christina appeared from the kitchen. Njaal bustled past me. Linda had all the radiance of when she was happiest, I noticed, a glow of sociability about her, particularly visible in the luster of her eyes, which was stronger than usual, but also in the skin of her cheeks, which had a slight blush to them. Her entire being smiled. I straightened up and we hugged each other.

"I missed you," she said softly.

"Good to have you back home," I said, my head lowered to her neck.

"Hi, Karl Ove," said Christina, and looked up. She was crouching in front of Njaal, asking what he'd been up to.

"Hi," I said. "Good to see you."

She got to her feet and we hugged fleetingly. Behind us, Linda and Geir did likewise. Njaal tugged at Christina's dress, wanting her to go into the living room with him. She smiled at me apologetically and went with him.

"Were they all right when you picked them up?" I asked.

Linda nodded and put her hand against my hip.

"So when did you get back?"

"About an hour ago, I suppose. I bought them each an ice cream."

"Good idea," I said. "I haven't got the prawns yet. I was thinking I'd pop out."

I went to the kitchen, took the coffeepot and the filter holder over to the sink, and tipped the used filter into the bin before emptying what was left from earlier into the sink, rinsed the pot a few times, and then filled it with fresh water, which seen through the unwashed glass didn't look fresh at all but took on a faint yellow tinge.

Linda sat down at the table and took an apple from the big, almost flat blue dish we'd once borrowed from her brother and never returned. It was ceramic and decorated with an Arabic-looking pattern in black that set off yellow apples and bananas especially well.

"Helena and Fredrik give you all their best," she said, biting into the apple.

"Thanks," I said. "Are they doing all right?"

She nodded as she munched.

Geir went through the hall, glancing at us as he passed, before going into the living room and by the sound of it sitting down on the sofa.

"It's nice to be home again though," she said. "I've never been away from the children that long before."

"That's positively sick," I said. "You were only away three days. That's nothing."

"It was enough for me," she said. "Anyway, I got talking to a man on the train. It turned out he was head of a school. He wants me to be a substitute teacher. I got his number. I've got a job!"

I poured the water into the coffeemaker, put a filter in the holder, measured out six heaped spoonfuls, then switched it on.

"Is that what you want?" I asked. "I thought you wanted to write, and make radio programs."

"But I never really get going with any of it. It's so incredibly taxing, making a radio program all on your own. I need something simple. Something more clearly defined. With this I'd go to the school, teach, and then go home again."

"What are you going to teach?"

She gave a shrug.

"Whatever they give me. As long as I can read through the syllabus beforehand, I should be all right."

"True," I said.

"You don't sound very convinced," she said.

"Yes, I am," I said. "It'd be fantastic if you had a steady job, of course it would."

I took an apple, too, and sat down opposite her at the table.

"You can't think about much apart from those e-mails, can you?" she said.

"Not really," I said.

"You mustn't worry."

"I can't help it. It won't go away. I know it's irrational. But it feels like someone died. The intensity of it, I mean. Something terrible that's there all the time. Even when I'm not thinking about it, it's there."

"You've got to shake it off. You can't write four books in a year and then let yourself be totally swallowed up by this as well."

"But I can't help it, that's what I'm saying."

"Do you want me to read what he's written? Maybe it would help, make it easier to talk about?"

"Yes, if you want."

I got to my feet and went to the bedroom, where the computer was still switched on, put the apple down on the desk, and opened the browser. Linda came in just as the first message appeared on the screen.

"This is the first one," I said, picking up the apple again. "You can scroll up to the others."

She nodded and sat down. I went into the living room, where Vanja and Heidi were playing with some Playmobil on the bed we used as a kind of divan up against the wall, with a blue-and-white-patterned throw to cover it, while Njaal stood with a plastic sword in his hand, making fencing moves in front of Christina, who turned her head toward me and smiled, a bit uneasily, I sensed.

"Have you seen John anywhere?" I said.

"I think he's asleep," she said. "He was before, anyway."

Njaal was directing all his attention to her, presumably in reaction to the complication of Vanja's and Heidi's presence. They had each other, he was on his own, and so he fenced with his mother instead.

"I think there's a pirate's eye patch in the toy box over there," I said. "And a hook for your hand. Is that right, Vanja?"

"I don't know," she said.

"Come and look then."

"But we're playing!"

"Njaal can find them," said Christina. "Can't you, Njaal?"

"Haa!" he said, lunging forward and striking her thigh with the flat of the sword. It wasn't made of plastic or wood, but of some other material a bit like foam rubber, only harder, and it had started coming apart all the way up the "blade."

I went into the other room, where Geir sat leafing through a book.

"Do you want some coffee?" I said.

"Yes, please," he said.

"It'll be ready in a minute," I said, and sat down in the chair across the table while munching what was left of my apple. Usually I ate them whole, core, stalk, the lot, and had done so ever since I was a boy, and there was something about that, to do with the slightly bitter taste of the stalk and the seeds, and the stringy consistency of the core, that for some reason always reminded me of childhood, as if the deviance of that action, for that was how I perceived it, as a rather deviant thing to do, opened up new spaces of experience compared to the norm, which was the taste of the white, succulent flesh of the fruit. These spaces were not large expanses, more like tiny stabs of the past prickling the consciousness, the feeling of fingers passing over the surface of a dark blue down jacket on the road outside the house in the dim light of morning, or the rain as it began to fall on a Sunday morning, patches of snow still left here and there at the roadside, bicycle wheels plowing through a sludge of gray mud on the gravel track.

"What are you reading?" I asked, placing my arms on the armrests and, since he wasn't looking at me, staring out the window at the small section of the balcony and the rooftops beyond it that was visible through the slats of the blinds.

"Daniel Defoe. About the Great Plague in London. Have you read it?"

He looked up, and I glanced toward him.

"What do you think?" I said. "The chances of your picking a book out here that I've actually read aren't that great."

"Here it is, Njaal," I heard Vanja say from the next room.

"Thank you," said Njaal.

The next minute Heidi was standing in the doorway. She was wearing a white summer dress with a red print on it.

"Can we watch a movie, Daddy?" she said.

"Not when we've got visitors. Play with Njaal. We'll have some nice dinner soon."

"What are we having?"

"Prawns."

"Prawns?"

"Yes."

"Are they nice?"

"I think so."

She gave me her skeptical look. I loved it when she did that.

"Njaal's playing with Vanja," she complained.

"Come on," I said. "Two minutes ago you were playing with Vanja. It can't have changed that much since then. Join in."

"What?"

"Go and play."

She turned her head and stared into the other room. I got up and went to the kitchen, where the coffee stood black in the pot. I closed off the filter so it wouldn't drip after I took the pot away, then poured the coffee into the thermos, the red Stelton we'd been given as a present by Axel and Linn, though what the occasion had been I could no longer remember.

Linda came through the hall.

"Do you want some coffee?" I said when she came in.

She nodded. Her face wasn't as lively as it had been only minutes before. Now she looked drained, paler.

"It's awful," she said. "How can he say such things? I'm afraid for you, Karl Ove. He wants to hurt you."

"Come on!" I said. "I pissed him off, that's all."

"No, he's lost it. He's lost control of himself. It feels dangerous. He's completely unstable."

"No, no. It's unpleasant, that's all. Everything's going to be fine. I promise. Did you want some coffee?"

She nodded, and then I remembered that she had already nodded in response to the same question. I got four cups out of the cupboard, they were brown on the outside, with a faint tinge of red and white on the inside, and the four saucers that belonged to them were also brown. They were meant to go with some kind of Italian coffee, as far as I remembered, but they were just as good for regular filter coffee, and if I was displaying my social incompetence in that respect it was only to Geir and Christina, whom I'd never suspected of laughing at us behind our backs after they'd been to see us, though of course you could never be certain.

No, I was pretty sure they hadn't.

I took the thermos and the cups with me into the other room, where Geir was sitting, put them out on the table, and sat down. Then I remembered Linda needed milk, so I got up again and went back into the kitchen to get it, got the carton out of the fridge and checked the expiration date, which said it was on its last day, so I opened the carton and smelled inside, just as I heard Geir ask Linda if she'd read Gunnar's messages, and since there seemed to be nothing wrong with it I took it back with me into the other room and put it down next to the thermos on the table, while Linda told him how awful she thought it all was.

"What if it goes to court?" she said. "You might have to stay in Norway all autumn. What am I supposed to do then? Imagine this place. Am I going to be left on my own with the kids? And how will you deal with the pressure?"

Geir gave her one of his most sardonic smiles and glanced at me as she went on. Linda noticed, of course, and I could see how a sudden rage welled up in her, which the presence of guests meant she had to keep inside, and her eyes clouded over. She flashed me the blackest look before getting to her feet and going out into the hall. I sent Geir a look of reproach, but it seemed like he misunderstood and thought it was Linda I was annoyed with; whatever the reason, he simply smiled again, or maybe he was just smiling at the whole thing.

"Help yourself to coffee," I said, and went after Linda, who was already in the bedroom by the time I got to her.

The spring Linda and I got together we went out a couple of times with Geir and Christina, it was when we were still obsessed with each other, kissing and touching, unable to keep our hands off each other, and even when I met Geir on my own, for instance in the place I had then, I was still immersed in the thought of her and just sat there blushing with joy, listening to whatever Geir was going on about without any of it actually seeping in, for I was no longer a person, or so it felt, I had become something else, a creature floating in the sky, high above the world and everything in it. I was the sky man, she was the sky woman, and together we were going to have a sky baby. But then we came back down. The sky life stopped and something else began.

Linda wrote about it in a short story, the two lovers lying in bed talking, she saying she had once seen a strange bird in her childhood, and describing it to him, never before had she seen such a bird, and never since, and it turned out that he had seen one exactly the same in his own childhood, for this is how it is to be a sky man and a sky woman, everything joins up, everything becomes meaningful. But in the story this was the conclusion of something, and she compared that conclusion with the last day spent in a summerhouse, when everything is packed away, the windows closed and the door locked. And this was how it was, too. We had been somewhere together, a place filled with light, and now we were going somewhere else. She was afraid of that, it

340

was a darker place. And because she was afraid of it she tried to keep me where I was. This was new to me, something I hadn't known before, and it made me afraid, too. We started arguing, and the walls of her apartment, into which I had moved, closed in on me, its rooms became smaller and smaller. Our arguing turned her into my father, I was afraid of the loudness of her voice, her sudden fits of anger, and had no idea how to handle it, so I was cowed by her, and when it passed I would be on my guard, trying to act in ways that would placate her, wary of the slightest sign of displeasure, and it was that subjection, the fact that I was always trying to assuage and appease, that made our relationship increasingly difficult, because at the same time I was trying to get away from it, I needed to gain some measure of independence, to become my own person, find my own space, and I started getting just as angry with her whenever we argued, maybe even angrier, because I needed to come free of myself, too, the bonds within. She went to college, I tried to write, on weekends we tried to be like before. One Sunday we ran into Geir and Christina in a restaurant, Linda and I were going somewhere else afterward, we invited them along, and they came with us, Linda hissed in my ear that Geir was doing it on purpose, hadn't I noticed he was doing it on purpose, he wanted to ruin things for us. I didn't understand what she meant, we spent nearly all our time together, wasn't that enough for her, couldn't we ever see anyone else?

One time, Geir came over to her apartment, we were going out, he walked around the place, shamelessly examining everything in it as if he wanted to tell her he could read her like an open book. I could see how angry it made her, it was a provocation, but I didn't know what to do, surely a person could have a friend as well as a partner without them wrecking things between them? Geir had grown up with a mother who suffered from anxiety, a woman who had lost her father when she was still a child, and for the rest of her life she clung to those closest to her, she was a master of the art, Geir said, shunning no means to get what she wanted, and making people feel guilty was the least of them.

So the fact that I was suddenly less available than before, the fact that I suddenly needed to stay in all the time, was something he interpreted in the context of that same pattern. He had needed to break free, and now he despised everything to do with intimacy, everything that smacked of commitment and bonds. At the same time, he committed to Christina. And Christina was in many ways like me, someone who endured and stuck things out, a person who pleased others, at the same time, like me, being essentially solipsistic or solitary, she could have been the last person on earth and been quite happy with that. I could, too. Inside me was this enormous distance from other people, at the same time as I was hugely impressionable and open to influence, and could allow myself to be tied to someone and remain incapable of freeing myself. A friendship never ties, because if it does it ceases to be a friendship. But a relationship ties, because its foundations are deeper, rooted in the emotions, in the very fulcrum of life, and a relationship is in every respect a common bond; if we are not bound to each other, then what we have is not a relationship but a friendship. Whenever I got an engagement somewhere, Linda would say what about me, have you thought about me, left on my own here, what am I supposed to do? Even when there had just been the two of us, I would turn things down and back out of things because she couldn't be on her own, and when the children came along it became ten times worse, and if I did go away regardless, I would have to carry the responsibility for her being on her own and having to cope with the children without me, I would be one of those men who ran out on his family, the kind who think only about themselves, their jobs and careers. I didn't want that, and so I would decline and stay at home. Even the shortest absence was a problem, like the two hours I spent playing football every Sunday; when Linda wasn't feeling good she would be angry at me before I left, it was unfair of me to leave her on her own with the children, I was leaving her with far too much of the burden, she worked her fingers to the bone, she was exhausted, it was touch and go whether she could manage anymore. I told her it was the only thing I did outside the house. I never went out at night, never went to the cinema, never met up with any friends, we were together twenty-four hours a day, and those two hours of football were something I looked forward to all week. But she never did anything on her own, she said, that was a luxury denied to her, to be able to just go out whenever she felt like it. It was a poor argument, I could come back at her and say there was nothing I wanted her to do more than that. Feel free, I would say. You can go away three days a week, if you want. I can look after the kids on my own. It's no problem. I can do that. To which she might then say it was easier for me to have the kids, that they demanded less of me than of her, that I could just sit there and read the paper while I was on my own with them, whereas if it was her they wouldn't leave her alone. That's true, I might say, but that's no argument. What you're saying is that even if we have the children an equal amount of time, even if we're completely democratic about that, your burden is always the heavier because you're together with them in a different way than I am. But then what do we do? Does that mean they should be with me 70 percent of the time and you 30 percent, so as to even things out? Well, that's fine with me. I can have the kids 100 percent of the time. I can have them all the time. It's fine. And you know that. Fine for you, maybe, she might say then, but not for them. And then she could change tack and say I was always playing football on the weekends when the kids weren't at the nursery, and that we ought to be doing things together. True enough, I would say in response, but I'm back by twelve o'clock, which gives us the rest of the day to do stuff. And anyway, we spent our whole time together, all of us, the entire rest of the week besides, apart from when they were at the nursery, so the two hours I was playing football couldn't possibly harm. But that was different, she would say, because that was ordinary weekdays full of obligations, over the weekend we had the chance to do something nice together, as a family. If we didn't, I understood, we weren't a family. And so it could go on. Sometimes I got so angry I consciously

343

tried to punish her, to make her feel guilty and show her how miserable everything could be if all we had were obligations, but it would only rebound on the kids. Sometimes I went off and played anyway, of what she said, which meant I was a bad husband and father who ignored his responsibilities and left his family in the lurch, and when I got back it was usually to an apartment full of tantrums and chaos, and Linda would imply: look at this, this is what happens when you're selfish. One such Sunday, after I'd been playing football for two hours in the pouring rain and I got on my bike to cycle back, already in low spirits at the prospect of going home, I was suddenly struck by the liberating realization that Linda wasn't there. Her mother was with us that weekend. And that fact, the relief I felt at being able to go home to her mother and not to her, was the same as admitting that we had come to the end of the road. No husband should ever dread coming home. I had to get out. I was in shreds, not when I was on my own, but with Linda, and why should my life have to be like that? I could put up with not feeling up to the mark, but this was worse, I was in a terrible state. I was taking care of pretty much everything at home for long periods, at the same time as I was trying to work, something she didn't have to worry about, and here she was saying things weren't equal, because her share of the burden was more demanding. But I've got a job besides! I could almost yell at her. I've got to earn money! She could have had a job too, but because she'd had three children she'd been away from the labor market so long it was almost impossible for her to get back in. This was a sensitive area, and I had to tread carefully. It was true she'd been at home the first six months with Vanja, but the next six months it had been me who had taken over. She'd stayed at home with both Heidi and John, but we had three children by then and she had to concentrate on the little one, meaning there was plenty for me to do too, and as luck would have it I worked from home and was always on hand, and besides, I confined myself to working only five hours a day, which she didn't have much respect for. I wasn't a pilot or a surgeon with regular working hours and clear obligations to fulfill, I was a writer who'd been writing the same thing for years without getting anywhere. Her referring to this as career building was an insult to careerists. And the idea that she was being kept out of the labor market, and denied any way into it ever again, kept out by a male society hostile to women, wasn't exactly true either, because for as long as I'd known her she'd never been anywhere near any labor market. She was a writer and a trained radio documentarist, and the fact that she hadn't made a documentary since leaving college wasn't just down to her having stayed at home with the kids, because now they were in the nursery and she still wasn't making documentaries. Life with the children drained the energy out of her, she couldn't manage having to work as well, yet we spent equal portions of time looking after the kids, and I somehow did manage to work. Was this a woman trap? Did she spend more time changing diapers or going to the playground than I did? She believed yes, and no matter how much I did, regardless of how far I went to accommodate her, it was never enough. My frustration at the way my life was being dominated, and the shame of that, was enormous, and I couldn't tell anyone I knew, because they wouldn't believe that I was in a relationship that didn't allow me the time to play football two hours a week and where even the minutes I spent sitting on the balcony with a cigarette were something Linda would deny me or use against me in her arguments to the effect that all I ever thought about was myself, since those few minutes of peace were not available to her, she had to be there all the time inside, whereas I could just sneak off on a break whenever I felt like it. That I should yield to that and allow myself to be boxed in by it felt demeaning and was certainly not a matter I would wish to air with anyone. Anyone, that is, apart from Geir. He listened to it all. I assumed Linda knew, and that she maybe even guessed Geir was advising me to get out, since the life he lived was exactly the opposite, elevated above day-to-day obligations, but it wasn't like that at all, because what he told me, and was constantly reminding me about, was that it was all anxiety talking, not Linda. Anxiety eats people up from the inside, it's bigger than them, monstrous even, impossible to appease, and it eats away at relationships because the only thing it wants is for everyone to be snuggled up close all the time.

"It's anxiety, it's not Linda," he said. "Linda's intelligent, capable, talented. She knows the score. My mom was proud of me when I finally broke loose. And she was proud when I went parachuting or went off somewhere and drank myself senseless. Because she could see why. That was a side of her too. But the anxiety was that much greater. She was terrified and did everything she could to make me stay with her. Those were emotions I couldn't take into consideration, cry as she might. I think it probably had an effect on my empathy. Fortunately, my dad doesn't suffer from anxiety at all. I don't even think he knows what it is. I've never seen him scared or anxious about anything. But they're still together. I wasn't married to my mom, and we didn't have children, so I could just leave, which was the right thing to do. It's different for you. You and Linda are married. When Linda's feeling on top of things you can do what you want. When she isn't, when the anxiety gets to her, she needs you there. It's tearing you apart. But you're still there."

That was basically what he would say. It helped me see things from the outside, and to see the difference between the roles we occupied and the people we were. She was always Linda, the woman I'd been more in love with than any other, with whom I had three wonderful children, and when she was on a high she never saw a problem in anything, she was generosity personified, of course, get yourself away, my gorgeous footballing man, we'll be fine, maybe we'll go over and see Jenny or Bodil, or someone else perhaps, or go for a walk in the park, why don't you give us a call when you're finished, we could all go somewhere and do something nice? Or maybe you'd like to do some work? When she was on a high she had no difficulty working either, she would write while the kids were at nursery, and I would read what she wrote, it was as buoyant and exuberant as she was herself, and had the same kind of unfathomable depth, which I no longer tended to see, since it vanished so easily in our everyday routines, but which, whenever I caught sight of it and the person she was, either in something she had written or in herself, when we were together, seemed to come back. But there was no balance between these two aspects, either in her life or in ours, for the frustration I felt with respect to the one grew increasingly in strength, I was living a life of compulsion, and whether it came from inside or out made no difference, it was compulsion all the same, obligation, and that wasn't how I wanted it, and this not wanting was sooner or later bound to become a not being able. I was approaching that limit, and I supposed I was merely waiting for some factor that would finally give me release. In our arguments I'd already begun to threaten her with leaving. It would mean our sharing everything equally, down the middle, she would have the children 50 percent of the time, I would have them the other 50 percent, and she would have to earn her own money, and I mine. When I said this she would fall apart and beg me not to. Don't go, please don't go. And I didn't because I knew it would destroy her life, how would she ever manage on her own? And then, when the argument was over, there would be hope. Always a promise of change.

Her reacting the way she did to the look Geir gave me on this particular day in August 2009 had to do with all of this. Geir's look said, I see what you mean, Karl Ove. She's relating Gunnar's threats to herself, what am I supposed to do, how am I going to cope, and, by extension, how could you do this to me? In that look, she recognized the way I saw things and felt herself left bare. Geir and I were ganging up on her. It wasn't like that at all, but she had been left bare, certainly, since I confided in him the way I did. It wasn't a betrayal because I had to be able to talk to someone outside our relationship, but it felt like a betrayal in the way it had been made visible all of a sudden. Another thing I sensed she was reacting to was that I allowed Geir to influence me to such an extent that his opinions became my opinions, that to a degree he was brainwashing me, and that the distance that had opened up between Linda and me, which was due to my frustration, was a part of that. Geir was whispering in my ear about my life and her role in it, and before long it would make me leave her. I didn't know if this really was what she was thinking, or whether it was my own paranoia that had led me to such ideas, but there was no way to find out because there was no way we could talk about it other than when our arguments were coming to a head, at such a point she once yelled at me that she couldn't understand why I didn't just move in with Geir seeing as how I spent the whole time on the phone with him, words that as soon as the argument was over and we'd made up again, she in tears, I with my anger stuck like a stone in my chest, she said she hadn't meant. She actually liked Geir. I believed her because now, finally, after seven years, I had begun to understand her. She liked him when she was feeling strong and had the energy in her to be relaxed and casual about things, including her feelings for me, whereas when she was down things looked different to her, because then she was afraid everything was going to be swallowed up and she was going to lose all that she had, and that feeling was so powerful it affected all her opinions, assessments, and perceptions. So there was nothing underived other than anxiety or joy, emotions so powerful inside her that they could turn good into bad and bad into good in the space of a moment. It had torn so much apart that I no longer cared, I'd used up so much energy to accommodate it, regardless of how unreasonable it could appear to me, that all of a sudden I could do so no longer: she could weep and be as despairing as a person could be, and all I could do was look at her and tell her I wasn't going to say anything until she stopped crying. She could scream at me, and I would say, Are you done yet? That I was no longer tangled up in the emotions, but detached, standing there looking at them, perhaps made her feel even more scared, and the fear she felt was justified, because I was reaching a point where I couldn't handle it anymore, I felt myself to be at the very limit of what I could endure, so removed from the life I wanted to live that I could hardly think about anything else.

Then the e-mails started coming in, the pressure from outside, and I no longer stood with my back to her and the family, looking out, I swiveled around, quickly, in the space of an hour, and was then standing with my back to the world, facing them, Linda and the children, for the first time in a very long time. She went off to visit Helena, I missed her because I needed her, I needed to feel her warmth. Only then it got torn apart by the look Geir sent me, all that was contained in it, and I despaired, all of a sudden it felt like it was too late, as if somehow the dynamics of destruction carried on without me after I stopped. I had stopped too late, swiveled around too late, and it had taken on its own momentum. This was the feeling I had when I followed Linda into the bedroom that afternoon in August 2009, but there was more, so much more than that: I had put all my frustration into the writing, it had filled an entire novel, it was about us, she and I, and although I suddenly needed her again, suddenly wanted her again, suddenly wanted to live my life there again, my past, my frustration, and my yearning to get away wedged itself in between us, because soon she would have to read that novel, soon it would be published.

She was at the computer when I entered the room, staring stiffly at the screen as if in deep concentration, but I recognized that look, it was a sign of the opposite, an inner turmoil she was trying to conceal.

"What's the matter?" I said, sitting down on the bed.

"Nothing," she said.

"Why did you come in here, then?"

"To check my e-mail."

I felt I should get up and put my hand on her shoulder, but I knew she would react as if it were something alien and just leave it there to show me how removed she was from me, and not, as she normally would have done, since such signs of affection had become so infrequent and would always come as a surprise to her, return the gesture.

It pained my heart. I had denied her the only thing she really needed from me.

"Was it that look Geir gave me?" I said.

She glanced at me, then turned her attention back to the screen in front of her.

"No, not at all," she said. "I didn't see any look."

"What is it then?"

She sighed.

"I got such a bad feeling from those e-mails. And I can see how much it's getting to you. I just started thinking about what the autumn's going to be like. If it goes to court. There won't be room for anything else. And there's you and Geir sitting there, and . . . well, wallowing in it, in a way."

"I wouldn't call it wallowing exactly," I said.

"You asked what the matter was. That was it. I don't want to discuss it."

"Okay," I said, and got to my feet. "Are we friends?"

She nodded.

I put my hand on her shoulder. She didn't react.

"It'll pass," I said. "It's just right now, that's all. And I won't be able to cope without your help. I can't fight on two fronts. It'll do me in."

"I'll do my best," she said, looking up at me and putting her hand on mine.

"I'm glad," I said.

Njaal and Vanja came bombing in from the hall. Linda took her hand back.

"I'll go out and get those prawns, then," I said. "Is there anything else we need? Wine, bread, lemons, mayonnaise, prawns."

"We've got mayonnaise, I think, don't we? In the fridge?"

"It'll be ancient if we have. I'll buy some more. Is there anything you'd like?"

The children started bouncing on the bed.

"Maybe those yellow berries, that fruit or whatever it is they've got there, you know," said Linda. "In those small baskets. I can't remember what they're called. Do you know what I mean?"

I nodded. Somewhere Heidi was on her own and sad, I thought to myself.

"Okay," I said. "I'll get some ice cream and strawberries as well, I think."

"Get some candy for the children, then."

"Will do," I said, and went through into the hall. I stopped in the doorway of the children's room; John was fast asleep on his belly, spread-eagled, his head resting on one arm, saliva dribbling from his mouth. I stood looking at him for a moment, then went back into the living room, where Heidi was sitting on the toy box, Christina must have put the lid back on, with a doll in one hand and a small blue plastic comb in the other.

"Do you want to come shopping with me, Heidi?" I asked.

She shook her head.

"Yes, come on," I said. "It'll be nice."

"No, I said."

"Okay," I said, and smiled, then went into the other room, where Geir was sitting on the sofa reading, while Christina was sitting in the chair across the table, skimming through a photo book.

"Just popping out to get the prawns," I said.

"I'll come with you," said Geir, getting to his feet.

"No need," I said. "Just buying prawns, that's all."

I didn't want him to come, it would be too much the two of us, seen from where Linda was. But I couldn't say no to his face. He would have to grasp the intention.

"It'll be nice to get out," he said, looking at Christina. "Is there anything we need?"

"I don't think so," she said.

Linda came in from the hall. From the look on her face and her movements I could see she wasn't upset anymore.

Maybe she and Christina could have a chat for a bit if we went out.

"I'll pop out for the shopping, then," I said.

"Can you take Heidi or Vanja with you?" she said.

"Heidi didn't want to go. I can ask her again, though."

I poked my head around the door.

"Put your shoes on. We're going shopping."

She looked up at me.

"Do I have to?" she said.

"Yes," I said.

"Why doesn't Vanja have to?"

"Because I want you to come. Come on."

She got to her feet and went past me, put her sandals on, and stood waiting by the door while I put my own shoes on, patted my back pocket to make sure I had my wallet with my cards in it, then my front pocket, feeling its lumpy nest of keys, grabbed my sunglasses off the hat shelf, and opened the door.

Heidi was shy with Geir being with us in the elevator, she looked down at the floor. She could be shy with me, too; sometimes if I caught her eye and smiled, she could look away with a sheepish little grin on her face. She was hardly ever like that in social situations and had been confident right from the start, but often in what was almost the opposite situation, the more intimate context, when the attention of a single person was directed toward her. With Vanja the opposite was true, she liked attention from one person and would even go looking for it, whereas in new social situations she would be shy and withdraw.

Shyness is a protective mechanism, and the interesting thing was that they were protecting different aspects of themselves. Did those aspects need protecting because they were particularly fragile or because they were particularly precious?

It was interesting, too, that they should both protect themelves by lowering their gaze, bowing their heads, turning away. Shyness was directly linked with the eyes, it was always their eyes they hid from view. They could respond if someone asked them something, but with their eyes cast down. So what were they protecting themselves against, what was it about being seen by another person? It wasn't being seen as such, since there they were, in plain sight, their physical selves present in the space, rather it was being seen to be who they were, and that was contained in the eyes. They were protecting themselves against someone looking into their eyes and seeing who they were, what was inside them, and the eyes were the entrance to that, for which reason they had to be concealed. Animal young behaved differently; if, for instance, a person suddenly came into a room full of kittens, the kittens would scurry away and hide, but what they hid would be their physical selves, since they were vulnerable to attack and could be killed and eaten. Perhaps the children's instinctive reaction to such intrusion was the same, yet in some more cultivated version, translated from the physical to the social world, from the body to the soul, which trembled with the fear of being taken.

Down on the ground floor, Geir pressed the button to open the elevator doors and Heidi took my hand as we walked the few meters to the front door, which closed slowly behind us, the barely audible buzz it made before clicking shut gradually drowned out by the sounds from outside, cars rumbling through the traffic lights, the voices of the customers sitting outside the Chinese takeaway, each with their own little box of noodles or rice in front of them, the voices and footsteps of those passing by, on their way to and from the city center.

"It's that way," I said, pointing across the square. The air felt warm, the sun angling down from above the Hilton hotel, a bit fuller in color now, a richer yellow than earlier in the day.

"I like Malmö," said Geir. "I wouldn't mind living here."

"What's stopping you?" I said.

Heidi took a little skip at my side. I gave her hand a little squeeze, and then another, and smiled when she looked up at me.

"Moving costs money. And money's in short supply, as you know."

"Everything's a lot cheaper here," I said.

"True," he said. "But we'd have to do an apartment swap, rather than buying, so there's not much chance, I'm afraid."

"I can see that," I said.

We went down the steps and crossed the square in front of the fountain, following the sidewalk along the street where the buses and taxis passed, then taking the first left toward the shop we were going to. It was called Delikatessen and apart from prawns they also sold lobsters, oysters, mussels, fish, and crabs, as well as meat from selected suppliers, poultry, game, and well-hung beef, and cheeses too, and just about everything else one might associate with good eating, such as exclusive olive oils, red and white wine vinegars, olives, herbs and spices, salt flakes from France, freshly baked French bread and baguettes. On Saturday mornings the place was always full of people, Malmö's upper echelons, or so I imagined, getting the shopping in for their social gatherings in the evening, but when we opened the door and stepped inside, the place was empty apart from two assistants in chef's hats and white aprons, busy clearing away before closing time, so it seemed.

"I want to sit there," said Heidi, pointing at the tall bar stools that surrounded two tables by the window.

I pulled one of them out and lifted her up onto it, nodding at the same time to one of the assistants who had stepped up behind the glass counter ready to serve us.

"We'd like some prawns," I said.

"Certainly," he said. "How many were you thinking of?"

"We're four adults and four children," I said. "The children won't eat much, so maybe two and a half, three kilos? Something like that?"

"I'd say two and a half ought to do it," he said, snatching a white bag from a pile behind the counter with one hand, picking up his scoop with the other.

"Let's make it just over two and a half, then," I said.

"Right you are," he said, and began scooping the prawns into the bag while I cast a glance at Heidi, who was sitting with both hands flat on the tabletop, watching the assistant. Geir stood with his hands behind his back at the counter, looking at the oysters.

I went over to Heidi, lifted her up, and carried her over to the counter just as the assistant put the bag down on the shiny scales. The pointer shot up to a kilo and a half and dithered there for a moment.

"Can you see the lobsters over there?" I said. "They live at the bottom of the sea."

"I know," she said.

"Aren't they splendid?" I said.

She nodded.

Hauled up from the depths of the ocean and placed on display here, with their black peppercorn eyes and long, bright red tentacles.

"What's that?" she said, indicating the red plastic nets full of mussels lying on their bed of crushed ice.

"Mussels," I said.

"What?" she said.

"*Musslor*," I said. "*Blåmusslor.*"

"Are they alive?"

"Yes."

"But they don't have eyes!" she said.

"No," I said. "The shell is like their house. They live inside it."

The assistant put a second bag on the scales. It weighed in at 1.3 kilos. His powers of assessment were impressive, I thought to myself, putting Heidi down and stepping up to the till on the counter at the other end of the narrow room.

"Anything else?" he asked.

"Some bread, perhaps. One of those baguettes over there. And maybe one of those," I said, pointing at one of the large, stone-shaped loaves.

"Certainly," he said, dropping each into a separate bag. I took my card out of my back pocket.

"Can you think of anything else we need?" I said to Geir.

"No," he said. "Unless you were thinking of a crème brûlée for dessert?"

I shook my head.

"Ice cream and fruit."

"As ever," he said.

"Are you getting tired of it?" I asked him, glancing at the assistant as he entered the amounts into the till.

"Tired, me? Not at all. I'm a traditionalist. As long as you've got those wafers you always buy to go with it, that'll do me."

"You can't get them in Malmö. They're a Stockholm thing."

"I might have known," he said.

The assistant told me the amount.

"Okay," I said, and put my card into the reader. I entered my PIN, which was no longer 0000, but nearly as easy to remember, since it consisted of the four figures in the top right corner of the key pad, 2536, took the two bags he handed me across the counter, waited for the message to appear on the display telling me the transaction was accepted, pulled out my card, put it in its little wallet, and slid it into my back pocket again as the assistant tore off the receipt and handed it to me.

"Thanks, have a nice day," I said, and stuffed the piece of paper into my other back pocket, which was a kind of archive for all my receipts.

"Same to you," he said.

"Come on, Heidi," I said. She was still standing at the shell-fish counter looking at the display, but turned and came running to put her hand in mine, and we went out onto the sidewalk, where the air between the four-story buildings was warm and still.

"Where to now?" said Geir.

"The liquor store. Then Hemköp after that," I said.

"No need to break the bank for our sake," he said.

"It doesn't matter," I said. "Besides, I like spending money. The more the merrier."

"Tell me about it," he said.

"What's a sausage at slaughtering time," I said. "That's what

Mom used to say when we did the Christmas shopping and there was something I was pestering her for. She never had much money, but if there was ever anything I needed, clothes for instance when I was at the *gymnas*, or later, when I was in college, she always gave me the money for it. I never understood that. If she didn't have any money, how come she could suddenly afford to give me some? Now I've figured it out. Money's relative. It's an incredibly vague entity. Whenever I buy clothes for the kids I always buy a great big pile, because they can't go without. Then I'll grab a couple of CDs while I'm at it, because I need music when I'm working, and that's where the money comes from. Or I might blow a couple of thousand on a fantastic pair of shoes. What happens then is there's no more money left in the account, or very little. So I go through all our pockets, all the cupboards and drawers, and scrape together what I can find, maybe pick up the deposit on all our bottles or something, and then I buy some milk, bread, and spaghetti, and ignore all the bills. After a while, the reminders start coming in, and if I've got the money I pay them off, if I haven't I'll ignore them until the next step. It's not that long ago that someone came around with a statement of claim or whatever it's called, which I had to sign. Eventually, it'll come to enforcement and they can seize your property. But long before that happens I'll have money coming in again and be able to pay. I never connect the clothes for the kids or the CDs with suddenly having no money left, or someone coming to the door with a claim, that's something else entirely."

"We could never live like that," said Geir. "In our house everything's planned and by the book."

"That doesn't surprise me," I said. "But it does make things a whole lot easier. It takes it out of you, not being able to manage things properly."

We came onto the square and Heidi let go of my hand and ran up to the fountain. Geir and I followed her.

"I'm not sure you're right about that," he said. "I'd love to just let things go sometimes. But I can't."

Heidi had put an ice-cream wrapper in the water, it bobbed gently up and down on the ripples made by the fountain. I recognized the wrapper, it belonged to an ice cream called Strawberry something. Strawberry Delight? Strawberry Dream? Pink ice cream with a white chocolate coating.

"To will is to have to will, as Ibsen put it," said Geir.

"Now is the time to shut up! was something else he said. But there's a saying I believe in. Or not a saying, exactly, more a popular belief, to the effect that losing money is a good sign, meaning more will be coming your way. I totally believe that. The more you tighten your finances, the narrower the channels become that the money goes through. If everything's wide open, there's always going to be room for more."

"If you ever get the Nobel Prize, it won't be for economics," he said.

"It's not a bad theory, is it? I could actually be on to something! I could write about the emotions of economics, instead of the mathematics of economics."

"You're the most optimistic person I know," he said. "A depressed optimist. That's what you are."

"It's got nothing to do with optimism. It's all about accepting the way of things. This is how it is. Either you've got money, in which case you buy stuff, or else you haven't, in which case you don't."

"But you've just been talking about all the stuff you buy when you haven't got any money."

"But I have got money! If I'd saved it to pay the bills next week, I wouldn't have had any."

Heidi floated her ice-cream wrapper all the way around the fountain. When she appeared again she waved at us.

"Come on," I said. "We've got to get going."

"I'm all wet," she said.

"You'll dry in the sun," I said, taking her hand in mine and walking on just as a double-decker bus stopped outside the entrance to the Hilton.

"I still remember what a fantastic feeling it was to find an ATM in Bergen that wasn't connected to my own bank, so I could take out money I didn't have. It was like Christmas. Or when someone unexpectedly agreed to lend me a couple of hundred kroner."

"Or twenty thousand."

"You'll get it back as soon as my advance comes in. Don't worry."

I had borrowed twenty thousand Swedish kronor from him, which he had taken from a savings account of his that he never touched, money set aside for harder times. Linda had borrowed a similar amount from her friends, who also had money put away for the future. When Linda and I started a joint account together, we arranged for an amount to be transferred automatically into a savings account once a month, but either there wasn't enough money in the account for the transaction to go through, or else we spent the savings as soon as they went in.

Linda wanted so badly for us to have a savings account with money in it to support our future and our children's future. It had enormous symbolic value to her. It was what proper families did, and she wanted more than anything else that our family should be a proper family. Her romantic dreams were about ordinary life.

We stopped at the crossing. Over by the Hilton, retirees from the bus were shuffling off along the sidewalk. A classic American convertible with the top down came cruising along Södra Förstadsgatan, its engine purring. In Arendal in the seventies American cars were as cool as you could get. Here it just looked out of place, some clueless idiot out showing off.

"Linda's right, too," I said. "Even if you don't think so. But if it's going to be hell for me, it's going to be hell for everyone else, too."

"Why wouldn't I think so?"

I gave a shrug.

The light changed to green and we ambled over the road in a little throng of pedestrians.

"I saw the look you gave me when she started talking about how awful it's going to be for her," I said. "I suppose that's what I meant."

"What sort of look was that?"

"You know, kind of a telling look."

"You think I'd give you a telling look about something relating to Linda while she was there? I'd never dream of such a thing."

"Well, it looked like it to me, anyway," I said, letting go of Heidi's hand for a second while I wiped my palm dry against my trousers, then taking hold of it again. "She saw it too, I think. That's why she went off like that."

I pushed open the door of the Systembolaget, the state-run liquor store, gave it an extra shove so Geir could come through too, grabbed one of the gray baskets with the black handles, and went through the little automatic barrier, already scanning the signs above the aisles to see where the white wine was.

"I can understand it's not going to be much fun for her if everyone in Norway hates you all of a sudden and you're in the hot seat like some criminal. But she's not the one getting the worst of it, is she? So yes, that's the way I look at it."

"Daddy?" said Heidi.

"Yes?"

"Is this soda?"

She pointed to a display stand with various shelves that could be spun round. They were full of green bottles of Jever's nonalcoholic beer.

"No," I said. "It's beer. Do you want soda?"

She nodded.

"All right, we'll get some in Hemköp after we're done here. Okay?"

She nodded again. We found the white wine section and stopped in front of the shelves. They were arranged according to price, the cheapest on the right, then more expensive the farther left you went. It suited me fine; I knew nothing about wines, so whenever we had guests for dinner I just went with one a bit left of center and hoped for the best.

I put three bottles of Chablis in the basket and looked at Geir.

"Will that be enough?"

"I should think so."

I looked around for the cognac, locating it in one of the intersecting aisles closer to the checkout. I went over and stood there for a moment looking at all the labels, unable to recall the system of quality grades, the O's and the X's, and the differences between them, and ended up putting a half-bottle of a brand I hadn't tasted before in the basket before joining the line behind a man of about fifty who gave off a blend of the characteristic sportiness a polo shirt and a pair of khaki shorts can lend to a tanned frame, and the alcoholism his fatigued features and lackluster eyes otherwise seemed to indicate. He bought two cartons of white wine.

"First came the volcanoes, then the dinosaurs," said Heidi.

"That's right!" I said.

"And then came the people."

"Yes."

"But the dinosaurs didn't know they were called dinosaurs."

I looked down at her. She was staring at a man in a wheelchair who had joined the other line, his basket resting in his lap. It sounded like something I could have said. But I couldn't remember having done so.

"Who told you that?" I asked her.

"What?"

"About the dinosaurs."

"No one. Why is he sitting in a wheelchair? Is he sick?"

When we had traveled home after spending last Christmas in Jølster, Heidi had suddenly fallen ill on the journey, and by the time we got to Flesland, Bergen's airport, she was so feeble we had to borrow a wheelchair for her. She still talked about it. It was one of the events that stood out in her life so far.

"I don't know," I said, and put the basket down on the little

361

counter before the checkout as the man in front of me placed the divider bar behind the second of his cartons on the conveyor.

"I don't suppose prawns are anything special to you, are they, now that I come to think of it?" I said to Geir as he went past the till, presumably to bag the wine as it came down the conveyor. "It's probably all you eat when you're on Hisøya."

"You might have thought of that before," he said.

"Paying by card?" said the assistant.

"Yes," I said.

"Six hundred and twelve, then," he replied.

"Yeah, it was a bit stupid of me," I said, inserting my card into the reader. "You might have said so, though."

"We're here to spend time with you. We could have boiled onion and it wouldn't make any difference. For goodness' sake, man."

Two people in the other lane looked across at us.

I didn't care for this, and turned away so all they could see was my back.

We were speaking Norwegian, that must have been it. Unless they happened to think we were a pair of gay men out with our surrogate child. Or our niece. Weren't gay men often close to their nieces?

"Thank you," said the assistant.

Why on earth would they think that?

It was enough me looking like an idiot, with the beard and the long hair. I looked like a has-been heavy-metal musician rapidly heading for his fiftieth birthday. Oh, the fleshy face, the chubby cheeks, the deep furrows, and that wispy beard.

Heidi clung to my leg all of a sudden. I looked around. There was an old terrier sitting against the wall in the bagging area at the end of the checkout, its leash wrapped around the leg of a chair.

"It's all right, I'm sure he's friendly," I said. "Walk on the other side of me as we go out."

She did as I said. As soon as we were outside she changed sides again.

We strolled along the sidewalk, the flagstones cast into shade, the warm air seeming even warmer now after the air-conditioned environment of the liquor shop, then passed into sunlight as we crossed the side street, which was edged by leafy deciduous trees. They were invisible in the same way as all the parked cars were invisible, something one usually failed to notice, apart from at the end of April and the beginning of May when they blossomed white, as if dressed with snow, all the way down the street.

My anxiety suddenly intensified, it felt like it came streaming from every extremity to lump together in my abdomen, and I looked down at Heidi walking beside me, the small steps she took as she gazed toward the windows of the shopping center on the other side of the road. I was in pain, such terrible pain. It was like everything had come apart. And although I knew the reason, the book I had written and the reaction it had provoked, I had no idea why the emotions it sparked should be so powerful, it was as if they had been separated from their origin and were now running wild. This was the anatomy of guilt. Guilt was in everything, spreading vaporously through my organism, pervading my very fabric with its ruin and destruction. It was a guilt that could no longer simply be traced back and attributed to the terrible thing I had done, it was now rampant in its own right.

We passed between the sidewalk advertising on one side and the bike racks on the other, then went into the supermarket, where, to our right, the cell phone provider 3 had set up a stand that seemed to be mostly made of cardboard, manned by two young men of about twenty who stood there trying to grab the attention of passersby so they could ask them which provider they used. If they asked me, I invariably mumbled something vaguely dismissive, I wasn't at all comfortable, their energy was so incredibly cheerful and positive, mine so dismissive and negative. Who was that? Vanja always asked. What did they say? What did they want?

Now they were both engaged in discussion with a woman of about fifty, and we walked past without hindrance into the big store, with its checkouts on one side and the combined kiosk, gambling station, and post office on the other. I grabbed a basket, went through the barrier with Heidi, who looked up at the TV monitor that hung from the ceiling as we came toward the camera.

"Do you want a banana?" I said.

She nodded, let go of my hand, and stared up at the monitor's reaction as she put first one, then the other arm in the air. I picked up one of the ripe bananas whose skin was speckled brown, which they had put out for children to take in a small box next to the regular, hard, yellow-green bananas, peeled it, and handed it to her.

"We need lemons, mayonnaise, soda, and mineral water," I said.

"Don't forget the ice cream and the fruit," said Geir.

"You're right," I said.

"You don't look that well, are you okay?" he said.

"Does it show?"

He laughed.

"You look worried to death."

"I'll be all right," I said. "It's probably just that I'd much rather it all wasn't happening. I don't want to upset people. I don't want to offend anyone. I don't want to wreck anything for anyone."

I put five lemons in one of the smoky bags, which seemed immediately to yield to them, suppressing its faint transluscence in favor of the yellow of the fruit where it bulged against the plastic, bringing even the pores of the outer rind to the fore.

"I know," said Geir. "But it's done now."

"Yeah, and it hurts like hell," I said, looking away to see where Heidi was. "Come on, Heidi!"

She came running, curled her hand into mine, and walked at my side as we went down the aisles, past the fish counter and the ready-made meals, the cheese and charcuterie counter, with its cheeses the size of barbell weights, salami sausages like baseball bats, past the island displays of bread, the rows of cookies, to the slanting shelves of carbonated drinks, where I put two one-and-a-half-liter bottles of Loka mineral water, one with citrus, the other without, into the basket, followed by four glass bottles of Fanta.

"It makes no difference your telling me I've done nothing wrong," I said. "I can tell myself that. I've written about myself and my life with my father, what can be so terrible about that? That's what I tell myself. But it doesn't help in the slightest. It has no bearing on the matter. Arguments don't help. Legal arguments don't help. Literary arguments don't help. I've overstepped a mark, and it's got to me."

"If the sociologists could understand that, maybe the discipline would have a future," said Geir.

"Understand what?" I said, looking up from the tubes of mayonnaise, which reminded me of my childhood, and the jars of mayonnaise, which I considered somehow more sophisticated.

"Social boundaries, the things that regulate what we do and allow us to exist side by side with each other, aren't abstract. They're not thoughts. They're concrete, as you say. If you overstep the mark, it hurts. That's what you're sensing now."

"Sensing? But it hurts like I killed someone. Oh! And not just anyone, but someone close to me. That kind of feeling. Like something irreparable has happened."

I glanced around. Heidi was nowhere to be seen.

"Jar or tube?" I said. "Real or light? French or Swedish?"

"Take one of each," he said. "A tube of Swedish light, and a jar of real French."

"You're a genius," I said. "I'd never have thought of that."

"Where's Heidi got to?" he said.

"She'll either be at the ice cream or down by the pet toys."

We set off toward the middle aisle. A child screamed somewhere, but it was a baby, six months old at most. As we got to the corner I looked up the aisle. There she was, with a pet toy in her hand, the kind that squeak when you press them, just as she was doing.

"Come on, Heidi," I said. "We've got to pay now."

She put it down and came running back to us.

"Can we have a rabbit?" she said.

"We already had a rabbit," I said. "It didn't really work out that well."

"Can't we have another one?" she said. "One that's nicer?"

I laughed.

"You were so afraid of it," I said.

"No, I wasn't."

"A little bit," I said.

"I wasn't."

"We'll have to see," I said.

The rabbit had come from one of the nursery staff. It was Linda's project. Cage and rabbit were transported home and put in the corner of the kitchen. The rabbit was frightened, and we were too. None of us dared take it out of its cage. John dropped all sorts of stuff in there. After two days we had to take it back. Hopefully, the episode had had no adverse affect on Vanja and Heidi. The arrangement had been that we could borrow it and see how it went, so it wasn't that big a failure, not like the aquarium, when all the fish had died one after another over the course of the spring.

It hurt to think about it. The things we did were their childhood.

I stopped at the ice cream, picked out a tub of Carte d'Or with real vanilla, which I supposed was what the little black specks in the yellowish ice cream were, shards of vanilla pod, and put it in the basket. I looked at Heidi.

"You can decide what kind of ice creams you want. Have a look in there," I said, indicating the other counter where they had popsicles, too. "Look at the poster and see which ones you want."

She studied the various sorts.

"That one," she said, pointing to a Piggelin. "No, I mean that one," she said, and pointed at a Daim.

"That's the biggest one they've got," I said. "Are you sure?"

She nodded, and I put three Daim and an ice-cream sandwich in the basket.

"There we are," I said. "Now we can go up and pay."

"Fruit?" said Geir.

"I'll get some from the stall outside the apartment. It's cheaper there. And better, too."

We got in line, there were about ten other people in front of us. I put the basket down on the floor.

"Wait a minute," I said. "I forgot the wafers."

I hurried over to the far side of the supermarket and stared at the rows of wafers, there had to be fifty different varieties, but none of the fluted kind I wanted, or at least I couldn't see any. Maybe they had some more on the other side? Then, suddenly, on a lower shelf I hadn't noticed before, at a right angle to the other shelves, and separated from them by a two-meter-wide passage, in their blue-and-white packaging, were the Belgian wafers I'd only ever seen before in Stockholm.

Perfect.

I grabbed two packs and hurried back to the checkout, where Geir and Heidi were now sixth in line.

"Your evening's just been saved," I said, putting the wafers in the basket. "Belgian waffle wafers."

"Now I'm a happy man," he said.

I picked up the basket and kept hold of it in my hand as step-by-step we progressed slowly toward the till; there was no way in the world I was going to end up the sort of person who shoved their basket over the floor with their foot while they flicked through a newspaper they had no intention of buying, putting it back in the rack as soon as it got to be his turn. I took four light-bulbs from the shelf next to the conveyor; the bulb in the hall by the kitchen had gone, I remembered, and the one above the toilet in the bathroom.

Heidi slipped off to the end of the conveyor as our turn approached, clambering up onto the counter that was intended for bagging your purchases, then looking up at me in case I shook my head. I didn't, so she stayed put, watching the first items bought by the man in front of us come sailing along on their black conveyor-belt river, gently sliding ashore onto the sedate metal, there to be buffeted by the items that followed, in patterns of movement not unlike those made by sticks and plastic detritus in the quiet pools that came after swift-flowing sections of water, only much slower.

He placed the divider bar on the conveyor, thereby signaling that it was our turn, and I lifted the basket up onto the ledge that was there for the purpose, putting the items one by one onto the conveyor, the big bottles of mineral water upright so they could be easily scanned, but the motion caused them first to wobble, then to fall, one against the other, like a pair of drunks. The assistant was the young man with the funny voice and the crutch, he glanced up at me and uttered his mechanical *hej*. I infused my own with a degree of enthusiasm, thinking vaguely it would add some touch of humanity to his plight, this conveyor-belt reality he occupied, but forgetting to take into account my otherwise dismissive and disinterested body language that completely invalidated any hint of warmth there might have been in my voice.

"*Hej,*" I said, taking my Visa card out of my pocket.

"One hundred and sixty-five, ninety," he said.

"Okay," I said, noticing the top edge of the Hemköp customer card I hadn't used for some days, pulling it out and swiping it through the reader, though I wasn't sure why, it verged on the compulsive, because although I'd spent vast amounts of money there over the past few years and saved up tons of bonus points, as the monthly statements I received in the mail informed me, I'd never cashed them in, and since they ran out after a certain time the action of swiping the card had become fairly meaningless. On the other hand, I thought I might as well start now.

I inserted my Visa card, entered my PIN, and accepted the amount.

"A bag might have been practical," Geir said.

"Damn, I forgot," I said, and tried to catch the assistant's attention, though he seemed not to notice.

"Can I have a bag as well, please?" I said.

Would he say it was okay and dismiss the extra cost with a wave of his hand, or would he enter the amount and make me get my card out again?

"That'll be two kronor," he said.

You little shit. Fuck you.

I did my shopping there every single day.

"Okay," I said, inserting my card again, entering my PIN again, accepting the amount again. By the time it was done, Geir and Heidi had filled the bag with our items and we could go back out into the warm, late-summer afternoon.

We bought strawberries on the square, and Heidi carefully carried one of the overfilled cardboard cartons all the way to the elevator, Geir and I trudging along behind with our shopping bags. In the elevator I realized I'd forgotten to get flowers. A bunch of white roses would have been nice for the table, setting off the fiery red of the prawns and the yellow of the lemons. Never mind, we would have to do without. I couldn't be bothered to go out again, even if the florist's was only across the square.

The elevator came to a halt and I shoved the door open with my elbow, holding it there for Geir and Heidi, who still had the little box of strawberries in her hands, cautious as if she were holding a small animal. Geir opened the door and as soon as I was inside I dumped the bags next to the row of shoes and went off to the bathroom, the one farthest inside.

"Mommy, Mommy, I carried the strawberries," Heidi called out.

I felt a brief tingle of happiness in my chest, at the same time registering that Vanja and Njaal were still in the bedroom as I pressed the bathroom door handle down. I dropped my pants and sat down on the toilet seat. Next to me was an issue of the Swedish football magazine *Offside*. Argentina was due to play in the

Andes, where the air was so thin it was by no means unusual for players to pass out, they even had oxygen tanks ready to go!

I could hear Vanja's voice next door, then Njaal's. I guessed that Vanja was showing him her computer game, the one she got for her birthday. It was about dogs, and the idea was to get them to do various things. Most of the functions were still too difficult for her, but some she managed, like making the dog jump on and off a log to snatch different objects as they came flying through the air. Heidi had been given the matching version with cats, but she was still too little to get anything out of it and was happy enough watching her older sister play.

A small silverfish had paused on one of the floor tiles, perhaps twenty centimeters in front of my feet. It looked like a trilobite or some other small fossilized creature from prehistory. Such a simple creation. There was something crude and matter-like about it, as if it were a tiny blob of clay or a catfish that had been given feet.

I leaned forward to squash it under my finger, but the moment I moved it darted away toward the wall and vanished through a gap under the baseboard.

There were probably quite a few under the laundry baskets. And most likely in all the dust that had collected under the window in the corner, too. A little colony of silverfish.

Footsteps sounded in the hall, and since Vanja and Njaal were still in the bedroom it had to be Heidi. The children hardly ever used this bathroom, so even though the door was unlocked there was no reason to fear they would come in. It did happen on occasion, because they were by no means entirely predictable, though only rarely. With Linda it was different, if I heard her coming I would grip the door handle and press it upward in case she tried to press it down and come in. The first time Yngve had come to see us here he had asked for a key, finding it unthinkable to go to the toilet without being able to lock the door. It had been just as unthinkable for me, too, or at least deeply alien, and for the first few weeks I had felt exposed and vulnerable, but then I got used to it. Somehow I always knew where everyone was and if anyone approached I would hear them. That we didn't have a key was because of Vanja and Heidi, so they wouldn't lock themselves in. It was about the only safety measure we had when it came to the children; all the sockets were open, all the shelves and cupboards unsecured, and the stove too, and the sharp knives and scissors lay within easy reach in one of the bottom drawers. Nothing had happened so far, and nothing would, because parents have a keen sense of what their children might conceivably get up to, and one thing I was certain I would never see was Vanja or Heidi with a big kitchen knife in their hands, or John crawling about on the stove like a little monkey. Moreover, I always knew exactly where they were, and almost always what they were doing. Of course, all these assumptions could be invalidated in the space of a few horrible seconds, but I didn't believe that would ever happen, and I never felt less than comfortable about their safety at home.

Outside the door, Heidi passed by and went into the bedroom. I picked the magazine up again and carried on reading. Once, we caught a ling in the sea off Torungen, I suddenly remembered. It had been windy, but the air had been warm; it must have been sometime in the summer. We were in the boat Dad bought when I was eleven or twelve, a seventeen-foot Rana Fisk with a twenty-five-horsepower Yamaha outboard. Yngve was with us, his hair blown to the side, and of course Dad, that dark figure of which I was so watchful. Waves chopped and dashed against the yellow fiberglass hull. The line, running barely visible through the air, down into the blue water. The first glimpses of a fish, which instantly lent depth to all the blue, rather like the first stars in a sky still light in early evening. A dense green shape, now here, now there, whiter with Dad's every pull.

What was it?

A long, regular body, yellow-gray and white, with a hideous face and wide, bulging eyes.

"It's a deepwater fish," Dad said. "A ling, I think."

Inquisitive and filled with pity, I stared at it. Its stomach had burst, he said, and dropped it onto the floor of the boat, where it lay lifeless, before he cast his line out again, and then I remembered I was holding one too, and tugged it hard, gripping it tight between my fingers.

The feeling of floating on the surface of such enormous depths.

Dad.

What had I done to him?

A stab of distress and terror went through my chest. A moment later, when I turned on the tap and looked at myself in the mirror, I saw no sign of my inner turmoil. If I hadn't seen that same face, those same eyes, so many times before, and associated them so closely with who I was, they could just as easily have belonged to someone else.

My eyes looked sad, my features stark and, with the deep furrows that lined my cheeks and brow, masklike.

I twisted the thin pole with the little knob on the end and opened the blind, looked across at the hotel, above which the evening sun angled down, there were people sitting on the steps of the square and on the half-meter-high wall my children always wanted to balance on whenever we went to the park just along the road, and at the same time I took the towel from the peg and dried my hands. There was no getting away from the guilt I felt, it had transplanted itself from the abstract reality of the mind, where it could be countered by abstract means, to the physical reality of the body, where it could not be countered at all because the body had no means of defense but itself, and could only run, walk, sit, sleep, and a few other such things. It felt as if I were a room, and inside that room with me there was something horrifying. It was no use running, because if I ran, the whole room ran with me. There was no escape, for the simple reason that it was there. It didn't matter if what I'd done was reasonable, if I was within my rights or not, because it was *there*, indisputable, inescapable, and all I could do was wait until it was something that was there no more.

The door behind me opened, and I spun round.

It was Heidi. There were tears in her eyes.

"What's the matter, *lilla tjejen*?" I said, hanging the towel back on the peg.

She came up and wrapped her arms around my legs. I lifted her up and kissed her cheek.

"Won't they play with you?" I asked.

She shook her head and stared stiffly into space.

"Come on, you can stay with me and we'll make some dinner."

"I don't want to," she said.

I went out with her on my arm.

"How about a film, then?" I said. "Or *Bolibompa*? It'll be on in a minute."

She nodded.

I went through the hall and into the living room, where I put her down on the sofa – I could hear Linda, Christina, and Geir talking in the other room – and looked around for the remote. Normally it was on the bookshelf where the children couldn't reach it. But it wasn't there.

Oh, for crying out loud.

John started wailing in the bedroom. I heard Linda get to her feet, and a second later I caught a fleeting glimpse of her as she passed the open doorway while I scanned the long windowsill that ran the length of the far wall. It wasn't there either.

Heidi looked up at me.

"I can't find the remote," I said.

She stared toward the table in front of her. There it was, half-hidden under the newspaper Linda must have been reading while we were out.

"There it is," I said. "Now, let's see!"

Linda came in with John on her arm. He was curled up like a little monkey, pressing his cheek to her chest.

"Put *Bolibompa* on," she said.

"That's what I'm doing," I said.

When the sound came on and the picture appeared, John

turned his head to see. Linda put him down next to Heidi, and he accepted this without protest. TV was like a drug to them.

"What time do you think we should eat?" said Linda.

"I don't know," I said. "Around seven, maybe?"

"What about the children? I can't see them shelling prawns."

"That's a point," I said. "I didn't think of them when we were shopping. Do we have anything? I can have a look," I said.

Njaal and Vanja came charging through the hall.

"Is *Bolibompa* on?" Vanja called out.

"In a minute," I called back, went into the kitchen, and opened the fridge. There were some eggs. Carrots, potatoes, yellowing broccoli. Half a bag of fish cakes. The freezer next to it was mainly full of things Linda's mother had made for us, and various cuts of meat she'd bought, besides some peas, a few half-empty bags of chicken drumsticks, a couple of loaves of bread we'd frozen and forgotten about. But oh, thank goodness, there on the bottom shelf was a pizza! I looked up at Linda, who was standing behind me.

"They'll be more than happy with pizza, don't you think?"

She nodded.

"I'll make it for them now," I said. "They can eat in front of the TV."

I took the pizza box out and put it on the counter, switched the oven on, found the scissors in the drawer, tore off the long strip along the side of the box, tipped it so the pizza itself, round and surprisingly heavy, slid out into my hand, snipped open the see-through plastic it was wrapped in, which was stiff and had a kind of crinkly crispness about it, nothing like the see-through plastic of the bags we bought our fruit in, which were looser in some way, or the thin cling film for wrapping food up before putting it in the fridge. Nor was it anything like the slightly thicker, more durable plastic that covered the corn-on-the-cob we sometimes bought, or the six-packs of beer.

"In that case we might as well eat after they've gone to bed," said Linda.

"Sounds good to me," I said, taking the pizza out through the opening I had made in the wrapper and allowing it to rest in my palm, as if my hand were a serving plate, while with the other I pulled out the metal drawer underneath the stove and took out a mottled brown or, more accurately, blackened baking sheet on which I placed the pizza before sliding it into the oven, crumpling the wrapper and taking it to the bin under the sink, which was so full I had to press the garbage down with my fists in order to make room. Just as I had done so and was about to close the cupboard door, momentarily occupied by the thought of the garbage rising slowly up to the lid again, the phone rang.

I went warily into the hall. Someone had intruded into our home, he or she was here now, ringing their presence out into the room. I paused at the table under the mirror and picked up the phone. It was an 04 number, meaning it was from someone in Malmö.

"Yeah, hello?" I said.

"Hi, Stefan here."

"Hi, Stefan!"

"How's it going, all right?"

"Fine," I said, noticing the two bags of groceries I'd dumped next to the shoes and forgotten all about. "How about you?"

"Fine, too. We were thinking of going to the beach tomorrow. Would you like to come with us? We can just take Vanja along, if that's better for you."

"Sounds great," I said. "Only we've got visitors at the moment, so I think we're going to be spending the day with them, I'm afraid."

"Oh, I see. It's short notice, I know. Still, not to worry."

"Some other time."

"Definitely. Speak to you soon, then."

"Yeah. Take care."

"Thanks, same to you. *Hej då*."

"*Hej då*."

I hung up, took the two bags with me into the kitchen, and

put them down on the table, put the paper bags of prawns in the fridge and the two loaves on the big cutting board, bent down to the oven and looked at the pizza that lay inside, illuminated in its little compartment as if it were on TV, but of course it was no-where near ready yet, I had only put it in a few minutes ago.

Bolibompa's signature tune came from the living room. I went and stood in the doorway. Christina was sitting in a chair with Njaal in her lap, Linda on the sofa with John in hers, and Heidi snuggled up to her, Vanja on a chair in the middle of the floor. All the blinds were down, but there was still so much sunlight in the room it was hard to see the picture on the screen.

I ought to have sat down with Vanja in my lap. But I couldn't let Geir sit on his own in the other room. I could see what it would look like from his point of view, each of us sitting there with a child in our lap, watching children's TV. It didn't look good.

I went up to the back of Vanja's chair, put one hand on her belly and kissed the top of her head. She didn't so much as look up at me, concentrating all her attention on the television, and so I stepped past the table and went into the other room, where Geir was standing at the bookshelf.

"Going out for a smoke?" he said as he turned around.

"Good guess," I said. "Are you coming with me?"

He nodded, poured himself a cup of coffee, and stepped outside. I filled my own cup with what was left and followed him out. He had taken my chair again, and again my inner being protested at the way everything was wrong with the angle at which I now had to sit. Maybe it was the fact I had my back to the door that made me so uncomfortable. I put my feet up on the railing and lit a smoke.

"Njaal and Vanja are getting along all right," I said.

"Yes," he said. "They're doing great together. Christina's happy too."

"Is she?"

"Yes, she likes being here. Plus it's a joy for her to see Njaal having such a good time."

"I don't understand that," I said. "About being here, I mean."

"I like it here too."

"It must be the mess of the place."

"Yeah, it's that as well. There's a nice, relaxed feel about things. It feels free."

"I'm glad you think so," I said. "Personally, I'm anything but relaxed."

"You're not stressed by us being here, are you?"

"No, not at all. It's all this business about Gunnar."

"There's nothing you can do about it. Just let it go. What happens happens."

"Yes," I said.

Our top-floor neighbors in the building farther along were sitting out on their balcony eating. They were perhaps twenty meters away, but up here among the rooftops it was close enough to be encroaching, and when I was on my own and they were sitting out I could hear everything they said if I concentrated and they didn't lower their voices the way they might if they knew I was there. On the other side, at the end of our own building, I could stare right into the kitchen of an elderly couple, they often sat there smoking, and after three years their habits were nearly as familiar to me as my own. I assumed they looked at me in the same way; at any rate, our eyes occasionally met and we always looked away. Such visual encounters were strange, our entering fleetingly into each other's minds in that way, they into mine, certainly, they meant we somehow knew each other, balancing continually between seeing and knowing on the one hand, and looking away and not wanting to know on the other. Opposite, in the apartments belonging to the same building as the balcony couple, I could likewise gaze in on the private lives of families, couples, and singles, usually without interest, merely noting what I saw, but every now and then something happened that insisted on occupying me for a moment, for instance the time one couple, the corner of whose kitchen was as much as I could see, suddenly were a family with a little baby. When the child

377

was visible, half seated, half lying in its baby bouncer, it was as if it were presiding over them, because everything they did was in some way related to its wants and needs, which was a completely new thing.

"You've done nothing wrong," said Geir.

"But I have, obviously," I said. "I'm trying to live with it."

"Your dad's dead. Your grandma's dead."

"And your empathy's dead."

"Look who's talking."

"Imagine there's a life after this," I said. "If we take that thought seriously. Only the body dies. The soul lives on in the world to come, in whatever form. What if it's true? I mean, really true. It struck me the other day. What if there is life after death? It'd mean my dad's out there somewhere waiting for me. And he's going to be angry as hell."

Geir laughed.

"You can relax. He's dead as a dodo."

"Gunnar isn't, though."

"But what can he do? Okay, he can sue you. But for what? Defaming your father's name? He wasn't exactly Jesus, was he?"

"Gunnar says I'm a Judas. In which case he must have been Jesus, since he's the one I'm betraying."

"If he was Jesus, that makes your grandmother the Virgin Mary. And your grandfather was Joseph, the carpenter. Besides, Jesus didn't have a son to betray him."

"I wonder if it was actually Brutus he meant. He was a kind of son. Brutus Juliussen. Et tu, Brute? No, I only ate one."

"You don't have to say everything that comes into your mind, you know. Kids do that. Adults can put their utterances through quality control first."

"I remember crying when I read about Julius Caesar. His death. I always did whenever I read biographies. Because of course they all die. Thomas Alva Edison. Henry Ford. Benjamin Franklin. Marie Curie. Florence Nightingale. Winston Churchill. Louis Armstrong. Theodore Roosevelt."

"You read Theodore Roosevelt's biography when you were a kid?"

"I did, yes. There was a series. About twenty of them, I suppose. One on each. Most were about Americans. A lot of presidents. Walt Disney, I remember him. Robert Oppenheimer. No, I'm joking. But Abraham Lincoln, at any rate. And when they died, no matter how, I always cried. But in a good way."

"Because it wasn't you!"

"No, no, it wasn't that. It was more that they'd overcome all this injustice in their lives and eventually succeeded in what they wanted to do. It would have been a lot sadder if they had died before achieving what they were meant to. Like Scott. Scott was bad, I was out of it for days."

"He probably wasn't happy about it either."

"Whereas Amundsen's death was a bit more ambivalent. He did what he set out to. And then there was something decent about him vanishing while trying to save someone else."

I stubbed out my cigarette and got up.

"But what about Nansen, what did he actually do? I mean, what did he achieve? Were there any discoveries? Did he reach somewhere first? I never actually got what it was about him."

"You may as well ask," he said, getting to his feet. "He crossed Greenland on skis, and was frozen in by the ice on board the *Fram*."

I opened the door and went inside.

"I think I got frozen in one winter," I said over my shoulder. "The house was like a fridge."

"Then there was all that stuff about his refugee passports," Geir went on behind me. "And Quisling, of course."

"There we go again. Gunnar called me a quisling too."

"Who's Nansen, then?"

"I suppose he is," I said, and sat down again. "It can't be my dad, anyway. He was useless on skis."

When *Bolibompa* was finished, I moved the IKEA camp bed that Njaal had slept on the night before into the children's room so we could sit in the living room in the evening and not have to worry about waking him up. After that I got started on the dinner while Linda and Christina put them all to bed and Geir sat on a chair in the kitchen so we could keep on gabbing. I put the prawns in a big green bowl, sliced the lemons, and laid them out on a green dish, cut the bread and arranged it in a basket, took four plates and four wineglasses out of the cupboard, got the butter and mayonnaise from the fridge, carried it all out onto the front balcony, where the sun was still shining in that hazily unreal way it does on a summer evening when the shadows grow long and the day draws to an end, yet the air is still warm. When people finish their jobs and turn toward home with the sun still blazing, yet slowly sinking in a great blue sky.

The children's voices drifted through the half-open window of their room and out onto the balcony. They were loud and giggling, as boisterous as they were only at bedtime. I set the table, then stood for a moment with my hands curled around the metal railing, looking down on the square below. The shadows of the buildings opposite almost covered the entire area. But the wall beneath me was lit up, the windows sparkling in the sun.

In the kitchen I rinsed the strawberries and put them in a white bowl, and got the wine and mineral water out of the fridge.

"That's about it," I said. "A glass of wine while we're waiting?"

Geir nodded and followed me out. As I opened the door and stepped out onto the balcony, a great big seagull took off from the table, twisting its body away as it flapped its wings, and the next second it was airborne and gone. In its beak was a prawn, and a few others lay scattered next to the bowl and on the wooden decking.

"Did you see that?" I exclaimed.

"How could I miss it?"

"The cheeky bastard."

"What do you expect? A bowl of prawns left out on a deserted sixth-floor balcony. It's an open invitation, isn't it?"

I sat down, pressed the corkscrew into the cork and twisted it a few times before pulling it toward me until it released from the neck of the bottle with a gentle *thwop*. The dark green glass misted. It was such a fine color. Cool green, bottle green, fjord green. And then the pale yellow of the wine in the shiny glass.

"*Skål*," said Geir.

"*Skål*," I said, taking a sip and lighting a cigarette. The taste that assailed my palate as I bent my head to the unmoving flame of the lighter reminded me of summer nights in Kristiansand when I was still a teenager and filled me with the urge to drink until I dropped.

"Nice wine," I said.

"Lovely," he said.

That was one of the things Gunnar had accused me of, drinking and smoking dope when I was still at *gymnas* in Kristiansand. Partly, I supposed, he believed it to be a sign of poor character, meaning I was unreliable and possibly also deranged, certainly not a decent human being, and partly it was meant to explain why I apparently hated Grandma enough to write six books about her to tarnish her name. I understood what he'd written, it was all somehow within the bounds of a logic I knew, but he hadn't written to me, he'd written to the publisher. Did he think they would pull the novel because its author had drunk beer in his youth, and maybe even smoked dope, and for that reason was surely a despicable person? It didn't matter, I still felt that was what I was, a despicable person, but it was my emotions that hadn't changed since I was sixteen, not my reasoning. My reasoning saw things differently. I knew who I was and what I was worth. I knew, too, that being human meant being inadequate, to be human was to err and never quite be good enough. When I looked around me, that was what I saw. Weakness everywhere, shortcomings and flaws, often congealed within a character in the form of self-righteousness, smugness, and conceit. Humility, a word so often bandied about in public contexts, was something hardly anyone knew the meaning of anymore. Only those who had every reason to be conceited, those of real caliber, showed no trace of conceit, only they were humble. Conceit and self-righteousness were part of a defense mechanism without which a person would be crushed under the weight of their own weaknesses, shortcomings, and flaws, and that fact underlay almost every discussion I witnessed, verbal as well as written, in newspapers and on television, but also in my immediate surroundings, in the private sphere. Such weakness could not be admitted, since so much would be lost, and the form of those discussions and the power of the media resolved it by endowing it with their strength. That was why opinions were so important in society, through opinions we appropriated a strength and supremacy we did not possess. That was the function of form here, to obscure the weakness of the individual. Any joining together, around a set of morals, a bureaucracy, an ideology, obscured the weakness of the individual. I knew this because it was what I saw, but when I encountered such things myself, that knowledge was preempted by my emotions, which mechanically fell in with them, slinging me off into the nightmare of feeling myself guilty or inferior. In my dealings with the tax authorities, the bank, or credit companies, I was consumed with guilt. Sneaking around the subdivision gardens I was consumed with guilt. Dropping off and collecting the kids from nursery I was consumed with guilt. I knew that I was not inferior to anyone I met there, my weaknesses and shortcomings were no greater than theirs, but they weren't representatives of themselves, they were representatives of a system in which there were rules, and those rules were very simple: if you followed them you were a good person, if you didn't you were a bad person. I tried to follow them, but because I was undisciplined I often found myself breaking them. I knew the reason, it wasn't because I was bad, sloppy, or lackadaisical, but knowing why could in no way make up for what the eyes of the system saw, which was someone who didn't follow the rules, and this I incorporated into the person I was. Whenever I saw a real work of art or read real literature, all this was brutally shoved aside, for there was another dimension to being human, something quite different, of a different quality, dignity, and significance, it was what had inspired medieval man to build such enormous cathedrals against whose magnificence they became what they actually were: lowly, insignificant, and inconsiderable beings. Tiny little farts of life, one could say. Yet they had built them! They were creators of astonishing, otherworldly beauty, but they were farts, too. This was the truth of being human. It was important and unimportant at the same time. Weakness was important, and greatness was important. But not what lay in between. The kind of weakness that hid away in the crowd and believed itself to be strength, that saw neither weakness nor greatness, was what I, driven from counter to counter, allowed myself to be intimidated by and to which I submitted. The yearning to drink until I dropped was the yearning to remove myself from it all, if only for a few hours, and the yearning to write something fantastic, something truly splendid and otherworldly, was part of the same thing. It wasn't an escape from trivial everyday things, because life itself is trivial, but an escape from trivial life's invasion of my self, which forced on me the idea that I wasn't a good and decent person but a fool, conceited and inadequate, and which had been forcing that same idea on me ever since I was sixteen and started drinking in Kristiansand, under my uncle's ever-watchful eye, or so it felt. What I yearned for and had been oblivious to at that time, but which twenty years later I had managed to identify and which was totally unrealizable, was what Hölderlin had expressed when he penned that simple plea: "Come out into the open, my friend."

What was "the open"?

It was freedom, it was utopia.

But what did it mean?

Certainly not that we should talk about everything, account for everything, abolish the borders between ourselves, others, and the world, because that would only be to set up new borders somewhere else and to let the human prevail, and what would happen then, and happen soon, was that reality would be gone.

What Hölderlin meant no one can know for sure anymore. Like all the other Romantics, Hölderlin was a child of the French Revolution, of liberty, equality, and fraternity, and that radical transformation of the old societal order must to them have seemed like a sudden opening through which a whole new potential was revealed. The prevailing order, society's order or the world order, makes all other ways by which life might be organized seem threatening, dangerous, or corrosive, for which reason such possibilities are not real alternatives, until its own inconsistencies bring it toppling down, to be replaced by a new order, which then becomes the prevailing order that for all the world must not be tampered with. But reading Hölderlin it is difficult to understand "the open" as a political category, concerned with class, relations of production, or material conditions of life. No, the open as Hölderlin sees it was, I imagined, an existential category. Hölderlin was a poet, and what was utopian to a poet was a world without language. Poetry tried to enter into the space between language and the world so as to stand before the world just as it was in itself, but conveying that insight, which perhaps was the oldest of all insights, or committing it to paper, could only be done by the intervention of language, and what had been won was then Orpheus-like and instantly lost. In the world outside language, one could only ever be alone.

But what kind of world was that?

A world without language was a world without categories, where every single thing, no matter how modest, stood out in its own right. It was a world without history, in which only the moment existed. A pine tree in that world was not a "pine," nor was it a "tree," but a nameless phenomenon, something growing up out of the ground, which moved when the wind blew. Indeed, if one stood on top of a hill one could see how these living organisms swayed this way and that as the wind passed over the flat ground, and one could hear the rushing sound they made. This sight, and this sound, could not be conveyed. As such, it would be as if they didn't exist. But they did, and do. All it takes is one step and the world is transformed. One step and you enter the world of no names. It is blind, and you see the blindness. It is chaotic, and you see the chaos. It is beautiful, and you see the beauty. It is open, this is the open, and it is meaningless, this is the meaningless. It is also divine, indeed this is the divine. The little blue box with its red sun and the coarsened black surface of its sides, inside, the white matchsticks with their red, bead-like heads of phosphorus rest as if in a bed, is divine as it lies there motionless on the kitchen shelf with its thin covering of dust, faintly illuminated by the light of day outside the window, which slowly darkens as a black blanket of cloud drifts in over the city, and the first electrical charges snap through it at hurtling speed, following their unpredictable paths, thunder rumbling heavily in the sky. The wind as it picks up, and the rain that begins to fall, this is the divine. The hand that grasps the box, pushing the tiny bed out with the tip of an index finger to extract a matchstick, is a divine hand, and the fiery flame that flares up as the hand strikes the red phosphorus bead against the coarse surface, becoming, in the space of a second, a steady, much gentler flame, is the flame of the divine. Yet it burns in the shelter of our language, it burns in the shelter of our categories, it burns in the shelter of all the relations and connections those categories establish. The thought that a state of human innocence once existed, an uncomplicated nearness to the world, in what mythology calls the Garden of Eden, the place from which we come and to which we long to return because there we were at one with our surroundings and with God in a kind of original state of nature, is treacherous in that it implies time, a before and a now, whereas in reality only the now exists, in reality there is but one time for everything: the flame of the divine is burning now, the Garden of Eden exists now, all it takes is one step and you are there. But that step is impossible for us to take, for we are humans, and it is a step that can lead us only into the inhuman.

To be human is to be several. To be social. The social world is a community. The boundaries of the community are the boundaries of the language. When Hölderlin finally stepped into the open he vanished into madness. In his poems he is not mad, but nor are they in the open, they stand within the social world, looking in at the open. This is what religion has always done. Olav Nygaard called his collection of poetry *Ved vedbande*, which is to say at the boundary of the divine. Not within the divine, but at its edge. When religion is dismissed as superstition, and poetry becomes marginalized and no longer believes in its own significance, the open vanishes from the sphere of the human, which closes in on itself, since nothing outside it any longer exists.

Is that a loss? As long as what is outside the human sphere remains impossible to reach, as long as the world in its essence can never manifest itself to us, but merely reveal itself in our language and categories, in other words as something within the human sphere, and the world without language, outside the sphere of the human, is a utopia in the actual sense of the world, a non-place, why should we strive toward it? Why not simply turn away?

The reason is that it is where we are from, and where we are destined to return. It is because the heart is a bird that flutters in the chest, it is because the lungs are two seals through which our air smoothly passes, it is because the hand is a crab and the hair a haystack, the arteries rivers, the nerves lightning. It is because the teeth are a stone wall and the eyes apples, the ears mussels, and the ribs a gate. It is because it is always dark inside the brain, and still. It is because we are earth. It is because we are blood. It is because we must die.

Death, that great restorer of stillness, is outside the sphere of the human too and cannot manifest itself to us, for as it comes to us we cease to exist, much as language ceases to exist as it comes to that which is without language. Death is what the human sphere borders, the absence of language is what our human world borders, and it is against its darkness that we and the world shine. Death and the material world are the absolute, unattainable to us, for as we become them we cease to be ourselves. Our world, shining against the darkness of the it, is however not absolute, but relative and inconstant. Natural science is relative, morality is relative, social science, philosophy, and religion are relative, everything within the sphere of the human is relative. The distinction between discovery and invention is not great, and when it comes to their consequences is nonexistent. Did red and white blood cells exist in the seventeenth century? Yes, they did, but not to the human mind. They were in other words a part of the world but not of our reality. That reality is our world, and for that reason the world of the seventeenth century was different from the world of today, though the sky and the earth and the twinkling stars are of the same nature and material now as then. Darwin wrote a book, and whereas biological nature before Darwin existed spatially, after Darwin it existed temporally. The world was the same, reality changed. To describe the world is to establish reality. This is the same thought Harold Bloom expresses when he writes that Shakespeare invented man. When Shakespeare's characters step forward on the stage and reason with themselves, as if aside from the action yet still a part of it, haunted by doubt or stricken by love, at odds with themselves or astonished at themselves, man is then no longer merely a creature of action, a seat of emotions, but also a locus in which these emotions are confronted by a reflective self. It is the appearance of this self that arises from Shakespeare, in Bloom's opinion, prompting him with some justification to claim that Shakespeare invented humanity, since only when something becomes visible to others besides the single individual does it become real. Reality, our human reality, consists of all that is visible and may be perceived within and between us. Whenever that changes, reality changes too. This is why Greek Antiquity has been such a point of reference in Western civilization for more than two thousand years, and continues to be; so many of our conceptions about the world and about humanity were founded in that culture. History, philosophy, politics, natural science; everything comes from there. The only aspects of our own culture that don't come from there are religion, which is Jewish, and the machine, which is our own. That a culture as supreme as the Greek, with all its theoretical advances, looked on religion with such mild disdain is not surprising, though their dismissive attitude toward technology most certainly is, not least given their increasingly skilled craftsmanship. Yet if we accept Arendt's idea that the ancient Greeks sought freedom in the public domain and found the essence of humanity to be there, in what could be laid out in front of everyone, whereas in everything concerning day-to-day subsistence, the material needs of human beings, they saw constraint and necessity, their lack of interest in mechanics and technology, in practical knowledge, becomes easier to understand. The Greeks invented democracy but were unable to conceive of the water closet. Quite as extraordinary is the fact that these people who invented history were unfamiliar with the diary. Still, it surely was not the case that everything to do with the home lay in shadow, a kind of unarticulated zone of reality, with only what went on in public having actual existence by virtue of being formulated there for all, because the private sphere, too, enjoyed its own stage in Ancient Greece, in drama, more precisely the comedies, which dealt with the less elevated stuff of life and were founded on recognition. The freedom that lies in laughter is quite different from that which lies in the expression of virtues, which is perhaps why Arendt doesn't mention it, since it strives toward nothing, establishes nothing, changes nothing, distinguishes nothing, but exists simply for the moment, having no other purpose than to make it tolerable.

What do we laugh at in comedy? The answer is everything we deem to be base and normally conceal: the life of the body, excrement, copulation, bodily noises, and all human properties that pretend to be something they are not, impossible for a person to admit to: envy, conceit, avarice, self-righteousness, self-effacement, unscrupulousness, ambition, demanding esteem when none is appropriate. The striving to be something other than what one is, is the theme of comedy. Comedy exposes, and the humor lies in the gap revealed between the world as it wants to be and the world as it is. In that exposure lies an insight to the effect that the social world is a game that proceeds according to certain rules, some things are hidden, some are shown, and that in a way we live an illusion. The game depends on everyone taking part, the illusion that everyone believes in it. Comedy breaks that contract and as such it is the truest and most realistic of all genres. It is liberating in the sense that what it says is: this is what it really means to be human, and all of us are human. Yet it also constrains, a hindrance to anyone who wishes for something else and who believes it possible to elevate himself above this lowly world of excrement, copulation, envy, conceit, and constant misunderstandings, in other words anyone who insists on *ought* and *should* instead of *is*. Laughter is in this respect a powerful social force, one of the strongest corrective mechanisms of all; few things are more humiliating than being laughed at in public, and in order to avoid it a person must keep his head down and stay with everyone else. In this way, laughter on the one hand exposes the social game, and on the other keeps it going. Laughter is counterrevolutionary and anti-utopian: he who laughs at everything laughs also at the dictatorship of the proletariat, and if everyone laughs at the revolutionary there will be no revolution. If everyone had laughed at Semmelweis, mothers and newborn infants would still be dying of childbed fever. If the Germans had laughed at Hitler, he and his ideas would have been rendered harmless. But they did not laugh, they were earnest, they wanted something, the supreme, and in the supreme tragedy prevails, and tragedy is no laughing matter.

But if comedy is the truest and most realistic of all genres, drawing all things and all people into the real world, the body and its illusionless reality, how are we then to understand tragedy? Tragedy concerns the same thing as comedy: the rise and the fall. So why is the fall comical in the comedy and tragic in the tragedy? How come we don't laugh at Oedipus? He thinks he's something other than what he is. How come we don't laugh at Hamlet? He doesn't know who he is or what to do; ignorance and restlessness are his plight. How come we don't laugh at little Hedvig who shoots herself? Hasn't she misunderstood everything?

In that which is at one with itself there is no distance, and since distance is laughter's and comedy's point of departure, nonidentity its prerequisite, the only thing comedy and laughter cannot disturb is identity. That which does not pretend, which is not something else, that which is what it is. Dostoyevsky's masterpiece *The Idiot* is about just that. The novel was born as a comic genre with Cervantes's *Don Quixote*, in which the author allowed the idea of the great, cultured world to be played out in the small, mundane world, which is to say the world as it was, with windmills, sheep, decrepit steeds, donkeys, and drunken bandits, through which rode a thin and ailing old man and his fat little companion. With *Madame Bovary*, Flaubert pursued that novel's demystifying, reality-oriented aspect; in this case it is the idea of romantic love that collides with the world as it actually is, and which drives the main character to her death. Both *Don Quixote* and *Madame Bovary* are cynical novels insofar as they do not believe, yet scorn those who do. That what *Don Quixote* and *Madame Bovary* believe in is made so clearly illusory, thereby positioning the novels on the side of truth, and that both are lovingly portrayed, recognizing the universally human nature of their weaknesses and flights from reality, does nothing to alter this. *The Idiot* is the opposite of *Don Quixote* and *Madame Bovary*. *The Idiot* is an anti-comedy. It turns the logic of comedy on its head, exposing the cynical world, scorning those who laugh at the emptiness of life, doing so by means of its confrontation with the unaffected human. Oh, what is it about the unaffected as a human quality that causes everyone in its vicinity to despair, unease to swell, chaos to loom, for no other reason than its mere existence? Prince Lev Nikolaevich Myshkin believes that what he sees, what is shown to him, is what it is, and that whatever is said is meant sincerely. He is oblivious to the ulterior motive, he does not understand irony, he is blind to the roles people play. He has no idea that the social world is a game. He is at one with himself, and assumes everyone else is, too. But they are not, and his ignorance of this is sufficient on its own for the game to disintegrate, in that he gives them a vantage point from which to view it from the outside, a place outside the social world from where it becomes visible to them, thereby exposing its arbitrary nature. Roles are meaningful within the framework of the game, but as soon as the game is revealed to be just that, a game, they become meaningless. Who do you then become? The person you are? What does that mean? Myshkin is himself, the person he is. He is genuine. He is indivisible, no one's twin, no doppelgänger. For that very reason he is doomed to remain outside humanity. A society comprising genuine individuals taking everything at face value is a society in which nothing can be concealed, nothing kept secret, no real variation established. In other words, the genuine is the opposite of the social. The social world classifies and groups, excludes, suppresses, elevates. The social world is a system of differences, a world in which everything and everyone is graded and differentiated. The idiot nullifies all differences, in his realm everyone is equal. It is not his goodness that causes the social world such problems, but his authenticity. From a revolutionary perspective in which the complexity of the literary character is seen to develop from Odysseus's simple, archaic smartness to explode, as it were, in Hamlet's wild and contradictory Renaissance self, heralding the modern individual we know, Dostoyevsky's Myshkin represents a regression, something deeply reactionary and unmodern, if not directly archaic, a kind of pre-Homerian man, on whom both Odysseus's ingenuity in fooling the Cyclops with his clever name game and Plato's cave allegory would be lost. Indeed, is Myshkin not somewhat reminiscent of that Cyclops, the one-eyed enemy imprisoned by his literal understanding of language, unable to comprehend that Odysseus is not being straight with him when he tells him his name is Nobody? Dostoyevsky was a deeply reactionary author, firstly in the fact that he was searching for meaning, in all seriousness and with eyes open, secondly in the fact that he was searching for it not in politics or ideology, in science or philosophy, but in religion, and that he found it there, in simplicity. The great threat in all of Dostoyevsky's novels is nihilism, the spinning, flashing tombola of the social world on the fairground of meaninglessness, in the black night of emptiness, and what he defends himself so fiercely with, time and again, is the holy and the simplicity of the holy. Dostoyevsky cherishes simplicity. His novels are hugely complex and chaotic, a tumult of characters and voices, not a quiet moment in one of them, quite without the slow and sleepily hypnotic passages, the lazy days of summer in which little or nothing happens, that occur in Proust, for instance; Dostoyevsky is all pace, a series of highly intense, near-hysterical scenes on the brink of madness, but in all his depictions of a violent and uncontrolledly spiraling world, in his best books there is always, sooner or later, a light, and surrounding the light is silence. Dostoyevsky's light is not dim and soft like an oil lamp, nor bright and dissecting like our modern strip lighting, but white and almost all-obliterating, like flaming magnesium, one might imagine, which burns away details and nuances and gives one the feeling that it is not what is illuminated that is important, but the light itself. That difference, between the light and what is illuminated, is the difference between premodern reality and modern reality, and where the former is singular and simple, the latter is plural and grotesquely complex. Dostoyevsky turned toward that light, he wanted to believe in it, but the will of that wanting, which only a person living in the complexity of the illuminated knows, made it impossible, it being the very opposite of belief. Wanting to believe is impossible, a contradiction in terms. Had he believed, he would not have written. But he could feel it.

What was it he felt he wanted? What is the light in Dostoyevsky's novels? It is grace. And grace is the undifferentiated, that which is without difference. It cannot be grasped by language because language is in its very nature differentiating. In that way, Dostoyevsky's grace resembles Hölderlin's concept of "the open," but whereas Hölderlin's open pertains to the material world of rivers and clouds, Dostoyevsky's grace pertains to the social world. In that world grace nullifies all distinctions, in grace all are equal. The radicalism of this is huge and almost unthinkable. Yet it is this, and nothing else, that Christianity is about. There is no difference between anyone. The most despicable person is as worthy as the best. Jesus said, whosoever shall smite thee on thy right cheek, turn to him the other also. He is a man, as you are a man; he is you. Strike him not. Such a thought is inhuman in that it comes from outside the social world. Indeed, it is a divine thought. Adolf Hitler is as worthy as the Jews he gassed to death. In this our identity dissolves, being established by our very differences, and this is what makes Christianity unfeasible, we cannot think ourselves into oblivion, it would be too much to lose, since it is all we have. Nor can we remain the same without losing everyone else. The undifferentiated is not a category, it is a place in which all meaning vanishes; regardless of what you possess and how inalienable it is to you, it has no value there. This is what none of us grasps. And no matter Dostoyevsky's intentions when he wrote his masterpiece, what Myshkin brings with him none of us wants, it is almost a nightmare vision. The idiot is he who gapes and laughs with those who laugh at him, his face a question mark. The idiot is the cynic's antipode. Between them lies the choice. The cynic asks, But who will forgive? The idiot replies, I will.

♦ ♦ ♦

The sun that shone directly down on the balcony where we sat was so warm that beads of sweat trickled from my hairline, though it was well into evening, and so bright I wondered whether to go in and get my sunglasses. I wondered, too, if I should pinch a couple of prawns, their faint salty smell and the sight of the pink, armored creatures in itself awoke in me an urge to taste their fresh oceanic flesh. But I decided not to. Wearing sunglasses during a meal was bad form, and digging in before everyone had come to the table was even worse.

Geir sighed.

"What are you moaning about?" I said.

"Who's moaning? That's your department."

I lit a cigarette and leaned forward in my chair, resting my forearms against my thighs.

"All right, so I'm moaning. Can I make amends with a joke?"

"Jokes and moaning, it's all the same in your case."

"What did Stevie Wonder say when he walked past a prawn trawler on the quayside?"

"I don't know, what did he say?"

"Hi, girls!"

Geir grinned and put his feet up on the balcony. I leaned back in my chair and swept the perspiration into my hair with my middle and ring fingers, making sure the burning cigarette between my index and middle fingers didn't make contact.

The sounds from the children's room had died down; most likely they were listening to a story. I took a sip of the wine. I'd never told anyone that I preferred a soft drink. Nor that I favored drinking tea with prawns, even in the summer, the way I'd done when I was growing up, ever since then I'd always felt the two things went together.

A prawn's eye had separated from its head and lay on its own on the side of the bowl. It looked like a peppercorn. Their tentacles, strewn about their chubby bodies, resembled whiskers. That live prawns were pale and sleet-colored, bordering on the transparent, much like dirty windows, hardly seemed credible when you saw them cooked, their color being such a strong and splendid characteristic you could hardly imagine that nature should squander it on something dead. The lobster, on the other hand, in its somber, steely armor not unlike certain suits of armor in the Italian Renaissance, black and articulated, was certainly finer living than when the boiling water so swiftly extinguished its life and the red-orange color seeped into the shell. To be sure it was a delicate thing to behold, and more elegant, but compared to the beauty of the black and all its associations with power and strength, the refinement of red was nothing. How different in the case of the prawns. Alive they looked almost like office workers of the ocean, in death like a company of ballet dancers.

Below us a bus stopped with a sigh at a red light. The traffic that streamed along the street, which continued out to the grassy coastline and the beach, slowed to a halt on the other side of the lights. Now it was the turn of those coming from the north, but the street on that side was deserted. The pedestrian crossing, ticking with the appearance of its green man, or green person as I supposed it was called now, was deserted too. A sliver of the feeling that could come over me at night, when the lights changed in the empty streets without anyone there to see them, implanted itself in my mind like a note slipped under a door. The image it conjured, which I could so vividly entertain, was of a world without people. All the houses empty, all the streets deserted, no cars, no buses, just the lights changing back and forth at the crossing down below, and at other crossings throughout the city. There would be movement, vegetation creeping forth everywhere, albeit at its own inimitably slow pace, pushing up through the concrete and the asphalt, gradually subsuming everything around it, and there would be animals in the streets. But none would heed the lights and their ticking men. They would belong to an empty system. The beings that once inhabited that system, which had created these lights in order to regulate their own movements, existed no more and would never return.

I leaned forward and stubbed my cigarette out against the upright of the railing in front of me, dropping the end at my feet for want of an ashtray, the discreetest thing I could think of to do with it. It lay there like a man under a tree, I thought to myself, and downed the rest of my wine, putting the empty glass on the table next to my plate, then looked up: at the other end of the balcony, some ten meters away, the door had opened. It was Christina. She smiled and raised her hand halfway in the air, as if we wouldn't be able to understand she was there if all we saw was her body, and she needed a gesture to convince us.

She closed the door behind her with one hand, sweeping her long hair to the side with the other, and came toward us.

"How nice," she said. "And such a lovely evening for sitting out!"

"Is he asleep?" asked Geir.

She shook her head and sat down on the chair up against the wall, blinking at the sun.

"But he's in bed at least. It's such an adventure for him to sleep with the other three."

"Do you want some wine?" I said, holding up the bottle toward her.

"No, thanks," she said. "I'd like some Ramlösa, though."

I put the wine down, picked up the bottle of mineral water, and poured. The glassy, bubbly liquid, fizzing faintly, settled itself in the transparent receptacle. Some of the bubbles released from the surface leaping four, five centimeters in the air, visible in the light of the sun which made them sparkle.

She put the glass to her lips and drank.

"Are mine in bed too?" I asked.

She nodded and swallowed, lowering the glass, though without putting it down on the table, holding it in one hand, her elbow resting against her thigh.

"Yes," she said. "But John's standing up in his crib and wants to join the others."

Christina had a reserved quality about her, not in the substance of what she said or talked about, more in the way she spoke; it was as if she didn't want to let go of her gestures, I sometimes thought. The same was true of her facial expressions, which she always seemed like she wanted to keep under control; not that they were forced in any way or false, because they weren't, it was more like she was wary of giving too much away, as if that would be dangerous, and was always holding some part of herself back, something she kept inside. In many ways she was Geir's complete opposite, he was much more casual about himself, his body language, and his expressions; his need to control had the external world as its object, which he organized meticulously, the material aspects, where nothing was left to chance, as well as the immaterial, the realm of ideas, where he was unable to write anything at all without accounting for its origin in a footnote.

Christina was always well-dressed, not in a showy way but classy and elegant. It wasn't surprising, seeing as she was a trained fashion designer. I always studied what she was wearing when we met, it filled me with a kind of satisfaction, perhaps it was the sureness of her choices that did it, the way everything complemented each other without calling attention to itself, because that would have been an unnecessary demonstration, the way the little details, like a scarf or a belt, brought out the maximum in all the other elements, raising them and presenting them, as it were, at the same time as they were foregrounded, by the chunkiness of a buckle, for instance, and yet backgrounded in that the buckle also served to set off something else. Color, cut, material, pattern; all were measured against each other with a sureness that could only be intuitive. This was something she was good at, something she didn't need to make an effort to achieve. In that respect she managed what few people can, which was to erase the discrepancies between what was new and what was old, between what was expensive and what was cheap, by looking away from those properties and looking instead at the inherent properties of each item, each accessory. Labels didn't exist for her; brand didn't come into it when I thought about her clothes. Of those I'd seen, I was especially fond of a light brown leather jacket she sometimes wore, there was something extremely appealing about it, though I had no idea what exactly. What was the source of that feeling? It was something I vaguely associated with the seventies, even if it wasn't especially seventies-looking in itself. Perhaps it was more the warmth of its tone, and the cut, but at the same time it possessed an almost aggressive quality, as leather jackets often do, and that combination might have been what I found so appealing. Big buttons. Feminine, in an unfrilly kind of way. Elegant. Yes, that was the word. The jacket was elegant.

She dressed Njaal in the same way. Nearly all other kids were H&M kids, or KappAhl kids, their clothes followed the seasons and the tastes dictated by those stores, ours too. If Njaal wore anything from H&M, it never stood out as H&M but was absorbed by other, independently selected and subtly coordinated items. He was elegant, too, though quite unlike any Little Lord Fauntleroy, on the contrary, he looked like a child of our time but in his very own way, just as Christina was a woman of our time but in her very own way. Twenty years from now, if we looked at photographs from today, she and he, mother and son, would clearly belong to the first years of the new millenium, the same way as everyone else, none of us would be able to escape that, but in a purer, more stylish way, much like John F. Kennedy and Jacqueline Kennedy are so obviously fifties and sixties, but with a completely different air of significance and elegance about them from our parents, uncles, and aunts from the same era, despite their being contemporaries.

The sureness of Christina's dress sense didn't correspond well to the way she came across as a person, in the sense that she wasn't nearly as sure of herself, or as superior, as she was in her choice of clothes. I didn't know her that well, and naturally we'd never talked about what went on in her mind, or about her appearance, but from what I'd seen I imagined the relationship between her inner and outer selves to be less than harmonious, I had the feeling her inner life was much greater and more expansive than her outer self suggested. She was cautious about how much of herself she revealed, not necessarily consciously so, most likely not, but her unwavering reticence seemed to indicate this was the case; she didn't want her inner self to be made visible to others, brought forward where it could be exploited by other people's attentions and thoughts. Why not? Was she hiding something? Was there something she felt ashamed of? Or was she just a very private person?

I recognized the same characteristic in myself. I had no way of knowing if that sense of recognition was relevant, for all I knew she might feel and think quite differently, but if it really was like I thought, then I knew exactly how she felt. If that was so, she had grown up in a family from whom part of the person she was had to be hidden. If that was so, her childhood had been all about freeing herself from that, enabling her to exist and act in her own right, to accept that part of her that was hidden and allow it to come out into the open, but so powerful is that dynamic, so deeply integrated in the singular identity of the self, that it's as good as impossible to eradicate: it is you. Because what happens, or at least what happened in my own case, is that the part of you that cannot be expressed, which has to be hidden, leads its own life inside, and this inner life, to which you grow accustomed, becomes a way of living, something good, you become more than sufficient in yourself and have no need for others. What ought to unfold, folds inward. For Geir, to whom she was married, there was no such imbalance between what he thought and what he said, between what he did and what he felt. He was a social being through and through, he lived his life with others, even when he was on his own. For that reason Geir needed Christina a lot more than she needed him. She could live a whole life alone if she had to, that was my assumption. He, however, could not; without the constant emotional exchange that went on between his self and the social world, he would perish. He needed the outer world, she did not; she had all she needed inside herself. She was a person who felt a strong sense of duty, she did what was asked of her; he was not, he did what he wanted. I, too, felt a strong sense of duty, that was what the outer world basically was for me, obligation, whereas my inner world to a much greater extent was freedom. Only during the past few years had I begun to understand that retreating into the self was perilous, something that removed me from life. And only during the past few years had I begun to understand that it was something I shared with my father. He was a fundamentally lonely person when I was growing up, in the way he kept to himself in the house, shutting himself away in his own little studio in the basement, and in the fact that he had no friends. The social world was a game he mastered but took no part in; perhaps he found nothing of value in it, nor, I suspect, in anything else. The things that make a difference, those that are replete with meaning and significance, were, I think, wholly absent from his life. He bore the mark of remoteness in everything he did, and the only thing which countered that were the upsurges of rage and resentment that would come over him, which so agonizingly brought him close to me, physically and mentally, and which, one could imagine, to him had the very purpose of keeping everything at bay, maintaining remoteness.

In a diary we found among his things after he died, he wrote about "the solitary individual." He wrote that he could tell the solitary individual apart from others, and it would seem he counted himself as one. He wrote, too, about conventions in more southern cultures, which were more inclusive and social than the Scandinavian, and it was impossible to read this as an indication of anything other than that he longed for such a life. The fact that he started drinking must have had something to do with that. Freedom, independence, community. The most radical difference in his lifestyle before and after he left our family, besides his alcohol consumption, was social contact, all the new people who suddenly came into his life. It was a new beginning, one last try, but the alcohol was not only a blessing, a bestower of grace, because soon he felt the desire for it when he got out of bed, or rather not desire, it was a need, he was compelled by it. On weekends he drank from the time he got up until he went to bed, during the week he managed to keep more of a grip to begin with, refraining from alcohol in the mornings, popping home at the lunch break to drink a bit, then drinking all evening, gradually it became harder and harder to resist, and eventually he gave in to it completely and no longer cared. But it started down there in his studio, the urge he felt to be alone, to keep the nearness of the world at bay, so impossible to reconcile with his longing for the social world, which could not be admitted or even acknowledged, not until the very end, when everything was already gone. He was trapped, increasingly confined, and he lost everything, due also to an outwardly directed aggression and destructiveness, as I understand it, which eventually he turned inward, and that was his decline, totally removed from society, back in the house where it all began, alone with his mother, in a steady flow of alcohol. The priest who held the funeral service said something I'll always remember. One must fasten one's gaze, he said. One must fasten one's gaze.

One must fasten one's gaze.

He could have said the little things are important; but he didn't. He could have said that loving thy neighbor is most important of all; but he didn't. Nor did he say what that gaze must be fastened upon. All he said was that it must be fastened.

It made sense to me then, as we sat in the chapel and wept that morning, his body lying there in its coffin a few meters away, and it makes sense to me today, as I sit here writing these words. I know what it means to see something without fastening one's gaze. Everything is there, the houses, the trees, the cars, the people, the sky, the earth, and yet something is missing because their being there means nothing. It could just as well be something else that was there or nothing at all. This is what the meaningless world looks like. And we can inhabit the meaningless world quite adequately, it being a simple matter of endurance, and indeed we do so if we must. It can be beautiful, though we may wonder in relation to what, it being all that we have, without such a thought making any difference, without it really bothering us. We have not fastened our gaze, we have not connected ourselves with the world, and could just as well, taking things to their logical conclusion, depart from it. The connections that hold us back, which cause us to thrash in our chains, as it were, have to do with expectations and obligation, with what the world asks of us, and sooner or later we come to a point where we realize the imbalance of our honoring the world's demands while the world fails to honor ours. At that point we become free, we can do as we please, but what has made us free, the meaninglessness of the world, also deprives that freedom of its meaning.

But if the world is meaningless, what good does it do to fasten our gaze on it? What kind of foolish middle-class delusion is that?

The question is how we define meaning. If we take the challenge of fastening our gaze seriously, it must be the case that it is not the object itself that is important, nor the person, in fact it can be any object or any person, in any place, at any time. The important thing is the eye, not what it sees: the link between the person seeing and what they see, regardless of what that might be. This is so because nothing means anything on its own. Only when an object is seen does it become. All meaning comes from the eye seeing. Meaning is not a property of the world, but something we attach to the world. The eye internalizes the extrinsic, but since the extrinsic remains so to the eye, something outside the self, it often believes that the meaning it sees belongs to the object or the phenomenon, which it then denounces, elevates, or remains indifferent to without understanding that what it denounces, elevates, or remains indifferent to is something within itself. It is by way of this internalization of the world that meaning becomes possible. All significance arises in the eye that sees, all meaning in the heart. Attaching meaning to the world is peculiar only to man, we are the givers of meaning, and this is not only our own responsibility but also our obligation. My father failed to live up to his obligation and he fell. It was not a punishment, but a consequence. That's pretty much how I look at it today, thirteen years after he died. I believe the priest was right, it really is all about fastening one's gaze, but I believe, too, that such a plea is related to the similar plea that calls on us to be good. No one disagrees about this, though for many it remains unattainable, related to the equally utopian though more popular call underlying so much in our society that tells us we must be rich. Certainly. It's easy to be rich if you've got lots of money, and being good is easy enough for those who are whole, but for those who are not whole, good isn't even within their horizon; indeed, perhaps no horizon exists for such people, no up, no down, no good, no bad, only anger or pain or loathing, because something inside them is broken, truly fucked up, and they are so deeply entangled in all sorts of unmanageable emotions, struggling for life with their backs to the wall, unless they've resigned themselves and given up completely. So many struggle for life, so many give up, and the rest, who know nothing of such pain or anger, watch TV in the cozy warmth of their own goodness. When I think about that, about what we have made of the world, a single great living room in which we sit and stare at what other people are doing, I think of what Dad once said, spitting sarcasm, as we sat outside at the barbecue, he, Mom, and me, the very incarnation of family happiness and *hygge*: "Now we're living the life, aren't we, eh!" And when I think about that, I think to myself that he did the right thing. To hell with meaning, to hell with everything, I'm going to drink until I drop. Drink myself into a stupor, drink myself into darkness, drink myself into the empty void, for desperate diseases need desperate remedies. I drink and I fall, I fall and I drink. Everything stinks, everything is shit, people are morons, to hell with them, I'll drink myself stupid, stupider than them. People are small, but I'll drink myself smaller. Because when I drink, as I shrink and become smaller and smaller, my shadow on the wall gets bigger and bigger, until the moment I die, slumped there in the chair with my nose broken and blood on my face and shirt, and from then on I will be nobody and my shadow will be everything.

My father failed to fasten his gaze, and he was not a good man. But he was his own person, and if he'd wanted to, wanted to fasten his gaze and be good, I think he could have done so. Something inside him was broken right from the start. To me it doesn't matter: he was the way he was. I've never been able to see my father as a person in his own right, the way I see myself, he exists only by virtue of his relationship to me, as my father, and his actions are mysterious to me and yet sovereign. Whether he suffered or not isn't something I wonder about. My father was a king without a country, and who cares for a king to suffer? That he died a clown, his nose reddened by blood, in his mother's armchair, changes nothing. To me, he will be king until the day I die. He comes to me still in dreams, in all his former splendor, the terrible ruler of the basement, for insights are worthless to the subconscious; it's like one of those boxes filled with crushed ice in which they transport living hearts, kidneys, lungs, livers, from the hospital where the donor died to the one where the living body waits. In this box, from which dreams rise in the night, dead emotions live on outside the body in which they once grew, and there among them my father still reigns.

The relationship between parents and children is a bit like that between customs officers and airline passengers; the customs officers watch the passengers through a window as they come through arrivals and can study everything they do, while the passengers, glancing at the same window from the other side, see only themselves. A child can learn nothing from his parents; the best he can hope for is not to repeat their mistakes. Dad wrote in his diary that he had been beaten as a child, and now he was a father who beat his own children. More than any other, such a statement stands as an argument against the idea that humans are rational beings. He experienced the pain and humiliation of being beaten at home, so why did he pass that pain and humiliation on? Perhaps the very ability to empathize, the ability to recognize that others feel the same as oneself and that those feelings can be just as important and may be taken as seriously as one's own, gets beaten away. To begin with we are near the world, I believe, but if our trust is broken we seek refuge deep within ourselves, cut off from what goes on outside, and the remoteness thereby established is then so very, very difficult to surmount. But a connection of that nature, between abuse in childhood and remoteness from the world in the later personality, only seems obvious in a system in which the rules of reasoning alone are valid, not in reality, which is quite differently open and oblivious to logic. My own aversion to intimacy and all outbursts of emotion, and the fact that all the relationships I've been involved in have sooner or later seen me occupy the middle ground of detachment and levelheadedness, has little to do with that aversion being in any way metaphorical, a symptom of a relationship to a father or a mother having broken down. No, my aversion to intimacy and outbursts of emotion is due to my actually being averse to intimacy and outbursts of emotion, I can't stand them, don't want to be anywhere near them, and the remoteness I crave in such instances is a blessing, occasionally even the highest conceivable blessing. Sexual desire is the only thing that displaces that need for boundaries and distance, only in that desire am I able to surmount my fear of intimacy and need for remoteness and thereby be close to another person. At the same time, and this seems fairly obvious, that fear of intimacy rears up again, doubly potent, in that the person this sexual desire is meant to overcome my remoteness to is the person to whom I am nearest, with whom I share my life, since then there is no longer any remoteness and sex then becomes infused with resistance. Socially I can overcome my remoteness to others when drunk, then it goes away, but in no other circumstances. A hug is anathema to me, a pat on the shoulder or back a threat. But in such cases it is not remoteness that is the problem, and lack of empathy is not a defect, the problem is the intimacy; I genuinely cannot deal with it, and the same goes for people's empathy. Why can't they just stay away and leave me alone, I think to myself. Is that too much to ask? The loneliness Dad wrote about is not something I know. As such, I am more broken than he, in that I entertain no expectations of interpersonal closeness and empathy, this not being something I crave, which, I suppose, makes it easier for me than it was for him, and less likely that I will end up following in his footsteps and drinking myself into the grave. Why on earth would I drink if I had all my time to myself?

Swallows flitted back and forth high up in the sky. I knew it was a sign about the weather, but that was all. Either it would be fine when the swallows flew high, or else it would rain. That much I could work out. I knew, too, that they were flying that high because that was where the insects were. But had the insects sought such heights because there was an area of low pressure or an area of high pressure on its way? And what did they actually do up there?

"How's the novel coming along, Karl Ove?" Christina asked. "Or maybe it's finished?"

"Pretty much," I said. "I just need to change some names."

"And then write four more," said Geir.

"Some minor complications have come up," I said, looking across at her. "I don't know if Geir said anything?"

"He has mentioned something about a relative not wanting it published. Is that it?"

"Yes. He keeps sending e-mails to the publisher, threatening to go to court and the newspapers. He's got the idea my mother's behind it all and made me write the book to get back at my father's family for him having left her."

She smiled gently and put her glass down on the table, shoving a plate aside to make room for its foot, which partially vanished from sight beneath the slightly elevated rim of the plate, whereas the slender stem that connected it to the bowl of the glass was a thin column of light in the sun.

"They can't be taking it seriously then?"

"No, not that. That's just a kind of background theory, it's not the main issue. The main issue is he finds the novel libelous. He says it's a pack of lies, that none of it's true."

"He's pissed off," said Geir.

"Yes, he is," I said.

At the other end the door opened again. Linda came out and, after closing the door behind her, stood for a second, shielding her eyes with her hand as she peered toward us. She was wearing a blue-and-white-striped sweater and dark blue shorts; with the wooden decking and her saluting gesture it made her seem quite nautical. I smiled.

"Is there a chance he can actually stop the book?" Christina asked.

"I don't think so," I said. "He might give it a try, I don't know." Linda stood beside us.

"This is looking nice," she said, and pulled out a chair at the opposite side of the table from me.

"Why don't we get started?" she said. "Just dig in."

"Thanks," said Christina. "It looks delicious."

"Come on," I said. "It's prawns."

"I haven't had prawns all summer," said Christina. "We usually do."

She laughed and looked up at Geir. "We have them at your dad's."

"We do," said Geir. "They like their prawns down there."

"Up," I said. "You're in the south now, remember."

"Were you talking about your book?" asked Linda.

Christina grabbed a couple of prawns and put them on her plate. The shells were so slippery and frictionless they slid on the smooth surface, and one of them ended up with its curling tail hanging over the opposite side from where she'd put it. Geir took a piece of bread, glanced around for the butter, located it, and picked it up. I lifted the bottle of wine and poured some into Linda's glass, nodding in reply.

"It's awful, really," I said.

"Thanks," she said.

"Weren't you expecting it?" Christina asked.

I shook my head, dropped a piece of bread onto my plate, and took a sip of wine while I waited for Geir and the butter.

"No," I said. "Nothing even close. I thought maybe he might be a bit peeved, but I hadn't anticipated anything like this. I've been really naïve, as it turns out. I thought I was writing about stuff that happened, and I hadn't imagined people could object. I realized it might annoy a few people, I was prepared for that, and maybe they'd want their name taken out, but I never envisaged anyone would want to stop it. Or get so ridiculously worked up."

"I've read the e-mails," said Linda to Christina. "He comes across like a madman. He scares the life out of me, anyway."

"He's not dangerous," said Geir. "If he was dangerous he'd have tossed an ax in the trunk and driven down here long before now."

"Don't say things like that!" said Linda.

"The worst thing, though, is that he's saying what I've written isn't true. That things didn't happen the way I describe them. Not just that it's innacurate or whatever, but that I'm lying. He says he can prove it."

Geir took a handful of prawns and dropped them onto his plate. I picked up the butter dish and put it down in front of me, drawing the knife toward me across the dark yellow surface which by now had been softened by the sun, then spreading the small curl that had gathered on the flat of its blade over the bread. The crusts were brown, verging on black, quite smooth on top, with a powdering of flour here and there, though porous in the cross section, tightly enclosing the soft white substance of the bread itself. I picked up the slice so as to find a better angle with the knife, whose remaining deposits of butter I wanted to spread onto the bread, just as one of the hotel's three external elevators began to glide upward through its transparent tube taking it to the very top of the building. Christina sat leaning forward, as if absorbed in some piece of sewing, shelling her prawns. I knew the feeling of tiny, delicate prawn eggs on one's fingers, they had their own very particular consistency, not unlike wet sand, and quite as hard to brush away, only a bit stickier. Linda, who as yet didn't seem to be ready to concentrate on the meal, as if she'd decided to rest for a moment on its outskirts, perhaps still with the rumpus of headstrong children whirling about inside her, raised her glass.

"*Skål*, and welcome!" she said.

"*Skål*," said Geir.

"Thanks for having us," said Christina.

We clinked our glasses and drank. I put my glass down and made sure to make eye contact with the others, as I had learned was customary only after arriving in Sweden seven years previously, an insight that was accompanied by the realization that, in all the years before that, people had sought eye contact with each other during every toast, apart from me, who had sat there completely oblivious, my ignorance exposed on every occasion without my even knowing.

"I don't want to spoil the evening going on about my uncle," I said, and noticed that the elevator had now stopped, the doors then slid aside, and a fat man and a slightly thinner woman got in at the same moment as one of the other elevators began to ascend. "But just to finish up what I was saying, about him claiming he can prove I'm lying."

I took a fistful of prawns and dropped them next to the bread, then picked one up between my fingers, pinching my thumb and index finger together at the seam of the head and body, and removed the head.

"It was as if suddenly I no longer knew what was true and what wasn't. It was really unpleasant – is really unpleasant. We're talking about things I've lived through. All of a sudden I start wondering if I'm just making them up. Do you know what I mean?"

She nodded. I pinched the shell that covered the belly of the prawn, bulging with its roe, most of which I managed to squeeze onto the edge of my plate before gripping the top of the shell and removing it with a swift upward movement, the way you might lift up a visor and put it to one side.

"The only thing I'm completely sure of is that my dad drank himself to death. If I'd written it like that, it wouldn't have mattered. As a simple fact, I mean. But I've gone into detail in describing the place where it happened. That was his childhood home. I've written about my grandmother, right down to the smallest detail, and she was his mother. He grew up in those rooms. Of course it's an infringement, because it's a private space. His space. And there I am, turning up for a few days, then writing an entire novel about it. A novel that might even be lies. Or a distorted truth. I can't trust myself. I don't know what's true and what isn't. And now I'm doing this to his brother. I've always looked up to him, he's always been an important person in my life, a representative of something."

I passed my thumb over the underside of the little grub-like scrap of prawn meat to remove the few remaining specks of roe, then placed it on my bread, at the very corner, before beginning the same process all over again with a new prawn.

"That's what makes it all so agonizing. Because everything he says resonates against something I carry inside me. It's already there. And when it comes from outside, it just consumes me."

"What's happening in purely practical terms, then?" Linda asked. "You're changing all the names, of course. But is there anything else you have to do?"

"No."

"I don't even think you should change the names," said Geir. "Why should you?"

"You'd understand if you thought about it," I said. "It's his name. I've no right to exploit it for my own purposes."

"Okay, so maybe in his case," Geir replied. "Though basically I think you should keep them all. But what about your dad's name? And your grandmother's? That's not okay."

"That's as far as I can go," I said, placing the second prawn next to the first. The transformation from living creature to waste was remarkable, the little pile of shells, heads, roe, and the antenna-like tentacles that lay next to the fine and delicious shellfish.

"Let's say it goes to court, then," said Geir. "Where's the case against you? That you wrote about your dad? Why should he be protected? Why should his name be kept untarnished? What if an incest victim wrote a book about his dad, would the court be supposed to stop them publishing because the dad's brother doesn't want his name dragged through the mud? As if it wasn't already sullied by what he did?"

"But that's a criminal matter," I said. "That's different."

"True. But he still did what he did to you. Are you supposed to keep quiet just because it can rub off on your uncle, because they were related? That's absurd. What's worse, the action or the description of the action? Is the description of the action an offense but not the action itself?"

"I don't think that's what Karl Ove means," said Christina. "I think it's the description of the space it took place in that's causing the offense. The fact that your door's being opened and everyone can look in."

"That can't explain why he's so angry," said Linda. "There must be something else besides."

"Why does he think your mother is behind it all?" Christina asked. Her bread was almost covered by pale fleshy prawns with their streaks of red. They lay there on the thin layer of butter, like people on a beach seen from a plane preparing to land, I thought to myself.

"I've no idea," I said. "But he was still a child when Mom and Dad got together. Ten years old, something like that. His big brother got married and moved away. That must be quite an upheaval for a boy that age. Who was she to him? Presumably the same person she was to his parents. My guess is they didn't want Dad to marry her, that they didn't think she was good enough, or right for him. At any rate, they didn't go to their wedding. That's a statement. I remember Dad making an issue of it when he married for the second time and they still didn't go. It was obviously something that had affected him. It meant a lot. Gunnar must still carry all that with him, their rejection, and the reason for it. Maybe not in the form of arguments or thoughts as such, but emotionally, and thereby as a kind of truth: that's how she was. Then after they got married and had children they must have been able to tell that Dad wasn't happy. That's certainly something

411

I can see now, looking back. And because he was theirs and came from them, the obvious thing for them to think must have been that it was her fault."

"So he lost a brother?" said Linda.

"Yes," I said, placing another prawn on my bread, which would soon be covered. My mouth was watering and I removed the shell as quickly as I could. "And then he lost him again when he started drinking."

"And a third time with you writing about him."

"I hadn't thought about it like that," I said. "But you're right. I've taken him away from him, and now I'm saying he was mine, that he was like this and like that."

"Did they get along at all, your mom and your dad's parents?" Christina asked. She lifted her bread to her mouth and took a bite, and her movements were so small that for a moment there was something squirrel-like about her, but then, perhaps because I was looking at her, or perhaps because she felt some sudden twinge of happiness, she smiled and everything that was small dissolved.

I smiled too.

"Can I just ask you something?" Linda intervened.

Christina nodded.

"How come you're not having any wine?"

Christina laughed and put her hand in front of her mouth. Geir grinned, the biggest smile he had. And Linda smiled too.

"We're expecting," said Christina.

"I knew you were!" said Linda.

"Seriously?" I said, looking across at Geir. "You never said!"

"We're saying it now."

"I can tell, too," said Linda. "There's a bulge."

Christina looked down at her tummy and placed her hand on it. When she looked up again, her eyes were full of joy.

"When's it due?" asked Linda.

"Late December," Christina replied.

"That's fantastic," said Linda.

"Congratulations," I said, raising my glass.

"We were inspired by you two," said Geir. "When we were here New Year's Eve and saw John. The thought of having another little one like him. He was such a little bundle of happiness, reaching his hands out to us."

"It'll be good for Njaal," said Linda.

"Yes," said Christina. "It'll be great for him being a big brother."

"Have you told him yet?" said Linda.

Christina shook her head.

"We've told my parents. And Geir's dad."

"Have they found out if it's a boy or a girl yet?" Linda asked.

"No," said Christina. "We don't want to know either."

"We're keeping the excitement," said Geir.

"I can't get over you being here two days already and not saying a word," I said. "Or maybe I can, come to think of it. Do you remember me telling you we were having Heidi?"

Geir nodded.

"You were expecting Njaal, but you still didn't let on. Not for another two months, in fact."

"And?"

"That's far too disciplined for me. We could never keep anything like that secret. How long did it take before we told everyone we knew?" I said, looking across at Linda.

"Two days, maybe," she said.

"It's the Strays looking at the Hamsuns," said Geir.

"And you're the Strays, I take it?" I said.

"Of course," said Geir. "We look on everything you do with wide eyes. We're the ones with our house in order."

"I'm so pleased for you both!" said Linda, looking at Christina.

As I looked at her, the radiance inside her now visible in her eyes, everything fell into place; of course, that was it! She had been withdrawn, but not like she had turned herself away from the world, from something in it she didn't want, more as if there was something good there inside her.

"We've even got the names ready," said Geir, his eyes looking into Christina's.

"Are you sure you're ready to divulge, after six months?" I said.

"If it's a girl, she's going to be called Frøydis," said Geir. "And if it's a boy, he'll be called Gisle."

As we sat there, on our narrow ledge above the city, eating and drinking, the sun gradually sank in the sky, redder and redder, the darkness rising and enclosing us imperceptibly from the streets, where the air seemed to become grainier, the colors of everything there, the cars, the people, the buildings, fading slowly into gray. We talked about the baby they were expecting, we talked about the children we had, we talked about what were now already the old days, the time we lived in Stockholm, and we talked about Gunnar and his e-mails. I was hesitant about the latter, but the unease I felt about the whole situation had to be calmed, and the only way I knew of doing that was by talking about it. After the wine had been drunk and the food eaten up, Linda and I cleared the table and took the things into the kitchen. I put the coffee on and got the ice cream out of the freezer.

"What a lovely evening," said Linda.

"Yes," I said.

"Are you all right?" she asked.

"Yes, fine," I said. "Well, sort of. But it's nice to have company."

I put my arms around her. We stood there for a moment, then she went to get the lantern she had once given me as a birthday present, an old-fashioned kind made of metal and with little windows of glass, inside which a fat candle can burn, or in this case, because we'd run out of candles, an array of tea lights.

I stood in the living room and watched her go past with the lantern glowing in her hand in the dim light. Then I carried the ice cream out, and the fruit, the wafers, and the coffee, all on a tray, together with the cups, plates, and spoons.

The darkness in August is the finest darkness of all. It lacks the luminous transparency of June's, the sheer ripeness of its potentialities, yet is quite unlike the impenetrable depths of autumn's or winter's darkness. What was with us before and now is gone, spring and summer, lingers on in August's darkness, whereas what is to come, autumn and winter, is a time into which we can only peer, a time of which we are not yet a part.

The light of the lantern flickered on the table, shimmering in our faces and eyes. The darkness swelled, and the streets below were quiet. The elevators went up and down, the traffic lights continued to change, and now and then people came walking from the pedestrian street, ambling families or young people on their way out, perhaps to a park where they would sit and drink, or to some outdoor café. There was a force field of excitement about them, or perhaps it was me, because what they were doing was so familiar to me, and I could still feel the pull, to be out on the town with the feeling that tonight anything at all could happen.

But that feeling also belonged to the darkness of August, I thought to myself. In that darkness, too, there was promise and expectation. Something closes, something else opens. Life is there for the living. Through autumn and winter, spring and summer, fuller with every turn. Wasn't that what was happening? Never had the darkness of August felt more replete than now.

Replete with what?

The beauty of time passing.

After we finished dessert and I had fetched the cognac and drunk a glass of it, I went inside to piss. On the way, I poked my head around the door of the children's room where they lay sighing like little animals in their own little worlds. The voices of the others drifted in from the balcony, I heard Linda's voice, and her laughter, too, and I thought about what it must be like to be a child and fall asleep to the sounds made by one's parents. The sounds of life outside themselves. I pissed, and it felt good. I looked at myself in the mirror as I washed my hands. The deep furrows in my brow, the lines that ran down my cheeks, the wrinkles around my eyes, none had been there when Vanja was born. But I felt the way I had always felt, the same now as when I was twenty, and perhaps that was the reason that what I saw in the mirror was not a forty-year-old man, though my age was clear and conspicuous, but myself, Karl Ove.

I dried my hands on the towel, went into the bedroom, and opened my e-mails, as always with my heart pounding and gripped by an intense feeling of dread.

There was a message from Amazon, and one from Tonje.

I opened Tonje's.

Dear Karl Ove,

I'm sorry I haven't sent word before now. Your assumptions are quite right. I had a pounding headache and a nerve in my eyelid twitched for three days while I read your novel. Since then I've tried to figure out where that reaction came from. To begin with it was the fear of being held up in full view. Gradually, the reading itself became a burden. All the little stories I'd forgotten about suddenly came to life again, as you did too, the person you once were to me.

After having read it I found I could relax a bit more. Tore is right, I am a princess, if only in the book. But I'd like to try to see it in terms of principle, if I can. After all, I've no idea what you're saying about me in Book 5. And I can't just say everything's fine as long as you stick to writing nicely about me. So I've decided not to intervene in any way. It's your project. Use my full name by all means, all or nothing. I don't feel I can give you any viewpoints on the book, I'm sure you understand that. But it touched my heart to read it. Dearest, dearest Karl Ove.

All my best,
Tonje

My relief as I read her message was so immense, and the last line so unexpectedly warm and loving, that tears welled in my eyes. I closed the message and sat for a moment in front of the computer. I wanted the emotions to subside a bit before going back out to the others. The mere fact that I'd received an e-mail from Tonje felt like I was deceiving Linda. As if I had a secret life outside the family. But I did, too, I'd had a life before them, and though I wasn't in the habit of thinking about it, I certainly had while I'd been writing the first book. I had resurrected the life I once led, I had resurrected all the people I knew and was connected to back then, resurrected them in my mind, and with the past come to life in that way, I had gone about among them, my family, without saying a word about it, without letting on in the slightest, and yet there it was in their midst.

After maybe ten minutes I got to my feet and went back. I would have to send Tonje's e-mail to the publishers, partly because they needed to be sure of everyone's response now that the fuss concerning the manuscript had spiraled the way it had, and partly because I wanted them to see that I wasn't totally unreliable, because although Gunnar's letters were out of control I couldn't help but assume that the publishers were thinking there was never smoke without fire and that there was most likely at least a grain of truth in Gunnar's accusations. I was a writer, I made a living out of making things up, and most likely, so I imagined them thinking, Gunnar's reaction to my description of those real-life circumstances was tainted by my novelist's temperament, which tended toward exaggeration, perhaps even strongly so. I especially suspected Geir Berdahl of such thoughts. The accountant's veracity versus the writer's unreliability. That Tonje had reacted the way she had, and had sufficient faith in me to give me free rein as to how she and our relationship would be described in the books that followed, was no proof of anything, but it was at least a different take.

Still, it would have to wait until tomorrow. Now I was going

417

to sit out in the dark with Linda, Christina, and Geir, illuminated by the light of the lantern, drinking cognac and talking about whatever subject happened to crop up.

When I returned to them Linda was telling a story. It was about the first summer after we moved here. The apartment, the balcony, the city, all had been new to us. Nearly every evening we sat out here after the children had been put to bed. The summer had no end; well into September we were still sitting outside in the evenings. We'd bought a baby alarm, the transmitter was in the children's room, the receiver on the table between us. Whenever they stirred, whenever they made a sound, the receiver came on and we could hear it. One evening it crackled with the sound of a child crying. I went into their room, but whoever it was, Vanja or Heidi, must have settled again right away, because when I came in they were fast asleep. I went back outside, only for it to start again. This time Linda went in. The same thing happened: they were asleep. It was creepy, the sound of a child crying, coming to us through the hiss and crackle of the receiver, a small, distant voice. I found myself thinking it was like a dead child crying from the afterlife, its sound waves picked up by the transmitter. I didn't mention the thought, Linda was already beside herself, she bustled back to the children again, this time with receiver in hand so she could see with her own eyes that the crying she was hearing wasn't from one of her own. While she was away I tried to figure out what was going on. We were in the middle of a city, with hundreds of people in our immediate vicinity, and somebody among them clearly had the same make of baby alarm as us.

I told Linda when she got back. It calmed her down. But then a moment later she looked at me and said, But there's no one taking care of that child.

As she told the story, the creepiness we had both felt at the time was gone. It had become a story. But Linda had just written a short story about that very incident. In it the creepiness was intact, perhaps even more intensely. That was how she was, it was her talent, she could distill life down to points of extreme intensity and densely concentrated meaning. I often felt tears come to my eyes when I read the things she wrote, and this particular story was no exception because the person she was so immediately became apparent to me.

"We bought that baby alarm before we went to Gotland," I said. "Do you remember? Our trip there?"

"Yes," she said. "I remember you used to run to the shop with your backpack on to get breakfast in the mornings."

"Run?" said Geir. "How far?"

"Ten kilometers," I said. "For a few months there I was in superb shape. Only I didn't realize. Everything's relative. You manage one thing, but there's always something else you can't. So I focused on that."

"Vacationing with kids and no car, it's a genre on its own," said Linda.

"A sonnet of life with small children," I said. "It doesn't get much harder than that."

"It was lovely, though," she said. "I was pregnant with Heidi. And Vanja was so little! To us she was a big girl. But she was just a tiny tot!"

"She was," I said. "It's horrendous how time flies! It feels like such a long time ago, back in my boyhood almost."

We spent two weeks there in a rented house on the edge of the woods, and in the middle of those woods, which reminded me in every respect of the woods at Hove, pine trees that went all the way down to the shore, in the middle of those woods were these peculiar white rock formations they call *raukar*. Oh, what an exhilarating sight they were! Every afternoon, while Linda and Vanja were at the house, I would run there to look at them. Like statues they stood, tall as a man, white among the straight, upright pine trees. There was something totem-like about them, and the associations they had for me were of indigenous peoples and a world without cars, without asphalt, without concrete, without glass, without machines. A world consisting only of what grew and people living among it. I ran there and it filled me with emotions, and then I ran back to my little family.

Now it was no longer something that had just happened, but something that had happened a long time ago, the same way as this, this evening on the balcony, years from now will be something I look back on, removed from the life I will be living then. A memory is a ledge on the mountainside of the mind; there we are, drinking and chatting, and on the ledge below us my dad sits in his chair, dead, his face smeared with blood. And on a ledge below him we are sitting in a rest stop somewhere in the Agder region, Mom, Dad, Yngve, and I, we've been picking berries all morning, now we're eating our picnic, and next to us is a river, its waters green and white and icy cold, descended from the high fells to our rear, and on the other side, at the edge of the road, coated with dust, stands our red Opel Kadett.

But as yet it was not a memory, not some constituent of the past, but still simply the point to which we had come, an evening that was now drawing to an end.

"You must be tired," said Linda to Christina, who nodded, yes, she was, and with those words it was over, for we were all tired and the children would be waking up at five o'clock in the worst case, half past five at best, so the time had come to clear the table, load the dishwasher, turn off the lights, brush our teeth, and go to bed.

I lay on my back under the covers, waiting for Linda to come in from the bathroom. When she did, and lowered herself into the bed, as if into water it seemed to me, I put my arms around her and held her tight, feeling her body against mine, her warmth, sensing her smell.

"I love you," I said. And for some strange reason I cried as I spoke the words. But I did so silently, my eyes simply filling with tears, and she knew nothing of it.

The next day we went to the beach. Linda made meatballs and buttered some bread, I made an omelette and filled a thermos with coffee and another with squash, we put it all in a cooler, packed a big blanket, towels, and bathing suits, and the girls' inflatable armbands that were so very important, helped them into their summer dresses and sandals, gave them each a cap to put on, rubbed their sunscreen in, put John in the stroller, and set off. Until that summer Ribersborg had been synonymous with the beach for us, but there was no shade there anywhere, and Linda – who was sensitive to the sun and hid herself under wide-brimmed hats and behind sunglasses all summer, as well as always choosing the shady side of the street and always sitting under the parasols if we were out at a café, unlike me who couldn't get enough of the sun – had taken us all to the beach at Sibbarp instead one day when the summer began, because although it was quite a bit farther there were trees there that grew right down to the beach, and pools of deepest shadow under their leafy crowns, and since then we'd always gone there whenever we wanted to swim. Sibbarp was too far to walk, we had to take the bus from Bergsgatan by the Konserthuset; it took just under half an hour to get there. Njaal, Heidi, and Vanja went first, then came Linda with the cooler bag slung over her shoulder, Christina with a backpack on her back, and Geir carrying a tote bag in his hand, while I brought up the rear, pushing John in his stroller with a big bag full of clutter. It was hot and there was no shade at the bus stop, so it was a relief when the bus came after ten minutes. It was almost full. Geir and Christina found seats at the front, Christina sat with Njaal on her knee, while Vanja and Heidi found two next to each other farther back after the open area in the middle of the bus, and Linda and I sat behind them, Linda with John on her lap. We passed through the city, skirting the hospital and the concourse area on the other side of the Pildammsparken, where the old and particularly striking sports stadium was, shaped like an elongated bowl or a flat-bottomed boat, built in the days of functionalism, unfortunately rather unsuited to football because of its running track and the insufficient incline of its stands, which was why a new stadium had been built next to it. In the same area was the Baltiska Hallen, as well as another big indoor arena with artificial turf. I'd been there a lot the first winter we lived in Malmö, there were some journalists who met a couple of afternoons a week to kick a ball around there and they'd let me join in.

I wiped the sweat from my forehead and realized we were crossing Bellevuevägen. I was so unfamiliar with the city I didn't even know yet how the various districts were connected. We must be near the subdivision garden, I thought to myself. The very thought of the place plunged me into darkness. I looked at Linda and John. His face was sweaty, his eyes kept opening and shutting like the mouths of a pair of expiring fish. In a few seconds he would no longer be able to resist the compelling onslaught of sleep, so overpowering at that age.

Vanja twisted around and found my gaze and asked when we'd be there. A few minutes yet, I said. How long is a minute, she wanted to know. Sixty seconds, I said. How long is a second, she wanted to know. From now until now, I said. That wasn't long, she said. Don't start counting, I said. She looked at me. Why not? she asked. I shrugged. You can if you want, I said. She began to count. When she got to thirty-eleven I corrected her. We came through the center of Limhamn, the main street was full of cars, the sidewalks on both sides filled with milling people. What comes after thirty-nine, Daddy? said Vanja. Forty, I said, turning my head to Linda. Is he asleep? I asked. She nodded. We carried on along the shoreline and soon wide-open areas of green appeared, dotted here and there with clusters of darker deciduous trees, and a moment later the bus swung into its terminus. Linda carried John to his stroller, he woke up and started wailing, I lifted the stroller out, she tried to get him into it, he kicked and struggled, I took over, and he calmed down after twenty seconds or so and I managed to get his legs into the stroller and was able to pick up the bag and follow the others while he laid his head back and immediately fell asleep again. I broke into a trot and caught up with Linda. Vanja, Heidi, and Njaal walked in front of us, scurrying along like three little dogs. The harbor was packed with small boats, and there were lots of people on and around the jetty. The grass we crossed was popular too, people were strolling, some were playing games, I heard the buzz of a radio-controlled plane, others were sitting around on blankets. The air was teeming with ladybugs, a couple landed on my white T-shirt and I flicked them away. We crossed the open lawns, passed the kiosk, and followed the gravel path that led off along the inside of the beach to the northern end where the trees were. We went past a woman in a bathing suit, she walked in that cautious way you do when you're not used to having bare legs, and three young men, perhaps twenty years old, visibly wearing underpants under their low-slung bathing shorts. Linda was walking beside Christina now, the children were already way up ahead, running to see who would get there first. Geir stopped and I came up to him.

"Did you see her?" he said.

"Who?" I said.

"That woman in the bathing suit. It was all wet around her breasts. Soaking wet. But dry everywhere else. So she hadn't been swimming. It was milk. Breast milk."

"I didn't notice," I said.

Something kept crunching under my feet and I stopped to see what it was. Ladybugs. They were all over the ground. Dead ladybugs on the path and on the grass. The air was alive with them. I walked over to the trees, spread the blanket out in the shade, and started helping Heidi with her bathing suit and her water wings while Linda got Vanja changed. John was fast asleep in the stroller, chin against his chest and hat over his eyes. Three ladybugs had settled on his T-shirt, one on the brim of his hat. I felt them crawling in my hair and shook my head.

"Do you want to go out and swim with them while I get things organized?" I said to Linda. She nodded and got changed while I turned to the picnic. The blanket was already covered in ladybugs. I looked up. Great swarms filled the air. I looked down at my chest, four more had landed there. I flicked them away, picked up the blanket and gave it a shake before spreading it out again and setting out the containers with the sandwiches, meatballs, salad, omelette, and olives.

"I've never seen so many ladybugs," I said.

Geir batted at the air. Christina walked to the shore holding Njaal's hand. Now that I knew, I could see she was pregnant. She flapped her free hand. Njaal copied her. Linda shook her hair. Heidi and Vanja stood hand in hand at the water's edge and stared out at the sea. The blanket was crawling with ladybugs again.

"We can't eat here," I said. "They're everywhere. Look at them," I said, indicating the swarms that seemed to be swirling all around.

"Maybe it's better over there," Geir said. "It's more exposed, so there'll be more wind."

We went over to where the grass came to an end, only to find the air just as thick and the ground covered with them.

"We might as well stay put," I said. "They're harmless enough."

Back in the shade I tried to ignore them as best I could. I lit a cigarette and poured myself a cup of coffee. Seconds later, a ladybug was floating in it. I picked it out, inhaled and blew a cloud of smoke out in front of me, wondering if ladybugs like mosquitoes would be repelled by cigarette smoke. Geir had gone down to the shore, now all five of them were there. Linda stepped cautiously out into the water with Heidi and Vanja on each side of her. They reached up to her hips. Her skin was white as marble. The air was alive with flitting black dots. They were settling on the containers, and on the blanket again. They crawled on my shoes, shorts, and T-shirt. It was creepy. Ladybugs were among the most appealing of insects. So delicate and flowerlike in their beauty, they were the very antithesis of the monstrous. Mosquitoes could occur in huge swarms and be everywhere, there was nothing unnatural about that, but with ladybugs there was something ominous about it, as if something had gone wrong, as if something that ought to have been closed had been opened, and as I looked out over the sound, where the gigantic structure of the Öresund Bridge rose up disconcertingly near us to the south and the contours of the Barsebäck nuclear power plant were visible to the north, the blue sky above the glittering blue sea teeming with tiny black dots I knew to be ladybugs, I thought to myself: this is how the world ends.

THE NAME AND
THE NUMBER

S ome months ago I received an anonymous threatening letter in the mail, it was written to my brother, so what I got was a copy, though my brother wasn't mentioned by his actual name but by our mother's maiden name. Yngve Hatløy, it said. The sender no longer considered him worthy of the name Knausgaard and had given him another name instead. I myself had been deprived of a name entirely, being mentioned throughout by my profession only, albeit sarcastically. "The storyteller," that was me.

The writer of this letter stated the following:

How bitter the thought that an abortion in 1964 could have given so many people a simpler life in 2010. We would have been spared the Hatløys. And your father would have been alive today.

Yngve was born in 1964. The contention that everything would have been better if Yngve had been aborted then, and that Dad would have still been alive if that had happened, was not only conveyed to Yngve. The writer also wrote to Yngve's daughter, a child. The book I have written is the reason we are no longer worthy of the Knausgaard name. I am not, my brother is not, our children are not.

Great is the power of the name.

The strange thing is that names have always been an issue in our family. When my father was young he experimented with different spellings of his name, writing his first name with an *i* or a *y*, an *å* or an *aa*. I've seen this in books and papers he left behind. Later, he took another surname and was known by it for the last ten years of his life. My mother took my father's surname when she married but subsequently reverted to her maiden name. So when I was eighteen both my mother and my father had different surnames to the one my brother and I shared.

When I began writing this novel I did so with the intention of writing about Dad, and since the nature of fiction is to make what applies to one person apply to all, in the sense that a certain dad becomes "Dad," a certain brother becomes "brother," and a certain mom "Mom," I used his own name. At first his original family name, then his assumed family name. After a time I sent the manuscript to those concerned. My father's family, represented by my father's brother, threatened to take me to court and stop the novel coming out if the names weren't changed. I did as they wanted, changing the names of my uncle, his family, and everyone else on my father's side. But I couldn't change the name of my father. If I called him, say, "Georg Martinsen," then it would no longer be my father I was writing about, the way he was to me, a body of flesh and blood that was also my own flesh and blood, because the name is the only element of reality that can exist unchanged in the novel, everything else is a reference to something, a house or a tree, not in themselves a house or a tree; only the proper name can be the same in the novel as in reality. I could change the names of everyone else, but not his. It was also because I was writing about myself and my own identity: who would I become if my father was someone called Georg Martinsen? What effect would that have on my own name and identity? So I refused. On the day of the publishing house's annual press conference I had met with the publishing director, Geir Berdahl; he had written a letter to my uncle and itemized all the changes we had made in the novel on his insistence. The final point stated that my father's name would not be used. The evening before, the culture editor at the *Bergens Tidende* had called Berdahl, apparently they knew each other from some earlier time, he had got wind of the issue and my uncle threatening to take the matter to court. I had been incautious and mentioned it in an e-mail to a person I knew well who was employed by that newspaper, who had then passed it on. This was the situation when Berdahl read his letter to me. Until then I had refused to give up my father's name. But at that point I felt I could stand firm no longer; on the other side of the door of the office in which we sat, the room was filling up with journalists, and I was so scared of the consequences of what I had written that it seemed to me the only possibility I had was to say okay, you can send the letter, I'll change my father's name.

But I could not change it. I could not call him by any other name. So I solved the problem by not using his name at all. Neither his first name nor his surname appears in the novel. In the novel he is a man without a name.

◆◆◆

When I see the names of those I grew up with, they bring back to life not only the entire landscape there, and all the days and evenings we spent running around in it, filled with autumn's heavy darkness or spring's gossamer light, but also the individuals they were. Geir Prestbakmo, Karl Martin Fredriksen, Dag Lothar Kanestrøm, Marianne Christensen, and, later, Per Sigurd Løyning, Arne Jørgen Strandli, Jan Vidar Josephsen, Hanne Arntsen. In each case the names represent them and the time in which I knew them, and form a kind of capsule in the mind in which all sorts of things, important and unimportant, are stored. But that is what their names are to me. To those people themselves the same names are perhaps something else entirely. Whenever they speak or write their names they are referring to themselves. This "self" is something apart from what everyone else sees when they present themselves, it is the inside of the seen, full of thoughts and emotions to which no one else has access, the inner life as it unfolds from birth until death.

A name is intimately connected with this secret and particular self; so entwined are the name and the individual's sense of identity, in fact, that one thinks of the name as belonging to the self, even if it was not given with that purpose in mind, there being no need for a person to refer to themselves by name in order to know who they are, but in order to represent what they are to others. Instead of saying "that little crybaby with the buck teeth" they said "Karl Ove." And since the proper name points both inward and outward at the same time, it is an exceptionally sensitive thing. There is a remnant of magical thought in the fact that the word is what it refers to, or may awaken it. I *am* my name, my name *is* me. If anyone abuses it, they abuse me. The most basic form of teasing among children is for the teasers to twist the name of their victim, knowing full well that doing so strikes at the very core of who they are. One of the biggest social blunders a person can commit is to admit to not knowing the name of the person they are talking to, for although one might be perfectly aware of who they are, and recognize their face, their dialect, their gestures and expressions, and can recall any number of situations one might have experienced together, it doesn't help; if you can't remember the name, you can't remember her, since without a name she is no one.

The vast majority of the people we see are nameless, all those sitting behind us on the bus or the subway train, those who pass us on the street or stand in line in front of us at the supermarket checkout. We know each has a name, because everyone has, we just don't know what it is. In the event that one of them becomes our friend, he or she is then moved from the nameless masses into the sphere of the named, by whom we are all most closely surrounded. Yet there is another sphere outside that one, comprising names known by everybody: the famous. We say of any member of this group that he or she is a name. Such a name cannot merely be taken, but is something bestowed, which can only happen by virtue of a person becoming particularly prominent in some way. Anyone who runs, cycles, or skis fast enough may thus be bestowed with a name, anyone who sings beautifully enough, or who is sufficiently good at playing the guitar, anyone excelling in their field, the history of ideas, for instance, and anyone graduating to any important position in society. Such a name does not primarily represent the person themselves, but rather their achievements or role. Yet as soon as a person's name has become public because of some achievement, curiosity is at once aroused as to what else that name represents: the private self. It is a characteristic of our time that public selves have increasingly come forward to present to us their private selves, which thereby have become public, too. This is not to say that we are witness to a degeneration of the public sphere, as is often suggested, but rather to a wholly necessary regulatory mechanism in any media society.

Apart from material necessities, the most important need of any human being is to be seen. Anyone who is not seen is no one. The worst punishment in old Nordic culture was to be proclaimed *fredløs*, which is to say cast out from society, forbidden to associate with others. If such an outcast ever showed themselves in public they would be shunned, perhaps even killed; the outcast was a nobody, and it meant nothing whether they lived or died; but why kill a person as long as they could merely be shunned? We strive to be seen. Yet to be seen can involve a number of things; in a peasant society, being seen would be something else entirely compared to a media society. Whoever is seen in a media society is seen by all. And when being seen means being seen by all, it gives rise to an impossible craving, since being seen by all is the preserve of the few. When the few display not only what makes them prominent and which is unreachable for the vast majority of us, in other words their public personalities, but also their private personalities, which are not unreachable but by contrast are an embodiment of the ordinary, the sphere in which all of us live, the public personality is then no longer unreachable, no longer merely an object of admiration and desire, but a person with whom we can identify, and the gap between ordinary private life, in which the name denotes the individual and nothing else, and public life, dissolves almost completely: essentially, they are just like us. We see ourselves in them, and this is another way of being seen. In this there is security, for while the desire to be seen is great in all of us, it is countered by an equal force pulling in the opposite direction, which is the desire to be like everyone else. To be like everyone else is to be one among the crowd, and to be one among the crowd is to be safe. As humans have experienced throughout their existence, in any flock facing danger the important thing is not to be seen, not to attract attention. To be seen is vital, but not to be seen is vital, too. Nothing feels more perilous to us than to be exposed to the attention and gaze of others. By opening up the private side of their name, the ordinariness shared by us all, a person becomes both a part of the community and one of the select few seen by all.

The notion that to be seen is to be seen by many, in the media, as a name with a particular aura, has become so prevalent that almost everyone I know has begun to treat their name as something that not only denotes who they are, replete with meaning beyond their control, but also as an advertisement of their own idea of who they are, setting up profiles on Facebook and furnishing their name with a certain air by inserting it in certain contexts, not unlike the way in which a brand is built up or a pop star constructed. To be surrounded by media doesn't just mean that we look at images of other people in other places and in that way keep ourselves abreast of what is going on in the world, it also has an effect on the way we see ourselves and seeps imperceptibly into our identities, which gradually recalibrate toward the expectation of an observing "everyone" or "all," eclipsing the particular gaze in the particular situation, where everything is tangible, with all the consequences that implies with respect to the image we hold of ourselves.

While the expectation of being seen by some specific other – the neighbors, for instance, or what Tor Jonsson called "the village beast" – may be shut out physically by lowering the blinds, or dealt with by going away, the expectation of the abstract other, the all of society, is impossible to eliminate, since it lives inside us and is something to which we continually relate even in our innermost dwelling spaces, which we furnish to satisfy that expectation, the kitchen, formerly a place in which to prepare and eat food, now being done up at huge expense to look like a showroom despite hardly ever being seen by others. This inner all, whose flame is kept alive by the presence of TV screens in every room and which ensures that we are always seen and are somehow held under our own surveillance, means also that we begin to resemble each other more, it being the same god to which we submit and to whose requirements we adapt ourselves in a system of social control far subtler than that imagined by Orwell in his famous dystopia.

The name has always occupied a space between the concrete and the abstract, the individual and the social, but when it begins to be shaped and charged with meaning in places removed from the physical world, in that way entering the world of fiction, albeit unseen by the majority, at the same time as this fictional world is expanding and taking up an ever greater part of our lives – the TV screens are now not only in our own rooms, but also on the walls of our trains and under the luggage bins of our planes, in the waiting rooms of our doctors' offices and the halls of our banks, even in the supermarkets, quite apart from our carrying them around in the form of laptop computers and cell phones, in such a way that we inhabit two realities, one abstract and image-based, in which all kinds of people and places present themselves before us with nothing in common but being somewhere other than where we are, and one concrete, physical, which is the one we move around in and are more palpably a part of – when we arrive at a point where everything is either fiction or seen as fiction, the job of the novelist can no longer be to write more fictions. That was the feeling I had: the world was vanishing because it was always somewhere else, and my life was vanishing because it, too, was always somewhere else. If I was to write a novel it would have to be about the real world the way it was, seen from the point of view of someone who was trapped inside it with his body, though not with his mind, which was trapped in something else, the powerful urge to rise out of such fusty triviality into the clear, piercing air of something immeasurably greater. Ascent was art, fiction, abstraction, ideology; confinement was in the world of things and bodies, the material soon-to-be-rotting universe all of us comprise. That was the idea, or the urge: reality. And the sign of such reality, its only transferrable component, was the name. Not as dream or image, but as the sign of the individual human. I was of course aware that the novel, being composed of signs, could not be reality itself, but merely invoke reality, and that the reality it invoked would be just as abstract as the one from which I was trying to escape; and at the same time I knew, too, that what the novel can do, and which perhaps is its most important property, is to penetrate our veils of habit and familiarity simply by describing things in a slightly different way, for example by being insistent with respect to some particular state of affairs, let's say describing a child's pacifier over a whole page, whereby the real child's pacifier would subsequently present itself differently, in that its pacifying – that aspect of it that makes us see only its function and not its form, which is quite sensuous in its combination of soft, droplet-shaped rubber with the hard plastic of the grip, this blend of nipple imitation and toy, created to satisfy the cravings of the child, who likes both to suck and to chew, and to look at and grasp objects with bright and simple colors and rounded forms – would thereby be modified, or by juxtaposing things not normally juxtaposed, since it was not reality that had vanished, but my attention toward it. I could not relinquish my grip on it, this was my intuition, or my explanation of the fundamental lack of meaning I felt in my life, and it may well have been just another explanation, another theory, in itself abstract, but it did not feel that way, and if there's something I've learned to trust over the course of the forty-two years I have lived, it is my feelings. In the novel I began to write, the authentic names were therefore the key. I was aware that a number of people could not be named, since they would not wish to be associated with the events I was going to describe, my uncle being one, and I had no problem at all giving up those names, although for a short time I resisted when one of them didn't want to be in the book in any way at all, not even under another name, because at that point I had no idea how the novel was going to be received, viewing it simply as an experiment in realism that would reach only a very small number of interested readers and be hurled against the wall out of sheer boredom and frustration by anyone else who might venture into its pages. I was, however, totally against changing the names of those in the next most immediate sphere, those I played with as a child, for instance, or went to *gymnas* with. The whole point of the novel was to depict reality as it was. A growing-up shaped by the boy who lived here and did this, the girl who lived there and did that, the boy I heard about at that particular time, the girl I kissed that Friday night, not shrouded in literature's pall, not ingeniously illuminated in prose's darkened studio, but described in full daylight, swathed in reality. I wanted to get to what was raw and arbitrary about that reality, and to that end the name was essential. Obviously, reality would be altered into something else in the process of being depicted, but my hope was that what was fantastic about the phenomenon itself, the fact of existing alongside a certain collection of people where everyone knew each other or had heard of each other, in a certain period of time in a certain geographical area, and where basically anything at all could happen, but where things eventually turned out according to reality's own exactness and precision, that some of this, the starry luster of growing up, familiar to us all, would shine through the literary form. Every name that went from being real to being fictional weakened that feeling and pulled the novel into the shimmer of enfeebled reality it had been written to engage against. Geir G. said it didn't matter to the reader, he or she wasn't going to connect the names with anyone anyway and wouldn't know if it was authentic or not. But the authentic is a timbre, impossible to imitate.

In a novel the name works like a face: on the first encounter it's new and unfamiliar, but spending even a short time in its presence you start associating certain characteristics with it, then gradually, if it remains near to you over time, a history, eventually an entire life, in that the faces with which you're familiar absorb all that you know about them without you necessarily being aware of the fact; in the case of an old friend walking toward you, that knowledge is patent, melted into the face, each and every aspect that to you comprises "him" or "her." In the best instances the name of a character in a novel is so precise as to summon something essential to the epoch, and in exceptional cases may even become an emblem of the universally human. The inauthentic life of Emma Bovary, the ruthless ambition of Lucien Sorel, the loss of meaning felt by Hamlet, the ideological unyieldingness of Brand. The Austrian writer Ingeborg Bachmann points out in an essay how the literature of our own time strikingly comprises no such names. Don DeLillo is one of the best novelists of our time, yet how many recall even a single name among his many characters? Bachmann writes that Thomas Mann was the last great conjurer of names: Hans Castorp, Adrian Leverkühn, Tonio Kröger, Serenus Zeitblom. These are names that sponge up characteristics and meanings that belong not merely to the individuals they denote, but also to the culture of which they are a part. Thomas Mann was the last great bourgeois novelist; together with Marcel Proust he marks the end point of an entire epoch, perhaps also, and certainly in the case of Proust, its consummation. In no other work of the bourgeois period does the name play so great a part as in Proust's *In Search of Lost Time*.

Here the name is no longer an instrument by which to achieve some particular effect, and no mere furnishing of the novel's interior; rather it is a major theme, and thereby it loses its innocence. However, this loss of innocence occurred not only in Proust's novel; while Proust was working on *In Search of Lost Time* in Paris, Kafka was writing his novels and stories in Prague, and in them the name has changed radically; he called his main character Josef K, or more simply K. The abbreviation of the name removes everything that the name usually brings with it, the individual and the local, which thereby become plain in its absence. The individual and the local are what we can identify with, a name inspires first and foremost a form of intimacy, and when the intimacy of the name is gone, our intimacy with the character is gone too, and the character is left surrounded by uncertainty and mystery: the name in Kafka is an anti-name. At the same time, the character bearing the name leaves a very clear and definite impression, he is a "someone" rather than a "no one." The reduction is by no means arbitrary, the particular things that vanish with the name, everything that binds the character to others and itself, and to places, represent his history. If history is gone, only the moment remains, and what is a human being in the moment? What is a character without its history? What is this something we sense, this impression of another human, when it is unattached to action or origin? The question is not entirely adequate in light of what goes on in Kafka's prose; this we see if we compare it to that of another, slightly earlier author, Knut Hamsun, who in his first novel also writes about a person without history or home, who exists in an environment to which he is fundamentally unattached. Hamsun's character is nameless, but this does not mean that he is an anti-person, merely that his name is not given. The difference between Hamsun's unnamed and Kafka's anti-named character is palpable and determines how the two novels are read. Hamsun's urge toward individuality was great, occasionally immense, and what he opposed most of all in his first phase was literature's reduction of the individual, the unique never being allowed to be simply unique, but always a sign of something general and universal, and that the two were connected by means of formulas and schemata. "A man who deals in horses, for example," he wrote in his manifesto *From the Unconscious Life of the Mind*, "A man who deals in horses is nothing else but a horse dealer. He is a horse dealer in every word. He cannot read a folktale or speak of flowers or take an interest in cleanliness; no, he must always brag, always pat his wallet, curse like a barbarian, and smell of the stables." Literature as Hamsun saw it was simple, schematic, structural, cohesive, harmonious, explained, whereas the life he saw around him was complex, unsystematic, incohesive, arbitrary, unharmonious, unexplained. How could the writer transport the language out of the system into life as it was lived? This was the question Hamsun posed in Lillesand in the autumn of 1890. It was a confrontation with realism or an attempt toward a new, truer realism, and what he did to that end was to remove all categories he found establishing particular connections and which in themselves steered the reader's understanding of the character: so no childhood, no parents, no native soil, no friends, no environment, no history – and no name. He was striving for the unique, and sought therefore to move toward the now, the world prior to meaning, *prior* to interpretation, which is to say toward the forever as yet unexplained. If the name is the character's face in the novel, then the character in Hamsun's novel ought to be faceless, yet he is not; his "I" is so strong, so willful, and brings together so much in its being that it becomes like a name itself, with which the reader quickly becomes intimate, though without at any point becoming ensnared in the emblematism Hamsun so despised. He wanted the character not to be representative of time or epoch, but of itself, and if there was any semblance of representation in that it was of the unique human. Kafka's design in removing origin, history, and environment from his character was almost the exact opposite; what he endeavored to demonstrate was not the individual's uniqueness, its development and individuality, but the forces by which it was constrained and governed, not in terms of the near, the personal, and the intimate, but of the common and the general, in which they appear quite as faceless as his main character. The K is like a blindfold. Josef K, we say, and think not of a certain person's character, the way we do when we say Othello or Odysseus, but of a certain state, dim and obscure, labyrinthine, unfathomable, faceless.

The main character in Hamsun's next novel was just as removed from his history as the I of *Hunger*, and quite as alien to his surroundings, but did possess in contrast a name. Yet the name, Nagel, signified no particular place of belonging, neither in terms of class nor geography, and was perhaps first and foremost an anagram – certainly it would seem reasonable to take it to be a play on the Norwegian *galen*, mad. Whereas Emma Bovary's fate consists of her confusing the romantic and the real, Nagel's is that he sees through the romantic, sees through art, sees through the circus of small-town life and the drama of the wider world: everything is pretense, this is his insight. Including death, into which it all propels him; it, too, has an element of performance about it, not in the form of tragedy, more like a farce. The notion that nothing can be taken seriously is an infrequent starting point for a novel, which presumably on some level has to take itself seriously in order to be written. *Mysteries* is perhaps not the most successful of novels, yet it does contain some quite unrivaled passages in which Hamsun ventures still further into the now and describes the almost completely unattached stirrings of a human mind at any given moment. Of all that goes on in Nagel's mind, little may be traced back to a particular self, or rather it would seem hard to say what this self in actual fact consists of, not least because so much of what runs through it comes from outside, in the first instance by the fact of being language, which is the same for everyone, and in the second by being made up of fragments of general culture, and what reveals itself then, perhaps for the first time, for never before have I seen a stream of consciousness so rendered with all it contains of high and low, important and unimportant, is how the world flows through the individual to such a remarkable extent that one has to wonder if anything like individuality even exists, and, if it does, in what ways it might manifest itself. And if it does not exist, what does a name then represent?

"Names! What's in a name?" Joyce asks in the ninth chapter of his *Ulysses*, the part that takes place in the national library in Dublin, where Stephen Dedalus, the young man with the rather less than realistic-sounding name, discusses Hamlet and Shakespeare with some intellectual acquaintances. This question of the name was originally posed by Shakespeare. Shakespeare, says Stephen, was not Hamlet, but Hamlet's father, the dead king who appeared as a ghost before his son. Hamlet's mother, Queen Gertrude, was then Anne Hathaway, Shakespeare's wife, who according to Stephen was unfaithful, while Hamlet himself was Hamnet Shakespeare, dead son of William Shakespeare and Anne Hathaway. Underlying this discussion is the fact that the novel opens by describing a conversation between two young men in a tower, one being Stephen, who has just lost his mother. The other, Buck Mulligan, says to him, "The aunt thinks you killed your mother," to which Stephen replies, "Someone killed her." The tower is the castle at Elsinore, Dublin Bay the strait between Denmark and Sweden, and Stephen is Hamlet. But Stephen is also Telemachus journeying in search of his father, Odysseus, which is to say Leopold Bloom, the Jew. And Leopold Bloom is, besides Odysseus, also Virgil when in the night he walks side by side with Stephen, which is to say Dante, through the streets of Dublin, which is to say Hell, and he is the writer Henry Flowers, who sends audacious letters on the sly to a woman whose acquaintance he has made by way of an advertisement. But he is moreover the father of a son who died, which in this universe makes him Shakespeare, father of Hamnet. And his wife is not only Penelope, who is besieged by men in Odysseus's absence, but also Anne Hathaway, which is to say Queen Gertrude, since just after four o'clock that day she is in bed with her impresario, making a cuckold of Bloom. *Ulysses* is a novel about change, but also a novel about everything always being the same, and the dimension with which it is most concerned, the mystery it grapples with so unrelentingly, is time. The action takes place during the course of a single day in Dublin, and the now is a kind of gateway standing open to the past, which rises and falls imperceptibly in everything, and to the future, which is slung through it. "Hold on to the now," Stephen tells himself in the library, "the here, through which all future plunges to the past," words that contain at once a philosophy of life and a poetics. In the discussion of Plato and Aristotle there, Stephen suggests that Aristotle would have considered Hamlet's musings on death, this "improbable, insignificant, and undramatic monologue," to be quite as shallow as Plato's. The apotheosis of ideas, the heaven of shapeless spirit, is anathema to Stephen; what he believes in is the material world in all its abundance, and what Joyce does in *Ulysses* is to investigate how ideas and the immaterial manifest themselves in the material, proceeding from the idea that they are found only there, in the now, in the bodies and objects that exist here at this moment. If life is a journey forward through time, the past is its phantom. "What is a ghost?" Stephen asks. "One who has faded into impalpability, through death, through absence, through change of manners." That such a transition occurs through death is the normal understanding, through absence a logical extension, but in the last phrase, "through change of manners," we leave the individual death and enter the collective: a ghost is that which time has abandoned. This is Joyce's overarching theme, treated first in the small and, compared to *Ulysses*, relatively intimate format of the short story "The Dead," toward the very end of which he uses the same expression as he would later have Stephen think: "His own identity was fading out into a gray impalpable world." The gray impalpable world into which his own self vanished was that of the dead. The palpable world the dead had once built up and inhabited, dissolved and disappeared. In *Ulysses* that thought is launched into the world, we might say, transplanted from the framed confines of the closet drama into teeming, ordinary life, on an ordinary day in an ordinary city, in which it is active on all levels and in every context, though without dominating any, since with the action taking place during the course of a day, and the text unyieldingly in the moment, nothing is overriding and everything is dissolved in the now. This is true of history, it is true of mythology, true of the dead, true of philosophy, true of religion, and especially, perhaps primarily, true of identity. None of these categories is splintered or dissolved, but simply viewed through the prism of the moment, which can only handle little bits at a time. A glimpse of the dead mother here, the smell of the room in which she lay, a thought from Thomas Aquinas there, a sparkle of sun on a pane, the rush of the waves, a brewery horse on its way down the street, a sentence in a newspaper, a snippet of an aria, a fawning librarian, the books on the shelves thought of as coffins. This is what it is to exist in the world. To understand it or think about it, you have to step back from it. So, too, with *Ulysses*. All the little bits, all the structures dissolved in the now, come together in bigger bits, which is Joyce's answer to the question: What does it mean to be human? The novel has three main characters: Stephen Dedalus, the young man on his way up; all his energy is spent on wrenching himself free of what holds him down, his father, a drunken charmer, his mother, whose death weighs on his mind and racks him with guilt, his friends, against whom he competes, and his education, which is familiarity with the thoughts of others – his adventurous suggestion of Hamlet's mediocrity is a way of elevating himself in what we refer to, with some measure of resignation, as youthful arrogance, in actual fact but a necessary vigor; Leopold Bloom, the middle-aged man (who in our day would be considered relatively young, would wear sneakers and regularly shave his head; he is thirty-eight years old), in the middle of life, an advertising agent with no upward trajectory, an ordinary man doing the best he can; and Molly Bloom, singer, some years younger than her husband, spending most of her time in bed and merely referred to, until concluding the novel in her own voice, a long inner monologue completely unlike everything that has gone before. Leopold Bloom is in many respects Stephen Dedalus's opposite; whereas the younger man is introduced at the top of a tower, high above the world, hooked up with Hamlet, Ancient Greece, and Christianity, the reader meets Bloom right in the middle of his everyday life, in a kitchen, associated closely from the start with the mortal world and bodily pleasures; first the faint smell of urine from fried kidneys, then the pleasing waft of his excrement after moving his bowels. When later in the day he visits a museum and looks at the statues there, it is Aphrodite that captures his attention, for reasons quite apart from the noble and artistic. Leopold Bloom's mind, too, is filled with fragments of immaterial reality, though in its lowest form, as it appears in newspapers and advertisements, signs and leaflets, he misconstrues and is often naïve, but in contrast to Stephen he is a whole human being, a complete human being, a true human being, so when finally they meet and go through the city together at night he is indeed Virgil to Stephen Dedalus's Dante. That Molly Bloom should be lying above them with her head full of thoughts as they seat themselves in the kitchen is something of which both are unaware, just as they are oblivious to her superiority over them, in the sense that she sees her husband so much more clearly than he sees her, and sees Stephen as a diligent schoolboy, the son of his father.

Few characters in the history of literature are depicted with as much complexity as these three. Yet the novel could not have carried any of their names as its title; it could not have been called *Leopold Bloom*, as Flaubert's novel was called *Madame Bovary* or Shakespeare's play was called *Hamlet, Prince of Denmark*, for the novel is greater than them, which is to say that the characters are not the principal focus of its theme. Everyone knows Madame Bovary's conflict, Hamlet's conflict, Don Quixote's conflict, it is what we think about when we hear the names, but who knows Stephen Dedalus's conflict? He is more intelligent than Hamlet, finds Hamlet's ruminations about death shallow, and his field of reference is broader, he too has lost one of his parents and feels guilty about it, yet the fact remains that as a literary character he is not in Hamlet's league. Is that because Elizabethan England had a different view of greatness from that of Dublin at the beginning of the twentieth century? Joyce strives to portray the lives of quite ordinary people, and the contrast to the greatness of Odysseus and Hamlet is a continual point; if the same thing happens in *Ulysses*, it happens on a smaller scale. Prometheus's impressive and wild transformations are represented in Dublin by a dog and Stephen's imagination, as Olof Lagercrantz observed. The modest life, meaning the ordinary and down to earth, is the foundation of *Ulysses*, and through such life the novel's great characters and themes wander ghostlike. Of course, it is far from unusual for an ordinary person, one deemed by others to be insignificant, to make a great character in a novel; Emma Bovary is no princess or duchess but the jilted wife of a country doctor. The difference is that Madame Bovary, Don Quixote, and Hamlet reside in history, whereas in the case of Leopold Bloom, Molly Bloom, and Stephen Dedalus the opposite holds and history resides in them. The new in Joyce and modernist literature is in the weakening of the boundary between the self and the outside world, so radical that the relationship becomes near osmotic. People get bigger in a way, embracing both history and the stream of events of contemporary existence, but they also get smaller insofar as what is unique and unexampled about them, collected in the name, the person they are, becomes dissolved in it.

Yet while Joyce achieved these insights, and they were achieved simultaneously in many other fields of culture, they have never been for everyone, the way the *Odyssey*, for instance, once was for everyone, as one must assume it was, something children and adults alike, women and men, poor and rich listened to. *Ulysses* has only ever been read by the few, a fate it shares with many other trailblazing works of modernism, not just in literature but also in philosophy and psychology, the work of Husserl and Freud to mention but two, because although many of their ideas have spread and been accorded universal validity, the exactness on which they depend and which only direct reading can provide, has been lost along the way. *Ulysses* has become the myth of the difficult book, eight hundred pages about a single day, Freud is associated with the subconscious, with stretching out on a couch and talking about your childhood, and with jokes about cigars and trains going through tunnels, Husserl is Heidegger's forerunner, Heidegger himself a Nazi. The fact that Joyce writes about this, the way culture's every expression is broken down to live among us only barely understood, as misconstruals, assumptions, half-truths, myths and surmisals, bits of this and fragments of that, as if to show that culture is this, the human and living is that, God but a shout in the street, is perhaps ironic in view of he himself becoming the very epitome of literary elitism and obliviousness to the world, though quite understandable given the fact that in order to get there, in order to penetrate into this, he had to shun that same quotidian culture's ways of communicating.

What they actually comprise becomes clear in the way the American writer William Faulkner exploits the name. In his novel *The Sound and the Fury* names are presented without accompanying information as to those they denote, who are taken for granted, hardly a characteristic or note of origin to go with them; Faulkner's names leave us utterly in the dark.

In her essay on the name in literature Ingeborg Bachmann writes about Faulkner, and her examples are telling: one minute we're reading about someone calling for Caddie, the next about someone called Caddy, no information is given, one is associated with the verb "hit," perhaps we're dealing with a golfer calling his caddie, but something else is triggered by this too; later the name Caddy appears, the time is another, the connection unclear. Then a character named Quentin is introduced, and one minute the name refers to a woman, the next to a man. In a way, Faulkner goes further than Joyce in his approach to reality, attempting to describe the world the way it appears to his characters and making no effort at all to describe the characters to us, their gazes are as such unconveyed, and in that lies the realism. Reading *The Sound and the Fury* is like going into the house of a family you don't know, where everyone's talking about their relations and paying you not even the slightest attention; all you get is a number of names connected to various events and occurrences everyone knows about except you, which is why they are never related in their entirety but merely alluded to. Or rather, no, it's like going inside the mind of one of those sitting there and being party to the way he or she experiences the conversation, the allusions and references being even more oblique; no one explains to themselves what they already know. The names are closed to us, but not in the same way as in Kafka, where they are relieved of their surroundings and history; on the contrary, in *The Sound and the Fury* the names are woven into the surroundings and history, and since both are closed to us, the names, too, are closed. The lack of openness points directly inward toward the core of the novel, the fulcrum around which it revolves: something happened once, something no one can talk about, not even think about, but which nevertheless is present in the various streams of consciousness. It cannot be conveyed, it cannot be confronted, it must be concealed. The word "incest" appears, apparently it has to do with that. Incest is one of the oldest of all taboos, and the whole novel, the mood it creates, does indeed have something archaic about it. In Faulkner the past is like a void and unclear, differing radically from Joyce's past, which above all is the past of culture, that which is devised and created, Odysseus and Circe, Dante, and Shakespeare, a past to which one relates through the intellect, whereas the past in Faulkner's work is nameless and without language, and may only be sensed or felt. The difference is reflected, too, in the titles. Both are intertextual, Joyce finding his in Homer, Faulkner in Shakespeare, but while Joyce uses a name, Ulysses, and brings a culture to life, Faulkner uses a phenomenon of the world, sound/noise/commotion, and another from the domain of the human, fury/rage/anger, both timeless. The name does not address the archaic, but the social. The distance between the archaic and the social is brought about by Faulkner through the unfamiliarity that is infused into the name, the rejection of familiarity. Thus, an existential depth is invoked, which neither Joyce nor Kafka are anywhere near. This is not about the presence or absence of the contemporary, and the idea of "existential depth" is perhaps misleading, since the archaic is not behind anything, and not inside anything, the difference being not a matter of rungs, but of the eye, and through the eye the experience, which is unreachable by language and therefore must be evoked. While the secret is not in itself unreachable in *The Sound and the Fury*, it cannot, for social and psychological reasons, be named, much as in Ibsen's plays, the only difference being that there it rises to the surface to be perceived and recognized in a kind of culmination alien to Faulkner's own characters. Faulkner's, Joyce's, Flaubert's, Proust's, and Kafka's books inhabit the social domain, the novel is its literary form, concerned with interpersonal relationships and how the reality we make up and by which we are surrounded is communicated. This is the case even in Dostoyevsky; the fulcrum of his novels is never the spiritual or the religious in itself, but the reactions to it of the surrounding world. This is the novel's basic constraint, chained as it is to life in the social domain, the way people are to each other, and the minute the novel departs from that human world and ventures into the non-human or the beyond-human of the divine, it dies. As long as Dante is writing about an inferno populated by people, his epic poem lives; as soon as he proceeds upward to heaven to depict the divine, it withers away in his hands. Music can express it, and painting, too, since their forms are wordless, their language another and nameless, as removed from the I that employs it and the I that perceives it as figures in a mathematical formula. Reading a novel after having listened to Bach's cello suites is like leaving a sunset to descend into a cellar. The novel is the form of the small life, and when it's not it is because it's being deceitful and is no true novel at all, since no I exists that isn't small, too. The only literary form that can exceed it is the poem. The poem is akin to the song and exists somewhere between music and the word, which is to say that it is capable of reaching beyond the word and thus to break out of the social, which is another term for the world as we know it. This means poetry is related also to religion, which has always been rooted in the human domain, staring out at the nonhuman, in whose icy winds we are unknown and strangers to all, not just to each other, but also to ourselves.

A poem of Rilke's begins like this:

> *They had, for a while, grown used to him. But after*
> *they lit the kitchen lamp and in the dark*
> *it began to burn, restlessly, the stranger*
> *was altogether strange.*

The situation is the washing of a corpse, and the poem concludes thus:

> *And one without a name*
> *lay clean and naked there, and gave commands.*

The name is what joins the body to our social life, the name collects all judgments and assumptions as to a particular personality, and what happens when a person dies is that the name is no longer connected to the body, which decomposes and disappears, whereas the name lives on in the social world.

Can we imagine a person without a name?

It would certainly say something quite different about being human. Without a name the human would be a locus for the beating of a heart, the wheeze of lungs, the tumult of thought, its identity residing in the unique moment, which is to say akin to animal.

But we are that, too.

Rilke's corpse had always been strange, in the sense of unknown, but only when dead and nameless could it be seen as such. And the commands it gave were commands to life outside the social world, commands of flesh, earth, water.

That perspective is ever present in Rilke's poems; not without reason was he a pupil of Hölderlin's, the poet of the divine perspective, for whom the social world does not exist; in Hölderlin everything is existential, and the fact that at the end he abandoned the social context completely in his life, vanishing into madness, beyond the grip of the self, is hard not to understand as a consequence of the worldview expressed in his poems. Rilke is closer to the social, his poems wash in and out of the two different worlds, and the fact that he wrote so often about angels must be seen in that light, angels being the very connecting figures between the divine and the human. In one of his Duino Elegies he writes:

> *For it seems that everything*
> *hides us. Look: trees do exist; the houses*
> *that we live in still stand. We alone*
> *fly past all things, as fugitive as the wind.*
> *And all things conspire to keep silent about us, half*
> *out of shame perhaps, half as unutterable hope.*

The poem moves between what is, the silent, nameless world, and we who see it. That the silent world tries to hide us means that it knows us; and it does so because we issue from it, which in turn is to say we have left it, yet at the same time we continue to belong to it, our hearts beating without word, and I believe it is that very movement he is describing, inward toward our being, outward away from it again. Religion strives inward toward being, and art strives toward that same place. Religion and art combine in the angel. "Every angel is terrifying," Rilke also writes. Why is the angel terrifying? Because its presence renders the human figurative in the same way as death. Yes, the angel looks at us with the eyes of death. Rilke's angels have nothing to do with Christianity.

In Christ man was made God, and what he opened up to us he opened up in the social world: your neighbor is you, turn the other cheek, everyone is of equal worth. The social world is about establishing and maintaining differences. In one swoop he annulled them. Forgiveness is the uniformity of the divine implanted in the human. It is as if the gaze is turned from the stars to the eyes.

But as hard as it is for us to exist in the uniformity of the divine, it is quite as hard to do so in that of forgiveness. We are too small, we creep and crawl in and out of our houses and through our streets, terrified for a moment by the vacuum of death yet shaking off our fears to keep on crawling, in and out of our houses, up and down our streets, with a vitality we cannot hope to make shine in the way of the all-obliterating light of the good, no matter that this is what we wish, for our vitality hits a wall, is thrown against a ceiling, hurled toward a floor, it steers us this way and that, in the small and intermittent dislocations that characterize not only the human body, but also its soul and mind.

We lose ourselves, and we lose ourselves in each other.

When I read Rilke's poem it was Dad I thought about, the time I saw him lying dead on a table in the chapel in Kristiansand, in the summer of 1998.

> *They had, for a while, grown used to him. But after*
> *they lit the kitchen lamp and in the dark*
> *it began to burn, restlessly, the stranger*
> *was altogether strange.*

That was what I saw. Not that he was a stranger, but that he had always been a stranger. If I had spoken his name then he would not have reacted, it would have glanced off him, for it was no longer his. He was a corpse and as such outside the name. His body had slid out of its name and lay there without, nameless.

For the remainder of that week I saw in short glimpses everything else around me in the same way, outside the name. It was a secret world I saw, and if I did not understand it then, I understand it now, the kinship of death and art, and their function in life, which is to prevent reality, our conception of the world, from conflating with the world.

So much of Dad was collected in his name. He spelled it differently when he was young, and changed it sometime in his forties, and as he lay there dead and nameless, the name the mason chiseled into his headstone was spelled incorrectly. The stone is still there, in the cemetery in Kristiansand, with its misspelled name, on top of the interred urn containing the ashes of his body. And when, ten years later, I began to write about him I was prohibited from referring to him by name. Before that I had never given a thought to what a name was and what it meant. But I did so now, accentuated by the events that followed in the wake of the first book, and I began to write this chapter, first about the name itself, then about various names of literature and their function there, starting out with a piece of thinking I found in the writing of Ingeborg Bachmann concerning the decline of the name in literature, contained in a short essay in a book published a few years ago by Pax. The essay on the name began on a right-hand page. On the left-hand page were some lines of a poem my eyes absently scanned when at some point during the spring I sat down with the book in front of me, intending to see if anything of what I had written had been unwittingly drawn from Bachmann's essay.

So
there are temples yet. A
star
probably still has light.
Nothing,
nothing is lost.

These were the words I read. I guessed they were from a poem of Paul Celan, knowing that Paul Celan and Ingeborg Bachmann had been friends and furthermore enjoyed a certain literary kinship. This is the kind of thing one knows without it necessarily having any bearing on anything, a relationship of some sort that is simply there. That Paul Celan knew and corresponded with Nelly Sachs, for instance, and that Nelly Sachs fled to Stockholm during the war and remained there for the rest of her life. Both were Jewish, and both wrote poetry that had to do with the extermination of the Jews. Both lived in exile, Celan in Paris, Sachs in Stockholm. I had never read any of their poems, apart from Paul Celan's "Death Fugue," which I found astonishingly beautiful when I was introduced to it as a nineteen-year-old student in the writers' academy in Hordaland. "*Svart morgonmjølk me drikk ho um kvelden*," as Hauge's Norwegian translation went, "Black milk of daybreak we drink it at sundown," and "*døden er ein meister frå Tyskland*," "death is a master from Germany." It was a poem I would later feel shame at having found such beauty in, since its theme was not the exquisite and the sublime, but the exquisite and the sublime's antithesis, the extermination of the Jews.

I skimmed back a few pages in Bachmann's book. Indeed it was Paul Celan. The six lines cited at the end of the essay were from a poem called "Engführung," or "The Straitening" as it is called in one celebrated English translation. I had not heard of it before, but I did have a collection of Paul Celan's poetry in Øyvind Berg's Norwegian translations, it had remained unread on my bookshelf since sometime in the midnineties and I found it immediately. Something in those six lines had appealed to me. Perhaps it was the sequence "Nothing/nothing is lost" that seemed so positive at first sight, only then to turn itself almost inside out and become the opposite; "nothing is lost" can mean that everything goes on as before, if one reads the words in their most immediate sense, meaning that nothing has been lost, but if they are read in the sense of "nothing" being what is lost, the poem then opens out toward something else entirely, since "nothing" is not simply nothing, it is also the end point of all mysticism – the Kabbalists wrote that God resides in the depths of his nothingness. The idea that God is nothing belongs to negative mysticism; by saying what God is not, the divine may be approached without reduction. I had no idea if Paul Celan's poem had anything at all to do with such things, but in the preceding lines temples were mentioned, the houses of religion, and a star, which is only there in darkness. "A/star/probably still has light," it said. Why "probably," why "still"? The existence of the temples, too, was qualified by a "yet." Did it have something to do with Rilke's poem? He, too, used the word in a sense that seemed to deviate from the expected, when he wrote "the houses/that we live in still stand." All this made the poem potentially very interesting, but the most important reason for me picking it out and skimming through it was because I was looking for something I could use in my essay about the name. I found it.

> *The place where they lay, it has*
> *a name – it has*
> *none.*

I read.

Something had a name, but what this name might be wasn't mentioned, and then the fact of it having a name was taken back.

With that in mind I noted there wasn't a single name in the entire poem. Not of a person, not of a place, and not of any time.

Why would that be?

Whatever the reason, I found myself drawn in by it, for this was not a world in which the reason for the name not being mentioned could be that it wasn't important, which is to say not the nameless essence of reality, the world beyond language, true and authentic; this seemed rather to be a world in which the name more simply could not be mentioned. It was as if the very foundation of the name was broken.

What was the foundation of the name?

In what way was it broken?

I read the poem, understanding nothing, it was closed to me, almost completely mute. This was no infrequent experience of mine. I couldn't read poetry, and had never been able to. At the same time I had always, from when I was nineteen and had been introduced to the leading modernist poets at the writers' academy, considered poetry to be the pinnacle. What poetry was in touch with was something I was not in touch with, and my respect for poetry was boundless. This is no exaggeration. I have written about it earlier, too, in this novel, the way the poem, which I took to be the highest form of expression, refused to open itself to me. When I grew older I became familiar with all the names of the poets and knew enough about them to be able to mention them in what I was writing or talking about, as with the example of Paul Celan above; he was from Romania, his parents died in a German concentration camp, he lived in Paris, wrote in German, and committed suicide sometime in the sixties by drowning himself in the Seine. His poems were mysterious, belonging in a way to the same tradition as Hölderlin and Rilke, but at the end of it, because with Celan the language came apart.

I knew who they were, but not what they had written.

Could it really be the case that poets and readers of poetry comprised some esoteric sect? Surely not only the initiated could read poems?

For some reason that was exactly how I had perceived it. The sense of others possessing insights I have no idea about, of everyone else being able and knowledgeable, has pursued me all through my adult life, in almost every respect. And, I think to myself now as I sit here at the age of nearly forty-three, most likely with justification. I suspect there are vast areas of human erotic life about which I know nothing and which I associate with darkness and fervency, an almost limitless sophistication into which other people, though by no means all, are initiated. When I meet people I often think this to myself, that to them I must come across as naïve and innocuous, a bit like a child. The same applies to poetry.

Poetry expresses the innermost secrets of life and the world, some people relate to it with the greatest of ease, others are excluded. That I got nothing out of the poetry I read merely confirmed this to be true. It was as if poems were written in code. I felt excluded by many other languages too, that of mathematics, for instance, yet the language of mathematics did not possess the aura for me of leading to the grail, was not shrouded in such dim mists, with half-turned faces, derisive sneers, scornful eyes. This feeling, of being outside what was important, was degrading, since it made me simple and my life shallow. The way I tackled it was to ignore it and pretend it didn't bother me. The deep secrets of erotic life and the esoteric insights of poetry were meant for others, whereas I, constrained by the stupid thinness of my life, struggled to accept that life was just that, stupid and thin. At the same time, something happened when I entered my thirties, in that some semblance of confidence came to me in the way I engaged with literature, though it was difficult to pin down, most of all a feeling of being able to see that little bit further, think that little bit further, and that what previously had been closed to me suddenly seemed possible to prize open. Though not unconditionally; I could read *The Death of Virgil* by Broch with some return, but not *The Sleepwalkers* by the same author, a novel of which I still hadn't the faintest understanding. It was at that time I got a job working as a consultant on the Norwegian revision of the Old Testament, and since I had no grounding in the linguistic, cultural, or religious aspects that were involved, I had no option but to work hard and meticulously, nothing was going to come to me on a plate, and what revealed itself then, when I went through the first sentence of the creation word for word, for instance, was the way in which entire worldviews might be encapsulated in a comma, in an "and," in a "which," and, with those insights, how different the world becomes if its description is coordinate with rather than subordinate to the metaphor, for example, or the way a word not only has lexical meaning, but is also colored by the contexts in which it appears, something the writers of the Bible exploited to the full, for instance by allowing a word at the beginning to apply to the sun's relation to the earth, and then to let that same word many pages on apply to man's relation to woman. The word is merely there, in the two different places, and the connection is as good as invisible, yet decisive. People have been reading the Bible as holy Scripture for a couple of thousand years, and every word it contains has been considered meaningful, a dizzyingly tight mesh of different meanings and shades of meaning have thereby arisen, which no single human can ever possibly command. What happened when I started working on those texts was that I learned to read. I began to understand what it meant to read. Reading is seeing the words as lights shining in the dark, one after another, and to engage in the activity of reading is to follow the lights into the text. But what we see is never detached from the person we are; the mind has its limitations, they are personal, but cultural, too, in that there is always something we cannot see and places we cannot go. If we are patient and investigate the words and their contexts carefully enough, we may nonetheless identify those limitations, and what is revealed to us then is that which lies outside ourselves. The goal of reading is to reach these places. This is what learning is, seeing that which lies outside the confines of the self. To grow older is not to understand more but to realize that there is more to understand. Yet the secrets of the Old Testament were to begin with so remote as to be unthreatening. The secrets of erotic life and poetry were menacing, in contrast, having to do with my identity, and what kept me outside was not the alien nature of their culture but the chasm within my own, which was to do with the very remoteness of such things. I realize this probably comes across as somewhat hysterical, and I don't know how to put it in order to make it clear just how inhibiting it is to feel excluded from that which is significant. To me this was exactly the aura in which Paul Celan's poetry was shrouded. His poems canceled out what was given about the words, and thereby what was given about the world. As such, it was not so much existence that was on the line as identity. The name had to become visible in the nameless, much as the all became visible in the nothing, so I imagined on the basis of the four words, "nothing/nothing is lost," which I had read and puzzled over. And that surely was how it was with regard to the poem as a whole. It was not composed of mysteries, but of words. So all that was required was to read them. To note down all possible meanings of the first word, then the next, and then consider the connections between them.

The first word was "Driven."

Driven into
the terrain
with the unmistakable track:

grass, written asunder.

Aside from its everyday, transportational sense, "drive" means to propel, to force to go into or penetrate. It suggests the existence of an outside, a place from where what is propelled comes. The German original has "*verbracht*," and that contains the same element of force. Another English translation has "deported," suggesting forcible removal from one place to another.

Something is driven in from outside, not tenderly and with caution, but firmly, without consideration, harshly and mechanically even; this seemed like a plausible interpretation. But driven into where? Into "the terrain with the unmistakable track." This could be the poem's own terrain, the place established by its very designation, and yet that place seems to exist already, whatever is driven in is already driven, now an element of that terrain.

The terrain is characterized by way of "the unmistakable track." Like "driven," "unmistakable" has something unaccommodating about it, something firm and incontestable. The unmistakable is hard fact, something a person can do nothing about. If "driven" and "unmistakable" are words suggestive of disregard or lack of consideration, carrying with them a more or less direct sense of

459

power or enforcement, then "asunder" is more manifestly suggestive of this in that something is patently said to have been damaged. Yet we understand that this is not a physical force, but a force inflicted by language, the grass being "written" asunder. So it is the way the grass is considered that is damaged, rather than the grass itself.

This damaged way of considering is driven into a preexisting terrain characterized by an unmistakable track, and, one might suppose, damages the way of considering that terrain; this is what is driven.

The first three lines are not just nameless, they are also lacking in pronouns. Only actions are described, as if they occur on their own, at the same time as the element of force attaching to the words "driven" and "asunder" associates them with a will, a certain origin, something not arbitrary. Actions without agents often relate to weather. "It's raining," we say, "it's blowing" or "it's snowing," but what exactly is doing the "raining," the "blowing," the "snowing"? The rain is, the wind is, the snow is; the actions are their own agents, conflated with the subject, and to denote that we use the pronoun "it." "It" points toward a force that exists outside of us and over which we have no control. When actions in the human domain are described without pronouns, as in this case, those actions share that same meaning, it is as if they stem from some force we cannot control, the impersonal and nameless itself: "driven," "written."

> grass, written asunder. The stones, white,
> with the shadows of grassblades:
> Do not read any more – look!
> Do not look any more – go!

The next entity, the white stones with the shadows of grassblades, belong either to what has been driven or to the terrain as it was before; presumably the former, since a connection exists between the two, grass and grassblades are much the same thing, and the writing and the shadows are also connected, because what would constitute a shadow of grassblades if not the word "grassblades"?

The first six lines establish an ambivalent space in that they contain elements that simultaneously establish the space and undermine that of which it consists, which is language.

Into what kind of terrain may "grass, written asunder" be driven? No truly tangible one, the way terrain is in the real world with its concrete objects and physical materiality, in such terrain the asunder-written grass would likewise be an object, characters on a page. But it can be driven into the consideration of that terrain, into that which goes before the gaze of the eye that sees it and colors its perception of it. The terrain as it is considered, into this the asunder-written grass may be driven, and into its recollection. In the poem the terrain exists as a terrain prior to the writing asunder of the grass, and as a terrain after the writing asunder of the grass. At the same time the poem is itself writing, thereby itself carrying that which inflicts the damage. Yet only the grass is written asunder. And only in this terrain, which the poem opens before us, does the written-asunder grass, the damaged way of considering, obtain. It is not driven into all terrains, but into this one, characterized by the unmistakable track. So what kind of a terrain is it? Where is the poem?

The opening sets out a terrain and a situation, and leads into a plea. Do not read any more, it says. Why? Because what we read, writing, writes the world asunder? Look instead, we are told. But then the plea is expanded: we are not to look either. Why? Perhaps because looking and reading are so closely connected. In characters on the page and in the gaze of our eye the world may emerge to us. To the eye the world exists merely in the fleeting now of the moment. What the eye sees is unique and can never return. Language ties the moment down and turns it into something else. Language is not, and can never be, the same as what it represents, but will always comprise its own shadow world pointing toward the real one, so what we see when we read is language, not the world itself. The question is whether language colors our vision and thereby our perception of the world. The grass being written asunder does not necessarily mean that the grass is damaged only in the writing, but also when we lift our gaze from the writing to look at the world. Therefore the plea goes on. Do not read, do not look, but go. To read and to look are in a certain sense passive actions by which we perceive the world; to go, however, is to actively perform, to penetrate into the world. We must not contemplate the world, but act within it. We must not read, and we must not look; instead we must go. Go toward something, perhaps; something whose nature is as yet unknown to us.

> Go, your hour
> has no sisters, you are —
> are at home. A wheel, slow,
> rolls out of itself, the spokes
> climb,
> climb on a blackish field, the night
> needs no stars, nowhere
> does anyone ask after you.

"Your hour has no sisters." What does that mean? Perhaps that every moment is unique and stands alone, or that only this hour does? This hour, which thereby is the last? It says "your" hour, rather than any hour in general, not time as such, but your time, it belongs to you and has no sisters. It stands alone and is unique. Perhaps it is the hour of death, though this could also be marked out in some other way.

"You are —," it goes on, the dash a slight hesitation or uncertainty, as if something as yet were being kept open. "Are" as in existing? Yes, but something has to follow. If the hour that has no sisters is your last, then what lies in the "are" is death, this is the conclusion: your hour has no sisters, you are dead; this is the eventuality the dash suspends in the air. And yet you are not dead, you are at home. It is as if that assertion is postponed, by means of the dash and by the repetition of "are." You are – you are at home. Is saying you are at home the same as saying you are dead? That death is a coming home to the darkness from which we once arose? Why not just say it outright, you are dead, you are home? Is the poem unable to say "dead"? If so, why? Because no one knows what death "is"? Because it "is" not, whereas the act of naming it, death, turns it into "something"? Or are you simply at home? Where, in that case, is that? In memory, its own memory, or in language, this language?

The lines that follow add depth to the terrain. In the terrain is a wheel, it "rolls out of itself," which is to say turns slowly of its own accord, its spokes climb up a blackish hill. The night needs no stars, it says; does that mean the stars are there but superfluous, since the night in question is deeper and of another nature than any through which light might penetrate, or does it mean that there are no stars at all in this night, but simply darkness?

After the wheel and the night, it says: nowhere does anyone ask after you. You are either forgotten or someone who cannot be asked after. Because you are dead? Because they who do not ask want to forget you? Or because they are dead?

Nowhere does anyone ask after you.

Who are you then, when you are absent in the minds of others? In your own eyes you are alone, in the eyes of others you are no one. But why "nowhere," why not just "nobody"? "Nowhere does anyone ask after you" – in this no person is mentioned, no name, simply the absence of any place in which someone asks after you. And what is required when someone asks after someone else? A name; there is no way of asking after someone other than by a name. That name is not asked after. The object of the asking after is unnamed.

Until now the poem has been without human presence, apart from the "you" who "goes" – we have been given a track, grass written asunder, white stones with shadows of grassblades, a turning wheel, a blackish field, a night that needs no stars, places in which no one asks after you – yet people are there nonetheless, the agents behind the act of driving, the writing asunder, the not asking after you. Such is the home of the "you."

In such an unwordy poem, in which almost nothing of the world is named, each word and each named element is lent extraordinary weight. A wheel mentioned in *Ulysses* means practically nothing. A wheel mentioned in this poem insists on meaning. But how is it to be understood? The wheel is one of the oldest symbols known to us. It is the sun, it is repetition, it is the serpent that bites its tail, it is time, cyclical and repeating of ages, it is eternity. Here the wheel is mentioned immediately following the hour, yet the two are unconnected, they are next to each other, the wheel turning on its own, of itself, climbing on the blackish field. What makes this image of the wheel remarkable is that the wheel is in motion, in a particular terrain, seen in the now and in a particular space, seen here. As a symbol or an allegory, the wheel represents something else, and it is this other to which the wheel refers that then becomes primary, that which the wheel "is." The more tangible and specific the wheel, the weaker its symbolic force, since being made concrete individualizes it, until eventually the realism becomes consummate and the wheel becomes merely this wheel, the way it is here and now, without any other meaning than its own. The wheel in this poem exists between the all of symbolism and the one of realism. It is not a purely symbolic wheel because it turns on its own in the field at night, nor is it a realistic wheel because no real wheel can ever turn on its own in the field at night.

How are we to understand it?

The wheel is apparently something other than a real wheel, it carries more meaning than its own self, and perhaps the concretization of it, which gathers the meaning closer around this particular wheel in this particular poem, in a way individualizes its symbolic meaning, making it an idiosyncratic symbol, something valid only here, in this poem, whose meaning in that case arises in relation to, and is regulated by, the context in which it appears, the other words and images in the poem.

But the space opened by the ambivalence between realistic and symbolic has been opened before, often in works of literature from ages of crisis caught between two different worldviews or two different aesthetic paradigms, frequently two sides of the same coin. An immediate example here would be the Book of Ezekiel in the Old Testament, its depiction of the revelation of the divine.

Ezekiel first sees a burning cloud in the sky above; in it he sees four creatures, each with human form, each with wings, each with feet hooved like a calf's, and each with four faces: a man, a lion, an ox, and an eagle. Fire blazes among them, and lightning flashes from the flames. I beheld the living creatures, he writes, and behold, by each was a wheel upon the ground.

Until this point the creatures have been in the sky above him, but now they are next to wheels on the ground. The wheels are tall and terrifying and rimmed with eyes. They looked like they were made of golden beryl, he writes, and whenever they moved, no matter in which direction, they moved without turning. Above these mysterious wheels is a canopy, above the canopy something reminiscent of a throne that seems to be made of sapphire, and on it a figure resembling a human being, immersed in fire and with a radiant light surrounding him. The figure is God. But what are the wheels? Clearly, they are allegorical, rimmed with eyes, yet also tangible, moving this way and that on the ground as though of their own accord.

In the oldest Scriptures of the Old Testament, God's appearance to man is always in the guise of some external phenomenon. God appears as a burning bush, a whirlwind, a pillar of fire, and as a man who comes wandering across the plain outside Abraham's tent. Ezekiel's revelation, too, is described in terms of an external phenomenon, something in the sky above him, but what he sees is not merely a medium by which the divine reveals itself, as in the instance of the burning bush, but the divine itself; moreover, other revelations follow, clearly visions: lying on the ground with eyes closed he is transported to the temple of Jerusalem, where he sees the same four figures and the same four wheels. This is what makes Ezekiel's revelations so odd and so ambivalent: what he sees is not simply inside or outside his own being, it is at the same time the divine itself. Ezekiel found himself caught between two different modes of perception of the religious, where in the former a chasm existed between the human and the divine, while in what was to come there was a connection between them, by way of man's inner experience, which is to say the mystical. Midway between them are the wheels with all their eyes, moving this way and that on the ground beneath the throne of God.

Is there anything in Paul Celan's poem to justify employing Ezekiel's ancient vision in its reading? What, in a poem, decides whether the reader's association is relevant or tenuous?

The key word in the verse is "no." No sisters, no stars, no place. "No" denotes an absence. In that absence, that which is not, exists that which is. You, a wheel, spokes, field, the night, are characterized by this absence, and it is against the background of this absence that they are presented to us. The night is characterized by the absence of stars. The wheel turns on its own, this is emphasized, and seems not to belong together with anything else. The sky beneath which it slowly turns is empty. Read positively, as it stands, there is no connection between the wheel in the poem and the wheels in Ezekiel's vision. But read negatively, in terms of what it lacks, the wheel is a symbol without context, where the lack of context together with the emptiness of the sky expresses something extremely important, linking up with the "no" of the hour, the "no" of the night, and the "no" of the nowhere: something is no longer. And in that: something is no longer possible.

The wheel that rolls slowly, out of itself, and which is tied up with the darkness of the night and the emptiness of the sky, has to come from somewhere, too, and that place, one might imagine, would be a place of cohesion, where things hung together and meaning was apparent. In the here of the poem, wherever it might be, the you is alone, the wheel on its own, the sky empty, and if all cohesion is absent, the reason is not because it has been written asunder like the grass – that terrain was centered upon what was written and the eye that saw, for the grass that is written asunder has been left behind; the you did not read in order to come here, did not look in order to come here, but went. This is not the terrain with the unmistakable track, this is home.

What is home? Home is the place you belong, the place you know, often the place you come from. This home is something to which the you comes. The you thereby returns; time has passed. There is a before, and there is a now. This home is empty, and there is no one there who knows the you. Nowhere does anyone ask after you. Where are they who might have asked after you, and who were they? The way they are mentioned, impersonally, without even a "they," connects them with whoever drove, whoever wrote the grass asunder, in the sense that they are quite as remote.

"Nowhere does anyone ask after you." In the original German this is "*nirgends fragt es nach dir,*" in the Norwegian translation "*ingen steder spørres det etter deg.*" What is the "*es*" in the German? The "*det*" in the Norwegian? The vague, impersonal agent: it's raining, it's snowing. The human is as remote as can be without having vanished completely. Even the act of asking after you is unperformed, visible only in its negation. No one asks after you, and as such they who do not ask are presented to us. Yet they were here once, this is implied; once they asked after you. Now all there is here is a wheel, a field, a night sky devoid of stars. The terrain being empty, the emphasis of absence, means that the one entity to be named is accorded special weight indeed. The wheel that rolls "out of itself," of its own volition.

A wheel appears in Dante's *Divina Commedia* too; Dante is in the Earthly Paradise and witnesses a procession, and this is also allegory. He sees twenty-four elders, representing the books of the

Old Testament; he sees four animals, representing the Evangelists; he sees a griffin, representing Christ; he sees a chariot, representing the universal church; he sees two wheels, representing the two Testaments, or the active and the contemplative life, or justice and devoutness. But the allegory is no abstract vision, it is a tangible occurrence, the procession comes toward him as a physical reality, so physical even that the wheels leave ruts in the ground. The image is a poetic monstrosity in that when the allegory materializes and is accorded particular time in particular space, the griffin is not primarily Christ, but a griffin, the wheels not primarily the two Testaments, but wheels. What happens in Dante is that the timeless construct of the medieval world, the untouchable and schematic system to which all things and powers are subordinate, present for instance in the *Divina Commedia* in the form of all manner of devilish cycles and heavenly spheres centered upon the number three, is implanted into time and space, where the symbolic level is pervaded by the concrete in an impossible equivalency.

The terrain at the beginning of Celan's poem is, like the terrain of Dante's epic poem, bound up with death or nonexistence, though only implicitly so, by way of suggestion, in the wording "your hour has no sisters," and in the caesura between "you are –" and "you are at home." But if we take this in the sense that this starless, blackened terrain is the terrain of death, through which the "you" of the poem proceeds, the wheel is something that reveals itself. In the poetry of the death realm this is a trope: he who wanders through the kingdom of death sees something, and what he sees is shown to him so that he may tell of it when he returns to the land of the living. What the wanderer sees is meaningful. In the first fifteen lines of Celan's poem perhaps the most obvious trait is the archaic, the fact that everything that is named is in some way timeless – terrain, track, grass, stones, grassblade shadows, wheel, field, stars. No name can assign time to the space or assign to it any particular culture. We are in what is always the same. And perhaps this is why the wheel turning on its own through the empty night comes across so forbiddingly, or so fore-bodingly. A wheel turning by itself is not something that should be unfamiliar to us, given that we are surrounded by wheels turning by themselves, from the cogs of clockwork and machines to the wheels of cars and trains. The forbidding aspect here comes from it being a wheel on its own and that its movement is the only movement, indeed the only thing at all to exist in this terrain, and that in every respect it appears so archaic. The wheel turns of itself. This gives rise to associations of God's wheel, seen by Ezekiel, which like this wheel also existed tangibly in a tangible terrain. It gives rise to associations of the culture infusing the wheel with meaning; the wheel of life, rolling on unalterably, and the wheel that gives order to chaos and gives form to the formless. But in these cases the wheel is everything; here in the poem it is an entity surrounded by everything. And it gives rise, too, to associations of the mechanically driven wheel, which in such case is not only an image of time, but of our time. The wheel is archaic and religious but not to us, since to us the archaic aspect of the wheel has dissolved into the modern age in which the wheel now exists, and the two levels are made to converge here, the single wheel in the timeless terrain is the archaic wheel, while its forward motion, which is not connected to the divine, the sky above it being empty, renders the archaic strange to us, and the ambivalence renders it forbidding. And forbidding it is, certainly. No one is there to steer it, no one in control; it rolls slowly "out of itself." It is beyond the human. The grass, written asunder, and the agent of not asking after the you, are beyond the name, faceless, invisible higher powers, almost though not quite, for they still belong to the human sphere. The wheel does not.

Does it leave a rut in the terrain, like Dante's wheels?

The poem says nothing about this. But the word "track" appears only a few lines above. "The unmistakable track," it says. A track is at once something in its own right and a sign of something else. A track is language. Usually, tracks are temporary, while that of which they are a sign is more permanent. Animal tracks in the snow or sand are blown away and disappear. This track is different, it is unmistakable, the way for instance a railway track is unmistakable. The poem doesn't say railway track, and it says nothing of the wheel turning the way the wheels of a train turn. There is no mention of machinery, nothing to do with mechanics. All we have are the words "unmistakable" and "out of itself." And the fact of the grass being written asunder, which is to say that something is damaged. The line of progression goes from the damaged to what is at home, where a single wheel slowly turns, the night prevails, and no one asks after whoever has come. This is the terrain of the poem, this is the home of the you, accorded more depth in the verse that follows:

◆

Nowhere
　　　　　　does anyone ask after you —

The place where they lay, it has
a name – it has
none. They did not lie there. Something
lay between them. They
did not see through it.

Did not see, no,
spoke of
words. None
awoke,
sleep
came over them.

This is the first time someone other than "you" appears directly in the poem. They are without name, referred to simply by the pronoun; they are "they."

Who are "they"?

And what is meant by the fact that they "lay"? Were they dead, were they buried, or were they asleep? In which case, where? The place has a name, but the name is unstated, and then the very fact of it having a name is withdrawn – it has none. "They," too, are unnamed. Their namelessness, their being referred to merely as "they" or "them" is disquieting, for while the "it," the agent of driving and writing asunder and not asking, is so remote as to defy association, the pronoun here draws "them," whoever they may be, closer, and their namelessness, which is the facelessness of language, becomes menacing in a different way altogether, much like the eyes of a blind person, one might imagine, the absence of the human in the human gaze. Disquieting also because they are surrounded by negation – none, not, no, none – it is almost as if they do not exist at all, as if they are on the very brink of erasure, at the same time as the neutral aspect, the remoteness of the nonpersonal, lends to their presence an aura of representation, something solemn and ritual; as if they were kings or gods. But "they" are not gods, they do not see and barely exist; we are told that "none awoke," so they were asleep even before "sleep came over them." The sleep of sleeps is death. But the poem does not say death, nor does it say sleep of sleeps, but: none awoke, sleep came over them. Why?

They are tightly bound to each other, they slept in life, they did not see and did not awake from it, for the next sleep came over them. Their not seeing stands in direct opposition to their speaking of words: they did not see the true world but the world that points toward the true world, that of words. This can be understood in existential terms, as if they were living a life that was inauthentic, unseeing of that which is genuine, but in the space between "none awoke" and "sleep came over them" lies the possibility of an unuttered "before it was too late." This, along with the failure to see, "they did not see through it," the repetition of "not see," the reinforcement of "spoke of words"; all this implies neglect, and the consequence of that neglect was that the other sleep came over them. They died, though the poem cannot state as much, since death would then become "something" and the dead "someone." Death is nothing and the dead are no one, and it is the absolute nature of this loss, the complete irreversibility of it, that the language has to deal with; this is what it has taken upon itself, at the same time as it must remain true to the unique and individual, which is to say separate it from the undifferentiated void without at the same time maintaining that identity and making it something that "is." The poem stands at the very borderline between language and the unspeakable, but this is not what it points toward, this is no language game; the poem is out there in the night of nights in order to evoke the unevokable, that which is so brittle and fleeting, so ghostly and indefinite that the slightest glimpse of an eye or a fleeting thought would cause it to recede and vanish; indeed, in a way it is that very movement it seeks to express.

The question posed is this: how to name that which is nothing without making it something? This is the very negation of religion's great puzzle: how to name what is infinite without making it finite? Even the "all" is finite. How do we name what is beyond humanity without drawing it into the human domain, given that language in itself is human? How do we refer to God?

In orthodox Judaism, God's name is unuttered, or uttered only by the high priest in the temple of Jerusalem, which no longer exists. And if the name is written down it cannot then be erased or defaced. The name appears in the Torah, the collection of holy Scriptures that for non-Jews is the Old Testament, in the form of four letters, YHWH, known as the Tetragrammaton, "the four letters." Instead of reading this name of God in prayer, the faithful read it as "Adonai," meaning "my Lord," while mention of God's name in conversation generally requires the form "HaShem," literally "the Name." Adonai and HaShem are thus names of the name. "The name has a name!" as the Jewish philosopher Emmanuel Levinas exclaims in a reflection on God's name. The name is revealed and is hidden. It is as though the name itself were God.

A normal name is the name of something or someone, here the name is itself something besides. "God" in Hebrew is Elohim; YHWH is the name of the one God, God's own name. Its correct pronunciation is no longer known with any certainty; the oldest Hebrew alphabet contained no vowels, these having been added to the Scriptures at some later date, though not in the case of YHWH. Insofar as the name must not be pronouced, this would not seem to matter. But what does this name that cannot be pronounced actually say?

In the Bible, when Moses asks God his name, God replies "I am that I am" or "I am who I am," more simply "I am." The Canadian critic Northrop Frye writes that some scholars believe a more correct translation to be something along the lines of "I will be what I will be." What is important though is the fact that the name is derived from a Hebrew word meaning "to be," a verb. The name of that which cannot be named is given by God himself to Moses in the form of flames rising from a burning thornbush on Mount Horeb. The Bible says, "There the angel of the Lord appeared to him in a flame of fire out of a bush; he looked, and the bush was blazing, yet it was not consumed." Moses approaches and suddenly he sees not the angel of the Lord, but the Lord himself, calling out to him. "Moses, Moses! Come no closer," the Lord says. "Remove the sandals from your feet, for the place on which you are standing is holy ground. I am the God of your father, the God of Abraham, the God of Isaac, and the God of Jacob." Moses hides his face, afraid to look at God. And thus, barefoot and with eyes lowered, Moses is given his task, to lead the Israelites out of Egypt. Moses replies, "Who am I that I should go to Pharaoh, and bring the Israelites out of Egypt?" And God says, "I will be with you," and he tells Moses he will receive a sign that God is with him; and when he has brought the people from Egypt they are to worship God on that same mountain. But not belonging to the people he must lead, Moses needs a sign now, rather than later, for how else might he persuade them to go with him? For this reason he says to God,

"If I come to the Israelites and say to them, 'The God of your ancestors has sent me to you,' and they ask me, 'What is his name?' what shall I say to them?" To which God replies, "I am who I am. Thus you shall say to the Israelites, 'I AM has sent me to you.'"

The name God gives Moses is not a name, because it defines nothing, locates nothing, yet it is a name nonetheless, but of that which defies definition, location, determination. The inexhaustibility of this name, which is not a name, contrasts strongly with the context in which it is revealed. As in so many other instances in the Old Testament there is something comical about the occurrence, the reason for this being that the highest, the divine, the extra-human comes so close to the human as to become almost snared up in it. God or the divine revealing itself in the form of some heavenly phenomenon might be sublime, but not in a burning bush, there being something almost trivial about such a thing, at which one might stand and stare in perplexity but never tremble in fear. God asking Moses to take off his sandals diminishes the revelation yet further: sandals or no sandals is a particularly human deliberation, one would think. And when Moses speaks to God, a misunderstanding arises, Moses asking for a sign to bolster his credibility in the eyes of the Israelites, God however promising him a sign once it is all over, meaning Moses has to be more exact and explain: but if I come to the Israelites and say to them that the God of their ancestors has sent me, and they ask me what his name is, what am I supposed to say? Moses's approach is reminiscent of a trick, asking for God's name by asking for the answer to a hyopothetical question the Israelites might ask him. The answer, the name, points away from the trivial toward the nature of the divine. The two levels intermingle throughout the Old Testament, as when God sews clothes of animal hide for Adam and Eve in the Garden of Eden, or when God gets himself into an argument with Sara, wife of Abraham. The same occurs in other ancient texts, for instance in Homer's *Iliad* and

Odyssey, where gods and the divine move in and out of the human domain, not in any metaphorical sense but tangibly so, with physical bodies in the physical world.

Gershom Scholem writes of the three phases of religion, the first occurring when the world itself is divine, populated by gods humankind may encounter anywhere, who can be won over to one's cause without trepidation: the human and the divine are not separated in any fundamental way. Everything is connected: man, nature, the gods. So too in Homer, where the names of the gods are likewise anything but unmentionable, flourishing in daily conversation. The second phase occurs with the emergence of the great religions, which open a vast and absolute abyss between the divine and the human, Scholem writes, bridgeable only by the voice: God's voice, instructional and legislative, and man's voice in prayer.

Some of the texts of the Old Testament carry with them fragments of earlier periods, such as the fairy-tale nature of the incident when Jacob encounters a stranger in the twilight and wrestles him all through the night, until the stranger beseeches Jacob to release him because dawn is approaching. Jacob refuses, only if the stranger blesses him will he let him go. The stranger does so and tells Jacob that from that moment on his name shall be Israel, for he has striven with God and prevailed. Then, although the stranger has made himself known as God, Jacob asks his name. God replies, "Why is it that you ask my name?," blesses him, and is gone. That God may physically be encountered and even wrestled with – the physical nature of the meeting being made plain in the detail of Jacob's hip being put out of joint during the struggle – brings to mind the world of which Scholem writes, shared by humans and gods alike, and God's wish to end the struggle before the dawn draws the encounter into the world of the folktale and the ancient reality of myth, in which the troll turns to stone in daylight. Northrop Frye writes that the world is characterized by what he calls a metaphorical language in which words are substantial in their own right, invoking their objects, the entities or phenomena they denote, much like hieroglyphics, posessing powers used in spells and evocations, as for instance is shown by the account of the creation when God's word becomes real: Let there be light, and there was light. Names may create, and names may rule. In such a world to know the name of God would be to possess the power of the divine, one might imagine, it hardly being accidental that Jacob measures himself against God, eventually even prevailing, before asking for his name. "Tell me your name!" he demands with some presumption. "Why is it that you ask my name?" asks God, and vanishes into the shadows of the night.

According to Scholem, mysticism arises in the third phase of religion, once religion has assumed its classic expression in communities of faith, and when the new religious impulses that occur, rather than stepping outside the prevailing context to establish something new, instead remain to shape themselves within the old religion, where the abyss between the divine and the human is considered a mystery that inner experience of the divine may resolve.

Mysticism is free of the practical sides of religion, the morality, the obligations, the tasks, directed entirely inward toward the experience of the divine and its nature. The original revelations, the burning bush seen by Moses, for instance, or the winged creatures with the heads of animals that appeared to Ezekiel, are to the mystic somewhat obscure and poorly developed, Scholem suggests.

His definition of mysticism is approached firstly by way of a quote from Rufus Jones as "the type of religion which puts the emphasis on immediate awareness of relation to God, on direct and intimate consciousness of the Divine Presence," subsequently by reference to Thomas Aquinas, who defined it as *"cognitio Dei experimentalis,"* the experiential knowledge of God. The great canonical revelations are placed side by side with the individual's own experience. As Scholem states:

With no thought of denying Revelation as a fact of history, the mystic still conceives the source of religious knowledge and experience which bursts forth from his own heart as being of equal importance for the conception of religious truth.

The heart is the very symbol of the innermost human self, our deepest emotional being, in direct contrast to the rational intellect and the outer world. And it is here, in the perception of and meditation upon the nature of the divine, present in our souls, in the ecstasy of the heart, that language becomes a problem in religion. Religious ecstasy contains all manner of vast and formidable emotions; they are wordless and cannot be represented, cannot be described, cannot be repeated, at one with themselves, and only in the very particular experience is the presence of God real. And what reveals itself, what is perceived, the divine, is outside the human sphere, drawn into it only by the very nature of language. A strong tradition in mysticism is therefore the negative; only by stating what the divine is not may it be approached without reduction. Can it be said that God is living? Scholem ponders, citing Maimonides. Would that not imply a limitation of the infinite nature of his being? The sentence "God is living" can only mean "He is not dead," which is to say that he is the opposite of the negative, the negation of negations. But what is he then? Can we say that God is anything at all? It is to this progression that the Kabbalist notion of God resting in the depths of his nothingness belongs. God is nothing. This is not to say that Celan's poem explores any sort of mystical experience, merely that the language employed in it has certain things in common with the language of mysticism, the issue being the same: how to approach that which is not, without turning it into something that is. But if the abyss of religion is that separating the divine from the human, bridgeable only by that which is without language – the heart, ecstasy, delight – and the challenge in the texts of mysticism for that reason lies in giving words to the wordless presence, then the challenge of Celan's poem lies rather in approaching wordless absence. The poem's unutterable word is not God, but death, since death is nothing, whereas the name of nothing is something. This awareness of the impossibility of representation is fundamental to the poem; it is as if the relationship between the world and its linguistic representation has broken down, and the poem exists, ruin-like, within that destruction at the same time as being about it. Its basic distrust of language reveals itself firstly in the image of the grass written asunder in the opening lines, then in the opposition between seeing and speaking about: they saw not, and spoke of words. The words exist between them and reality, and they do not see through them, but see them, and speak of them. This again has to do with being asleep.

> *The place where they lay, it has*
> *a name — it has*
> *none. They did not lie there. Something*
> *lay between them. They*
> *did not see through it.*
>
> *Did not see, no,*
> *spoke of*
> *words. None*
> *awoke,*
> *sleep*
> *came over them.*

Yet the poem itself consists of words, the poem "speaks." This can hardly be understood in any other way than that the image of the grass written asunder and of the sleeping who speak of words are not an expression of misology, it is not the language itself which is distrusted, but the conceptions that attach to it, the fact of language not only evoking what it names, but also the idea of what belongs to "the word," which is to say the community of language, and not the "thing" or the "phenomenon." This becomes especially clear when language names that which is not, the past, which language makes present, and death, which language makes into "something." The poem turns this latter point to its own advantage, since by naming nothing, the nothing emerges as something, to exist in the text, then to be withdrawn, not existing after all, here and not here at one and the same time. The first instance of this strategy being used is in connection with the name, that which turns the open, indefinite, diverse, and heterogeneous into one, the emblem of place, the place name, which seems almost to accommodate both the terrain itself and the history of the terrain, in that way becoming an existence in the language, which is to say the culture, and not in the world. "The place where they lay, it has/a name – it has/none." The place does and does not have a name. The fact of it having or not having a name is no more significant than the name itself, but the name cannot be mentioned. Mention the name, and the place and those who lay there become something they are not. Then the poem, too, would speak of words, and sleep.

Up until now the poem has been about a "you" in a world in which other people at first are discernible only as powers unrepresented by pronouns, then, in the movement of the "you" toward "home," expressed as "they" and "them." These "they" are unpositioned within the space; to begin with they lay "there," only then to be called back, "they did not lie there." They are, however, positioned in time, for while the poem's "you" is described as being in the present, in the terrain of the now, "they" are assigned to the past. They lay, they did not wake, they slept. This makes it possible to read their presence as a memory, something on which the "you" thinks back. "They" exist in a time remote from the "you," but the place where they lay/did not lie exists in the same time, since it "has" a name.

The place where they lay, it has
a name – it has
none. They did not lie there.

Then comes the poem's first turning point. Until now the poem has proceeded steadily, from the terrain with its track, via the call not to read, not to look, but to go, into a deathlike landscape in which the thought of the "they" who once were arises. In the next verse an "I" speaks for the first time, and like the "you" it speaks in the present, about the "they" of the past.

> *It is I, I,*
> *I lay between you, I was*
> *open, was*
> *audible, ticked at you, your breathing*
> *obeyed, it is*
> *I still, but then*
> *you are asleep.*

◆

It is I still –

The original German has *"Ich bins,"* a contraction of *Ich bin es*, a colloquial expression often used when answering the phone, *Ich bins*, "It is I." After the mysterious introductory stanzas from which little meaning may be extracted, the everydayness of the introduction of this "I" seeems striking, there is almost something childlike about it, the way it insists, the "I" being named three times in the course of four words. *Ich bins*, *ich*, *ich*, at the same time as the time shifts, *ich bins*, *ich lag*, *ich war* – I am, I lay, I was – then shifts back again, *ich bin*, I am – *noch immer*: still. The movement is thereby from I am to I was and back to I am again. Present, past, present.

Péter Szondi, who has provided the classic and probably most detailed analysis of this poem, now a standard reading, believes that it is time speaking here, time personified. This may be so, but there is another possibility, that the writer is the "I" and that the situation described, when I lay between "them" and was open, is a memory. Both the sudden childlike presence in the text and the wording "I lay between you" make me think of a child lying between its parents. The significance of time in this verse is plain, but so, too, is "I," whose presence is conspicuously emphasized in the forceful repetition I, I, I. Regardless of how this "I" is understood, the "they" the "I" lay between may be the same "they" mentioned in the previous stanza, of whom it is predicated "something lay between them." They were sleeping, and the movement of the "I" from am to was and back to am again is something from which they are excluded; they, too, "are" still, but sleeping, which is to say dead. That which "is" becomes "was" through the "I," who turns it into "is" by the evocation of memory – identical with the poet's evocation of reality, the two things, the past and the written, memory and literature, coincide here – but that possibility does not exist for those he was with at that time, they slept then and they sleep now, their "still" being of a different character altogether, unchangeable, uniform, of death and the timelessness of the nothing. Death is not a state or a quality, it is an absence of states and qualities, and as such it has no time, only non-time. Non-time, too, has no "is" of existence other than in language, which abstracts the world, and in abstraction nothing, too, may be accorded form. The gaze of the eye may exist only as an "is," in the now, whereas the language may strive toward "was," through memory, where the differences between tangible and intangible are wiped out: in memory the space was the same, the world and its people faded into impalpability, as Joyce defined the ghost.

If we ignore the "I" and the "they" and the question of who they are and what relation exists between them, or rather, who they are to the "I," given that the "I" is not something to them, then the most significant thing occurring in this stanza is the time that flows through the verbs and thereby through the I. You cannot step twice into the same river, as Heraclitus says in one of his fragments, the ninety-first, perhaps his best known quote, now a cliché. But there is another fragment of his concerning the same thing, the forty-ninth, in which he puts it rather differently and thereby makes a quite different statement:

We step and do not step into the same river; we are and are not.

Time and identity are drawn together in "are," we are and yet we are not, and what is "are" then? In Celan's poem time opens up the same distance in the I, which does not say I am, I was, I am, but shades and complicates it by subtle means, impossible to reproduce in translation to Norwegian, to do with the interplay between *ich* and *bin* and *es*. In English *Ich bins* has to be rendered as "It's me" or "It is I," but another meaning becomes apparent if, leaving aside the idiomatic, one shadows the syntax of the German more closely. That gives us "I am it," then "I am it still," and finally "am it still." This latter nuance is important insofar as it deprives the everyday "It's me/It is I" of its notional subject, leaving us with "it's/it is" and thereby drawing attention to that very constituent. What is the "it" that is? "It," apparently, is "I," but then what is the "it" that the "I" is? The question projects back to the opening, no longer quite as quotidian, the "I" containing an "it." The German looks like this:

Ich bins, ich,
ich lag zwischen euch, ich war
offen, war
hörbar, ich tickte euch zu, euer Atem
gehorchte, ich
bin es noch immer, ihr
schläft ja.

◆

Bin es noch immer —

Translating the first assertion as "It is I" preserves, more so than the literal "I am it," some measure of the colloquialness of the original, the unencumbered everydayness about the wording that keeps the I firmly within the bounds of the social: It's me. But then the final line would strictly speaking have to be "It is still," them-ing "it," the assertion thereby extending beyond the social. I am it, it is I. This points toward something outside the "I" that encompasses itself. "I am another," said Rimbaud, but while this is dissolving of the identity it remains within the realm of the social. "I am I" goes beyond the social, beyond the name, into the nameless, "it" being the mark of the impersonal. "It sleeps," "it laughs," "it grieves" – no person would be referred to in such a way: "it" pertains not to the human, but to the nonhuman. And yet it is an "I" that is "it." Taken positively, the "it" might be that through which existence presents itself, that which is common to us all, bound up with the authentic, in contrast to that aspect of human existence that is joined up with the social world, which is to say all our hierarchies and laws, norms and rules, what Heidegger called *das Man*, the derivative and inauthentic, the very opposite of the authenticity and independence of pure existence. This pure self of Heidegger's, open toward existence, is in turn related to the self of the mystics, that which comes together with the divine in the forgetting of the self, the I-less I. It seems beyond doubt that the I of the poem has to do with this, though not in any positive sense; the I is what is left of the person when the name is gone, the I is what dies when the person dies and the name lives on. The I is not erased in ecstasy, filled with the meaning of life, but in its opposite, being erased in the shadow of death, filled with its nonmeaning.

> *It is I.*
> *It is.*
> *It.*

But "it" is not what the poem invokes. What the poem invokes is "I." Three times in succession it rings out, I, I, I, almost as if it were trying to wrench free of its "it." The fact that it is, whereas they were, is another way of saying I am alive and they are dead. The constituents are the simplest possible: you, they, I, it, is, was. Being and not being. Being is a matter of existence, we are dealing with being in itself. This is Hamlet's question, to be or not to be, and it concerns the notion of being without identity. In such being, one is not someone but something. This is where the line goes between being someone and being nothing. But being is also a matter of identity. One is, in such an instance, someone, and the line goes between being someone and being no one. Something/someone, nothing/no one. The first, something/nothing, is that which stands outside the name and the social realm, the second, someone/no one, exists within the name and the social. One can be something in relation to nothing. But one cannot be someone in relation to no one: one can be someone only in relation to others. A you, a they, which together make a we. But here there is no we, only an I/you and a they. The they is absent and no one asks after the you/the I. This is what is at stake here; who is the you, since no one asks after them, since no one knows them or knows about them? In such an instance the you is not someone, but no one/something.

Who is the I? Is the I a part of "them," does it belong among them, is that what is meant by "home"? Is that the connection that has been lost? The important thing in the verse is what separates I from them, which is time: once, I and you existed together in a present, now only I remain there, while you are in a past. That time, that division, that abyss, is expounded upon in the next verse:

Years.
Years, years, a finger
feels down and up, feels
around:
seams, palpable, here
it is split wide open, here

it grew together again – who
covered it up?

◆

Covered it
        up – who?

The insistence, the repetition of the word three times, joins "I" and "years" together. The space between is and was, present and past, has been opened, within or by the I. Into it the I now enters. Years, years, years; time here is a space, something within the same, the movement is down, up, around. The finger that feels around is connected to that which ticks in the previous stanza, Aris Fioretos suggests in his reading of the poem; German "*ticken*" can mean both "tick" and "touch with the fingertip." The ticking finger that joins the notion of the I as the person writing with that of the I as the voice of time. A finger feels and finds. What does it find? Seams. What are seams? Seams are made of stitches. Stitches join together wounds. The wound is grown together again and is thereby absent and yet present, unmentioned, yet apparent in the mention of that which covers. The wound does not emerge in its authentic form, hardly anything does in this poem, and yet this is somehow different, because here "someone" has covered, the covering is active and has a particular cause, and the question concerns who covered up the wounds, rather than what covered them.

To cover something up involves something coming between one thing and another, an intervention, and so far in the poem this has been expressed in terms of the grass written asunder and the speaking of words, and time separating the I from them. The attention has been on the what, the act of covering, but here it is directed not toward the what, but toward a who.

Who covered it up? And why is "who" so important that their identity has to be asked for in a question?

Thus, cautiously and without naming anything that might propel it back into the darkness from which it is lifted ghostlike, the poem approaches its center or zero point.

> *Came, came.*
> *Came a word, came,*
> *came through the night,*
> *wanted to shine, wanted to shine.*

The repetition of the word is of the same intensity as that of "I" and "years": three times a "came." And it is intensified further still, mentioned twice more. Came, came, came, came, came. The effect is much like that of an incantation, a ritual recitation. The word that came represents the opposite of the covering up, it came "through" the night, that which covers up or makes things the same, thereby canceling it out. The word is the opposite of the nothing, the word came forth as something against the darkness of the nothing, and for this reason it is recited. It is, therefore, a different kind of word from those of which "they" spoke, for those words prevented them from seeing, and were the very hindrance. In that instance there was a contrast between seeing and the words, a negative relation: they who spoke, spoke of words, and they did not see. Here it is the similarity between seeing and the word, a positive relation: the word wanted to shine in the night. And light makes visible. But the word did not shine, it wanted to shine, and in this lies the idea of the light being an insubstantiated possibility. The word could shine, but it could not shine here, the poem appears to say.

Why not? What is it that prevented the word that could shine from shining?

It is the night.

What kind of night is it? At the beginning of the poem it is described as a night that needed no stars. This is a different night to that which ends at dawn: it is tempting to think of it as an image of death: the night needs no stars, needs no light, for there is nothing there to illuminate, there is nothing. This night is of a different quality, there is something in it the words lack strength to illuminate. Night is darkness, darkness is undifferentiated, the opposite of words, which by their nature are differentiating, establishing of distinctions. Whereas the first night did not need stars or light, this one does. Why? The poem has predicated a moving forward, and in that moving forward it has approached something, and in that approach this something, at first distant and remote, has gradually become clearer in shape, and in this, the gradual uncovering of something whose nature is still unknown to us, the intensity of the poem has increased and is now so acute that the words are repeated with the forceful effect of the incantation. Came, came, came, came, came. This incantation comes immediately after the ascertainment that the wound, unmentioned and unshown, present merely by virtue of the "it" that "grew together," is covered up, and immediately after the question as to who covered it up. The words repeated are repeated in a time other than that of their occurrence: came a word, it says, in the poem's present, in the time of the you and the I, whereas the will to shine, and the lack of ability to do so, is in its past: wanted to shine.

Is it so because the night is the very force that makes present past, that it is this, the darkness of what has been lost, that is meant, in that case also comprising the light of the words, and turning their want into a wanted, by virtue of their being words, immobilizing what is and transforming it, inevitably, into something that was? Or is the night connected with the covering up of the wound and the writing asunder of the grass, the language then being a part of the night, a part of what covers up – something that lies in the description of those who "spoke of words" and did not "see"? Would that be why the words cannot shine, nor, thereby, make it possible to see, because they offer only darkness themselves? The desire that lies in "wanted to shine, wanted to shine" suggests that it is not the language in itself that darkens, but a particular kind of language, spoken by "them," and that some other language exists, but even that language cannot penetrate this night. This night is associated with events, they who did not wake before sleep came over them, and they who caused a wound, and they concern the I who once lay between them, who opens up the space between the absence of the wound in the present and the presence of the wound in the past.

"Came a word, came/through the night," and yet in vain, the word wanted to shine but could not. The will is without subject, the poem says only "wanted to shine, wanted to shine," according weight to the will, which is strong, yet futile.

Wanted to shine, wanted to shine.

Why can the words not shine here? What is it that makes the night so undifferentiated that no word can make a difference in its darkness?

> *Ash.*
> *Ash, ash.*
> *Night.*
> *Night-and-night. – Go*
> *to the eye, the moist one.*

Ash, it says three times, night three times, though without a verb, nothing "came," there is no motion of any kind, no "through."

Ash, ash, ash.

Ash is the form of that which has been incinerated without it bearing any similarity to its former state, ash is nothing, yet it is what is left of an object when that object has gone, at the same time as it is something in itself, a blackish-gray dust, the same in any instance of incineration. In a poem in which nothing came from nothingness, the ash can be read as an actualization of that which is not, the physical form of absence. And it can be read as the material instantiation of the undifferentiated. Ash is nothing, yet it is something, and it is the same for everything.

After the ash, night and night follow night. In this night even the undifferentiatedness of ash becomes undifferentiated.

Ash.
Ash, ash.
Night.
Night-and-night.

Why the "and" in night? Separated by a comma it might be the same thing, night, night, night, an insistence, an incantation, but the "and" inserts a relation, which is to say a distinction, and in so doing introduces a course of events. Night-and-night. Night follows night, but so closely joined, the hyphens connecting the two nights in a single word, "night-and-night," that nothing exists between them, no light, no dawn, no day.

Then the "go" is resurrected, the plea from the beginning of the poem, at that point open, general, a simple "go" instead of "reading" and "looking." Now "go" is directionally specified: "to the eye." And further: "to the moist one." This is at the end of the poem's fifth section, and since the poem consists of nine sections in all, it comes exactly midway, at the very center.

Came, came, came a word, came, came, wanted to shine, wanted to shine, ash, ash, ash, night, night-and-night, go to the eye, to the moist one. From the word, that which is general, and its light that is not possible, to the ash and the night and to the eye, but not to the eye that sees, it carries on, to the moist one.

Do not read, look, do not look, go, go to the eye that weeps.

"Ash" and "night" enter into the series of words that are given weight by being repeated three times and which establish particular places in the poem where meaning becomes concentrated. I (identity), years (time), came (incantation), ash (absence, destruction), night (undifferentiatedness). These words make up an axis of meaning within the poem. Another axis consists of the pronouns, you-I-they-who. A third is comprised of the imperatives, read, look, go, which to begin with lead into the deathlike and the terrain, empty of both people and stars, down into the past and up again to the here, where for the first time a direction is specified. The weeping eye is the midpoint of the poem around which the entire text revolves, for after the eye, and the long way toward it, the poem radically changes character.

Until now the human presence has been a "you," an "I," and a "they." The significant aspect of the relationship between "I" and "they" has been their separation from each other. By time, sleep, death, darkness. The gaze of the eye and the word have been likewise separated from the world. This latter separation, from the unnameable wound, which is a wound no longer, but covered up by someone, was followed by the coming of a word and its failure to shine. From the ash and the night, nothing may be extracted but ash and night. There is nothing to read, nothing to see. But there is something to feel. This eye does not separate, does not divide, it is not primarily connected with the external and with seeing, but with the internal and with feeling; indeed, it is hard to understand "to the eye, to the moist one" in any other way.

In mysticism the source of innermost truth is the heart, locus of the ecstatic coming together of all things. Celan's eye can be understood conversely as a place whose wordless concentration is not of joy and expanded awareness, but of grief and the implosion of awareness. Both places exist outside the social world, and outside the name.

The heart is full of the all, the eye of the nothing. The heart, filled with what is, is blind and sees nothing; the eye, filled with what is not, sees, and sees nothing.

Here, at the place of grief and the weeping eye, the poem turns away from its now to face a then, not what grew together and was a wound, but that which went before. The time of the "we."

> *Gales.*
> *Gales, from the beginning of time,*
> *whirl of particles, the other,*
> *you*
> *know it, though, we*

> *read it in the book, was*
> *opinion.*
>
> *Was, was*
> *opinion. How*
> *did we touch*
> *each other — each other with*
> *these*
> *hands?*

Gales are specified in two different ways here. Firstly as being from the beginning of time, which is to say archaic, immutable, the same then as now. Secondly as a whirl of particles, something known by a "you," because "we" read it in "the book": it was opinion. The next stanza emphasizes the past nature of that opinion. Was, was opinion.

What is a gale? A strong wind, a force of nature, arbitrary, violent, destructive, chaotic, something of the "it" we name when we say "it's blowing outside." But also "the other," the whirl of particles, the explanation in that, the resonance of science in "particle," something broken down into its smallest elements, and thereby also the concept, though not unconditionally; the "whirl" is that which has been whirled together into something beyond concepts, something more and other than the mere whirling together. The word "particle" points toward something invisible to us, but which nonetheless we know to be there. This line of thinking stems from Democritus and the atomic theory of the ancient Greeks, as pursued by Lucretius in his poem *De rerum natura*, in which poetry meets science; it seeks to explain a phenomenon, to command and delimit, whereas the word "gale" points to a phenomenon. The significance of this distinction becomes clear in what comes next: the whirl of particles was in "the book," it was "opinion." Knowing something is associated with reading, which in turn is associated with opinion. But that opinion no longer exists, as suggested by the emphasis of past time in the repetition.

491

Was, was. Opinion, opinion. The plea not to read any more might be directed toward this time, the time when what was written was opinion. In other words, that opinion is now lost. But the emphasis is not so much on the reading itself as on what "you" and "we" read. There is a community there, and the fact of opinion now being of the past, and perhaps no longer valid, is followed by a question that has to do with the connection between those who comprised the "we," and it is hard indeed not to construe this in such a way that it is the socially cohesive aspect of the opinion that is at stake, the common foundation shared by people belonging to the same culture: "we" read, "we" touched each other.

Who are "we"?

Seemingly, the "we" would refer to something in the past, a community no longer in existence and which now in some sense defies understanding. How did we touch each other, is the question, though it does not stop there, but continues with a specification: – each other with these hands? These hands exist now; what they touched, which comprised the "we," exists in the past, the verb form being "touched" rather than "touch," and this is the abyss the question spans. "You," "you," "they," "we," and "our" are all past, only the "I" is present, so what happens is that something of what has been lost is separated out. The difference between being an I looking toward other I's that existed once, and being an I looking toward the "we" the living and the dead once comprised, is huge. Not only has the community of those particular people been lost to time, but what made that community possible then, the very conditions of its existence, has been lost too. It is within the field of this loss that the poem is written. It is as if what this entails, what "we" represents, cannot be stated until after the plea to go to the eye, to the moist one; only then can the lost "we" be named; and this is the most painful thing of all.

Another of Heraclitus's fragments, the twenty-sixth, concerns the relationship between the living, the sleeping, and the dead:

Man kindles a light for himself in the nighttime, when he has died
but is alive. The sleeper, whose vision has been put out, lights up from
the dead; he that is awake lights up from the sleeping.

The states described exclude each other – when sleeping, one cannot be dead, when awake one cannot be asleep – and yet are connected by the very ambivalence of those states, the borderlands between them. Man is in the nighttime, which is to say the darkness, where nothing is visible and nothing may be differentiated. He kindles a light, but the light cannot make visible, his eyes are put out and cannot see, he is himself darkness. Man is dead, but is alive, which is to say that he is sleeping. The sleeper lights up from the dead. He that is awake lights up from the sleeping, he is outside sleep, even further from death, yet the border is by no means absolute; like the text, we pass through the various states, consciousness waxing and waning within us, and when it wanes something else comes into view, unknown to those awake; the shores of the dead.

But this proceeds in one direction only, from the living to the sleeping to the dead; the dead do not look back.

There is another of Heraclitus's fragments likewise concerning death and sleep, the twenty-first:

All the things we see when awake are death, even as all we see in
slumber are sleep.

In both fragments seeing is pivotal, and both relate to sleep and waking, life and death. Both fragments are opaque, and to begin with seem to point in different directions. In the first, he who is awake lights up from the sleeping, but not the dead. In the second, death is all that he who is awake can see, while the sleeper sees only sleep, i.e., that which is his, not that of the other. But they may also be understood as expressing the same thing. When we are awake we see death, in the sense of absence and nothingness; when we sleep we do not, in sleep death is sleep, too. There may also be a point relating to a qualitative distinction in the act of seeing; to be awake is to see clearly, faithfully, we see that death is all around us, a fundamental condition of our lives, while to sleep is to not see clearly, in that we see only that which is ours, sleep, which hushes us up. The authentic life, which recognizes death, and the inauthentic life, lived as if death does not exist.

All these various levels are present in Paul Celan's poem, those that distinguish between gradations of awake, asleep, and dead, and those that distinguish between gradations of authentic and inauthentic. From the poem's beginning:

> *The place where they lay, it has*
> *a name – it has*
> *none. They did not lie there. Something*
> *lay between them. They*
> *did not see through it.*
>
> *Did not see, no,*
> *spoke of*
> *words. None*
> *awoke,*
> *sleep*
> *came over them.*

They do not light up, but slip away. At first it is the place where they lay that slips away, it has a name and then does not, and they lay there no longer. This is what they are to those who write, who in their woken state seek to "touch" them. Then we are told what they were in themselves, unseeing. They saw not, because they spoke of words, in a sleep. The agent of the writing is awake, and if it is to "touch" them it cannot speak of words. The name of the place is such a word, something that lies between. It existed, and it exists, but not to them, nor therefore to the poem, which by naming it would have included them within it. The world of the name is the world of opinion, it belongs to the we that was, but which is no longer. Here the world of the name has become still, deactivated, because its foundation, the we, is no longer viable or must be established anew. This stillness of the name exists on two different levels. Nowhere does anyone ask after you, it says, and as such you are something concealed, outside language. The wound is covered up by someone unknown to the I, it is kept under cover. In both instances we are dealing with agentive forces outside the terrain opened up by the poem. The first, the no one asking after you, may also be down to "you" being dead, or because all others in the terrain in which you are present are dead and cannot ask after you, no longer know that you exist. But the covering up is not ambivalent in this way, merely vague. The second level exists in the relationship between those who write and what is written, between "you" and "they," "I" and "we." "They" did not see, they spoke of words. "You" know this, we read it in the book, it was opinion. Was, was, opinion, opinion. And then:

> Spoke, spoke.
> Was, was.

To speak is to be within language, and the pervading mistrust of what the poem says on all levels is attached to being. Is what it deals with the language of being? Or are the two things separate?

> Yes.
> Gales, whirl of part-
> icles, there was
> time left, time
> to try it out with the stone – it
> was hospitable, it
> did not cut in. How
> lucky we were:
>
> Grainy,
> grainy and stringy. Stalky,

dense;
grapy and radiant; kidneyish,
flattish and
lumpy; loose, tang-
led –: he, it
did not cut in, it
spoke,
willingly spoke to dry eyes, before closing them.

Spoke, spoke.
Was, was.

Gales, whirl of particles, these have already been established as being within the opinion-community of the book and the society; this is the time in which "we" was meaningful and was good. This is before it becomes lost, and before the grieving over it, but it is written after, and remodeled not into the now of the I, but the now of the poem. It stands on the very brink of meaning, not because it has no meaning in itself, a stone has no meaning, merely a state of being, but because it has no meaning to anyone but the I.

But try what out with the stone? How is the stone hospitable? What does it mean, that it did not cut in? Stones are among the commonest and least meaningful of entities; a stone is a stone, neutral and moreover most usually unspecific, a stone looks much like any other stone. In itself it is unchanging, or changes only unimaginably slowly, without conveying any trace of its age to anyone but a geologist, thereby in a way existing beyond culture, history, and time, or in a time other than our historical time, but the fact that whenever we see a stone we are confronted by something infinitely older than humanity, which existed here before even the beginnings of life, is something we rarely if ever think about, a stone is simply a trivial phenomenon of nature, no, not even a phenomenon, an object of simple existence, something we skim across the water's surface without thought, for the pleasure of our children, for instance, or in the case of larger ones, something on which we sit down to drink coffee on picnics in the woods.

In ancient religions stones were used as a symbol of the continuous and everlasting; raised in circles at certain places they enclosed what was deemed to be sacred and were often associated with the heavenly bodies. The laws given to Moses were inscribed on tablets of stone, rendering eternal and unalterable the otherwise transient script of God's commandments to humankind. In religious life the stone was in contrast to the tree: whereas the tree symbolized life and rejuvenation, the stone was the symbol of eternal being. Not much remains of that world in our day and age, the tree and the stone are no longer opposites by which we make sense of our lives, but here and there we find remnants of its very tangible mode of thought, not least in the funeral ritual, in which we continue to erect stones over the dead, while the coffin is of wood. Into the stone we inscribe the name of the deceased. While the body decomposes in the earth below, the name stands in stone for all time, belonging no longer to the social world alone, but also to matter.

There are no traces at all of ritual or religion in Celan's poem, on the contrary, the stone is shrouded in the quotidian, it is something we must "try it out with," it is "hospitable." "Try it out with" preserves the stone quality of the stone, an object we move or share, whereas "try it out at," as the German might also be interpreted, makes important the place of the stone and would seem to make it a question of proximity to it. "Hospitable" is a radical anthropomorphization, hospitable being a human quality, not even animals can be hospitable, yet the stone is hospitable in the poem. To be hospitable is to be accommodating toward others. In this case "we." What made it hospitable was the fact of it not cutting in, of it being accommodating of the "we." But what it did not cut into was the discourse that was conducted outside it, meaning perhaps, in the logic of the poem, that it was not seen through words. Was it then with its property of absolute duration that it exists outside the fleeting community of the human?

That it did not cut into language with its radical otherness? An otherness to which "we" then also belong, since our bodies contain not only our beating hearts, but also our skeletons, that part of us which remains when we die, along with the names on our stones. The stone belongs to "it," the nonhumanity of the world, is that what did not cut in? Because it was woven into the veil of language? The puzzle deepens in repetition:

> *he, it*
> *did not cut in, it*
> *spoke,*
> *willingly spoke to dry eyes, before closing them.*

To speak here is in other words the opposite of cutting in. And not only does "it," the stone, speak, it is also drawn into "it," which must be all things indirectly referred to after it: grain, grapes, kidneys. It is this that "speaks."

Earlier in the poem speaking was placed on an equal footing with not seeing, and with sleeping, which is another way of not seeing, though stronger since the person asleep is wholly turned away from the world in which he or she lies. But sleeping and not seeing apply to humans; not cutting in, which is to say speaking, applies in this instance to things. What the things speak to are eyes. To speak to eyes is to be seen. But not in the way those awake see, for they do not cut in. They are seen sleeping. The eyes that see are dry, in contrast to the eye at the poem's midpoint, which is moist. That was before the grief, of the poem's we. But to go to the eye, to the moist one, may of course be read less sentimentally, moist can point simply to a property of the moist, that it flows, runs, is not firm in its form, is never the same. The contrast between the dry and the moist is found in other places in the poem too, for instance between the "unmistakable track" at the beginning and the "water-level traces" at the end. A track is something that points to something else, an imprint, and that imprint must have duration in order to be meaningful. Water does not have duration, it forms itself according to the now, so a water-level trace contains at one and the same time the trace and the dissolution of the trace. The entire poem rests here, between the traces in time and the tracelessness of time. The traces are not themselves that which once was, but signs of what once was, at the same time as they are something in their own right. When the trace is water, the traces are more transitory, their mistakability drastically increased. But the trace is not merely water, it is groundwater, something that lies below the surface, pervaded by that which comes from above, all that seeps through the soil. The moist, the liquid, belongs to the eye, which sees the now, whereas that which pegs down and gives form belongs to writing. The fact of the eye never seeing the same thing, the seen always in flux, is something the poem addresses on a number of levels, not only in tracks and traces, but also for instance in the way the nouns are transformed into adjectives, from entities into properties of entities – not grain but grainy; not stalk but stalky; not grape but grapy; not kidney but kidneyish. Thereby the poem describes, rather than specifying membership of any class or category. Together these properties make up an "it," which along with that of the stone does not cut in, but speaks to dry eyes before closing them.

Why are the eyes dry? Is it because they are untouched by grief, or because they see only the immutable and invariable? Is it because the grapes and the grain and the stone do not cut in? It does not cut in, the speaking, the talk of words is compared earlier on with sleep, and their closing their dry eyes might also be sleep, or death, or a mere doze, but in any case it has to do with not seeing. "It" is active, it "closes" the dry eyes; the unseen closes the eyes of the unseeing, who then becomes "it," dead? But while the dry eyes are outside the "it," the poem is not; the poem calls it forth, in a time and in a form that is the poem's own. The poem sees. The poem sees the eyes of the sleeping, they are dry but good, in the stone, the grain, the grape; yet it sees the stone, the grain, the grape as well.

Good, but is it true?

The question the poem does not pose directly, though it may be read as a response to it, is how reality is to be represented when language by its very nature renders general all objects and phenomena, depriving them of time and thereby veiling their uniqueness, and moreover is bound up with a society and a history attaching to that society, which has charged and depleted them in slow ebbs and flows of meaning, in the sense of ways of seeing, and which, more than merely concerning the existential and the social, is what actually makes the existential social. For "blood" is not simply blood, "soil" not simply soil. One way of getting away from that would be to create a new language altogether, freed of history, wholly constrained in respect to its generality, but that would not be a language at all; the wholly particular cannot be communicated, but requires community, a you, to create a we; this is the foundation of language. The poet would understand the poem, but no one else would, and so the question would then be what the poet understands, in a solipsistic world.

Another way of getting away from it would be to change languages. But for one thing all languages generalize and are laden with culture and history, and for another this poem goes so far into the particular that it becomes hard to read as an instance of the specific language, German, or the specific culture, the German; its crisis goes deeper, to the very foundation of our understanding of what a human being is, what a language is, what reality is, what memory is, what death is, what time is. Such questions can be neither posed nor answered in the language in which the general understanding of the concepts is seated without losing their own particularity and radicality. But at the same time it cannot step outside the language and become one with its own particularity and radicality, since then it would reveal itself to no one. It is through language that reality reveals itself to us, not as it is but as it is revealed by language, and if that language is to be genuine it must reveal to us the singular reality of the own, in its own singular language, but without severing either the connection with reality or the connection with others who share that language. "Engführung" inhabits that borderland. And existing at the very limits of meaning means the question of what meaning actually is becomes inevitable, at the same time as each single word is accorded quite extraordinary weight. That weight comes not from meaning, but from the basis of meaning. "Stone" is such a word. It is there, almost like a stone in the poem, unconnected with its surroundings, and if we try to draw in aspects of the stone's connection to the human sphere, to give it meaning in that way, it does not "answer." It is within language, and yet outside the contexts of language.

In the unique lies the own, in the own the private; the path that evades generality passes through here. And perhaps the stone in Celan's poem is laden with something unknown to the reader, at which he or she cannot even guess. In the afterword to his Norwegian rendering, Øyvind Berg writes that Celan's parents, Friederike and Leo, German-speaking Jews resident in Romania, died in a German work camp known as the Stone Pit. "This brings to mind a poem such as 'Engführung,'" Berg writes, "though at the same time it is important to keep some measure of air between biographical background and the poems that transcend it: historicizing interpretations deprive the poetry of contemporary interest." What Berg points to here is the fundamental hermeneutic issue: where exactly is the line between what is in the poem, what is in the poet, and what is in the reader? Celan writes the word "stone." Was he thinking about his parents? Are they contained in the word "stone"? We will never know. Now I know that Celan's parents died in the Germans' quarry, or stone pit, and I can read that connection into the word "stone," but is it right to read the poem in that way, or am I forcing something upon it that it does not contain? How much is outside and how much inside the poem?

The key words of the poem, besides "no one" and "nothing," are "night," "words," and "ash." When Celan wrote "came a word through the night, wanted to shine," was he addressing the beginning of the Gospel of John? There we find the classic connection of word and light, the word there is God, God is life, and life is man's light shining in the darkness. If this was indeed what Celan was thinking about, does it then "exist" in the poem, as opposed to if he was not? If he was not and it does not "exist" in the poem, but only in me, a reader, am I then understanding it "wrongly"?

> *In the beginning was the Word, and the Word was with God, and the Word was God. He was with God in the beginning. Through him all things were made; without him nothing was made that has been made. In him was life, and that life was the light of all mankind. The light shines in the darkness, and the darkness has not overcome it.*

> *Came, came.*
> *Came a word, came,*
> *Came through the night,*
> *wanted to shine, wanted to shine.*

If one hears the tone of the Gospel of John in those four lines of Celan, one will also hear the tone of God in the word they evoke, which wants to but cannot shine. But God is not only the word, he is life, and life was the light of mankind; that tone, too, then fills the words; just as light is a word that cannot penetrate the undifferentiatedness of night, there may be people who cannot penetrate the undifferentiatedness of death. Yet the opening verse of the Gospel of John not only associates the word with God, and God with the light of mankind, it also tells us we are "in the beginning," in the manner of the creation narrative. Thereby it becomes an echo of the Old Testament's account of the creation, which also starts with the words "In the beginning." Whereas in the Old Testament the creation is of the material world, the sky and the earth, which to begin with are empty and desolate places in the midst of an expanse of darkness, gradually gaining light, land, life, and which in keeping with all accounts of creation are brought from chaos to order, the beginning in the Gospel of John is not the dawning of a day and land rising out of eternal darkness in the material world, but the word. What begins here is the human world, and it emerges in the word, which establishes differentiation in the undifferentiated, meaning in the meaningless, order in the chaos. If a person falls out of language, he or she falls out of the world. A world without language is a world without distinction, and a world without distinction is a world without meaning. Instead it is chaos, the expansion and collapse of all things. But language is not above the world and the people in it, a ring-binder system of distinctions and differences, but something existing in every one of us, by whose means we understand ourselves, our fellow humans and the world in which we live. Language is the human. In language I exist, but only if there is also a you to which the I of the speech act can relate, because if not, how then should the I separate itself and find form? The you-less I is no one and everyone.

What does a language look like without the other? Not like Joyce's inner monologues, for although the language in them purports to come from the most particular own, it listens to it at the same time, and it is this presence in the entire, quiet flood of memories, thoughts, fragments of life, and an I that pass through a mind, as for instance in Molly Bloom's concluding monologue in *Ulysses*, that is the other to whom the inner human being relates, no longer enclosed within itself. Joyce's merit was precisely in knowing how tightly the innermost I was bound up with the other and to the culture through language, and in his next novel he proceeded further along the same path, where language was no longer decoded within the one, he wrote of an "all," or within an all, which is to say the language in itself, without sender or receiver, an I or a you, but a gigantic we extending in all directions, for every single word has part in another, all words are open toward one another, and all that they contain in the way of history and culture and centuries of meaning flows through them, and thereby they come to exist at the second limit of meaning: the first is where the I disappears into the own, which cannot be communicated without losing its character of ownness and becoming the other, therefore ultimately being without language. The second limit, at which *Finnegans Wake* is written, is that where the I disappears into the self of the language. In the instance of our crossing the first limit, the you ceases to exist, and the I becomes it; in our crossing the second limit, the you ceases to exist, and the I vanishes into an "all"; in both instances meaning departs the language, which accordingly becomes mysterious.

But what is the mysterious? It is that which cannot be understood. But then what is meant by understanding? Do we "understand" a stone? Do we "understand" a star? Do we "understand" water? The most important concept in the first verse of the Gospel of John is "*logos*," the word. "*Logos*" is Greek, and in the Greek culture, from Plato onward, language is abstract to a greater extent than in the Jewish culture, where, according to Northrop Frye, if I have understood him correctly, the word, "*dabar*," is taken more tangibly, as if closer in some way to what it denotes, almost as if words were entities or actions in themselves. If the Gospel of John is not a presence in Celan's poem, the Greek certainly is, and not only in the suggestion of reference to Democritus, where the physical world is divided up into its smallest component parts, but also in the abstract, relational, all-connecting language world that was the prerequisite of the we that no longer is possible: without connection, the stone lies in language. What does the stone mean? This is a question for language, for the "stone." We know what it looks like, we know how it is built up, and we know what kind of properties it has. But as for what it is, in itself, we have no conception. "It," we can say. "It is a stone." "It is a star." "It is water." "It is I." Or, perhaps, "I am it." What is "it"?

It is what has no name.

Understanding and meaning are not the same thing. The Israeli-American sociologist Aaron Antonovsky defines meaning as a feeling or experience of coherence. Religion sets up such states of coherence, drawing the stone and the tree into the human sphere, where they are what they are, tangible objects in their own right, and moreover represent aspects of the sacred or divine, which is to say that which lies outside the human. Science, which took the place of religion, also sets up such states of coherence, placing the stone and the tree within an enormous system of differences and similarities that man has established and is himself a part of. And the social world establishes connections and coherences, an intricate system of rules as to what may and may not be done, what is desirable and what is not, what can be said and what not, organized in a hierarchy in which the individual may ascend or descend according to how finely the society's various strata are divided. Meaning is not something in itself, but a feeling that may arise, and the coherence on which it is dependent is relative and may be based on misunderstanding as well as understanding, superstition as well as true belief, illusion as well as reality, immorality as well as morality. Meaning is a sense of coherence, and the greater the coherence, the greater the meaning. Affinity with the all of the universe and with the divine, as experienced in ecstasy, is the strongest feeling of coherence a person may experience. Love is a coherence-bringing emotion. And the sense of community that arises when we are together with other people in a shared experience is also coherence-bringing and fosters meaning. The great insight of whoever wrote the Gospel of John was not only that the human world arose in the word, but also that mankind itself arose in the word, and that all meaning that may exist in that world derives from the word. The word is a light that illuminates our world, beyond that world is but darkness, and this is so because the word creates differences while the dark is without difference. In Paul Celan's poem the darkness and the undifferentiated are not something belonging outside the human sphere, our perimeter, at which we stand when we encounter death or the divine, but something that has pervaded the very core of humanity itself, which in this understanding is the same as language.

If language falls, darkness invades our world, flooding in like an ocean.

But what does it mean for language to fall? How can language fall? Or, put differently: why did the word not shine when it wanted to shine? In the Gospel of John the word is God, and this can be understood as saying that God is what gives the word meaning, that in which meaning resides and from which meaning emanates, which is to say a securer of coherence. In the poem there is no such meaningful coherence. Words relating to the world destroy the world, the grass is written asunder and the wheel turns of itself, unconnected with its surroundings, a symbol detached from context, where perhaps that very detachment is the most important aspect, certainly it is emphasized, for the night sky under which it turns is without stars. Stars are lights in darkness, lights are words, the word is God. The evocation of the word as light immediately afterward must be understood as a longing for another kind of word, the wish to establish another coherence after the one that has broken down, and when that does not occur, and that light does not shine, the poem collapses into ash, ash, ash, night, night-and-night, and the call to go to the eye, not the one that sees and distinguishes, but the one that weeps.

However, coherence or meaning are not exclusively found where the word comes from, but also where the word is going, which is toward a you. To this you, absence of meaning is meaning, too. Without this you the poem would have been mute. It would not have collapsed into ash and night, which are proximate to the language-less, but into the language-less itself. The you is the poem's hope, the poem's future, the poem's utopia. But the poem's you is not the same as me, reading it now, but a semantic role into which I can insert myself or not. If I do, I must do so with caution, since this is what it means to read, to give up the self and yield to the alien voice, obeying it, in this instance a voice created by a Paul Celan, a human being long since dead but who in these words and their fine shades of meaning emerges into view, an

I directed toward a you, which I, more than fifty years after it was written, endeavor to identify with. If I bring too much of myself into that endeavor, I turn the you of the text into my own I, and the poem then becomes a mirror, its potentials in terms of yielding insight constrained by my own limitations, since I know what I know. That prejudice operates not only in respect to my own personal self, but also in relation to the culture as a whole, which is also a part of my reading self, and quite necessary; without it I would be blank at every word. The "you" that exists in Paul Celan's poem, to whom the poem is addressed, is denied all words that are creative of such common prejudices, precisely because the perceptual space in which it is written is concerned with the inadequacy of those prejudices in relation to the world it strives to reach, and this is why the poem is so difficult to grasp; it moves away from points of commonality, and when nevertheless it approaches them it is somehow free of the usual associations and resonances: a stone is a stone. This idiosyncrasy is the method employed by the poet in order to write about something other than words that awaken words, and this forces the reader to read idiosyncratically, complicating all associations between the image of the poem and that which the image "represents," that which it "in essence" is an expression "of." The poem expresses itself. But it does so using the words of the community. That makes it difficult to interpret, but not to understand, for while the associations the words give rise to are denied space and rejected by the other words in their vicinity, no such rejection occurs of the moods and emotions awakened by the same words. Nor is it the case that the poem's true and absolute meaning lies, beyond its language, in the heart and the weeping eye. It is where the "you," which may well be a personification of the reader, is urged to go. Not read, not look, but go to the eye, the moist one. On the other hand, the eye that does not see but that weeps, is a kind of equivalent of the light that wanted to shine, an image in this darkness of futility, the fall of language. Language has fallen, since the "we" from which it both arises and issues has fallen, but it is not only to show this that the poem has been written, it is itself an attempt to find a way out and as such reestablish meaning, if only here, in this poem, and if only negatively, by way of making the loss of meaning visible. The figure for this loss is not the night that conceals, nor the word's lack of force, but the ash, into which everything has vanished. Ash is the form of absence. Religion, which in its laws and rules relates everything in the human world to God, thereby rendering it significant, has incorporated the ash, too, in its delineation of the borders between our social reality, our physical reality, and the divine reality of God; ash is mentioned particularly in the Law of Moses, given by the Lord to the Israelites through Moses, where it is the object of certain rules. Not ash in itself, but the ashes of burned offerings. The priest must be clad in linen when he removes the ashes, and he must place the ashes beside the sacrifice. Then he must put on different garments before carrying the ashes from the camp to a clean place. The ritual of sacrifice consists of a series of transitions, an animal is slaughtered and brought into the sphere of the holy, becoming holy in itself, becoming God's own. The ashes are still within the holy and therefore holy in themselves. The priest changing clothes marks a transition, completed by the ashes being removed from the temple and taken out of the camp, returned to the world once more. But even in the differentiation of the holy, ash is a remnant that in contrast to life cannot be brought to conclusion – it being already dead – and which is carried away, thereby becoming unholy.

The question is what this dimension of ash has to do with Paul Celan's poem. Ash, ash, ash, it says, as if insisting on it being merely that, ash, and nothing else. At the same time, the burned offering of which the ashes are a remnant is called *holocaust* in Greek. And in a poem written by a German Jew in 1959 it is hard to read "ash" and "holocaust" in any neutral way. But is such a reading historicizing? To turn the issue on its head: what else would "ash" and the wound suggested by "seams" and "grew together" point to, relate to, if not the Holocaust? Is it reductive?

In a way, for it is exactly the reduction of the name the whole poem, with its fierce negative force, tries to avoid, for the simple reason that it would close what the poem strives to keep open. But it is precisely this and nothing else that is going on in the poem. It addresses something quite specific that it cannot name, and in that it strives beyond the specific, that which applies in historical time, to reach into the fundamental existential categories where what is important is the relationship between language and reality. Without the human catastrophe of the Holocaust, the poem would very likely have been able to speculate as to the difference between words and stones, and to circle about the nothingness of death, but I can hardly imagine it would have been able to lament the absence of light from on high, the divine light, to bewail that it did not shine.

"Engführung" is clearly no exercise in language, clearly not an academic excursion into presence and absence, it is an elegy and a requiem to those who perished, but also to what was lost with their death, which is to say "we." It was in Celan's native tongue, German, that the Jews were first separated from the "we" of the language to become "they," and subsequently, in the extermination camps, "it." The Jews were deprived of their name; in the name lay not only their identity, but also their humanity; they became "it," bodies with limbs that could be counted, but not named. They became no one. Then they became nothing. All that was left when they were gone was ash.

A short while ago I watched a documentary film about the extermination of the Jews, Claude Lanzmann's *Shoah*, which deals exclusively with what was left, exclusively with what exists now; no old photos, no old footage, just people in the present time, relating, one by one, what they saw and experienced during that time. Trains, forests, faces. Some spoke frivolously of what they had seen, without understanding, they didn't know what they were saying, others were mute, others broke down under the weight of a single recollection, abruptly unbearable. As a viewer I could understand what it was about, that this and that event had occurred, I could assess the accounts of the various people in the film and place them into perspective with everything else I knew, and in relation to their own psychologies and character types, but only twice during the course of the nine hours the film lasted did the reality of what had happened, in all its horror, come home to me, two glimpses of insight, by which I mean that I grasped what it was telling me emotionally rather than intellectually. In both instances this lasted two, perhaps three, seconds, and was then gone. One of these glimpses of insight I related to Paul Celan's poem.

A railway official who had been working at a station next to a German camp in Poland in 1942 spoke of something he had experienced there one afternoon. The camp had been under construction for a short time, there was talk of what it might be for, perhaps he asked some of the Germans, I can't remember, but the assumption, for whatever reason, was that it was a labor camp for Jews. That afternoon he was just about to knock off work when a train came into the station. It was made up of many wagons, all crammed with Jews, and as he cycled home the soldiers began to empty the wagons and herd the Jews into the camp. The station being so close by, everyone at work there heard the murmur and commotion of this great number of people passing through the area as evening fell: the shouts, the cries of the children, the hum of voices. But when he came back the next morning all was still. He could hardly comprehend how still it was. Where had they all gone? They had not been transported on, he knew that, so they had to be there, in the camp. But how could so many people be so quiet?

That stillness, in which every human distinction is erased, is what Paul Celan was writing about. That stillness is nothing, but in that nothing resides a something, all those who have disappeared within it. That stillness, and the darkness of that stillness, is what makes the poem's I lament the word that came and did not shine, and what compels that I to write: wanted to shine, wanted to shine, and then ash, ash, ash, night, night-and-night. All distinctions are erased, everything has become nothing, and what it once was cannot be called back, is lost forever, and not even in language can it be called back, for in the empty dominion of this undifferentiated void a word cannot make a difference. The only thing left behind is stillness, which is to say the wordless, which is to say night, and ash. The one's entire differentiated world: ash. The past, the future: ash.

Perhaps a cynical person might say that a life is a life, and that a child dying in a gas chamber is no more terrible than a child dying in a car accident; the grief of the bereaved is the same; grief is grief, it is not increased by multiplication, people are not numbers, grief is not arithmetic. This indeed is true. To lose a child is always the same. But the accumulated number represents more than just one added to another; the dead were a community in themselves, a collective entity. When a person dies in a society his or her memory lives on among the others and their physical belongings are divided up among the next of kin. A we has lost a you, which in death has become it.

The Holocaust saw whole societies wiped out in one swoop, in such a way that not only what they were became nothing, but also what they had been. All memories and stories were wiped out with them. What they were when they died, their own "is," ceased to exist, but also their "was," and that nothing, which is absolute, in which no one and nothing is left, creates a distinction between is and was which death in itself does not establish, for the we never dies, it lives on, all our institutions, all that we build and all that we do is directed toward the continuation of the we, more resilient than any of its individual parts, which all will die, remaining for a short time in the memory of the closest we, which in turn dies too, until the we, fundamentally the same, eventually comprises completely new individuals.

This is what culture is.

The culture not only bears the deaths of the you and the I, but exists to overarch and build on them. And the most important element in that endeavor is language. Language belongs to the we, it is ours, but what we express through it is our individuality. That individuality, expressed again and again in language, through the centuries, is the cacophony of the we. In language and culture we overcome death, and this is perhaps their most fundamental function. When Mallarmé wrote about his son and his son's death, his writing edged toward the brink of the nothing, staring into its darkness, but the fact that the language broke up had to do with his venturing out to language's very perimeter, and at that exact point it came apart, faced with the fact that it was powerless, but it is not intrinsically so, for if the language shifted itself from there toward the center, toward life and the social world, it would again become meaningful and whole. Mallarmé remembered his son. In the Holocaust, the child and those who remembered the child perished.

But this is not what sets Celan's death poem apart from Mallarmé's death poem, though the absence of memory makes the undifferentiatedness of the nothing that much greater. No, what sets them apart is that the dissolution of meaning in Celan's death poem does not apply to the outermost zone of the language, that which language cannot grasp, the negation of the problem of God's name, but applies to language as such, the language in itself. Not the individual words of the language, like stone or grass, but the foundation of coherent meaning established by the language's we, since it was this we that had separated you after you from the community of the we and recategorized them as a "they" and then an "it," expelling them from the language and from the domain of the human.

Can an I who has seen this then say "we"? And if it cannot, how then to write and speak at all?

Language is a social activity, all language presupposes an I and a you, together a we.

The reality of language is thereby a social reality, it is the reality of the I, the you, and the we. But language is no neutral phenomenon giving expression to the existent; the I, the you, and the we both color and are colored by the language they create and are created within. Identity is culture, culture is language, language is morality. What made the atrocities of the Third Reich possible was an extreme reinforcement of the we, and the attendant weakening of the I, which lessened the force of resistance against the gradual dehumanization and expulsion of the non-we, which is to say the Jews, bolstering the we still further. This dehumanization took place in the language, in the name of the we, where morality, too, is found, and within only a very few years the voice of conscience in Germany went from Thou shalt not kill to its reverse, Thou shalt kill, as Hannah Arendt points out.

In this language, where morality, ethics, and also aesthetics were perverted, Paul Celan uttered an "I." To utter the word "death" in the same language would be to say something other than the absence of life, something other than nothing, for Nazism, which had pervaded all parts of the culture, was a death cult; to say "dead" was not to say "nothing," but to say sacrifice, fatherland, greatness, fervor, pride, courage. To say "soil" was to say history, belonging, heritage. To say "blood" was to say rage, purity, victim, death. Death in the gas chambers was another death, its nothing was something else, referred to as one refers to the extermination of insects or vermin, an elimination of the undesirable, something other than human, and how was it possible to refer to that death, which was without identity, without awakening the fluttering banners or the teeming rats that lay in the very word "death"?

Seven years earlier, in 1952, Paul Celan published another poem concerning the Holocaust, perhaps his most famous, "Death Fugue." The theme is the same, but the world described is very different, not least because the poem contains names. Germany is mentioned five times, Margarete with the golden hair four times, Shulamith with the ashen hair three times. Death is personified, a master from Germany, violence is exemplified, "he grabs at the iron in his belt he waves it," "he strikes you with leaden bullets his aim is true," "he sets his pack on to us," the violence is directed toward Jews and is associated with music, "he whistles his pack out/he whistles his Jews out in earth has them dig for a grave/he commands us strike up for the dance," and above him, the master from Germany, flash the stars. "Death Fugue" is a suggestive and hypnotic poem, its beauty is wild and compares with that of Hölderlin's poetry. And it is not untrue, Nazism was wild, barbaric, and carnivalistically grotesque in the extreme, it sought the sublime in its banners and uniforms, its parades and posters, invoking history and history's depths, holding German culture, including Hölderlin, proudly before it, its I dissolving in the we of the masses, and the dissolution was good, for it was to dissolve itself in something greater than the self, to leave behind the strangulating narrowness of class and enter the proud all of us, blood, nation, Germany, and then night fell, brutal and perverted, its darkness lit by fires of violence and destruction.

This strident evil, as base as it was solemn, permeates "Death Fugue." Identity is not destroyed, but gathered in three names, Germany, and Margarete, her golden hair against Shulamith's ashen, the Aryan against the Jewish. Death is not nothing, the past not absent, not impossible to represent, the language is not broken, but gives meaning still. All this is gone in "Engführung," fallen to the ground. In "Engführung" all is silent. Not a name remains. The poem penetrates the space between the name of the world and the world itself, but what it seeks is not pureness of being, in the sense of freedom from civilization and culture, which is to say the so-called authentic, for the absence of the name is a loss in the poem, as the absence of the name's differentiating power is a loss, beseeched in vain, impossible. Even nature as it is, authentic and true, behind language, as it were, is colored by the ideology of the we, the project of striving to establish common meaning, including the Nazis' own, in which it was one of the dominant ideas, evident not least in Hitler's *Mein Kampf*, where the idea of nature in itself is perhaps the most important element of all, but also in the philosophy of Heidegger, in whose work Celan immersed himself, going so far as to meet him in person, an encounter not entirely without controversy, Heidegger having aligned himself to Nazism, so not even the idea of the world as it "is," outside language, was unaffected by the ideology and the worldview, it was woven into all things, and this lack of innocence, or this discovery of the loss of innocence, is, the way I read it, the very point of departure of Celan's poem.

The biggest difference between "Death Fugue" and "Engführung" derives not unnaturally from the years that separate them, though is not merely a result of Celan's writing having developed, matured, and deepened, for something else happened, too, during those years, concerning the way in which Nazism and the Holocaust were perceived by the culture, which is to say the we, for while in 1952 that must all still have been gaping open in its unfathomable atrocity, in a society laid waste, in 1959 it was quite differently shut, an episode that could be referred to, a period of history in which each single event, each single life, each single moment was locked tight in the emblem of the name – Auschwitz, for instance.

"Who covered it up?" the poem asks. Designation is another kind of disappearance. Therefore the poem cannot describe the deportation of the Jews, the transportation in cattle trucks through the Polish countryside, the herding into the camps, the stripping naked, the processions prodded into the gas chambers, the extermination inside the gas chambers, where in panic they scrabbled toward the doors, their corpses tumbling out when those same doors were again opened, the incineration in the ovens or on the grids over the pits, the ash. This description, which we may say is made up of facts, and which we associate with the word "Auschwitz," has nothing to do with reality, in part because its perspective indicates a consummate course of events, which is a fiction for the simple reason that no single person witnessed this sequence, but only parts of it, and that those who were there and who did witness that course of events in its entirety are either dead, without ever having related their experience, or, in the case of those who survived, experienced it from the inside, whereas the description is always as seen from the outside.

The perspective has never existed, it belongs to writing and is possible only there. Auschwitz, the way we think of it, does not exist, it belongs to the past, which is gone, and it did not even exist there either, because what we imagined happened there, in the way it was told to us, did not happen in that way, the story lies, forgetting the one, whose perspective is the only perspective possible, and this very forgetting of the one was what made the extermination possible.

◆ ◆ ◆

When I was growing up, playing at the age of ten in the German bunkers in the woods on Tromøya, or sitting on their artillery emplacements with my legs dangling as I stared out over the sea, only some thirty years had passed since they had been in use. But the world in which I played was peaceful and orderly, and when for the first time I visited Flensburg in northern Germany, nine years old, tagging along at the heels of my father, who walked quickly and had such an odd expression on his face as we passed through a narrow street with scantily clad women sitting in small booths on each side, presumably the reason I remember the place at all, I saw that same peacefulness and orderliness there, too. Whenever we drove over the fells to my grandparents in Vestland, the majority of tourists we encountered were Germans. Many of them must have been there before, during the war. The war was something we learned about at school, mostly that small part of it that had taken place in Norway, but also, gradually, what had gone on in the rest of the world as well. In the newspapers it was present in reports of war criminals being discovered in various parts of the globe and brought to trial. The weekly magazines, perhaps *Vi Menn* in particular, were full of colorful stories about war treasure, so-called Nazi gold, and German war criminals hiding away in Argentina or Brazil. But the biggest sources of knowledge about Nazism were the comic books I read, such as *På vingene* and the *Vi vant* series. There, the Germans, or Fritz as they were called, were evil and unscrupulous, the "yellows" or the "Japs" even worse. All this, the books, the comics, the newspaper articles and the magazine stories, as well as our history lessons at school, seemed to be situated in a radically different age, in a radically different place, more like the forest in which Hansel and Gretel got lost than the one that became smaller and narrower as it approached the pebble beach, eventually to come to an end altogether out at Hove, where the German artillery positions were still plain to see.

In the spring when we were in the seventh grade, I was thirteen years old, I saw pictures from the extermination camps for the first time. I was standing in the library, which was housed in the school's basement, and it was a complete shock, I froze inside, but it was not the numbers of the dead or their suffering I was reacting to, because I had learned about the Holocaust and knew what it was, it was the image itself, a woman so emaciated she barely resembled a human, she was naked, but there was nothing sexual about her, and then there was a picture of a pile of corpses, heaped and stacked like timber, the picture had been taken from a distance and the limbs and bodies were tangled up, but I could still see very clearly that they were humans. The coldness it filled me with, the horror that went through me and left me in a state of alienation for some hours afterward, had nothing to do with their suffering or the terrible nature of what had taken place, it had to do with the bodies, the way they were arranged and what that expressed, something I had never seen before and had no idea even existed.

At university I encountered the war and the Holocaust in a quite different form, for instance the way Horkheimer and Adorno write about it in their *Dialectic of Enlightenment*, where in order to grasp the collapse of civilization in that ultimate barbarity they provide an analysis of the *Odyssey*, as far as I understood it in order to demonstrate how light and darkness hung together and that light had always tried to free itself from the dark, in several instances almost succeeding, only in each case to be sucked back again. The way enlightenment became blind to itself, what began as a de-enchantment from reality, designed to make man free and his own master, ending up in re-enchantment, at the same time as progress, with all its advances and technologies, marched on, making man unfree and slavelike, and eventually it collapsed completely.

Adorno's solution was more enlightenment, as I understood it. "What is at issue here is . . . the necessity for enlightenment to reflect on itself if humanity is not to be betrayed," he wrote. And: "What is at stake is not conservation of the past but the fulfillment of past hopes." Where the connections were between light, darkness, enlightenment, myth, Nazism, and Bergen – the city I lived in – I had no idea, because the issue did not exist. Everything had its place then. Adorno was in one place, the *Odyssey* in another, my life in a third, the war in a fourth. When those categories became mixed up, as in Sørbøvåg one night when I was watching TV with Grandad and the politician Jo Benkow appeared on the screen, prompting Grandad to point at the TV and say, "What's that Jew doing there?" I did not know they had got mixed up, did not think about enlightenment, did not think about myth, did not think about Adorno, did not think about Arendt, but about Grandad, who I knew had never been a Nazi, assuming by extension that his prejudice stemmed from the age from which he came and did not in any way express anything significant about the person he was inside.

The fact that in the years that followed I read many books about Nazism had less to do with an attempt to understand than with the enormous fascination the events of that time exerted on me. The unbounded was a much-discussed concept at the time, vague and theoretical, applied to texts, usually modernist texts, whereas the unbounded in reality, in the same way as the transgressional, another academic-intellectual buzzword, was not something anyone wanted to know about. For where did the unbounded and the transgressional exist in our culture? Drug addicts were unbounded, shunning no means of getting their hands on drugs, and pornography was transgressional, like the political direction no one approved of, the suburban pseudolibertarianism of the Progress Party, Fremskrittspartiet, like racism and the glorification of violence.

What consituted the unbounded in literature? What was transgressional there? Mostly it was genre, the traditionally low appearing in the traditionally highbrow, or philosophy turning up in creative texts, or the poem approaching prose. For my own part, the transgressional was associated with an enormous sense of freedom on the one hand, and enormous shame on the other, played out in a rather unsophisticated fashion in a few too many beers followed by a couple of hours of undesirable yet delightfully unfettered behavior as a result. It was low and vile and wretched, even if it didn't necessarily feel like it, whereas the crimes that took place in the Third Reich were transgressional in a radically different and fundamentally incomprehensible yet no less compelling sense altogether. It was as if they exceeded the very limits of what was human. How was that possible? The allure of death, the allure of destruction, the allure of total annihilation, of what did it consist? The world burned, and they were joyful.

I read about it, I wondered about it, and never without feeling some small measure of that same allure myself as I sat there far from war and death, destruction and genocide, on a chair in Bergen, surrounded by all my books, usually with a cigarette in my hand and a cup of coffee next to me on the desk, the dwindling hum of the evening's traffic outside the window, sometimes with a warm cat asleep on my lap. I read about the final days of Hitler, the utterly demented atmosphere far beneath the ground where he lived with his attendants and those closest to him, the city above them, bombed to rubble by the Russians, a blazing inferno. At one point he ascended to inspire some boys of the Hitler Youth, I had seen the footage that was shot, he is ill, tries to stop his hand from shaking as he goes from one boy to the next, it must have been Parkinson's disease. But in his eyes there is a gleam, something unexpectedly warm.

Surely it couldn't be possible?

When Dad died, Yngve and I found a Nazi pin among his belongings, a pin with a German eagle to put in the lapel of a jacket. Where did he get it from? He was not the type to have bought something of that nature and therefore he must have been given it or come across it in some way. When Grandma died, a year and a half after Dad, and we went through the house to divide things up, we found a Norwegian edition of *Mein Kampf* in the chest in the living room. What was it doing there? It must have been there since the war. It was a fairly common book at the time, with thousands of copies sold, someone might have given it to them as a present, without it having any significance for them, but nevertheless it was still strange that they hadn't got rid of it after the war, for they would hardly have been unaware that it was incriminating. After the initial sensation the discovery of something so illicit gave rise to, I thought little more of it. I knew the people they were, Grandad and Grandma, and I knew they were from another age, in which other rules applied. Then came a period, perhaps a year later, when I began to read up more systematically about Nazism, it was just a subject I began to explore, the way I had previously explored other times and places in history. I read Shirer's work on Nazism, Kershaw's first book about Hitler, Gitta Sereny's book on Speer, Speer's Spandau diaries and his memoir, *Inside the Third Reich*. This was what I was reading when Tonje and I broke up and I moved to Stockholm. There, alone in a very feminine one-room flat I'd borrowed in the city's Söder District, I read the Swedish translation of Gitta Sereny's book about Treblinka, *Into That Darkness*, it made me unwell for a couple of weeks, and after that I read no more about it, it was a path on which I could proceed no more, where everything closed in on itself, everything emptied itself.

Seven years later, in the spring of last year, I bought a copy of Hitler's *Mein Kampf* in Norwegian. Or rather, because I had since made a name for myself as a writer, and because the interest surrounding that name was as great as it was, I took no chances ordering the book from the antiquarian bookshop myself, I was paranoid and scared it might get out, so I asked Geir to order it for me. He paid the two thousand kroner the two volumes cost and sent them on to me. Unwrapping them and standing with them in my hands filled me with distaste, to say nothing of the near-nausea that came over me when I started reading the first volume and Hitler's words and Hitler's thoughts were thereby admitted to my own mind and for a brief time became a part of it. I was due to go to Iceland for two days and had thought of reading the book on the plane, seeing as how I was intending to get started writing the first book of this novel when I got home again, and because it shares its name, *My Struggle*, with Hitler's book, and because Hitler's book and the Nazi pin were unexplained mysteries in that story, or perhaps not mysteries, but more exactly fields of the past that manifested themselves in the present and which I felt unable to trace back to anything I knew in that past, I had decided to write a few pages about Hitler's book.

I usually always sniff the books I buy, the new ones as well as the old, putting my nose to the pages and breathing in their smell because I associate that smell, and the smell of old books in particular, with something good, that element of childhood that was unconditionally pleasurable. The adventure, the abandoning oneself to other worlds. But I could not do that with *Mein Kampf*. The book was evil, in some indefinable way. I was unable, too, to have it on my shelf or on my desk, and instead I put it out of sight in the bottom drawer. Reading it on the flight, as I had imagined I would, was unthinkable, I realized that the moment I sat down in my seat after boarding. One of the female flight attendants congratulated me on my books, the other winked and said she knew who I was, and two passengers in the row in front of me were reading the same article about me in *Aftenposten*. Being that visible made reading Hitler's book out of the question, but it would have been just as impossible even if I had been anonymous, since the book in itself is stigmatizing, and if anyone had seen me reading it there in public a mood of distaste would have spread through the cabin and people would have thought there was something wrong with me. I left it in my bag for the duration of the flight and even when, having reached my destination, I stretched out to relax on the bed of my hotel room before the event I was scheduled to take part in, I left it there and turned on the TV instead, the embarrassment was simply too great. But why? I had read the Marquis de Sade, another stigmatized writer, but that was literature, hailed as pioneering and revolutionary by all the great French philosophers of the postwar period and used as a point of departure for their analyses of power, sex, language, and death. But with Hitler's book it was different. Hitler's book is no longer literature. What later happened, what he later did, the axioms of which are meticulously laid out in that book, is such that it transforms the literature into something evil. Hitler's *Mein Kampf* is literature's only unmentionable work. To say that this fact makes it interesting is impossible, regardless of the fact that it is interesting, since in that case one is deemed to lack respect for all those sent to their deaths by the system to which the book directly gave rise. Six million Jews, only sixty-five years ago. Almost all literature is simply text, but not *Mein Kampf. Mein Kampf* is more than text. It is a symbol of human evil. In it the door between text and reality is wide open, in a way quite unlike any other book. In Germany it is banned to this day. In Norway it has not been printed since the war.

Shortly after the war ended, in 1947, a book came out by a German-Jewish philologist, Victor Klemperer, entitled *LTI – Lingua Tertii Imperii: Notizbuch eines Philologen*, later published in English as *The Language of the Third Reich*. Klemperer was a professor of Romance languages at the Technical University of Dresden, an assimilated Jew, married to an Aryan woman. When the Nazis seized power in 1933 he therefore considered himself safe enough to remain in Germany. Soon, however, he lost his job, his house, his right to borrow books from the library; he was stopped from listening to the radio, refused the right to read books by non-Jewish writers, and eventually prohibited from speaking to anyone other than Jews – and, indeed, from writing. He lived under the constant threat of deportation, a fate he avoided only by virtue of his wife's lineage and because he had fought for Germany as a volunteer in World War I.

LTI is an eyewitness account of the Third Reich as seen from within – not of how life inside it harshened and became ever more brutalized throughout the 1930s and on into the 1940s, but rather of how the language changed. Klemperer kept a diary, its first entries are dated the spring of 1933, at the time he still holds his professorship and thereby a prominent position in society, and while his entries exhibit concern, such concern is mild in nature: a mere disquiet. Gradually, all that is Jewish is separated from the German, and the German bolstered everywhere. In Leipzig a commission is established for the nationalization of the university. A bulletin board in Klemperer's department carries the words: "If a Jew writes in German, he is lying." The word *Volk* – most simply "people" in English – is all over the place, in every context: *Volksfest* (public festival), *Volksgenosse* (ethnic comrade), *Volksgemeinschaft* (ethnic community), *volksnah* (in touch with the people), *volksfremd* (alien to the people), *volksentstammt* (descended from the people). Hitler himself is *der Volkskanzler* – the people's chancellor – and the elevation of the nation becomes the National Socialist revolution. A ceremony is held at the grave of "Rathenau-eliminators." By summer Klemperer senses that the people are weary of Hitler, as if they are exhausted by all the propaganda. On August 22 he writes:

Frau Krappmann, the deputy concierge, married to a postal inspector: "Professor Klemperer, by 1 October, the 'Hospitality' club of the postal

workers of section A 19 will be brought into line [gleichgeschaltet]
by the Nazis. But they will not receive any of its capital; a sausage
dinner will be organized for the gentlemen, followed by coffee and
cake for the ladies." Annemarie, clinically blunt as ever, relates the
remark of a colleague wearing an armband with a swastika: "What
is one supposed to do? It's like a lady's sanitary towel." And Kuske,
the grocer, recites the new evening prayer: "Dear Lord, make me
dumb, so that to Hohnstein I never come." Am I deceiving myself if
I derive some hope from all this?

Three days later Klemperer writes that his vice-chancellor has politely asked if he might hold back on publishing an article he has written; instead he approaches another publishing house, receiving a speedy rejection on the grounds that the piece is lacking the necessary national angles (*völkische Gesichtspunkte*). On August 28 he writes that he does not believe the people are going to go along with things much longer. He tells of going on a bus trip, a "mystery tour," some eighty people in two busloads, "the most petty-bourgeois company imaginable." During a coffee stop entertainment is laid on, a *compère* recites a pathos-ridden poem in praise of the Führer, the savior of Germany, and the new national community; the audience is silent and apathetic, the applause that follows entirely without enthusiasm. To top things off the man tells a funny story about something that happened at the hairdresser's, a Jewish woman wants a permanent, only to be refused, for as the hairdresser says, "The Führer solemnly promised on the occasion of the boycott of the Jews that no one is to harm a hair on a Jew's head." The story meets with laughter and enthusiastic applause. Three weeks later he relates some scenes from the party rally at Nuremberg that he has seen at the cinema. Hitler blesses new members of the *Sturmabteilung* by allowing them to touch the *Blutfahne*, the Blood Banner, from the failed coup attempt of 1923. Other Nazi banners are touched by the *Blutfahne*, thereby becoming consecrated, and cannon are fired in celebration. Klemperer reflects upon the name: "Blood Banner."

He ponders the way that whatever has to do with the National Socialist party is elevated from the political to the religious sphere. He descibes those in attendance, how devout they appear toward the scenes that are played out before their eyes. The rallies are cult ceremonies, a ritualistic action, he writes, National Socialism is a religion. He learns of Jewish colleagues dismissed from their jobs. A colleague of Klemperer asks if Klemperer and his wife can receive a guest, "an enemy of the state" unexpectedly released from prison, the man had written about Marx and was deemed "politically unreliable" (*politisch unzuverlässig*). Klemperer notes that the philological journals are pervaded by Third Reich jargon: "science on a National Socialist footing," "the Jewish spirit," "the Novembrists." Deductions are made from his salary, a "voluntary winter charity" donation; he reflects on the the words "tax" and "charity," the way the latter appeals to the emotions. October 29, a sudden directive: every Tuesday afternoon the students are to gather for military sporting exercises – *Wehrsport* – instead of attending lectures. He notes the same word used for a brand of cigarettes: Military Sport brand (Marke Wehrsport). He hears about some communists who have been interned in a concentration camp. He reflects on the word *Konzentrationslager* ("concentration camp"). When he was a boy, he writes, the word had an exotic, colonial, and quite un-German ring to it, he heard mention of it in talk of the Boer War conducted by the English, after that the word disappeared from common usage, but now suddenly it had reappeared to describe a German institution, a permanent peacetime establishment directed against Germans, and he considers that the word will henceforth through all time be associated with Hitler's Germany.

He asks himself if it is heartless of him, a manifestation of some pedantic schoolmasterly streak, that he keeps returning to this philology of misery? He searches his conscience, he writes, and comes to the conclusion that it is not heartless, but a matter of self-preservation.

Disconcertingly few students find their way to his lectures. The

Jewish students carry yellow cards, the stateless blue, the German brown. He lectures in French, in itself unpatriotic, and he is a Jew; attending his lectures requires courage, he writes. Besides, the students are more interested in "military sports exercises" or else are helping out with propaganda or taking part in demonstrations and rallies ahead of the upcoming referendum. He rages about Hitler's "unified list of candidates" (*Einheitsliste*) and maintains that it means the end of the Reichstag as a parliament. All wear little buttons with the word *Ja* on their lapels, he writes, and one cannot turn the button sellers away without being viewed with suspicion. He calls it such a "rape of the general public" that it must surely work against itself. But he has held this belief for some time; Goebbels addresses an intoxicated common herd, Klemperer is an intellectual and has been wrong all along. He mentions having a Jewish couple he refers to as "K" over for coffee. He finds Frau K snobbish and uncritical, a person who repeats the dominant opinion in any circumstance, but has more respect for her husband. When Herr K says that he is intending, in line with the central committee of Jewish citizens, to vote yes in the referendum, Klemperer loses his temper and thumps his fist on the table. His voice raised in anger, he demands to know if the man considers the policies of the government to be criminal or not. The man replies with composure that he has no right to ask such a question. The woman says that one must acknowledge that the Führer is a most brilliant and captivating man whose extraordinary charisma cannot be denied. Later, while intending to apologize for his behavior, he hears similar judgments from other Jews in his circles, from all walks of life, including intellectuals.

"Some kind of fog has descended which is enveloping everybody," he writes. At that time the Nazis had been in power for only a few months.

The new came not from without, but from within, and not in the guise of the unfamiliar, but as an amplification of the already known. And it came not as a negative force, and was not associated with destruction and death; reading accounts from early 1930s Germany, there is a striking optimism radiating from everywhere. Something new has begun, enterprise is strong, and the new party assuming power brings with it new career opportunities for a new people. Much is unproven, established and shaped as they go along; reading Albert Speer's memoir, *Inside the Third Reich*, the sense of empowerment and freedom it gives out is clear; as a young architect straight out of school he joins the NSDAP, is commissioned to renovate a party building in the provinces, does the job to everyone's satisfaction, receives further commissions, is noticed, entrusted with greater responsibilities, handpicked by the party's central offices, and one day finds himself standing before Adolf Hitler himself. The optimism of shaping one's own future blows like a wind through Speer's account of the era. The Nazis were of course continually on the lookout for young talent, there were positions to be filled, and many. The new optimism and momentum emanated, too, from all the parades, the marches, the rallies, and the meetings, which made the public space a stage, and what was shown on that stage came not from the outside, was not some alien element belonging to some other, it was the people themselves as they were in community, together, that found their form in these scenes.

But it was not the case that the people were deceived, that they were unaware of the propaganda, of the fact that behind what they were seeing and hearing there was a will and a particular intention, and that this was directed toward them in order to make them act or think in a certain way. That aspect was so obvious it was impossible not to be aware of it. It is similar to advertising in our day; we know full well it is trying to manipulate us and make us buy some product, but this does not prevent us from watching the ads, which can be good or funny, subtle or just plain silly, but even if we dislike them we do not necessarily dislike advertising in itself, and although we know there is no difference between this or that product and that all the glamor associated with one and not the other belongs to the image and not the product, which can be a different thing altogether, we nevertheless still buy what we associate with the glamor. We know that someone always will, and we know that the association between a product and its advertising is arbitrary, so buying the product or not buying the product is entirely up to us. No one has deceived us.

What is peculiar about advertising is that it works and does not work at the same time. The same is true of the propaganda of Hitler's Germany. They knew it was propaganda and seldom took it seriously, as is evident from Klemperer's notes, people regarded it more as a phenomenon, easy to see through, and yet they could be taken in by it, and when it came to the matter of the Jews it was an exaggeration, a hang-up Hitler had, any reasonable person knew this even if not necessarily distancing themselves from what it involved. Klemperer despised the propaganda, but was also affected by it; his emotions reacted even though his mind shunned the idea that there might genuinely be something inferior about him. Klemperer is interesting, too, because he was both Jewish and German, which is to say he was born into Judaism, but converted later to Protestantism, so he considers what is going on around him as both an intellectual German citizen and a Jew.

This is how he describes one palpable instance of propaganda in 1933:

> 10 November, evening. I heard the apogee of propaganda this afternoon on Dember's radio (our Jewish physicist, already dismissed, but also already negiotiating for a professorship in Turkey). On this occasion the organization by Goebbels, who also served as the compère of his own show, amounted to a masterpiece. The emphasis is on work and peace in the service of peaceful work. First the sound of sirens wailing across the whole of Germany and then a minute of silence across the whole of Germany – they have picked this up from America of course, and from the peace celebrations at the end of the Great War. This is followed by the framework around Hitler's speech, perhaps not a great deal more original either (cf. Italy), but executed to

absolute perfection. A factory floor in Siemensstadt. For a few minutes the noise of all the machines at work, the hammering, rattling, rumbling, whistling, grinding. Then the sirens and singing and the gradual falling silent of the wheels as they are brought to a standstill. Then quietly, out of the silence, Goebbels's deep voice with the messenger's report. And only after all of this: Hitler himself, he speaks for three quarters of an hour. It was the first time that I had heard one of his speeches from beginning to end, and my impression was essentially the same as before. For the most part an excessively agitated, hectoring, often rasping voice. The only difference was that on this occasion many passages were declaimed in the whining tone of an evangelizing sectarian. He advocates peace, he proclaims peace, he wants the unanimous support of Germany not out of personal ambition, but only in order to be able to defend peace against the attacks of a rootless international clique of profiteers, who for the sake of their own profit unscrupulously set populations of countless millions against each other . . .

All of this, together with the well-rehearsed heckling ("The Jews!"), I had of course been conversant with for a long time. But in all its hackneyed overfamiliarity, its deafening mendacity – audible surely to the deafest of ears – it acquired a special and novel authority from a peculiarity of the foregoing propaganda, an aspect which I consider to be the most outstanding and ultimately decisive among its succesful individual ingredients. The advance notice and radio announcement stated: "Ceremony between 13:00 and 14:00. In the thirteenth hour Adolf Hitler will visit the workers." This is, as everyone knows, the language of the Gospel. The Lord, the Savior visits the poor and the prodigal. Ingenious, right down to the timing. Thirteen hundred hours – no, "the thirteenth hour" – sounds too late, but he will work miracles, for him there is no such thing as too late. The Blood Banner at the rally was of the same order. But this time the dividing line separating it from ecclesiastical ceremony has been broken down, the antiquated costume has been shed and the legend of Christ has been transported into the here and now: Adolf Hitler, the Redeemer, visits the workers in Siemensstadt.

The present is charged with the weight and suggestive force of the myth, the proximate, normally trivial, becomes meaningful and ultimately sacred. The quotidian becomes a magical world. It is elevated. Like Klemperer, one can see through it, but not without being touched by it at the same time. The sound of sirens is magnificent; once a month they are heard in this country, too, and when they sound out it is hard not to stop what you are doing and look out the window if you are inside, or up at the sky if you are out; their sound pierces everything, ominously they pervade the air, as if it were doomsday itself. The sirens call out, call out to us, to all who hear them. Collective silence works in much the same way, within it we are never alone.

After the two invocations of this great "we" come Goebbels's and Hitler's speeches about peace. The footage I have seen of Hitler's speeches, two generations on, shows a screeching, gesticulating man, his face contorting as he spits out his words to an audience that receives everything he says with huge enthusiasm. But those images are part of a course of events, containing a before and after, which show something else. I once saw one of Hitler's speeches in its entirety, it, too, began with Goebbels bellowing slogans, arms gesturing, eyes flashing, a warm-up man, and when finally he introduced Hitler the crowd erupted in exultation. Suddenly Hitler is there, utterly impassive on the stage. He mumbles some politeness into the microphone, ladies and gentlemen, perhaps, or dear countrymen, something like that. He seems ill at ease, as if he wishes he could be anywhere else but there. He fidgets uneasily with some papers on a table at his side, sips water from a glass, hitches up his trousers. He says nothing, but stares down before this enormous crowd whose attention is directed entirely toward him. His silence is almost unbearable, what can be wrong, has he lost his nerve? Is he really that nervous? Why is he not saying anything? He takes another sip of water. And then he leans forward toward the microphone. He speaks quietly, slowly, hesitantly. But everyone is listening, the silence is total, everyone wants him to succeed. I, too, wanted him to succeed. Even before he has spoken, he has established a very strong feeling of identification with himself on the part of his audience, the crowd is on his side, he is one of them. After that there is only one way, his speech rises and rises again in intensity, gripping each and every individual present, soon he has them all in the palm of his hand, they obey his every motion, he can say anything and they will never deny him but give him whatever he might ask them for. The important thing about Hitler's speeches was not what he said, the nature of the arguments he presented, but his winning over the crowd. The people were with him.

Albert Speer was twenty-eight years old when he saw Hitler for the first time, at Hasenheide, a beer hall in Berlin, where Hitler was to speak to the students of the university. In his autobiography Speer writes that he was expecting a caricature, a shrieking, gesticulating demagogue in uniform with a swastika armband. What he saw was something quite different. Hitler was dressed in a neat navy-blue suit, giving an impression of respectability, and when he started to talk he spoke softly and self-effacingly, Speer writes, and what he then witnessed was more like a talk on history than a political speech. Sober, self-conscious, respectable, these are the words Speer uses to describe Hitler. After a while the shyness and hesitancy vanished, his voice became more forceful, he stressed his words and spoke with great persuasion and more and more hypnotically, and this enthusiasm washed away all reservations, all skepticism, Hitler was no longer speaking to persuade and convince, yet nor did he seem to be saying what his audience expected of him. Speer writes that he had forgotten what Hitler had said only hours later, whereas the mood stayed with him, the passion and the optimism: he had seen the new, he had seen the future. All this was written in hindsight, and certainly with the aim of exonerating Speer himself, portraying him as someone who had been pulled along by something of considerable substance rather than by something lesser, thereby in a way being duped – at the same time there are many other sources that say exactly the same thing: there was something more to Hitler than the historical caricature.

Hitler himself knew he could never win over the people through argument alone. The written word was of no use to him, it led to nothing. What he wanted was palpable action, he strove for transformation, and transformation took place in the moment, among the people. An opinion in the newspaper, hitting out against this or that, prompting a response in kind, an endless debate washing this way and that, was meaningless, nothing but words. Even in his book, *Mein Kampf*, he returns time and again to his distrust of the written word. *Mein Kampf* is about how a society can be changed starting at the very bottom, and in that it is pragmatic rather than fanatical. At one point he writes:

> *How hard it is to upset emotional prejudices, moods, sentiments, etc., and to replace them by others, on how many scarcely calculable influences and conditions success depends, the sensitive speaker can judge by the fact that even the time of day in which the lecture takes place can have a decisive influence on the effect.*

This is the goal: to work other thoughts in behind the protective wall formed by prejudice, which is to say general, unreflected opinions. That protective wall cannot be penetrated by argument, for it is not made of arguments. It is made of a sense of what is right and wrong, what is decent, what is appropriate. To reach behind it into where such opinions reside and may be changed, one must proceed via the emotions. This requires great attention to the audience, whose self-image must not be violated, what is said must not appear alien – in such cases it will be rejected – but familiar, as something already belonging to them, something that is them. Hitler writes:

> *How hard it is to upset emotional prejudices, moods, sentiments, etc., and to replace them by others, on how many scarcely calculable influ-*

ences and conditions success depends, the sensitive speaker can judge by the fact that even the time of day in which the lecture takes place can have a decisive influence on the effect. The same lecture, the same speaker, the same theme, have an entirely different effect at ten o'clock in the morning, at three o'clock in the afternoon, or at night. I myself as a beginner organized meetings for the morning, and especially remember a rally which we held in the Munich Kindl Keller as a protest "against the oppression of German territories." At that time it was Munich's largest hall and it seemed a very great venture. In order to make attendance particularly easy for the adherents of the movement and all the others who came, I set the meeting for a Sunday morning at ten o'clock. The result was depressing, yet at the same time extremely instructive: the hall was full, the impression really overpowering, but the mood ice cold; no one became warm, and I myself as a speaker felt profoundly unhappy at being unable to create any bond, not even the slightest contact, between myself and my audience. I thought I had not spoken worse than usual; but the effect seemed to be practically nil. Utterly dissatisfied, though richer by one experience, I left the meeting. Tests of the same sort that I later undertook led to the same result.

This should surprise no one. Go to a theater performance and witness a play at three o'clock in the afternoon and the same play with the same actors at eight at night, and you will be amazed at the difference in effect and impression. A man with fine feelings and the power to achieve clarity with regard to this mood will be able to establish at once that the impression made by the performance at three in the afternoon is not as great as that made in the evening. The same applies even to a movie. This is important because in the theater it might be said that perhaps the actor does not take as much pain in the afternoon as at night. But a film is no different in the afternoon than at nine in the evening. No, the time itself exerts a definite effect, just as the hall does on me. There are halls which leave people cold for reasons that are hard to discern, but which somehow oppose the most violent resistance to any creation of mood. Traditional memories and ideas that are present in a man can also decisively determine an impression. Thus, a performance of Parsifal in Bayreuth will always have *a different effect than anywhere else in the world. The mysterious magic of the house on the Festspielhügel in the old city of the margraves cannot be replaced or even compensated for by externals.*

Mein Kampf was published in 1925, after *Growth of the Soil, The People of Juvik, Kristin Lavransdatter, Ulysses,* and the first volumes of *In Search of Lost Time,* but before *The Castle, Being and Time,* and *The Sound and the Fury.* It is the most infamous book of our time, not because of what it says in itself, but because what it says was carried out in real life, and it is impossible to read *Mein Kampf* today without immense distaste, for something terrible and repulsive is attached to it, as if it were written by the devil himself. But at the time of its writing, its author, Adolf Hitler, was an ordinary man, he had not murdered anyone, had ordered no killings to be carried out, had stolen nothing and burned nothing to the ground. Had he not risen to power in Germany nine years later, nothing of what he wrote would have had any particular significance or overtone, the book would presumably be long since forgotten, existing only in a limited number of dusty volumes on the shelves of university libraries, borrowed on rare occasion by a doctoral student writing about the historical period and finding the work illustrative of some of its typical characteristics, not least the paranoid hatred of Jews. But Hitler did rise to power in 1933, and *Mein Kampf* now occupies a place apart in literature, wide open to the world: not only were the words on its pages transformed into real life, but what happened there, in real life, stains its each and every word; not a sentence can be read or quoted without thinking about the Nazis' industrial extermination of the Jews and the millions who perished in World War II. It is almost impossible to read the book for what it once was, the work of a political fanatic outlining his personal background, analyzing society, and detailing what needs to be done in order to change it in the direction he wants. There is nothing gripping about it, nothing hypnotic or suggestive, and what little it says about its author and his life mutates into lengthy political ventings after barely a few lines. It has a smug, opinionated quality about it, for regardless of what aspect of society its author touches upon there is always something wrong with it, and moreover he knows exactly what it is and what needs to be done in order to put it right. Even the lambasting to which he often resorts gradually becomes rather mechanical. *Mein Kampf* is written in a tone of righteous indignation so powerful it must surely scare away anyone whose indignation by comparison falls short.

That the book takes the form of a bildungsroman, in which we follow the author from birth, through the first character-shaping years of childhood, and further into youth and the discoveries and fundamental insights of the young adult, has to do with the same thing: Hitler makes himself one with his politics, makes himself one with his role; what he believes and what he is are inseparable. Hitler builds up a persona in *Mein Kampf,* and that persona is his political platform. He is of the people, this is his message, and he knows the people's problems, having experienced them himself; gradually he devises a comprehensive political solution, a vision thereby bound up with both the people and his own person, concentrated in the name, the signum of the work, Adolf Hitler.

Invariably, the personal experiences he describes are hooked up to the political, and if the book has any biographical axis at all, it is considered from such a remote distance that everything personal and private, relating only to him, to his own person and character, the idiosyncratic, vanishes from sight. These are the book's first sentences:

> *Today it seems to me providential that Fate should have chosen Braunau on the Inn as my birthplace. For this little town lies on the boundary between two German states which we of the younger generation at least have made it our life work to reunite by every means at our disposal.*

> *German Austria must return to the great German mother country, and not because of any economic considerations. No, and again no:*

even if such a union were unimportant from an economic point of view; yes, even if it were harmful, it must nevertheless take place. One blood demands one Reich. Never will the German nation possess the moral right to engage in colonial politics until, at least, it embraces its own sons within a single state. Only when the Reich borders include the very last German, but can no longer guarantee his daily bread, will the moral right to acquire foreign soil arise from the distress of our own people. Their sword will become our plow, and from the tears of war the daily bread of future generations will grow. And so this little city on the border seems to me the symbol of a great mission.

Like any other memoir or autobiography, *Mein Kampf* begins with the main character's birth. But no sooner are we informed of it than this "I" recedes into a "we," so essential that the first thing it does there is to define its borders.

"We" is the people, and the people's we stands above the we of the state by which it has been divided. The necessity of the we becoming united again stands above practical everyday politics and has its foundations in morality, finding its force in the body, that which is outside of language, nonargumentative, tangible, and physical: the blood. So essential is this that reunification takes precedence over the damage it will entail. Once this, the book's utopia, has been accomplished, the practical consequences of it, the damage done, the country being unable to feed its people, will be rectified by way of the moral mandate that comes with being a united people, which is to say the conquering of new land. In less than half a page then, Hitler has both outlined his political program and associated it with his own person, born in Braunau on the Inn, a border town and thereby symbolic of this great task, the reunification of the two countries' peoples into one, which he, child of the borderland, will carry out. This goal stands above everything else, and such is the symbolic and moral power of the reunifying act that it can transform a sword into a plow, tears into bread, war into peace.

After a page in this vein, the author returns to his point of departure and carries on the story of his origins:

In this little town on the Inn, gilded by the rays of German martyr-dom, Bavarian by blood, technically Austrian, lived my parents in the late eighties of the past century; my father, a dutiful civil servant, my mother giving all her being to the household, and devoted above all to us children in eternal, loving care.

Hitler was born in 1889 in a town far from the world, provincial and unimportant in every sense, into an ordinary family of the lower middle class. He did not feel himself particularly attached to the place, the family moving elsewhere when he was three years old. Its description as being gilded by the memory of German martyrdom, with Bavarian blood running through its veins, places us partly in the obscure and magical world of myth, partly in the late-nineteenth-century Austrian provinces. The outline of his mother, her looking after the household and devoting herself lovingly to the care of her children, is the only thing said of her in the entire book. There is no mention of the fact that she was related to her husband by blood and pregnant when she married him some six months after his first wife had been put in her grave. Nor are we told that the three children to whom she gave birth before Adolf all died, one, a girl, at the age of two, or that the boy she had after Adolf, Edmund, died when he was six. How many siblings Hitler had, what their names were and what kind of feelings he had toward them, are all passed by. They are men-tioned merely as "us children." The father is the only person in Hitler's life, during his first thirty-five years, to be described in more than a few words and accorded some biography. Like every-one belonging to Hitler's closest family in *Mein Kampf,* he appears without a name.

Of "my father," Hitler writes that he was from poor circum-stances, son of an impoverished cottager, who ran away from home at the age of thirteen, determined to make something of himself and become a civil servant, the most respected position he had heard of, succeeding at the age of forty, retiring at fifty-six to purchase a small farm at Lambach in Upper Austria. The book tells us nothing of his relationship with his family or Hitler himself. Where the mother is loving and devoted in relation to her children, the father is "a dutiful civil servant." His social trajectory is described in sentimental terms. He is the "poor boy" from the village with "all the tenacity of a young man whom suffering and care had made old while still half a child." Moreover he was born outside wedlock, a bastard child, to all intents and purposes a nobody. Hitler does not deny his father's poor circumstances and low social status, instead making a point of it in a narrative about the power of will and independence. Certainly, Hitler makes no explicit mention of illegitimacy. The description of his father returning after a long and hardworking career to the life his own father had led is part of the same embellishment of the gilded German town of Hitler's birth. This is an idea of lineage, which basically means being born of somebody else, there is in essence nothing qualitative about the concept, nor in the expression to be of "one blood," since blood is in all of us and all of us are born into some lineage. "Lineage" and "blood" create similarity and in this instance elevate, into these concepts vanish the miserable circumstances of life, the low social status of the illegitimate child, and this, too, is the sense such words are ascribed in Hitler's politics, erasing social divides and making everyone a part of the same thing. Lineage and blood are nature; class and status are culture, and in Hitler's image of the world the former governs. As he later writes when discussing the issue of rapidly increasing population:

> *While Nature, by making procreation free, yet submitting survival to a hard trial, chooses from an excess number of individuals the best as worthy of living, thus preserving them alone and in them conserving their species, man limits procreation, but is hysterically concerned*

that once a being is born it should be preserved at any price. This cor-
rection of the divine will seems to him as wise as it is humane, and
he takes delight in having once again got the best of Nature and even
having proved her inadequacy. The number, to be sure, has really been
limited, but at the same time the value of the individual has dimin-
ished; this, however, is something the dear little ape of the Almighty
does not want to see or hear about.

For as soon as procreation as such is limited and the number of
births diminished, the natural struggle for existence which leaves only
the strongest and healthiest alive is obviously replaced by the obvious
desire to "save" even the weakest and most sickly at any price, and
this plants the seed of a future generation which must inevitably grow
more and more deplorable the longer this mockery of Nature and her
will continues.

Here, mankind is reduced to numbers, the aggregate being decisive, determinative of power, expressing the will of nature, which is the same as the divine will, and the nameless individual who succumbs to hunger or sickness has no right to life. Keeping such individuals alive is "humane," and thereby counter to nature. Such a perspective was by no means unique to Hitler, it was everywhere in the age and would not have been possible without Darwin and his unprecedentedly influential book, *On the Origin of Species*, in which all living creatures were considered through the same lens of evolution, this mighty power which through its very few laws has conveyed life from its monocellular origins in the great oceans to the huge complexities of the human. The fittest live on, and thus our life-bearing properties are steadily improved and refined, and since life is one long struggle the fittest are often the strongest, and that thought, translated to the social and the civilizational, comprises a pillar of *Mein Kampf*, one of the immovable premises from which the rest of its ideology issues. Nature is above culture. In nature the sick die, the weak die, the tardy die, the injured die. The brutality and cruelty of according this same principle so very central a status in culture lies in the worth of the human, the humane, being so radically diminished. A single human life is of little value in *Mein Kampf.*

But what is of value? The ideal a person can express, or be an expression of, this is of greater value than life. This is what lies behind dying for a cause, the idea that there is something greater, something one lives for and which is understood to be of such manifest importance that a person would be willing to give up his life for it.

Life is not primary.

Hitler wrote his book in 1924, six years after four million young men had slaughtered each other in the trenches of Europe, a shadow that lay over all that was to be thought and written in the years that followed. In the autumn of 1914 a human life was infinitely more worthless than in the autumn of 1913. World War I was an abyss, a near-unfathomable crisis of civilization, and one of the most important issues that needed to be addressed in its wake was precisely the worth of the human being. To understand *Mein Kampf,* one must understand this.

This is the overarching societal perspective to which the book belongs and by which it is steered, but there is a personal perspective too, the I of its writer, the close and proximate world in which he grew up and by which he was formed, with his conscientious father, the civil servant, and a mother who gave "all her being to the household, and devoted above all to us children in eternal, loving care." In this proximate world death, too, was close, and if the three children who died before Hitler was born were mentioned only rarely during his childhood and upbringing, they must surely have been present in the minds of his parents, in particular his mother, who sources unanimously describe as serious and mournful. Child mortality was high in those days, to lose three children was by no means unusual. August Kubizek, Hitler's childhood friend, likewise had three siblings die before he was born, and the fact of death being so common must have made life seem at once more and less valuable. Less valuable in the sense that death was something to be reckoned with; the death of one's first three children must have made the death of the fourth a perilously proximate possibility. More valuable in the sense that the one who survived would be the only one, correspondingly precious.

Adolf Hitler was Klara Hitler's fourth child, he was sickly, and yet it was he who survived, and his mother, according to his friend Kubizek, was forever fretting and worrying about him. When the fifth child, Edmund, died, Hitler was eleven years old, old enough to grieve over him and to remember him for the rest of his life.

According to the ideology expressed in *Mein Kampf*, Hitler's younger brother died because he was too weak and therefore unworthy of life. What Hitler himself thought and felt as an eleven-year-old boy is a matter of conjecture, but it would not seem unreasonable to suggest that he was affected by his brother's death and that he pondered on why it had happened. Why him rather than another? As a teenager Hitler distanced himself from the Church; his mother attended devoutly every Sunday, his friend and his friend's family likewise, but not Hitler, who would stand outside and wait for them, suggesting that he was certainly not looking for any religious explanation of the brutality of existence.

In *Mein Kampf* everything belonging to Hitler's own biography is related to his ideology. It is not his father's life as such that is significant to him, the person he was in real life, the man whose smell could be described in such and such a way, who walked and stood and sat like this or like that, who expressed himself in this way rather than that and who filled a room with his very own presence, but rather what he in his life represented. His father is presented as a man who worked his way up from the humblest beginnings, in other words he belongs to the strong, and in this way Hitler turns his problematic social background to his advantage, at the same time as he keeps private that which would ruin the trajectory, the striving to surmount, that which takes place in the material world among real people, who not only belong to a lineage, but also belch and shit and yell and lash out, and with a certain regularity drink themselves senseless; who slurp and spit and reek of piss and sweat, who drag their sons here and there by the hair, behavior that presumably cannot have been unusual in the home of a customs official at the end of the nineteenth century – all this vanishes, too, in the ancestral circle closed by his father's passage from cottager's son to farmer.

But while Hitler translated his father's history into an example of vitality and strength, there is something else in that history that Hitler is not sensitive enough as a writer to be able to control. Almost everything that follows on the subject of his father concerns the disparity between him and his son. The conflict is very much toned down and yet occupies some considerable surface area, and in this asymmetry there is tension.

> *It was at this time that the first ideals took shape in my breast. All my playing about in the open, the long walk to school, and particularly my association with extremely "husky" boys, which sometimes caused my mother bitter anguish, made me the very opposite of a stay-at-home. And though at that time I scarcely had any serious ideas as to the profession I should one day pursue, my sympathies were in any case not in the direction of my father's career.*

In his own self-image, Hitler is a child of the outdoors, playing with "extremely 'husky' boys," "rather hard to handle," and "a boy who in reality was really anything but 'good' in the usual sense of the word." In other words, he is indignant, obstinate, unruly, perhaps also aggressive, all of which is directed toward his father, no one else being named in this context, his father who could "achieve no understanding" of the "youthful ideas" in his son's head and was thereby made to feel "concern." As a result, his father begins "the relentless enforcement of his authority," this by later accounts involving beatings and harsh corporal punishment. But Hitler lends another side to this depiction:

I had become a little ringleader; at school I learned easily and at that time very well, but was otherwise rather hard to handle. Since in my free time I received singing lessons in the cloister at Lambach, I had excellent opportunity to intoxicate myself with the solemn splendor of the brilliant church festivals. As was only natural, the abbot seemed to me, as the village priest had once seemed to my father, the highest and most desirable ideal. For a time, at least, this was the case. But since my father, for understandable reasons, proved unable to appreciate the oratorical talents of his pugnacious boy, or to draw from them any favorable conclusions regarding the future of his offspring, he could, it goes without saying, achieve no understanding for such youthful ideas. With concern he observed this conflict of nature.

As it happened, my temporary aspiration for this profession was in any case soon to vanish, making place for hopes more suited to my temperament. Rummaging through my father's library, I had come across various books of a military nature, among them a popular edition of the Franco-German War of 1870–71. It consisted of two issues of an illustrated periodical from those years, which now became my favorite reading matter. It was not long before the great heroic struggle had become my greatest inner experience. From then on I became more and more enthusiastic about everything that was in any way connected with war or, for that matter, with soldiering.

But in another respect as well, this was to assume importance for me. For the first time, though as yet in a confused form, the question was forced upon my consciousness: Was there a difference – and if so what difference – between the Germans who fought these battles and other Germans? Why hadn't Austria taken part in this war; why hadn't my father and all the others fought?

Are we not the same as all other Germans? Do we not all belong together? This problem began to gnaw at my little brain for the first time. I asked cautious questions and with secret envy received the answer that not every German was fortunate enough to belong to Bismarck's Reich.

This was more than I could understand.

Both fascinations are embellishments of reality. The splendor of Church ceremonial, in which he delights, is theatrical and external, whereas the narrative of the heroism of war is an internal transformation, the character of the soldiers, their courage and self-sacrifice giving luster to an otherwise trivial and quotidian reality, not in itself, but in the sympathetic insight into their heroism the books about them make possible, the viewpoint thereby established, the notion that this ordinary landscape could be transformed and become uniquely significant. Both fascinations are associated with his father; the first making Hitler's idealization of the abbot natural, a reflection of his father's veneration of the village priest in his boyhood days. A male ideal to any boy of such age is the ideal of his father, and to Hitler's father nothing was more natural since he had no father of his own. Hitler, however, does, and his idealization of the abbot must be seen in that light. It is this "conflict of nature" in his son's character that makes his father feel anxious. He seeks what is furthest from his father. In the description of his infatuations with war, the two realities, the one in which he grew up and the one he dreamed about, are brought even closer together, the nearest the book gets to an accusation without tearing away the veil of euphemism by which it shrouds all things proximate. Why did Austria not fight? Why did my father and all the others not fight in that struggle?

It is a childish accusation, for there were any number of good reasons for his father not having fought, but the childish nature of it suggests that it preys on him during the time about which he is writing; nothing else in the first three or four pages seems to be so, everything is controlled, held in the same grip and tone as is used throughout the work.

The suggested conflict escalates when a decision is to be made as to what kind of school the eleven-year-old Adolf is to attend. Hitler himself prefers the classical *Lyceum*, whereas his father wants him to attend the non-classical *Realschule*.

Then barely eleven years old, I was forced into opposition for the first time in my life. Hard and determined as my father might be in putting through plans and purposes once conceived, his son was just as persistent and recalcitrant in rejecting an idea which appealed to him not at all, or in any case very little. I did not want to become a civil servant. Neither persuasion nor "serious" arguments made any impression on my resistance.

I did not want to be a civil servant, no, and again no.

All attempts on my father's part to inspire me with love or pleasure in this profession by stories from his own life accomplished the exact opposite. I yawned and grew sick to my stomach at the thought of sitting in an office, deprived of my liberty; ceasing to be master of my own time and being compelled to force the content of a whole life into blanks that had to be filled out.

The odd thing is that the book says nothing of how it turned out, what happened, how the conflict ended. Instead, this is merely suggested, a dozen lines on: "In this respect my attendance at the *Realschule*, which now commenced, made little difference."

He describes an absolutely intractable conflict, he is eleven years old, for the first time confronting the wishes of his father, who is harsh and strict and high-handed, nothing can break down his opposition – and then, although nothing apparently happens, Hitler has given in and is in the midst of everything he so fiercely rejected.

The narrative is clearly hiding something, but what? Is it his defeat itself and the way it must have altered his relationship with his father? His father broke his will, and insofar as he had been open in his opposition and squared up to him in a battle of strength, that defeat must have been humiliating indeed. Yet there is something odd about this entire depiction. That a father should have plans as to his son's education is only natural, but the son being so farsighted in respect to his future as to invest, at the age of eleven, all his strength in opposing his father's will in the matter of something as far off in time as a civil servant's position sounds strange.

Why was it so urgent for Hitler to say that he was sent to the *Realschule* in Linz against his will? It was a highly respectable school, Ludwig Wittgenstein, born in the same year as Adolf Hitler, went there, and he was from one of the wealthiest and culturally most well-endowed families in Austria, if not the whole of Europe. Wittgenstein and Hitler both did poorly at the school, Hitler especially so, failing in several subjects and having to re-take his first year, then failing again in his third year with the result that he was not allowed to continue before improving his grades at another, less prestigious school. Could it be that this whole story of his father forcing him to attend was something he made up, allowing him to state that he could have passed had he wanted to, but that what he wanted was something else, for which reason he saw no reason to make an effort? It sounds like a rather circuitous route.

The conflict surrounding the civil servant's position is escalated further. Hitler attends the *Realschule* against his will, forced to give in to his father's wishes, but in his own words he is "persistent and recalcitrant" and instead of standing firm on *Lyceum* over *Realschule*, he redoubles the conflict a year later:

> How it happened, I myself do not know, but one day it became clear to me that I would become a painter, an artist. There was no doubt as to my talent for drawing; it had been one of my father's reasons for sending me to the Realschule, but never in all the world would it have occurred to him to give me professional training in this direction. On the contrary. When for the first time, after once again rejecting my father's favorite notion, I was asked what I myself wanted to be, and I rather abruptly blurted out the decision I had meanwhile made, my father for the moment was struck speechless.
>
> "Painter? Artist?"
>
> He doubted my sanity, or perhaps he thought he had heard wrong

or misunderstood me. But when he was clear on the subject, and particularly after he felt the seriousness of my intention, he opposed it with all the determination of his nature. His decision was extremely simple, for any consideration of what abilities I might really have was simply out of the question.

"Artist, no, never as long as I live!" But since his son, among various other qualities, had apparently inherited his father's stubbornness, the same answer came back at him. Except, of course, that it was in the opposite sense.

And thus the situation remained on both sides. My father did not depart from his "Never!" And I intensified my "Oh, yes!"

The consequences, indeed, were none too pleasant. The old man grew embittered, and, much as I loved him, so did I. My father forbade me to nourish the slightest hope of ever being allowed to study art. I went one step further and declared that if that was the case I would stop studying altogether. As a result of such "pronouncements," of course, I drew the short end; the old man began the relentless enforcement of his authority. In the future, therefore, I was silent, but transformed my threat into reality.

His brother Edmund dies of the measles in February 1900. Hitler begins at the *Realschule* in Linz in September that same year. How his brother's death affects him is impossible to glean from his own writings about the period. Some biographies describe a transformative impact on his personality, suggesting that Hitler went from pleasant and outgoing to argumentative, sullen, and introverted, but even if this was the case we have no way of knowing what might have occasioned it, all we can do is note that at some point during this time he left one milieu for another, going from a small village school to a big city school where he knew no one and made no friends, and that his brother died some months before. But then again, it was his younger brother who had died, it must have left a crater, and was bound to have darkened his mind and his life in general. Everything his little brother was in life, and then his ceasing to exist, no longer being alive among them, would perhaps be more difficult for an eleven-year-old to accept than to understand. And when the child of a family dies, the grief of its parents is unfathomable; in that grief those who do not die must live on. The parents must have been quite differently attached to him than to those who had died at birth, the future must have been meshed into their gaze whenever they looked at him. The death of a child is a crisis greater than any other, and how can an eleven-year-old relate to that, other than to dwell on the injustice of it? This tragedy resonates through Hitler's years at the *Realschule*, his disinclination to apply himself, his impudence and self-confidence; he is his own person, with no reason to give a damn apart from his father's attempts to thrash sense into him. The beatings cannot have been decisive in shifting his character, he had been beaten before, it was a circumstance of his life, as doubtless it was for many other children of the time, certainly in that environment. He writes nothing about his mother, nothing about his siblings, nothing about friends, only about his father. If we are to believe his account, the way he sabotages his schooling to demonstrate to his father that he was wrong, then certainly there is something self-destructive about his behavior here. Only a darkened mind would pursue the thought, refuse to work, make him see what he has done, when no other opportunity exists but this to take revenge, no other way to hurt the one you hate. While this entire elaborate operation may conceivably be a concoction designed to excuse Hitler's poor grades and lack of schooling, it is nevertheless descriptive of the remoteness that existed between father and son, a deadlock, though there seems to be no obvious reason to consider it fictitious, since it clearly seems to have been working at various levels and is confirmed by other sources. "The old man . . . as I loved him" would seem to be a rather kind way of referring to an obstinate, cantankerous, and bitter customs official who beats his children senseless, but the representation here is not of Hitler's father, but the more abstract "father," a presence in almost any life, to be looked up to and respected, hence the form Hitler uses slightly further on, "the old gentleman."

Few had much good to say about Alois Hitler, born Schicklgruber. In her book *Hitler's Vienna* Brigitte Hamann cites one of his acquaintances, Josef Mayrhofer, as saying this of him: "In the bar he always had to be right and had a quick temper . . . At home he was strict, not a gentle man; his wife didn't have an easy life." Yet the picture is by no means unambiguous; the obituary in the Linz *Tagespost* describes a cheerful and sociable man, "always . . . happy" and "of a downright youthful joyfulness even," Hamann quotes, and also "a friend of song." "Even though a rough word may have escaped his lips once in a while, a good heart was hiding behind a rough exterior," the obituary went on. Basically, then, he would seem to have been a jovial sort socially, a pig at home. To his secretary Hitler later confided that he had not loved his father, and moreover had been frightened of him. "He had tantrums and immediately became physically violent. My poor mother would always be very scared for me." Hitler's older brother, Alois Junior, draws much the same picture, adding that Adolf was spoiled and protected by his mother, Alois Junior's stepmother, who pampered him from morning till night. But Alois Junior, too, states that Adolf was beaten, on one occasion so brutally he thought him to be dead.

Undeniably the most important source about Hitler's early days in Linz, and to a certain extent in Vienna too, is August Kubizek's book *The Young Hitler I Knew: The Memoirs of Hitler's Childhood Friend*, which came out in 1953. Kubizek was nine months older than Hitler and they first met at the theater in Linz when they were both sixteen. This means that Kubizek never met Hitler's father, but he became a friend of the family and writes that Alois was still very much a presence in their lives. A large portrait of him adorned the most prominent place on the sitting-room wall; the long pipes he used to smoke were still arrayed on a shelf in the kitchen, and Kubizek writes that they were in some strange way a symbol of the father; often when Frau Hitler spoke of her late husband she would gesture toward his pipes "as though they should bear witness how faithfully she carried on the husband's tradition."

According to Kubizek, the father's colleagues at the customs office described him as precise, dutiful, and strict, proud of his rank, though an unpopular superior. The most notable trait highlighted by Kubizek is a near-manic restlessness. He changes address twelve times during the years he lives in Braunau, twice when living in Passau, and seven times after his retirement. Adolf himself recalls seven different homes and five different schools. The moves had nothing to do with the quality of the dwellings, often he would move to a poorer habitation. Kubizek's explanation is that his temperament required constant change, and since his job demanded stability his restlessness had to find another outlet. Kubizek interprets his starting three different families in his life in the same way; while married to his first wife, a considerably older woman, he was unfaithful with the woman who would become his second wife, and the same thing happened again when he embarked on his affair with Hitler's mother. "This strange and unusual habit of the father's, always to change his circumstances, is all the more remarkable as those were peaceful, comfortable times without any justification for such change."

Kubizek finds exactly the same restlessness and unease in the sixteen-year-old Hitler's character and he sees the civil-servant conflict between father and son as described in *Mein Kampf* in this very light. The father's volatile nature is kept in check by the demands of his position, the discipline that gave direction and meaning to his unstable character, the uniform of the state official served to conceal his stormy private life; the authority to which he thereby submitted allowed him to steer clear of the dangerous reefs and sandbanks on which his life might otherwise have foundered, Kubizek suggests. The father must have seen the same traits in his son and for this reason would have been more than unusually keen to direct his son's future career. It is by no means certain that Hitler's father was aware of the inner reason for his attitude, Kubizek writes, but his insistence on imposing his point of view would seem to indicate that he indeed realized how much was at stake for his son. "So well did he know him," Kubizek writes.

This idea provides a more sympathetic picture of Hitler's father than is normally presented, and it is neither untrustworthy nor improbable; on the contrary, the traits parents tend to be most implacable toward in their children are often those most similar to their own, and in acts of brutality toward children there is always an element of self-loathing even if one is unaware of its existence, perhaps especially so when the emotions that well to the surface are so powerful and all-consuming as to eliminate any semblance of reason. A will as strong as this, in which the father invests all his power and authority, contains solicitude too, however impossible for a child to understand or recognize, in that it firstly seeks to subjugate the child without listening to his objections or even trying to put oneself in the child's place, and secondly is quite bereft of the language by which love more generally is communicated. Whether such love existed or did not, we have no way of knowing. Hitler's own feelings for his father lay somewhere between hatred, terror, and respect for his authority. The changes of address, the infidelity, the age gaps in the marriages would point toward a troubled and restless soul, and it seems likely that Alois recognized this in his son's rebellious manner. The idea that he knew his son better than his son knew himself shifts the whole conflict away from responsibility and subjugation, or from the mechanical aspect of such responsibility, such subjugation, into something essential, unknown to those involved, who were helpless against themselves.

Where did the notion of becoming a painter come from? There were no artists in the family or its milieu; the closest Hitler came to art must have been what he saw in the churches and what he read about in books. Yet this is what he wants to be when he grows up.

Not a soldier, not a priest, not a teacher, not a civil servant, but the absolute opposite of a civil servant, an artist. That Ludwig Wittgenstein should become a philosopher is not in the slightest bit odd or surprising, his world was awash with art and culture, the very finest the contemporary age could offer. But Hitler could draw, and may have been encouraged, he wanted something quite different from the life that surrounded him, so perhaps art seemed to him to be a way out.

His father died suddenly from a violent hemorrhage when Hitler was thirteen.

> *The question of my profession was to be decided more quickly than I had previously expected.*
>
> *In my thirteenth year I suddenly lost my father. A stroke of apoplexy felled the old gentleman who was otherwise so hale, thus painlessly ending his earthly pilgrimage, plunging us all into the depths of grief. His most ardent desire had been to help his son forge his career, thus preserving him from his own bitter experience. In this, to all appearances, he had not succeeded. But, though unwittingly, he had sown the seed for a future which at that time neither he nor I would have comprehended.*

The word "hale" echoes Hitler's use of "husky" to decribe the boys with whom he played, and by association himself, making the notion of robustness a governing one, contrasting with his mother, who is "anguished," and with a sedentary indoor life as a "stay-at-home." "Hale" evokes his father's vitality, a man not in any way sick or in decline.

In the text Hitler's father is the very antithesis of art, the pattern being: indoors/reading/mother/stay-at-home versus outdoors/in the open/friends/combative, and ecclesiastical ceremony/art/freedom versus father/coercion/strength/vitality. "Hale" is an honorific here, held up as a positive, but beneath it flows the nonrobust. The only place where there is a bridge between them is in the description of his reading about the war, where the active, vigorous, and robust aspects of soldiers' heroic lives meet the passive, dreamy, mother-bound stay-at-homeness of reading and art.

His father dies, but Hitler does not leave school to begin with, his mother wishing him to continue. "Then suddenly an illness came to my help and in a few weeks decided my future and the eternal domestic quarrel. As a result of my serious lung ailment, a physician advised my mother in most urgent terms never to send me into an office." The fact of the doctor advising "in most urgent terms" suggests her having to be persuaded, and her having to be persuaded suggests that it was no easy task. The illness seems to have been minor, an excuse to which his mother surrendered. The fact that she gave in to the will of her son is hardly surprising in that she had been witness to her husband's beatings of the boy without being strong enough to step in, he was twice her age and a man of authority, and she had lost four children. Hitler is the survivor, nothing is too good for him.

> *The goal for which I had so long silently yearned, for which I had always fought, had through this event suddenly become reality almost of its own accord.*

> *Concerned over my illness, my mother finally consented to take me out of the Realschule and let me attend the Academy.*

When Germany entered Austria in 1938, Hitler ordered the Gestapo to remove all documents relating to himself and his family from the public archives. Seemingly he wished to wipe away all traces of his past. Nevertheless, a wealth of material concerning his life during those years still remains, and hardly a single person who entered his sphere has not been interviewed. The past resists control, it lives on in memory, in recollections and stories, rumor, letters, diaries – and whereas normally such things might never be brought together but remain solely with each individual, spread out in the way fate and destiny spread out the people of any generation, the progress of a single individual may cause them to converge and condense, as in the case of Adolf Hitler. *Mein Kampf* is by no means an unambiguously credible source, but in giving us a picture of Hitler as he saw himself in 1924 it nevertheless tells us a lot. He describes his childhood the way he wanted it to be, though with elements of his childhood the way it was, intact, in the sense that some key characters and events are included, albeit not all and not necessarily the most significant. The five years that pass between the deaths of first his father, then his mother, are treated in nineteen lines, the two years he lived in Linz with his mother and sister without attending school are dealt with in a single sentence: "These were the happiest days of my life and seemed to me almost a dream; and a mere dream it was to remain. Two years later, the death of my mother put a sudden end to all my high-flown plans."

These two happy, though in *Mein Kampf* silent, years are dealt with in Kubizek's book. It is the single most important source as to Hitler's life between the ages of sixteen and twenty, and provides at the same time the best documentary insight into Hitler's personality, Kubizek being the only real friend he had in his life.

As in the case of other accounts provided by contemporaries of Hitler, Kubizek's motives and the reliability of the picture he draws must be scrupulously assessed. This indeed has been the case with Kubizek's book. Having pointed out some minor errors, Brigitte Hamann concludes: "Yet altogether, Kubizek is reliable. His book is a rich and unique source for Hitler's early years, not even counting the letters and postcards by young Hitler that it includes."

Ian Kershaw, author of Hitler's two-volume biography, *Hubris* and *Nemesis*, is more critical, stating:

> *Kubizek's postwar memoirs need to be treated with care, both in factual detail and in interpretation. They are a lengthened and embellished version of recollections he had originally been commissioned by the Nazi Party to compile. Even retrospectively, the admiration in*

which Kubizek continued to hold his former friend colored his judg-
ment. But more than that, Kubizek plainly invented a great deal,
built some passages around Hitler's own account in Mein Kampf,
and deployed some near plagiarism to amplify his own limited mem-
ory. However, for all their weaknesses, his recollections have been
shown to be a more credible source on Hitler's youth than was once
thought, in particular where they touch on experiences related to Kubi-
zek's own interests in music and theater. There can be no doubt that,
whatever their deficiencies, they do contain important reflections of
the young Hitler's personality, showing features in embryo which
were to be all too prominent in later years.

The reasoning here is typical of Kershaw's work, which is marred
by his describing everything, and I mean everything, about Hitler
extremely negatively, even such aspects as relate to his childhood
and youth, as if his whole life were tainted by what he would become and do some twenty years later, as if in some way he were
evil incarnate, or as if evil were some core inside him, immutable
and irremediable, and thereby an explanation of why things
turned out the way they did. Such an understanding of Hitler is
immature, and makes Kershaw's books, renowned as the definitive
Hitler biography, almost unreadable. Is it possible for everything
a person does, even when that person is sixteen years old, to be
appalling and bad? Kershaw's descriptions of Hitler's youth are
invariably thickly strewn with negatives. He writes of the father's
aversion to his son's "indolent and purposeless existence," he
writes that "Alois had worked his way up through industry,
diligence and effort from humble origins to a position of dignity
and respect in the state service," whereas his son "from a more
privileged background saw fit to do no more than dawdle away
his time drawing and dreaming." Given the evidence to suggest
the father would beat the daylights out of his son and was in every
sense a domestic tyrant, casting the father as the hero and the son
as the villain in this way appears severe indeed.

The transformation in Hitler's character that would seem to have occurred in his adolescence is described by Kershaw in the following manner: "The happy, playful youngster of the primary school days had grown into an idle, resentful, rebellious, sullen, stubborn, and purposeless teenager." Of the time between Hitler leaving school at sixteen and his mother's death when he was eighteen he writes, "In these two years, Adolf lived a life of parasitic idleness – funded, provided for, looked after, and cosseted by a doting mother."

> *He spent his time during the days drawing, painting, reading, or writing "poetry"; the evenings were for going to the theater or opera; and the whole time he daydreamed or fantasized about his future as a great artist. He stayed up late into the night and slept long into the mornings. He had no clear aim in view. The indolent lifestyle, the grandiosity of fantasy, the lack of discipline for systematic work – all features of the later Hitler – can be seen in these two years in Linz.*

How great the disdain in the inverted commas dashed around "poetry"! And how conservative the negative inflection concerning his staying up late and sleeping into the mornings! How often he states that the boy was "indolent" or "lazy," that his existence was "purposeless" or "parasitic," and how negatively charged the words "daydream," "fantasize," "dream"! Together with the idea of drawing being a "dawdling away" of one's time, all this is the very expression of the mind-set and attitudes that Hitler's life at that time would seem to be protesting against. If we substitute "Hitler" with "Rilke," for instance, and imagine someone writing of the young Rilke that he was indolent, lazy, and parasitic, with no aptitude for systematic work, that he stayed up late and lay in bed in the mornings when he was sixteen; if one read such a damning rant in a biography of Rilke, one would be left perplexed at the author's outlook on life and art. Kershaw views everything even verging on art negatively, art being construed as the opposite of actual work. Of course, it might be objected that

Hitler was no true artist, and that such damnation thereby is justified, but when a boy is sixteen years old no one can possibly know what he will become or not become, and it is by no means a given that artistic talent was what primarily distinguished Hitler and Rilke when they were sixteen.

Kubizek's picture of Hitler is drawn from within this reality, of which Kershaw is so disdainful, and it is a picture of a young man fired with enthusiasm for life. Hitler lives for the opera, for the theater, for music, for poetry, for painting, for architecture. He writes poetry, he draws, he paints watercolors, he draws and designs buildings as he sees and imagines them. Instead of wondering about where such vigorous interests could come from and what they might express, as striking and conspicuous as they are in the young Hitler's life, such a powerful presence in his first twenty-five years, Kershaw sees them as an expression of Hitler's personal, and thereby base, character. But he is sixteen years old, his poetry is bound to be poor, the buildings he draws in detail cannot possibly match the work of a trained architect, obviously he is a dilettante, but what sixteen-year-old is not?

Kubizek's description of his friendship with Hitler, and of the time and milieu in which that friendship occurred, where music, art, and literature provide the very fulcrum of youth, is reminiscent of the picture Stefan Zweig gives of his formative years in Vienna in his memoir *The World of Yesterday*. Zweig was ten years older than Hitler, and what he writes about Austria in the years prior to the outbreak of World War I, that it was a period characterized by stability and liberal idealism, a "Golden Age of Security," as he calls it, must also have been true of life in Linz in 1905–6.

Zweig's description of his youth in Vienna emphasizes how obsessed he and his friends were with everything to do with culture. They line up outside the theaters for every opening night, the poems of Rilke are stuck between the covers of their Latin grammars at school, they sneak-read Nietzsche and Strindberg under their desks, they keep up with literary criticism and follow all the discussions, and if one of them should spot Gustav Mahler on the street one evening, the event would be proudly reported at school the very next morning.

A première of Gerhart Hauptmann's in the Burgtheater had our entire class on edge for weeks before the rehearsals began. We slipped in to the actors and understudies to be the first – before the others! – to know the plot and learn about the cast. We had (I do not hesitate to report upon absurdities) our hair cut by the barber of the Burgtheater, so that we could gather secret information about Wolter or Sonnenthal, and a pupil in one of the lower classes was particularly spoiled by us older boys and bribed with all sorts of attentions, merely because he was the nephew of one of the lighting inspectors at the Opera, and through him we were sometimes smuggled on to the stage during rehearsals – the shock of treading on that stage exceeded that of Virgil when he mounted into the holy circles of Paradise. The radiant power of fame was so strong for us that even if it were seven times removed from us, it still forced us to respect it; a certain poor little old woman seemed like an immortal being to us because she was a grand-niece of Franz Schubert, and on the street we gazed respectfully at Josef Kainz's valet because he had the good fortune to be close to the most beloved and most genial of all actors.

Stefan Zweig was a Jew born into Vienna's upper bourgeoisie. He wrote his memoirs under the shadow of the brutal and destructive regime of Nazism before committing suicide "in despair at the fall of European culture," as it says on the cover of the Norwegian edition of *The World of Yesterday*. Few have provided a better or more fascinating picture of the lost reality of prewar Europe than Zweig in that book. This is the golden age of the middle class, a time of wealth, continuity, caution, harmony, and security, so staidly sedate that the ideal to which its youth aspires is middle age; he writes that anyone wishing to get along in life was compelled to conceal his youth in every conceivable way. Young men of twenty-four and twenty-five grew impressive beards and acquired paunches, strolled leisurely in long frock coats, and wore glasses even if their vision was perfect.

Thomas Mann's first novel, *Buddenbrooks*, published in 1901, provides the same double exposure as Zweig's memoir: on the one hand the staidness of commercial prosperity and an unfluctuating bourgeois existence, on the other the children of this bourgeoisie and their fascination with art and the culture of the great emotions, who in Mann's universe invariably have something fragile and almost destructive about them. Citizen and artist, these are the two figures both Mann and Zweig hold up for scrutiny. Mann's Munich and Zweig's Vienna were among the great centers of European culture at the twentieth century's beginning, but although Hitler was to live in both cities, at the same time as Zweig in Vienna and Mann in Munich, he was separated from the culture of which the two were a part by what amounted to an abyss. Hitler's Vienna was a slum, Hitler's Munich not much better. Yet despite the great social divide between them, Hitler still frequented the same world; during his time in Vienna he attended Gustav Mahler's stagings of Wagner's operas, which he admired greatly, and on his arrival in the city he carried with him a letter of recommendation to the famous Alfred Roller, not only a professor at the academy of arts, but also Mahler's collaborator and scenographer, a person Zweig and his friends would have turned their heads to look at on the street. This recommendation had come about through the owner of the Hitler family's apartment in Linz, a woman who had taken a liking to the young Adolf; she knew Roller's brother and wrote the following about him to a female friend in Vienna, quoted in *Hitler's Vienna*:

> *The son of one of my tenants is becoming a painter, has gone to school in Vienna since the fall, he wanted to attend the Austro-Hungarian Academy of Visual Arts, but was not accepted and went to a private institution instead (Panholzer I believe). He is a serious, ambitious young man, nineteen years old, more mature and settled than his age*

indicates, nice and sensible, from a perfectly decent family. His mother died before Christmas, suffered from breast cancer, was only forty-six years old, the widow of a higher-up official at the local main customs office; I liked the woman very much, she lived next to me on the first floor; her sister and her daughter, who is in high school, are keeping the apartment for the time being. The family's name is Hitler; the son, in whose behalf I'm asking your help, is called Adolf Hitler. We happened to talk about art and artists the other day, and among others, he mentioned that Professor Roller is a famous man among artists, not only in Vienna, but one could even say he has world renown, and that he reveres him in his works. Hitler had no idea that I am familiar with the name Roller, and when I told him that I used to know a brother of the famous Roller and asked him if it might be helpful to him in his endeavors if he received a recommendation to the director of the Court Opera's Scenery Department, the young man's eyes started glowing; he flushed crimson and said he would consider it the best luck he ever had if he could meet that man and got a recommendation to him! I would love to help the young man; he simply has no one who could put in a good word for him or help him by word and deed; he arrived in Vienna a complete stranger and alone, and had to go everywhere alone, without anyone giving him direction, to find entrance. He has the firm intention of learning something solid! So far as I have got to know him, he won't "operate in a low gear," since he is focusing on a serious goal; I hope you won't waste your good offices on someone unworthy!

Roller replied by return of post in a three-page letter, writing among other things, "Do tell young Hitler to call on me and to bring some of his works so I can see how he is doing. I surely will advise him as best I can. He can meet me every day in my office at the Opera, entrance Kärntherstrasse, Principal Offices staircase, at 12:30 and at 6:30 p.m."

But Hitler never appeared. Later he would say that his courage had failed him. He had gone to the Opera some days after arriving in Vienna, but had not found it in him to go in and had turned around instead. After much deliberation with himself he conquered his fear and went back, only with the same result, he was too scared. On a third occasion he had been standing outside Roller's office when someone asked him his business and he had muttered an apology and fled. After that he destroyed the letter of recommendation and never returned. At this point he had been turned down by the Academy, so there was much at stake for him; an introduction to Roller would clearly have been invaluable to a provincial teenager wanting to become a painter. If nothing else Roller could have cast an eye over Hitler's sketches and pictures and told him what aspects of his work he should try to develop, what was good about them and what was lacking, thereby equipping him better in case he should try again for admission to the Academy. Hitler's problem was that he was self-taught and had little if any contact with other artists or artistic communities. This meant he was most likely unaware of what was required, unaware of what was important, and to anyone wanting to get into one of the major institutions, such ignorance would be fatal; these places were the very seat of the cultural establishment

But still he lacked the courage. Why? One reason is shyness, and Roller was a man he admired greatly, he had seen two of Mahler's Wagner operas to which Roller had contributed, *Tristan* and *The Flying Dutchman*, to speak to him must have been to speak to a god; another likely reason is that he feared rejection. The artist identity was so important to him, he had gone through so much in order to keep it alive, defying his father's will, then his mother's, and, after they were dead, the forceful wishes of his remaining family and his guardian. Everyone expected him to get a normal job, to grow up, earn his own money, start a family. Shortly before leaving home for Vienna he was offered a job at the local post office by a relative. He turned it down, presumably not without contempt, for according to Kubizek there was always contempt in his voice when he spoke of "bread-and-butter" jobs. Art was Hitler's opposition to civil life, and so strong was the dream of art inside him that he found himself unable to run the risk of Roller deeming him without talent and advising him to go back to Linz and get himself a job like anyone else. He could not risk having to face such a fate, even if it were to become reality. Better then to live on with the dream.

A typical trait of Hitler's, revealing itself on many occasions described by Kubizek, seems to be that he lives a vital inner life, intensely nourished by fantasies he goes to great lengths to preserve from any confrontation with reality. Perhaps the most typical example of this is his four-year infatuation with Stefanie, a young Linz girl who catches his eye on a number of occasions on the Landstrasse in the center of the city, where Linzers would stroll in the afternoons and evenings, to see and be seen, to stop and chat with friends and acquaintances, to look in the shop windows, enjoying provincial life as it was lived at the time. One evening in 1905 when Kubizek and Hitler are out taking their usual stroll, Kubizek writes, Hitler suddenly grips his arm excitedly and asks him what he thinks of the slim blond girl walking arm-in-arm with her mother along the boulevard.

I am in love with her, Hitler says.

It transpires that he has never spoken to her. The evening strolls along the Landstrasse were occasions for flirting, for glances and smiles, yet the formalities were strict; if he wanted to speak to her he would first have to be introduced, a matter that lay beyond his reach, as Kubizek explains. Hitler asks him what he should do, Kubizek tells him he should approach the mother, introduce himself and ask her permission to address the daughter and escort them.

> Adolf looked at me doubtfully and pondered my suggestion for quite a while. In the end, however, he rejected it. "What am I to say if the mother wants to know my profession? After all, I have to mention my profession straight away; it would be best to add it to my name –

'Adolf Hitler, academic painter' or something similar. But I am not yet an academic painter, and I can't introduce myself until I am. For the mama, the profession is even more important than the name."

Hitler never takes that step, never approaches the mother to introduce himself, consequently he does not exchange a single word with the girl during the four years that ensue, a time in which according to Kubizek she is Hitler's great love. He makes do with looking at her from afar. Now and then their eyes meet, now and then he receives a smile, making him certain that her feelings for him are just as great as his own for her. He plans out a future down to the smallest detail; he even draws up plans for the house in which they will live; for a time he is utterly absorbed in the project. He writes poems about her, "Hymn to the Beloved" is the title of one, according to Kubizek's account. Stefanie is a near-dreamlike, perfect, and utterly idealized woman, perhaps best related to Wagner's mythological heroines, and when the real world, so compelling that it cannot be denied forever, intervenes, Hitler's reaction is one of anger. He has asked Kubizek to investigate her background, and Kubizek has spoken with an acquaintance who is a friend of her brother's. Her family is of the upper middle class, he finds out, and she lives with her mother, a widow, and likes to dance; the previous winter she had attended all the important dances in the town along with her mother. As far as Kubizek's acquaintance knew, she was not engaged. Hitler is highly satisfied with the report, apart from one thing, the fact that she dances. The thought does not accord at all with his image of her, nor with the life he leads himself.

Kubizek describes Hitler as an exceptionally serious person, dedicated to his interests, which at the time are mostly art and architecture. He doesn't drink, doesn't smoke, has no interest in sports, no interest in provincial social life. Dance is completely alien to him. The fact of her dancing, and thereby belonging to that life, troubles him intensely.

After having been his butt for so long, at last I had a chance of pull-
ing his leg. I proclaimed with a straight face, "You must take dancing
lessons, Adolf." Dancing immediately became one of his problems. I
well remember that our lonely perambulations were no longer punc-
tuated by discussions on "the theater" or "reconstruction of the bridge
over the Danube" but were dominated by one subject – dancing.

As with everything that he couldn't tackle at once, he indulged in
generalizations. "Visualize a crowded ballroom," he once said to me,
"and imagine that you are deaf. You can't hear the music to which these
people are moving, and then take a look at their senseless progress,
which leads nowhere. Aren't these people raving mad?"

"All this is no good, Adolf," I replied. "Stefanie is fond of dancing.
If you want to conquer her, you will have to dance around just as aim-
lessly and idiotically as the others." That was all that was needed to
set him off raving. "No, no, never!" he screamed at me. "I shall never
dance! Do you understand! Stefanie only dances because she is forced
to by society on which she unfortunately depends. Once she is my wife,
she won't have the slightest desire to dance!"

Contrary to the rule, this time his own words did not convince
him; for he brought up the question of dancing again and again. I
rather suspected that, secretly at home, he practiced a few cautious steps
with his little sister.

To extract himself from this torment, Hitler came up with the
idea of kidnapping Stefanie. This was something he seriously con-
templated, Kubizek writes. When for a time she seemed un-
friendly and would avert her gaze, passing Hitler on the street as
if he did not exist, he began to despair, proclaiming that he would
commit suicide, an act as meticulously detailed in his imagination as all his other plans. Sometime later, however, she takes part
in a festival parade and tosses him a flower. Kubizek writes that
he would never again see Adolf as happy as he was at that moment. "I can still hear his voice, trembling with excitement, 'She
loves me! You have seen! She loves me!'" When Hitler moves to
Vienna after his mother's death two and a half years later, in

February 1908, with the letter of recommendation addressed to Roller, he sends Stefanie a postcard saying that he is to begin at the Academy and that she must wait for him, he intends to ask for her hand as soon as his studies are completed and he returns to Linz. He leaves the card unsigned, and she has no idea who on earth might have sent it to her.

The ambivalence of not putting his name to his words is the same failing as emerges in his inability to act on his introduction to Roller – he lacks the courage to take the final step. The world he dreams about, his future as an artist, his future with Stefanie, exists partly within him and partly without – he seeks her out, he sees her, she exists, the future is possible, in the same way as he sketches and paints and puts his work forward to the Academy with a view to acceptance – yet he is too afraid to actually join these two planes of reality together. What reality does, and brutally so, is to correct. And a prominent trait of the young Hitler's character is precisely an unwillingness to accept correction. It is anathema to him. Even the slightest contradiction incenses him and leaves him indignant.

It is hard not to see his inner strength and its expression as a means of defense. But against what? Seemingly against the social world. Hitler takes no part whatsoever in any social life, he is completely uninterested by it and looks with disdain on his contemporaries as they have fun, drinking and dancing, playing sports and flirting. He has no friends either; Kubizek appears to be the exception, but their friendship is basically monological: Hitler talks, Kubizek listens. Hitler is primary, Kubizek secondary. Kubizek knows this and accepts it since he admires Hitler and feels advantaged by his friendship; moreover, so he writes, he understands that Hitler needs him.

> Soon I came to understand that our friendship endured largely for the reason that I was a patient listener. But I was not dissatisfied with this passive role, for it made me realize how much my friend needed me. He, too, was completely alone.

At one point Kubizek has to attend a funeral, his former violin teacher having died, and to his surprise Hitler decides to go with him. Hitler had no association with Kubizek's teacher, so why would he want to go to his funeral? Hitler replies, "I can't bear it that you should mix with other young people and talk to them."

He wants Kubizek for himself, which in a way is touching, revealing vulnerability, yet disturbing, too, in that he almost wants to own him.

What is it then about Hitler that Kubizek so admires?

Above all, perhaps, it was his standing apart from his contemporaries, to Kubizek's mind radically so. Most had their lives mapped out by the time they were sixteen; Hitler had not, he was "just the opposite" as Kubizek states. "With him everything was uncertain." His shunning of middle-class life appealed to Kubizek, who worked in his father's upholstery workshop and was expected by everyone to eventually take over the family business, whereas what he himself wanted, a wish he hardly dared utter to anyone, was to train as a musician and conductor. When Hitler moved to Vienna, he insisted on Kubizek following, approaching Kubizek's parents himself and managing to convince them to allow his friend to leave.

Hitler, then, represented something Kubizek himself wanted to become. However, they were by no means alike. Kubizek hardly spoke when they were together and had none of his friend's restless energy, though he possessed the patience Hitler lacked. Kubizek practiced and was admitted to the conservatory in Vienna at the age of eighteen, whereas Hitler practiced nothing, had no patience, threw himself into the loftiest projects without ever completing them, and would never gain admittance to Vienna's Academy.

Hitler's most striking trait, acccording to Kubizek, was his holding forth on everything he saw and thought about, usually involving some form of change: a building in one style, he might suggest, ought to be pulled down to make way for another in a different style, Linz needed an underground railway, a pension scheme required an overhaul, a traveling opera had to be set up to bring Wagner to the outlying districts. Seemingly there were no limits to what he might take an interest in and hold an opinion about. Describing this aspect of his friend's personality, Kubizek emphasizes the restlessness of which it was an expression, his need for things to happen, and this gives an impression of Hitler as being in some way menaced, as if there were something he needed to get away from, and since the things that caught his attention in this way were so external, there always being some element of his surroundings with which to take issue, it is easy to think that there was something inside him that he wanted to escape or get rid of. A conspicuous aspect of what is revealed of Hitler's inner life in *Mein Kampf* as well as in Kubizek's memoir is his almost dreamlike remoteness from reality, as if he were turned toward another age, another place, whether rooted in the intense experiences the two friends shared at the opera, which they frequented, in what he would read of German history and mythology, or in what he would relate of his own life, which never was concerned with what it was but what it would become. To this picture belongs the wholly asocial nature of his character, his disinterest in social life, and his strikingly serious demeanor.

> *I have often been asked, and even by Rudolf Hess, who once invited me to visit him in Linz, whether Adolf, when I knew him, had any sense of humor. One feels the lack of it, people of his entourage said. After all, he was an Austrian and should have had his share of the famous Austrian sense of humor. Certainly one's impression of Hitler, especially after a short and superficial acquaintance, was that of a deeply serious man. This enormous seriousness seemed to overshadow everything else. It was the same when he was young. He approached any problem with which he was concerned with a deadly earnestness which ill suited his sixteen or seventeen years. He was capable of loving and admiring, hating and despising, all with the greatest seriousness. But one thing he could not do was pass over something with a smile.*

Kubizek finds the same earnestness in Hitler's mother. When he meets her she is forty-five years old. He writes that she still looked like the only known photograph of her, but that "the suffering was more clearly etched in her face and her hair had started to go gray." He felt sympathy for her, stating that she made him feel like he wanted to do something for her. "Every smile which crossed that serious face gave me joy," he writes. She was disinclined to talk about herself and her worries, yet found relief in confiding to Kubizek her concerns about Adolf and the uncertainty of his future.

> Her preoccupation with the well-being of her only surviving son depressed her increasingly. Often I sat together with Frau Hitler and Adolf in the tiny kitchen. "Your poor father cannot rest in his grave," she used to say to Adolf, "because you do absolutely nothing that he wanted for you. Obedience is what distinguishes a good son, but you do not know the meaning of the word. That's why you did so badly at school and why you're not getting anywhere now."

The family lived in a small flat comprising two rooms and a kitchen. Hitler had one room for himself, while his mother, his half sister, and his younger sister shared the other. He never helped out at home, his mother did everything for him, and there is no doubt he was spoiled. At one point he announced that he wanted to learn the piano, his mother bought him one and paid for lessons, all presumably beyond her means. After four months Hitler gave up, enraged by his teacher's insistence on "stupid" finger exercises. Music was about inspiration, not finger exercises, he declared, and laid his ambitions to rest. Placing the blame for his inadequacy on his music teacher was typical of him. He read all he could lay his hands on about Wagner and identified almost entirely with him; the adversity he encountered in his young life was the same as the young Wagner had to battle against. "So you see," he would say after quoting from some letter or essay, "even Wagner went through it just like I have. All the time he had to tackle the ignorance of his surroundings." Kubizek found these comparisons somewhat exaggerated, Wagner having led a long and productive life with plenty of ups and downs, whereas Hitler was only sixteen years old with hardly any experience at all. Nevertheless he spoke "as though he had been the victim of persecution, fought his enemies and been exiled."

There is something of the poseur about this side of Hitler in the sense that it is the role itself that seems to appeal to him, an impression accentuated by his inability to invest the role with the necessary practice and talent, and by the way he dresses, the young dandy in black coat and white shirt, the ivory-handled cane, on occasion even a black top hat, and yet the matter is not as simple, he does not do this to impress or to be seen, since basically he is on his own, and the intensity with which he absorbs himself in the operas they attend, for instance, seems anything but affected or shallow and would seem to saturate his entire being. The same is true of the frenzy he exhibits when devoting himself to his architectural drawings, which often lie scattered about his room. He is impassioned, burns with enthusiasm, is willing to put everything else aside for their sake. Why? Both Hitler and Kubizek believe in the supreme position of art in human life, and in that belief they express a rather typical attitude of the age in which they live, in the provinces shared only by a small handful of young people, certainly, yet highly prevalent in Vienna and the other major cities. From the picture Kubizek paints of Hitler this would seem to be not simply a fad but so much a part of his character as to be imperative. "His intense way of absorbing, scrutinizing, rejecting, his terrific seriousness, his ever-active mind needed a counterpoise," Kubizek writes. "And only art could provide this."

Noticeable in Kubizek's descriptions of Hitler are the elements of mania he exhibits; Hitler talks incessantly, he is quick-tempered and irritable, he harbors grand designs and seems never to doubt that he will see them through to completion, and he can work frenetically on a project for nights on end. On the other hand, and such loftiness always has its counterweight, there are periods where Hitler does not appear to speak at all but withdraws and goes for long walks on his own in the environs of Linz, dejected and dispirited. Art is somewhere outside this, and he seeks it presumably so that something else may fill his soul and that he may express himself in it.

Another obvious reason for art being so important to him as a teenager was that it was the only way he could see of moving beyond the social class from which he came. This becomes apparent in his remote infatuation with Stefanie. Why does he not approach her? He is bashful and clearly lacks the courage. Perhaps he has no will or feels unable to try his fortune, knowing at some level that to make his desires known to her would be for reality to intrude on the dream and that the perfection and ideal of the dream is preferable to inadequate reality. Moreover, there is the fact that he is a nobody. Pressed by Kubizek, this is what he says, that to introduce himself to the mother he needs to be someone, to have a profession, and not just any profession, a postman, for instance, would not impress her, the widow of a high-standing official, but an academic painter would fit the bill admirably.

In a certain sense art is classless insofar as it is available to all; in Linz in the first decade of the twentieth century there were no such things as television, radio, gramophones, or cinemas; music had to be heard live, though it cost little, and these two sixteen-year-olds of the lower middle class frequented the theater and the opera and attended all manner of concerts, absorbing everything, and on their way home they would be fired with enthusiasm, discussing what they had seen and heard; admission to art galleries was cheap, too, and then there were books. In another sense art, too, is a class issue. The fact that it exists and is available does not mean that it is actually accessible to all; anyone growing up in a home without books, without pictures, without music, among people who never speak of art and do not care for it, perhaps even think it to be a waste of time and money, has no easy path in art's direction. And even if they discover that path and venture along it, they will more than likely find themselves lacking the basic means possessed by those belonging to more elevated classes, the self-assurance with which they embrace culture and its expressions. Hitler, who came from a home quite without books and with no interest at all in art, overcame this first hindrance, though would never wholly surmount those that remained. His taste in art, and his understanding of it, was throughout his life always provincial and conservative, even though at the time he lived in the provinces and opposed the petty bourgeois with all his might, his attitudes and ideas must have seemed radical to those in his surroundings.

This radical streak is what Kubizek finds so striking about Hitler when they first meet. They notice each other at the opera and strike up a conversation in the intermission of a late performance, and from then on it was as if Hitler monopolizes him completely. Whenever Kubizek is late for an appointment, Hitler will go at once to fetch him from his father's upholstery workshop; he has no understanding of the fact that his friend must work, insisting that they stroll through the town together, more often than not with Hitler holding forth.

Kubizek is surprised that Hitler has so much time on his hands, does he not work? Of course not, Hitler snaps back, the very idea of a "bread-and-butter" job is beneath him. Kubizek is rather impressed by this, yet finds it somewhat puzzling. Perhaps this Adolf is a student at a school somewhere? "School?" Hitler snorts back at him in a first outburst of temper. The mere mention of the word incenses him, school is a red rag. He hates it, hates the teachers, hates his classmates.

Kubizek tells him how little success he had at school himself.

Hitler demands to know the reason for this, apparently dissatisfied with his new friend having done poorly. This self-contradiction confuses Kubizek but is something he will soon get used to; self-contradictions are a characteristic of Hitler. In this first instance in the upholstery workshop, however, it seems innocuous enough. Self-contradiction arises when two incompatible utterances collide, and in this case they are easy to identify: Hitler's experiences apply to him alone, they are his, perhaps precious and inalienable in that they define his character, he hates school and the very notion of it, and this makes him what he is, an independent man with no need of what school could possibly give him, no intention of assimilating himself into the society it represents, the petty bourgeois world of Linz, for he is destined for greater things in the wider world. Kubizek sharing that same experience would mean Hitler was no longer unique, and this he cannot tolerate.

However, this simply does not exist for him as an insight, he is completely blind to it; for Kubizek different rules apply, Hitler does not regard him in the same light as he regards himself, but wholly from without, and in that external light not doing well at school looks like failure. Is his new friend a failure? A failure in the eyes of his teachers and the other students? No, he does not care for the thought; Kubizek doing badly at school is not good at all.

What this little scene reveals is the gap between Hitler's inner and outer selves, how distinctly they are separated, and this separation is significant in that the inner self is thereby beyond reach and unamenable to correction. Self-insight is the ability to apply the outer perspective to the inner, it is the presence in the ego of the voice or gaze of the indefinite other, and if that is prevented, then the two will be unconnected, there will be no accommodation within the ego, which then will be left to its own devices, and this abandonment means that interaction with and understanding of others essentially becomes an external phenomenon, occurring outside the I, without empathy, without involvement of the inner self, which is empathy's first and to all intents and purposes only condition.

Hitler was by no means wholly unable to empathize with others, but his empathy was weak; everything Kubizek writes suggests it. He was ruled by emotions, almost in their thrall, they could overpower him, overcome him completely; this, too, is in the pattern of the abandoned ego. His asocial nature, too. And not only was he asocial, he avoided moreover all points of potential confrontation between his inner and outer selves, as the examples of Stefanie and Roller show. Nor would he tolerate any kind of dissent from Kubizek or his mother. On the other hand, he was only sixteen years old, at a stage of his development when a person is perhaps the most challenging of life, hurtling on, and in turmoil.

Later Hitler would refer to the two years in Linz as the happiest of his life. Just as Kubizek was a frequent visitor in his home, Hitler spent much time in Kubizek's. Kubizek's mother was fond of him, he was polite and well brought up, Kubizek's father being rather more skeptical, he had hoped his son might find a more stable and dependable friend, sensing perhaps the direction in which he was going, the lure of the upholstery business pale compared to the world of music that now seemed to open itself to him even more.

On weekends, Hitler and Kubizek enjoyed going for long walks together into the countryside, often meeting up with Kubizek's parents, who would take the train to some appointed place and treat them to a meal at a local inn. Hitler was fond of them and attentive to their well-being; as late as 1944 he would send Kubizek's mother a present on her eightieth birthday.

The provincial prewar life Kubizek describes seems quite as sleepy and secure as Zweig's descriptions of his young days in Vienna ten years earlier. Evening strolls along the boulevard, Schiller at the theater, and Wagner at the opera, bandstand concerts, long walks and outings in the surrounding countryside. There are no cars, no planes, hardly any engines of any kind, no telephones, no radio or television, barely an electric light. They are, however, anything but wealthy; Kubizek's father toils to keep his tiny business running, Hitler's mother scrimps and saves to make her widow's pension last. Poverty is no abstract concept, something that only applies to others: Hitler's mother came from the humblest of circumstances in one of Austria's poorest regions, one of twelve children. The young Hitler's contempt for the petty bourgeoisie must have grown out of a strong though probably unarticulated class consciousness; he came from quite a different background to the vast majority of his classmates in the *Realschule*, it took him an hour to get there in the mornings and there was something rural and unsophisticated about him, and when later he moves to Linz with his mother, he refuses even to talk to them – Kubizek mentions an episode when Hitler is approached by a former schoolmate who asks him sincerely how he is doing, Hitler instantly flies into a rage and tells him it's none of his business – but his sense of being better than them, these representatives of the provincial bourgeoisie, who complete their schooling and take on normal work, must find articulation in some way, and this is a problem: how to rise above something basically unfamiliar to him, how to abandon and leave behind a level for which he has never really qualified himself? He dresses like a student or a young artist and insists he will never take on ordinary work as long as he lives, he is certain of it. He despises middle-classness and yet is its captive.

> *Adolf set great store by good manners and correct behavior. He observed with painstaking punctiliousness the rules of social conduct, however little he thought of society itself . . . It is most revealing that the young Hitler, who so thoroughly despised bourgeois society, nevertheless, as far as his love affair was concerned, observed its codes and etiquette more strictly than many a member of the bourgeoisie itself . . . It was apparent in his neat dress, and in his correct behavior, as much as in his natural courtesy, which my mother liked so much about him. I have never heard him use an ambiguous expression or tell a doubtful story.*

The young Hitler is acutely aware of the importance of dress and behavior in assessing a person, and while he couldn't care less about the bouorgeoisie, in actual fact he has no choice, being wholly without qualifications: if he dressed like an ill-bred peasant or an ignorant son of the lower middle class, there would be nothing separating them, he would be exactly that in the eye of the beholder, and with justification, so if he is to elevate himself to the status he believes he deserves, he has no other means than correctness, which, with a little dash of effort, can be embellished with the panache and flair of the dandy, the young artist.

The Young Hitler I Knew was published more than forty years after the events it portrays. As Ian Kershaw points out, no one can remember exactly what was said in a given situation decades later, the way Kubizek pretends when quoting both Hitler and Hitler's mother. But memoirs are no exact science, readers understand this and know from their own lives how later events twist and turn what happened at some earlier time, adding new shades, illuminating from new angles according to where we are in life. We need to be alert whenever events shape themselves into narratives, for narratives belong to literature and not to life, and occurrences of the past seep into and absorb expectations of the future, for the true present stands open and knows as yet no consequence. So when Kubizek allows the story of Hitler's infatuation with Stefanie to coincide with the death of his mother, in a scene where the funeral cortège passes Stefanie's house and she at that very moment opens the window and leans out to see what is going on, we should have every reason to doubt that this was how it actually happened. And when Kubizek describes how deeply affected Hitler was by a performance of Wagner's opera *Rienzi*, about a Roman demagogue –

> *Adolf stood in front of me and now he gripped both my hands and held them tight. He had never made such a gesture before. I felt from the grasp of his hands how deeply moved he was. His eyes were feverish with excitement. The words did not come smoothly from his mouth as they usually did, but rather erupted, hoarse and raucous.*

From his voice I could tell even more how much this experience had shaken him.

Gradually his speech loosened and the words flowed more freely. Never before and never again have I heard Adolf Hitler speak as he did in that hour, as we stood there alone under the stars, as though we were the only creatures in the world.

– there is no doubt that they saw the opera and that it made an impression on them both, but the definitive and fateful aspect the description lends to the moment, the sense that Hitler gazed into the future and found his destiny is obviously constructed after the event, as Kershaw points out. Much of what Kubizek writes about Hitler is in this way colored by what was to happen, which does not mean to say that what he writes did not take place, only that those events were not accorded any such weight at the time, were not in any way inclined toward fortunes at which neither could as much as hazard a guess. But the advantage of Kubizek's memoir is that the period with which it deals is sufficiently short, and the events sufficiently small and quotidian, as to hinder the construction and development of any larger narrative, at the same time as the temporal constraint, the fact of Kubizek never having met Hitler until he was sixteen years old, and not meeting him again until almost thirty years later, frames the events portrayed and renders them clear. Hitler's presence was a unique and brief occurrence in Kubizek's life, and Hitler himself was such a curious character as to make it likely indeed that Kubizek should remember him well. In his recollection Hitler is an unusually ambivalent figure, his memoir is certainly no hagiography, and the traits he describes of his friend's character are fully in accordance with what emerges from other sources, only clearer, because no one before or since came as close to him as Kubizek did. The fact that Kubizek values Hitler greatly and sees him as if through a veil of admiration, does little to detract from what is a many-sided and nuanced portrait. The following description is typical:

But although he was often brusque, moody, unreliable, and far from conciliatory, I could never be angry with him because these unpleasant sides of his character were overshadowed by the pure fire of an exalted soul.

Hitler vanished from Kubizek's life in the summer of 1908, and he neither saw him nor heard anything of him until 1933 when Hitler became Reich chancellor and Kubizek sent him a letter, a reply to which arrived some months later.

> *My Dear Kubizek,*
> *Only today was your letter of 2 February placed before me. From the hundreds of thousands of letters I have received since January it is not surprising. All the greater was my joy, for the first time in so many years, to hear news of your life and to receive your address. I would very much like – when the time of my hardest struggles is over – to revive personally the memory of those most wonderful years of my life. Perhaps it would be possible for you to visit me. Wishing yourself and your mother all the best, I remain in the memory of our old friendship,*
> *Yours,*
> *Adolf Hitler*

In 1938, during the so-called Anschluss, Hitler crosses the border of Austria at the town of his birth, Braunau on the Inn, thereby fulfilling the ambition he had set out at the beginning of *Mein Kampf.* This attention to the power of the symbolic was typical of him. That same evening he spoke from the balcony of the city hall in Linz. Kubizek was unable to attend, but when Hitler returned in April that same year Kubizek visited him at the Hotel Weinzinger. There was a huge crowd on the square outside, the guards took him for a madman when he asked to see the Reich chancellor, but after showing them the letter he was led into the foyer, where, he writes, the activity was like a beehive. Generals, ministers of state, Nazi Party bosses, and other uniformed officials came and went, all buzzing around one man, Adolf Hitler, now separated from Kubizek by a wall of power. He is told by a senior adjutant by the name of Albert Bormann that the Reich chancellor is feeling unwell and will not be receiving guests that evening, but that he should come back the following afternoon. The adjutant then invites him to take a seat for a moment so that he might ask him a few questions.

Had the Reich chancellor always slept in so late, he wishes to know. Hitler it seems never goes to bed before midnight and sleeps until well into the morning, while his entourage, who presumably have been required to stay up just as late, are obliged to be up bright and early the next day. The adjutant, brother of the more familiar Martin Bormann, goes on to complain about Hitler's outbursts of temper, which nobody could calm, and about his peculiar diet, vegetarian based on flour and plenty of fruit juices. Has he always been like that? Kubizek replies that indeed he has, except that he used to eat meat.

When he returns the next day the excitement and activity is unabated, the whole city has taken to the streets, he writes. He fights his way through the crowd and is led into the hotel foyer by some officials. He holds no illusions, expects nothing more than a brief handshake and a few warm words, and is nervous as to the form of address to use, fearing that any breach of protocol will send Hitler into a rage. But he is given an hour. Hitler appears in the corridor, recognizes him immediately, and cries out with joy, "It's you, Gustl!" and when he grasps Kubizek's hand with both of his and looks into his eyes, he is quite clearly as moved by the occasion as Kubizek himself. Hitler leads him to the elevator, which takes them up to his suite on the second floor.

The personal adjutant opened the door; we entered and the adjutant left. Again, Hitler took my hand, gave me a long look and said, "You haven't changed, Kubizek. I would have recognized you anywhere. The only thing different is that you've got older." Then he led me to a table and offered me a chair. He assured me how much pleasure it gave him to see me again after so many years. My good wishes had pleased him especially, for I knew better than anybody else how difficult his path had been. The present time was unfavorable for a long talk, but he hoped that there would be an opportunity in the future. He would contact me. To write to him directly was not advisable, for all his mail was dealt with by his aides.

"I no longer have a private life and cannot do what I like as others can." With these words he rose and went to the window, which overlooked the Danube. The old bridge with its steel bars, which had so annoyed him in his youth, remained in use. As I expected, he mentioned it at once. "That ugly footbridge!" he cried. "It's still there. But not for much longer, I assure you, Kubizek." With that he turned and smiled. "All the same, I would love to take a stroll with you over the old bridge. But I can't, for wherever I go, everybody follows me. But believe me, Kubizek, for Linz I have many plans." Nobody knew that better than I. As expected, he drew forth from his memory all the plans which had occupied him in his youth just as though not thirty, but no more than three, years had passed since then.

After describing his plans for Linz in detail, Hitler questions Kubizek about his life, what he has become. The reply, *Stadtamtsleiter*, displeases him: "So, you are a civil servant, a clerk. That doesn't suit you. What did you make of your musical talents?" Kubizek tells him the war had thrown him off course and that in order not to starve he had to change horses. Hitler nods gravely. "Yes, the lost war." He looks at him, and adds, "You won't be ending your career as a municipal clerk, Kubizek." He asks him about the orchestra he runs, and enthuses, instructing him to make out a report detailing anything they might be short of and he will make sure they get what they need. He asks if he has any children. Kubizek tells him yes, three sons.

"Three sons!" he cried emotionally. He repeated the words several times and with an earnest expression. "You have three sons, Kubizek. I have

no family. I am alone. But I would like to help with your sons." He made me tell him everything about them. He was delighted that all three were talented musically and two of them were skilled sketch artists.

"I will sponsor the education of your three sons, Kubizek," he told me. "I don't like it when young, gifted people are forced to go along the same track that we did. You know how it was for us in Vienna. After that, for me, came the worst times of all, after our paths had separated. That young talent goes under because of need must not be allowed to happen. If I can help personally, I will, even if it's for your children, Kubizek!"

I have to mention here that the Reich chancellor actually did have his office foot the bill for the musical education of my three sons at the Linz Bruckner-Conservatoire and on his orders the sketches of my son Rudolf were assessed by a professor at the Munich Academy.

Later they meet again, Hitler inviting him to the Wagner festival in Bayreuth in 1939 and 1940. The question is how reliable are the descriptions of these meetings and the picture of Hitler they provide? No one else was there, we have no other account to go by than Kubizek's own. One thing though is certain, the portrayal of Hitler is by no means opportunistic. Had Kubizek's book come out while the Nazis were still in power, in 1938 or 1942, for instance, the picture would have been different, there would have been grounds for suspicion, since any suggestion of anything negative or ambivalent in the portrait it paints of Hitler would have been impossible or at least highly precarious. But the book was published in 1953, and at that time the opposite held: the opportune thing to do then would have been to demonize Hitler, emphasize his negative aspects, whereas writing about his kindness, for instance, might be seen as an expression of Nazi sympathies, something not many people would wish to admit to after the war.

Kubizek was contacted by the Nazi Party in 1938 and asked

to put his recollections of Hitler's youth on paper for the NSDAP archive. He joined the party in 1942, was to all intents and purposes ordered to write his memoirs by Martin Bormann, and in 1943 was given a better-paid position in order to complete the task. When the war ended, however, he had managed to write only some one hundred and fifty pages. He was arrested by the Americans because of his connections with Hitler and was interned for sixteen months under repeated interrogation. His manuscript and memorabilia remained hidden in his house, forming the basis of the book he eventually published in 1953, but the differences between the manuscript and the published work are nevertheless notable, Hamann writes. All passages expressing admiration for the Führer had been deleted, those describing their lives together in Linz and Vienna were retained. Some of the stories, such as Hitler's infatuation with Stefanie, have been expanded and reworked, many dates are incorrect, and in some places his memory fails him – for instance at one point he writes that their landlady in Vienna was Polish, whereas in actual fact she was Czech, and that they lodged at number 29 rather than number 31 – but otherwise everything that can be checked is correct. An exception is a number of episodes purporting to reveal Hitler's anti-Semitism, yet there would seem to be no evidence to support the suggestion that Hitler was an anti-Semite in his youth; on the contrary, his acquaintances in Vienna included several Jews and he expressed interest in Jewish culture. Mahler, whom he admired, was Jewish. The anti-Semitic episodes in Kubizek's book do not exist in the original manuscript, but were added in its later version. Hamann writes:

Here Kubizek is clearly trying to promote himself. The Americans had questioned him exhaustively about his anti-Semitism, and now he is forced to maintain his line of defense. Thus he claims that Hitler had joined the Anti-Semitic League, filling out an appliction for him,

Kubizek, as well, without his permission: "This was the high point of the kind of political violation which I had gradually got used to with him. I was all the more surprised since otherwise Adolf eagerly avoided joining any associations or organizations."

However, before 1918 there was no Anti-Semitic League in Austro-Hungary. The Austrian anti-Semites were so at odds with one another, politically as well as ethnically, that an organization similar to the German Anti-Semitic League of 1884 never came about. Kubizek could have only joined the Austrian Anti-Semitic League, which was founded in 1919 – and voluntarily at that, without Hitler's help. This issue is important because of all those early eyewitnesses who can be taken seriously, Kubizek is the only one to portray young Hitler as an anti-Semite, and precisely in this respect he is not trustworthy.

Another noticeable aspect that separates the two versions is that the first, completed during the Nazi period, is comparatively poorly written, while the second, published eight years after the war was over, is comparatively well written. Kershaw explains this by suggesting the second was ghostwritten, whereas Hamann points to "a skilled editor." Both however agree that the memoirs are the most important source of insight into Hitler's early years. And if it seems contrived that the circle should so neatly be closed with Hitler's return to Linz and his declaration that he will re-design the city according to the plans of his youth, it is nonetheless an incontrovertible fact that Hitler, in his final time in the bunker, with the world aflame above him and the Russians already well inside Berlin, only days before he shot himself, could sit for hours and ponder over a model of Linz built on his instructions by his architect Hermann Giesler and shown to all his visitors no matter the time of day or night. A bell tower one hundred and fifty meters tall with a mausoleum containing his parents' graves at its foot, a gigantic hotel for up to two thousand guests at a time, a music school called the Adolf Hitler School of Music, an opera house that was to be the biggest in the world, seating thirty-five thousand, were the most prominent buildings, according to Bengt Liljegren. Moreover, a technical university was planned, and a huge hundred-thousand-capacity arena, housing areas for workers and artists, homes for SS and SA invalids, a railway station connecting to an underground transit system, access to the autobahn, and heavy industry, steelworks, and chemical factories besides. The focal point of this new cityscape, in addition to the mausoleum with its bell tower, was to be a giant art museum. So determined was Hitler that his extensive art collection be donated to Linz that he explicitly mentions it in the will he draws up prior to his suicide, Liljegren writes. And throughout Hitler's entire period in power Linz was favored over Vienna. Hamann cites Goebbels's diary entry of May 17, 1941: "Linz costs us a lot of money. But it means so much to the Führer." This in contrast to Vienna, which during Hitler's years of government is given no priority whatsoever. Goebbels's diaries again, March 21, 1943: "The Führer doesn't have any particularly great plans for Vienna. On the contrary, Vienna has too much, and it might rather lose something than gain anything."

Hitler made it clear to Kubizek almost from the very outset of their friendship that he would live in Vienna. Linz was too small and provincial. To begin with he made a short trip there in May 1907 and enthused at what he saw. Back in Linz after this four-week sojourn in the capital, however, he is impossible to reach, withdrawn and silent, he wanders alone in the daytime and night in the city's environs, presumably in crisis at the prospect of uprooting, though it seems certain that it is his decision to make the move to Vienna that brings him back to normal again a couple of weeks later.

The idea that he, a young man of eighteen, should continue to be kept by his mother had become unbearable to him. It was a painful dilemma which, as I could see for myself, made him almost physically ill. On the one hand, he loved his mother above everything: she was the only person on earth to whom he felt really close, and she reciprocated

his feeling to some extent, although she was deeply disturbed by her
son's unusual nature, however proud she was at times of him. "He is
different from us," she used to say.

On the other hand, she felt it to be her duty to carry out the
wishes of her late husband, and to prevail on Adolf to embark on a
safe career. But what was "safe," in view of the peculiar character of
her son? He had failed at school and ignored all his mother's wishes
and suggestions. A painter – that was what he had said he wanted
to become. This could not seem very satisfactory to his mother for,
simple soul that she was, anything connected with art and artists
appeared to her frivolous and insecure.

Hitler's brother-in-law, Raubal, wants him to start working like
any other young person, and tries to win Hitler's mother over. He
finds Hitler spoiled, a manipulator who twists his mother around
his little finger and needs to shape up and get a job, learn something decent. "This Pharisee is ruining my home for me," Hitler
says of him. Raubal appeals to Frau Klara's reason, stepping into
the role of her deceased husband. It is by no means difficult to
imagine his arguments: Hitler sleeps late, earns no money, wanders around with his head in the clouds all day, she can't go on
paying his way, he'll never learn to look after himself and his
family otherwise, it's for his own good, surely you can see? Hitler's guardian, Mayrhofer, wants him to become a baker and has
arranged an apprenticeship on his behalf. The other tenants in
the building have their opinions, too, Kubizek writes; none is
in Hitler's favor. His mother despairs. For Hitler's own part,
staying is out of the question, he has made up his mind, there is
no alternative to Vienna and an artist's career there.

He had come to hate the petit-bourgeois world in which he had to live.
He could hardly bear to return to that narrow world after lonely hours
spent in the open. He was always in a ferment of rage, hard and
intractable.

The feeling of everyone being against him is not new in Hitler's life. But he and his mother are close – despite the pressures of others she can refuse him nothing. She is also ill. In January of that year the family physician, Dr. Bloch, discovers a lump in her breast. She undergoes surgery, and since the family has no health insurance, the bill, somehow settled by Hitler himself, then aged seventeen, must have been a considerable strain on their finances. She was in the hospital for a month; Hitler visited daily. After her release her frail condition meant she was no longer able to cope with the stairs and the family was forced to move. Their new apartment was on the ground floor of a building in the suburbs, owned by the woman who a few months later would write Hitler's letter of recommendation to Roller. Undeterred by the resistance of those closest to him, Hitler uproots to Vienna that same summer in order to become an artist.

Kubizek writes that Hitler came to see him the evening before his departure, asking him to see him off at the station, not wanting his mother to come.

> *I knew how painful it would have been for Adolf to take leave of his mother in front of other people. He disliked nothing more than showing his feelings in public. I promised him to come and help him with his luggage.*
>
> *Next day I took time off and went to the Blütgengasse to collect my friend. Adolf had prepared everything. I took his suitcase, which was rather heavy with books he did not want to leave behind, and hurried away to avoid being present at the farewells. Yet I could not avoid them entirely. His mother was crying and little Paula, whom Adolf had never bothered with much, was sobbing in a heartrending manner. When Adolf caught up with me on the stairs and helped me with the suitcase, I saw that his eyes too were wet.*

Hitler leaves for Vienna to seek admission to the Academy of Fine Arts; confident of his own talents he considers it a formality that he will be given a place. But he is turned down. In view of all the pressures at home, all those who held that his artist dreams were folly and who wished only that he would pull himself together and get himself a proper job, the rejection must have been crushing, and in fact he told no one. Neither Kubizek nor his own mother heard from him in those first weeks, not a word was sent, and a worried Kubizek went to see Frau Klara to find out if her son had been in touch. She offers him a chair and unburdens herself.

> *"If only he had studied properly at the Realschule he would almost be ready to matriculate. But he won't listen to anybody." And she added, "He's as pig-headed as his father. Why this crazy journey to Vienna? Instead of holding on to his little legacy, it's just being frittered away. And after that? Nothing will come of his painting. And story writing doesn't earn anything either. And I can't help him – I've got Paula to look after. You know yourself what a sickly child she is but, just the same, she must get a decent education. Adolf doesn't give it a thought, he goes his way, just as if he were alone in the world. I shall not live to see him making an independent position for himself . . ."*
>
> *Frau Klara seemed more careworn than ever. Her face was deeply lined. Her eyes were lifeless, her voice sounded tired and resigned. I had the impression that, now that Adolf was no longer there, she had let herself go, and she looked older and more ailing than ever. She certainly had concealed her condition from her son to make the parting easier for him.*

Frau Hitler's condition deteriorates while her son is in Vienna: according to Hamann she visited the doctor once again on July 3, and again on September 2. Kubizek is busy; if not working in his father's workshop, he spends all his time practicing, so with Hitler's absence he does not return to visit Frau Klara until later that autumn. When he does he is shocked by what he sees. She is lying in bed, thin and pale, her face worn. Immediately she begins to talk of her son's letters, he seems to be doing well in Vienna.

Kubizek asks if she has told Adolf how unwell she is. She has not, she does not wish to burden him, but if her condition fails to improve she will have to send for him. The doctor has advised her to go to the hospital and be admitted. Before leaving, Kubizek makes her promise to write to her son. When he gets home again he tells his parents. His mother immediately offers to help Frau Hitler, but his father thinks it bad manners to impose without being asked.

On October 22 in his office, Hamann writes, the doctor, Eduard Bloch, informs the family – Klara, Adolf, and his younger sister, Paula – that Frau Klara's illness is incurable. The next day Hitler appears at the upholstery workshop. Kubizek describes him as looking terrible. His face is so pale as to be almost transparent. His eyes are dull, his voice hoarse. Without a greeting, without word of what he has been up to in Vienna, and with no question about Stefanie, all he utters is, "Incurable, the doctor says."

His eyes blazed, his temper flared up. "Incurable – what do they mean by that?" he screamed. "Not that the malady is incurable, but that the doctors aren't capable of curing it. My mother isn't even old. Forty-seven isn't an age where you give up hope. But as soon as the doctors can't do anything, they call it incurable."

He says he will stay in Linz and look after his mother and the housekeeping. Kubizek asks him if he can manage, knowing his friend's distaste for the necessary chores others have always carried out on his behalf, how disdainful he is of such monotonous work. Hitler replies that a person can do anything if they have to. For the next month he does exactly that. Not a word does he say about the issues on which he normally holds forth; politics, architecture, art, none of these things seems to occupy him any longer, only his ailing mother, close to death, and the grief of that. He moves her bed into the kitchen, the warmest room in the apartment, and sleeps on the couch next to her. He reads to her, cooks her food, helps his younger sister with her homework. One day Kubizek finds him scrubbing the floor, Frau Hitler smiles on seeing his surprise and says with pride, "There, you see, Adolf can do anything."

> *I had never before seen in him such loving tenderness. I did not trust my own eyes and ears. Not a cross word, not an impatient remark, no violent insistence on having his own way. He forgot himself entirely in those weeks and lived only for his mother. Although Adolf, according to Frau Klara, had inherited many of his father's traits, I realized then how much his nature resembled his mother's. Certainly this was partly due to the fact that he had spent the previous four years of his life alone with her. But over and above that there was a peculiar spiritual harmony between mother and son which I have never since come across. All that separated them was pushed into the background. Adolf never mentioned the disappointment which he had suffered in Vienna. For the time being, cares for the future no longer seemed to exist. An atmosphere of relaxed, almost serene contentment surrounded the dying woman.*

December is cold and bleak, a damp mist hangs over the river; the few hours in which the sun shines allow no warmth. Kubizek visits them daily; on one occasion he is not admitted, Hitler comes out instead and tells him his mother is suffering terrible pain. Snow falls, dusting the rooftops white, Christmas approaches. On the morning of the twenty-first of December, Hitler appears at the Kubizek home. From his distraught expression they realize what has happened. She has died, he tells them. Her final wish was to be buried next to her husband in Leonding. Hitler is beside himself and barely able to speak.

Kubizek writes nothing of the doctor's presence during the final weeks of Klara Hitler's life, yet according to Hamann he was there in daily attendance from November 6. He administered morphine and treated her with iodoform, a treatment "typical of the time and extremely painful" – cloths containing the substance were laid on the open wound to "burn it out," resulting in excruciating thirst and the simultaneous inability of the patient to swallow.

In 1941, Bloch published an article in *Collier's* magazine detailing the course of the illness and the circumstances surrounding it, in which he stated that Hitler was tormented by his mother's treatment and expressed gratitude to him for administering the morphine. Bloch's version confirms Kubizek's account.

> *In the practice of my profession it is natural that I should have witnessed many scenes such as this one, yet none of them left me with quite the same impression. In all my career I have never seen anyone so prostrate with grief as Adolf Hitler.*

Bloch also briefly described his general impression of Hitler:

> *Many biographers have put him down as harsh-voiced, defiant, untidy; as a young ruffian who personified all that is unattractive. This simply is not true. As a youth he was quiet, well-mannered, and neatly dressed. He was tall, sallow, old for his age. He was neither robust nor sickly. Perhaps "frail-looking" would best describe him. His eyes — inherited from his mother — were large, melancholy, and thoughtful. To a very large extent this boy lived within himself. What dreams he dreamed I do not know.*

On December 23, Kubizek and his mother visit Hitler's home. The weather has changed, the snow in the streets turned to slush, the air a mist. Frau Hitler is laid out in her bed, her face waxen, Kubizek writes that death must have come to her as a release from terrible pain. Paula, who is eleven years old, is crying, but not Hitler. Kubizek and his mother go down into the street. The body is placed in a coffin and brought down into the hall. The priest blesses the deceased and the small cortège begins its progress. Hitler follows the coffin, wearing a long black overcoat and black gloves, carrying a black top hat in his hand. He is stern and composed. To his left is his brother-in-law, Raubal, and between them Paula. His half sister, Angela, heavily pregnant, follows in a closed carriage. The rest of the cortège comprises only a few neighbors and acquaintances. Kubizek describes it as miserable.

The next day is Christmas Eve, Kubizek invites Hitler to spend it with his family, Hitler declines. Nor does he wish to join Raubal and his sister, who from now on are to look after Paula. Instead he wanders about the streets of Linz through the night, if what he later tells Kubizek is true.

Little mention is made of any of this in *Mein Kampf*. Of his mother's death and the circumstances surrounding it, Hitler writes as follows:

> *It was the conclusion of a long and painful illness which from the beginning left little hope of recovery. Yet it was a dreadful blow, particularly for me. I had honored my father, but my mother I had loved.*
>
> *Poverty and hard reality now compelled me to take a quick decision. What little my father had left had been largely exhausted by my mother's grave illness; the orphan's pension to which I was entitled was not enough for me even to live on, and so I was faced with the problem of somehow making my own living.*
>
> *In my hand a suitcase full of clothes and underwear; in my heart an indomitable will, I journeyed to Vienna. I, too, hoped to wrest from Fate what my father had accomplished fifty years before; I, too, wanted to become "something" – but on no account a civil servant.*

The little "but" in the sentence concerning his mother and father, "but my mother I had loved," more than suggests that he did not love his father, and by dwelling so little on his mother's death and immediately directing the text toward the future, and so optimistically, in such a way as to close the circle of what, if *Mein Kampf* is to be believed, has been the predominant and governing conflict in his life so far, his refusal to become a civil servant, he gives the impression that the grief of losing his mother was transient, an impression reinforced by the fact that she is hardly mentioned at all in the text and that the two years they spent together are passed over in a single sentence. This gives a sense of vigor and drive, a new beginning, pockets empty, his own devices being his only resource. In the chapter that follows he goes back in time, writing:

> When my mother died, Fate, at least in one respect, had made its decisions.
>
> In the last months of her sickness, I had gone to Vienna to take the entrance examination for the Academy. I had set out with a pile of drawings, convinced that it would be child's play to pass the examination. At the Realschule I had been by far the best in my class at drawing, and since then my ability had developed amazingly; my own satisfaction caused me to take a joyful pride in hoping for the best.

He gets through the first part of the exam, but fails the remainder. "I was so convinced that I would be successful that when I received my rejection, it struck me as a bolt from the blue. Yet that is what happened."

This happens before the death of his mother, and since he has already described that event, and the previous chapter concludes with his moving to Vienna, his rejection by the Academy is tacked on to the description of his arrival in Vienna following his mother's death, meaning that the rejection and his mother's death are reported in reverse order and separated. This gives the impression that while his mother's death was a blow it was also a release in that it brought with it a sense of future, though in real life it must have seemed quite different: his mother is gravely ill, he leaves for Vienna to take his entrance exam, fails, his dream thereby in ruins, and with that failure he returns home to his mother, who then dies. In this there is no future, but quite the opposite, his life closes in on him. She was the very center of his existence, and he of hers. His mother's condition deteriorates, he returns from Vienna, they both know she is dying, she is concerned as to his future, and he never tells her he failed the entrance exam to the Academy.

◆ ◆ ◆

The first eighteen years of Hitler's life are described in only fourteen pages of *Mein Kampf*, and the narrative is furthermore dotted with reflections on nationalism, history, and his own theories on a number of subjects. The period in which he lived in Vienna, the five years from 1908 to 1913, takes up all of ninety-eight pages. But there is hardly a sentence that touches on his personal life, and what little he writes in this respect is general in nature.

> *To me Vienna, the city which, to so many, is the epitome of innocent pleasure, a festive playground for merrymakers, represents, I am sorry to say, merely the living memory of the saddest period of my life.*
>
> *Even today this city can arouse in me nothing but the most dismal thoughts. For me the name of this Phaeacian city represents five years of hardship and misery. Five years in which I was forced to earn a living, first as a day laborer, then as a smaller painter; a truly meager living which never sufficed to appease even my daily hunger. Hunger was then my faithful bodyguard; he never left me for a moment and partook of all I had, share and share alike. Every book I acquired aroused his interest; a visit to the Opera prompted his attentions for days at a time; my life was a continuous struggle with this pitiless friend. And yet during this time I studied as never before. Aside from my architecture and my rare visits to the Opera, paid for in hunger, I had but one pleasure: my books.*
>
> *At that time I read enormously and thoroughly. All the free time my work left me was employed in my studies. In this way I forged in a few years' time the foundation of a knowledge from which I still draw nourishment today.*

Nothing of this is untrue. He was poor, often hungry, and eked out a living painting for tourists or frame makers, a "meager" time indeed. In *Mein Kampf* he makes this out to be a necessary apprenticeship, a time in which, from his lowly position in society, he learned what it meant to be poor, what it meant to live in social misery, experiencing firsthand the dissolution of shared values and the collapse of the Habsburg Empire. He presents himself as a manual laborer, describing how he involves himself in workers' politics, the violence and the suppression of opinion that occurs at society's lower levels, and he puts forward his visions of how all this may and ought to be dealt with. He tells of his visits to the parliament, giving rise to his disdain for parliamentarism and democracy. And he describes his first encounters with Jews, not personal but in the form of strange figures he sees on the streets. He gives a picture of a world disintegrating on all levels and in every imaginable way. Everything he experienced, even the misery in which he lived, is in this way given meaning: he observes, perceives, reads, thinks, and though his circumstances are poor, his life at this time is a school he would not have wished to have done without. He has entered the school of life, nothing of what he can do comes from any university, nothing of what he takes in and writes about is down to any theory, but is alone the result of practical reality.

The pride in this account hides how badly he wants to enter the Academy and is clearly a rationalization after the fact. Everything points forward to the person he is now. But if we are to understand the kind of life he led in those five years, all Hitler's future must be discarded. Nothing of what he did then pointed toward anything else. The misery into which he gradually sank was indeed misery. He was seen standing in line at a soup kitchen for the homeless; everything indicates he slept in the parks for a time. He had no friends, hardly any acquaintances, and what little social contact he had consisted of the fellow destitutes he encountered at a flophouse. Moreover, the five years he spent living in this way are perhaps the most crucial of all in a person's life, those between the ages of eighteen and twenty-three. Hitler was destitute, nothing of what he had believed in had turned out to be right, his dreams had fallen short, he was a person no one wanted and no one needed. He had lost his grip on reality, had practically no footing at all in the real world. If he had frozen to death in the night, no one would have cared. He was, in every sense, a nonentity, vanished into total anonymity, in the very gutter of society.

Yet it began in a different place altogether. It began well. Arriving in Vienna he had with him his mother's money, enough to keep him going for a year providing he was thrifty. He could re-apply to the Academy. And he was not alone in the big city, Kubizek came with him.

In his Hitler biography Ian Kershaw provides this depiction:

> When he did return to Vienna, in February 1908, it was not to pursue with all vigor the necessary course of action to become an architect, but to slide back into the life of indolence, idleness, and self-indulgence which he had followed before his mother's death. He even now worked on Kubizek's parents until they reluctantly agreed to let August leave his work in the family upholstery business to join him in Vienna in order to study music.

Kubizek himself was for the rest of his life grateful that Hitler had talked his parents into allowing him to pursue his desire to study music. Self-indulgence was undoubtedly one of Hitler's most prominent traits, yet it was this very eruptive, near-manic side of him, too, that meant he would throw himself with great abandon and urgency into whatever subject or issue might capture his imagination at a given time, this often being followed by periods of despondency, though such moods, too, could be quite as restless and insistent. What Kershaw is perhaps alluding to is that this urgency was never directed, would never follow any plotted course or plan. While Hitler's relatives most likely would have endorsed the description of him giving himself up to "indolence, idleness, and self-indulgence," Hitler himself must certainly have seen things differently, there was something he wanted to become, something never quite within reach, that never quite turned out, which of course is by no means unusual for a young man of eighteen years old with ambitions of becoming an artist. Hitler was in every respect an autodidact, and like so many of his kind he became gradually more opinionated, a development exacerbated by his essentially solitary nature, inclined never to seek the company of others; he had a favorite bench in one of Vienna's parks, slightly out of the way, where he would sit and read whenever he was not seated at one of the city's many cafés poring through the newspapers, or else immersed in one of his many projects in his lodgings, whether drawing up plans for apartment buildings, opera houses, and concert halls, or writing plays and short stories – these all being matters to which he devoted himself during this time, all abandoned before completion, all witnessed by Kubizek, who lived by his side.

Kubizek arrives at the railway station in Vienna late one evening in winter. Hitler is waiting for him, elegantly clad, the ivory-handled walking stick in his hand, seemingly acclimatized and at ease with the hustle and bustle, already the city dweller. Hitler kisses him lightly on the cheek in greeting, they take a handle each of Kubizek's heavy bag and head out into the city, "such a terrible noise that one could not hear oneself speak," Adolf eventually leading them down a side street, Stumpergasse, to his rented room in a rear courtyard building.

> In the small room that he occupied, a miserable paraffin lamp was burning. I looked around me. The first thing that struck me were the sketches that lay around on the table, on the bed, everywhere. Adolf cleared the table, spread a piece of newspaper on it, and fetched a bottle of milk from the window. Then he brought sausage and bread. But I can still see his white, earnest face as I pushed all these things aside

*and opened the bag. Cold roast pork, stuffed buns, and other lovely
things to eat. All he said was, "Yes, that's what it is to have a mother!"
We ate like kings. Everything tasted of home.*

Kubizek is tired after his journey, his senses already bombarded, the hour is late, but still Hitler insists on showing him the city. How could someone just arriving in Vienna go to bed without first having seen the opera house? They go out. Kubizek writes that it feels as though he has been transported to another planet, so overwhelming is the impression. They proceed to the Stefansdom. The evening mist is so dense they cannot see the spire: "I could just make out the heavy, dark mass of the nave stretching up into the gray monotony of the mist, almost unearthly, as though not built by human hands."

Kershaw describes the same events as follows:

*Adolf met a tired Kubizek at the station that evening, took him back
to Stumpergasse to stay the first night, but, typically, insisted on immediately showing him all the sights of Vienna. How could someone
come to Vienna and go to bed without first seeing the Court Opera
House? So Gustl was dragged off to view the opera building, Saint
Stephen's Cathedral (which could scarcely be seen through the mist),
and the lovely church of Saint Maria am Gestade. It was after midnight when they returned to Stumpergasse, and later still when an
exhausted Kubizek fell asleep with Hitler still haranguing him about
the grandeur of Vienna.*

Kershaw's only source as to this evening is Kubizek's book, which says nothing of Hitler "haranguing" him, and the sense, on seeing the opera, of having been transported to another planet, and of the cathedral appearing unearthly in the mist, as Kubizek writes, charging the experience with positive energy, is ignored by Kershaw; in his version the mist is negative, making the spire scarcely visible, and this is so in order to make Hitler out to be an unreasonable, self-indulgent, and egotistical young man oblivious to the needs of his friend. But if this had been the case, if the experience had been unambiguously negative, why does Kubizek not say so? Kubizek is a friend, his arrival has been greatly anticipated, Hitler is eager to show him all the things he has seen himself, all that is marvelous about the city, and can anyone blame him for that? How can we say that Hitler's enthusiasm was in fact disregard for his friend, when at the same time his friend has described what happened as a positive experience? Was Kubizek duped? Was he too stupid to realize that Hitler was using him? Did he not understand that viewing a cathedral in the mist is a washout, not an unearthly experience?

Or, conversely, on what basis does Kershaw overrule the account of his only source with a version of what *in fact* happened?

The issue with biography as a genre, and this is as true of autobiography as it is of the memoir, is that the author purports to be omniscient, a sole authority, he or she knows how it all turned out, and as such it is almost impossible not to accord emphasis to any sign, be it character trait or event, that points in that one direction, even if, as in this instance, it is merely one trait, one event among many others that in no way called attention to themselves. Of course, the truth of any past situation is elusive, it belongs to the moment and cannot be separated from it, but we may ensnare that moment, illuminate it from different angles, weigh the plausibility of one interpretation against that of another, and in that experiment endeavor to ignore what later happened, which is to say refrain from considering one character trait, one event, as a sign of something other than what it is in itself.

This "in itself" is both riddle and solution at the same time. If we view Hitler as a "bad" person, with categorically negative characteristics even as a child and a young man, all pointing toward a subsequently escalating "evil," then Hitler is of "the other," and thereby not of us, and in that case we have a problem, since then we are unburdened of the atrocities he and Germany later committed, these being something "they" did, so no longer a threat to us. But what is this "bad" that we do not embody? What is this "evil" that we do not express? The very formulation is indicative of how we humans think in terms of categories, and of course there is nothing wrong with that as long as we are aware of the dangers. In the night of pathology and the predetermined there is no free will, and without free will there is no guilt.

No matter how broken a person might be, no matter how disturbed the soul, that person remains a person always, with the freedom to choose. It is choice that makes us human. Only choice gives meaning to the concept of guilt.

Kershaw and almost two generations with him have condemned Hitler and his entire being as if pointing to his innocence when he was nineteen or twenty-three, or pointing to some of the good qualities he retained throughout his life, were a defense of him and of evil. In actual fact the opposite is true: only his innocence can bring his guilt into relief.

The day after Kubizek's arrival in Vienna the two friends begin their hunt for a room he can rent. The task is a difficult one, most rooms being too small for the piano he needs, and when they do find one big enough the landlady refuses to hear of having a lodger practice such an instrument. Kubizek's impression of Vienna is not good, the city seems to him full of indifferent, unsympathetic people, gloomy courtyards, narrow, ill-lit tenements and stairs. Despairing and miserable, he happens on another "room-to-rent" notice in the Zollergasse; they ring the bell and a maid opens the door and shows them into an elegantly furnished room containing magnificent twin beds.

> *"Madame is coming immediately," said the maid, curtsied, and vanished. We both knew at once that it was too stylish for us. Then "madame" appeared in a doorway, very much a lady, not so young, but very elegant.*
>
> *She wore a silk dressing gown and slippers trimmed with fur. She greeted us smilingly, inspected Adolf, then me, and asked us to sit down. My friend asked which room was to let. "This one," she*

answered, and pointed to the two beds. Adolf shook his head and said curtly, "Then one of the beds must come out, because my friend must have room for a piano." The lady was obviously disappointed that it was I and not Adolf who wanted a room, and asked whether Adolf already had lodgings. When he answered in the affirmative she suggested that I, together with the piano I needed, should move into his room and he should take this one. While she was suggesting this to Adolf with some animation, through a sudden movement the belt which kept the dressing gown together came undone. "Oh, excuse me, gentlemen," the lady exclaimed, and immediately refastened the dressing gown. But that second had sufficed to show us that under her silk covering she wore nothing but a brief pair of knickers.

Adolf turned as red as a peony, gripped my arm, and said, "Come, Gustl!" I do not remember how we got out of the house. All I remember is Adolf's furious exclamation as we arrived back in the street. "What a Frau Potiphar!" Apparently such experiences were also part of Vienna.

These are a pair of inexperienced young men from the sticks; the man of the world he thought Hitler was vanishes in the blushing cheeks that also give us a picture of Hitler's chastity and fear of women. He is eighteen years old and utterly unversed, Kubizek tells us there were no women in Hitler's life in the four years they spent together and he did not masturbate. This latter point is of course impossible to verify, yet it fits well with what we know of Hitler's sexuality from *Mein Kampf* and various other sources. Womanhood was associated with purity and exalted, a part of the ideal world he so cultivated, and his later romantic relationships were all with very young and innocent women. His obsession with purity and the way that obsession also pertained to sexual matters reveals itself in several episodes in Kubizek's book. On one occasion, after they had been to a performance of a play the press had made infamous for its supposedly immoral nature, Hitler takes Kubizek by the arm and leads him to the red-light district so that he might see with his own eyes how depraved and morally corrupted humanity has become. The prostitutes sit in illuminated rooms in low, one-story houses along the street, men amble back and forth, stopping to conduct whispered interchanges with the girl of their choice, after which the light inside would be put out. Hitler and Kubizek pass down the length of the street, but as they reach the end Hitler turns to go back. "Sink of iniquity" is a recurring phrase, and when Kubizek suggests that seeing it once is enough, Hitler drags him back past the windows with him. The prostitutes try to win their attention, one rolls down her stockings and shows her bare legs as they pass, another casually takes off her chemise as if to change, and as soon as they are out of the area Hitler rages against their "tricks of seduction." Back home in his room in the Stumpergasse he proceeds to hold forth and deliver a lecture on these new impressions and what they mean. Now, he declares, he has learned the customs of the market for commercial love and the purpose of his visit has thereby been fulfilled.

The episode makes plain three of the young Hitler's various modes of relating to the world around him: at first he is within it, filled with unmanageable feelings of attraction and disgust, lust and shame; then he rages against it, eventually, at due distance, to analyze it. Analysis is the preferred mode, and the remoteness it requires is one of the most striking elements of Hitler's character and cannot be underestimated.

Hitler and Kubizek live in the middle of one of the world's biggest cities, they are eighteen years old, and Hitler at least is completely free in the sense that both his parents are dead, he has no family to tie him down, and in principle he can do whatever he wants. The possibilities are many, the world stands open. Yet he associates with no one, does not so much as look at a woman, takes no part in the life that is going on around him. The seriousness with which he approaches life is immense, he has only disdain for anyone having fun, enjoying oneself is superficial and in some way beneath him. He sees much hardship and misery in his surroundings and possesses a strong sense of social indignation, he speaks often of the little man and of poverty; at one point he makes an excursion into the poorest district so that he might know what he is talking about, but the poor themselves, the people who live in such poverty, are anathema to him, he ignores them, will not speak to them or even be close to them, his dislike of contact is immense and conspicuous. The same applies to women, he can speak of them, idealize them, or consider them depraved, but he cannot have them close to him, expressing relief that women have no access to the area where he and Kubizek usually stand at the opera.

The strict morals he champions and according to which he conducts his life, these harsh rules he follows in all their rejection of the physical body, would clearly seem to be a way of controlling his inner self, which by all accounts is chaotic in the extreme. And since the outside world too is chaotic, which is to say complex and expanding in every way, as the city and culture were in the first decade of the twentieth century, marked by rampant poverty, political chaos, prostitution, and sexual liberation – it has to be remembered that Freud was living and writing in the same city, and that Gustav Klimt was painting there too – it is hardly surprising that he should apply to society the same rules he has applied to himself, rules of abstinence and control, the two things, individual and society, meeting and leveling out in the emotions, which in his case are powerful. The contempt of his "Frau Potiphar!" or "tricks of seduction" stem clearly from emotions thereby occasioned inside him, lust and disgust, perhaps, and applied to society as a whole, the "sink of iniquity." He is manically obsessed with cleanliness and a well-groomed appearance, dressing always as neatly as possible, another way of controlling his inner chaos. And this must be why he is so interested in art, it affords him peace in which to devote himself to something else, something grand and beautiful and majestic.

When he listened to Wagner's music he was a changed man: his violence left him, he became quiet, yielding, and tractable. His gaze lost its restlessness; his own destiny, however heavily it may have weighed upon him, became unimportant. He no longer felt lonely and out-lawed, misjudged by society.

These emotions that so uplift him are his too, they belong not to the music, not to Wagner, but to him, and the feeling of being elevated by the music and language of the stage, of being permeated by the exquisite, is so important to him that he even forgoes eating so as to have money to buy opera tickets.

His immense energy, construed by Kershaw as indolence insofar as it exists outside any academic framework or meaningful enterprise whatsoever, is hard not to read into the same pattern, for when he is most deeply immersed in a project, he vanishes completely, and the only thing that exists is his urgent industry: his thoughts, plans, and sketches. His behavior is eruptive, obsessive, on the threshold of normal. Indeed, if Hitler's personal morals and those he applies to society at this time are strongly constraining, his artistic industry is quite without boundary. There are simply no limits to what he will apply himself to, nothing can stand in his way, everything is wide open. "It is not the professor's wisdom that counts," he says to Kubizek, "but genius," and begins promptly to compose an opera. He can play no instrument, has no knowledge of harmony or orchestration, and yet he pushes such limitations aside as technicalities, striving to delve into his fiercest emotions and express them in the language he admires most of all. He experiments with an ill-fated system attempting to combine sound and color, works out a prelude and asks for Kubizek's opinion of it. Kubizek tells him the basic themes are good, but that he has to realize that on such a basis alone it will be impossible to write an opera, at the same time declaring his readiness to teach him the necessary theory. "Do you think I'm mad?" Hitler shouts at him. "What have I got you for? First of all you will put down exactly what I play on the piano."

They proceed accordingly. Kubizek tries to make it clear to him that he must keep to one key. "Who is the composer, you or

I?" Hitler rants back. Eventually he decides that the opera, based on a legend of Germanic mythology, should be performed in the musical mode of expression pertaining to the period in question. He asks Kubizek if anything remains preserved of Germanic music. Kubizek tells him there is nothing save for a few instruments, drums, bone flutes, and horns. Hitler reminds him that the skalds had sung to the accompaniment of harp-like instruments and proposes they do likewise. To make the thing tolerable for the human ear, as he puts it, Kubizek talks him out of the idea. Reverting to more conventional instrumentation they forge ahead, however slowly. Hitler designs the scenery and costumes in detail and pens the libretto. He eats nothing, goes without sleep, hardly drinks. Throughout, he demands that Kubizek not only be party to the process, but quite as devoted as he is, and berates him repeatedly. Hitler is the roommate from hell.

> It would have been easy for me to take as an excuse one of our frequent quarrels to move out. The people at the Conservatoire would have been only too pleased to help me find another room. Why did I not do it? After all, I had often admitted to myself that this strange friendship was no good for my studies. How much time and energy did I lose in these nocturnal activities with my friend? Why, then, did I not go? Because I was homesick, certainly, and because Adolf represented for me a bit of home. But, after all, homesickness is something a young man of twenty can overcome. What was it then? What held me?
>
> Frankly it was just hours like those through which I was now living which bound me even more closely to my friend. I knew the normal interests of young people of my age: flirtations, shallow pleasures, idle play, and a lot of unimportant, meaningless thoughts. Adolf was the exact opposite. There was an incredible earnestness in him, a thoroughness, a true passionate interest in everything that happened and, most important, an unfailing devotion to the beauty, majesty, and grandeur of art. It was this that attracted me especially to him and restored my equilibrium after hours of exhaustion.

Like so many of Hitler's projects, his opera comes to nothing. He is far too restless and has far too little patience to see such a demanding enterprise through to completion, and furthermore we can assume that his frustrations at his own musical shortcomings must eventually have wearied him.

Other projects on which he embarked in this period included a grand attempt at solving the housing crisis in Vienna, a task that involved him redesigning the entire city as well as meticulously drawing plans for the new workers' units he envisaged. Another idea was that the music he so cherished should be taken to those living outside the city, a "mobile Reichs-Orchestra" whose organization and repertoire he planned down to the smallest detail, even the color of the orchestra members' shirts, Kubizek recalls. All these projects were pipe dreams, remote from reality and basically meaningless, yet they tell us a lot about Hitler's character, the way he could dedicate himself, the boundless belief in his own abilities, and the way he thereby found out how he might connect his internal and external existences without having to pass through the social domain he seemingly either feared or loathed, and which, regardless of all else, always broke down his inner dreams by confronting them with external reality, presenting to him, in other words, their real-world consequences. Our internal existence is abstract, external reality tangible, and in these grand yet unrealistic designs the two aspects collide in a way he is unable to manage.

Kubizek and Hitler lived together in Vienna for five months over the spring and summer of 1908. Hitler never let on that he had been turned down by the Academy, and he led his life in such a way as to make his friend believe he had been accepted and attended its lessons. They shared a room; after the incident with Frau Potiphar they had decided it was convenient. Hitler made inquiries with his landlady, Frau Zakreys, who agreed to move into Hitler's old room, while the two friends moved into hers. Kubizek took the conservatory's entrance exam the following day.

He passed and was admitted, but Hitler seemed anything but pleased on his behalf. "I had no idea I had such a clever friend," he remarks baldly. He was often irritable during this period, and Kubizek considers this the reason he does not wish to hear about his studies. Kubizek is puzzled by a number of aspects of his friend's behavior, among them the fact that he spends so little time painting, devoting his attention to any number of other things instead; he writes a play, he reads books that have nothing to do with painting. Kubizek clearly senses that all is not well, but he is used to Hitler's obstinacy and eccentric manner and puts it down to that, besides him having only recently lost his mother.

> His mood worried me more and more as the days went by. I had never known him to torment himself in this way before, far from it. In my opinion, he possessed rather too much than too little self-confidence. But now things seemed to have changed round. He wallowed deeper and deeper in self-criticism. Yet it only needed the lightest touch — as when one flicks on the light and everything becomes brilliantly clear — for his self-accusation to become an accusation against the times, against the whole world. Choking with his catalog of hates, he would pour his fury over everything, against mankind in general who did not understand him, who did not appreciate him and by whom he was persecuted. I see him before me, striding up and down the small space in boundless anger, shaken to his very depths. I sat at the piano with my fingers motionless on the keyboard and listened to him, upset by his hymn of hate, and yet worried about him.

They argue a lot in these first weeks about how to arrange themselves in the apartment; Kubizek wants to practice, Hitler wants to read; when poor weather forces them both to stay in, the mood can be tense. At one point Kubizek fixes his schedule to the cupboard door with a thumbtack and asks Hitler to do likewise so they can see when the other one is going to be out. But Hitler has no schedule, he doesn't need one, he says, he keeps it all in his head. Kubizek shrugs his shoulders, unconvinced. Hitler's work is anything but systematic, mostly he works at night and sleeps until late in the mornings. To see his friend doing so well cannot have been easy for Hitler. And now, with the schedule on the cupboard door a clear and visible symbol of his friend's progress, he explodes with rage.

"This Academy," he screamed, "is a lot of old-fashioned fossilized civil servants, bureaucrats devoid of understanding, stupid lumps of officials. The whole Academy ought to be blown up!" His face was livid, the mouth quite small, the lips almost white. But the eyes glittered. There was something sinister about them, as if all the hate of which he was capable lay in those glowing eyes! I was just going to point out that those men of the Academy on whom he so lightly passed judgment in his measureless hatred were, after all, his teachers and professors, from whom he could certainly learn something, but he forestalled me: "They rejected me, they threw me out, they turned me down."

I was shocked. So that was it. Adolf did not go to the Academy at all. Now I could understand a great deal that had puzzled me about him. I felt his hard luck deeply, and asked him whether he had told his mother that the Academy had not accepted him. "What are you thinking of?" he replied. "How could I burden my dying mother with this worry?"

I could not help but agree. For a while we were both silent. Perhaps Adolf was thinking of his mother. Then I tried to give the conversation a practical turn. "And what now?" I asked him.

"What now, what now," he repeated irritably. "Are you starting too – what now?" He must have asked himself this question a hundred times and more, because he had certainly not discussed it with anyone else. "What now?" he mocked my anxious inquiry again, and instead of answering, sat himself down at the table and surrounded himself with his books. "What now?"

He adjusted the lamp, took up a book, opened it, and began to read. I made to take the schedule down from the cupboard door. He raised his head, saw it, and said calmly, "Never mind."

That Hitler can construct and live such a lie instead of admitting to his friend that he has failed must surely have been a great strain on his life and tells us something about his ability to deny the real world in favor of illusion, but most of all it is revealing of his pride. Their friendship is based on Hitler talking and Kubizek listening, Hitler acting and Kubizek tagging along, in short Hitler dominating and Kubizek submitting. During that spring a fundamental shift occurs in this power structure, for not only does Kubizek gain admittance to the music conservatory, with Hitler having failed the entrance exam to the Academy, he also makes great strides in his studies. Soon he is entrusted with teaching, and as part of the conservatory's end-of-term festivities he conducts the first-night concert, with three songs of his own composition being performed on the second night as well as two movements from his sextet for strings. Hitler is in attendance and witnesses the congratulations Kubizek receives from his professors and even from the director of the conservatory. Hitler is enthusiastic and proud, though, as Kubizek writes, one can well imagine "what he was thinking in his heart of hearts." His friend's success throws his own failure emphatically into relief. And while he may still dominate him when they are on their own together and appear totally superior, when things are boiled down, the fact of the matter is that he is outshone and overlooked.

Summer arrives, and they have been living together for five months; Kubizek returns to his parents in Linz for the holidays, after which he is to undergo eight weeks of training in the Austro-Hungarian army reserve before coming back to Vienna to continue his studies. Hitler remains in the apartment, having no money to travel anywhere and no one to visit. He sends Kubizek postcards and letters while his friend is away, all is fine, and in the main he is occupied by the building projects going on in Linz and wants Kubizek to keep him informed as to their progress. Kubizek does as he asks while putting in hours in his father's workshop, sending his share of the rent to their landlady in Vienna; he departs for his military training and writes to Hitler announcing his arrival back in Vienna so that his friend might meet him and lend a hand with his luggage. By then it is November.

I had, as I had written to him, taken the early train to save time, and arrived at the Westbahnhof at three o'clock in the afternoon. He would be waiting, I thought, at the usual spot, the ticket barrier. Then he could help me carry the heavy case which also contained something for him from my mother. Had I missed him? I went back again, but he was certainly not at the barrier. I went into the waiting room. In vain I looked around me: Adolf was not there. Perhaps he was ill. He had indeed written me in his last letter that he was still being plagued by his old trouble, bronchial catarrh. I put my case in the left-luggage office and, very worried, hastened to the Stumpergasse. Frau Zakreys was delighted to see me, but told me immediately that the room was taken. "But Adolf, my friend?" I asked her astonished.

From her lined, withered face Frau Zakreys stared at me with wide-open eyes. "But don't you know that Herr Hitler has moved out?"

No, I did not know.

"Where has he moved to?" I asked.

"Herr Hitler didn't tell me that."

"But he must have left a message for me – a letter, perhaps, or a note. How else shall I get hold of him?"

The landlady shook her head. "No, Herr Hitler didn't leave anything."

"Not even a greeting?"

"He didn't say anything."

Thirty years would pass before Kubizek again laid eyes on Hitler. He had vanished and did not wish to be found. Had he wanted to keep in touch, Kubizek reasons, Hitler would have asked for his address from their former landlady, his parents in Linz, or the music conservatory. He never did, so there was no doubt he wanted to be left alone. Kubizek looked up his half sister the next time he was in Linz, but she knew nothing of his whereabouts or what he might be up to.

There are many conceivable reasons why Hitler would take such a drastic step as to sever all contact with the only person in his life. The most obvious of these is pride: while Kubizek was undergoing his military training in September Hitler had again taken the Academy's entrance exam and had once again failed; this time he was rejected after the first round. From what Kubizek tells us of his character and nature it would not be unreasonable to assume that his failure this time was too great for him to be able to tell Kubizek. Another reason has also to do with pride; after a year in Vienna punctuated by the death of his mother, his funds were beginning to run out, he could no longer afford to keep up the room in the Stumpergasse, nor did there seem any likelihood of him earning money without degrading himself by taking on what he so disdainfully referred to as "bread-and-butter" work; another loss of prestige in relation to Kubizek. Another reason still was that Kubizek represented his only contact with Linz and Hitler's family there; through Kubizek's parents they could easily find out where Kubizek – and therefore Hitler himself – was living. By vanishing the way he did, all ties to his family, which is to say the family of his half sister, were broken.

With Kubizek out of the picture we know little about Hitler's life in the year that followed. This is telling indeed, given that his life as a whole is one of the century's most thoroughly charted and dissected. From the public records we know he moved out of the Stumpergasse into cheaper lodgings not far away in the Felberstrasse. The form required by the local police authority states his profession as "student" – on his arrival in Vienna he had registered as an "artist." He remained in the Felberstrasse for a year, until the following summer. What he did during that time is not known. The only existing information tells us he canceled his membership in the museum association in Linz on March 4, presumably in order to save the cost of the subscription. In August 1909, after a year, he moves to even cheaper accommodation, a room on the outskirts in the Sechshauserstrasse, where he registers himself as a "*Schriftsteller*," or "writer." He lives there no more than three weeks before moving out again, at which point all trace of him is lost. On the registration form a hand has written "moved, no known address." Everything points to him now being homeless, sleeping out through the autumn and winter. It was not possible to rent a room without registering with the police, and even though everything relating to Hitler was removed by the Nazis from the Austrian archives following the Anschluss, the documents were not destroyed but kept in the archives of the NSDAP, and tell us nothing. Another indication that he now lived on the streets consists of a sighting of him, the only one reported during this time, by a relative of his first landlady, Frau Zakreys, who recognized him standing in line at a soup kitchen for the destitute: "His clothes looked very shabby and I felt sorry for him, because he used to be so well dressed."

The next time he appears in police archives is in December 1909, when he found his way to a flophouse in Meidling. There he made the acquaintance of a tramp, Reinhold Hanisch, a man with a police record for a variety of misdemeanors including fraud and theft. Later, Hanisch would publish a memoir, in which he writes that Hitler, then twenty years old, looked in a sorry state, depressed, tired, and hungry, and with sore feet. His blue-checked suit had turned purple due to rain and the disinfectant with which anyone staying at the hostel was obliged to delouse their clothing. He had no possessions, presumably having sold everything he had brought with him from Linz. According to Hamann, Hitler told Hanisch he had been thrown out by his landlady, that he had sat around in all-night cafés the first few nights until his money ran out, and that since then he had been sleeping on park benches. He had not eaten for some days and told of approaching a drunken gentleman one night and begging him for money, only for the man to hurl insults at him. Hanisch shared some bread with him and put him in the know as to where to get free soup and medical attention.

This is not the Vienna in which Stefan Zweig and Ludwig Wittgenstein grew up; and if Hitler belonged to the lower social strata when renting his room in the Stumpergasse with Kubizek, he had now definitively fallen through the floor into the gutter. This was rock bottom. He has no work, nowhere to live, no money, no food, no friends, barely an acquaintance. He owns nothing, his clothes are shabby, he is cold and he is hungry. That he should be indolent, a layabout, as Kershaw suggests, accords poorly with the fact that he remains in Vienna. To be indolent is to choose convenience, to be indolent is to proceed by the easiest route. The life he is now living, at a minimum level of existence, depending on the charity of others, is no convenient life, but the most strenuous life imaginable. Knowing as we do that Hitler had offers of work at the time of his leaving Linz, from one of his former neighbors and from his guardian, that he had relatives in the countryside whom he visited in the summer with his mother, and that his brother-in-law was a state official in a secure tenure, with whom he almost certainly would have been able to stay for a period of time if only he would bow his head in humility, the fact that we now find him here, in such extreme destitution, indicates the opposite of convenience and indolence, it is a life far from that of the layabout. His rejection of bourgeois existence is no convenient rejection, but an absolute rejection, a "no" for which he is prepared to pay quite a high price.

One must ask oneself why. What was it he wanted? He has sought admittance to the Academy of Fine Arts, not once but twice, John Toland suggests three times, that he reapplied in September of that year, but the fact remains that he has his whole life set on it. "Artist," he calls himself when registering as tenant of his first lodgings, "student" the second time, "writer" the third. His talk was of becoming a painter, then an architect, and in the meantime he has written plays, stories, and an opera. None of these ventures has been successful, but he is undeterred, for next time may be different. Another headstrong young man from the lowest levels of society with an unbounded, and in the eyes of others unfounded, reservoir of self-confidence, lived similarly from hand to mouth for many years with no other ambition than becoming a writer, something he achieved at the age of thirty with the publication of his first novel: *Hunger*. Van Gogh was another artist of that time who lived in extreme poverty, wanting nothing else than to paint, even though in his lifetime he sold not a single canvas. We have no way of knowing if this was what Hitler was doing, but if it was not, his "no" must then have been all the more emphatic, all the more obstinate, since in that case he was rejecting society itself and all that came with it of work, career, marriage, children. Rather than being a part of that, he chose to live in the gutter. This is not an expression of indolence, but of something else entirely. Could he simply have allowed himself to drift? Nothing would indicate to us that he struggled against it in the way of a man possessed by a particular goal, rather he seems to have positioned a framework of circumstances about his life that slowly but surely sent him to the subterrain, to the flophouse in Meidling at whose doors the subterraneans flock: down-and-outs, tramps, beggars, winos, criminals, the jobless, the poor, hustlers, and fraudsters.

◆◆◆

The social problems that existed in Vienna around the turn of the century were huge. Poverty was rampant, the housing shortage severe, several hundred thousand people existed in the most abject circumstances, and still more continued to join them, migrants flooding from all corners of the great empire to converge on its capital. The cost of housing rocketed, and landlords exploited the situation to its limit; the workers' district of Favoriten, Hamann writes, housed an average of ten persons per rental unit, which consisted of one room and a kitchen with no running water. Child mortality was astoundingly four times greater here than in the city's more affluent areas. Almost all basements were utilized for habitation, and beds unused during the daytime were rented out to so-called *Bettgeher*, literally "bed-goers," homeless people permitted to use a bed for some eight hours or so but not to stay in the apartment the rest of the time. In 1910 the city contained more than eighty thousand of these bed-goers. No system of social security existed, the only poor care being charity-based in the form of soup kitchens, shelters, hostels, and children's homes, all private sector, many of them established by Jewish philanthropists. Some of the needy were lucky enough to be allowed to take leftovers from the taverns and hospitals, and whenever a baker gave away unsold bread, Hamann writes, hordes would descend and fights could break out. The housing shortage became increasingly acute and the so-called shelters, overcrowded with bed-goers during the daytime, began to stay open at nights. The worst conditions, however, were in the illegal sublets. Hamann cites the report of a journalist at the time: the flats are crammed with people unknown to each other, many are children, often they sleep in the same bed, crawling with lice and vermin, inhabiting a single room for cooking, washing, living, sleeping, studying, and carrying out work to earn money; he mentions a stable deemed unfit for animals, inhabited by ten people with three children among them. A two- or three-room apartment in a crumbling, condemned tenement could house eighty or more people, men and women, able and infirm, alcoholics, and prostitutes, and children. "Everything around me was a confused mass of people, rags, and dirt. The room looked like a humongous dirt ball." These places were infested with rats, and disease spread quickly – cholera, tuberculosis, syphilis. Begging generated little income and for many prostitution was the only option, and it was prevalent, too, among children.

Outside the flophouse in Meidling, which could take in about a thousand people, and where Hitler duly appeared in December of 1909, the destitute lined up in long lines each evening, watched by the guards deployed to prevent rioting among those for whom there would be no room. The newspapers would mention the place only in the case of some tragic incident such as a child freezing to death outside the hostel gates or someone being denied medical assistance and dying there. In 1908 the opposition on the city council moved to establish shelters and to open up tram sheds to the homeless, but the authorities pointed merely to existing measures, though these were practically nonexistent, claiming, according to Hamann, that no one could possibly be homeless in Vienna without bearing the blame themselves. There was no help to be had from the city, and in this unregulated social mire the immigrant population, in this case Slavs and eastern European Jews, ranked lowest; many citizens were of the opinion that the hospitals ought only to accept Austrian natives and turn everyone else away.

Hitler himself describes housing conditions for casual laborers as follows:

> *Even more dismal in those days were the housing conditions. The misery in which the Viennese day laborer lived was frightful to behold. Even today it fills me with horror when I think of these wretched caverns, the lodging houses and tenements, sordid scenes of garbage, repulsive filth, and worse.*

This was the situation in all of Europe's major cities of the time, and had been ever since the great tides of industrialization and urbanization in the first part of the nineteenth century. This was a new kind of poverty, concentrated in the urban conglomerations where the lowest classes lived so densely, and were so many in number, and so faceless as to be conspicuously referred to throughout the available sources as hordes or masses or armies of poor.

In 1903 the American writer Jack London published a firsthand account of life in the slums of east London, *The People of the Abyss*, referring to that inner-city area as a ghetto, a place "of remarkable meanness and vastness . . . where two million workers swarm, procreate, and die." Some 1.8 million people in London are estimated to be very poor, he writes, one million exist with one week's wages between them and pauperism. The misery he describes is difficult to take in and comprehend, but the consequences of the extremely high mortality rate and the extremely poor housing conditions are nonetheless clear: here, inside the ghetto of the poor, life is worth less than life outside. It is worth less because death is a constant presence and because the inhuman circumstances in which the poor live are practically insurmountable. In the city's West End, he writes, 18 percent of all children die before the age of five; in the East End 55 percent of all children die before the age of five. In other words, every other child. "And there are streets in London where out of every one hundred children born in a year, fifty die during the next year; and of the fifty that remain, twenty-five die before they are five years old. Slaughter!"

And should the child survive, work awaits in trades that are not merely unhealthy but lethal. In the linen trade wet feet and wet clothes, a result of the preparation of the flax, lead to bronchitis, pneumonia, and severe rheumatism, and the women, who start work at the age of seventeen or eighteen, break down and are physically destroyed by the time they reach thirty. Laborers in the chemical industry, "picked from the strongest and most splendidly built men to be found," live on average less than forty-eight years. In the potter's trade dust gradually settles into the lungs until eventually a case of plaster is formed, making breathing more and more difficult, until finally it ceases.

Jack London wrote his book in 1903 in London, thirty-five years after Karl Marx published the first volume of his *Das Kapital* but only eighteen and nine years respectively after the posthumous publication of volumes two and three. Jack London was a socialist, *The People of the Abyss* an attempt to raise awareness by entering into a world usually viewed from some great distance, and to describe that world from the inside. It contains no analysis, but a wealth of emotions; indignation and resignation being the most dominant. *Das Kapital*, on the other hand, is an analysis of the fundamental preconditions of the misery Jack London describes: commodities, labor, and capital. Theoretical as it is, the work includes lengthy statistically based descriptions of conditions among the lowest class, the same people London would later visit, which at the time, in the 1850s and 1860s, were not much different to those in the first decade of the twentieth century. In his Chapter 25, "General Law of Capitalist Accumulation," Marx tries to outline the circumstances that led to the "intoxicating augmentation of wealth and power" that industrialization had brought about for the privileged classes, not in this instance conditions in the workplace, in themselves appalling, with working days of sixteen, seventeen hours or more in cramped spaces with little light or ventilation, but conditions outside the workplace, the standards of diet and housing of the most poorly situated workers. In 1855, the official list of paupers in England numbered 851,369 persons, these being people without employment and relying on public alms for their survival, while in 1864, due to the crisis in the cotton industry, that figure rose to 1,014,978 persons. These are people living below the very minimum level of existence.

These enormous numbers of poor were an unmanageable problem for society insofar as the colossal changes in production circumstances of which they were a result, the massive industrialization that had taken place, found no counteraction in any form of societal planning or governance; poverty's bottomless pit, concentrated as it was in huge ghetto-like areas of the inner city, arose over a period of only a few decades, and many considered it to be the result of some kind of natural law or force of nature, not least in the wake of Darwin's breakthrough theory of the survival of the fittest, whose axiom was applied equally to the social domain, and the apparent moral and spiritual decline that accompanied it was seen to derive from a kind of human inferiority, self-inflicted, irremediably mushrooming among the lowest classes.

It was as if a whole new society or societal order had arisen within the framework of the old, and the huge pressure it applied to its structures cannot be underestimated. Prior to industrialization, in rural society there were no classes at all but status and strata, and poverty found quite different forms, dealt with in different ways altogether. Marx's analyses, as an instrument by which to understand the enormous upheavals that had taken place in society, were of course invaluable. He had experienced the consequences of poverty at first hand, three of his own children having died when they were still small, and he had seen misery with his own eyes in the great English industrial areas from whence it had spread, seemingly systematically, as if according to its own laws, to large parts of the world.

Industrialism knew no boundaries; nor indeed did the misery that followed in its wake, and the fierce political strife that divided Europe at the beginning of the twentieth century was in the main a matter of a horizontal, transgressional solution versus a vertical, national solution. In other words, identification with class or with place. Hitler, who came from a small petty-bourgeois environment in a relatively homogenous town, source of all his ideals, accorded much emphasis to the poverty issue in *Mein Kampf*, written at a time when the decay of which he had been a part no longer threatened to consume him. His understanding of it was primarily structural:

> *If I did not wish to despair of the men who constituted my environment at that time, I had to learn to distinguish between their external characters and lives and the foundations of their development. Only then could all this be borne without losing heart. Then, from all the misery and despair, from all the filth and outward degeneration, it was no longer human beings that emerged, but the deplorable results of deplorable laws; and the hardship of my own life, no easier than the others, preserved me from capitulating in tearful sentimentality to the degenerate products of this process of development.*
>
> *No, this is not the way to understand all these things!*

Hitler recognized poverty as a major political problem and he was just as distraught about its inhumanity as Karl Marx and Jack London, but in Vienna it had not only emerged within a relatively homogenous working class as in London, but was exacerbated by great numbers of immigrants from all corners of the empire converging on the city in the hope of finding work, and the ethnic conflicts that were so rife there in that period are crucial to Hitler's way of understanding his surroundings and the time in which he lived. He was born a German in Austria, his father was a German nationalist, albeit moderately so, loyal to the Kaiser, while many of his teachers at school and the majority of students cultivated a more radical German nationalism, and the idea of the supremacy of the nation, not merely in constitutional terms but almost as if it were some kind of metaphysical entity, pervades every conception in *Mein Kampf*, and also, if we are to go by Kubizek's memoir, everything else he thought as a young man when it came to politics. When Hitler observed such gross social injustice he did not look firstly toward class relations in search of a solution, but to relations between peoples. In the Greater Germanic Reich of which he dreamed there would be no division between burgher and aristocrat, but between German and non-German. It was on this basis that he was already at the age of eighteen a confirmed anti-Marxist. The international orientation of Marxism went against everything he stood for. He was anticapitalist for the same reason. And the fact that he knew what it meant to be poor, and had seen firsthand the huge and inhuman poverty that existed in Vienna, was surely significant in the formation of his viewpoints on social misery as expressed in *Mein Kampf*, where rather than being seen as a problem of class structure, it is understood as a combined consequence of the disintegrating Dual Monarchy and international capitalism. That his meticulousness and overarching need for control moreover may be seen as a kind of embodiment of the wish to delimit and localize even the biggest structures into more manageable units, in the same way as his fear of everything that spreads, everything that crosses boundaries, like disease and flotsam, may be seen as a kind of embodiment of all the great currents and forces that were at work in his time and which knew no boundaries of nation, is not quite as tenuous and forced as it might appear, for if there is something going on in *Mein Kampf* it is precisely an interpretation of the external world on the basis of the feelings and temperament of the internal being.

After the turn of the century, Vienna was, socially speaking, one of the most backward cities in Europe.

Dazzling riches and loathsome poverty alternated sharply. In the center and in the inner districts you could really feel the pulse of this realm of fifty-two millions, with all the dubious magic of the national melting pot. The Court with its dazzling glamor attracted wealth and intelligence from the rest of the country like a magnet. Added to this was the strong centralization of the Habsburg monarchy in itself.

It offered the sole possibility of holding this medley of nations together in any set form. But the consequence was an extraordinary concentration of high authorities – in the imperial capital.

Yet not only in the political and intellectual sense was Vienna the center of the old Danube monarchy, but economically as well. The host of high officers, government officials, artists, and scholars was confronted by an even greater army of workers, and side by side with aristocratic and commercial wealth dwelt dire poverty. Outside the palaces on the Ring loitered thousands of unemployed, and beneath this Via Triumphalis of old Austria dwelt the homeless in the gloom and mud of the canals.

In hardly any German city could the social question have been studied better than in Vienna. But make no mistake. This "studying" cannot be done from lofty heights. No one who has not been seized in the jaws of this murderous viper can know its poison fangs. Otherwise nothing results but superficial chatter and false sentimentality. Both are harmful. The former because it can never penetrate to the core of the problem, the latter because it passes it by. I do not know which is more terrible: inattention to social misery such as we see every day among the majority of those who have been favored by fortune or who have risen by their own efforts, or else the snobbish, or at times tactless and obtrusive, condescension of certain women of fashion in skirts or in trousers, who "feel for the people." In any event, these gentry sin far more than their minds, devoid of all instinct, are capable of realizing. Consequently, and much to their own amazement, the result of their social "efforts" is always nil, frequently, in fact, an indignant rebuff; though this, of course, is passed off as a proof of the people's ingratitude.

Such minds are most reluctant to realize that social endeavor has nothing in common with this sort of thing; that above all it can raise no claim to gratitude, since its function is not to distribute favors but to restore rights.

I was preserved from studying the social question in such a way. By drawing me within its sphere of suffering, it did not seem to invite me to "study," but to experience it in my own skin. It was none of its doing that the guinea pig came through the operation safe and sound.

This passage, so typical of *Mein Kampf*, begins by sketching the divide between Vienna's rich and poor, viewed as if from afar, from the viewpoint of an impersonal "you," which is to say in general terms, though not objectively; the multinational state has a "dubious magic" and the many nationalities held together by the centralizing power are a "melting pot." The preliminary conclusion is that no other city would seem to be as well suited for the study of social issues. However, such a study is possible only at first hand, and, moreover, only by someone "in the jaws of this murderous viper," in other words someone who has actually lived in poverty. What this says is: I was there, I know what I'm talking about, unlike almost everyone else. In this way Hitler lends ethos to his text, the same ethos as is evoked at intervals at the beginning of the book, and gradually, by way of meticulous insistence and the fundamental lack of other perspectives, that ethos becomes increasingly self-propelled, jettisoning "This is true because I say so, having seen it with my own eyes" in favor more simply of "This is true because I say so."

To what purpose does the text employ this legitimacy? It pursues no analysis, presenting only a sudden outburst against those who condescendingly "feel for the people" and who fail to realize that their false charity is degrading to its recipients. Hitler shares this same perspective with Marx, but in Hitler's case, judging by the sudden intensification of mood and the closeness of association of subject matter to writer, signaled by the use of the first-person pronoun, it would seem to have its source in his own experience, entangling moreover with more general misogyny. His conclusion, that genuine social activity consists not in handouts but in the reestablishment of a more just system, was likewise shared by Marx.

In Jack London's depiction of London's East End ghetto, life there is described as raw, brutal, and base, words like barbaric and primitive are employed, and to those who live such a life, at the very bottom of the world, in the most wretched need, men abandoned to drink, for instance, who batter their wives and neglect their children, or women who lose their babies to disease and sickness and who themselves cough and hack and shiver from cold and hunger, no crack of space exists between themselves and their misery to allow them a more generous perspective on their fellow human beings or to insist on maintaining some kind of human-centered mind-set, as Jack London is able to do as he wanders about and observes them as if they were a part of some abominable freak show. Humanity requires at least some minimum of material comforts. As Mackie Messer says in Bertolt Brecht's *Threepenny Opera*, "Erst kommt das Fressen, dann kommt die Moral" – first food, then morals. The same is true of human worth. For this is what happens in these vast slums, the value of human life, to those who live there as well as to those outside, diminishes. Thus, Jack London:

No more dreary spectacle can be found on this earth than the whole of the "awful East," with its Whitechapel, Hoxton, Spitalfields, Bethnal Green, and Wapping to the East India Docks. The color of life is gray and drab. Everything is helpless, hopeless, unrelieved, and dirty. Bathtubs are a thing totally unknown, as mythical as the ambrosia of the gods. The people themselves are dirty, while any attempt at cleanliness becomes howling farce, when it is not pitiful and tragic. Strange, vagrant odors come drifting along the greasy wind, and the rain, when it falls, is more like grease than water from heaven. The very cobblestones are scummed with grease.

Here lives a population as dull and unimaginative as its long gray miles of dingy brick. Religion has virtually passed it by, and a gross and stupid materialism reigns, fatal alike to the things of the spirit and the finer instincts of life.

It used to be the proud boast that every Englishman's home was his castle. But today it is an anachronism. The Ghetto folk have no homes. They do not know the significance and the sacredness of home life. Even the municipal dwellings, where live the better-class workers, are overcrowded barracks. They have no home life. The very language proves it. The father returning from work asks his child in the street where her mother is; and back the answer comes, "In the buildings."

A new race has sprung up, a street people. They pass their lives at work and in the streets. They have dens and lairs into which to crawl for sleeping purposes, and that is all. One cannot travesty the word by calling such dens and lairs "homes." The traditional silent and reserved Englishman has passed away. The sidewalk folk are noisy, voluble, high-strung, excitable — when they are yet young. As they grow older they become steeped and stupefied in beer. When they have nothing else to do, they ruminate as a cow ruminates. They are to be met with everywhere, standing on curbs and corners, and staring into vacancy. Watch one of them. He will stand there, motionless, for hours, and when you go away you will leave him still staring into vacancy. It is most absorbing. He has no money for beer, and his lair is only for sleeping purposes, so what else remains for him to do? He has already solved the mysteries of girl's love, and wife's love, and child's love, and found them delusions and shams, vain and fleeting as dew-drops, quick-vanishing before the ferocious facts of life.

Marx quotes from a report on living standards drawn up in 1863 by one Dr. Simon:

It must be remembered that privation of food is very reluctantly borne, and that as a rule great poorness of diet will only come when other privations have preceded it. Long before insufficiency of diet is a matter of hygienic concern, long before the physiologist would think of counting the grains of nitrogen and carbon which intervene between life and starvation, the household will have been utterly destitute of material comfort; clothing and fuel will have been even scantier than food — against inclemencies of weather there will have been no adequate protection — dwelling space will have been stinted to the degree in which overcrowding produces or increases disease; of household utensils and furniture there will have been scarcely any — even cleanliness will have been found costly or difficult, and if there still be self-respectful endeavors to maintain it, every such endeavor will represent additional pangs of hunger. The home, too, will be where shelter can be cheapest bought; in quarters where commonly there is least fruit of sanitary supervision, least drainage, least scavenging, least suppression of public nuisances, least or worst water supply, and, if in town, least light and air. Such are the sanitary dangers to which poverty is almost certainly exposed, when it is poverty enough to imply scantiness of food. And while the sum of them is of terrible magnitude against life, the mere scantiness of food is in itself of very serious moment ... These are painful reflections, especially when it is remembered that the poverty to which they advert is not the deserved poverty of idleness. In all cases it is the poverty of working populations. Indeed, as regards the indoor operatives, the work which obtains the scanty pittance of food is for the most part excessively prolonged. Yet evidently it is only in a qualified sense that the work can be deemed self-supporting ... And on a very large scale the nominal self-support can be only a circuit, longer or shorter, to pauperism.

The intimate connection between the pangs of hunger of the most industrious layers of the working class, and the extravagant consumption, coarse or refined, of the rich, for which capitalist accumulation is the basis, reveals itself only when the economic laws are known. It is otherwise with the "housing of the poor." Every unprejudiced observer sees that the greater the centralization of the means of production, the greater is the corresponding heaping together of the laborers, within a given space; that therefore the swifter the capitalistic accumulation, the more miserable are the dwellings of the working-people. "Improvements" of towns, accompanying the increase of wealth, by the demolition of badly built quarters, the erection of palaces for banks, warehouses, etc., the widening of streets for business traffic, for the carriages of luxury, and for the introduction of tramways, etc., drive away the poor into even worse and more crowded hiding places. On the other hand, every one knows that the dearness of dwellings is in inverse ratio to their excellence, and that the mines of misery are exploited by house speculators with more profit or less cost than ever were the mines of Potosí. The antagonistic character of capitalist accumulation, and therefore of the capitalistic relations of property generally, is here so evident, that even the official English reports on this subject teem with heterodox onslaughts on "property and its rights." With the development of industry, with the accumulation of capital, with the growth and "improvement" of towns, the evil makes such progress that the mere fear of contagious diseases which do not spare even "respectability," brought into existence from 1847 to 1864 no less than 10 Acts of Parliament on sanitation, and that the frightened bourgeois in some towns, as Liverpool, Glasgow, etc., took strenuous measures through their municipalities. Nevertheless Dr. Simon, in his report of 1865, says:

"Speaking generally, it may be said that the evils are uncontrolled in England."

And Hitler:

In a basement apartment, consisting of two stuffy rooms, dwells a worker's family of seven. Among the five children there is a boy of, let us assume, three years. This is the age in which the first impressions are made on the consciousness of the child. Talented persons retain traces of memory from this period down to advanced old age. The very narrowness and overcrowding of the room does not lead to favorable conditions. Quarreling and wrangling will very frequently arise as a result. In these circumstances, people do not live with one another, they press against one another. Every argument, even the most trifling, which in a spacious apartment can be reconciled by a mild segregation, thus solving itself, here leads to loathsome wrangling without end. Among the children, of course, this is still bearable; they always fight under such circumstances, and among themselves they quickly and thoroughly forget about it. But if this battle is carried on between the parents themselves, and almost every day in forms which for vulgarity often leave nothing to be desired, then, if only very gradually, the results of such visual instruction must ultimately become apparent in the children. The character they will inevitably assume if this mutual quarrel takes the form of brutal attacks of the father against the mother, of drunken beatings, is hard for anyone who does not know this milieu to imagine. At the age of six the pitiable little boy suspects the existence of things which can inspire even an adult with nothing but horror. Morally poisoned, physically undernourished, his poor little head full of lice, the young "citizen" goes off to public school. After a great struggle he may learn to read and write, but that is about all. His doing any homework is out of the question. On the contrary, the very mother and father, even in the presence of the children, talk about his teacher and school in terms which are not fit to be repeated, and are more inclined to curse the latter to their face than to take their little offspring across their knees and teach them some sense. All the other things that the little fellow hears at home do not tend to increase his respect for his dear fellow men. Nothing good remains of humanity, no institution remains unassailed; beginning with his teacher and up to the head of the government, whether it is a question of religion or of morality as such, of the state or society, it is all the same, everything is reviled in the most obscene terms and dragged into the filth of the basest possible outlook.

When at the age of fourteen the young man is discharged from school, it is hard to decide what is stronger in him: his incredible stupidity as far as any real knowledge and ability are concerned, or the corrosive insolence of his behavior, combined with an immorality, even at this age, which would make your hair stand on end.

What position can this man to whom even now hardly anything is holy, who, just as he has encountered no greatness, conversely suspects and knows all the sordidness of life, occupy in the life into which he is now preparing to emerge?

The three-year-old child has become a fifteen-year-old despiser of all authority. Thus far, aside from dirt and filth, this young man has seen nothing which might inspire him to any higher enthusiasm.

But only now does he enter the real university of this existence.

Now he begins the same life which all along his childhood years he has seen his father living. He hangs around the street corners and bars, coming home God knows when; and for a change now and then he beats the broken-down being which was once his mother, curses God and the world, and at length is convicted of some particular offense and sent to a house of correction.

There he receives his last polish.

And his dear bourgeois fellow men are utterly amazed at the lack of "national enthusiasm" in this young "citizen."

Day by day, in the theater and in the movies, in backstairs literature and the yellow press, they see the poison poured into the people by bucketfuls, and then they are amazed at the low "moral content," the "national indifference," of the masses of the people.

It seems unlikely Hitler came close to any such family in Vienna; at the time he was living outside history, in the sense that we have no eyewitness accounts of his life then, firstly in a room on his own for a year, then in the weeks and months of homelessnesss before his appearance at the flophouse, when it seems reasonable to assume he was sleeping rough in the parks rather than in some overcrowded basement lodging with a family he did not know. His description is an example, a concretization of something otherwise abstract, the decline of working-class youth in the face of social circumstances. Hitler provides many examples throughout *Mein Kampf*, though practically no narrative such as this, and certainly he never seems to empathize with his examples the way he does here, where moreover he appeals to the reader's sympathies in a way that seeems quite out of keeping with the tone of the book as a whole. There is also an element of identification.

Ian Kershaw suggests there might be a touch of autobiography here, writing:

> *A passage in* Mein Kampf, *in which Hitler ostensibly describes the conditions in a worker's family where the children have to witness drunken beatings of their mother by their father, may well have drawn in part on his own childhood experiences. What the legacy of all this was for the way Adolf's character developed must remain a matter for speculation. That its impact was profound is hard to doubt.*

If indeed he is giving vent to experiences from his own childhood here, as if under cover of the example's neutrality he somehow were able to write about himself, then it is the only instance that occurs.

Respect for human life need not necessarily be diminished by the baseness of what Hitler saw in Vienna, though this may certainly happen, and apparently did so in Hitler's case, even though he clearly states in *Mein Kampf* that it did not, emphasizing that the individual is without blame in his or her misery, which rather is brought about by a miserable system. But how does he express this?

> *Then, from all the misery and despair, from all the filth and outward degeneration, it was no longer human beings that emerged, but the deplorable results of deplorable laws; and the hardship of my own life, no easier than the others, preserved me from capitulating in tearful sentimentality to the degenerate products of this process of development.*

This is a treacherous statement, typical not only of Hitler but of the times. By saying it is not the fault of the individual that he or she has become brutalized, but of the system within which the individual exists, one thereby expresses a humanistic attitude by which it is emphasized that it is the conditions under which the people live that are unfit and wretched, rather than people themselves. However, one consequence of this is that the individual is thereby seen to be a manifestation of class, and if class is the important category here, then the life of the individual diminishes in value, being seen in relation to the common goal. Not the face or the name, but the mass and the number. The reduction or absorption of the individual by the mass was indeed a new phenomenon, a direct and highly perceptible result of industrialization and urbanization: hordes of poor, in which the individual was an expression not of itself but its poverty; droves of workers filing in and out of factory gates in the mornings and evenings; armies of protesters taking to the streets, converging into surging crowds marching on the squares and parks. Baudelaire was fascinated by the city's rivers of people in which the dandy so to speak bathed, Chaplin juxtaposes herded sheep with workers milling toward a factory in *Modern Times*, and Hamsun, primarily and in everything the individualist and therefore never one to hold the worker in contempt, only the mass in which the worker himself was everyone and no one, the rabble, had his protagonist in the 1920s, August, come to a grisly end, swept under by a tide of sheep. A recurring motif in the literature of the Weimar Republic was the human mass, and a frequently employed perspective was that of remoteness, in which the human world seemed to consist of busy swarms of insects or great flocks of teeming animals. The reduction of the human that such a perspective entailed was not unambiguous, since at this time, perhaps more than any other, the power of the masses and the potential they held for change began to be understood.

Another consequence of the mass perspective is that it propels the human in the direction of biology, the biological human.

Jack London's urban exploration of 1903 construed man as a cow, and in describing how the ghetto is constantly drained of its best stock he uses for his metaphor the image of blood being drawn from the body. This was a common way of thinking, such metaphors were in frequent usage, no one found them to be suspect, no one was anxious about their use, as yet they were unladen with cruelty, still neutral in a way. The fact that blood became the great symbol of the national socialist movement has to do with man as a mass as well as with man as biology, for blood is the same for all of us, the same blood in the rich as in the poor, in the educated as in the uneducated, and in its being bound up with the people, *das Volk*, whose institutional expression was the nation-state, blood moreover separated out those who did not belong, according to the racial theory of the day, which again was in no way frowned upon, issuing as it did from those most elevated seats of learning, the universities.

Hitler never formulated any ideological manifesto apart from what may be gleaned from the various reasonings, assertions, and analyses that go to make up *Mein Kampf*, and which in actual fact cannot be extracted from it without turning them into something else, for the most unusual aspect of the book is that it is so characterized by impulsive notions, so inextricably bound up with the temperament of its author and with its time by virtue of the psychology that is transported backward and forward throughout its pages, and also so intent on building up a persona by way of this peculiar plainsong, as we might call it, of indignation, self-assertion, and obdurate resentment, that any superstructure would ring false, so no, there is no superstructure here, nor any kind of consolidated whole, the sheer centrifugal force of pettiness and rhetorical crudeness being so strong as to prevent this.

Language, more so than the image, is intimately connected with the social environment, and while the Nazis' meticulous orchestrations were able to mobilize the seductive power that lies in the mythological and in the past, and while they managed to make tangible the idea of the nation as rendering each and every individual significant, Hitler's own language is stuck in prosaic experience, which is to say the hum and sputter of the linguistic reality that surrounded him in Vienna, where for instance anti-Jewish sentiment was rife in the press, and where the air was thick with political agitation and propaganda as if the great political issues of the day had been taken out into the streets and deprived of any Olympian perspective, construed there as manifestations of the own, the local, the private: What are the Czechs doing here? What are the Jews doing here? The housing situation is critical, poverty rampant, inflation spiraling. There are mass protests and riots, windows and streetlights are smashed, trams and motor cars vandalized, troops are deployed, violence spreads through the workers' districts. What will happen if a revolution comes? The violence escalates, tangibly at street level, in clashes between police and protesters, police and homeless, police and the poor, and within families, but also at the structural level, in the shape of a societal order that looks after the well-to-do and completely ignores everyone else. Parliament has ceased to function and is in a state of near-dissolution; with its myriad of political parties from the disparate countries and cultures of the Dual Monarchy it can barely muster a quorum, representatives fighting for attention with whistles, children's trumpets, and rattles, Hamann writes, as indeed Hitler himself witnessed during his first year in Vienna, when he would often drag Kubizek along with him to spend entire days in the parliament, barely able to contain his excitement, according to his friend. Hitler immerses himself in political reading, mostly newspapers, pamphlets, and journals, and it is in the secondary, popularized form he becomes familiar with the works of some of the great and most controversial thinkers of the age, such as Darwin, Nietzsche, Chamberlain, and Schopenhauer, so Hamann tells us. Inherent in the zeitgeist was dwindling esteem for academia and scientific knowledge, while idiosyncratic and autodidactic thinkers seething with distrust of the establishment flourished, and what we know of Hitler's preferences at the time, of which he later offers glimpses, points, according to Hamann, almost exclusively in the direction of such unorthodox, unscientific renegade figures. So in the year he lived alone in his room, socializing with not a soul, we can assume theirs were the works he read, and without academic or even human context of any sort everything was then down to his own judgment and instinct, and this lack of opportunity for correction was perhaps the most characteristic aspect of his private world of thought. What few books he might have owned must have been sold when his money ran out, because when Hanisch encounters him in Meidling in December 1909 he owns nothing but the clothes on his back.

That evening, when after a year and a half hidden from the light of history he once more steps into it by joining the line outside a flophouse two and a half hours on foot from the city center, thereby to have his name registered in the police archive, tired, cold, and hungry, in a shabby purple suit, pale and thin, twenty years old, with eyes that in Kubizek's words dominated his features with the piercing look Kubizek's mother found almost frightening, he is not the all of everyone, nor is he the nothing of no one, for though he is unimportant in the eyes of others, to all intents and purposes socially nonexistent, there is no reason to believe that the grandiosity of his self-image, this boundless belief in his own abilities, has been entirely lost. Weakened it must surely have been, however, for this is the nadir of his life, quite intolerable for a young man of Hitler's self-confidence and pride, yet in the picture Hanisch paints of him he appears meek and without resistance.

The hostel plays an important social role, a source of information about places to keep warm in the day and sleep at night, favorable begging pitches and possible openings as to a chance of work. To Hitler, Hanisch became a kind of helper; they began to hang out together. In the daytime they would look for work, in the evenings they bedded down in one of the establishments that existed, a night shelter in Edberg, for instance, and another in Favoriten, perhaps then to return to Meidling again. According to

Hanisch Hitler was unsuited to physical labor; once, some men were needed for ditch digging, but Hanisch advised him against it, realizing it would be too much for him. Instead, Hitler hung around the railway station offering to carry luggage for people, or, when winter came, he stood in line to shovel snow, though without a winter coat, freezing and coughing miserably – he did this only a few times, Hanisch reports. So helpless and frail was he that he was even considered poor compared to the other destitutes who at least could labor for a day's wages. Hitler "thought of all sorts of jobs, but he was much too weak for hard physical work."

This is in stark contrast to Hitler's own account of this period in *Mein Kampf*.

> *The actual business of finding work was, as a rule, not hard for me, since I was not a skilled craftsman, but was obliged to seek my daily bread as a so-called helper and sometimes as a casual laborer.*
>
> *I adopted the attitude of all those who shake the dust of Europe from their feet with the irrevocable intention of founding a new existence in the New World and conquering a new home. Released from all the old, paralyzing ideas of profession and position, environment and tradition, they snatch at every livelihood that offers itself, grasp at every sort of work, progressing step-by-step to the realization that honest labor, no matter of what sort, disgraces no one. I, too, was determined to leap into this new world, with both feet, and fight my way through.*
>
> *I soon learned that there was always some kind of work to be had, but equally soon I found out how easy it was to lose it.*
>
> *The uncertainty of earning my daily bread soon seemed to me one of the darkest sides of my new life.*

This may not be untrue, but knowing that he earned money carrying luggage at the railway station and shoveling snow, a young man who in his adult life so far has set his sights exclusively on becoming an artist, but has failed and withdrawn from all human company, tormented and grossly humiliated, a loser in the eyes of all others, the comparison with the pioneers in America, who worked the soil and made fields and built houses, seems eccentric to say the least. But this is what *Mein Kampf* is like: Hitler construes his poverty in words that fall sorely short of its actual consequences, yet rather than denying it he instead turns it into something immensely powerful and productive, weaving it into a political viewpoint that finds much of its force in, and indeed practically bases itself on, this distortion of his life.

A person such as this, in whom a pervasive sense of inner nobility buffers all outer abjection, was of course the main character in Knut Hamsun's novel *Hunger*, published seventeen years before Hitler's own wretchedness in Vienna. Like Hitler, Hamsun's character exists from hand to mouth in a city where he knows no one, has no friends, no job or income of any sort other than the money he occasionally earns writing a piece for a newspaper. He harbors the ambition of becoming a writer, the idea of which is the only thing that keeps him going. Applying for work at a fire station he is met with rejection, and subsequently makes no further effort to find a job, instead spending his days drifting about the streets, trying to write, trying to think, moving to increasingly shabbier lodgings, disgusted by the poverty that surrounds him. He never mentions the place he grew up, his childhood or youth, his parents, brothers, or sisters, it is as if they do not exist. He is himself only, and though in the profoundest material need, he never once doubts himself.

Hitler possessed the same self-belief and some measure of the same feverish imagination; at the hostel in Meidling he is reported by Hanisch to have claimed that science would soon eliminate the force of gravity from objects, allowing even the heaviest iron blocks to be moved from place to place without difficulty, and that people would in future nourish themselves with pills alone.

His mode of survival, too, is highly reminiscent of Hamsun's hero; not short pieces in the newspapers, but small paintings he sells in inns and drinking establishments.

Selling paintings was Hanisch's idea. Hitler lied and told him he had attended the Academy. Hanisch suggested he paint to earn a living. Hitler buys the necessaries and starts work; since the shelters are overcrowded he sits painting at cafés while Hanisch hawks the canvases around. They do brisk business and before long can move into a new, permanent men's hostel a cut above the ones for the very poorest; here they pay a modest sum each week for a small private cubicle with a bed and a daily meal. The hostel is big, housing some five hundred residents, for some it's a permanent home, though for most a temporary measure. About 70 percent of the residents are under the age of thirty-five. Seventy percent are workers and tradesmen, the remainder coachmen, shop assistants, waiters, gardeners, unskilled men, and unemployed, with a smattering of fallen aristocrats, unsuccessful artists, divorcés and bankrupts, Hamann writes. The ethnic backgrounds represented were quite as diverse. Hitler lived for three years in this environment. He had his own cubicle, where he could relax between the hours of eight in the evening and nine in the morning. There was a dining room and two reading rooms, one for smokers, one for nonsmokers. There were newspapers and a small library for the use of the residents, where Hitler according to Hanisch spent most of his time. He would read the papers in the mornings, paint during the day, and read in the evenings, provided he was not attending one of the many public debates and discussions that still went on all around the city, where the political challenges were so great and so conspicuous. Selling his canvases meant Hitler and Hanisch made just enough money to pay for rent and food, though not enough for clothes, and by Hanisch's account Hitler kept his coat on indoors for a period, having a hole in the seat of his trousers and no shirt to cover it. To make ends meet Hitler needed to paint a picture a day. Hanisch kept him to the grindstone, Hitler eventually becoming so annoyed with him that after a year and a half, in June 1910, he turned to another occupant, Josef Neumann, and asked him to take over the sale of his pictures. Hitler had previously disappeared from the hostel for a whole week in the company of Neumann without informing Hanisch and was obviously quite friendly with him. Liljegren writes that they toured the art galleries together.

Eleven years Hitler's senior, Neumann was, moreover, a Jew, so if Hitler did hold any anti-Semitic views at this stage they most certainly cannot have featured as prominently in his mind as they would later. Nothing suggests that he did. His political views were, however, nationalistic, he was against the Social Democrats, and anti-Marxist, and according to Hanisch held the workers in low esteem, saying repeatedly that they were "an indolent mass that cared about nothing but eating, drinking, and women," in other words possessing no sense of life's finer cultural values, interested only in its material level. Yet one must assume Hitler's own self-image at this time to have been somewhat muddled; certainly he painted, in the region of seven or eight hundred pictures during the period, but there is little reason to believe he saw any prestige at all in what was entirely a matter of earning money for his survival; in 1939 he would prohibit their continued sale, presumably embarrassed and unpleasantly affected by their circulation.

But if he was not an artist, not an architect, not a worker, and not a layabout, what was he then? Did he consider this to be a gap, an interlude while waiting for better times? And what did he expect such times to bring?

What separates Hamsun's young alter ego in *Hunger* from Hitler is that Hamsun would later write the book he imagined he would and break through as a writer, whereas in Hitler's case nothing happens. Why not? For want of talent? For want of drive? Was he not strong enough to cope with the lack of artistic environment his marginalization entailed? Did he give up and allow himself to drift aimlessly wherever his fortunes might take him?

His youthful reveries about art were perhaps more to do with the life of the artist than with art as such; in contrast to the civil servant, the artist's life is an expression of the self, a person is an artist by virtue of being that self, with that particular talent, and such a thought must surely have appealed to him. He saw no need to work for the sake of achievement, it was sufficient simply to be the person he was. Only one figure could transcend the rigid framework of bourgeois culture and elevate himself above it, one figure of whom this moreover was expected, and that figure was the genius. The one against the mass's many. This was an idea born of the understanding that the one should manage the culture of the many, and this by its idealization, by evoking the sense of there being something the many could reach out and long for, by distilling the insights of the many into one: such is our life in this world. This is the mandate of Goethe and Wagner. What happened in art at the end of the nineteenth century was that this figure, the artist genius, altered character. The one no longer represented the all, but went against them. An example is Munch. He went beyond the social world – not positively, but negatively. He was met with scorn and disdain. To do this, to not be a part of the all but to express his particular self, which so deviated from the accepted mainstream, he had to either go against it, which required enormous strength, or be unattached to it. In Munch's case, as in the case of many artists, he chose to be unattached, living for long periods of his life within himself, having little or no contact with family and practically no friends. Only then could he go beyond, for Munch was not Hans Jæger, and lacked his strength and will. Jæger lived in the social world, cavorted with the social world, went to the wall in the social world. Munch turned away, turned in, painted. Such solitude and lack of social attachment was not dissimilar to the way Hitler was living during this period of his life, but in Hitler's case this transgression of the bourgeois was only social in nature, not artistic. On the contrary, his æsthetic was identical with that of bourgeois culture, sharing with it the imperative that art should be splendid, beautiful, ideal.

The foremost shaper of such a conception of art, to many still so obvious as to resemble a law, was perhaps G. E. Lessing, who put the idea into words in his *Laocoon*, originally published in 1766, in which he writes of the difference between ugliness and beauty in art. The ugly form "wounds our sight, offends our sense of order and harmony, and excites aversion without regard to the actual existence of the object in which we perceive it." Lessing divides art into two: imitative art, which seeks to reproduce reality the way it is, and art that strives for beauty. "Painting as imitative skill can express ugliness; painting as a fine art will not express it. In the former capacity its sphere extends over all visible objects; in the latter it confines itself to those which produce agreeable impressions." To Lessing's mind, ugliness in art was a threat also to order and harmony in society as a whole, and he wished to forbid representation of ugliness altogether in favor exclusively of art that presented beauty. "The object of art . . . is pleasure, and pleasure is not indispensable. What kind and what degree of pleasure shall be permitted may justly depend on the law-giver."

With the advent of realism in the middle of the nineteenth century, which represented ugliness as well as beauty, the hideous as well as the sublime, Lessing's view of art fell into decline, though no more so than that the bourgeoisie reacted with repugnance and rage at the direction in which painting was going at the turn of the century, which they believed had nothing to do with art, since it did not elevate or make agreeable, but was the expression merely of the sick mind of the artist.

Hitler, who wished to transcend the bourgeois by following the path of genius, almost brims over with the same ideas:

Thus, the saddest thing about the state of our whole culture of the pre-War period was not only the total impotence of artistic and cultural creative power in general, but the hatred with which the memory of the greater past was besmirched and effaced. In nearly all fields of art, especially in the theater and literature, we began around the turn of the century to produce less that was new and significant, but to disparage the best of the old work and represent it as inferior and

surpassed; as though this epoch of the most humiliating inferiority
could surpass anything at all. And from this effort to remove the past
from the eyes of the present, the evil intent of the apostles of the future
could clearly and distinctly be seen. By this it should have been recog-
nized that these were no new, even if false, cultural conceptions, but
a process of destroying all culture, paving the way for a stultifica-
tion of healthy artistic feeling: the spiritual preparation of political
Bolshevism. For if the age of Pericles seems embodied in the Parthe-
non, the Bolshevistic present is embodied in a cubist monstrosity.

In 1907 and 1908, when Hitler applied for admission to the Academy, painting was exploring its forms of expression in hitherto
unprecedented ways, as for instance in the Expressionism of
Munch, Kirchner, and Nolde, the Fauvism of Matisse, Derain,
and Vlaminck, the Cubism of Braque and Picasso, the radical
simplification and nascent abstractions of Burliuk and Kandin-
sky, the Primitivism of Jawlensky, to mention but a few examples
of the hugely radical currents that ran through European culture of
the day, Vienna being one if its most important cities.

The question that arises is of the kind of relationship that exists between the contemporary age and its art, whether art is simply a weather vane occupation, a fashionable way of life whose
purpose is to do what everyone else is doing, though not "everyone else" in the sense of anyone at all, but a defining elite, the
happy few, the standard-bearers of the arts, those on everyone's
lips in all the cafés, culture then being a locus of ingratiation?

Hitler looked on these currents as a sign of decay; the latest
thing, the new, the next has nothing to do with art in Hitler's
eyes, to him art is the expression of something everlasting and
timeless. He shows no understanding of how inextricably the everlasting and the timeless in art is bound up with the contemporary and the social, or how crucial that dynamic, between what
is living and what is dead, is to its power of expression and to its
significance, and the reasons for this failure to comprehend are
presumably the same ones as make it impossible for him to con-

ceal the low and small-minded aspects of his person in his writing, which is to say a poorly developed sense of form, according to which content and the feelings it gives rise to are the only things of real importance.

But his failure as an artist is not down to being out of touch with the zeitgeist. That none of these currents is present in Hitler's pictures is hardly surprising and tells us little else about him other than that he was the product of the lower middle class and excluded from what was happening at the vortex of the culture, or else he excluded himself, in that he chose to adhere so firmly to the preferences of his class, these not yet having been deemed void nor necessarily entirely forsaken; the Academy to which he sought entrance, held in such great esteem, guarded the same neoclassicist and realistic aesthetic that formed the basis of his own painting. That he was not accepted to study there would seem more due to the lack of expressive force in his painting, the almost exclusively decorative nature of his canvases, which possess no element of self. On the other hand he was only seventeen years old when he applied there, and only a couple of years older when he was painting his other pictures. A relevant comparison could be Hamsun's early attempts at the novel, for instance, *Bjørger*, which in the same kind of way lacks originality and is without soul, an image of what its author saw to be literature, where the idea of the literary stands between himself and the world, much as the way Hitler's idea of what art was and should be stood between him and what he painted. The presence of such an idea is destructive enough in itself, but in Hitler's and Hamsun's cases its destructive thrust was compounded by its provincial and homely nature. Their social points of departure were not dissimilar, though Hamsun was from more humble circumstances by far, his parents near destitute, with no education, and he himself, in contrast to Hitler, had not even finished school. Hamsun taught himself everything, Hitler did too, but whereas Hitler gave up painting, Hamsun stuck at his writing, eventually finding success as a novelist. What Hitler lacked as a painter and Hamsun gained for himself as a writer was intimacy with the form of his art. Hitler's weakness as a painter was that he found no way of expressing his own inner being, or else lacked the will to address it, and perhaps this was the reason he gave up and settled for painting as a simple means of making ends meet.

But what actually was his own inner being?

The writer Ernst Jünger, Hitler's senior by ten years, who came from a considerably more elevated social background, and who in the interwar years came out on the extreme antiliberal and antidemocratic right, published a number of essays in the Nazi Party journal, writing as follows in 1929:

> *And I also know that my basic experience, what finds expression through life's events, is the typical experience of my generation, a variation on the motif of the times, an exotic species perhaps, but one that still displays the characteristics of the genus.*

Reading biographies of the period, patterns emerge, certain recurrent connections and types, perhaps this is what Jünger means by "a variation on the motif of the times," for the very structure of society and the views by which it is characterized set up spaces that are astonishingly alike, and those who inhabit them go through the same experiences, which become typical for them. Hitler was not the only person in the Habsburg Empire with an authoritarian father and a loving mother, with siblings who perished and dreams of becoming a metropolitan artist. No, the age was full of them. An example is Alfred Kubin, born in 1877, twelve years before Hitler, who grew up in a small town in Austria called Zell am See. He, too, had an authoritarian father he hated, a loving mother who died, and he, too, left for the city as a young man in order to become an artist.

The many resemblances between Hitler's and Kubin's biographies might lead us to wonder if similarity of background and experience begets similarity of mind, whether what each on his own considers and understands to be unique, particular failures

and shortcomings, longings and urges, experiences and preferences, hopes and fears, might not in fact merely be variations on
a common theme, in Jünger's sense, arising out of an age and a
place and a class. Not that Hitler and Kubin were alike in temperament or talent or character, but the feelings that streamed
through them, the things they held back or allowed themselves
to show, the things they despised and the things by which they
were attracted, looked to be, or in certain cases perhaps even were,
the same. It is tempting to entertain the thought in this instance,
since the pictures Kubin painted as a young man are so full of
death and fear of women and possess such remoteness from the
human aspects of what they depict, their figures being seen as biological entities, lending them a repugnant, distasteful quality, as
if he thereby were expressing directly what Hitler suppresses and
which with all his might he tries to eschew.

Hitler wishes to elevate the world, Kubin describes it the way
it is, which is to say the way he perceives it, sunken into hell, as
in his drawing of a powerful woman standing naked with both
hands raised in the air, sprinkling something onto the ground;
her belly is large, grotesquely shaped, perhaps she is pregnant, and
on the ground about her feet are the severed heads of men, some
with mouths gaping. She is Mother Earth.

Another drawing depicts a huge vulva into which a tiny man
dives from the woman's knee, which from his perspective is as tall
as a mountain. There are others, too, of masses on their way to hell,
seen from such distance that nothing of any individuality may be
discerned, and there are drawings of death in the shape of a great
skeleton leaning over a house and sprinkling something on it from
a pouch, the title being *Epidemic*. Elsewhere, an ape holds a
woman tightly from behind and paws at her genitals, there are
men with the heads of birds, a vast congregation of helmeted soldiers gathered beneath the towering sculpture of an ox, chopped-
up animal carcasses, severed heads on stakes, the state depicted
as a trundling machine in a field, suicides, dogs frothing at the
mouth, a man with his head between a woman's legs, she in a coffin

and thin as a skeleton, another is an actual skeleton, though with a pregnant belly rising like the top of an egg. These are fin de siècle pictures, yet they are filled with a horror of the body, with an extravagance and a mood of man as mass that distinguishes them radically from fin de siècle elsewhere, in other countries; Kubin would have been unthinkable in England, for instance, and also in America, and while some of his pictures come close to the French pastelist Odilon Redon, their mood is nonetheless radically different, finding their like only in other areas of German Expressionism of the day, with the exception of some of Goya's darkest and most apocalyptic drawings, in which Kubin most likely found inspiration.

Kubin also left his mark on literature, publishing a single novel, *The Other Side*, in 1908. The novel tells of an imaginary realm, a city called Pearl, inhabited by some sixty-five thousand souls, located deep in eastern Uzbekistan, separated from the rest of the world by a vast wall and governed by a godlike figure by the name of Patera. The city's inhabitants have come from all corners of the world, many from sanatoriums and health resorts, particularly sensitive individuals full of mad ideas, hyperreligious, obsessed with reading or gambling, neurasthenics and hysterics; to all intents and purposes homeless, these people have entered into the world of the imagination, of which the city is a physical, tangible manifestation. But the presence of Patera, who rules with an iron fist, makes this dream kingdom more of a sinister underworld, a kingdom of the dead devoid of all hope rather than a haven for the escapist.

Kubin wrote his novel following the death of his father, and the father's presence in the name – Patera so closely resembling *pater* – and the omnipotence of that figure, while remaining so elusive, is of course an image of paternal authority. It is not surprising that Kafka held Kubin in high esteem and was influenced by his work; the dreamlike otherworldliness of his universe, the impenetrability of bureaucractic process, its incessant deferments and adjournments, so vague and slippery and unassailable, and the authority of the father figure, are of course all important themes in Kafka.

Kafka was six years younger than Kubin and six years older than Hitler, but Prague belonged within the same empire, and as a native speaker of German Kafka related to the same culture as both Kubin and Hitler. He refers to Kubin several times in his diaries. On September 26, 1911, for instance, he writes of Kubin's meeting with Hamsun.

> *The artist Kubin recommends Regulin as a laxative, a powdered seaweed that swells up in the bowels, shakes them up, is thus effective mechanically in contrast to the unhealthy chemical effect of other laxatives which just tear through the excrement and leave it hanging on the walls of the bowels. He met Hamsun at Langen. He (Hamsun) grins mockingly for no reason. During the conversation, without interrupting it, he put one foot on his knee, took a large pair of scissors from the table, and trimmed the frayed edges of his trousers. Shabbily dressed, with one or so rather expensive details, his tie, for example. Stories about an artist's pension in Munich where painters and veterinaries lived (the latters's school was in the neighborhood) and where they acted in such a debauched way that the windows of the house across the way, from which a good view could be had, were rented out. In order to satisfy these spectators, one of the residents in the pension would sometimes jump up on the windowsill in the posture of a monkey and spoon his soup out of the pot. A manufacturer of fraudulent antiques who got the worn effect by means of buckshot and who said of a table: "Now we must drink coffee on it three more times, then it can be shipped off to the Innsbruck Museum." Kubin himself: very strong, but somewhat monotonous facial expression, he describes the most varied things with the same movement of muscles. Looks different in age, size, and strength according to whether he is sitting, standing, wearing just a suit, or an overcoat.*

Kafka read both Kubin and Hamsun, who met each other in Munich in the company of Hamsun's publisher Langen, probably in

1896. Kubin met Jünger and corresponded with him for a decade, while Hamsun met Hitler in 1943, penning his infamous obituary of him in May 1945. Of these figures, Hamsun hailed from the lowest social rank and from the very periphery of Europe, and belonged moreover to the previous generation, whereas of the others, all of whom were of the same generation and belonged to the same language area, Hitler was from the lowest social rank, with Kubin next above him, then Kafka, then Jünger, who as the son of a factory owner hailed from society's upper echelons. When it came to that generation's overriding experience, the First World War, Hitler and Jünger had served at the front in the German army, Hitler as a corporal and orderly, Jünger as a lieutenant in the infantry, whereas Kafka and Kubin were both exempt from service. When the Nazis were elected into the Reichstag, Hitler offered Jünger a seat in the parliament, which he declined. Hitler, Jünger, Kubin, and Hamsun were right-wing radicals, a fact that influenced their writings to various degrees, whereas Kafka kept himself well out of politics, well out of the sphere of the ideological, this being obvious in his diaries, which reveal him to be as near-dissolved in the trivialities of the quotidian as to quote Kubin's reference to "laxatives which just tear through the excrement and leave it hanging on the walls of the bowels," something neither Hitler, Jünger, Kubin, nor Hamsun could ever have put to paper. That ease within unease, the proximity to his own life in its truest nature, from where everything, even the most imaginative of events, issues, makes his writings much more valid beyond his time than both Jünger's and Kubin's, though perhaps not Hamsun's, whom he admired. In character and temperament Hitler and Hamsun were not unlike each other, and are similar particularly in their being self-made and in the grandiosity of their self-images, though Hamsun, who rose from quite impossible beginnings, was a much more sympathetic social being and an incomparably greater artistic talent. When he met Hitler, a couple of years before the latter's downfall, he saw him as his equal and treated him as any other person he respected, without trepidation or fear, which to Hitler was an affront, only Göring was permitted to challenge him and never without being subjected to his wrath, albeit always forgiven, and Hitler was enraged by the time Hamsun left. Hamsun was from the generation of Hitler's father and was quite as stubborn and authoritarian, so it is hardly odd that Hitler should become so enraged. Kafka, Hitler, and Kubin all struggled with the authority of their fathers, they were loners, tormented to a greater or lesser extent by the fear of contact and, each in his own way, by inhibitions relating to women. Moreover, for all their individuality, all three belonged to the same cultural type. Psychology is also epochal, the mind, too, has its directions of style, which change through the years.

Hitler was a resident of the Vienna hostel for three years. That he stayed there so long does not mean he found it pleasant; the moment he reached the age of twenty-four and received the final installment of his father's inheritance he went into town, bought himself new clothes, collected his scant possessions, and boarded a train for Munich. The resoluteness of his actions would seem to indicate that he had considered the matter for some time and decided that as soon as he got the money he would leave the city which he would gradually come to despise as if it were the very source of his ill fortune. Traveling with him on the train, which he presumably hoped was going to take him to a new and more prosperous life in the country he loved, at the same time as allowing him to avoid an imminent call-up to the Austrian army, was an acquaintance from the hostel, Rudolf Häusler, a nineteen-year-old who shared Hitler's interest in art, a kind of Kubizek Junior he could lecture and impress, and whose parents, which is to say his mother, took a liking to him. They rented a room together in Munich, in the house of the Popp family, where Hitler registered as an "architectural painter."

There he carried on the life he had lived in Vienna: as soon as his inheritance was spent he began to paint again, wandering the beer halls in the evenings to sell his canvases. Häusler moved out after a few months, leaving Hitler to a life on his own; on the occasions he was invited to supper with the Popp family he declined. In Toland's account, Frau Popp found him an "Austrian charmer," though something of an enigma too: "You couldn't tell what he was thinking," she would later state. Nor could she recall Hitler ever receiving visitors in his room. He would paint in the daytime and read at nights. Frau Popp asked him once what his books had to do with painting, to which he replied, "Dear Frau Popp, does anyone know what is and what isn't likely to be of use to him in life?"

He lived like this for a year in Munich and then the war broke out. Hitler joined up the same day and was sent to the trenches on the French front, where he would remain for four years.

It changed everything.

One of the most famous images of Hitler is from those same days in the summer of 1914. He is in the midst of a great crowd on Munich's Odeonsplatz, beaming a huge smile, one of thousands who have gathered there following the declaration of war on August 2, his face recognized and enlarged in the 1930s after he became Reich chancellor of Germany, but at the time utterly anonymous. A young man wearing a white shirt and dark suit, lifting his hat in the air, hair parted at the side, cheekbones pronounced, sporting a thick black moustache, eyes plainly gleaming with elation. It is a very suggestive photograph, for he is merely one of the crowd, a face among thousands, a fate among thousands, full of the collective zeal that swept through the cities, towns, and villages of Europe in that summer of 1914. To himself, naturally, he was everything, immersed in his life and destiny, a twenty-five-year-old semi-artist with no family and no friends, living in Munich with no direction but with an inner fire now ignited, fed by the fuel of high politics which had so interested him since early youth and by the declaration of war that so unexpectedly provides him and every other member of his generation with the opportunity to act in accordance with the ideals and dreams they have felt so fiercely from as far back as childhood and which bourgeois society, centered as it was around preservation and security, business and commerce, had until then denied them.

The European summer of 1914 was exceptionally balmy, an area of high pressure lingering over the continent for months. Under blue skies and a blazing sun the forests lay "dark and profuse in their tender green," writes Stefan Zweig, who found himself in the small town of Baden outside Vienna when news of the assassination of Archduke Franz Ferdinand of Austria filtered through. The impression he gives is of carefree abandon. What the war that now lies ahead will bring, no one yet knows, and even if they did, even if they had sensed that it would proceed with such destructive force as to wipe out almost an entire generation of European men, the darkness in which the future lay shrouded would not have endured more than fleetingly in the lethargic, time-steeped tranquillity that emanated from all things: the leafy trees that lined the rivers, the undulating green fields, the cool brick of the village churches, whose lazy bells laid their acoustic cloaks over the old houses, the way Marcel Proust describes life in the French countryside in a book that came out the year before. Ruminating cattle and sheep, horse-drawn carts, the smoke of steam locomotives billowing into the sky. The smell of warm earth and warm grass, the tart, dry taste of cold white wine or the bitter-sweet of cool ale sipped under the parasols of a hotel patio or in the shade of a leafy tree at the side of a road. The dust of the road, the dark currents of the river that sweeps under the bridge, the silvery glimpses of darting fish. The way the summer connects itself to all previous summers, the body and weight of repetition exuded by the landscape, its structures and people in the social domain, making any radical upheaval so hard if not impossible to imagine, though it lies but weeks ahead.

Stefan Zweig leaves Baden and travels to Le Coq, a small seaside resort on the Belgian North Sea coast. People are just as carefree there, he writes; they doze on the beach and soak up the sun, they bathe in the sea, the children fly kites, young people dance on the dikes in the evenings. He moves on to visit a friend, the painter Verhaeren, tension mounts, the threat of war ever growing.

> *At once an icy wind of fear blew over the beach and swept it bare. People by the thousands left the hotels and stormed the trains, and even the most optimistic began to pack their bags with speed.*

Austria declares war on Serbia, Zweig is on the last train into Germany. On the German side of the border the train suddenly comes to a halt in the darkness. The edgy passengers peer through the windows and see cargo trains passing one after another; beneath the tarpaulins they glimpse the ominous outlines of cannon. Zweig goes on:

> *The next morning I was in Austria. In every station placards had been put up announcing general mobilization. The trains were filled with fresh recruits, banners were flying, music sounded, and in Vienna I found the entire city in a tumult. The first shock at the news of war – the war that no one, people or government had wanted – the war which had slipped, much against their will, out of the clumsy hands of the diplomats who had been bluffing and toying with it, had suddenly been transformed into enthusiasm. There were parades in the street, flags, ribbons, and music burst forth everywhere, young recruits were marching triumpantly, their faces lighting up at the cheering – they, the John Does and Richard Roes who usually go unnoticed and uncelebrated.*
>
> *And to be truthful, I must acknowledge that there was a majestic, rapturous, and even seductive something in this first outbreak of the people from which one could escape only with difficulty. And in spite of all my hatred and aversion for war, I should not like to have missed the memory of those first days. As never before, thousands and hundreds of thousands felt what they should have felt in peacetime, that they belonged together.*

That Zweig, a pacifist all his life, would not have wanted to miss the sense of togetherness that pervaded those first days of August 1914 is telling indeed of the force with which the war swept through the land. Adolf Hitler was not the only one to lift his hat in joy, eyes gleaming, when the declaration came. The enthusiasm was all over Europe, the war was welcomed and celebrated by almost all. The Swedish historian of ideas Svante Nordin, who in his book *The Philosophers' War* examines the stance of the intellectual community in respect to the war and its outbreak, notes Sigmund Freud's words of July 26 in Vienna: ". . . for the first time for thirty years I feel myself an Austrian and feel like giving this not very hopeful Empire another chance. Morale everywhere is excellent."

On July 27, the British ambassador in Vienna reported: "This country has gone wild at the prospect of war with Serbia, and its postponement or prevention would undoubtedly be a great disappointment."

The poet Rainer Maria Rilke, ten years older than Hitler, also a native of Austria-Hungary, applauded the war's outbreak:

> *For the first time I see you rising,*
> *hearsaid, remote, incredible War God*

The otherwise levelheaded and unsentimental Thomas Mann, fourteen years Hitler's senior, wrote the following of those same days some six months later:

> *War! It was purification, liberation that we experienced, and an enormous hope . . . It set the hearts of poets aflame . . . How should the artist, the soldier in the artist, not have praised God for the collapse of a world of peace that he had his fill, so completely his fill of?*

Kafka, too, got carried away. Though on the day of the war's outbreak his diary notes matter-of-factly, "Germany has declared war on Russia. Swimming in the afternoon," four days later he writes,

"I discover in myself nothing but pettiness, indecision, envy, and hatred against those who are fighting and whom I passionately wish everything ill," then, in a letter to Felice seven months later, "In addition, I mostly suffer from the war because I myself am taking no part."

Of course, not everyone was as enthusiastic about the war. Kafka's friend Max Brod, five years Hitler's senior, reflecting on the war's outbreak, despaired at the apolitical indifference that had allowed it to catch them unawares:

> War to us was simply a crazy idea, of a piece with, say, the perpetual motion machine or the fountain of youth . . . We were a spoiled generation, spoiled by nearly fifty years of peace that had made us lose sight of mankind's worst scourge. No one with any self-esteem ever got involved in politics. Arguments about Wagner's music, about the foundations of Judaism and Christianity, about Impressionist painting and the like seemed infinitely more important . . . And now, overnight, peace had suddenly collapsed. We were quite simply stupid . . . not even pacifists, because pacifism at least presupposes a notion of there being such a thing as war, and of the need to fight against it.

This indifference was widespread, not least in academic circles, where an intellectual such as Martin Heidegger, born in the same year as Hitler and Wittgenstein, making him twenty-five years old when the war broke out, carried on regardless, immersed in debates about nominalism in medieval philosophy.

One of his student friends, Ludwig Marcuse, described the mood at the university in Freiburg during those days in July 1914 in the following way, as cited by Safranski in his Heidegger biography:

> Toward the end of July I encountered one of my most respectable seminar colleagues, Helmuth Falkenfeld, on Goethestrasse. He said

despairingly, "Have you heard what's happened?" I said, full of contempt and resignedly, "I know, Sarajaevo." He said, "Not that, tomorrow Rickert's seminar is canceled." I said, alarmed, "Is he sick?" He said, "No, because of the threatening war." I said, "What's the seminar got to do with the war?" He shrugged sadly.

Falkenfeld, Safranski writes, is sent to the front only weeks later, from where he sends Marcuse a letter:

> *I continue to be all right, even though the battle in which I participated on October 30 nearly deafened my ears with the roar of twenty-four artillery batteries. Nevertheless . . . I still believe that the third Kantian antonomy is more important than this whole world war and that war is to philosophy as sensuality is to reason. I simply do not believe that the events of this material world can, even in the least degree, touch upon our transcendental components, and I will not believe it even if a French shell fragment were to tear into my empirical body. Long live transcendental philosophy.*

This indifference toward politics, however, is not the same as that recalled and condemned by Max Brod. Brod was deeply involved in the cultural life of the day and simply dismissed politics as unimportant without thereby turning his back on the world. The apathy of these students was altogether more ideological, they saw philosophy as the antithesis of life in society, a space in which the authentic revealed itself beneath the veneer of the social, outside history. According to George L. Mosse in his book *The Crisis of German Ideology*, academic milieux produced intellectuals "whose ideal was to view the world *sub specie aeternitatis*," which is to say from the perspective of eternity, Schopenhauer's motto. "Their concern was hardly with mundane, day-to-day affairs," Mosse writes.

This fundamental ideological standpoint, that the social, political, and societal were superficial phenomena behind whose pragmatic façade something more important existed, at least potentially, was widespread throughout prewar German culture, which more than anything cried out for essence and unity. It manifested itself in the wild paintings of the Expressionists, who in their powerful subjectivity, their powerful primitiveness strived for the life that lay beneath the sheen of civilization and culture, where instinct and basic human drives prevailed. But it came out, too, in another, almost diametrically opposed orientation, in which the answer to the rising social unrest and instability that had come with industrialization and modernity was sought and focused in overarching, ahistorical notions such as that of the people and the rootedness of culture. Alienation entailed a loss of meaning that could not be offset by the material. If a single idea recurs throughout the mind-set of the age it is a distaste for the pragmatic and what Wagner in an essay called "soulless materialism." Modernity was characterized as rationality, therefore they turned toward what was not rational, not purposeful, but which transcended such tendencies and found meaning in notions considered timeless and nonpragmatic. "The people" was one such notion, bringing together concepts of home, nature, culture, and religion, against whose immutable core the constant shifts of industrialism and modernity could only flake away, against whose profound depths, evoked by history, mythology, and religion, the entertainment industry and increasing commercialization of the day appeared abjectly shallow and banal.

The infatuation with art that Zweig describes as so strongly affecting his youth, and which also ran through Hitler's teenage years, was not faddish but genuinely meaningful. Wagner, Hölderlin, Rilke, Hofmannsthal, George, all those writers and poets cultivated by German youth, celebrated the great, the divine, the essential, and they lauded death, too, which lay beyond it all. *Stirb und Werde*, die and become – something to die for means something to live for. The people, the earth, the war, the hero, death. The local, the own, the great, the eternal. These were the predominant concepts of German culture prior to the outbreak of

World War I, and many of those who saw it coming looked on it as a catharsis, long-awaited and good.

What was singular about the enthusiasm many made manifest was that it was not politically but existentially motivated. Thomas Mann expressed pleasure at the collapse of a peaceful world, so full of loathing. Freud regained his belief in Austria as a nation. Rilke wrote of war being a god. Kafka envied the soldiers who were fighting. Georg Simmel saw the war as a great opportunity for Germany and proclaimed his unconditional love of his homeland. But neither Mann, Freud, Rilke, Kafka, nor Simmel took any part in the war, their enthusiasm was that of the onlooker. Ernst Jünger on the other hand, only nineteen years old when war broke out, joined up as a volunteer like Hitler. He kept a diary throughout, publishing in 1920 perhaps the best book about World War I, *Storm of Steel*. This is how he describes the mood of his generation in the summer of 1914:

> *We had come from lecture halls, school desks, and factory workbenches, and over the brief weeks of training, we had bonded together into one large and enthusiastic group. Grown up in an age of security, we shared a yearning for danger, for the experience of the extraordinary. We were enraptured by war. We had set out in a rain of flowers, in a drunken atmosphere of blood and roses. Surely the war had to supply us with what we wanted; the great, the overwhelming, the hallowed experience. We thought of it as manly, as action, a merry dueling party on flowered, blood-bedewed meadows. "No finer death in all the world than . . ." Anything to participate, not to have to stay at home!*

The hallowed dream of greatness and glory, this was what the war was about. Carefree dueling on blood-bedewed meadows, this was the vision. In his biography of Ernst Jünger, *Into the Abyss*, Thomas Nevin points to some of the origins of this mind-set, noting essay assignments given to students of the gymnasium schools in the Hanover District in the spring of 1914, topics to be discussed including "The Kaiser's words, 'I am a citizen of the German Reich,' words of pride and duty," "War is as terrible as plagues from heaven, but it is good, it is a fate like them," "How authentic is the saying of Frederick the Great, 'Life means being a warrior'?" "The bow when bent first shows its power," "My favorite hero in the *Nibelungenlied*," "A nation is worthless if it doesn't set everything upon its honor."

Jünger's conceptions of war, Nevin writes, came mainly from his readings of Homer, whose influence was acknowledged by the school's director, Dr. Joseph Riehemann, in his speech to graduating students, who were told that "apart from the light of Christianity, nothing will penetrate your future life with a brighter and warmer glow than Homer's sun."

Europe had been at peace since 1871, and in the war between France and Germany that ended that year, the machine gun as yet to be introduced, transport taking place by means of horse and cart or sailing ship, some 150,000 people lost their lives. In 1914 most believed that this new war would be conducted in much the same way and last no more than a few short months.

◆ ◆ ◆

In the waning summer of 1914 Hitler, too, was afraid the war would be over before he got there. In *Mein Kampf* he writes:

> *For me, as for every German, there now began the greatest and most unforgettable time of my earthly existence. Compared to the events of this gigantic struggle, everything past receded to shallow nothingness. Precisely in these days, with the tenth anniversary of the mighty event approaching, I think back with proud sadness on those first weeks of our people's heroic struggle, in which Fate graciously allowed me to take part.*
>
> *As though it were yesterday, image after image passes before my eyes. I see myself donning the uniform in the circle of my dear com-*

*rades, turning out for the first time, drilling, etc., until the day came
for us to march off.*

*A single worry tormented me at that time, me, as so many oth-
ers: would we not reach the front too late? Time and time again this
alone banished all my calm. Thus, in every cause for rejoicing at a
new, heroic victory, a slight drop of bitterness was hidden, for every
new victory seemed to increase the danger of our coming too late.*

Two weeks after Germany's declaration of war against Russia,
Hitler joined the 16th Bavarian Reserve Regiment in Munich,
where he underwent a seven-week stint of basic training. Before
being moved on to Augsburg for more intensive training, he
visited his landlady's family asking them to pass on word to his
sister Angela should he fall in battle. In the event that she did
not wish to inherit his few possessions, the Popp family would be
welcome to them. He hugged the two children, and Frau Popp
wept as he left, Liljegren reports. The regiment marched west for
some eleven hours in pouring rain, Hitler writing in a letter to
Frau Popp that he had spent the night in a stable, soaked to the
skin and unable to sleep. The following day's march took thirteen hours, after which they bivouacked in the open, so cold that
another sleepless night awaited. Reaching their destination the
next day, they were "deathly tired, ready to drop," Toland writes.
There, in the camp at Lechfeld, they trained for two weeks, until
October 20, when in the evening they boarded the trains that
would take them to the front in Flanders. "I'm terribly happy,"
Hitler wrote to Frau Popp that same day. "After arrival at our
destination I will write immediately and give you my address. I
hope we get to England."

Mein Kampf tells us nothing of this, no names are mentioned,
no faces appear to us, no detail is described. All we have is Hitler
and the war he has entered.

*At last the day came when we left Munich to begin the fulfillment of
our duty. For the first time I saw the Rhine as we rode westward*

along its quiet waters to defend it, the German stream of streams, from the greed of the old enemy. When through the tender veil of the early-morning mist the Niederwald Monument gleamed down upon us in the gentle first rays of the sun, the old "Watch on the Rhine" roared out of the endless transport train into the morning sky, and I felt as though my heart would burst.

And then came a damp, cold night in Flanders, through which we marched in silence, and when the day began to emerge from the mists, suddenly an iron greeting came whizzing at us over our heads, and with a sharp report sent the little pellets flying between our ranks, ripping up the wet ground; but even before the little cloud had passed, from two hundred throats the first hurrah rose to meet the first messenger of death. Then a crackling and a roaring, a singing and a howling began, and with feverish eyes each one of us was drawn forward, faster and faster, until suddenly past turnip fields and hedges the fight began, the fight of man against man. And from the distance the strains of a song reached our ears, coming closer and closer, leaping from company to company, and just as Death plunged a busy hand into our ranks, the song reached us too and we passed it along: "Deutschland, Deutschland über Alles, über Alles in der Welt!"

Four days later we came back. Even our step had changed. Seventeen-year-old boys now looked like men.

The volunteers of the List Regiment may not have learned to fight properly, but they knew how to die like old soldiers.

This was the beginning.

The List Regiment, to which Hitler belonged, numbered 3,600 men on arrival at Lille on October 23. After the first four days of action at Ypres only 611 were left. Five out of six had perished. The risk of being killed during the push forward was considerably greater than the chance of surviving. The mental effect of such losses on those who survive, with comrade after comrade falling in their midst and every minute potentially one's last, is something known only by those who have been to war. The Battle of Ypres was one of the most comprehensive in the war's initial phases; the British in their efforts to break through the German lines there in October and November lost 58,000 men. Writing to an acquaintance by the name of Ernst Hepp in Munich, Hitler describes the first engagements:

> *Now the first shrapnel hisses over us and explodes at the edge of the forest, splintering trees as if they were straws. We watch with curiosity. We have no idea as yet of the danger. None of us is afraid. Everyone is waiting impatiently for the command, "Forward!" . . . We crawl on our stomachs to the edge of the forest. Above us are howls and hisses, splintered branches and trees surround us. Then again shells explode at the edge of the forest and hurl clouds of stones, earth, and sand into the air, tear the heaviest trees out by their roots, and choke everything in a yellow-green, terribly stinking steam. We cannot lie here forever, and if we have to fall in battle, it's better to be killed outside . . . Four times we advance and have to go back; from my whole batch only one remains beside me, finally he also falls. A shot tears off my right coat sleeve, but like a miracle I remain safe and alive. At 2 o'clock we finally go forward for the fifth time, and this time we occupy the edge of the forest and the farms.*

The regimental commander is killed and his deputy seriously wounded. The new commander, Lieutenant Colonel Engelhardt, taking Hitler and another man with him, ventures forward to observe the enemy lines. Detected, they are sprayed with machine-gun fire, Hitler and the other man pulling Engelhardt to safety in a ditch. A thankful Engelhardt tells them he intends recommending the two men for the Iron Cross, but the very next day he is badly wounded when the regimental headquarters tent takes a direct hit from a British grenade, killing three and wounding three of its occupants. Only moments earlier, Hitler, together with three other enlisted men, had been told to vacate the tent to make way for four company commanders, as a result of which perhaps he was saved. "It was the most terrible moment of my life," Hitler would write to Hepp. "We all worshipped Lieutenant Colonel Engelhardt."

The new adjutant, Lieutenant Wiedeman, recommends Hitler for the Iron Cross, First Class. The recommendation is turned down, but Hitler is instead decorated with the second-class award, prompting him again to write to Herr Popp, this time with news of the happiest day of his life. "Unfortunately, my comrades who also earned it are mostly all dead." He asks Popp to save newspaper reports of the battle. He is promoted to the rank of corporal and begins his duties as an orderly, a position he holds throughout the four years of the war. His job is to take dispatches from regimental headquarters to the soldiers in the front line. It is a perilous assignment, not only because it involves crossing open land, either by bicycle or on foot, and, unlike the men in the trenches, unprotected by any cover, but also because he is an important target for the enemy. The dangers faced by dispatch runners pale in comparison with those of assault troops, who rush forward across no-man's-land to break into enemy positions, but are considerable nonetheless; Kershaw reports that three of the eight runners attached to the regimental staff were killed and another wounded in a confrontation with French troops on November 15. Where possible, dispatches are sent via two runners, increasing the chances of their reaching the lines. But death is not just in the trenches or between the lines; shells burst everywhere and at any time, in the camps to which the men withdraw for rest, in villages kilometers behind the front and in the various makeshift headquarters that are the domain of the highest-ranking officers.

Of all the depictions of the war in the trenches, Ernst Jünger's *Storm of Steel* is the most closely detailed and therefore also the most appalling, alongside the Englishman Robert Graves's *Goodbye to All That*, which provides a view from the other side. Jünger describes everything at eye level, from the moment he arrives at the front until he leaves it again four years later, and the sense of chaos is never absent from his account; this is a world devoid of any privileged vantage point, a disordered, tumultuous world in which lives are reaped by the minute.

Joining the front in Flanders in December 1914, Jünger is oblivious to what lies ahead, and the eyes by which he sees become ours. His company base is a staging point, Orainville, a village of some fifty houses grouped around a château in parkland. Wide-eyed, he observes the hectic comings and goings of ragged soldiers with weather-beaten faces, the glowing field kitchen with its smell of pea soup, men jingling their mess tins as they wait to eat. He spends the first night in a barn, eating breakfast the next day in a school building, when suddenly they hear a series of dull concussions. The more experienced soldiers rush out, those just arrived follow them without knowing why. There is a curious fluttering and whooshing sound above their heads, those around him cower or fling themselves to the ground. "The whole thing struck me as faintly ridiculous," he writes, "in the way of seeing people doing things one doesn't properly understand." Immediately afterward he sees dark figures emerge onto the empty village street, carrying black bundles on canvas stretchers. "I stared, with a queasy feeling of unreality, at a blood-spattered form with a strangely contorted leg hanging loosely down, wailing 'Help! Help!' as if sudden death still had him by the throat."

This takes place far from the enemy lines, at a place for recreation and rest, and it is Jünger's first experience of the war.

It was all so strange, so impersonal. We had barely begun to think about the enemy, that mysterious, treacherous being somewhere. This event, so far beyond anything we had experienced, made such a powerful impression on us that it was difficult to understand what had happened. It was like a ghostly manifestation in broad daylight.

A shell had burst high up over the château entrance, and had hurled a cloud of stone and debris into the gateway, just as the occupants, alerted by the first shots, were rushing out. There were thirteen fatalities, including Gebhard, the music master, whom I

remembered well from the promenade concerts in Hanover . . . The
road was reddened with pools of gore; riddled helmets and sword belts
lay around. The heavy iron château gate was shredded and pierced
by the impact of the explosive, the curbstone was spattered with blood.
My eyes were drawn to the place as if by a magnet; and a profound
change went through me.

They are moved to the trenches, where life between the fighting is cold, wet, muddy, sleepless, marked by routine, harsh and dull. In a stream only a stone's throw away lie the irretrievable, rotting corpses of soldiers from a French colonial regiment, their skin turned to parchment by the water that flows over them. Exhausted and mostly unused to physical work, Jünger and his comrades dig their trenches still deeper, and the merry dueling on flowered meadows has never been more distant. After four months they take part in their first major battle, at Les Éparges. Shells come down with dull thumps in a clump of firs, and when they get to the spot bloody scraps of cloth and flesh hang from the bushes around the crater, "a strange and dreadful sight that put me in mind of the butcher-bird that spikes its prey on thornbushes."

In the ensuing battle Jünger is wounded for the first time. The artillery fire intensifies, flashing about them, clouding the air with the dust and debris of detonation, splitting the ear with its dull clamor. Jünger describes it all as being as distant and peculiar as events on another planet, and he is unable to distinguish between the Germans' own gunnery and the shells of the enemy, everything is a tumultuous confusion, the wounded lie slumped around him, shrieking and wailing, and the reader can vividly imagine this inferno, so utterly detached from the familiar world, and then suddenly he describes happy, ardent birdsong, as if the birds were inspired or even encouraged by the bombardment, and one understands that the battle is being fought in an ordinary forest, on the edges of an ordinary village, in the middle of an ordinary day.

This brief glimmer of everyday life, continuing as before, proceeding according to its own laws and habits, makes clear to us that this is a construction, that the forest, presently set ablaze, the twittering birds, the sun in the sky, and the grass in the fields are nature, and that the wave of unprecedented destruction that takes place within it is civilization, regardless of the savage and primitive gash it gouges in those who fight, regardless of how blind the rain of metal lashing down.

Men have come together at this place, on each side of a hypothetical line, an invisible chalk mark, in this theatrical distortion of reality in which the familiar is uprooted and life removed to its furthest limit, so relentlessly transgressed, as if they were the gods themselves, since what awaits beyond, on the other side, is death, which is to say nature. The existence of an inside the war, in which lives are emptied out into the void, and an outside the war, in which lives go on as before, together with the mechanization of weaponry, something that further cements the link between war and culture, the large-scale industrialization and modernization of ways of killing, reinforces this impression. Trains crammed with living bodies are sent in, the bodies are destroyed, buried, new trains with new living bodies follow in their wake, their bodies, too, are destroyed, buried. Some eight million living bodies perish in this celebration of death beneath the persistent sun.

In a way, this is the zenith. For nothing is more precious than life, and here it falls to the ground like hail in a storm. Clearly it is a sacrifice of unprecedented dimensions, but for what purpose? The birds inhabit a world that to them is complete, a repertoire of actions they must carry out every day, throughout their every year, in an interplay of events and instincts with no other significance than keeping them alive, sustaining them in their state of existence. They see the world, and they are familiar with it, though only as effect, not as cause. The sun is warm, the rain is wet, the air consists of various strata through which they fly. They are locked inside their birdness, through which the world appears to them.

That we should similarly be locked inside our humanness has always been a natural thought, our religions issue from it and seek to define what is beyond, that which is concealed from us yet visible in its effects, and they do so in images that simplify for us what we feel to be complex. None of these images is useful here. No god descends from on high to appear before them in the clamor of their war, no only begotten son to whose heaven death is the entrance. The only things here that are not human are the burning trees, the stream running through the forest and fields, the birds sitting on their branches in song, their calls and sorrowless ardor, heard perhaps through a sudden lull in the thunder of cannon.

And then Jünger is hit in the thigh by a sliver of shrapnel, his blood begins to trickle, he drops his haversack and runs to the trench, the wounded from the shelled woods converging on the same place from all sides, the pattern of a star.

The trench is appalling, he flees to a nearby copse, where he is found after some hours and taken to a hospital in Heidelberg. After two weeks of convalescence, he visits home for a short period of leave before being sent to the front again.

He was twenty years old and had gone to war almost straight from school. What he saw and experienced there, the immense battles in particular, like the most violent forces of nature, was so radically removed from ordinary life as to alter forever his outlook on the quotidian. What Jünger saw in World War I was so powerful that it must have been impossible for him to think of it in terms of a haphazard occurrence, an expression of some peripheral idiosyncrasy of the human being, an accident, arbitrary and exceptional. On the contrary, in the years of war he found himself at the very core of the human, with all its exterior fallen away and only the simplest and most basic elements remaining: life and death. That he should have experienced things in this way is not hard to understand in view of the fact that one minute he was a nineteen-year-old living in a world of friends and family, school and literature, an occasional and fleeting romantic infatuation, a chess-playing father who whistled Mozart in the bath and a mother who read Ibsen and had actually met him, and who took her children on pilgrimages to Goethe's Weimar; while the next minute he was in a world of military camps, mud, cold, hunger, exhaustion, and abrupt death, beneath a sky filled with fire and metal. The first of these worlds had contained the second, in the shape of the wars he had read and heard about, but German culture was as classical as it was militaristic, so a nineteen-year-old such as he would be familiar with Homer and Caesar, as well as with Napoleon and the German generals of the war with France in 1870, whereas the second world, that of the trenches, did not contain the first. *Storm of Steel* does not concern itself with the superstructures of war, neither the most primary structures, which is to say the political structures that determined it all, the very reason they were there fighting, nor the militaristic structures that directed them here and there, but only with his own tangible experiences, the things he sees and feels himself. He's the one who must make the decision to get to his feet and stumble out into the hail of fire; no state, no army, no kaiser, no general can do so on his behalf. And he's the one who is hit in the chest, whose mouth fills with blood as he stumbles into a crater certain he will die, filled by an intense feeling of happiness amid the inferno of explosions, artillery fire, battle cries, and shrieks of terror. What he sees is in the same way connected to him, in the sense that it is he who has to understand it, give meaning to it, or deprive it of meaning. Death is the background from which life emerges. Had death not existed, we would never have known what life was. War is the only activity contrived by man that consciously approaches the line between them. If the processes that lead to war are a scheme, war itself is not, for death is absolute.

Death is not modern.

By our thoughts we try to release ourselves from that fundamental, inevitable circumstance, an endeavor short-circuited by our own demise. In all the efforts of our mind to extricate ourselves from the fact of death, our yearning toward heaven and a life beyond our own, which finds expression so variously depending on the age and culture in which we live, death is ever present.

As indeed is the heart, for like death the heart is always the same. The heart is not modern either. It is neither reasonable nor unreasonable, neither rational nor irrational. The heart beats, and then it does not. That's it.

This is the insight of war. All existential thought, any quest toward authenticity, stems from here. The occurrence of death opens up a new reality within our preexisting reality. It is our existential circumstance, and yet we seek to conceal the gate that is opened by death. Not so in war. In war the gate is opened and opened again, everywhere. Eventually the living become used to it, death becomes the norm, opening itself anywhere and at any time. Within this zone it is as if the distinction between the living and the dead shrinks, consisting in little but the fact of the living being animate and the dead not, the living by way of their animation being free in respect to the earth, while the dead have so to speak become bound to it and are ground down into it, little by little.

At the time of writing, it is ninety-seven years since World War I began. Considered from such distance it is a war that appears utterly senseless. World War II does not, being essentially a war of defense against Nazism. But what was World War I about? Politically it was meaningless, there being nothing to make real enemies of Britain and Germany, nothing for which they should fight; on the contrary, they had everything to gain by cooperation. Territorially it was meaningless, since nothing was conquered, and even if one of the countries concerned had broken through and conquered the other, it would have been hard put to find any benefit; what would Britain have done with Germany, or Germany with Britain? As such, it was quite as meaningless in human terms, too; those who gave their lives did so for nothing.

This meaninglessness exists in the superstructures, whereas in the nearness of the soldier's everyday life zones of meaning arise, so vivid as to demolish any question concerning the war's justification or the legitimacy of its carnage. Jünger sees three things in the war. The first is the archaic, the immutability of man, Homer's sun, whose logical conclusion is death and whose notion is universal and extrahuman. The second consists of the values on which soldiers depend for survival, such as courage, will, and endurance, what could be called the life force, perhaps a universal property of man, but a mere potential of the single person and thereby in itself individual. The third consists of the new machines, the mechanical means that have now increasingly taken over the conduct of war, which are an expression of civilization.

It, I, we/they.

These are the fundamental elements of life, which from their hiding place in the complexity of civilization emerge in the simplicity of war, and which, by virtue of their concerning the most essential, must be acknowledged. If instead they are suppressed, life becomes nonlife, an escape from life's very foundation, as essential as it is grave. Why would anyone wish to escape from the circumstance of existence, one might wonder, why would anyone choose the nonessential? The reason is that the price is such a heavy one to pay. If we accord the highest value to the life of the individual, if we understand life to be a quantitative concept that must be maintained for as long as possible, then death is our foremost enemy and war becomes absolutely meaningless, absolutely undesirable. If we do not accord the highest value to the life of the individual, but to some element of that life, a property, or to something outside it, an idea, then we consider life as something qualitative, something more than the sum of cells and living days, in other words, we hold that there is something more hallowed than life, and then the equation is simple and one might choose to die for it.

But what could be more hallowed than the life of the individual? The life of the all, or one's own all, one might surmise, this being the legitimization of the majority of wars. Nonetheless, it is an abstraction, and must surely mean nothing in the instant of rising to one's feet to charge forward into a hail of bullets.

To commence an assault on enemy trenches as one's comrades

are falling before one's eyes would seem inconceivable on the basis of some abstract notion of collective benefit. In the first edition of Jünger's memoir there is little mention of patriotism and none at all of defending any other grand notion. In the second edition the author has added some lines toward the end where he is sitting on a train on his way to Germany after his war has come to an end, and here he has "the sorrowful and proud feeling of being bound to the land more intimately for the blood shed in battle for its greatness," and moreover, according to his biographer Nevin, is filled with the sense that "Life has deeper meaning only through sacrifice for an idea, and that there are ideals compared to which an individual's life or even a people's count for nothing." This second edition ends with the exclamation, "Germany lives and shall never go under!" All this is gone in the third edition, published in 1934; nationalistic rhetoric had become the property of the Nazis, and Jünger wished not to be associated with them. What remains is the war as an expression of an essentially internal state: "The true springs of war are deep within us, and all that's atrocious, occasionally flooding the world, is only a mirror image of the human soul."

Mein Kampf was written in 1923, in the Great War's shadow, and is impossible to understand without this being taken into account. There was not a single family in Germany left unaffected, no one who had not lost a son, a brother, an uncle, a neighbor, a colleague, or a friend. Their grief was invisible, yet it touched everyone. Visible were the war invalids, hundreds of thousands of them, faces on the streets with cheekbones shot to pieces, bodies without arms or legs, eyes flaring in terror at any sudden noise, any abrupt movement, profoundly confused men in loud conversation with themselves. Those who had survived brought back with them experiences that could only be shared with others who had been there too, for what they had lived through defied words. What they had witnessed left its mark on them for life, not merely in the form of darkness or the shadowy, suppressed images that came over them in dreams or when least expected in their waking

hours, but also with respect to the way they related to their surroundings after they got back. A person who has seen others die
by the hundreds over a number of years sees life differently. The
dead were not anonymous, they were people one had lived with
and lived among, whose lives and suffering one had shared in
that tight-knit social sphere, the close bonding that comes of
war; perhaps you had shown them photos of your loved ones, they
were your comrades, and one by one they fell, abruptly and arbi-
trarily. To anyone who has been through that experience the attachment of human relationships can never be the same again, for
even if you know death is no longer likely to strike like a lightning bolt from the sky, the experience of losing a friend in the
space of a split second, and of knowing that it can happen again
to any other friend at any moment, and moreover to oneself, too,
is so fundamental that it cannot be erased, not even by an entire
lifetime of peace. In such instances people become withdrawn,
there being simply too much to lose. This inner disablement, this
emotional paralysis, was as invisible as the grief of the sufferers'
parents, it was never talked about, and yet it was there, the catastrophe all too great, all too brutal not to leave those who had been
through it scarred for life. To the generation born between 1880
and 1900, World War I was the single overriding event of their
lives, and the question they asked themselves when it was over was
why it had occurred at all. Millions of young men had perished,
but for what? For this? For entertainment, cabaret, cinema, self-
indulgent art? Had they given up their lives for such systematized
emptiness? Was this what they had fought for? This is the way
Hitler saw it, and he was not alone.

They had been to the very perimeter of life, inhabited the borderland between all and nothing, and the intensity that had saturated them there, the carnage they had witnessed, could never
be meaningless or empty, could never be nothing; this they knew
above all. From a political perspective the possible consequences
were basically twofold: never again could there be such an appalling and meaningless waste of human life, or else a new war would

render meaningful the sacrifice of those two million German soldiers. To Hitler, only the second of these possibilities was real. For if everything that had gone before the war had been reduced to nothing by it, then the same would hold for the war to come:

> *Thousands of years may pass, but never will it be possible to speak of heroism without mentioning the German army and the World War. Then from the veil of the past the iron front of the gray steel helmet will emerge, unwavering and unflinching, an immortal monument. As long as there are Germans alive, they will remember that these men were sons of their nation.*

It is this, the mythology of war, the Wagnerian or Homerian tale of heroism from the depths of time, that Hitler knew and cultivated, this was his condensation of meaning, and it was this to which he aspired, not only in relation to the war, but in relation to everything in his time, which from that perspective, in the great, echoing chambers of the past, became hallowed and was accorded unity and cohesion, which is the same as meaning. Certainly, that meaning was absent from the war to anyone who had fought in it, for the war was anything but the expression of unity and cohesion, yet there is no reason to believe that Hitler was being calculating in describing it the way he did, and every reason to believe he did indeed experience the war as profoundly meaningful. He risked his life for what he believed in, and did so as part of a great community that provided him with arbitrary comradeship with no obligations as to close friendship or intimacy in a situation in which all were fighting for the German nation, to which ever since childhood he had dreamed of belonging, and also – at least if we are to believe those passages in *Mein Kampf* where he writes about the impression left on him by reading his father's book about the Franco-German War of 1870–71 – of fighting for.

This mythologization of war is no dream of war but an essentialization, and the fact of it offering not a glimpse of its everyday reality is typical of the romantic I, the inner being's exaltation of the external, something Hölderlin's poems in particular express rather strikingly, they too being devoid of quotidian triviality, elevating and exalting, saturated with existence, always bordering on the ecstatic, the way life is when charged to the brim with meaning. Romantic infatuation, the state of being in love, can charge up a life in such a way, as the mystical-religious experience can too, and death as well. All three states of being have to do with the transcending of the I. The sense of there being something close to divine in Hölderlin's poetry has to do with the same thing, any distinction between the world and the I all but absent, the poem being almost one with its evocations of deep, green shadows and baking-hot sun, thunder rolling in over the high ground, rivers gushing ice-cold from the mountains, everything being significant and meaningful: the identity of the I and the world is the ultimate meaning. If no such identity exists, the world becomes alien, and before the alien the I stands isolated and detached, as if expelled, alien moreover unto itself and its surroundings. This is what the second creation narrative concerns, the fall that knowledge entails being a fall into the alien. The yearning for nature and the natural is a yearning for identity, unity, the absolute meaning of oneness. The Romantic period's solitary I with its longing to transcend the self is an expression of the same thing, following directly from the dissolution of the religious view of the world, after which only the human remained. The young Karl Marx's notion of alienation is existential rather than political; only later would it be linked with the specific and mechanical nature of labor under capitalism. Wagner's tales of heroism, his great storms of emotion, are to do with the same thing, exaltation and the transcending of the self. The I of *Mein Kampf* expresses itself in terms of the same model, elevating war and the singular life of the self to something untainted by the quotidian, a hallowedness meaningful in itself, but unlike Hölderlin, Rilke, Trakl, Wagner, Beethoven, and almost any other German artist of the Romantic and late-Romantic periods, Hitler's I is constrained by its feeble mastery of form, an inability to mold the language into any true expression of the I and the emotions by which it is pervaded, all he can do is seek to copy the formal qualities of others, in the simplest of ways, a cliché. "Then from the veil of the past the iron front of the gray steel helmet will emerge, unwavering and unflinching, an immortal monument," he writes. He is constrained, too, by his very mind-set, which confines itself to the culture in which he has lived, full of prejudice and approximate insight, half-truths, rumor and generally unreliable assumptions, which, as Hamann demonstrates, surprisingly often is in line with the Viennese newspapers of the day as well as more populist publications, in such a way that what to him appeared grand and meaningful was not depicted as such, in the way of Hölderlin, for instance, but rather as something inauthentic, since the idea of greatness, or the desire for greatness, is the only element of the grand that comes out, this then pointing back to the I and its petty-bourgeois nature, which by its very presence disqualifies any quest for the sublime. Reading Hitler's endeavors toward exaltation in *Mein Kampf* is like looking at a poor painting of a steep and splendid mountain.

The fact that his prose renders everything small is not to say that Hitler's feelings in respect to the things he described were small, nor indeed that those things in themselves were small. Hitler's talent lay elsewhere, he even underlines this several times in *Mein Kampf*, the inferiority of writing compared to the spoken word, which he so definitively held in his power and was so adept at exploiting to make his audiences feel what he felt or what he wanted them to feel. In this the mythologization of the essentially quotidian again comes into its own, and the exaltation of a real world in which work, fundamentally dull and monotonous and bleak, becomes heroic and hallowed, and where the past is repeatedly resurrected in parades with horses and medieval banners, in rites and oaths, grand works of architecture reminiscent of Antiquity, a sublime rendering of the present, a reconjuring of society, whose aesthetic elements were largely culled from the world of the military and war: uniforms, ensigns, parades, all unifying. The workers became worker-soldiers, schoolchildren became child-soldiers, sportsmen became athlete-soldiers, and what was unique about it all was that everyday reality was thereby elevated and made significant, not by its interpretation in art, by art's selection of individual constituent parts within it, the world as read in the poem, as heard in music, as seen in the painting, but by the direct and unmediated reshaping and modeling of reality itself. Hitler turned Germany into a theater. What that theater expressed was cohesion, and through cohesion identity, and through identity authenticity. It was not a matter of invention, of constructing an identity by means of costumes, flags, and rallies, but rather of giving expression to something that had always been there, which modern society had held in check and diffused, and this is why so many of its elements came from history: something had been reestablished.

Nor was Hitler a fanatical, militaristic theater director enforcing his will on the people; the strings he played were genuine, the emotions he aroused were in everyone. Anyone who has seen footage of the rallies of Hitler's Germany knows what feelings they evoke, the sheer might of the uniformed, I-less community, the strength of the collective, and oh, how one might long to be a part of such a we. Some of the images of the age express an almost savage beauty, the endless ranks of soldiers viewed at eye level, a sea of steel helmets extending into the beyond, totally symmetrical, the same human being repeated and repeated as if into infinity itself. Or the hush as Hitler walks the several hundred meters toward the burning flame beneath the monument to honor the fallen, surrounded by thousands of soldiers in rank, uniformed, helmeted, invulnerable. Everything he strove to awaken through the prose of *Mein Kampf,* and which in that context failed, is accomplished now in these human tableaux. An iron front of gray steel helmets rises before us, awakening the past from its slumbers, and yet they are in the present, they are immortal. As one soldier cries out during the Nuremberg rallies: They did not die! They live on in Germany!

Who would not wish to be a part of something greater than the self? Who would not wish to feel their life to be meaningful? Who would not wish to have something to die for?

The tranquillity, satiety, and calm that fills our lives, or with which we strive to infuse them, our foremost aim being satisfaction, a state in which hardly a cloud smudges the sky, is reminiscent of the life Stefan Zweig describes in his memoir *The World of Yesterday*, a life that came to such an abrupt end in those days of August 1914. The question we must ask is whether the war was caused by political circumstance and historic, societal factors, unthinkable in our own postwar societies, or whether it came about because of a release of certain forces that have always been present in man, a part of our makeup as human beings, present in every one of us, and which may be released again at any time from now. In that case the only thing we might say with certainty is that it will come in a different way, in a different form, because the form in which it came in 1914, and again in 1939, has now long since been identified and all conceivable outlets blocked. There will be no marching in the streets, no seas of steel helmets on the city squares. Yet in my mind, as I sit here in the spring, in a room in Glemmingebro outside Ystad, the sun pouring onto the greening landscape I have blotted from view by means of a travel rug so as to concentrate on my work, though not without interruption by the children, who run in and out of the house with the same eagerness and joy, the same urge to express themselves and their existence as I remember from my own childhood, while my mother is in the garden weeding the flower beds, Linda at the shop buying food for the Easter dinner, her brother hammering nails into the pent roof that collapsed under the weight of snow in the winter, her mother at work next to him trying to straighten a thick bush that also collapsed at the same time, I can feel a yearning for something else, and that yearning, I assume, must be felt by others, too, because surely people of the same culture cannot be so different from one another that an emotion can exist in one person only? I don't know what this yearning represents, but I do know that it does not involve any dissociation from what is here, from that which is mine and in which I live, that's not it at all, there is nothing I despise about any of that, and I realize and understand the value of the unwavering regularity of this existence, and its necessity too. And yet, a yearning. For what?

Or more than a yearning it is perhaps a want. A feeling of something not being here. In the midst of life and the living, as if swathed in the chirping and wing-beating of all the birds building their nests nearby, beneath the sun, surrounded by vegetation in every direction, something is wanting.

Is the want in me?

Am I simply unable to grasp hold of my own time, my own place, to see it the way it is, the way it really is, to know that it is everything, and to be filled with joy by that knowledge? For an entire world opens up inside even the smallest plant one stoops to inspect, a living organism bound up with everything else that is living too, growing on the brink of the dizzying precipice of time at which we, too, stand. Is it my responsibility to validate that world, to fill it with value? Is that possible? Or is it empty, a simple, ongoing state of serial reproduction, copying itself and copying itself again, on and on into infinity? An emptiness that moreover is the foundation of our own biological reality, our life as human beings? If so, why do we imitate the emptiness of serial life in the culture we create? Should our culture not instead establish difference, which is the stuff of all worth, in which value resides and from which it is released, and thereby of all meaning? Does that meaning not exist? Or is it concealed? Concealed then by what means? Concealed by our social existence, whose differences exist in order to keep in place, not to set free, and which indeed keep us in place within our particular lives, our routine lives, from whose viewpoint the entire world dissolves and becomes the same?

But if this is so, where does the idea come from that it might ever be different? We don't believe in God, which means God does not exist and never did. If this is so, then he existed only in our human minds, as a kind of existential tool, and what was necessary for that to be meaningful was that the insight of this instrumental aspect should not become conscious. It became so only when material reality was identified as instrumental, and from then on there was no turning back, since meaning precludes the deception of open eyes, faith is to know, and just as they knew that God was real, we know that God is not real. The link with the authentic, which resided in religious ecstasy, was broken because the authentic did not exist; ecstasy, too, that fervent emotion of the human, was false, a delusion.

But the sun beats down, the grass grows, the heart pounds in its darkness.

"But the sun beats down, the grass grows, the heart pounds in its darkness."

Why did I write those words?

Such language is hollow. It looks like the language of the Nazis. Yes, the sun is actually beating down, the grass is actually growing, the heart actually pounding in its darkness, but the factuality of these things is not what is significant about their linguistic expression, what is significant is what that language evokes, that the sun, the grass, and the heart are in a way elevated, made to be something more than themselves, as if somehow they become bearers of actual reality. It is the same language that says civilization is detached from our basic urges, our sufferings and the brilliance of genius, whereas the sun, the grass, the blood are connected to the authentic, whose two great expressions are war and art, as Mann wrote in 1914.

This language is hollow, and it became the language of the Nazis, but is it untrue?

Paul Celan's poem was a response to that language, which had destroyed the entire culture. It did not first arise in *Mein Kampf*, but was gathered and concentrated there and through the author of that book disseminated into an entire society with the aim of turning it completely on its head. Everything that language brought with it we have since discarded. All thoughts of the hallowed, all thoughts of the authentic have been eliminated from our minds. We live our lives surrounded by commercial goods, and spend great swaths of our waking hours in front of screens. We conceal death as best we can. What do we do if out of all this a yearning arises for something else? A more real reality, a more authentic life? Such a yearning would be founded on false precepts because all life is quite as authentic, and the hallowed is a notion belonging to life, not life itself. Yearning toward reality, yearning toward authenticity expresses nothing other than the yearning for meaning, and meaning arises out of cohesion, in the way we are connected to one another and our surroundings. This is the reason I write, trying to explore the connections of which I am a part, and when I feel the pull of the authentic, it becomes another connection I feel compelled to explore. That war and art are related, as Mann wrote in 1914 though of course later dissociated himself from, is something I am convinced of, since both seek the very extremity of existence, which is death, against the backdrop of which life gleams radiant, suddenly precious and inalienable, which is to say meaningful. I have always felt this in art, a powerful sense of meaning, almost always in paintings of the period from the seventeenth century to the end of the nineteenth century, though seldom in modern art, albeit with some shining exceptions, the paintings of Anselm Kiefer, for instance, to which I have always felt a strong sense of connection. But then four years ago, on a trip to Venice, it was as if all of this suddenly fell apart. I was looking at the paintings at the Accademia and found them "saying" nothing to me, as if somehow they belonged to a room outside the one in which I existed. What applied there did not apply here. This felt strange, for death is death, life is life, man is man regardless of culture, was that not how it was supposed to be? We had hurried through the exhibition rooms, the children impatient, though Vanja noted the forbidding gruesomeness of all the skulls, the rearing horses and crucified figures, and when we came out and had found a place to sit at a quiet café with a view of the lagoon, and were drinking our Sprite with ice, I was struck by the thought that what those paintings represented, in their age and beauty, which for so many years I had held so highly and striven in so many ways toward, its allure seeming to me to be not merely necessary, but absolutely vital, was perhaps, when everything boiled down, without worth. Suddenly it felt like a burden we bore, a kind of shadow that had fallen upon us, dead and cold. The beauty of the paintings was the beauty of death, the insight they awoke in us was in what was dead and nothing else.

The same day I saw something utterly sublime and quite different to anything else on that trip. I was out with John in the area surrounding the apartment in which we were staying, walking through the narrow, dark, and damp passages where little bags of rubbish with knots tied in their tops had been left outside every door and clothes had been hung out to dry on washing lines that ran up above between the houses, it was late afternoon and we were approaching the square facing the lagoon where the vaporettos came in, when an enormous ship suddenly appeared above the rooftops, gliding slowly away. We emerged onto the square, from where the sea opened out and the very special light that is always in Venice, under cloud or sun, in autumn as well as in spring and summer, made everything, the walls and roofs of the buildings, the paving stones and the surface of the water, shimmer.

The ship was indeed gigantic, towering above the city, passengers milling on all its decks. A loudspeaker voice blared out tourist information, and the air was a glitter of flashing cameras. Something welled inside me. A shiver ran down my spine.

"Look, John," I said, crouching down beside him. He smiled and nodded, and pointed to one of the many pigeons strutting about the square. "Dah!" he said. I rose to my feet again, looking up once more at the vessel, which was now just far enough away for me to be unable to pick out the features of the faces that filled the decks, all I could see was a blur of human figures and the camera flashes momentarily lighting it all up, and then I turned the stroller around and headed back through the passage to a tiny café where John had a bread roll and I had an espresso.

Why did the sight of a cruise ship send a shiver down my spine? What was it that made me think it so sublime?

In classical aesthetics the sublime lay in the beholding of something that rocked the very foundations of the beholder on account of its magnificent or unfamiliar nature. A volcanic eruption, a sinking ship, a tall and rugged mountain, an event, a state of affairs, or an entity before which the beholder has a distinct sense of feeling small or inconsequential. Beauty, synonymous as far back as Antiquity with proportion and harmony, which is to say something within the scope of human control, was incorporated into the notion of the sublime in the Romantic age, perhaps because the idea of the divine had ceased to be a fulcrum of human existence, something all concepts, all human thinking issued from or strove toward. But the sublime and the divine are two different things, the revelation of nature's alienness is different from the revelation of the nearness of the divine, since the nearness of the divine makes conspicuous not only remoteness, not only the gruesome, nagging realization of nature's blindness and inhumanity, but also the opposite, a promise of cohesion and belonging. A we. The divine, or the holy, indicates the boundaries of this we, at the same time as it accords it meaning, not individually but as a collective, a whole. And the nature of the revelation must also have been radically different, for the experience of the divine or the holy was of something transcending an otherwise regular reality, and one can imagine how terrible and fearful that must have been. To stand before an almighty creation that is neither human nor animal, a creation that conceals itself and yet is present where you stand. Rudolf Otto wrote that religious emotion can fill the soul with almost insane force and endeavored to describe the numinous in all its various phases. The sweeping, tide-like moods of tranquil worship that can pass over into a more set and lasting attitude of the soul, continuing, vibrant and resonant, until at last it dies away, the soul resuming its more profane, everyday, nonreligious mode. The strong, sudden ebullitions of personal piety from the depths of the soul, with spasms and convulsions, leading to the strangest excitements, frenzy, transport, ecstasy. It may sink to almost grisly horror and shuddering. The numinous has its crude and barbaric antecedents, Otto states, which may be developed into something beautiful and pure and glorious. "It may become the hushed trembling and speechless humility of the creature in the presence of – whom or what?"

When I read Rudolf Otto or Mircea Eliade, both of whom circle around the experience of the divine or the holy, in order to gain an understanding of that experience and to define it, and when I read the writings of Christian mysticism or the Church Fathers, pervaded as they are with the rapture of religious excitement, I find myself confronted by something utterly alien to me, which does not occur at all in my life or in the world around me, other than the occasional glimpse offered by TV into some ecstatic religious movement. This weakens an otherwise fundamental conviction of mine that says the emotional life of the human is constant, that the feelings that stream through us have always streamed through all human beings, and that this is the reason why it makes sense for us to consider even the oldest works of art, or to read even the oldest texts of literature. To be human has forever been the same, I tell myself, quite independently of the ways in which our cultures have evolved. But the kinds of experience that were once the most important of all, meditations on God and the divine, holy rituals and cults, visions and raptures occurring in lives wholly devoted to God and the divine mystery, this resolve to seek meaning, this fervor, with all its spectra of intuitions, moods, and emotions, is no longer sought or, if it is, then only on the peripheries of society, outside our field of vision, perhaps occasionally evoked in respect to some odd and obsolete phenomenon in TV entertainment: So, you're a *monk*? What's it like not having sex? When we closed the door on religion, we closed the door on something inside ourselves as well. Not only did the holy vanish from our lives, all the powerful emotions associated with it vanished too. The idea of the sublime is a faint echo of our experience of the holy, without the mystery. The yearning and the melancholy expressed in Romantic art is a yearning back to this, a mourning of its loss. This at least is how I interpret my own attraction to the Romantic in art, the short yet intense bursts of emotion it can discharge in my soul, the sudden swell of joy and grief that can arch up inside me like a sky if I happen to encounter something unexpected or something commonplace in an unexpected way.

A cruise ship thick with people, an industrial landscape mantled by snow, the red sun that illuminates it through a curtain of mist. An old man in blue overalls tossing a cardboard box onto a bonfire, this, too, in a landscape of snow in which all is still apart from the old man's movements, with which I am so familiar, he being my mother's father, and the fire's cautiously flickering flame. The flame, the fire, what else is this but something opening into the world? Something that occurs is here and then gone? Always and yet never the same. When I see the image in my mind's eye I am transported there, and with all my being I become aware not only of my own existence, but of my own self. For a brief moment it floods my consciousness, and in those few moments I am quite oblivious to my own problems, the things I have done or need to do, the people I know, have known, or will know in the future, and everything that connects me to the social world is gone. For five seconds, perhaps, or ten, maybe even for as long as thirty seconds, I exist in that state, in the midst of the world, watching a bonfire burn and a man step back from it in a soundless, snow-covered landscape, and then it is gone, the magic broken, and everything is as it was before, me included.

But so small and insignificant that experience is compared to the rapture of the mystics, so sad my own quest for meaning, forever interrupted, compared to their lifelong devotion, so pathetic my rituals in front of the television screen, compared to those that once took place in the world. Oh, I can hardly bear to speak of it, the difference between the stirring emotions that run through me when a Norwegian skier wins the world championship, and those that run through a person kneeling before the holy itself, whose soul is elevated by that experience.

Oh, for crying out loud, what do I even know of the divine? What gives me the right to even use the term? I, a secularized man of the West, forty years old, as naïve as he is unschooled, one of the world's multitude of unspiritual and unremarkable individuals? Did I not seat myself, two days after seeing the cruise ship, at a Venetian sidewalk café and drop my fork on the ground, prompting the waiter to bring me a clean one, which I declined – no, it's all right, I've got one here, look – oblivious to the context of my fork having been on the ground, for which reason it was to the waiter's mind dirty and unusable? Indeed I did, and in the company of Espen and Anne to boot, who smiled overbearingly before Espen hesitantly suggested that the waiter might have wanted to give me a clean fork because mine had been on the ground and was dirty. How could such a clumsy creature even contemplate letting a phrase such as "the divine" pass his lips? A man who moreover did not believe there to be a God, nor that Jesus was the son of that God; why in all the world should he poke about in such matters?

What was I even looking for?

Meaning. Most likely it was that simple. In my day-to-day life I was filled by a sense of loathing, quite bearable, never threatening or destructive in any way, most of all a kind of shadow that blanketed my existence, the logical conclusion of which was what might be described as a passive yearning for death, so on a plane, for instance, I could find myself thinking I wouldn't care if it crashed, though I could never dream of ever actively doing anything that would put my life at risk. In this state of loathing, meaning could detonate inside me. It would be as if I were suddenly brought to the threshold of something radically significant into which I was then absorbed, only to be expelled again. As if the meaning I was looking for was there all the time, and what kept me from it was *me* and *my* way of seeing things.

Was that it? Was there something out there, something objectively true and real, a constancy of life and the living, there always, to which I only seldom, hardly ever, had access? Or was it just something inside me?

I could have knelt, put my hands together and directed trembling prayers and lamentations to God, Our Father, but I was living in the wrong age, for when I looked up toward the sky all I saw was a vast and empty space. And when I looked around me I saw a society we had fully and completely organized to lull us all to sleep, to make us think about something else, to entertain us. The quick and easy, the soft and comfy, that was what we wanted, and it was what we got. The only remaining space where life was taken seriously was art. In art I looked only for such fullness of being. Beauty and fullness of being. On occasion I found it, and when I did it consumed me, yet the experience led to nothing, was perhaps nothing but the projections of an overtense soul, little lightning flashes in the darkness of the mind.

I see a cruise ship thick with people gliding past, high above the rooftops of an ancient, sinking city, and a shiver goes down my spine. So what? Is that all?

James Joyce, brought up in Catholicism, familiar with the great Fathers of the Church, typically for him called such moments epiphanies, a word originally used to denote the revelation of the divine nature of Christ to the three wise men that starry night in Bethlehem, but which for him stood for the worldly revelations of life in the streets around him. In his sketchy, unfinished novel *Stephen Hero*, he defines epiphany as "a sudden spiritual manifestation." Joyce takes as his point of departure here Thomas Aquinas's definition of beauty, or what is required for beauty in any object, yet shifts the focus from the properties of the object itself to our own perceptions of them. This is a three-stage operation: first, the object must be lifted away from everything else, and then we perceive it as *a* thing (Aquinas's "integrity"); then it must be analyzed, considered in whole and in part, in relation to itself and to other objects, the mind recognizing then that it is indeed a *thing* (Aquinas's "wholeness"); finally, and this is the moment of epiphany, we recognize that the object is *one* integral thing, that it is *that* thing (Aquinas's "radiance").

Joyce calls this the soul of the object, its whatness.

The starting point for this reflection, which Stephen details in a conversation with his friend Cranly, is a little intermezzo he witnesses one evening in Eccles Street, where a young lady was standing on the steps of a house and a young man was leaning on the rusty railings below:

> *The Young Lady – (drawling discreetly)* . . . O, yes . . . I was . . . at the . . . cha . . . pel
> *The Young Gentleman – (inaudibly)* . . . I . . . (again inaudibly) . . . I . . .
> *The Young Lady – (softly)* . . . O . . . but you're . . . ve . . . ry . . . wick . . . ed.

To apply a concept denoting the revelation of the divinity of Christ to such a mundane occurrence as this is blasphemy, the distance between the two domains being as great as it is, yet there is surely an equally great distance between the occurrence and the scholarly aesthetic into which Joyce lifts it up, making fun of the gap between reality and its academic interpretation, at the same time as he is without doubt circling in on something important concerning his own aesthetic. What he is describing is the mundane, everyday world as we know it, and what he wants to probe into are the things going on around him here and now, for everything is local, to everyone, for all time. But in Joyce's epiphanies there is nothing else, this is what characterizes them, they are an expression of themselves only, and the author's task is to view them in exactly that way, in their own right. The examples he cites of epiphanies are certain modes of expression that crop up in conversation, certain ways of gesticulating, certain thoughts that pass through the mind, in other words, fully and completely attached to the human sphere, more particularly to our social existence, life the way we live it in relation to ourselves and to one another. There is something almost anti-essentialist about his aesthetic, so unconcerned with the authentic and indeed the transcendental, seeking all meaning and significance in the river of movement and language that flows through our lives each day. The language in which he captures this is itself a river, and like all rivers it has a surface, that part of it that first catches our eye, and below the surface its depth, words beneath the words, sentences beneath the sentences, movements beneath the movements, characters beneath the characters. Everything in *Ulysses* is moreover always something else, not because the world is relative, but because the language through which we see it is. The transcendency of *Ulysses* lies in the language, it opens up a chasm in the now, which is thereby no longer epiphanic – neither isolated, whole, nor particular – and if Joyce's portrayal of the world is true in its relativity and in its massive intertextuality, it is then cerebral and at root scholarly in its determination toward systematics and cohesion, hurtling away from physical reality and the realistic novel, much as the medieval Church Fathers detached themselves from the Bible and the concrete, action-oriented, physical reality found in it, and arced into the hugely abstract, bodiless canopy of speculation and reflection they stretched out over their lives. In that one may lose oneself, as one may lose oneself in *Ulysses* and the other great works of modernism, with all the intellectual enjoyment and aesthetic pleasure they have to offer, for their turning toward form and language makes them all the more works in their own right, something in themselves, at the same time as they have so plainly lost something too, for as Henry James once suggested, *in art, the emotions are the meaning*.

To those who consider art from that perspective, form means

nothing in itself, possessing meaning only as the bearer of something else, and modernism, which is to say most of what has taken place in art from the beginning of the last century to the present day, has abandoned that dimension. The work of those who do not consider art in that way is tinged with the Romantic. Hermann Broch, for instance, in his *Death of Virgil*, one of the most hardcore modernist novels of the nineteenth century, whose opening, in which the dying Virgil is lying in a boat on its way into a Roman harbor, contains one of the finest sentences of prose written in Europe during the last two hundred years:

> *Steel-blue and light, ruffled by a soft, scarcely perceptible crosswind, the waves of the Adriatic streamed against an Imperial squadron as it steered toward the harbor of Brundisium, the flat hills of the Calabrian coast coming gradually nearer on the left, and here, as the sunny, yet deathly loneliness of the sea changed with the peaceful stir of friendly human activity, where the channel, softly enhanced by the proximity of human life and human living, was populated by all sorts of craft – by some that were also approaching the harbor, by others heading out to sea and by the ubiquitous brown-sailed fishing boats already setting out for the evening catch from the little breakwaters which protected the many villages and settlements along the white-sprayed coast – here the water had become mirror-smooth; mother-of-pearl spread over the open shell of heaven, evening came on, and the pungence of wood fires was carried from the hearths whenever a sound of life, a hammering or a summons, was blown over from the shore.*

A singular joy comes over me every time I read this. It is sublime. But why? What is it about this passage in particular that can give rise to such strong emotions? What the sentence describes, a boat entering a harbor one late afternoon, is trivial and recognizably commonplace, at least to anyone who grew up near the sea, at the same time as it takes place in Ancient Greece, to us a lost and unreachable world. Is that why? The interplay of the general, true of any harbor, and the specific, true only of this harbor, long since lost. Yes, this does give me joy, awakening personal memories of the smells, the sounds, the light, and not least the gusting wind as the sun moves slowly across the sky, the way it can fill a person with its thriftless extravagance, but it is not sublime. The sublime comes not from familiarity, but from the opposite. The sublime in this passage is the movement from the sea toward the land, "here, as the sunny, yet deathly loneliness of the sea changed with the peaceful stir of friendly human activity."

The sunny, yet deathly loneliness of the sea – I have never thought about the sea like this, and yet I must have felt it because when I read those words something inside me, faintly, as if from some remote distance, recognizes what they are saying to me. It is a recognition of something whose more exact nature has eluded me. And a recognition of the vast and to us unknown quantity that is death. The transition from there toward the peaceful stir of human activity is what the sentence describes, and what it detaches, because besides applying there, in Broch's imaginary scene at the harbor in Brindisi some time in the last century BC, as well as in the physical reality the sentence evokes, it also applies to the place in which I am seated at this moment, on June 2, 2010, at one minute past four in the afternoon, in the study of this sixth-floor apartment on the Triangeln Square in Malmö, the stir of human activity all around me, which is to say the traffic going past on the roads outside, the people on the street below, their occasional shouts and cries, the blaring horns of this year's high-school graduates on their parade, their music systems thumping and pounding as they make another tour of the city, the elderly black saxophonist sitting leaned up against a pillar, playing the same piece over and over again. This stir of human activity, which is the social world, is what we approach in the opening scene of *The Death of Virgil*, sailing toward it in anticipation of entering into and becoming a part of it, and as long as we see it in this way, as something gradually emerging before us, so far only in the form of sounds and smells, we see it for what it is, which is to say a haven. During the time Broch was writing about, people were few in number, towns and cultures were separated by great distances, and crossing the divides between them was a slow and perilous business. Everything has changed now, and the stir of human activity, our haven from an indifferent and mortal universe, is no longer local and constrained, but exists wherever we care to look, no longer is something we leave and approach, but something that's all around us, all the time, regardless of where we are or what we are doing. This does not mean that the circumstances of life have changed from that time, only our perception of them. This is why Broch's opening passage has such a powerful effect, since it directs attention toward a fundamental circumstance we increasingly tend to ignore. That it does so in such a simple way, by relating it to a physical landscape in the world, to a particular moment, an early evening outside the harbor in Brindisi, the elements of which, the steel-blue sea blushed by the sun, the rose-colored tinge of the sky, the white-sprayed coast, the glittering houses there, bringing forth similar recollections from the depths of the reader's memory, means that the moment and its potential for creating awareness become something *experienced*. An experience is what is seen, colored by emotion. Reason ignores emotion, addressing only the mind, but to the mind the fact of endless numbers of people having lived and died before us, and the fact that we who are alive now will also soon be dead, is a banal insight, something we have known since we were five years old. Only by experience, by feeling the gaping void in even the most trivial of surroundings, do we *grasp* it. Only then does it become an insight. This insight is to all intents and purposes inarticulable, so vast is its content. Since it is so fundamental, so completely central to our lives, Broch could naturally have produced reams on the subject, discussing numerous aspects of death in nature and the havens we make to safeguard ourselves from it, but he wrote this when he was at the height of his career, keenly aware that what the text says in words and what those words awaken in the reader are two different things. He wrote about the sea with only the merest intimation of death, and about the peaceful stir of human activity toward which a boat slowly came drifting, so simply as to allow us to see each element for what it is, and with such meticulous concretion as to allow the image to pass into the reader's imagination, there to unfold and be fleshed out in the wealth of human mood and emotion.

Day passes toward night, soon we are in our final hour, which is the time of Broch's novel. In the boat immediately after Caesar's lies Virgil, poet of the *Aeneid*, the mark of death on his brow. He is acutely conscious, sensitive to everything, knowing it will all soon be gone. Day passes toward night, everything blazes up before him one last time. In Nordic mythology the realm of death is Hel, a word deriving from *hylja*, meaning to hide or cover up, an apt name indeed, since the realm of the dead is beyond our sight, and yet, I think to myself now, it can also mean the opposite, that the world of the living hides from the dead. Only a few weeks before we went to Venice we were in Norway, in Vestland, and besides seeing my mother and having John christened, we drove out one day to visit my cousin Jon Olav, he had bought a summer retreat not far from the place where he grew up, a small farm to be more exact, on a ridge above the Flekkefjorden, with some land, a bit of woodland, and a small stretch of coast. We drove there in the morning, one of many gorgeous days that summer, the sky was bright blue, the fellsides lush green, a blaze of dazzling sunlight flooding the landscape. The water in the fjords and rivers glittered, the peaks shimmered with snow, the leaves of the trees winking and fluttering in occasional breaths of wind. Mom drove first with Linda and Heidi in her car, while I followed behind with Vanja and John in the backseat. There was hardly any traffic. The car I was driving was one we had borrowed from my mother's sister Kjellaug, Jon Olav's mother. An old Toyota. After the new driving-school and rental cars I'd been driving it felt like a vehicle from another age, the mechanical twentieth century. It was as if I were seated just above the surface of the road, everything rattled and shook, even the slightest acceleration could be felt. The other cars I had driven were dark and sleek, like something out of a computer game, as if the traffic surrounding us were just a projection on a screen, speed, whether 100, 110, or 130 kilometers an hour, merely numbers on a display. This was something else entirely, and I was enjoying it. We came around a bend in the road and there was a river, cool and green, rapids hurtling over the rock, an effervescence of white. We came through a tunnel, and there was a fjord beneath us, its blue expanse with farms dotted about the shore on one side, steep, treeless fells on the other like slabs of iron in the haze. There were no people any-where to be seen, only old and sagging structures, the occasional flashy home from the 1980s, agricultural machinery lying around, fields and enclosures, forest, fjords, fells. And Vanja's voice from the backseat:

"How much farther, Daddy?"

"It won't be long now. Just be patient!"

"I'm bored!"

"Look over there, look! A waterfall on the other side!"

"I know, I can see."

"Do you want some music on?"

"Yes."

I put Dennis Wilson on. Vanja calls it car music when we lis-ten to it at home. In the mirror I could see her lean back in her seat and stare out with an empty look in her eyes. John was fast asleep next to her.

We came down into Dale, its two gas stations making it a me-tropolis in this scarcely populated wide-open place where I had spent so many weeks of summer when I was growing up. On the other side of the town a minute later, the steeply sloping ridge of the esker rose up to our right, crowned by Kjellaug and Magne's farm. Shortly after, as we got out of the car at Jon Olav's place, everything was still. I heard bees, a busy hum wafting back and forth, rising and falling in the quiet air. I opened the door on Vanja's side and unfastened her seat belt, she climbed out and looked up at me. John was still asleep and started to cry when I bent over him and began to extricate him from his belts and buckles, but when I lifted him out he hushed and put his head against my shoulder. The house was set back from the road at the top of a steep meadow running down to the deep-blue fjord, whose waters lapped lazily against the shore. The trees on the other side shimmered.

We were there all day. I dived into the fjord in my underpants as Vanja and Heidi stood and watched me from the rocks, we rowed out in a little boat with Johannes, Jon Olav's eldest son, guiding us, and when the afternoon came I took Vanja fishing with a rod we borrowed. Vanja had never been fishing before, now I had to teach her, and so that she wouldn't be disappointed, neither the weather nor the time of day being especially suited for fishing, I kept telling her we probably weren't going to catch anything. As long as you know, I said. Yes, I know, she said. We pushed through some bushes, picked our way over the rocks, and came onto a little point of land that jutted out into the water, where I cast the spinner. It glittered in the sunlight as it arced through the air and landed with a little splash, and as it sank I handed the rod to Vanja so she could reel it in. Is this right, Daddy? she asked. Yes, that's fine, I said. I've got one! she said. You're joking, I said. A moment later a fine codfish lay flapping at our feet. Your very first cast! I exclaimed, and she beamed with pride. It was the only bite of the day. Back at the house, Linda took a picture of her with the fish in her hands. For once I felt like a real dad. Liv and Jon Olav were busy making dinner, his whole family was coming, Ann Kristin with her two girls, and Magne and Kjellaug. An hour later, as the sun nestled on the treetops to the west, we numbered eight children, five parents, and three grandparents, all of us seated on the slope, each with a plate in our lap, eating sausage stew and rice. On the outside it was just like any other cozy family get-together, but beneath the surface it was a different story. Magne, whom I had known all my life, was terminally ill. He had always been a strong and vigorous man, a focal point in any gathering, a man of immense charisma, impossible to ignore. Sitting there now he was hardly recognizable. Physically he wasn't much changed, but his presence had gone. He was hardly there, and it pained me the whole time, even when he was out of sight, I couldn't grasp it, that such a total transformation could be possible, I'd always equated his presence with *him*, the person he was, to me they were the same. Now he was a shadow of himself. He chatted a bit, ate a little, occasionally gazing out over the fjord, surrounded by his children and grandchildren, on what was perhaps the most beautiful day of that whole summer.

Everything he saw would soon be gone to him, and would never come back.

Not just his family, whose fates and destinies he would never know, but also the fjord and the fell, the grass and the humming insects. And the sun. He would never see the sun again.

These thoughts tainted everything I saw that day. The beauty of the world became enhanced, and yet it seemed crueler too, for one day it would be gone to me too, and continue to exist for those who remained, as it had done since the beginning of time. How many people had sat where we were sitting and looked at the same view? Generation after generation stretching back in time, all here once, all gone now.

When evening came and it was time to go home, Vanja wanted to go with Heidi and Linda, so I drove with John, who slept, an hour and a half beneath the towering fells, through the valleys where the shadows of approaching night grew long, past the racing rivers and gushing waterfalls, and all the time I sang out loud, drunk on the sun and death.

What else could I do? I was so happy.

It was the same sun Broch had written about in the thirties, the same sun that sank into the sea off Brundisium that evening in the year 19 BC. And it was the same sun Turner let shine upon his picture of an ancient harbor, painted some hundred years before. Turner found his motif in Virgil's epic *Aeneid*, more specifically in the story of Dido, who falls in love with Aeneas and takes her own life when he parts from her. However, it is not so much the drama of the events Turner is interested in as the place in which they unfold. His painting depicts the harbor at Carthage on the northern coast of Africa and appears markedly Romantic in both its exoticism and its rubble-strewn *ruin lust*, the many monumental, half-collapsed buildings that fill its canvas. At least this was what I thought the first time I saw it. On closer inspection though, I realized these were not ruins at all, but the opposite. The great chalk-white buildings of Antiquity were actually under construction, and what the painting shows is a city rising rather than falling. It's a splendid painting. On the right of the picture a cliff thick with vegetation drops steeply away to a river, which then opens out into a harbor. On the other side of the river, in the left of the picture, a building is under construction, and below it are some people, figures made small by the imposing cliff and the buildings. A woman in white, Dido, stands in the midst of a group of men, one of whom, seemingly a soldier, is turned away from the beholder, and most likely this is Aeneas. Building materials lie scattered about, and in the background a number of men seem to be at work, hauling something ashore from a boat. A cluster of boys, almost detached from all this activity, are gathered at the water's edge, they are naked and have either just climbed out of the water or are about to jump in. While they may be detached from the goings-on at the riverside, they are not detached from their surroundings, on the contrary, the feeling I get when I look at the picture is that everything seems to hang together, the boys are in some way joined up with the vegetation and the water, with the people behind them and the mighty buildings, and the masts of the boats in the background seem almost to melt into the haze that pervades the activity taking place at the river on this particular day.

While cold light makes everything sharp and separates things out, warm light blurs contours and makes the elements of the scene seep into each other. This was primarily what Turner was interested in, I imagine, since so many of his paintings display this feature, the one of the train, for instance, almost completely blotted out by the snowstorm, hardly a definite line or contour in the picture, everything a blur, everything in flux. Seeing in color, this is what we see, the objects vanishing, or their functions, and the eye that puts aside all it knows, that puts aside all preexisting insight, is the eye that can see the world anew, as if it were emerging before it for the very first time. Turner was interested in the relationship between the inconstant and the immutable, the solid and the fluid, and in that way the train becomes an expression not of anything else, one of the many categories into which it might be placed to do with modernity, industrialism, civilization, and the man-made, but only of what it is in itself, in pure physical terms, an enormous iron object proceeding along an iron track, almost obliterated by the snow, which would obliterate almost any other object in the same way: a sailing ship, a horse-drawn carriage, a funeral procession, a bear. When it comes to *Dido Building Carthage*, his interest lies similarly in the near endless ways in which light alters the landscape, from its shimmering in the river to the haze that absorbs it into the horizon, and this focus naturally affects the scene unfolding there. Dido is perhaps seeing Aeneas for the first time, something is beginning there, yet something is coming to an end too, for what she sees will soon lead her into death. The fact of there being so little difference between what is built up and what comes crashing down, the fact that the buildings under construction could just as well be ruins, compounds this impression. The tropical vegetation also plays a part, growing so wildly, so blindly, and with such vigor as to pose a threat to the civilized world, which by comparison is so neat and orderly as to be reminiscent of death. All this exists in Turner's painting, and yet none of it is central, for its principal motif is the sun.

The first time I saw the painting, which hangs in the National Gallery in London, I was filled with a sense of welling emotion, it was all I could do to remain standing in front of it, so huge was the impression it made on me. This was of course down to its sheer beauty, but also to the way in which the sun is presented, the way it actually dazzles the beholder. The sun is the primary subject, suspended high above the scene, its rays pervading everything, illuminating all surfaces, either directly or indirectly, conjuring forth all colors, warming the air, making it thick and consuming all distinctions, in a way tying the various elements of the scene together, though without any of the people present even being aware of it. How can this be possible, I thought to myself as I stood there. How can they go about beneath something as mighty and immense, such an insanely creative principle, this enormous sphere of gas aflame in the sky, and yet ignore it so completely? They do not see the sun, but Turner did and, thanks to him, we do too. The sun in this painting is so predominant it is hard not to think of it as holy, and that Turner was worshipping it. Indeed, he valued this particular canvas highly, so highly that an early version of his will declared that he wanted to be buried with it. Later he abandoned this bizarre wish, donating it instead to the National Gallery on condition that it be displayed next to a painting by Claude Lorrain, also of an ancient seaport, a picture he greatly admired and on which his own canvas can be taken to comment. And so it came to pass: in Room 15 of the National Gallery, Turner's painting now hangs next to Lorrain's. The similiarities between the two are striking. Both motifs are classical and centered around a female figure – in Lorrain's instance the Queen of Sheba – both are set in a port lined by ancient buildings, far below that which so dominates both canvases: the sun and the sky. But this similarity serves only to make their differences all the more marked and significant. The most obvious of these is that Lorrain's harbor opens out on the sea, whereas in Turner's painting the sea is not visible at all, the harbor all but enclosing the river. And whereas the light in Lorrain's painting is sharp and clear, in Turner's it is thick and always somewhat hazy. This makes the effect of the two canvases quite different. In Turner's, life is hemmed in, there is an inertia about it, in the sense that it rises and falls in the same place, with no way out.

This is emphasized by the motif, which on the one hand is death – Dido burying her husband – and on the other, life: Aeneas, the great survivor, has come, and with him love, which is to say the vital force of life and the future, which for Dido, bereaved and emotional as she stands there at the river, is to be her death.

This claustrophobic sense of being hemmed in is essential to the feeling or understanding of life the painting manifests or explores. The sun, too, is part of this, its static aspect being likewise compounded, and while it may give life to everything, it precipitates decay too. In Lorrain's seaport, depicted some hours later, at evening, the breezy air of passing day blowing in from the sea, everything by contrast appears wide open and in motion. The motif here is the Queen of Sheba's embarkation, but around this event all sorts of other things are going on too, boats putting in and rowing away, sailors clambering up a ship's rigging or leaning against the gunwales, people going about the quayside, pausing to chat, gazing out at the royal vessel or keeping an eye on a scampering child at the water's edge, and all of this with the open, sun-drenched sea stretching out toward the horizon. The majestic pseudo-antique buildings, the finely dressed people and the many boats in the harbor in front of them are clear and distinct. This has a particular effect on the main event, the embarkation of the queen, which becomes just one of several things going on, significant to those who are a part of it in that precise location, but nowhere else, paling as one shifts one's gaze outward to the sea or inward to the town. Entities that vanish in the open, existing only locally, are a frequent phenomenon in Lorrain's work.

Recently I visited the Metropolitan Museum in New York, and there was a painting by him entitled *The Trojan Women Setting Fire to Their Fleet*, another scene from the *Aeneid*, where this very aspect is perhaps even more pronounced. It shows a war fleet at anchor near the shore, some women are standing with flaming torches, some are in a boat on their way out to the ships, but the intense drama of the scene, its momentousness, seems to be taking place among these people only, while the landscape stretches out beyond, unmarked by these events, submerged in the deep slumber of uneventfulness, and above them is the immutable sky with its still-burning sun. Was it viewed in that way when it was painted, four hundred years ago, in Lorrain's own time? To us the local aspect of any major event is hardly ever present, both because every part of it is focalized and because it is made to exist in all places at once.

No matter where we happened to be on September 11, 2001, we heard about or saw the same thing, the two planes crashing into the twin towers. This event was in all our minds, there was no outside – apart from the place one happened to be, physically, wherever in the world. This bipartite operation, so characteristic of our age, where something is on the one hand almost completely focalized, and on the other almost completely spread out in all directions, was of course unknown in Lorrain's day, the technologically unsophisticated seventeenth century, when an event was for those who happened to be there when it took place. When Lorrain interprets a scene from the *Aeneid*, he brings it across to us in a way not unlike that of a news photographer in our day and age, as a kind of witness – the fact of the former being a fictive witness, and the latter being an actual witness, makes no difference to the form – but he shows us something more besides, which has to do with the time and space in which the event took place. The great, eventless landscape that surrounds what is going on makes it so obvious to us that it is going on only in the scene's here and now, and that this is the most important, essential aspect of any event. Oh, how simple and plain an insight, yet it is one thing to know the nature of something, quite another to feel and experience it. How hidden the actual nature of events has become to us is something we understand only when we see something unexpected happen in front of our own eyes. Only then, at such a moment, do we realize how unimaginably few unexpected events unfold in our world, how incredibly systematized and regulated our every movement, even in our largest cities, and, moreover, and this is perhaps the most shocking aspect, the way such an event vanishes again the same moment it occurs.

Some years ago, when we were living in Stockholm and I kept an office on Dalagatan, I was out walking with Linda, we had eaten lunch together, she was on her way home, I wanted to stop at a record store before getting back to work. It was snowing, the street was full of slush, the sky above us gray and leaden. The cars with their yellow headlights and red taillights, their growling engines and swishing wiper blades, the people on the street with their heads bowed to the sidewalk, beneath the vertical faces of the buildings, made the moment a cacophony without my thinking of it in that way, everything was simply how it was supposed to be. Suddenly, something happened, there was a thud, my eyes were drawn to the middle of the road. A car braked, and a man flew through the air above it. He landed heavily on the road surface, and a short distance away a bicycle hit the ground the same moment the car jerked to a halt. The other cars behind it stopped. On both sides of the street pedestrians stood motionless on the sidewalks, eyes fixed on the middle of the road. The man, wearing a thick blue down jacket, sat up slowly. He had a big, bald head. He sat there, looking emptily into space. Blood trickled from his forehead and down his nose. Great flakes of snow whirled in the air around him. The thought occurred to me that I should do something, and I opened my bag to get my phone, but then I saw a young man just in front of us with his own phone pressed to his ear, I heard him say there'd been an accident, so I put mine away again just as the car door opened and a man got out. He crouched down in front of the cyclist, said something to him, gripped him under his arms, helped him up, put him in the front seat of the car, clicked the seat belt into place, slammed the door shut, climbed in behind the wheel, shut his own door, and drove off.

The street had opened like a flower, now it closed again. Apart from the bike, which was still lying there on the road, everything was exactly as before.

The young man on the phone said there was no need for an ambulance after all.

I looked at Linda.

"What happened?" I said.

"I'm not sure," she said. "It all went so fast. I suppose he took him off to the hospital?"

"I suppose so," I said.

The young man swiveled to face us.

"He drove off with him," he said.

"Yes," I said.

"I called an ambulance. No need now, though."

"No," I said.

"He drove straight into him. It was the driver's fault. He might not be taking him to the hospital. He could just leave him somewhere and clear off."

"No, I can't imagine that," I said.

"Why else would he be in such a hurry?" he said, then walked over to the bike and leaned it up against a lamppost, raised his hand to Linda and me in a wave, and went off toward the center while we ambled away in the opposite direction. Linda went home, I turned around and went back to the office.

I felt shaken. But why, exactly? There was nothing puzzling about what I had seen, and it was hardly spectacular either. It was a minor accident, that was all, a motorist knocking a cyclist off his bike in busy lunchtime traffic. The next day I checked the paper to see if there was anything about it. There wasn't. Of course there wasn't. Not a word. But still I felt shaken. It wasn't because I felt for him, or because there had been blood, it was something else, something to do with the very nature of the occurrence. Fifty meters away no one knew what had happened, and to the few people who were there it was all over and done with as quickly as it took place. Had there been some mention in the paper, I would probably have calmed back down, order would have been restored. The newspapers are full of that kind of thing, events deviating in some way from the norm, and our reading about them there lends

697

them a kind of fixedness they don't have in real life, where they are over the moment they occur and no one who witnesses them can quite grasp what actually happened. That fixedness is a fiction, but we understand it to be reality, and thereby the real world remains under our control, and this is our haven. The event is lifted out of its physical environment and its particular moment and goes from being without continuity to becoming a part of an ongoing system, so-called news. Anything that cannot be explained, any unexpected accident or catastrophe, any instance of sudden death or incomprehensible malice is gathered here in the form of small narratives, and the mere fact of their being told is sufficient to put us at ease, to assure us that order exists. This system is completely irrational, such order being but fiction, and in this it resembles other systems people have seemingly always sought to establish. Order operates in the social domain but relates to what lies outside that domain. The fear of natural forces, inorganic as well as organic, has always needed to be assuaged, and since the human is what is known to us, and such forces are alien to us, they have been incorporated into the human sphere, still as alien, yet alien within our own domain. The classic trope here is the ghost, death in human form. One of the places where this aspect of the relationship between man and nature is clearest is in the work of the author Olav Duun. One of his most important books is called *Menneske og maktene* (published in English as *Floodtide of Fate*), the original Norwegian title evoking the human struggle against the tide of inhuman forces, a theme that runs throughout his work. His masterpiece, the six-volume saga *The People of Juvik*, is steeped in it. Though Duun was only ten years older than Broch and they wrote and published their novels during the same period, *The People of Juvik* is so unlike *The Death of Virgil* that they could be attributed to different civilizations if one did not know any better. Broch's opening scene, with its Imperial Adriatic squadron and the dying Virgil, is worlds away from this:

The first Juviking they can tell us about came from the south, from Sparbu or Stod or wherever it was. His name was Per. He had been married, it was said, and had had house and land, and he brought his mother with him. What had driven him out the Lord only knew. He leased a piece of land from Lines.

Whereas Broch's novel takes place in the very epicenter of power, with the empire's greatest poet as its main character, and explores the relationships between ethics and aesthetics, politics and literature, Duun's novel is set in the very margins of civilization, a tiny and in every respect insignificant village community on the coast of Nord-Trøndelag in preindustrial Norway, with a family of uneducated farmers and fishermen as its main characters, the political upheavals and transformational occurrences that might take place in the wider world washing up onto their shores only in the aftermath, like historical driftwood. Naturally, this is not the way they see things themselves, to them this is the center of the world, and so closely does Duun zoom in on them that the reader feels this too, following the family's tale as individual existences are established and eked out, a society formed and maintained. Land is cleared and cultivated, houses are built, children are born. This is the foundation of their lives, on which they could stand so firmly if not for the crackling force field that exists between them, the invisible sphere of emotions, jealousy and resentment, love and benevolence, greed and arrogance, suspicion and fathomless naïveté that drives them here and there, lumping together in great knots, dissolving, lumping together, dissolving, and lumping together again. The narrow horizon within which this takes place and the long period of time the saga covers make it seem like it's the place itself that finds expression in its people, as if they are their place more than they are themselves, in contrast to Hamsun – probably the most obvious writer to compare with Duun – in whose work such an idea could never arise. Hamsun's characters are alien, belonging to no place, they are tourists of the mind, somehow, without a past, without origin. Hamsun's characters come barging in. Emotions occur within rather than between individuals, in contrast to Duun. The difference reveals itself, too, in their understandings of irrationality. Both Duun and Hamsun are interested in the notion. In Hamsun the irrational is often fine and delicate, a reflection of the nobility of the nerves, romantically maniacal, as rich as it is a thing of beauty. In Duun the irrational is bound up with popular belief, superstition, misunderstanding, and darkness, a thing that occurs between people, often helpless and impoverished. When Per Anders, the first of the saga's series of protagonists, dies, Duun describes it like this:

> *The maids dared not lie down to sleep that night. They sat downstairs in the parlor and slept. For they heard a braying outside. They heard queer noises in the old house. Ane sat half-covered up in her shawl. She was reading a hymn, or perhaps the Lord's Prayer itself.*
>
> *Then he jumps to his feet and listens out: "Hear, the buck!," only to lie down again smiling: "Oh, never mind, it's only the ladder and the birch. They don't frighten me."*
>
> *There was something terrible outside the house, this they felt. There sat an evil spirit, riding on the roof. It was a night of ill fortune.*
>
> *Per Anders had a dire fit of coughing and rattling of the throat. Then he said: "Come now, Ane. Give me the staff."*
>
> *"Pray to the Lord, pray to the Lord!" she whispered anxiously.*
>
> *"M-m. If I have never prayed to him before, why – "*
>
> *It was the last he said. Ane opened the door, that the soul might depart, and then she laid out the body the way it was supposed to be done. She noticed little Anders standing in the doorway. At the same moment, Valborg saw him too, and both of them asked him: "What are you standing there staring at, Anders?"*
>
> *The boy pointed to the foot of the bed. "Who was that man there?"*
>
> *"There?" They looked at each other. Their knees trembled. Valborg took the boy and put him to bed.*

Death in Duun's writing is shrouded in terror and superstition. They open the door to let out the soul of the deceased, they see a ghost sitting at the foot of the deceased's bed, or perhaps it is the devil himself come to collect him. The next morning they burn the *likhalm*, the straw on which the corpse has lain on the bier, and when the wind blows the smoke back toward the farmhouse they are gripped with fear, taking it to be an omen of impending death. When the son rings the church bell for the deceased, it feels unusually heavy and sluggish, a bad sign, he lies and tells his mother all went well. The corpse is laid out on straw inside the farmhouse, his hymnbook under his chin and a coin on each eye, one of which slips from its place, the deceased staring at them all, a couple of the women gasping in fear. He lies there a week before the wake and the burial. "The women dared hardly go outside after dusk, they thought they had a white one at their heels wherever they went; and all sorts of ugly noises were to be heard in the evenings." On the day of the wake a crow settles on the roof of the farm, they chase it away, but it keeps coming back; again they take it to be a sign that someone else is soon to die. Yet the deceased makes them think of other things, too, besides ghosts and spirits. Per Anders's son Per visits the corpse daily.

> It seemed to him like it wanted to tell him something. But when he was there it told him nothing: it slept as before.
>
> Ay, he thought, here lies the last. Of them.
>
> And when he came out, he said out loud to himself: "And so the fell ends at the sea. It wants no further. And as death has drawn this face, so does evening lift hills and fells toward the sky: still and stone-dead, so far removed from life and all that lives and moves."

It is the sunset Duun is describing, when evening rises in the landscape and all becomes still and dark. The foreboding of death Broch invests in his glittering sea is effectuated here to the full, though without the landscape losing its beauty. "So does evening lift hills and fells toward the sky." That we are bound up with stillness and the dark, and seemingly become one with them when we die, is the oldest mystery of all, for we are here one moment and gone the next, never to return, but to remain there, blind and still, for all time. The endeavor of Duun's characters is to give voice to this blindness, this stillness, thereby drawing the unknown into the known. The smoke of the *likhalm* is a sign, it *tells* them something. The sluggish church bell tells them something. The black crow tells them something. And the corpse, when the coin slips from its eye, tells them something. When this dark and silent world speaks, a path is opened between the living and the dead, which in itself is meaningful. The inexplicable, such as a person in the prime of life, wholly involved in human reality, suddenly being struck down without anyone being able to do anything about it, snatched by death or else spared to recover, makes any occurrence a meaningful sign: the smoke blowing back to the farm, the omen of what was to come. Order exists, nothing in the world is arbitrary. The order Duun describes is a blend of Christianity, paganism, and homespun fatalism, and much of the story's value lies in the way he shows how the great superstructures that exist independently of the people there are adapted to the real-world lives they live, hauled down into praxis, a day-to-day existence of plows, fishing nets, livestock, and outhouses, by which they are changed. In their pure form myths are complete depictions of reality, closed upon themselves, yet the way they work, what they do, resembles what Duun's characters do. Myth lends a face to the unknown, giving it body, place, and time, establishing connections between the human world and nature, between death and life, between past and future, creation and destruction. When a figure such as Odin dangles from the branches of Yggdrasil, half dead and half alive, to obtain its knowledge, or when Eve is coaxed into eating the fruit of the Tree of Knowledge, thereby becoming mortal, in both cases a connection is established between the tree, death, and knowledge. Of what does that connection consist? The roots in the ground, the branches in the sky, these are the world and life, which is endless, forever sprouting anew from dead stubs. Knowledge comes from the dead, everything we know we have learned from them. Life is the life of the one and the life of us all. Death is the death of the one and the death of us all. The sun is forever being seen for the first time, always a new pair of eyes squinting up at it, and forever being seen for the last time, other eyes closing, losing sight of it once and for all. These connections are what our myths and rituals manage and administer, and the same applies to them, they are already there for us. They are a language, a different language, and what they communicate can be communicated in no other way. In this respect the Enlightenment, resting on the idea that myth, ritual, and religion were a form of superstition, represented decay. We call the mythological view of the world unenlightened, and obviously, four hundred years after the beginning of the Enlightenment, we now know more about the material world and how it works than those who lived before that time. And not just more, but unimaginably more. But what is knowing? Throughout the *Völuspá*, the *völva*'s questions are repeated in what seems like a refrain of reluctance: Do you know enough yet, or what? Knowledge is concealed, connected to Hel, the dead and the past, out of sight, and access to it comes at a price. "Do you know enough yet, or what?" says the *völva*, and in that lies an evaluation of those listening in, their thirst for knowledge, at which she sneers. To drink from Mimir's Well, Odin sacrifices an eye, quite unthinkable to us, since what we know is so bound up with what we see. For us knowledge comes from sight, this was the essence of the revolution that was the Enlightenment, no longer were we to be tied to the authority of religion's ancient scriptures, the texts of philosophy. In myth this is not the case, in fact the opposite holds, for in myth knowledge is bound up with what we cannot see, that which is secret and concealed. Moreover, the price to be paid for it is great. In the Bible's creation myth the fall of man is down to Adam and Eve eating the fruit of the Tree of Knowledge. "The oldest of our religious traditions considered knowledge to be guilty; we had thought it to be innocent," writes the French philosopher Michel Serres. The rituals, myths, and folktales that have been handed down through the generations, as far back as our collective memory can reach into the dark depths of history, of whose lives we are unknowing, are referred to by Serres as social or cultural technologies, industries that worked to "secrete time," as he puts it, "from whose compost the different traditions appeared." Language, which we take for granted, came once from nothing. The insight that the community lives on even when the individual dies, which we take for granted, came only gradually. Responsibility toward the future, of which they themselves were not a part, was not given but was won. There is a light in this, but it is directed toward what it means to be human, rather than toward the components of the human and how they work together. Our myths see us in terms of time, the Enlightenment sees us in terms of space.

Our world is very much about the space we inhabit, practically all our technology, industry, and science is organized according to its principles. The space we inhabit is seen, mapped, and explained, and subjugated at an increasing rate. The space we used to inhabit, and which Duun describes, characterized by repetition through generations, where people toiled by the sweat of their brows, made love, gave birth to children, and died, in other words the space in which they felt themselves at home, but which they also feared, surrounded as it was by the darkness of ignorance, no remoter to us in time than to be inhabited by the parents of my own grandparents in Vestland, who were fishermen and farmers, is now gone. We do not believe in omens, we do not believe in God, in fact we believe in nothing; instead we know. We know the wind's direction is determined by meteorological phenomena, and that smoke blowing toward a house means nothing other than that, a movement of air caused by differences of atmospheric pressure. We know the soul dies when we die, so we no longer open the door to let it out. We know there are no such things as ghosts, and that devils do not exist either; if a boy sees a figure in the half-light at the foot of the bed, it is a product of his imagination. We know that a sluggish bell cannot determine how the year will proceed. We know birds are not omens; a crow settling on the roof of a house where a person lies dead is a matter of coincidence, the whim of a bird; perhaps the roof gave it a better view of what it was after? Everything has a sensible, rational explanation, we know this and live our lives according to that knowledge. For that reason, we are not afraid of the dark and not afraid of death.

But what do we actually know?

In Duun's world everyone believed in God, this was a matter of course, anything else was unthinkable. But few had any real idea of what it was they actually believed in, few had anything more than a superficial knowledge of religion, that was what the priests were there for, they knew everything there was to know about the Scriptures. For ordinary people it was sufficient to know there was a god, and a son of that god, who took all their sins upon himself, and that there was a life after death. This applies to us, too. We know how everything works and hangs together, nothing remains unexplained. Yet few of us know exactly what it is that we know, few are in any way genuinely familiar with the sciences. We know about atoms and electrons, we know about the theory of evolution and the big bang, yet would be hard put to explain any of these things ourselves; as long as we know someone else knows, we trust in that knowledge, that the world is organized in that way, and this puts our minds at ease and makes us feel secure. Duun's world revolved around repetition, time was mythical and static, whereas our world revolves around the new changing times, progress. The new is in everything; the things we use, for example, are continually being redesigned, cutlery made in the eighties is different from cutlery now, a house built in the 1950s is different from a house built in our day, but such change is for the eye only, visual rather than functional: a knife has a handle and a blade in 2010 as it had a handle and a blade in 1710 or 1310. In any mythological understanding of reality the eye does not count, meaning resides in what the eye cannot see, whereas any rational understanding of reality is visual, and that shift, which occurred in the sixteenth and seventeenth centuries, comprises the very nucleus of the revolution that was the Enlightenment. The most important technologies developed in that age were the telescope and the microscope, without these two optical instruments the gradual insights of science would have been inconceivable. And perhaps the emphasis placed on design in our own age should be understood on that basis? Time is invisible, time can be neither enlarged nor diminished, evading all spatial technologies by virtue of that invisibility, but in design it is captured, in design it appears to us: the seventies looked like this, the eighties looked like this, the nineties looked like this. The old becomes the new in a system that in principle is the same as that of our former rituals, where each spring was a new beginning, though with the important difference that what we see is not the same, we do not see the repetition, only the new. The same is true of news, which removes events from their original time and their original place, inserting them into a flow of other events, the same from one day to the next, from one month to the next, from one year to the next, in that planes will continue to crash, people will continue getting killed, workers will always be on strike somewhere, there will always be car accidents, maritime disasters, elections, famines, and within this continuity, in which individual events are different but the form always the same, time is again static and mythical. Oh, our world is indeed a mythological world, above us a sky of images in which nothing ever changes and everything is the same. We have made a myth of reality, but unlike the people whose lives were determined by a mythological understanding of the world, we are unaware of it, thinking what we see and relate to to be reality itself, the world the way it really is. It is in this light that I understand the experience of the sublime, or the epiphanic, more particularly that something in the world emerges before us, passes through our conception of it and for a brief moment reveals itself the way it is. The things themselves are the same, only our perception of them changes, because in being unusually grand, unexpected, or in some other way departing from the norm, for a few seconds they contrive to put our expectations out of action. This is why Turner's sun, or the event depicted by Lorrain, or the sea and the harbor in Broch's opening passage, appear so intense and awaken such vigorous emotion. This is the truth of art. The truth of science is of a different nature, quite differently bound by time; practically all scientific research of the eighteenth and nineteenth centuries is unreadable today, certainly it has lost most of its relevance, whereas the art of that period still speaks to us and is laden with meaning. Indeed, across the chasm of familiar and unfamiliar time it speaks to us; a cave of paintings tens of thousands of years old leaves an impression on us and in a certain respect cannot be surpassed, the same is true of the first creation narratives, even though we know little if anything about those who wrote them or how they lived. Compared to the swell of generations who lived through the hundreds of thousands of years before the advent of Enlightenment philosophy, the ensuing four hundred years of rationality are but a ripple on the surface, a scratch on the rock of a fell, and from such a perspective concepts like "rational" and "irrational" are not particularly fruitful. It is all a matter of different ways of relating to the unknown. We have succeeded in exorcising the unknown, and we are at ease and secure, the first culture in history not to tremble in the face of our circumstances, life is under our control. But the price of such security is high, for it is a presence in our lives. And it reveals itself in death. We are no longer afraid of death, having lifted everything to do with it into the sky of images above us, because if one thing is prevalent there it is the image of people dying. In the world of images people die all the time, they are shot in the head or in the chest, they plunge from cliffs and waterfalls, they drown or crash in their cars, they perish in air disasters, they die on the battlefield, or fall victim to a suicide bomber at a checkpoint in the Middle East or Iraq, they are hacked to death with ice picks, slashed by knives, run through by swords or pierced by lances, they are gassed to death, they freeze to death and are incinerated in fires. They stumble and crack their heads open on the edges of bathtubs and doors, they fall on the steepest ski slopes and bleed to death when their arteries are severed, they die in childbirth, in their sickbeds, of cancer and plague, brain hemorrhages and heart attacks. They die on the cross, in the electric chair, on the gallows, and strapped to a table with poison injected into their blood. This death, which is visual and unattached in time or place, floating freely and weightlessly in our sky of images, is a surrogate, a substitute for real death, absorbing our fear and anxiety, while real death, the physical death of the body, the way it occurs in a certain place at a certain time, is hidden away as much as possible. And when it occurs, when we encounter it in the real world, the way it really is, when it descends from heaven to earth in all its chthonic longing, its lust for mull and humus, darkness and damp, and the corpse lies there in front of our eyes, stiff and dead, it is as if a veil is drawn aside, for we are not modern at all, we are old as the dolmens and barrows, kin to the grass and trees, the worms and snails that slither as best they can, one day simply to lie there, immovable beneath the sky, to disintegrate and be gone, a speck in all the world's jagged edges and swirling forms, made from dust, returned to dust, earthly in marrow and bone, hands and feet bound to the now that we today, despite all promises to the contrary, depart. But we cannot part from death, death will never betray us, death comes to us always, and with it life.

I saw a cruise ship thronged with people pass slowly through a sinking city, a loudspeaker voice blaring out, a glitter of flashing cameras, and was it death I saw?

Indeed, and it was sublime. The sublime is everything, though now, in our fracturing world, it has become almost extinct. We live under the hegemony of constituent parts, and death, too, is under its jurisdiction. It is the death of the individual that matters, we are snatched away one by one, hidden from each other's gaze, and only the specified death matters. Not Death, but the death of constricted arteries and overexerted hearts, the death of lungs eaten up by cancer. The same applies to beauty. The covers of chunky art books almost always show a small section of a painting, a hand, the gaze of an eye, a bird, a sky, a figure in the background, seldom the painting in its entirety. Inside their covers the painting appears together with various sections of it, often with an X-ray for good measure so we can study for ourselves the processes that went into making the finished painting. Aha, so he moved the hat? In the case of a famous painting, lesser-known paintings from the same period are shown alongside it, and in the accompanying essays the issues raised are most usually social in nature – the people in that Renaissance painting, what clothes are they wearing? What class do they belong to? What sort of economic system was the artist a part of? Where did they get their paints, did they leave any fingerprints anywhere? What currents made the perspective possible or necessary? Was the painter a homosexual, and in what ways does this show in what he chose to paint? Why were there so few women painters, and how has this affected the way we perceive quality? This atomization of everything, this is also a result of the primacy of the visual, since it is no longer the impression art or death or the divine awakens in us that applies, but what it looks like – in the case of the body, what kind of memories precede our expiry; in the case of art, not the impression itself, but the preconditions of that impression. This atomization, which Broch and many around him believed to represent a degeneration, but which of course may also be seen as an enormous revitalization of a slowly withering culture, something to which not least the paintings of the Baroque attest, the world there almost exploding in detail and the own beauty of our physical reality in everything from pheasant feathers to dead hares, apples, blunderbusses, skulls, and shells, was met by another, seemingly contrary tendency, a universal science, *una scientia universalis* to use the words of Francis Bacon, achieved through principles of observation, probability, and verification. It is impossible to think of a science that is local, that a phenomenon or object, for instance, should display properties that applied only in one place, only then. Seventeenth-century debate about the wonder or miracle, which until then had been fully believed in, the improbable event that occurred only once, in one place, never to be repeated, perhaps illustrates better than anything the new line that was drawn through the world, as well as its impact. In his *Religio Medici* from 1635, Thomas Browne writes:

> *That Miracles are ceased, I can neither prove, nor absolutely deny, much lesse define the time and period of their cessation; that they survived Christ, is manifest upon record of Scripture; that they outlived the Apostles also, & were revived at the conversion of Nations, many yeares after, we cannot deny, if wee shall not question those Writers whose testimonies wee doe not controvert, in points that make for our own opinions; therefore that may have some truth in it that is reported by the Jesuites of their Miracles in the Indies; I could wish it were true, or had any other testimony than their owne Pennes.*

On the one hand he argues in favor of the unchallenged authority of Scripture, doubting not for a moment the existence of miracles as a phenomenon, these being described in the Bible and therefore necessarily true; on the other hand he is troubled by doubt as to whether the miracle exists in his own time, Scripture in this instance falling short, requiring him to seek independent testimony. This new way of reasoning, based on observation, was gradually to displace faith and the idea of the holy, though the two viewpoints were nevertheless not dissimilar, since what characterizes the holy, its exclusion of all that is not holy, in like manner characterizes the rational, which excludes all that is not rational. This state of affairs still holds. Religion and art are no longer midpoints in our ways of perception, but exist at the periphery, without power or influence. While religion has become a personal matter – if a person is Christian, it is his own, private belief – art has turned to addressing issues that arise in the social domain in which our lives are played out, and on the odd occasion it chances to home in on that middle point of meaning where our world is defined, which is to say in the laboratory and the observatory, it invariably comes across as rather amateurish and undignified. At once ignorant and ingratiating, it talks big about string theory or quantum physics. A new path for the novel? For humankind? Party afterward? Anyone?

When I was a boy I wanted to be a surgeon. It was a wish that probably came from watching the medical programs shown on Norwegian TV in the seventies, long sequences of actual operations that had me completely captivated. The body was never shown in its entirety, only the parts of it that were cut into, the rest was covered up by material of the same kind and color as the aprons and masks worn by the surgeons and nurses. It was a smooth, pristine material without folds or stains, against which the white skin that lay like a crater in the middle with all its irregularities seemed almost obscene. When the scalpel was inserted and the section of skin cut open by the faceless surgeon under the light of a powerful lamp, it seemed as if a little ditch appeared. When held open by clamps it was seen to be full of fluids and pulsating organs impossible to distinguish from one another, much less identify, yet they gleamed like membranes in the light, and clearly some order did exist, for the rubber-clad fingers set to work swiftly and with obvious experience. And so it was I saw the heart, the blind beast that moves in the chest, and the blood in which it bathed. Many of my drawings from that time are of surgeons operating on patients, they were gory and full of blood, and my mother worried about me: perhaps there was something wrong? But surgery was part of a pattern; my other interests were diving and space exploration, all three areas having in common the fact that they served to open up the world, in the first instance the human body, in the second ocean life, in the third the vastness of the cosmos. I was fascinated by everything that was hidden to the human eye, longed to see into life's secret rooms, to be admitted into the unknown. Of those rooms, the human body was perhaps the most exciting in that the unknown was inside me and in everyone I saw, always there no matter which way I turned, and yet not, for the body's gurgling, blood-drenched inner realm remained out of reach, impossible to enter. Every summer we penetrated the surface of the sea and could glimpse the shimmering, darting life that existed there. The black universe of space revealed itself to us with twinkling stars on the clear nights of winter and autumn, when even planets might be visible too. Only the room of the body remained closed. The small gray sacks of the lungs; the spongy growth of the brain on its spinal-cord stalk; the tubes that transported the blood this way and that, through all the flesh and tissue of the body; these were things I had never seen. The closest I got were those images of operations on the TV screen. I have no idea how many such programs were broadcast, but presumably it was two or three series at most. Yet the impression they made remained, the fascination with the body's internal workings, the strangeness of that secret life never left me, though it became gradually more ambivalent, often merging with revulsion; the sight of the body's insides was at once revolting and alluring. As an adult I became absorbed by the exploration of the body that came with the Renaissance, when the physical human being was methodically mapped out for the first time, primarily by way of the dissection of fresh human corpses, often executed criminals, though sometimes bodies would be taken from churchyards, laid open behind closed doors or frequently in public in the context of anatomy lectures at the universities, in the so-called anatomical theaters. It was state-of-the-art science. Thomas Browne traveled from England to continental Europe at the beginning of the seventeenth century so as to study anatomy at Montpellier, surgery at Padua, and pharmacology at Leiden. But it was also a spectacle and a form of popular entertainment, the internal physical body was a sensation, a fairground of flesh and blood.

Four hundred years on, what seems strange is not the phenomenon itself, but that such fascination did not emerge earlier. What prevented the people of the Ancient World or the Medieval Age from exploring the inner body? The ancient Egyptians were familiar with it due to their culture of embalming, but they were never fascinated by the workings and interplay of the human organs, their practice being completely focused on death and respect for the deceased. The Greeks, who took the practice of medicine from sorcery to rational science, based their knowledge of the internal human body on what they could observe and understand from the insides of animals and, one might imagine, on what was revealed by accidents or war, when the body revealed itself in various ways: the brain inside a shattered skull, the colon spilling from a slashed belly, the jutting bone and ragged tendons and arteries of a severed foot or arm. The idea that they might dissect a corpse themselves and study it at their leisure did not occur to them. The thought must have been impossible, for their thirst for knowledge was in every other respect insatiable.

Why was that thought so impossible?

Perhaps they regarded the body and life as one, so that the notion of dissection made no sense to them; perhaps they did not understand that the life of one body could be prolonged by the knowledge gained from dissecting another; perhaps they saw no worth in prolonged life. Or perhaps they simply considered the inner body to be sacrosanct. Whatever the reason, they did not cut up the bodies of the dead and consequently knew little about the functions of the internal organs. Their writings on medicine and biology, full of approximations and guesswork yet nonetheless surprisingly reliable in view of the absence of empirical observation, were standard through the hundreds of years before the Renaissance, when they continued to carry such weight that both Dürer's and Leonardo's anatomical studies, made with human corpses in front of them, contain errors, details of medical literature rather than the medical body, indicating that what they knew occasionally overrode what they actually saw. The same was true of Charles Estienne's anatomical drawings from 1546, which include details of Galen's text that were in fact nonexistent. But the new paradigm quickly replaced the old, the best anatomical drawings of the seventeenth century are so exact as to still be useful for teaching purposes. Naturally, such a radical modification of our human knowledge did not occur without opposition. In the mid-sixteenth century Paracelsus for instance wrote as follows on the matter of dissection:

> *It is in no way sufficient to view the human body, to dissect, then to view again, and finally to boil it and look at it once again. To view in this way is to be compared with the unlearned peasant reading psalms: he reads only the letters and there is nothing more to say about him.*

Paracelsus's alternative was magic. Only in the relations between the heavenly and the earthly, the concealed and the unconcealed could the true nature of things be explained. His arguments proceeded from a medieval conception of reality, a world consisting of correspondences between what was visible and what was not, between the microcosmos of the human and the macrocosmos of the universe, a God's book whereby everything was a sign of something else and nothing existed simply on its own terms. To describe what was evident in the material world was meaningless until rendered otherwise by demonstrating or establishing its connection to the immaterial world. Paracelsus, with his to our mind chaotic hodgepodge of natural science, morals, magic, and metaphysics, in a world populated by spirits bound respectively to the elements of fire, earth, water, and air, connected with the human sphere in a near-infinite number of ways, was oblivious to the significance of anatomy to medical science, and from the perspective of his writings the practices of a figure such as Leonardo da Vinci, two generations older than Paracelsus, come across as empty exercises, whereas to Leonardo himself his work must have felt like an adventure, a second Creation no less.

In his notebooks Leonardo seems almost obsessive in his urge to delve into our physical reality, and he makes no distinction between the human and the material, the living and the dead, he wants to describe and capture it all, to understand. How come the fossils of mussels and sea creatures can be discovered at the top of a mountain? How come older people see things better from a distance? How come the sky is blue? What is heat? He attempts to describe the causes of laughter and crying, the nature of a sneeze, a yawn. He wants to know all about the falling sickness, spasms, paralysis. Why do we shiver when we are cold, and why do we sweat? What are fatigue, hunger, thirst, lust? He wants to explore our beginnings in the womb and to discover why an eight-month-old fetus dies. He wants to detail which muscles decay when we grow fat, and which become pronounced when we are thin. He wonders why the spots on the moon change when observed over time, and explains them as being caused by clouds rising from its waters, coming between the sun and those waters, by their shadow depriving them of the sun's rays, the waters thereby remaining dark and unable to reflect the solar body. In all his observations and speculations he proceeds from what he sees with his own eye, and only that. Leonardo describes a world without transcendence, and yet it does not in any way appear closed, on the contrary, for not only is the richness of what his eye is drawn toward overwhelming, his very gaze is moreover so fresh that everything he sees, even the sun and the moon, the rivers and the floodplains, seems almost to engage and take part in the vigor and clarity of the new. The old world with its dizzying transcendence is quite absent, albeit still perceptible, in the will of the new. Little or nothing of that from which the need wrenches away is expressed, but it is found in the very sensation of that detachment, which is the sensation of freedom.

Oddly, Leonardo's paintings seem quite apart from that sensation. They are masterworks of course, but at the same time too saturated in a way; their vital sense is that of harmony and clarity, his technique of rounding shapes, allowing them to glide off into their surroundings without losing substance and solidity in the process, may have something to do with it, but also the regularity of his compositions, so perfect as to lose all tension and become . . . well, rather *lazy*. Leonardo's paintings are never arresting to me in the way his notebooks are arresting. I suppose it has to do with the simple fact that as a painter he belonged to a tradition and saw things with the eyes of that tradition, painted with its techniques, whereas as an anatomist, biologist, physicist, geologist, geographer, astronomer, and inventor he was forging his own path. "The tears come from the heart and not from the brain," he suddenly writes. Or, in one of his many strange prophecies, "Men will come out of their graves turned into flying creatures; and they will attack other men, taking their food from their very hand or table. (As flies.)" That tone, that temperament, which is not without wildness and which is quite as unpredictable as it is exact, is wholly absent from his paintings, with one remarkable exception: *Lady with an Ermine*. I bought a poster of it on a trip to Italy with Espen more than ten years ago, it's on the wall in my living room now and I still haven't tired of looking at it. The motif is simple, a young woman holding a white-coated stoat, an ermine, to her chest; the animal is looking the same way as she, right of picture, and her right hand rests against its back. It's a disturbing picture. Why, I don't know, but the background is completely black, there is nothing else but this woman and this animal, and perhaps what is disturbing about it lies in this very juxtaposition. The woman's face is sharper than any other of Leonardo's female faces, and the hand that rests on the animal's spine is thin and bony, slightly out of proportion to what we can see of the rest of her body, slightly too big, and while the model he hired may actually have had big hands, our gaze is nevertheless drawn toward it in such a way that along with the head of the animal it forms the focal point of the picture. The hand, placed there to soothe and comfort, makes plain to us the animal's unease. Its rather bony appearance emphasizes its physiological aspect, a rare occurrence in Leonardo's paintings, which are nearly always more immersed in their colors and forms, their saturatedness, and together with the animal's intensely nonhuman presence, seemingly outside the sphere of the woman's attention, it appears almost as if her body splits in two before our eyes, one part belonging to the physiological, biological, bestial, the fingernails on her hand, for instance, corresponding with the claws of the animal's foot, the animal's eye the same color as the woman's eye, the other part belonging to the human, that which has to do with her serenity, the fact of the animal being outside her consciousness, her mind concerned with something else, perhaps with what she is looking at, perhaps with something within herself, but whatever it is, she is serene. Her dress, the pearls around her neck, her hair band, these things belong to that sphere, outside of which is the animal. Part of what is disturbing about the painting lies in the exactness with which the animal is depicted, quite unlike other animals in Leonardo's paintings, his lions, for instance, his horses and lambs. The ermine is neither biblical nor mythological, it doesn't belong to the battle or to any idyll but is there in its own right, as this one, particular animal. One might imagine this to be themed in the shape of fauns, half human, half animal, or a Pan figure, or perhaps centaurs, mythology is full of all sorts of creatures existing in the space between human and animal, but that would have made the picture an illustration, and this is precisely what Leonardo shuns here, the illustration of a thought or notion: the picture *is* the thought.

His anatomical sketches exhibit nothing of this, although the encounter they represent, of art and the body, is the same as in *Lady with an Ermine*. Perhaps this is because in the sketches the two aspects are compounded, the sketches representing the body in themselves, whereas the painting exists in the space in between. Of course, the difference between the drawing and the drawn is quite as big in both cases, but when it comes to sketches of the human body, an enormous number have been produced since Leonardo's time, and what was then a new phenomenon is now so common we no longer see it as a phenomenon at all, or even as drawings done by a certain artist, they are merely a part of the anonymous flood of textbook illustrations and instructions in which we paddle for the first time in childhood and never really step out of again, where everything that exists and occurs is conveyed by diagrams, like the elements of the molecule, the chlorophyll production of trees, the orbit of the planets around the sun, or the components of the inner ear. It was most certainly different for Leonardo, he draws everything like it was for the first time, and so new and controversial is the practice of drawing the inner human body from the study of corpses that he feels the need to defend himself in the introduction to his anatomy notes, swiping at a fictitious *you* who claims there is more to be had out of watching the dissection itself than studying one of the drawings:

> *And you, who say it would be better to watch the anatomist at work than to see these drawings, you would be right, if it were possible to observe all the things that are demonstrated in such drawings in a single figure, in which you, with all your cleverness, will not see nor obtain knowledge of more than some few veins, to obtain a true and perfect knowledge of which I have dissected more than ten human bodies, destroying all the other members, and removing the very minutest particles of the flesh by which these veins are surrounded, without causing them to bleed, excepting the insensible bleeding of the capillary veins; and as one single body would not last so long, since it was necessary to proceed with several bodies by degrees, until I came to an end and had a complete knowledge; this I repeated twice, to learn the differences.*
>
> *And if you should have a love for such things you might be prevented by loathing, and if that did not prevent you, you might be deterred by the fear of living in the night hours in the company of those corpses, quartered and flayed and horrible to see.*

What Leonardo is pleading here is the utility value of simplification in a world unfamiliar with the diagram. His fictional opponent believes it better to watch the dissection as it takes place, since the dissection itself is closer to reality, whereas Leonardo holds that reality, in this case the body, is too complicated and is best understood when conveyed by means of a drawing, which brings out its essence; ten corpses were required before he knew enough about the blood vessels to be able to draw them. The line of progression is from the chaos and confusion of reality to the order and functionality of the diagram, but also from the truth of the particular instance, local and tangible, this particular body, to the truth of all instances, the universal and general, all bodies. Leonardo's drawings are not diagrams, he does not simplify what he sees, but rather endeavors to depict what he sees as accurately as possible, but in order to do so he must isolate the individual parts so that they may be presented more clearly, and as such he both removes himself from and steps closer to the reality he depicts, a progression that resembles a law: the closer you get to a true picture of the physical world, the more remote it becomes.

What makes Leonardo's anatomical drawings so interesting is that they are there at the very outset of that progression, or are perhaps even its instigation, at the same time as they are there, too, at another point of intersection, that between art and science.

What exactly is going on when a painting such as *Lady with an Ermine* generates all manner of emotions and moods, opening itself to the beholder, who more than six hundred years on cannot help but find it dense with meaning, while a picture of the inner body drawn by the same artist at much the same time is experienced as something neutral, a fact closed upon itself, apart from the vague impression it gives of the age in which it was produced, over which the artist has absolutely no control?

Art is what the institution deems to be art, that is a tenet of modernism, but such a distinction is of no use here, because although we might consider the anatomical drawings to be art, this says nothing of their radical distinctness vis-à-vis *Lady with an Ermine*, which so plainly is something else entirely. Nor is it helpful to suggest that one has more quality than the other, or that one is reductive, the other not, because such reduction is conspicuous, too, in *Lady with an Ermine*, the pure black of the background removing the motif from its context, and only its core elements, the female subject's upper body and the wriggling animal, being depicted. Yet one can stare and continue to stare at such a painting, which comes alive in the beholder's gaze and seems inexhaustible, whereas the drawings of the inner body saturate the senses in a different way entirely, constraining our gaze and the emotions that follow on: what we see is what there is. In other words, the painting contains more. But what is this "more"? What does the painting have that the drawings don't?

In Jorge Luis Borges's renowned first collection of stories and essays, *Labyrinths*, there is a short story called "Pierre Menard, Author of the *Quixote*." According to its narrator, Pierre Menard was a recently deceased, lesser-known French author, a symbolist and friend of Paul Valéry. The narrator wishes to honor his memory, which is already receding, and lists his few works, among them a number of sonnets and monographs, one of the latter concerning Leibniz's *Characteristica Universalis*, another on the subject of Ramon Llull's *Ars Magna Generalis*, which gives us an indication of where Borges is heading, before concentrating on Menard's most important work, described as perhaps the most significant of our time, comprising the ninth and thirty-eighth chapters of the first part of *Don Quixote*, as well as a fragment of the twenty-second chapter. Menard did not merely copy these chapters, as anyone could have, instead he created them anew, an achievement characterized by the narrator as heroic, indisputably greater than Cervantes's own in writing the novel in the first place. It is one thing to pen a chivalric satire and have a decrepit nobleman ride off into the villages of seventeenth-century Spain, easy enough as a Spaniard living in the seventeenth century, but quite another to do so as a Frenchman at the beginning of the twentieth century. The very premise is an improvement, the narrator opines, comparing two brief passages from the two works.

It is a revelation to compare Menard's Don Quixote *with Cervantes's.*
The latter, for example, wrote (part one, chapter nine):

. . . truth, whose mother is history, rival of time, depository of
deeds, witness of the past,

exemplar and adviser to the present, and the future's counselor.
Written in the seventeenth century, written by the "lay genius"
Cervantes, this enumeration is a mere rhetorical praise of history.
Menard, on the other hand, writes:

. . . truth, whose mother is history, rival of time, depository of
deeds, witness of the past,

exemplar and adviser to the present, and the future's counselor.
History, the mother of truth: the idea is astounding. Menard, a con-
temporary of William James, does not define history as an inquiry into
reality, but as its origin. Historical truth, for him, is not what has
happened; it is what we judge to have happened.

By juxtaposing the idea of originality with that of its repetition, which is impossible and therefore naturally ranks higher than any renewal, Borges rearranges the hierarchy between new and the same, bringing the two concepts into the light. The idea that *Don Quixote* cannot be written again is so obvious it probably never occurred to anyone before Borges wrote his story about Menard's fabulous achievement, and for that very reason it is significant: what we see but are not consciously aware of seeing, the invisible world of laws and rules in which we move about and by which we are governed, the time and space of the given, is our cage as well as our home. Art is what cannot be done again, Borges reminds us, and is as such akin to the miracle. That someone else by coincidence should happen to paint *Lady with an Ermine* exactly as Leonardo did is an impossible thought, whereas that of someone drawing the same picture of the heart or the chest or the arm with its exposed tendons and blood vessels is not. The painting has a time and a place, it is a situation encapsulated, with all its properties and details, whereas the drawings of the body are timeless and placeless. What matters in the painting is the particular woman, the particular animal, the unique and local, whereas in the drawings it is all bodies, the general and universal.

Art is unique and local, striving always toward the unique and local, resisting everything that seeks to pull it from that trajectory. Its entire value resides in this. Even a painting by someone like Malevich, whose simple geometric figures or wholly monochrome surfaces seemingly aim toward total generality, is unique and local, for rather than being the expression of those figures in themselves, the painting is Malevich's depiction of them, and this presence of another human being fixes the painting in time: it could not have been painted by anyone else. When this is copied, and inevitably any bold style will be absorbed by others, the art is no longer unique, it becomes less local, and anemic. Without exception the paintings of the Norwegian and Swedish Cubists pale beside those of Picasso and Léger. It is this notion of the unique that "Pierre Menard, Author of the Quixote" is about. Art is what cannot be done again, but unlike the miracle, art extends in time and spans the generations, and it is into that temporal space Borges directs Menard when ingeniously he finds a way out of his own age and into the past without losing sight of either, enabling himself to perform the feat of making the copy original without alteration, the twentieth century's entire mind-set going back with him and exerting its own pressure on the sentences Cervantes once constructed, altering them as if from within, because what we know always shapes what we see. So enthusiastic is Borges's narrator about this new literary invention that he suggests the method be applied to other works, concluding with the question: "To attribute the *Imitatio Christi* to Louis Ferdinand Céline or to James Joyce, is this not a sufficient renovation of its tenuous spiritual indications?"

Nothing is coincidental in Borges's work, not even the choice of reference. The *Imitatio Christi*, or *Imitation of Christ*, is a collection of fifteenth-century texts attributed to the monk Thomas à Kempis, one of Christianity's most widely read books, renunciant of worldly life in its standpoint and holding up the life of Christ on earth as its ideal, hence the title, primarily motivated by a quote from Matthew:

Then Jesus said unto his disciples, If any man will come after me, let him deny himself, and take up his cross, and follow me. For whosoever will save his life shall lose it: and whosoever will lose his life for my sake shall find it. For what is a man profited, if he shall gain the whole world, and lose his own soul? Or what shall a man give in exchange for his soul? For the Son of man shall come in the glory of his Father with his angels; and then he shall reward every man according to his works.

The idea of denying oneself and living a life in imitation of another is even more radical and impossible than Menard's, and yet this was a genuine endeavor, not in detail, obviously, though the occasional wound may well have opened miraculously in someone's hand or side at various intervals throughout the Middle Ages, but in spirit, and this, the devotion of one's life to another, is the greatest sacrifice a human can make. The thought of Céline or Joyce, the two great idiosyncracies of twentieth-century literature, having written such a work is of course a joke, for if anyone ever invested themselves in their writing, and if anyone were ever as oblivious to the idea of humility, it was they. Their souls would have been damaged by it.

For us, the one true life is our own singular life, unexampled and individual, while imitation is false and submissive. In the *Imitatio Christi* imitation is the ideal, the possibility of withdrawing from life and devoting oneself fully to Christ being ever present, always hallowed, never anemic or strange. And while Scripture was paramount, governing people's understanding of everything, the material as well as the immaterial, while it was the form into which everything had to fit, a dizzying system of correspondences and connections devised in its name, an unparalleled instance of universalism, the body was always there, at the center of it all, the body of Christ, the flesh and blood of the Son of Man, which although dissolved in the text and in the language, was the point from which all theological abstractions radiated. This was evident not least in the relics that filled medieval churches, monasteries, and cathedrals. These were ranked according to a system based on physical proximity: first-order relics were everything that derived from the bodies of the saints or disciples – hair, nails, fragments of bone, even whole skeletons; to the second order belonged objects they had used or carried about their persons; the third order comprised things that had come into contact with them in some other way or had been stored in proximity to first-order relics. The most precious were those associated with the body of Christ and his life on earth, the holiest of all being those connected with the crucifixion: splinters of the cross, thorns of the crown, the head of the lance with which he was prodded, cloth from the garments of people who had been present, and, of course, the shroud itself. The adoration of all these objects, which could take on hysterical forms, many of them associated with miracles and healing, comprises the very core of Christianity, expressing its innermost truth and authentic nature: that God in Christ became man, was born into the human world, a living body, a person who for some thirty years lived *here* among us, in *our* world. The idea is so radical as to be impossible to take in, much less understand, other than in fleeting, emotional moments of insight. The relics opened that insight, the divine was local, could be associated with places to which one could travel and see with one's own eyes, and with identifiable people who once, not that many generations before, actually existed. The Old Testament was local too, almost all the places mentioned in it were still in existence, and if one cared to investigate one would find that all were close to each other. The River Jordan, the Sinai Desert, the Dead Sea, Mount Gilboa, the brook of Zered, the plains of Moab. Jerusalem, Bethlehem, Hebron, Gaza, Beersheba, Ezion-Geber, all inside an area no bigger than a Norwegian *fylke*.

For us this sense of the local trails off into the exotic and remote, everything in the Bible takes place far away, the narrative is all about others and their country. But what if it had been about us and our country? The local aspect would then have been plain to us. Moses and the children of Israel might have come into the Setesdal, having wandered about the Hardangervidda for forty years. Moses could have received the Tablets of the Law, inscribed with the Ten Commandments, on the Gaustatoppen, and the Promised Land he was allowed to see but not to enter might have been Aust-Agder. The Lord's speech to him about the Promised Land, following the Golden Calf incident, might have gone like this: "I will send an angel before you and drive out the Setesdalers, the Arendalites and the Frolanders, the Hisøyites and the Tromøyites. Go down to the land flowing with milk and honey. But I will not go with you, because you are a stiff-necked people." And Deuteronomy's magnificent finale might have been as follows:

> *And Moses descended from the plains of the Hardangervidda into the Setesdal and went up into the hills there, over against Valle. And the Lord shewed him all the land: from Byggland unto Evje and Åmli, from Birkenes unto Hægebostad, and all of Agder unto Arendal and the utmost sea to the south, and Grimstad and Lillesand, all the land of the south unto Kristiansand. And the Lord said unto him, This is the land which I sware unto Abraham, unto Isaac, and unto Jacob, saying, I will give it unto thy seed: I have caused thee to see it with thine eyes, but thou shalt not go over thither. So Moses the servant of the Lord died there in the Setesdal, according to the word of the Lord. And he buried him in the Setesdal, over against Bykle: but no man knoweth of his sepulchre unto this day.*

But it is not just the geography that draws the texts of the Old Testament toward the sphere of the local, the people in them do too. Those who had in common the fact that God had appeared before them are named, they possess their own, clear character traits and personalities, from the fearful Lot to the cunning Isaac, and if nothing remains to testify to their existence outside these texts, it is not necessarily because they were figures of mythology created in the depths of popular imagination, but because the age in which they lived is so very remote. The way in which their stories are told reinforces the local aspect and anchors them in time, for there are no abstractions or systems, practically no mythological or fairy-tale-type constructions, everything conveyed is conveyed through descriptions of concrete events in the concrete world. Soil, sand, roads, houses, blood. Journeys, births, battles, flight.

Explanation is anathema in these texts, all meaning must be extracted from the events portrayed, which are not relative, only unfathomable. Why are they unfathomable? Events are not a language, though they may be conveyed by one. When we understand an event, we do so by virtue of the culture in which the event takes place. If that culture no longer exists, our understanding fails and the events are left behind, as mysterious to us as the statues on Easter Island. The stories of the Bible are ancient, and in them are traces of stories even more ancient.

When I started school at Sandnes primary in 1975, Christian studies was still one of the most important subjects, together with Norwegian, math, and the combined studies of science, history, geography, and social studies, and for the most part it consisted of our teacher, Helga Torgersen, telling us stories from the Bible, and our drawing or talking about them afterward. It was a pastoral world we entered, dramatic and full of light. Being Christian was about being good and kind. All of us wanted that, but gradually, one by one, we fell by the wayside as we approached puberty. I held out for a long time, to me mopeds were bad, one-armed bandits were bad, even cola and peanuts were tinged with badness. To this day I remain wary of such deviations; driving above the speed limit fills me with guilt for days; killing a fly or watching a plant in the apartment die because I've forgotten to water it pains me unspeakably, for the desire to be good and decent has kept itself alive in me through all these years. What I know now, which I did not know then, is that there are forces inside us oblivious to good and bad, and emotions that can be so powerful as to override everything without our even knowing that we are in their grip, for the ego, the I, that thin sliver of light at the edge of our consciousness, contains our whole identity, colors our understanding of all the other forces, desires, and emotions that exist within us, much as the age in which we live colors our perception of the past, for there is no natural outside, neither in the body nor in society, and to arrive at such a place, from where we can see ourselves or the age in which we live, requires an effort, and that effort is huge, for the forces that pull on our self-awareness and on the contemporary age, drawing everything into their domain, are not gravitational, but centripetal. The Bible, however, is one such outside, particularly the texts of the Old Testament, simultaneously remote and proximate, familiar and strange. They are ancient and we are separated from the lives they portray by a chasm of thousands of years. At the same time they belong to our culture, our grandparents, great-grandparents, great-great-grandparents, and the generations before them, all the way back to the first millennium, read the same texts, which shaped them and their culture, in which we continue to live to this day, albeit its form has since become somewhat modified. A story such as that of Cain and Abel carries with it not only our prehistory but also the fifth century of Augustine of Hippo, the thirteenth century of Thomas Aquinas and Dante, the seventeenth century of Shakespeare and Bacon, as well as our own childhood and contemporary age. In translating that story into modern language, much of its strangeness disappears, whereas sticking closely to the Hebrew original makes it incomprehensible. A compromise might look like this:

And the man came to Eve, his wife, and she conceived and bore Cain, and said, The Lord has given me a man. And she bore his brother,

Abel, and he was a shepherd, and Cain a tiller of the earth. One day, when his work was done, Cain brought grain from his field in offering to the Lord, while Abel brought the fattest cuts of the first lamb of his flock. And the Lord regarded Abel and respected his offering, yet ignored Cain and his. Cain was enraged and his face fell, and the Lord said to him, Why are you angry? Why has your face fallen? Lift it up and you will be accepted; if not, sin will gather at your door and you shall be its desire and rule over it. And Cain talked with his brother Abel; they were in the field, and Cain rose up against his brother and killed him. And the Lord said to Cain, Where is Abel, your brother? And Cain replied, Am I my brother's keeper? And the Lord said, What have you done? The voice of your brother's blood cries to me from the ground. And now you shall be banished from the good earth that has opened her mouth to receive your brother's blood from your hand. Tilling the land will no more yield its grain to you, henceforth you shall be a fugitive and a vagabond on earth. And Cain said to the Lord, My punishment is greater than I can bear. Behold, you have driven me out this day from the face of the earth, and from your face I shall be hidden; and I shall be a fugitive and a vagabond, and anyone who finds me may kill me. And the Lord said to him, Therefore, whoever slays Cain, vengeance shall be taken on him sevenfold. And the Lord set a mark upon Cain, lest anyone finding him should try to kill him. And Cain went from the presence of the Lord and settled in the land of Nod, east of Eden.

It is a simple story, yet strange. A man kills his brother and God sends him away, at the same time placing a mark on him to prevent anyone from killing him. What does it mean? Oh, the blood and the earth are everything here. The Lord respects the lamb, the blood sacrifice, but not the grain. Cain kills Abel, blood is shed, the Lord curses Cain but does not kill him, and wishes him not to be killed by any other, for Abel is dead, and it is Cain who lives and may pass on the blood. And the blood is bound up with the earth, firstly through their father, who bears its name, *adama* in the Hebrew, which is to say through a creature of God, then by way of the blood that is shed, death, and the blood's return to the earth. The voice of the blood cries from the ground, the mouth of the earth opens to receive it. But neither the blood nor the earth are driving forces in the narrative, merely stations between which the story passes. What drives the narrative is the face and the gaze. The Lord regards Abel. Cain's face falls. The Lord admonishes him, he must lift his face, otherwise sin will gather at his door. He disobeys, kills his brother, and from then on he will be hidden from the face of the Lord. And since surface and face are the same word in Hebrew, his banishment from the face of the earth may be taken literally, the face, or gaze, of the earth.

Cain was enraged and his face fell.

Cain is ignored, the Lord does not regard him, this is the story's starting point. Ignored and unregarded, he is no one, and if he is no one he is dead, and if he is dead he has nothing to lose. What might he have lost? Might he have lost face? But his face was already lost. The crux lies in the void between Cain's face not being regarded and his lowering his face so that it can no longer be seen. The fallen face is directly associated with evil, for God says, "Lift it up and you will be accepted." See and be seen. If not, "sin will gather at your door and you shall be its desire and rule over it." To turn away, which is not merely not to see, but also not to be seen, is perilous, for there, in that gap, that uncorrected reservoir of space, sin gathers.

And his face fell.

Lift it up.

The face is the other, and in its light we become. Without that face we are no one, and if we are no one we are dead, and if we are dead we can do as we please. With that face, which sees us and is seen by us, we cannot do as we please. The face puts us under an obligation. This is why God says lift it up. Take that obligation upon yourself. But Cain does not lift his face, he does not take that obligation upon himself, he oversteps the bounds of the social and kills his brother. The transgression affects them deeply, since the person he kills is his brother, which in this archaic world is to say his own blood. And such violence against the self is the most dangerous of all, since it is almost impossible to guard against; it comes from the we, not from the alien without, not from any them, but from the you of the fallen face.

Fratricide is still going on around us, brother killing brother someplace in Africa, in Asia, in Europe; yesterday, today, tomorrow; it occurs, and then the occurrence is gone. Nothing of being human has changed since biblical times: we are born, we love and hate, we die. But our archaic aspect and the things we do are sucked up by our quotidian lives in the contemporary age we have created and which we comprise, where reality is above all horizontal and the vertical only seldom glimpsed and acknowledged. Yet all we have to do is to look up to grasp it, for above us is the sun, blazing, the same sun that blazed for Cain and Abel, Odysseus and Aeneas. The fells before our eyes are of similar dizzying age. That we are but the latest in a line of ancestry reaching back thousands of generations into the past, emotionally the same as them, for the heart that beat in them beats also in us, is a perspective we are unable and unwilling to take upon ourselves, for in it our uniqueness is erased and we become merely a locus of feelings and actions, much as water is the locus of waves, or the sky of clouds. We know each cloud to be unique, each wave to be unique, yet we see only clouds, only waves. Mythology points directly into that space, since each myth is about the one, yet what it expresses applies to us all. Cain is enraged, his face falls. Cain is assailed by hatred and is made blind, he assails his own brother and kills him. The myth is about forces in the human that cannot be subsumed into the individual's identity or the sphere of the social, instead breaking loose and running riot. It is about something out of control in the human itself, which we fear and tremble before, not unlike the way we react when confronted by the sublime in nature. This is the sublime in human nature, the wild and uncontrolled, the destructive aspect of our makeup that can be bridled neither by the individual nor by the structures of our social world, arising in one human being, who is all of us. The sublime in the one. But the sublime is also in the all, when we are one together, congregated in teeming numbers. The roar of a football crowd, the flow of mass protesters in the streets. Common to these two instances of the sublime in human nature is that both edge toward the place where what is individual and peculiar to the one ceases to exist. The place where our humanity dissolves into other forces of nature and loses itself. This is the boundary of the I, and it is the boundary of our culture, and as such it is justifiably feared. When the archaic is sucked into the quotidian and the sun that blazes in the sky is our sun, we live within culture, which relentlessly toils to confirm that idea, relentlessly drawing everything in toward the already known, whereas art quite differently is adjusted to what is beyond the boundary of the I and culture, the unfamiliar, and what used to be called the divine. Death is the gateway to the land from which we come and to which sooner or later we must return. It lies beyond language, beyond thought, beyond culture, and cannot be grasped but merely glimpsed, for example by our turning toward the mute and blind in ourselves. It is there always, even when we are having breakfast on a normal Tuesday morning and the coffee is a bit too strong, the rain is running down the windowpanes, the radio is sending out the seven o'clock news, and the living-room floor inside is littered with toys, even then the heart beats, the very muscle of the archaic, pumping its blood around the body. Culture is created to avoid that perspective, so that we might look away from the precipice at whose edge we exist, but contemporary culture, whose perspective belongs only to a couple of generations and which relates only to the most proximate history, what used to be called living memory, has never been absolute, for another age has always existed within it, the age in which nothing changes, where everything stays the same, the age of myths and rituals. That this aspect of our understanding of reality is gone does not mean that it is gone from reality. What did Hitler do when he withdrew into himself as a young man?

He saw no one, and no one saw him. Not even as an adult did he attach himself to any you; when he was seen, he was seen only by a crowd, by the mass of an all, and the same was true when he wrote: *Mein Kampf* contains an I, contains a we, contains a they, but does not contain a you.

And his face fell.

Lift it up.

The story of Cain and Abel is about the elimination of the you as the source of violence, and the reader may stop there or continue, for it does not simply concern one brother killing another, but relates also to sacrifice: Cain slays Abel after God accepts Abel's offering, an animal sacrifice, while ignoring Cain's offering of grain. The French anthropologist René Girard reads the story as expressing the function of the sacrifice in respect to the act of violence. Sacrifice brings violence into relief and steps into its place as a way of controlling its otherwise unbound forces within society; Cain does not have the violence-outlet of animal sacrifice at his disposal, and kills his brother. The surrogate function of sacrifice is made plain in the narrative of Abraham offering his son Isaac in sacrifice to God, when God yields and asks him to sacrifice a ram instead. This ram, Girard writes, is in Muslim tradition the same ram as once offered by Abel. The sacrifice is a ritual, it is collective, and it construes violence as collective.

The concept of sacrifice is mythic, central to primitive cultures, abandoned in those more developed, such as our own, where violence is understood to be something individual, arising in a particular situation, among particular people, and dealt with by a judicial system that punishes the guilty individual. The most important aim of the process of socialization in any society is for the individual to control his impulses, emotions, and actions, to avoid what destroys and corrodes all structures and communities, violence among like kind, and if the individual is unable to do this, and kills one or more of his own kind, he will be punished by the community through the apparatus of law. The forbiddance of violence among like kind occurs in all societies, indeed one cannot imagine a society without it. In primitive societies the distinction between the I and the we is less clear, discriminating and legislative institutions do not exist, and the insight of violence among like kind, the peril of internal disturbance, is therefore greater perhaps, the community being that much more vulnerable to its consequences. Girard believes that the wish to deal with violence among like kind lies behind all notions of taboo, which is a means of avoiding anything that might bring it about. If this is so, rituals stand for the very opposite, being a means of venturing to the point where forces are controlled, the repetitions of the ritual nullifying the arbitrary and constraining emotion.

But repetition is also tabooed, the emulative and the echoic, imitation, mimesis being likewise associated with peril, and according to Girard this is quite fundamental. In some primitive cultures twins are killed at birth. Mirrors, too, are often associated with danger; some cultures forbid the imitation of others, whether by gesture or the repetition of utterances; the doppelgänger has always put fear into people; many religions prohibit the depiction of their deity.

One might imagine that the fear of duplication, facsimile, imitation has to do with the notion of identity, the individual becoming lost in its image in the event that identity is unstable, open to the world, and susceptible to impregnation, but Girard believes the opposite to hold, that likeness represents a threat to the collective in that the act of violence cannot then be construed individually, related back to its perpetrator nor even associated with its results, being viewed not as a completed event, but instead, and to a much greater extent than in our own culture, in terms of process, seeing in it symmetry and likeness: two rivals facing off, between them an object, the bone of contention, and on either side of it they are alike. If not stopped, this likeness will be reproduced serially, in retaliations, representatives of the first taking vengeance on representatives of the second, and such violence, the violence of the blood feud, can go on through generations, the original conflict long since forgotten, consumed into the seriality.

In any small community such escalation is catastrophic, and it is its fundamental pattern, one against the other, that gives rise to duplication taboos, the manifest and mysterious fear of symmetry. Violence is imitative and repetitive. If taboos are an avoidance measure in this respect, sacrifice confronts it, not only by being its imitation and by re-creating it serially in ritual, but also structurally, the sacrifice on the one side, the members of the community on the other, though not divided, the surrogate victim as scapegoat bearing the division, but collectively: the all against the one, which is then duly killed. And when it is done, only the all remains, a single, stable whole.

On the other hand, imitation may also be a desirable phenomenon in a culture, nearly all learning and development occurring by way of repetition and duplication, directly, too, in the imitation of role models, though never without some degree of ambivalence, since imitation of the one by the other is down to the one wanting what the other one has, and this, in Girard's terminology mimetic desire, is no stable concept. When the final commandment of the Old Testament decrees that you shall not covet your neighbor's wife, his ox, or anything else that belongs to him, the reason is of course that doing so would be a source of conflict, two facing off over an object desired by both; where two individuals confront each other in a state of mimetic desire, the object becomes the one subject by virtue of the imitation or duplication, which brings about an imbalance in the relation, whether it be the depiction eclipsing the depicted, or vice versa. The association of imitation with power, or lack of power, and in essence with violence, is according to Girard the reason for Plato's loathing of mimesis, the concept being unresolved in his writings, and he interprets the crisis of the we's collapse into the I as seen in schizophrenia as the expression of a lack of ability to imitate the other, something society is rooted in, and this is what manifests itself in the occasionally grotesque, parodic exaggerations often displayed by schizophrenics.

Girard's thinking concerning sacrifice and imitation is non-psychological, seeking explanation not in the particular I, but in the collective, and construing violence as a structural entity. This aspect of violence has all but disappeared in our time, insofar as its containment has consisted of relating the act of violence itself, as well as the emotions that give rise to it, to the individual in a system whereby the community steps in as soon as the trangres-sional act takes place, thereby regulating it and preventing its escala-tion, a fact that has led us to consider it in terms of the individual and accordingly made us blind to its collective aspect. But when any group emerges in society, placing value outside the individ-ual and declining to identify with the authority of the state or with areas in which that power is weak, symmetrical, serial vio-lence occurs once again; the Sicilian Mafia or the inner cities of the northeast of the United States are examples of environments in which the blood feud has recently been pivotal, and the gangs that populate the run-down areas of American cities gun each other down according to the same principle of retaliation. They destroy one another utterly, but the power of destruction lies not in their hands, it spirals out of control, and this was what primi-tive cultures sought to manage by their taboos and rituals, which nearly always ended in sacrifice. Their myths, and gradually their religions, were the expression of the collective, treating and con-cerning the whole, and as those cultures evolved, doing so in in-creasingly sophisticated ways. The Pentateuch, the Five Books of Moses, is the narrative of that evolution, from the emergence of man, the separation of culture from nature, to the establishment of a homogenous and civilized societal unit with laws, rules, forms of governance, and religion. What the sacrifice does is to estab-lish differences in culture. Between life and death, animal and hu-man, human and divine, but also differences within the human sphere, where the destructive power of likeness is separated out and dealt with by its transformation into unlikeness. The sacrificial offering is a language without words in which the unspoken is made manifest, not so much in order to be perceived as to be controlled, by being brought into existence. The sacrifice is a means of naming the unnameable, of giving form to the formless. The formless is likeness, there lies the point of departure of all creation narratives, including those of science. The first chapter of the Book of Genesis says, "And the earth was without form and void; and darkness was upon the face of the deep. And the Spirit of God moved upon the face of the waters." The void is nothing, emptiness is nothing, darkness is likeness, the deep is the boundless, the Spirit of God is the universe, the waters the undifferentiated. Then, by its very predication, land is separated from sea, night from day, sun from moon. God said let there be light, and there was light. When everything in the material world was separated, the animals that swim in the sea, creep on the land, and fly through the sky were created.

What is the nature of this first picture of life?

"Let the waters bring forth abundantly the moving creature that hath life," it says. "And God created great whales, and every living creature that moveth, which the waters brought forth abundantly, after their kind, and every winged fowl."

The emphasis here is on quantity and movement: "abundantly," "moveth," "living creature," the "moving creature." Against this blind abundance of life stands the categorization of "after their kind," but so unspecifically is life described, primarily in terms of its living abundance only, that its categorization becomes secondary, much like the rattling pots that enclose the living, crawling lobsters as they are lifted into a boat.

Then comes evening, and after it the morning of the sixth day, and God creates the animals of the land, and creates man, the male and the female. And to them he says, "Be fruitful, and multiply, and replenish the earth, and subdue it: and have the dominion over the fish of the sea, and over the fowl of the air, and over every living thing that moveth upon the earth."

While the message in his commandment is that man is superior to all other living creatures, and thereby separated from them, distinct and on his own, the parallels in the choice of words pull the human irresistibly toward that abundance of life: "Be fruitful," it says, "and multiply, and replenish the earth"; in other words man is considered as a mass, surrounded by the other masses of life, characterized by their movements, life that moveth, teeming, creeping, crawling.

And God says:

> Behold, I have given you every herb bearing seed, which is upon the face of all the earth, and every tree, in which is the fruit of a tree yielding seed; to you it shall be for meat. And to every beast of the earth, and to every fowl of the air, and to every thing that creepeth upon the earth, wherein there is life, I have given every green herb for meat: and it was so. And God saw every thing that he had made, and, behold, it was very good.

The weight given to expansion is huge in this first chapter of the Old Testament, the idea of life extending out being presented as its fundamental condition. In this lies the notion of repetition, for what spreads is the same, life in its various forms, and it does so singly, the leaves of the deciduous tree that unfold every spring being the same leaf over and over again, as it does so together, the deciduous trees growing up in community, great forests extending ever deeper. Humanity is a part of this expansion, bound, too, by the imperative of multiplying and replenishing the earth, this being the very urge of life, to increase, and man is in this sense construed as life on the same level as all other living things.

But then something happens. In the second chapter of the Book of Genesis the narrative shifts from the remote to the near, and is no longer about the abstract universe, about the earth viewed generally, the sky viewed generally, life viewed generally, but about the particular place, this earth, this sky, the creation of these two particular people. Adam, whose name is associated with earth, and Eve, whose name is associated with life. Having breathed the breath of life into their nostrils, God places them in a garden, to the east, in Eden. And from the garden ran four named rivers: Pison, Gihon, Hiddekel, and Euphrates. After what happens there, when they eat the fruit of the Tree of Knowledge and are banished, several names appear. Adam and Eve's son Abel, who dies, and all the descendants of their son Cain: Enoch, Irad, Mehujael, Methusael, Lamech, Adah, Zillah, Jubal, Tabulcain, Naamah. Then come the descendants of the third son, Seth: Enos, Cainan, Mahalaleel, Jared, Enoch, Methuselah, Lamech, Noah, Shem, Ham, and Japheth. In the lifetime of these four latter persons, all life on earth is destroyed in the Flood, and a new lineage begins. After Japheth, Gomer, Magog, Madai, Javan, Tubal, Meshech, Tiras, Ashkenaz, Riphath, Togarmah, Eishah, Tarshiss, Kittim, Dodanim. After Ham, Cush, Mizraim, Phut, Canaan, Seba, Havilah, Sabtah, Raamah, Sabtecha, Sheba, Dedan. After Shem, Elam, Ashur, Arphaxad, Lud, Aram, Uz, Hul, Gether, Mash, Salah, Eber, Peleg, Joktan, Almodad, Sheleph, Hazarmaveth, Jerah, Hadoram, Uzal, Diklah, Obal, Abimael, Sheba, Ophir, Havilah, Jobab. After Peleg, Reu, Serug, Nahor, Terah, Abram, Nahor, Haran.

These names connect historical time with the mythic, illuminating as it were the darkness of history and forging a path directly into the moment of creation. The connection is real, if not factual, since there must be some particular point in time at which humanity emerged, and some particular place. Viewed in relation to the age of the earth, that time is not far from the present, some two hundred thousand years, somewhere in the region of ten thousand generations. It occurred on the African continent, where creatures resembling humans had already lived for millions of years, and for a time they must have lived alongside each other, perhaps until only forty thousand years ago. The first humans cannot have been many in number, a few small flocks at most, and they must have kept to the same places until some of them, about a hundred thousand years ago, began to wander, the species gradually spread across the globe.

When in the 1990s scientists began to identify and map our DNA, the paths these early humans wandered could suddenly be followed, deposited in our living bodies here in the present, an unfathomably long chain of inheritance enclosing us all in our history, or exposing us to the very depths of time: not only are we like them, in a sense we are them.

The emergence of the human being was a local occurrence, it took place in a certain geographical area; the idea of the Garden of Eden and man's dispersion from it expresses no more than that. Some caves, plains, forests, some lakes or rivers.

By the time the narrative gets to Abram we are somewhere between historical time and the void of prehistory, and what emerges from Abram are the foundations of a family, a people, and a nation, governed by the will of a single God, who gradually bestows on them laws and statutory instruments, which is to say civilization and religion. The relation between the divine and the nondivine, between man and the world, and between individuals, is regulated within those systems. And the future is a promise of descendants, for God brings Abram forth and says to him, "Look now toward heaven, and tell the stars, if thou be able to number them. So shall thy seed be." And when Abram, who after his covenant with God becomes known as Abraham, is later instructed to sacrifice his only son, God intervenes with that same promise: "That in blessing I will bless thee, and in multiplying I will multiply thy seed as the stars of the heaven, and as the sand which is upon the seashore."

The stars and the sand are the mass, the many, but the many are also alike. The promise of God does not apply to all people, it is not humanity as such that is to multiply so infinitely, but Abraham and his kin, which is to say a singular we, and this is what makes God's words a promise and a utopia, since the expansion of a single family, a clan, a people, brings with it power and wealth. By virtue of sheer numbers, land may be conquered and empires won. The Bible's negative representation of innumerableness consists in the swarms of grasshoppers, the great clouds of insects consuming all in their path, unstoppable and merciless.

This distinction between we and they is consistently of the greatest significance throughout the biblical narrative. The Old Testament can be seen as a story issuing out of the various tensions that distinction creates. All the men of Abraham's family shall be circumcised, this being the sign of their belonging, their we, and in the covenant he enters into with God, the promise of their own land is the utopia the later stories seek, until it comes to fruition when before his death Moses sees the Promised Land, overflowing with milk and honey, and his people then cross the river to enter it. Until that point they have been slaves in Egypt, powerless, their lives in the hands of others, and in such a situation, possessing nothing of their own and without influence on their own days, not even on their own children, the only thing that keeps them together is their sense of particularity, the idea of their own, guaranteed to them by God, who is the one God.

The Egyptians murder all male children born to the Hebrews, but when Moses is born he is hidden in an ark among the bulrushes at the river, where he is found by Pharaoh's daughter, who takes him as her own. Not only is he then able to live safely among the Egyptians, he also enjoys the foremost privileges as a member of a hallowed, godlike family, yet so strong is the bond to the people from whom he stems, the slaves, that he renounces all of this, not in any planned or calculated manner, but in an act of passion, his blood brought to the boil when he sees an Egyptian beating a Hebrew; Moses kills the man, buries the body in the sand and flees the country, whereupon God appears before him and a new covenant is entered into. Led by Moses, the Hebrews escape from Egypt into the desert. There the laws and rituals by which they must abide are delivered to them. And they are counted.

That laws are delivered to them is by no means surprising, this being a narrative of foundation, but counting and stating their own number is conspicuous indeed. One could conceive of it as some kind of bookkeeping exercise, an archaic urge to account completely for the situation at hand, where their number must have played a significant role given that they were in the desert at the time, in a landscape where food and drink must have been scarce, and because they were about to invade another land and the number of soldiers at their disposal would be one of the most important factors in determining the outcome. Nonetheless, the preciseness of the number stated seems odd, such exact detail occurring only seldom in the Scriptures, which elsewhere can report a people's suffering through centuries or the destruction of a city in only a single sentence.

The only other place where the text displays such exactness, allowing not a detail to escape, is in the listing of the laws and rituals the priests are to perform. But the laws are universal, immutable, and meant to apply through all time; the Hebrews' number is the opposite, capturing an inconstant entity at a certain point in time, applicable only to them, in that place, when Moses gathers the Israelites in the Sinai Desert. They are many, though not in the way the stars or the grains of sand at the shore are many; in total they number 603,550 able-bodied men spanning twelve tribes and with the following distribution:

The tribe of Reuben: forty and six thousand and five hundred.
The tribe of Simeon: fifty and nine thousand and three hundred.
The tribe of Gad: forty and five thousand and six hundred and
fifty.
The tribe of Judah: threescore and fourteen thousand and six
hundred.
The tribe of Issachar: fifty and four thousand and four hundred.
The tribe of Zebulun: fifty and seven thousand and four
hundred.
The tribe of Ephraim: forty thousand five hundred.
The tribe of Manasseh: thirty and two thousand and two
hundred.

The tribe of Benjamin: thirty and five thousand and four hundred.
The tribe of Dan: threescore and two thousand and seven hundred.
The tribe of Aser: forty and one thousand and five hundred.
The tribe of Naphtali: fifty and three thousand and four hundred.

Seen from the outside, as when later they conquer the new land, killing everything in their path, they are a faceless horde, but seen from within, all are bound to the familiar in lines of descent going back through families and through history, which in sum comprise the people.

Reading this ancient text today, perhaps the most remarkable aspect is the way the foundation of the religious merges into the social, as if they were two sides of the same coin. For the number's freezing of the multitude in time is just one aspect of this, what the number represents is another, and it is this that joins number and law together. The number stands open to the boundless, the uncontrollable, the identityless, the infinity of sand and stars; the names constrain and control in the identity of the name, the face of the language. Similarly, the law constrains and controls action; killing is forbidden, being a trangression of life, lying is forbidden, being a transgression of truth, adultery is forbidden, being a transgression of marriage. The punishment is expulsion from life, which is to say death, or, if the transgression is deemed to be minor, a sacrifice in place of death. And the boundary that emerges in this, which separates this people and their existence from all that is holy, is the most important of all, testified to by the text's richness of detail in describing the various rituals, the exactness required when the priests step into the hallowed space and dash blood on the sacrificial stone or burn animals or corn or oil. The sacrifice is not merely a reminder of the price of transgression, is not merely a symbolic act, but is in itself a price, in the way the ox whose head is severed is not merely a symbol of life and blood, but is in itself life and blood. That the language of the Old Testament is so specific, so proximate to physical reality and the events that take place within it, to body rather than spirit, is undoubtedly an aspect of the same thing. What is to be found beyond the holy, the boundless and infinite, is also nameless, indefinite, its identity construed by a verb, which is to say action or movement. I am what I am. The image of the nameless human is a grain of sand or a star, the loss of identity in the mass merely ostensible, for the number of stars or the number of grains of sand is not infinite, but finite, and only from a distance are they the same, seen up close each grain of sand is different, each star unique. They may be counted, and they may be named. The image of the nameless God, however, is infinite and identical, for it is fire. Its manifestations are always the same – to name an instance of fire would seem meaningless, to name a grain of sand would not – and yet each is different. Fire cannot be counted, cannot be named, cannot be delimited; doused in one place, it will burn in another. The stars and the grains of sand express the idea of the one and the all, the individual and the mass, whereas fire establishes identity between the two, the one being simultaneously the one and the all. Beyond the boundaries of law and ritual stands the boundless God, beyond the name stands boundless biological life, only concerted effort can prevent us from disappearing into or being consumed by its depths.

Religion, whose rituals gather together all time, tying it down in their gravity to only a single point in time, lay in this rural past close to the social world, whose horizons lay mere generations backward and forward in time, but whose practices, bound up with the land and the seasons, were mainly associated with repetition. They were distinct from one another regarding the local and the universal, where that which applied to all, that which for example regulated the total population of the earth, existed beyond the reach of humans and was identified in terms of external forces, fate and destiny, so strong that not even the thought arose of their being controllable other than by prayer and sacrifice. In the face of drought, floods, cold, and epidemics, man was vulnerable, fragile, and helpless. The relationship between the local and the universal, between individual and whole, was one-sided in that these mighty and impersonal forces intervened in individual lives, whereas the individual could never encroach on the universal. The universal was religious, rather than social.

When science becomes the language by which man construes the material world, the religious stepping aside to apply only to the spiritual aspect of life, the relationship between the local and the universal becomes radically displaced and ensuing technological progress, which in such an astonishingly short space of time completely alters the circumstances of production and distribution, causes our populations to skyrocket compared to the demographic calm of preceding centuries and millennia. Whereas there were some 250 to 400 million people in the world in 1350, and between 465 and 545 million in 1650, that figure rose to between 835 and 915 million in 1800, between 1 billion 91 million and 1 billion 176 million in 1850, between 1 billion 530 million and 1 billion 608 million in 1900, to 2 billion 416 million in 1950, in the region of 4 billion in 1980, and now, in 2011, to some 6 billion people. We have indeed replenished the earth and subdued it as the account of the creation would have it, and have become as many as the sand upon the seashore and the stars of the heaven.

In a way, such a radical rise in population changes nothing. What it means is simply more of the same. More births and deaths, more mouths and more food, more clothing, more houses, closer together and spread over greater areas of land. Humanity advances in much the same way as a forest, for whose trees the number of other trees changes nothing. The local does not cease to exist as a concept even if connections extend from there into the global, such as when the global market came into being with the Industrial Revolution, when goods began to be produced in one place, to be transported from there out into the wide world, for as the sociologist Bruno Latour puts it in his book *We Have Never Been Modern*, by following the process step-by-step "one never crosses the mysterious *lines* that should divide the local from the global." When does the train depart the local and pass into the global, Latour asks, and replies: never. All large organizations and associations comprise local units, armies are for instance organized in much the same way as armies were organized in Roman days, only multiplied, and the same is true of bureaucracy, the apparatus of state, the great commercial and international businesses. They comprise a single person with sweat blotches under his arms and his tie askew in an office to the power of a thousand or hundreds of thousands. It is not the number in itself that has altered man's circumstance, but our perception of that number.

In the 1680s an anatomy professor of Oxford University, Sir William Petty, wrote a book called *Political Arithmetic* in which he endeavored to understand or capture society on the basis of mathematical terms, in other words to quantify and measure the sphere of the human. He wished thereby to establish laws to govern what was human, much as Newton had established laws to govern nature. That there should exist an absolute order, a firm set of rules behind the world's apparent chaos of variability and arbitrariness so exact and predictable they could be calculated and accounted for mathematically, was an irresistible thought in the seventeenth century and one that would moreover confirm the greatness of God; as if some hidden plan had existed all along, relating to the world the way a technical drawing related to an invention, in a system in which all fluctuation occurred according to a predetermined pattern where nothing could change and where all constituent parts worked together in a single glorious expression of the wholeness of the universe. Man, belonging to this universe, was a part of the same system, not only in the form of the individual human, with its blood and lungs, its brain and nerve paths, its muscles and tendons, which like cables enabled the arms to be raised and lowered, the legs to walk, but also as a mass, in the structures within which human beings lived, such as villages, cities, and states, where their numbers could be determined precisely, not just those who were living, but also those who died and those who were born – for in viewing such a whole one could see there were rules that governed it. The annual numbers of births and deaths, for instance, were not arbitrary; true, those numbers rose and fell, but they did so on the basis of parameters that could be identified and determined. The same was true of life expectancy.

But what drove society, what drove the people who lived in it, what decided their actions, made their bodies do one thing rather than another? Were there rules for such things that applied to everyone?

If the comparison between the body, society, and clockwork, as made explicitly by both Descartes and Hobbes, seems almost brutally simplistic to our minds, the clock not being a particularly sophisticated machine to us, the mind-set it revealed – the foundation of medical science on the one hand, whereby the body is made up of functional parts that may be exchanged quite mechanically, and the foundations of statistics and societal planning on the other, by which all human activity may be measured and quantified, captured in numbers, providing significant background for political decision-making. The list of numericized phenomena in society is almost endless, and they are broken down in all sorts of ways so that currents within people may be read and either diverted in the case of their being undesirable, or reinforced in the case of their being desirable. One may also see connections between the various parts. These statistics have a cutoff point; it would be meaningless to compile statistics of the number of people within a family killed in traffic or who have died from cancer, for instance, since such occurrences cannot be understood as the expression of anything quantative, because while Johannes belonged to the segment of young men most likely to die in traffic, to his family he was not representative of anyone, he was Johannes, who picked his car keys up off the table in the hallway one afternoon only a month ago and never came back. Not even in a small society, in one of the many village communities that line the coast of northern Norway, for example, with their two or three hundred inhabitants, where everyone knows each other, would the viewpoint of statistics make sense; he was Johannes. But at some point statistics do become meaningful. This is the point at which the observer loses overview of the "we" and can no longer identify the individual within the mass; a teacher in a school of five hundred students knows all those in his class, but not all those in the school, and while in the first instance it is meaningless to compile statistics of what marks the students have been given, the teacher knowing perfectly well how each student has performed in the different subjects, in the second instance, that of student performance in the school as a whole, statistics would indeed be meaningful. The tipping point between the individual and the individual within the mass is the tipping point between the I and the we, though not the personal we, this one borders on another, greater we, which is impersonal, no longer represented by any name, but by a number, and which thereby approaches the "it."

If we imagine humanity in terms of a scale, it would have to begin at one end with the impersonal, the materiality of the body, where in principle all parts are exchangeable, being the same for everyone, and where for that same reason the notion of the individual makes no sense – the human concept would thus proceed from the impersonal I, or the "it" of the I, shading in turn into the personal I, the personal we, and eventually the nonpersonal we, or the "it" of the we, humanity as a mass, the individual as a number.

The boundaries of both the I and the we in respect to the it are fluid and unclear, but nonetheless they are real, for in the it-zones humanity is characterized by sameness, predictability, and near-mathematical regularity, whereas in the I-zones and the we-zones it is quite differently free and individualized. The world of the inner "it" is that of biology, where thoughts are interactions between cells, emotions are chemical and electric impulses shooting through the nerve fibers, existing alongside all other bodily processes, which lie beyond their scope and cannot think or feel on their own, unless communication between the DNA spiral and the cell is a form of thinking at the most fundamental level of life, the one's duplication in the other, but no matter what it is or what it is called, it takes place at such depths within us that we neither feel, sense, understand, nor see it other than as a result, which is to say that which is brought forth within us.

These systems are uniform, what applies to one, applies to all, and they are continuous in the sense of their being transmitted as copies down through the generations. Their process is mechanical, a kind of biological-material industry, immeasurably finely tuned of course, and yet material, for which reason it has always been just a matter of time before human industry and its mechanical technology became sufficiently finely tuned to be applied inward, to ourselves. Its tentative beginnings were sometime in the Middle Ages, proceeding with astonishing velocity when religion no longer accounted for nature and man could intervene and take matters into his own hands, familiarize himself with nature's laws and principles, and its first practical results were crude Prometheus-like machines, monsters of iron and steel into which coal was shoveled, clouds of vapor and smoke billowing from their innards, but which were quickly refined and reduced in size until reaching such a level of sophistication as to be able not only to isolate our human cells and strings of DNA, mapping our entire microscopic genetic material, but also to intervene and modify it, altering and eventually manufacturing it too. These systems, which comprise the foundations of our self-awareness and our spirit, are biological and thereby mortal, and in them the I expires, which is not necessarily to say that I thereby am "it": we may feel the heart to be ours, but if our heart should falter, it has been shown that we can insert a new one, from a dead person, and go on living. We are not our hearts, we are not our arm, all we need to do is chop it off and look at it there on the table, what could such a blood-drenched object possibly have to do with me? We are constrained by this darkness of flesh and brightness of eye, by the insensitive beating of this simple heart, by the air inhaled and exhaled by the dismal gray twins that are these lungs, we are unthinkable without them, yet they live within themselves and do not know us, for they know no one, and the muscles cannot tell if their twitching occurs in someone dead or someone alive.

The difference between the "it" of the I and the "it" of the we is considerable. Whereas the former occurs in the material domain, the latter is relational, and while the former is therefore mortal, the latter is immortal in the sense that it lives on even when the individual dies. What they share is predictability and regularity, which in their different ways exclude the individual, and which in their different ways are associated with the extra-human, characterized by the forces or phenomena that pervade great totalities, previously understood as powers, in the former instance those which give rise to life's beginnings and life's course, in the latter instance fate, by which it is steered.

When does here become there? asks Michel Serres. To which might be added, when do we become they? The notion of the local is geographic, but social too. The geographic sense, the space of the local, is defined by constraints. The walls of a city are such a constraint. The hedge around a house. And property rights attach people to place: room, house, farm, manor. Mine, yours, ours, theirs. Through the ages our world has been rural, consisting of small, bounded societies where all social structures were centered around the notion of the local, where people normally died in the same place they were born, rarely having ventured far from the area in which they lived their entire lives. In such a society, a German village in the fourteenth century for instance, knowledge was local too; since only a minority could read and write, that knowledge was transmitted orally and through practice, residing in the memory of the mind and the memory of the hands, bound up with the circumstances determined by its particular landscape, whether the occurrence of a certain type of rock in a quarry or a mine, the quality of the soil, or the types of trees in the forests. The idea that some kind of scientific industry could arise in one such place, a German village in the fourteenth century, or that some kind of machine, a combustion engine perhaps, a sewing machine or a microwave oven, could ever be made here is unthinkable, precisely because of the local nature of the circumstances and the shape they accorded all knowledge there. Constrained by the limitations of individual memory, the theory required would have been impossible to attain, each and every person would have had to start from scratch, on the basis of their own capabilities alone, and nearly all knowledge gained would be lost again when its host died. All text, all theory and philosophy was in such a world gathered in the hands of the few, all manuscripts were copied out by hand and existed only in very few locations, usually monasteries, and from the thirteenth century onward in the new universities of the major cities. From these environments came the alchemists, who like Paracelsus dabbled in this and that, and the itinerant Faust figure, whose knowledge was indeed systematic but bound to a community so narrow that all experimental endeavor was undertaken alone and without connection to other such endeavors, a circumstance that could hardly lead to anything but the repetition of each other's errors.

The new has to be required or desired, it must afford clear-cut advantages, and when the impulse toward the new arises, communities must be found in which it may be developed and maintained. Within local boundaries the new would be extinguished like embers on a stone. The new is possible only in structures where the local is dissolved. In the case of knowledge, the great advance occurred in Germany in the fifteenth century with the invention of the printing press, which enabled the reproduction of any book or any treatise, as well as its dissemination into the world, and then everything no longer hinged on the one or the few. Knowledge could be accumulated in ways until then unknown, to the point where no single individual could ever acquire even a fraction of that circulating in his or her lifetime. A theory put forward in one place could be strengthened or invalidated in another, no longer was it a matter of having to start from scratch every time, and once a small number of principles concerning verifiability and universality, and thereby comparison, were established, this overarching system meant that inventions could be made that no individual would ever have been able to create on his own, the train for example, or the machine gun. Nature was released from religion, knowledge was released from the local, and once freed these forces blew like the wind through the domain of the human.

"All people" was no longer a religious concept, but biological and social. The realization of biological sameness, the body as materiality, consisting of calculable and thereby manipulable parts amenable to instrumental and gradually chemical intervention, was without issue, posing no threat to the old religious division between body and soul; on the contrary this seemed consolidated: the I belonged to the flesh, and if its life could be prolonged by someone cutting into the chest and cleansing the heart of calcium, then all the better for it. The realization of social sameness, man as mass, it too consisting of calculable and thereby manipulable parts, it too amenable to intervention, was however not without issue, since the threat it posed to the I concerned not moderation but extinction, and in a strange way set previously well-defined concepts such as worthiness and goodness in flux.

All these currents through the centuries, and everything they brought with them, which can be seen as the dissolution of the local, were for the good. But with it all, in the midst of the human domain, came a shadow, something not for the good. Societal structures change, urban centers balloon, the young pack their belongings and leave for the city to seek their fortunes, and this goes on everywhere. One by one they have made the decision, but together they form a mass, each becomes another face in the

751

flow, on their way to and from the factories, where they perform tasks that can be performed by anyone, or to and from their rooms, which are as good as identical. Smoke pours from the factory chimneys and settles in clouds upon the cities and towns, the streets are full of people, many are poor, and in the districts they inhabit, which are occasionally slum-like, hunger ensues, and the deepest hardship. Hunger is nothing new, nor the sense of powerlessness in its presence, but in previous times it was something inflicted from the outside, in the shape of floods, droughts, or cold, whose forces were ascribed to fate or to the heavenly powers, and as such were a part of man's given circumstance. This new circumstance, this new hardship, comes from people themselves, and thereby fate and the heavenly powers are drawn into the human domain, which in a way has taken on their responsibility: illness need not be fatal, it may be cured by human intervention, epidemics can be prevented, famine need not decimate a population, there being more efficient ways now to cultivate the land, making it possible to increase food production to the extent that there is now a safety margin, reinforced by a hugely improved infrastructure that means humans are no longer as dependent on local conditions. Poverty is no longer down to the heavenly powers, but to the people. This culpability cannot be isolated, cannot be attributed to this or that person or a particular group of persons, nor may it be localized to any particular place, for the consequence not only runs over from the actions of the one into those of the all, it also runs over from the local into the global, the invention of the spinning wheel being one example, basically a local occurrence, an idea conceived by a small number of individuals somewhere in England, quite innocuous on its own but with shattering consequence for all corners of society, its ramifications felt throughout the Western world, where the same thing occurs, the population explodes, the cities swell, work becomes mechanized, the market turns global – all these processes apparently unstoppable, unmanageable, incalculable, happening seemingly on their own. The blame for poverty, need, sickness belonged to no one, it was contained in the system, and if its consequences were to be prevented or modified, the system itself had to be identified and changed.

This was what Marx and Engels did: they identified the system, anchored it in history, and oriented it toward a utopian future. But a system is not human, it has no face, and "all" is by no means an unproblematic quantity, not even when divided into classes. There is no doubt that poverty and need were structurally determined, the work of a large societal group benefiting a small societal group, because if "all" is primary, "all" in the sense of a class of people living under the same circumstances and conditions, which is to say defined on the basis of what is common to them, their sameness, if it is the good of this "all" that matters, their common conditions that must be improved and changed, measured statistically in terms of average life expectancy, average child mortality, average income, average working hours, average living area, average food consumption, which are the parameters employed in *Das Kapital* to show and account for the inhuman conditions under which the working class lived, if the circumstances of the one are of secondary importance, then it is the good of the community that counts, the individual workers construed as a class or sum, and all atrocities that later took place in the name of communism, whether under Lenin, Stalin, or Mao, are a consequence, however unpredictably brutal, of that thought. The collectivization of agriculture was meant to benefit everyone, any hardship suffered by the individual in that context was of secondary importance. The same is true of the relocation of intellectuals during the Cultural Revolution.

How can the idea of a society in which everyone is equal and enjoys the same rights lead to the Gulag? Was the indignation Jack London felt on seeing the extreme poverty of the London slums misguided? Are we not to feel solidarity with others and try to help them in their need?

When hardship rises above a certain level it becomes unmanageable for the individual: even if London or Marx had spent their entire time working for the improvement of the slums and had donated their last pennies to the cause, their efforts would have been little more than a drop in the ocean. The poverty, violence, and need they saw were structural and could only be tackled and managed structurally. The premise of Marxism was that society's enormous problems, with large numbers of the population living in deplorable conditions, had to do with the distribution of social assets; as such the solutions it proposed were materialistic in nature. The issue consisted not of the forms of mass production, but of who controlled the means of production, which was not only determinative of inequality in terms of economic opportunity and huge differences in living standards, but also the alienation of the individual, which was a function of the extent to which the individual could dispose of his or her own labor. The idea was that a radical upheaval in the conditions of production would precipitate an equally radical upheaval of social conditions, evening out all economic inequalities and ensuring equal distribution of privilege, making each individual equal. However, if the main problem of industrialism was not the distribution of material wealth but was instead concerned with the reduction of the human, in a staggering process of shrinkage toward the material that all but appropriated the life of the individual, Marxism's solution was not utopian at all, but a continuation of the nightmare by other means.

Marxism was also a matter of identity in which the association of the I with the we lay not in the local dimension, following geographical boundaries, but in the new working class, which by the middle of the nineteenth century had spread throughout the Western countries, and the aim was for the revolution, the process of overturning the "they" and incorporating them into the "we," to span the world. The communist I located itself between the international we of the workers and the national they of the bourgeoisie, for while the wealth of the ruling classes knew no bounds, the self was certainly more constrained – it is by no means coincidental that the swelling I of the Romantic age, the genius and unrivaled human, emerges at the start of the nineteenth century, at the very outset of industrialism: people are becoming increasingly numerous and more alike, the unique and the local are diminishing, the concept of the mass human appears, and as if to counter this threat to the individual the grand I steps forth. The Gothic horror fiction of the same period concerns this very theme.

E. T. A. Hoffmann, who sensed more clearly than most the depths of the collective nightmare, wrote about automata so human in their appearance one could fall in love with them, and moreover about doppelgängers; Bram Stoker wrote about a person unable to die; Mary Shelley wrote about a scientist who created a human. The gripping fear of sameness encroaching upon the unique is the same fear of the inhuman encroaching upon the human, of nonlife encroaching upon life. Boundaries create distinctions, distinctions create meaning, and it is for this reason man's primeval fear is of the undifferentiated: in the domain of the undifferentiated everything is erased. To consider the unprecedented emphasis placed by the Romantics on the singular I, to which concept its construction of the genius belongs, as a way of compensating for the absence of God from the world, as well as of facing the increasing pressure of a growing sense of undifferentiation, is perhaps speculative, though not without justification; the works of Stoker, Shelley, and Hoffmann, expressions of their age, are about the boundary between the human and the nonhuman, and consider the distinction to be under threat. These two great shifts of identity in the nineteenth century, toward the unique in the one instance and the undistinguished all in the other, were mutually exclusive, an impossible equation. Not the I and the we in themselves, but the perspectives on the human each entailed. The construal of man in terms of the mass, with its accentuation of sameness, arises out of the external and is conveyed by the external's language, which is the language of mathematics and the natural sciences, whereas the construal of man as unique and grand arises out of the internal I and its language. The signficance of the national is part of the same identity complex, where the concepts of nation and people not only constrain and make manageable the we, but also aggrandize that we in their turning toward history, which is consistently heroic. As such it is a direct reply of sorts to the dissolution of the structures of the local, the heroic occurred here rather than there, within a people from whom we descend, so belonging to us, as opposed to something that occurred there, among them.

The grand I of the Romantic age reinforces the name. The mass human of industrialism reinforces the number. The opposition has always existed; the line of motion from teeming, crawling life to the two named humans is all about this: differentiation, distinction, the accordance of meaning. The function of the sacrifice is of a different quality, not undermining the collective, not turned toward the individual, as in the case of the name, but establishing difference within and according meaning to the collective as a whole. But the function of the sacrifice changes too. The primitive nature of Abel's offering and Cain's fratricide, expressing in a single image the violence that issues from sameness, becomes cultivated and complex in the story of Abraham's offering of his son, there no longer being anything absolute about either the sacrifice or the God to whom it is offered, since God rejects the offering, and what's a rejected sacrifice worth? There are many signs that primitive cultures initially sacrificed humans, but later substituted animals, though not just any animal, they were always domesticated and thereby proximate to man's daily life. The story of Abraham seems almost to express that very transition. But there is more to it than that. There is no explicit involvement of the collective here, only Abraham, his son, and their God. God, the almighty creator of the universe, its very gestalt, who in demanding human sacrifice has demanded the inhuman, and Abraham, willing to sacrifice his son, thereby placing something else, God's name and honor, higher than death, and in that way overcoming death by not allowing it to be the ultimate end. Something in life is greater than death, therefore life may be sacrificed.

Had he killed his son, he would have done so out of love – for God, but also for his son. When God rescinds the command and Abraham aborts this sacrifice of his dearest to the highest, his son thereby living on, another love arises, that between father and son, not concentrated in any pillar of fire, the very flash point of life and death, but spread out over endless days, so much time that it is continually being erased, and so near as to hardly be noticed, for in his son a father sees himself, and in his father a son sees himself, what belongs to one and what to the other is not always easy to say, and he who was below will one day be above, and he who was above will one day be below.

The story of Abraham's sacrifice of his son is one of the strangest in the Bible, not only because it is so unfathomable, for all mythological narratives are unfathomable, but because it departs from the absolute, generally a fundamental of mythic and religious narratives, a departure that is not merely peripheral to the story but that manifests itself at its very center. God is an absolute being, the sacrifice an absolute action. But here the sacrifice is not an absolute action, it is rescinded. God's command to Abraham is a test, and the locus of significance is displaced, shifted from the sacrifice itself to the willingness to sacrifice, which is to say from the connection between the human and the divine to the human. Sacrifice is never merely a loss, for something is always gained by sacrifice, so what did Abraham lose when the command was rescinded? What he lost was the absolute, and triumph over death. In other words, he lost the uttermost meaning of life. What then did he gain? What he gained was the innermost meaning of life, his son's life, properly inalienable, but this in a world where "properly" conceals itself in the open and is not given like the offering, but instead must be taken. It is a conquest, too, of human worth, as the Old Testament is a narrative on the same subject. That the relationship between the divine and the human is so ambivalent, the worldly weight of the mortal earth, pulling the divine toward the terrestrial amid the whirling sand and dust of the antiabsolute, which may also be seen as the opposite, the endeavor of the trivial toward the hallowed, forever halted in midflight, rescinded, half workday, half festival, half man, half god, petty at one moment, almighty the next, is what makes Judaism a religion of doubt, hesitancy, and postponement – and of ambivalence, for the forces of the opposite are always present too, in the symmetry of this clearest image of revenge: eye, eye, tooth, tooth.

If, with Girard, one considers the narrative of the life and teachings of Christ to be the consummation of the long story that is the Old Testament, it is in this respect particularly that the line of progression comes to an end, for what the New Testament means above all is the discontinuance of the notion of vengeance, the end of uncontrollable violence. Turn the other cheek, says Jesus, and this is the symmetry of the good, the one no more faced against the other, but turned toward his neighbor, which is to say that the other is no longer construed as a threat or danger, but as a part of the self.

The New Testament scene that measures up to the story of Cain and Abel, or that of Abraham and Isaac, is when Jesus stands up to the crowd as they are about to stone a woman accused of adultery. For Girard this scene is the conclusive curbing of the forces of mimetic violence. Jesus finds himself in the scapegoat's position, the one surrounded by the all, but instead of being destroyed by them he turns to face them, dispersing the crowd by means of a single utterance. Stoning is the manifestation of retribution and based on duplication, both ritual insofar as stoning is employed in all such cases of transgression, and individual insofar as everyone takes an active part. What Jesus says to them is simple: "He that is without sin among you, let him first cast a stone at her." By that utterance he redirects responsibility for the act of violence to each and every one of them as individuals, and the collective dissolves. There is no all, only the one, responsible for his or her own actions.

But the good, and solicitude for one's neighbor and the dissolution of violence in forgiveness is indeed good, is not an expression of civilization, but of something radically different. The good does not solve the problem of violence, it is not instrumental in the way civilization's laws and institutions are instrumental, but the very opposite, a socially solvent force. The antithesis of violence is not the good, but the social. That equation does not work out, for violence exists within the social, embedded in the differences inherent to the domain, but it is the best we can do, and the violence on whose basis Girard construes his notions of taboo and ritual, the violence within, which tears the community apart from the inside, is something we control, the systems we have established deal with it, and it no longer poses any real threat to us. The control of such violence was made possible by transferring responsibility to the individual, in turn leading to the disintegration of our knowledge of the collective, for this was no longer neeeded, but with the huge population swell that occurred toward the end of the nineteenth century, flooding at the tidelines of the new structures of industrialism, came its violence, unprecedented in scope within that system – at no point in our world history have so many been systematically oppressed as at the close of the nineteenth century – utterly out of control, yet deriving from a single point, in itself insignificant and innocuous, the assassination of an archduke by a lone fanatic, sparking first regionally, a crisis in Austria-Hungary, then nationally, then internationally, and in the space of weeks the whole of Europe was at war, a war no one wanted and no one needed, profoundly destructive at every conceivable level, with no one able to prevent it, its avoidance beyond the scope of any single individual, and the violence it brought with it escalated out of all control. People who otherwise cooperated and collaborated, whose interests and goals were shared, destroyed each other with such attention to detail, such savagery, and in such numbers as to eclipse all previous wars – and at last, when it was all over, it had taken eight million people with it. It was a storm of destruction impossible to command, as if it were taking place outside the domain of the human, and yet it was not, these were the very forces of human nature manifesting themselves, the same forces of which ancient cultures had been so fearful, for if they found form they would reproduce themselves and spread, and threaten to destroy everyone and everything entirely. This was the violence within, violence among like kind, but on a whole new scale and with new, serially manufactured weapons that redefined death in its image: serially manufactured, industrial.

◆◆◆

The Hitler we know was created by World War I. Nothing he became or did afterward can be explained without reference to that background. The war became a home to him; he did not apply for leave until he had lived in the trenches for two years, not because he was ineligible but because he didn't want to.

When Germany capitulated in November 1918 he was receiving treatment at a military hospital in Pomerania. He was shattered by the news. He wanted to fight until the last, anything else would destroy the foundation of everything he believed in. When the peace came, without defeat in battle, he saw it only as an act of faithless villainy. This is how he describes it in *Mein Kampf*:

> *The next few days came and with them the most terrible certainty of my life. The rumors became more and more oppressive. What I had taken for a local affair was now said to be a general revolution. To this was added the disgraceful news from the front. They wanted to capitulate. Was such a thing really possible?*
>
> *On November 10, the pastor came to the hospital for a short address: now we learned everything.*
>
> *In extreme agitation, I, too, was present at the short speech. The dignified old gentleman seemed a-tremble as he informed us that the House of Hollenzollern should no longer bear the German imperial*

*crown; that the fatherland had become a "republic"; that we must pray
to the Almighty not to refuse His blessing to this change and not to
abandon our people in the times to come. He could not help himself,
he had to speak a few words in memory of the royal house. He began
to praise its services in Pomerania, in Prussia, nay, to the German
fatherland, and – here he began to sob gently to himself – in the little
hall the deepest dejection settled on all hearts, and I believe that not
an eye was able to restrain its tears. But when the old gentleman tried
to go on, and began to tell us that we must now end the long War,
yes, that now that it was lost and we were throwing ourselves upon
the mercy of the victors, our fatherland would for the future be exposed to dire oppression, that the armistice should be accepted with
confidence in the magnanimity of our previous enemies, I could stand
it no longer. It became impossible for me to sit still one minute more.
Again everything went black before my eyes; I tottered and groped
my way back to the dormitory, threw myself on my bunk, and dug
my burning head into my blanket and pillow.*

*Since the day when I had stood at my mother's grave, I had not
wept.*

His rage and ignominy at what he saw as a breach of faith formed
the engine of hatred that drove his later political ideas and actions;
without it they are unthinkable. The scene in which he buries his
face in his pillow and weeps transforms into an ominous, heavily
laden picture of the consequences of that breach:

*And so it had all been in vain. In vain all the sacrifices and priva-
tions; in vain the hunger and thirst of months which were often endless; in vain the hours in which, with mortal fear clutching at our
hearts, we nevertheless did our duty; and in vain the death of two
millions who died. Would not the graves of all the hundreds of thousands open, the graves of those who with faith in the fatherland had
marched forth never to return? Would they not open and send the
silent mud- and blood-covered heroes back as spirits of vengeance to*

the homeland which had cheated them with such mockery of the high-est sacrifice which a man can make to his people in this world?

This host of spirits, these two million dead soldiers covered with mud and blood, were indeed to come home and haunt Germany, it was in order to restore their honor and accord meaning to their sacrifice that Hitler rearmed the nation in the thirties; defeat was to be avenged, the old enemies and the traitors who had worked for peace were to be crushed, but it was also because the war in itself had been so significant to him and so many of his generation. Nazism was also a death cult and a warrior cult; this gruesome image, the graves opening, the fallen rising up, bloodied and smeared with mud, as spirits of vengeance, was later to find further expression in the skull-and-crossbones symbolism of the SS.

In contrast to the majority he had nothing to come back to when the war ended, so what he did was to remain in the military, for besides meaning and direction the army had given him food, lodgings, and a well-defined job of work to carry out for four years. He went back to Munich and reenlisted with the reserve battalion of the infantry regiment with which he had served.

After returning to Munich, Hitler was assigned duty as a prison-camp guard for two months, subsequently carrying out guard duty at the city's Hauptbahnhof, and was selected as a representative of his company. In the spring of 1919, following a period of civil unrest, he was picked out by the officer in charge of an army information department, a captain by the name of Karl Mayr, whose job it was to monitor suspicious political elements, which is to say the radical left, and to combat subversion within army ranks. Hitler was undergoing an anti-Bolshevik "instruction course," Kershaw writes, and it was on this occasion his rhetorical talents first came to notice. A lecturer on the course, a Professor von Müller, mentioned these and pointed him out to Mayr, who recognized Hitler immediately as "Hitler from the List Regiment." Later,

Mayr would write, "he was like a tired stray dog looking for a master . . . ready to throw in his lot for anyone who would show him kindness," Toland reports. The most remarkable thing about this description of Hitler, however, is that at this time he was "totally unconcerned about the German people and their destinies." This was hardly the fact of the matter; what Mayr observed was that Hitler was not talking about it. Introverted, silent, troubled, pale, without purpose – a stray dog hungry for kindness. Mayr gave him that kindness, or at least a small measure of purpose: toward the end of the summer Hitler was giving his own pro-nationalist, anti-Bolshevik "course" at a military camp outside Augsburg. In Hitler's own words:

> One day I asked for the floor. One of the participants felt obliged to break a lance for the Jews and began to defend them in lengthy arguments. This aroused me to an answer. The overwhelming majority of the students present took my standpoint. The result was that a few days later I was sent into a Munich regiment as a so-called "educational officer."
>
> I started out with the greatest enthusiasm and love. For all at once I was offered an opportunity of speaking before a larger audience; and the thing that I had always presumed from pure feeling without knowing it was now corroborated: I could "speak." My voice, too, had grown so much better that I could be sufficiently understood at least in every corner of the small squad rooms.
>
> No task could make me happier than this, for now before being discharged I was able to perform useful services to the institution which had been so close to my heart: the army.
>
> And I could boast of some success: in the course of my lectures I led many hundreds, indeed thousands, of comrades back to their people and fatherland. I "nationalized" the troops and was thus also able to help strengthen the general discipline.
>
> Here again I became acquainted with a number of like-minded comrades, who later began to form the nucleus of the new movement.

That he ever held the position of "educational officer" is a misrepresentation, and the number of students he lectured is grossly exaggerated, but his teaching was undoubtedly a success and his talent for winning over an audience was demonstrable. Professor von Müller describes the moment he first saw Hitler hold forth:

> *[A small group were] riveted to a man in their midst who, with a strangely guttural voice incessantly and with mounting passion, spoke to them. I had the peculiar feeling that the excitement generated by his performance at the same time gave him his voice. I saw a pallid, gaunt face under strands of hair hanging down in unmilitary fashion. He had a close-cropped moustache and strikingly large, light blue, fanatically cold, glowing eyes.*

Hitler's task was to give lectures to his fellow soldiers and to monitor the teeming numbers of political parties that had arisen in Munich at that time. It was in this latter capacity, in the autumn of 1919, that he attended a meeting of a small party called the German Workers' Party, whose political program was a blend of nationalism, socialism, and anti-Semitism, combating internationalism and Judaism its two primary causes. Shortly after this meeting Hitler applied for membership of the party, which would soon change its name to the German National Socialist Workers' Party, swelling from a few dozen members at the time of Hitler joining to become the largest political party in Germany in the space of little more than a decade.

Four days after his membership was accepted, Hitler was ordered by Mayr to respond to an inquiry the department had received from a former participant in one of the instruction courses asking for a clarification of "the Jewish Question." Hitler provided a lengthy and meticulous reply, writing that the Jews were a race, not a religion, and that anti-Semitism had to be based not on sentiment but on fact. An emotional reaction would lead to pogroms, whereas anti-Semitism based on reason had to lead to a systematic removal of the rights of the Jews. The "final aim," he concluded, "must unshakeably be the removal of the Jews altogether."

❖ ❖ ❖

Three years later, in autumn 1922, the American ambassador to Germany dispatched a man to Munich to compile a report on the new and prospering National Socialist party and its leader, Adolf Hitler. The attaché's name was Truman Smith and his specific brief was to meet Hitler and provide an assessment of his character, personality, abilities, and weaknesses, as well as to investigate the strengths and potentialities of his party, the NSDAP. The United States consul in Munich, Robert Murphy, informed Smith that Hitler was a "pure and simple adventurer," though nevertheless believed he was "a real character and is exploiting all latent discontent"; still it was questionable whether he was "big enough to take the lead in a German national movement," as Toland reports. At the invitation of the newspaper editor Max Erwin von Scheubner-Richter, a member of Hitler's inner circle who assured him that the party's anti-Semitism was purely propaganda, Smith witnessed Hitler's inspection of storm troopers in front of the new party headquarters:

> *A remarkable sight indeed. Twelve hundred of the toughest roughnecks I have ever seen in my life pass in review before Hitler at the goose step under the old Reichflag wearing red armbands with Haken-kreuzen. Hitler, following the review, makes a speech . . . then shouts, "Death to the Jews!" etc. and etc. There was frantic cheering. I never saw such a sight in my life.*

Three days later, on the morning of November 22, Smith meets Hitler in person, and is given an outline of the party's politics. During the meeting Hitler states that "only a dictatorship can bring Germany to its feet," and that it was

much better for America and England that the decisive struggle be-
tween our civilization and Marxism be fought out on German soil
rather than on American and English soil. If we (America) do not
help German Nationalism, Bolshevism will conquer Germany. Then
there will be no more reparations and Russian and German Bolshe-
vism, out of motives of self-preservation, must attack the Western
nations.

While also discoursing on other subjects, Toland writes, Hitler avoids mentioning the Jews at all, until Smith asks him outright, Hitler disarmingly replying that he merely favors the withdrawal of citizenship and their exclusion from public affairs. By the time their meeting ended, Smith was convinced Hitler was going to be an important factor in German politics. Before leaving, Smith accepted a ticket from the party press secretary, Rosenberg, to a speech Hitler was giving that same evening. As it turned out, he was unable to attend, being called back to his embassy and having a train to catch, for which reason he passed his ticket on to Ernst Hanfstaengl, a Munich contact of Warren Robbins, who was a counselor at the embassy; the two had studied together at Harvard. Hanfstaengl's father was German, his mother American, both families belonging to the highest echelons of their respective societies. His mother was of old New England stock, his maternal grandmother was the cousin of General Sedgwick, who fell in the Civil War, his maternal grandfather was General William Heine, originally from Dresden, also a Civil War veteran, and a pallbearer at the funeral of Abraham Lincoln. Hanfstaengl's mother remembered the funeral and her father being visited in Dresden by Wagner and Liszt. On his father's side, two generations of Hanfstaengls had served as privy councillors to the Dukes of Saxe-Coburg-Gotha, and the family were well-known patrons of the arts; his grandfather founded an art publishing house and had moreover photographed three German Kaisers, Moltke, Liszt, and Wagner, as well as Ibsen, and the family home in Munich was a favored rendezvous for such luminaries as Richard

Strauss, Fridtjof Nansen, and Mark Twain. Hanfstaengl was in other words a person for whom the world stood open, a member of Munich's cultural glitterati as well as that of the American northeastern seaboard; during his time at Harvard he had met two American presidents, the then-incumbent Theodore Roosevelt, as well as his later successor, Franklin D. Roosevelt, not to mention the poet T. S. Eliot, a fact he makes abundantly clear in the blustering introduction to his memoirs, first published in the United States in 1957.

It was Hanfstaengl who took Smith to the train in Munich that November evening in 1922, meeting Rosenberg, who gave Hanfstaengl Smith's ticket to the evening's event and accompanied him to the venue. Hanfstaengl describes Rosenberg as "a sallow, untidy fellow, who looked half-Jewish in an unpleasant sort of way." They take a tram to the Kindl Keller beer hall, which is packed. Hanfstaengl sits down at the press table and asks one of the reporters there where Hitler is. The man points; Hitler is seated next to Max Amann, a sergeant from his old regiment, and Anton Drexler, founder of the party Hitler joined three years before. Hanfstaengl's first impression is this:

> *In his heavy boots, dark suit, and leather waistcoat, semistiff white collar and odd little moustache, he really did not look very impressive — like a waiter in a railway-station restaurant.*

When Drexler introduces Hitler, a roar of applause goes up. Hitler straightens up and walks past the press table to the platform with a "swift, controlled step, the unmistakable soldier in mufti." The atmosphere is electric, Hanfstaengl writes, and the speech Hitler proceeds to give is brilliant.

> *No one who judges his capacity as a speaker from the performances of his later years can have any true insight into his gifts. As time went on he became drunk with his own oratory before vast crowds and his voice lost its former character through the intervention of microphone*

and loudspeaker. In his early years he had a command of voice, phrase, and effect which has never been equaled, and on this evening he was at his best.

In a quiet, reserved voice he drew a picture of what had happened in Germany since November 1918: the collapse of the monarchy and the surrender at Versailles; the founding of the Republic on the ignominy of war guilt; the fallacy of international Marxism and Pacifism; the eternal class war leitmotif and the resulting hopeless stalemate between employers and employees, between Nationalists and Socialists.

As he felt the audience becoming interested in what he had to say, he gently moved his left foot to one side, like a soldier standing at ease in slow motion, and started to use his hands and arms in gesture, of which he had an extensive and expressive repertoire. There was none of the barking and braying he later developed, and he had an ingenious, mocking humor which was telling without being offensive.

Hitler criticizes the Kaiser for being a weakling, he criticizes the Weimar Republicans for accepting the victors' demands, which were stripping Germany of everything but the graves of those who perished in the trenches. He compares the separatist movement and religious exclusivity of the Catholic Church in Bavaria with the comradeship of the soldiers on the front line, who never asked a wounded comrade his religion before leaping to his aid. He speaks at length on the subjects of patriotism and national pride, highlighting Kemal Atatürk in Turkey and Benito Mussolini in Italy as examples to be followed. He hits out at war profiteers and receives roaring applause as he tears them apart for wasting valuable foreign currency on importing oranges from Italy at the same time as half the country goes hungry because of inflation. He attacks the Jews, who are becoming fat on the misery of others, and he lashes out against the communists and socialists for wanting to disrupt German traditions.

I looked round at the audience. Where was the nondescript crowd I had seen only an hour before? What was suddenly holding these peo-

ple, who, on the hopeless incline of the falling mark, were engaged in a daily struggle to keep themselves within the line of decency? The hubbub and mug-clattering had stopped and they were drinking in every word. Only a few yards away was a young woman, her eyes fastened on the speaker. Transfixed as though in some devotional ecstasy, she had ceased to be herself and was completely under the spell of Hitler's despotic faith in Germany's future greatness.

When the speech was over Hanfstaengl went up to introduce himself to Hitler, who was still standing on the platform.

Naïve and yet forceful, obliging and yet uncompromising, he stood, face and hair soaked in perspiration, his semistiff collar, fastened with a square imitation-gold safety pin, melted to nothing. While talking he dabbed his face with what had once been a handkerchief, glancing worriedly at the many open exits through which came the drafts of a cold November night.

"Herr Hitler, my name is Hanfstaengl," I said. "Captain Truman Smith asked me to give you his best wishes." "Ah yes, the big American," he answered. "He begged me to come here and listen to you, and I can only say I have been most impressed," I went on. "I agree with 95 percent of what you said and would very much like to talk to you about the rest some time."

"Why, yes, of course," Hitler said. "I am sure we shall not have to quarrel about the odd 5 percent." He made a very pleasant impression, modest and friendly. So we shook hands again and I went home.

There are many descriptions of Hitler's speeches from this time. Hanfstaengl's is special because he belongs to the apex of society, not the usual beer-hall crowd that is most often Hitler's audience, and the fact that he is so taken by Hitler's gifts indicates that the vulgar and tasteless, brutally simple strokes of *Mein Kampf* were absent from his public appearances. Hanfstaengl recognizes that Hitler is petty bourgeois, but also that as a speaker he is unconstrained by the fact, rising above it by virtue of his magnetism and oratorical skills, the almost hypnotic charisma he so obviously possesses, and is thereby able to capture the imagination of almost every member of the crowd, regardless of class. At the same time his petty-bourgeois nature is a crucial factor, for as Hanfstaengl thinks to himself that night, unable to sleep after listening to Hitler for the first time:

> *Where all our conservative politicians and speakers were failing abysmally to establish any contact with the ordinary people, this self-made man, Hitler, was clearly succeeding in presenting a non-Communist program to exactly those people whose support we needed.*

Once Hitler is encouraged to speak in public, finds the confidence and discovers that he is able to, and that people are interested in what he has to say, he is for the first time free to explore his abilities. He is now able to mine his inner being without the destructive checks and balances of the brain, existing simply in the moment, and that feeling of control, of mastery and skill, must surely have filled him to the brim. He is thirty years old and yet to experience success in anything to which he has applied himself. In fact he has failed in every endeavor, until now, stepping onto the platform and looking out at the crowd of people in the room in front of him. His sensitivity, which is so great and which compels him to sever himself from other people completely, either by withdrawing, avoiding the gaze of others, keeping to himself, or by talking incessantly to keep everyone at arm's length, this sensitivity, so unmanageable in the face of an individual you, now comes into its own, perhaps for the first time in his life, for while he is so aware of that you as to shut it out entirely, with near-autistic compulsion, his awareness of the we is quite as intense, and to this we, which is unthreatening, he is able to open himself. He opens himself to the we, heedful of what it says, sensing every nuance of its mood and playing on its strings, for he is not himself a part of this we, but stands outside it, rousing it, stirring it into life, taking it here, taking it there, and he is able to do so because he has always stood outside it. In order to see something, one must see from outside.

Only someone who stands outside the social world knows what the social world is; to those within it, it is like water to a fish. Hitler rejects the singular you, and stands outside the we, and yet he longs for it, and it is this longing his audiences sense when he speaks, the longing for the we being the very foundation of the human, swelling in times of crisis, swelling in chaos, as it did in the Germany of the 1920s, and in Hitler it burns fiercely indeed. There is no need to listen to what he says, his audience were oblivious too, but to the way he says it, the emotions by which he is filled, this is what they react to, this is what they feel, and they drink it up like water. Oh, this longing for community, this longing to be equal, this longing to belong. The simplest is the truest, and this is the truth of Hitler, his longing to be a part of the we touches something deep within that we itself – all accounts of his speeches from this time focus on the same thing, the way his raucous beer-hall audiences, for all their shouting and scuffling, their whooping and howling, hush and fall calm, and become as one. The simplest is the truest, and hatred of the Jews represents the simplest thing of all, the we's need of a they, the basic mimetic structure of violence, the one against the other, duplicated in ritual, us against them, the sacrifice of a they in order that the we may prevail. That need, too, swells in crisis, swells in chaos, one of the fundamental forms of culture, a condition to which we continue to return. For Hitler, longing for the we is also a longing for the war, and the role it played in what later occurred cannot be underestimated.

Ernst Hanfstaengl recognizes this more clearly than most, writing:

> *We all knew, but overlooked the deeper implications of the fact, that the first flowering of his personality had been as a soldier.*
> *When he talked of National-Socialism what he really meant was*

military-Socialism, Socialism within a framework of military disci-
pline or, in civilian terms, police-Socialism. At what point along the
line his mind took the final shape it did I do not know, but the germ
was always there.

When Hitler joined the German Workers' Party it was hardly a party at all. Its first public meetings in 1919, with Drexler speaking, were attended by audiences of ten, thirty-eight, and forty-one respectively. With Hitler speaking these numbers improved dramatically. In 1920 he spoke at more than thirty public meetings, drawing audiences of between 800 and 2,500 in every instance, Kershaw reports, party membership figures increasing similarly, from 190 in January 1920 to 2,000 a year later, and 3,300 six months after that. Hitler was being noticed, at first by other party members, subsequently by Munich's general public. Those who saw him speak at those first meetings had need of him and took care of him accordingly, which was a further boost to his confidence, extending his radius, bringing him into contact with new people in new contexts. An early member of the party, Dietrich Eckart, was especially important in this respect. Eckart was a poet, translator of Ibsen, a morphine-addicted anti-Semite who quickly took an interest in Hitler and became a mentor to him. He was twenty years Hitler's senior, as educated as he was cultivated, though often blunt in manner. He gave Hitler his first trip in an airplane, took him to the theater, bought him a coat, taught him writing, published his first articles, introduced him to circles he had not previously had access to, and generally paved his way into Munich's right-wing radical environment, as well as nourishing his anti-Semitic and anticommunist opinions and providing him with arguments in their support. "This man is the future of Germany," he would say of Hitler, according to Timothy W. Ryback. "One day the whole world will be talking about him." Eckart became a father figure to Hitler, who was flattered by his attentions and absorbed everything he taught him. Three years before Eckart was introduced to Hitler, he had found cause to proclaim:

We need someone to lead us who is used to the sound of a machine gun. Someone who can scare the shit out of people. I don't need an officer. The common people have lost all respect for them. The best would be a worker who knows how to talk. He doesn't need to know much. Politics is the stupidest profession on earth. Any farmer's wife knows as much as any political leader. Give me a vain monkey who can give the Reds their due and won't run away as soon as someone swings a chair leg at him. I would take him any day over a dozen educated professors who wet their pants and sit there trembling with their facts. He has to be a bachelor, then we'll get the women.

Few could fit that description better then Hitler. When Hanfstaengl, born in 1887 and two years older than Hitler, met him, Hitler was thirty-four. For the first time in his life he was succeeding at something, for the first time in his life he was of worth to others and not just himself, but the portrait Hanfstaengl paints could quite as easily have been the young man Kubizek describes from his time in Linz and Vienna. After that first evening in the beer hall, Hanfstaengl attends another meeting and hears him speak a second time, and on this occasion his impression of Hitler is moderated somewhat, Hitler going further this time, with thinly veiled incitements to guerrilla warfare in the case of a French incursion on the Rhine, this sounding to Hanfstaengl like the language of a desperado. He finds Hitler's views on foreign politics alarming, disproportionate and extravagant. Yet he remains both captivated and intrigued, asking himself what might be at the back of this curious man's brain, and on attending a third meeting at which Hitler speaks he introduces him to his wife and to the wife of the Norwegian illustrator Olaf Gulbransson, and invites him to his home. Before long, Hanfstaengl is drawn into Hitler's inner circles, Hanfstaengl's wide network of contacts being of particular use to them. He pays for a new printing press for their weekly newspaper, facilitates the publishing of some articles on foreign affairs, and endeavors in his own words to influence Hitler's views on foreign politics, which he finds too continental and narrow-minded, and overly determined by Rosenberg and his associates, whom he despises and whose anti-Semitism and anti-Bolshevism positively disgust him. Hitler listens attentively to what he has to say, Hanfstaengl writes, though would later become more indifferent; when it came to the United States, Hitler wanted to hear about skyscrapers and was more fascinated by details of technical progress than by political matters, though he was particularly interested in the Ku Klux Klan, which he thought to be a political movement much like his own, and in Henry Ford, not so much as an automobile manufacturer and industrial innovator but more as an anti-Semite.

In Hanfstaengl's home Hitler made a good impression, being especially taken with his wife, sending her flowers, kissing her hand, giving her adoring looks, and he played with the couple's son with the kind of spontaneity a child likes in an adult. His ill-fitting suit, his respectful diffidence and adherence to formal manners of address were all revealing of his class background, Hanfstaengl writes; Hitler spoke the way people of lower rank spoke to people of better education, title, or academic attainment. His table manners were good, though his tastes were occasionally curious; Hanfstaengl states that he had the most incredible sweet tooth of any man he had ever met. At one meal Hanfstaengl treats him to "a bottle of Prince Metternich's best Gewürtztraminer" and coming back into the room after being called out to the telephone catches Hitler spooning sugar into his glass.

Hanfstaengl visits Hitler in his tiny flat at Thierschstrasse 41, where he lives extremely modestly, "like a down-at-heels clerk." His lodgings here comprised a single room with a large bed, too wide for its corner and with the head obscuring the single narrow window. The floor covering was cheap, worn linoleum, with a couple of threadbare rugs, on the wall opposite the bed was a makeshift bookshelf, the only other piece of furniture in the room apart from a chair and a table. The landlady, a Frau Reichert, was Jewish and found Hitler an ideal tenant.

> *He is such a nice man, but he has the most extraordinary moods. Sometimes weeks go by when he seems to be sulking and does not say a word to us. He looks through us as if we were not there. He always pays his rent punctually in advance, but he is a real Bohemian type.*

In the hallway there was an upright piano, and on one occasion when Hitler was due in court as a witness he asked Hanfstaengl to play something to calm his nerves. Hanfstaengl obliged with some Bach, to which Hitler sat nodding his head with vague interest. But when Hanfstaengl moved on to the prelude of Wagner's *Meistersinger*, Hitler switched on immediately:

> *This was it. This was Hitler's meat. He knew the thing absolutely by heart and could whistle every note of it in a curious penetrating vibrato, but completely in tune. He started to march up and down the hall, waving his arms as if he was conducting an orchestra. He really had an excellent feel for the spirit of music, certainly as good as many a conductor. This music affected him physically, and by the time I had crashed through the finale he was in splendid spirits, all his worries gone, and raring to get to grips with the public prosecutor.*

Kershaw describes the same occasion, and since this was a meeting that took place between Hanfstaengl and Hitler alone, there are no other sources than Hanfstaengl's memoir. Kershaw's account is as follows:

> *Hitler was taken by Putzi's skills as a pianist, especially his ability to play Wagner. He would accompany Putzi by whistling the tune, marching up and down swinging his arms like the conductor of an orchestra, relaxing visibly in the process.*

In the passages where Hanfstaengl is the source he is consistently referred to by the diminutive "Putzi," and Hitler's interest in Wagner comes across as comical and bizarre, as if only Hitler could find something so absurd to be relaxing. But Hanfstaengl does not portray Hitler as foolish, on the contrary he emphasizes his knowledge and his feel for the spirit of the music. The fact that he is able to whistle entire Wagner symphonies may indeed appear unusual, but the same was true of Wittgenstein, who could whistle Wagner to perfection and would often exploit his talent as a party trick to entertain his guests. It is hard to imagine the author of a Wittgenstein biography belittling the great philosopher's passion for music, even if it did manifest itself peculiarly in the form of whistling, but when it comes to Hitler the way Kershaw portrays him, everything he does is either sinister or ridiculous. Another example, Hanfstaengl writing:

Hitler's intimates were nearly all modest people. As I got to know him I started attending the Monday evening Stammtisch at the Café Neumaier, an old-fashioned coffeehouse on the corner of the Petersplatz and the Viktualien Markt. The long, irregular room, with built-in benches and paneled walls, had space for a hundred people or so. Here he was in the habit of meeting his oldest adherents, many of them middle-aged married couples, who came to have their frugal supper, part of which they brought with them. Hitler would speak en famille and try out the technique and effect of his newest ideas.

And Kershaw's version:

Certainly by the time Putzi Hanfstaengl, the cultured part-American who became his Foreign Press Chief, came to know him, late in 1922, Hitler had a table booked every Monday evening at the old-fashioned Café Neumaier on the edge of the Viktualienmarkt . . . In the long room, with its rows of benches and tables, often occupied by elderly couples, Hitler's entourage would discuss politics, or listen to his monologues on art and architecture, while eating the snacks they had brought with them, and drinking their liters of beer or cups of coffee.

Hitler's audience, his oldest adherents, middle-aged married couples of modest background, are in Kershaw's rendering "elderly couples" who "often occupied" the benches and tables, so not only does he alter their age, he also gives the impression they were simply customers there and Hitler knew them as no more than that. Why? Middle-aged couples of modest background gathered around Hitler in a cozy café lends an air of respectability and decency to Hitler that goes against Kershaw's image of him. This is why Kershaw's version also departs from "frugal supper" in favor of "snacks" and "liters of beer." The source text has no mention of beer or snacks, this is something Kershaw has added, presumably to enhance the impression of the place as a drinking joint, though certainly beer would also have been served there, and in the context of the juxtaposition the "cups of coffee" seem equally negative.

Hanfstaengl goes on to describe Hitler's inner circle at this time, all of whom are present at these Monday-evening political and social meetings.

While Hanfstaengl perhaps might not be the most reliable source, having been close to Hitler for some ten years, for which reason he might well be considered a Nazi, with all that this entails as regards the need to explain things away, his memoir nonetheless does provide a balanced portrait of Hitler and his supporters, simply by not tending to any one side. It is this balanced nature of Hanfstaengl's account that makes it credible, and also what makes it interesting, in the picture it paints of Hitler and in its contribution to our understanding of his appeal, which cannot have been the appeal of a criminal, a clown, or someone of shallow nature, but must surely have been of a wholly different character, for how else would he be able to lead an entire nation with him into the abyss? He was human, the people around him were human, his party comrades were human. This is not the same as to say they were good, for the bad and the brutal too are human. Christian Weber, a burly horse dealer who enjoyed knocking communists about, has another side to him too. Hanfstaengl writes that Weber is flattered to be invited into the home of a person of the upper classes. How much this says of his sense of class belonging. All he really wants is a secure job and a measure of dignity in his life. And Hanfstaengl writes that Weber, this thug, possesses "an oddly intuitive sense of the bottomless pit of Hitler's mind" and realizes fully what Hitler is capable of – this is perceptible, at least to someone who knows, perhaps from himself, what humans are capable of and how that potential finds expression. Another who senses this is Eckart, Hitler's mentor, who "was already beginning to regret it." Why? And Drexler, the union man, who strongly disapproves of the violence that is becoming a growing factor in the party's activities. Those who accompany Hitler home from these Monday-night meetings are armed, Hitler himself carries a pistol in his jacket pocket, even when speaking. These evenings are strange in the way they bring together decent folk from meager backgrounds and raging fanatics, one of whom is perhaps mixed up in the most significant political murder to have taken place in the Weimar Republic, the assassination of the foreign minister, Rathenau. Hitler is the radial point of the group. He can whistle entire symphonies while air-conducting, he lacks the courage to approach a woman of his own age, he loves cakes and anything sweet, he holds the Iron Cross First Class, for bravery in combat, he lives a shadowy Bohemian existence in a shabby apartment, never keeps an appointment, is often seen in the show-rooms of automobile dealers, and when in the company of others talks incessantly. He cannot tolerate anyone other than himself dominating any situation in which he is present, and in such instances will readily lie in order to regain others' attention, he always knows better, wears carpet slippers indoors, and has a nice line in impersonations, his take on Göring's wife and her Swedish accent being particularly funny, though he can do equally good ones of Max Amann in a rage and Quirin Diesl insulting a political opponent, his star turn however being the semiprofessorial, politically aware nationalist babbling on about Siegfried's sword and the German eagle in insufferably pompous fashion, Hanfstaengl writes, adding that Hitler had learned off by heart the greater part of a dreadful poem written to him by an admirer, containing endless half-rhymes on Hitler, which he recited with such passion he would have his audience in tears of laughter. Moreover he registers as a "writer" when checking into hotels, he has no eye for nature, never reads novels, admires Cromwell but most of all Frederick the Great; he is attracted by death, idealizes war, writes poems about his mother, hates the Jews and all things Jewish, he is interested in eugenics and reads everything there is about the biology of race, has never read Nietzsche, though he holds his prose to be the most splendid German, has in fact read Fichte and Schopenhauer, and his favorite motif in painting is Leda and the Swan. This man it is who sits at the Café Neumaier every Monday night, surrounded by party comrades and supporters, with a pistol in his pocket and a militarized group of young men watching out for him who beat up communists and other opponents. He has written a letter in which he states that the Jews should be removed, and he has spoken out against them in all his numerous speeches. It is an opinion he shares with many, most prevalent among the lower classes, those higher up, where power normally resides, find it inappropriate and vulgar, a breach of a norm that is primarily aesthetic or founded on notions of class. Thomas Mann, who is in the same city, perhaps only a few streets away from the Café Neumaier, does not hate the Jews, such a notion would be unthinkable to him. He hailed the outbreak of the war, its blood stood for the authentic and significant, in contrast to the inauthenticity and insignificance of civilization, this, too, an extreme standpoint in our time, yet within the bounds of the acceptable not least because he took it all back after the war. But Hitler and Mann in the same city, at the same time. Is Hitler more evil than Mann? When neither has yet done wrong? What is evil? Anti-Semitism? What made Mann recoil from anti-Semitism while Hitler embraced it? Education? Is anti-Semitism a class issue? Or is it a question of personal decency, a qualitative difference between people who are unlike each other? Nazism plainly came from the bottom, Drexler was a blacksmith and a trade unionist, Weber was a horse dealer, most of the others were lower middle class like Hitler himself, functionaries and office workers, all in one sense or another having failed or been marginalized in some way. The exception is Eckart, but he is a deviant, not many poets were morphine addicts and Jew-haters, whereas figures such as Rosenberg and later Himmler and Goebbels are fanatics. The sympathizers, those middle-aged couples, also belonged to the working class and the lower middle class and were of slender means, those who suffered most from the crisis that had struck Germany. They took their frugal suppers with them from home to the restaurant. Such are the people closest to Hitler in 1922, before he took a step up and became a name throughout the land. But the simple fact of Truman Smith being dispatched to meet him, and Hanfstaengl joining his inner circle, indicates that the movement had started. Every premise of what would later occur is in place here. In Hitler, who has shown himself to be a brilliant orator, but who must also, on the basis of what Hanfstaengl writes, have revealed frightening sides of himself; in Drexler, who wanted decency, and in Hanfstaengl, who wanted the return of a strong and stable German Reich, and in Rosenberg, who with his Estonian background despised Russia, and whose eastern European anti-Semitism, according to Sebastian Haffner, surpassed that of the West in its brutal and violent expression, and in the anonymous middle-aged couples of the lower middle class. Of this conglomeration, Toland writes:

> Such were the men close to Hitler. His movement cut across all social classes and so all types were drawn to him – the intellectual, the street fighter, the fanatic, the idealist, the hooligan, the condottiere, the principled and the unprincipled, laborers and noblemen. There were gentle souls and the ruthless, rascals and men of good will; writers,

painters, day laborers, storekeepers, dentists, students, soldiers, and priests. His appeal was broad and he was broad-minded enough to accept a drug addict like Eckart or a homosexual like Captain Röhm.

Hitler never underrated a follower, Toland writes, no matter how humble, no matter how wretched he or she might be, he opened up the new party offices to down-at-heel and unemployed followers and party members who needed refuge from the cold. At the same time he looked upward, seeking out wealthy industrialists sympathetic to his cause to drum up financial support, and through Hanfstaengl he was introduced into upper-class society. Hanfstaengl introduced Hitler to William Bayard Hale, a classmate of President Wilson at Princeton and chief correspondent in Europe for the Hearst newspapers, to the artist Wilhelm Funk, whose salons were frequented by Prince Henckel-Donnersmarck and a variety of wealthy, nationalistically inclined business figures, Hanfstaengl reports, never concealing his own attraction to nobility and fame; he takes Hitler with him to visit Fritz-August von Kaulbach's family, patrons of the arts, Hanfstaengl hoping they would connect in that common interest and that Hitler would be influenced by their refinement; he takes him with him to visit the Bruckmann family, who run a large publishing house in Munich and published Houston Stewart Chamberlain, the well-known anti-Semite. Elsa Bruckmann, formerly Princess Cantacuzène, would take Hitler under her wing as a protégé, but when later she extends her patronage to Rosenberg, Hanfstaengl makes a point of no longer attending her salon, finding it unworthy that a woman from "a family which had entertained Nietzsche, Rainer Maria Rilke, and Spengler" should be taken in by such a charlatan.

There is something naïve and wide-eyed about Hitler in these contexts, he writes, particularly after a dinner given by the Bechstein family, the famous piano makers, where Hitler in his usual ill-fitting blue suit feels embarrassed in such splendidly elegant company. Frau Bechstein convinces him to acquire a dinner jacket and a pair of patent leather shoes, which he does, though apart from the shoes, which for a period barely leave his feet, he hardly ever wears the outfit, an appalled Hanfstaengl warning him that no leader of a workers' movement should be seen going around in the garb of the upper classes.

Both Frau Bechstein and Frau Bruckmann show maternal concern for Hitler, and Hanfstaengl mentions other such women in Hitler's life, much the same age as his mother would have been, to whom he is obviously drawn, presumably because they are maternal and caring and because sexually they represent no threat to him. He knows no other women, is uninvolved in any relationship, and, Hanfstaengl writes, has no sex life. He is taken with beautiful women, and develops an infatuation for some, Hanfstaengl's wife among them, but always platonically and without commitment.

One thing that became borne in on me very early was the absence of a vital factor in Hitler's existence. He had no normal sex life. I have said that he developed an infatuation for my wife, which expressed itself in flowers and hand-kissings and an adoring look in his eyes. She was probably the first good-looking woman of good family he had ever met, but somehow one never felt with him that the attraction was physical. It was part of his extraordinary gift for self-dramatization, part of hidden complexes and a constitutional insufficiency which may have been congenital and may have resulted from a syphilitic infection during his youth in Vienna.

At this early period the details were unknown to me and one could only sense that something was wrong. Here was this man with a volcanic store of nervous energy, with no apparent outlet except his almost medium-like performances on a speaker's platform. Most of his women friends and acquaintances were the mother-type, Frau Bruckmann and Frau Bechstein. There was another woman in her sixties I met, named Carola Hoffmann, who was a retired schoolteacher and had a little house in the Munich suburb of Solln, which he and his cronies used to use as a sort of sub-headquarters, where the good lady mothered Hitler and fed him with cakes.

His rage, not without lust, when he took Kubizek into the red-light district in Vienna, seemingly as terrifying as it was enticing; his total rejection of brothel visits and Frenchwomen in the trenches, his sustained, remote infatuation with Stefanie in Linz, whom he never found the courage to approach, his tirades against the declining sexual morals of the day, his abstention from masturbation, his horror of germs and infection, his physical and moral meticulousness, not to say prudery. On the bottom shelf of the bookcase in his apartment he kept a small collection of semi-pornographic books, Hanfstaengl writes, and this is the essence, woman as pure, woman as image, an object he can admire and dream about as long as he can do so from a distance, but which poses an immediate and alarming threat as soon as it comes close to breaking into his world in the form of some physical reality. His fear of intimacy is immense, and with it his fear of sex; it is the bodily, physical nature of it he cannot stand, and the nearness of another. Woman as *it*, alluring and delightful in dreams, but never as *you*, in his intimate sphere. The few women he became involved with had in common that they were all much younger than him, barely of age. One such was Maria Reiter, whom he met along with her sister in 1926, just after the publication of *Mein Kampf*, she was very young and they met in a park where they were all walking their dogs. They chatted for an hour, Hitler invited them to attend one of his speeches, a closed event, glancing often at Maria as he spoke, accompanying her home afterward, placing his hands on her shoulders, about to draw her toward him when suddenly in a fit of rage he felt compelled to thrash his misbehaving dog with the whip he was in the habit of carrying at the time. According to Liljegren they saw each other again on a number of occasions; Hitler asked her to call him Wolf, and he called her Mizzi. They visited her mother's grave, they went on picnics and for drives in the countryside. Hitler was thirty-seven, she was sixteen. Later she related that he had kissed her once. When her birthday came he gave her a yellow armband and the two volumes of *Mein Kampf* bound in red leather, with the inscription "Read these books and you will understand me." Her father, who was a social democrat, did not approve of his daughter being involved with the leader of the Nazis. In a letter to her, Hitler wrote:

Even if fathers sometimes don't understand their children any longer because they have got older not only in years but in feelings, they mean only well for them. As happy as your love makes me, I ask you most ardently to listen to your father.

Less than a year later Hitler had started to lose interest in her, and when she discovered he had stayed the night in his Munich apartment without getting in touch she tried to hang herself with a clothesline, only to be saved by her brother-in-law, Liljegren writes. The relationship was by all accounts never consummated, nor was another discreet love affair a few years later with his niece Geli, who his sister Angela had been pregnant with at the time of his mother's funeral.

Geli was nineteen years old when she moved to Munich to study; at first she became involved with Hitler's driver, Emil Maurice, the couple going so far as to become engaged, which made Hitler furious. In a letter to Maurice, however, Geli writes that "we shall be able to meet and even be alone together, Uncle A has promised. He's a dear, as you know." Nevertheless, Maurice, who had been with Hitler as a minder and all-around gofer since 1921, was given the boot. Later, he would state that "Hitler loved her, but it was a strange kind of love to which he would never admit." Hitler himself would say, "There is nothing finer than to educate a young thing as one wants: a girl of eighteen or twenty is as malleable as wax." When Hitler moved into a larger apartment in 1929, Geli moved in with him. He hid her away, gave her what she wanted, unless it was freedom – if she was going out she would be escorted, and she enjoyed no social contact with anyone her own age, only Hitler's party comrades. After two years of living like this she committed suicide, Hitler was on his way to Bayreuth when she shot herself in her room with his pistol. The bullet went through her heart. Questioned by police, Hitler said the two had argued before he left, she wanted to go to Vienna and take up singing lessons, Hitler refused, but she had been calm and wished him a pleasant trip when he left. Hitler's housekeeper Anni Winter, however, claimed Geli had found a letter in Hitler's jacket pocket when they had been cleaning his room earlier in the day. The letter was from another young and innocent-looking girl he had started courting. She was eighteen years old, her name was Eva Braun, and she, too, would end up committing suicide.

When Hanfstaengl first met Hitler he was involved with no one; whether this means he was physically impotent, as Hanfstaengl suggests, is impossible to say, but there are many indications that he lacked interest in or was perhaps even afraid of sex. Hanfstaengl's wife called him sexless or asexual, which tells us something about the way he came across, his attentions were pantomimic and unphysical, a representation of courtship, a representation of desire, not desire itself, which was kept wholly under wraps, suppressed. There was something effeminate about Hitler too, as can be seen in the film reels of his speeches, his gesticulations are often delicate and womanly, the way he sweeps his hair to the side, his body thin and unmanly, his voice often ascending into the higher registers. At the same time he found his place in a supremely male environment and would adorn himself with masculine accessories, whip, pistol, Alsatian dog, military boots, uniforms, and this is hardly strange, since a masculine environment such as the army shuns intimacy, in favor of remoteness, is centered around action and the handling of situations, without hugging, touching, confiding, as such perfect for Hitler in that he thereby discovered he could be with others without being touched by them, physically or emotionally. His great sensitivity, to which he opened himself only in his boundless and unflagging fascination with Wagner, belonged also to his feminine side, as did his whole passion for art; much can be said of his painting watercolors during lulls at the front, but it was not the usual pastime of the hardened soldier in the trenches.

Hanfstaengl's wife puts her finger on what both of them find odd about Hitler, stating succinctly, "Putzi, I tell you he is a neuter." Hanfstaengl ruminates on the theme, noting how many homosexual men there are in Hitler's inner circle – three or four, of whom Röhm, who displayed "a normal" interest in women during the war, were not discovered to be homosexual until the late 1920s – and writing:

> *But even if he [Röhm] was not yet an active pervert there were plenty of others around who were. Heines and one or two other patriotic organization leaders became notorious for their tastes in this direction. And when I thought of my earliest contact with a Nazi recruiting agent, it occurred to me that there were far too many men of this type around Hitler.*
>
> *Part of the curious half-light of his sexual makeup which was only slowly beginning to preoccupy me was that, to say the least, he had no apparent aversion to homosexuals.*

The utterance is interesting on several counts, not least in revealing Hanfstaengl's own problems in respect to homosexuality, which was indeed prohibited by law when he wrote his book in the 1950s, but "active pervert" and "a lunatic fringe of sexual perverts," as he goes on, are wordings full of disgust and, by contrast, reveal Hitler's own lack of problems with the issue. What Hanfstaengl is reacting against is the very fact of Hitler failing to react as strongly as he. On the contrary, Hitler wants men without family in his ranks, considering them more likely to put their hearts into the struggle. Does this mean Hitler is a homosexual, or does it mean he is sexually indifferent? Hanfstaengl is right in his musings insofar as Hitler's apparent lack of aversion is striking, since normally he is so extremely petty bourgeois in his opinions, reacting hatefully against any deviation from the norm, opposing anything that goes beyond, apart, that is, from this supposedly abhorrent deviation, taken to be the very antithesis of the masculine ideal Hitler so flaunted. Presumably his stance on the matter was determined by the fact that it did not encroach on him personally in any way – his fear and loathing of other forms of transgressive behavior, particularly promiscuity, touched more obviously on his own emotional life, as witnessed by his linking together of the Jewish and the sexual in *Mein Kampf,* where he writes:

> *With satanic joy in his face, the black-haired Jewish youth lurks in wait for the unsuspecting girl whom he defiles with his blood, thus stealing her from her people. With every means he tries to destroy the racial foundations of the people he has set out to subjugate.*

While it is Hanfstaengl who removes himself from homosexuality and Hitler who accepts homosexuals in his ranks, this is reversed in the case of the Jewish issue, Hanfstaengl holding that anti-Semitism is untenably prejudiced and despicable, with Hitler the fanatical Jew-hater, though the congruence is far from unambiguous, Hanfstaengl's contempt for the most hard-core anti-Semites in the party stemming in part from their own unpleasantly "half-Jewish" appearance.

Hitler is an embodiment of conflict as he passes through the Munich streets in 1922 in his dark overcoat and hat, always with his Walther pistol in his pocket and his whip in hand, flanked by his Alsatian dog Prinz and his bodyguard Ulrich Graf, boiling with his hatred for the Jews, his fear of women, and his yearning for simplicity. In the latter he was not alone, it was in the air, as if the times had suddenly been overwhelmed by complexity and confusion and were reeling under the impact.

The crumbling of norms against which he reacts so strongly in his speeches and in *Mein Kampf* is of course not only going on out there, in the culture, but also inside him. There is an abyss between his inner emotional life and his outer behavior, and the rational explanations he gives as to his opinions and actions are clearly squeezed by other, baseless, yet by no means unfelt motives.

The great theme of the Weimar Republic, alienation, was illuminated and described from all angles, from the right and from the left, and the notion of life as a struggle was by no means confined to Hitler. Walther Rathenau, the Jewish Social Democrat minister of the Weimar government assassinated by right-wing extremists in 1922, wrote in 1912 of humanity that it

> *builds houses, palaces, and towns; it builds factories and storehouses. It builds highways, bridges, railways, tramlines, ships, and canals: water, gas and electricity works, telegraph lines, high voltage power lines, and cables; machines and furnaces . . .*
>
> *What then is the purpose of these unheard-of constructions. In large part, they directly serve production. In part, they serve transport and trade, and thus indirectly production. In part, they serve administration, domicile and health care, and thus predominantly production. In part, they serve science, art, technology, education, recreation, and thus indirectly . . . once again production.*
>
> *Labor is no longer an activity of life, no longer an accommodation of the body and the soul to the forces of nature, but a thoroughly alien activity for the purpose of life, an accommodation of the body and the soul to the mechanism . . .*
>
> *Labor is no longer solely a struggle with nature, it is a struggle with people. The struggle, however, is a struggle of private politics; the most risky business, practiced and nurtured less than two hundred years ago by a handful of statesmen, the art of divining others' interests and using them for one's own ends, to have an overview of global situa-*

tions, to interpret the will of the times, to negotiate, to make alliances,
to isolate and to strike: this art is today not only indispensable for the
man of finance alone, but, in an appropriate measure, is indispens-
able to every shopkeeper. The mechanized profession educates one to
become a politician.

Peter Sloterdijk cites Rathenau here in his book *Critique of Cynical Reason*. Rathenau's analysis allows man two options: either to be consumed by production, thereby becoming a part of it, on a par with its machines and conveyor belts, or to stand up for himself and his own individuality, albeit using the system's own economic and political means, which in that way are pulled down from the superordinate structure into the sphere of the individual. The connection between the local and the global established by the new world-embracing modes of production and trade is something by which we, a hundred years after Rathenau was writing, have learned to express ourselves, indeed our lives have become as such in the peculiar interplay of individuality and mass consumption in which we live. The issue of authenticity, so precarious and acute in the period from the turn of the last century until Germany's collapse in 1945, has been solved by way of a grand flanking maneuver, a textbook display of pragmatics made possible by the two wars themselves. Each and every one of us lives as though we were our own statesman at the center of the world, where all that we believe and think is accorded the greatest weight, quite regardless of the fact that everyone else believes and thinks exactly the same thing. Culture's unprecedented and extreme cultivation of the individual, which takes place in the most equalizing culture the world has ever known, is a response to the problems that first appeared toward the end of the nineteenth century, which at the time were likewise perceived to be new. We simply close our eyes to the possibility of there being any discrepancy between the widespread perception of the one's unique individuality and the striking sameness of the all. In the 1920s, the sameness of the all was a dystopia.

Throughout culture the threat of the mass human found expression, masklike faces and uniforms amid huge cogs of clattering machinery in a world from which all individuality had been erased.

Rathenau:

The intellect, still shaking from the excitements of the day, insists on staying in motion, on experiencing a new contest of impressions, with the proviso that these impressions should be more burning and acidic than those that have been gone through . . . Entertainments of a sensational kind arise, hasty, banal, pompous, fake, and poisoned. These joys border on despair . . . The devouring of kilometers by the automobile is a graphic image of the deformed way of viewing nature . . .

But even in these insanities and over-stimulations there is something mechanical. The human, simultaneously supervisor of the machine and machine in the global mechanism, under growing tension and heating, has surrendered his or her quantum of energy to the flywheel of the world's activity.

The war that came two years after Rathenau wrote these words meant that the idea of the unique I came under further pressure, catastrophic to the individual self, since the medium through which it then might express itself, heroism, was closed off by the mechanization of weaponry; courage, ingenuity, cunning, resourcefulness, all were futile in the face of the machine gun or in the hail of shells: death was random, its forces unmanipulable, the heroic departure of the one became a mass slaughter. The war was a war of machines, and men were but one device among others. In 1932 Jünger described a society in which everyone was a worker, all subordinate to machines, in a world without borders, without individuality, only movement and dynamics, bodies and machines; life in the total state. In a strange, paradoxical way it is toward just such a world Hitler and his party are heading as their movement gains momentum in 1921 and 1922. Strange because it is this very de-individualization Hitler fears in Marxism and capitalism, and which he believes has led to cultural decline and chaos in society. That he finds this decline so marked means there is no longer any concord between his feelings as to the way things should be and the way they are. In the case of such concord existing, inner morals give meaning to the external world so imperceptibly that one understands them to be natural, while external actions and events likewise give meaning to the inner being. In the case of such concord being absent, it must be established and at almost any price, its absence representing a direct threat to our identity, which is to say the relationship between the I and the we.

Hitler is clearly a damaged individual, presumably by a process that began in his childhood and which because of some innate dynamic became reinforced in his youth and early adulthood, but that part of him that is damaged, which is the ability to approach and be close to another, the ability to empathize with another, which is to say to see the other in himself, himself in the other, has placed him outside himself, alienated him from his own emotional life, which is to say that an unbridgeable divide has opened up between his emotions and his understanding of his emotions, whereby he has been deposited outside the sphere of the social.

The damage was in the times, and many of those who suffered it became artists, for in art the divide could be bridged. Hitler tried but received no acknowledgment, was not strong enough or talented enough to overcome the resistance and would have spun away into the oblivion of the great social void had it not been for the fact that he at least in part overcame himself, firstly in the war, then in politics, where he was acknowledged from the outset and helped along, and where he fulfilled a need. When the emotions are so radically disjointed, when the inner being is in chaos, one looks for order, rules, boundaries. The order, the rules, and the boundaries Hitler knew were those he had grown up with in Linz, but that was a world he had hated ever since the age of sixteen, when he began to dress like a Bohemian artist, and it was a world too that was on its way out, whose morals and rigid structures were not applicable to what he saw and experienced in Vienna and Munich, which to a far greater extent were characterized by the new age and the massive social problems that had come with it. The confusion triggered by the radical nature of the new was especially vast in Hitler's case and could find no outlet, certainly not in the social sphere; he read and thought, striving to establish some other concordance between himself and the world he lived in, inflamed with resentment by the dereliction of morals he saw to be a fundamental expression of a societal form and an outlook on life that he despised. He forbade himself all manner of enjoyment, retreating into asceticism, descending into depression for long periods, emerging urgently again, manically active, living only in art, in his dreams, and in the ideal, until eventually finding himself in a place where he could be unburdened of all that he contained, that place being the army, the radical simplification of his life.

The organization he was a part of building up in Munich in the 1920s, with its storm troopers, uniforms, and weapons, was an extension of the military, and the politics he put forward, with its starkly defined enemy and all its muscular aggression, was an extension of the war by other means. That his appeal should be so vast that he could draw many hundreds of thousands, indeed millions of people along with him seems unfathomable to us today; we read the arguments and the perils are plain to us, the idiocy, the sheer contempt for fellow human beings, yet it was not by arguments he won over the people, but by that very abyss that ran through his soul, or by what it generated within him, for what he thereby expressed, his inner chaos and his yearning for that chaos to stop, were curiously congruent with society's inner chaos and its yearning for that chaos to stop. His chaotic soul strove toward the boundaries by which it was constrained, his hometown morality and the order provided by the military, which is to say the petty bourgeois and the Prussian or Wilhelmian, both belonging to the past, which in the hardships of the Weimar years was where the majority, Hitler among them, turned. What made

Hitler so different, however, was the flame he ignited in all who listened to him speak, his enormous ability to establish community, in which the entire register of his inner being, his reservoir of pent-up emotions and suppressed desire, could find an outlet and pervade his words with such intensity and conviction that people wanted to be there, in the hatred on the one side, the hope and utopia on the other, the gleaming, almost divine future that was theirs for the taking if only they would follow him and obey his words.

Hitler was the great simplifier, a mirror to his own yearning, but rather than merely paying lip service to that yearning in his political convictions he exploited it cynically as a rhetorical trope, even hitting out against sophistication and complexity in his speeches. On one occasion, on his way home from the Café Neumaier with Hanfstaengl one evening in 1922, he was almost apologetic about this:

> *Herr Hanfstaengl, you must not feel disappointed if I limit myself in these evening talks to comparatively simple subjects. Political agitation must be primitive. That is the trouble with all the other parties. They have become too professorial, too academic. The ordinary man in the street cannot follow and, sooner or later, falls a victim to the slap-bang methods of Communist propaganda.*

Hanfstaengl saw his role in respect to Hitler as saving him from Rosenberg and the fanatical anti-Semites, providing him with a wider, more international perspective than the provincialism Hitler and his party comrades otherwise stood for. He believed Hitler's political radicalism and leanings toward brutality derived from lack of education and would be consumed once he was introduced into the higher circles of society, the barons of industry he brought him together with, whose conservatism was the same as Hanfstaengl's own, extending no further into the utopian than the society their parents and grandparents had inhabited. Hanfstaengl believed they could make use of Hitler to reach down into the depths of the people, thereby failing to understand that he was uncorrectable, a revolutionary utopian and a fanatical racist. That this latter trait, specifically his anti-Semitism, could be moderated along the way as he gained in power and influence was a frequent notion of Hanfstaengl's. Hitler listened to him and needed him, but did not care for the things he said. For instance, whenever he tried to impress on Hitler the importance of a future alliance between the United States and Germany or spoke insistently about other issues of foreign politics, Hitler would lead him back to Clausewitz, Moltke, and Kaiser Wilhelm. Prewar Europe was his frame of reference for foreign politics, and as such it was not a question of whether Germany with him in charge should go to war, but rather of when. This was his position as early as 1922. Everything that happened in Hitler's life following the first war was a repeat of what had happened and existed in his life before it, only on a much grander scale and in reality, and the only true aim, to which everything had to lead, was a new war, bringing the first to its rightful conclusion. That he could achieve such a feat from the starting point he had in 1918 is hard to believe. But the very fact that all the odds were stacked so heavily against him, that he was such an underdog, was an important factor, certainly in the final years before he rose to become chancellor, it being widely held across a number of political parties that what would be most damaging to Hitler would be to hand him genuine power, because then he would be politically dead in no time, being nothing more than a charlatan, a bluffer, a simple little man of the lower middle class. Indeed, it is strange. That he, of all people, so alienated from his own emotions, sensing them only as they washed through his organism, blinding or darkening his soul and all his being, should become sovereign over those of all Germany.

Hitler would spend between four and six hours writing a speech, which he would then condense into ten foolscap pages with no more than fifteen to twenty words on each. As the meeting approached, Liljegren writes, he would pace the floor as if rehearsing in his mind the various points of his argument. At intervals he would speak on the telephone with someone inside the venue itself, asking how many people had come, what kind of mood they were in, whether opposition could be expected. He would dish out instructions as to how the audience was to be handled while waiting for him. Half an hour after the meeting had started he would call for his coat, hat, and whip, and go out to the car, preceded by his bodyguard and driver. On the speaker's platform he would place his sheets of paper with their cues on a small table on his left, moving each to another table on his right when he had finished with it. His pistol was in his back pocket. After the speech, which normally lasted some two hours or more, the national anthem would be played. Hitler would salute right and left, leaving the venue while the music was at its height, and was generally back in the car again before the singing was over. If he was speaking outside Munich he would go directly to his hotel. There he would take a bath, change, rest on the sofa, perhaps with Hanfstaengl at the piano, his entourage in the room next door. He made no contact with anyone in his audience either before or after his speech. It was him and the all, and no one else.

Hans Frank, then a young law student, saw him speak in 1919:

> *The first thing you felt was that there was a man who spoke honestly about what he felt and was not trying to put something across of which he himself was not absolutely convinced. He made things understandable even to the foggiest brain . . . and went to the core of things.*

The *Münchener Post* reported one of his speeches in 1920, Toland writes, and was amused by his imitations of Jews:

> *Adolf Hitler behaved like a comedian, and his speech was a vaudeville turn . . . One thing Hitler has, you must give him credit, he is the most cunning rabble-rouser in Munich practicing such mischief.*

Kurt Ludecke saw him in 1922:

Presently my critical faculty was swept away. Leaning from the tri-
bune as if he were trying to impel his inner self into the consciousness
of all these thousands, he was holding the masses, and me with them,
under a hypnotic spell by the sheer force of his conviction . . . His ap-
peal to German manhood was like a call to arms, the gospel he preached
a sacred truth. He seemed another Luther . . . I experienced an exal-
tation that could be likened only to a religious conversion . . . I had
found myself, my leader, and my cause . . . I had given him my soul.

What was it about Hitler's speaking that awakened such emotion?
That he came across as honest and genuine was important here, a
person at long last who presented the unvarnished truth, unlike
other politicians. Hardship was plain, discontent rising, verging
on despair. Hitler gave direction to that discontent. The shame
of Versailles, the November Criminals, the worldwide Jewish-
Marxist conspiracy, these were the three points around which
Hitler gathered his rage, and in this he was clearly not alone, but
his special gift was to draw forth that rage and hatred in his audiences in a way that seemed utterly unmanipulative but true and
obvious in the same way as that which may not be said but which
nonetheless is known appears true and obvious. His charisma as
a speaker lay very much in the sense he gave that here was a man
who said things the way they were, and the trust he thereby gained
from his audiences, who in expressing their enthusiasm for him
were also expressing their enthusiasm for themselves, the unity
he created this way, was an unprecedented force he discovered
himself able, like a magician, to direct wherever he wanted. This
was power. Not the formal kind that came with a job or position,
constrained by laws and regulations, those in writing and those
unspoken, but real power, revolutionary and above the notion of
the law. This probably only dawned on him gradually, for as
Sebastian Haffner writes, he seemed for a long time to be satisfied merely with being his party's speaker, whose job it was to
mobilize the masses, and the idea that he could become his party's
and even his country's uncontested leader – an idea with a long

German prehistory – did not become manifest until *Mein Kampf*, and became real only after the subsequent relaunch of the party in 1925.

But just as important as saying things the way they were was the way he did so. The language he employed was that of his audiences. Hanfstaengl writes that without stooping to slang, except for special effect, Hitler caught the vocabulary of the day as it rose from the people around him. Outlining the problems of a housewife without money to buy food for the family at the Viktualienmarkt, for instance, he would use just the words and phrases she herself would have used to describe her difficulties if she had been able to formulate them.

In this ear for voice, register, and sociolect, that which rises from the people and which differs from generation to generation, lay Hitler's talent. In it his sensitivity came into its own, the fact that he could not only listen to the voices of his day, but also convey them to his audiences in ways that were finely tuned, addressing each audience according to its own nature, depending on whether they were students or workers. He excelled too in the art of improvisation, pausing for instance if someone shouted a comment, folding his arms across his chest and delivering a bitingly satirical response that would have his audience in stitches. Always he spoke from within, in the language of the inside, rather than from above, in the manner of other politicians and speakers.

About a quarter of his audiences were women, and this, too, he would exploit to his advantage; often there would be opponents ready to heckle and interject, and in his search for initial support he would turn to the women, directing attention toward their everyday problems and domestic difficulties, the very proximate realities they lived and experienced, thereby, according to Hanfstaengl, eliciting his first bravos, breaking the ice between him and his audience. But all this is rhetoric, what he says and the way he addresses his audience, his ability to tune in to the will of the we and to stand as its rightful voice was certainly immense, but not immense enough to account fully for his success, neither at that particular time, having already spoken to a crowd of 6,000 in 1920 at the Circus Krone, nor later, when entire stadiums were filled to the brim with people wanting to hear him speak. More important than what he said and the way he said it must surely have been the fact that it was *he* and no other. In other words, his own personal presence, his appeal, what we call charisma.

Charisma is one of the two great transcendental forces in the social world; beauty is the other. They are forces seldom talked about, since both issue from the individual, neither may be learned or acquired, and in a democracy, where everyone is meant to be considered equal and where all relationships are meant to be just, such properties cannot be accorded value, though all of us are aware of them and of how much they mean. Moreover we attach value in our human sphere to that which is made, produced, or formulated, not to what is merely there to begin with; in other words, what is made, produced, or formulated is important, and what is merely there to begin with is not. In a university lecture hall, male attention is centered not on the woman with the most compelling arguments, she who speaks engagingly and with insight about Adorno or de Beauvoir, but on the woman deemed to be the most beautiful, and so it is in every space in which men and women are gathered, on every street and square, in every restaurant and café, on every beach and in every apartment, in every ferry queue and train compartment; beauty eclipses everything, bedims all else, it is what we see first and what we consciously or unconsciously seek. Yet this phenomenon is shrouded in silence inasmuch as we refrain from acknowledging it as a factor in our social lives, driving it out instead by our social mechanisms of expulsion, calling it stupid, immature, or unsophisticated, perhaps even primitive, at the same time as we allow it to flourish in the commercial domain, where it quietly surrounds us whichever way we turn: beautiful people everywhere. Beautiful people on TV, beautiful people in magazines, beautiful people in films, beautiful people in the theater, in pop music, in advertising, indeed our entire public space is packed with beautiful faces and beautiful bodies yet, at the same time, we consider beauty to be superficial, unconveying of the authentic, which is the inner being. Beauty belongs to the body and the face, which are masklike outer expressions of the I, and its immutable, inevitable nature, the fact of it being given rather than chosen, is what disqualifies it, since after Nazism we can no longer attach value to what is innately human, the Nazis' division of the human into categories of the innate being what eventually led them into the final catastrophe. Which is to say: we attach value to it but do so in silence. This is similar to the relationship between individuality and sameness: the two things are mutually exclusive, but only if the connection between them is made – and so we refrain from making the connection. It is as if we live in two different cultures existing parallel to each other. One is the culture of commerce, in which everything is superficial, face, outer beauty, uniformity, sameness, properties we understand to be inauthentic, shadow-values existing only for the purposes of our entertainment; the other is the culture of the social, consisting of unique individuals, inner beauty, changing properties, diversity, things we understand to be authentic, values we take to be true. The untrue world is a place to which we escape in dreams, the true world is where we live. The sense of the untrue world becoming increasingly dominant in our lives, to the extent almost of becoming the world we live in, is what brings about the forceful craving for reality that has begun to emerge in the culture around us. But what is reality, if not the body? And what is the body, if not biology? Here we are within the realm of the given, to which all yearning inclined in the Weimar era, becoming apparent for the first time in the period leading up to World War I, when the pressures exerted by the inauthentic, by the many new and increasingly mechanized expressions of civilization, were displaced in favor of the authentic, which is to say the innate, which in turn is to say the body, blood, grass, death.

Charisma, which resembles beauty in that it cannot be learned or acquired, no matter how much we might practice or train, transcends the simple dichotomy of the inner and outer I, as well as that of the biological and the cultural in the human sphere, and may possess such force as to occasionally cancel out all other categories, causing them to disintegrate completely.

The charismatic human is truly unique, an individual who cannot be replicated, not because of his or her skills in argumentation but because of his or her presence alone, making plain the nonuniqueness, the ordinariness, of all others. So what kind of a value is charisma? And why are we so attracted by it? If a charismatic woman had been sitting next to the one talking about Adorno and de Beauvoir, and the other one, the one who was strikingly beautiful, all attention would have been on her, and not only all male attention, but all female attention too. Charisma is an unusual property, and what it consists of is almost impossible to say, and yet we recognize it instantly the moment we see it. If I see it in a woman, I desire her. If I see it in a man, I desire him too, in a comparable though not identical way, since what a charismatic man awakens in me is a wish to be there, in his presence, and to subordinate myself to him. There is an element of tenderness and affection in these feelings, there being an element in the charismatic, not of weakness, weakness is not the word, but vulnerability perhaps. The wish to be near, tenderness, affection, subordination; these are strong, direct emotions. But I cannot submit to them, cannot allow myself to want to be in the presence of a man as if I were in love with him, and I certainly cannot subordinate myself to him. Therefore I keep my distance, but not without observing the effect he has on everyone else in his presence, and in that I am consumed by jealousy, sometimes to unreasonable degrees, because I want to be him. This inner tussle goes on, I suppose, in the presence of all charismatic individuals, whether it is acknowledged or not. The charismatic I is so strong as to pose a threat to all other I's in its presence, who must fight to keep themselves afloat, or else give in and become, well, what? A part of the stronger I's we? A disciple, a follower, a yes-man. The aura of the charismatic individual contains an element of disinterest, of detached ease, an independence verging on the sovereign and somehow discouraging; to be seen or even liked by the charismatic individual is to be bestowed with favor, a gift with no ulterior motive, hugely covetable. Indeed the charismatic individual is free of the bonds of the social world, standing in a certain sense outside its domain, and this sense of boundlessness is what lends such force to their presence: the charismatic person is unrivaled.

As with all other human properties, charisma occurs in different degrees; many possess some small amount, few an abundance, hardly anyone has nothing but. Jesus was an extraordinarily charismatic person, his presence was so overpowering it illuminates the Gospels, which were written a hundred years after his death, and has continued to dazzle through the centuries that have passed. He, and what happened to him, cannot fully be understood without taking this into consideration. People stopped what they were doing to follow him. Enormous crowds gathered to hear him speak. He could disperse an angry mob by his sheer presence. His favor is a blessing, his disfavor a punishment. He demands of his disciples that they leave their families and friends, their entire social spheres, to live with him. When his mother and brother come to see him he sends them away. He is angered by the most trivial matters, like when he curses the fig tree outside Jerusalem, causing it to wither, or when he storms into the temple courts and sends the money changers scattering in all directions. His inner darkness as he sits in the Garden of Gethsemane, the self-destructive urge he feels within him becoming ever stronger, weighing him down during the days of Easter in Jerusalem, where he does nothing to save himself but follows the path that has been mapped out for him until, maimed and mutilated, he expires on the cross. Perhaps he was the most charismatic person ever to live. Someone must have been. Certainly his charisma continues to shine through to us today, two thousand years after his death. And it is not theology that has kept it alive; on the contrary, for theology is anticharismatic by nature, being abstract.

Nothing in Hitler's life before he reached the age of thirty indicates that he possessed any such remarkable charisma. Quite the opposite, for the descriptions we have of him from this time, from the flophouse in Vienna and the front in Flanders, suggest he is an odd little man with a somewhat unpleasant air. Captain Karl Mayr saw him as a tired stray dog looking for a master. But this changed drastically from the moment he began speaking in public. From then on the descriptions seem almost to be of a different person altogether. Socially, too, he was transformed; Rosenberg, Hess, Streicher, and soon Goebbels, all were in awe of him and more than willing to subordinate themselves to him. Yet Hitler himself was unchanged, his character and personality remained the same throughout. It was as if it were the very crowds themselves that conjured forth in him what they found so appealing. Without the crowd he was a nobody, a lonely failure of a man with an unjustifiably high opinion of himself, but in front of the crowd, in its gaze, his loneliness turned to independence, and the unjustified became justified as if by some covenant: he gave the crowd what it wanted, his I, independent of the we, and the crowd in turn gave him what he wanted, its we, dependent on the I. They saw him, and were drawn toward him. That pull was also of an erotic nature, the tension between him and the crowd is plainly sexual, though not unambiguously so, for he stands there not in absolute masculinity, and without absolute strength, which would have been cold and autocratic and forbidding; no, he is feminine too, which is to say ambivalent, and it is in that unclarified space that the tension exists and interplay with the mass becomes possible. It feels personal to watch him.

So it is with charisma, it becomes instantly personal. Watching a charismatic performer like Elvis in footage that might be forty years old, the way he relates to us feels personal, not because of his charm, or his sex appeal, or his good looks, or his body language, but because of his charisma, his unique presence, for which we can feel a kind of solicitude, and from which we could allow almost any indiscretion if we happened to be in its proximity. But those feelings might be peculiar to me alone, and other people might react less emotionally to watching Elvis in a forty-year-old TV show, because I had exactly the same feelings in relation to my father, seeing the same synthesis of remoteness and vulnerability in him, his unapproachability being so immense given that we occupied the same modest living space in the house on Tybakken all those years ago. But yes, there was something almost awkward about him that in the midst of all his forceful severity, so dislocated from my own existence, seemed to be asking for solicitude. I suppose I wanted to accommodate him in that, so it occurs to me now, though I have no idea how I would have reacted if any such thing had ever happened. But either it is the case that the state of subservience in which I existed at that time, that happy subordination, has meant that these feelings well up in me all too easily whenever I encounter the disinterested, independent type of person who is quite inaccessible, but who also exudes the opposite and thereby instills in me some sort of hope of community, of favor and blessing, or else I'm simply trained to see it like that, and am especially aware of it.

The summer has come. Warm streets outside the apartment, green parks, lightly dressed people. All winter and spring I've been getting up at three and four o'clock in the morning to write so I'd be finished in time for summer. I've promised Linda this, that the summer will belong to the family. Last summer we booked a holiday in Corsica, but Linda was ill and we couldn't go. I've always wanted to go to Corsica, so we booked again in the spring. The plan was to go away as soon as the novel was done. Now it looks like it's not going to work. But the holiday is paid for and they're going without me, taking Linda's mother instead.

I'm listening to Midlake, *The Courage of Others*, I've listened to it every day for months, and the last time I drove out to the house and listened to it in the car, the mood of Kubizek's book spread through me like a memory, as if it all stemmed from my own life. In a way it does, the books I've read are as inseparable a part of my history as everything that's ever happened to me. Hitler's *Mein Kampf* is no exception. It's different from all the other books I've read. I'm not sure why, but it stands out. Kubizek's memoir, in which Hitler is the main character, does not. In that book Hitler is seen from the outside and is an ordinary young man, albeit extremely serious and unusually strong-willed.

When Hitler writes himself, appearing in his own right, the reconciling aspect of Kubizek's viewpoint is gone. There is a consistent pettiness throughout *Mein Kampf*, a complete lack of the grandeur we have come to expect of literature, philosophy, and art, where the deepest and sincerest, often hard-won insight is forgiveness for everyone, the recognition of the human in us all, the absolute equality of others with ourselves. There is no such universality in Hitler's book, in which everything gushes through his mind to be manipulated at his own convenience according to whatever emotions are awakened in him, and in which not a single face occurs, in the sense of any unique person, rather the mere representative of a type, a political standpoint or a public role, apart from his own. But if we lift our gaze, if we elevate ourselves to where the particular characteristics of others can no longer be differentiated, *Mein Kampf* is a book in two volumes published in 1924 and 1928 respectively, written by a man born into the lower middle class in a monarchy on the verge of dissolution due to major internal tensions of both ethnic and cultural nature as well as staggeringly huge social problems, where the old values, the slow-paced bourgeois world with all its little securities so vividly described by Zweig, stood in sharp contrast to the explosively increasing poverty among the lower classes, which the book's author, whose faith in others must have been small to start with, as is often the case with children who have been ill treated, and whose belief in meaning and justice in life must have been undermined by the deaths of first his brother, then his mother, not only saw with his own eyes but also came to experience himself. He cannot have felt that he owed anyone anything. Grace, forgiveness, understanding, sympathy cannot have been part of his repertoire.

A generous person would have been able to express himself from there too, but the author of this particular book was not a generous person, he was embittered, vindictive, conceited, and, when eventually he had the chance, callous and without mercy. But even in that he fell short, unlike Homer's or Shakespeare's or Snorre's heroes, who can be callous and without mercy and still display greatness; in that too he was petty and grudging. But for this very reason *Mein Kampf* does still express something significant, for while it was written by a certain man of a certain character, it is also pervaded by the time in which that man lived, and the problems of that time, and the fact that he never raises himself above his own person and his own time, being so small-minded and unyielding that he fails even to see the possibilities, means that all that is base and bad about that time gushes through the book as it gushes through him. He is indeed the little man writing about the great age.

Mein Kampf received terrible reviews. It was totally destroyed wherever it was given attention. The *Frankfurter Zeitung*, under the headline End of the Road for Hitler, called it political suicide. One Berlin newspaper expressed doubts as to the author's mental stability, according to Ryback. And the *Bayerische Vaterland* dubbed the book *Sein Krampf* ("His Cramp"). Hitler's book was ridiculed in many circles. In his memoir Stefan Zweig writes that hardly anyone read it, and the few who did refused to take it seriously because it was so poorly written.

Hitler himself was proud of his book, handing out signed copies to all and sundry and sending a copy to his family in Austria, although he had not been in touch with them since well before the war. The terms of his prison sentence included a ban on public speaking that prevented him from engaging in political activities, and on his release he rented a cottage in the Alps and began work on a second volume, *Mein Kampf II*. Completed in the summer of 1926, the book was ignored by the newspapers and a year after publication it had sold only some seven hundred copies.

But Hitler carried on writing. Following *Mein Kampf,* which had been put out by a small-scale local publishing house with only limited distribution, he contacted the publishers Elsa and Otto Bruckmann, presumably because the book he was now planning to write was not intended to be political but to deal with his time at the front, much in the style of Ernst Jünger's *Storm of Steel,* a book he admired. Jünger had sent him a copy with the inscription "To the national Führer Adolf Hitler," and the volume is full of Hitler's underlinings. Ryback, who saw it, writes that what Hitler was interested in, judging by his marginalia, were the emotional and spiritual aspects of the war rather than more descriptive passages detailing concrete events, though with two exceptions, both concerned with moments in which sensory impressions become so fierce as to make everything shimmer, all sound vanishing at once. In a letter to Jünger, Hitler wrote, "I have read all your writings. In them I have come to value one of the few powerful conveyors of the frontline experience." In August 1927, in a letter to her husband concerning Hitler, Elsa Bruckmann writes that "he is already reflecting on the form of his war book, and says it is becoming more vivid and alive in him." In December a date is fixed for publication the following spring. But Hitler never delivered the manuscript, and it was never found. Most probably it was burned in the spring of 1945 along with all the other private documents Hitler ordered his adjutant to collect and destroy. Ryback, however, unearthed a manuscript intended as a third volume of *Mein Kampf,* kept in a safe on premises belonging to the Eher Verlag in Munich and handed over to the Americans after the war by an employee. Unfinished and running to 324 pages, it was presumably written in the summer of 1928, when Hitler was thirty-three years old, as political events in Germany were gathering pace and he and his National Socialist party were moving in on the epicenter of power. While the first volume of *Mein Kampf* dealt with Hitler's life up to his joining the German Workers' Party, and the second concerned the party itself and its history, the unpublished third volume focuses, according to Ryback, on Germany's place in history. After

1928 Hitler seems to have given up writing completely, and his image of himself as a writer, which must still have been very much intact during the four years he spent producing two published books and two manuscripts, with ambitions in one of the latter of going beyond the political, was eclipsed by his political involvement, at the same time as he began to recognize his limitations in the field. Reportedly he once complained to his personal solicitor, Hans Frank, praising Mussolini for his splendid mastery of Italian in speech and writing, while regretting that he himself was incapable of matching him in German. "I just cannot keep my thoughts together when I am writing," he remarked, according to Ryback. And again to Frank, on another occasion: "If I had had any idea in 1924 that I would have become Reich Chancellor, I never would have written the book."

For a modern reader, and by that I mean someone reading it today, as I have, on May 4, 2011, society is in almost every conceivable respect far removed from that in which *Mein Kampf* was written, though not without occasional ties – as I write these words today the last surviving soldier from World War I has died. Claude Choules was his name, he fought on the side of the British and was 110 years old. It is three days since Osama bin Laden was killed in Pakistan by U.S. special forces, a man often compared to Hitler, as so often happens with important enemies of the West and Western values, but even if there are some similarities, in their irreconcilable hatred of international capitalism, in the victim mentality expressed by terrorism, where the cause is always greater than the individual, who not only gives up his life in its service but does so gladly, the differences are at the same time so vast that any comparison is irrelevant, be it in the case of Bin Laden or anyone else who wears and has worn the face of evil since Hitler's day, for instance Idi Amin, Papa Doc, Saddam Hussein. We are used to it always being the others, always the not-us, whereas Hitler was one of us, he pursued his will from within us, from our own European culture, and he did so as the leader of a community big enough not just to start a world war but to keep it going for five years, until twenty million human lives had been lost and the genocide of six million people had very nearly been completed, against which everything else simply pales. The most alien aspect of Hitler's writing is not the politics, for although such radical nationalism is anathema to us, it is not unrecognizable or impossible to relate to, rather it is the hatred of the Jews, set forth with such vigor it is hard to conceive, in the sense that to us today it seems unthinkable that someone could actually mean what Hitler writes about the Jews in *Mein Kampf*.

The other striking thing about *Mein Kampf* relates indirectly to the first and has to do with the often unpleasantly base style its author employs, normally absent from the writing of the day, which is to say the age of the Weimar Republic. Style is little more than self-awareness, not in the singular I, but in the I of the text, arising in assumptions about the receiver of the communicative act. These assumptions exist as a kind of horizon of expectation against which the I defines and molds itself. Style is to the written text as morality is to behavior, setting the boundaries of what may and must be said or done, and how. If I write the word "cunt," I am overstepping the boundaries set by normal style; if I do so fully cognizant of this it is because I am trying to achieve a certain stylistic effect, albeit not necessarily tastefully; as a provocation the word is devoid of meaning, mostly coming across as adolescent and almost impossible to use without it rubbing off adversely on the I of the text, unless of course it was being used as an example of a certain kind of language, to represent a character, to "say" something about that character. (After writing this, I added the word "cock," so that the sentence instead began "If I write the words 'cunt' and 'cock' . . ." and the reason I did this was because it struck me that "cunt" could arouse suspicions that I might be a misogynist, perhaps even afraid of women, having chosen that particular word, as if it were the most readily available, and in that way I might infelicitously be associated with Hitler – infelicitously because it might look like I was not aware of the fact, that I was blind to it, and around this point, my presumed misogyny and fear of women, a highly intricate web might then be spun out of whatever other indications might be discovered as to my lack of social intelligence, my sad and lonely life, and what I wrote about blood and grass, and all sorts of other things besides, could all be clustered around one single point of identification: Hitler. If such language occurs in a way that can be perceived as blind or unconscious, the entire credibility of the I may fall or be undermined, but if it occurs in a way that is clearly intended, and thereby calculated, it may in that case be perceived as heightening the relevance of the Hitler figure, perhaps even fleshing out the singular I of the text. Within that space, what the text knows and does not know about itself, tensions crackle always, though less so in texts in which the I is stylistically certain, precisely since it complies with all kinds of expectations the words create, having them under its control, knowing how to play on them, and that play, which takes place between reader and writer, two entities emerging in the very act of writing, becomes more invisible the more sophisticated the writer happens to be. That such play occurs is often impossible to discern before a certain time has elapsed, when what belongs to the age is no longer taken for granted, which is to say when the reader of the text is no longer a part of what the writer seeks to go toward. The writer's motion toward, which begins in the expectation of the I, does not find a way to implant itself in the reader, and the very gesture of proceeding toward meeting a reader in a text becomes plain. The epochal mood exuded more or less by all writing, which for instance makes all texts from the 1950s similar in style, is to do with this. When I typed the word "cunt" and intuitively realized it could be read in a certain way in respect to the text as a whole, which is to say that I "felt" a certain viewpoint, "sensed" a certain line of thought directed toward unrecognized or suppressed misogyny, I added the word "cock" in order that the two words together might be a better signal of the rather stupid transgression I was trying to illuminate, without the gender imbalance that could arouse suspicions [probably justifiably, though that would be another discussion], until I realized that it was the very process I was seeking to describe that was at work here, the considerations one makes when writing, the boundaries the very act of communicating establishes, which make up the morality of the text.) If I were to type "nigger" or "spade," the vast majority of cultured readers would turn away, such words being unacceptable, not because what they refer to, black people, cannot be named, but because they cannot be named in that way, with words so laden with contempt, used only by people who know no better because they grew up in parts of society that are largely uncultured in this sense, perhaps having been mistreated, now full of aggression toward just about anyone and anything, which comes out in such expressions of the language, or else by people more cultured who know what they are doing, and who do so calculatedly, which is to say out of malice or spite, something which seldom occurs, no scientific paper would ever contain the word "golliwog" used in this way, no essay or newspaper article would contain the word "nigger," no novel the word "spade" in this sense, other than to provide a picture of people in uncultured, which is to say socially deprived, areas of society. If someone from such areas of society is to express themselves in public, they must learn to command the style that is prevalent there, and if they do, its implicit moral judgments come with it, meaning such thoughts and notions as prevail in the uncultured domain are invariably kept out and suppressed, not by some dedicated strategy but as a result of the mechanisms society always has at its disposal to control what is undesirable and make sure it never gets a chance to rise to the level at which political decisions are made.

The boundary between what may not be said and the ways in which it may not be said is so unclear that sometimes they look like two sides of the same coin.

Nearly all the literature of the Weimar years that is still read today, a striking number of classics coming out of Germany in the period 1919–33, is tasteful indeed, at the very highest cultural level in terms of style, and while to us the mind-set of that writing can be both outrageous and unacceptable, for instance Carl Schmitt's definition of politics as the business of distinguishing between friend and foe, the consequence of which has to be the physical elimination of the foe, or Walter Benjamin's notion of divine violence, we nonetheless accept that literature, studying it and discussing it in the same way as the unoutrageous, though taking care to state that such thinking is dangerous, that the texts in which it occurs are an exception, that they were produced in politically turbulent times. The mind-set is dangerous, but the style is exquisite, and for that reason we allow ourselves to handle them.

Hitler's *Mein Kampf* exhibits no style whatsoever, not even low style, its I simply gives vent to its opinions on a variety of different matters without at any time showing the slightest sign of being able to see itself; in other words it is uninhibited and excessive, seeking no legitimacy anywhere other than in its own self, which can say exactly what it wants because that is what it is, and because it knows no better. The I of *Mein Kampf* is self-congratulatory, self-centered, self-righteous, unrestrained, hateful, and small-minded, yet considers itself just and reasonable and grand, and it must have been this that resulted in such dismal reviews and meant that the book was never taken seriously, Hitler was showing his face without realizing it, revealing himself to be nothing more than an uncultivated, crude, and brutal man of the masses, who with his limited knowledge took a little here and a little there and stirred it about until ending up with something he thought was politics, but which was nothing more than a series of prejudices, anomalous opinions, and pseudo-scientific assertions. His strong anti-Semitism was another expression of the same thing. Anti-Semitism was widespread, although, as Hitler points out, in the quality newspapers and magazines it was nonexistent, they were above it, often to such an extent that they would refrain from addressing it, even though it was one of the major issues of the time. The newspapers and magazines in which it did find expression belonged to the lower levels of society, the vulgar and unrefined, and often, though not always, displayed contempt for all that was considered intellectual and high-cultural, not what belonged to the conservative middle class with its Wagner, but the culture of the growing avant-garde.

When the "Jewish question" was discussed at levels above these bubbling cauldrons of prejudice and stereotype, the language employed was without hatred and disgust, without visible emotion, but rational and investigative. In 1930, for example, toward the end of the Weimar period, the *Süddeutsche Monatshefte* devoted a special issue to *"Die Judenfrage."* The editors justified the move by stating that the matter was one of the most pervasive and complex issues since the war: "The diversity of explanations, interpretations, and attacks directed toward the Jewish person from without corresponds to what seems to the outsider to be a confusing diversity of ambition in Jewish society itself." The editors wanted as many voices as possible to be represented, Jewish as well as non-Jewish, Semitic as well as anti-Semitic. "We believe this to be the first time Jews and anti-Semites have collaborated in a single publication," they noted.

Ernst Jünger's contribution, *Über Nationalismus und Judenfrage*, concludes that the Jews in Germany were faced with the choice "either to be a Jew or not to be," Heidegren writes, by which he meant that the Jews needed to retain their particular Jewishness in order to remain Jewish, and that the values that lay in that particular identity were under fire from the equalizing mind-set of economic liberalism. Like Hitler, Jünger saw international capitalism and Marxism as posing a threat to Germanness, both were nationalists, but the crucial difference was that for Jünger this sense of the individual, rather than being restricted to what was German, also pertained to others, including the Jews. Jünger holds up this notion of particularity and differentiation, the qualities deemed peculiar to an area, a culture, a people, a nation, as a counterweight to sameness and undifferentiation, and in that respect the problem becomes more the assimilation of the Jewish into the German, comparable to the assimilation of the German into the international, rather than Jewishness in itself. But even in this brief, rational, and stylistically formal essay, as far removed from Hitler's prose as it is possible to get within the same culture, there are traces of anti-Semitism.

> *In order to be able to become dangerous, infectious, corrosive, it was necessary for him to first have a status that enabled him to be in his new figure, the figure of the civilized Jew. That status was created by liberalism, by the grand declaration of the independence of the spirit, and it likewise will be destroyed again by nothing but the complete bankruptcy of liberalism.*

That the Jew was "dangerous, infectious, corrosive" was by no means an outrageous claim in 1930, for such assertions were common. Jünger ties this to a shift in culture whereby Jewishness lets go of itself and becomes German as a consequence of liberalism rather than of anything inherent in Jewishness itself, its nature or essence, and this is the big difference between Jünger's utterance here and those of Hitler in *Mein Kampf*, yet it is impossible not to view them in the same context, for the elements are the same, Jewishness viewed as infectious and bound up with liberalism, and only that context – in which Jewishness was considered a problem, not only in the realm of the vulgar but also in that of the cultured, albeit far from universally so, and even among Jews themselves – for there were indeed anti-Semitic Jews – and Jewish identity, and what comprised it, was discussed without end throughout the interwar period – makes it possible to understand that a man such as Hitler, who had written such a book as *Mein Kampf*, in which anti-Semitism was the core from which everything radiated, could eventually end up chancellor of the Reich.

If we compare Hitler to one of the most important intellectuals of the same period, the Jewish philosopher Theodor Adorno, this aspect of *Mein Kampf* becomes clear, for what would Adorno have made of it? He would have been unable to challenge it with his rational, finely tuned, unimaginably precise and subtle arguments, for there is nothing there to challenge, Adorno is at a level so far above *Mein Kampf* that he would not have been able to take it seriously, to consider it worthy of his attention. Had he done so, he would have elevated it to something it was not, lending it legitimacy by his very interest. He could have ridiculed it, as it was ridiculed elsewhere, but doing so would not have served any purpose; the only sensible strategy would be to pay it no heed. *Mein Kampf* was too base to be made the object of rational discussion, and as such could simply be rejected without argument.

Had Hitler not been self-taught, had he, say, studied philosophy during his time in Vienna and formulated the ideas put forward in *Mein Kampf* within that horizon, it would have been fair to discuss it, analyze it, dissect it, but that would not have been possible unless it had vented something other than was the case, the main thing about the book being that it has no such horizon, that its I does not direct itself toward any singular you, only toward a we, and stands furthermore outside that we. It is in the singular you that the obligation exists, and it is that obligation, which comprises a community, that makes a discussion possible. Hitler's I lacks a you, is unbound by any obligation, and so ultimately is immoral, or devoid of morality in any sense. Jünger's I possesses a you, meaning it can be argued against, for example by saying that the word "infectious" not only denotes something that spreads between humans, but also has strong connotations with sickness and disease, something pathological, and that the connection between liberalism and Judaism is too weak for the pathological aspect of the argument not to cling to the particularly Jewish, or to the Jew, who precisely in this way is construed as corrosive and dangerous, or disposed to be so, and in other words to be qualitatively apart from you and I, who are non-Jews, and surely you cannot claim this to be the case? But indeed I can, he would then be able to counter, or no, that's not what I mean at all, but whatever he might say, the text and the opinions it makes manifest would be amenable to discussion, and Jünger and those who agreed with him would, in principle, be able to accept the counterargument and change their opinion accordingly, or adjust their arguments so as to reduce the risk of misunderstanding. In that process, which should not only be taken literally but also figuratively in terms of the conscious or unconscious reflection any text invites, between the singular I and its you, the boundary is set for what is possible and what is not possible to say in any day and age; this is where contemporariness exists, and crossing that boundary, which is also the boundary of obligation and morality, is only possible by transcending the you of the I, which presupposes that it is weak or nonexistent. Jünger did not, his assertion was good seen from the perspective of what was acceptable in society at the time, and yet it was dubious. But dubious in respect for what? The law? The courts? Public opinion? Societal norms?

An utterance being anti-Semitic cannot be relative, but the way we understand the anti-Semitic may indeed be relative. We explain Jünger's utterance in terms of him being a right-wing nationalist, a glorifier of war, and a person held in esteem by Hitler, without that necessarily meaning he was a Nazi himself, and yet there is a connection, and on the basis of that contextualization we think to ourselves that he was indeed morally dubious, and consider his utterance about Jewishness in that light. But how are we to understand another person of the same generation, one of the twentieth century's most significant literary figures, Franz Kafka, a Jew, writing disparagingly about the Jews? In a diary entry from August 6, 1914, he writes:

Patriotic parade. Speech by the mayor. Disappears, then reappears, and a shout in German: "Long live our beloved monarch, hurrah!" I stand there with my malignant look. These parades are one of the most disgusting accompaniments of the war. Originated by Jewish businessmen, who are Germans one day, Czech the next; admit this to themselves, this is true, but were never permitted to shout it out so loudly as they do now. Naturally they carry many others with them. It was well organized. It is supposed to be repeated every evening, twice tomorrow and Sunday.

The utterance is by no means anti-Semitic, but "Jewish business-men" is nevertheless associated with "malignant" and "disgust-ing," and their identity construed as something they choose according to whatever is most advantageous, and this, that Jews are businessmen ready to abandon almost anything for personal gain, even their identity as Jews, is a standard trope of anti-Semitism, and even though Kafka does not state that it is a property of all Jews, but only these particular Jewish businessmen, his utterance might certainly have been used as evidence to that effect if it had been presented as something the likes of Jünger or Hamsun had written. If it had occurred in a book by Jünger or Hamsun, we would have deemed it inappropriate but, if we held those authors in sufficiently high esteem, perhaps explained it as being a mere expression of political naïveté in confusing times, whereas if we had not held them in esteem we would have taken it to be another indication that they were bad and immoral indi-viduals, yet coming from Kafka's pen we construe it quite differ-ently. This suggests that the morality of an utterance is not absolute, but is determined also by its style and its signature, and may change as its framework of interpretation, which is to say culture, changes. *Mein Kampf* did not mean the same in 1924 as it did in 1934, and it did not mean the same in 1934 as it does today. Both Kafka's and Jünger's utterances were fully acceptable in their day, they were by no means outrageous, whereas Hitler's utterances in *Mein Kampf* were definitely so. They were not for-bidden, and were not even controversial, in the sense of causing scandal, they were merely vulgar, simple, tasteless, and malicious.

The story of *Mein Kampf* is the story of how, from being some-thing to disassociate oneself from in 1925, it becomes transformed into something to espouse in real life in 1933. Hitler himself did not change, he held the same opinions in 1925 as he did in 1933 and 1943, but the people around him changed, and that change is perhaps the most significant thing of all about the Nazi movement in Germany, that what was previously wrong with the movement became right, what was previously immoral became moral, and that this did not occur by any change in legislation or any other instrument at the disposal of the formal institutions of society, but by a change in the very community, which is to say in the social world, the societal we, whose expression in the individual is called conscience.

If Hitler's I is lacking the singular you, both in life and in literature, this does not mean that he lives or writes in a vacuum, only that what he does, thinks, says, and writes is unconstrained by obligation to anyone else but himself and what he believes to be right. He does so within a system where "the other" exists only as "the others," either in the great we, the community of nation, the Germans, or in the great they, the enemies of the nation, the Jews. Inside this system, ideas and notions circulate, lifted from various aspects of life in society, put together in totally idiosyncratic, often idiotic ways, which is one thing that can happen when an individual is unamenable to correction, another being that moments of genius may occur, and what emerges from all this, in a text that pays no attention to what ought or ought not to be said, to what is decent and what is offensive, is the blind side of society, that part of it we try to avoid and which the power structures of style and taste keep hidden away in the dark. In 1910 it would have been unthinkable that a man who had written a book such as *Mein Kampf* could become a head of state.

Heads of state were either monarchs, as in Britain or Germany, the ministers they appointed coming from the upper reaches of society, from the finest families and the finest schools, cultivated individuals held in the highest esteem for this very reason, or else they were presidents, elected from the same elevated and culturally and economically affluent circles. This system was suppressive, keeping the lower classes in their place, but suppression is not unambiguously an ill as we are taught to think, the exercise of power is not the same as the abuse of power, which is to say that abuse of power can have other functions besides maintaining the privileges of a certain class. It excludes what is undesirable, and the undesirable is of course that which undermines the privileges of the ruling class, but also that which is destructive of the values and stability of the society the ruling class is entrusted with governing. Revolution overturns the structure of society, destroying the values on which it is built, and doing so by violence. Revolutionary violence may be construed as a reaction to the structural violence inherent within a societal system – the need, poverty, and gross injustice it generates – but is nonetheless unlawful, for revolutionary violence is also violence among like kind, which no society can tolerate, and the first thing that happens when revolutionaries seize power is that they set up new laws quite as inviolable as the old, with the same purpose, to control that violence within and ensure order and stability in society. This was what happened in France in 1789, in Russia in 1917, and in Germany in 1933, the difference being that the revolution in Germany was not simply a class revolution from below, but involved the lower, middle, and upper classes at once, though primarily the lower middle class, and set the law aside largely without bloodshed. This was possible because societal structures had already broken down or were in the process of breaking down. The state apparatus belonged to the old monarchy, parliamentary democracy was weak, and when inflation and unemployment rocketed with the Depression in a context of humiliation following the debacle of the war, democracy became a paradox, voting for its own dissolution, which is to say handing power to Hitler and the National Socialists, who were antidemocratic. What had existed only as a miscellany of phenomena and shifting currents at the bottom of society only ten years before was suddenly the ideology of a supreme governing party, no longer base and contemptible, but elevated and noble.

Hitler expressed what the average German thought but declined to say, and he did so compellingly and with such conviction as to make it legitimate, and the more people who followed him in that direction, realizing that what one thought in one's own mind yet was perhaps wary of expressing could indeed be expressed, the more legitimate it became. The opinions Hitler expressed were clear and unambiguous, he concealed nothing, and they could easily have been repudiated, he and his party having no power on their own, such power being granted by those who listened to them and who in doing so heard themselves, their own voice of reason, the voice that said this is the lay of the land. That nothing suppressed that voice, those hitherto quiet thoughts, and that the structures to reject such baseness had ceased to operate became Germany's tragedy.

This is the lay of the land, said Hitler, this is the lay of the land, said the people and cheered Hitler, and in doing so they cheered themselves and their own. Hitler gave self-righteousness a voice, we could say, but only if we are above that voice, only if our taste is superior, our judgment superior, only then is it the voice of self-righteousness. If one is a part of it, it is righteous. And who is to say where the boundary lies between righteous and self-righteous? Who is the arbiter of a society's morals, who decides what is acceptable and what is not? Not the one, but the all. Morality does not exist outside society, outside its institutions, in the form of something absolute that we humans may invoke at any time, no, it is a part of us at this very moment and moreover was different in the time of our parents, as it will be different in the time of our children, though perhaps not by much, for the most desirable thing for a society is for its moral structures to remain the same and to appear for as long as possible to be absolute and extrasocietal. This, however, is not feasible, as events in Germany after World War I made abundantly clear. The philosopher Hannah Arendt writes of this issue in her book *Eichmann in Jerusalem*:

> *And just as the law in civilized countries assumes that the voice of conscience tells everybody "Thou shalt not kill," even though man's natural desires and inclinations may at times be murderous, so the*

law of Hitler's land demanded that the voice of conscience tell every-
body "Thou shalt kill," although the organizers of the massacres knew
full well that murder is against the normal desires and inclinations
of most people. Evil in the Third Reich had lost the quality by which
most people recognize it – the quality of temptation. Many Germans
and many Nazis, probably an overwhelming majority of them, must
have been tempted not to murder, not to rob, not to let their neigh-
bors go off to their doom (for that the Jews were transported to their
doom they knew, of course, even though many of them may not have
known the gruesome details), and not to become accomplices in all these
crimes by benefiting from them. But, God knows, they had learned
to resist temptation.

Conscience is morality as it appears in the individual. For an individual such as Hitler, who was bullied and beaten by his father and lost his siblings and his mother, who grew up to adulthood in a society whose enormous transformation dislodged forces that were to exert such tremendous pressure on its structures as to gradually cause them to cave in and collapse, and who lived through the mass slaughter of World War I and all its subsequent turbulence, who was surrounded by violence on all sides – for such a person conscience did not speak in the same way as it speaks to those of us who have experienced none of the above. But it did speak to others of his generation, for none of the things Hitler experienced were unique to him, and nothing of what he wrote in *Mein Kampf* was unprecedented, which is to say that everything that exists in *Mein Kampf* also existed elsewhere in society at that time. One of Hitler's most important sources of inspiration in writing *Mein Kampf* was Henry Ford's book *The International Jew*. Ford, the American industrialist and car manufacturer, was famous throughout the world, and his book caused a stir when it was published in Germany. According to Ryback, *The New York Times* could report in 1922 that Hitler had a framed photograph of Ford on the wall next to his desk, and paid tribute to him in speeches at the time. Ryback cites

Baldur von Schirach, a teenager when Ford's book came out, who claimed that he became an anti-Semite on reading it. "In those days this book made such a deep impression on myself and my friends because we saw in Henry Ford the representative of success, also the exponent of a progressive social policy." Other books Hitler read prior to writing *Mein Kampf* included Hans F. K. Günther's notorious *Racial Typology of the German People*, while Otto Strasser, a member of Hitler's staff, according to Ryback identified the main concepts of *Mein Kampf* as stemming from conversations Hitler conducted with Feder, Rosenberg, and Streicher and, most significantly, with Eckart, conversations in which books by authors such as Chamberlain and Lagarde were a staple topic.

None of this is mentioned in *Mein Kampf*, whose anti-Semitism and attendant theorizing are presented as something Hitler arrived at himself, long before he entered politics. He construes his anti-Semitism as something near a revelation, as if some crucial piece of a jigsaw had fallen into place, allowing him at last to grasp the great scheme of things. In *Mein Kampf* he ties this revelatory experience to his first autumn in Vienna, but since there is no evidence of any anti-Semitism in his life at that time, this can hardly be correct. However, the actual structure of his epiphany, the way it occurs, may still be an accurate account of the way he later experienced it. This is how he describes it:

> *Today it is difficult, if not impossible, for me to say when the word "Jew" first gave me ground for special thoughts. At home I do not remember having heard the word during my father's lifetime. I believe that the old gentleman would have regarded any special emphasis on this term as cultural backwardness. In the course of his life he had arrived at more or less cosmopolitan views which, despite his pronounced national sentiments, not only remained intact, but also affected me to some extent.*
>
> *Likewise at school I found no occasion which could have led me to change this inherited picture.*

At the Realschule, to be sure, I did meet one Jewish boy who was treated by all of us with caution, but only because various experiences had led us to doubt his discretion and we did not particularly trust him; but neither I nor the others had any thoughts on the matter.

Not until my fourteenth or fifteenth year did I begin to come across the word "Jew," with any frequency, partly in connection with political discussions. This filled me with a mild distaste, and I could not rid myself of an unpleasant feeling that always came over me whenever religious quarrels occurred in my presence.

At that time I did not think anything else of the question.

There were few Jews in Linz. In the course of the centuries their outward appearance had become Europeanized and had taken on a human look; in fact, I even took them for Germans. The absurdity of this idea did not dawn on me because I saw no distinguishing feature but the strange religion. The fact that they had, as I believed, been persecuted on this account sometimes almost turned my distaste at unfavorable remarks about them into horror.

Thus far I did not so much as suspect the existence of an organized opposition to the Jews.

Then I came to Vienna.

Preoccupied by the abundance of my impressions in the architectural field, oppressed by the hardship of my own lot, I gained at first no insight into the inner stratification of the people in this gigantic city. Notwithstanding that Vienna in those days counted nearly two hundred thousand Jews among its two million inhabitants, I did not see them. In the first few weeks my eyes and my senses were not equal to the flood of values and ideas. Not until calm gradually returned and the agitated picture began to clear did I look around me more carefully in my new world, and then among other things I encountered the Jewish question.

I cannot maintain that the way in which I became acquainted with them struck me as particularly pleasant. For the Jew was still characterized for me by nothing but his religion, and therefore, on grounds of human tolerance, I maintained my rejection of religious attacks in this case as in others. Consequently the tone, particularly that of the Viennese anti-Semitic press, seemed to me unworthy of the cultural tradition of a great nation. I was oppressed by the memory of certain occurrences in the Middle Ages, which I should not have liked to see repeated. Since the newspapers in question did not enjoy an outstanding reputation (the reason for this, at that time, I myself did not precisely know), I regarded them more as the products of anger and envy than the results of a principled, though perhaps mistaken, point of view.

I was reinforced in this opinion by what seemed to me the far more dignified form in which the really big papers answered all these attacks, or, what seemed to me even more praiseworthy, failed to mention them; in other words, simply killed them with silence.

I zealously read the so-called world press (Neue Freie Presse, Wiener Tagblatt, etc.) and was amazed at the scope of what they offered their readers and the objectivity of individual articles. I respected the exalted tone, though the flamboyance of the style sometimes caused me inner dissatisfaction, or even struck me unpleasantly. Yet this may have been due to the rhythm of life in the whole metropolis.

These newspapers, however, frequently disgust him in the way they grovel to the Court, presenting themselves in glorified colors and reminding him of "the mating cry of a mountain cock." He finds them "a blemish on liberal democracy." Moreover, they wage war against the German Kaiser, Wilhelm II, whom they criticize "with supposed concern, yet, as it seemed to me, ill-concealed malice." The fact that the same press "made the most obsequious bows to every rickety horse in the Court" simultaneously airing doubts about the Kaiser and "poking its finger around in the wound" as if it were a scientific experiment, soon made him lose faith in them, whereas he found the *Deutsches Volksblatt* more decent in such matters. Another issue he had with the big newspapers was the way they cultivated admiration for France, which he found repugnant, writing:

A man couldn't help feeling ashamed to be a German when he saw these saccharine hymns of praise to the "great cultural nation." This wretched licking of France's boots more than once made me throw down one of these "world newspapers." And on such occasions I sometimes picked up the Volksblatt, *which, to be sure, seemed to me much smaller, but in these matters somewhat more appetizing. I was not in agreement with the sharp anti-Semitic tone, but from time to time I read arguments which gave me some food for thought.*

When he first arrived in Vienna, he writes, he had felt opposed to the city's mayor, Dr. Karl Lueger, and to his Christian Socialist Party, finding both the man and the movement "reactionary." However, he came to change his opinion as he became more familiar with their politics, judging him more fairly, his attitude eventually growing into admiration. Lueger and his party were anti-Semites, and this, along with his lack of faith in the press, was what swayed him.

My views with regard to anti-Semitism thus succumbed to the passage of time, and this was my greatest transformation of all.

It cost me the greatest inner soul struggles, and only after months of battle between my reason and my sentiments did my reason begin to emerge victorious. Two years later, my sentiment had followed my reason, and from then on became its most loyal guardian and sentinel.

At the time of this bitter struggle between spiritual education and cold reason, the visual instruction of the Vienna streets had performed invaluable services. There came a time when I no longer, as in the first days, wandered blindly through the mighty city; now with open eyes I saw not only the buildings but also the people.

Once, as I was strolling through the Inner City, I suddenly encountered an apparition in a black caftan and black hair locks. Is this a Jew? was my first thought.

For, to be sure, they had not looked like that in Linz. I observed the man furtively and cautiously, but the longer I stared at this foreign face, scrutinizing feature for feature, the more my first question assumed a new form:

Is this a German?

As always in such cases, I now began to try to relieve my doubts by books. For a few hellers I bought the first anti-Semitic pamphlet of my life. Unfortunately, they all proceeded from the supposition that in principle the reader knew or even understood the Jewish question to a certain degree. Besides, the tone for the most part was such that doubts again arose in me, due in part to the dull and amazingly unscientific arguments favoring the thesis.

I relapsed for weeks at a time, once even for months.

The whole thing seemed to me so monstrous, the accusations so boundless, that, tormented by the fear of doing injustice, I again became anxious and uncertain.

The crucial argument that according to *Mein Kampf* removed that uncertainty and turned him conclusively into an anti-Semite has to do with Zionism and the attitude to it of liberal Jews, who rather than disowning the Zionists as non-Jews, as they perhaps would have done had it been purely a matter of faith, instead made sure that all Jews "remained unalterably of one piece."

In a short time this apparent struggle between Zionistic and liberal Jews disgusted me; for it was false through and through, founded on lies and scarcely in keeping with the moral elevation and purity always claimed by this people.

The cleanliness of this people, moral and otherwise, I must say, is a point in itself. By their very exterior you could tell that these were no lovers of water, and, to your distress, you often knew it with your eyes closed. Later I often grew sick to my stomach from the smell of these caftan-wearers. Added to this, there was their unclean dress and their generally unheroic appearance.

All this could scarcely be called very attractive; but it became positively repulsive when, in addition to their physical uncleanliness, you discovered the moral stains on this "chosen people."

In a short time I was made more thoughtful than ever by my slowly rising insight into the type of activity carried on by the Jews in certain fields.

Was there any form of filth or profligacy, particularly in cultural life, without at least one Jew involved in it?

If you cut even cautiously into such an abscess, you found, like a maggot in a rotting body, often dazzled by the sudden light – a kike!

What had to be reckoned heavily against the Jews in my eyes was when I became acquainted with their activity in the press, art, literature, and the theater. All the unctuous reassurances helped little or nothing. It sufficed to look at a billboard, to study the names of the men behind the horrible trash they advertised, to make you hard for a long time to come. This was pestilence, spiritual pestilence, worse than the Black Death of olden times, and the people were being infected with it! It goes without saying that the lower the intellectual level of one of these art manufacturers, the more unlimited his fertility will be, and the scoundrel ends up like a garbage separator, splashing his filth in the face of humanity. And bear in mind that there is no limit to their number; bear in mind that for one Goethe, Nature easily can foist on the world ten thousand of these scribblers who poison men's souls like germ-carriers of the worst sort, on their fellow men.

It was terrible, but not to be overlooked, that precisely the Jew, in tremendous numbers, seemed chosen by Nature for this shameful calling.

Is this why the Jews are called the "chosen people"?

He goes on to link the Jews with prostitution and the white slave traffic in Vienna, declaring that he no longer hesitated in bringing up the Jewish problem, but was determined to bring it to light, and that now that he knew what signs to look for he would constantly discover new connections and manifestations, until suddenly coming upon Jews in a position where he had least expected to find them:

*When I recognized the Jew as the leader of the Social Democracy, the
scales dropped from my eyes. A long soul struggle had reached its
conclusion . . .*

Gradually I began to hate them.

*All this had but one good side: that in proportion as the real lead-
ers or at least the disseminators of Social Democracy came within my
vision, my love for my people inevitably grew. For who, in view of
the diabolical craftiness of these seducers, could damn the luckless victims? How hard it was, even for me, to get the better of this race of
dialectical liars! And how futile was such success in dealing with people who twist the truth in your mouth, who without so much as a
blush disavow the word they have just spoken, and in the very next
minute take credit for it after all.*

*No. The better acquainted I became with the Jew, the more
forgiving I inevitably became toward the worker . . .*

*Thus I began to make myself familiar with the founders of this
doctrine, in order to study the foundations of the movement. If I
reached my goal more quickly than at first I had perhaps ventured to
believe, it was thanks to my newly acquired, though at that time not
very profound, knowledge of the Jewish question. This alone enabled
me to draw a practical comparison between the reality and the theoretical flimflam of the founding fathers of Social Democracy, since it
taught me to understand the language of the Jewish people, who speak
in order to conceal or at least to veil their thoughts; their real aim is
not therefore to be found in the lines themselves, but slumbers well
concealed between them.*

*For me this was the time of the greatest spiritual upheaval I have
ever had to go through. I had ceased to be a weak-kneed cosmopolitan
and become an anti-Semite.*

The first phenomena he attributes to the Jews are all concerned
with cultural decay. The decay of the press, the decay of literature, the decay of art, in other words decay within the public domain. This decay, perceived by many, could be seen either as the
expression of moral decay or as the cause of moral decay. Hitler

believed the latter, and his implication of the Jews in this respect may similarly be understood in two ways, as the expression either of the base morals of the Jewish people or of an attempt to corrupt existing moral structures, in other words to destroy the people from within. Hitler seems to believe it to be a combination of the two and that it is through the policies of the Social Democrats that the categorization and calculation applied to send those areas into decay, absent in other areas, become visible. Opinions, beliefs, and morals, whether expressed publicly or by the individual in private, in a work of art or a political utterance, are by such reasoning relative notions, like degrees of good and bad on a scale of morals. Eventually he shifts this relative boundary in toward the absolute, by posing the question: "Have we an objective right to struggle for our self-preservation, or is this justified only subjectively within ourselves?" Or, put differently, are culture and morality relative, something we decide for ourselves, or is their basis objective? Is there something external that lends credence to our moral beliefs, something external that defines our culture, something fundamental and given? He believes the answer to be yes, setting the boundary between nationalism and Marxism, which is basically an expression of the boundary between the German and the Jewish, in a notional space he calls the handiwork of the Lord. He writes the following:

> *The Jewish doctrine of Marxism rejects the aristocratic principle of Nature and replaces the eternal privilege of power and strength by the mass of numbers and their dead weight. Thus it denies the value of personality in man, contests the significance of nationality and race, and thereby withdraws from humanity the premise of its existence and its culture. As a foundation of the universe, this doctrine would bring about the end of any order intellectually conceivable to man. And as, in this greatest of all recognizable organisms, the result of an application of such a law could only be chaos, on earth it could only be destruction for the inhabitants of this planet.*

If, with the help of his Marxist creed, the Jew is victorious over the other peoples of the world, his crown will be the funeral wreath of humanity and this planet will, as it did thousands of years ago, move through the ether devoid of men.

Eternal Nature inexorably avenges the infringement of her commands.

Hence today I believe that I am acting in accordance with the will of the Almighty Creator: by defending myself against the Jew, I am fighting for the work of the Lord.

The most significant rhetorical turn in this line of reasoning, forming the kernel of Hitler's political ideology as it is formulated in *Mein Kampf*, and thereby the point from which all subsequent actions performed by the Nazis issue, including those which in sum comprised the most comprehensive disaster in our human history, the Holocaust, is its arguments to the effect that anti-Semitism is not emotionally founded but the very opposite, a rational standpoint at which he has arrived by way of common-sense reasoning. This is a crucial distinction. Crucial for Hitler himself, in that if the hatred he felt toward the Jews had no rational foundation, which is to say if it were not accountable for by reference to something inherently Jewish, then it would necessarily come from him and be the expression of his inner feelings, whose existence he barely acknowledged, and crucial for those he was addressing, since by stating that his first, intuitive emotion in respect to the Jews was that anti-Semitism was a terrible thing, he thereby preempted an important and very human objection, that the Jews were people like them, with joys and sorrows, children and parents, friends and colleagues, and so one could not possibly hate them, could not turn against them, it being unreasonable and wrong. This is what you feel, Hitler says, and there is nothing wrong in feeling it, I did too. Anti-Semitism is outrageous. The pogroms are a terrible thing. But these feelings, which are deeply human, cloak the true state of affairs. And it is thus, concealed as if in disguise, that the activity of the Jew, which is directed toward destroying precisely what is good, precisely that which gives rise to the feeling that anti-Semitism is wrong, is taking place. It must be exposed, and this can only occur by way of rational arguments such as those he provides in his book. This is the rhetorical crux: I say things as they are. Germanness is associated with differences: the individual has value as a person, in that they belong to a race and are a part of that race's political expression, which is the nation-state. The value of what is German resides in its spiritual ideals.

Jewishness, equated with Marxism, is associated with sameness: for the Jew and the Marxist alike there are no individual differences between people, the individual is expendable, of value only in belonging to the mass, and there are no differences of race, which is to say no *Volk* and no nation-states. Jewish-Marxist value is material and monetary. Everything is the same in the Marxist world, and that lack of differentiation, that reality of no distinctions, is akin to chaos. Germanness is founded on values that form the basis of moral distinctions, good and bad, which is to say the qualitative, whereas the Jewish-Marxist domain is based on numbers and masses, which is to say the quantitative. Germanness finds its legitimacy in nature, which is to say the living world, the biological, which natural science has divided into classes, families, and species, and whose principle, the very principle of life itself, is the survival instinct, the right of the strongest. The Jewish-Marxist domain, too, finds its legitimacy in nature, but in that part of nature that is lifeless, which is to say in the material, that which is dead. The consequence of the Jewish-Marxist view is chaos, sameness, eventually death and the absolute void, which is the final and most undifferentiated state of all.

A biological mind-set comes out on several levels of the text; when Hitler writes about areas of cultural life in which Jews feature strongly, they are likened to an abscess into which "you cut," a dissection that reveals, like a maggot in a rotting corpse, a Jew. The activities of the Jews are likened to a pestilence, worse even than the Black Death, a poison. All this, filth, plague, poison, decay, comes from outside the human sphere to spread within it, eventually to destroy it. To Hitler's mind, the body is at the outset pure, morally and physically, and may remain so by maintaining its remoteness from other bodies in a meticulous system of constraints regulated by morals. Syphilis, he later states, diseased sexuality, comes of prostituting love, which in turn is the fault of the Jews. "This Jewification of our spiritual life and mammonizing of our mating instinct will sooner or later destroy our entire offspring," he writes. Money converts all values into pecuniary values, even the most hallowed of all, love, and the consequence is not just decay of the spirit, but also decay of the flesh, which becomes sick and riddled with disease. The image of the Jew as a kind of sprinkler spraying filth into the face of humanity would seem to adequately sum up Hitler's mind-set, the threat of transgression, diffusion, disease, and chaos, the worst imaginable scenario, finding simple, striking, yet absolutely ambivalent expression.

But thus far in his reasoning the distinction between the Jewish and the German is yet to be conceived as absolute, Marxist-Jewish understanding of the human domain as being amenable to quantification, capable of being weighed and measured, expressed in numbers, is yet to be construed as an expression of Jewish nature, that is as a part of the racial makeup of the Jews, but as belonging to their culture. The right to fight for one's moral beliefs and culture is something Hitler finds in nature, where the strongest prevails, which makes the struggle absolute, though as yet it is not the object of his endeavor. This changes, however, as he proceeds to racial anthropology toward the end of the first volume of *Mein Kampf,* following his account of the capitulation and the resentment and hateful darkening of his soul it precipitated.

What racial anthropology does is to transpose elements of nature onto culture. Nature is the biological world of animals and plants, of all things living, and it expresses nothing other than itself, refers to nothing other than itself; it is a godless universe

Hitler writes about, though by no means valueless, for the principles that govern nature, its biological laws, are in themselves generative of value, and among those values the survival and development of the species is primary. That value is regulated by two principles, delimitation and selection.

There are some truths which are so obvious that for this very reason they are not seen or at least not recognized by ordinary people. They sometimes pass by such truisms as though blind and are most astonished when someone suddenly discovers what everyone really ought to know . . .

Thus men without exception wander about in the garden of Nature; they imagine that they know practically everything and yet with few exceptions pass blindly by one of the most patent principles of Nature's rule: the inner segregation of the species of all living beings on this earth.

Even the most superficial observation shows that Nature's restricted form of propagation and increase is an almost rigid basic law of all the innumerable forms of expression of her vital urge. Every animal mates only with a member of the same species. The titmouse seeks the titmouse, the finch the finch, the stork the stork, the field mouse the field mouse, the dormouse the dormouse, the wolf the she-wolf, etc.

Only unusual circumstances can change this, primarily the compulsion of captivity or any other cause that makes it impossible to mate within the same species. But then Nature begins to resist this with all possible means, and her most visible protest consists either in refusing further capacity for propagation to bastards or in limiting the fertility of later offspring; in most cases, however, she takes away the power of resistance to disease or hostile attacks . . .

The consequence of this racial purity, universally valid in Nature, is not only the sharp outward delimitation of the various races, but their uniform character in themselves. The fox is always a fox, the goose a goose, the tiger a tiger, etc., and the difference can lie at most in the varying measure of force, strength, intelligence, dexterity, endurance, etc., of the individual specimens. But you will never find a fox who in his inner attitude might, for example, show humanitarian tendencies toward geese, as similarly there is no cat with a friendly inclination toward mice.

Therefore, here, too, the struggle among themselves arises less from inner aversion than from hunger and love. In both cases, Nature looks on calmly, with satisfaction, in fact. In the struggle for daily bread all those who are weak and sickly or less determined succumb, while the struggle of the males for the female grants the right or opportunity to propagate only to the healthiest. And struggle is always a means for improving a species' health and power of resistance and, therefore, a cause of its higher development.

This is a duplication of Darwin's notion of the survival of the fittest, laden with values. Delimitation, purity, development, these are Hitler's key concepts, first establishing them in nature, then transposing them onto the culture on the premise that man is first and foremost a biological being, but also that man's ideas and conceptions are keyed to the biological in such a way that superior ideals may be developed only by superior races, and that the survival of these ideals is a function of the survival of the race. Such an ideal is unselfishness. All living organisms possess the instinct of self-preservation, which in the case of the most primitive species operates entirely on the I. What makes the Aryan race superior, according to Hitler, is not that the instinct of self-preservation is stronger than in other races, but that it expresses itself in a more advanced manner, rising above simple egotism, allowing its own needs to recede into the background so that it may work for others, make sacrifice for others, working for the good of a community greater than itself.

The Aryan is not greatest in his mental qualities as such, but in the extent of his willingness to put all his abilities in the service of the community . . .

This state of mind, which subordinates the interests of the ego to the conservation of the community, is really the first premise for every truly human culture. From it alone can arise all the great works of mankind, which bring the founder little reward, but the richest blessings to posterity. Yes, from it alone can we understand how so many are able to bear up faithfully under a scanty life which imposes on them nothing but poverty and frugality, but gives the community the foundations of its existence. Every worker, every peasant, every inventor, official, etc., who works without ever being able to achieve any happiness or prosperity for himself, is a representative of this lofty idea, even if the deeper meaning of his activity remains hidden in him.

What applies to work as the foundation of human sustenance and all human progress is true to an even greater degree for the defense of man and his culture. In giving one's own life for the existence of the community lies the crown of all sense of sacrifice. It is this alone that prevents what human hands have built from being overthrown by human hands or destroyed by Nature.

Our own German language possesses a word which magnificently designates this kind of activity: Pflichterfullung *(fulfillment of duty); it means not to be self-sufficient but to serve the community.*

The biological perspective on the human applies in other words not only to the purely physical, is not simply a question of hair color, eye color, skin color, height, and strength, but also of less tangible properties and ideals, which is to say of what traditionally is thought of as the spiritual side of man: this, too, is a matter of biology, race, and blood.

The objection that nature and culture are two separate entities, and that culture is superior to nature in exploiting it to its own ends, managing and mastering it, is countered by Hitler in the following argument:

Here, of course, we encounter the objection of the modern pacifist, as truly Jewish in its effrontery as it is stupid! "Man's role is to overcome Nature!"

Millions thoughtlessly parrot this Jewish nonsense and end up by really imagining that they themselves represent a kind of conqueror of Nature; though in this they dispose of no other weapon than an idea, and at that such a miserable one, that if it were true no world at all would be conceivable.

But quite aside from the fact that man has never yet conquered Nature in anything, but at most has caught hold of and tried to lift one or another corner of her immense gigantic veil of eternal riddles and secrets, that in reality he invents nothing but only discovers everything, that he does not dominate Nature, but has only risen on the basis of his knowledge of various laws and secrets of Nature to be lord over those other living creatures who lack this knowledge – quite aside from all this, an idea cannot overcome the preconditions for the development and being of humanity, since the idea itself depends only on man. Without human beings there is no human idea in this world, therefore, the idea as such is always conditioned by the presence of human beings and hence of all the laws which created the precondition for their existence.

And not only that! Certain ideas are even tied up with certain men. This applies most of all to those ideas whose content originates, not in an exact scientific truth, but in the world of emotion, or, as it is so beautifully and clearly expressed today, reflects an "inner experience." All these ideas, which have nothing to do with cold logic as such, but represent only pure expressions of feeling, ethical conceptions, etc., are chained to the existence of men, to whose intellectual imagination and creative power they owe their existence. Precisely in this case the preservation of these definite races and men is the precondition for the existence of these ideas.

If there are superior races, there must also be inferior races. And if high ideals and noble qualities are associated with biological race, lack of ideals and poor qualities must be too. In this system, where everything is biology and heredity, the big threat is therefore the degeneration of the race, which can happen from within, as a result of superior individuals mating with inferior, and from without, by means of an inferior race merging with a superior. Hitler gives an example of such blood-mingling and its dangers by pointing to the differences in North American and South American cultures, where in the former instance the population is largely made up of Germanic elements intermingled with inferior peoples only to a small extent, whereas in the latter instance the population is largely made up of Latin immigrants who often mixed with the original inhabitants, on a large scale, as he puts it.

Hitler divides mankind into three categories: founders of culture, bearers of culture, destroyers of culture. The Aryans represent the first, the Jews the last. The Jews possess a strongly developed instinct for self-preservation, but their readiness for sacrifice extends only seldom beyond the purely egotistical instinct of individual preservation. Their sense of solidarity, seemingly so robust, is in Hitler's view nothing but the primitive instinct of the herd.

> *In the Jewish people the will to self-sacrifice does not go beyond the individual's naked instinct of self-preservation. Their apparently great sense of solidarity is based on the very primitive herd instinct that is seen in many other living creatures in this world. It is a noteworthy fact that the herd instinct leads to mutual support only as long as common danger makes this seem useful or inevitable. The same pack of wolves which has just fallen on its prey together disintegrates when hunger abates into its individual beasts. The same is true of horses which try to defend themselves against an assailant in a body, but scatter again as soon as the danger is past.*
>
> *It is similar with the Jew. His sense of sacrifice is only apparent. It exists only as long as the existence of the individual makes it absolutely necessary. However, as soon as the common enemy is conquered, the danger threatening all averted and the booty hidden, the apparent harmony of the Jews among themselves ceases, again making way for their old causal tendencies. The Jew is only united when a common danger forces him to be or a common booty entices him; if these two grounds are lacking, the qualities of the crassest egoism come into their own, and in the twinkling of an eye the united people turns into a horde of rats, fighting bloodily among themselves . . .*

So it is absolutely wrong to infer any ideal sense of sacrifice in the Jews from the fact that they stand together in struggle, or, better expressed, in the plundering of their fellow men.

Here again the Jew is led by nothing but the naked egoism of the individual.

That is why the Jewish state – which should be the living organism for preserving and increasing a race – is completely unlimited as to territory. For a state formation to have a definite spatial setting always presupposes an idealistic attitude on the part of the state-race, and especially a correct interpretation of the concept of work. In the exact measure in which this attitude is lacking, any attempt at forming, even of preserving, a spatially delimited state fails. And thus the basis on which alone culture can arise is lacking.

Hence the Jewish people, despite all apparent intellectual qualities, is without any true culture, and especially without any culture of its own. For what sham culture the Jew today possesses is the property of other peoples, and for the most part it is ruined in his hands.

If this is the case, that human properties and race are connected, that culture and human ideals are in essence expressions of biology, that the lowest, the Jewish, exists within the highest, the Aryan, with no clearly defined boundaries between the two biological entities, then racial intermingling indeed represents the system's greatest peril, overshadowing all other issues. The struggle to maintain racial purity overrides all other struggles.

Everything on this earth is capable of improvement. Every defeat can become the father of a subsequent victory, every lost war the cause of a later resurgence, every hardship the fertilization of human energy, and from every oppression the forces for a new spiritual rebirth can come – as long as the blood is preserved pure.

The lost purity of the blood alone destroys inner happiness forever, plunges man into the abyss for all time, and the consequences can nevermore be eliminated from body and spirit.

Only by examining and comparing all other problems of life in the light of this one question shall we see how absurdly petty they are by this standard. They are all limited in time — but the question of preserving or not preserving the purity of the blood will endure as long as there are men.

For Hitler, the Jewish question was in other words the single most important political issue in Germany in 1924, more important than poverty, more important than the Armistice and the Treaty of Versailles, inflation, and unemployment, because, in contrast to all those other issues, it was bound up with the notion of the authentic and the most fundamental of all things, life itself, human life. As such, the body was drawn into the very center of the political field. The body was an expression of the state, whose purpose it was to keep the body pure and ensure it developed in a desirable manner, physically and morally, and that it did not propagate with those inferior to itself. The biological perspective was superordinate to the individual, the human being as a body came before the human being as a person, and the properties of the individual were unimportant, for regardless of how good and unselfish a Jew might be, regardless of how hardworking and innocent, he or she was nonetheless guilty by virtue simply of being a Jew. In this way, the individual Jew was absolved of guilt, he or she being unable to do anything about it, whereas the Jews collectively were condemned, associated with a whole range of properties they could never escape, and without having any say in the matter.

This is exactly how we have always regarded animals, which are condemned to expressing themselves by way of the properties of their species, a relationship they are unable to escape, a cat or a rat always at first being a cat or a rat and only then perhaps the cat or the rat. To conduct court proceedings against a cat or a rat would be meaningless, for they possess no guilt, are mere expressions of their species, without a say in the matter, a concept such as morality would be equally meaningless when applied to their lives. In the event of their doing something we find undesirable, making a nuisance of themselves in some way, nothing stands in the way of our removing them, for since they cannot possess guilt, they accordingly have no individual rights. Animals are outside the law, unless as a collective, a protected species for instance, but this, too, is independent of inherent properties, provided they are not directly harmful to man.

The biological perspective, whereby the human primarily is regarded in terms of race, a collective with certain properties, characteristics, and ideals and, secondly, in terms of individuals deemed worthy or unworthy according to the race to which they belong, and only then as people with particular names and faces, would, if it were to be applied in any future state, require the introduction of new legislation and a new system of law, the notion of individual responsibility and personal guilt standing so firmly in culture, with roots going back to the beginnings of civilization. The only exception to this rule of civilization would be war, only in war could individual responsibility and personal guilt be abolished, for in war every soldier on the other side was firstly an enemy, representative of a collective, who could be killed as a matter of course, and only then an individual. It is this collectivity that is signaled by the uniform, and which marching makes manifest: the one, the individual, the personal name and face are always subordinate to the community, the all, the name of the nation, and the flag. These two aspects, both canceling out the individual, one by construing the human in terms of biology, bound by the laws of nature, the other by seeing the human as a creature at war, a state in which the laws of civil society are nullified, are what makes Hitler's reasoning as to the Jews in *Mein Kampf* possible. Both perspectives were common in the society in which he wrote, directly and indirectly. Alongside Henry Ford's *The International Jew: The World's Foremost Problem*, Günther's *Racial Typology of the German People*, and the writings of Chamberlain, Eckart, and Rosenberg, the American writer Madison Grant's book *The Passing of the Great Race* was likewise important to Hitler at this time. Ryback states that Hitler referred to it as "my Bible" and traces several lines of argument in *Mein Kampf* back to its pages.

But such racial thinking was more than paranoid, pseudoscientific theory, it was also widespread in serious scientific environments in academia, where it was presented as objective truth on a footing with other scientific truths, thereby lending legitimacy to Ford's, Grant's, and Hitler's thoughts, for if they carried its consequences to the furthest extreme, they could nevertheless claim their ideas to be based on an accepted notion that race was a relevant compartmentalizer of human beings, and that racially pure and impure existed, based on facts that could be expressed in figures. In 1926, the year after *Mein Kampf*, a work came out in Sweden called *The Racial Characters of the Swedish Nation*, published by scholars of Uppsala University affiliated to the Swedish State Institute for Race Biology. It was a far-reaching and prestigious publication, setting standards for similar works that would subsequently see the light of day elsewhere. In one of its essays, "An Orientating Synopsis of the Racial Status of Europe," Rolf Nordenstreng defines "race" as follows:

> *The meaning of the word race, from a scientific point of view, is a group of individuals of one and the same species, which differ from other individuals of this same species in showing a peculiar combination of certain hereditary characters. A race is always a product of selective factors in cooperation with still unknown factors, which in some way or other transform the hereditary characters.*
>
> *A race is a purely anthropological concept, its characteristics are above all physical. To be sure, there must also be mental differences among the races, and these are by no means less important; but they are exceedingly difficult to find out and to prove. At present they are little more than guesswork, and though the attempts that have been made to define the mental characters of the races are likely to contain a great deal of truth, based upon good and sound observations, they also contain a considerable quantity of prejudiced and arbitrary state-*

ments. In time there may be developed something like a scientific racial psychology – at present nonexistent.

As rather certain we may venture to state the existence of the following five greater races: 1) the Nordic, 2) the East Baltic, 3) the Mediterranean, 4) the Alpine, and 5) the Dinaric. To these may be added, though they are not in the proper sense of the word European, but mainly Asiatic, the Anatolian (Armenoid, Anterior-Asiatic), and the Semitic (Araboid) race, the latter name being a bad one, because it is also a linguistic term, but inevitable, as no better one has been suggested.

The name of the Nordic race is not quite appropriate, the adjective being in many languages used also as a linguistic term, meaning "Scandinavian"; most persons of this race speak languages that are not Scandinavian. But the term is customary, and North Europe together with North Germany is the distributing center of the race, and it is in the northern countries, on the Scandinavian Peninsula, that it is found most commonly and in its relatively greatest purity. This race it is which one often hears called the "Teutonic" or "Germanic," and it has also been termed the "Kymric." German archaeologists sometimes call it the "row-grave-type," Reihengräbertypus. Its characteristics are a light, translucent, rosy skin; a fair, sometimes reddish, soft, often wavy or curly hair; a rich beard-growth; clear blue or blue-gray eyes; a tall stature, with proportionately long legs and a firm, elastic gait with stretched legs; a strong frame; a long and rather narrow face with a narrow, usually high, straight, or somewhat bent nose, often with a little bump at the transition from the nasal bone to the cartilage; a narrow, high nasal root; very slightly or not at all prominent cheek-bones; nonsalient jaws with the rows of teeth standing nearly vertically, each against the other; somewhat thin lips; a strongly projecting chin; a narrow, somewhat sloping forehead; weak, but quite perceptible eyebrow ridges; rather deep-set eyes; a long and rather narrow braincase (head length about 195 mm, cephalic index about 77) with a nearly horizontal crown line and strongly elongated occiput. It must, however, be observed that both the color of the hair and the shape of the nose vary a great deal. Nearly every imaginable

shade of fair hair color occurs, from flaxen yellow through reddish yel-
low to light golden-brown and through light ashy-blond to the
darker grayish-blond. And together with the straight and the bent
noses there are somewhat cocked ones, with the tip turned a little up-
ward and the bridge somewhat depressed in the middle — a shape
widely distributed over the whole sweep of this race.

    The Semitic *race, which perhaps also might be called the* Araboid
race, because its characteristics seem to be more common among the
Arabs than anywhere else, is considered to be an offshoot from the
Mediterranean race. It differs from this race mainly in having a
higher, more bent, but also thin and narrow nose; fuller, though not
thick lips; a rather light, though never rosy complexion; and an almond-
shaped eye (the inner angle of the eye being more rounded, the outer
angle more pointed). The hollow between the chin and the lower lip
lies higher than in other races. There is a great deal of Semitic blood
in the Sephardic Jews and less in the Ashkenazic ones, and very likely
there must be some of it in the population of most South European
countries.

Cephalic index is the percentile relation between head breadth
and head length, German *Kopfindex*, not to be confounded with
the corresponding relation for the cranium, German *Schädelin-
dex*, as is stated in the introduction to one of the book's chapters,
full of tables, graphs, and diagrams detailing the results of the
scientists' fieldwork throughout the country. *The Racial Characters of the Swedish Nation* measures the cephalic index in all Swedish *landskap* (provinces), all Swedish *län* (counties), all Swedish
rural and urban communities, the latter including the four biggest cities, mapping distributions according to occupation and
social class and drawing comparisons across the other Scandinavian countries, and this is repeated for all other anthropological characteristics — trunk length, arm length, leg length, head
breadth, head length, face breadth, morphological face height,
morphological face index, jugo-frontal index and jugo-mandibular
index, nose, ear, nasal bridge profile, eye color, eyebrow color,

pubic hair color, all broken down into the various geographical and social divisions, all then correlated in a dedicated section on the relations between anthropological characters and indices revealing, for example, the relation between face height and arm length, rural community and province. The final part of the book consists of full-page plates, photographs of naked racial types, children, women, and men, a farmer from Norrbotten for instance appearing in the section *East Baltic Types, Relatively Pure*, a nomad from Jämtland in the section *Lapp Prototype, Relatively Pure*, a working man from Lappland in the section *Race-Mixed Types, East Baltic-Lapp*.

The most important difference between these texts and Hitler's has to do with their style. The racial theory expressed in Nordenstreng's article is penned in the objective, matter-of-fact style employed by all scholarly discourse, a style we take to indicate truth. Truth, objectivity, meticulousness, overview, certainty, insight, all these things are inherent in the style. The figures, the tables, the Latin terminology, everything connotes truth and absolute reliability. This is reinforced by the text delimiting and keeping apart what it can state with certainty and what it cannot state with certainty. A link between race and psychology, a biological connection, is likely but cannot yet be asserted on the available evidence. In this way, the text suggests that everything else it says about race may be asserted with certainty on the available evidence, at the same time as it opens the possibility of race and psychology indeed being biologically linked. The immediate association of truth with the style employed here, its rhetorical figures and tropes, is plain to us now that the content has been so discredited, not only as speculative and unscientific, but also as dangerous and, at root, evil.

But wherein does this evil lie for us? In the scholarly, scientific style there is solicitude too, for what is presented here is knowledge, insights gained by these scientists, not on their own behalf, but on behalf of the community, and this knowledge is what they impart to us in their articles and papers. Solicitude and also a clear notion of progress; the field is new, no one has studied these things before, no one has considered them before, but with the giant strides taken in biology in the latter part of the nineteenth century, with Darwin's groundbreaking explanatory theory of the origin of species, and before that Linnaeus's all-encompassing taxonomy, this advance, the establishment of an institute of racial theory and the opening up of an entirely new field of research, we approach deeper insights into the human species that will yield obvious opportunities for further progress, for only a small step from this racial biology lay eugenics, the new theory of racial hygiene, whereby the health and procreation of entire peoples could be steered in whichever direction was found to be desirable, for instance by sterilizing undesirable elements such as schizophrenics, the mentally ill, habitual criminals, vagrants, and Gypsies, as actually took place in Sweden, Norway, the United States, and Germany in the 1930s and 1940s.

This occurred on the basis of this research, under state auspices, pushing back the boundaries of what the state was and could be: the concept of public health goes back to this period, for the idea that the state should be responsible for the health and well-being of the individual is by no means a given, and its attendant notions of healthy minds in healthy bodies, of poverty and darkness and poor health being swept away as the sun shone in on hardship and abjection, which then would jump up invigorated, of poor children being sent to the countryside in summer, of health visitors and vaccinations, were all about the conjugation of body and state. And it was carried out by decent people with decent intentions, the thought that it might be wrong to sterilize a woman suffering from delusions and unable to look after herself being not at all obvious, since there was a risk, if she became pregnant, that she might pass on her affliction to the detriment of her child, and thereby also burden society as a whole.

The division of human beings into the racially pure and the racially impure, superior and inferior by implication, belongs to the same paradigm, and it is this scientification or biologization of the human, and nothing else, that makes Hitler's racial theory, and his subsequent racial policy, possible. Without it, anti-Semitism is just an irrational emotion, an obvious scapegoating, a paranoia within the culture that can be taken more or less seriously, but never be employed as the basis of any political program. Hitler kept up with international research in eugenics as it was conducted in Europe and the United States, before and after he became Reich chancellor. He was familiar with the work of leading American eugenicists such as Leon Whitney, director of the American Eugenics Society, Charles Davenport, a Harvard-educated biologist and prominent representative of the American sterilization program, and Paul Popenoe of the Human Betterment Foundation. Ryback quotes the following from a speech given by Hitler in the mid-1930s:

> *Now that we know the laws of heredity it is possible to a large extent to prevent unhealthy and severely handicapped beings from coming into the world. I have studied with interest the laws of several American states concerning prevention of reproduction by people whose progeny would, in all probability, be of no value or be injurious to the racial stock.*

According to Ryback, Hitler also met the American eugenicist and fiercely anti-Semitic racial theorist Lothrop Stoddard in 1939, when Stoddard was working as a correspondent in Berlin and received a personal invitation from the Führer on account of his work in the field. Stoddard promised Hitler that he would not make reference to their meeting, but he would later state that Hitler's handshake had been firm, though he had not sought eye contact, subsequently writing more generally of Germany's relationship with racial hygiene:

> *The relative emphasis which Hitler gave racialism and eugenics many years ago foreshadows the respective interest toward the two subjects*

*in Germany today. Outside Germany, the reverse is true, due chiefly
to Nazi treatment of its Jewish minority. Inside Germany, the Jewish problem is regarded as a passing phenomenon, already settled in
principle and soon to be settled in fact by the physical elimination of
the Jews themselves from the Third Reich. It is the regeneration of the
Germanic stock with which public opinion is most concerned and
which it seeks to further in various ways.*

The scientification of racial thinking, the entire scientific apparatus that was set up around it, with its specially constructed instruments for cranial measurement, its tables and graphs, its Latin
terminology, and technical vocabulary, lent such thinking legitimacy, and although Hitler's book contains no trace of the scholarly style, it is nevertheless *Mein Kampf* that makes the connection
between culture and nature possible, the coupling of state and
body, politics and biology, all so central to Hitler's ideology. *Mein
Kampf* is an extreme version of that mind-set, and while many
found it exaggerated and bordering on the paranoid and could not
believe he meant it seriously, certainly not as he approached the
corridors of power and thereby became outwardly more respectable, they did not question the fundamental goal of such a policy,
which was to improve the stock, the race, to lift it upward into a
resplendently healthy, morally unassailable future.

Hatred of the Jews was nothing new, it was prevalent in the world
of Faust; Martin Luther hated the Jews, and their persecution
went far back into history, as ancient as themselves, an integral
part of their own self-image and of the cultures that surrounded
them, as though somehow it were embedded in the villages and
forests, a mythical fabric from long before the Enlightenment,
yet still in force, for example in the great impoverished rural
areas of Poland, where the familiar prejudices relating to the
Jews – that they were rich, that they hoodwinked and cheated people, that they took care of their own – were ingrained in the
culture and explanatory of the indigenous population's hardships

and miseries. The Jew-hatred of Hitler and the Nazis, however, was new in the sense that it was related to modernity, to the cities and the mass human, not to the Jewish peddler Papst encountered in Hamsun's *Wayfarers* but to international finance and international Marxism. Racial theory was new as well, and provided the mind-set with a legitimacy that removed it from the mythical and placed it firmly within the realms of the rational and the modern. Most striking, however, is the coming together of the mythical and the modern in propaganda, where the images of that ancient hatred – the Jews portrayed as rats, the Jews portrayed as pigs, the Jews portrayed as evil – are projected through the new technology, in moving pictures on cinema screens, living voices on the radio, drawn thereby into a world of automobiles, neon lights, factories, telephones, and films, as its antithesis and primitive prelude.

Hitler was just as forthright about his thinking on propaganda in *Mein Kampf* as he was about his anti-Semitism, his antidemocratism and his Lebensraum ideology, whose consequence could never be anything else but war.

But whereas his anti-Semitism and nationalism were idealistic in nature, amalgamated by racial biology, his thoughts on propaganda were pragmatic. Propaganda was the most important means of carrying through his idealistic aims, and so convinced was he of its power that he was quite open about it. As Peter Sloterdijk notes, Hitler was so sure of himself when it came to the potency of propaganda that he felt he could afford to reveal his recipe. Hitler referred to propaganda as a weapon, "a frightful one in the hand of an expert."

The second really decisive question was this: To whom should propaganda be addressed? To the scientifically trained intelligentsia or to the less educated masses?

It must be addressed always and exclusively to the masses . . .

The function of propaganda does not lie in the scientific training of the individual, but in calling the masses' attention to certain facts, processes, necessities, etc., whose significance is thus for the first time placed within their field of vision.

The whole art consists in doing this so skillfully that everyone will be convinced that the fact is real, the process necessary, the necessity correct, etc. But since propaganda is not and cannot be the necessity in itself, since its function, like the poster, consists in attracting the attention of the crowd, and not in educating those who are already educated or who are striving after education and knowledge, its effect for the most part must be aimed at the emotions and only to a very limited degree at the so-called intellect.

All propaganda must be popular and its intellectual level must be adjusted to the most limited intelligence among those it is addressed to. Consequently, the greater the mass it is intended to reach, the lower its purely intellectual level will have to be. But if, as in propaganda for sticking out a war, the aim is to influence a whole people, we must avoid excessive intellectual demands on our public, and too much caution cannot be exerted in this direction. The more modest its intellectual ballast, the more exclusively it takes into consideration the emotions of the masses, the more effective it will be. And this is the best proof of the soundness or unsoundness of a propaganda campaign, and not success in pleasing a few scholars or young aesthetes.

The art of propaganda lies in understanding the emotional ideas of the great masses and finding, through a psychologically correct form, the way to the attention and thence to the heart of the broad masses. The fact that our bright boys do not understand this merely shows how mentally lazy and conceited they are . . .

The receptivity of the great masses is very limited, their intelligence is small, but their power of forgetting is enormous. In consequence of these facts, all effective propaganda must be limited to a very few points and must harp on these in slogans until the last member of the public understands what you want him to understand by your slogan. As soon as you sacrifice this slogan and try to be many-sided, the effect will piddle away, for the crowd can neither digest nor retain the material offered. In this way the result is weakened and in the end entirely canceled out. Thus we see that propaganda must follow a simple line and correspondingly the basic tactics must be psychologically sound.

The most crucial aspect of propaganda, however, is not its simplicity, that it may be understandable even to the least intelligent member of the crowd, but rather that it is entirely subjective, without so much as a hint of objectivity about it, and displaying not the slightest form of nuance as to any subject.

What, for example, would we say about a poster that was supposed to advertise a new soap and that described other soaps as "good"?
We would only shake our heads.
Exactly the same applies to political advertising.
The function of propaganda is, for example, not to weigh and ponder the rights of different people, but exclusively to emphasize the one right which it has set out to argue for. Its task is not to make an objective study of the truth, insofar as it favors the enemy, and then set it before the masses with academic fairness; its task is to serve our own right, always and unflinchingly.

What is intriguing about this section of *Mein Kampf* is that Hitler is telling it like it is, propaganda is manipulation, often presenting pure lies so repeatedly and so insistently as to make them truths. One would think that for a politician to write something of this nature would be to undermine his entire credibility and kill him off politically, yet Hitler ventures to do so for two reasons: firstly because propaganda is a means to an end, that end being so important and so just, so beneficial to society, that any means are permitted in search of its achievement, including lies – pragmatism exists for the sake of idealism and is its servant, not the other way around; secondly because he is so certain propaganda works and is so robust in itself as not to be threatened by any such synopsis or admission; this is what he is saying, that the complex, the objectivized, the nuanced will never reach a wide segment of any audience and find effect there, this moreover being true of his own words here.

The dialectic is anything but unfamiliar to us in our day, everyone knows that advertising, which exists all around us to such an extent that it fills our lives almost to the brim, is manipulative and untrue, that the picture advertising paints of the world is a lie, which nevertheless does not stop us from being influenced by it and doing what it wants us to do: I know that drinking Coca-Cola is not going to turn me into an unworried American teenager, but I still prefer it to Jolly Cola when I am out buying in the supermarket, and I know, too, that Dove soap is basically the same as any other brand, the only difference being in the packaging and advertising budget, but whose soap do I put in my basket? Advertising seems immune to any critical insight into its nature, and in this respect Hitler was right. As such, advertising is indeed related to beauty and charisma: we may want complexity and knowledge, but in the final analysis other, simpler, more immutable forces prevail. The difference between our society and Hitler's is that we have banished all such forces and all that we associate with them to an unthreatening domain, one which is least accountable to reality, the world of fiction and images, which is to say entertainment culture, refusing to allow them into other domains that are highly accountable to reality, such as politics, education, administration, or the private sphere, unless in the guise of the inauthentic. The fact that we operate with one compartment for the authentic, another for the inauthentic, to which advertising and the power of advertising belong, is perhaps what saves us from some of the forces that were set free in Europe three generations ago. Though not forever, there being an element of the unknown in this, the system always containing something that cannot be said although it is true, and at some point, one might speculate, the power of truth will prevail. In a society without physical hardship, where violence among like kind is regulated, it is hard to imagine that this could happen; never has a society been further from revolution as our own, never has any human population been so comfortably dulled in *hygge* as our own, but our world, too, has its downside, the so-called Third World, where structural violence is quite as merciless and destructive as it once was in Europe, and if it were to be set in motion against us, it is by no means certain that the good and the bad, the moral and the immoral, the true and the untrue could be kept apart from each other as they are today.

Hitler's insight was that emotions are always stronger than arguments, and that the power that resides in a we, the yearning and desire for community is unfathomably greater than that which resides in solicitude toward a they. Propaganda directs itself to emotions, not to intellect, which it insults, and some of this same dynamic applies to what he writes about the precedence of the spoken word over the written; the spoken word goes at least potentially directly to feelings and so works from within, since what a person feels always eclipses what they might think, an emotionally based opinion is felt to be exactly what it is, something one *knows*, as opposed to a rationally based opinion, which is quite differently relative in nature, being open to objective, reasoned argument and thereby capable of being changed by such argument.

The written word complicates, the spoken word simplifies, at least when directed toward moods and emotions, something the written word, or at least the political and argumentative written word, cannot. This is why firstly music and secondly painting are Hitler's preferred art forms; both communicate without words, through emotion. That he understood this, and understood how to exploit it politically, was what set him apart from all other politicians of his day.

When Hitler was appointed Reich chancellor in 1933 and the Nazis assumed power, a shift occurred in public language in a number of respects. It became simpler, the same words repeated over and over again. Victor Klemperer traces this back to Hitler and *Mein Kampf*, published eight years earlier, which he sees as establishing every characteristic of Nazi language use. With the Nazi takeover in 1933, what previously had been group-speak became the language of the people, a *Volkssprache*, Klemperer writes, and the significant thing about that shift was that this language took possession of the entire spectrum of German life, its private as well as its public aspects. Politics, the courts, the economy, art, science, school, sport, family, nurseries, the armed forces. The Nazis intervened in everything, and they did so by means of their language. It was simple, uniform, and based on speech. The new technologies such as radio and film turned communication between the one and the all into something that happened in the moment – as opposed to the printed word, which could be read at any time, in any place, and as many times as the reader wished – and meant that the message reached everyone, even those unable or unwilling to read. Klemperer writes of how the Nazis erased the distinction between written and spoken language, turning everything into oration, address, exhortation, invective. There was no difference between the propaganda minister's speeches and tracts, and no longer any divide between public and private. This is what Klemperer describes, the shift that occurs, starting in 1933, not only in the language of the state but also in the language of the individual. The state speaks in the guise of the one, one voice penetrating into the all, and the one among the all soon begins to speak in the manner of the state, becoming its own expression. All newspapers, all magazines, all radio programs, all novels, all poems, all textbooks are colored by this language, which does not stop there, but spreads everywhere and to all.

I listened to workers while sweeping the streets and working in the machine room: it was always, be it printed or spoken, from the mouths of the educated or the uneducated, the same clichés and the same tone. And even in the case of those who were the most persecuted victims and of necessity mortal enemies of National Socialism, even among the Jews, the LTI [lingua tertii imperii] was ubiquitous – in their conversations and letters, even in their books, insofar as they were still able to publish, it reigned supreme, as omnipotent as it was wretched, omnipotent indeed in its very poverty.

As an assimilated Jew, Klemperer stands from the very first on the outside; what this language does, by building up an enormously strong sense of community, a we that cuts across all political and class distinctions, by embracing the most destitute of vagrants and the wealthiest families of upper-class society within the same overarching whole, which is to say Germany and Germanness, is to exclude Klemperer and the other Jews; the we does not include them, instead it expels them in just as many ways as it includes the others. The Jews become they. Jews with German-sounding forenames are compelled by the state to add a supplementary Jewish name, such as Israel or Sara, so that their Jewishness may be plain in all circumstances, the opposite being introduced for Germans, who are now forbidden to bear Jewish-sounding names. No German child was to be called Lea or Sara. When letters of the alphabet were to be made clear over the telephone, it was no longer permitted to say "D for David" – this was actually banned by the authorities in 1933. Before long, Jews were forced to wear the yellow Star of David with the word *Jude* in lettering reminiscent of Hebrew. The designation *J* appears in official documents; Klemperer writes that eventually the full word "Jew" occurs some sixty times in every tiny section of his ration card. They are singled out immediately through language. The name, the badge, the letter. The Germans become correspondingly more German; the names of the newborn shift toward the Germanic. Dieter, Detlev, Uwe, Margit, Ingrid, Uta are among those Klemperer notes in the birth announcements of a Dresden newspaper. Place-names, too, are changed, the Slavic giving way to the more Germanic. In Pomerania 120 Slavic place-names, in Brandenburg 175, in Silesia 2,700, in Gumbinnen 1,146. Street names, too, are replaced, often with historical references. Klemperer comes across one such in Dresden, Tirmannstrasse, with the explanation underneath: "Magister Nikolaus Tirmann, Mayor, died 1437."

The German, the local and the historic, are cultivated in the language, which with the advent of new technologies and the total state is no longer either local or historic, as can be seen in slogans of the time, the modern and the medieval melting together in "Fallersleben, Site of the Volkswagen Plant" or "Nuremberg, City of the Reich Party Days." The old suffix *–gau* is added to denote a province, Klemperer writes, harking back to ancient Germanic custom, border regions similarly being dubbed *mark*, as in Ostmark for Austria and Westmark for the Netherlands, thereby establishing connections to these countries that would later legitimize their invasion and occupation. All these changes are about creating identity. Klemperer stands outside this identity, though not entirely so, being married to an "Aryan" and thereby in principle assimilated, meaning his identity is with neither the we nor the they, and consequently he sees the formation of both clearly. The transformation of identity that the systematic, all-encompassing, all-pervading language of the Nazis establishes and reinforces day by day, week by week, month by month, impacts directly on his life.

In 1933 Klemperer was still a professor at the university. He tells of one of the staff there, Paula von B, an intelligent, good-natured woman "no longer in the first flush of youth," assistant to a professor in the German department. She hailed from an officer's family belonging to the old nobility, and Klemperer finds her obviously liberal and European, "despite the odd wistful reminiscence of the glorious Imperial era," and nothing to suggest that politics is an issue for her. On the day of Hitler's ascent to Reich chancellor he bumps into her in the corridor. Usually so serious, she is now suddenly cheerful with a youthful spring in her step.

"You look radiant!" Klemperer says. "Has something good happened to you?"

"Something very good!" she replies. "Do I really need to explain? I feel ten years younger, no, nineteen: I haven't felt like this since 1914!"

"And you are telling me about it? You can say all this even though you can see, read, and hear how people who used to be close to you are being denounced, how books which you once respected are being condemned, how people are rejecting the very intellectual things that you used to – "

She interrupts him, alarmed, and yet lovingly, he writes:

My dear Professor, I hadn't expected you to overreact so nervously. You should take a couple of weeks' holiday and not read any newspapers. You are allowing yourself to get upset at this moment, and allowing yourself to be distracted from what really matters by minor embarrassments and blemishes which can scarcely be avoided during periods of such radical change. In no time at all you will judge things quite differently. Can I come and visit the two of you sometime soon?

With that, and a heartfelt "kind regards to your family," she exits through the door "like a bouncy teenager," Klemperer recounts. Over the following months he doesn't see her, until one day she turns up at their place. As a German, she feels it her duty to make an open confession to her friends, she says, while hoping that she could still be considered a friend of theirs.

"Duty as a German is not something you would have said in the past," Klemperer interjects. "What has being German or non-German got to do with highly personal or universal human questions? Or do you want to discuss politics with us?"

"Everything is related to the issue of being German or non-German," she replies, "this is all that matters; you see that's what I, what we all, have either learned from the Führer or rediscovered having forgotten it. He has brought us home again!"

"And why are you telling us this?"

"You must recognize, you must understand that I belong entirely to the Führer, but I don't want you to think that as a result I have renounced my affection toward you."

"And how can these two feelings be reconciled? And what does the Führer say concerning your former boss Walzel, the teacher you admired so much? And how can you reconcile this with the humanitarianism of Lessing and all the others about whom you had essays written? And how . . . but it's pointless asking any more questions."

In response to each sentence he utters she merely shakes her head and has tears in her eyes.

"No, it really does seem to be pointless," she says, "because everything you are asking is based on reason, and the accompanying feelings stem from bitterness about insignificant details."

"And what are my questions supposed to be based on if not reason? And what is significant?"

"I've told you already: that we've really come home! It's something you have to feel, and you must abandon yourself to your feelings, and you must always focus on the Führer's greatness, rather than on the discomfort you are experiencing at present . . . And our classical writers? I really don't think they are at variance with him in any way, you just have to read them properly, Herder, for example, and in any case they would certainly have been convinced sooner or later!"

"And where does this certainty come from?"

"Where all certainties come from: faith. And if all this doesn't mean anything to you, then – yes, then the Führer is right after all when he comes out against the . . ." Here Klemperer states that she just manages to swallow the word "Jews" before continuing: ". . . against the sterile intelligentsia. Because I believe in him, and I had to tell you that I believe in him."

"Well in that case, Fräulein von B, the best thing is to postpone our friendship and the discussion about faith indefinitely . . ."

He sees her again five years later, in 1938, when opening the door of a bank where everyone inside was standing stiffly erect each with an outstretched arm listening to a voice on the radio proclaiming the annexation of Austria to Germany. She was, he writes, in a state of total ecstasy, her eyes sparkling, not simply standing to attention like all the others, the rigidity of her posture and salute more like a rapturous convulsion. Later, he hears it reported with a chuckle that she is one of the Führer's most devoted followers, though utterly harmless. The first woman, who gave him an apple, was ambivalent with regard to the Nazis, whereas the second, this assistant to Professor Walzel, was a true believer. Both were ordinary people, and both made Nazism possible in their own ways. Klemperer fails to understand them, seeing in Hitler only the yelling monomaniac, in Nazism an untenable constraint upon the human. It is what we see too. Yet clearly others must have seen something radically different that gave them hope and a belief in the future and aroused in them such fervor.

It seems no coincidence that Paula von B should compare the spring days of 1933 with the summer days of 1914, the enthusiasm in Germany for Hitler's coming to power being so reminiscent of the tide of emotion that washed across the land at the outbreak of the war. In his biography of the philosopher Martin Heidegger, Rüdiger Safranski describes the buoyant mood in academia during those months, when even Jews allowed themselves to be carried away. Eugen Rosenstock-Huessy, in a lecture given in 1933, opined that the National Socialist revolution represented Germany striving to realize Hölderlin's vision. And in Kiel, Safranski reports, Felix Jacoby begins a lecture on Horace in the summer of 1933 with the following words:

As a Jew I find myself in a difficult position. But as a historian I have long learned not to view historical events from a private perspective. I have voted for Adolf Hitler since 1927 and I am happy that in the year of the National Rising I am allowed to lecture on Augustus. Because Augustus is the only figure in world history that may be compared to Adolf Hitler.

This was after the boycott of Jewish businesses that came into effect on April 1 that year, and after the dismissal of Jewish public employees on April 7, Safranski notes. Heidegger, who along with Wittgenstein was among the most prominent and significant philosophers of the century, became a Nazi himself, a fully fledged member of the NSDAP. What he and others saw in National Socialism, and in Hitler, was a political movement that penetrated the membrane of politics, reaching in to the authentic, the deepest seat of all that was human, the locus of emotions, community, truth, and morality, far beyond administration, bureaucracy, and day-to-day pragmatics, and so very much greater. Heidegger had described public life as the antithesis of the authentic in his concept of *das Man* (often rendered as the "they"), the inauthentic being who expressed the mean, where individual modes were regulated and to a certain extent subsumed by the others. He referred to this as "the dictatorship" of *das Man*.

> In this inconspicuousness and unascertainability, the real dictatorship of the "they" [das Man] is unfolded. We take pleasure and enjoy ourselves as they take pleasure; we read, see, and judge about literature and art as they see and judge; likewise we shrink back from "the great mass" as they shrink back; we find "shocking" what they find shocking. The "they," which is nothing definite, and which all are, though not as the sum, prescribes the kind of Being of everydayness . . .
>
> Distantiality, averageness, and leveling down, as ways of Being for the "they," constitute what we know as "publicness." Publicness proximally controls every way in which the world and Dasein get interpreted, and it is always right – not because there is some distinctive and primary relationship-of-Being in which it is related to "Things," or because it avails itself of some transparency on the part of Dasein which it has explicitly appropriated, but because it is insensitive to every difference of level and of genuineness and thus never gets to "the heart of the matter." By publicness everything gets obscured, and what has thus been covered up gets passed off as something familiar and accessible to everybody.

The dictatorship of *das Man* sanctions and reduces the unique, who become trivialized to such a level as to become amenable to commentary by all, though in a form beyond recognition, radically deconstructed, diluted, and essentially without quality. In mass society, through the mass media that atunes itself to the mean, this happens every day. From such a perspective, the business of politics, whose players pursue their own agendas and lobby according to personal interest, at the same time as leveling down to *das Man*, allowing nothing to remain unique or unexampled, is the very arena of the inauthentic. Heidegger's existentialism, in which the state of being, in its true and authentic form, is construed as something beyond language, moreover, one must assume, inaccessible to language and rational thought, approaches mysticism, standing at the *vedbande*, the forest fringe, to use Olav Nygard's expression, which is to say at the fringe of the holy. Our being in the world is something we grasp with our rational minds, but the rational mind comprehends by representation, and the sense of being we grasp this way is thus a simulation. The moods we feel, always a part of us, are another fundamental way in which we relate to the world. We do not know where they come from or what they mean, only that they are always there. They are given to us, as our existence is given to us. In such a system, speech, or *logos*, is neither language nor reason, Heidegger's Norwegian translator Lars Holm-Hansen writes, but the articulation of what is understandable, that which is possible to understand. Speech is not the same as language, but is the foundation of language. Language is a representation of what is already articulated in speech. Speech also suggests listening, and that we may also refrain from speech. In these instances we are quite beyond the rational. Moods, silence, listening, all that cannot be articulated by language but nonetheless is present in speech, the speech of being. Here, in this extrarational space, in the realm of our moods and emotions, in the borderland of religion and mystical ecstasy, far, far removed from the newspapers and their self-important political editorials, fashion shows, cabarets, and sporting events, was where Heidegger came together with Nazism. True being against untrue being. The nonlinguistic expression of feelings against linguistic rationality.

Safranski describes the mood as follows:

> *There were overwhelming demonstrations of the new community spirit, mass oaths under floodlit cupolas, bonfires on the mountains, and the Führer's speeches on the radio – people would assemble, festively attired, in public places to listen to them, in the great halls of the universities and in taverns. There was choral singing in the churches in honor of the Nazi seizure of power. Generalsuperintendent Otto Dibelius, in his sermon in Saint Nicholas's church on March 21, 1933, the Day of Potsdam, said: "Through north and south, through east and west, there marches a new will to a German state, a yearning, to quote Trietschke, no longer 'to be deprived of one of the most noble sensations in a man's life,' that of the enthusiastic pride in his own state." The atmosphere of those days is difficult to describe, writes Sebastian Haffner, who experienced it himself. It formed the real power base of the new führer state. "It was – there is no other way of putting it – a widespread feeling of deliverance, of liberation from democracy."*

We can gain some sense of this aspect of the Third Reich – the popular demonstrations, the torchlit parades, the songs, the sense of community, all of which were unconditional joys to anyone who participated – by watching Riefenstahl's films of the Nuremberg Rally the following year, 1934, where all these elements are present. The spectacle is staged, but its content far eclipses the fact, because emotions are stronger than all analyses, and here the emotions are set free. This is not politics, but something beyond. And it is something good.

The philosopher Jaspers visited Heidegger in his office in May 1933, describing their meeting as follows, in Safranski's account:

> *Heidegger himself seemed to have changed. Straight away on his arrival there arose an atmosphere dividing us. National Socialism*

had become an intoxication of the people. I went to Heidegger's room
to welcome him. "It's just like 1914 . . ." I began, intending to continue:
"again this deceptive mass intoxication," but when I saw Heidegger
radiantly agreeing with my first words, the rest stuck in my throat . . .
Face-to-face with Heidegger himself gripped by that intoxication I
failed. I did not tell him that he was on the wrong road. I no longer
trusted his transformed nature at all. I felt a threat to myself in view
of the violence in which Heidegger now participated.

The yearning for simplicity proved quite as vigorous in Heidegger as in his contemporaries, Hitler and Wittgenstein, but whereas the latter drew a boundary as to what could truthfully be said by means of language, construing this in terms of mathematical quality, Heidegger found his own truth on the other side of that boundary, that which could not be spoken. Speaking in Tübingen on November 30, 1933, Heidegger said the following, once again according to Safranski:

To be primitive means to stand, from an inner urge and drive, at
the point where things begin to be primitive, to be driven by inter-
nal forces. Just because the new student is primitive, he has a calling
to implement the new demand for knowledge.

In National Socialism, philosophy and politics come together at a point outside the language and beyond the rational, where all complexity ceases, though not all depth. It can be seen as such: the rational and objective, analysis and argument, associated with the written word, moves horizontally, between people, is always external to them, always between them, always in motion, in networks of overwhelming complexity and of such scale as to correct and mold the I, and this to an infinitely greater degree than it may be corrected and molded by the I; whereas emotion and mood, associated with speech, the tangible presence of the one in the face of the other, are vertical in nature, associated with the biological and ultimately with death, but also with all else that is biological and mortal, in ways that cannot be predicated, but merely sensed: we are alone, we are one and one, but in the voice, always concrete, always bound up with a particular human in a particular place, our solitude is overcome, this is the promise it brings with it, and in that voice, in its final consequence, death too is overcome. All flags and banners, symbols and rituals are directed, wordlessly, toward this. A torch burning in darkness can make a soul shiver, the cheer of a crowd send it into transports of elation, and in that instance it is the elation of existing and belonging it recognizes and reacts to. Oh, we all know this, it is the heart beating and the blood rushing, it is life and the world, the rivers, the forests, the plains, the wind in the trees. What can the rational mind do that could ever measure up to this? The difference between a poem and the hundred different analyses of a poem, this is what I am talking about. Or as Hitler said, speaking in Potsdam on March 21, 1933:

> *The German, at odds with himself, with deep divisions in his mind, likewise in his will and therefore impotent in action, becomes powerless to direct his own life. He dreams of justice in the stars and loses his footing on earth . . . In the end, then, only the inward road remained open for German men. As a nation of singers, poets, and thinkers, they dreamed of a world in which the others lived, and only when misery and wretchedness dealt them inhuman blows did there perhaps grow up out of art the longing for a new rising, for a new Reich, and therefore for new life.*

The language employed by the Nazi state was also directed toward the emotions; what was important in that language was not its lexical meaning, not its analytical and argumentative side, but everything else, that which was said without being said, that which resided in the tone of the language, its voice, in speech. "You are nothing, your people is everything," ran a Nazi slogan of the time, Klemperer notes, and this was the message, directly and indirectly repeated and repeated again. The people, came the cry, Germany, came the cry, we, we, we, everywhere.

Personally I have never felt myself to belong to any we; right from when I was small, I have always felt myself to be on the outside. Not because I have thought myself better, quite the opposite, I have never felt good enough to be a part of any we, never felt like I deserved it. Nor do I have any clear feelings of belonging to a particular place; we were newcomers to Tromøya, where I grew up, and so I had, and still have, no right to say that is where I am from. This feeling of being on the outside was most acute during my time at the *gymnas*, everyone could see I was not good enough, and my realization of that served merely to reinforce my outsideness, there was something odd about me. Oh, how I tingled with joy when the others let me in, like on the day of our graduation parade, and yet I knew that I did not really belong with them, but on my own. Always, I have had only one friend at a time, never more, never any *we*. I reconciled myself to this when I was a student, stopped hoping for anything else, tagged along with my brother, played in his band, knowing it was the only reason I was allowed to be in it. The role of the writer saved me; being on my own became legitimate, I was something special, an artist.

This summer I experienced something different for the first time. It was paradoxical, because I was on my own when it happened. Nevertheless, I felt myself suddenly to be a part of a we, and that feeling was so enormous and so good that I wept. At least that was one reason I wept. There were many others, for what I am writing about now is the Utøya massacre, when a Norwegian man only a few years younger than myself went through the woods on that tiny island shooting the young people who were gathered there one by one, sixty-nine lives in all. I wept as I would not have wept had sixty-nine youngsters been killed by a bomb in Baghdad or died in an accident in São Paolo, but the feeling that overcame me was that what had taken place had taken place at home, and this, the feeling that I actually possessed a feeling of home, was something I had never felt before. I wept when I saw the images. I called Mom, I called Linda, I called Geir, who was in Norway. No thoughts or feelings existed for anything other than what had happened. Now and then the full reality of what had taken place on the island, and its consequences, occurred to me in all its horror, but then it would go away again. It seemed all to be engulfed in darkness. It was the darkness of grief, but also the darkness of atrocity, and the darkness of death. But the broadcast images showed light, and I knew that light, it was the light of a Norwegian fjord on a rainy day in July. Indeed, all the images that came out from there were recognizable to me, the dark green of the pine trees that extended down to the water, the white-gray of the rocks, the water itself, heavy and motionless below, also gray. There, amid all that was so familiar to me, lay dead bodies, covered by plastic sheeting. From the land came images of the survivors. Some were lying on the ground receiving treatment, some were boarding buses, some were walking away, wrapped in woolen blankets. Some stood and held each other. Some were calling out, some were crying. These were ordinary Norwegian children. The ambulances were ordinary Norwegian ambulances. The police cars were ordinary Norwegian police cars. And when pictures of the man who had done this, who had gone around the island shooting all these people one by one, appeared in the media, they showed an ordinary Norwegian face with an ordinary Norwegian name. It was a national tragedy, and it was my tragedy too. I felt the need to be there, a powerful urge, for the people, the Norwegian people were gathering in huge, silent demonstrations, hundreds of thousands of people standing in the streets clutching roses in their hands. What I felt was the pull of the we I knew, the pull of belonging, of being a part of what is good and meaningful. More democracy, greater openness, more love. This was what Norwegian politicians said, it was what the Norwegian people said, it was what I said to myself as I sat and wept and watched it on TV, the pull it exerted on the emotions was so strong, so vigorous and strong, and the feelings I felt were real and authentic, they came from the heart; this had happened at home, and those gathering in the streets were my people.

Now that I am removed from them I have difficulty grasping those feelings. They seem false, induced only by the power of suggestion, I knew none of the dead, how could I grieve for them as I did? How could I feel such a strong sense of belonging? And yet the feelings were quite incontestable, and swept everything else aside during the time of the tragedy.

Only afterward did I realize that these must have been the same forces, the enormous forces that reside within the we, that came over the German people in the 1930s. That was how good it must have felt, how secure the identity they were being offered must have appeared to them. The flags and banners, the torches, the demonstrations: that was what it must have been like.

Against this *we* stood the *they* of the Jews. The language by which the we was conveyed, and of which it consisted, constitutive of the new identity, may be understood in two ways, as a language invoking grandeur, the emotions that lie beyond the language, having to do with ideals and nearness to the world, but conversely also as an enormous depreciation of the possibilities of language, a violent constraint, a *straitening*, in which the human itself is rendered mute. Klemperer saw it like this:

> *And here a more profound explanation for the impoverishment of the LTI opens up from beneath the obvious one. It was poor not only because everyone was forced to conform to the same pattern, but rather – and indeed more significantly – because in a measure of self-imposed constraint it only ever gave expression to one side of human existence.*
>
> *Every language able to assert itself freely fulfills all human needs, it serves reason as well as emotion, it is communication and conversation, soliloquy and prayer, plea, command, and invocation. Regardless of whether a given subject properly belongs in a particular private or public domain – no, that's wrong, the LTI no more drew a distinction between private and public spheres than it did*

between written and spoken language – everything remains oral and everything remains public. One of their banners contends that "You are nothing, your people is everything." Which means that you are never alone with yourself, never alone with your nearest and dearest, you are always being watched by your own people.

Something is denied a place in the language, on the one side the individual and the unexampled, on the other that which makes complex, which accords subtle differences, the tentative, the uncertain, and the slow, and when everything belonging to this is silenced, no longer finding space in which to articulate itself, it disappears. Whether it disappears only from the language or if what gives rise to it disappears too, ceasing to exist, is perhaps the most burning question of all raised by Nazi rule, pointing as it does toward a problem of identity that is by no means neutral, which is to say of a technical or instrumental nature, but directly tied up with the dreadful shadow cast over humanity by the Holocaust.

No one among us can say what the reason was for the Holocaust, any link between, for example, the brutalization of human minds that occurred in the trenches of World War I, the *Völkisch* preoccupations of prewar German culture, the flourishing nationalism of the interwar period, the stock market crash of 1929, inflation and mass unemployment, the growth of racial biology, Hitler's pathological hatred and charisma, Germany's humiliation with the Treaty of Versailles, and the extermination of the Jews is impossible to draw, for the simple reason of not being real. The Holocaust came of society, an occurrence within it, but was something to which society would or could not give name, and which already at that point, as the first trainloads of Jews trundled eastward, was something barely real, taking place at the very margins of humanity, mute and practically invisible to the eye, for if there is one thing shared by the few who witnessed it, it is that they turned away. The silence described by the Polish railway official interviewed in *Shoah* is telling. That silence was the exter-

866

mination of the Jews. The sound of the human suddenly ceasing to exist, the stillness that cloaked the landscape in which it had echoed only a moment before. The occasional rush of wind in the trees, a faint hammering in the distance, the sounds of emptiness. How was it possible that so many people, more than a thousand, could fall so silent? Where were they? That stillness is the stillness of the void, descending when what *was* no longer *is*, and it is this that makes what took place so impossible to comprehend, for the extermination of the Jews is that which *is not*. Indeed, it is nothing. How are we to relate to it in any real way? If we select someone to represent it, an individual with a name and history, family and friends, we are addressing it through the fate of the individual, thereby lending it dignity, for the person in question was indeed dignified by virtue of being human, yet it was precisely that human dignity that was absent in the Holocaust, and that absence which made it possible. If we do not select someone to represent it, we are depriving the victims of their names, construing them as the six million, generalizing the atrocity, and thereby falling quite as short, since it was not six million Jews who were exterminated, but one and one and one, six million times. The two perspectives cancel each other out.

Shoah, which not once in its nine-and-a-half-hour entirety abandons its obligation to that problem, resolves it in what is presumably the only way possible, by considering the Holocaust as a contemporary occurrence on the basis that we can only fully relate to those parts of it that still exist around us, to the places as they are now, all but Auschwitz long since gone, and to the recollections or nonrecollections of those who were close to it, as guards, survivors, neighbors, railway officials, bureaucrats, and nothing else, pure present time, of which such recollections are a part. Absence thus becomes the form itself, people talking about what is not, in what is, and the impossibility of this, on every level, is the film's theme. How can we talk about what cannot be talked about? How can we talk about something that escapes designation by language insofar as designation itself makes it something it is not?

The extermination of the Jews took place outside the language, undesignated by any linguistic form, a silent occurrence, and the Jews themselves were outside the language too, banished to their bodies, to the "it," the nameless nothing, which eventually was itself destroyed. One of the most telling scenes in *Shoah* is the interview with Czeslaw Borowi, who lived next to the railway station in Treblinka during the war, then a young man who saw the trains come every day with their wagonloads of Jews, saw them wait their turn, after a time fully aware of what was going on only a few hundred meters away. As he describes what he saw he suddenly recounts the voices of the Jews from the packed wagons. Ra ra ra ra, he says. Ra ra ra ra. It sounds like animal noise, bird noise. This was their language to him.

Richard Glazar, who was on board one of those trains, in a normal carriage with passenger seats, as if on a holiday trip, recalls that after the station at Treblinka the train moved very slowly, at walking pace, through the forest, it was summer and the weather was hot, and there through the window they saw a boy gesture to them, a slice of his hand across his throat, as if to indicate decapitation. Glazar didn't know what he meant. Two hours later his fellow passengers were ashes. Glazar himself was spared, they needed labor and he survived.

Czeslaw Borowi uses the same gesture during his interview, a slice of his hand across his throat, and likewise, in quick repetition, two brothers who lived on the farm next to the camp and would hear the screams of terror and smell the rotting, burning corpses daily as they plowed the soil and tended their livestock, the smell hanging in the air even kilometers away. It must have been one of these brothers Glazar saw from the train, the gesture, if not directly sadistic then at least full of *Schadenfreude*, was the only communication that took place between them and the Jews. Ra ra ra ra was the language from the Jews to them, the slice of the hand across the throat was the language from them to the Jews. What is apparent in that particular scene is that those interviewed are oblivious to what they reveal. They are clearly anti-Semites, and although they are among a very small number of witnesses to the extermination, they are ignorant of what this means and display no perspective whatsoever on the dimension of that human disaster. The fact that they put their fathomless ignorance on show in this way is extremely painful to watch, because they do so in all innocence. They simply have no idea.

Quite as powerful is another scene in which some inhabitants of Chelmno are interviewed. Chelmno was where the industrial extermination of human beings first took place. Human beings have been exterminated throughout history, but what occurred in Chelmno represented a qualitatively new step, something that had never occurred before. Those who were to be killed were transported to a castle where they were forced to strip naked before being herded along a corridor onto a ramp and into a truck. The doors were closed, and a tube attached to an exhaust pipe filled the truck with carbon monoxide. When everyone was dead, the truck drove into the forest outside the village. There, the bodies, gathered around the doors they had instinctively tried to prize open, were tipped out onto the ground, and thrown into mass graves. After a time a huge incinerator was set up in the forest and the corpses that had been buried were dug up again and burned, all other bodies from then on simply being incinerated. What was new about this was that it was not a single occurrence, but took place several times a day over a period of two years. Today the castle has been demolished, the incinerators dismantled, and the only thing that remains is some rubble in a clearing.

Dark is the forest, and still. A river runs by below. Here the flames leaped into the sky, Simon Srebnik recalls, a boy of thirteen in 1941, who worked at the incinerator. More trucks were deployed to increase capacity, and after a while the arriving Jews were gathered in the church rather than the run-down castle. It is outside this church that the people of the village are interviewed, Simon Srebnik, whom they all remember, in their midst:

he sang for the German soldiers, was almost their mascot, they taught him German songs, and as they stand there gathered around him, the boy now a middle-aged man, it is with the obvious joy of reunion. They recount what happened in detail, the things they saw. How the church behind them was filled with Jews, the vestry piled up with the suitcases they had brought with them, the number of trucks required before the church was emptied. One of them steps forward and recalls a rabbi he heard about at the time who said the Jews were to blame for the death of Jesus, that his blood was upon them, and when the interviewer asks him if he believes it was the Jews' own fault, he replies that he is merely repeating what the rabbi said. More accounts follow, in the same detail, and more villagers congregate in front of the camera, which they stare at with ill-concealed interest and glee, like children. Soon after, a procession comes out of the church and the villagers busy themselves making sure no one gets in the way of the camera, holding the children back so that it can film the procession, a proud tradition of the village. They are oblivious to what they are showing us, have no idea what the camera sees, no grasp of what happened there, it is something they regret, naturally, that much is understood, but nothing of it has sunk in. As all this is taking place, in front of the church where hundreds of thousands of Jews spent their final hours, in the midst of this flock of villagers, stands Simon Srebnik. It is impossible to tell what he is thinking. His face is unfathomable.

Later he says the only thing he wanted when he was tending the incinerators, thirteen years old, was five slices of bread. He had no understanding of what was going on, he was too young, he says, and used to people dying in the ghetto, people dropped dead all the time. When the Germans left, they shot him in the head, but he survived, and in the film he returns for the first time, sitting in a boat on a narrow river singing the old German soldier songs. In another village those now living in the former homes of the Jews are interviewed, one of them proud of her child's education, another saying that the Jewish women stole their men, and one of the men saying that he is pleased the Jews have gone but not that they went the way they did. Most of all they seem simply to be flattered by the attention. All these people were there at the time, from their midst, their local communities, the Jews were collected and taken away, in their districts they were gassed and burned. The interviews took place in the late 1970s and early 1980s. By then some thirty years had passed, and what happened had become an occurrence among other occurrences. The obvious anti-Semitism they display has an element of innocence about it, since they have absolutely no idea what they are revealing of themselves, or rather to whom they are revealing it. It is small-minded, socially inherited, a function of poverty and no education. But is it evil? Were the people evil who appropriated the houses of the Jews and were glad of the improved living standards that came with them? Are they evil, these people who so eagerly swivel round to point to where the suitcases of the Jews were piled up, excited at the prospect of being on television? They know not what they do, for they are innocent. They would not be capable of perpetrating such crimes as they witnessed. The extermination of the Jews organized and carried out by the Germans was qualitatively apart, something other and far greater than popular Jew-baiting.

To organize something of that nature first of all requires an enormous volition; we know what resistance the human being feels to killing its own kind, even for the soldier at war, faced with an armed enemy and in danger of being killed himself, the effort required to overcome that resistance is great, but in this instance we are dealing with unarmed people who never raised a hand against them, even toddlers of two and three years old, boys and girls, young women and men, the elderly and infirm, and over a period of some two years on a scale three times that of the total number of Germans killed in World War I. This is not something that simply happens. It can occur only on the basis of an immense will, since so much human resistance must be overcome in order for it to take place, yet if we look at the sequence of events, how it came about and was carried out, that will seems almost entirely absent, it appears more like something that just happens, wearily and without exertion, something to be gone along with.

The peasants of the Polish village had not understood what had taken place and what it meant. The question is whether we have. For it was not the simple peasants of the Polish village with their uninformed anti-Semitism who exterminated the Jews. It was the Germans, from Berlin, Munich, Dresden, Frankfurt, the big cities of Europe, a modern and in every respect informed society, technologically and culturally among the most advanced, this being true also in Hitler's own generation, only three generations older than ours. We might posit that the circle of individuals governing Germany at the time were barbaric and brutal, ruthless criminals, and indeed they were, but they were but a tiny handful in a population of sixty million, they were in power because they gave expression to what the people wanted, they were their representatives. But restricting the blame to Germany, the suggestion that the cause lay in some degeneration of things German, would be something of a simplification. It was not German but Norwegian police who identified, tracked down, collected, and dispatched the Norwegian men, women, and children who were burned to ashes in Auschwitz. And the Norwegian men, women, and children who were burned to ashes there had neighbors, acquaintances, colleagues, and friends. They bowed their heads, they looked away as if it was not happening. So it was in Norway, so it was in Germany, so it was over the entire continent. It was not happening, or only barely so. No one knew what was going on. No one saw. It scarcely happened. And then it was over. Then we realized that what had taken place had not been inconsequential at all, but the opposite, something so extreme and so huge in scale that nothing like it had ever happened before.

How are we to make sense of this? That while it is happening it is scarcely of consequence, since it happens namelessly and imperceptibly, and those who see it do not know what it is they see, whereas afterward, when it has happened, it is understood to be the very end point of humanity, our outermost boundary, something that must never, ever be repeated. How can one and the same event give rise to two such different perspectives? And how can we know what we must never, ever repeat, when we did not even know what was happening when it happened? Why was it seen only when it was over and there was no longer anything left to see? At that point all the people were dead, the barracks bulldozed and the incinerators dismantled, trees planted, and traces removed.

We still don't know who died. They lost their names and became a number, and their names have yet to be reclaimed, they remain a number, six million. I don't know the name of a single person who perished at Chelmno, first gassed to death in a truck, then burned to ashes in an incinerator and scattered into the river there, the remains of those who were not burned, the largest bones being crushed to bonemeal and likewise scattered into the river, all I know is, their number, 400,000. Nor do I know the name of any one of those gassed and incinerated at Treblinka, only their number, 900,000.

But I do know the names of the most important figures in the German Nazi Party. Hitler, Göring, Goebbels, Himmler, Bormann, Hess, Speer, Rosenberg. Not only that, I also know their faces and quite a lot about their lives and what kind of characters they possessed. The imbalance is striking. Hitler is a name known by everyone and triggers associations in us all. The people he exterminated could be exterminated only by expelling them from the language, taking away their names, making them one with their bodies, severing their connections to the social world, which is the human world, in a process of reduction that ended in them becoming nothing, which is to say a number, their status to this day. The power of the name becomes plain if we bring them together. Hitler on one side, six million Jews on the other. Hitler resurrected two million Germans from their graves in *Mein Kampf* and led them back to Germany, covered with mud and blood, to remind the population of the sacrifice they had made for their sake. If in our minds we resurrect from their graves the six million people who were exterminated under cover of World War II, bring them together on the plains of Poland, and place Hitler in their midst, the true relationship between them becomes apparent, for his name is then but one among millions of names, his voice one among millions of voices, his life one among millions of lives. The nature of this vast multitude changes according to how far away or how close we stand to observe it. If we are far away, looking at it from high above, we see simply a mass of bodies – limbs, heads, eyes, hair, mouths, ears – man as the creature he is, the human being in terms only of its biology and materiality, and this was what made it possible to incinerate those people, and what their incineration moreover revealed, as if it were some new perspective on the human, our worthlessness, our interchangeability, life rising up in a well. Human life as a cluster of mussels clinging to rocks in the sea, human beings as beetles and vermin, man as a shoal of writhing fish brought gasping to the surface in nets. If, however, we stand up close to each individual, so close as to hear each name as it is whispered, to look into each pair of eyes, where the soul of every human is revealed, unique and inalienable, and listen attentively to the story of a day in the life of each and every one of them, a day in the company of loved ones, families, and friends, an ordinary day in an ordinary place, with all its joy and delicacy, envy and curiosity, routines and spontaneity, imagination and boredom, hate and love, then the opposite becomes apparent, the one, not as I, but as the I's necessity. Which is you.

When Simon Srebnik, the thirteen-year-old boy with the beautiful singing voice, who bundled dead bodies into the enormous incinerator so the flames leaped into the sky in the forest gloom, thought about the future he would see two things in his mind's eye. One was five slices of bread, the only thing he wanted. The other was that when all this stopped he would be on his own. That there would not be a single person left on earth but him. So it was that he went about his work beneath the sky, dragging the corpses, singing his delightful songs in the fields, without feeling anything else but that beyond all this, if he survived, nothing would be left. And Richard Glazar recounts the moment they began burning the bodies at Treblinka, it was dark and the forest rose like a wall outside the camp, the flames leaped into the sky, and one of the other Jews who worked there, an opera singer, began to sing, "My God, my God, why hast thou forsaken us?" That moment, described to Gitta Sereny in *Into That Darkness*, her book about Treblinka and the camp commandant there, Franz Stangl, and related also to Claude Lanzmann, is not shocking in the way the atrocities themselves are shocking, since they, in all their inconceivable vileness, are perpetrated by "them" and are impossible to entertain as belonging within the realm of one's own capabilities, for which reason we refer to them as evil; no, that moment shocks in a different way entirely, since in its very monumentality, its invocation of God, and, in that, its overwhelming beauty, it betrays our human truth in favor of divine truth. In that moment, God dies. Not because he has abandoned them, but because the divine belongs to the very perspective that made the Holocaust possible.

As I write about the Holocaust I sense its unmentionable nature. It feels as if there exists some right of ownership to it that means not just anyone can write about it, one has to have earned the right in some way, either by having lived through it or by writing about it in a manner that is morally binding and unambivalent. To write about the Holocaust one has to be irreproachable, only then is it possible. One's motives have to be unselfish, uncommercial, unspeculative, good and decent. A writer can say what he or she wants about God in a novel, it may be condemned as blasphemous, but not in all seriousness, for the moral indignation entailed by blasphemous violation no longer exists. But when it comes to the Holocaust the writer certainly cannot say what he or she wants, indeed it is the only phenomenon in our society to which the notion of blasphemy remains applicable, in the sense that the indignation brought about by any violation is unanimous and fierce. There lies the boundary. But what kind of boundary is it? Why is it there and not somewhere else? And why is it so fragile?

When we condemn any joking about the Holocaust with such moral force it is because we are defending and protecting something, a value we consider to be inviolable. But what is it exactly that we are protecting in this case? What do we achieve by making that event so invulnerable? What value exactly are we talking about? The British historian David Irving was sent to prison for claiming the gas chambers did not exist. This is an opinion, not an action. What other opinions can we be sent to prison for expressing? Not many, certainly. In fact, I can't think of any.

The Holocaust has taken on all the characteristics of a taboo. The taboo is society's way of protecting itself against undesirable forces. It is a way of making them plain by negation, fencing them in by a *not*, thereby turning them into something that exists outside our daily lives, outside the zone in which normal life, by virtue of its very existence within the field of the normal, unfolds in a continuous flow of possibility. What is particular about the Holocaust is the opposite of what we have made it. What is particular about the Holocaust is that it was trivial, proximate, and local. The Holocaust was families being singled out and made to assemble. It was trains leaving the ghettos in Poland, Germany, the Netherlands, Belgium, Greece, Czechoslovakia, Lithuania, Latvia – all countries under Nazi control – trundling through Europe, coming to a halt at tiny stations outside Polish villages, Treblinka, Sobibor, Auschwitz, Belzec, where those inside were bundled out if they came from the east or instructed to alight if they came from the west. The places they arrived at were what they believed to be relocation camps or work camps. Here they were segregated, women and children to the right, men to the left, made to strip naked, then led through a corridor into a chamber where they were gassed to death, their bodies removed and incinerated or buried. These camps were small, Treblinka was six hundred by four hundred meters in area, and those who worked there were relatively few, a hundred and fifty Ukrainian soldiers, fifty German SS. Treblinka moreover housed a thousand so-called work Jews who carried out hard labor, before they too were gassed and incinerated. On any normal day in what Glazar refers to as the peak periods ten thousand Jews would arrive at the camp by train. Hours later their bodies were gone. This industrial destruction went on for two years. In that time somewhere between 800,000 and 1,200,000 people were murdered there. No human being is capable of grasping this figure and the events it represents. Yet at the same time it was commonplace, a routine, what they referred to themselves as production, though production of death. The production of death at Treblinka was primitive compared to what took place at Birkenau, according to Franz Suchomel, an SS soldier assigned to the camp.

What I am trying to say is that all this was real. And in being real, it was tangible. And in being tangible, it was local. And that it was incorporated into the realm of the normal. So wholly incorporated, in fact, that it could take place and scarcely be noticed. All horror converges on this. The first people to be gassed to death in the Third Reich were not Jews, but people with mental and physical disabilities. They called it euthanasia and it was an extension of legislation passed in 1933 sanctioning the sterilization of people with serious hereditary illness. According to Sereny, the Nazis commissioned an opinion from a professor of moral theology at the Catholic university in Paderborn, Joseph Mayer, seeking support before implementing this "merciful" program. Mayer's hundred-page report firstly provided an historical review, then moved on to discuss the pros and cons, before proceeding to cite the Jesuit moral system of probability:

> there are few moral decisions which from the outset are unequivocally
> good or bad. Most moral decisions are dubious. In cases of such

dubious decisions, if there are reasonable grounds and reasonable "authorities" in support of personal opinion, then such personal opinion can become decisive even if there are other "reasonable" grounds and "authorities" opposing it.

On which basis Mayer concluded that euthanasia was justifiable, as there were reasonable grounds and authorities both for and against. The report, which according to Sereny was found in five copies only, has never come to light, does not exist; like almost everything else to do with this it has either been destroyed or is merely rumor, initiated with the purpose of legitimizing or whitewashing something incriminating. The silence surrounding these murders and their administration is near total. But the euthanasia program was effectuated, more than a hundred thousand people were exterminated. It was about racial purity and was founded on science and law, it began with sterilization and continued with the gassing of people so badly afflicted and helpless it can be assumed it was seen as a blessing to themselves and those who cared for them.

In *Mein Kampf* the Jewish question exists in principle within the same sphere, racial purity versus racial impurity, the control of the state over the biological body, racial hygiene, and public health, but whereas sterilization and euthanasia were within the bounds of the law and what the authorities and ordinary people found acceptable, albeit controversial, the matter of wiping out an entire people was of course utterly unprecedented and quite as unthinkable. When the decision to exterminate the Jews was taken, probably somewhere toward the close of 1941, almost certainly in the form of a spoken order given by Hitler to Himmler, and the first death camps were set up that winter, most of the central figures involved were drafted in from the euthanasia program. Killing people on that scale had never been done before, there was no precedent, nothing to refer back to other than the gas chambers of the euthanasia program, and these were accordingly taken as the blueprint. The murders of Jews on the Eastern Front, which were pure executions, not only of men but of women and children too, were too costly in terms of time and personnel and would have been impracticable. What they were looking at was a question: how to kill as many people as possible, in as short a time as possible, using as few human resources as possible? Much trial and error was involved before the system became effective. No budget existed, the whole endeavor financed by the confiscation of the personal assets of the victims. An ordinary travel agency took care of the practicalities of chartering trains in exactly the same way as they dealt with such matters normally. Ordinary railway staff were deployed to organize the logistics of the transports, plotting train times into the schedules, passing information on through the system. The camps were built, personnel received their orders, the industry began. Some of the soldiers must have been picked out on account of their brutality, many being obvious sadists who could find outlets and indulge themselves here, while others were ordinary and, in any other context, considerate men doing a job.

Two years later they tried to remove all traces; having demolished Treblinka's every structure, they built a farm on the site and instructed the Ukrainian family they installed in it to say they had lived there always. The same occurred in Sobibor, Belzec, and Chelmno, all traces gone. All around, life went on as if nothing had happened.

What had happened?

I think it would be correct to say that what happened was not inhuman at all, but human, and that this is what makes it so terrible and so closely bound up with our own selves and our human lives that in order to see it, and thereby take command of it, we must remove it and place it beyond ourselves, outside the boundaries of the human, where it now stands, sacrosanct and inviolable, mentionable only in certain, meticulously controlled ways. But it began in a we, and came together in an I, who concentrated its essence into a book, from where it swelled into the social sphere, unfathomably silent in its seeping pervasion, thought morphing into action, a tangible, physical presence in the world we inhabit, questioned by none of those involved, but carried out and done.

Train after train, transport after transport, human being after human being.

Clickety-clack. Clickety-clack. Clickety-clack.

◆ ◆ ◆

During these past weeks writing about *Mein Kampf* I have been contemplating what I know about evil. Before I started I never gave it a thought, it was an issue belonging to my teenage years, my Bjørneboe period, when I felt personally reponsible for all humanity. The question of the possible existence of God belonged to the same period. I still remember a page from my diary when I was sixteen, starting with the question "Does a God exist?" and ending in the conclusion that it did not. Now I am forty-two and back at the start. I am no longer the same person; what for so long seemed so near, my teenage years, exists now on the other side of a vast ocean of time. And what I related to then only instinctively or emotionally, the social world, whose power I felt whenever my cheeks burned with shame or I was consumed by self-reproach because of something I had done that made me feel so inadequate, so awkward, so indistinct, so totally stupid and foolish, but also unprincipled and dishonest and fraudulent, I now see more clearly, not least after having written these books, which in their every sentence have tried to transcend the social world by conveying the innermost thoughts and innermost feelings of my most private self, my own internal life, but also by describing the private sphere of my family as it exists behind the façade all families set up against the social world, doing so in a public form, a novel. The forces that exist within the realm of the social reveal themselves only when they are exceeded, and they are powerful indeed, almost, no, *absolutely* impossible to break away from. I imagined

I was going to write exactly what I thought and believed and felt, in other words to be honest, this is how it is, the truth of the I, but it turned out to be so incompatible with the truth of the we, or this is how it is meant to be, that it foundered after only a few short sentences. I came to understand what morality is, and where it is found. Morality is the we within the I, which is to say a concept of the social world, and it stands above the truth. The "ought" of morality is the voice of decency that saves us. But it is also the voice of I-constraint, the antithesis of truth and freedom, the voice that stands in our way. It is this latter dimension to which Heidegger alludes with *das Man*, the dictatorship of the we, the tyranny of the mean, the middle-class mind-set that transforms everything into its own image. That he failed to see through Hitler, so petty bourgeois in everything he did and thought, and Nazism, which was the revolution of the petty bourgeoisie, but was instead duped by their symbols of greatness and constructs of authenticity, unseeing of the fact that greatness and authenticity were the same as death, is astonishing. When Jaspers asked him how such an uneducated man as Hitler could ever govern the country, Heidegger replied infatuatedly, *Education doesn't matter at all, just look at his wonderful hands!* Only decency could have saved him, as with all others who followed Hitler. Jaspers was saved by decency, Jünger and Mann likewise. But not Heidegger. And certainly not Franz Stangl, the commandant of Treblinka. To him, decency was remaining at one's post and making sure ten thousand people were gassed to death and incinerated every day, ensuring the system ran smoothly and without backlogs. How treasonable the social world could be, and how powerful its forces, revealed itself in Stangl as it did in nearly all other Germans under the Nazi regime. Had he possessed the strength to break the bonds imposed on him by the social world, he would never have found himself in the diabolical madness in which he stood, would never have had the lives of 900,000 people on his conscience. In the Third Reich the voice of human conscience did not say it is wrong to kill, it said it is wrong not to kill, as Hannah

Arendt so precisely observes. This was made possible by a shift in the language, displayed in its purest form in *Mein Kampf*, which contains no "you," only an "I," and a "we," which is what makes it possible to turn "they" into "it." In "you" was decency. In "it" was evil.

But it was "we" who carried it out.

To protect ourselves we use the most potent marker of distance we know, the line of demarcation that passes between "we" and "they." The Nazis have become our great "they." In their demonic and monstrous evil, "they" exterminated the Jews and set the world aflame. Hitler, Goebbels, Göring and Himmler, Mengele, Stangl, and Eichmann. The German people who followed "them" are in our minds also a "they," a faceless and frenzied mass, almost as monstrous as their leaders. The remoteness of "they" is vast and dashes down these proximate historical events, which took place in the present of our grandparents, into a near-medieval abyss. At the same time we know, every one of us knows, even though we might not acknowledge it, that we ourselves, had we been a part of that time and place and not of this, would in all probability have marched beneath the banners of Nazism. In Germany in 1938 Nazism was the consensus, it was what was right, and who would dare to speak against what is right? The great majority of us believe the same as everyone else, do the same as everyone else, and this is so because the "we" and the "all" are what decide the norms, rules, and morals of a society. Now that Nazism has become "they," it is easy to distance ourselves from it, but this was not the case when Nazism was "we." If we are to understand what happened and how it was possible, we must understand this first. And we must understand too that Nazism in its various elements was not monstrous in itself, by which I mean that it did not arise as something obviously monstrous and evil, separate from all else in the current of society, but was on the contrary part of that current. The gas chambers were not a German invention, but were conceived by Americans who realized that people could be put to death by placing them in a chamber infused with poisonous gas, a procedure they carried out for the first time in 1919. Paranoid anti-Semitism was not a German phenomenon either, the world's most celebrated and passionate anti-Semite in 1925 being not Adolf Hitler but Henry Ford. And racial biology was not an abject, shameful discipline pursued at the bottom of society or its shabby periphery, it was the scientific state of the art, much as genetics is today, haloed by the light of the future and all its hope. Decent humans distanced themselves from all of this, but they were few, and this fact demands our consideration, for who are we going to be when our decency is put to the test? Will we have the courage to speak against what everyone else believes, our friends, neighbors, and colleagues, to insist that we are decent and they are not? Great is the power of the we, almost inescapable its bonds, and the only thing we can really do is to hope our we is a good we. Because if evil comes it will not come as "they," in the guise of the unfamiliar that we might turn away without effort, it will come as "we." It will come as what is right.

◆ ◆ ◆

Reading texts written in the decades leading up to World War II is like reading the legislation of a former society whose laws no longer apply. The ideas expressed make up a system which in itself is comprehensible and meaningful but which is no longer connected to any practical reality. The notions of what constitutes a human being, what constitutes a society, and what is most important in our human life are inapplicable to the society in which we live today. No student of any high school today would lay down his life for his country, no twenty-five-year-old today would find any value at all in the deaths of two million people. The phenomenon is simply inconceivable, other than as an abnormality. Anyone today who suggested democracy was an expression of decay, liberalism a disgrace, would be hung out to dry in all our media. Antidemocratic sentiment is a taboo in the original sense, something society regards as untouchable. When it is approached, it is approached in ways that shield us from its content, much like the rituals of primitive societies, in this case by the texts of the era being accorded a particular status where, in the same way as the holy excludes that which is unholy, all but their purely textual properties are ignored. In this way we are able to approach notions like divine violence, central to an essay written by Walter Benjamin in 1921, which, because he is one of the most recognized thinkers of the Weimar period, perhaps of all modernity, must be rescued from its antidemocratic implications, and we may also investigate ideas concerning the arbitrariness of law without lending them any significance other than that which they command in the internal world of the text, whose propositions go back to Antiquity, to Plato, Aristotle, or even to the Presocratics, as far forward as to Nietzsche, back to the Romans and Roman law, further to Heidegger, back to Augustine and Thomas Aquinas, on to Benjamin, back to Descartes, and all the way up to Kierkegaard, but never at any point reaching into our time and our society, never in any binding sense, for the insights gained in such texts find no consequence in the reality outside them. The problems they raise are addressed and aired, but their validity is restricted to their own delimited context, exactly as rituals once addressed the chasms within their own societies. The best example is Nietzsche, one of the most influential figures in the field of the humanities, referred to in almost every discussion of society and culture, yet the reassessment of values that takes place in his philosophy, which absorbs and fascinates generation after generation of students, never genuinely impacts in the sense of any obligation being established between the texts and the present-day reality of the reader. All thoughts in this respect, relating to the undemocratic, to qualitative differences between human beings, to the nihilistic, to the amoral, and to the arbitrariness of law, are treated as text, and any fascination or relevance made a matter of internal fascination or relevance.

This distance between the text and the world emerges in exemplary fashion in an essay by Girard in which *Hamlet* is construed as a drama dealing with Hamlet's attempts to put an end to vengeance, which is the fundamental trope of mimetic violence. Hence the postponements, the doubt, the hesitation, the lack of initiative, the impotence. In this essay Girard disqualifies almost all previous interpretations, such disqualification eventually becoming a point in itself as he considers how so many scholars of literature, so many professors over the past hundred years and more, could have construed Hamlet's reluctance to avenge his father as a failure, an expression of faltering will and faltering ability, even going so far as to pathologize Hamlet's resistance to such an act. When these texts on Hamlet are read a thousand years from now, in another culture, their readers will surely think that professors and other scholars of literature were a bloodthirsty and vengeful lot. *Hamlet* is a portrayal of a human being, professors and other scholars of literature are human beings too, yet this identification is never touched on, the connection is simply never made, for the morals and ethics of *Hamlet* are morals and ethics applying within the text or system of texts, not to the human beings who read those texts in their own lives. The question professors and other scholars of literature ought to ask themselves in order to understand Hamlet is this: What would I have done if my father died and I suspected someone of killing him? Would I have gone to the person I thought had killed him, who it turned out was my uncle, and avenge my father's death by killing him? No, nobody would, to do so would be quite atrocious, a deeply archaic and absolutely immoral act. What we would do would be to go to the police and allow the law to preside. This is Hamlet's dilemma, Girard tells us, he is one of us, a so-called modern man caught up in an archaic system of vengeance and violence. To his mind this system is not anchored in anything absolute, it is arbitrary, and if it is arbitrary it is also a game, and if it is a game then indeed everything else is a game too, the social world is nothing but counters on a board that may be moved in one direction if this set of rules applies or in another if another set of rules applies. Such arbitrariness only becomes clear the moment we step outside the system, or when the system goes from following one set of rules to following another. Both before and after such a transfer, the social world and the system of rules are one and the same, difficult to separate, as if the rules are not applied but come from within, from the social world itself, like nature, with the same conditions as exist between the laws of nature and natural matter.

The question of what I would have done and thought had I been Hamlet is one of identification, and identification concerns likeness. In an essay about Rembrandt, Jean Genet describes a train journey he once made and how he was seated in a carriage opposite a particularly loathsome man with bad teeth, who smelled awful and spat tobacco on the floor, and how all of a sudden it came to Genet, out of nothing and with the force of every revolutionary idea, that all men were of equal worth. This is an idea that is more than familiar to us, and we are brought up to believe it to be right, but what Genet describes is the abrupt insight into what it actually entails, its utterly wild radicality. Was this wretched and despicable person on the seat opposite *equal* to him? Are you *equal* to me? It is an impossible thought. Genet stares at him and their eyes meet. What he sees in the man's eyes, what reveals itself to him there, in that fleeting moment, makes him wonder if there is something in our identity, far within its depths, that is absolutely the same. In other words absolute identity. Genet does not link this idea in any way to Rembrandt, but it is rooted in Rembrandt's paintings, and this I know to be true; I saw a self-portrait by Rembrandt in a London gallery, and the powerful sense of nearness in its gaze, as if risen through the four hundred years that have passed since it was painted, now to meet our own, told me exactly what Genet was talking about. While I have never put it into words, I have nonetheless felt its truth.

I am you.

This has nothing to do with the social we, for only the unique I can express it, and all art, in conveying and communicating what is shared within a culture, concerns this. Any art that expresses only the social we is art that becomes isolated by time, a hundred years later it is the expression only of its era, of what was going on in the social world at that particular time and nothing else. This social we was what Nazism destroyed, and what Paul Celan's poem is a response to. "Engführung" is the end of what began with Hitler's *Mein Kampf*, written in the remains of the language the Nazis destroyed, not with the intention primarily of displaying that destruction, though in 1959 that must also have been important, but to forge a new path from language into reality. To do so, Celan went to the most basic components of the language, its very foundation, which is I, you, we, they, it – and is, was. Against the void of death and absence they discharge new meaning, which is unexampled, which is to say inimitable, valid only here, in this single poem. The boundary of meaning is also the boundary of community, and to that place only the one may go. So far does the poem reach into the idiosyncratic that no name can be mentioned, the name being a superordination, something general, unaffected by time, always the same, and yet steeped in time, whose associations flow steadily through it. Thus Celan approaches the it of the I, though not in the form of the body's namelessness, not in the form of the silence of biology, but that part of the human self which is the same in all of us. The poem's archaic feel, the historic events addressed as something outside the name, which is to say in the undifferentiated, which is always the same, or borders on sameness, comes from this. In a strange though absolutely significant way, the namelessness of the Jews who were executed in World War II seems at variance with the namelessness within the poem, which is not in any way bound to the body, not deadlocked by silence, but on the contrary seeks to give the silence that is the relationship between the nothing and the all, between the linguistic conception of the world and the world itself, a voice. That voice is the voice of the one, and it is the voice of the all. It is I, it is you, it is we, it is they, it is it, and it is time, flowing through it all.

I am you.

Jesus said, Your neighbor is like you. The consequence of that idea, so wildly radical, is that Hitler is worth as much as the Jews he ordered to be unprecedentedly to death and incinerated. Genet said, Your neighbor is you. From this too there is no exception, not even in the case of someone such as Adolf Hitler. We are opposed, and rightly so, to everything he stood for. Hitler is our antithesis. But only in respect to what he did, not in terms of the person he was. In that, he was like us. Hitler's youth resembles my own, his remote infatuation, his desperate desire to be someone, to rise above the self, his love for his mother, his hatred of his father, his use of art as a space of great emotions in which the I could be erased. His problems forming relationships with others, his elevation of women and his anxiety in their company, his chastity, his yearning for purity. When I watch him on film, he awakens the same feelings in me as my father once did. In that too there is likeness. He represented conservative middle-classness in so many respects, and this too I know, it is the voice, trembling with indignation, that says you are not good enough. He also represents the defiance of conservative middle-class values, the young lad sleeping until midmorning, refusing to look for a job, wishing instead to write or paint, because he is something more and better than the others. He was the one who opened a we and said you are one of us, and he was the one who closed a we and said you are one of them. But above all he was the man who emerged from the bunker, with the world in flames and millions of people dead as a result of his volition, to greet a line of young boys, his hands shaking from sickness, and there, in a fleeting gleam of his eyes, revealed something warm and kind, his soul. He was a small person, but so are we all. He must not be judged for what he was, but for what he did. What he did, however, he did not do alone. It was done by a we, that we was put under pressure, it gave way and something collapsed. Only those who were strong enough in themselves could withstand it. They were the self-willed and the disloyal, who refused the ideology, which is the community's idea of how the world should be. Paul Celan's poem is a nonideological poem, expressing the antipode of ideologies. Even a name is expressive of ideology, an idea of a person, at the same time as it is that idea that saves a person from extinction within the mass: the name is the one. Hitler made his name the all, emptying from it any semblance of individuality, as Hess once said, You are Germany. After the Holocaust his name remained, his face endured, whereas the six million Jews who perished remained nameless, faceless nobodies. This too is a theme of Paul Celan's poem. A story ended there, in that zero point, in that oblivion, desolate and forsaken, all that is human obliterated, worthless. Another story began there, our story. Who covered it up, Celan asks in "Engführung," who concealed the uniquely and authentically human of this catastrophe in the general, emblematic, and common language if it had not broken down?

A story ended there, but it was not a story of evil. The time from the beginning of the twentieth century to the end of World War II was a period when the fundamental building blocks of our human existence and organizational structures were in flux, not to say disintegrating, and the unprecedented radicality of those fifty years, which gave rise to the last two great utopian movements, Nazism and Communism, can only be understood on the basis that the societal order suddenly, because of a massive buildup of pressure arising in industrialism's changes – in time, extremely compressed while in volume expansive, no longer could be taken for granted, it began to crack and appeared increasingly arbitrary, governed by rules imposed from without, in a civilizational system at odds with its people, from which they, or many of them, felt utterly alienated. Those who experienced this strove toward a new foundation, a new society, and since this was not self-evident the way democracy and liberalism are self-evident to us, they endeavored to find it in what presented itself as such in the realm of the human, in other words the absolute. The core, the essence, the authentic.

Our society and culture, which not only surround me on all sides as I sit here in a room inside an apartment in the city of Malmö in southern Sweden, listening to Iron & Wine in the early morning, alone, with Linda and the children vacationing in Corsica, but also pervade me completely, as they pervade my language and pervade my thoughts, shaping my instincts and ideas, setting my boundaries as to what may or may not be done and thought, in short, all that which comprises my particular self, and which also connects me to all other selves, were founded in two crises of massive upheaval, two periods of extremely compressed structural transformations within our human existence, the first occurring with the advent of the scientific revolution in the sixteenth century, the second with the advent of industrialism in the mid-nineteenth century, which sent the world spiraling into fifty years of chaos culminating in the fall of Hitler's Germany in 1945. The human world exists not as an abstract, but in the sum of individual human beings, and it was there, in every single one of them, that the transition from the religious to the secularized occurred from the sixteenth century onward, which is to say in the self, in the I's understanding of itself in relation to the it, the we, and the they.

In the fourteenth century it was impossible for any person to dissect a human corpse in order to see what it looked like inside, the way the internal organs functioned and were ordered. This was so not because it was forbidden in the sense of being punishable by law, what made it impossible was not the fear of reprisal but the fact that it was quite simply unthinkable. In the fifteenth century Leonardo was dissecting corpses and meticulously drawing what he saw, by then it was possible, albeit only to a certain extent; he cut up his bodies in the night, in secret, alone with the dead, but for him the boundary could be exceeded. Today dissecting corpses has not only become institutionalized, it comprises one of the most important foundations of our medical science, and is an absolutely uncontroversial practice.

This is the case because the idea of what we are has changed, and with it the idea of what we can and must do. That change is not instrumental, although the practices that come with it are that too; as Latour writes, there is no such thing as science, only scientists, fragile and small in themselves, shuffling about in laboratories in their slippers, with their freezers and microscopes, their test tubes and computers, drinking coffee with their colleagues, going home after work and wondering whether to barbecue or if the clouds above the hills mean it's going to rain. That this is so means "science" is something that cannot be localized without violating that singularity, but which at the same time obviously exists, as the sum of activities performed by scientists.

Here, in the transition between the one and the all, resides the problem of our time. On the one hand, we live in a society in which a whole set of evaluations in one way or another deemed threatening to the status quo and associated with violence, revolution, and utopia are treated as taboo in the sense that they may only occur in contexts of ritual, moored only figuratively in reality; on the other hand, we live in a society that is changing in ways we cannot consider to be anything but revolutionary, along lines of flight that are directly connected with those taboos, which then are of such form and nature as to preclude that connection. We can talk about the one thing, but only as something outside ourselves, inside a closed system; the other, happening in our midst, is hard for us to see, since the correspondence between those events and our understanding of ourselves is so great, and the door of the external perspective closed.

In practice this means we live in a society which on the one hand has made the utopian and the revolutionary impossible, and which moreover resists any real change to its system on the basis that it is as good as it can get, certainly better by far than the alternatives, all of which degenerated into systems of escalating inhumanity and ended in disaster, but which on the other hand renews itself so swiftly and with such radicality as to be essentially revolutionary, leading directly toward the utopian, construed as the next place. That passage occurs as if in secret, because it is fundamentally undemocratic, for although it affects every one of us, the decisions made along the way are made by the individual. The individual is neither a utopian, nor a revolutionary, nor an antidemocrat, but a devoted democrat and citizen of society, and if there is any trace of revolt in him or her, any suggestion of an urge toward societal change, it is directed toward the distribution of wealth, which at any time is either more or less fair. Together and in this way we venture into still new areas, some so new to us as to require new legislation, not to prohibit or exclude such advances, but to include them in the existing order. We have cloned animals, we have mapped the human genome and are able to modify its genes, we have transplanted hearts and lungs, we have created children outside the womb, and we have even created new species, creatures without origin with properties we alone have decided.

To us these appear to be minor matters in that the industry that has brought them about is made up of small units in which the rest of society is uninvolved, but also because after Nazism and the genocide of the Jews we have suspended the validity of the grand scale, consistently avoiding points at which several values converge into a single trope, such as the idea of the genius, the idea of the sublime, the idea of the divine, the idea of the chosen people, in a construal of the world that leaves no room for a concept such as veneration, this sounding too hollow, or, even more hollow, veneration for the human; this is rhetoric, we consider, it refers to something bigger than us, a trope that with Nazism showed itself to be destructive.

The consequence of this is that there is no longer anything bigger than ourselves, no longer anything to die for, and therefore no longer anything at which to stop in veneration. But to clone an animal, to manipulate human DNA, to create a new creature, is no minor matter. To split the atom is no minor matter. It is to exceed a boundary never before exceeded, it is to intervene in the very constituents of life, though we are ignorant of its origins and have always through all time considered it to be a gift and a mystery, something inviolable. That mystery is not solved by our manipulations, but its boundary is violated. The inviolability of individual life is the very foundation on which we build our society. What does it mean to violate an individual life? It means to kill it, to abuse it, to steal from it, to rape it, to torture it, to victimize it. To act against it in a manner contrary to its own wishes. That boundary is something we protect by means of the bonds that tie together the social world, and if those bonds are broken and the boundary exceeded, we impose sanctions.

But who protects the inviolability of human life when understood not in terms of the individual, but in terms of the collective life, the all? Previously it was religion and the laws of religion. But what about now, with religion gone? The state? The state is an instrumental entity, a more or less pragmatic steering mechanism of the community, whose success is largely measured in terms of gross national product and rates of unemployment, and because science is instrumental too, and its pushing back of the boundaries profitable, there is little motivation for the state to legislate to the effect that life be held sacred and that its boundaries remain unviolated.

We have gone beyond the absolute, for it led us to unprecedented atrocities, but without the absolute everything is relative, a matter of good or poor argument, negotiable, within the domain of reason. Reason is to us the same as profitability. What happens to that which is outside reason? In a world governed by profitability, lack of profitability has no bearing, and the absolute is that which is not exchangeable, neither in money nor in arguments. The absolute is neither reasoned nor unreasoned, it is what exists outside categories. The absolute may be reached only by the emotions. The absolute belongs to religion, mythology, and the irrational. The absolute is what propels someone to die for a cause greater than himself, faith in the absolute was once the foundation of law. The absolute is death, emptiness, nothingness, darkness. The absolute is the background against which life is lived.

The absolute is eternity. The relative is day-to-day existence. These are the two fundamental tropes of our lives. We hold the absolute at bay, firstly by leveling down the bigness of our existence, that which has to do with the very boundaries of life and materiality, to the commonplace, addressing the issues that concern us all, the great collective, mankind, only in the quotidian; secondly by ritualizing the absolute in an unreal world of images: death is to us not the physical death of the body, but the figurative death, as it occurs in images, in the same way as violence is not physical violence, but figurative violence. Heroism is no longer a possibility, there being no arena for it, those arenas have all been shut down, for the heroic belongs to the bigness we do what we can to shun, yet in the world of images, which any one of us may enter at any time, the heroic lives on: entire worlds and societies have emerged in Internet gaming, where anyone can pick up a machine gun and venture out into the world to shoot the enemy for a few hours. Practically all the films we watch are about exactly this: heroism, violence, death. And the people we watch carry out these heroic deeds in our name, in our place, are all physically beautiful or charismatic, or both. Indeed, that world, growing and expanding with every year that passes, celebrates all the worlds we otherwise reject. Outer beauty, charisma, heroism, violence, and death are not relative, they belong to the pure, the unambivalent, the simple. Our need for this, to see the magnification of our existence and what borders the absolute, is insatiable.

But since the two systems, relativized reality and absolutized pseudo-reality, are mutually exclusive and can exist only separately, the question is what happens if they are measured against each other, if a person not simply applies the yardstick of the absolute to relative reality, but moreover acts on that basis. This is what happened in Norway this summer, when a man only a few years younger than me went out to an island and began indiscriminately shooting and killing young people. He acted like a figure in a computer game, but the act of heroism he thought he was performing, and the carnage he brought about, did not belong to the world of images, was not abstract and without consequence, did not occur in some other place, detached from the time and place of his physical body; it was real, tangible, absolute. Every shot he fired lodged in human flesh, every eye that closed was a real eye belonging to a human being with a real life. Only remoteness can make such an act possible, since in remoteness consequence ceases to exist, and the question we must ask ourselves is not what kind of political opinions this person held, nor if he was mad, but more simply how such remoteness could ever arise in our culture. Did he feel a yearning for reality, for an end to relativity, for the consequences of the absolute? We must assume he did. Do I feel such a yearning? Yes, I do. My basic feeling is that of the world disappearing, that our lives are being filled with images of the world, and that these images are inserting themselves between us and the world, making the world around us lighter and lighter and less and less binding. We are trying to detach ourselves from everything that ties us to physical reality; from the bloodless, vacuum-packed steaks in the refrigerated counters of our supermarkets, the industrially produced meat of cooped-up animals, to society's concealment of physical death and illness, from the cosmetically rectified uniformity of female faces to the endless flow of news images that pass through us every day and which together, in sum, erase all differences and establish a kind of universal sameness, not only because everything is conveyed in the same language, but also because what thereby is so incessantly conveyed inexorably, albeit gradually, re-creates what is conveyed in its own image. The symbol of this trend is money, which converts everything into monetary value, which is to say numbers. Everything we have is mass-produced, everything is the same, and our entire world, which is commercial in nature, is based on that serial system. The values in our sky of images are Nazi values, though everyone says differently. Beautiful bodies, beautiful faces, healthy bodies, healthy faces, perfect bodies, perfect faces, heroic people, heroic deaths, the same images prevalent during Nazism, the only difference between theirs and ours being that we refrain from letting them loose on reality, but keep them there, in the domain of the unbinding, and say it is not the value of the image that counts, but the value of the human, which is different. Yet the gap between them is so vast, and the rush of the authentic, which here is fictitious, so compelling, that someone sooner or later is bound to bring the sky down to earth and let it apply here. The perpetrator of the Utøya massacre did so, unbound by any relationship to reality, to the physical bodies he killed, but bound to the image of reality, in which no real consequence exists. In the days following that horrific event a story came out about a boy who had swiveled to face the killer, who in turn had looked into his eyes and told him he was unable to shoot him. And he did not. He shot everyone else he could, with this one exception. Why? Because he saw his eyes, and in doing so his actions became binding. A similar story, reported by Liljegren, exists from Hitler's life. In his time as Reich chancellor, Hitler became attached to a child, a blue-eyed little girl by the name of Bernhardine Nienau, whom he invited out of a crowd and treated to strawberries and whipped cream. So taken was he by the child and the conversation they had together that he told her she could come and see him whenever she wanted. They exchanged letters after this first meeting, but investigations initiated by Martin Bormann found the girl's grandmother to be Jewish. Hitler was annoyed, Liljegren writes, and commented, "There are some people who have a positive genius for spoiling all my little pleasures." However, they continued to correspond until 1938, and Bernhardine visited him on several occasions at the Berghof, again according to Liljegren. All this says nothing about Hitler's evil or goodness, and nothing about the ferocity of his hatred for the Jews, but rather a lot about its anatomy: Hitler was consumed by hatred and had been ever since he was growing up, and he had established a world for himself in which it was important to maintain remoteness from others, a world without family, close friends, and romantic attachments, an irreparable system in which all that was inside him found outer manifestation, including his hatred, which following Germany's defeat in World War I he directed toward the Jews and everything they stood for in his system. There, in that system, his hatred was absolute. But when something encroached upon it and entered the space between his own I and his convictions, a space which, besides whatever passageways there may have been within it that were unfamiliar to him, was quite empty, his hatred did not apply. His hatred applied to the others. In that space was the memory of his mother, for instance, and that it had remained so strong becomes plain to us in the fact that every Christmas, the time of his mother's death, he would descend into silence and dejection, as he did in 1915 at the front, and in that space too were the Jewish doctor, Bloch, and this ten-year-old girl, therefore his kindness to both. To Bernhardine's eyes he could maintain no remoteness, she was real, in that space together with him. The yearning for reality, for the authentic, and for nature is not dangerous. The dangerous force of Nazism was the exact opposite, remoteness to the world and the regimentation of the human that all ideological thinking creates. But if our culture removes itself from physical reality by placing the image before it, and if it levels out all differences in its extreme seriality, then it must be judged in the same way as Hitler, according to what it does and not what it is. The fact is that it does not exterminate people, either literally or metaphorically, that it does not persecute people or prevent their voices from being heard, and the question is then whether this culture, when all is said and done, provides an adequate response to an insoluble problem of the modern world that relates to the one and to the all. There is a difference between a country waging war and trying to wipe out an entire people in its name, and a lone killer taking the lives of sixty-nine children. We endeavor continually to safeguard ourselves against the former, but cannot safeguard ourselves against the latter. Both are to do with violence among like kind, and both arise out of remoteness, but there the similarity ends. Remoteness is the opposite of authenticity, and it is not the yearning for authenticity that is the problem, but the remoteness that gives rise to it. The unique is what cannot be replicated, existing only in a particular place at a particular time. It is the art of the one, and the life of the one. What took place in Germany was that the one dissolved into the all, the sky of ideals descended to earth, and the image of the absolute, which is without consequence, became a point of reference for human action. The absolute, in this case construed in terms of race, biology, blood, soil, nature, death, was not only set against the relative, construed in terms of the stock market, the entertainment industry, democratic parliamentarism, as occurred throughout the period leading up to World War I, but was also carried through into life itself, as action: Nazi Germany was the absolute state. It was the state its people could die for. Watching Riefenstahl's film of the rallies in Nuremberg, its depiction of a people almost paradisiac in its unambiguousness, converged upon the same thing, immersed in the symbols, the callings from the deepest pith of human life, that which has to do with birth and death, and with homeland and belonging, one finds it splendid and unbearable at the same time, though increasingly unbearable the more one watches, at least this was how I felt when I watched it one night this spring, and I wondered for a long time where that sense of the unbearable came from, the unease that accompanied these images of the German paradise, with its torches in the darkness, the intactness of its medieval city, its cheering crowds, its sun, and its banners, whether it was something I imposed upon them, knowing how this paradise arose, what it would become and at what cost, and what happened to it, but I came to the conclusion that this was not the reason, that it came not from what was in me, the knowledge I had of what lay behind the images of those days, but from something in the images themselves, the sense being that the world they displayed was an unbearable world. Not that it was a false world, because this was obvious, its every image meticulously created from scratch for that particular occasion, it was more that this false world, one of the few pure utopias to be established in the last century, in which everything was exactly the way it was supposed to be, was unbearable in itself. What was unbearable about it lay in its undifferentiatedness. Everything affirmed one and the same thing, and when this is the case no other thing exists but that one, and without the other the one dissolves into itself and vanishes. The one without the other is nothing. The society Riefenstahl portrayed, this utopia of the one, had to establish an other in order for its own simplicity, its own undifferentiatedness, to be maintained, and this is what lies beneath those peaceful and harmonious images and fills them with such foreboding: the inevitability of war. It was not the absolute values of Nazism that led them to war, for birth and death, homeland and belonging are characteristic of all people and all peoples, it was the utopia of the one and the same. It was the fall of the name into the number, it was the fall of the differentiating into the undifferentiated.

If we say that our present culture was founded in the seventeenth century, in the sense that all the elements that characterize our age appeared for the first time in that century, then two particular portal figures flank its door: Hamlet and Don Quixote. The creators of these figures, Shakespeare and Cervantes, died in the same year, and their understanding of the human condition, as radically dissimilar as they might appear in respect to each other, form two poles in the way we understand ourselves. In their day, the absolute, familiar to them under the name of the divine, was drawn increasingly closer to the relative, which is to say the interhuman domain, the social world. Hamlet doubts, and seemingly finds doubt to pervade everything. Don Quixote does not doubt, he believes, but what he believes in, and what he sees, since it fills his vision, is not real, belonging not to the world but to fiction. He sees sheep, aims his lance and attacks, imagining he sees an army of enemies. He sees a windmill, aims his lance and attacks, imagining he sees a giant. Don Quixote is a hero in a world without heroes, or in a world where heroes and the absoluteness of their lives belong to the pseudoworld, irreconcilable with the relative reality of the quotidian. Don Quixote is a comic hero. Hamlet is a hero too, but for the opposite reason, he doubts and relativizes in a world of absolutes. Hamlet is a tragic hero. Don Quixote sees the old world as if for the last time. Hamlet sees the old world as if for the first time. Through them we see ourselves, for our culture is founded on doubt, and our scope extends from the relative reality of the quotidian to the skies of our grandest conceptions. Hitler eliminated doubt and lowered the skies of our grandest conceptions to the relative reality of the quotidian, which is to say he inserted fiction into material reality and made reality a play, binding the individual to the mask.

As early as 1934, the Jewish philosopher Emmanuel Levinas wrote the following about Hitler and Hitlerism:

> *The body is not only a happy or unhappy accident that relates us to the implacable world of matter. Its adherence to the Self is of value in itself. It is an adherence that one does not escape and that no metaphor can confuse with the presence of an external object; it is a union that does not in any way alter the tragic character of finality.*
>
> *This feeling of identity between self and body, which, naturally, has nothing in common with popular materialism, will therefore never allow those who wish to begin with it to rediscover, in the depths of this unity, the duality of a free spirit that struggles against the body to which it is chained. On the contrary, for such people, the whole of the spirit's essence lies in the fact that it is chained to the body. To separate the spirit from the concrete forms with which it is already involved is to betray the originality of the very feeling from which it is appropriate to begin.*
>
> *The importance attributed to this feeling for the body, with which the Western spirit has never wished to content itself, is at the basis of a new conception of man. The biological, with the notion of inevitability it entails, becomes more than an object of spiritual life. It becomes*

its heart. The mysterious urgings of the blood, the appeals of hered-
ity and the past for which the body serves as an enigmatic vehicle,
lose the character of being problems that are subject to a solution put
forward by a sovereignly free Self. Not only does the Self bring in the
unknown elements of these problems in order to resolve them; the Self
is also constituted by these elements. Man's essence no longer lies in
freedom, but in a kind of bondage . . . Chained to his body, man sees
himself refusing the power to escape from himself. Truth is no longer
for him the contemplation of a foreign spectacle; instead it consists in
a drama in which man is himself the actor. It is under the weight of
his whole existence, which includes facts on which there is no going
back, that man will say his yes or his no.

This is man at one with himself, unified and whole. It is man as the one. Levinas, who became the philosopher of the other, turned in this reasoning as much to Heidegger as to Hitler, according to the Italian philosopher Giorgio Agamben, who cites the passage in his book *Homo Sacer: Sovereign Power and Bare Life*. For it is here, in the human construed as the one, at one with itself and its body, with no division between the being of the I and its ways of being, that Heidegger and Hitler come together, Agamben believes, where all anthropological distinctions – between spirit and body, sensation and consciousness, I and world, subject and properties – are abolished.

Dasein, the Being-there who is its There, thus comes to be placed in a
zone of indiscernability with respect to – and to mark the definitive
collapse of – all traditional determinations of man.

The relative in our existence – all that may be chosen – is bound to that which is not relative but absolute and unambiguous, which in the case of the I is the biological body. Thereby the I approaches its "it," where all voices fall silent and the darkness of the undif-ferentiated prevails, and this movement toward life's absolute, its "it," is what makes it possible to separate the Jewish from the

German, for the important distinction between they and we was drawn in the body, in race, which is to say in the immutable, whereas all other distinctions, such as those of language, thought, and culture, which may be learned and adapted, moderated and discussed, were absolutely invalid. Everything was pressed in toward the body, everything gathered in the body, and the final consequence of the human being at one with itself, which we tentatively call the monophonic human, at one with itself and shoulder to shoulder in unbroken series, for the next was not the other but the one again, the final consequence of this turning of the I toward the body, which is uniformity and unvariedness, was the extermination of the Jews, in which the Jew was body and limbs only. By the time they arrived at the extermination camps and were bundled from their cattle wagons they were no one. Deprived of their civil rights, deprived of their human rights, deprived of their names. They were the "it." On leaving the wagons, they were ordered to strip. Those then herded toward the gas chamber, which in Treblinka was situated on a small hill, were without citizenship, without name, without clothes. They were the naked human, without anything but its body, in the midst of what Agamben calls "bare life." What emerges before us in this image, which is not a metaphor, but an actual event, is what a human being is, and what it becomes. The human being, naked and bare, is this not the true and authentic human? The natural human, the human as a biological creature, as it is beneath the cloak of civilization and culture? If we imagine a world without language, without countries, without names, we would all have lived a life such as this, naked, nameless bodies in a nameless world, until death came and transformed the naked body into a corpse to be cast into the world of the dead, which is the world of decomposition and erosion. Such a life would take place in the very midst of the world, among its trees, waters, fells, and dales, upon the soil of the earth and beneath its sky, and yet it would be a life lived outside. Outside what? Outside the human world. For it is this that emerges before us in the image of the naked human; it is outside the law, outside the social world, outside the name. Only then, in that absence, are we able to see the nature of the law, the social world, the name. The law regulates violence among like kind, according responsibility for it to the individual, moreover at the same time institutionalizing it for the purposes of self-preservation in the police and military. The social world regulates the community; in it, all those it comprises are gathered in groups of greater and smaller we's, both formal and informal; and the name guarantees the individuality of the individual in the community of the all. If a person stands outside the law, they may be killed. If a person stands outside the social world, they are no one. If a person stands outside the name, they are a number. The Jews who were not immediately killed in Auschwitz were identified by a number tattooed on their forearm. But the matter is not so simple that we may say the Jews could be killed because everything belonging to the human domain was taken away from them, that civilization was negated in them and their fate, for the forces that took them there, outside the community of the human, were forces within that community, which is to say within civilization, our we. The bringing together of the I and the being of the body, drawing the human closer to the "it" of the I, thereby removing it both from history and from the moment, masks the human in uniformity and sameness, the play, which has always represented the possibilities of man, no longer a play but life itself, the way it unfolds. This bringing together occurred in parallel with, and was perhaps only possible by virtue of, a similar movement toward the it within the collective; the we, too, was drawn toward the it, which is to say the number. In bureaucracy the human is a number, and in the mass the human is a number. This dehumanization of the we, whereby the other may be reduced to a number, is necessary in war if the enemy is to be killed, and it is necessary in the administration of large numbers of people even now, for a modern state without statistics is unthinkable, but in Hitler's Germany the state became a total entity, the we merged completely with the state, they were one and the same, and in much the same way as the I was bound to the body and possessed no space of its own outside, the we was bound to the state and possessed no space of its own outside, and in much the same way as this made it possible to push the Jewish I into the "it," reducing it to body alone, it also made it possible to push the Jewish we into the "it," reducing it to number alone. Neither the I of the body nor the we of the state contained any singular you. It was for this reason that millions of Jews could be sent to the gas chambers before the eyes of everyone, without anything happening other than that they looked down, they looked away, for what was there to see? There was nothing to see. They saw nothing, they heard nothing, they said nothing. The it of the body: undifferentiated. The it of the we: undifferentiated. Outside the language they were driven into the terrain, along the unmistakable track, and became, in undifferentiated night, ash.

Nowhere does anyone ask after you, for "you" does not exist.

◆ ◆ ◆

It's evening already. I'm on my own at home, Linda and the children are still in Corsica with Linda's mother. Heidi has lost a front tooth there, she told me proudly on the phone. I'm looking forward to seeing her smile when she comes home. John has got a new air bed in the shape of a crocodile and fell and hurt his knee, as far as I could make out from his incoherent and breathless report. Vanja didn't want to talk on the phone, but she cried when I said goodbye to them on the train platform and walked away, and she's never done that before. Since they left, four days ago now, I've spent every day and evening writing, watching *Shoah* into the night, apart from yesterday when I read Sereny's book about Treblinka. *Shoah* doesn't get to me, either because I'm keeping a distance or because it works through insight rather than feelings. Which isn't entirely true because suddenly, out of nothing, a scene made me weep, a single stab of empathy, and that was it, I carried on watching as before. Sereny's book, which almost paralyzed me the first time I read it, left me unmoved too. But that's when I'm awake. When I'm asleep, I dream about it.

Earlier today I was sitting on the balcony, smoking and looking out over the rooftops as I always do. The sky was pale blue, typical for May, and the usual sounds rose from the city below: the rumble of buses, the squealing of brakes, the hum of tires moving over the road surfaces, an occasional shout. On the roof of the apartments opposite some Polish builders have a project going, they've been there for months now, putting in roof terraces and converting the loft space into living units. Suddenly a child laughed somewhere. It was such a joyful laugh, so overwhelming and gleeful and utterly abandoned to the delight of the moment that I felt it too. I smiled, and got to my feet to see where it was coming from. It sounded like a young child, maybe three or four years old. There was a man's voice in there too, and I imagined it was a father tossing his child into the air, again and again. But there was no one there when I looked down into the street below, no one in the parking spaces, or outside the garage. Then there it was again. I guessed it had to be coming from the little passage connecting the pedestrian street with the street behind our building, and that they were hidden from sight by the building in between. I sat down again, poured myself some tepid coffee from the thermos, and lit another cigarette.

PART TWO

When the alarm clock rang it was still dark outside. I turned it off and got up. Linda lay still in bed, her face on the pillow almost completely obscured by her hair, which spread out in all directions. It was half past four, and my whole body ached with tiredness, I had lain awake for so long before I fell asleep. That seldom happened; if there was one thing in my life that worked it was my sleep. I was what they call a sound sleeper. I could sleep on the floor without any problem, and with children screaming a meter away from me, it didn't make any difference; if I was asleep, I was asleep. Once I had thought it was a sign that I wasn't a real writer. Writers slept badly, had ravaged faces, at the crack of dawn they sat at the kitchen table staring out the window, tormented by their inner demons, which never rested.

Who had ever heard of a great writer who slept like a child?

To think that was a bad sign, I reasoned. Because tomorrow my third book was coming out. Reviews in all the newspapers.

I grabbed the clothes I had laid out the night before and padded into the bathroom to shower. The sight of them triggered a fit of nerves. My hand holding the showerhead shook with unease as I clambered into the bath. I turned on the water and shivered as the hot jets hit skin which had just emerged from the warm depths of the duvet and would have preferred to stay there.

But then, after only a few minutes, everything changed, and getting out of the shower was what would make me shiver.

After the thrum of the shower, everything was silent. Not a sound from the streets outside, not a sound from our apartment or the apartments below. It was as though I was meant to be alone in the world.

In the harsh light I rubbed myself down with a large towel, and once my skin was relatively dry I wiped the steam off the mirror and put styling gel in my hair and deodorant under my arms while observing my reflection, which slowly became less and less sharp as the water molecules, or whatever they were, attached themselves to the glass again.

I donned my Ted Baker shirt, which stuck to my still-damp shoulder blades and would not hang straight at first, then I got into my Pour jeans with the diagonal pockets, which usually I didn't like, there was something so conventional about them, all Dockers trousers had slanting pockets, but on a pair of jeans there was so much else working against the Dockers look that they actually looked good, for then it was the jeans style that was being challenged and as a result a kind of tension grew, not much, but in a world where all denims looked identical, it was enough to make these just that little bit different.

I wiped the floor with the used towel and draped it over the side of the bathtub, went into the kitchen, put on the kettle, spooned some Nescafé into a cup, and looked out the window while waiting for the water to boil. The window faced east and a patch of something brighter in the distance had begun to emerge from the darkness. Impatiently I lifted the kettle before the water had started to bubble, and the crescendo of noise was interrupted and replaced by a soft murmur as the coffee rose inside the cup, at first a golden brown from the powder, visible as an earthy clump at the bottom, until over the next few seconds it completely dissolved and the surface became an impenetrable black with some lighter-colored froth at the edges.

Cup in hand, I went out to the balcony, sat down, and took

out a cigarette. A plane passed high above like a small ball of light; it was still too dark for me to distinguish the fuselage from the sky around it. In an hour and a half I would be sitting up there myself, I reflected, and then I thought of the Cortázar short story which so often surfaced from my subconscious when I was sitting here because it shifted perspective in such a dizzyingly abrupt way between someone on board a plane and someone on the ground, to be precise on an island in the Mediterranean. Cortázar was the master of giddy shifts of perspective, and even if his short stories occasionally bore a likeness to those of Borges, in this respect he was unrivaled.

The man reading about the man reading about the man reading. The line of faces which disappeared into the illusory depths of the mirror when, as a boy, I had stood in front of it holding another mirror to reflect the image. Smaller and smaller and smaller, deeper and deeper into the distance, into all eternity, for it was impossible to stop this movement, it could only become so small that it could not be distinguished from its surroundings.

I drew the smoke deep into my lungs. I was cold, partly because I was wearing only a shirt, partly because I was tired. And partly because I was afraid.

But there was nothing to be afraid of, was there?

The plane was no more than a tiny dot now while daybreak seemed to have come closer to the town, and the darkness in the air between the buildings below me was filled with a kind of light so hazy that it was as if someone had stirred the gloom, causing the light hiding at the bottom to mingle and rise to the surface.

Ever since I was in my teens I had imagined that the universe might well be microscopic and perhaps encapsulated in an atom belonging to a different universe, which in turn was enclosed in an atom in a different universe, and so on ad infinitum. But it was only when I read Pascal and saw the same idea there that it gained validity and authority as a distinct possibility. Yes, that was probably how it was. The fractal system, on which so much in our world is based, was like that: an image within an image within an image, ad infinitum.

I stubbed out my cigarette in the ashtray, chucked the rest of the coffee over the railing, heard it hit the roof far below as I opened the door and went in. Placed the cup on the counter, put on my new suit jacket and new shoes, packed a tub of hairstyling gel, an extra pair of underpants, and a shirt in my backpack, passport, plane ticket, cigarettes, and lighter in the outside pocket, hung one strap over my shoulder and was about to open the door when Linda came in.

"Are you off?" she said.

"Yes," I replied.

"Well, good luck," she said.

We kissed briefly.

"See you tomorrow!" I said.

"Yes, looking forward to that," she answered.

I walked out to the elevator. She closed the door behind me, I averted my eyes from the mirror on the way down, lit a cigarette as I emerged onto the street. There were two taxis outside the hotel, I ambled toward the traffic lights and crossed over to them. The driver in the first car was asleep. I leaned forward and knocked on the window with one knuckle. He didn't give a start, as I had expected, but instead opened his eyes without moving his head or body, evincing a kind of out-of-place regal dignity.

The window slid down.

"Are you free?" I asked.

"Yes," he replied. "Where do you want to go?"

I opened the rear door and got in. Actually the plan had been to catch a taxi to the railway station and then the train to Kastrup, but it didn't feel right to wake him up for such a short trip, which would earn him no more than a hundred kronor, besides which I needed the immense feeling of power and luxury it would give me if I went by taxi all the way to the airport, something I had never done before, apart from once with the children when we were

912

going to the Canary Islands and had so much luggage we didn't feel like lugging it all onto the train.

"Kastrup," I said. "Is it a set price?"

"Yes," he said, flashing his left indicator.

It cost four hundred more. Almost as much as the plane ticket. But what the hell. The novel was coming out tomorrow. I would be getting at least sixty thousand kroner for it. Surely I could indulge myself. Besides, I was going to do a lot of interviews, so it was important I was rested and my energy levels were up, after all, this was my job.

I leaned back in the seat and looked at the town, its lights glinting in the gray dawn, and another wave of nerves surged through me.

For nearly two years I had worked as a language consultant on the new Norwegian translation of the Bible, and I had caught the plane from Kastrup to Gardermoen so often, there and back in a day, that what I had previously considered unremarkable, though it was certainly unusual, a kind of travelfest, had now become routine, as commonplace as catching the bus. I collected my boarding pass from one of the machines in the departure hall and walked up to the first floor and over to the security control in the long corridors there. My jacket over my arm and belt in hand, I put the backpack on the carousel when it was my turn, picked it up on the other side, surrounded by besuited men in their fifties and equally professionally dressed women, some cheery and outgoing, others withdrawn into themselves, standing like trees. I presumed that I would give the same impression if anyone looked at me when I looked at them. I put my belt back on and then my jacket as I walked through the tax-free shopping area to the café at the entrance to the B gates, where I would usually sit after buying Norwegian and Danish newspapers in the big kiosk there, and had a coffee at the bar.

I had hardly talked to anyone about the novel, apart from those closest to me, and they saw me and themselves in it with none of the objectivity a normal novel required, so I knew little about how it seemed from the outside, to people who had nothing to do with me. It was difficult to predict what questions the journalists would ask. But as soon as they began, a certain way of regarding the book would be established because they always thought alike, always asked the same questions, and once I had said something to one of them, then I said the same to the next, it became a kind of platform for the book, which in turn became the book because what was written in the newspapers the following day was further reinforced by a fairly large circle of readers and interested parties, who discussed it on the basis of this same platform. The next time I did interviews the journalists had prepared by reading earlier interviews and reviews. In the process everything apart from a couple of points was filtered away, and these were then so squeezed and wrung dry until the book completely lost any signs of life and lay dead and buried in a warehouse somewhere outside Oslo.

But one thing was certain this time, and that was that they'd ask about the autobiographical element. Why did I write about myself? What was it that made me so interesting that I could write not only one novel based on my life but six? Was I a narcissist? Why did I use people's real names? That would be fine, they weren't impossible questions to answer, but if they honed in on individual names, my father and his mother, for instance, and their various relatives, and were bent on talking about the novel's depiction of reality in specific rather than general terms – Grandma and Dad and those days in Kristiansand – it could turn out to be a nightmare.

A clue as to what they would be asking about was given in the three interviews I had done in Malmö: one for *Dagbladet*, one for *Dagens Næringsliv*, and one for *Bokprogrammet* on NRK. Both *Dagbladet* and *Dagens Næringsliv* had been preoccupied with what I had written about myself, about the person I was now. About having no friends, no interest in social life, and about getting so drunk that I lost all self-control. These matters had been almost impossible to talk about. Who would want to state in the newspaper that they don't have any friends? When I was writing this wasn't a problem since what I wrote was how things were for me, sitting alone in my room. This novel was tightly drawn around me and my life, but as soon as it all came out into the open, everything changed. An immense distance appeared within this private world that belonged to me and my family, it became an "object," something public, while in reality that which we moved about in, without this ever being formulated, was not a thing, admittedly in the novel it had been given form, but the big difference between a novel and a newspaper article was that the first belonged to an intimate sphere – it was closely associated with an "I," a specific voice – which the novel reached beyond, as it also addressed itself to one or more readers, although it never left what was its own and what was personal; a newspaper article, on the other hand, had no such personal ties, and therefore it changed everything that was in the novel and turned it into something else, something public and general, with the power of a judgment: Knausgaard has no friends, Knausgaard loses control of himself when he drinks, Knausgaard yells at his children. And that was how it was with everything I wrote in that novel. The novel is an intimate genre and its intimate nature doesn't change even if eight thousand copies are printed, because it is read by only one person at any one time and would never leave the private sphere. But when the newspapers discussed what I wrote, there was no longer any connection with this private sphere, there was no longer any connection with the intimate sphere, it was objective and public, detached from the "I," and even though it was still related to me and my world, it was solely via my name, its exterior, "Knausgaard," one object among other objects – and only then did what the novel was about become a "thing." I had decided not to read any of the interviews I was going to do, or any of the reviews, they would make me die of self-hatred when I saw my inner self from the outside like that, but the *Dagens Næringsliv* journalist, a young Sørlander, had insisted I read his review before it went to print, which I did, and I would never do that again. In an e-mail to him

I compared my experience of this to an animal being transfixed in the beam of a searchlight.

I enacted various scenarios in my head as I sat in the airport, trying to find an answer to any questions that might crop up – while looking out the window at the planes standing in readiness and the small airport vehicles darting to and fro like toys against the backdrop of the vast, now sheer blue sky and the sun, which, shining from the other side, made the glass and metal sparkle wherever its rays struck; I gazed, too, at the throng of people, more here than anywhere else – until it was time to board, at which point I got up, put the newspapers in my backpack, and walked down the corridor to the gate, when another colossal surge of nerves, like a torrent of fear, quivered through my body as I sat down.

I had no doubt that *Fædrelandsvennen*, the newspaper in Kristiansand, would get as close to the truth as they could. They would probably be indignant, for one did not write about one's private life, and it was extremely likely they had spoken to Gunnar and would push me as hard as they could on that. Court case, lack of regard for the facts, unscrupulous exploitation of innocent people for personal gain.

I got up, I couldn't sit any longer, and went to the toilet, forced out a dribble of dark yellow pee, washed my hands, put them under the hand dryer or whatever they called the little hot-air machine attached to the wall next to the mirror. After coming out, I wandered down the corridor to a duty-free shop, cast an eye over the goods for a few minutes and walked back, the line for the plane had formed, the airline employee behind the gate desk had opened the door to the jet bridge and was busy checking passports and scanning ticket bar codes.

As the plane lifted from the runway and rose into the sky I scoured the land beyond the strait, searching for the house where we lived. It wasn't difficult; it was directly opposite the Hilton, which was the second-highest building in Malmö. It was incomprehensible that only two hours earlier I had been sitting there and looking up here, and also that everything down there had felt as big as up here, because from where I was now I could not only make out the balcony where I usually sat, I could also see all the square kilometers of buildings around it where several hundred thousand other bright sparks sat looking at the world as if they were the only ones in it.

Linda and the children must be up by now, I thought, and recognized first Landskrona, then Helsingborg below me, after which the countryside became anonymous and featureless and somehow homogenized: fields, yeah, right; roads, yeah, right; villages, yeah, right. I took out the newspapers and read until the plane started its descent toward Gardermoen, and I looked down on the sunlit woodlands, dark green with the scattered reds and yellows of autumn, like cries from more unruly trees rent with yearning and happiness and death amid the tranquil, paternal spruces and firs.

A river, dark, some fields, yellow. Some cars, which seemed lonely even when in long lines of traffic. Everything below bore all the signs of waiting for winter not even the Indian-summer sun could erase.

Slowly the plane descended from the sky until the wheels hit the ground and began to roll along the runway, the flight attendant's voice welcomed us to Oslo and asked us to keep our seat belts fastened, which almost everyone ignored, we knew it wasn't dangerous anymore, no one would punish us if we didn't obey, that was what you call freedom.

Click, click, click, everywhere. I usually waited until almost everyone had left the plane before I got up, but now I was short of time, so I pushed my way into the aisle, shrugged on my backpack, and switched on my phone, as everyone around me was doing. I hadn't received any text messages of course, I never did, but no one else knew that.

I put the phone in my inside pocket and met the gaze of a woman in her fifties, she had just lifted a bag down from the overhead bin and was twisting around to place it on the floor.

"Fantastic books you write," she said. "Thank you very much."

Embarrassed, I returned her gaze, my cheeks warm, my lips forming a half smile.

"*A Time for Everything* is the best book I've read in years," she continued.

"Thank you," I said. "That's nice. I'm happy to hear that."

She gave me a warm smile and then turned to face the front again.

A stranger had never addressed me to talk about my books before. If that wasn't a good sign, I didn't know what was.

An hour later I got out of a taxi in Kristian Augusts gate, paid, and walked through the gateway of the building where Oktober had its offices. The publishing house had just extended its premises and now occupied two floors; I assumed it was the money that Anne B. Ragde's books had generated that had made this possible. I rang the bell, fortunately someone buzzed the door open without asking who I was, I hated standing in front of those little boxes and introducing myself. When I got up to the first floor there was Silje, waiting for me. I was given a cup of coffee, we went up to the floor above and I sat down on the black leather sofa just inside the door where the first interview was to take place and lit up. Geir Berdahl came in to say hello, perhaps it had been the smell of cigarette smoke that had reached him in his office at the other end. He told me the book hadn't arrived yet. It was supposed to have been here the day before, but the truck had been involved in an accident in Sweden; as far as he understood, it had gone off the road to avoid a wild boar. He laughed, I smiled. Then he turned serious, as was his wont, reined himself in after all his merriment and said this wasn't good, tomorrow it was being reviewed in all the newspapers and there wasn't a single copy in any of the bookshops. But he would personally drive a consignment to the big bookshops in Oslo early tomorrow, he said with a fleet-ing smile, and returned to his office after wishing me good luck. I sat back down on the sofa, Silje came in with a thermos of coffee, a cup for the journalist, water, and some glasses. I visual-ized a truckload of books between lines of trees in a Swedish forest, the driver climbing down from his cabin, a phone pressed to his ear, smoke rising from the hood, total silence after the door has slammed shut. Then I pictured Geir Berdahl with di-sheveled hair and tousled beard driving through the streets of Oslo in a small Toyota crammed with books. That must have been how he worked in the seventies when Oktober was a Marxist-Leninist publishing house with its own chain of book dealers through whom they distributed translations of Marx and Mao to the Norwegian population. I knew next to nothing about that period, everything was wreathed in myth, and I decided I would ask him the next time an opportunity offered itself. In fact I had given him nothing but trouble; I owed the company a lot of money because I hadn't had a book published for five years – although I had no idea how much; it could be anywhere between three and seven hundred thousand kroner, and now that I had finally fin-ished a novel he had to deal with my uncle, who was sending him malicious, rabid e-mails, and talk to him on the phone, as well as having to engage a firm of lawyers to scrutinize my man-uscript and all the details of the case. That this should happen to me was actually pretty damned idiotic and unbelievable. I had never gone looking for trouble in my life, as far as possible I tried to be kind and friendly and polite and decent, I just wanted ev-eryone to like me, that was all, and here I was, in such a storm of aggrieved people and lawyers, not through ill fortune but fol-lowing a reasonable response to an act I had committed. I wanted nothing more than to write and be an author, so how could I have ended up in a situation where lawyers had to read everything I wrote? I had their observations at home along with the usual consultants' reports I had received over the years, and it was remarkable how different the lawyers' ones were. In normal circumstances this would have been interesting because the law was language, and when it had to be applied, it wasn't in any absolute way, it was always a question of an assessment, which had to be formulated with as much precision and exactitude as possible. The lawyers had to describe whatever the case might be, in other words what had happened, and in court this was of course often the crux of the conflict: what had actually happened? And once this was established, with what motives? And to what effect? It was not unlike a novelist's work.

The difference was that the lawyers not only had to understand the acts in themselves but also how they applied to the law, which furthermore was in writing, formulated on the basis of expectation regarding future events, thus as a kind of prognosis – based on thousands of years' experience of mankind, which indicated that theft, embezzlement, and murder would continue to occur while some of the more culture-specific laws died as the culture that had necessitated them also died. Actions were language-less, while the law and its interpretation were language-based. A law without language was as inconceivable as a poem without language. Law and poetry were connected; they were two sides of the same coin.

One of the other editors walked past, smiled, congratulated me on my book, and disappeared into his office. Silje talked me through the schedule, I listened with half an ear; it was a long time since I had dreaded anything so much. The doorbell rang, that would be the journalist, and I went into the bathroom for a pee and to put some more gel in my hair, there was to be a photo session after the interview.

When I returned, the journalist from the Norwegian News Agency had arrived. She was dressed in a way, or had an air about her, that I associated with motorbikes. We shook hands, she said the photographer was on his way, we sat down, she began to ask her questions, it was going very well, I thought, and the questions were of a general nature except when they concerned me. Half an hour or so later I was in the backyard being photographed and then I was ready for the next item on the agenda, the telephone interview with *Bergens Tidende*. I spent the intervening minutes in Geir Gulliksen's office; he had come while I was doing the interview with the NNA journalist. We talked about the next novel. We had edited the first one together here, he had sat with the manuscript in front of him, I had the computer, and we had worked through his suggestions, most of which were deletions. Apart from the opening, which we considered removing because the tone was so different from the rest of the manuscript, and the long passage about the new year's party, which he wanted to take out, I did exactly what he recommended. I could see at once it was better. The text was tighter and had more force. Now, sitting there, him on his swivel chair by the desk, me on a chair up against the wall, I asked him when we should begin editing the second volume. It had been ready for a while, but when all the fuss surrounding the first started I realized it couldn't come out in its present form, it was far too aggressive and in some parts almost slanderous, I had been frustrated and angry when I wrote it, and the frustration and anger had occasionally infused it in ways that would damage both me and those I had written about. I had deleted the worst of it, but the balance was still wrong. The idea was that I should write about my life as it was now and then go back in time, through my childhood, up through my teenage years into adulthood, to end with meeting Linda in Sweden, in such a way that our love story, which was so intense, would cast its light back on the events of the second book. But the patience this required was inhuman, the picture I painted of us too one-dimensional, and it felt as if what was supposed to provide depth and perhaps give a rationale was too far ahead for it to work. So one morning, only a week earlier, I had sat down and written the story of when we met and what happened between us. Almost exactly twenty-four hours later I had finished, the story had turned into fifty pages and exuded the light the novel needed so that all the rest would not be incomprehensible. I had an hour's sleep, then I left to do an interview with *Dagbladet* in the café in Malmö Art

Gallery, exhausted in a way I felt only when I had been drinking the night before.

"We don't need to do any more," Geir said now. "We'll publish it as it is."

"Do you mean that?" I said.

"Yes, I do," he said.

"Are you sure?"

"As sure as I can be."

"No deletions? Nothing?"

"The little there is we can do at the proofreading stage."

"I'll have to trust you," I said.

"Yes, you will," he said with a laugh. "By the way, how did it go with the NNA?"

"It went pretty well, I think. But now it's *Bergens Tidende*. I'm dreading it."

"It'll be fine," he said. "I talked to him yesterday, as I told you. What was his name? Tønder?"

"Yes."

"First off he said he just wanted a bit of background info about you. But I knew right away he had an agenda."

"What was it then?"

"Well, it was all about the biographical details."

"So he knew about Gunnar?"

"He did."

"What did you tell him?"

"I told him I couldn't talk about your book in those terms. I think he understood. He just asked about this and that. I don't think you have anything to fear."

"I hope not," I said.

Silje knocked on the half-open door and popped her head in.

"You can call him from an office on the floor below," she said.

"Now?" I asked.

"Yes, I think he's probably ready and waiting."

I got up and followed her down the stairs. The office was at the back to the left. The coffeepot and my cup had mysteriously moved to the desk there. Beside the phone lay a pen and a pad. Silje passed me a slip of paper with a phone number on it.

"Here's his number," she said. "Dial zero first."

"Thank you," I said, and sat down. She left and closed the door behind her. It went through my head that I didn't have to call. I doodled on the pad. Then I pulled myself together, lifted the receiver, and dialed the number.

The voice at the other end spoke Bergen dialect, and whenever I've heard anyone speaking Bergen dialect since, I have heard that voice resonate and it's sent shivers down my spine. It is the most unpleasant voice I have heard in the forty-nine years I have been alive and it was the most unpleasant conversation I have ever had. It wasn't what the voice said, I don't remember that very clearly, no, it was the tone it was said in, which fluctuated between flattery and condemnation, though without ever relinquishing a sense of self-righteousness, however insidious or covert.

During the two years that have passed since the first volume of this novel appeared I have met a lot of journalists, and I have always had something good to say about them, there has always been something conciliatory about them, whatever they have written and however stupidly or nonsensically or uncompromisingly they have described me, but there was nothing conciliatory about this voice, it was just hideous, and I never want to hear it again. After the interview was over I felt nauseous, and repulsive to myself, the voice had been in my ear, in my head, and I had never realized before that a voice was an alien force that could penetrate your body and fill you with its being. The worst thing about this voice was that it seemed to be trying to lure me into a trap, a bit like the way you can imagine the police interrogate their suspects, switching between everyday topics in order to gain their confidence and give them enough scope to slip up, to say more than they should, only then to ask a question that can nail them. You weren't there, were you? You were actually there, weren't you? You can tell me. I know what really happened.

The voice was like that. It asked me why I hadn't written about my mother in the novel. That is a strange question to ask a novelist who has written about his relationship with his father and his father's death. Why did Kafka write letters only to his father and not to his mother? The voice didn't ask the question because it wondered why my mother wasn't in the novel, it knew that very well, underlying the question was an accusation, unformulated but obvious, and all it wanted was for me to admit it. I didn't, of course. Instead I said it was a book about my father and my father's death, not about my mother and my mother's death, and the voice, which didn't believe a word of what I said made a mental note to be used later when I contradicted myself and was beginning to fall into the trap. It was an interrogation, not an interview. The voice assured me it had really enjoyed the book and asked some relatively harmless questions. It wanted to know in what way the novel related to reality. After my answer he said that I had claimed the novel was about reality, but it was also at odds with reality, and he wanted to know how I could explain that.

"You write that your father lived for two years with his mother. But that's not true, is it? He stayed there for only two months, didn't he?"

"I did not write that," I said. "That's not in the book. It doesn't say anything about how long he lived there."

"Yes, it does. It says he lived there for two years."

"No, it doesn't. I took it out. You couldn't have read that. It's not there."

The voice was silent for a few seconds. Then, in a confidential, deeper tone, it said:

"As you know, I've spoken to your family."

"You've spoken to Gunnar?"

"Yes. He says what you've written doesn't correspond with the facts. In the book you're presented as a hero. But actually you're not such a fine fellow. You didn't really clean the whole house, now did you. You don't know how to clean, isn't that the truth of the matter?"

I said I had cleaned the house exactly as I had described, and that cleaning was about the only thing I could do well, but it wasn't possible to talk about the novel in this way, discussing whether it was me or my uncle who had cleaned the house, this was absurd. Again I could tell the voice wasn't taking in a word of what I said, and I had myself lived with the image it had of me ever since I hit puberty, I was an untrustworthy little shit with a high opinion of myself, no morality, no self-restraint, none of the common decency necessary to be a respectable person. And I had written that I had cleaned my grandmother's entire house after my father's death to present myself in a favorable, honorable light whereas in fact it had been my uncle who had cleaned the place. And I had turned my father's death into something verging on the grotesque and transformed what had been an ordinary heart attack into the result of a self-destructive hell on earth and, not content with that, I had even dragged my ever-kind, sweet old grandmother through the mud and mire, which was mine and no one else's. And behind all this towered my mother, the Knausgaard-Avenger, who had turned her son's head.

Why hadn't I written more about my mother? Why had I described her in such positive terms and my father in such negative ones? Why had I written that my father lived with my grandmother for two years when the truth was that he had stayed there for two months, and barely that? Why had I written that I had cleaned the whole house when I barely knew anything about cleaning and had actually got in the way?

It wasn't just that the voice obviously believed everything that Gunnar had told it, including the theory that it was my mother who had indoctrinated me, which upset me so much I felt nauseous sitting there with the phone in my hand, it was also the insidious way this was expressed, faintly acknowledging I was good at writing while at the same time maintaining I lied and was mendacious, an immoral person, yes, that voice spoke to me as if I were a criminal. It was one thing for Gunnar to do this, after all he was deeply involved in this business, and I was the one who had involved him, against his will, so regardless of whatever accusations he came up with, I was to blame. But this voice wasn't involved, I wasn't to blame for any of its accusations, yet it passed judgment on me, with all the moral legitimacy and self-righteousness the post of journalist at Bergen's biggest newspaper could accord while nonetheless wanting something from me and needing me, for the sake of the news story. It knew: no me, no article, so it both condemned and begged me at one and the same odious time.

Yes, it was an odious voice.

I knew it had believed Gunnar. Berdahl, who had also spoken to Gunnar on the phone, said he came across as collected, sensible, and moderate. It was only in his e-mails that he unleashed his fury. The crime correspondent at *Bergens Tidende* had spoken to him on the phone and believed him. Gunnar was an accountant, a respectable citizen, as was the voice, I could imagine, and when my novel was read with that in mind he saw exactly what Gunnar saw: I was untrustworthy, mendacious, and had written the novel because I hated the Knausgaard family and, prompted by my mother, wanted to take revenge on them. With that Gunnar had deprived me of all my independence and individuality: even hating was not something I did of my own accord but on behalf of my mother. He had turned my novel into a burlesque, something unworthy and contemptible. *Bergens Tidende* agreed with him about everything. I had lied, and what I had written was not a novel but trivial and socially unacceptable, an attack on living people in book form.

I didn't think any of this during the conversation with that insidious, half-begging, half-condemning voice because it had taken over, I had more than enough to do defending myself, and not even when the interview was over did I think about it. The sense that I was a criminal and the fear of the consequences of what I had written, which was now beginning to make itself felt, shut out everything else. It was these same feelings that had raged inside me throughout the end of summer. Completely under their sway, my mind in turmoil, which can happen when a catastrophe beckons but still hasn't struck, I left the room, went up to the floor above and into Geir's office. I felt sick and my insides were trembling. But just sitting there helped. I told him what had been said and when Geir Berdahl came in I repeated it. Geir told me the journalist had said the same to him the evening before: my father hadn't stayed for more than two months with his mother and I hadn't cleaned the house as I had written. Geir had thought the journalist was testing this out on him and wouldn't make the same allegations in an interview with me.

"But I soon realized he wasn't interested in the novel. He was only interested in this. It was his news story."

"Fortunately I told him I wanted to read everything connected with Gunnar," I said. "So he said he would e-mail it to me in the course of the day."

"That's good," Geir said. "It'll be coming out soon and we'll have to take a stand on it. I'm not sure it's going to be much of a problem."

"Actually Siri Økland was down to do this interview," I said. "Einar Økland's daughter. But then they put him on it. Slightly heavier artillery. He's a former crime correspondent, you know."

"That's right. You said."

"Oh, shit," I said.

Geir laughed.

"It'll be fine, Karl Ove," he said.

"That's the most unpleasant conversation I've ever had. He flattered and humiliated me at the same time. My God, and in such a creepy way."

"Yes, he was unpleasant. I thought the same."

"And now it's *Fædrelandsvennen*'s turn. This is the one I've dreaded most. If *Bergens Tidende* rang around my family what do you think they would have been up to?"

"I don't think they'll have done anything," Geir said.

"I hope you're right," I said, getting up. "That *BT* interview was the worst experience of my life."

I went down into the street with Silje, where the sun was

shining, bright and clear, past the National Gallery and down Karl Johans gate. On the way I stopped outside a newspaper kiosk and picked up a copy of *Morgenbladet*. Silje, who understood what was going through my mind, said there wasn't a review section today. I put it back on the stand, we entered the Grand Hotel, where Ibsen used to sit with a mirror in his top hat, and took the elevator up to the bar at the top, where the journalist and the photographer from *Fædrelandsvennen* were waiting. I sat down with the journalist at a table on the terrace. She had made a point of wearing sunglasses so that she didn't have to look into my eyes. The book had shaken her, she said. From the way she spoke I realized she hadn't made any moral judgments. I talked about what she wanted to talk about, as warily as possible, beneath the blue, cloudless September sky, and afterward the photographer took pictures of me on the other side of the terrace. I did another interview, this time with a journalist from *Morgenbladet*, and I sat smoking and drinking Farris mineral water and coffee while answering his questions. His name was Håkon, I seemed to remember, or it might have been Harald, he came from almost the same place as me, had grown up on the other side of the bridge, and wanted to talk about it, and that was good because as a result there was some distance from both me and the book.

After lunch I took a taxi up to NRK. I arrived twenty minutes early, so I sat down on a rock outside and was having a smoke in the sunshine when I heard a Swedish voice from somewhere, I turned and saw Carl-Johan Vallgren, a Swedish writer I had met a couple of times in Stockholm, getting out of a taxi and walking toward the reception desk. He was about to launch his latest book in Norway. I stubbed out my cigarette and followed him. He was standing with his back to me as I entered, so I placed my hand on his shoulder, which normally I would never do to anyone, but somehow circumstances had colluded to bring me in here. He turned and when he saw who it was he smiled. He was wearing a suit, and his seventies shirt with large collar points was open at the neck. We shook hands, I said I had enjoyed his last book, he said all the writers in Oslo had been talking about me ever since he arrived, and their voices were not without a touch of envy. He was laughing as he spoke and turned to face the lobby, where someone was coming to fetch him. See you, I said, yes, see you, he replied, after which I went out for another smoke and to call Linda. Meeting him had put me in a better frame of mind, he was the kind of person who lifts your mood when you meet them, some people are like that, not many. I definitely wasn't one of them.

Linda was sitting outside at a café in Malmö, where the weather was good too. The morning had gone well, she said, her mother had arrived and in the evening my mother would be arriving. I said the interviews had gone fine and there were two more to do before I left to see Axel and Linn. Sounds good, I'm looking forward to tomorrow, she said. I answered that I was too, and then we said goodbye and hung up.

The interview with *Søndagsavisen* went pretty well. Afterward Siss Vik met me in reception and we went up to her office and did the interview for *Ordfront*. For the first time that day I spoke about literature. What I said was vague and not very good, but it was about literature and that in itself felt cathartic. I imagined it was a bit like how a shy plumber might feel after having to speak all day to the media about himself and his feelings, his family and friends, when at long last, late in the afternoon, he was able to talk about pipes and washers.

I took a taxi from NRK to Axel's, he didn't live that far away, and when I arrived he had made *fårikål*, lamb and cabbage stew, the whole apartment was full of a smell that took me straight back to the autumns of my childhood. He said he figured I didn't get much of this stew in Sweden, at any rate that had been his experience when he lived there, it had been one of the things he missed. He was right about that, apart from once during the first autumn Linda and I were together, when I was busy explaining to her who

I was and where I came from and therefore made both *fårikål* and *pinnekjøtt*, mutton ribs, I hadn't tasted it since I moved to Sweden.

Linn, Axel's wife, had to go somewhere after work. I sat in the kitchen with Axel's sons, Erik and Johan, eating lamb stew and drinking beer. I had arranged to visit them for exactly this reason, being with a family was balm for the soul, there was something good about it, maybe also something innocent, certainly uncorrupted. If I had gone to a hotel room after the interviews everything that had been said and done in the course of the day would have still been there, washing back and forth inside me, and it was not beyond the bounds of possibility that I would have ended up lying on the bed crying, it had happened before. Geir Angell had laughed when once I told him this, he said that was just like Arthur Arntzen, the comic, performing as Oluf, he ordered sandwiches and milk to be brought up to his hotel room and then, after the shows, he sat there crying and eating. I'd laughed too, but when I was caught up in it I didn't laugh, I had more than enough to do just trying to survive. What actually upset me I had no idea, it was utterly indefinable, but it was as though all the malice I had in me opened up and had free rein on days like that. At the interviews it was all about pinning something down, giving form to something, in a way, in order to keep it at a distance, while that which was given external form created ever greater turbulence internally. When, some years ago, a TV channel ran a series of twenty-four-hour interviews with people in their own homes, including one with Jan Kjærstad, I discussed this with Tore, who told me I would have maintained the mask if they had done one with me, answering good-humoredly and politely throughout the day, but the minute they went out the door I would have gone to bed and burst into tears. I had never told Tore I cried after being on live TV, and I occasionally did so after run-of-the-mill literary events as well, so I gaped at him in puzzlement, how had he worked that out? Was I so easy to read?

So this, stew and beer, at a kitchen table in Oslo, with Axel and his sons, the sun low and the air cold outside, was exactly what I needed.

I had met Axel in Stockholm four years earlier, one evening Helena's actor friends had called her, they had a football team and were short of players and asked if Jörgen, her partner, could play for them. He phoned me and asked if I felt like coming out. I did. On a soft shale pitch somewhere outside Stockholm, in a sort of industrial area, it was cold and dark, the floodlights a bright yellow. I hadn't kicked a ball for many years and was put at left back, where I could cause the least damage. The team consisted entirely of actors, and it was comical, at half-time most of them talked about their own performances, what they had or hadn't done, with no regard for the team as a whole, in a cacophony of egocentricity. The coach, a man of around thirty who played at center half, gave his instructions in a dark Stockholm accent. He and the other center half came over to me after the game, it turned out they were both Norwegians. The coach's name was Axel, an Østlander, the other was Henrik, a Kristiansander, they had gone to acting school in Stockholm together and both lived in the capital. Karl Ove, Henrik said. You wouldn't be Knausgaard, would you? Yes, I said, and they laughed because they had both read my books and they must have thought the odds of bumping into me out here on a muddy field on the edge of Stockholm in the autumnal gloom were fairly low. I continued to play for them and then one Saturday Axel texted me, wondering whether I would like to go to his son's birthday party. I was sure he had made a mistake, sent the text to the wrong person, and I politely declined. But it hadn't been a mistake, he still got in touch now and then, we met a few times outside the football context, and when he and Linn came on the occasion of Vanja's second birthday, Linn was surprised to see a poster for a short film for which Linda had written the script and asked how it came to be hanging there. It transpired that Linn had produced the film. Their children were the same age as ours and we started seeing each other regularly.

Axel was a friendly, considerate person, but on the football field I had seen another side to him, an aggression and a drive that seemed alien to his usual self; once we had been to see a football match in Råsunda, on the way back we were in the crowd catching the metro when a man sat down on the seat I was about to occupy, Axel almost flew at him in a rage. I couldn't get these sparks to tally with the person he normally was because if anything typified his personality it was gentleness, and it was genuine, an innate quality from what I could see, not something he had learned. Linn was also considerate, although inside her there was an edge too, she wasn't afraid to be direct and she couldn't care less what others thought about what she said or did. As far as family life was concerned, they were on a different plane from us, they had a house and a car and order in their finances. She worked as a TV producer for SVT; he worked as a freelance actor. They had met on set while making an ad; that was one of the first things he told me. Sometimes we had lunch at my regular place next to the office, often we got together over the weekend, and every Monday during the season when we played a match. We kept in touch even after we moved to Malmö and they moved to Oslo, though the intervals between seeing each other were becoming longer and longer. Axel and Linn were generous sorts who invited us to all kinds of things and resolved all the practical details along the way. One Easter they asked us to stay with them at a mountain cabin his father owned, and once they invited us to Berlin, where he had been given the use of an apartment. We hadn't invited them to anything, how could we, there were no cabins or houses in our family and we didn't have the money to rent one. But they didn't seem to keep a tally.

After eating we flopped down on the sofa with a beer to wait for Linn to return so that we could go out. I was so tired that I barely knew what I was saying. It had been a terrible day. And tomorrow everything would be in the papers.

Sometime later, walking toward the center along the streets

in the western part of town, the night sky was dense and star-spangled. Leaves lay under all the trees. The air was crisp, crystalline, though not cold, it still retained the heat of the day, which died away very slowly. We sat down at a table outside Tekehtopa, just by the hotel, had a couple of beers and chatted. As I had to do a reading at the Opera House the next day and the last thing I needed was a hangover, I left after an hour to go to bed. Axel accompanied me into the hotel as Silje had promised they would drop off two copies of the book when it came out, and the receptionist passed me the packet with a smile and glanced over furtively as I opened it. I signed one and gave it to Axel, said goodbye, and took the other up to my room, where I put it in my backpack, then undressed, switched on the TV, and lay watching until I could no longer keep my eyes open. At some point in the night I must have woken up and switched off the television because when I opened my eyes at around six the screen was black and silent. I showered, dressed, and went down for breakfast. All the newspapers were laid out on the table, but I gave them a wide berth, I didn't want to know. Got myself some scrambled eggs, bacon, sausages, and some bread, a little juice and a cup of tea, sat down, glanced across at the pile of newspapers. What I didn't want to see was the interviews. They were in *Dagbladet Magasinet*, *Dagens Næringsliv*, and *Dagsavisen*. But the reviews? I had decided not to read them. But I had to find out whether they were a catastrophe or had gone well. I had an agreement with Geir that he would text me when he'd read them, to say how they were. But it was only seven o'clock, he could be hours yet.

What the hell, a quick look at the intro couldn't hurt.

I got up and picked up *Dagbladet*, carefully avoiding the magazine section, flicked through to the culture pages. There it was.

I was burning inside as my eyes ran down the lines.

It looked good.

It had gone well.

I wondered if it had gone just as well in *Dagens Næringsliv*?

I put *Dagbladet* back and picked up *Dagens Næringsliv* instead, went to the table, did the same, avoided the interview and flipped through to the review.

This one had gone well too.

Phew.

With a cup of coffee in my hand I had a smoke outside the hotel entrance and watched the few people walking along the street at such an early hour. The sky was as blue as it had been yesterday and the sunlight was already streaming down over the roofs and spires.

The reading at the Opera House was part of a kind of book day organized by the book clubs. I didn't want to read anything from the first volume and had instead chosen a passage from the second, it was about a Rhythm Time baby class I had once been to in Stockholm, and I had selected this because I hoped it would make people laugh. I had done two readings from Book 1, the first at the invitation of Ingvar Ambjørnsen, who was the honorary resident writer at Bergen International Festival, on which occasion I chose the opening I had just written; the second was at a Litteraturhuset event, when I chose the scene where Yngve and I arrived at the house in Kristiansand. Both passages were about death, and if there was anything that dampened the atmosphere at a function it was of course a reading about death and decay, and as this was an autobiographical novel and not something I had made up I felt as though I was forcing myself and my gloomy personality on them and ruining their evening by my mere presence. After the last time at Litteraturhuset I had decided I wouldn't do it again. Hence comedy, hence the Rhythm Time scene. Book 2 was a comedy, but a comedy deep, deep below the surface. It was about a man who was trapped in his own self-delusions and a family which was also trapped in its self-delusions, and this led them into highly undignified situations, which would have resolved themselves if they had only looked at each other and said they had been deluding themselves, this is the reality and it didn't matter. But they couldn't, it was precisely this that was impossible, they did the opposite, they looked at each other and said it mattered.

The hotel was around the corner from the publishing house, and after a while I strolled over to print out the passage I was going to read; my printer at home hadn't worked. Geir Berdahl was there packing the books he was going to deliver by car with his daughter Maria, with whom I had only a passing acquaintance, I had never spoken to her. It was irritating that on the very day when the papers were full of reviews the book wasn't on the shelves, because this focus and interest lasted for only one day, by the following week all the attention would already be on the wane, unless the book was nominated for some prize or other, in which case it might be rekindled for a few days. When my debut book came out the publishers had gone for a very small print run, and when it sold out they printed another two hundred copies, no more than that, and so it went on, with the result that for the whole of December, the sole month when books actually do sell in Norway, it wasn't in any of the bookshops. Sales figures in themselves meant nothing to me, but money did, especially now that there were five of us in the family and the royalties from the books were our only source of income apart from my scholarship.

I put the printout in my backpack, said goodbye to Geir and Maria, and walked down to the Opera House. I hadn't seen it before, except for its anonymous façade from the railway station and, standing in front of it, I was surprised. It really was a magnificent edifice. All that white stone gleaming, ablaze almost, in the sun next to the cool blue sea from which it rose. I walked up onto the roof, surveyed the harbor area as I smoked a cigarette, an hour to go to the reading. Leaning against a wall I took out a half-liter bottle of Pepsi Max, had a swig, got out my phone, and called Linda. She had packed and would soon be off to Kastrup, she said. My mother had also arrived; right now they were with the children at a playground. I said I was nervous and that it would be wonderful to go out in Prague this evening. She wished me luck and we hung up. I switched off the phone and put it in my backpack. Once when I was being interviewed onstage it had rung and the audience laughed; it was just the sort of thing audiences laugh at. Audiences wanted to laugh, they zeroed in on anything comical and always burst into laughter when there was something funny, almost irrespective of how trivial. An audience over a certain size has its own dynamics and its own mind-set regardless of the individuals that constitute it. Something they would never have laughed at on their own, they would never have found amusing in a million years because it was so petty, could, in an auditorium, generate howls of laughter. And when they sat there in silence, this silence could be indicative of a variety of very distinct moods. Boredom, indifference: then it was as though what was said dispersed and disappeared like smoke. Responsiveness, interest: what was said hung in the air and it was as though there were a greediness in the room, which was a fantastic and exhilarating response to have. I often read the same texts, but the atmosphere is never the same; sometimes a particular passage makes everyone laugh, at others there is total silence. A scene can be explosive one evening and appear flat and meaningless the next. Some of this depends on my delivery: as I come across as very serious, and occasionally also somber, it's as if my very presence seems to stifle the comedy, whereas when I am able to chat first the laughter comes more easily. But for the most part it comes down to the audience, its particular makeup and the atmosphere of the venue.

I threw my cigarette down, stepped on it, and made my way toward the entrance. The plaza outside was thronged with people. Right in front of the door I bumped into Vetle Lid Larssen. We had the same publisher once, but I had never spoken to him or even said hello. So what should I do? Pretend I hadn't seen him? That might seem haughty or dismissive. But greeting him didn't seem natural either; we didn't know each other.

"Hi," I said.

"Hi," he said. "Congratulations on the reviews!"

"Thank you," I said.

"See you," he said, slipping inside the door. I followed him, plowed my way through all the people, located a young woman who appeared to have something to do with the event, she did, just a minute, she said, and went to find someone else who took me backstage. Narrow corridors with black walls, sudden high-ceilinged areas full of wires and hoisting equipment, doors all over the place, and then a makeshift room behind some half-walls where we were to wait before going onstage. A bowl of fruit, some pots of coffee, and bottles of mineral water. Cathrine Sandnes, who was the emcee, was there, she gave me a hug and said something and laughed, she was one of those rare people who laughed all the time, and Dag Solstad, who was going to read after me, sat there with the head of a book club and some others I didn't know. I said hello and poured myself a coffee. I asked Cathrine how her children were doing, she told me a bit about them and showed me some photos on her phone, she asked after mine, I said they were fine. I couldn't remember when I had met her first, probably it had been with Espen and Frederik, I seemed to recall we were watching a football match and she was there, and someone told me she was the Norwegian champion in some martial art. She worked for *Dagsavisen* then. She had also interviewed me once; afterward, walking to the hotel, I remember we had talked about the mysterious expression "in form" – the immensely successful phase sportsmen and -women can experience when all the shackles fall off them – with respect to writing. As a writer you can also go through a phase where nothing works and then all of a sudden you are in the zone, and everything works. It is all in your head. Football, writing, tae kwon do. Cathrine was now editor in chief at *Samtiden*, married to Aslak Sira Myhre, whom I remembered from Bergen, initially I knew him only from a distance, as an ultra-left-wing student politician, afterward I got to know him better because he had been Tore's best friend when they were growing up in Stavanger and was an obvious model for the most important minor protagonist in Tore's novels about Jarle

937

Klepp. I had written an essay for *Samtiden* and had a little to do with Cathrine then. Over the years we had run across each other a few times and she hadn't changed in the slightest. Her most prominent character trait, at least the one that was most obvious, was that she was completely fearless. She wasn't affected by the terrors and tensions that abound in the art world. As was the case now, standing in the midst of a crowd of people, chatting and laughing with them on all sides.

She led me onto the stage, explained what she had planned: first of all, a brief introduction, then I would come on, stand there, she would ask a witty question about the title, and then I would read.

The blood drained from my head as I stood on the stage gazing at the empty auditorium in front of me. My face must have gone white with fear. We went back through the corridors and into the makeshift dressing room. I poured myself another cup of coffee, glanced warily at Dag Solstad, who was sitting on a chair a couple of meters away. I had met him several times before, most often in a publishing-house context, but I had never managed to say a word to him, not even about the weather. I wasn't afraid of him, it wasn't that, it was that I couldn't view him as a man of flesh and blood. He was already a writer when I was born, and not only that, he had already been hailed as the greatest writer of his generation. Throughout my life he had been "Dag Solstad," the great writer; so as a social fixture he was as well established as Gjensidige Forsikring insurance, the Ringnes Brewery, or the cup final, a status which incidentally he shared with Jan Erik Vold, who had also always been there, on TV and in the classroom, they were in a sense representatives of the writing fraternity, iconic images – the mild-looking man with the strange voice who read the poem about the loaf of bread and the bespectacled man with the unruly hair who mumbled and snuffled when he was asked about something. So there was an immense distance to be covered when I grew up and started reading their books in earnest, as works relevant to the present, and the wonderful part about this, when the iconic image breathes with life because you suddenly invest yourself and your experience and knowledge in it, can be compared to how your perception of your own parents changes when you become a parent yourself: suddenly their distant lives, their incomprehensible behavior, reflect something deeply human and universal, and they come to life. In this way "Dag Solstad" had come to life, but not as a person, only as a writer, for if there was one thing that characterized Dag Solstad's literary work it was that he wrote iconic books; they expressed something unclear and invisible in such a way that they became clear and visible, not just once but again and again. So the unmasking of "Dag Solstad" that the reading of his books brought about led only to another mask, for as icons the books weren't a reflection of the writer but the writer's time, and perhaps also contributed to forming it. One of his books opens with a person who is alone and out of shame raises his hands to his face. Reading that, I thought I had done a much better job and with greater profundity in my debut novel, in which the main character is constantly ashamed and no stranger to the gesture and impulse that occasions the shame. In my hubris I even suspected Dag Solstad of having lifted it from my book. Back then I hadn't understood the value of the iconic, it was too alien to me, nothing in my life and writing coalesced to form an image, everything overflowed its banks. Now I understand. The iconic is the pinnacle of literature, its real aim, which it is constantly striving to achieve, the one image that contains everything within but still lives in its own right. The lonely man raising his hands to his face: the shame. The man who sets the scene for his own paralysis: inauthenticity. And the most pregnant and terrible of all of Solstad's images: the father witnessing his son accepting money to drive his friends around. That must be why Solstad was so preoccupied with Thomas Mann and Henrik Ibsen in his later books: they are the last great iconic writers. Mann's sanatorium in *The Magic Mountain* is the perfect setting for a novel, it is both a symbol and a place, in the same way that *Peer Gynt* and *Brand* are symbols and characters. All literature wants to go there, to the one essential symbol that says everything and is at the same time everything. *Heart of Darkness*, *Moby-Dick*, *Riverrun*.

I lifted my cup to my mouth and sipped the hot coffee, then lowered it as, to my mortification, tiny brown drops were running down the outside. I looked out at the auditorium, took another sip, wanting to chat with "Dag Solstad," but I didn't know about what. Once someone had said I just wanted to chat with the greats; ever since then I had been reminded of that remark whenever I was standing next to one of the "greats." Was it true? Did I want to chat only with them? Not *only* perhaps, but I had to admit I did want to, they had a magnetic appeal, being in a position to say something to them was a privilege, that was how it felt. On the other hand, it was also fawning. There was no doubt about it. Fawning and crawling.

I sought his eyes and met them.

"Do you have any opinions on Peter Handke?" I said.

It sounded a bit abrupt. But "Dag Solstad" didn't appear to notice. He shook his head and said actually he didn't. He had read some of his books, but that was a long time ago and he couldn't say he was particularly interested in Handke, no.

"I'm in the middle of reading a fantastic book by him now," I said. "*My Year in the No-Man's-Bay*, it's called. Have you read it? Think it came out in the eighties or maybe the nineties."

"No, I haven't. It's good, you say, is it?"

"Yes, it is."

That was it. There were a lot of people around, conversation flowed, people drifted in and out and soon it was time to go on-stage. Solstad didn't move, he wasn't on until half an hour after me, and when the technician had attached a mic to me I stood behind the curtain, beside the flashing mixing desk, waiting for the applause to die down and Cathrine to introduce me. Then I walked across the stage, she asked her question, the audience laughed, I waffled something trite, she took a few steps back, and I started reading. After I had finished I went backstage, removed the mic and hurried into the foyer, which was still full of people, crossed the plaza, and dashed up onto the footbridge, also crowded, in some places so packed that I had to stand and wait, until, on the other side by the train station, I found a taxi and gave the driver the address of Thorenfeldt's photographic studio in west Oslo. We drove through the glittering, sunlit autumn streets and after I had paid and got out I saw a man waving at me from a doorway around fifty meters away. I half ran over, was led into the studio where Hanne Ørstavik and Ingvar Ambjørnsen were waiting, the former wearing a vintage dress, from the 1920s or the 1930s perhaps, and the latter a white dinner jacket with a white top hat. Thorenfeldt himself appeared and shook hands, he was a portly man who obviously laughed a lot, at least he was now. I was given a pile of clothes, all white, stepped into a cubicle and put them on. The trousers were much too big, they hung off me like a sack, but with suspenders they were fine, the assistant said when I emerged, and away we went. We lined up for the photo, Thorenfeldt played some Frank Sinatra at full blast, laughed and shouted as we three squeezed together and posed, with and without hats, and finally Hanne was given confetti, which she threw into the air as a kind of finale. It was all over in ten minutes. The photos were for a chain of bookshops, as far as I could make out, and at first I had been dubious, which was my way of declining, it meant nothing to me since I had my literary credibility to think about, which this would undermine at a stroke. I wasn't that type of writer, I had thought, but then I allowed myself to be persuaded after all, it was important for the book, and "no" was one of the words I found hardest to say, I was too weak for that word, the thought of disappointing someone always outweighed any consideration of my credibility, so there I was, in the studio of a photographer who was used to working with celebrities, dressed up as some kind of literary revue artiste. And it had been fun. It had been fun to dress up, it had been fun to have my photo taken, it had been fun to stand there posing amid the laughter and blare of music. It helped that I was doing it with Ingvar Ambjørnsen and Hanne Ørstavik, I respected them both, and if they had signed up it couldn't have been that bad. It was a sellout. Yes, it was, but what had I actually sold? My soul. But I had already lost that anyway.

After the photo shoot I had a cup of coffee with Hanne at a nearby sidewalk café. We first met in the mid-nineties, I had done an interview with Rune Christiansen for *Vagant*, and he had invited me to the Oktober summer party. Espen was there, he was an Oktober writer, Mom's brother Kjartan was there, he was an Oktober writer, and at the table where I was assigned a place Hanne was there, who was also an Oktober writer. We chatted during the meal, but as I felt so inferior, being the sole nonwriter there, I moved to Espen's table as soon as we had finished eating, and stuck close to him for the rest of the evening. The next time I met Hanne was just after I had made my debut and she reminded me of that evening, of how impolite I had been, moving away from her as though she wasn't worth talking to. Since then we had met at various literary events at the publishing house, after I had moved from Tiden to Oktober. She was a novelist to her fingertips, uncompromising with regard to her books, and incorruptible. Rare qualities, both of them. As a person she was sensitive and there was something vulnerable about her, and perhaps it was the impossible equation, the uncompromising, incorruptible essence versus the openness to impressions of the world that made her novels so perfectly rounded and yet so testing. We had never talked at length apart from on one occasion a few weeks earlier, at a dinner held by Oktober after a press conference, when all our social inhibitions were suddenly thrown to the wind and we got down to the nitty-gritty. I talked about what my life was really like; she talked about what her life was really like. The openness had been restricted to that moment, now we just talked about our books for the most part and after a quarter of an hour I got up, the plane would be going soon, and I took a taxi to the train station, from where I caught the express to Gardermoen, checked in at the last moment for the Copenhagen flight, and finally plumped down onto a seat, alone.

The desperate rush through the departures hall reminded me of another time when I'd had to run to catch the plane home. At that time I had been carrying Vanja. She couldn't have been more than twelve months old. I had been invited to my uncle's child's confirmation ceremony, which was to take place outside Oslo, and as Linda was pregnant with Heidi and didn't want to fly, I had gone with Vanja. I wanted to show her to the family. Everything had gone well, except on the plane home when she had screamed without interruption for half an hour, and even my suit jacket was soaked with sweat. Now, the race across the airport having jogged my memory of the previous occasion, it struck me that that was probably the last time I had seen my family. Admittedly I had seen Gunnar and his sons once since then, in Mom's garden in Jølster, but that had been only for a few minutes. The confirmation had lasted all day, and all the people I had known all my life behaved in their own idiosyncratic ways, which I knew so well. The dynamics between the two brothers, all the wordplay, all the hackneyed phrases. Their children, who were becoming adults. Representing Dad and having Vanja with me made the occasion an enjoyable experience.

Holding Vanja in my arms, sensing the person she was, filled me completely as I sat in the stationary plane waiting for our turn to take off. My love for her seemed to collect in one point, overwhelming and uncontrollable, it hurt so much tears came to my eyes, and then it relinquished its hold on me and sank back into the depths as the plane began to taxi onto the runway. The sun was low, the shadows were long, I leaned back and closed my eyes in an attempt to doze. Of course it was impossible; too much had happened in the past two days. But now it was all about getting off this plane, onto the next, off again, a taxi to the city center, and then I would have a different world around me.

When we were up in the air and the Østland forests beneath us were becoming more and more distant, the passenger in the seat next to me, a woman in her late twenties or early thirties, blond with muscular arms, picked up *Dagbladet*, took out the magazine section, and started flipping through it. As soon as I saw that, I turned away and looked out the window. A few seconds later, in a diversionary move intended to appear as if I was opening the air vent above the seat, I glanced at the page she was holding steadfastly in front of her and discovered to my despair that she was reading the article about me. I glimpsed a photo of me before turning away again with my cheeks burning. She couldn't have realized that the man who was featured in the interview she was reading was in the seat beside her, otherwise she would have looked at me and said so, wouldn't she? If the krone dropped during the flight she would know why I had turned away so obviously and the situation would be embarrassing for both of us; she would have unmasked me, I would have been unmasked. But I couldn't tap her on the shoulder either and say: That's me you're reading about! That would have sounded completely stupid. If she had kept flipping through, it wouldn't have been so bad, but now she was reading every single word while I sat beside her, only a few centimeters away, with my head averted as far as possible. When she finished the interview I would have to continue hiding because the predicament was not over, even if the reading was.

She spent at least ten minutes on the interview, I was able to confirm after several sidelong glances at the silly magazine. It was odd that she didn't notice as my body must have been giving off all sorts of signals. But no, while I stared out the window for the long hour from Oslo to Copenhagen she quietly occupied herself, reading a bit, eating a bit, reading a bit more. Oh, what a relief it was when the plane landed, came to a halt, and she got up and went down the aisle and I could finally straighten my neck, breathe out, and relax.

Linda was waiting in the arrivals hall when I came out. She had dressed smartly and was happy. We kissed, checked in, and spent the hour before the plane departed having a beer in the café where I had been that morning. It felt decadent, I never drank when I traveled because there was always something I had to do on my arrival, and Linda and I seldom drank together anymore either because we always had children around us.

It was a feeling of freedom. For the next two days we could do exactly what we wanted. No children, no writing, no readings, no interviews. Just us two. The cloud hanging over everything, the book I had written about us that Linda hadn't read yet, I cast from my mind. There is a time for everything. She would get the manuscript on our return. For the moment she knew nothing and the weekend would be spent within that nothing.

The sun had gone down when we boarded the plane. The atmosphere in the bright cabin was quite different from what it had been on the Oslo-bound plane because the language on all the signs and advertising stickers was foreign, the faces of the cabin attendants another type, but also because of the darkness which, as we rose through the air, soon shut us in and defined the space with such incredible clarity: here we were, high above the ground, on our way down Europe to one of its old capitals while nameless, unknown towns lay like luminous jellyfish in a sea of darkness beneath us, and what the sharply defined space said was "travel," in the same way that a train compartment said travel, a ship's cabin said travel and for that matter a cabin on a zeppelin said travel. Not travel as movement but travel as mythology. Travel in the twenties and thirties; travel in the fifties and seventies. And not Europe in the sense of geography, but Europe as mythology. It was fantastic that the towns had been there in the Middle Ages, indeed that they had been what was the Middle Ages, what was the Renaissance, what was the Baroque, not to mention the world wars in the previous century, it was fantastic that they were still there, scattered across the continent beneath us, and they were so different, had such different auras and meanings, permeated by time, each in its own way. London and Paris, Berlin and Munich, Madrid and Rome, Lisbon and Oporto, Venice and Stockholm, Salzburg and Vienna, Bucharest and Manchester, Budapest and Sarajevo, Milan and Prague, just to name a handful. Prague, it was Golem, the man-made man, and it was Kafka. It was the Faustian Middle Ages and the nineteenth-century dual monarchy, it was the communist 1950s and the capitalist 2000s of the unsophisticated and vulgar Eastern European variety.

What was the difference between reality and our perception of it? Did reality exist, was it beyond our reach? For perception-less reality was also a perception.

What did the moods and impressions these names evoked mean? They meant nothing. But neither did our lives, if we took away our perceptions of them.

The hotel was by the river, beside the old bridge, and our room had windows overlooking the water. It wasn't luxurious, no minibar or TV, but it was classy in the same way that the old hotels along the fjords in Vestland are classy, those that have retained the interior from the turn of the previous century, as they had done here, unless they had re-created it, that is. We put down our luggage and went out to eat. It was nearly ten, so we chose the first – and the best – restaurant, on the other side of the bridge, with tables along the river illuminated by small lantern-like lights. It was hard to grasp, at least for me, that we were here, beside the black flowing water with the old bridge arched over it, the castle towering up behind us, it was as though everything that moved around us was somewhere else, even when we were crossing the bridge a short time before and had our feet on it, that had been the feeling.

We ordered a bottle of red wine and clinked glasses. Linda's dimly lit face blazed in the darkness, her eyes glittered, she placed her hand on mine and a warmth spread through me. The food arrived, we ate, from behind us came the sound of Norwegian voices and the feeling that we were completely free was gone, suddenly there were people who could see us. Linda noticed the change in me and asked what was wrong. I said there were Norwegians here and that I was beginning to weigh everything I said on their scales, hear everything with their ears. She said that sounded terrible and I had to stop doing it. I said I would try. Then I told her about what had happened on the plane. She laughed at me. We paid and wandered around the town before going back to the hotel. The next morning we woke up early and were unable to sleep in, even though we tried, our circadian rhythms were in tatters after five years with small children, instead we had breakfast and went out into the morning-empty, Sunday-quiet town which was slowly getting warmer, had a coffee at a café and on our way back a few hours later we bought tickets for a ballet that evening, Tchaikovsky's *Swan Lake*, which we thought must be wonderful here in old Eastern Europe. In the evening we dressed up, I put on a white shirt, a tie, and suit, Linda a dark dress, and then we left for the theater. I imagined marble staircases, balconies clad with red plush, men in tailed coats and women in white evening gowns. I had found instructions for how to get to the theater on the computer in the lobby, but I didn't print them out, and when we arrived in the area we walked around for a while, unable to find the street. With only ten minutes before the performance was due to start we began to run. Linda asked a woman in a kiosk where the theater was, she didn't understand, Linda showed her the ticket, she pointed, we set off in the direction she indicated, nothing, we came into an open square, no theater, we crossed it and ran down a narrow street where there was nothing but apartment buildings, turned, ran back, crossed the square again, Linda asked someone else, this time a fat man with a dog, he spoke English and said it was in the parallel street, we rushed off in that direction, found the name of the street, ran up and stopped, there it was at last. But instead of the large palatial theater I had imagined, something like the opera house in Proust's novel, we were standing in front of a building that looked more like a cinema of the run-down, lugubrious variety. Surely this couldn't be it? But, yes, it was, the name on the elegant, ornate tickets we had been given matched the name above the door. We entered, and the shabby music-hall feel of the building became even stronger. The auditorium was small and dowdy, the stage tiny, there was no orchestra pit, let alone an orchestra. The audience was meager and seemed for the most part to consist of disoriented tourists, but not as disoriented as the two of us, who had dressed up and were attracting interested looks as we made our way along the row of folding chairs to find our seats. Oh no, I said to Linda, what have we got ourselves into here? The dancing might still be all right, she said, taking my hand as we sat waiting. Around us the lights dimmed, but not much, and in front of us, on the stage, the lights came on at the same time as someone put on the CD they were going to dance to. The music came from two loudspeakers on a stand on either side of the stage, and after a few minutes without anything much happening two young ballet dancers jumped out, they must have been sixteen or seventeen, probably students, and from their dancing bodies came nothing, all their movements seemed to stay inside them as they gyrated and jumped and sallied back and forth across the stage, every step a thud on the floor. I was none too fond of ballet, I was there for Linda's benefit and squirmed with embarrassment at all the awkwardness and lack of grace unfolding in front of our eyes. Linda had spent so much time in front of the mirror preening herself. It was the only full evening we had in Prague and we were going to spend it here of all places. I looked at her. She looked at me. Then she smiled. I think it's the worst show I've ever seen, she whispered. And that's saying quite a bit, I've seen a lot of bad dancing. Shall we go, I whispered. Let's wait until the interval, she whispered. And we did. We found a bar instead, where we sat for the rest of the evening chatting and getting drunk. The next morning we slept in, had lunch somewhere at the foot of the hill where the castle stood, in a courtyard, and then we walked up to the castle, visited an art exhibition, and afterward went to an outdoor café on the margins of the castle precinct, overlooking a forest below. It was warm, like in summer, we both had a cold beer, suddenly she took out a pen and wrote down the song she had sung at my fortieth, six months earlier, after which she passed it to me. I had asked for it some months ago but had forgotten. I'd had a party at home, there were twenty-odd guests and I had let it be known that I didn't want any speeches. Espen, Tore, and Geir had taken no notice, so when Linda stood up I was expecting another speech.

"Vanja once said there are no grown-ups in this family," she said. "But I think you're well on the way to becoming one and I hope I'm not far behind. But I'm not going to make a speech. I was thinking of bursting into song. And as I never learned to play an instrument I was thinking of playing the ukulele."

She took a few steps back, and when she reappeared she was holding a ukulele. I knew she couldn't play and feared the worst. But it transpired one of the parents at the nursery school had taught her, she had learned the chords of a song, and whenever I had been out during the previous month she'd practiced.

So there she stood, playing and singing a song to me. It was the one she handed to me in the castle café and I read it with tears rolling down my cheeks.

Only once I saw that man
My eyes were transfigured
He moved like the wind
Swift and bold, master of his fate
He looked at me and smiled
He saw me blush and smiled
And he walked on by
But he did walk by

Then I saw the man again
My eyes were transfigured
He beamed like the sun
He was to turn my life around
He touched me and smiled
He touched my hand and smiled
And he didn't walk on by
No, he didn't walk by

The days have turned to years
And my eyes are transfigured
Such a man, such a man is he
A touch of his hand made my life complete
He looked at me and smiled
I saw his lion heart and smiled
Karl Ove, my beloved
I love you so, I love you so.

I had never even entertained the idea of having a party on my fortieth; it had been absolutely out of the question. But in early autumn the previous year, September 2008 to be more precise, when we had been visiting Yngve in Voss, Linda and Yngve had brought up the subject. We had been sitting on the veranda in the evening, after the children had gone to bed, each of us with a glass of red wine in hand. The sky above us was pitch-black and ablaze with stars. The air was cold and clear.

"We've been talking about your fortieth birthday," Linda said, looking at me in the faint light from the veranda door.

"Have you?" I said.

"Yes, we have. We've decided you should have a big party and celebrate it properly."

"Invite everyone you know," Yngve said. "And maybe Lemen and Kafkatrakterne could play."

"But that's the last thing I want," I said. "I couldn't imagine anything worse."

"We know that," Linda said. "But you've been hiding out for long enough, haven't you?"

"But there's nobody to invite."

"There are lots of people," Yngve said. "You know more people than you imagine. If you give it some thought."

"Possibly," I said, looking at Linda. "If it were up to me I'd celebrate it with you, like any normal birthday. That's nice, too. You come in with candles and presents and sing 'Happy Birthday.' That's enough celebration for me."

"Of course," Linda said.

"But this isn't for you," Yngve said. "It's to give everyone you know a chance to make a fuss over you. And to have a party. If you send out invitations in plenty of time so people can plan, book hotels, and planes, and so on, I'm sure everyone'll come. I'm definitely up for it anyway."

"That I don't doubt," I said with a smile. "But you didn't celebrate your own fortieth."

"And I regret it."

"So what do you say?" Linda asked.

"No," I answered.

Something about the suggestion did appeal to me though, it was true what Linda had said, I'd been hiding out for long enough.

Why had I done that?

It was a form of survival. In my terrible twenties I had tried to involve myself in the life around me, normal life, the one everyone lived, but I'd failed, and so strong was my sense of defeat, this glimpse of shame, that little by little, unbeknown to myself as well, I shifted the focus of my life, pushed it further and further into literature in such a way that it didn't seem like a retreat, as though I were seeking a refuge, but like a strong and triumphant move, and before I knew what was happening it had become my life. I didn't need anyone else, life in my study and the family was sufficient, actually, more than sufficient. It wasn't because I had problems with the social world that I withdrew from, no, it was because I was a great writer or wanted to be one. That solved all my problems and I thrived on it.

But if it was true that I was hiding, what was I frightened of?

I was frightened of other people's judgments of me, and to avoid this I avoided them. The thought that anyone would like me was a dangerous thought, perhaps the most dangerous one for me. It never occurred to me, I didn't dare think it. I didn't even think that Mom might actually like me. Or Yngve or Linda. I assumed they didn't, not really, but that the social and family bonds we were entangled in nonetheless meant that they had to see me and listen to what I had to say.

If I had been responsible for only myself there would have been nothing to consider. I would manage whatever the circumstances. But I had three children with Linda and didn't want them to grow up in a home that was hidden away, didn't want them to believe that hiding was an acceptable way of engaging with the world. All I could give them was what I was giving them now, and this wasn't given through what I said but what I did. I wanted them to be surrounded by people, I wanted them to become independent and fearless, able to develop their full potential, by which I mean to be as free as possible within the unfree limits of this society. And, most important of all, I wanted them to feel secure in themselves, to like themselves, to be themselves. At the same time they had the parents they had, I thought, and we couldn't change our personalities in any fundamental way, which would have been both senseless and catastrophic: having two parents who pretended to be something they weren't would obviously just bring more misery. This was about our living conditions. They were fixed, but not immutable. The way I had behaved during the first three or four years of having children, when, much too often, I took out my frustrations on them, must have affected their self-esteem, the one thing in them you, as a parent, mustn't fuck up. I had got out of this, it hardly ever happened anymore, we never argued in front of them now and I never lost my temper, but I said a silent prayer almost every day that this hadn't left any marks, that what I had done wasn't beyond redress. I imagined that their self-esteem was a beach, I had left my footprints there, but then the waves washed ashore, the sun shone, the sky was blue, and the water, so fantastic at adapting to its environment, covered everything, erased everything, salty and cold and wonderful.

I thought about this, but I knew I should never intervene directly, I should never let these concerns, which all parents feel, take on a form that they would notice and react to. Vanja wasn't even a year old when she began to close her eyes if strangers visited, and where did that come from? Was it genetic, a shyness so great that it forced her to shut out everything? Or had she picked it up from us, the atmosphere in the house, the way I behaved with other people? It continued, she hid from strangers, and if she couldn't do that she closed her eyes, the last occasion at the age of three and a half years old in the stroller one afternoon, we met one of the parents from school, Vanja slid down and pretended she was sleeping. It didn't matter, but it bothered me nonetheless, I just wanted her to be happy. The worst that could happen was that she noticed my unrest. I shouldn't tie them to me, shouldn't allow my concerns to be noticeable, I should just try to fix everything quietly. I had to snap out of my prevarications, my evasive looks, my reclusiveness, my life closeted in the study.

Linda had much of the same in her. But with her it was changeable: an introverted, depressed, and passive period in the daytime when she was unable to do anything but lie on the sofa and watch undemanding films was followed by an extroverted, enthusiastic, and very active period when she suddenly would swing the children around as if nothing in the world could be more natural. So there were two of us with problems adjusting to our surroundings. A mother and a father. Their mother and father.

When we got married, in the spring of 2007, the wedding had been as minimal as possible. Linda's maid of honor, Helena, my best man, Geir, and his girlfriend Christina, Linda's mother, Ingrid, and my mother, Sissel. Five people attended our wedding in the town hall, lasting two minutes, plus Vanja and Heidi. An hour later only five people sat around the table we had booked in Västra Hamnen and ate with us. No speeches, no dancing, no fuss. That was how I wanted it, I hated being the center of attention, even with people I knew.

Did Linda want it like that?

She said she did, and I believed her, but later I realized that she might have wanted a bigger wedding. For me the fact that we were marrying was the most important; for her the emphasis was more on the way we did it.

In the evening we went to Copenhagen without the children, stayed at the Hotel d'Angleterre, had dinner at a nearby fish restaurant, and the next day flew with the children to the Canary Islands, Linda pregnant with John, and spent two weeks there, at a terrible holiday center for Scandinavians where they showed the Norwegian nine o'clock news on TV in the bars and sold *Dagbladet* in the lobby. We arrived absolutely exhausted, schlepped the enormous pile of luggage, double stroller to the waiting buses, the children hungry and thirsty and snarling with irritation, drove through the barren, desert-like landscape, from which the holiday bunkers and shopping malls had extracted all hope, and arrived an hour later at the place where we were going to stay. Rows of two-story concrete blocks, a parched lawn, asphalt, and two big hotels, all inside high fences, next to a pile of rocks, full of Scandinavians and Brits, this was the location for our honeymoon. I was so wound up with frustration and Linda was so exhausted that she began to cry when I growled at her for not being able to find the key when we were standing outside the door. Vanja got angry with me; I shouldn't talk to Mommy like that. Heidi looked frightened. We went inside, the two rooms were dark, but there was a balcony, which was something at least. I ventured out to buy some food, close by there was a sort of supermarket. When I returned Heidi and Vanja were in their swimming suits. For them this was a fairy tale come true, so, I realized, if I pulled myself together, they would be happy.

For us it was anything but a fairy tale. In fact, the very antithesis. There was nothing enchanting about it, there was no magic, not so much as a hint of allure. We fell into a rhythm: out of bed at half past five when Heidi woke up, play a movie on the laptop to kill the first uneventful hours, shop for breakfast when the extortionate supermarket opened, eat, go down to the pool

and swim with the children until lunch, have lunch in the restaurant there, which catered for several hundred customers and
served hamburgers, sausages, and spaghetti, with waiters who
hated us, then take Heidi home for a nap while one of us went
with Vanja and sat in a café drinking coffee while she drew with
crayons and ate ice cream. Go swimming again when Heidi woke
up, play for a while in one of the two small playgrounds, eat at
one of the four restaurants, and then take part in the evening entertainment for the children. This was provided by a happy young
Swede, maybe nineteen years old, who played songs on a stereo
that the children were supposed to sing along to, he threw in a
few comments about a clown coming later and asked if they were
enjoying themselves. The clown was the star turn, he came, danced
around, and handed out lollipops to everyone, then he was gone.
A couple of times we took the children to the Teddy Bear Club,
they were too young to be left on their own and too shy to do
anything but stare at the young person dressed up as a teddy bear
or draw pictures.

One evening toward the end of the first week there was to be
a birthday party for the clown and all the children were invited.
Vanja who, along with Heidi, stared wide-eyed at the clown
every evening, and didn't see that behind the mask was a Swedish kid with, at best, one semester of drama under his belt, was
really looking forward to the party. She put on her nicest clothes
and went there with her mother full of excited anticipation while
I strolled with Heidi along a path beside the sea. We had arranged
to meet up at the evening event. Heidi sat calmly in the stroller
looking into the distance. Her eyes were large, in photos her face
was all cheeks and eyes, in character she was gentle and outgoing. When she was born Vanja clung to her mother with a passion
and Heidi was left to me, I carried her around the apartment, first
the one in Stockholm, then the one in Malmö, so often that she
never really weaned herself off it, she still wanted to be carried. I
wanted it too, there were few things I liked more than having her
in my arms, and even if I knew she should walk as much as

possible, to become independent and self-reliant, all it took was a pair of outstretched arms for her to be back. As was the case this afternoon as well. With the stroller under one arm, Heidi in the other I walked toward the café on the headland, only twenty meters or so above the breakers, which both she and I stared at hypnotically as we passed. At the café she had an ice cream, and the concentration she ate it with was a relief because no matter how close I felt to her there was always an element of self-consciousness or perhaps even shyness in my relationship with her, which was also true of Vanja when I was on my own with her, just different, as she was older and more verbal. It felt as though I always had to perform with her, we couldn't just walk in silence, so I filled it with little comments and questions. What a relief when she laughed! Only for the pressure to return in the ensuing silence. All this was emotion, but rationally I knew it was okay to go through quiet periods with your children, that they absolutely did not have to be entertained all the time, they had to learn it didn't matter if nothing happened, and that expectations of something special didn't come from them but from me.

What kind of person is shy with his own children? And what does it do to the children?

Getting really close to Heidi, which I did this evening when she suddenly placed her soft cheek against mine and smiled, was too much to endure. I walked faster and almost ran down the narrow asphalt path beneath the tropical trees, the wind from the Atlantic gentle and fresh against my face and the lights from our holiday center glowing far ahead of us in the falling dusk.

The clown's birthday party, which Vanja had been looking forward to all week, had not been as she had imagined. At first the staff refused to allow Linda in, the whole point of the exercise was that parents would not be present, the idea was that they should have a few hours on their own, so if Linda had time for Vanja, this was not the place to be.

"They didn't want to be seen," Linda said. "They didn't want us there because it would've shown them up."

"The clown wasn't there, Daddy!" Vanja said. "He didn't go to his own birthday party."

The children had each been given a party hat and sat around a table drawing a picture for the clown's birthday. They were then given a glass of soda and a hot dog and a piece of cake, which they ate in silence. They asked the staff when the clown was coming, he would be there soon, they were told. Then they played for a while, without the clown or any real enthusiasm since they didn't know one another and despite encouragement from the staff. Vanja didn't want to join in, she sat on Linda's lap and kept asking when the clown would be coming and why he wasn't there already. Finally the party was over, they trooped out, over to the stage where all the other children were sitting waiting for the clown, who did finally make an appearance, performing his standard routine with one exception, he collected the drawings from the children who had been at his party.

Vanja didn't understand this. How could the clown not turn up for his own birthday party?

We couldn't of course tell her the truth – that the pathetic tour operators didn't give a shit about the kids and didn't want to waste resources on them – so we said that Coco, which was the clown's name, had been pleased with the drawings, and the cake had been good, hadn't it?

And so the days passed on our package tour. Even though we disliked it intensely, both of us, something developed that we only became aware of later, when we talked about it, and the atmosphere on those evenings, sitting on the balcony reading and talking while the children slept indoors, suddenly became something we longed for and would happily experience again. The lapping of the sea, the immense dark sky above us, strewn with stars, the sounds of the tropical night. I read Gombrowicz's diaries there, they were fantastic, and this merged into the world of Scandinavian strollers, worn-out parents of small children, and pee-warmed swimming pools in a strange, almost alluring way: this was life too! This is how it could be too. Embrace it! But while we were there ennui was the dominant mood apart from two moments, one when I was on a dolphin safari with Vanja, out at sea, and the beautiful creatures playfully plowed through the water just below the railing where we stood, and not only I, but Vanja too, thought it a magical sight. When we talked about it afterward it turned out that her attention had been caught as vividly by the man who, on our return journey, went white in the face, rushed to the railing, and threw up. I could still feel how she had placed her little head in my lap and fallen asleep, and the rush of pleasure it gave me. And the picture of the Knossos dolphins I had seen once in a museum on Crete came to mind, the simple but almost unbelievable joie de vivre that lay in that fresco. Such simplicity was difficult to imagine in northern European art from that period, which was ornate to a far greater degree, and in the preornate era, in the Stone Age with its simple rock carvings, the simplicity of the line drawings was only on the surface, for humans and animals were interconnected in other, profound, and to us incomprehensible ways, the thinking behind this art was ritual and magical, whereas the Knossos dolphins were only dolphins. This fact basically ripped the bottom out of the theory I had just read, and loved, because it turned one perception of the world on its head, namely, the Italian nuclear engineer and pseudo-historian Felice Vinci's idea that Homer's *Odyssey* actually took place in the seas between Norway, Sweden, and Denmark. Like so many others, Vinci had been puzzled that the geography in the *Odyssey* was so much at variance with the real geography of the Mediterranean area, even if the names were the same. Ithaca was described in a way that did not fit Ithaca as it was, and it was the same everywhere. When Vinci for some reason looked north he discovered that the geography there fit the descriptions to a tee. Aeaea was Håja in northern Norway, Thrinacia was Mosken in Lofoten, Scheria was Klepp in Rogaland, the Peloponnese was the island of Sjælland in Denmark, Naxos was the island of Bornholm, the northern part of Poland was

Crete, Faros was the Swedish island of Fårö, and Ithaca was the little Danish island of Lyø. If you went to Lyø you would see Homer's description perfectly matched the topography of the island. The notion was beguiling and it couldn't be rejected out of hand either as it solved a number of problems regarding the epic poem, for instance the fact that they light a fire in midsummer, which is odd when you know how hot the days are in the Mediterranean at that time of year, or the fact that the sea is often ascribed hues that are alien to the Mediterranean as we know it but more normal in northern waters. Vinci also had an explanation for how the whole transformation from the north to the south had come about: the people Homer describes lived for a long time in the north, but then, because of the change in climate, they were forced south, down to the Mediterranean, where they simply gave places the same names they had used in their earlier home. Hence the geographical mismatches between the book's Ithaca – which was Lyø in reality – and the real Ithaca. Ithaca was "Ithaca" or New Ithaca. But what really flew in the face of the notion, I now realized, with Vanja quietly breathing on my lap and the wind blowing straight into my face, surrounded by that strangely intoxicating mix of gasoline and salt, and slightly seasick though happy nonetheless, were the cultural differences between places. It is not only people who define the culture of a place; the place itself also defines the culture of a people. There is a direct line between the Knossos dolphins and the horses in the Parthenon friezes or between the smiling kouroi and the magnificent bronze statue of a bearded man, presumably Zeus, which was found at the bottom of the sea off the coast of Greece in 1928, or between the first Doric temples and Aristotle's philosophy. I am talking about the joy of experiencing the world as it is, as it presents itself to the eye. For that is what the Greeks did, they set the world free. The radical nature of Greek art, which deals with the world as it is, with no links to any secret world or any deeper truth, can in consequence probably only be compared with the idea that man was the son of God. One of the most interesting things about the development of Greek art is how the demand for authenticity seemed to increase, as though every move to make the world more visible was bound up in a new way with the invisible, which only then was made apparent and subsequently rejected. The archaic statues, with their inscrutable smiles, were created from the same matrix, whereby the identical, nonindividual aspect is also a nonhuman dimension, and if you imagine them in front of a temple or a grave, out in the world among people and not in a museum, they must have had a formidable, intimidating effect, for the nonhuman in human form, that is death or the divine. Their time is not ours. Their place is not here. The classical statues the Greeks made some centuries later are individual through and through, with none of those frightening nonhuman qualities about them, they point neither to death nor the divine, but are wholly human. There is however a dignity and beauty about them that in a sense places them outside time, they are elevated, ideal, representatives and universal, which later generations attacked in the Hellenistic Period, when attention was focused on divergence, including its ugly or unattractive sides, and nothing was elevated, take for instance the bronze bearded boxer sitting on his own with cuts to his arms and legs and a broken nose, apparently at rest after a boxing match, his head cocked, looking to his right, scowling almost or a little aggressive, as though his peace has just been disrupted by a call or a sarcastic remark. He looks slightly stupid, but the strength and latent brutality of his body seem to eclipse that, stupidity is not what defines him. Here, in this statue, made by one Apollonius in the last century before Christ, there is nothing that points to anything beyond this particular moment, what we see is everything, nothing is hidden, neither death nor the divine, nor man as an idea or ideal, this is the world as it is, no more, no less. But is it art?

What is art?

The conflict between what we know and what we don't is played out in all art, that is what has driven it over the centuries, and that situation is never fixed, never stable, because the moment we find out something new, something else new appears of which we know nothing. In their art, the Greeks were the first to ignore completely what they didn't understand, they concentrated on what they knew. There aren't any mysteries in Greek art. The Pyramids are an enigma, but not Doric or Ionic temples. Onstage this became a theme: Sophocles's *Oedipus Rex* is about a man who doesn't know and about what happens to him as he is gradually enlightened and finally discovers the truth. The question of whether the tragedy lay in ignorance or knowledge is central because this was Greek culture's own great issue. But in the play there is both what Oedipus knows and what he doesn't know, and the emphasis is on his reaction to the unknown, not on the unknown itself. And Greek mythology, the whole pantheon, consisted of gods it was impossible to take completely seriously, they were too human for that, and the allure of the underworld, which is so strong in many other mythologies, not least Norse, is quite insignificant in Greek mythology, where the dead are shadows, in other words a darkness we are familiar with. What we see is what we are. But Plato, doesn't he look to a world behind this? Yes, in a way, but that world is no different, it is the same one, only stronger, as an object is stronger and more real than its shadow.

I found it difficult to imagine that an art such as Greek art could have been spawned in Polish forests or the Danish heathlands. Why, I didn't quite know. Many people have gone into this in the past, indeed I have myself read several interpretations of the southern and the northern temperament and climate by the great Swedish poet Vilhelm Ekelund, and even though it might be frowned upon to speak in these terms now, to say that culture was influenced by climate, as those who maintained this seldom did so without hailing northern clarity and simplicity as opposed to southern deviousness and peacock-like vanity, that was how it was, I thought to myself, only vice versa: clarity belonged to Mediterranean culture, lack of clarity to northern European culture. A forest where everything is hidden, everything is connected, and everything is always a sign of something else is not conducive to ideas of openness, clarity, and simplicity. That Norse culture became obsessed with ornamentation and interwovenness and American Indian culture with animals and always balked at objects in themselves is not in the least surprising and demolishes Vinci's otherwise fascinating idea that Odysseus ravaged the Skagerrak and the Baltics. This was what was going through my mind on the boat, which was full of tourists, while a voice announced over the loudspeaker that a whale had been spotted in the vicinity, but it had dived a few minutes ago and probably wouldn't resurface before we were back in the harbor. I told Vanja this when she woke up and we were about to disembark, she was disappointed, she wanted to see a whale so much, but contented herself with the thought that it had been out there with her. I praised her for going to sleep when she felt seasick, no one else had done that, I said, she was very clever, I said, and for the whole of the following year she remembered that and returned to it several times, the others hadn't gone to sleep, so they had been sick, but I went to sleep, do you remember that, Daddy?

We walked through the harbor area to the little beach in the middle of the town. I had swimming things in my backpack, but Vanja didn't feel like a dip, she wanted to go home to Linda and Heidi, so after she had polished off an ice cream in a café and I had bought her a pair of heart-shaped sunglasses we got on the bus and were soon speeding along the road, as it wound its way like a shelf around the cliffs over the sea, the sun burning high above us. Before I had paid for the sunglasses in the shop I spotted a clothes stand at the other end, and as I made my way there with them the assistant shouted, almost screamed, at me, the sunglasses, you have to pay for the sunglasses! That annoyed me because pilfering was not in my nature, to put it mildly, and I also had a child with me, so why did she think I was stealing? When I said this to her she didn't even apologize.

"Why weren't there any sharks?" Vanja asked, not looking at

me, she was staring out to sea, so vast and blue and deserted, quivering with the reflections of the sun.

"I suppose they must have been somewhere else," I said. "And they might be a bit scared of dolphins, don't you think?"

I had the idea that dolphins held sway over sharks from *The Phantom*. He had two dolphins on the island of Eden, which pulled him along on his water skis. One of them was called Nefertiti, but the other one? Dolphi? Anyway, if sharks came, they drove them away.

"Why are they frightened of dolphins?" Vanja asked.

"I don't know," I said. "They're stronger, I think."

She accepted that. I studied her, the little head, her blue eyes, the slight squint as she stared out to sea. Was she thinking about sharks, dolphins, and whales? If she was, what were her thoughts? She was three and a half years old, her vocabulary was limited, and what she didn't know or understand was endless. How did that feel?

I smiled and tousled her hair. She was so lovely.

She looked at me seriously. Then she smiled, too, and looked out the window again.

Had she done that to humor me?

I stared at the craggy mountainside flashing past the windows on the right like a film. Maybe her thoughts were basic and undeveloped, but they must have filled her mind in the same way mine did. They must have been just as important for her as mine were to me. So it couldn't be the understanding that thoughts produced that was the point of them, their objective content, but just their interaction with feelings, sense impressions and consciousness. Whatever was connected with the sense of oneself. So why push your thoughts so far and measure yourself by that yardstick? Intelligent, not intelligent, brilliant, not brilliant?

That awful sales clerk.

I stretched a leg out into the central aisle and leaned back. The trip had gone well. Vanja was happy, and the unease I had felt in the morning, that she might get bored and yearn for Linda and Heidi, had completely gone.

Something important, close to me, flagged itself up.

What was it?

Something I had been thinking about.

I looked out the window.

Something out there.

The sun?

The dark blue sea?

The slightly curved horizon? The feeling of being on a planet whirling through space?

No, no. The boat we had been on, Vinci's theory about Homer. That was it.

What was so important about that?

Let's see . . .

The bus braked sharply, I looked ahead, there was a big white semi in front of us on the bend. We backed up.

"What's the matter, Daddy?" Vanja said.

"We have to back up because of a truck," I said. "Feel like some chewing gum?"

She nodded.

"It's adult chewing gum," I said.

"Does it taste like toothpaste?" she asked.

"Yes, just like it," I said, putting one of the small tablets into her outstretched hand. Popped three in my mouth as the truck slowly passed the windows. The peppermint taste spread like a miniature storm in my mouth.

Ah, yes. It made no difference to Vinci's theory that Mediterranean art had got close to the world in its representation of it and torn it free from all fetters. If Odysseus's adventures had taken place in the north, the accounts of them need not have been written there. And was this not what constituted the battle in the *Odyssey*? A battle between the mythical world represented by the Cyclops, Circe who turned the crew into pigs, the song of the

Sirens, in other words a magic reality, and the new, as yet unrealized, nonmagical world from which Odysseus with his reasoning powers and ingenuity comes and which he brings with him? Horkheimer and Adorno had understood this conflict as the very dialectic of enlightenment, the place where reason liberates itself, and the barbarism of the Second World War as the place where it comes crashing down again. They were clear-sighted, it was brilliant, but I had never gone along with the implicit idea of progress in it, that the enlightened world was better than the unenlightened world, reason better than unreason, perhaps only because my own thoughts were obscure, unclear, superstitious while, at the same time, intelligible and sensible. I felt the irrational was always as important, or as dominant, as the rational. Inside me all of this ebbed and flowed, and all my thoughts, even at their most precise, were invariably colored by feelings and urges. Oh, the Sirens, they also sing for us, death lures us too, the song of decay and destruction never ceases, for in it lies the new, that which is to come, this is how life is organized. We can develop culture, we can elevate it higher and higher and we can shut out the song of the Sirens. But people are not identical with the culture in which they live, although it is easy to believe they are, as we are born into it and grow up in it. A sophisticated culture has to be sustained, it requires a great effort from all and sundry, as though they are living beyond their capabilities, until the culture's structure is strong enough to carry itself, which is treacherous as a lack of effort makes the construction invisible and we merge into the culture in which we live. Then it becomes natural, it is the only option, there is no beyond anymore, which is where the Sirens are, and barbarism becomes incomprehensible, evil, nonhuman. How can a brilliant literature professor become one of the worst war criminals in the Balkans? It's a mystery! Incomprehensible!

Knut Hamsun knew this. In almost all of his novels the enchanted and disenchanted worlds lie side by side, with the insight that is gained thereby, that all of this is of no real consequence since in the end life is empty and meaningless. But this, too, can be celebrated, and maybe this is what his books do.

"I've finished, Daddy," Vanja said, taking the chewing gum out of her mouth. I put out a hand and she placed the gum in it. I tore off the outside of the packet, wrapped the strip of paper around the gum and put it in my pocket. Far below us lay a little town of newly built hotels and holiday homes, shimmering white in the bright sunlight.

"Is it much farther?" Vanja said.

"No," I said. "Half an hour maybe?"

"How far away is it?"

"As far as the first part of *Bolibompa*."

"What's Heidi been doing?"

"How should I know! I've been with you all day."

"Did she get an ice cream?"

"I would think so. But you did, too."

"Yes."

We came into a biggish town full of dirty white-brick houses, unlit neon signs, and northern Europeans in holiday mode. Sand dunes were visible between the outermost rows of houses, above them the sea, blue and calm. The last kilometers were built up all the way: houses, supermarkets, garages, hotels, a whole forest of hotels. The bus was going fast, soon we would be heading down the hill to the last bay before our hotel, where we had gone for a walk one afternoon when we could no longer stand being in the compound and found a restaurant right by the sea. The waves had foamed and crashed against the terrazo wall, the wind made everything flap and bang, the shadows were long and sharp, the connection between the light over the countryside and the slowly sinking, burning globe in the sky hard to understand. The restaurant, overlooked by a hotel, was from the fifties or maybe early sixties and already in disrepair. Both Linda and I liked it, the atmosphere of transience and slow demise was irresistible, we sat down and ordered, but the girls were restless and irritable, so it was a case of gulping down the food and getting out as fast as possible.

The sixties, that was forty years ago. Not exactly ancient history. Nevertheless, even mass tourism was lent an aura of passing time.

Up the hill, into the right-hand lane and down to the big hotel complex where we were staying.

"There are Mommy and Heidi!" Vanja shouted.

And indeed, there they were, walking up the hill, Linda with her big belly, pushing the double stroller, in which Heidi sat leaning back in one of the seats with her legs dangling, wearing a brightly colored summer dress. The bus stopped, we got off, and Vanja ran up the hill to meet them. I was curious to hear what she would say, often it turned out that she had experienced quite different things from me, but this time it was just that she had seen some dolphins and had fallen asleep to stop herself being sick.

"How did it go for you?" I said, coming to a halt in front of them.

"Fine," Linda said. "We've had a good time."

"Are you tired?"

"A bit. Nothing serious. I had a nap with Heidi."

"Okay. Shall we go and get something to eat?"

She nodded and we strolled down toward the center, where the restaurants and shops were. They were concentrated around a kind of patio, half covered by a roof, with a little fountain in the middle. The floor inside the shops was the same as on the patio, terra-cotta tiles, and the lack of any distinction made me feel uncomfortable, in the same way that the sight of lawn turf being laid does. We found a table in the restaurant at the top end, ordered spaghetti bolognese for the children, I had a hamburger, Linda a pizza. The sunlight glinted and glistened on the metal railings running around the restaurants. People wearing swimming trunks and suits, with Crocs on their feet, *Foppatofflor* in Swedish, walked to and fro beneath us, many pushing strollers.

The low sound of Euro-disco music came from the speakers above our heads. Vanja banged her knife against her glass and then Heidi followed suit. I told them to stop. Children plunge into everything, sound too, it never bothers them; if you have a lot of children in one room, such as at a birthday party, they can shout and scream and laugh amid a total cacophony, a noise level that is unbearable for adults but that they don't even notice.

Over the past few years I have become more and more sensitive to noise, it was as if the slightest little bang or clink went straight to my soul, which shook and trembled, and one day it struck me it must have been the same for Dad because if there was one thing he reacted to, if there was one thing he couldn't stand, it was noise. Footsteps across the floor, doors banging, cutlery clinking against crockery, children chomping their food. Mom, on the other hand, had never been bothered by noise. Perhaps she was more at peace inside herself, perhaps she was more closed to the world, perhaps it was only that her tolerance levels were higher. But Dad really lived on his nerves, nothing was at peace inside him, one sudden noise and he exploded.

Now it was my turn.

Not so loud! No, no, no! Stop it! DO YOU HEAR ME? BE QUIET!

Vanja slipped down from her chair and crawled under the railing. Heidi followed her, and soon they were both lying on their stomachs by the fountain splashing the water with their hands. I took out a pack of cigarettes and lit up. Linda sent me a miffed look.

"I am pregnant, you know," she said. "Couldn't you at least go and sit somewhere else?"

"Take it easy," I said. "I'm going."

I got up and headed for one of the tables farthest away. If I was sensitive to noise, Linda was sensitive to smells. It was like being married to a bloodhound. In her present state smoke for her was torture. But I was still annoyed that she had been so miffed. She didn't have to be so pissed off, for Christ's sake! I had barely had a chance to have a cigarette all day. How many had I actually smoked? Three? Yes. One in the morning, one in the café with Vanja, one now.

A waiter with a tray in one hand stopped in front of our table and put down the glasses of mineral water and soda. Linda looked up at him and smiled.

Down by the fountain Vanja and Heidi were giggling. Vanja dipped her hand into the water and flicked it at her sister, whose dress was already drenched at the top.

"Vanja!" I shouted. "Calm down now!"

She looked up at me. Several other people did too.

But at least she stopped, and the next time I looked over they were hanging from the metal railing on the other side.

After eating we went to the exit at the other end of the shopping center, past the restaurants, clothes shops, and souvenir boutiques, at Vanja's request we stopped in front of a big amusement arcade with plane simulators, car simulators, war-game machines, and one-armed bandits, continued past a couple of empty retail outlets, stopped again by a long counter where tickets for activities and excursions were sold. We had talked about getting out of the compound the following day, perhaps finding a good beach somewhere. An amiable-looking man of about my age came over to us.

"Do you know of a good beach nearby?" I asked.

Yes, he did. Taking out a brochure and showing us pictures of a magnificent beach, he said it was some distance away, but there was a minibus going there the following morning. I asked how much it cost. He replied that it was free. Free? I echoed in surprise. Yes. The beach actually belonged to a hotel, it was new, and all we had to do to get the free trip and the beach chairs was to commit ourselves to viewing the hotel and promise to tell our friends about it when we got home. That was voluntary too, of course, but it would be a great favor to him if we did, he said, as he would a get a bad reputation if everyone he sent just went straight to the beach.

"Please have a look at the hotel first and then you can go to the beautiful beach."

I exchanged glances with Linda.

"What do you think? Shall we? So that we get out a bit tomorrow?"

"Sure, why not?" she said.

The salesman handed us a form, we filled in our names and address, he gave us a ticket, we said goodbye, and returned to the compound, to the fenced-in playground behind the main hotel, where we stood side by side watching our two children go down the slide and play on the swings while people in sodden swimming suits with wet towels over their shoulders came past in a steady stream on their way back from the pools. In an hour's time they would go out again, couples dressed in short-sleeve shirts and cotton dresses, red-faced from the sun and the party atmosphere, on their way to have dinner at one of the restaurants, some of them holding their children's hands, some alone. The thought that many of them probably considered being here fantastic, indeed almost like paradise, and might have saved up for ages for this very holiday, moved me, there was something wonderful about it, as well as something sad, because the place was terrible, constructed only to shovel in money from sun-starved Scandinavians, a kind of advanced form of exploiting the unwary. The worst part was what it turned me into. Was I – someone who despised all this – any better than they were? Wasn't I actually the idiot here? They were happy, I was unhappy, but we'd paid the same money.

In the evening, after the children had gone to bed, I put on my running shoes and jogged up the hill, across the footbridge to the barren lava-black plain beyond the interchange. The idea was to get into the mountains and then run a little there to see something different from roads and hotels on my holiday. I followed a narrow asphalt road. The heat rose from the ground. The sun shone onto the mountains ahead of me. There wasn't a soul in sight. I was out of shape and ran slowly. In front of me a bus rounded the bend and came toward me. As it passed I saw it was full of elderly tourists. Where on earth had they been? My breath coming in pants now, I continued upward, the road went into a tunnel, another tourist bus came toward me, the roar of the engine reverberated against the bare rock face. At the other end was a little valley. There were more buses in a large gravel parking lot by an enclosed area that turned out to contain a Western town, as I had seen them on TV when I was growing up. If I hadn't known where I was, the deserted, sun-scorched countryside and the run-down wooden buildings could have tricked me into believing this was somewhere in the Wild West and not an island in the Atlantic off the coast of Africa.

I kept running. My T-shirt was slowly getting soaked, the sun sank into the sea, and when I returned to the compound it was almost completely dark. In the hall of our apartment I opened the door to the bedroom where Vanja and Heidi lay asleep. Their regular breathing, their limp arms and legs, and their total lack of awareness to their surroundings, where almost anything could happen without them reacting, had fascinated me from my first moment with them. It was as though they lived a different life, were connected to another world – to the dark, vegetal realm of sleep. It was so obvious where they came from, the unseeing existence inside their mother's body, and they clung to it long after their birth, when they just slept and slept. Their state wasn't dissimilar to when they were awake because their hearts were beating, their blood was circulating, nutrients and oxygen were being supplied, blood corpuscles created and destroyed, in their insides fluids and organs gurgled and pulsated, and even their nerves, the lightning of the flesh, shot through their own dark pathways as they slept. The sole difference was consciousness, though even this was present in sleep, except that it was turned inward rather than out. Baudelaire wrote about it once in his diaries, I recalled, what courage it took to cross the threshold into the unknown every night.

They lived as trees live, and, like trees, they didn't know. Tousled and heavy with sleep they would open their eyes the following morning, ready for another day, without giving a second thought to the state they had been in for almost twelve hours. The world was wide open for them, all they had to do was run out into it and forget everything, as the premise for openness is forgetting. Memory leaves trails, patterns, edges, walls, bottoms, and chasms, it fences us in, ties us up, and weighs us down, turns our lives into destinies, and there are only two ways out: insanity or death.

But my children were still in the open, free stage. And then I go and obstruct them! I was strict, said no, told them off! Why was I so eager to destroy the best thing they possessed? Which they would lose anyway.

I closed the door, took off my shoes, and was about to open the bathroom door when I changed my mind and, instead of taking a shower, took a beer from the fridge and joined Linda on the balcony, where she was reading. She put her book aside when I appeared. I sat down and lit a cigarette, but my lungs, which had just put in a hard shift, weren't up to it and I coughed for a long time.

"Why don't you stop smoking, Karl Ove?" Linda said.

I scowled at her and took a swig of beer.

"I want the children to have a father for as long as possible," she continued.

"I do, too," I said. "Grandma said once I'll live to be a hundred. I believe that implicitly."

At last my lungs adapted and I was able to draw the smoke deep down.

We chatted about what had happened that day and what we would do on the next. Linda was sleepy, the dual life, the child in her belly, was taking its toll, and after a while she went to bed while I sat up reading. I was reading Witold Gombrowicz's diaries, and although I hadn't exactly been looking forward to it all day, it had been at the back of my mind as a vague presentiment of something good. I underlined sections as I read, which I seldom did anymore, but so much in these diaries seemed significant to me, and that was so rare, that I kept thinking I ought to reread them to remember and reflect on later. At regular intervals I put the book down, lit a cigarette, and gazed up at the enormous vaulted sky or down at the lights from the row of bungalows or at the trees along the avenue leading to the two swimming pools whose still surfaces were not visible from where I was sitting, but the mere thought of it had a calming effect. The reflection from the streetlamps lent the green of the treetops an artificial tone, as though nature here, and not just the architecture, was man-made. But my mind didn't follow my eyes, didn't take note of either shapes or colors, drunken Brits or young Scandinavian families on their way home across the lawn – it drifted off on its own, in the dark shadows of consciousness, excited about Gombrowicz, to whom it didn't give another thought, didn't muse on but treated like a dog treats its owner after a long day's loneliness. Wagging its tail, licking, barking happily. With my heart and soul I knew these writings were important and my own writing had to go in that direction, into the emerging, the developing, the ever evolving. So I had to go down beneath the surface, beneath the ideologies, which you can only stand up to by insisting on your own experience of reality, and not by denying it, for that is what we do, all the time, deny the reality we have experienced in favor of the reality we have learned, and nowhere was the betrayal of the I, the unique and individual I, greater than in art, as art has always been the privileged domain of the unique. It almost seemed as though the prerequisite for creating art was to renounce art. In which case, that would be the most difficult of all because the creation of art wasn't loaded with value beforehand, and no one, least of all the artist, could know whether what was produced was just shit or something original and priceless. In the last years of his life Van Gogh suddenly became a name, the enormous progress he made from painting to painting was plain for all to see, and the light, which no reproduction in the world can re-create, given that it would miss its very essence, was ultimately rendered with an almost morbid abandon and beauty, which everyone who sees these pictures knows to be true to life, knows is demonstrable: this is exactly how it is. He hardly ever painted people, the rooms and landscapes are unpopulated, but not accidentally so, it is more as if the beholder is lost to them, hence dead. The way the dead see the world, that is how Van Gogh painted it. In order to get there, to the stark nothing of our lives in the midst of a world ablaze with color, he renounced everything. As he wanted only to paint, he renounced everything when he did that. And who, hand on heart, can say that he or she is willing to renounce everything? For everything does truly mean everything.

Well, I certainly couldn't, that's for sure.

Gombrowicz?

No, not everything. A lot, but not everything. He writes that the flight of art has to find its counterpart in the sphere of normal life, in the same way that the shadow of the condor spreads across the ground below. He writes that Gordian knots should not be solved with our intellect but with our lives. He writes that the truth is not just a question of argument but of attraction, that is, the power to attract. And he writes that an idea is and remains a screen behind which other, more important, things go on. There were no complicated truths. And they must have come at a price. The price was high, it was isolation, but the payoff, freedom of thought, was high too. In the ruthlessness of his thoughts he was akin to Nietzsche, and like Nietzsche's texts Gombrowicz's were descriptions of a path, not the path itself. If he had written about his sexual escapades with young men in the Buenos Aires harbor quarter, the joys and humiliations of these nocturnal adventures, the shame and the seduction, about waking up one Sunday in his filthy accommodation with the South American sun shining in through the window, about his many jobs, including one as a bank clerk, about his wounded pride, about his fantasies of nobility, in short, if he had described all the circumstances from which his thoughts – and through them his soul – rose, and in practice connected the highest (for even thoughts about the lowest rank among the highest in the diaries) with the lowest, that is, the fluff in his navel, the worm up his ass, the blood in his piss, the wax in his ears, or just an autumn day strolling in a park in Buenos Aires with a book by Bruno Schulz under his arm, he would have been the world's greatest writer, the modern-day Cervantes and Shakespeare, all rolled into one.

But he couldn't. He was free in thought but not in form, not quite.

Could I?

Fuck off, Karl Ove. You stupid little shit. I didn't even reach Gombrowicz's boot laces. The mere idea of saying something as honest and true about Norwegian literature anywhere near as honest as he did about Polish literature gave me a stomachache. Yes, my hands trembled at the very thought, that I could actually describe everything as it was. That all I had to do was just go ahead and do it.

What a treacherous thought!

"Just" my ass!

But Gombrowicz pointed, and said: that's how it is here, better go that way.

Perhaps I could do that?

If only I'd had a really profligate, sleazy past in the docklands of Buenos Aires, lived at the bottom like a crab, and gorged myself shamelessly on everything I came across, preferably killed someone with a rock to the head, as Rimbaud may have done, and, like him, fled to Africa and made a living as an arms smuggler, yes, anything but this, on a hotel balcony in the Canary Islands with two small children and a pregnant wife sleeping on the other side of the sliding-glass door, and all that this loaded the future with in terms of propriety and responsibility.

But there, too, Gombrowicz had given me a little hope, lit a barely perceptible flame in the great darkness of my banality. Didn't he write, "Physical comfort can sharpen the sensibilities of the soul, and behind the cozy curtains, in the suffocating sitting rooms of the middle classes, engenders a toughness of which those who attacked tanks with Molotov cocktails could never dream."

Oh, to hell with everything.

It would soon be four years since my last novel came out and I hadn't written anything of note in the meantime. Fuck all, in fact. For close to a year I've been fiddling around with an opening to a novel in which Henrik Vankel, the protagonist in my first novel and the intended writer of the second, wakes up in a hospital after a suicide attempt. I had left him in a bathtub in a house on an all-but-deserted island at the end of the previous novel, just after he had slashed his face and chest, and the idea was he would complete what he had started and cut an artery and slowly his blood would drain away, and his life, too. I described how his eyesight was overrun, how there was something vegetative about the waning clarity, something growing and spreading inside him, it was death, and then the knocking at the door. Far, far in the distance, like outside a dream. Later it transpired it was the neighbor's son, one of the island's four other inhabitants, who had dropped by for a cup of coffee. A naval vessel lay anchored just off the coast, he contacted it, they took Henrik on board, and saved his life. I didn't believe in this story for a second, the part about the ship was particularly dubious and stupid, but there really had been a ship anchored up when I was living on the island, and it had made a great impression on me because it was somehow completely faceless, it just stood there in its world, with its cannons, not a single person to be seen on board. One day a little rubber dinghy was launched, it came into the bay in front of the house where I lived, four men in uniform pulled it ashore and ran inland. The dinghy lay there, beached, the whole day. In the evening it was gone. The next day the ship was gone too. All this was charged with meaning, so to speak, because both the ship and the crew of the dinghy stood out so incredibly clearly in an otherwise uneventful life on the island, they were out of the ordinary in every sense, although I didn't know what the meaning was.

The events arrived sender unknown, out of nowhere, and the mysteriousness of the clarity fascinated me, it was like a poem. At the time a Russian submarine had sunk somewhere in the Barents Sea, the members of the crew were alive, but the boat couldn't be saved, and they died within a few days. While I stood brushing my teeth and surveying the mist-wreathed island with its yellow grass, dark brown rocks and crags, the surface of the water black and still, there were several hundred young Russians in a death trap somewhere out there at the bottom of the sea. At this very moment. When I joined my neighbor in his boat to go to the main island to buy some provisions, I saw the front pages of the newspapers as openings in the world. *Kursk, Kursk.* Every radio program started with an update on the situation. They were going to die in days, hours, minutes. I walked around the island, I sat reading, they were trapped in the deep. So all hope was gone, they must be lying there, every last one of them, at the bottom of the sea, like dead fish. Did they bang their fists against the walls in their last moments of life? Did they stagger around screaming with rage and despair? Did they lie there, motionless, waiting for the inevitable?

They died, and then they were forgotten, new accidents and disasters captured the world's attention. I, too, forgot all about it until I began to write about Henrik Vankel's last days on the island. Then I reflected that the events represented two diametrically opposed phenomena. One was the openness of our times, in which we are informed about everything, even about those dying at the bottom of a distant sea, *while it is happening.* The feeling this produced was one of constriction, a sense that we are never left in peace, we are always seen, there is no longer anywhere we can be alone. The way these incidents were dramatized created a familiarity with them. The second event, concerning the naval boat, wasn't dramatized at all, it was just something I saw, unprocessed, there was nothing familiar about it, it was an absolute mystery. From all this I concluded that writing had to move toward the unfamiliar, what we know but cannot describe.

Actually that was true for everything because even if everything were explained and understood, it would always exist as a phenomenon as well, something in itself, closed off and apart.

The world had to be closed again.

But I was getting nowhere. I began to write about what happened in the grandmother's house when Henrik Vankel's father died and he was there with his brother, Klaus, but I didn't have an ounce of faith in it, everything was artificial and for show. I spent three weeks describing how Henrik took his luggage off the carousel at the Kristiansand airport, when Klaus went to pick him up, then I rejected it.

That was how far I'd got. For this reason, reading Gombrowicz was humiliating, the standard was so high, and to make things worse I agreed with just about everything he wrote.

I picked up the book and resumed reading. I had got to the last part, where Gombrowicz has left Argentina and moved to France. All the power, all the tension, and all the radicalism had disappeared from his prose, suddenly his style is drained of life and any remaining sharpness seems a little tired, mechanical, and repetitious.

What happened? Had he got old or was it the loss of exotic surroundings that did it? Europe is an old continent and that is where he came from, where he grew up, it was in him. In those days he was on familiar ground, he was strong, he was young. Could it be that this vitality, which otherwise would have died along with his curiosity, in his forties to judge from others, could it have been prolonged by his foreign adventures? Or was it just that he was dying in a dying culture, a bit like the composer in Thomas Mann's *Death in Venice*?

I read for an hour. Then I went indoors and got into bed, in my running gear, I couldn't be bothered to change. The next morning I put on a film for Vanja and Heidi, *The Little Ghost God-frey*, showered, had a smoke on the balcony, and went down with the others to the hotel entrance, where a minibus pulled up ten minutes later. We showed the tickets we had been given, placed the folded stroller and the bag of swimming things in the back, and got in. There were two other couples with us. Soon we were whizzing along the same cliff road Vanja and I had been down the day before. No one said anything, I gazed across the sea, squinting. Heidi started to cry, her face was ashen, was she carsick? She lay with her head on Linda's lap, Linda stroked her hair until she fell asleep while, luckily, Vanja was unaffected by any potential jealousy and stared across the sea, which lay like a floor beneath the roof of the sky.

Less than an hour later the minibus drove up a paved road to a resplendent luxury hotel on a hill, alongside verges of flowers, rows of palm trees, and lustrous green lawns. The driver stopped the vehicle, opened the door, and we – the motley package-tour family from Malmö – got out into the already oppressive heat. A woman with a name badge on her chest stood at the entrance looking at us. I unfolded the stroller, ashamed of all the stains on the canvas, looked over at her, and smiled politely. We're just going to the beach, I said. But we were supposed to take a look at the hotel first, I understand?

"Come this way, please," she said.

Vanja and Heidi stood looking around, slightly wary in these strange surroundings. Linda had her eyes fixed on me. She smiled when I met them.

We walked through the swinging door and into the reception area. The dark tiles on the floor shone in the light flooding through the enormous panoramic windows, the air was cool, the people working behind the counter wore suits or uniforms. Elevators went up and down all the time, not inside invisible shafts, but on the outside of the walls in glass tubes. Inside, there was a kind of shopping arcade with small, exclusive boutiques on both sides. It resembled an ocean liner, I thought, one of the gigantic luxury liners where no expense is spared and everything is available on board.

The woman with the name badge showed us into an area to the left of the reception desk with sofas and chairs, where a few lost tourists in holiday garb were sitting, and a counter where we were given a form to fill in. Name, address, telephone number.

What on earth was all this about?

We filled in the information, gave back the form, they said we could sit down and wait, we would be called when the time came.

Called?

Vanja and Heidi climbed up onto the stone ledge running along the inside of the window, crawled along on all fours, stood up suddenly like monkeys, and pressed their hands against the glass. Don't do that, I said, you'll leave marks. They ignored me, shouted to each other, crawled farther along. I checked to see if they had caught anyone's attention, they hadn't, and I sat down beside Linda, who was leaning back with her hands over her protruding belly. A TV screen hung from a column not far away, showing pictures of what I presumed to be the hotel where we were, probably the lower floor because there was a beach, the people there were suntanned and slim and seemed to be having a good time. Behind them was a building with terraces all the way up, filmed from a distance. A palace, a golden beach, and in the sea beyond a water-sports paradise.

Heidi knelt in front of a large flowerpot picking up the Leca pebbles from inside. I walked over to her, moved her away, and put the pebbles back while Vanja pressed her lips against the window, and I walked over to her and lifted her down. Can't you two come and sit with us for a bit, I said, but they couldn't, they wanted to go to the other end of the concourse where the avenue of shops started, there was an aquarium, and I went there with them, picked them up in turn so that they could see the fish close up, while glancing behind me from time to time to see what was happening. The people who passed us looked affluent, and I wondered what it was that made me think that, because it was the morning, they were on holiday and walked around wearing everyday shorts or skirts. Could it be something about their self-confident posture? Whatever it was I felt inferior and, with the children's arms and legs all over the place, lacking in authority and dignity.

That's Dad, Heidi said, indicating an unmoving yellowy-brown fish with an enormous lump above its head. And that's Mom, Vanja said, pointing to an elegant orange fish with a long veil tail. And that's me! Heidi cried. She directed a little finger at a tiny blue and yellow fish, beautiful as a jewel. That's me! Vanja said, and pointed to a red and white clownfish. Nemo! I'm Nemo!

"Okay," I said. "Now we should go back. Come on, you little clowns."

They ran after me, taking their own illogical routes across the floor, and pulled up right behind the sofa where Linda sat, very abruptly in fact, for there, only a few meters away, stood a teddy-bear-like creature – as tall as a man with an enormous head – which, when it caught sight of us, started to walk our way. Ill at ease and probably afraid, but also fascinated and excited, they stared at it with innocent blue eyes and mouths agape. He stopped in front of them and stretched out a hand, but neither Heidi nor Vanja realized that they were supposed to hold it. He held a paw in the air as though he had suddenly remembered something, turned, and shuffled over to a table, then came back with two disposable cameras, which he handed to them.

"Mommy, Mommy, what's this?" Vanja said after he had gone.

"A camera, I think," she said.

"Can I see?" I said.

Vanja passed hers to me. It was a disposable underwater camera.

"You can take pictures underwater with this," I said.

"Can we?" Vanja said. "I want to do it! When are we going swimming?"

"Soon," I said.

"Why did we get it?" Vanja asked.

"I don't know," I answered. She raised the camera to her eye. Behind her a middle-aged man wearing jeans and a blazer came toward us. He was semi-bald with dark hair at the sides and holding a thin folder in one hand.

"Linda and Karl Ove?" he said.

We nodded, he stopped and shook our hands, told us in faintly accented Swedish to follow him and he would show us around. We walked down the arcade, he paused in front of a wall full of pictures, all of celebrities. Norwegian, Swedish, and the occasional American.

"They've all stayed here," he said.

"You don't say," I said.

He stretched out a hand, and we went down a long corridor. Tiles, mirrors, gilt balustrade.

"What do you do back in Sweden?" he asked.

"Karl Ove's a writer," Linda said.

"Linda is too," I said.

"How interesting," he said. "Might I have heard of you?"

"Karl Ove's quite well known," Linda said with a smile.

Why did she say that? Jesus Christ, how foolish.

"Ah!" he said. "Then we'll have to take a picture of you afterward and hang it on our celebrity wall."

"I'm not sure about that," I said.

He laughed out loud.

"I was only joking, sir," he said.

Red-faced with embarrassment, I looked down at the floor in front of me.

"I realized of course," I said.

"But perhaps you *will* be famous one day, you know. Then we'll hang up a picture of you. I promise you. If you become guests of ours here, that is!"

"Mm," I said.

He came to a halt by an elevator and pressed the button, which glowed dimly. Heidi stared at the light. Pressed the button. At that moment the door opened and an expression of shock spread across her face.

The elevator was almost completely covered with mirrors. I

inadvertently glanced at myself for a brief instant. I looked like an idiot. The white T-shirt, bought for 49 kronor at Åhléns two years before, loose at the neck and a bit too tight around my waist where the fat bulged out, and the military-green three-quarter-length trousers with all the pockets and dangling laces, also bought at Åhléns, for 149 kronor, which in my imagination I had seen as pretty cool gear, and the worn-out Adidas, once white now gray, which I wore without socks, became in these luxurious surroundings a sort of curse, it was impossible not to feel deferential, undignified even, as the elevator sank to ground level.

"Where on the island are you staying then?" he asked.

Linda gave him the name of the hotel complex. He nodded.

"How much did you pay in all? For everything?"

"Twenty-five thousand," I said. "Then costs for food and so on top of that."

"That's not cheap," he said as the elevator came to rest and the doors slid open. The heat hit us as we exited. We were at the foot of the hotel, right next to the beach.

"Let's go this way," he said. "To that island. It was made when the hotel was built."

"Really?" I said.

"Yes," he said. "No expense spared here. Our prices are still low though. It's based on an entirely new holiday concept. It's a standard hotel in one way – you can rent a room – but it's also possible to buy a room or a suite if you want. Forever. You pay a one-time sum and then you can stay here every summer for the rest of your life.

"Oh?" I said.

"Yes," he said. "It's brilliant. It costs a lot less than an apartment would cost here. And at the same time you get so much more for your money. We're talking real luxury here."

Heidi had had enough. She stretched her arms up to Linda.

"I can't carry you, you know, my love," she said.

"Baby in your tummy!" Heidi said.

"That's right," Linda said.

"How old are your girls?" he asked. "How sweet they are!"

Vanja turned her head away, I lifted Heidi up and started to walk across the terrace, past an Italian café and ice-cream parlor, where two elderly ladies with wrinkled suntanned skin were sitting in bikinis drinking coffee, both wearing sunglasses and sun hats.

"Vanja's three and a half," I said. "Heidi's one and a half."

"And when are you expecting the next one? You are, aren't you?"

"Yes, we are," I said, with a glance at Linda. "In the middle of August, right?"

She nodded, walking a few paces behind us, holding Vanja's hand.

"And you live in Sweden?"

"We live in Malmö," Linda said.

"It's a nice town," I said. "Big enough and a little offbeat. But what about you? How come you speak Swedish?"

"I worked in Sweden for many years," he said. "In Stockholm."

"Oh!" I said. "We did too. Where did you live?"

"In Nacka," he said.

"In Nacka!" I said. "We've been there a lot. Some friends of ours live there."

"It's a small world," he said with a smile. "It's very nice there. I love Sweden."

"Mm," I said, putting Heidi down. "Now you can walk yourself. We want to go over there. Vanja, can you hold Heidi's hand?"

When we were on the island, which was like a park with trees and fountains, he wanted to know if we'd heard about the hotel. We hadn't. What about the concept then? It was in fact Norwegian, he said, and mentioned the name of the entrepreneur. I shook my head, then, to my surprise, Linda said she had heard of it. I looked at her. Had she really? He wanted to know where she'd heard about it, whether some friends had told her, she said she had seen a TV program. Was she making that up? If so, why?

He started to talk about the hotel, how elegant and luxurious it was, how the sand on the beach had been transported all the way from the Bahamas, the restaurants and shops were top class, all the rooms were magnificent, even those in the lowest price range, and there were always lots of Norwegians and Swedes here. All the time he was talking, beneath the dark blue morning sky, the sun beating down with such intensity that my shoulders, cheeks, and the bridge of my nose were burning, and the light seemed to neutralize all the nuances of the countryside around us, all this time I was keeping an eye on Vanja and Heidi, who wandered ahead of us and behind us. And the longer he was with us the more unkempt and dirtier I felt. He was silver-tongued and pleasant, had a kind of management air about him, and could well have been if not the hotel manager then perhaps his deputy. It was beginning to pain me that he was spending so much time on us. The idea was of course that we would talk about the hotel to our friends. But it was inconceivable that any of our friends would stay at this hotel, certainly not mine anyway, so we were wasting his time. I didn't know how to express this to him. At the same time it was as if he trusted us, as if he realized the way we dressed didn't convey the whole truth about our personal qualities, and I tried to reinforce this by being as friendly and jovial as I could. And, I told myself, I really *would* mention this hotel to people when we got home. We owed it to him, I thought, as we strolled along side by side. The sun didn't seem to have any effect on him; apart from a shimmering film of moisture on his forehead and above his top lip, the heat left him untouched.

At the far end of the island he stopped and turned. From here you have a wonderful view, he said. The best apartments are at the top, all with large balconies, as you can see. The less expensive ones are farther down, but they are all spacious and of a high standard.

"Yes, it really looks wonderful," I said. "Absolutely fantastic."

Linda looked at me.

"What do you think?" I said.

"Yes, it's very nice."

There was a negative tone to her voice and I felt a twinge of irritation. But he probably didn't notice anything. Only those closest to her could interpret the tiny variations of mood and temper that constantly emanated from her. No, not even them. Only I could.

"Perhaps we should go back," the man said. "Then you can see one of the apartments from the inside."

"I'm not sure that's necessary," Linda said. "We've formed a picture of what they're like now."

He looked at me, and I smiled apologetically.

"It wouldn't do any harm, would it?" I said. "We can have a little peep, can't we? Don't you think?"

She nodded, reluctantly it had to be said, but she assented, and I called the children, who of course didn't want to go. Vanja was beating the surface of the water in the fountain with a little stick she had found, Heidi was lying on her stomach with her hands deeply immersed in the water.

"Hey, girls, we're going now. We just have to see one room. There's an ice cream for you afterward."

"Don't want one," Heidi said. I grabbed her around the waist and lifted her up.

"No!" Vanja said, and ran away. Heidi kicked and struggled. I laid her over my shoulder and ran after Vanja. Fortunately Heidi was laughing, that wonderful bubbly laughter she had come out with ever since the first few months of her life. I put her down, took a few quick steps, and caught up with Vanja, who had become jealous of her sister.

"I want Mommy," she said.

She always wanted Mommy, regardless of what I did. Sometimes I thought it was because I was so hard on her and unreasonable; sometimes I thought that was just the way it was.

"She's over there!" I said now. "All you have to do is walk!"

She squinted into the sun, and her mouth opened as though connected with her eyes in a secret, to her unknown, pact. I knew the mannerism from Linda. When I had been most in love and my insides burned like a forest fire it had been as though the slight movements of her lips passed straight into my soul. I had never been as open as I was then. The whole world streamed through me.

Vanja turned and ran over to Linda, grabbed her hand, and snuggled up to her. Heidi had sat down on the ground; I lifted her up and followed the others.

In a corridor at the top of the hotel the man asked us to wait, he just had to check if the room was empty and had been cleaned.

"I want to go to the beach," Vanja said.

"Soon," I said. "We just want to have a look at this room."

"Why?" Vanja asked.

"Good question," Linda said, and smiled at her.

At that moment the man reappeared and waved us into a room. Open windows, curtains fluttering in the Atlantic breeze, light colors, shiny stone floor, the feeling of trespassing as Heidi and Vanja walked around, no sandals on the sofa, do you hear me, don't pull at it, no, be careful now, you might break it! He took us onto the large balcony, the sea blue and heavy and glittering in the sun, the sky vast and deep, the cliffs along the coast to the south in shade. The cars on the road there tiny, like busy insects. He said all this could be ours if we wanted, and without it costing us that much. I asked how much. He repeated that you pay a one-time sum and you could be here for a few weeks every year. It was like buying a stake in an apartment or in a mountain cabin, he said with a smile to me. No maintenance, no cleaning, everything taken care of, so we could have a luxury holiday every year for the rest of our lives. As parents of small children we deserved that, he said. Live in a paradise like this every single summer. And if you prefer to buy a stake in one of the smaller apartments you retain all the rights and the full service, of course.

He asked us to follow him. Making us such an offer meant that he actually believed we could afford something like this. That was why he was spending so much of his time on us. So at least he hadn't thought we were a traveling flea circus, as Linda was wont to call us. In the corridor he told us how much the cheapest apartment cost, and the most expensive. The price wasn't out of the question, at least not for the bottom of the range.

We were ushered into a huge carpeted conference room full of men in shirts and ties and women wearing blouses sitting in front of computers, many of them engaged in conversation with clients like us. There were several TV screens showing pictures of the hotel and the countryside around, there was a lounge with brochures displayed on a low table, the air was cool, almost cold, the atmosphere one of professionalism and efficiency. He guided us to a high table where there was a thick folder he asked us to peruse. It turned out that if you bought a stake you didn't have to come here every year because there were other equally luxurious hotels all over the world where we, if we paid the one-time fee, could stay free of charge. We wouldn't have that option if we bought the standard holiday home or mountain cabin. Now he would leave us alone, there was something important he had to do, but he would be back.

I thumbed through the folder, Linda took care of the children. My eyes lingered on a hotel in the Alps. The photo had been taken in the autumn, before the snow had fallen, and the sight of the countryside, the steep rock faces with the green conifers and the melancholic glowing foliage at the bottom, the fences and country roads, and the old, white-walled hotel awakened a great yearning in me. Oh, to be there. I turned the pages, there were hotels in Mexico, Italy, France. We could travel around the world every summer or autumn, the whole family, it would be a magnificent experience, at least for the children. Perhaps my mother could stand security so we could get a loan? Or I could get a bigger advance from the publisher?

I called Linda and showed her the photo of the hotel in the Alps. I suppose she must have seen how excited I was because she said it was lovely, but that we couldn't afford it. Don't say that, I said. We can probably wangle it somehow. It is actually a good opportunity. Not the hotel here necessarily, but all the others. And it's not a lot of money. Not really.

"We don't have any money," Linda said. "And I have a problem with the feel of this place. I've had enough of the upper crust in my life."

We sat down. It felt as though we were in a large prestigious law firm or at the European headquarters of a multinational company. The man who had shown us around appeared at the other end of the room a few minutes later and beckoned us over. Our relationship changed when we sat down on one side of the desk and he, with all his piles of papers and folders in front of him, on the other. We were his clients. He asked us what we thought of all we had seen, was this for us? So he assumed that we were affluent enough to enter into a deal. It felt good that he could see past our clothes and style. He was taking us very seriously. I said we were definitely interested. Perhaps not in this particular hotel, but all the others and the fact that you could move around. You could, couldn't you? I had to know for sure, I said. Yes, that was correct, he said. So would we be able to manage the financial side? I wasn't sure. It depended. Would you like us to look at it together? he asked. Yes, we can do that, I said as the children began to move around in territory that grew bigger the more secure they felt. What is your income? he asked. I told him how much I earned, the scholarship plus my monthly consultancy fee, and added that in the good periods, when I came out with a new book, it was much higher. Then I could earn several hundred thousand in one go. One way of doing this was to take out a loan now and then pay it off as the money came in. That is one option, yes, he said. How much are your monthly expenses? I told him, and he wrote it down and looked up at me. Do you have any savings? If not, it will be hard for you to get a loan on this. No, we don't have anything else, I said. But it would be possible to get someone to stand surety for us, I think. Do you think you could arrange that now? You can call from here free of charge.

I looked at Linda.

"That would be a bit stressful," I said. "Can't we do this when we get back home? Just take some papers with us and then read them at our leisure?"

He shook his head and smiled.

"What I'm giving you now is a special offer. You're entitled to it because you're here. It requires you to make up your minds rather quickly. There's a lot of interest, you know. We can't reserve it just for you."

"But we can't tie this up here and now," I said.

"Do you think you have the means to go through with this? If you know you have, you can sign now and juggle the finances when you get home. But you have to be absolutely sure."

"We can't afford it," Linda said. "Nowhere near."

He gave a sigh of resignation and leaned back.

I looked at her.

"We can try," I said. "We can do it if we want."

"But do we want to? I couldn't imagine coming here every summer for the rest of my life. It sounds like a nightmare to be honest."

The impoliteness of what she said cut me like a knife.

"I think it's really nice here," I said. "But the hotel here isn't the point. It's all the others we gain access to. Actually, I think it's a very good idea."

"But we can't make up our minds now. We have to think it over!"

I looked at him.

"Can we think about it? And then contact you from home?"

"As I said, the offer is only valid for today. But who was it you thought could stand surety for a loan?"

"My mother possibly," I said.

He pushed the phone over to me.

"You can give her a call now," he said. "Then we can clear this up right away."

"We need more time," I said. "We have so little money that

such an outlay has enormous consequences for us. We'll have to think about it."

I spoke in an almost pleading voice so that he would understand I wished things were not as they were. But it didn't help. When I said that, he seemed to change personality. All his amiability was gone, his kindly eyes went black, he rose to his feet, his movements stiff with irritation.

"If you don't have any money, what are you doing here?" he said.

"I'm sorry," I said.

"If you go out and turn right you'll come to a *terraza*. Take a seat and a colleague will come and take care of you."

He turned and walked over to one of his colleagues. I felt like running after him and apologizing again. Or telling him we were joking, of course we had the money, give me the contract and we'll sign. Instead I stood up, lifted Heidi, and we made our way to the exit with the defeat stinging and aching inside me.

"Let's just get out of here, no?" Linda said. "We don't need any more of this."

"We promised we would wait for his colleague," I said. "Out there, didn't he say?"

I nodded toward a *terraza* behind a glass partition. We went out, sat down at one of the tables. No one came, Heidi was tired, it was her bedtime and she whined while Vanja nagged us for an ice cream and to go to the beach.

"Let's go," Linda said. "Come on."

"No," I said. "We promised we'd wait. So we wait."

The man who was to take care of us was young, wore black Prada sunglasses, a white shirt, and a tie. He had the same folder as his older colleague, placed it on the table in front of him and said in English he had an offer for us. We could have a two-week stay at the hotel at a much reduced price, almost half price in fact, he said.

"We came here for the beach," Linda said. "We were promised

tickets for beach chairs today. We've already been here for two hours."

He looked at me.

"We don't have the money, I'm afraid," I said.

It was true, I had five thousand kronor left in my account, at most. It had to last us for the next four days.

He got up. His movements, too, showed signs of irritation.

"Then I'll get you your precious tickets," he said, and was gone.

"I'm utterly exhausted," Linda said. "And hungry."

"I understand," I said. "But we can eat at one of the cafés down there and then you can relax on the beach afterward. Heidi's fallen asleep. And I can take care of Vanja."

The salesman didn't return for half an hour. Mute, a scornful grimace on his young face, he placed the tickets on the table and left. We had something to eat, Heidi slept in the stroller, I went for a swim with Vanja, who used up the whole roll of film in thirty minutes. Even though the sand was fine-grained and golden, and the water in the lagoon an exotic green, it felt as if we were there on sufferance and could be thrown out at any point. We hadn't shown ourselves to be worthy enough. But we couldn't go home, not until the taxi came for us and the other Swedish couple, who were now lying a few beach chairs away and, unlike us, seemed to be enjoying life.

"I would never have believed I'd be glad to get back here," I said as, some hours later, the minibus turned off the main road and drove down to the hotel. "But I am."

"Me, too," Linda said. "Imagine you actually considering buying a time-share!"

"Yes, it's unbelievable. But the worst is that I didn't catch on. I didn't get what was happening until afterward! But you did, right?"

"Yes. I wondered what you were up to."

"I was taken in hook, line, and sinker. Oh, the thought of it is so painful! Accepting the tickets in the first place without realizing what was going on. An hour in a taxi. Who would pay for that without any hope of gain?"

Linda laughed.

"Yes, go on, laugh," I said. "We won't breathe a word of this to anyone, okay?"

"Okay!"

In the evening, after we had been to see Coco the clown on the stage by the pools, and the children had gone to bed, we sat on the balcony and talked at length for the first time in ages, me with my feet on the railing and a bottle of beer in my hand, Linda with her hands folded over her voluminous belly. We decided never to go on such a vacation again, it was pointless, neither one of us enjoyed it, everything was done for the children, based on some notion of the family and the ideal of a normal, healthy father and mother and two children by the pool, on a beach, in a Spanish restaurant, suntanned and happy, all of which, however, paled the closer we came to the reality of it, and in the end, once we were actually there, went up in smoke. We should have rented a house, I said, somewhere we liked, it wouldn't have been any more expensive. I agree, Linda answered. I don't like this any more than you do. But the worst, I said, is that I find myself on two levels the whole time. One level is the children's because they are having a really good time, they can't see through all this, for them Coco is a genuine clown, a fairy-tale figure. They have no idea that the waiters despise us or that they show Norwegian TV and sell *Dagbladet* in the kiosk, for them this is a fantastic place, and I have to keep thinking that too, if you see what I mean. This is a world for children, not for adults. And then I think that almost our whole culture is too. That it's actually for children.

I looked at her.

"But that doesn't bother you?"

"Yes, it does. Of course it does. Was I inattentive?"

"A bit. But it doesn't matter. You have other things on your mind. I understand that."

"Not at all," she said.

"What were you thinking about?"

"Heidi. It feels almost unfair for her to have another sibling when she's so small."

"It's only good for her."

"Maybe."

"It is as it is anyway," I said, on my feet to get another beer from the fridge. The effect of the two I had already drunk lay like a veil of well-being over my consciousness, and another one, I knew, would charge it with a faint sense of anticipation, which a couple more would dispel, whereafter everything would be good. A couple more and I would convert my mood into actions, anesthetized against any objections and common sense, and then, if I went out, everything inside would be glittering and sparkling.

Oh, how I loved drinking.

I loved it.

The longing to do so came only when I had drunk a little, then I seemed to remember what it was like and realized what I really wanted, which was to drink copious quantities, drink myself senseless, unconscious, as deep down in the shit as I could go. I wanted to drink myself out of house and home, drink myself out of family and friends, drink myself out of everything I loved and held dear. Drink, drink, drink. Oh my God, just drinking and drinking, night and day, summer and autumn, winter and spring.

I opened the fridge door, held the cold, slim beer bottle, whipped off the cap, and took a couple of long swigs before going back to the balcony.

"Do you remember when we saw each other for the first time?" I said, sitting down. "What would you have thought if you'd known you were going to marry and have three children with him? That foolish Norwegian?"

"My heart would have melted," she said with a smile.

"Come off it," I said.

"But you're right about you being 'that Norwegian.' Ingmar

had talked a lot about you beforehand. Almost all of it was about you and your book, so I was well aware you were coming."

"But you didn't want me," I said.

"Of course I did. Just not at that moment. I was heading somewhere else. If it had happened then, we wouldn't be sitting here now."

"No," I said. "I remember going into the common room, the one with the big fireplace, everyone was there, and I just had to leave. I couldn't take being in the same room as you or rather I couldn't stand seeing you talking to others and having a life beyond me."

"I didn't even know you!"

"No. But that didn't matter. So I left and sat on the steps outside the hut where my room was, and prayed to God that you would follow me out. I never pray to God – I haven't since I was a child – but I did then. Make Linda come to me, I said. Dear God, can you do that? And then the door opened! And you came out! Do you remember?"

She shook her head.

"I thought I was dreaming. You came out, you closed the door behind you, you started to cross the yard, over to where I was sitting. At that moment I believed in God. I thought he had intervened. But then you didn't turn in my direction, you just kept going, to where you were staying. You said hi. Do you remember?"

"No."

"You were just going to get something."

"Oh, Karl Ove," she said. "Now I'm starting to feel bad!"

"I'm not surprised."

"If I'd gone over to you, we wouldn't be sitting here now."

"Are you sure?"

"Yes."

"Because you fell ill? Because you went to the hospital?"

"Yes."

"Maybe I would've been there with you. Have you considered that?"

"Maybe. But I didn't want that. I was a very different person then."

"You were. When I met you next, in Stockholm, that was my first thought. Your whole personality was different."

"In what way?"

"There was none of the hardness in you. The performance side of you was gone. Mm, how should I explain it? You'd been tough, cool, self-confident. Yes, you'd had your own very distinctive personality. That was the feeling I had. And when I met you again that was gone."

"My own what?"

"Your own distinctive personality. You were enough as you were."

"You didn't recognize me?"

"No, but I'm not talking about who you actually were. I'm talking about how you appeared to me. I was utterly defenseless against that. As you know."

"Yes, but that wasn't what you got. I'm sitting here now with an enormous belly. And those two children in there. It doesn't feel as if I have anything of my own."

"I know. It's better though. It's so, so much better."

She fell silent.

I drank up the beer and fetched myself another.

"A penny for your thoughts," I said. We had switched off the light outside, so she was sitting in near darkness, the glow from the window like a faint stripe across one side of her face.

"I'm thinking about everything I've lost," she said.

"Better to think about everything you've gained," I said.

"There's so much contempt in you," she said. "I know you look down on me."

"Look down on you? I certainly do not!" I said.

"Yes, you do. You think I do too little. I whine all the time. I'm not independent enough. You're sick of this life of ours. And of me. You never tell me I'm beautiful anymore. Actually I don't mean anything to you. I'm just someone you live with who happens to be the mother of your children."

"No, that's not true," I said. "But you're right that sometimes I think you don't do enough."

"My friends can't understand how I manage to achieve all I do. Two children and pregnant with a third. I don't think you have any idea how much that really is."

"Your friends don't know anything. You shouldn't listen to them. They're just trying to comfort you. It's like the time Jörgen came home, you know, you told me about it, when you and Helena were sitting on the sofa drinking tea. 'Sitting here whining again, are you,' he said. Do you remember that?"

There was a hint of a smile, but her eyes were cold.

We said nothing for a long time. The faint sound of the sea lapping against the shore hung like a veil over the artificial landscape below us. Muted voices from the balconies beneath and the odd shout or gale of laughter from the restaurants farther down.

I lit a cigarette, took a swig of beer, and grabbed a handful of peanuts from the bowl on the table between us.

This was what she usually said when we had a fight and she tried with her frenzied attacks to rip the heart out of my chest. That I looked down on her and I should leave her and find myself another woman, someone who was nice and independent enough to leave me in peace. That I was staying with her out of pure duty and it wasn't enough for her. She knew what she was worth and she was worth much more than this.

But this had not been a fight. She hadn't tried to rip the heart from my chest. She had said what she said calmly and firmly, as if it were a fact of life. And I had only objected as a matter of form.

I knew she would soon get up and go to bed. I felt a kind of panic grip me, the air had to be cleared, Linda placated, the situation could not remain unresolved.

She placed a hand on the railing.

"I'm sorry," I said.

"What about?"

"Everything."

"You shouldn't be," she said. "Right now I'm actually enough as I am. But of course this changes. Sometimes being pregnant makes me feel strong and I think I can manage everything alone if need be."

"That's the first time I've heard you say that," I said.

"And then it completely goes and I feel I'm utterly dependent on you. Then I get so frightened. Do you understand? I feel I have nothing myself. If you go, everything goes. It's a terrible feeling. And I see that is *precisely* what you like least of all. And if you did go, that would be the reason. But I can't do anything about it."

"I know."

"And you're longing to get away."

"I am not. I want to be here. Hand on heart."

She didn't say anything.

"I read something in Gombrowicz yesterday that I've been thinking about," I said. "It's about why we don't allow ourselves to be surprised by anything, how we can walk round a corner without being curious to know what is waiting for us there. How we can sit in a restaurant and not be curious about the soup we've ordered, how it will *taste*. That's what my problem is. Do you understand? I take everything for granted. And it's a poison. I don't look down on you, I think you're wonderful, but when I take everything for granted and there's no reaction it gets on my nerves. That's what I mean. It gets on my nerves."

"Do I get on your nerves?"

"Come on, you know. When I'm grouchy and pissed off, of course that's what happens."

She got up and went inside. I followed.

"Surely you understand what I mean!" I said. "I'm not making some great statement. I'm just trying to explain something."

She undressed without looking at me and got into bed. I sat on the edge beside her.

"What do I do that gets on your nerves?" she said after a while.

"It's not something you do," I said.

"You have to tell me and I'll stop doing it," she said.

"But it's nothing specific, don't you understand?"

"Is it all our life together?"

"Oh, come on! You know what it's like to feel out of sorts. There's something inside you. Right? That's what I was trying to describe. It's something inside me."

I stroked her back. She lay perfectly still, looking into the distance.

"What shall we do tomorrow?" she said.

"I don't know," I said. "But I'm not that keen to spend the whole day here."

When she lay on her side like that you could see her stomach wasn't just a stomach, there was something inside, an object, and the biological reality, she, this human female, was duplicating herself piercing the veil of notions that her personality, the woman she was for me, all we had experienced and thought together – cast over everything. As though we lived one life in our language and ideas and another in our bodies.

"No," she said. "Couldn't we go on the trip to Las Palmas we'd talked about?"

I nodded and got to my feet.

"Yes, let's do that. Sleep tight."

"Don't stay up too long."

"No."

"Sleep tight."

I walked through the apartment, switched on the balcony light, sat down, and gazed into the distance. I wasn't thinking about anything special, but I was filled with the emotions aroused by what Linda had said and the way she'd behaved. After a while, maybe twenty minutes or so, I took out Gombrowicz's diaries again and looked for the passage I had mentioned to Linda.

For some time now (perhaps because my life is so monotonous) I've occasionally been seized by curiosity with an intensity I've never experienced before – a curiosity as to what might happen the next moment. Right in front of my nose – a wall of darkness out of which at any moment a menacing apparition might reveal itself. Around the corner . . . what is lurking there? A person? A dog? If it is a dog, what size, what breed? I am sitting at a table and in a minute the soup will be served . . . but what kind of soup? Art hasn't yet addressed this basic experience in any comprehensive way, man as an instrument to transform the Unknown into the Known does not figure among art's greatest heroes.

He wrote that one Wednesday in 1953. I associated it with something I had once read by Deleuze while I was a student in Bergen and it had become a sort of landmark for me, which I came back to again and again: the idea that the world is permanently in the making, that it is constantly evolving around us, but that this ceaseless creation from moment to moment merges into what we already know about the world. Of the two forms of understanding we have developed – science and art – science pertains to certainty and calculation whereas art, by emerging from nothing, pertains to the moment and the uncertainty that lies in its constant creation. No artist had worked more with this than Cézanne, it was his principle and vocation, and the reason for his immense influence on his contemporaries. With a predetermined concept of what space is you can paint various objects without the space being changed, the system is invariable and unshakable, this is how we see, and hence this is how space is. In Cézanne's paintings the opposite is the case, here it is the objects that make the space, space is something that is made, and its making is relative. Then it is as much about the eye that beholds as what the eye beholds; the convention of space, which is usually invisible, becomes visible.

For fifteen years I had been doing this, seeking out thinkers who confirmed this idea, especially Nietzsche and Heidegger, but also Foucault, who was more preoccupied with social rather than existential structure and thereby deepened the discussion. The problem was that I hadn't moved any further, hadn't budged from the spot in the fifteen years that had passed since I studied literature and the history of art in Bergen. Basically it flew in the face of everything. Inception, creation, emergence, the eternally new – just not in me or in my understanding.

I got up and went to the bathroom for a piss. My urine was light-colored, almost completely clear, and I was reminded of my father's, which I had seen whenever he had forgotten, for some reason or other, to flush in the morning. It had been dark yellow, almost brown. It was frightening. I had connected the color with his mind. And with masculinity. My own pale, almost colorless, urine was feminine, his dark urine masculine. His temper was also masculine. My terror was feminine.

I flushed the toilet and returned to the balcony, stood for a while and gazed across the lawn.

No, I didn't look down on her, she was wrong there. But she demanded so much of me, so unutterably more than any other person ever had, and she didn't realize. Sometimes it was so exasperating that it threw me into a state akin to insanity. I became so angry that nothing else existed apart from anger, without my being able to give vent to it, I held it inside me, and the way I was then, when my fury engulfed me and was absorbed into my body, when my movements rumbled with rage, could of course be confused with contempt. No, it *was* contempt. For a while it was, but the moment would pass and then something else was waiting. Was this something else the true state of affairs? Did we actually get along? Did I really love her? Christ, no, everything shifted and changed and ebbed and flowed, one thing was no truer than anything else. We got along fine and we got along badly, I loved her and I didn't love her.

The night before our wedding I asked her to wash the kitchen floor. I had already washed every single one of the other one hundred and thirty square meters. On her knees with a rag in her hand, she looked up at me and said this was not how it was supposed to be, that she had to wash the kitchen floor the day before her own wedding. No one else would put up with it, she said. It was unfair, she said. I answered that it was our floor and we were the ones who had to wash it, wedding or no wedding. I said nothing about this being only the second time she had washed a floor in the five years we had been together. If I had she would have lost her temper, would have said she had done all sorts of other things, she was the one who held the family together and she did more than anyone else she knew. I would have replied that she was living a lie, and then it would have gone on and on, so I said nothing. The following day I said *Yes* to her and she said *Yes* to me and we gazed at each other with tears in our eyes.

It is through feelings we connect with one another and it is the feelings which are good and bad, not the days.

I seemed to sense something behind me and turned at once, but the room was empty.

May as well go to bed, I thought.

Sink into a world that was beyond the world, the wonderful void.

I woke up in a bad mood. I always did, but as long as I had the critical first half an hour in peace, got a cup of coffee down me, and smoked a cigarette, it passed of its own accord. It was half past five. I pulled on the T-shirt and trousers I had worn the day before, walked barefoot into the living room, where Vanja and Heidi were sitting with bowls of muesli in front of them, Heidi on a high chair, Vanja on a normal one, which made her so low her chin barely reached over the table. Linda stood at the counter slicing an apple. Without saying a word I poured water into the kettle, sprinkled instant coffee into a cup, poured milk and muesli into a bowl, took it with me to the balcony, closed the door and sat down to eat, with my back to them. The sky was gray, more fog than mist, the air cold. After I had gulped down the breakfast mixture I went back in, filled my cup with boiling water, got my cigarettes and lighter from the shelf in the hall, and went back out. My body was cold, my joints were cold, my soul was cold.

Behind me someone banged on the window, I turned, it was Vanja, and she pushed the glass door open.

"Go back in," I said. "I'll be along soon."

She squeezed through, stood by the railing, and looked across the empty lawn.

"Go back in, I said."

"No," she said with a pout. "Why is no one out?"

"Because you get up so early. No one else gets up at this hour. It's still nighttime."

"It's morning," she said.

"Okay, okay," I said. "But it's very *early* morning. You'll realize how early it is when you're an adult. Where are your glasses by the way?"

"Inside."

"Go and put them on. Then you can both watch a movie."

She did as I said, and soon they were on their chairs in front of the laptop. Where movies were concerned they were insatiable, they could sit without moving for hours devouring whatever was on the screen. When Vanja was eighteen months old she watched her first movie from beginning to end. I remembered that because we traveled to Gotland the day after, it was the summer of 2005, the movie she saw was *Pippi on the Run*. I watched it with her, dropping off now and then, so it took on a dreamlike quality, and ever since, as we had seen it many, many times, I connected it with a kind of dreaminess, the way all the impressions from those days, when we lived in the apartment in Regeringsgatan, came back to me in all their detail. Watching films with her, I always had my eye on the background in the picture, the houses, the forest, the road, the beach, and I found just enough of interest in it to watch a ninety-minute children's movie without getting bored. If it was a film from the seventies, such as *Karlsson on the Roof* or *Elvis! Elvis!*, my interest increased because the times, which were discernible in everything, were the first I could remember, they were when I grew up, they were my whole world, and now they were gone. The seventies, that sad, unsophisticated, restaurant-less, impoverished decade with rest stops and gravel roads, VW Beetles and the Citroën DS, one TV channel and one radio channel, when everything was state-owned and almost nothing commercial, when the shops closed at four and the banks at three and no one who earned money from sports was allowed to participate in the Olympics, those times were gone, and, seeing how the world had moved on, it was incredible to think that once upon a time all this existed. Even a tiny glimpse of that world filled me with pleasure and sadness. Pleasure that I had been alive then, sadness that it had disappeared. The beginning of *Karlsson on the Roof*, where Svante is playing in Tegnér Park in Stockholm, muddied the waters because I walked through this park almost every day and recognized all the houses and streets, they were the same, yet they weren't, they were no longer in the 1970s but the 2000s, and the question I was unable to answer was: where had the seventies gone? In my head, apparently, in the heads of all the others who had once been alive then, but only there? What was time in a film? What was time in a photograph? It became even more puzzling when we watched *Elvis! Elvis!* because Linda's mother had been in that film, she played the teacher, a woman in her midthirties, and it was impossible, absolutely impossible, to connect the woman in the film with the woman who was our children's grandmother. Her appearance was different, her body language was different, even the sound of her voice was different. Was it the same woman?

Nostalgia is an illness, but it belongs to the person through whom time is filtered, unpredictably and individually, with all the flaws and defects inherent in human beings. The era that had passed is located in pockets of consciousness, some hidden and unseen, like ponds in remote forests, some bright and familiar like houses on the forest edge, but all of them fragile and changeable, and they die when consciousness dies. Films were a curse because they belonged to everyone, and they were mechanical and unchangeable, storage space for an era, corpses passed from one generation to the next, and still so new that the consequences were unpredictable. Already there were thousands of films in which all the people who had taken part in them were dead. This was a new way to be dead, with your body, life, and soul captured on camera forever while the body had decomposed long ago and was gone. Films were a graveyard, a necropolis, but still a work in progress, for what would they be like in two hundred years, in five hundred years, in a thousand years? In my grandparents' time it had been only actors and famous people, by and large, who were immortalized on film, and that was easy to relate to, that *their* images would live on. But now everyone filmed everyone else, every day thousands of films were posted on the Net, and after we were gone how would it feel to our successors to be able to see us all the time? They would be swimming in dead bodies in quite a different way. This would inevitably change the whole view of death, the perception of what it meant to be dead, and ultimately the view of what it meant to be alive.

And time? What would happen to time if the past piled up? Would it eventually be so overwhelming that it would drive out the present? We could already see one consequence of this, that trends from earlier eras were returning, that the eighties, which in a different world would only have existed in individual consciousness, bound up with individual life, were re-created in collective forms of expression: fashion and music.

Despite these feelings, we still let the children watch almost as many films as they wanted. I wasn't proud of it, and I didn't like it, but the calm that settled over the apartment was too wonderful to resist. Besides, in my defense, I thought, they learned a lot from what they saw.

Well, maybe not from *The Little Ghost Godfrey*.

If the island were a person and the road an artery, we got on the bus on one of the fingers, I mused a few hours later as I gazed inland at the black rocky landscape; the road was narrow and the roads crossing it were also narrow and disappeared between the mountains in this deserted region. And the activities that took place here, in low brick buildings behind wire fences, were of no interest to anyone except for those involved. Then the road widened, there were more cars, we came to large intersections with bridges and roads that wound around and met others, the traffic infrastructure grew, the complexity increased, the intervals between signs became shorter, soon there were buildings and life everywhere, we were approaching the center, the place all and sundry flocked to, the heart of the island. We glided past sidewalks thronged with people, surrounded by cars, in streets that became narrower and narrower until we arrived at a large concrete bus station, where the bus came to a halt and we alighted.

The transition from the deserted, uneventful countryside to the center of a town is the same everywhere, whether it is from Tromøya to Arendal, Jølster to Bergen, Cromer to Norwich, or Norwich to London. It was like falling, the speed increased the closer you came to the hub, and even though it was an external phenomenon, it was impossible not to experience subjectively, which seemed to cause your insides to vibrate with activity too, that is how open we are to the world, it flows ceaselessly through us and leaves its mark not only on our thoughts and ideas, but also on our moods and emotions. There is no other way I can explain the pleasure that arose in me as we strolled into town and sat down at a sidewalk café, Linda and I with coffee, the children with ice cream; it was as though I had come out of myself, as if after a long, hard winter, everything suddenly was wonderful and carefree, I started chatting away, I might even have been laughing in the sunshine, why? Everything was the same. Linda was the same, the children were the same, the sun in the sky was the same one that had been there for the ten days our holiday had lasted. What wasn't the same were the surroundings. Parks with wizened old men dressed in dark suits sitting on benches in the shade, often smoking, always elegant; small, crooked seventeenth-century brick houses, cobbled streets, big dilapidated churches in open squares, priests and nuns fluttering past, old women in black, either skeletal or voluminous, sitting on a chair outside a door or on doorsteps inside an archway. Avenues of palm trees, buses full of tourists rumbling past, semis, trucks carrying cement mixers, tradesmen in pickups or small vans, boxlike cars from the eighties, sparkling new aerodynamic sedans, mopeds – endless mopeds. Functional sixties and seventies architecture, resplendent eighties architecture, restrained nineties architecture, almost dystopian with its great expanses of dark stone and glass.

The town wasn't big, but it was a capital, and it was Spanish, though separated from Spain by a sea and hence different, not in anything major but in the minor detail. You saw signs of the old days everywhere, as though time hadn't wrought such great changes here, hadn't flooded the town and changed it radically, as it had done in other Spanish cities, where the past was fenced off, preserved in specimens, but here it had just seeped in all over the place. In addition, the fact that the sea made its presence felt everywhere made me think that Las Palmas was like the old South American colonial towns, where I had never been but whose atmosphere I nonetheless believed I could recognize and which I had longed to see all my life.

I said as much to Linda. We were ambling across a cobbled square in front of a white church, Vanja ran over to a marble lion and climbed up it while Heidi crouched down in front of the water in a little fountain.

"There's something South American about the atmosphere here, don't you think?" I said. "It's as if you can imagine this is Buenos Aires. Not that I've been there, of course. It's just the feeling you get. A bit offbeat, slightly run-down, colonies, palm trees, but also modern. Spanish, but not Spain."

"I know what you mean," she said. "It's wonderful."

"It is."

"You're so happy. That makes me happy too."

"I'm sorry," I said. "I should be like this all the time. There's no reason to be any other way."

"We're not going to move to Buenos Aires then?" she said.

I laughed.

"No, seriously. Why not?"

"There's nothing I'd like to do more," I said. "But for someone who fears the slightest change I can think of better alternatives than moving to Argentina with three small children."

"It doesn't *have* to be like that," she said. "It might be fantastic. It might be just what we need."

"I'd do it at the drop of a hat."

"That's agreed then? We move there? At some point in the future, I mean."

"If you're fine with it, there's no reason not to," I said.

We followed one of the narrow, shaded streets, discovered a museum devoted to Columbus's expeditions to America, and entered, it was like an augury. An atrium with the sun flooding in, flowers along the walls, a little fountain with a murmur of running water in the middle. The museum was located in the surrounding rooms, we walked through them, dark and cool after the bright light outside, full of charts, models, a few artifacts from ships or the days of sailing glory. Heidi was tired, she shrieked at the slightest thing, so after a quick circuit we agreed I would go for a walk with Heidi in the stroller to get her off to sleep while Linda and Vanja stayed there.

I walked down the shady side of the street, which opened, in narrow shafts, onto sun-filled yards or dark, tableau-like shop-windows where it wasn't always easy to establish which branch of commerce it was: a wooden torso dressed in servant's livery, was this attire an antiquity or an item that was sold to hotels? We emerged into a square, went to the right, and crossed a wide boulevard with trees that afforded some shade. Heidi was quiet, but her eyes were open.

"You need to sleep now, my girl," I said.

"No," she said.

"Well," I said, pushing her across another street into a park and out on the other side, where the modern center started. Something about the light above the part of town we had just left reminded me first of Stavanger, then Bergen. Not the light itself,

I immediately realized, but the proximity to the sea, the feeling of how close it was.

What effect did this have on my thoughts?

The streets, the market squares, the houses, the apartments, the shops, the cafés, all the people occupying them and who occupy your mind as well.

Then the exoticism all around you.

How frightening it must have been for Columbus and his men when they docked at the harbor here, the last outpost before the unknown. They didn't know what lay out there. How terrified they must have been!

I leaned forward and looked at Heidi, who still had her eyes open. I placed my hand on her chest.

"You can sleep if you like," I said. "You're tired, aren't you?"

She didn't say anything, she didn't react to my touch, just sat still staring at everything around us. H&M, Sony, Adidas, Zara. Glass gleamed, music blared from the open doorways, and as we passed them I could also feel that particular coldness that air-conditioning has. There were people everywhere. But no one with a stroller. I was the only person pushing one!

No, I wasn't. There was one. Black and attractive, with a little infant inside wearing a lace dress. The woman pushing the stroller was young and walking beside another woman, perhaps her sister, they were talking earnestly and intensely about something in the midst of a stream of besuited men and shorts-clad tourists. Then they were gone. I walked the length of the pedestrian street and by the time I reached the café where we had been that morning, next to the park, Heidi was asleep. I parked the stroller by a table, ordered a double espresso, and flipped out a cigarette, retrieved the Gombrowicz book from my backpack, but only managed a few lines, it felt wrong to read where there was so much to look at.

A suntanned man in his sixties with thinning sandy hair was reading a newspaper at a table close by. It was *Verdens Gang*. He looked up and met my gaze.

"Are you Norwegian?" I said.

"Yes," he said.

It was so rare for me to initiate a conversation with a stranger. Apart from when I was drunk, of course. Now I felt so light and carefree that it was the most natural thing in the world.

"You, too?" he said.

"Yes. Well, I live in Sweden, but I'm Norwegian."

"Here on holiday?"

"Yes. I take it you aren't?"

"No, I live here. The climate, you know. Sun and warmth all year round. I was sick of shoveling snow."

"I can understand that," I said.

He took a long swig of beer and lit a cigarette.

"And it's so lovely and cheap here. Buying a packet of cigarettes doesn't spell financial ruin."

"Do you live here in town?"

"Oh, no, no. I live farther north. I have a place in a little town there." He wore a lightweight gray jacket, a blue shirt, and a pair of Dressmann-style trousers underneath. He wasn't exactly scruffy, but nobody would call him well dressed. His shirt was wrinkled and I spotted a couple of dark stains on the breast of his jacket.

I told him the name of the hotel complex where we were staying and asked if his town lay nearby. He shook his head, took another swig of beer, and wiped his lip with a finger.

"I live on the other side."

"Many other Norwegians there?" I asked.

"There are a few of us, yes."

"So do you go home in the summer?"

"Many do. Not me though. I'm a resident."

There was an air of loneliness about him, perhaps also of unhappiness. The well-meaning friendly glint in his eye vanished as soon as he turned away.

"Are you happy here?" I said.

"Yes, I am," he said. "I don't have to shovel snow anyway."

"No, that's true," I said.

"We do actually get a little sometimes, but it doesn't settle, you know. It melts right away."

"Yes," I said.

He pulled another cigarette from the packet and raised it to his mouth. The hand holding the lighter trembled slightly.

I pretended to start reading again to give him some peace. But I was aware of his presence the whole time, whether I was staring toward the park, along the pedestrian street, or down at my book. He was my father's age, and although he hadn't reached the same state as my father, something about him was the same.

They came here to live in peace for their remaining years.

I looked down at Heidi, placed my hand on her head, just to touch her.

Once, a couple of years before he died, some friends of Mom's sister Kjellaug ran into Dad in the Canaries, in a bar, as far as I remembered, they had recognized him while he had no idea who they were. They'd started talking, he said he was a seaman but he'd come ashore now.

When Mom told me that, she had smiled because, as she put it, there was a lot of truth in what he said.

In the park a girl came up the dusty path, a boy on a bench sat up straight, he was almost glowing, and sure enough the very next moment they stood in an embrace, then they sat down next to each other, full to the brim with conversation and gestures. I glanced at the man beside me, he was reading the sports pages, then he looked up at the waiter, who placed another beer on his table.

I leaned back, stared up at the cloudless blue sky, lit a cigarette, inhaled, and blew the smoke out with relish. I always smoked Chesterfield abroad, it was my favorite brand, but they weren't sold in either Sweden or Norway apart from at Sørensen Tobakk on Torgallmenningen in Bergen, where they had been so expensive I could only afford them when my student loan arrived.

A beer would have been a pleasure.

But not with Heidi asleep in the stroller.

Anyhow, I would have to get back to Linda and Vanja soon. Another quarter of an hour.

I caught the waiter's eye, he came over, I ordered another double espresso, took my notebook and a pen from my backpack, described the trees in the park, first the shadows they cast over the parched, dusty ground, tried to make out what color the shadows *really* were, if the green of the sparse grass or the faintly reddish soil rubbed off on them, then I made a note of the dry, cracked, and probably brittle bark on one tree, the smoother, shinier bark on the second, and then the way the trunk seemed to cleave into branches, thinner and thinner until they became the small, trembling twigs at the farthermost ends. The way the sunlight seemed to be poured out over the leaves at the crown, as if from a bucket, and trickled down through the layers of foliage until it dripped down onto the ground below.

When I moved to Stockholm I went for a walk in Haga Park one morning with Geir, my new friend, it must have been mid-May because it was warm, but I still hadn't got together with Linda. We had walked from the Copper Tent and down the hill, along the big grassy slope where people lay sunbathing everywhere and into a more wooded area. I had started talking about all the fantastic trees that grew here. How individual they were, each with its very own shape, yet how alike, they shared the same features, both as trees generally and within the various species. How alive they were, just standing here in our midst, although we never thought of them as such, as living beings, or ever talked about them. Most of them were much older than we were, I said, some of these are from the nineteenth century, maybe even the eighteenth. Isn't that incredible? They are here, like us, but in a very different state. A very different form of life. We wonder whether there is life in outer space, what sort of weird and wonderful forms of life might exist there while we walk around among these fantastic creatures every day!

Geir burst into laughter.

"You know what everyone looks at these days, don't you?"

I shook my head.

"There are women lying all over the place. Many of them are beautiful. And most have only a bikini on. And there's you, looking at trees! Wake up, my boy!"

"There's no contradiction in that, surely?"

"Yes, there is. One is biology within the human domain. The other is biology outside the human domain. You're human."

"That's someone talking who can feel the sap rising. The difference is not as great as you imagine."

"Oh yes, it is. I don't know anyone who effuses about trees. No one! And over time I've gotten to know a lot of people."

"It doesn't mean I don't think about women."

"Are you offended?" he said with a laugh.

"A bit maybe," I said. "I don't think it's as unusual as you make out. There's even a weekly magazine about it."

"Oh?"

"Yes. *Woman & Tree.*"

"Ha ha ha. I can remember someone who used to run around this park hunting for trees. A friend of mine in sociology. He had to organize a stag night and the idea was they were going to play volleyball here. He ran around with a tape measure looking for two trees exactly the same distance apart as the net posts on a volleyball court. He's the biggest pedant I've ever met, so he wouldn't accept any approximations. No, the measurement had to be exact. I hardly need to tell you it took him an incredibly long time to write his thesis."

"He's an aberration. Talking about trees as you walk past them isn't."

"Sure it is. He stayed within the human domain. A game, a relationship between two entities. You talk about trees per se. To me all life is social. I'm not in the slightest bit interested in what lies outside. It's pointless."

We'd had this discussion at regular intervals over the four years that had passed since then. The material world with its stones, grains of sand, and stars or the biological world with its lynxes, beetles, and bacteria didn't interest him in the slightest unless it could tell him something about humanity. I, on the other hand, was always drawn to those realms where consciousness and identity were no longer operative, both inside the body – where the self appeared to go in two directions, toward the particular, in other words, all the processes that sustained themselves, as though humans consisted of many different animals, coordinated by one of the oldest and most primitive parts of the brain, and toward the general and shared, as all these organs and processes were the same for all – and outside the body, that is the world the body became part of the moment it ceased to exist. Geir did not accept any of this, and if his voice or facial expression didn't become weary with impatience whenever I talked about it, this was purely a result of his interest being focused on *me*, the social creature preoccupied with such matters.

The man at the neighboring table got to his feet, folded up his newspaper, tucked it under his arm, and glanced over at me.

"Have a good holiday," he said.

"Thank you," I said.

He walked briskly down to the pedestrian street, stood slightly stooped waiting for a green light at the crossing, and the next time I looked he had been swallowed up by the town.

On the way back to the museum I kept an eye open for a restaurant where we could have lunch, found a nice old one full of elderly islanders, but its rustic charm was outshone by the neighboring restaurant which had a little *terraza* where customers were served, beside a busy main road admittedly, however that was compensated for by the shade from the trees and the crooked walls of the building, against which a waiter leaned with a cigarette between his fingers while his colleagues ran in and out with trays full of food and drink.

When I entered the atrium of the museum Linda and Vanja were sitting on the bench by the wall squinting into the sun.

"Well, we've been having fun and games," Linda said as I pressed down on the stroller's brake.

"Oh yes?" I said, sitting beside her.

"Would you like to tell him, Vanja?"

"I dropped my shark down the cannon," Vanja said.

"No, you threw it down on purpose," Linda said. "We couldn't get it out," she said, turning to me. "And you know how attached she is to it."

"Yes, I do," I said.

"Then we went in to see if we could get someone to help us."

"In those cannons there?" I said, nodding toward the two big verdigrised cannons by the opposite wall.

"Yes, exactly. Columbus's cannons."

"Are they?"

"Yes. The cannons that were on the ships that discovered America. That's where our daughter dropped her shark hairbrush."

"What happened then?"

"There was a huge fuss and palaver. All the staff came out to help. They lifted the cannon down and it banged against the wall and the cannon cracked. But in the end the shark came out. You should've seen their faces when they saw that what we'd lost was a hairbrush!"

"Good thing I wasn't here. I would've died of shame."

She laughed.

"But they didn't seem to mind. They were just happy to help. You know what it's like with children here. They love children so much they'd do anything for them."

"Are you sure? They're not inside now, fuming? I mean, cracking Columbus's cannon?"

"I got my shark back!" Vanja said, narrowing her eyes and smiling.

"But now I'm starving. Shall we go and get something to eat?" Linda said.

I nodded, got up, and wheeled over the stroller. Vanja jumped up and then our little cavalcade trundled out of the museum.

Throughout our meal the wind tugged and tore at the tablecloth. The paper napkins flew into the air several times, but one of the waiters always managed to pick them up before I could get to my feet. We talked about the future awaiting us in Buenos Aires, and it was nice, perhaps the nicest time since we had moved to Malmö the summer before, and everything, including our lives, was bathed in the light of newness. After we had eaten and were waiting for our coffee, I told her about the restaurant next door, how beautiful it was with its thick brick walls and wooden benches and, with Heidi in her arms, she went in while I sat with Vanja, who was busy blowing down her straw, making her soda bubble and froth, but she didn't seem to be doing it for fun, her expression was rather one of preoccupation and stubborn perseverance.

I racked my brains for something to say to her.

Cars whooshed past on the road. A nun appeared at the entrance to a street and was gone again. The tall, slim conifers swayed in the wind. I took an apple from my backpack and placed it on the table between us.

"Did you know that some apples can talk?" I said.

She looked up at me without moving her head. Her eyes were skeptical, though not totally dismissive.

"When I was walking with Heidi I heard a voice in my backpack, you know. I'm not sure, but I think it was the apple. If so, we're so incredibly lucky because there are hardly *any* apples that can talk. But I think this one can. Do you know how small the chances are of that?"

She shook her head, her eyes fixed on me.

"They can't speak human language. That's obvious. You didn't think they could, did you?"

She shook her head again.

"They speak applish. Look, if I shake it a bit, it might say something. Shall I try?"

She pushed her glass away.

"It can't speak," she said. "You're teasing me."

"No, I'm not. It's very unusual. That's probably why you've never heard of it."

I gave a start.

"There! Did you hear it?"

She stared at the apple, shaking her head. I lifted the apple to my ear and made big eyes.

"It said something," I said.

"No, it didn't." She laughed. "It did not."

"Yes, it did. Here, *you* listen."

I held up the apple and she leaned over and put her ear to it.

"Can you hear anything?" I said.

She shook her head.

"Daddy," she said. "Apples can't talk."

"It just did," I said.

"What did it say then?"

"I'm not sure. It was applish. But I think it said, 'I'm so lonely.'"

"You can't speak applish."

"Yes, I can. Not very well. But I understand a little."

"How did you learn it?"

"I picked bits up here and there. There were lots and lots of apple trees where I grew up."

"You're teasing me."

"Listen. Did you hear that?"

She gave a tentative smile and shook her head.

"It said, 'What a lovely girl. What's her name?'"

"My name's Vanja."

"Vanja," I squeaked.

"That was you," Vanja said. "It can't talk."

I began to feel sorry for her.

"You're right, it was," I said. "Did you think apples could talk?"

"No." She laughed.

"Are you sure?" I said, lifting the apple to my mouth and taking a bite.

"Don't eat it!" she said.

"But I was just teasing you," I said. "It's only an apple."

"Okay," she said.

The waiter came with two cups of coffee and two bowls of ice cream. Vanja started hers as soon as he put the bowl in front of her. I said thank you and looked up, but he didn't meet my gaze, walked over with bowed head to the table beside us, set the plates on his right arm, stacked the glasses, which he carried in his left hand, and disappeared into the darkness of the restaurant.

"I want to blow," Vanja said.

I pushed the cup over to her, she blew, I took a sip. Linda appeared from around the corner, still carrying Heidi on her hip. She looked flustered.

"I fell over inside," she said. "Right onto my side. With Heidi in my arm as well."

"Did you hurt yourself?"

"A little," she said, putting Heidi in the high chair. I pushed her ice cream over to her. "It's a tiled floor. I think Heidi got a bang too. Or perhaps it was mostly a fright. Anyway, there was quite a commotion in there. Everyone rushed over to help me. Not so strange, I suppose. A pregnant woman with a child in her arm falling on the floor. I toppled over. Like a boat heeling to one side. Then all these kind people came running over to help me to my feet and they brushed me down and asked me how I was."

"Sounds very dramatic," I said.

"It was. And I felt so helpless. Suddenly not being able to walk. Do you know what I mean?"

"Yes."

"You don't see any children here. God knows where they are. Not here anyway. Then I come along with a child in my belly and one in my arm and right in front of everyone, bang. I felt so Scandinavian."

In the bus going home Vanja slept with her head in Linda's lap while Heidi sat limply on mine dozing. Her little body registered all the bus's jerks and jolts as at first we drove from traffic light to traffic light through the town, then onto the motorway along the coast where the blazing sun hung above the dark blue sea.

Happiness isn't in my nature, but happy was how I felt.

Everything was light and airy, my emotions were lofty and uncomplicated, the mere sight of a bulging wire fence or a stack of worn tires outside a garage opened my soul, and a rare warmth spread through my insides.

What effect does happiness have?

Happiness erases. Happiness erodes. Happiness overflows. All that is difficult, all that usually hinders or limits us, disappears inside happiness. In the long term it's unbearable because there is no resistance in happiness, if you lean against it, you will fall.

Where do you fall?

Into open space, my friend.

I looked at Linda, she had leaned back against the seat and closed her eyes. Vanja's face was covered with her hair; she lay like a tuft of grass on Linda's lap.

I bent forward a little and peeked at Heidi, who stared back without interest.

I loved them. This was my gang.

My family.

In terms of pure biomass, we were nothing special. Heidi weighed perhaps ten kilos, Vanja maybe twelve, plus Linda's and my weight we constituted something like one hundred and ninety kilos. That was considerably less than a horse, I imagined, and about the same as a mature male gorilla. If we lay close together our physical bulk was nothing to shout about either, a sea lion was bulkier. In terms of intangible factors, however – which was the essence of a family – in other words everything connected with thoughts, dreams, and feelings, the family's inner life, the aggregate was explosive, and spread over time, which was the relevant dimension to see the family in, it would cover an almost endless surface area. Once I met my great-grandmother, which meant that Vanja and Heidi and the new baby belonged to the fifth generation, and if fate was kind, they could in their turn witness three further generations, so this little pile of flesh numbered eight generations, or two hundred years, with all the concomitant changing cultural and social conditions, not to mention how many people it included. A whole little world was what was moving along the highway at great speed this late-spring afternoon, my own little family, which might eventually develop its own special characteristics, something typical only of us, as I had encountered many times in other families and always envied: their security and goodness and contentment.

When the children had gone to sleep we moved closer and were near each other in the darkness. Linda's eyes were wide open, the way I remembered them from the first weeks we were together, somehow bare and defenseless. Afterward we went onto the balcony, me with the beer that had become a habit during the ten days we had been there, Linda with a ginger ale. The darkness seemed to hover in the air, which became grayer and dimmer by the minute as stars appeared in the sky one after the other, hesitantly, a little shyly, as though they didn't really trust the memory of how they had shone the previous night, proud and firm and minerally unforgiving. But, bit by bit, the memory came back to them and soon the whole of the now black sky was full of sparkling lights.

"I think I'll go to bed," Linda said, getting up. "Thank you for everything today. Would you like me to switch on the light for you?"

"Please," I said. "Good night."

"Good night, my prince."

The light came on, her footsteps faded into the bedroom, I sat down on the chair and put my feet on the railing. What if Columbus had turned around when they discovered America? I wondered. What if they had said they would leave the continent intact and allow those living there to continue their lives in peace? What if they had said they wouldn't exploit its riches and its people? Then America would only have existed as a concept in old Europe, in Asia and Africa. There is an enormous continent out there, to the west, every new generation would learn. We have no idea what goes on there. Nor what it looks like, what species of plants and animals exist there, or what people think about life and existence. We know nothing of this and we won't find out.

I had never considered a more impossible thought. It would go against everything we were.

But it would have been so fantastic. A secret, undiscovered continent no one had opened up or exploited but had just left in peace. What an incredible shadow of ignorance that would have cast over our European brains.

I finished my beer, stubbed out my cigarette, and stood for a moment holding the balcony railing looking into the darkness behind the light from the bungalows, at the sea that stretched into the distance.

Then I, too, went to bed.

Two nights later the plane left for home, it was packed, and we felt stressed with all our baggage and our two small children, but we got on board and after a few minutes in the air both Vanja and Heidi fell asleep. We sank back in our seats. The plane flew through the black sky, lights flashing. The mood on board was strange, many passengers were feverishly drinking and talking in loud voices and laughing, probably trying to squeeze every last minute out of their vacation, others slept. After half an hour the captain made an announcement over the intercom, asking everyone to sit down and fasten their seat belts, we were entering a spot of turbulence. Vanja woke up and started crying. It wasn't a low, whiny cry, she screamed from the bottom of her lungs. That woke Heidi, who also started crying. Suddenly there was an inferno around us. Linda and I frenetically tried to calm them down, but nothing was any use, they were caught up in something they couldn't get out of and just kept screaming. People tolerated it for the first few minutes, but after a quarter of an hour the displeasure and annoyance around us were palpable. Why couldn't we get our godforsaken kids to shut up? Why were they screaming like that? Were we bad parents? It was unbearable, and when the seat belt sign was switched off I asked Linda to stand up so that I could carry Heidi into the central aisle, she did, I undid Heidi's belt and lifted her up, she resisted, twisted and squirmed, her whole body as tense as a spring, while Vanja was kicking the seat in front of her. I squeezed through the narrow gap between the seats, bent double, with Heidi held firmly to my chest, wriggling and screaming in my ear, finally emerged in the aisle, made my way through to where there was a measure of space, but Heidi wasn't happy, she didn't want to walk, didn't want to be carried, didn't want any candy, didn't want to see what was behind the curtain, she just wanted to scream and scream, her face bright red, legs kicking in all directions. People were no longer hiding their irritation, they were staring at me with obvious animosity, a man who couldn't control his child. I forced Heidi back into her seat, the man in front of us turned and told us to stop the kid kicking him, which infuriated Linda, she's four, she shouted, I placed a hand on her shoulder, a flight attendant leaned over us with some toys, Vanja threw them away, in a rage. I was drenched in sweat. The girls were caught in a fit and couldn't get out of it, and all I could think was: what must the other passengers be thinking. It was obvious we were bad parents, why would children scream like this otherwise? Their childhood must be terrible, traumatizing. Something *had* to be wrong. I had *never* seen other children behaving like this in public. The situation was acute, we had to get them to stop, but none of our methods was helping, it was like throwing gasoline on a fire. This situation was chronic, it was a symptom of something else, which chafed away incessantly behind my sweaty forehead. I felt like "white trash" on a charter trip to Gran Canaria with my neglected children. Everything was out of control, and in a very confined area to make matters worse.

They kept it up for a good hour. Then they stopped. First Vanja, afterward Heidi. They sat staring into space, sweaty and exhausted. I couldn't believe it was true and didn't dare move a muscle. A few minutes later they fell asleep, and seven hours later we were able to tuck them into their own beds in our apartment. Absolutely drained, we looked at each other and promised we would never, ever, under any circumstances, do anything like this again. But then, slowly and imperceptibly, all the hassle around the journey and the vulgarity of the holiday center was forgotten; what remained of the two weeks was the children's pleasure in the pool, the evenings on the balcony, the trip to Las Palmas.

John was born, and Linda stayed at home with him while I took the girls to school and brought them home every morning and afternoon, I worked at home during the intervening six hours, partly on a translation of the Bible, partly on a novel I was making no headway with, until the following spring, when I started writing about myself. Linda sat on the office chair, in the darkness after the children were in bed, listening to me reading from it, she said it was "heady stuff." At the end of the summer, which was John's first, we went to see Yngve in Voss, then my mother in Jølster, and plans for my fortieth had been forged behind my back. It was to be a small party – twenty or so people is not a lot – but for me it was overwhelming. We had set up a long table in the sitting room, and when all the guests had assembled in another room, glass of champagne in hand, and we were about to welcome them, I had thought of saying they were all characters in a novel I was writing and that everything they did and said over the evening would be used against them, but I didn't have the courage, I said nothing, Linda made the speech, I stood beside her, smiling. Tore spoke, Geir G. and Espen spoke, Linda sang, and Yngve was in despair when he realized that my wish for no speeches was being ignored and that he, as the brother, appeared to be neglecting his duty. I told him it didn't matter. Later in the evening he got together with Knut Olav, Hans, and Tore and gave a little concert, they played one Kafkatrakterne song, one Lemen song, and one ABBA hit. For the rest of the night we danced and drank, I danced for the first time in what must have been fifteen years, and when we went to bed, at about seven in the morning, I was happy and thinking this had been the beginning of something. On New Year's Eve, three weeks later, Geir and Christina got married in Malmö, and had their wedding party in our place, that too as low profile as possible: there were six adults and five children around the table. The idea was that they would stay with us for a few days afterward, but they left in the evening of New Year's Day, Linda's brother, Mathias, had called, he asked to speak to Linda, I said she was resting, he said it was important, their father had died, could I wake her up?

◆ ◆ ◆

Today is August 26, 2011. It is 5:59. I am writing this in an unfurnished loft in Glemmingebro, in what we have begun to call the "summer house" as it isn't insulated. I have just been to the main house to wake Linda up; in two hours Vanja and Heidi go to school. It is a stone's throw away and there are only thirty pupils in total in the four classes. We never planned to move here, it just happened, like so much else. The plan was that we would have the house as a summer residence, come here every weekend and holiday, but only eight months after we had taken it over we moved in. So now we live here, right out in the country. I get up at four every morning, have a cup of coffee and a smoke before coming over here, into the freezing-cold loft, then I write until eight, when I take Vanja and Heidi to school, and afterward have a thirty-minute nap before resuming my writing for the rest of the day. In the afternoon and evening I'm in the garden, I have been going wild cutting down trees and bushes in the central part, where, it transpired, there were beautiful flagstone paths, completely hidden by soil and undergrowth. I removed the worst, and last week I sowed grass, which has already started coming up. On the first afternoon I cleared away the branches and twigs, tore up bushes and plants, I couldn't stop; at nine the children were hanging out the window in their pajamas asking me what I was doing running back and forth, dragging whole trees after me, and I didn't stop until close to midnight, and it has been like that ever since; once I start working I don't want to stop, and I have to force myself to go to bed to ensure I have enough strength to write the following day. That was what my father did when I was a boy, he was always in the garden working, and I was never able to understand why – what could it possibly give him? – until now. Previously I thought it was boring, a duty, and when for example I helped my mother at home or when we were at the cabin it was a chore, I always preferred to sit and read. Now I understand. From the outside, and invariably I did regard my father and what he did from the outside, gardening is the very symbol of bourgeois stasis, utterly ridiculous and superficial, an artificial way of ordering the world's chaos by limiting the world to a lawn and a few bushes and subjugating them completely. The garden is also part of your private life others can see and therefore functions as a kind of display window for those around. In other words, a façade.

Yesterday I sat in the garden reading a text Yngve had written about the Aller Værste! and their album *Materialtretthet*, in which he also interviewed the surviving band members about that period. One of them, I think it was Harald Øhrn, described himself as a vagabond, a man who had lived the life of a vagabond. That instant the attraction was back: seeing the world open up before you, always traveling, no roots, only that, the world continuing to open. That was what I dreamed of when I was in my teens, but I didn't know what it was and I never realized the dream. The band they had in 1979 was about that, the freedom to do exactly what they wanted, completely unfettered by anything that had gone before. Chris Erichsen put it best, punk was about out with the old, all history, all the old heroes, all the bygones, and in with the new, what is here, right now, this is what counts, follow it wherever it may lead. This is what it is like being twenty, everything is open, but as that which isn't open still hasn't revealed itself, you don't know about it, what it entails, until it is too late, and then the next generation has the world at their feet while you putter around in a suburban garden with children and a car and perhaps soon even a dog, if our eldest gets her way, which of course she will.

That is how I felt yesterday as I read Yngve's text with Heidi swinging under an apple tree and occasionally shouting whatever came into her head at me, for example she asked me if I knew what she was going to be when she was big. No, I said. I'm going to be a pixie, she shouted. She laughed at that for a long time. I said it sounded like a good idea, and read on. Taking life into your own hands: not studying, not working, just jamming with a few pals in a band. Or traveling down through Europe, finding a job, earning some money, always on the move.

That was the attraction. It was about being open to the world, letting what happened, happen, and not being governed by the fixed structures that education, job, children, and a house constituted, this calcification of life that came with institutions: school for your children, hospital and a care home for your parents perhaps, a job for you.

So when I was running around the garden like a crazy man, with a petty-bourgeois fire burning in my insides, not dissimilar to my father, although his beard was thick and mine wispy, his upper torso strong and mine weak, it was hard to regard this as anything other than an escape inward. Yet there was something about it that I liked. The smell of soil, all the worms and beetles wriggling and crawling in it, the pleasure of a big branch falling to the ground and the light flooding across the previously overshadowed flagstones, the children wandering over sometimes to see what I was doing or to say something to me.

I'd had the chance when I was twenty. I hadn't taken it. Now they had the chance. Now it was their turn. It was their future.

This is the voice of resignation speaking here, but also of necessity and sudden insight: this is how it must always have been. I never knew. But someone has always known, for someone has always been there. *Ulysses* deals with this as well, the difference between being the son, which Stephen Dedalus is, and being the father, which Leopold Bloom is. Stephen outdoes Bloom in everything, but not in this. Leopold has nothing of Stephen's yearnings and aspirations, he doesn't want anything else, he's at home. Leopold is a complete person, Stephen Dedalus an incomplete person. Only Stephen can create, for to create is to want everything, to create is to want to come home, and the whole person doesn't feel that unrest, that urge, those yearnings. Hamlet, like Stephen, is a son and actually no more than that. It is his father's death that triggers his crisis and his mother's desertion that keeps it alive. Hamlet has no home. Jesus wasn't a father either, but a son, and he had no home. Hamlet, Stephen, Jesus, Kafka, Proust were all sons, not fathers. So there was something about being human that they didn't know and perhaps didn't know about either. But what was it? What is it to be a father? Being a father is a commitment, so it is possible to have children without being a father. But what are you committing yourself to? You have to be at your post; you have to be at home. Yearnings and aspirations are irreconcilable with this because what you hunger for is limitless and what home does is set limits. A father without limits is no father, but a man with children. A man without limits is a child, that is, the eternal son. The eternal son takes or gets, he doesn't give, and he takes or gets because he isn't whole and he isn't his own person. It is not some accidental detail that Dad moved into his mother's house before he died; he died a son. He had abrogated his responsibility as a father, and you can only do that if paternal duty is an external entity, a role you have assumed out of obligation. I believe that is how it was for him. He didn't want to be there. He became a father at twenty and must have suppressed all his urges to break with propriety, combated all the yearnings and aspirations because that aggression, that anger and frustration he had, which characterized my whole childhood, could only exist in someone who didn't want to be there, who didn't want to do what he was doing. If that was so, he had sacrificed his entire young adult life, the years between twenty and forty, doing something he didn't want to do but was forced to do. I was sixteen, as good as grown up, when he left the family, which suggests he took his responsibilities seriously. But he was no father, he was a son. He wasn't whole, he had no inner peace, none of the inner gravity adults have. Mom was also twenty when she became a mother, but she was an adult or grew into adulthood with the responsibilities that came. She was also his mother, in the sense that she set his limits, which was what he was unable to do himself, and no sons can. This is a simple explanation, but I believe it to be true. Linda's father was without limits in a very different way: he had been diagnosed as a manic depressive, which is as good as a complete disclaimer of any responsibility for his own life, since the self cannot control the mania's frenzied activity and the depression's inactivity, there is something inside that constantly drives the self up or down, which means it is never present, it either expands into the world or implodes, and of course the disclaimer applies to the lives of his children as well. Both Linda and I were the children of sons, and we had experienced firsthand fathers without limits, Linda from the time she was quite small, me from the age of sixteen, but actually also from the time when I was quite small, as what I witnessed and experienced with respect to Dad was a limitless man setting limits, which in the absence of any inner peace or gravity were defined by the outside, and for someone born in 1944, this was the authoritarian, rule-setting father. The mother of Linda's father died when he was thirteen and he alone had been responsible for his siblings. He had been in the hospital when she died, he had been lying beside her on the bed. He'd been very attached to his mother and perhaps it was as simple as this: his attachment never weakened because her life ceased before he had cut himself free. It remained strong inside him, I suppose. I don't know, I met him only three times. Once in our apartment in Regeringsgatan, once in his apartment, and once by chance on the street. He was a warm, open person, perhaps too open for his own good. In my life with Linda he was a distant figure, I imagined she had distanced herself from him long ago because she had no choice.

When she was in her mid-twenties she, too, was diagnosed with manic depression, or bipolar disorder, as it is called, and had spent more than a year in the hospital. Her increasingly intense life was suddenly out of control, as though she had fallen over the edge. She fell into the limitless. It was one of the options in her life, one of the paths that were open to her. When we met, the manic phase had passed and was over. At that time her father was living alone in an apartment only a hundred meters from ours, somehow outside the community, because he hadn't had a job for many years, from when he fell ill, and he had organized his life in the best way he could for himself. He died alone in a new apartment, just after moving in. It was New Year's Eve. By the time Linda found out, it was New Year's Day, she sat down on the hall floor with her back against the wall. The children were asleep. She wept. Christina and Geir packed their bags and left to give us some space. In the night I woke to Linda crying beside me, I stroked her back and fell asleep again. I didn't realize that for the next three weeks she went through exactly the same thing as I had gone through with my father, when he'd died eleven years earlier. She traveled to Stockholm, dealt with the undertakers, dealt with the solicitor, pored over her father's worldly goods in the apartment with her brother Mathias, and grieved. She mourned the loss of her father, but I, her husband, wasn't there for her. I was writing. And what was I writing about? I was writing about the death of my father, which at that time, eleven years ago, had consumed me totally, darkened my life, and it still consumed me. When it happened to Linda I saw it from a great distance, and my attempts to console her and be sympathetic were mechanical. When it came to the crunch, I failed her. I told myself my role was to take care of the children and I had to write, not only for my own sake, but for the family's, we needed the money. I was also angry with Linda and had been for a long time. But sometimes you have to be big enough to rise above the trivial and the mundane, all the pettiness and self-absorption in which we live our lives, or at least I do, because now, when it really counts, when it is a life-or-death situation, the minutiae don't matter and the person who clings to them is small-minded.

On the morning before the funeral we caught a plane to Stockholm. John was a year and a half old, Heidi was three and a half, Vanja approaching five. A friend of Linda's had given us the use of her apartment, which the children reduced to bedlam within seconds. Late in the afternoon Linda's mother, Ingrid, arrived, then Linda's brother, Mathias. We shared a bottle of wine and talked for a couple of hours. Mathias, a warm, attentive person, asked me how my writing was going. I said I was busy with an autobiographical novel and he was in it. His eyes widened. Linda said with a smile that she thought I was performing a character assassination on her in the novel. I countered that she had the right of veto, if she wanted something excised all she had to do was say so. Mathias said Linda could use the veto on his behalf as well. I had such a bad conscience about what I had written that I decided there and then to delete everything to do with them. They were so kind! And on the following day they were going to bury their father and Ingrid's ex-husband. Who was I to write about them in such a vulnerable situation? The whole time we were sitting there the children kept wandering in and out of the other room, where they were watching a film on a laptop. Heidi sat on my lap staring impishly at Mathias for long periods at a time; Vanja stayed with her grandmother and ignored Mathias, while John was devouring him with his eyes and only turned away for a second when Mathias lifted him in the air, then John burst into laughter as Mathias threw him up toward the ceiling.

Mathias and Linda discussed the final preparations for the following day, we talked briefly about whether we should let Ingrid look after the children for an hour while we adjourned to a nearby café, but we decided to stay, and after mother and son had left, we tucked in the children and went to bed early ourselves. That is, I sat up reading as everyone around me slept, Carl-Johan Vallgren's new novel *Kunzelmann & Kunzelmann*, a contemporary thriller I'd bought the day before on the basis of a review it had received on Swedish TV: Ingrid Elam had said, "I don't think much of this," which was a mark of quality for me. And it was great sitting there reading in the darkened flat, under the light of a single lamp, surrounded by the breathing of tiny people, without a thought for anything except the story, which was narrated so deftly and with such energy.

The next day I put on my black suit, and got the girls into their best dresses and their winter gear, which fortunately we'd had the presence of mind to bring along, outside a gale was blowing, a cross between rain and sleet, into the back of the waiting taxi, buckle the children in, twenty kilometers to Skogskyrkogården Cemetery, with Ingrid and Mathias, and Helena, who had come along to help us with John during the ceremony. We arrived an hour before the proceedings were due to start. Just inside the walls surrounding the chapel there was a little house, where we left our things while Vanja and Helena's one-year-older daughter, Blanca, ran between the trees playing, with Heidi bringing up the rear, a little hesitantly. Linda and Mathias went into the chapel to see what it was like and to speak to the undertaker.

While they were inside a vehicle stopped on the other side of the cemetery. One man opened the rear door, another came to help, together they carefully lifted a coffin onto a bier.

The coffin contained Linda's father.

Slowly the two men in black rolled the coffin along a flagstone path between the green fir trees, which swayed to and fro in the wind. The men came to a halt in front of the doors, opened them, and trundled the bier into the chapel. I just glimpsed them gently lifting the coffin onto the catafalque at the opposite end of the little room before the doors closed. I turned my head to look for the girls. They were running between the trees, easy to spot against the dirty gray snow covering the ground. The doors opened again, the two men in black came out, strolled over to the hearse on the other side of the fence, and got in. The rear lights went red as the engine started up. The sky above the green fir trees was a leaden gray.

The vehicle slowly passed down the road and was gone. It struck me that there was the quality of a monument about the stone chapel, despite its diminutive size. The aesthetics of the twenties, this spirit of Blood and Soil, Nordic forests and heroic deaths lay over the whole of the enormous cemetery grounds.

Linda and Mathias returned. I looked down, not wishing to intrude on their grief. Linda suggested the children should eat something, a banana or a mandarin. The fruit was in my backpack, which I had left at home.

"I forgot to bring my backpack," I said.

"WHAT?" Linda said, staring at me furiously.

"What did you put in it?" I asked. "Anything important?"

I thought maybe the book with the poem she was going to read or something vital for the ceremony. But no, only some food and diapers.

"That's just *perfect*," she said angrily. "Well, *no one* can rely on you!"

I was fuming, but the circumstances were a mitigating factor, even I understood that, in forty minutes her father would be buried, so I kept my mouth shut.

"Give me a cigarette," she said.

"I don't have any," I said.

"You're a smoker. Why don't you have any cigarettes today of all days?"

"Because you took them this morning. You put them in your jacket. I imagine they're still there."

"No," she said, patting her pockets. "Oh, yes, here they . . ."

Then she went out and disappeared behind the waiting room while Helena avoided looking at me.

"I'll take John and try to get him off to sleep," I said. She nodded, I pushed the stroller onto the path and walked back and forth with him – peering up from beneath a pile of clothes and blankets – for twenty minutes as the icy wind howled through the thin material of my suit and the slush I was trudging through soaked my flimsy shoes. On my return, with John asleep in the stroller, I was frozen, colder than I had been in years. The first mourners had arrived, I shook their hands, Linda's husband, I said, yes, we've heard about you, they replied. Fifteen of them, plus the children, stood gathered around the coffin later. Mathias laid a scarf on the coffin from the football club his father had played for in his youth, we sat down, a harpist played Bach, Vanja and Heidi stared with big eyes. But they knew they had to be quiet, and when Heidi wanted to say something to me she did so in a whisper. Mathias raised his head now and then, as though gasping for air, his face distorted in sudden grimaces. Linda had tears in her eyes, which occasionally coursed down her cheeks. When the first piece of music came, a dance band tune by Benny Andersson's Orchestra, grief also overcame me. I hadn't known him, but I knew his children, it was their grief that touched me. Vanja sat staring intensely at her mother, she had never seen this before, and sent her a smile from time to time, as if to console her. I had told her beforehand that Mommy would cry, and it didn't matter, that was how it was at funerals, you cried and were sad, you were saying goodbye to someone who would never come back. The priest gave a thumbnail sketch of the deceased's life, Mathias read out his commemorative speech, bursting into tears at the beginning and end, otherwise his reading was loud and clear. Linda read a poem. "Bridge over Troubled Water" was played. Then Vanja started sobbing. She was inconsolable and clung to Linda. Heidi, who was sitting on my lap, patted her. In the end it became so bad that I took them out and carried them down to the sentry-box house where John was sleeping. When we entered, Vanja immediately wanted to return, she wasn't crying anymore, she wanted to lay her flowers on the coffin, as we had planned to do. I carried them back, one on each arm, put them down outside, opened the doors, and went in as the ceremony was drawing to a close and the last people were laying flowers on the coffin. Afterward Linda said it had been so beautiful when the doors opened and we entered with the light behind us, the two small children laid their bouquets on the coffin, the final piece of music was played, everyone paused and bowed by the coffin on their way out, paying their last respects to the deceased.

At the restaurant to which we repaired after the ceremony, Linda's cousins told me how it had been when her father came to visit them in the summer, how he had filled their lives for a few days with his manic energy and lust for adventure and took them fishing or for a drive, incapable of standing still for a moment.

The next day we went with the children to the island of Djurgården. While we were at the aquarium there, Mathias came in. He told us he had been to a pub after the funeral to "get smashed out of his head," as he put it. His eyes were sensitive and kind, his voice was always cheery, he always tried to find something lighthearted to say, and as we were about to leave, he placed a friendly hand on my shoulder. He had lost his father and, sitting there, I thought, it wasn't the same father that Linda had lost because being a son or a daughter is not the same, and Linda and Mathias were so fundamentally dissimilar, also in grief, that they must have had a different experience of him.

In the afternoon we packed our things and caught the train to Arlanda Airport. We arrived three hours before the departure. But the children played and were in a good mood the whole time, even though the plane was an hour late and we didn't take off until half past nine. They fell asleep the minute we were seated on board, and when we landed in Kastrup at half past ten we had a problem: how to manage two suitcases, a backpack, a big bag, and three sleepy children? On top of which, the plane had parked at the farthermost gate, probably a fifteen-minute walk from the arrivals hall. Somehow we managed to get off the plane and into the endlessly long, empty corridor. Linda carried John and held Vanja's hand, I carried Heidi and managed the two suitcases, the backpack, and the big bag. After roughly a hundred meters Linda said she couldn't go on, it was too difficult. But you're only carrying John, I said. Surely you must be able to do that, for Christ's sake. But no, her arms hurt and she was in pain, she couldn't do it.

"Help!" she shouted in a loud voice. "Help us!"

"Shhh," I said. "You can't shout for help here, you know that."

A couple ahead of us turned and looked at us. I shook my head in an attempt to signal that it was nothing serious. If one of us had been having a heart attack I could have understood her calling for help. But just because she had her hands full? For God's sake. For God's sake.

I spotted a couple of trolleys.

I breathed a sigh of relief, placed the cases on the bottom of one, put Heidi on top, and set off without waiting for Linda. "Help." If we had got lost in the mountains or a boat had capsized at sea I might have shouted for help. But at a bloody airport?

I turned, grinned, and waited for them. The rest of the trip was fine, the children were cheery despite being tired, problems only came up at the taxi rank, Linda shouted at the poor taxi driver, who became so angry that he threw our luggage down on the road and yelled back. A kind, friendly driver came to our rescue as I was wishing the ground would swallow me up, the mortification and shame of it. He asked if we'd had a long journey, yes, said Linda, were we tired, yes, said Linda, I was in torment where I sat, watching the lights sweep across the hood as we approached Triangeln Mall in Malmö and could finally get out, take the elevator, put the children to bed, and then ourselves. The last thing I did was to put Heidi's dinosaur egg in a bowl of water. So that it would have cracked and a little dinosaur would have emerged by the time she woke the following morning.

◆ ◆ ◆

August 27, 2011, 8:06. I am sitting in an annex on the island of Møn, in Denmark, I have to appear onstage this afternoon and tomorrow afternoon, and I drove here from Glemmingebro last night. Linda's mother is at home with us helping out, she has been there all month. After I've finished here I'll go sit in my study in

Malmö and finish the novel. On Friday I am going to the literature festival in Louisiana, outside Copenhagen, with Linda. Some
aspects of her life are changing. She has started to come to terms
with them. She goes for a long walk every morning, she's stopped
smoking, she doesn't drink alcohol anymore, not even a glass of
wine with food, she eats healthily, and for more than a month she
hasn't been either up in the skies or down in the dumps, but present, inside herself, as it were.

Last night I woke to her screams.

"Help," she shouted, in a loud drawn-out cry, as though danger were looming.

I was awake at once, put my arm around her, and told her it
was only a bad dream. She mumbled that she knew and fell asleep
again. It was half past three, I went down to the kitchen and made
some coffee, went up to the loft in the other house and started
writing. I had written the passage about her father's funeral
straight after it happened and had promptly forgotten it. I remembered it then because she had called for help at the airport and
was doing so again now. At the time I had taken it literally, she
wanted help carrying John, but when I reread the passage it was
impossible not to think of something else, something greater, a
cry from her inner being, to me, I had to go to her rescue. I had
to put everything aside, she was in distress, I had to help.

I hadn't done that, I had lost my temper and was
embarrassed.

When she screamed in the night I thought I should help her.
I hope I can, I hope I am good enough. I hope I have learned.

◆ ◆ ◆

August 28, 2011, 4:56. Pitch-black outside. The house where I am
writing is by the sea, and the first thing I did when I woke an
hour ago was listen to the faint crash of the breakers below. Last
night I was woken by thunder and lightning so violent that the
whole countryside was lit up by the quivering electrical discharges.

Lightning flashed right outside the window, the sound of thunder came with the light – immense explosions. The rain followed, also violent, torrents fell everywhere. When I spoke to the hosts later that morning they told me water had flooded in over their kitchen floor. At just before two we drove to the venue where the performance was to take place, and at several points the road was submerged to a depth of between half a meter and a meter. The countryside around was absolutely drenched. I can't remember any thunderstorms from my youth or from later life being as intense or wild as this. When we moved to Malmö the late-summer leaden horizon could be permeated by sudden angled shafts of light and the sky would rumble and boom. Presumably the simple explanation is that atmospheric conditions are different here. Surely thunderstorms couldn't be increasing in frequency and intensity with every year that passes, could they?

Last night's performance went well. There were two hundred people in the audience and I spoke for two hours, first with the interviewer, who asked his questions, then with the audience, who asked theirs. My strategy in such situations is simple: I try to be as present as possible at the moment, by which I mean not repeat myself. I try to answer all the questions as if it were the first time they had been asked, to exercise no self-criticism at all, only to say what occurs to me on the spot. Afterward I can't remember what I've said, and I want to be alone because, in a sense, I have been on display up there, everyone has seen me, not just for a second but for more than two hours, and I have taken great risks by not pretending. It is odd that it should be so painful, but it is. When they laugh at something I say or when there is a kind of sigh, which means that I am confirming something they have thought themselves, it hurts me because I am fooling them, that is the feeling I have, they are falling for my tricks. Linda once called me an itinerant purveyor of earnestness, and that is an apt image. Mathias, who turned up at the Culture House in Stockholm when I was there two weeks ago, told his mother afterward that I had been fantastic and that he had never seen me so warm or sincere before. And this is exactly the point. When I am with Mathias or Linda or anyone else I am close to, I am the antithesis of warm and sincere. It is therefore as though I can only be warm and sincere in front of a group of strangers and not with kith and kin. That is why what I do is a kind of trick. When I am sitting on the stage talking to an audience there is a great distance. I can manage that and appear close and warm. When I am sitting at a table afterward and eating with the event organizers the distance to them is not as great, but inside me I feel it is. I say nothing and seem dismissive and cold, not open or warm, as before onstage. It is as though having a name enables me to be who I actually am and how I actually feel, but only in staged settings, not in normal social situations. That is why I feel so false afterwards, even though I have really been more genuine. The smiles, the friendliness, the admiration I encounter when I sign books is unbearable, not because it isn't well meant or honest, but because it is on false premises. Deep down, I have to reject it. At the same time, when the wind changes, when my star is on the wane and I have become yesterday's news, I assume I will miss the buzz when I enter a room – all the eyes surreptitiously turning to me and the waves of applause washing over me.

Another strong feeling I had afterward was that I had betrayed the novel by talking about it in public. It isn't public yet, it is still just mine, it is a place where I go and where I am every day, a part of me, my inner being, which, as soon as the book is published, becomes part of external reality and no longer a place where I go or am. Talking so much about it as I did yesterday doesn't feel good. The familiarity between me and the novel was broken in a way. And when I spoke about it, it sounded better, more interesting and important than it is. The *Mein Kampf* essay became more important when I spoke about it, in particular, it sounded good, four hundred pages about prewar Vienna, Weimar between the wars, how times and psychology, art and politics are closely linked, and the formula for all things human, I-you-we-they-it, this was easy to talk about and had an aura of significance in that context. I talked about it because they had made an effort to attend, and it didn't feel as if I could just sit there talking about myself and my life, I had to turn the occasion into something relevant for them, to create a "we," and that was what I did. To survive the moment and reap a short-term gain, I betrayed the novel. Everything is mixed as I sit here. Good and bad, false and genuine, literature and reality, private and public. As if that weren't enough, someone has sent me a copy of *Weekendavisen*, in which the fourth book, which has just come out here, is reviewed. I skim-read it when I came home. Bo Bjørnvig had written it. He said that for the first time in the series I hadn't been quite honest, and this was noticeable throughout the novel. A slightly false note, he said. I hadn't thought about the novel since I wrote it, but when I read that comment, it came back, and I knew that what Bjørnvig wrote was true. I had not been honest in that book. I wrote it when the pressure was at its peak, at that time the first two books were out and the debate about them was raging in the media, every single day there were several articles about them, everyone had an opinion, a newspaper like *Morgenbladet* ran its entire front page and several other pages inside on the immorality of what I had done and had published not only my father's name but also a photograph of a rhododendron bush he had planted and my grandparents' house. That house isn't in the novel, I located the action somewhere completely different, and their names are not in the novel either, but in this article everything became public. Other newspapers called all the characters from the novel they could track down. I spoke to Jan Vidar: as he came out of his house he had walked slap bang into two journalists who wanted to interview him about me. I spoke to Mathias: he had come home from nursery school in Stockholm with his son and was cooking when there was a ring at the door, two journalists from Norway who wanted to have a chat about me. Mathias, who wasn't even in the novel, said no, thank you, he didn't want a chat. As soon as he had shut the door he called his mother and warned her. There were journalists heading her way.

And sure enough, not long afterward there was a ring at her door. She didn't open up. They left but returned later that evening after she had gone to bed. They wouldn't give in, and she didn't dare go to the bathroom for fear that they would realize she was home and keep ringing. They called her ex-husband, Vidar, who is more than seventy years old and still lives in a house in the forest, and asked him what he thought about me and the way I had written about his former wife. They called my mother, Yngve, Tonje, and Tore, and, where I'd grown up, four of my old friends from school talked in the local paper about what I had been like and what we had done. They called all my ex-girlfriends, and my old teachers, one of them, the only man I had mentioned by name, Jan Berg, appeared on television and talked about how it felt to be described as "evil" in the hit novel of the autumn. Every single day there was something about the books in the papers, and my photo was everywhere. My entire private life had been turned upside down; there were no limits anymore: when I was at the Litteraturhus in Oslo a *Dagbladet* journalist ran after me and kept asking the same question, had I had sex with an under-age girl? That was Book 4 he was referring to, which I was writing then, and the question, which was actually like asking me if I was a sex offender, was posed because I had mentioned a conversation with Geir about this in Book 2, and I had said Book 4 would deal with my time in northern Norway. Personally, I saw or heard nothing of what was in the papers, nothing of what was said on the radio or TV, I found out secondhand, and I heard about all the journalists who had been buzzing around everywhere. They bombarded me with e-mails at the beginning, but that stopped fairly soon, then I seemed to find myself in the eye of the storm. *Verdens Gang* had interviewed the people working in the Chinese takeaway beside the entrance to our apartment, I heard, and those working in the café I frequented, and the mayor of Malmö, and the owners of our apartment, whom they asked how much I paid in rent. In this climate, with all the stones of my life apparently being turned over, I sat writing about the year

I had worked as a teacher in northern Norway. It was a little place where everyone knew everyone, and it had been such a sensitive situation because I went there as a teacher, and it was one thing writing about life in the family or in my closest circle and quite another writing about the children I met at school. Of course they had shown me a kind of total, unconscious trust then, although it wasn't actually shown to me but to my teacher persona, unaware that the teacher would one day write about them and their lives. Parents confided in me about their children and thus indirectly also about themselves. When I wrote the first two novels publication wasn't in my mind; usually what I wrote and thought stayed in the novel, even when I had written something outrageous – when the novel came out it was as though the outrageous passages didn't exist, as though I hadn't written them. In my debut novel I wrote about a man of twenty-six sleeping with a girl of thirteen, she was his pupil. No one took any notice. It was a risqué topic, but the novel made it innocuous. The novel sold seventy thousand copies in total, quite a large readership, but it still didn't exist, it remained with the readers. When I reached that point in the novel, it must have been the summer of 1997, I was living in a mountain farmhouse in Jølster, writing a film script with Tore. I told him what I had written and what I was thinking of writing about. I asked him for his opinion. This was a major challenge to conventional morality, I spent two weeks thinking about it, can I write about this, and if so, why am I writing about it? Tore thought I should. I came to the same conclusion, and I wrote it, uneasy and fearful, it was as though I were doing something evil. If I had been completely innocent, if this had been a theme I had plucked from the air, it wouldn't have been so bad. But then there would have been no point writing, it would have been something I had made up, a kind of thematic detail, calculated, a provocation, and therefore artistically dead. Precisely because it pained me justified my writing about it. The more painful it was, the more justified it was. It wasn't that I had slept with a thirteen-year-old pupil at that time, but I had articulated the thought, not just once but many times, and I had been filled with a desire that was strong and so secret that I managed to repress it completely as soon as I left. While I was writing the novel, it came back, I remembered, and I knew that the right thing would be to complete the thought and enact it in reality, which wasn't reality but fiction, because that is what writing a novel is, all the tendencies there are, wishes, desires, possibilities, and impossibilities crystallize in one point, an image, an act, where everything that is immanent, hidden, and veiled, reveals itself. So I did, I wrote about my alter ego, the teacher Henrik Vankel who had sex with one of his pupils, thirteen-year-old Miriam. Up to that moment I had written perhaps two hundred pages about his life in Kristiansand, much the same as my own biography, but it was only when I reached this point, the scene where they were lying together, that it became a novel and I became a novelist because there, through a simple act that never took place, I succeeded in expressing something that was true and that I had never even been able to think, on the contrary I had relegated it to the depths from which it came. This truth is the novel's truth. The novel is a place where that which cannot be thought elsewhere can be thought and where the reality we find ourselves in, which sometimes runs counter to the reality we talk about, can be manifest in images. The novel can describe the world as it is, as opposed to the world it ought to be. Everyone who has read *Out of the World* will understand that the emotions, urges, and desires that it contains are not something the author has made up but are something inside him. But the agreement between the author and the reader, the novel's pact, is that this conclusion should not be drawn, and if it is, only in secret. It should never be spoken aloud. The term "novel" is the guarantee of that. Only in this way can what is not said but which is true still be said. That is the pact, the author is free to say whatever he or she wants because the author knows that what he or she says will never, or at least should never, be linked with the author, with his or her private person. It is a necessary pact that the books, which provoked such a sensation and such anger, broke. I wrote them because my commitment to the novel wasn't enough for me, I wanted to go a step further and commit to reality, because the contravention of the norms that had allowed me to write a novel for the first time, when I expressed what was true through the novel, was at an end for me, it was empty, a gesture, it meant nothing or I couldn't make it mean anything, I felt that I could write anything at all. To be able to write anything at all is death for an author. An author can only write something specific, and what determines this something specific is, to be precise, commitment. My commitment was to reality, what I wrote about had really happened and it had happened as described. What the "I" of the novel felt was what the author of the novel felt, so the private space was nullified, and I personally had to answer for everything written there. Doing this was no problem in Book 1 and Book 2 because once I had broken down the barrier between my "I" and my author's "I," the barrier was down for good, and the relevant rules, that events should have happened and have been experienced in reality, were easy to follow. The books had come out to an unexpectedly warm reception from the public. And this meant that they had a life of their own and became real, beyond my control, and this was new because before I had been able to write whatever I liked, controversial or not, without it becoming real. It had always stayed in the novel. Now it didn't, it lived outside, in reality, with my photo attached, which increasingly began to resemble a logo. Nevertheless I was still able to write the third book without deviating from the categorical demand for truth because the distance from the events it portrayed, in my childhood, was so great. We, that is, the publishing house and I, still changed some names and deleted some features that might have caused offense, but not many. My mother hasn't read it yet, but she has found out quite a bit anyway; her private role as a mother has been discussed in public because of the book, as though she represented wives and mothers and as though people other than herself or her closest family were entitled to criticize what she did or didn't do. But Book 4 was different. I feared I might have started something that had got out of hand. I anonymized the village where I worked, calling it Håfjord instead of Fjordgård, as it was actually called, which the newspapers were not slow to pick up on. I gave different names to all the pupils and teachers and I also furnished them with made-up character-istics or idiosyncrasies, all to escape the commitment to reality I could no longer fulfill. In this book, therefore, I committed nei-ther to the novel nor to reality. For this reason it became a strange book, in which I do the opposite of what an author should, I cover over the truth. In *Out of the World*, which deals with the same theme, I wrote the truth by committing to the novel; in the first two books I wrote the truth by committing to reality. In Book 3 this link is weaker, only to fall away entirely in Book 4. However, everything I said about myself was true. The passages that seem most authentic because they are raw are nonetheless a kind of masquerade because I knew exactly what was going on when I was there, but not when I wrote about it. And there was one thing I wrote in the book that I had never told anyone, and this was that I hadn't masturbated, not a single time, until I was nineteen. I hadn't told anyone about the ignominy and the con-stant humiliation of premature ejaculation either, as it is so dread-fully tritely called. One doesn't talk about that sort of thing. But what was really dangerous, the feelings I had for a thirteen-year-old girl when I was eighteen, I didn't examine in sufficient depth, the mere mention of it meant I had to be so incredibly careful with all the rest, all those fathers and mothers, sons and daughters I had mixed with while I ached with desire in an inner world that was thoroughly sexualized. The publishing house was careful too, it was not unusual for the editor, Therese, to call me to discuss whether a character was anonymous enough or whether this or that character ought not to make such and such an utter-ance in such and such a way. The lawyers also read the manuscript and suggested changes. The public had me and the publisher in its grip, and the novel became a hostage to reality. This is not an excuse, and this is not my way of saying Book 4 is a poor novel, it is still full of the terrible banality and vigor of youth, it is a comedy of immaturity, and despite being conventional it is inimitable, for the simple reason that it arose under precisely the conditions it did. But it is not the truth.

August 29, 2011, 2:12. I am in the flat in Malmö, which shows signs of having been empty for close on three months: all the plants have withered, the air is dry, dusty, and there is a foul smell in the bathroom; water must somehow have been left to stand in the pipes. The rest of the family is in Glemmingebro. I talked to Vanja on the phone yesterday, she said, Dad, you're not allowed to be in Malmö until Friday, you have to come tonight. I said that if she gave me permission to stay in Malmö until Friday the book I was writing would be completely finished. She said, *Finished?* I said, yes. Then you'll have to work all the time, she said. You shouldn't eat or sleep, just work. I'll do that, I said. But when I sat down this morning, I had such a headache and felt so lethargic I couldn't work. It has happened a couple of times over the past three years, all of a sudden I'm unable to do anything, I find it an enormous strain to get out of bed, dress, and go to the kitchen to butter a few slices of bread, almost impossible. It lasts one, maybe two days and then it goes, and everything is as before. Once it lasted a week, Linda was so worried about me that she forced me to go to the doctor, although I never go. I was given a full examination and even an ECG. Nothing. I was fit as a fiddle. I knew I was, but I went in order to reassure Linda, who, I know, is sometimes afraid I might drop dead from a heart attack. It is an interesting phenomenon, standing outside everything you used to be inside, when things you normally do without a second thought become unattainable. That is what it's like to get old, I think with fear in my heart, only slower, your strength is gradually sapped until ultimately you stand outside the life you once lived and you no longer have the strength to recover, with maybe twenty years left to live. But what is living? It is doing things and being at the center of the world. If you are deprived of that, of acting, doing, being at the center of the world, a distance develops between you and the world, you observe it but you are not part of it, and this estrangement is the start of death. Living is being greedy for days, no matter whether they are good or bad. Dying is being weary of days, when they no longer matter or cannot matter because you are no longer inside them, but on the outside. Being whisked off by an illness or a sudden accident is another thing, a different death, more brutal for those around you, but perhaps more merciful for the life that comes to an end, because it happens when life is in full spate, you are in the midst of it, and there is no slow fade. But of course I don't know. The opposite might be true, that it is best to be sated with days and watch the world slowly become weaker and weaker, lighter and lighter, until eventually it disappears and ceases to exist.

In the time it has taken to write this book four people in my close family have died. Aunty Ingunn, Uncle Magne, my great-uncle Anstein, and my father-in-law, Roland. I liked all of them, they were fine people. Now they are no more. From the more distant family further uncles and aunts have died, of whom I have no more than vague memories. Geir's mother, Signe Arnhild, has died, Christina's mother, Eivor, has died, and two of Geir's friends, Marco and Peter. The latter two were young. The others were in their midsixties to midseventies. The births: my cousin Yngvild's son, Sigurd August, whose christening Linda and I went to in January in Brussels, Linda's girlfriend's first child, Annie, and Geir and Christine's second child, Gisle. Our three children, Vanja, Heidi, and John, have gone from being four years, two years, and six months old when I started writing, to being seven and a half, almost six, and four today. The remorseless wind of time, which takes away as much as it brings, has also swept through these pages.

I am not the same person as when I started either. That is I am the same person, but my relations with other people have changed. A lot was revealed when the books, and with them my private life, were made public. Everyone I know has been put through an ordeal. It hasn't been easy for anyone. It has been hardest for Linda. Being a relative, irrespective of what emotions are involved, is both a bond and a role. Yngve is a brother, Sissel is a mother, Ingrid is a mother-in-law. Whatever Yngve did, even if he killed someone and ended up in prison, he would still be my brother and I wouldn't be able to turn my back on him. Being a father myself, I understand what it is like to be a parent and I know that what applies to your brother applies a thousand times to your children. Whatever Vanja, Heidi, or John do, I will always forgive them and I will always be there for them. Anything else is inconceivable. I thought of the aftermath of the brutal massacre on Utøya in Norway on July 22, when the father of the perpetrator said his son should have killed himself. A man with children can say that, but not a father. For parents, children, and siblings there is a guarantee, that the bond between them cannot be severed. This is so because the role is not connected with acts but with the bond. At least this has always been guaranteed for me. Mom and Yngve might be hurt or saddened by what I wrote, they might be angry with me, and they might distance themselves from me, but they would still be my mother and brother the day they, or I, die. The bond is indestructible, and of course that is for good or ill. For my father, who was so closely attached to his mother, it was also problematic because he never really freed himself to become his own man. For my mother, when I was in my teens and we lived together, the most important priority was that I should be myself and feel free. The final consequence of this is my book, which completes a trajectory that started when I was sixteen. The question then was not so much who I was as where I belonged. Now the questions have merged into one and the same. And, as when I was sixteen, it has been about freeing myself. In this book I have tried to write myself free from everything that ties, perhaps first and foremost the ties to my father, but also the ties to my mother, not the emotional ones, they are indestructible, as indeed are those to my father, but from all the values and attitudes she has transferred to me, both directly and indirectly. She has had an immense influence on me, but she doesn't any longer.

Ties of friendship are different from family ones because they are formed in the social sphere and can be dissolved there. The role of friend can be for life, but it doesn't have to be. A love relationship is close to a friendship in that it too can be formed and dissolved, but the moment love involves children it becomes a family, as you will be connected with each other via the children. You can separate, live alone, but ineluctably you still belong together through them. Another decisive difference between a friendship and a love relationship is that friendship is limited, it is an exception, which is revealed in its declaration, it refers to another place, where real life takes place. Friendship is a place of refuge from which you can observe life or where something else, set free from its surroundings, can happen. You can drink, you can play football, you can go to concerts, you can go bowling, you can talk about life. A love relationship is not a place of refuge, it is *the* place to be. It means that you have greater commitments, for you share the place where you reveal yourself as you are and where neither partner can get away from himself or the other person. When I met Linda and fell in love with her, everything else faded into the background, there was only her. This was an exceptional state. When it normalized and everything else returned, the spell was broken. The limitless had limits, the abnormal became the norm, the holiday became the everyday, and we, the lovers, began to argue. We had children, that too was an exceptional state, during which everything else faded, then it normalized and everything else returned, and the everyday permeated the holiday like water permeating cloth. I had written about that. When I had written about friends or acquaintances I had described only a small part of them, the part they showed me. But nothing of what I wrote was harmful or could threaten them in any way. It might have been unpleasant, but that was because they were mentioned in a novel, not because what was written was revealing or in any way damaging. It was different with my family because they played a larger role in the novel, but the only person I examined in depth was my father, and he had been dead for almost ten years. My relatives also considered the description of my grandmother offensive, but, firstly, I did not agree, and, secondly, she was dead too, and it was her descendants who would have to react to my description of her and the publication of it, which they found insulting, but in that case it wasn't them I insulted but her memory. The description of Linda was different. We lived together, she was the mother of my children, and I knew virtually everything about her. Linda and I were a "we," it was "us two." But the "we" was not all of me, it was what I shared with her, and in all relationships you hold that which you don't share outside, that which belongs only to the "I." The moment you bring it in, it belongs to both of you. I hadn't written about our relationship but about my life within it, and in so doing brought it into the relationship, for now she had to consider my secret thoughts as joint, now we had those in common as well. They weren't secret in any criminal or underhanded way, they were secret in the sense that I didn't reveal them because they weren't relevant to what we shared. They might perhaps have had a negative effect on it. Everyone has such thoughts and everyone knows everyone has them, but in a tacit agreement they are not mentioned and constitute no part of what two people have together. The urge to crane your neck after a beautiful woman in the street, the urge to be alone, an indifference to the people your partner likes or is close to, everything that is done out of duty and not for pleasure. Beyond this, I also presented an image of her that she didn't know. She suspected it, she may even have known, but in what we shared it was not mentioned and it was therefore nonexistent, it was more like something vaguely threatening but unformed, I imagined. However, not only that, others would also read about it and form their own image of Linda as a result. They didn't know her, and that didn't matter, but the very knowledge that this is the image others would get from me would have to be integrated into her identity. Not only the new "This is how I am for Karl Ove when he is alone" but also "Now others can see this is how Karl Ove sees me," and the power of this was immense, especially for Linda, I knew, who was the kind of person who had dreams and could partly live in those dreams. The dream of love, the dream of family, the dream of a professional career, the dream of a role as writer. In the book love was pervaded with frustration, family life was a series of duties, and she was a character I criticized for not doing enough and burdening me with her limitations. I had asked her to read this and approve it.

How could I have done that?

The truth was that when I sat down to write the novel I had nothing to lose. That was why I wrote it. I wasn't only frustrated, the way you can become when you live as a parent with small children and have many duties and have to sacrifice yourself, I was unhappy, as unhappy as I have ever been, and I was all alone. My life was pretty dreadful, that was how I experienced it, I was living a dreadful life, and I wasn't strong enough, I didn't have the spine to abandon this and start anew. I often thought about leaving, sometimes several times a day, but I couldn't do it, it was no good, I couldn't bear the thought of the consequences for Linda and her life, because if there was one thing she was afraid of it was this: that I might leave her or I might die. I was also afraid of her anger. And I was afraid of her mother's anger. The terrible reproaches I would have to confront, the treachery I had inflicted on Linda and our children, I couldn't face that. But that was what made me decide to write a novel in which I threw caution totally to the winds and told it as it was. Only when the book was ready to be published did I realize what I had done and went through the manuscript and crossed out the worst. Not about Linda, but about the people around her. And then I added our love story, for that was what had brought me to where I was. How could two people who so clearly had such love for each other, whose hearts burned with love, end up in such darkness, in such misery? It wasn't the everyday grind that had darkened our existence, far from it. I didn't mind changing diapers, dressing and undressing the children, taking them to school, walking in the park and playing, cooking, doing the dishes and the laundry. What I couldn't cope with was doing all this and writing at the same time – and encountering nothing but criticism, always hearing that I didn't do enough, and whenever I wanted to do something else not being able to because she couldn't be on her own with the children. She offended my mother, she offended my brother, and she offended my close friends, and she could be so unpleasant that I was torn apart with conflicts of loyalty. But what made the whole thing so crazy was that her mental picture of what was happening was the exact opposite of reality, and that was the picture we lived by. In it she was the hub of the family, the person who drove everything and sacrificed herself. Even when I was in the bathroom scrubbing and cleaning, and she stood watching, she couldn't refrain from letting drop a critical comment, I was too fussy, at that rate I would never finish, and although she never did any cleaning, apparently she was the one who kept the apartment in order. Even when I had to take the children in two strollers to school, as well as John, because she was tired and wanted to sleep a bit more, and even though only three days before I had broken my collarbone, she was the one who wore herself out doing everything with the children. She often stayed in bed, and could lie there for days on end, she constantly had pains somewhere, either in her throat or her stomach or her head, it was always the same, she was ill, and then she couldn't do anything, on those days I had to do everything. As for me, I was rarely ill. And if I was, she refused to acknowledge it. Once, when I had a temperature of one hundred and four, she said I took to my bed for no reason, typical man, if she had the tiny ailment I had now, no problem, she would soldier on. I stared at her, mouth agape. What insanity was this? Were we living in Upside-Down Land? Me, who was never ill, whereas she, who had such a low threshold for anything disagreeable, never took to her bed for anything – was so egregious that I was speechless. Furious, I staggered to the nursery school with Vanja, hardly able to stand upright, we lived in Stockholm then, and for the rest of the day I lay delirious in my office. If anything went wrong at home, something as trivial as a lightbulb going, it would never be repaired or changed unless I did it. I could clean the whole apartment one Saturday morning and have the children at the same time, but if she had the children and I cleaned, she complained there was so much on her shoulders and so little on mine. I did all the food shopping, trudged home with all three children, and four or five shopping bags filled to the brim, I had to get everything in one trip to save time so I could write, and it was like that with everything, I didn't have a minute free because once the apartment and the children had been taken care of I had to write, apart from five minutes on the balcony, sitting alone smoking, for which she also berated me, she never had any breaks like that. It was as though she regarded the time I wrote as my own, leisure, something for me, and after I had finished and went out, I had to continue to do all sorts of things, for now she wanted her downtime. She didn't write when she could have, so it wasn't that, she didn't have a job either, and although she talked about it, she didn't do anything specific. I had no problem with that, for when she did write she wrote something essential and brilliant, and that was enough for me. The problem was that she had an image of herself as someone who was always working and constantly exhausted as a result, while I was someone who thought only of myself and never did anything. It was crazy, absolutely crazy, because I couldn't correct this picture if I tried, she just said I didn't "see" her and all she did, and that was typical of men, women did everything, but invisibly while what men did was visible. It was impossible to fight against this. Of course I saw what she did with the children, but I did exactly the same, plus all the other stuff. She also reproached me for not loving her enough and said I was selfish and prioritized writing above family life. I wrote perhaps for five hours a day while the children were at school, and I didn't write on weekends, which was strictly forbidden, so in reality I worked minimally at what brought in the cash and maximally at everything else. This situation lasted for many years. I couldn't stand it, but I had to if I wanted to keep everything in one piece. Occasionally I reached the breaking point. The first time I told her I didn't want to keep this up and I was going to leave her was the summer we moved to Malmö. We had been living for a few weeks with Linda's mother and her husband, in the mornings I went into town and worked on the Bible translation, returning in the afternoon while Linda was with her mother and Vanja and Heidi. One evening I didn't go back, I went out with Geir, that was fine with Linda, we went to the Södra Theater, the outdoor terrace there, and I got so drunk I couldn't stand up to walk to the train I had said I would catch. When I arrived back at two in the morning she was furious with me and shouted. I became so desperate that I started crying. I yelled that I couldn't take any more. I can't take any more, Linda, I said. I simply can't do this. I've had enough. I'm leaving. And I'm leaving now. After I had said that I marched into our room, threw my clothes in a suitcase, shut it, carried it outside, and set off down the forest path as Linda screamed for me not to go, I couldn't leave her, please don't go, don't go. Her tearstained face and her vow that she would change made it impossible for me to continue. I stopped, walked back, put down the suitcase, and stayed. When we were moving, only a few days later, while Linda was at Helena's, I worked nonstop for thirty-two hours packing everything we owned into cardboard boxes and finished half an hour before the moving van arrived. Then we all went by train to Malmö.

This autumn was the best we'd had since we first got together. It was the new town, the new apartment, the open sky and beautiful late-summer weather that did it, but perhaps it was also because the depths of my despair had revealed themselves to her, because our relationship opened as well, there was more room to maneuver, and once the first six months were over it became clear we were expecting another child, and the good times rolled on until they didn't, presumably they had been too much for both of us, and we were back where we had been. We argued and shouted, that was her way of solving disagreements, which I had to face, while mine was distance, the most frightening of all for her, and so the spiral wound downward again. I became unloving, dismissive, did what I had to do out of duty, took my frustration out on her, was ironic, sarcastic until she'd had enough and met it with a furious outburst, which was the most frightening response of all for me. It wasn't always like this, there were good days too, and whenever we had guests or visited someone we found each other again, then it was "us two," and the darkness that shrouded what we actually were, which was no small thing, namely soul twins, lifted. We also had children, whom we obviously both loved above all else, and we were almost of one mind with regard to who they were, what qualities they had and showed; we saw the same, thought the same, and felt the same. But the disharmony between us spilled over them too, of course, because we weren't above arguing in front of them, and when I was at my angriest with Linda but swallowed my anger and didn't want to talk, it was the children I took it out on. If Linda had stretched out on the sofa and said I should take them for a walk because they needed some fresh air, they didn't have to put up much resistance before I was shouting, almost frothing with rage, or shaking them. Once Linda and I had been yelling at each other in the kitchen, the children appeared in the doorway, in descending order of height, we saw them and quieted down. Then Vanja came in and reenacted what had happened, Dad shouted and banged the table, *there*, Mommy shouted and threw a cup on the floor, *there*. Linda and I looked at each other, her face was ashen, we both realized what we were doing. The situation could not continue like this, but it did. The only reason I could write about it was that I had reached a point where I no longer had anything to lose. It made no difference if Linda read this, she could do what she liked. If she wanted to leave me, she could. I didn't give a damn. I woke up unhappy, spent the day unhappy, and went to bed unhappy. If only I could have an hour, a day, a week, a month, a year alone, everything would be fine, I knew that. That is for me, not for her. For Linda it wouldn't be good, I knew that too. The very thought of leaving filled me with guilt and a bad conscience, in my mind I was living a double life. I was also afraid of facing all the fury and the abyss-opening fear that my departure would create. Linda was frightened, that was the point, she was afraid, whereas I was so conflict-averse that I would rather live in despair than say how things were. And as soon as the tide turned, and we were fine again, I thought, I love her, and perhaps it was difficult just now, but it would pass. When Linda's father died I was so emotionally blunted to everything that I couldn't give her any of what she needed. I was giving everything to the novel and the children, I was giving nothing to her.

Then there was a change, something out there turned against me and went on the attack. It was as though everything inside me was in jeopardy, as though the ground beneath my feet had gone. There was something out there, and to confront it I sought courage in what I had within, my real life, Linda, Vanja, Heidi, and John, and found strength there. I knew what I had. I knew what they meant to me. I saw Linda, who she was, and I saw our children. I saw my family. I didn't want to lose it. I didn't want to lose Linda. She was everything I had. And she kept me alive. If I turned away from life, if I wanted to retreat and disappear from the world, she tugged at me, I wasn't allowed to, I had to be there for her, in the midst of life. I needed her, and I needed the children, they made me a whole person. And she needed me, and the children needed me.

Such was the situation when, some days after we had returned from Prague, this topsy-turvy autumn, I gave Linda the manuscript. When I wrote it I'd had nothing to lose, when she read it now, suddenly I had everything to lose.

She was going to Stockholm to see a theater performance, up by train one morning, back the next day. The previous night I sat wondering whether to remove the passages that would hurt her most, it would be easy to do and wouldn't detract from the novel, but at the same time I thought it had to be truthful, if not it was utterly meaningless, all of it. I wanted to show her this because it was true. That the truth was not just in a letter to her, meant for her eyes only, but in a novel, meant for everyone's eyes, made what I was asking her to do actually inhuman. Fear and guilt accumulated in my chest like water behind a dam. I tried to subdue them by telling Linda there were a lot of terrible parts in the novel and she would be angry, but my intentions were not bad. She just smiled, she could take it, she said, don't worry. She put the manuscript in her bag, stood up straight by the open front door, we gave each other a kiss, again she told me not to worry and said everything would be fine, then she stepped into the corridor, closed the door behind her, and was gone. I went to the balcony and had a smoke, walked back to my study and worked on Book 3, strolled down to the kiosk and bought some more cigarettes, returned to my study and wrote a little more, but the thought of Linda reading the manuscript was burning inside me, there was no room for anything else, and the most difficult aspect of it all was that she was reading without any explanations, without any corrections, I had to soften the blow and dialed her number. It had been an hour since she left. She answered at once. I could hear from her voice that she was sad. She said she was on the train and had started reading. She thought it was good, terrible to read, but she was coping. I told her I had been frustrated, but I wasn't now. She said, Goodbye, romanticism. She said, One thing's for sure – all the illusions about our relationship have gone now. Her voice was unemotional as she spoke, and there was something hard there, as though she had told herself to resist. I'm sorry, Linda, I said. I'm sorry too, she replied. But it won't get any worse than this, will it? she asked. Yes, I said. It will. I'll survive that too, she said. Okay, I said. But now I'm hanging up, she said. Okay, I said. Talk to you later.

I ate, wrote, sat on the balcony smoking, washed some clothes, wrote a bit more, and then I couldn't wait any longer, I called her. She had cried, she said, but now the train was close to Stockholm and she was looking forward to meeting Helena and maybe thinking about something else for a few hours. We clicked off, I picked up the children, made them some food, they watched children's TV, I brushed their teeth, put on their pajamas and read to them, then went to bed not long after they had fallen asleep. I took them to school, wrote, talked to Linda on the phone, she was on the train home, she had just read my description of how we first got together and her voice sounded lighter. I told her the worst was still to come and she should brace herself. She didn't believe me, I could hear, there was a smile in her voice when she said she would.

An hour later she called.

"What happened on Gotland?" she shouted.

"Only what's written," I said.

"What did you do?"

"It's all in the manuscript. I knocked on the door."

"Who was she? Why did you do it?"

"I was drunk."

"When was it? I remember when it was. I was at home with the children. Heidi was sick. How could you do that? How could you? Who was she?"

"That doesn't make any difference."

"Why didn't you tell me?"

"You know why."

"How can you write that in a novel and let me read about it?"

"I don't know. It just happened like that."

"Well, I don't want to talk to you anymore."

She hung up. A few minutes later she called again.

"Who was she? I want to know who she was."

"I don't know what her name is, Linda. Nothing happened."

"You were banging on her door all night."

"Yes, I'm sorry. But that's how it was."

"Heidi was sick. I was all alone."

"Yes," I said.

She hung up. I went onto the balcony, smoked, trudged back inside, paced back and forth in the apartment, phone in hand the whole time. Surfed the Net, went back out and smoked, stood in front of the living-room window and gazed across at the hotel, went back into the study and surfed, out again and smoked, shuffled from room to room, finally stopped in the children's bedroom, the innocence there would do me good, I thought, but it didn't, everything just got worse and I went back out on the balcony. I didn't have a thought in my head, not one.

She called again just as I was going to pick up the children. She was calmer. She had read the manuscript now, she said. What shall we do? she said. She began to cry as she said that. What shall we do now, Karl Ove? And suddenly I snapped. I sobbed. I said, I don't know. I cried. I said, I don't know, Linda. I don't know.

An hour later I was in the kitchen frying fish cakes when I heard the sound of the elevator outside, it seemed to come all the way up and I called to the children to go and see if it was Mommy. They didn't need to be asked twice, they had missed her, as they always did when she was away, and now they were in the hall waiting for the door to open. They pressed against her, she knelt down and hugged them in turn, stroking their backs as she sent me an all-penetrating look. She was red-eyed and pale, but still full of warmth when she turned to the children. They didn't notice the glare she had sent me.

Look what you've done, it said.

Look what we've got and you're destroying, it said.

The children clung to her as she took off her shoes and jacket and put the little suitcase by the wall. I set the table, we ate, we said nothing to each other, conversation plied back and forth between us and the children. They were excited and happy to have her back. Afterward we sat in the living room to watch children's TV with them. After a while she looked at me and said, in English:

"The knife."

I didn't understand what she meant. She occasionally spoke English to me when she didn't want the children to understand, which I was unable to do and didn't like. That wasn't what I was thinking about at this moment, of course, only about her pasty face and red eyes, which in some way had something to do with a knife.

"In the novel," she said. "The knife."

"What are you talking about, Mommy?" Vanja asked.

"I'm just chatting with Daddy," she said. "About something he wrote."

A knife? What kind of knife? Had I written about a knife?

"What do you mean?" I said.

"The one Geir gave you," she said. "No one will understand why it's in the book if it isn't used. A pistol mentioned in the first act is fired in the fifth."

Geir? I puzzled. What did he and his present have to do with this?

"What pistol?" Vanja said.

"We're talking about a play. Drama," I explained.

"Quite a drama," Linda said.

When the TV program was over she read to the children. I sat on the balcony, my soul chilled. We would have to clear the air once the children were asleep. I had sensed her restrained anger and despair the whole time. She would give vent to them when the children were asleep.

I couldn't stay on the balcony. I didn't want her to come out thinking I was relaxing and didn't care. So I got up and returned to the living room, sat down on the sofa, heard her say good night to the children, their protests, she mustn't go yet, they weren't tired, they couldn't sleep. A banging noise reverberated through the apartment, it was Vanja lying on her back in bed and hitting her heels against the wall.

She went into the kitchen. Poured some water, opened a cupboard, I knew she was making tea. Just afterward came the roar of the kettle. Then she came in with a big cup in one hand and sat down on the sofa, on the other side of the table from me. She looked straight at me. I felt sick.

"What did you mean about the knife?" I asked.

"He gave it to you so you could stab me. He wanted to get rid of me. Don't you understand? He's a vampire. He hasn't got a life of his own. He lives through you. Do you think him giving you a knife was chance?"

"It was his prized possession," I said.

She snorted.

"This isn't about Geir," I said. "This is about you and me."

"With him looking over your shoulder," she said.

"No," I said. "He's the only person I can go to outside the family. It's the same for me as it is for you and Helena."

"We don't speak like you do. I say only nice things about you to Helena. I've never said anything else."

I didn't answer. I looked down at the floor. She lifted the cup to her mouth and drank. Looking straight at me.

There was one thing I had to ask her. Something she hadn't mentioned.

"What happens if I publish it?" I said.

"Do so by all means. It's a good book. I can see that. If it hadn't been, all this would've been impossible."

"Is there anything you want me to take out?"

"No. I mean, yes. One thing. The part where you write that Bergman patted me on the head and said I was a beautiful child. That's so incredibly embarrassing you'll have to take it out."

"Nothing else."

"There were some mistakes and misunderstandings. But we can look at them later. Otherwise nothing."

She put down the cup and looked over at the balcony door. It had got darker outside.

"Who was she?" she asked.

"Who?" I said, even though I knew very well whom she meant.

"On Gotland. What was her name? What did she look like?"

"Don't go there," I said. "No good will come of it. I don't know what her name was. I was drunk. I was out of control."

"And then you did it? While I was here with Vanja and Heidi, and Heidi was ill. I trusted you."

"I know," I said. "I'm sorry."

Again she glanced at the door. Then she jumped up. Her eyes were either furious or frightened or both.

"I can't stay here. I can't be here with you. It's awful. I'm off to Jenny's. You take the children tomorrow."

"Okay," I said.

"I can't believe you did it," she said, and ran into the hall as fast as she could, threw on her jacket, bent down and put on her shoes. Her hands were trembling as she tied the laces, she couldn't tie them quickly enough.

"I'll call you," she said.

And then she was gone.

Jenny was a costume and set designer. She had children in the same nursery school as we did, that was where we had met her, and then she and Linda had become friends. She lived in a house with a big garden outside the center, which she had bought with a girlfriend, and Linda had a permanent offer to write there if she wanted. Sometimes she did. Sometimes, when she needed to get away, she slept over as well. So when, the following morning, the children asked where Mommy was there was nothing strange about my answer, she had left early to go to Jenny's. We were late leaving for school, it was one of those mornings when everything was difficult, and just as we were finally outside and about to cross the street, Linda came walking toward us on the other side from a gaggle of people waiting for the bus. She looked drained and exhausted. She still hadn't seen us, and when she did, as the lights changed to green and we stepped off the sidewalk, it seemed to come as a shock. It was as if she were seeing ghosts. The children caught sight of her, Vanja and Heidi let go of the stroller and raced over, John stretched out his arms.

"I thought you were at school," she said without looking at me. "I hadn't expected to run into you here."

"Where've you been, Mommy?" Vanja said. "Were you at Jenny's?"

She nodded.

"I just had to run home to pick something up."

She stood up and looked at me for the first time.

"Will you be there when I get back?" I asked.

She shook her head.

"Can I call you then?"

"I'll call later," she said.

"Okay," I said. "See you."

"See you," she said, and we set off in different directions, me with the children toward school, her toward the apartment.

She came back in the evening, after the children had gone to bed. I made us some tea, we sat in the living room. Even though the despair was still present it wasn't as close to the surface as it had been. My insides were as chilled as they had been at other times in my life when I'd found myself in crises, when it is as though everything around me is burning with white heat and the only other thing left is feelings, which are completely out of control. Being in a crisis is being at the center because when everything is on the line, everything is vital. That is all that exists. This was that sort of crisis. Everything else had fallen by the wayside, there was only this, her and me.

I didn't know what to say. We drank our tea in silence. We looked at each other, we looked down.

"How are you?" I said.

"Better," she said.

"We should talk," I said.

"Yes, we must," she said.

"We must talk seriously. No pretense."

She nodded.

"I've had a terrible time," I said.

"I know," she said.

"I'm sorry you had to read about it in a novel. But the novel's not the point for me. It's life. That's what we should talk about. We can't be like this. It's impossible. We can't."

"No," she said. "I know."

"Not just for the children's sake. But for ours, too. We're as far away from where we were when we got together as it's possible to be. Do you remember what it was like then? Do you remember how fantastic it was?"

"Of course I do. I long for it too."

"But we're in a different place now. You say 'goodbye, romanticism.' But this isn't about romanticism. It's about this life. It's all we have. And we have to try to make it good. As good as possible."

I got up and sat next to her. Put my arms around her. She cried. She cried and cried. I cried too. We went to the balcony and sat down in the darkness, she lit a cigarette, so she had started smoking again, I lit up too. We went into the bedroom. We stayed there the whole night, in the dim light from the hall lamp. I sat with my back to the wall looking ahead in the gloom, she lay beside me. We talked about everything there was to talk about. We were completely honest. It was as though everything we had established between us, all the images, ideas, dreams, desires, and hopes had crashed, and all that was left was the core, which we talked about. Her and me. Who we were to each other. It was like when we lay in bed in the little Stockholm apartment in Bastugatan and talked and listened to music and were completely open, completely naked, completely honest, because there was nothing to hide, not only did we have each other, we wanted each other. I wanted her, she wanted me. We could never return to that, we were somewhere else now, but it was perhaps a better place, it had a deeper feel to it because we had our children, we were a family, it was real, it was us, we didn't need any dream between us and life. She had to accept me as I was. She had to leave me in peace. She had to trust that I, too, wanted the best for everyone. And I had to support her because she couldn't carry on as she was, she had lost herself, slipped into a darkness where she no longer knew what was up and what was down, what was children, what was her, what was me.

At last I was calm. What had happened, had happened. There were no dangers. I hadn't felt like this since we first got together. It was like that then. There had been no tensions and we had been utterly free. Everything had been open. Now we had done what we'd planned with such passion. We had started a family, we had children, and it was unbelievable that it had been that which would cleave me to her, and her to me. But that's what had happened.

We stayed there talking all night and when morning came she went back to Jenny's. She had more to ponder alone. At twelve she called and said she'd sent me an e-mail. I walked down to the Internet café because our connection still wasn't working and read it there, in the dark between all the bright screens and the shouts from the war-game players.

Darling Karl Ove. I feel this is the only thing I can say. It is as though someone has died. Was it me? Have I died? The person I was.

You have told me so often to live my own life.

I know you are right. I'm so frightened.

You know how frightened I am.

You say you don't want to be everything for me. I sense a way to go and I'm afraid. I'm standing at the bottom and know that I have to start living.

I know nothing about this life.

I see myself with the children. I see myself cycling in the wind.

I see myself abandoning things before I need to. I see the two of us in the evenings. I have to let you out of my sight and do something I want to do. I don't know what I want. I don't know what is good for me. I know that I have to make something of myself.

I want to take photos of the children. The mess in the apartment. I want to do something with the children.

You say we have to accept each other completely. I know this is right. Deep inside me I hear a clear voice. I want to quietly mourn the child I was. I want to be an adult now. What is the endless grief that pours forth when I see you breaking down this door?

I love you. I will love you till eternity. And I know that it's hard to bear all this love and all this yearning. I would like to be able to love you in a way that is good for us. I know I must let go. I am letting go, Karl Ove. I love you so much. You and the children are a miracle that has happened to me.

When she came back that afternoon and we cooked and ate as usual it felt as if we had lived through a year in the past two days. I was utterly exhausted, she was too, but at the same time something trembled inside me, and I knew that feeling, it was happiness. Whenever I felt myself tremble like this I tried to repress it, for if there is one thing I had learned in the forty years I'd been alive it was that it was so much easier to carry despair than hope.

◆ ◆ ◆

The whole of autumn 2009 and spring 2010 were like this, for if the two days had felt like a year, the year had felt like ten. I had three novels published that fall, and two the following spring. All of them had to be edited and marketed, three of them also had to be written, at the same time I couldn't let Linda carry the whole burden at home, so the solution was to write fast, I set a quota of ten pages every day, and if, an hour before I was due to pick up the children, I had done six, I had to write four in that hour and then go and get them. It worked fine, I liked the feeling that something new was happening all the time and never knew where what I was writing would end. The pressure to write so much made it possible, and although I didn't like what I wrote, I liked the situation, everything was open and there wasn't a gatekeeper in sight. The media pressure, which grew with every day that passed, was more difficult to manage for me, but by completely ignoring it, by instructing everyone I spoke with not to mention a word to me of what was in the newspapers, not so much as a hint, the problem solved itself. If they did despite my instructions, it was utter torture for me, such as the time I saw that my old teacher had commented on the book he was in. I read in *Weekendavisen* that he had appeared in their quotations column. The media furor had just started when we returned from our brief trip to Prague. The first novel, which had just been reviewed in the literature pages, was now being discussed in other sections, and while reviewers had read it as a novel with material from reality and had not made anything of the fact that the people I wrote about were not only characters in a novel but also existed in reality, the potential consequences of this dimension soon began to dawn on journalists, especially as this perspective had been so dominant in *Bergens Tidende*'s coverage. They had interviewed my uncle about the book and also censured it in an editorial written by Jan H. Landro. On Tuesday I called Geir Gulliksen, and at the end of the conversation he said he was about to debate my book with Landro in the culture program on NRK radio. I called him afterward to ask how it had gone. He said it had been fine but a bizarre experience. Landro hadn't quoted any concrete examples from the book to show what was wrong with it, apart from one, which did have some emotional force because it hurt someone, but ethically and legally it was insignificant. Somewhere in the book he said I had written that as a twenty-year-old I'd had a girlfriend I didn't really love. How might she be feeling when she reads that, Landro had said, according to what Geir told me. But she's anonymous, isn't she, Geir had said. Her name isn't even mentioned! If a writer can't write about a woman he went out with

heart. Once we had put an advertisement in *Dagbladet*, this was during the Christmas period toward the end of the nineties. It said, "The New Sentimentalists wish the Norwegian nation a merry Christmas and a very happy New Year."

"Do you remember the ad we put in the paper?" I said, sitting in a chair and smoking while he was trying on a freshly ironed shirt in the hall.

"Which ad?" he said.

I told him.

He laughed.

"Oh, yes, Jesus. That's true."

"Perhaps there's someone out there somewhere still trying to figure out what it meant," I said.

"Yes, it didn't exactly become a national movement, did it."

"Your division of books you cry over and books you don't is definitely up there too," I said.

"Tie or bow tie or nothing?" he said.

"Nothing," I said.

He put on a plaid jacket and a cloth cap.

"Shall we go then?"

I nodded, rose to my feet, and then we took a taxi to the café, where Frode Grytten had already arrived. He introduced us to his brother, who was a meteorologist or something else equally distant from cultural life. Tore and Frode had become friends. He had shown Tore respect, not all writers did, so I liked him for that reason alone.

People stared at me. As they had done at the airport. A girl came over to me outside, where I was smoking, she could hardly articulate what she wanted to say, something about me had intimidated her.

We did our readings, and afterward we went to Cementen and drank beer, Tore told me a terrible story about his life, it was grim and shocking, an abyss. There were such abysses in his life, but they were not apparent in his manner, the way he behaved, what he talked about, yet they defined him, at least to my mind, he was someone who believed he would sink into the ground if he stood still, so he didn't.

On the plane I reflected that I had given away all of myself, I had nothing left of my own, I was a no one. Perhaps it was because I had been drinking the night before that I had these thoughts, although I hadn't drunk much, but it was enough for me to feel angst, maybe because there had been so many people looking at me, and as a result I understood what I had actually done, everyone could read everything about me, even total strangers, and think what they liked. I had put Vanja, Heidi, and John in their hands.

I met Tore again not so long afterward, at a literature festival in Odda. I flew to Bergen, rented a car to drive along the fjord, appeared onstage with Tore, drove back to the airport the next day, and flew home. The festival organizer was Marit Eikemo, we had worked with her on Student Radio. Yngve and Asbjørn came to watch; Selma Lønning Aarø, whom I remembered from student days when she won a novel-writing competition, was there; and Pedro Carmona-Alvarez, I knew who he was, he played in Sister Sonny, sometimes wore makeup when he went out, I had never spoken to him, but I'd written about him in the summer, that is, about his latest novel, *Rust*, which had impressed me, he was there, and we sat drinking in the hotel bar, all of us, and there too I had the feeling that the nineties weren't over, they just kept going and going. At the actual performance Tore produced many old letters and e-mails I had sent him during that period, there was also one about my father, which he read out while we were all sitting onstage, and at first I was unable to comment on it because I couldn't remember ever having written it.

My father died two weeks ago. He passed away in an armchair in the house where he grew up, it is hard to believe, I can't believe it, and now I'm over it, now I'm here in Bergen and I'm writing to you,

Tore, my friend, in Iceland. Yngve called to say what had happened, I caught the next plane down to his, and together we drove to Kristiansand the day after. I cried every day for a week. I had often wondered: what if he dies – but I had never imagined this is how I would react. So what was I grieving over? I don't know. It has nothing to do with rationality, it was just feelings, they kept gushing up, I lay alone in my grandmother's house, in tears. Now I'm over it again, now it's as if it hasn't happened.

I was moved as I sat there because the voice came from August 20, 1998, and because it was still stricken with grief, perhaps without even knowing. It was there, onstage, that I really understood for the first time what it meant that Dad was dead. It was as though it was only then, in Odda, that he died for me. That was why the whole world suddenly became so incomprehensible.

The next morning I met the editor in chief at Spartacus, Frode Molven, in the hotel café. I'd sent him Geir's book, which after six years' toil was finally finished. It was called *Baghdad Indigo* and was a unique piece of work. It was about the human shields who had traveled to Baghdad to stop the U.S. invasion by occupying the most important bombing targets. Geir went with them, all the way from Istanbul to Baghdad, on board a red double-decker bus, and he was a human shield in Baghdad throughout the invasion. He interviewed all sorts of people in the war zone, even when the sky above them was exploding and the windows behind them were being blown out. What was war, and why was it so appealing to so many, even to those who had gone there to stop it? That formed the core of the book. Unlike the journalists, who were looked after by the regime and were either bused around town or sat in their hotel rooms, Geir was free to go wherever and whenever he wanted. When Baghdad fell and elite U.S. soldiers were standing by the waterworks where he and a handful of other activists were staying he grabbed his backpack and lived with them for a few weeks. He interviewed them; they had come straight from the fighting and were more than happy to talk. The book was more than eleven hundred pages long, and that meant the three months it spanned had enormous importance, like something beyond time. He had captured a fragment of time. Practically no one did this anymore; journalists' reports and books from the war zone were light, noncommittal, the authors had moved on even before the corpses had gone cold. The specifics of time and place disappear in their unspecific, similar voices; conflicts merge into one, regardless of whether they take place in Afghanistan, Libya, or Somalia. When I read Geir's book it was like reading something from the Spanish Civil War in the thirties, not because the conflict was similar, but because the approach was the same as in many books from that period, namely existential. *Baghdad Indigo* was an excellent book, of that I had no doubt, so I had told Geir it would be easy to get it published. He was skeptical, he didn't want to take anything for granted, and didn't listen to me. I thought it best to send the manuscript to a publishing house before it was finished, so that they could be involved earlier in the process, it was such unusually comprehensive material. Geir listened to me, and I sent it to Aslak Nore, the nonfiction editor at Gyldendal. He had read Geir's previous book, he said in his e-mail back to me, he liked it, was interested in the topic, and was looking forward to reading the latest. He also wanted to ask me a little favor while I was there, would I mind writing a blurb for the book? Just a couple of words. Of course I couldn't say no as his decision regarding Geir's book was so important. I wrote a recommendation, however Nore not only rejected Geir's book but also went on the attack with a vengeance, calling it immoral. The second person I sent the manuscript to was Halvor Fosli at Aschehoug, but he was halfhearted, lukewarm, he never read the book, which became apparent when he said it was anti-American, which it was not, he had only skimmed it, he must have read a few lines of the interviews with the peace activists and assumed they reflected the book's main thrust. Fosli said he would talk about the book at a meeting with the other editors, which of course produced nothing. So Geir gave up on this strategy and decided to wait until the manuscript was completely finished. Which it was now. I couldn't imagine that anyone would say no. I knew Molven a little from Bergen, he seemed flattered that I had contacted him now, and Spartacus was a serious publishing house. But when we sat down in Odda he initially wanted to speak about something else. No, he didn't want any blurbs; he had in mind a biography about Axel Jensen, however, and wondered if I would like to write it. I didn't say no, even though I would never write a biography about anyone for as long as I lived, nor did I say yes. When that was clear we spoke a little about Geir's book. He said it sounded interesting and he would like to read it. We shook hands, and I walked over to Yngve, who had been sitting nearby waiting, we were going to drive to the ferry. I decided not to tell Geir that Molven had asked me to write a biography for him. There was something unpleasant about everyone on all sides trying to get a chunk of me, I owed Geir so much and I didn't want his book to be about my name.

On the ferry Yngve and I had a coffee, on the quay on the other side we had a smoke, and then he drove to Voss while I made my way toward Flesland Airport. It was autumn, the air was cold, sharp, and clear, the sky cloudless and blue, the sun heavy and drunk with light. Yngve had lent me a CD, it was the first by Dire Straits, I had it on full volume in the rental car, it was the one we played when I was in fifth grade and he was in ninth at Tybakken, and the atmosphere of that time filled my head, the Norwegian seventies, the soft snow, quilted jackets.

Alongside the glinting fjord. Past red, yellow, brown, green trees. Up the mountainside. And then, ahead of me on the road, a dog. I jumped on the brakes, but ran over it anyway, there was a thud and the dog was thrown into the ditch. I stopped the car, switched off the engine, and got out, a man came walking across a yard toward me. I looked for the dog, but it wasn't there. The man pointed. The dog was running up a path on the other side of the road. How was that possible? I had been doing at least fifty kph when I hit it. I keep telling them they should keep the dog on a leash, said the man, who was in his forties, as he came to a halt in front of me. What happened? I said. How could the dog have survived that? You hit it with your bumper. It might be hurt, but it doesn't look like it, he said. Does it come from up there? I said, nodding toward the farm above the road. He nodded. I'd better go up and tell them, I said. He nodded again and accompanied me. The dog was lying in the yard when we arrived, it wasn't squealing or anything, seemed healthy and happy. An old man was there, I walked over to him, explained what had happened and apologized, the dog seemed to be fine though. Thank you, he said. And then I walked back down, got into the car, and drove on. I thought about Vanja, as she loved dogs more than anything else. She knew the names of most breeds and we had to read to her from a dog book almost every day. If we were out and came across a dog we had to ask if she could pet it. Sometimes she asked if she could borrow my phone and take pictures of the dogs we saw. She wasn't allowed to have a dog until she was twelve, which she negotiated down to ten. Now she was eight. I was looking forward to telling her about the incident. If the dog had died I wouldn't have said a word. But it had been fine. I could tell her.

At Flesland I parked the rental car, handed over the keys, checked in, and flew home.

In the following weeks I finished off the third novel. In Odda, Tore had promised to help me with it because it was long and shapeless, that is, its sole principle of form was chronology. Tore had read it, made a few suggestions, which I had accepted, but it hadn't been enough, something more radical was needed, some twist or other. While I was working in Malmö the evening before I had to hand it in, Tore was skimming through it in Stavanger, and he called when he found a turning point around which the whole novel could revolve, and sent me lots of texts throughout the evening and night. By the morning it was finished. I had followed his instructions to the letter. Just a few days later Book 2 came out. Geir called in the morning, and even though I had told him not to mention a word that was written about me, he insisted on reading the *Aftenposten* review. You've got to hear it, he said. Come on, you can take it. But it's not what it says or doesn't say that bothers me, I said. It's the fact that it's there at all. You know how it fucks me up inside. Come on, he said. Just this once. Never again. OK, I said. And he read it to me. All I remember from it is one sentence: "Well, is the case actually statute-barred?" and I was described as "the possible perpetrator." The reviewer was wondering if I was the perpetrator of a sex offense and if the case was statute-barred. I remember because Geir was laughing so much as he read and because he repeated it several times. Have they lost their minds? he said. Have they utterly gone off their rockers? A few hours later I received an agitated e-mail from Tonje. She quoted from the same review, in which the following appeared: "For example the writer's former wife appears by name, and you can only imagine how unpleasant this publication must be for her now," and Tonje asked what that meant and why she hadn't been given the novel before it came out, if it was about her. Previously I'd sent her an e-mail where I asked her not to read the novel. I had done that because it wasn't about her, but about Linda and my feelings for Linda, and it had occurred to me that it might hurt Tonje to read about how in love I was only a few weeks after we had broken up. Now Tonje thought I had kept this from her, that I had deceived her. All of Norway would be reading about her while she was left in the dark. That I might have done something to spare her was so naïve that she didn't believe me for a second. The pressure was so great, the phone calls from the media so incessant that it was impossible to maintain this perspective. The damage was done in the book, not when she read it. I hadn't written about her, but I had written about something of which she had no knowledge and which had happened while we were together: I had fallen in love with Linda. Wham. She was the one. An arrow to the heart. But what kind of heart? Everything was a blur during those days, I fell head-long, there was no reciprocation, Linda turned away, and I cut up my face, left everything, and traveled home. It was the most intense experience of my life. I had been in a place I didn't know existed. The world was a river of impressions and I was connected to them, that was how it felt, everything had significance, I could examine an acorn for ten minutes as though it contained the secret of the universe, which it did, that was why I stared at it. In that state I saw Linda and was hypnotized by her, but nothing happened, we didn't even touch. She was becoming manic; I was, without any doubt, manic. Writing a book about my life was in-conceivable without including the feelings I'd had then and what happened to me. But it was a torment for Tonje and I was the tormentor. I e-mailed and tried to explain, but that only made things worse, you cannot be both tormentor and consoler. She sent a furious e-mail to my editor, who had publicly stated that all the characters appearing in the novel had been given the manuscript to read beforehand. She had not. So, in the gloom of the Internet café reading her e-mail and all the others that had come in over the past two months, I found myself in a place I had never been before, in a world of lawyers who scrutinized every word I wrote, with threats of legal action and public accusations of lying, re-views calling me immoral and where everyone I had been or was close to suffered because of me. While I was writing I didn't think about them, but as the publication date approached they suddenly loomed large, as they really were, and the repercussions revealed themselves to me. The conflict was between the novels and their consequences. The approach I chose was to publish the novels, al-low whatever happened to happen, with all the pain I'd inflicted that brought, and hope the wounds could be healed. In general terms I was able to defend this approach as I knew what I was looking for and the value of it, but not in specific cases, regard-ing the consequences for every individual I had written about. No one has the right to inflict injury on another person. Sitting in front of the screen in the computer games bunker, I was afraid, desperate, and sorry, but I also knew these feelings would disappear when I wrote and would therefore come and go because in the written "I" the social "we" disappeared and the "I" was free. It was only when I got up and left my desk that the "we" returned and I was able to feel ashamed at what I had written and thought, with varying degrees of intensity, according to how deeply I was in the writing process. The social dimension is what keeps us in our places, which makes it possible for us to live together; the individual dimension is what ensures that we don't merge into each other. The social dimension is based on taking one another into consideration. We also do this by hiding our feelings, not saying what we think, if what we feel or think affects others. The social dimension is also based on showing some things and hiding others. What should be shown and what should be hidden are not subject to disagreement because they are connected with the "we." The regulatory mechanism is shame. One of the questions this book raised for me when I was writing it was what was there to gain by contravening social norms, by describing what no one wants to be described, in other words, the secret and the hidden. Let me put it another way: what value is there in not taking others into account? The social dimension is the world as it should be. Everything that is not as it should be is hidden. My father drank himself to death, that is not how it should be, that has to be hidden. My heart yearned for another woman, that is not how it should be, it must be hidden. But he was my father and it was my heart. I shouldn't write that because the consequences affect not only me, but also others. Yet it is true. To write these things you have to be free, and to be free you have to be inconsiderate to others. It is an equation that doesn't work. Truth equals freedom equals being inconsiderate and is on the individual side of the equation; being considerate and secrecy are on the social side, but only as an abstraction, like an inner entity in the "I" because in reality there is no such thing as the social dimension, only single human beings, our "you" in other words, also on the individual side. Tonje isn't a "character." She is Tonje. Linda isn't a character.

She is Linda. Geir Angell isn't a character. He is Geir Angell. Vanja, Heidi, and John, they exist, they are in bed asleep about a hundred kilometers away from where I am sitting at this moment. They are real. And if you want to describe reality as it is, for the individual, and there is no other reality, you have to really go there, you can't be considerate. And it hurts. It hurts not to be considered and it hurts not to be considerate. This novel has hurt everyone around me, it has hurt me, and in a few years, when they are old enough to read it, it will hurt my children. If I had made it more painful, it would have been truer.

It has been an experiment, and it has failed because I have never even been close to saying what I really mean and describing what I have actually seen, but it is not valueless, at least not completely, for when describing the reality of an individual person, when attempting to be as honest as possible is considered immoral and scandalous, the force of the social dimension is visible and also the way it regulates and controls individuals. Its power is enormous, for what I have written about have been exclusively everyday events, there has been nothing sensational about any of it, these things happen all the time, every single day, and everyone knows they do: alcoholism, infidelity, mental illness, and masturbation, just to cite some of what has found its way from the novels into newspaper headlines. The only unusual aspect in this case has been that normality has been associated with real names in a novel and communicated for what it is, something specific tied to certain persons. The novel is a public form, and therein lies the contravention of the norm, the specific and the personal have been transported into the public arena. It happens to all people in the public eye – actors, politicians, TV journalists, pop stars – but they have chosen it of their own free will and want nothing more than this. The only nonpublic people who find themselves thrust there are criminals. In this novel it has happened to ordinary people, who are not criminals. Accordingly their names have taken on criminal form, an ordinary name has crossed the bounds of normality and become so abnormal that journalists track down the person and write about them in the newspapers. What these people did, which was perfectly normal, also took on criminal form and found itself being judged. And I was the person who had turned them into criminals. But I didn't think about any of this at the time, during the many mornings I spent in the Internet café and my study, and the scant defense I was able to erect for my actions, such as that I was only writing about myself, crumbled as soon as one of the people I had written about turned and looked at me. They did it one after the other and I looked down, I looked away, I stared at a page in the novel and continued to write.

The same day that Geir read the *Aftenposten* review to me on the balcony, Asbjørn and Yngve came to Malmö. We were going to the Wilco gig in Copenhagen that evening and they would be staying with us over the weekend. I shook Asbjørn's hand, then Yngve's, and made a point of looking them in the eye, and I knew they were thinking that I was thinking about what I had written about this very thing. They'd brought candy for the children, and Asbjørn had framed the cover photo that he had taken in his capacity as a book designer and we had used for the first novel, and gave it to me along with a pile of books he had doubles of. Heidegger's *Sein und Zeit*, which I only had in English, Pascal's *Pensées* – I had the old, much-abridged edition – plus many more. They had also brought the day's papers with them. I held up a hand and turned my head away, but Linda took them, she was curious, and even though I said she shouldn't, she sat at the kitchen table reading them while Ingrid looked over her shoulder. I saw the front-page headline: Exposes Family – Alcohol and Mental Problems, and I saw the headline inside: Exposes Wife. Then I returned to Yngve and Asbjørn, who were putting their luggage in the living room. We went to the balcony and smoked a cigarette. Asbjørn said he'd been a bit wary when he heard that Linda's mother would be here, he wasn't quite sure what the atmosphere would be like between us after what I'd written. I said she was the larger-than-life type and it would be fine. But it was Ingrid rather than Linda I wanted to keep away from the newspapers. Because Linda was her daughter, and now the papers were saying I had hung her daughter out to dry with her mental problems. And *Alcohol*, that couldn't refer to anyone else but Ingrid. I knew how deeply this had hurt her as she had told Linda so, and she had also maintained it wasn't true. The pain was there, still smoldering and glowing. But a pile of newspapers was one thing, a book another, and an article in the press about it a third. It was getting closer all the time. For Swedes Norway was a distant country, but if the book came out in Sweden, in her own language – a decision hadn't been taken yet, but it was likely – it would impinge on her life and the consequences would be real.

Linda left to pick up the children, and when Asbjørn walked past the kitchen on his way to the bathroom, he saw Ingrid reading the newspaper, she looked up and gave him a thumbs-up. He laughed when he saw that. I wondered what she was thinking. That it was good for the book that it was receiving attention, and thus for the family, her grandchildren, who might finally get a house to live in? And a car to be driven around in?

Half an hour later, when the children came in through the door, they behaved differently from usual. As always when there was a visitor in the apartment, they reminded me of animals. Alert, watchful, cautious, they sniffed around. Hm. Unfamiliar shoes. Unfamiliar jackets. Best to be on your guard here. Vanja was the most guarded, Heidi the next, and John definitely the least. He smiled at everyone. We ate at the table in the living room, the children slipped down from their chairs after a few minutes and disappeared into their room with their bags of candy. I was happy, I always was when I was with Asbjørn and Yngve, although it was a bit odd because it was the two of them who were friends and formed a unit, I was more of a spectator or a distant associate, and not Yngve and I, who were brothers and had the same blood. The dynamics between us were exactly the same as they had been in Bergen when I arrived there in 1989, they were the experienced, worldly-wise ones, I was the novice who didn't know his way around, and nothing of what had happened in our lives since then had changed that. Perhaps that was what I liked, not being in charge, tagging along, being the little brother.

Heidi came in, sent Asbjørn a mischievous look, and asked him what his name was again.

"Asbjørn," he said.

"Isbjørn," Heidi said. Polar bear.

"No," Asbjørn said. "Asbjørn."

"Isbjørn," Heidi said, laughed, and ran off to join the others.

"Actually we're all characters in a novel sitting around this table," Yngve said.

"That's true." Asbjørn laughed.

"We should set up a web page for characters in a novel so that we can discuss our experiences," Yngve said.

"I can be the moderator," I said.

"What was it like to read that you'd been exposed?" Yngve said, looking at Linda.

"No problem," Linda said. "The worst part is being in the paper, if you know what I mean. Then people believe I've been exposed. Otherwise I'd just have been a description in a book. And, of course, that's not the same."

"In fact you two are the only ones who have censored me," I said. "Over such trivialities though. I wrote one thing about you," I said, focusing on Yngve, "I was sure you would be proud of. But no. So, out it went."

"What was that?" Asbjørn said.

"I can't tell you," I said. "But it was something to do with a note we once put on his door."

"Groupies must leave before breakfast?" Asbjørn said.

"Maybe," I said. "And Linda said she really hadn't whipped the donkey at the fun fair."

Ingrid laughed.

"I don't want that on my record, that I whip animals. Anyway, it didn't happen."

"No, it really didn't," I said. "I must've been trying to capture the atmosphere of aggression."

"Thank you for the meal," Asbjørn said, looking at Ingrid. "It was fantastic."

"It was," I said.

We got up and took our plates into the kitchen. Then we went to the balcony for a smoke, Linda and Yngve in the two chairs, Asbjørn and I standing with our backs to the railing.

"This vaguely reminds me of my fortieth," I said. "Wasn't everyone out here at some point? I just remember us standing here packed in like sardines. And I thought about that crack."

I pointed to the crack in the wall, which presumably was just on the surface because if not the whole balcony would have crashed down.

"Oh shit," Asbjørn said.

"Helena thought everyone at the party was so *rar*," Linda said in Swedish. "She returned to it again later. The man sleeping in the children's room, wasn't he fantastic? And the one who didn't say a word all evening, what was up with him? And the one . . . you've got the idea."

"Well, we are," Yngve said in Norwegian.

"Are what?"

"*Rar*, strange," he said.

"*Rar* in Swedish means nice," I said.

The Wilco gig took place in the old theater in Copenhagen, we had bought tickets separately, so I was sitting right out on the edge of a balcony close to the stage, but the sound probably wouldn't be very good, I thought as I took my seat, while Yngve and Asbjørn, I discovered after painstakingly scanning the audience, were like two birds on a perch under the ceiling, where the sound would probably be much better.

I sat back in the seat, which was upholstered in red velvet, and gazed across, not focusing on anything in particular. I was exhausted, and it was good to be surrounded by other people and to have peace and quiet. I hadn't been to a concert since I lived in Norway. It was a big thing when a band came to town then. Now David Byrne could play in a pub two hundred meters from our apartment and I wouldn't go. I had lost music, which had once meant so much to me, it was no longer relevant, a bit like watching TV. Now and then it returned with the force of an ax biting into ice, bringing a sense of grief for everything else I had lost on the path I had trodden.

The warm-up band was Norwegian. They stood in the middle of the stage, which wasn't theirs, they'd rented it, and for some reason I was reminded of a tent pitched in a parking lot, that was what they made me think of. Their sound was low and the lights remained on. But they were pretty good. Hukkelberg, I think that is what they were called.

I looked across the rows of seats and saw the two of them sitting at the top, glowing, sort of, they were the only two faces I recognized in a sea of strangers.

After reading Proust it was impossible not to see such an old theater as an underwater scene, a kind of coral reef with mussels or shells for seats and fishtails or jellyfish tentacles for women's dresses. The way he transformed everything and imbued it with magic is no longer possible, I thought, because everything has already changed, everything is already something else, pervaded by fiction as it were. We can strip down reality, layer by layer, and never reach its core, for what the last layer covers over is the most unreal of all, the greatest fiction of them all, the true nature of things.

The lights dimmed. A spotlight focused on the stage. Jeff Tweedy, chubby, almost a bit fat, came straight to the microphone, started playing at once and sang in a pure, clear voice, effortless. You could never count on this with English bands, at least not those I had seen live in my time. The exception was Blur, whom I saw with Tore at Sentrum in 1993. Everything they did was not only pitch perfect, but also full of the energy only young people have who want something and suddenly realize they can actually achieve it. But Wilco was American, the music wasn't for show, they were inside it. The other band members came on, they played for an hour and a half, maybe two, it was so peaceful sitting there, and at times the music had such an emotional intensity that I lost all control and just cried. Afterward, excited after this excursion back into early adulthood, we met outside and went and got drunk. I'd told them that trains ran all night, but when we arrived at the station, it was closed and we had to take a taxi the whole way to Malmö. Over the bridge the night felt like enclosing walls, the lights shivering as they lit up more and more meters of grayish asphalt, I felt as if I were in a dream. The next day the angst was immense, but I still went out with them, we ate at an Asian restaurant and Asbjørn regaled us with stories he'd heard from a doctor friend, who had told him about all the objects people stuffed up their asses when they were alone and then were unable to retrieve.

In late autumn my first novel was nominated for the Brage Prize and I flew to Oslo with Linda to attend the award ceremony. After we had dropped off our luggage at the hotel she went to the hairdresser's to have her hair done, or styled, maybe the term is, while I popped into the publishing house to talk to Geir. On my return I knocked on the door and Linda opened up sporting her new hairstyle.

"What do you think?" she said. "Honestly."

At first I didn't answer, I went into the room and sat down. Did she want me to confirm what she herself thought and say it was great or did she want, as she said, an honest answer?

I thought it looked terrible and had a feeling that she might think so too.

"It looks like what a fifty-year-old might consider nice," I said.

"Yes, doesn't it. Isn't it awful?"

"It is."

"Good. Then I'll wash it out and go as normal."

Elisabeth, who worked at the publishing house, came to pick

us up, then we took a taxi to the ceremony. Big building, lots of people, a room for the nominees. To my horror, I saw an *Aftenposten* journalist that I had written about in Book 2, and I hadn't minced my words. As soon as he saw me he came over and introduced himself. Did I remember him? Indeed I did, I said. He laughed and said it was an honor to appear in my book, even in the way he did. And then he said, But you were wrong about one thing. I'm not a privileged Oslo West kid. No? I said. I'm sorry. And then I noticed Kjartan Fløgstad, my old hero, the gentleman socialist writer I had also written about. I introduced Linda, he introduced his wife, we exchanged a few words while I kept looking around, I didn't want to be here, I couldn't stay here, I couldn't stand this. Ragnar Hovland, my old writing teacher, he was there. I stood around, and then I persuaded Linda to go out for a smoke by the entrance where people were still streaming in. The darkness was good, the rain was good, all the wet, slippery brown leaves on the grass were good, but not the feeling that you were being watched, that wasn't good. When we sat down at the front, where two seats were reserved for us, beside Kjartan Fløgstad and his wife, a photographer leaned over from the balcony and took a photo of Linda. She didn't see, I said nothing, maybe I was wrong. The show started, there was music, there were readings and sketches, and I was close to throwing up because I could see the stage and feel the audience at my back, and if I won I would not only have to go up there, but also say something. Unfortunately it was me who had to go up. The statuette was as heavy as a murder weapon. Holding it in my hand, I had planned to say that many people who had read the book probably imagined that I would shed a tear, but I didn't dare, so I mumbled something about a character in the novel I had met in the bar, and talked about the time I had moved away from home and what books I had been reading then, which had been written by the other nominees. It was true, Roy Jacobsen had just brought out *The New Water* that year, and I had bought it and the first book by Fløgstad I had ever read, *Dalen Portland*. I thanked Linda and said she was the most generous person I had ever met, and I was happy I hadn't said anything about shedding a tear, my voice cracked a little when I spoke to Linda, she had been looking up at me from below. Then I went back and sat down. I wished that Fløgstad had been the one to rise to his feet and go up and accept the statuette, a thousand times over, he could also receive awards with dignity, I assumed, unlike me, who only wanted the floor to swallow me up in my shame and humiliation. Afterward everyone repaired to a big Irish pub nearby. I sat with Linda and Frederik and some of his colleagues in the courtyard, the rain dripping down the walls and tent poles, or whatever they were called, the supports holding up the temporary roof. Frederik had met Linda the summer we got together, at the time he was visiting us with Kjetil and Richard and we all went on a pub crawl. They were talking now, I stared into the distance drinking beer, I occasionally answered a question from the others, that was how life had become, I was someone you asked questions. A well-known writer came over. We said hello, I was embarrassed, I knew he didn't like what I wrote. He had mentioned this once and been ironic, which made this even harder. But he didn't want to say just hello and congratulate me, he wanted to talk, and he spent at least five minutes refining his attitude to me and my books, he couldn't say straight out that he didn't like them, that they were bad in other words, but nor could he not say that, so what came out of his mouth was impossible to grasp. Why he was saying what he was saying? Was it something social that had to be cleared out of the way before we could talk? Or were there some aesthetic reflections which he thought it important to state, so that I wouldn't believe he was there on any other premise? He stood there for so long that his role imperceptibly changed from that of someone who had come over to say hello to someone who had a seat at the table. He was pleasant, he always had been, but why was he at my table? Did he like my books? Apparently not. Did he like me? Perhaps, perhaps not. But the odds of him coming over to my table because I was a reclusive author who tinkered with words in a valley in Vestland were low, I suspected, unless this reclusive author was considered the pick of his colleagues. Then he would have come. As indeed would I. Once I had been talking to a writer and her husband at a table in a restaurant in a tiny Norwegian town during a literary festival, and Lars Saabye Christensen sat down at the same table, I glanced over at him, didn't quite catch what my conversation partner said, and as soon as I got the chance I turned to him, didn't we have the same publishing house in England? I did that despite seeing that she had noticed my glances at Saabye Christensen and understood exactly how my mind was working. It still wasn't too late to save the situation, but my desire to talk to him was greater than the certainty that I was making a bad impression. At the same festival the emcee and I were rebuked by the wife of one of the writers because the emcee had devoted more time and emotion to my book than her husband's. This mixture of the highest and the lowest and most basic that literature can be is typical of the writer milieu, and it's hardly surprising, there are few areas of life where people invest so much of themselves to gain so little. The year I made my debut, late one evening I was sitting with Erik Fosnes Hansen in a hotel room, flattered to be talking to him, even if I hadn't read anything by him since he made his ridiculously young debut with *The Falcon Tower*, a novel I read when I was at *gymnas*, I happened to mention *Vagant* and it was like waving a red rag to a bull. *Vagant!* he yelled. He had sold hundreds of thousands of books, they were published all over the world, he received good reviews everywhere, but not in *Vagant*, they barely considered him a writer, this tiny literary magazine that in reality consisted of a handful of young people who gathered in cafés in the East End of Oslo. He despised them. Wishy-washy chitchat and academic intellectualism, he said. Why? He didn't say, but I imagine a lack of acknowledgment on their part might have played a role. When my first book began to sell I was worried about my status. For a while joining the editing team at *Vagant* saved me, and it was quite perfect from a strategic point of view, there I was both a big-time and a small-time writer, wriggling my way upward and meeting more and more names on the way, until one rainy autumn evening I ended up in one of Oslo's Irish pubs and the big names came to me. Knausgaard had become a trademark, a logo, the newspapers had been full of it that autumn, and now I could feel how much energy lay in its proliferation. People looked at me. People apologized to me before saying anything. People didn't dare speak. People came over when they were drunk. It was remarkable. And it wasn't the books I had written because they were pretty run-of-the mill – two sons who bury their dead father and a frustrated father of small children who strips himself naked for the reader – it was the name and all the resonance it contained now.

I liked it that a well-known author came over to our table that evening. It gave me a feeling of power. This feeling meant that I could say what I liked or refuse to say anything at all, it didn't matter, nothing would change as a result. When I met him for the first time I was a student in a writing course that he taught; when I met him for the second time I was a student with hubris, going around and interviewing all of Norway's famous writers. I had to put in an enormous effort even to be worth his time; when I interviewed him I had prepared for several weeks and done nothing else but. I had devised smart, probing, worthy questions which some years later I realized were totally transparent and laid me bare, and this was not only the case with him but everyone I met: final-year students, professors, writers, editors, and journalists, and as I was so immensely prestige-oriented, the bigger or more prestigious the name, the more I exerted myself. Oh, the time Professor Buvik not only remembered my name but also asked me a question during a lecture. The first time I met Jonny Halberg, Tone Hødnebø. Henning Hagerup. Eldrid Lunden. Thure Erik Lund. Ingvar Ambjørsen. Cecilie Løveid. Olav H. Hauge. Marit Christensen. Øystein Rottem. Kjartan Fløgstad. Ole Robert Sunde. Georg Johannesen. Kjersti Holmen. Erlend Loe. Åsne Seierstad. William Nygaard. Kjetil Rolness. Einar Økland. Frode Grytten. Trond Giske. I'd understood that the only way of managing was to act as if this didn't mean a thing, as if you were completely uncorrupted, while inside you were thrilled by the meeting and hoped someone would notice. It wasn't until I was sitting in this pub that I realized there was some movement and a goal, my name was suddenly so emotive that others were behaving toward me as I had previously behaved toward other emotive names. Not that I didn't understand what they were doing, I knew from my own experience, I knew all about the base, all-too-human art of fawning. That is why I also understood that it had nothing to do with me, for I had been the same, with my tongue hanging out of my mouth for all those years, making myself appear better than I was by behaving how the uncorrupted behave, which was no more than a more sophisticated form of corruption, I had been the same. All that had changed was the name and the associated image. I had always done readings for a fee of fifteen hundred kroner, but now I was being offered sixty thousand for a forty-five-minute gig. I turned it down, not because I didn't want the money, but because I wanted to have something that was worth more, namely integrity; not because I was someone with integrity, but because I was someone who was doubly corrupt. Yes, I was so corrupt that I no longer cared what *Vagant* might think about what I wrote, as, in the values hierarchy, not caring ranked higher than caring, and the hierarchy was all I cared about. That is how it was. I had sold my soul twice, it was nothing worse than that, I was at the top. If you showed you wanted to be at the top and basked in the glory, you weren't at the top after all because you were only at the top if your integrity was intact and you said no. No to newspapers, no to TV, no to social gatherings and performances. You were only at the top if you said no to the top, but not even that was the absolute top because there were those who really didn't care, who sat alone and unsung in some valley writing their stubborn, angry, uncompromising prose – if we are talking about authors at the pinnacle – and who would be happiest not even sending their work to a publishing house but burying it in the forest and starting on the next.

When the evening was over, Linda and I, holding the statuette in one hand, walked to the hotel arm-in-arm. She was hungry, I went down to the 7-Eleven to buy some food for her, and on the way back I burst into laughter, it came from nowhere, and I stopped and turned to the wall. Ha ha ha, I laughed. Ha ha ha. Then I carried on walking, through the rain and darkness, over the shimmering asphalt, to the hotel, which was the Savoy, where I stopped again and lit a cigarette, the last before going to bed. I didn't know what I had been laughing at, but just the thought of it made me laugh again. Ha ha ha. Ha ha ha. Ha ha ha.

I was still chortling when I entered our room. Linda had gone to sleep. I sat down on the bed and placed my hand on her brow. You wanted something to eat, didn't you? I said. But she was too far into the darkness of her soul, so I pulled a chair over to the window, sat down, ate her food, and drank a Pepsi Max looking out the window and watching the rain fall and the lamp hanging from a thin wire across the street swing back and forth in the wind.

♦ ♦ ♦

One weekend at the end of May 2010 I rented a car and drove to the cabin outside Malmö to sort out the chaos there. Linda had put the property up for sale, there had already been one viewing, but no one had been interested, and no wonder, nothing had been done to hide the neglect. The thought of it, how everything had gone to the dogs, had been on my mind for ages. After emerging from the last roundabout and entering the subdivision area, which extended on both sides of the street and consisted of several hundred small cabins with small gardens, almost all impeccably maintained, the thought weighed more heavily on me than before. The fact that I was actually here and would soon be coming to grips with the mess was like a light inside me. Not a flame or a shimmer, more like a clearing you approach in the forest, the expectation of it.

There was supposed to be another viewing the following day, and if I could tackle the worst of the neglect it was not impossible that someone might make an offer, they might even be drawn to its dilapidated state and the idea of fixing it up.

The sky was gray and wintry, and the people I saw along the road, some kids on bikes and a woman pushing a stroller and carrying a heavy Co-op bag, were not in contact with it, the way crabs are not in contact with the surface of the sea, it struck me as I drove along at thirty kph. The leaves on the trees had just come out, but without any sun it was difficult to associate them with the life that spring always ushers in.

I downshifted and turned into the large gravel parking lot. I had pains in my stomach. This was a place you were seen not as the person you were, whatever that might be, but as how you appeared. Here I was a man with long greasy hair and a beard, wearing old black clothes, with wild eyes and restless movements, and when this tramp-like figure arrived with our three children, I saw myself so clearly through the other cabin owners' eyes, and all my inner confidence and dignity simply vanished. If someone had called social services and told them to come and rescue the children from this terrible father, possibly a drug addict, definitely dubious, I would have been on the defensive, I would have felt there was something in that and would only have defended myself halfheartedly.

I drove to the barrier in front of the gravel road at the other end of the parking lot, stopped, got out, opened the barrier, swung it to the side, got in and drove forward a few meters, got out and closed the barrier, continued my journey at a snail's pace between the little wooden cabins. The gravel crunched beneath the tires and the car glided forward like a barge up the narrow canal-like road, past gate after gate until I stopped outside ours. It wasn't as clean and shiny as the others, but was covered with a layer of greenish algae or fungus. Nor was the fence free of foliage, like the others, as was stipulated in the rules: the hedge on the inside grew between the cracks in the fence and well above the top. I switched off the engine, took out the key, and noticed the sign that had appeared on the fence since I was last here. TILL SALU, for sale, it said in blue on white. I opened the car door, got out, and closed it again. I felt the chill air on my face and hands. The gravel was overgrown with weeds, thereby breaking another of the rules, and when I saw that I felt a pain in my stomach. I wished I could have made myself not care, say to hell with the idiots who sat scrutinizing other people's gardens, this feeble-minded bunch of wrinkled old folk with sagging skin who were unable to think about anything except what was right and fair and spent their remaining years and days, replete with all the experience a long and unique life had given them, keeping a lawn manicured and foaming with indignation when others did not. I wished I didn't care about them, but I did. The truth was that I feared them and really wanted to make peace with them.

I opened the gate and went into the garden.

Why hadn't she cut the grass? Overgrown beds was one thing, they would take weeks to clear, but the lawn? What had she been thinking when she put the plot up for sale. That the first impression wasn't important? That potential buyers would ignore the neglect and think, *actually*, this is a nice place?

I turned. From the window of the doll's house on the other side of the road an old dear was staring at me. Her husband had been the chairman of the owners' association. It was his responsibility to make sure that all the cabin owners behaved as they should. So when I caught the bus here to water the grass one Wednesday evening, after a few days of desert heat, he was the one who strolled over to the fence, by chance as it were, always by chance, to ask if I knew what day it was. Yes, indeed I did, it was Wednesday, wasn't it? Yes, it was. And we have a system here, you know, regarding watering. Odd numbers water on Mondays, Wednesdays, and Fridays while even numbers water on Tuesdays, Thursdays, and Saturdays. What are you? I was obliged to confess that I was an even number and therefore not entitled to do any watering. So it was a case of either catching the bus home or defying him and keeping the hose low behind the house, where no one could see me. Of course that was what I did, sitting on the doorstep and smoking, fearful that he would spot me. Or we all came here one Saturday afternoon and slept over, with the ulterior motive of cutting the grass, which was done all too seldom. And who happened to walk past our fence then but the chairman? You're cutting your grass, I can hear, he said. Yes, I am. It's gotten terribly long. Yes, he said. But you're not allowed to use any machines from four o'clock on a Saturday afternoon until Monday morning, because of the noise. We like to have some peace and quiet. However you can mow the lawn this afternoon and you'll know for next time. Oh, thank you very much, I said. That's very kind of you.

Then there were the pieces of paper they left in the mailbox after their rounds of inspection. A printed form on which they ticked various boxes according to what they had observed.

I rounded the corner of the house, and out of sight of the neighbors I sat on the doorstep, lit a cigarette, and tried to draw up a plan of action. From the highway to Denmark came a faint drone, in waves, as well as dull thuds and shouts from a football field nearby. I had never seen it, only the floodlights around it, which were switched on every evening and in the autumn and winter stood like a luminous hangar on the dark plain.

That autumn and winter I had been out here writing, alone in this great expanse of cabins, I collected water in a canister from over by the parking lot, went shopping in a supermarket a few kilometers away, knocked off page after page, three or four days in a row, returned home, stayed there for some days, then came back here. Where I was completely disconnected. No newspapers, no Internet, no TV, no radio, just a cell phone, but no one had the number. And not a soul around. In the evening and at night a hedgehog, which slunk through the garden and occasionally, if I was sitting still, nudged its snout against my shoe. During the day the birds. I sat in front of my computer wearing a hat and gloves, a jacket, a blanket or a duvet over my lap. The air was like smoke around my head in the cold light of my lamp. I wrote about my childhood and my teenage years. I had telephone conversations with Geir, whom I read to and I discussed things with, telephone conversations with Linda, who had her mother over to help with the children and who during the hours they were off at school never quite knew what to do or how to do it. The hours that stretched out before her were more frightening than rewarding, I knew. It had been like that for a long time. She had office space in a collective but was scared to go there, forced herself a couple of times but was absent for weeks at a time.

It was a nice office, she had a Mac with a voice-recognition program on the desk, pictures of the children beside it, books on the shelves for inspiration. Once she took Heidi with her and Heidi had been proud to go to work with Mommy, she had said hi to the others and sat drawing, and I could see how happy Linda was when she came home, for that day she had been like other parents, she had her child with her at work, she had shown her off to her colleagues and let Heidi see what she did for a living. Nevertheless, she went there less and less.

In Linda something weighed her down and lifted her up. She had to fight it because when it weighed her down everything was black and without hope, and when it lifted her up, it was bright and hopeful, and that colored everything, her whole existence, which kept changing dramatically in this way, even though it was the same.

When I met her for the first time she was on her way up, and at that time it didn't stop, it didn't turn, just carried on and on, there were no limits, she didn't sleep anymore, the day was endless, and finally a girlfriend found her in her apartment hunched up on a table, mumbling numbers. Linda has stars inside her, and when they shine, she shines, but when they don't, the night is pitch-black. She spent more than a year in a psychiatric hospital, and when I met her and we got together she hadn't been out long. We had children almost at once, we both wanted them. I never thought about her having been ill, I wasn't frightened of it, and that confidence was perhaps what made the thought of children possible for her or at least what made it easier.

In the maternity clinic she had to put a cross by "psychological illness" on all the forms, and I saw how that conditioned the midwife's view of Linda and me, although Linda was fine now. Her mood went in cycles, she plummeted and soared, but always within a normal range, I never thought about it, that was the way she was, temperamental, and I didn't react to her happiness when she was happy or the darkness when she was depressed or full of impetuous fury, I reacted to her, to what she said and did.

She tried all kinds of methods to stabilize her emotions because this took its toll on her, everything changing, the life we lived, which was so different from the one we had before, with the responsibility for the children and all that entailed, the feeling of not being in control was the absolute worst. She feared chaos more than anything else. She was petrified of anything that smacked of irregularity because with her volatile nature the rest of what we had, our home, had to be as solid and constant as it could be. Everything was a threat to her. My time spent writing was a threat. She knew it was my job, and it gave me meaning, and when she was fine it wasn't a problem, until her spirits sank and the fear came, then it became a threat as well, and she couldn't stand up to fear, it was insatiable.

It was at its height when she was pregnant with Vanja, she was terrified of losing her, she was terrified of the imminent responsibility, and she expelled her fear in great outbursts. I responded to these outbursts, which I considered unreasonable, while being afraid of them, they were so violent, I wasn't used to such strong inner forces, where I came from everything was controlled and rationalized. Vanja arrived, peace settled over us. Linda went to school, Heidi arrived, we moved to Malmö, John arrived. There was a lot of work, but it wasn't a problem for me, whatever it was; nor was housework a problem. You just had to get on with it. I took things as they came and wanted Linda to grit her teeth as well and tough it out.

What did she have?

She had her radio training, but that was already a long time ago, and she hadn't done any radio since, getting back into it, calling the station and saying she had an idea became more difficult by the day. She had bought a microphone and an editing program, that was as far as she had got.

She also had her writing. The oldest texts were from long before we met, the most recent ones she wrote last year. They were sensationally good. She sent them to her old publishing house. They were rejected, short stories were too difficult during tough times for publishers, they said. There wasn't a market for them, they didn't have the money. She sent them to three other houses, two of them never read the collection, the third said no. My two novels came out, the third was in the pipeline, and while I was writing the fourth Linda called Sveriges Radio and put forward an idea she had for a documentary. It was a big step and a turning point, the conversation was a commitment, the producer wanted to meet her, they met and she had faith in Linda. This time something would come of it. They agreed on a work plan. Linda was excited, full of energy and ideas, we sat on the balcony after the children were in bed and talked about everything she was going to do. She went to Stockholm to interview the Swedish astronaut Fuglesang, then up to Norrland, where she visited a commercial space station and interviewed the employees.

The documentary was based on the *Hindenburg*'s last flight, she had once come across some articles from the time in a Swedish paper, from which it appeared that a Swedish journalist had been on board and telegraphed reports of the journey several times a day. He died when the airship caught fire and burned up on the other side of the Atlantic just before docking at its destination. It was a brilliant story, which would be contrasted with one about space travel.

She was away for eight days doing research and called me full of enthusiasm from her hotel room. She had ridden on a dogsled, stayed in an ice hotel, wandered around an area full of space junk.

She had spoken to a lot of people and arranged to meet them, it almost seemed as though she was also friends with them as some of what she told me could only have been said in confidence.

Her voice at the other end sounded excited and full of life. I went to the balcony, sat down clad in a hat and coat, and smoked. The children were asleep. I felt a strange unease. It was as though I wasn't in actual communication with her.

"I walked around the area. It was enormous, covered with snow, and everywhere there were big chunks of metal. It was a space cemetery. Can you imagine that, Karl Ove?"

"Sounds exciting," I said. "Did you interview anyone?"

"No, I just walked around with the microphone talking about what I could see. But I know it was good. It was so fantastic there."

"Okay."

"And now the stars are so clear. Can you imagine what it's like up here?"

"Do you have to get up early tomorrow?" I said.

"Yes, oh, the man from the ice hotel, sorry, I just have to tell you this before I forget, he said we absolutely have to come up here together. We can have a room for free."

"An ice hotel? You're kidding."

"It's very special up here, you know. In a way, it's magical."

"Okay. Linda, I think I'll have to go to bed now if I'm going to have any chance with the kids tomorrow."

"Yes, I understand. Good night, my prince. I love you."

"Good night."

She came back home still excited by what she'd experienced and what she was going to do. She wrote a manuscript, the idea being that she would dramatize the zeppelin flight based on the journalist's reports. It was approved, a budget was set up. Linda hired actors, directed, and did the recording. She went to work at seven in the morning, came home at six in the evening. She was a changed person. I had seen her work as hard only once before, that was during the exam period at the drama institute, then she had given her all. But this was different. Now it was as though she was investing everything she had, her whole existence, as if it was now or never, not only for this documentary but for her whole life.

On the Friday evening after her first week of work we sat drowsily watching TV as the children slept.

"You'll take them tomorrow, won't you?" she said.

I looked at her.

"Why? What are you doing?"

"Working."

"Do you have to work on the weekend?"

"Yes, of course," she said. "It's important. There's a deadline."

Important? Deadline?

I started to fume inside. I looked at the TV screen for a few seconds. Then I turned back to her.

"Darling," I said. "You've always refused to let me work on the weekend because it's important we do something together as a family. I haven't worked one single weekend in seven years. And now you're going to work on the weekend?"

"How mean you are," she said. "You're so incredibly mean."

"So the family rule doesn't apply now that you've got a job?"

She got up.

"Where are you going?" I said.

"To bed," she said. "I have to be up early."

I stayed where I was, listening to her footsteps fade into the hall, I wanted to follow her and smooth things over, but I was still fuming inside, it wouldn't be a good conversation. Besides, I was actually happy that she was full of energy and determination, and in the long run perhaps there was a chance *I* would be able to work on the weekend.

Those were my thoughts. Actually it was good, actually it was as it should be.

She got up early the next morning and cycled to work. On Sunday we all went to Slottsparken, followed our usual route through the town to the first playground, which was really only a merry-go-round and a slide beneath some enormous deciduous trees whose crowns in the summer were like a ceiling, but now the branches were leafless beneath the gray sky, on to the second playground, across the park, which bordered a large residential area, where Linda and I stood beside each other in the wind keeping an eye on our children running around in their red all-weather jackets, Linda seemingly on her way down, inside herself for the first time in many weeks. At home the children watched a film while she rested and I read the Sunday papers. If she hadn't been obliged to work, with a schedule and a budget for what was a relatively large production, she would have been able to stay at home during the coming week, lie on the sofa, watch mediocre films, and sleep until the darkness and gloom disappeared. Now she couldn't, she had to work. On Monday morning she rose early and got herself ready while I took care of the children. I was rummaging through the shelves of clothes to find something for John to wear when she closed the bathroom door. Inside, she threw up. It lasted for several minutes. Then she opened the door, came out, went to the hatstand, where the coats were hanging, and put on her black leather jacket.

"Did you throw up?" I asked.

She nodded. Her face was white.

"But I'm going now. See you this afternoon. Don't know exactly when I'll be back. Six maybe."

She grabbed her bag and left while I continued to dress the children. After taking them to school, I returned, sat down, and worked on Book 4 all day, picked them up, cooked, and was eating with them when Linda arrived. She seemed drained. The next morning it was the same, she vomited in the toilet, then went to work, and the following morning again, and the one after that. I thought she was exaggerating, it was only a job after all, but of course I couldn't say that. After five years and three births, a life that consisted of nothing but children and childcare, with a few tentative attempts to get something up and running last year, this was her big chance, an opportunity for her to show what she was worth. Had it been anyone else she wanted to show I could have told her to take it easy, it wasn't that important, but she wanted to show herself that she had ability and there was nothing I could say to that. She was sick in the morning, went to work, came home in the evening, less and less confident. Her mother came down to help us and I was able to devote more time to writing.

At two o'clock on Friday I heard the front door open and ambled out to see who it was.

Linda, head bowed, was taking off her jacket without looking at me.

"Are you home already?" I said.

"I failed," she said. "I couldn't do it."

"Sorry?"

She was crying.

"I broke down in the control room," she said. "I realized I'd never be able to do it. It's just no good. It's no good, Karl Ove."

She went into the bedroom. I followed. It turned out the producer had said she should go home and take a couple of days off. The producer was strict and demanded a lot, she had understood what Linda was capable of, but perhaps not how fragile she was.

"I couldn't do it," she said. "I'm a fiasco."

Her mother came in, stopped in the doorway and retreated when she saw that Linda was crying.

"Are you sure?" I said.

"I can't get the two parts to gel," she said. "And now there's almost no time left. It won't work. It's impossible."

That was bad. A defeat after investing everything she had, it couldn't have been worse.

"Can't you make it simpler? Take a few shortcuts?"

She didn't answer. But after the children had gone to bed that evening she asked if I could listen to the little she had. Naturally, I said. In fact it was the last thing I wanted to do. I can handle my own failures, but not those of others.

She passed me the headset and pressed play.

1100

It was good. Of course it was good. There wasn't much, but the little there was, was good.

On Monday she forced herself to go back, ashen-faced and determined. Her radio program had become a fixation, a much larger entity than itself, and when the producer said it wasn't working and would have to be completely rejigged, she collapsed again. Like the last time I thought it was really over, that she had failed, her race was run. And like the last time she gave it another shot.

Eventually the program was finished. I was invited to Sveriges Radio as a kind of test listener, and there we sat in a run-down studio in Malmö, two producers, one technician, Linda, and I.

I was almost angry when I heard the program. It was brilliant. I had believed Linda when she said it was a disaster, she hadn't given me any reason to believe anything else.

Afterward she broke down. Over the following weeks, much longer than usual, she was in the grip of her darkness. She was quick to tears, watched films, said less than usual when we were alone together. With the children she made an effort to be as she always was with them, but I could see she was relieved when I took them out on my own. She would never do any radio again, she said. But when the darkness lifted, and light began to fill her, and her world became easier and easier, she started toying with the idea of other documentaries, she had a foot in the door.

I completed Book 4 after a week in the cabin, where I wrote night and day while the third book came out. All my old friends, to whom I had sent the manuscript, were keen to read about those days, all had consented to its publication. I received a lovely enthusiastic letter from my oldest friend, Geir Prestbakmo, whom I hadn't seen for thirty years. He described some scenes he remembered, among others, standing in a boathouse and holding a hose during a thunderstorm as we had heard that lightning didn't strike rubber. The spirit and tone of the letter were exactly as I remembered him. I spoke to Dag Lothar on the phone; he reminded me about the discussions we'd had about the connection between colors and the taste of hard candy and the summer we biked out past Eydehavn and played tennis. It felt as if I had given them our story, in a way, and not taken it. It was a good feeling. Everyone invited me back to visit them the next time I was in the area. The problems started again with Book 4. Instead of using authentic names and sending the manuscript to individuals, I used made-up names and just forged ahead with publication, I couldn't face another storm. But still people were angry. I wrote Book 5 in eight weeks, by then I really didn't give a damn, at the same time I found a tone that reminded me of the literature I used to read when I was the age I was describing, and it struck me this was the novel I had wanted to write when I was twenty, but I hadn't had it in me. Now I did. Last week Linda flew to Tenerife with our children, Helena, and her children, and I was finishing the book while the Winter Olympics were on TV, I sat on the sofa alone, cheering loudly when Northug, or "the wolf," as the Swedish commentators called him, won, and then I went into my study and carried on. When it was finished I sent it to the people I had described. Some were angry and said I had ruined their lives, I changed their names, some asked me to delete a couple of episodes as they contained a lot of dangerous things I hadn't understood at the time, and some said to leave it as it was. Tonje, who was the most important person in the book apart from Yngve, said to leave everything as it was. I asked Linda not to read it because it would be unpleasant to read about a love story with another woman. Similarly, but for a different reason, I had asked my mother not to read Book 3. After reading the second book she had texted me to say that it hurt to be demeaned. After reading Book 4 she called me and was as angry as she could be. I had written something that simply was not true, about what had happened between us when we lived in the house in Sandnes, to do with alcohol, and either I must have completely misunderstood or I'd made it up. I cut it. *Dagsrevyen*, NRK's evening news program, came and interviewed me, after it was over I returned home, got into bed, and could hardly move, I was paralyzed with fear, the interview would be on Saturday, all of Norway would see it, and I had barely managed to utter one coherent sentence.

The interviewer had shown me a magazine cover on which was written Knausgaard for Dummies, and I realized as the camera focused on my face that something had happened to me in Norway that I hadn't grasped. I had become big. Some of this I had sensed in Oslo before Christmas when I went into a bookshop to do a signing, it was an event, there were TV cameras, radio microphones, camera flashes, and the shop was full to the rafters, and the line in front of the signing table, where I sat with mics by my mouth, was endless. After the signing I walked up to Litteraturhuset, the biggest room was sold out, and another room, where they had set up video cameras, was also full. Tore interviewed me, we repeated what we had done in Odda, but at that time interest had been burgeoning, here it was hysteria. Afterward, on my way to the back room, a journalist followed me continually asking me whether I'd had sex with a thirteen-year-old. Then I went out with Tore and his girlfriend, we got drunk, and walking toward the hotel I saw the day's papers in a 7-Eleven. *Dagsavisen* had devoted its entire front page to a photo of me signing books. It was totally unreal and dreamlike, impossible to associate with me, so the cabin outside Malmö, where I headed the day after I came home, was as much a refuge as a place to write. Everything was as before, sitting in front of a computer screen. Three days there, home to the family, the Saint Lucia celebration in the school, Christmas with a full house, New Year's Eve. Out to the cabin, back to the family. No interviews, no papers, no TV, as it had been all autumn, and now I was doing the same all winter. *Dagsrevyen* was an exception, I had been awarded a radio prize for the first novel, I was due to receive it in Malmö, and for it I had to give an interview, and *Dagsrevyen* had asked if they could tag along. Thinking I had to do an interview anyway, I'd felt it didn't matter. When I was there, sitting on a chair with a camera trained on my face, it was as though the fear of everything I knew had happened but hadn't actually understood was gathered here, in this one place.

After the interview I lay in bed so frightened that I could hardly move, and I called Linda as soon as I heard her come home.

"Linda! Linda! Linda!" I shouted.

She came in, stopped at the doorway, and looked at me.

"You'll have to look after the children today," I said. "For the rest of the evening. I can't. I have to stay in bed."

She nodded.

"That's not a problem," she said.

I could see she was happy to be able to help me. After she had gone to get the children I sat up, switched on my laptop, which was finally online, and lay all evening watching a series of documentaries about the Second World War. The pictures were unique, many everyday shots of how the world's solidity and fortitude shone through the ravages of war, which made it real in a very different way. When Linda came to bed, I was asleep.

At Easter we traveled to Stockholm, rented a suite in a hotel, I had earned enough money for that, and the idea was I would make a start on Book 6 while Linda and the children visited her mother and spent time with her in various places such as the Junibacken Children's Museum, the Skansen Open-Air Museum, and the Children's Room at the Kulturhus. However, nothing went according to plan, Linda was down and couldn't manage, she called after a few hours and asked if I could take over, and I did. One day Helena and Fredrik invited us to his beautiful house. We caught the train to Uppsala, where he picked us up. Geir and Christina were also there, and after we had been shown around we sat and talked while the children were outside playing. Linda was on a high, so much so that I could hardly communicate properly with her, she was just floating, everything was fantastic. I knew that in reality she was depressed, and I was angry, I hated it when she was like this, so exaggeratedly happy, enthusiastic, and full of praise for everyone although she didn't feel it deep down. There was something false about it. I noticed the difference so easily, others didn't, they just thought she was wonderful. And she really was when she was in this state, the life and soul of every party, just not for me.

When we arrived back in Malmö I continued working on Book 6. So far I was no more than twenty pages in, but it wasn't going to take long anyway, and the plan was to finish it in six weeks. Geir's book had been turned down, it was too long and wordy for Spartacus to take the risk, Molven wrote. Now two large and two small publishing houses had said no, and we had to think in new ways. Geir had always said it would be like this, it was his experience of the world, while I kept saying it would be fine, that was my experience. How a book that was of international standing and radically different from other documentary accounts that had come out in Norway would not be published was beyond me. *Moby-Dick* wasn't turned down because it was too long and wordy. Or too immoral?

I called Yngve and asked him if he would like to start up a publishing house, e-mailed Asbjørn with the same question, both were enthusiastic about the idea, and so we founded Pelikanen, primarily to publish *Baghdad Indigo* but also with the idea of continuing afterward, translating books we liked and publishing them.

At this time I started sending the manuscript to those I had written about in Book 5. It was about the twelve years I'd spent in Bergen. The central figure was Tonje. I sat for a long time over an e-mail to her before I sent it.

When I sent you the first book to read, you wrote that it was a good portrait and you knew it might change later in the narrative; however, you gave me a free hand. That was then, afterward all that happened has happened — including Book 2, which you didn't get to read in advance — and now everything looks very different. What you once agreed to has developed into something else. I was thinking about that when I wrote Book 5, that is why I hardly go into who you are (to me) as a person, and almost exclusively describe you through the eyes of the lover. You have no reason to be ashamed of or to fear what I have written about you in the book, the only mistake (and it wasn't a mistake) you made was to get together with me. What you can fear is of course the newspapers and what they write. The headline "Knausgaard Suspected of Rape" is bound to appear. Naturally it's terrible for you to be associated with this. On the other hand, the book puts all the blame on me, nothing on you, every reader will understand that. If you like I can change the scene when you return from Kristiansand, remove the infidelity, and instead simply have you say it's over.

Not long afterward I received an e-mail from Jan Vidar, he was going to Copenhagen with his family, could they drop in? Of course, I wrote back, it would be nice to see you after all these years. I spent all day cleaning up the flat, going shopping, and cooking. They came in the late afternoon, Jan Vidar, Ellen, and their three children. I had only seen the oldest two when they were tiny tots, now they were big girls.

Linda wasn't well and wasn't feeling up to meeting anyone she didn't know, so she went to the bedroom as soon as she had welcomed them. I suspected Jan Vidar interpreted that as a rejection, that really she didn't want them to be there.

We chatted all evening. He hadn't changed an iota, he was as calm and relaxed as ever. We worked through everyone we had known in those days. Jan Vidar still lived in town and was in touch with many of them. We also talked about the books I had written, mostly about the hoo-ha around them. Jan Vidar told me he had refused all interviews up to a certain point, then as the attacks on me had increased and accusations of immorality were raining down, he gave up his resistance and defended me. I knew that, my mother had mentioned it, and I said I was pleased he had.

If there was anyone I had needed when I moved into the area as a thirteen-year-old it was him, I thought as we sat in one living room, while all the children were on the sofa watching a movie in the other. Loyal, incorruptible, considerate, independent. He had stayed, I had left. He had learned to play the guitar, I hadn't. He had three children, I had three children. The differences between us at that time had been minor, for when you are in your early teens age is decisive, the world that seems to be forming before your eyes is the same. Jan Vidar was the first person I got drunk with. He was the first person I went to parties with. He was the first person I experienced girls with. Predominantly talking about them because almost everything revolved around music and girls, but also cycling over to see them, each of us on a sofa, making out with a girl to the sound of "Telegraph Road" by Dire Straits, which was made for the purpose.

Now the small differences that existed had become bigger, but he was still the same person he had always been; the differences were in the layers of experience that time had deposited.

Jan Vidar said one thing that evening that I turned over in my mind after they had gone. It was about what my father had been for him. Jan Vidar and I were the best of friends, and for the first three years I lived there Dad had been around as well. While Jan Vidar's father became an important person in my life, always interested and present when I was at their house, Dad was nothing to Jan Vidar, a kind of shadow he knew existed and occasionally saw but with whom he never exchanged a word. He talked about a time I had just got off my bike and Dad came storming out of the house and gave me an earful for something or other. He realized he was strict and suspected I was afraid of him, but actually he knew nothing. We never talked about it. And that was odd to hear. Why did I never talk about Dad in those three years? Normally we talked about everything. Perhaps it was because there was nothing to say. That was how it was. Perhaps because there was no language to express it? I don't recall thinking about him either. I just think I reacted to him, kept him at bay, dealt with what he said and did out of a sense that everything he stood for and did was unchangeable, a bit like a power I lived under. And probably I was ashamed. That must have been why I never spoke to Jan Vidar about him. We were in our early teens, which is the age when it begins to dawn on you that there are other ways of doing things and other ways of thinking than those in your family.

At any rate I wasn't ashamed of Dad, but of the way I was. I can't remember that much about him during those years. His presence in my childhood is clear, then from thirteen until I was sixteen he is vague and indistinct, hardly there at all, he reappears full of vigor and gravitas when I was sixteen and he and Mom divorced.

In those three years he spent most of his time in the living room on the ground floor of the barn while Mom and I were in the house, and when he came in I invariably went up to my room.

No friends. No social life. Only his job, evenings at home. The occasional trip to his parents in Kristiansand over the weekend.

When we moved there he was thirty-eight. He must have felt he was a prisoner in his own life. And he must have been lonely. When I think of him, he is like a kind of shadow.

The autumn the first volume of this novel came out I received a letter from a man in Bodø who had once known my father. He didn't write much, he was more interested in writing about his own life and what the novel meant to him. When, a few weeks later, I was signing books in a shop in Oslo another man came up to me and said he had worked with Dad, and Dad had been an outstanding teacher. Then, not long before Jan Vidar and his family visited us, I got another letter from someone who had known Dad as a young man. He wrote that after reading the first four volumes he wondered how much of Dad's upbringing had affected his relationship with Yngve and me. He wrote that he had lost contact with Dad after *gymnas* as he'd moved to Bergen, where he has lived ever since, and Dad had moved to Oslo. He wrote that Dad's life had been full of bluff and lies when he had known him, and what I had written about this side of him was nothing in comparison to what he had seen. He wrote that Dad's father had been quick-tempered and moody, and ruled his son with an iron rod, often boxing his ears and not letting him go out. He also wrote about one incident when Dad had been beaten up by some kids his age and left lying on the ground, bleeding and with a split lip.

Reading that, I thought he had never had a chance. Something had been broken inside him at a very young age.

This is a dangerous notion because no one apart from ourselves has responsibility for what we do, we are humans, not creatures subject to forces that drive us here and there without offering any resistance. Unless of course being under the sway of others is part of the human condition, and being a good person is the same as being a lucky person.

My father died in a chair in his mother's house. The house was full of bottles, there was excrement on the sofa, his nose was broken and his face covered with blood. He was in the chair, dead, had been for more than a day, and during that time his mother was in the house. No one knows what she was doing. No one knows how Dad broke his nose or his face got covered with blood. But I do know for certain now that was what happened and what it looked like. If there should be a lawsuit on the basis of *My Struggle*, as my uncle Gunnar has suggested many times there will be, I have a document as proof. When I received it I was furious. I don't think I have ever been so furious. I had written about how Dad died, and then Gunnar said I was lying. What did that make me, lying about my father's death? How could he say I was lying about the circumstances surrounding Dad's death to journalists, to the publisher, and to everyone in my family, when I wasn't?

I called Kristiansand and asked them to send me a printout of Dad's medical records. Which they did. From the records it was clear that he had lived with his mother for a year and five months before he died. It wasn't quite two years, but it was a long, long way from the two months Gunnar had claimed Dad stayed there. How could he say Dad stayed there for only two months and that I was lying? And how could the *Bergens Tidende* journalist say that?

I had described what I had seen. After Gunnar's e-mail I had begun to doubt what I had seen. Now I was sure I had seen what I had seen. And that before we arrived Dad had been dead in the chair and Grandma had walked around him, he was dead, he was covered in blood, the place was full of bottles, and it had been like that for a considerable time. Then the ambulance came.

Who called it?

I called Kristiansand again and asked if such conversations were logged. They were, but the person I was speaking to didn't know how long they were kept, he would check it out, he said, and then contact me, but I never heard from him and assumed there was nothing.

Where did the blood come from? Had he fallen and then struggled up, sat down in the chair and died? That might have killed him, the bleeding from the nose, because he had an enlarged heart, which was the only detail I remembered from the autopsy. The undertaker had said the death was alcohol-related.

How could anyone say everything had been in order?

I was furious. Also because I knew I would never find out how he died. Grandma had given a variety of answers. In one she was sitting beside him and discovered that he was dead, we asked her if it was light or dark outside, she couldn't remember. In another she had fallen asleep and woken up and seen that he was dead.

But there wasn't just blood on his face, his nose was also broken, and how had he done that? There wasn't any blood anywhere in the room, I knew that, I had cleaned there, no matter what Gunnar maintained. Could he have gone outside, got into a fight, crawled home, and then died in the chair from the effort? Or did he fall indoors and hit his nose on the floor or perhaps the fireplace? That was most likely. But the blood? Grandma wouldn't have been able to clean it up, that's for certain.

I called Yngve and we talked. He said he could barely remember anything from those days. He couldn't even remember calling the doctor, which I had said he did. Could it have been me who called? I had no memory of it, I thought he had done it, but I wasn't sure. I mentioned the blood that wasn't there. Wasn't there any blood on the carpet? he said. Was there some? I said. No, I would have remembered that. No, there wasn't. I'm sure. Because the first time I realized there was some blood was when the undertaker warned us before we saw the body. Didn't he say something? Yngve asked. Didn't he just say his nose was broken? No, no, I'll never forget, it came as a shock, he warned us, there had been a lot of blood.

Yngve said he'd found another document among Dad's possessions, he had mentioned it earlier, but I'd forgotten. He went to get it from the cellar and called back. It was after a visit to the doctor. Dad had an incredibly high blood-alcohol concentration, and the doctor who had written this doubted everything Dad said, even that he was a *gymnas* teacher. There wasn't very much of the teacher about him. But he kept lying, it was typical of him to say he was about to start a job as an educational consultant.

What kind of death had he suffered?

When we were in Kristiansand and encountered the dreadful sight I immediately accepted it, that was how it was, but reading this document now, there was no longer anything to accept, I saw it from a distance, him, Dad, dead in the chair, broken nose, bloody face, surrounded by bottles, Grandma walking around. But he is her son. Her eldest son. Her beloved eldest son. Now he is dead, and he's been dead for a while, and she was with him, her dead son, she was walking around him. Is she making coffee? She had done that thousands of times. I knew exactly how she did it, I can visualize all her movements, and she, Grandma, who filled my chest with happiness whenever she paid us an unexpected visit and I smelled her perfume down in the hall, is pouring coffee into a cup and lighting a cigarette. Menthol, that was what she smoked, definitely.

Gunnar didn't want this story to be told. I can understand that. But I can't understand him saying I lied. Saying I had made it all up to avenge my mother, whom my father had left fifteen years earlier. I was so happy when they got divorced. I was so happy to get rid of him. I hated him, and I feared him, and I loved him.

That was how it was.

Now I had written a novel about him. It wasn't a good novel, but then he hadn't lived a good life either. It was his life, it ended in a chair in a house in Kristiansand because he had reached a point where he had given up all hope. There wasn't any hope. Everything was destroyed. So he died.

We could have traveled down to Kristiansand, forced him to go into a clinic, if it was possible, or somehow have got him out of the house. We didn't. I don't regret that. That was how he wanted it, and he was our father. I am his son. The story about him, Kai Åge Knausgaard, is the story about me, Karl Ove Knausgaard. I have told it. I have exaggerated, I have embellished, I have omitted, and there is a lot I haven't understood. But it isn't him I have described; it is my image of him. It's finished now.

◆ ◆ ◆

In the days before May 17, Constitution Day, the school was closed for several days, and to give myself some writing time, as I had a deadline hanging over me, I went with Heidi and John to Voss while Linda took Vanja to Oslo to visit Axel and Linn. The idea was that Yngve and his children would look after mine and I would be able to work. After that I would go on a short trip to Iceland and be interviewed at Nordens Hus, and then I would go to our cabin and finish the novel there. Mom and Ingrid would help at home while I was away and then it would all be over.

It didn't happen like that.

We had been at Yngve's for only a few hours when Linda rang. I was in the living room with John and Heidi running around me, chased by Ylva, when my phone began vibrating in my jacket pocket.

"Hi, it's me," she said.

"Hi," I said. "Have you arrived?"

"Yes, but guess what. I have some good news."

"What?"

"My book's been accepted."

"Really?"

"Yes! The phone rang just before we left. It was Modernista. The editor there. He said it was fantastic. He hadn't even finished reading before he called."

"How wonderful!" I said, gazing at the scenery outside the window, which at first fell away steeply to the water below, then rose up the mountain to the peaks on the opposite side. "Congratulations! That's exactly what you needed. Now you can really relax. About work, I mean. Now you're a writer again."

"Yes. I'm so happy."

"And when will it come out?"

"Next year. It takes a bit longer in Sweden. But I'll believe it when I see it. Do you remember when Bonniers withdrew their acceptance of my previous book?"

"That won't happen again. Relax. It's fantastic news, Linda." John stood below me and looked up. I lowered the phone.

"I'm talking to Mommy," I said. "Would you like to say hi too?"

He nodded, I passed him the phone, he put it to his ear. I could hear her excited voice, saw him nodding to everything she said. Then he passed me back the phone.

"We'll have to celebrate when we're back home," I said.

"Yes," she said. "We must."

"Great. I kept telling you how good your writing was."

"You did, but we're married."

"So it doesn't count?"

"Yes, of course it does. But you should've heard how enthusiastic he was."

The first of Linda's short stories I read was called "Universe," I had told her to send it to *Vagant*. This was several years before we got together. It had language and a suggestive power that went straight to your heart, something that was both naked and robust, helpless and supreme, beneath a bitterly cold winter sky. It was about the best thing I had read for many years, and when I noticed how happy she was when I said that I realized she had no idea how gifted she was. During the weeks when we became a couple she wrote a little essay about the Swedish poet Erik Axel Karlfeldt, and I thought this was the world she moved in. But it wasn't, the essay was an exception, she had barely come into contact with literary theory and she was ashamed of that. But that was precisely what was so good, her writing was her, and what she found inside herself possessed a different form of complexity from that which emerged when a writer was striving for it, as happens when you want the text to be something particular. Her problem was that she wrote very little and lacked confidence. Her writing came in bursts, a few hours of light, then it was gone.

An event from another world: we live in Regeringsgatan in Stockholm, we have one child, she is only a few months old and is asleep between us in bed. I read aloud to Linda from a book Yngve and I were given by my mother's parents when we were small, Asbjørnsen and Moe's collected fairy tales. I read "Valemon, the Polar Bear King." I love fairy tales, the darkness in the best of them, and Linda loves them too. Afterward we talk about it. Linda is particularly taken by the metal claws the girl is given to climb the rock face. A few days later she starts writing. She invests the whole of her being into this girl who wants and gets the bear. What she writes about belongs to what we cannot discuss, it's impossible, but it's still there, somewhere between us. It makes me think about what is actual, what is real, how dependent we are on language and form for it to exist. That which does not have language or form does not exist, even if it is there. And that was the problem for Linda and me, that what was there between us but didn't exist, grew weaker and weaker, more and more indistinct and nebulous, as the inexpressible dimension between us weakened.

So much in life is unspoken.

Linda called again that evening. She was still happy, it was as though the happiness was a wave washing through her. Everything was fantastic. Vanja, Axel and Linn, Oslo, May 17, Independence Day. I had a warning on the tip of my tongue, I wanted to tell her to take it easy, but I didn't have the heart, of course she should be allowed to be happy.

In Voss I didn't get much work done, Heidi and John wouldn't let me sit in the loft writing, at least not for long periods at a time. I had a whole day to myself when Yngve and his girlfriend, Tone, took all the kids to her mountain cabin, but that was it. In the house below Yngve's lived Espen, it was strange, this was how we had lived so many years ago in Bergen, him below and me above, and when I saw him in the garden I shouted to him and he came up for a cup of coffee and a long chat. He'd spent the last years writing a tome about dissection. We shared a fascination with the baroque and the physical, but our attitudes to it diverged: Espen was more rational; I was more irrational. He was a poet; I was a prose writer. Perhaps what was open in him was closed in me, and vice versa. Nevertheless we had been friends for twenty years, that was what mattered most. In the evening he came over with a bottle of red wine, we sat with Yngve and drank and listened to music from the eighties. The next morning I felt so sick I couldn't get out of bed. I threw up out of the children's sight, told them I had the flu, was unable to get up until late afternoon, when I took them to a shopping mall and bought some May 17 clothes. They didn't know what Constitution Day was but were happy anyway, they had a sense that it was an important day. At home Heidi got a splinter the size of a forefinger in her foot. She screamed so loudly it must have been heard all over Voss. She was afraid of everything that stirred in nature and everything to do with blood and pain, though felt perfectly at home in the social world. There was no question of my removing the splinter, she howled at the mere mention of it. But Ylva, whom she looked up to, was finally allowed to take it out, by the following day there was already a story Heidi could tell, on par with the time she was pushed through the airport in a wheelchair.

On May 17 we stood in the rain in Vossevangen watching the procession, Heidi and John with a Norwegian flag in one hand and an ice-cream cone in the other. I had written only a couple of pages, about Hermann Broch, of what looked like was going to become an essay. Tonje, who lived in Bergen, turned up one day with a tape recorder, she was going to make a documentary about being a character in my books, she asked if I would mind answering a few questions and I couldn't refuse. She had replied to my e-mail about Book 5 a few weeks earlier and said she didn't want anything deleted. I answered all her questions and read out some passages from the novels. She left, we stayed there a few more days, and then we flew to Malmö. A couple of hours after we arrived home the handle on the door started moving up and down and I realized that it was Vanja trying to open it.

"Here they are!" I called out. Heidi and John sprang to their feet in the living room and ran into the hall as the door opened and Vanja and Linda appeared. Vanja was full of her experiences she wanted to tell us about, but also how much she had missed her brother and sister, they had never been apart for so long.

"Hi," I said to Linda. "How was the journey?"

"It was fine," she said. "But I'm a bit tired."

"Have a rest, then," I said.

She nodded.

"But first we need to eat something. Do we have anything here?"

I shook my head.

"Shall we get Chinese takeaway?"

"Yes."

I took the elevator down, bought five boxes, brought them back up, placed the contents on five plates, called the children, who didn't come, so Linda and I sat eating at the table alone.

She was on her way down. The joy had gone, her energy had gone, she ate facing me, quiet. But, I reasoned, she might be tired after the traveling and the week away.

"I did hardly any writing up there," I said. "So I'll really have to go for it over the next few weeks. That's all right, isn't it?"

She nodded.

"At least when Mom and Sissel come," she said. "But that's after you go to Iceland, isn't it?"

"Yes," I said, looking at her.

"Do you have to go? Couldn't you cancel it?"

"Are you crazy? I can't do that. And it's only one day. One day, Linda."

"Okay," she said.

"If I can just get down to writing now, over the next few weeks, I'll be done for good. Then I'll have all the time in the world. I just need to stick at it. Then it's over."

"Yes," she said.

Before leaving for Iceland I had to sort out the details around the cabin, so I rented a car and drove there one morning at the end of May. Initially I sat down on the doorstep, smoked a cigarette, and studied the mess. The first job I had to do was to remove the pile of planks, drywall, pipes, and all the other scrap from the old bathroom. The car I'd rented was a Mercedes, it was brand-new, and I covered the bottom of the large boot with garbage bags before loading up with trash and driving to the dump several kilometers away. It took six trips to clear the pile.

I took another smoke break on the step.

The lawn which only two years before had been flawless was now riddled with weeds. There was no longer any separation between bed and lawn. Moss grew beneath the tall hedges, and elsewhere, the soil was like an open wound. The white wall of the cabin had a dark coating, several of the wooden boards were rotten at the bottom. The paint had peeled off the window frames. One pane was cracked. The pile of building materials and junk was gone, but the soil and sand the workmen had dug up when they were laying new pipes formed enormous bumps in the grass. By the hedge there were still two buckets of shit from the out-house days, and it had definitely ripened in the last year. I had to empty them today. And the boxes of apples in the cellar, which I'd optimistically stored two years before, had to be disposed of.

The grass had to be cut.

The hole had to be filled.

The heap of rotting garden waste had to be removed.

That would make a difference at least.

I flicked my cigarette into the hole and opened the door to the small shed where the lawn mower was kept. Took the coiled cord, put one end in the socket, the other in the mower, lifted it out, and started it.

It was Linda who had been behind the purchase of the cabin. During one of her sleepless energy-charged nights she had come across the advertisement online. The cabin had been built at the beginning of the twentieth century, it was really beautiful, a bit Swiss in style, while the garden was large and trim, with two old apple trees, rosebushes, a myriad of flower beds and massive, two-meter-high hedges around three sides. Linda had been saying for a while that we should have one; a couple at the nursery school had one, they went there every weekend of the spring and autumn, grew their own vegetables and berries, and spent large parts of the summer there. With three children and an apartment in the center of town, we had to take them for a walk in the park as if they were dogs, we absolutely should have a cabin in the country.

I should have loved her for that because she was dreaming

about our family when she was talking about it. About a happy life, hanging up the washing as the children played around her on a summer afternoon. About a woman's hands covered with soil, about children who had their own little vegetable patches, who had their own paddling pool, and about her husband who cut the grass with a push lawn mower in the evening. Somewhere in the open, our own plot, our own little house, that was what she dreamed about. I should have loved her for it, but I didn't, I was just annoyed.

She showed it to me in the morning. Sitting on the chair in front of the computer clicking on the photos. I leaned over her.

"Isn't it great?" she said. "So beautiful. Almost like a doll's house. But there are two floors. There are bedrooms upstairs. The inside has recently been done up."

She turned to me.

"What do you think?"

"Well, it looks nice," I said. "But we don't have any money. Have you considered that?"

"I can get some. I will get some."

"How are you going to do that?"

"I just will. I want that place."

"It's a lot of work though. *I* don't have any time. Out of the question."

"I do. I can look after it. You won't need to do anything."

"And if we could get hold of that much money," I said, "we should buy a car. We certainly need one."

"We don't need a car in town. And definitely not if we have a cabin."

"I can't talk you out of it, I can see. And it is nice. But, as I said, we have no money."

"Can't we go out and take a look at it at least?"

"Fine by me."

There followed a few days of hectic activity on Linda's part. She made an appointment at the bank, but that led nowhere since neither Linda nor I were credit worthy, that is, once we hadn't paid some bill or other and had ended up on a list that made it impossible for us to get a loan or a cell phone contract or to rent a car, except for with Europcar, who didn't check the list and whom I therefore used whenever we needed one.

It was humiliating to sit there in the bank, feeling as if I were a criminal with a record, while the lady wearing a pantsuit, blouse, and gold jewelery had no intention of giving us a loan. Linda called her father, who not so long ago had sold his place and was happy to contribute with a hundred thousand kronor as he had never given her anything before. I called my mother, she could take out another mortgage on her house, she said, checked, and called back the next day: she could lend us a hundred and twenty thousand.

So we were a hundred thousand short.

A hundred thousand!

Where were we going to get that from?

I received a monthly stipend of fifteen thousand. On top of which I read manuscripts for a publishing house, who paid ten thousand a month. That made twenty-five thousand, which was seventeen thousand after tax. Although that was a lot of money, it stretched just far enough to cover the rent for the apartment – ten thousand – and there were five of us in the family. If there was a crisis I could call the publishing house. I had no idea how much I owed them, I only knew that it was a lot because at various times I'd received a fixed monthly advance. But I didn't dare ask about my debt. It had been three years since my previous novel came out, and I was still nowhere near a new one. I closed my eyes to anything related to money and the future. By and large this approach worked, that was the main thing.

But a hundred thousand!

"Asking won't hurt anyway," Linda said. "The worst that can happen is they say no."

"Okay," I said, and e-mailed Geir Gulliksen.

We want to buy a cabin, I wrote, the idea being that I'll be able to work there, however we are a hundred thousand Swedish kronor short. I know I have had a large advance already, and I won't be upset if you say no. But please consider it.

Geir sent the inquiry to his boss, Geir Berdahl, who called me the following day to ask what kind of place this was. I explained. He said I could borrow ninety thousand Norwegian kroner. Would that be all right? Oh yes, thank you very much, I said. That's too much. Thank you again.

After I hung up, I was racked with guilt. The publishers were putting themselves out so much for me, they always had, and I was exploiting the situation, bringing family matters into the financial arrangements, allowing them to go out on a limb to help me buy a country cabin, which I didn't even want.

Now I would have to work there. That was for sure. I would have to write a lot there.

Linda was happy. We went to see the cabin, a woman in her midfifties met us, she had decorated inside the cabin with great taste, everywhere there were tiny maritime features, wooden sculptures of gulls and lighthouses, mobiles of seabirds, little ornamental cases of shells, balls of green yarn, and fishing nets. The furniture was simple and old, a nice couch with a lovely dresser, both painted blue and white, and two white wicker chairs, plus a dining table with chairs. It felt as if we were in a cabin on one of the skerries and not in the middle of an enormous subdivided community outside the third-biggest town in Sweden.

The girls loved it. After a few minutes hidden behind Linda's legs they thawed and ran around the garden. The owner said she had put so much work into the cabin and the garden, and she liked it so much she didn't really want to sell it. No, selling it was the last thing she wanted to do. But she was moving to another town and couldn't keep it any longer. She said she was pleased we had children, knowing that there would be children playing in her garden was a comfort.

She wanted 290,000 kronor for it. When we got home, we called her and offered 320,000. There were other people interested and I thought it was best to frighten them off right away to avoid a bidding war. She called back the same evening and accepted the offer.

And that was how we became cabin owners.

Linda pictured herself in a straw hat walking around the garden tweaking the flowers, I suspected, perhaps lying in a hammock in the shade and reading, the children around her, barefoot and happy, and on autumn evenings pulling up the carrots, almost colorless in the falling dusk, a pot of vegetable soup on the stove in the little kitchen. The children's excited voices and red cheeks before they fell asleep on the little mezzanine floor while she and I sat in the little living room with a glass of red wine. It wasn't like that, reality was bearing down on us like a juggernaut, all our dreams were crushed, we were arguing, the children were defiant, the garden was dug up to lay pipes and no one filled in the holes, so there were piles of soil and sand everywhere, and where there weren't any it was overgrown. The woman who'd sold it to us came back a few years later to say hello, and when she saw the state the garden was in her eyes had welled up, we were told. The neighbors scowled at us, the amount of work that had to be done increased to such an extent that we began to keep our distance because I'd been against the purchase from the beginning and made it a condition that I'd have nothing to do with it, Linda had to take care of it. She couldn't, it was beyond her now, and so there we were, with our shame and guilty consciences, her with a dream in tatters as well. Even the dream of barefoot children and a carefree life in the open air requires work.

On this afternoon in May 2010, as I pushed the mower down one side of the lawn, if indeed what I was cutting merited such an exalted term, we'd had the place for two and a half years, and nothing had gone as planned. It turned out to be difficult to have three such small children there. The staircase to the second floor was so steep that we constantly had to keep watch to make sure they didn't crawl up, and if we closed the door to be outside, one of us had to occupy John while the other kept an eye on the girls, so there was no question of relaxing, which despite everything we were able to do at home, where they had their rooms and toys and knew how to occupy themselves. Then I was always overcome by an immense feeling of claustrophobia there; I didn't like having people around me on all sides. In town I had no problem with other people, they had nothing to do with me, I had nothing to do with them. In town we were strangers to one another, here we were neighbors, we were supposed to greet one another and exchange a few words when we met, and it was impossible to do anything without being seen. To be seen as a random stranger was quite different from being seen as a particular individual, a stern forty-year-old father, and I couldn't bear that look, it made my brain boil, made it impossible for me to relax, I saw myself all the time, and if the children shouted, or cried and started fighting, it wasn't the shouts, the tears, or the fights I reacted to but being seen by others. I had internalized these other people, and I hated it. Oh, how I hated it. My head churned, I saw myself and I saw myself seeing my children, and nothing was as it was, everything was tied in knots, I was the most unfree person in the world. And I had voluntarily locked myself in here! On the other hand, it was a dream, Linda's dream, I owed it to her to live it out.

Up at six one spring morning, it is damn cold outside, the grass is wet, and there is nothing to do inside the doll's house, except wait for the hours to drag by until ten, then we can go to the shops and afterward maybe make some lunch.

If only the sea had been nearby! Or a forest. Some open expanse.

During the summer we were informed that sewage pipes were going to be laid for all the cabins. It would cost twenty thousand kronor. In the fall the whole garden was dug up and a pipe laid to the outside toilet, a small room with its own door. We had to get ahold of a plumber who could build a new toilet there and, somehow, find the money for this and the excavations. It definitely wouldn't come in at under forty thousand. Linda borrowed the money from the bank, her mother was our guarantor. The fence was taken down and the front garden dug up, in addition the lack of maintenance had already begun to have consequences. It wasn't my responsibility, I had been absolutely unambiguous in that respect: if we buy a cabin it is your responsibility, you are the one who will have to take care of it, I haven't got the time, I'd said, and because I'd said it, I wasn't going to go back on my word – except to cut the grass. As the neglect slowly spread I gloated, this was her responsibility and hers alone. I had washed my hands of the matter. No one could say I hadn't warned her! Or that I hadn't predicted it would turn out like this.

Linda's mother, who at this time was staying with us for long stretches, managed to turn up a gardener from the Balkans, who leveled the lawn and sowed new grass, and a plumber from North Africa, who was able to do the pipe job for a song, relatively speaking. How she found them I have no idea, but she was the kind who chatted to everyone, such as our neighbors, in a few days she knew them better than I did and I'd been there for more than two years. So by the spring the garden looked nice again, and we had a bathroom with a shower. I didn't care that when I turned on the hot-water boiler the shower wouldn't stop or that the pipes weren't discreetly tucked away alongside the wall, but stood out in all their chrome-metal glory and in places resembled the cryptic instruments in a Cronenberg film. We just had to accept it, we couldn't look after the place, we couldn't live out that dream, it wasn't for us. When would I ever sow carrots with the children? When would I ever weed the beds? The claustrophobia began to throb in me the moment we got into the bus to go there. We went there less and less, and in May 2010, when I was cutting the grass with the red cord wrapped around my shoulder, under a dry, gray sky, we hadn't been there since the previous autumn, and even then only sporadically, a few hours one sunny day perhaps, because it was a vicious circle: the more neglected it became, the less time we wanted to spend there, and the less time we were there the more neglected it became.

I felt an ache in my heart. We had failed.

As a family we had failed.

Or had we? Why not view the matter with a practical eye? We made a misjudgment, we bought a place we didn't have the time to keep in order, and when we realized that we put it up for sale. Why should that cause my heart to ache?

The heart cannot reason. The brain does that. And if there was one thing I had learned in life, it was that the heart is everything, the brain nothing.

That was why everything in life was always so horribly painful.

I stopped the mower and walked over to move the bench, the table, and the chairs, which were half under an apple tree. They appeared to be made of wood, but it was some synthetic material and completely weatherproof. Having done that, I restarted the mower, pushed it slowly across the uneven, undulating soft ground, which was so suffocated by moss that the blades mostly whirred over thin air. Only by the hedge, beside the overgrown flagstones, did they engage again.

The problem with people is that they are too sensitive. Almost everyone I knew or met or saw was too sensitive. Something had happened to them once and they hadn't got over it. If your father had lost his temper with you when you were a child and perhaps hit you, what does it matter now? If other kids locked you in the uniform closet in the gym, what has that to do with your present life? If you were a terrible bed wetter, a wussy little shit, or your mother drank or your father took his own life, or if your parents totally ignored you, you aren't them, you are your own person and you have your own time, which is now, so why on earth do you let the past have any influence on it? Why should what your parents did weigh so heavily on your life? Why didn't we leave it at that?

What good would all these feelings and musings do?

I saw it in my own children, how small things could grow to enormous proportions in them. At first they were like animals in the sense that their feelings were closely connected with the moment, from which tears or laughter or fear or well-being resulted, and the very next it was forgotten. Then they became human, that was when things lasted and expanded. Recently, for example, Vanja had started worrying that she couldn't say her *r*'s. When she was smaller it didn't matter, she said *j* instead, so when she had to say "*trädet*" for instance, she said "*tjädet*" or "*tjolleji*" instead of "*trolleri*," and even if it brought an occasional stab to the heart, because I hadn't been able to say my *r*'s when I was small, and I remembered the hell it had been, mostly I didn't think about it, it was part of Vanja, and everyone understood what she meant to say. Then she became aware of it. Dad, I can't say *j*, she said to me, looking up on our way to the school. Why can't I say *j*, Dad? Everyone else can. I answered that everyone had different *r*'s. Katinka, who spoke the Skåne dialect, had one; Mommy had a Stockholm accent and had another. And you have yours.

She was reassured by that, but not for long, now the seed was sown, now it was growing. There was such a thing as correct and such a thing as incorrect, something that was as it was meant to be and something that wasn't. One afternoon when she had been singing a song with all the letters in the alphabet, she paused just before the *r*, snorted with annoyance and started throwing things around. She went on and on about how she couldn't pronounce *r*. I could see it was terrible for her, but there was nothing I could do except say hers was good enough. But then Heidi happened to have the world's best rolled *r*, her tongue flapped against her palate and she pronounced all the words with an articulate felicity. Why can Heidi say it and I can't? Vanja said. She avoided words that started with an *r*. I remembered I had muttered about moving to England when I was older because they had an *r* I could pronounce. Not being able to say *r* had been a huge thing for me, it was as though it labeled me as a person. Now I was seeing it from the outside, and I wished I could communicate to Vanja that I loved her whatever she could or couldn't do, did or didn't do, but of course that was an impossible task, she had to resolve this herself. She had been wearing glasses for some years and had accepted it, now she was asking why so few children wore glasses and if she lost her temper they were always the first thing to go. Bang. Onto the floor with them. In school she was suddenly taken ill, she had a sudden need to sleep, the staff called and said she was sick, we knew better, something must have happened, we picked her up anyway, and at home, lying on the sofa with a blanket over her, watching a cartoon on TV, she let it slip, her best friend hadn't wanted to play with her that morning. Then she got it into her head that she shouldn't eat sugar, and refused sweets although she really wanted them. All the freedom there was in the first four to five years of life, which I had done my best to restrict, had stopped, now there was a new consciousness, and the complexity of relationships grew. I knew that none of this was important in itself, it was all arbitrary, but she didn't, for her this was everything. She was entering a system and didn't know she was.

She was six now. In three months she would be starting at real school. For the first time in my life with her I could remember what it had been like when I was her age. No longer vague or based on single memories, but clear and distinct, all the intensity of the world, which I had drawn down into my lungs with every breath as I ran around Tybakken, where everything, the smallest object and tiniest incident had a meaning all its own and rushed toward me as if seen through a magnifying glass, and where great emotion was invested in all the people I had around me. It felt as if everything was about life and death, life was stretched to the bursting point, and when I fell in love with a girl in my class, it filled me in a way I can no longer understand, least of all when I look at Vanja. Does she feel the world so intensely? I look at her and see a little girl going about her business within the framework we have set, we live here, in a city-center apartment, we send her to a parents' co-op nursery school every day. She draws and plays with the countless little animal and human figures she has; sometimes alone, sometimes with Heidi and John. She climbs trees in the park, she casts longing gazes after any dogs that cross her path. She reads her dog book, she has one of her school friends over or she goes over to their house. She swims at the Badeland complex, she has baths at home, she pushes the cart for me when we go shopping. I react to what she says and does, this is "Vanja," my daughter, whom I have seen almost every day of her life. I know everything looks different to her, inside her other laws apply, her laws, she is a person who sees the world and is filled by strong feelings for it, but hardly ever thinks about it, what it actually means. I am so numbed by all the routines we follow, by the system of coordinates that has been placed on my life, that I unconsciously assume everyone around me feels the same, not least the three small people with whom I share my apartment. Even their almost volcanic emotional outbursts I see in my terms, as irritating disturbances, desperate aberrations, obstacles in the way rather than as signs of distinct life inside them.

In this kind of life, as in everything else, there is probably a sense and a purpose: a life where you constantly relate to and empathize with those of others must be unbearable, and perhaps it is also harmful in the case of children, who need distance from the adult world in order to be able to see it and develop in relation to it. Be that as it may, this doesn't stop me thinking that I empathize too little with the lives of other people. Most conspicuously and persistently with regard to Linda. One of the many things she criticizes me for is that I don't see her. This is not quite true, I do see her, the problem is that I see her more or less in the way you see a room you know well; everything is there, the lamp and the carpet and the bookcase, the sofa and the window and the floor, but somehow transparently, no mark is left on your mind.

Why do I organize my life like this? What do I want with this neutrality? Obviously it is to eliminate as much resistance as possible, to make the days slip past as easily and unobtrusively as possible. But why? Isn't that synonymous with wanting to live as little as possible? With telling life to leave me in peace so that I can . . . yes, well, what? Read? Oh, but come on, what do I read about, if not life? Write? Same thing. I read and write about life. The only thing I don't want life for is to live it.

I put the lawn mower in the shed, which was empty as I'd had to clean it out when the bathroom was being built and I'd never put everything back. I walked over to the hedge and looked at the two buckets of shit. One had a lid, the other didn't, it was covered with a plastic bag. I had considered driving them to the dump, but first of all I was afraid the bucket without the lid might topple over or the contents would spill, because it was filled to the brim, and I suspected that even if the rental company were to allow the transport of bits of wood, drywall, and dust in the Mercedes, they might well feel differently about liquid excrement. And secondly the dump was packed with people from all over the district with their trailers, it was also full of people working there, and what section would shit come under? Garden waste? I could imagine myself carrying the buckets and one of the employees coming up to me and asking me what I was throwing away, because that is what they did, it was important that everything was disposed of in the right place. It wouldn't work. I would have to get rid of it here. The obvious option was to bury it. There was already a big hole where the pipe came in, under the bathroom. If I dug it deeper, I would be able to throw the garden waste in there as well. I had put aside some of the flagstones the plumber had taken up, they would stabilize it, I reasoned, and then I could cover the whole thing with earth.

I started digging. When I figured the hole was deep enough, I tossed branches, bushes, and rotting leaves in. Then came the shit. I grabbed the bucket with the lid first. It was heavy, so I had to use both hands. I breathed through my mouth. The stench when I removed the lid was still so pervasive that it triggered my gag reflex. The contents of the bucket were thin and liquid and dark brown. Agh, damn it. Oh shit. I poured it out, retched again. Fucking hell. I didn't have gloves, and my hands and the bottom of my jeans were spattered with shit. I turned on the hose and rinsed the bucket, washed my hands, put the hose by the edge, still breathing through my mouth, I could feel the nausea rising in my chest. I felt as if I were in an inferno, my brain was on fire, everything was bathed in a flickering light, and the whole time I was frightened someone would come and see what I was doing. But the worst was still to come because I would have to hold the bucket without a lid or handle close to my chest. Which I did, splashing even more shit over myself, but then it was done. The buckets were empty and rinsed, the hole glistened. I went to get more of the garden refuse and threw it on top. I shoveled some earth over, but I'd put in too many branches, they were springy and the earth wasn't heavy enough to keep them down. The stench was unbearable. My head was reeling. I put the flagstones on top, the branches sank under the weight and I covered it all with more earth. The branches were gone and the area was level, none of what lay beneath was visible. But the smell hovered above the ground and was apparent from meters away, and if you stepped onto the filled hole it moved beneath your feet.

I had to hope the stench would dissipate of its own accord and none of the potential buyers coming to the viewing the following day would stand just there.

I left the Mercedes in the multistory parking garage, put the keys through the door flap of the rental company, and walked home through the side streets. With my trousers stained with shit and my clothes filthy from soil and plaster, I wasn't going to risk walking along the pedestrian street, where I occasionally bumped into the few people I knew in Malmö. Sometimes I'd also been stopped by strangers, who wanted to say something about my books and the reflections they'd had. Back home, I went straight into the bathroom, tore off my clothes, put them in the washing machine and switched it on, then ran a bath and got in. Slowly the buzz of hysteria that had circled through my head for the past few hours ebbed away. For perhaps half an hour I lay in the bathtub staring up at the ceiling without thinking of anything specific, as the steam stuck like adhesive tape to the window and mirror, and in my imaginary world the bathroom turned into a tank, a room detached from everything else.

With reddened skin, fingertips crinkled like raisins, I got up, rubbed myself down, wrapped a towel around my waist, and padded into the bedroom, where I rummaged through the heap of clothes until I found a shirt, a pair of jeans, and a pair of matching socks and could finally join the others in the living room, the children on the sofa in front of the TV, Linda lying on the bed by the wall.

"How was it?" she said.

"Fine," I said. "It was a nightmare emptying the buckets of shit. Anyway, at least it's done now."

"Which buckets of shit?"

"At the cabin," I said. "Don't you remember what it was like before we got the toilet?"

"Did you empty them? Where did you do that?"

"Where they're supposed to be emptied," I said. "Have you eaten?"

"Yes," Linda said. "There's some for you in the kitchen."

After eating I began to pack for the trip. It was only one night away, so I didn't need much. But I took my laptop in case there was any time to write on the plane, and the first volume of Hitler's *Mein Kampf,* which I absolutely had to read before I went to the cabin to finish the novel. At least I had to skim through it so that I knew what it was about.

"Will you put the kids to bed?" Linda said when I'd finished and sat down on the sofa. "I've been with them all day."

"Will you sort out the cabin while I put them to bed? Or what were you thinking?"

She didn't answer, just looked at me for a few seconds. Then she turned to face the wall.

"Of course I will," I said.

"Can we have a bath, Dad?" Vanja said.

"Can you manage it by yourselves?"

"Yes."

"Then you can."

They jumped up and raced off to the bathroom.

"Do you have to go?" Linda said. "I don't know if I can manage with them on my own."

"Of course you can," I said. "It'll be absolutely fine."

"Can't you cancel it?"

I shook my head. I had canceled one trip to Luleå already, this was the second attempt, and to cancel it would have been inconceivable, it would have taken a natural disaster. I had also canceled an appearance at the Literature Festival in Lillehammer, the children were going camping with their classmates and Linda couldn't take them on her own by train and bus, so I had e-mailed the organizers and canceled, the children had been so looking forward to going, it was the high point of this half of the year. But I'd become so well known in the meantime that the cancellation was not received without a murmur as before, no, Mom called to say it was in all the papers and had been an item on the TV news.

"A deal's a deal," I said. "And it's only one day. I'm back the day after tomorrow. This is my job after all. You have to respect that."

In Iceland I hardly dared phone home, I was sure she would moan and say how difficult everything was and how badly things were going. And she did, that is she didn't complain, what she said was that this was no good. This is no good, Karl Ove, she said. This is no good. It has to be, I said. Stick it out.

I returned home late in the afternoon the next day. The children came running over as soon as they heard the door open. I gave them the presents I'd bought at the airport, three cuddly toys. Linda stood at the end of the hall, looking at me. She seemed scared.

I unpacked and put the suitcase on the top shelf of the hall closet. Vanja came over with a ribbon in one hand and scissors in the other.

"Can you make me a necklace?" she said.

"For me, too," Heidi said, close behind.

I cut off two long strips, tied one around the neck of Vanja's dog, the other around Heidi's neck.

"With a loop!" Vanja said.

I made a loop at the end for her hand, and did the same for Heidi. Then I went onto the balcony. The children seemed fine at any rate, I thought, things can't have gone that badly. Experience of an event wasn't the same as the event.

Linda opened the door.

"Can't you stay inside?" she said. "I've been on my own with them for so long."

"Coming," I said. "Just finishing a cigarette."

"Will you put them to bed?"

"Of course."

The trip had filled me with energy, so it was no effort brushing their teeth, finding their pajamas, a glass of water, reading a book, and resolving all the little squabbles. Besides, I was looking forward to the following day, when I would be at the cabin writing. It was mostly the thought of being completely alone and working that was appealing; when I did actually sit down and try to start, the resistance I felt was nearly insurmountable.

When at last they were in their beds and had reconciled themselves to the day being over, I went to Linda, who was on the balcony smoking in the darkness, wrapped up in the green parka I had once given her for her birthday.

She said nothing when I sat down. She gazed across the rooftops, one arm tucked into her body as though embracing herself or trying to hold herself in position, the other pointing straight ahead with a cigarette between her fingers curling smoke.

"How are you?" I said.

"Are you still going to the cabin tomorrow?" she asked.

I nodded.

"This is no good," she said. "Don't you understand? I can't manage."

"Listen," I said. "I have three weeks to finish the novel. That's very little time. I can't, by which I mean, I *cannot*, waste two more days."

"But I'm scared, Karl Ove," she said, looking at me. "I can't be with them on my own. I don't know what might happen. I can't do this. It's dangerous."

"It's just something inside you," I said. "Everything's fine. Everything's as it was before. The darkness is inside you. But we can't run our lives according to that. And I have to write."

"Don't go," she said. "Please. Don't go."

I didn't say anything. I could feel myself getting angry.

After a while, when I looked at her again, I saw tears running down her cheeks.

"Why are you crying?" I said.

"I'm so frightened," she said.

"There's nothing to be frightened of," I said.

"Sometimes when I've been on a high I've been completely out of control. I haven't known where the children were. Vanja was at a friend's house. Heidi at another friend's. John was asleep in bed. They could've been anywhere for all I knew. Do you understand?"

"That was a real high, yes. But everything was okay. Nothing happened. You dealt with it magnificently."

"And all the things I buy."

She sobbed.

"Come on, Linda," I said. "Pull yourself together now. We're adults. We can't stop working because we're sad. I'm going tomorrow, you're here with the children over the weekend, and then Ingrid and Sissel are here next week. You can let them take over. Two days. You can manage that. I have to finish. You'll manage fine with the children. I know you will."

"Not now though," Linda cried. "Not now."

"Yes, you will," I said. "You're strong, it'll be fine. I can deal with everything, so you can too. It's just that you've got it into your head that you can't. You give up. And that's no good."

She looked at me, despair in her eyes.

"You have to," I said. "Because I'm going anyway. And both your mother and mine are coming to help."

"Not tomorrow," she said. "I'll be on my own with them."

"That's true," I said. "And you'll manage fine. You just have to want to. And when I've finished we'll go to Corsica. It'll be great. But first of all I need to finish the novel."

I stubbed out my cigarette and went in. She stayed outside. I pulled out the big suitcase, packed my laptop, the keyboard, the headset, a pile of CDs, a handful of books, and some clothes. While I was doing that I heard the balcony door open and close. Linda stood in front of me.

"Don't leave me alone," she said.

I peered up at her and looked down again, at the zipper I was pulling on the side of the case, holding down the top with one knee.

"I have to," I said. "I have no choice."

She walked past me into the bedroom. I put the case in the hall and sat down on the sofa and zapped through the TV channels for an hour or so. When I went to bed she was still awake, lying perfectly still in bed and staring at the ceiling. I undressed and lay down beside her.

"You'll be fine," I said. "But I can't stay here. I've done it too often. And now I have the deadline hanging over me."

"Okay," she said.

"Good night."

"Good night."

"Sleep well."

"Sleep well."

I woke up once in the night, she was awake, staring at the ceiling, as she had been when I came to bed. I turned over and fell asleep again. The next time I woke it was morning. Linda was looking at me. When our gazes met her mouth opened and closed as if gasping for air. Her eyes were shiny with tears.

"You can't go," she said.

"No, I suppose I can't," I said, and sat up, put my feet into my jeans and pulled them on. "But the moment Ingrid enters the apartment I'm off. Just so that you know."

I closed the door hard behind me and went into the kitchen. Strangely enough, the children were still asleep. I got the newspapers from the front door, put the coffee machine on, and ate two slices of bread as I read the culture pages first, then the sports section. Outside it was raining, cold spring rain, it was pouring down. The children got up in the usual sequence, first John, then Heidi, last of all Vanja.

"Where's Mommy?" she said.

"She's having a rest today," I said. "She's not feeling herself."

"Me, too," Vanja said. "I want to rest today too."

"Nonsense," I said. "She needs some peace and quiet. Why don't we watch some TV? Okay?"

"Okay," she said, and joined the other two. They sat on the sofa watching TV all morning, they did that every Saturday. I closed the door to the hall, where the bedroom was, and told them not to go in. They were used to that, but if I didn't keep my ears pricked they would sneak in. Sometimes I felt like the pastor in *Fanny and Alexander*, the evil man who keeps the children away from their mother.

At ten we heard the voice of the preacher who stood in the square below every Saturday morning with a microphone in his hand. I opened the balcony door and looked out. The bare Christmas tree lay beside the door, with yellow needles scattered beneath it. All the flowers hanging in boxes under the balustrade were withered, as were those in the pots by the wall. The table and chairs, which had been left outside for three successive winters, were now gray and rotting. Some empty plastic bags, two big and two small deck chairs leaning against the wall, faded. A plant pole had blown down during a winter storm and other bits of debris had collected there.

I decided to clean it up, throw everything away and then buy some new flowers and perhaps a table and a couple of chairs. Partly because it was needed and partly because I wanted to show Linda how easy it was to occupy the children and do something constructive at the same time. The flaw was in her, not the world.

"All right, on with your boots and rain jackets!" I said.

"Why?" Heidi asked.

"Where are we going?" Vanja asked.

Only little John was up for some adventure, and he ran into the hall to wait for me to come and help him.

"We're going to buy some flowers," I said.

"Boring," said Vanja.

"Maybe," I said. "But we're going anyway."

"Is Mommy coming?" Vanja asked.

I shook my head.

"Don't want to go," Heidi said.

"I want to see Mommy," Vanja said.

"Oh, come on, poppets. I'm in charge. And I say, Get your gear on."

"No one is in charge of anyone," Vanja said.

Where did they get that from?

I took the remote and switched off the TV. Their furious little faces glared at me.

"We'll get some Saturday sweets too," I said.

"Okay," Vanja said.

"Okay," Heidi said.

A quarter of an hour later we were walking down the pedestrian street in the rain, Vanja in her blue rain gear, Heidi in her purple outfit, John sitting in the stroller like a frog in his green coveralls.

Outside the flower shop there was a metal table with two chairs, I was reminded of "*wrought* iron," a term I was acquainted with only on a literary plane, a bit like "*pock*marked," which I didn't fully understand either. They were meant to have a nineteenth-century feel about them, and were probably a bit kitschy, but I liked them anyway and bought them. I also bought six green plants. I balanced the table on the handle of John's stroller, carried one chair and some bags in each hand, and nudged the stroller forward with first one hand, then the other, while the two girls trudged beside me in their rubber boots. When they realized we were heading for the front entrance of our block, they protested.

"What about the sweets?" Vanja shouted.

"But we can't go into a shop with all this!" I said.

"You should've thought about that before," she said.

"We'll drop it off and then go out again. Okay?"

She nodded. I carried the table and the chairs onto the balcony while they waited in the hall, but when I returned they weren't there. Wet footprints led into the bedroom. I followed, they were standing around Linda as she lay looking up at them. She said something, but her voice didn't carry. She seemed barely able to talk.

Her face was expressionless.

"Now you come with me," I said. "Right now."

Vanja and Heidi did as I said, but John fell onto the bed. I grabbed his jacket by the collar, carried him into the hall dangling from my fist and put him down hard in front of the elevator. He laughed and looked up at me.

"Again, Daddy."

I smiled at him.

In the cheap furniture shop down from the florist's I found a white globe ceiling light that would fit the bill, and then we went to the mall in Triangeln, where there was a kiosk with a good selection of candy. After they had picked and mixed I bought them a chocolate bun in the café there while I ordered a coffee for me.

I had never seen Linda like that before. It was as if she were in a deep well and had to use all her strength to come to the surface, where the children were. There had been barely any life in her eyes.

Hmm.

I glanced across at Paparazzi, a little clothes shop which occasionally had nice stuff, Tiger and Boss suits, a Danish label whose name I never remembered, but I had bought some of their scarves and they had a good line of shirts.

"Could you sit here quietly for a moment?"

They nodded.

"I'm just going to that shop."

I got up and walked over. From the window I could see them, legs dangling from their chairs. I looked at the belts, chose a light brown one and flipped through a pile of black jeans, found my size, placed the belt and the jeans on the counter.

"You can try them on if you like," said the assistant, a woman in her fifties.

"I don't have time," I said. "My kids are over there."

When I nodded toward the café I saw John steaming toward me. I hurried out, caught him, and carried him into the shop in my arms.

"Stand here," I said. "I just have to pay."

I put my card in the reader, tapped in the code, she put the receipt in my bag with the trousers and the belt, and passed it to me.

"We have to do some shopping too," I told the girls when we came out.

"But I don't want to," Vanja said.

"I want to go home to Mommy," Heidi said.

"But we've got to, you know that. Come on. You can choose a movie each on the way."

There was a video and music shop at the other end of the mall. They ran over to the children's section as I flipped through some rows of CDs. I bought a Thåström collection, the first Järvinen record, and on a whim a Swedish band called the Radio Dept. and a Swede called Christian Kjellvander. The children came back with their movies, I paid, we crossed the street and went into Hemköp, I bought some pizzas for lunch, and bread, milk, and sandwich fillings for the following day. On our way home we

walked – to great protests – via Thomas Tobak, where I bought
some newspapers, the Danish *Politiken*, *Weekendavisen*, the Swedish *Expressen*, and *Aftonbladet*. Back home, they started arguing
about which movie they would watch first. I promised them they
could watch all three, and said it was fairest to start with Vanja's
since she was the eldest. They accepted that. After inserting the
DVD I went in to see Linda, who was lying on her side, her head
almost completely covered by the duvet.

"How's it going?" I said.

She turned around slowly and looked up at me. Her gaze
seemed to come from a great distance.

"Good," she whispered.

"Have you had anything to eat?"

"I . . . ," she said, and then came something I didn't catch.

"What was that?"

"I had a bite while you were out," she said.

"So you don't want anything now?"

She gently shook her head.

"The kids . . . ," she said.

"What about them?" I said. "They're fine. I bought some films.
They're watching them now. And I bought a table and chairs and
flowers for the balcony. And a ceiling lamp for the dining room."

She said nothing, just looked at me.

"I'm thinking of cleaning it up. Throwing out lots of the junk.
Is that okay? I'll tell the children not to come in here, but they
might anyway."

"That's fine," she said.

"Okay," I said. "It's pizza for lunch. You'll get up, won't you?"

She nodded slowly.

"Good," I said, closed the door, took my shoes to the balcony
door, put them on, and went out. I studied the Christmas tree
for a while, wondering whether to carry it down as it was, but I
doubted there would be any room in the trash container downstairs, and leaving it beside it wasn't an option either, that was
bound to lead to a full investigation. I went back inside, picked

up the saw and a black trash bag, cut it up into four parts, and put them in the bag, which I carried down to the cellar. Back on the balcony, I threw all the withered flowers into another trash bag, which I then carried down. When I returned, the sofa was unoccupied. I went straight to Linda's room. She was sitting up in bed, Vanja and Heidi were pulling at her, John was jumping up and down on the mattress, she looked dazed, as though she didn't know what to do, and utterly exhausted.

"What did I say?" I said.

"It's okay," Linda whispered.

"Come on now," I said. "Mommy needs some peace and quiet."

"Are you sick?" Heidi asked. "Do you have a temperature?"

"No, she isn't sick. Just a bit tired," I said. "Aren't you?"

"I can get up for a little now," she said.

"Yeees!" John said.

Linda sat on the edge of the bed fumbling around her.

"What are you looking for?"

"My sweater."

I leaned forward and flipped back the duvet.

"There it is," I said. "Come on, all of you, let's go to the living room. Mommy will be out in a minute."

They did as I said. I stopped in the doorway, looked at her. Her movements were so slow that it didn't seem as if she would be able to put on her sweater.

"You don't have to get up, you know," I said. "It'd be better if you rested."

She looked at me.

"But now you've told them you would," I said.

I went back to the balcony, stood in the gently falling rain surrounded by the sounds of the town seven floors down, picked up everything that was strewn around, dropped it in a garbage bag, and put the new plants in the old pots. When I walked in carrying the bag on my back, Linda was sitting on the sofa with John on her lap. She wasn't looking at the TV screen, I noticed, but staring straight ahead.

"I'll run down with this," I said. "Now it's looking all right out there anyway."

When I came back and sat down in the chair in the other living room to read the papers, I heard her get up, the sound of her footsteps, and the bathroom door opening. So that was where she was going.

A few minutes later it opened again.

I got up and stepped into the hall. She was standing still, looking at me. She was crying.

"I can't do it," she said.

"Go back to bed," I said.

"I'll have to," she said.

"Go on," I said.

I fitted the lamp, not without a fight because the screws were small and my fingers so big and clumsy, I heated the pizzas and made a salad, which we ate in front of the television, all together. Afterward they were allowed to have some candy and Linda went to bed. I brushed their teeth, they put on their pajamas but didn't want to go to bed without saying good night to their mother, so they charged in and Linda sat up to give them a hug. Her eyes, which were focused on the wall, were vacant as she stroked their backs and squeezed them tight.

I sat up for a few hours after the children had gone to sleep, browsing through the papers, watching a bit of TV, smoking on the balcony. Linda was asleep when I entered the bedroom, or at least her eyes were closed, and I lay down gently beside her and fell asleep at once.

The next day was Mother's Day. It was still raining, a steady drizzle over the town's buildings and streets. I took the kids to the playground. The verdant grass shimmered in the gray spring light. The colors of their rain jackets were almost obscenely bright as they walked around the playground equipment. After half an hour I dragged them with me to a furniture shop, where I examined sofas, the one we had was so dirty and worn after five years of children that it could only be used if we covered it with rugs. Then we made our way to Åhléns. I said it was Mother's Day and they could each buy a present for Mommy.

"Could you gift wrap these?" I asked the assistant in Norwegian.

"I beg your pardon?"

"Could you wrap them up?" I said, using a Swedish expression.

"Of course," she said.

The children had chosen a big towel, a pair of socks on which was written "The Best Mommy in the World," and I'd found two CDs for her. John wanted her to have a plane. They watched the girl wrap up the presents, then they headed for the toy department. I paid and was about to take the bag when my phone rang. It was the real estate agent. She had been trying to get in touch with Linda for two days now, she said.

I told her Linda was ill, and that she would have to talk to me from now on. My face felt hot, I was sure she would ask about the stench and why on earth the ground by the wall was springy. But she didn't say anything, just that there had been quite a few people at the viewing, one of them had started criticizing everything he saw and ridiculed the price, no one had made an offer afterward. There would be another viewing this afternoon and then next weekend. We hung up, I went to find the children. They were happy we were going to give presents to Linda. We had also bought some cinnamon buns and juice.

"Mommy, Mommy, we have some presents for you," they shouted as we came in.

"Hang on," I said. "First we have to *fika*."

Fika, that was the Swedish word for drinking coffee, an old slang word deriving from *kaffi*, with the syllables swapped around.

I put the buns in a basket, took out five plates, three glasses, two cups, mixed the juices, put the coffee on, Heidi and Vanja set the table.

"Now you can go and get her," I said.

Slowly she followed them through the hall. Perched on the edge of her chair by the wall. They stood in front of her, each holding a present. They handed them to her, one after the other. She slowly unwrapped them. The towel, the socks with "The Best Mommy in the World" on them. They watched her, full of expectation.

"Thank you," she said.

Her face was blank. Not a trace of emotion was visible.

Oh no, oh no.

Oh no, oh no.

"Heidi chose the towel, and Vanja the socks, and John wanted to buy you a plane, but I think it was because he wanted to play with it himself," I said.

"And then we bought some buns and juice. Heidi and Vanja have set the table. Now let's eat. Come on, everyone."

I'd spoken in such a loud voice, and quickly so that there would be so much going on around them that they wouldn't notice something was wrong and think about it.

Linda was crying when we were alone in the bedroom afterward.

"I can't do anything," she said.

"Well," I said. "That's now. It'll pass."

"I have an appointment with the doctor tomorrow," she said. "Can you come with me, do you think?"

"Of course I can," I said.

"It's awful," she whispered.

"It'll be all right," I said. "Everything'll be fine. You'll soon be better. The kids are fine."

She shook her head.

"Yes, they are. Their grandmothers are coming too."

"You have to write," she whispered.

"That'll sort itself out," I said.

After she made the radio program, Linda had been down for a long time. Then there had been a light patch, suddenly she didn't have a care in the world. It had been good for me as it meant her energy increased and I could have more time for writing. She did a lot of shopping, and if she didn't actually hide it from me, she wasn't very open about it either. Out of the blue there were two horrible large porcelain dogs in the children's room, for example, which she had bought for them, and the windowsill in our bedroom was full of similar ornaments. I knew her grandmother had been like that, presumably they gave her a sense of security. I didn't object to her buying them for herself, but I didn't much like her drawing the children into it. This wasn't her, usually she had good taste, now something else was coming out in her. Once she had seen a young girl begging in front of Hemköp and decided to do something, she called social services and told them about her. This may have been an act of kindness, but it wasn't something Linda would normally have done. If I said to her that she'd done a lot of shopping recently, she would snort, what she bought was so cheap, almost everything was from secondhand shops. One afternoon there was a ring at the door, and there stood an antique-shop owner, she had bought a lamp in the same mawkish, heavy, ancient-aunt style, and not because it was cheap, it wasn't, but because it was so beautiful. She spoke a lot to strangers, people sitting at the next table in a café, shop assistants, and at the nursery school, she was good friends with everyone. She beamed, chatted, and kept everything on a very superficial level. There was nothing wrong with any of this aside from the fact that I never had any real contact with her, and she never had her feet on the ground. When I said that, she looked at me and said she understood what I meant. Of course, she understood everything and everything was fine. She was happy, that was all there was to it, and everything worked, she was creative with the children, and they liked the mood she brought, things happened around her. I put my dislike of this to one side, after all there was nothing wrong with it, and what could I say, that she shouldn't buy such hideous things for the children? Oh, one afternoon the girls each had a used Barbie doll in their hands, and John had a soldier. Had *Linda* bought them?

I threw the dolls away after the children had gone to bed.

When the light period was over and she began to sink, she was full of shame for what she had done, even though there was nothing wrong with it, not in itself. It worried her a lot that her ups and downs had become worse. Once she attacked me, saying I should help her, every other man would. She wanted me to help her go back into therapy. Most of all she wanted us to go together. She had wanted that for many years. She knew I would rather die than go to couples therapy, and actually I meant it. If there were a choice between couples therapy and death, I would unhesitatingly choose death. I didn't want to subject myself to individual therapy either. But something about her desperate state made me call for an appointment with a psychologist the following day anyway. We had been there earlier that spring. Linda had started crying when she explained how she felt. The psychologist listened to what she said and then he asked me what I thought and I told him. He wasn't so much interested in Linda's mood swings as her life situation, the fact that she didn't have a job and wasn't earning money, and he asked her how this problem could be solved. He was right in what he said, but I didn't understand how him saying this would help her. Subsequently Linda went to see him on her own. Then she called a doctor for an appointment and had a session with her. At that time her mood was a great deal better. Now the situation was different, I had never seen her like this before, not even remotely. She had lost her grip and had fallen so far into her inner darkness that nothing around her had meaning any longer. That was how it seemed to me. She loved our children more than anything else, but not even for them could she come closer to the world.

After I had dropped off the children at the school the following morning, I made some breakfast for Linda and took it to her in the bedroom on a tray. I had often done that the first year we were together, as nothing made her happier. But then I stopped, I didn't want to put in any more effort to make her happy.

She sat up in bed. She ran her hands across the duvet, back and forth, it was uncanny, they were like the movements of an animal. Then with one hand she lifted the bowl of muesli, with the other she dipped in the spoon and transported it to her mouth. She was so slow that I turned, opened the blinds, and glanced over at the hotel.

Something had broken inside her, I reflected.

She ate half the muesli, then she put down the bowl.

"Are you full?" I said.

She nodded.

"Let's go then, shall we?"

She nodded again.

"Do you want to have a shower first?"

"I can't," she said.

"Okay," I said. "You don't have to."

I took her arm and helped her up. She stood looking at the open closet, where her clothes were. The same desperation appeared in her eyes now as when she had looked at the children.

I took a pair of blue jeans and a gray sweater and laid them on the bed by her.

"Is that all right?" I said.

She nodded.

"I'll be waiting in the hall," I said, and left.

We took the elevator and walked arm-in-arm to the taxis outside the Hilton. Her movements were heavy and slow, as if gravity were greater for her than for anyone else. And perhaps that was indeed how it was.

Something had broken inside her, I reflected again.

We got into a taxi, I said the name of the street and the number, the driver signaled to move into Föreningsgatan, which we followed as far as the Concert House, where we turned right, crossed the bridge over the canal, and came into the lower part of town, where we seldom went, we lived our lives between our apartment in Triangeln and the nursery school in Möllevangen.

Outside the door to the building I asked what the code was. She said it mechanically – she remembered all these things so much better than I did.

We took the elevator up, entered a large waiting room. Linda walked slowly to the reception window. I put a cup on the grill of the coffee machine, pressed the button for black, looked around while the cup filled.

Two people were sitting there, heads bowed, trying to occupy as little space as possible. One, a woman, perhaps fifty; the other, a man, perhaps thirty. The woman was pale, plump, dressed color-lessly. The man was also plump, had a sparse beard, greasy hair, and glasses. Beside them sat a woman talking loudly on her phone. A man came in, short hair, dressed formally, health sandals on his feet, presumably a doctor. He stopped in front of them as I took my cup for a sip, he said a name, the middle-aged woman got up, they shook hands, she followed him down the corridor.

"Would you like a cup of coffee?" I asked Linda, who had joined me.

She shook her head.

"Shall we sit down?"

She nodded. Slowly she took the few steps to the sofa, looked at me, I nodded, she sat down. I sat down beside her and held her hand in mine. The woman was still on her phone. There was a radio in the background, I looked up, a speaker under the ceiling. Someone was talking and laughed, it was one of those morning talk shows that were aired everywhere people worked: hairdress-ing salons, taxis, garages. I thought it inappropriate, it must cut straight into Linda's heart, the life she was excluded from.

I gazed at her. She didn't appear to notice.

I remembered once being in a taxi on our way to a hospital in Stockholm, Linda was terrified the child she would soon be giv-ing birth to was dead, and the radio was on in the taxi. Although I knew the light mood was an agony for her, in the zone of the ultimate horror, on the border between life and death, I didn't dare ask the driver to turn off the radio, I was afraid he would be offended.

I squeezed her hand. She was staring into the middle distance.

"Would you like some water?" I said.

She nodded.

I got up and filled a white plastic cup with water. The sides of the cup were so thin I could feel the water, cold and trembling.

She drank it in one swig.

Around the corner came a woman perhaps a few years younger than me. She stopped and looked at us, Linda got up, the woman smiled and held out a hand. Linda shook it.

"Hi," I said.

We shook hands, and then we walked down the corridor. She stopped outside a door, extended a hand, and we went in. A chair on one side of the table, two on the other. A desk beneath the window, a few unclear, neutral lithographs on the walls.

"Please, sit down," she said.

We sat down.

"How are you, Linda?" she asked, sitting with her legs crossed, a notebook in one hand, a pen in the other. Her eyes were friendly, her expression a little impersonal, perhaps because of the pad and the pen.

Linda studied her.

"Not good," she said at length, in an almost inaudible whisper.

The doctor asked several more questions, which I could see were meant to clarify the situation. Each time Linda answered with very few words after a long pause.

"Do you hear voices?" the doctor said.

Long pause.

Voices? I thought. She was way off target. Linda didn't hear voices.

Perhaps there was a list she had to go through and cross off.

"No . . . ," Linda said. "Only thoughts . . . I don't want to think them . . ."

"Do you think about suicide, Linda? About taking your own life?"

Linda stared at her. Then she burst into tears.

"But . . . but I . . . can't . . . I . . . can't do that," she said. "The children . . . I . . . can't do that."

"You think about it though?"

Linda nodded.

"Often?"

Linda nodded.

"I . . . I . . . think . . . about it . . . all the time . . . If only . . . if only I had . . . a disease and could die. That would make it . . . easier. For everyone."

Tears came into my eyes and I looked down. I took a slow, deep breath. I couldn't go there. Looked at the carpet, looked at the chair leg, looked at the wastepaper basket in the corner, swallowed.

"Does it feel as if everything is going more slowly?" the doctor said.

Linda nodded.

"You don't have the energy to do anything?"

"No!" Linda sobbed.

"Can you shower? Do you get out of bed at all?"

"No. Occasionally. The children . . . I can't manage . . ."

The doctor wrote something in her notebook. Then she looked at me.

"What's your perception of Linda now?" she said.

"I don't quite know. But I've never seen her as low as this," I said, looking at Linda. "This is completely new."

"You're obviously in a deep depression," the doctor said. "We'll have to try to turn that around. Naturally you'll be given antidepressants. But we don't want you too high when it lets go either, so we have to be careful. One possibility is going to the hospital, of course. Then you'll have peace and quiet around you. At home you have the children and normal life. There might be demands on you it would be best you didn't face. Have you thought about the possibility of going to the hospital?"

Linda stared at me, horror-stricken.

She shook her head.

"I think she'd be better off at home," I said.

"Linda?" the doctor said.

"I don't want to go to the hospital."

"I understand," the doctor said. "Of course you can be at home. It might be best for you. But then I want you to come here regularly. Is that all right?"

Linda nodded.

"It's important you try to get up as much as possible. Try to do what you normally do as much as you can. It doesn't have to be a lot. A little, so that you don't spend the whole day in bed. Could you manage to read to the children, for example?"

"I don't know," Linda said.

"Then you can sit with them and watch children's TV for half an hour. And it's important you get out for some light and air. You have to try to go for a little walk every day."

Linda nodded.

The doctor eyed her.

"I have such . . . terrible . . . fears," Linda said.

"You can take something for that. A tablet for when the fear comes. It works instantly. It might make you a bit sleepy. And we'll give you something for the depression. But I'd be a bit careful to begin with. We don't want you to pick up too quickly."

She got to her feet and sat down in front of the computer. I took Linda's hand and squeezed it.

"You can pick up the medication at any pharmacy," the doctor said, getting up. "And I've written down your next appointment. This Wednesday. Is that okay?"

Linda nodded and we stood up.

"I think it's best if you're not alone, Linda. Someone should always be with you."

"Of course," I said.

She accompanied us to the door, smiled, said goodbye, and gently closed the door.

"Do you think they can get a taxi for us at the reception?" I said. Linda nodded.

"Then I'll ask."

Linda waited by the door while I spoke to the receptionist. Down on the street I smoked a cigarette.

"It's going to be fine," I said. "It's good you don't have to go to the hospital. So you're there for the children at least, even if you don't feel up to much."

"Yes," she said.

"We can go for a little walk every day. And you can watch TV with them."

"Yes," she said.

"Is that the taxi, I wonder?" I said, looking up the road, where a black Passat was coming. It stopped beside us, and we got in.

"It'll be fine," I said. "You'll soon be free of it."

I knew the worst for Linda, the great nightmare, was going back to the hospital. The thought of the children exacerbated it, having a mother who had been admitted to a psychiatric institution, the stigma of it. I thought the same, hospitalization would define it and seal it as an illness, make it something institutional when it was actually only Linda, a darkness that filled her, and Linda, she was sitting beside me now, the mommy of Vanja, Heidi, and John. It was better for them that she was at home, that this didn't become something alien and dangerous, but something they could see.

As we sat in the taxi, on our way home, I wasn't sure. This was my responsibility. She wasn't in a state to make any balanced decisions, nor did she want to. That was why she had looked at me. If I had nodded and said, you absolutely must go to the hospital, she would have gone.

The doctor had advised this course of action. We had said no, it is better we do it our way.

"When's Ingrid supposed to be coming?" I said.

"I don't know," Linda said softly. "This afternoon sometime."

"That's good," I said. "Then she's here for the children, and they have something else to think about. They must have people around them now. I think that's important."

"Yes," she said.

The taxi slid in by the front of the Hilton and came to a halt, I paid, we got out, I held her arm as we crossed the road and headed for the pharmacy.

Back at home, she went to bed, and was asleep in minutes. I walked from room to room for a while, had a cigarette on the balcony with the door open in case Ingrid called, sat down in my study and switched on my computer, when she was asleep she didn't need me, but when I saw the essay I had been doing in Voss, about Turner and Claude Lorrain, I realized this wasn't the right time and turned the computer off.

I went into the bedroom to see her. The whole weekend she must have been lying there longing for death while we were in town shopping.

There was a ring.

I hurried to the hall, lifted the intercom receiver.

"Hello," I said.

"Ingrid here."

"I'll open the door."

I waited until I heard the elevator stop, then opened the door.

"How is she?" she said, coming out of the elevator.

"Not so good," I said.

I motioned to her suitcase, which she let go of so that I could carry it in.

"We've just been to the doctor's. She said it was a deep depression. And suggested that she ought to go to the hospital. But Linda preferred to be at home. I'd prefer that too."

"Was she a good doctor?"

"Yes, I think so."

"Ayayayaya," she said with a sigh.

"Yes," I said.

"Is she asleep now?"

"She is."

"And the children? Are they worried?"

"No, I don't think so. They haven't noticed much. They're at school as usual."

"That's good," she said, leaning forward to take off her shoes. I was a few meters away from her and wanted the conversation to end. She was angry with me because of what I had written about her in the second novel, and now there was this, with her daughter. At the same time she was dependent on me – I lived here and was the father of her grandchildren – as I was on her and the help she could offer.

She looked at me.

"I thought you could sleep in the living room," I said, turning to carry her suitcase there. "Is that all right?"

"I can sleep wherever I can," she said. "Also with the children, if Sissel wants to sleep in the living room."

"She can sleep in my office," I said.

"Ye-es." She sighed. "But it's good to be here anyway. It's going to be great to see the children."

"They're looking forward to seeing you," I said.

As I was about to leave to pick up the children that afternoon, Ingrid joined me, she wanted to surprise them, I suppose. In the elevator we said nothing. In the street we stopped and looked at each other.

"We can't leave Linda on her own," I said.

"I was thinking the same," Ingrid said. "You go and I'll stay with her."

How was it possible, I thought, as I continued up Södra Förstadsgatan? How could I have forgotten about her? How could I have forgotten that she shouldn't be on her own?

It was just as bad that I had been out so much over the weekend. It was as though the gravity of the situation hadn't hit home.

As though everything was normal and what was happening inside her as she lay in the room, excluded from the rest of the family, was only in parentheses.

"Did Grandma come?" Vanja asked. She had run over as soon as she had seen me behind the gate.

I nodded.

"She has, yes. She can't wait to see you."

I strolled across to the nursery school staff and exchanged a few words with them. Everything had gone well, they said, the children had been happy and content. I had thought of telling them Linda was depressed, so they would keep an eye on the children, in case something out of the ordinary occurred, but both Vanja and Heidi were standing next to me and I decided to wait until the following day.

We bought fruit, milk, and yogurt at Hemköp, they were impatient, wanting to get home now that Grandma was there. She would have presents with her, wouldn't she?

When she was with us she always cooked, did the shopping, and kept the kitchen clean. She stretched herself as thin as she could for us, of that there was no doubt. If I hadn't written the book everything in my relationship with her would have been good, but it lay there like a shadow, and we couldn't talk about it.

Strangely enough, it was John who was shy with her when we trooped in through the door. But it didn't last long. After they had unwrapped their presents they ran into Linda to show her. I followed, watching closely. Linda looked at them, sat up, and tried to smile. How nice, she said.

"Come on now, you little varmints," I said. "Mommy has to rest a little."

It wasn't difficult this time. I closed the bedroom door, and then the hall door. Ingrid was in the kitchen cooking.

"When would you like to eat?" she said.

"Anytime," I said. "Whatever suits you."

"Five?" she said.

"That's fine," I said.

I poured the coffee I'd made but forgotten into the thermos and was about to go onto the balcony when the phone rang.

It was an Oslo number and I took it.

It was Elisabeth from Oktober.

"Am I disturbing you?" she said.

"Not at all," I said.

"You're writing, I hope?" she said with a laugh. "But it's good I've managed to get ahold of you. We need to discuss the launch. Number five will be out soon."

"Yes," I said, closing the balcony door and sitting down.

"Have you thought about how you would like to do it?"

"Only in terms of as little as possible."

"In principle you can choose to do whatever you like. There is enormous interest, of course. But I have a suggestion. *Aftenposten* has been trying to get an interview with you for ages. What about doing that? And nothing else?"

"Sounds good," I said.

"I think it will be."

"There was one other thing. The Book Fair in Oslo this autumn. It would be great if you could come."

"When is it?"

"Mid-September."

"Should be possible," I said.

"Great! Now I know. We can sort out details later. Thank you, Karl Ove."

I put down the phone and poured myself some coffee. The last time Linda was ill it had lasted for more than a year.

I hadn't even thought about that.

What if it just carried on?

I stubbed out my cigarette and went back in. Checked that the children were fine before going into the bedroom. She wasn't asleep, she was lying in bed with her eyes open looking at the ceiling.

"How's it going?" I said, sitting on the edge of the bed.

She turned her head to me. Her eyes were as good as vacant.

"The kids are fine," I said. "They behaved as they usually do at school. And they're happy Ingrid's here. John was a bit shy at first, but he soon picked up."

She looked at me as though she wanted to say something.

"Do you have the energy to get up for dinner?" I said.

She gave a slight nod.

"And to watch *Bolibompa* with them afterward?"

She nodded again.

"That's enough," I said. "If you can do that, it's great."

I stood up. I felt unable to withstand her gaze.

"I'll come and get you when it's ready then," I said. "Okay?"

She nodded, and I headed for the living room, where I sat down with two of the morning papers I hadn't read yet.

The next day, when I returned home after taking the children to school, Ingrid was sitting on Linda's bed and talking with her. There was a tray of food between them. A bowl of muesli, an egg, fruit, a slice of bread, a glass of juice, a cup of coffee. Linda looked at Ingrid as she had looked at me the past few times, from somewhere deep inside herself. It was as though everything that was said disappeared in that gaze. Everything seemed to vanish into endless space, where it was so small it made no difference, yet it was all she had and therefore clung to. She looked and saw me, then she looked and saw Ingrid.

"They're off at school now," I said, stopping in the doorway.

Ingrid got up.

"Are you done?" she asked Linda. "If so, I'll take the tray with me."

I knew she didn't want to impose, and our bedroom was a boundary she would cross only with extreme reluctance, but I hadn't been at home and she had gone in because Linda was her daughter.

"Would you like to go for a little walk?" I said after Ingrid had left.

1157

Linda nodded and slowly got to her feet.

"Shall I find you some clothes?"

She nodded again.

I laid out a pair of trousers and a sweater and went into the hall to wait. Passed her a jacket, put out some shoes, took her arm when she was ready, and walked beside her to the lift. She stared at the floor as the elevator descended, probably to avoid the mirror.

Outside, the sun was shining. The trees between the market square and the road were green, thick with leaves. People walked to and fro across the flagstone square, cars whizzed by. We ambled toward the park.

"I love you, Linda," I said.

She gave a start and looked at me.

"Things are terrible now, but they will be good. I promise you. You just have to hold on tight."

She continued to stare into the distance.

"I know it's absolutely unbearable, but you have to stick it out. Then you'll be fine."

We went over the road at the crosswalk, walked along the sidewalk, past the Mexican restaurant, the hairdresser's, the denim shop. The sky was blue, the grass in the park over the road green. People sat dotted around, some with bikes by them.

"You're a fantastic mother, Linda," I said. "I know you think you're letting the children down, but you aren't. You can't do anything about this. It's just something that happens inside you. I promise you."

She looked at me with the same semi-absent, semi-imploring gaze. She said nothing. We crossed the road, entered the park.

"Why don't we sit down for a bit over there?" I said, nodding toward the stone wall beneath the trees in the middle of the park.

"Everything's going to be fine," I said.

An elderly woman with a dog strolled past, behind her came a young woman on a bicycle, she had a backpack on her back and gave us a wide berth. From the playground came the voices of children. Three or four parents were with them, I saw.

We sat down on the wall.

Linda burst into tears. She sobbed aloud, her shoulders shook. I put my arm around her and rested my head against her neck.

"It's going to be fine. I love you. It's awful now, but it'll pass."

The people sitting on the lawn around us glanced over. A gust of wind blew, the leaves on the trees rustled. Linda sat bent over, crying with all her heart, something seemed to have crashed inside her.

I stroked her back.

What darkness are you in now, Linda?

What darkness are you in?

"I love you. You're a brilliant person. You're a wonderful mother. This is going to be fine. You have to hold on."

Gradually the tears subsided. I held out my arm, she slipped hers inside, and then we got up and walked down the gravel path, as slowly as an elderly couple. I was racked by restlessness.

Ingrid came into the hall as we took off our coats.

"Well done, Linda," she said. "It's so good that you managed the walk."

"Do you want to rest a little?" I said.

She nodded. I accompanied her into the bedroom.

"Would you like a radio? Then you'll have something to listen to while you lie here." She shook her head.

"I just want to sleep," she said.

She lay down, pulled the duvet half over her head, and closed her eyes.

"Okay," I said. "I'll come back in half an hour to check you're all right."

I went for a smoke. I looked down as I passed the kitchen, where Ingrid was sitting with the newspaper open on the table in front of her, I didn't want a conversation. I knew she liked me, but I presumed what I had written overshadowed that, and I knew she probably drew a straight line between what Linda was going through and what I had done. I didn't know she was thinking that, but I had a strong suspicion she was.

We talked about what we would have for the evening meal. We talked about Linda, how we should try to get her out of bed as often as possible. We talked about the children and who should do what for them. But we didn't talk about her, we didn't talk about me, and we didn't talk about what I'd written about her.

Looking down, I slunk past, telling myself Linda was the priority for both of us now.

Sitting on the balcony, I caught the sound of the phone ringing. I rushed in and answered it. It was the real estate agent. She had just done another viewing. There had been seven people, but unfortunately there had been no offers. She would be doing another viewing this weekend. She said it would probably sell. I said that was good. She said there seemed to be something wrong with the shower, one of the people at the viewing had turned it on and they weren't able to turn it off, and then water had spurted out from the pipe. I said that was right, there was something wrong with the shower and the pipes. I would have to get someone to look at it. Good, she said, and we hung up.

I looked in on Linda. She was asleep, I came back out, went to my study, where I could be at peace. Switched on the computer. Flipped through the book of Claude Lorrain pictures I had bought in New York when I'd been there only a few weeks earlier. It felt like several years ago. I had fainted at a venue in Manhattan after doing a reading. I hadn't eaten all day, was so nervous, and I had drunk a beer with my American publisher, and when we were standing outside and she introduced me to an elderly Egyptian writer, who was holding court, suddenly I couldn't stand upright but had to go to the steps and sit down. I held my head in my hands and felt the blackness gathering inside me and rising, a wave of inescapable numbing weariness and giddiness. The elderly

Egyptian, who was a great poet and justifiably held everyone's attention, came over to me, friendly all of a sudden, put his arm around my shoulders and asked if I was all right. I said I was, and he went back to his circle. Now I couldn't even sit, so I stood up and staggered over to the publisher and said I had to go home, at once, and she said she would find a taxi. I couldn't even wait, so I lay down on the sidewalk and closed my eyes and was gone. I came to again when she placed her hand on my shoulder and I realized I couldn't have been out for more than one or maybe two minutes. But people were staring at me where I lay. I managed to struggle to my feet, she opened the door of the waiting taxi, gave the address to the driver, and then off we drove through this immense town.

I had seen a picture by Claude Lorrain in New York, and I was writing about it now. Strangely enough, I wrote with ease and focus, everything else vanished until, after lifting my head and looking at the blinds covering the window in front of me, shimmering with spring light, I suddenly thought about Linda. I switched off the computer, got up, and poked my head around the door.

She was sitting up in bed. She was scratching at the duvet and looked up at me. Leaning forward and scratching at the bedcover. Then she seemed to be brushing something away. All this frightened me, her movements were so unfamiliar.

"I have such fears, Karl Ove," she said. "I'm so afraid."

"Can't you take one of the tablets you were given?"

"Yes, but the effect doesn't last very long. And then it just gets worse."

"I can go and get one. What were they called again?"

She told me. I went into the kitchen, one shelf was completely taken over by her medication, I found the box she wanted, poured a glass of water, and carried them in to her.

She took a tablet and leaned back.

I lay beside her.

We didn't say anything. I held her hand. I thought about what

I had written, and the feelings Lorrain's pictures evoked in me filled me with a kind of peace, which I then immediately repressed, what sort of monster was I to think about that while she was lying beside me wanting to die?

"Would you like anything to eat? Fruit or something?"

She didn't answer. I looked at her.

"Grapes?" I said.

She nodded, I got up, went into the kitchen, which fortunately was unoccupied, put a small bunch into a bowl, and took it back to her.

"Still no radio?" I said, putting the bowl down beside her.

"I'm not up to listening to anything."

"Not even music?"

"No."

She pulled the duvet over her and turned her head to the wall.

On our way home from school Vanja wanted to know if Mommy was still sleeping.

"Yes, she is. She's not feeling well, you know. But it'll soon pass."

"It'll never pass," Vanja said. "She's always sick."

"No, she isn't," I said. "But right now she is. So she needs her rest."

"I do too," Vanja said. "I want to rest with her."

"I'm sure you could," I said. "If you keep still and stay quiet, that would be fine."

"Me, too," Heidi said.

"That's okay," I said. "But just one at a time. Shall we say that?"

But this didn't go too well. Vanja started nagging Linda to get up, and Heidi was no better.

Vanja refused to leave the room and it ended with me having to carry her out. I tried to turn it into a joke, some fun, but she was very angry.

I sat her down in her room. She wanted to run back and tried to dodge past me.

"Vanja," I said. "It's true that Mommy's ill. She needs some peace and quiet. It'll soon be over. I promise you."

"It won't," she said, and looked down at the floor.

"Come on. Let's go and watch a film."

"I don't want to."

"What do you want to do then?"

"I want to see Mommy."

"I understand. And you will be able to. But not right now."

She sat down and started moving all her toy figures around as though I didn't exist. I watched her for a while, then left.

The next day we went back to the doctor. She asked more or less the same questions she had on the previous occasion. Linda was equally monosyllabic.

"What we have to do is reverse the depression," she said after a while. "One way to do that is through ECT, electroconvulsive therapy. I know it sounds terrible, but the fact is it works. In a sense it applies a brake to the process and gives the brain a kind of new start. Is that perhaps something you could imagine trying? It's thoroughly safe, you know. And it will stop this."

Linda turned to me when the doctor said this, and her expression was the same as when she had looked at me the first time the doctor had suggested going to the hospital.

Her mouth opened and closed as though she were gasping for air, and her eyes streamed with tears.

"No," she said. "No."

"I don't think so," I said. "I think we'll just have to ride this one out."

"I understand," the doctor said, looking at Linda. "The most important thing is you have to get out of bed for a while every day. You've been walking, so that's good. If you have the strength it would be good if you could do some of what you normally do."

"I don't do anything," Linda whispered.

"I beg your pardon."

"I don't do anything."

"It's not so easy to see when you're depressed," she said. "It's like you don't do anything and so you're not worth anything. But I imagine there's something you like doing more than anything else, isn't there?"

Linda shook her head.

"You don't have any hobbies, something you particularly like doing?" Linda shook her head again.

"You like films," I said. "And reading."

"They're too much for me," she said.

"Well," the doctor said. "I wasn't thinking about big things. If you can put on the dishwasher, even if it's only for a couple of glasses, that's good."

Linda nodded.

"How's it going with your children? Do you spend any time with them?"

Linda shook her head.

"Yes, you do," I said. "You've watched TV with them."

"That's good, Linda. Perhaps you should try to read to them as well. Do you think you could manage that?"

"Yes."

She read to them that afternoon, one after the other, as she didn't have the energy to deal with all three of them at once, and they would only have vied for her attention. First she read for John while Heidi was in the hall waiting her turn, then Heidi, and last of all Vanja. After that she slept. A pattern was beginning to crystallize in these new days of hers: while I took the children to school, she had breakfast in bed, then she got dressed and went for a short walk with either Ingrid or me, slept, got up and had lunch, started the dishwasher, slept, read to the children when they came home, slept, got up and had her evening meal, watched TV with the children, slept. Every so often I wrote a little, but not much, just a few lines every day. Elisabeth called, she had an agreement with *Aftenposten*, they would send a journalist next week.

"The journalist's name is Siri Økland," Elisabeth said.

"But she works for *Bergens Tidende*. Wasn't it supposed to be someone from *Aftenposten*?"

"Yes, it was, but they work together. The big regional papers. They often print the same articles."

"Okay," I said.

I had actually decided I would never do any more interviews for *Bergens Tidende* because of the way they had behaved toward me when the first volume came out and because of the way they had treated me and my books since. Everything they had written had a negative slant; sometimes it was sarcastic to the point of mudslinging, sometimes morally indignant. I hadn't read the paper myself, but both Mom and Yngve lived in the area *BT* covered, so I had an impression of the tone they used. When I was in Odda I had received an inquiry via the event organizers regarding an interview for *BT,* and the journalist had assured them it would be done with propriety, it wouldn't be slanted in the way things had been so far. This was so outrageous that my jaw dropped when I read it. First of all they pissed on me, then they asked if they could have an interview, and promised they wouldn't piss on me again.

But I really didn't want to create problems for anyone. I trusted Siri Økland and, besides, the deal was already agreed. Publishing an interview she had conducted couldn't be damaging.

Linda wasn't getting any better. Whenever I was alone with her I told her the same, I said I loved her, I knew she was having a terrible time, but it would pass and everything would be fine. It was as though everything I said disappeared inside her, it just dissolved in the darkness and was gone. She never answered, nor did she look at me as I spoke. We walked to the little park, sat there for a while, walked back. I realized this was probably going to be long term, and the next time we went to the doctor I asked for a sick note so that we could cancel the trip to Corsica and get our money reimbursed. She read to the children every afternoon and was worn out afterward, but I was so happy she could do it, this was like a lifeline, a vital minimum for the children, which meant they weren't marked by what was happening to her. That is to say, this was the case for Heidi and John, they accepted everything as it was, while Vanja, on the other hand, was filled with a mass of conflicting emotions she didn't know how to handle. One evening she had a furious outburst. Linda was sitting in a chair in the living room and Vanja started hitting her as she shouted.

"You're ugly! You're ugly! You're ugly!" she yelled.

I lifted her off Linda, she kicked and wriggled and tried to hit me. I had to sit down with her and hold her tight for several minutes before she quieted down and was still. Afterward, sitting alone in my study while everyone was asleep, I cried. I don't know why, I just cried. At school they said everything was fine, they couldn't see any difference in their behavior. Vanja was the oldest child there now and had come into her own. She also had a new best friend, they would start in the same class in the autumn, we had chosen this school for precisely this reason, and they talked forever on the phone in the afternoons. And she had a strong attachment to her grandmother.

Children do what is necessary for them, they take what they need, compensate and counterbalance, all without realizing this is what they are doing.

One morning Linda came into the kitchen. She was trembling and in tears. She held a credit card in her hand.

"I found this on the floor," she said. "It was on the floor."

She cried as she said it.

"You don't keep things clean," she said. "Everywhere there's chaos."

"It's my credit card," Ingrid said. "It must've fallen out of my pocket."

"It was on the floor," Linda said in a trembling voice. "You're so messy."

She turned and slowly shuffled back to her bedroom. I followed her.

"It doesn't mean anything," I said. "I appreciate that you think everything's in chaos. But it isn't. Everything's under control. Completely. Don't give it another thought."

She was shaking. I wondered if it was a side effect of all the medication she was taking.

"You'd better get some sleep," I said. "But the credit card doesn't mean a thing. It's not what you think. Everything's under control."

"No, it isn't," she said, lying down.

"Yes, it is," I said. "It is. Actually everything's fine. We have three great children. They're beginning to grow up. They're doing very well. You've had a book accepted. You're a writer. We have money. We could buy a house if we wanted. You see, everything's fine. Everything is actually good."

She looked at me as I said that. Her eyes were large. It was as though she knew nothing of what I had told her. As though it were new to her.

Then she closed her eyes, I got up and said I would be back soon. I went into the kitchen, tipped some coffee into the filter, and switched on the machine.

That evening Ingrid asked me if I had the second novel in audiobook format. I nodded. She asked if she could borrow it. That was the last thing I wanted. Why would she want to go through it? What else could I do but find her a copy and hand it over.

She always turned in early, about the same time as the kids, closed the door, and was on her own until the next morning, when she got up and made pancakes or baked bread for the children. I usually watched TV for an hour after everybody had gone to bed unless I was in my study leafing through one of the art books. This evening I could hear she hadn't fallen asleep as she usually did. When I turned in, she was still awake. The next morning she said she hadn't slept a wink all night. She had been listening to the novel I had written. She said I had sent it to her just before it was about to go to press, she hadn't had time to read it and hadn't understood the Norwegian. That was why she had told me what I'd written about her was fine. She had trusted me.

As she said this she was standing in front of the stove making pancakes. I stood with a cup in my hand, on my way out to smoke a cigarette. I was afraid of her. But I couldn't go, nor could I defend myself, I had to stand there and listen and concede she was right. And she was, too. It was her prerogative. She was furious with me. But in the bedroom we had Linda, whom she loved and who she feared would die, in the living room we had her grandchildren, whom she loved and for whom she would do anything, even sacrifice her own life, of that I was sure. Linda was my wife, her grandchildren were my children. She was distraught, and so was I. I couldn't make excuses for myself. I couldn't defend myself, all the right was on her side. The only argument I had was that she had been given the book to read in advance, and she had approved it, but now that was invalid because it was true what she said, she'd only had a few days because the manuscript had been sent to the wrong address.

That was all she said, but I knew her, she was furious, sad, and afraid.

Beneath everything lay the unspoken reproach that it was because of what I had written that Linda had lost her bearings and was in bed. I felt it all the time. It came from both me and her. She was lying in there, and I was keeping everyone away from her. I was keeping the children away from her, and I was keeping Ingrid away from her. It was a terrible feeling, filled with gloom, because it was my fault she had ended up there, in the bedroom, in bed. I hadn't taken care of her. Had I done so, this wouldn't have happened. But I had done the opposite. I had made sure the pressure on her had been unbearable. What she was struggling with was her identity, who she was. Once before, when the pressure in her life had been immense, everything had unraveled, and she had fled into a kind of fantasy version of herself and then plummeted into the darkness. There was no connection between the person she was and the person she wanted to be or thought she was. The difference between the Linda I first set eyes on and the Linda I met two years later was enormous. She had caught up with herself, I had thought. She was whole or "wholer." Having children was something she could feel at ease with, what had to be done and who she had to be were obvious, there was no choice, that was how it was and that was how she was. Then I had written that life was an illusion, a notion, inauthentic. And not only that, I had talked at length about life to everyone. Her life, our children, our problems. And not only that, this particular book exploded in the public arena and was on everyone's lips. It hit her where she was most vulnerable, in the question of her identity, who she was. I held up a mirror, and not only did she see herself there, but so did everyone else.

After the books had come out her therapist had called her once from Stockholm, I answered the phone, her voice was ice-cold as she asked to speak to Linda. She knew Linda inside out, she knew exactly what she was struggling with and understood how dangerous my experiment was.

Every time I walked through the hall into the bedroom I had the same feeling, that I had damaged her and now she was hiding. We had lived together for almost ten years, and my premise was that we were like everyone else and our conflicts were like everyone else's and Linda had to manage as everyone else did. I had seen her outbursts, I had seen her attempts to control me, but I hadn't seen her fear of losing everything, the feeling that she was standing on the edge of a precipice. I had seen buckets and cloths, washing machines and bags of diapers. I had seen strollers and children's clothes, baths and cots. I had seen how close Linda was to the children, she gave them everything they needed, but I hadn't seen what it had cost her. Now I could see, for she had lost her grip and was sinking. She was sinking deeper and deeper, and she was drawing further and further away. Everyday life was beyond her reach now. She could see it from the depths of where she was, and if she exerted herself to the maximum she could stretch out a hand and touch it, be there for a few minutes, have a child on her lap, no more though, nothing of what a life consists of, and which is so easy, so unbelievably easy, giving them some fruit, telling a joke, asking them about something that interests them, dressing them, going with them to the park. All this is easy, and therefore nothing we appreciate while it is happening; it is only later – when the children are bigger – that it can hit us, what we did when they were two or four, both they and we are different people now, and the people we were then are lost forever.

This is how it is. Life is easy, life is a game, until the bottom falls out, and you fall, you are in the hospital and you plunge into the darkness, then it is suddenly impossible, then it is suddenly unattainable. Linda could see this but was unable to do anything about it, her thoughts, even when her children were jumping around in there, were about her not being worthy of life, we would be better off without her, she was destroying everything, and she continually fantasized about dying, which was so radically removed from us, who wanted to live, this was unbearable.

Ingrid accompanied Linda on walks to the park, I saw them, the daughter with her head bowed, her plodding movements, her empty eyes, the mother with her arm entwined in hers, encouraging, chatting, positive. I accompanied Linda on walks to the park, I told her I loved her, she was having a terrible time now, but it would pass, and everything I said disappeared inside her, there was no resistance, her inner life was like an abyss and the darkness so dense that nothing could lighten it. Nothing. Not even those she loved most – Vanja, Heidi, and John – could lighten the darkness.

My mother came, we had arranged a long time ago that the two grandmothers would be at home and help while I sat in the cabin writing the end of the novel. That was no longer relevant, but we still needed them, for now we were in dire need.

Mom and Ingrid had always got on well together, as different as they were, and they did so now too, as the tensions at home increased, because almost everything that lay between us was unsaid and unprocessed, bordering on unconscious, traces were evident in our body language and our voices, impossible to pinpoint yet hugely present.

In the evenings, when everyone was asleep, I sat up talking to Mom. It felt like betrayal. It shouldn't have felt like betrayal because I was being torn to shreds and needed someone to talk to, but it still felt like betrayal because I was guilty of what I was being torn to shreds over, and it was not me who was suffering but Linda, so I had no right to the relief I gained from talking to someone who was unconditionally on my side.

Mom said Linda was in a much worse state than she had imagined. She sat on the sofa knitting while I sat in the chair with my feet on the table and a cup of coffee in my hand. She didn't say this was what she had feared when Linda and I had got together, but I knew it was the case and thought it strange I had never been afraid of this outcome. I had been sure everything would be fine. My philosophy had been to follow your heart. Not your mind, not rationality, not money, but your heart. My first thought when we got together had been that I wanted to have children with her. Not one, not two, but three. And we had them. When I wrote about us, I had also followed my heart. It was cold then.

I called the travel agent and canceled the trip to Corsica. The plan had been that we would be there for a week at first, just Linda, Vanja, Heidi, John, and I, then Yngve and his kids, and Asbjørn and his family would join us there the following week. The departure date was the day after the deadline for the novel, the trip was supposed to be the reward for everything. Now I could forget the deadline, the novel had been set aside, it meant nothing. The real estate agent called regularly, she was doing viewings during the week and on weekends, she put ads in the papers and on the Net, people came, saw, and no one wanted it. I went for a stroll in the park with Linda, she put plates in the dishwasher, slept, watched TV with the children, read to them. Sometimes the fear in her grew so strong that she turned white and was incapable of moving, then she took an extra tablet and entered a kind of twilight state where she could sleep. Oh, Linda, Linda. Enough was happening around the children, with two grandmothers there, by and large they were happy, they had already got used to their mommy being ill. I didn't know what to do. Occasionally my anger spilled over, it rose inside me, couldn't she pull herself together, get up, and take hold of her life? I love you, it's terrible now, but it'll be fine. We went for a walk, she put on the dishwasher, had lunch with us, watched TV with the children, read to them. I knew that all her thoughts were black. I knew she wanted to die, but she couldn't.

Evening meal in the kitchen. Ingrid, Sissel, Vanja, Heidi, John, and I. Linda in the bedroom. Without looking at me, Ingrid said:

"Have you considered the consequences of writing about your children?"

"Yes," I said.

"How it will be for them when they grow up? Everyone knowing who they are? Have you taken that into account? That they're vulnerable?"

This is her daughter, I thought. Let her be angry at me.

"I don't think there's any danger," I said. "I don't think that any of what I've written is dangerous."

It sounded hollow, she looked at me, we continued to eat, the children slipped down from their chairs, they hadn't noticed anything unusual, there hadn't been any raised voices.

The next day was a Saturday, the sun was shining and we were all going to the park, we had packed a picnic basket and taken a large blanket, it was the first time Linda had been out with the children since I came home from Iceland. Ingrid and Sissel and the children were waiting for us outside, I didn't know that, I was walking arm-in-arm with Linda through the corridors in the cellar and emerged at the back of the building, which was closer to the park. I assumed they were already there.

After waiting for a quarter of an hour, Linda's mother had lost her temper and cursed me, Mom told me later that night, when everyone was in bed. Mom was also angry, it was her son Ingrid had cursed, but I said it didn't matter, and I understood Ingrid. She had every right to be furious with me. But she also liked me, and that was perhaps harder to understand.

All this was kept from Linda. When she came all the tensions between us ceased, then we concentrated on her. Of course I said nothing about it when we were alone, even if that was exactly the kind of thing we discussed normally, other people, the relations between them. Linda saw other people – that was a gift she had. Now there was nothing left of it in her. She rarely spoke, the little strength she had she devoted to the children. Nor did I tell her that Book 5 was due to come out soon. I was expecting a storm because I had written about a rape allegation I'd been subjected to once, and bearing in mind all the other trivialities I had written that had ended up as front-page stories I considered it inconceivable that this would not suffer a similar fate. I had also received some furious e-mails from people I'd written about and whom I had accordingly made anonymous. But the woman who said I had raped her, she existed, she lived in Bergen, and it wouldn't have surprised me if someone had located her and interviewed her, although neither her name nor anything else was mentioned that might identify her.

For this reason, the day I was to be interviewed by Siri Økland I said nothing about it to Linda, who was in bed after going out for a walk with her mother, this time all the way to Pildamm Park, only that I had an interview and it would take an hour, maximum two. She said okay, and then I left for the Art Exhibition Hall, where I had done almost all the interviews for the first four books. Siri Økland was waiting there with a photographer. The interview went well, although I was constantly on the defensive, constantly entrenched, it was obvious that what I had done was wrong. Afterward there were photos outside, in the street, and then I came home. Ingrid was out picking up the children, Linda was asleep, Mom was in the living room reading. She looked up when I entered.

"So how's it going here?" I said.

"Well, it's been good," she said. "Linda got up while you were out. She joined us in the kitchen. She talked for an hour."

"Really?"

"Yes. She cried and talked about how she felt."

"What did she say?"

"She said she couldn't do anything and she wasn't doing anything. She said she was utterly useless. She couldn't handle the children on her own, she didn't have a job, and it didn't look like she was going to get one either. She was desperate."

"But she talked," I said.

"Yes, she talked."

One morning Linda had made her bed and was sitting on the duvet with her back to the wall when I went in, and although the look she sent me was still desperate, she appeared to be different and stronger than the day before. I couldn't put my finger on what it was. Perhaps it was that not everything just vanished inside her, not everything just streamed inward, but that something also came out. She'd made her bed, she was sitting on the duvet, and she met my gaze.

"I tried to read a little," she said.

"Oh yes?" I said.

"Can't do it."

"That doesn't matter," I said. "It's good you're up. Feel like going for a walk?"

She nodded. We ambled through the small park, crossed the

road, followed the wooden fence along the old stadium into Pildamm Park, turned, and strolled back.

Instead of lying down and sleeping as soon as we arrived, she asked me to put a radio in the bedroom. I did, found a channel with classical music, closed the door behind me, and went into the study. Not long afterward the phone rang. It was Yngve. He said *Bergens Tidende* had a big spread about Book 5. Well, several spreads. Including an article about the rape allegation.

"They close the article by saying *BT* has her name," Yngve said.

"What the hell do they mean by that? Is it a threat?"

"I don't know," he said.

"Anyway, the book hasn't come out yet," I said. "There's a release date."

"Doesn't look like they've taken any notice of that," Yngve said. "And it's the same negative slant."

"I'll give the publisher a call. See you."

I called Elisabeth. She said that what had happened was that they had given a copy of the manuscript to Siri Økland, as she would be interviewing me. The condition had been that the manuscript was only to be used for that purpose. They had promised and then proceeded to break their promise. Elisabeth had spoken to Siri, she was very sorry, she said she had nothing to do with it, they'd ordered her to hand over the manuscript. Elisabeth was livid. It wasn't unusual for a newspaper not to stick to the release date, *Verdens Gang* never did, for example, and as a result they didn't receive the books to be reviewed in advance. But this time *BT* had been given the manuscript because they were the only ones to have a prepublication interview, and they had made an agreement and given their promise. Which they broke without a second thought. Why? They probably reckoned they had the right to treat me as they liked because in their eyes I had done something deeply immoral.

"But they haven't printed the interview yet?" I said.

"No, they will on the launch day."

"I'll pull it in that case. What do you think?"

"I think we should. I'll call them at once."

I hung up, strode to the balcony and took out a cigarette, then went back to the bedroom, where Linda was lying with her eyes closed. She opened them when I entered.

"How did it go with the radio?"

"I can't take anything in. Not even music."

She cried.

I lay down beside her.

"You're better already, Linda. You're closer now than you were only a few days ago. It's a question of letting go. I'm sure of it."

"I'm so afraid," she said.

"I know," I said. "But everything's fine. Everything's fine."

She lay back and pressed her head against the mattress.

Her movements were quicker; there was something new about her now.

I picked up the children from school, walked through Triangeln Mall and out the back, where the playground was only a block away. Vanja and Heidi stopped by the railing alongside the parking lot, which they wanted to climb, I took a deep breath and said yes, John sat with his head back staring up at the sky, where the white vapor trails from two planes formed a cross.

My phone rang. It was Elisabeth.

"I've spoken to them several times today," she said. "The last time the editor in chief called. They're going to publish the interview anyway."

"But I want to pull it!"

"That makes no difference. They're invoking the right to freedom of expression."

"What! Are they crazy?"

"Dad, Dad, look," Heidi shouted. She leaned back, held on with only one hand, and theatrically threw the other out to the side. I smiled and gave her a thumbs-up.

"Freedom of expression? They've committed a breach of contract. They've ignored the release date. And then they want to publish on the basis of freedom of expression?"

"Yes, that's basically it. They've got lawyers and the whole box of tricks. They're going to publish anyway. We can't do anything."

"I'm never going to do another interview with that newspaper for the rest of my life. I never want anything to do with them."

"I absolutely agree," Elisabeth said. "And I doubt they'll get any interviews with other Oktober authors for a while either."

"Anyway, thank you," I said.

"We'll talk later. The reviews will be in soon. But you never read them anyway, do you."

"Geir will brief me, I imagine. All right, bye."

"Okay, bye."

I hung up and put the phone in my pocket.

"Come on," I said, and started to walk. Stopped, turned. "Come on now!"

They slowly balanced their way toward me.

What two-faced bastards. Oh, how I hated it. Oh, the righteous indignation. Oh, fucking hell. Freedom of speech my ass.

May they burn in hell.

At the playground Vanja and Heidi headed straight for the tree they called the "climbing tree." John wanted to go on the swing, I pushed him, occasionally grabbing him by the feet when he came back, then he laughed, and he laughed even more when I raised him by the feet and swung him back as hard as I could. Now it was out, I thought, now everyone knew. Tomorrow the papers would be full of it. Knausgaard Suspected of Rape. I had told the events of those days only to those closest to me. I had been so frightened it would be in the papers. It never had been, but now I had written about it, they could just help themselves. But if I hadn't, some people would have known that I was going easy on myself, I was holding back on one of the most consequential incidents of my life, and by writing about myself I had given everyone else the right to write what they liked about my life. It would have come out sooner or later.

I lifted John from the swing and put him in the sand. He didn't want to play on his own, and walked beside me to the bench on the other side of the pit. I lifted him up and sat him on my lap, wrapped my arms around him, and rested my head on his neck.

"My little Johnny boy," I said.

"Don't, Daddy," he said.

"Okay," I said, straightening up. "Can you see the girls?"

He pointed. They were sitting among the leaves.

What were they doing?

Talking perhaps. I could dimly hear Heidi's characteristic laugh and Vanja's put-on voice.

A quarter of an hour later we made for home. Linda was in bed when we arrived, but after the children had taken off their shoes and run into the bedroom she got up.

"Mommy, can you read to me?" Vanja said.

She nodded, took a book from the pile on the desk, sat down, and the three children were a jumble of limbs around her.

The next morning I was sure there would be journalists outside. *Bergens Tidende* had written about the rape allegation, it was out there, and even though no journalist had, so far, been here to see me – the nearest they had come was to take photos of the apartment and interview people in the vicinity – they had contacted everyone I knew and I assumed it had to be only a question of time before they came here. And now there was a story that would lure them out.

I dressed the children, put John in the stroller, checked on Linda, who was dozing, said we were off, leaned over and kissed her on the brow, rushed back to the children, opened the elevator door, pushed the stroller in, and pressed the cellar button. If there were journalists outside I would meet them with the children, and there was a rear entrance to the building they wouldn't know about, I thought, pushed the stroller along the corridors, dragged it backward up the steps, opened the door, went out, followed Föreningsgatan, and took the backstreets up to the nursery school.

On the way home I stopped before the market square and scrutinized the area around the entrance. No one resembling a journalist there. I felt a little stupid. I wasn't so important that they would keep a watch on the apartment building where I lived.

I had become paranoid, I mused, walked over to the fruit stall and bought a couple of kilos of grapes and some apples, took the elevator up, sliced an apple for Linda, put it in a bowl with some grapes, and took them in to her. She sat up.

"How's it all going?" she said.

Oh, how happy that question made me.

"Fine," I said. "Eat now and rest a bit, then let's go out for a walk, shall we?"

"Okay."

"I'll just give Geir a call first."

"Angell or Gulliksen?"

"Angell," I said, taking the phone with me onto the balcony and calling him.

"Do you know what's in *Dagbladet* today?" he said.

"No," I said. "Damned if I want to know either."

"It says you can get ten years in jail."

"Oh."

"Yes, you can say that again. First *Aftenposten*'s reviewer wants to have you imprisoned and now *Dagbladet*."

"Right now I wouldn't mind," I said. "Being in prison, I mean."

"I thought you already were."

"Ha ha."

"How's it going down there actually?"

"In fact, better. Linda's a bit better. Not much, but the little bit suggests it's on the turn."

"Poor Linda," Geir said.

"Yes," I said. "She's been through hell."

I hung up. When I returned to the bedroom Linda was in the shower. I lay down on the bed. She came in, took some clothes from the cupboard, and dressed. We walked in the park, it was raining, we sat on the stone wall beneath the dripping trees without saying anything, and then we headed for home and had lunch. She filled the dishwasher, turned in, and lay listening to music, I wrote a few lines about Olav Duun. After half an hour I got up and went in to see Linda.

"Would you like some water or anything?" I said.

She turned her head slowly and looked at me.

"No, thank you," she said.

"What's the music?"

"I don't know."

There was a clatter in the kitchen.

"It's good you're listening to music," I said. "A few days ago you weren't up to it. You're making progress. Slowly but . . ."

I smiled. She looked at me.

"It's all going to be fine," I said.

She looked at me.

"I love you," I said.

She looked at me. Everything I said and did disappeared into that look.

She turned her head back and stared at the ceiling.

"I'll go and do a bit more writing," I said. "Back soon."

My mother traveled home, Ingrid traveled home, it was summer. Linda got up several times a day, read books, managed to do more with the children, and almost imperceptibly slipped back into a life she shared with us, and even if there was still something dejected and gloomy about her, there was a big difference, she was no longer outside the family, for which she had a few moments at the end of the day, but inside it. I went online and searched for a holiday home in Österlen. We had to get out of the apartment, we wouldn't manage a long journey though, so Österlen was perfect, it was only an hour away by car.

I found a vacancy and phoned the owner of the house, transferred some money into her account, rented a car for a week, and then we packed it to the gills and drove to the east coast. The town was called Hammar, the house stood beneath a steep hill; on the side away from us, out of sight, lay the sea. We parked the car outside the house, met the owner, who showed us the three small rooms we would be staying in, I unloaded the luggage, and then we climbed up the hill to have a look around. The sun was out and the sky was a cloudless blue. The hill was green, and from the top of it the sea that stretched out below us was glittering and misty. We clambered down the steep, thirty-meter-high, sandy slope. Linda didn't want to at first, but I held her hand and led her down. We sat next to each other on the beach, it stretched for kilometers in both directions, while the children paddled in the water, there wasn't a soul around.

Linda was silent, but she was here, she had walked here. The hill was too steep for the children and Linda to climb back up, so we trudged along the beach until the incline was gentle enough and then along a path up the grassy slope, climbed over a fence, and reached the top again. The countryside beneath us was completely flat, full of fields and farms as far as the eye could see. Seeing this and driving through it made me feel happy. Over the past year we had been here quite often, renting a car over the weekend, at first driving around, then we had started going to viewings. We were looking for a place that we could use on weekends and during school holidays. I loved this countryside, not just what was here with the rolling fields and long low houses, but also farther inland, the forests and lakes. It wasn't mine, it didn't exist in me, and perhaps that was the reason for the attraction.

We walked back down and had something to eat, the children were in bed, and Linda and I sat outside as the dusk thickened around us, and crows occupied a tree only a stone's throw away, they came flying in from all sides, there must have been more than a hundred of them, the whole tree was black, the air was filled with their shrill cries.

We went to the beach the next day and were there for a couple of hours before we drove to Simrishamn and had lunch. Beside the restaurant there was a real estate agent's, we went in and were given a brochure of all the houses that were for sale in the district. On the way home we drove to one, it was nice, but it stood alone in the middle of a plain and made a cold, desolate impression. Once home, we had a barbecue and then watched the World Cup before going to bed. This became the pattern for the week. Beach, town, viewing, barbecue, football.

On the third day, on our way to Simrishamn, Linda started laughing in the backseat.

I turned around quickly.

"Long time since I've heard that sound," I said.

On the fourth day, on our way home in the afternoon, we drove to a house in a village a few kilometers inland. As we came onto the road where it was supposed to be, I decided this place wouldn't work, it was obviously a residential area and we wanted a holiday home, alone and free, nothing that could remotely remind us of our subdivision hell.

We parked by the house, Linda said there was no point going in, there was nothing for us, I said we might as well take a peek while we were here.

We got out of the car and walked around the corner.

Christ, this is the one, I thought.

Two houses stood at right angles to each other, like a little L. There was also a third house, much smaller than the other two. Between the houses was a large well-established garden. It had to be at least fifty years old. In some places it was completely overgrown, but it was beautiful and perfect for the children as it had a variety of nooks and crannies that were connected in a labyrinthine way.

"What do you think?" I said, looking at Linda.

"It's lovely," she said.

"I think it's brilliant," I said. "Shall we buy it?"

"Maybe," she said. The slightly indifferent tone to her voice had more to do with her mental state than the house, I thought. John left his water pistol in the garden and that was a sign we'd have to go back. I arranged a viewing with the real estate agent and two days later we were there again. We said we would give it some thought. We drove home, were there for a couple of days, and then we flew to Norway and stayed with my mother for two weeks, and by then Linda was on the upswing, toward a lightness and joy, she talked a lot, laughed a lot, had lots of ideas and great energy, and it was fine, it wasn't too much.

I called the real estate agent and put in a bid for the house. There was a bidding round, I didn't give a damn about the money, I wanted the house, and two days later it was ours. We would take it over in October.

Earlier that summer Mom's cousin Hallstein had called her to ask if I would do a reading at an event they were having, I'd said yes because I had imagined a kind of book day in the old dairy that was now an art museum opposite Mom's house, with an audience of maybe sixty or seventy. The villages around Lake Jølstravannet were small and more than twenty kilometers from Førde, the center of the district, which was no great size either.

The day before the reading arrived, I hadn't given it a lot of thought, but hours before it was supposed to begin cars started parking outside. When I put on my shoes, walked around the house and crossed the road with the book in my hand, I ran straight into a large gathering of journalists and photographers. I was greeted by TV cameras and flashes. They had been waiting for me.

"What have you spent all the money on?" one asked.

"I've bought a washing machine, a tumble dryer, a dishwasher, and a TV," I said.

Hallstein shook my hand and led me in. The room was packed.

"Do I have time for a cigarette?" I said.

"Of course," he said.

The journalists flocked around me again. More questions. Behind them came Mom, Linda, and the children crossing the road. They stood at a distance watching what was going on. The children were wide-eyed. Heidi thought I was going to sing, she said. *Verdens Gang* took a photo of the kids without me seeing and printed it in the paper the following day. I called Elisabeth and asked if they were allowed to do that. I couldn't do anything myself because I had written about other people and so I no longer had any rights as far as my own life was concerned. I could accept this, but I didn't like it. Elisabeth called back, she had spoken to *Verdens Gang*, they had promised never to use the photo again. Mom had bought the papers, wanting to see what they said, and Vanja caught sight of the photo of herself, she was angry, she looked ugly with glasses on, she said. You're the prettiest girl in the world, I said, but to no avail, her eyes narrowed and didn't light up until all thoughts of newspapers and TV dissolved in the real world down on the little beach where they swam in the water on their inflatable dolphins.

The previous evening I had done the reading and talked a little about my relationship with Jølster, where I'd written parts of all my books and which also came up in everything I'd written. While I was talking I saw Vanja standing at the back looking at me. Hallstein asked a few questions, then I signed books and walked back across the road where those members of my mother's family who were there had gathered.

It had been absurd, I had been there every summer for nigh on twenty years and no one had ever been interested in what I wrote or said, and then all of a sudden the place was bristling with cameras the second I crossed the road.

Linda and I drove up into the mountains the next day to spend the night in a cabin. The river in the middle of the valley, the mountains on either side, the white peaks under the gray sky, the water that was perhaps three kilometers away. Not a soul around, just Linda and me sitting at the table outside the cabin, the dense forest stretching upward, spruce and fir trees.

I told her about the summer before I started at the Writing Academy, when I had been in that very place for a week on my own trying to write. I told her this was where Grandpa had courted Grandma for the first time. The sun set, we sat outside the cabin chatting in the dusk, surrounded by the faint roar of the waterfall high up in the forest.

Linda had been captivated by the nature in Vestland from the first moment she ever saw it and had almost fainted at the beauty of the fjords and mountains; she had been visiting my mother to produce a radio program about the seventeenth of May. She talked about it now. They had seen porpoises in the fjord, that had been a good sign according to Mom, and they had seen deer in the forest, that had been a good sign, too. She had been pregnant with Vanja then, but hadn't known. Anfinn, who was married to Grandma's sister Alvdis, was the son of a horse dealer and as compact and powerful as a bear, and he had told her about the time when he went hunting whales and had shown her all sorts of weird and wonderful objects he had kept from those days. We had visited them every summer since, they'd been at both Vanja's and John's christenings, but that winter Anfinn had died. It was their cabin we were borrowing. I told Linda about another of Grandma's sisters, Borghild, also dead now, who had known all there was to know about everyone in the family, both those who were alive now and those who weren't. And how Tore and I had written a screenplay here and we had gone down to visit Borghild, and she stared at Tore through a magnifying glass, which made her eye enormous.

It was precisely this countryside I had described in *A Time for Everything* and where I had set the story of Cain and Abel and Noah. The mountains before Ålhus in Jølster and Sørbøvåg by Mount Lihesten in Ytre Sogn. My maternal grandparents were in it, and Linda's mother and Linda and Yngve and I, however all with biblical names I had taken from a family tree and no longer remembered.

I had known this landscape for as long as I could remember, but it had never been mine, I had never belonged here. Perhaps because I demanded too much from what it meant to belong. I didn't feel I belonged to Kristiansand either and although I related to the countryside on the island of Tromøya, I never felt I had the right to call it my own, we were newcomers. And I had missed that all my life, coming from one place, belonging to a place, being able to call a place home. Geir used to say the definition of home was a place where no one could deny you access. And then we used to discuss whether "Hell is home" or "Home is hell." Connecting home with a landscape and not a state of mind was my most reactionary feature, but it was also the most deeply rooted.

The following day we drove into the valley behind Mom's house with the kids, parked the car where the road ends, and walked until they couldn't take any more. We stopped, had a bite to eat and drank some coffee, and then we hiked back. They had grown up in Malmö, unused to mountains and waterfalls, yet they took it all as a matter of course, although there was also something inadequate and helpless about them as they stood beneath the immensity of the mountains and the depth of the sky.

Linda began to feel depressed again, she talked less and less, by the time we visited Jon Olav and Liv at the end of the holiday she was hardly speaking. On the way home to Malmö we dropped in on my old friend Ole and his girlfriend Brita in Bergen, I hadn't seen them since I moved to Sweden, the only thing to detract from the joy of talking to Ole again was that Linda was feeling low. But she was still a long way from how she had been. A few hours before the plane was due to depart I called for a taxi and the woman on the switchboard inquired whether I was Knausgaard, the author. I said I was and hated myself for it. The taxi was a minibus, which the children considered exciting, having it all to ourselves. At Flesland Airport people looked at me, some came over to say something about my books. One of them, a woman in her late fifties, said she'd been to all the places I had described in Sørland.

"How big Vanja and Heidi are!" she said, and laughed.

"Yes," I said.

"But I won't pester you anymore. Have a good journey home. I suppose you're going to Malmö, aren't you?"

I nodded.

"Bye," I said with a smile.

Vanja looked up at me.

"Do you know her, Dad?" she said.

"No," I said. "Never seen her before."

"But how did she know who we were?" she said.

"I've written a book about us," I said.

"You've written a book about us?" she said.

"Yes."

"What's in it?"

"All sorts of strange things," I said. "You'll have to read it when you're older."

We passed through security, people stared at us. Once through, we went to a Narvesen kiosk to buy the children something for the flight. My face was everywhere. On the new paperbacks, which I hadn't seen, Thomas's photo of my face was on the cover.

"Dad, that's you!" Heidi said, pointing.

"Oh it is. What do you know," I said.

Once home, I got back to work. Vanja would be starting school in a few weeks and had been given permission to attend the nursery school until then. We had promised her she would have her own room when she started school and as the only extra room we had was my study, I'd moved my desk and all my books into a living room. That was as far as I'd got. The room had to be painted, a desk, bed, and wardrobe needed to be bought, as well as pictures she could hang on the wall. The plan was to paint one weekend and then go to IKEA the next. Vanja was nervous it wouldn't be ready, but I assured her that everything would be ready the night before she started.

Linda's depression lifted after a few days and everything was as usual at home. She said she would take the children to school and pick them up so that I could work straight through. I was happy about that. I got up at six in the morning, went right to the living room, closed the doors, and knuckled down, barely hearing the others getting up and leaving, I surfaced to say hi to them when they returned, ate with them, and worked until ten.

Linda had a friend from Stockholm staying, they had known each other for fifteen years or so, from when Linda worked at the Stadsteater in Stockholm. Her friend was a stage director and had recently made a short film from a script Linda had written. She had her one-year-old son with her and they planned to stay for a week. Locked in the living room from morning till night, I hardly saw them. An autumn publication was still a possibility if I hit the deadline.

"She's absolutely fantastic," Linda said about her friend one evening when we had a few minutes alone. "She gets stuff done. When she decides to do something, it always happens. That's the exact opposite of me. But we can help each other. We've already come up with lots of ideas. It's wonderful having her here."

"I'm so pleased," I said.

"And you can work as much as you like at the same time," she said.

"Yes," I said. "You're generous to me. Don't you go thinking I don't realize that."

One afternoon, on my way to check my e-mails in the bedroom, I met them in the hall, they had been out shopping.

"They were all on sale," Linda said. "And I didn't buy a lot."

"Relax," I said. "I didn't say a word."

"When I'm with her," she said, nodding toward her friend, "I feel totally secure. She knows me so well. She knows exactly where the limits are, what's good or bad for me."

Her friend smiled.

"Linda charms the pants off all the shop assistants. Once I had to leave the shop, I was so embarrassed," she said.

Linda laughed.

"Was that why you left? Really?" she said, and looked at me. "Nothing expensive, nothing over-the-top. Would you like to see?"

"No, I can take a look later," I said, and went into my study.

The place was a mess again, the living-room floor was almost totally covered with toys, clothes, and towels, the same was true of the children's room and the hall. Of course I couldn't say anything, it was my responsibility as well, and normally I would have thought the mess can stay where it is until we have a blitz, because I had to work, I couldn't waste even a couple of hours, but when we had visitors it was different, I was ashamed of the way we lived.

I said so to Linda.

"Don't give her a thought," she said. "She's used to mess. It doesn't bother her *at all*. And we're working too. We have lots of plans. And they will come to fruition. She always achieves what she sets out to do. She's so good for me."

There was a tone she had that always emerged when she was on a high, but which in some way or other was more obvious now. A breezy, noncommittal tone, which brought with it an infantile side, not much, just a touch, but enough for me to find it irritating, for at these moments I wasn't in communication with her, we were not operating from the same base. Sometimes I told her, then she just smiled and said she understood what I meant and she would try to be more present. When she was growing up she always had an element of the adult child in her, the child who saw through adults and retained her composure amid their chaotic lives, I'd gathered from what she told me, but especially from what she had written, where the adult child was a recurring figure.

Now she was an adult, and it was as though the opposite was happening: she wasn't assuming an adult role as a child but a child's role as an adult. Oh, it wasn't so much in evidence, only a tiny, tiny bit, something in her had stopped caring about any consequences, was no longer so careful about what was said, whether it was true or not, small dislocations of reality to make her appear funnier, grander, more entertaining. If she said something in front of the children that they shouldn't know or hear and I reproved her, she immediately corrected herself: Dad's right, that was silly of me.

I hadn't been aware of this element in her personality, I had never seen it until this spring, it suddenly emerged and it wasn't good for us because then I had to assume a role toward her, I became the person who corrected and set limits, and that was the last thing on this earth I wanted to do. There could be days, perhaps a week, when she was as light as light itself, and then it was gone from her character, like a comet leaving the firmament. Then she became "normal" again, then she became "Linda." It was easier to relate to the periods when she sank into the darkness because it didn't touch the person she was, we could communicate even though she was depressed. She was distraught that this was how she was, continually being raised to the heights and dumped back down, it made it almost impossible for her to work, for example, and forced her to go to places she didn't want to be.

I was, like Linda, pleased that she had her friend staying, she was a few years older than me, I imagined, and a responsible adult who really liked Linda and had seen enough in her life to appreciate the unusual qualities she possessed. In all the mess they had a really good time, I heard them chatting and laughing together, discussing and planning. Linda did everything with the children, trying to make up for the time when she had been so depressed she hadn't been able to do anything, I supposed.

Some slightly disturbing incidents took place. Twice Linda talked about me to her friend, she didn't know I was within earshot and would never have said what she did otherwise, the tone was confidential and the confidences were addressed to her friend not to me. Above all else I hated other people talking about me, so that was unpleasant in itself, but it wasn't disturbing. The disturbing element was that she didn't know I could hear. The first time was in the hall outside our bedroom while I was in bed on the other side of the door, actually she knew that, how could she possibly have said something in secret about me in a loud voice three meters away from where I was? The second time was similar, they went to the balcony, I was in the second living room, I heard Linda tell her friend in a loud voice to leave everything where it was, it was Karl Ove's problem. It didn't matter that she said that, it mattered that she said it as if they were completely alone. She had begun to ignore the consequences of her actions.

The next morning, when I was working in one of the living rooms, I suddenly heard a din in the other. Linda had put on a record. It was a quarter to six, and she had turned the volume up loud. "Forever Young," the old eighties hit, she was playing it at full blast at an unearthly hour.

I ran out to the stereo and turned it off.

"What are you doing? Do you know what time it is?"

She looked at me.

"Almost six. Relax. It wasn't on that loud."

She looked at me as though she were a teenager and I were the most narrow-minded middle-class parent she had ever seen. And perhaps she was right about that.

"Why are you up so early anyway? Didn't you go to bed late last night?"

"Yes. I couldn't sleep. I have so much on my mind. There are a few projects I've started. And you get angry when I lie awake and toss and turn, and then the children come in and want a glass of water or to sleep with us."

"I don't get angry. I'm asleep."

"You sleep through everything. I don't. And then you go to the kitchen to eat in the middle of the night and slam doors."

"But can't you lie down here, in the living room, at night? Alone? Then you might be able to sleep."

"The children find me anyway," she said. "They don't want you at night. Just me."

"That's not my fault, is it?" I said.

She looked at me and rolled her eyes.

"Do you know what it's like not to be able to sleep?" she said.

"No," I said. "I'm afraid I don't."

This was one of our most done-to-death topics of conversation.

"I have to work now," I said. "Couldn't you try to sleep a bit more? At least until Johnny wakes up?"

"Yes, I suppose I can," she said as though she were doing me a favor.

She went to bed late, got up early, and was still full of energy. She glowed with it. I walked past the kitchen at nine in the evening, she was sitting there with a black bowler hat on her head and wearing some clothes I had never seen before. She looked like she was in *Cabaret* or some musical or other. She smiled at her friend and when she noticed I was there turned to me with glittering eyes.

I went to bed and fell asleep at once, I had worked all day, then woke up to a bang, it was Linda coming in.

"Can't you be a bit quieter?" I said. "I was actually asleep."

"Can you believe this guy?" she said. "That's the best I've heard yet."

She flounced back out and slammed the door hard.

I got up and rushed after her. She was lying beside Vanja in her bed. I stopped in the doorway. She looked at me with eyes that shone white in the darkness.

"Come and lie down, Linda. I didn't mean what I said. I was asleep and woke up a bit abruptly."

"No," she said. "I'm sleeping here tonight."

"Come on. Come and sleep with me."

"No."

When I got up the next morning she was sitting in the kitchen with a cup of tea in front of her. It was five o'clock.

"Haven't you slept?" I said.

"No," she said. "I'm so tired now. I'm dying for some sleep."

"I can understand that," I said.

"I have an appointment with the doctor today," she said. "Maybe she'll give me a stronger sleeping tablet."

"Yes," I said.

"Will you come with me?"

"Is it vital?"

She looked at me.

I nodded.

"Of course I'll go with you. When is it?"

"At eleven."

"Okay," I said.

We set off at a little before half past ten. In our small covered entrance she lit a cigarette, looked at me, and slowly blew out the smoke.

"Ready to go?" she said.

I nodded.

She strode out, I had to walk almost as fast as I could to keep up. Her face was determined, closed, her strides quick.

Along the pedestrian street, over the bridge, and into the little park on the right.

"I've been thinking about something," she said, lighting another cigarette. "It might be a good idea to go to the hospital just for one night. They can give me some stronger medicine. And I'd have peace and quiet there. No children. What do you think about that? It'll be like going for a health cure. I'd get food and a bed and someone would make sure I sleep."

"Is it that bad?" I asked. "Are you so tired?"

"I long for sleep so much it's unreal," she said.

"Then do it," I said. "I'm sure it'll be good."

"I think so," she said.

We were a bit early and had a coffee at a 7-Eleven nearby. She was still as determined, I was reminded of the image she often used when she wrote, she was a soldier. Black leather jacket, black jeans, black shoes. A small black backpack on her back. Wan, determined face.

"So you can just tell the children I'm sleeping at Jenny's tonight," she said.

"Yes, that's probably best," I said.

Her friend was leaving that afternoon, so it was good timing.

"I suppose we'd better go now," I said.

The doctor came out the moment we sat down in the waiting room. She radiated the same qualities she had the first time I met her. Friendliness, caring, impersonal professionalism. I was also the same, I assumed, but Linda was a very different person. Then everything had been slow, every movement an effort. Now she was bristling with energy and impatience when she sat down. Nothing could go fast enough. She started talking long before the doctor had taken a seat.

"You said there would always be someone here I could talk to," she said. "But I called and you were on holiday. And there was no one else to talk to! That's not good enough! I needed you! I really needed you!"

She began to cry.

I didn't understand a thing and looked at her, then at the doctor, who was taking notes on her pad.

"I'm very sorry about that," the doctor said. "There was a misunderstanding. You should've been given my colleague to talk to."

"That's not good enough," Linda said. "I've been so frightened."

She sobbed.

"I've been so frightened!" she repeated.

The doctor looked at her without saying anything.

"How are you?" she asked at length.

"Things are moving faster and faster," Linda said. "It's as though soon I won't be able to hang on, if you understand what I mean."

"Are you sleeping?"

"No. I hardly sleep. Can I be admitted to the hospital and have some sleeping tablets? For one night only."

The doctor nodded.

"I think that's a good idea," she said. "I can sort it out right away, so that you can go straight there, if you like."

"I just have to go home and pack first."

"Of course. But it's a good idea, Linda. I think it'll do you good."

I tried to understand what was going on as they talked. Why did she burst into tears? She hadn't said a word to me about her fears and hadn't shown any of what she was showing now.

The doctor told Linda which ward she would be in. She was given a slip of paper with the address on it. They set a new appointment, which was also put on a piece of paper.

"If there are any problems, ask them to call me," she said. "But I'll arrange everything from this end, so they know you'll be coming."

We rose to our feet, shook her hand, and went down to the street.

Linda was happy again.

"I'll come home tomorrow morning. The children won't even notice I've been away."

"That's not a problem," I said.

We hurried through the streets, she was excited, I was bewildered but in a way also reassured, perhaps because of the way the doctor had reacted to her. It had been accepted without question that she could sleep one night in the hospital and surely that was how it should be.

Linda packed a few things into a backpack, said goodbye to her friend and me, I didn't need to accompany her, she would take a taxi, then she was in the elevator with a smile on her face, and gone.

I started to clean up the apartment. Linda's friend helped me. We had never actually talked, now we did. I told her what Linda had said, about her house being a mess and how that didn't bother her. She laughed and said that was probably how Linda would have liked it to be, but she was only projecting her own desires onto her. Once Linda had visited her in Stockholm, she said, many years ago, then she had been as high as she was now, she'd taken a bath with her friend's little daughter and more or less demanded to be treated like her.

What I didn't understand was how she could accept that. She'd accepted it at the time and had accepted it here. But this clearly wasn't Linda. And I refused to give any room to what wasn't Linda. I didn't want to see it. But her friend obviously didn't have the same demands for authenticity.

We worked our way through the rooms as we talked about Linda's mother and father, me and my father. She knew something I didn't, I thought. Everything related to Linda's excesses was beyond me, it was part of the unknown, and I felt prejudiced, limited, and very, very ordinary.

When the place was clean and tidy, she packed her things, lifted up her son, who had been playing on his own while we were busy and had hardly got in our way, put him in his stroller, and headed for the train station.

It was a strange feeling to be alone. Usually I liked it, but now Linda wasn't out somewhere, she had been admitted to the hospital, and for some reason or other this made me feel lonely.

For the first time it struck me that usually I wasn't alone, I always had Linda there.

I went through the fridge, tossing out everything that had passed its sell-by date, and I did the same in the cupboards. Then I took out a bag of chicken fillets from the freezer, left them to thaw on a plate, emptied the dishwasher, and had a smoke on the balcony before going to pick up the children. It was Friday, our ice-cream day, and I took them to the café in the mall as usual.

"Mommy's not at home," I told them. "She's sleeping at Jenny's tonight."

"Why?" Vanja asked, putting the little orange plastic spoon and its heap of blue ice cream with thin red stripes into her mouth while studying me.

"She's working," I said.

"Is she coming home tomorrow?" Vanja asked.

"Yes."

"What are we doing tomorrow?"

"I don't know," I said. "What would you like to do?"

"Go to the park," Heidi said.

"No, that's boring," Vanja said.

"It is not," Heidi said.

"We can do that," I said. "But we don't need to make up our minds until tomorrow."

"Carnival," John said.

I smiled.

"You don't miss a trick, do you," I said.

"Yes, the carnival," Vanja said.

"Yes. Me, too," Heidi said.

"That's decided then," I said.

After I had put them to bed the peculiar feeling of loneliness returned. I watched some TV, retired early, woke up to sounds from the kitchen, which turned out to be John banging around, he had dragged a chair to the counter, turned on the water, and filled the sink with washing-up liquid.

I made him some breakfast, saw to Heidi when she got up, and last of all Vanja. It was Saturday, their TV morning, while I sat beside them in a chair reading the newspapers. At half past seven the phone rang. It was Linda.

"How was it?" I asked.

"It was fantastic," she said. "I've never slept so well. And they've been so nice to me. There are some fantastic people here. How's it going at home?"

"Fine. When will you be home, do you think?"

"Ah, that's what I was going to tell you. The doctors here say they'd like to keep me in for one more night. To get the best possible effect. I don't think that's such a stupid idea. Then I'll be able to rest properly."

"Yes, that sounds wise," I said. "But what should I tell the children? It might seem a bit odd if you're at Jenny's for two nights and don't come home in between."

"Can't you just tell them I'm in the hospital?"

"Yeah, but then they'd want to know why."

"Tell them the truth. I'm here to get some sleep."

"Okay. I'll do that."

"I love you so much, Karl Ove."

"I love you too," I said. "You enjoy the day, okay?"

"Okay. Give the kids a kiss from me."

I pressed off and went in to see them. All three sat staring at the TV without taking any notice of me.

"Mommy just called," I said. "She won't be home until tomorrow."

"Why not?" Vanja said.

"You know she's been sleeping badly the past few nights, don't you? Now she's in the hospital so that she can get some help. She'll be there tonight."

"Can we visit her?"

"Well, it's only one night. She'll be home tomorrow. Let's go to the carnival, shall we?"

Folkets Park played a major role in the lives of our three children. It had a big pond, in which they splashed around and paddled during the summer and on which they skated during the winter. And a large terrarium where the parrot in the Pippi Longstocking film was spending the autumn of its life, plus a few motionless crocodiles. And a little ice-cream stall and a mini zoo with rabbits and pigs. As well as a riding center, where Vanja sat on a horse for some months of her young life, and a wonderful big playground. Not forgetting a café with a dance floor and a rock 'n' roll club. But the biggest attraction of all was the carnival. It was second rate, but the children couldn't see that and whenever we went to the park in the summer months we had to agree before starting out that there wouldn't be any discussion of the carnival today. This day was one of the few when I didn't say that. Instead I said that they could each choose three rides. If there was the slightest protest we would go home, was that understood? Yes, it was. Standing outside the entrance to the fair they would have promised me anything under the sun.

"I want to go on the mewy-go-wound!" Vanja said.

"Merrrrry-go-rrrrround," Heidi said.

Vanja flew at her, I had to grab her arms and lift her up.

"Come on, let's go for a walk and have a look around before we decide. Who wants to go on the caterpillar roller coaster?"

"Me!" John said.

"Not me," Vanja said.

"What about the bumper cars?"

"Can I?" Vanja said.

"Yes. But you'll have to go on your own. I have to look after Heidi and John. Do you dare?"

She nodded. And immediately she drove around the oval track with an expression that was part terror and part joy. Afterward we all had a ride on the caterpillar. And then I drove one of the veteran cars on rails with John while Vanja and Heidi stood watching. Finally they got on two separate merry-go-rounds. Once that was done we walked to the playground, where they ran into two friends from class. I stood with the parents for a while, they kept an eye on the three of them while I went for a coffee, on my return we talked a bit about football, the man from one family supported Hammerby, which had sunk down the table like a lead weight after winning Allsvenskan, the Swedish premier league, the previous year. I liked him but couldn't meet his eyes, he was mentioned in Book 2 in a way that was not uncontroversial. He congratulated me on its success and I realized he had not been curious enough to read the Norwegian version anyway.

I spent half an hour trying to encourage the children to make a move homeward.

Vanja was unusually quiet.

Not far from Hemköp I found out what was bothering her.

"Why can't I say *r*, Dad?" she said. "After all, Heidi can. And I'm bigger than her."

"I couldn't say *r* when I was little either," I said.

"When did you learn then?" she said.

"At about your age," I lied.

"I don't want to start school," she said. "I want to stay in nursery school."

"Of course you do," I said. "But when you start school, you won't want to stop there either. It's the same as with nursery school. You're a big girl now."

We did some shopping, then wended our way home, they watched a film, had pizza in the evening, and then took a bath. As I was about to tuck them in a chorus for Mommy rose.

"She'll be back tomorrow," I said.

"Do you promise?" Vanja said.

"I promise," I said.

The next morning I was woken by the phone ringing. It was six o'clock, I saw, and hurried to pick it up.

"Hi, it's me," Linda said. "Good morning."

"Hi," I said.

"How's it going at home? What did you do yesterday?"

"We went to the carnival," I said.

"What are they doing now?"

"They're asleep."

"Oh, right, it's still pretty early."

"It is. How are you? When are you coming home?"

"It's going very well here. I just need a few things from home. Especially my laptop."

"I asked you when you were going to come home."

"I don't know. We're taking one day at a time."

"You're not coming back today?"

"They say I ought to stay here for another week. Then we'll see."

I said nothing.

"There's Nanna. Hi, Nanna. She's fantastic. Strict but good. Motherly. Well, you know. Solid as a rock whatever happens. She's on nights."

"Linda, are you going to be there for another week?"

"I think so. It's voluntary, though, so they can't keep me. If I want to go, I can. But it's so good for me here. It's exactly what I need. A few days of peace and quiet. It doesn't matter, does it?"

"No, of course it doesn't."

"I'm so hungry. I'm waiting for breakfast. That's why I called. I get a bit restless. If only I had my laptop, then at least I could write."

"Right," I said.

"Now they're bringing breakfast. I'll call you back. Bye, my prince."

I turned the phone off and went into the bedroom, lay down on the bed. From the children's room I heard a strange sound. A few seconds passed before I realized what it was. Someone was jerking the door handle up and down as fast as they could. I got up. Someone was knocking on the door and shouting Dad! Dad! I opened it. It was John. He had tears in his eyes.

"Couldn't you open the door?" I said.

"No!" he said.

"Come on. Let's have a little breakfast."

I was frozen inside as I sat down and watched him eat. I hadn't understood a thing. I had actually assumed she was there to sleep. Like a naïve child. I had imagined they would administer some strong medicine in slightly more controlled circumstances and she

1201

would come down from her high as soon as she'd had a good night's sleep. God knows where I'd got that idea from, but that was what I had imagined.

She had been admitted to the psychiatric hospital, she was all alone there, and I had barely considered that.

I was her husband, for Christ's sake. Her closest next of kin. I had to go there, I had to talk to the doctors, and I had to see her. Just to let her know I was there for her, for her and for the children.

What an idiot I had been.

I was utterly brain-dead.

But how could I go there? I couldn't take the children with me. Obviously that wouldn't work. And I didn't know anyone in town who could take care of them. Or yes, I did, but they had their own kids to look after. And I didn't want to ask anything of anyone.

John had lost interest in food, now he was pushing a cornflake through a pool of milk on the wax cloth.

"Are you full?" I said.

"Yes," he said. "Thank you."

"You're going to do well, with such wonderful manners," I said, lifting him out of the chair. Removed his diaper and threw it into the bin under the sink. "Do you want to be in the buff for a while?"

He nodded and trotted off into the living room. I found the children's channel on the TV, went into the other living room, and phoned Linda.

She answered at once.

"Hi, *Hem*," she said.

She used to say that because *hem*, Swedish for home, came up on her phone whenever I rang.

"Hi," I said. "I should've been up there to see you by now, to talk to the doctors and so on, but now I'm wondering whether it would be all right if I came early tomorrow morning. Right after dropping the kids off."

"Yes, of course," she said. "They'll be pleased to meet you. I've told everyone what a wonderfully handsome husband I have."

"I'm sorry about all of this, Linda."

"There's nothing to be sorry about. I'm absolutely fine. It's like being in a mountain hotel. And I get proper sleeping tablets. I pass out like a clubbed seal."

"That's good. You have to sleep and rest. I'll see you tomorrow. Call me if you feel like it. I'll take my cell if we go anywhere."

The chill in my guts didn't leave me that day, it returned at regular intervals.

I was Linda's closest relative, I was her husband, and she was alone in a psychiatric hospital and I hadn't lifted a finger to help her. She had been there for two days now. With no help, no support, all on her own.

As soon as Vanja got up, she asked me when Mommy was coming home.

"She just called. She said she has to stay in the hospital for a while yet."

"But you promised!"

"I know. But she's there to sleep the right way. Do you remember when she was so tired this spring and slept all the time? Now it's the opposite, now she can't sleep at all. It's not a problem, but she has to be there for a few more days. But do you know what?"

"What?"

"We'll visit her in the hospital tomorrow. That'll be nice."

"Is that definite?"

"Yes, of course."

After I had dropped off the children at school the next morning, I walked the few hundred meters to the big hospital complex. I had been there only once before, that was when John was born, almost three years ago to the day. Then I'd rushed home to get Vanja and Heidi, and they had laughed and fooled around in the hotel room for relatives, patted John's head and placed a rubber dinosaur on top of it, which I took photos of, and they remembered for that very reason.

Linda had given me directions, which I'd written down on a Post-it. It was a long block reminiscent of the sixties, right at the end of the complex. I walked in, took the elevator up, and rang the bell outside the door, which was locked. While I was waiting a woman came down the stairs. She looked at me.

"Aren't you a writer?" she said.

"Yes," I said.

"You wrote *Min kamp*, didn't you? Imagine seeing you here."

"Yes," I said. "Nice to meet you."

The door opened, a nurse stared at me. She was wearing a white uniform.

"Hi," I said. "My name's Karl Ove Knausgaard. I'd like to visit Linda."

"Hi," she said. "Come with me. She's over here."

I followed her down the colorless corridor.

I had worked in a ward like this when I was eighteen, and I recognized the style. A refectory, a cage-like office with a big window, a recreation room, a long corridor with doors on both sides. Gray linoleum floor. Furniture with the unmistakable imprint of institution.

Four or five patients sat watching TV. Trembling, taciturn, pale. A couple paced to and fro, filled with a nervous, restless, aggressive energy. They were young; the ones watching TV were middle-aged and old. Linda came out of one room. She lit up when she saw me, gave me a big hug and a kiss on the lips.

"This is my husband!" she said loudly to everyone there.

"Well, you do have a handsome man, Linda!" a lively old lady called out.

"He's the best writer in Norway," Linda said. "It's absolutely true."

The patients sitting there, disabled or slumped, all with dark, vacant eyes, looked across at us.

"You should see my room," Linda said. "It's so cozy."

She led me into a room. There were two beds, on one sat an overweight woman; she got up as soon as she saw us and left. Linda said her name and smiled.

"This is where I live," she said, extending her arms. "But I need a few things from home. I've written a list. Or perhaps you can bring them with you next time? Look there!" she said, pointing to the wall where two drawings hung.

"Two twins drew them," she said. "They remind me of myself when I was young. They're twenty at most. Princesses of the night. They don't sleep either. They're acrobats. They're absolutely terrific."

She pressed against me.

"Isn't it cozy here?" she said.

"Yes," I said, taking a step toward the window. "But I was going to talk to the senior nurse. Don't you think it would be best to do that right away?"

"They'll come and get you," she said, patting the duvet. "Sit down."

I sat down beside her. She put her arm around me and wanted to kiss me. I leaned away.

"I'm not in the mood."

"Never mind," she said. "I understand. Look here."

She got up and took me by the hand to the window. She wanted me to see all the ornaments on the windowsill. Porcelain dogs, porcelain cats. A photo of Vanja, Heidi, and John. A Robyn CD, stood upright to show the cover, some stones, some toy rings.

"And that's my cuddly toy. A Moomin. I cover him with the duvet every night before I go to bed."

She pointed to a little box on the floor where a cloth figure lay.

There was a knock at the door. The same nurse who had opened the door for me escorted us to the office. There were four people inside. Linda and I sat down on chairs between them. The doctor responsible for Linda, as far as I could judge, wearing a brown suit, extremely jovial, asked her some questions in broken Swedish. One of the others was also dressed in normal clothes, the remaining two wore white uniforms. Linda answered all the questions with wit, in detail, and at great length. They smiled, all of them, I could see she was a kind of favorite.

"There's just one thing I *have* to say," Linda said. "I know this won't sound good because it'll give the impression that I'm an elitist, or something like that, but if you ask me how I'm getting on it's an inescapable fact that some of the nurses in the ward are so . . . well, I'll have to be careful now, but they're a bit on the slow side, they don't always understand things right away, and that can be wearing for me. I'm a writer, I do radio, I'm a professional woman, and I'm used to a certain level, if you see what I mean. But there's practically no one to talk to here."

I felt a strong urge to duck, I didn't, I retained my composure and watched her as she spoke.

"It is as it is, Linda," the doctor said. "But now your husband's here. He may have a few questions to ask. Do you?"

"Two," I said. "And they're of a practical nature. We have three children. They have to see Linda of course. How shall we do it? I'm not so keen for them to come here."

"You could meet in the park," the doctor suggested. "That would be all right, wouldn't it? Otherwise there's nothing to stop you, Linda, going out every other day, or every day, and going home. Perhaps not today, perhaps not tomorrow, but in the foreseeable future."

"And that's my second question. How long is she going to be here, do you think?"

I looked at Linda as I said that, it didn't feel good to refer to her as "she," but I couldn't find a way around it. She just smiled as if to say, Look what a clever husband I have.

"It's impossible to say, my dear man," the doctor said, getting up. "But we'd like to stabilize you a bit, Linda, before you go home."

"The medicine isn't working," Linda said, looking at me. "From what I understand I'm being given big doses, but they're not working at all."

"Well, there's a lot of energy in you."

"Okay," I said. "We're not talking days then?"

"Probably not," the doctor said. "Now I'm going on holiday, so there'll be another doctor coming tomorrow. But she's even better than me, so that won't be a problem."

"Are you going on holiday?" Linda asked.

"Yes," he said.

"And just as I was beginning to like you," she said.

He laughed, shook hands, and the whole entourage followed him out.

"I wanted to talk to you," the senior nurse said. "Could you come to my office for a moment?"

"Yes, of course," I said, looking at Linda.

"I'll wait in the room," she said.

I accompanied her to the office.

"Do you need any help?" she said. "You have a right to some social help. Someone could go to your house, do the shopping, cook and clean for you."

"No," I said. "No, no, no. I don't need it. Absolutely not. I'm fine."

"Okay," she said. "If you should change your mind, let me know. How's it going with the children?"

"Fine."

"Do they know she's here?"

"Sort of. We've told them she's in the hospital to sleep."

"Okay. I think it's a good idea for you to take them to the park and meet Linda there, as we mentioned."

"Is today okay? Actually I've promised them they would see her today."

"That's fine. Come here after school. When do you pick them up?"

"At three. No, I'm wrong, half past three. So if we say a quarter to four here?"

"I'll make sure she's waiting at the entrance."

"Thank you," I said, and went to Linda's room, knocked, and

opened the door. Linda came toward me and took my hand, pulled me to the bed.

"What do you think of the doctor? Isn't he great? Eastern European. Hungarian or Romanian or something like that. Shame he's going on holiday. Typical."

She looked at me. I bit my lip to stop myself from crying, got up, and stood in front of the window.

"Karl Ove, shall we go out for a cigarette?" she said.

"Sure," I said. "Okay."

"They've got coffee here. Visitors have to pay five kronor, but I'll see if I can get you a free one."

"I don't mind paying," I said.

She filled two cups, poured milk in one, called for a nurse.

"We're going out for a cigarette," she said. "Open up, open up."

We walked along the corridor with him, to the opposite end of the building from where I had arrived, he unlocked the door and we took the elevator down, came to a paved area with a shed where two old men were smoking.

Linda stopped and lit up. I did too.

"I'm so happy to be with you," she said. "You make me so happy, Karl Ove."

She stood up on her toes and we kissed. She clung to me, I took a step back, she let go, glancing down the road to where a vehicle was coming.

"I'm well looked after here," she said. "Don't you think?"

"Yes," I said. "But you mustn't stay too long."

"No," she said.

An ambulance drove slowly past.

"They're in and out all night," she said. "It's exciting."

"Mm," I said.

I watched the ambulance, she held my face and straightened it as if to say I had to look at her.

Our eyes met. She stretched up and kissed me.

"I'll have to go soon," I said.

"Yes, I know you have a lot to do," she said.

"But we'll see you this afternoon," I said. "I'll bring the children and we can meet outside."

"It's nice sitting in the park," she said.

"We can buy ice cream," I said.

"Yes!" she said.

"Bye," I said.

"Bye," she said.

As I turned I welled up. I cried all the way home, almost blinded by tears, but when I was at home, sitting on the balcony and smoking, my eyes were dry. A situation had arisen and it had to be dealt with.

I was booked to do a four-day reading tour around Gothenburg, I would have to cancel that. I had lots of gigs at the Oslo Book Festival, I would have to cancel them. I had two spots at the Louisiana Literature Festival, I would have to cancel them. And then I would have to call Ingrid and Mom and ask if they could come to stay for a while, not because I needed any help, but because I wanted the children to have someone else apart from me. Anything that would divert attention from Linda's absence was good.

I went inside and called Ingrid. I told her how the land lay, that Linda was ill and I would have to cancel everything for the next few weeks.

"It wouldn't be possible to arrange to do all the jobs on one day and organize a babysitter for that day?"

"Yes," I said. "That should work."

I e-mailed Stefan at Nordstedts and asked if he could cancel the arrangements I had. No problem. I e-mailed the organizer in Gothenburg and said I would have to cancel the tour. They e-mailed back and said it was fine, but couldn't I make one of the days, the one in Gothenburg? They had already advertised it and would prefer not to cancel. I wrote back and said that was fine. I didn't contact Louisiana, in fact I wanted to do that one, and Copenhagen was so close I could travel back in the evening.

I called Ingrid again, she was happy to come and help, but not before the end of the week. I called Mom, she would manage to get away somehow and come down too, but probably not before the following week.

Heidi ran toward me as I entered the gates to the school.

"Are we going to see Mommy?" she shouted.

"Yes, we are," I said.

John saw me, pulled himself off the wooden tricycle, and ran over too.

I lifted him up, put him down, and turned to the staff.

"How has it been today?" I said.

"It's been fine. The older children have been to the theater."

"Oh that's right," I said.

"John slept for an hour, more or less. But it was almost impossible to wake him today."

"He gets up very early," I said.

Vanja was on the swing with Katinka. I walked over to them. Heidi came along, holding my hand.

"We're going to see Mommy!" she cried.

"I know," Vanja said.

"Are you coming?" I said.

"I just have to get a drawing," she said, and ran inside.

I put John in the stroller in the meantime. I wondered what she had drawn. When Linda had been depressed Vanja had drawn a little girl and a mother with a heart between them and written, "I love you, Mama." This time it was a house with a tree beside it and a flower bed, drawn in the way I remembered from my own childhood.

We walked up to Södervärn and into the hospital complex. Vanja had been there several times before, to see the optician, and had positive associations with the place.

"Where's she staying?" Heidi said.

"Over there," I said.

"Do they sleep here?" Heidi said.

"Yes, they do."

"Are there lots of people who can't sleep?" Vanja said.

"Not so many," I said. "But there are some."

Linda was leaning against the wall beside the door. When Vanja and Heidi caught sight of her they set off at a run. I lifted John from the stroller so that he could chase after them.

"My children," Linda said, and bent down to embrace all three of them. "Vanja, Heidi, and John. How I've missed you!"

Linda straightened up and looked at me.

"Hi," she said. "Shall we go and get some ice cream?"

I nodded, and we set off. There were buildings on both sides of the road, but behind the psychiatric department there was a lawn. We walked past, turned left, at the end of the road there was a kiosk.

"What have you been doing today?" Linda said.

"We've been to the theater," Vanja said.

"Not me," Heidi said. "I was at school all day."

"You're so lovely," Linda said.

"Why can't you sleep, Mommy?" Vanja said.

"I don't know," Linda said. "But it's not serious. Look, there's the kiosk."

She opened the door and went in. As soon as her attention wandered from the children her face assumed an extremely distant expression. I could see she wanted to be somewhere else. She wanted to be with the children, but when they were there, she wanted to be somewhere else.

She bent down to them as they stood by the chest freezer.

"I want a Daim," Vanja said.

John pointed to a cone. Heidi to a tub.

She took the three ice creams, placed them on the counter, and paid.

Then we moved on. It was as though Linda was holding back almost everything she had inside her. I could see the glow in her eyes, but the children noticed nothing, I could see that too. We sat down on a bench by a little pool at the other end of the hospital complex. The children sat beside us eating their ice cream. When they'd finished they played by the water's edge, John carried over a big branch he had found, which he threw in. Heidi crawled onto Linda's lap, she sat caressing her and staring into the distance.

"I want to sit on your lap too," Vanja said. Linda put Heidi down and lifted Vanja. Usually this would have led to a spat, but not today.

I moved to another bench and had a smoke. After I'd finished the cigarette I got up and put the ice-cream wrappers into a nearby bin.

"We have to go now," I said.

"Has it been half an hour?" Linda said.

I nodded.

She got up, I put John in the stroller, and then we set off.

"My room's up there," Linda said, pointing to the top of the long building.

"Is it nice?" Heidi said.

"Yes, it is," Linda said. "It's really nice."

"Can we see it?"

"I don't think they allow any children up there," I said. "It has to be very quiet."

"That's true," Linda said. "Perhaps it's better if I meet you at home."

"How long are you going to be here?" Vanja said.

"I don't know," Linda said. "But I'll see you tomorrow."

"Bye, Mommy," Vanja and Heidi said.

The following day I arranged with the senior nurse for Linda to come home for an hour. She wasn't allowed to walk on her own, so I dressed the kids and we went to pick her up. As on the previous occasion, she was waiting outside the ward. She was heavily made-up. And a little unsteady on her legs, so I supported her with one arm and pushed the stroller with the other. Must be the medicine, I thought. She had such energy, they had said, medicines were ineffective against her mania, and they were giving her as much as they could. The children were chatting away as usual as we walked, past the big building site which would be the new underground train station – where people cycled and walked over the gravel-covered asphalt along the wire-netting fence after a day's work – past the end of the hotel first, then the side, across the road, through the door, and up and into the elevator.

Linda watched children's TV with them for a few minutes. She had John on her lap, with Vanja and Heidi snuggled up beside her. I made the simplest meal I knew, spaghetti and meatballs. After a little while Linda came out and headed for the hall. I thought she was going to the toilet, but she opened the door to the bedroom.

When the food was almost ready I looked in on her.

She was sitting in front of her laptop writing on Facebook.

"You've only got forty minutes left," I said. "Can't you stay with the children?"

"Soon," she said. "Just doing this."

I returned to the kitchen. Soon afterward she walked into the hall. I heard the balcony door open and close. I set the table, filled a water jug, cut some tomatoes into boats and placed four on each plate. I tipped the meatballs into a bowl, poured water into glasses, and emptied the spaghetti into a dish.

"Food's up!" I shouted.

No one moved.

I made a beeline for the TV and switched it off. The children followed me into the kitchen and sat down. I went to the balcony, where Linda was sitting with her feet on the balustrade smoking.

"Food's ready," I said.

"Coming!" she said.

As we ate she spoke to Vanja, Heidi, and John as she always did. I could see she had to pull herself together to do so and radiated a nervousness and desperation when the conversation flagged.

After the meal we all went into the living room. The children snuggled up to Linda, she put her arms around Vanja and Heidi and had John on her lap. But her eyes were frantic. She put John down on the floor and got to her feet.

"Where are you going, Mommy?" Heidi said.

"To the bathroom," she said.

She didn't come back, and I strode out to see what she was doing. She was writing on Facebook.

"We have to go now," I said. "It'll take a bit to dress them and so on. And you have to be back by seven."

"You don't need to accompany me," she said. "It's absolutely unnecessary. How far is it? A kilometer? Not even that. I can do it on my own."

"But they said you shouldn't walk on your own. They expressly said I had to be with you."

"That's just standard procedure," she said. "A rule for people who really can't look after themselves. I can. I'll walk back on my own so that you and the children can stay here."

"Okay," I said. "Let's do that then."

I went into the living room.

"Come and say goodbye to Mommy," I said.

John slipped off the sofa and ran into the hall. Heidi followed.

"Vanja?"

"Bye, Mom!" she shouted.

Linda bent down and hugged Heidi and John. With an unsteady step and a bag hanging off her shoulder, she walked into the living room, where she leaned forward and kissed Vanja on the head.

When she opened the elevator door she looked at me and winked, kissed her fingertips and blew me a kiss.

At just after nine the hospital rang.

A nurse introduced herself and asked me if I was Linda's husband. I confirmed that I was.

"Is she with you now?" the nurse asked.

"Linda? No. She left for the hospital two hours ago. Hasn't she arrived?"

"No. But didn't you accompany her? That was the deal we made, wasn't it?"

"Yes, it was. But she seemed so centered. And we don't live that far away."

"She'll be refused any leave if the rules aren't adhered to."

"I understand."

"Now you know," she said.

"Yes," I said.

I hung up and called Linda's mobile. It wasn't on. I tried again a little later, and since it was still off then as well, I went to bed.

The next morning I called her ward. Linda was there. She had arrived at around midnight, the nurse said. She called Linda, and Linda came to the phone.

"Hi," I said.

"Hi," she said. "I've got a new nurse. You should meet him. Turns out he's read *Mein Kampf.* Hitler's, that is. I think he does martial arts and has a combat dog. But he's nice. I think he might become a good friend here."

"Linda," I said. "Yesterday you were supposed to go straight back to your ward."

"Oh that," she said. "I've already discussed that with the nurse. I just wanted to go out for a little walk. Nothing dangerous. I'm here of my own accord, you know. They can't actually stop me."

"Where did you go?"

"Møllevangen. Around there. Are you going to visit me afterward?"

"Yes, after I've taken them to school."

"Good! It'll be good to see you again. Could you bring some money with you? I've run out."

"Okay," I said. "Will do."

I rang the doorbell upstairs in the gray building. A young nurse opened up. We shook hands, I followed her in. Linda was sitting at a table in the dining room with a bearded man around thirty years old. I realized this was the man she had been speaking about.

She stood up beaming with pleasure when she saw me, came over, and put her arms around me.

"This is Mats," she said. "I suppose you two have a lot to talk about."

"Hi," I said, shaking his hand.

"Hi," he said, and he must have noticed my obvious lack of interest because the first thing he said was that he had to go and do something.

We went into her room. The ornaments on the windowsill had multiplied. The photos of the children she had brought with her when she first came suggested she'd known her stay wouldn't be for one night. No one else had thought that except for me. Me and the children.

She talked about nurses and patients as though they were people she had known for many years. She talked about the ward as though it were a romantic sanatorium in a Thomas Mann novel. She talked about all her plans, everything she was going to do, and showed me a notebook in which she had already written quite a number of pages.

"What was it like being at home yesterday?" I said.

"It was great to see the children," she said. "But I can't manage so much all at once. There's something in me that wanders off. There are such strong forces in me and I can't resist them."

"You were wonderful with the children, Linda. It makes me so happy. I can see how much it takes out of you. But you have to carry on doing it. Do you think you can?"

She nodded.

"Are you coming here this afternoon?"

"Yes. Let's do what we did last time."

"Do you have any money on you?"

"Yes, but not very much. Two hundred. Is that enough?"

"No, not really. But I'll take it. Shall we go and have a smoke?"

We stood outside for ten minutes smoking, Linda found it impossible to stand still, I saw that she could hardly wait for me to go.

"See you later then," I said.

"Yes, see you," she said, and turned to two other patients standing there as I set off. At home I took my bike out of the cellar, it was a DBS I'd chosen from a selection of probably better bikes, only because the name reminded me of my childhood, the spring light, the smell of the sea between the spruce trees. I cycled to Flüggers Färg on Köbenhavnervägen and bought some paint, brushes, and foam rollers. When I got home I put the first coat on Vanja's room while crying so much I could barely see the wall. I painted three of the walls light blue, as Vanja had wanted, and the fourth white. Then I painted the long wall in what would soon be Heidi and John's room light green. That had been Heidi's suggestion. I cleaned the brushes and rollers, called Linda and asked how she was doing, she said very well, but she was bored. I said that was the point of being there, she was supposed to get bored and not do so much. She said she knew.

After the brief conversation I went to the balcony, surrounded by the sounds of the city and the warm August air, I inhaled the smoke into my lungs and thought about what was happening to Linda. It was clear she had complete awareness of herself, she agreed to everything I said to give me the impression she was closer to me than she was in reality: as soon as I was out of sight she changed direction and wandered into town. She would say she loved me, but as soon as I was there she felt an obligation she couldn't deal with, because it tied her and it was these bonds she was fleeing.

She had been as low as it was possible for any human to be, she'd been unable to articulate this and was overcome with thoughts of death, an unbearable state that lasted for weeks. It was obvious she wouldn't be able to control the light inside her afterward, which made everything easy and good, but she had to follow it because beneath the light, at the end of the wave carrying her further and further upward, was the darkness. She knew that. Once she had told me that a nurse had said to her during a manic spell, Remember that really you are sad. But what was the "really" and the "not really" in this? What was Linda, what was depression, what was manic?

That afternoon Vanja came rushing up to me as I opened the nursery school gate.

"Dad! Dad! I can say *r*!" she shouted.

"Wow," I said. "Is that true?"

"Rrrrrrrrrrrrrr," she said. "Crown prince!"

"How did you do that?"

"I don't know. I just did."

She had tried to make a kind of gurgling Skåne *r* at the back of her throat without success, and she had tried a tip-of-the-tongue *r*, which sounded like a whistle, closer to *th* than *r*, the one I'd had to use until I was sixteen, which had deeply shamed me.

Now she had suddenly succeeded.

"Absolutely wonderful, Vanja," I said. "And just as you're starting school!"

I didn't say anything about the painting I had done, I wanted to surprise them. They were really pleased, especially Heidi, she lit up when she saw the room. Vanja, as usual, was a thought ahead.

"I'd like a picture of a dog on *that* wall," she said.

"Yes," I said. "Tomorrow I'll do a second coat and when it's dry we can buy some pictures."

"I'd like one of a cat," Heidi said.

Painting their rooms felt as if I was betraying Linda because it was an unconditional blessing, and I had no right to it, something good was happening here while she was in need, it was like going behind her back. Yet I had to do it for my own sake, it was an obvious compensation, and for the children's sake, who had to be kept as far away as possible from Linda's needs.

On the way home from school we stopped by a picture-framing shop. Vanja chose three pictures of a dog, Heidi chose one of a cat and one of Babar in a red plane, and then I chose a motif from

Tove Jansson's *Who Will Comfort Toffle?*: Snufkin under a blue sky. We hung up the pictures, had something to eat, and set off to get Linda from the hospital. She swayed a little as she walked and seemed exhausted, spent. At home we watched kids' TV, she saw half the program before going to her bedroom, checking her e-mails, and logging on to Facebook. Afterward she went to the balcony for a smoke. When she came back in, we had to go. She rushed to pack her things, the children put on their shoes rather reluctantly, and then we set off for the hospital, John in the stroller, Vanja and Heidi on either side, Linda at the front. She gave them a hug each, and when she straightened up I saw her eyes were moist. We said good night and walked home.

The following morning we had another meeting with the doctor. Linda put on another show, she was charming, lively, made everyone laugh. She showed great self-awareness and joked about her manic state. She just wanted everything to move faster. Faster, faster, faster. She couldn't sit still, she couldn't stay on the same topic, had to interrupt, intercede with something new. If I said anything she stared at me impatiently, finished my sentences for me, knew what I was going to say long before I said it, presumably also before I knew it myself. In that sense she was brilliant, in an elevated state, special to her, magnificent. But the fact that she didn't care about what lay beneath, the slowness and the dull-wittedness, the sluggishness and the ugliness, or didn't want to see it, meant her brilliance was a cover-up and became a place for herself, the only place she could bear to be. Thoughts of the children belonged there and perhaps also of me. But when she was with the children these two levels conflicted and it was intolerable for her, I saw how she had to fight to keep everything together when we visited her. Everything in her personality was in turmoil, her ten-year-old self could manifest itself, her teenage self could manifest itself, her erotic self, which was usually hidden and only revealed itself to me, could manifest itself, her boundless star-spangled-poet self could manifest itself, her boastful, excessive self could manifest itself, for her personality was no longer under control, there was nothing to keep the various elements in check, the center had lost its hold, her manic forces hurled everything out, she wanted to rise, everything in her wanted to rise, and she rose higher and higher while becoming more and more exhausted. In all of this, the rising higher, the light that caused her to rise, there was one thing she never rose above, and that was her commitment to her children.

A lot became clear to me during these days. What Linda dreamed of was to live a perfectly ordinary life with a perfectly ordinary family. To have an ordinary job, go to the cabin on the weekends, and work in the garden with the children running around her. But she was no ordinary person. She was the least ordinary person I had ever met. During all the years of childbearing, breast-feeding, and having little ones she had fought. Her struggle had been very different from mine; hers had been life or death. I had written that I was living an inauthentic life, I was living the life of someone else, and I might well have been, and this tormented me, but it didn't threaten me. It did threaten Linda. Her whole personality, the one I had settled down with, and her whole language had been erased in the life we'd lived. That wasn't the case with me. I had written, I'd had my language and, not least, my distance. She hadn't had any such distance until now, rising above all the ties and obligations and wanting to be utterly free. But the freedom was false, the freedom was a deception, the freedom was a circus in daylight. She saw it perhaps as glittering lights, she saw it perhaps as magical, but when I looked at her what I saw was the exhaustion, the unsteadiness on her feet, the worthless, the false, the hospital tristesse, all the people who had no hope and therefore had nothing.

I informed the staff at the nursery school that Linda had been admitted to the hospital and we had told the children she was there to sleep. They said they hadn't noticed any changes in the kids, they were as they always were. One of the staff said that our children had strong personalities. But no one adapts as quickly as children, and for them it was nothing special that their mother was in the hospital to sleep and they visited her every afternoon. They treated the subject of sleep as the most natural thing in the world, at first they had lots of questions, what did they actually do in the hospital, gradually their curiosity waned, that was how it was.

The school staff told me just to ask if I required any assistance. Also the parents we knew and had told that Linda was ill offered their help. It wasn't necessary, I said, and this was true, apart from one afternoon when I was going to Gothenburg to do a reading and needed a babysitter. A woman at the nursery school was happy to lend a hand, so after I'd taken the children there, visited Linda at the hospital, and made a sausage stew for the evening meal, I caught the train north. The babysitter brought them home, fed them, put them to bed, and was sitting up for me when I returned at midnight, a bit annoyed that I'd arrived two hours later than I'd said, which I attempted to compensate for by paying especially well. If I had said how late it would be she might not have wanted the job, I had thought.

I had read a passage from the first novel, about inauthentic life, how I could lose my temper with the children and shake them, almost completely out of control. The moment I began to read I realized it was a mistake. I could sense what people were thinking, that no child should be treated like that, and I was a bad father who thought I was better just because I admitted how bad I was, I was seeking absolution in literature. Fortunately I was able to leave the event as soon as I'd done the reading, disappear into a waiting taxi and then a train compartment.

On the way back home, the real estate agent called. Not a nibble yet. We agreed to drop the price even further. I could hear that she, too, was heartily sick of the cabin.

In the midst of all this John's third birthday loomed. Both Vanja and Heidi had been allowed to have parties with guests from the start, while up to then John had been forced to celebrate with us. He hadn't known any different when he was one or two, but now that he was three I had been wondering for a while whether to invite some children over from the nursery school, to give him a party, but I came to the conclusion this was far too ambitious. Instead he would celebrate it at school in the usual way, with one of the parents bringing a cake and making a fruit salad, and then at home with cake and presents after the evening meal. Linda wanted to join us at the school, she had asked the doctor, who had said it was fine. I was not convinced it was a good idea. There was a shrill side to her now, which came out in social situations, and I was not keen for Heidi and John to see it.

She rang the doorbell of the apartment at eleven.

She'd had a haircut and dyed her hair black. She wore heavy green eye shadow, a red skirt, purple tights, and high heels. She was smiling, but looked utterly drained.

"What do you think of my Frida Kahlo look?" she said.

"You look good," I said.

"Shall we go and get some cake? And fruit?" she said.

"Can we have a cup of coffee first?" I said.

"Yes, of course," she said.

I wondered how to tell her. After seeing her, I knew there was absolutely no question of her organizing the birthday at the school.

"How are you?" I said.

"I'm very well. A bit tired though maybe."

On one wrist she had an enormous watch.

"You bought yourself a new watch?" I said.

"Yes! I took the biggest they had to remind myself to be punctual. Otherwise I can't handle it. They get so angry with me then."

"And the green strap?" I said, nodding toward her wrist.

"That's to symbolize that I'm totally free. Whenever I look at it I think about it. About being completely free."

"Very nice," I said. "Mm, Linda?"

"Yes?"

"It might be best if you don't go to the school. It'll be very

1222

intense, you know. And what you need is peace and quiet. It's much better if I go, and then you can come in the afternoon and celebrate at home. What do you think?"

"Yes, it'd be wonderful not to have to go," she said.

"That's good to hear," I said.

"But can I buy him some presents? I can do that, can't I?"

"Of course. We can do it together."

"Actually I've discussed everything with Jenny."

"Okay."

She was back after a couple of hours, several bags in hand.

"There might be too many, but they're lovely," she said. "And I've bought something for the girls too."

"Good," I said. "I'll put them in the closet. Would you like a cup of coffee?"

"No, Jenny's waiting downstairs. See you this afternoon."

She came and we decided to skip the meal, John wanted to go straight to the cake. I lit the candles, we sang for him, the girls stood on their chairs, as they did at school. He blew out the candles. We ate cake, they were each given a present, and then John got the rest of his in the living room. Linda came in with a flurry of packets, ribbons, and plastic bags, she sat down with him and helped him to open them. Suddenly, in the middle of unpacking a large present, she got up and went to the balcony.

"Mama!" John cried. "Help me!"

I sat down with him. Luckily he accepted that, and we unpacked the present and opened the box it was in. Linda moved to the bedroom and logged on to Facebook, she was writing when I entered.

"It's gone very well," I said.

"I couldn't stand any more," she said. "I can only take a little at a time."

"I know, but that's enough."

She didn't look at me, her fingers clattered across the keyboard.

"I think it's time to go," I said.

"Yes," she said. "I just have to finish this."

Afterward she stood up and went into the hall.

"It's John's birthday," she said. "It doesn't feel right that they have to come with me. Couldn't you just stay here and carry on with the birthday?"

"Do you remember what happened last time?"

"Yes, yes. But I'm not there now. I'll go straight to the hospital. I promise. I can't risk not being able to go out."

"Are you sure?" I said.

"Absolutely," she said.

"Okay," I said.

She looked at me.

"It's always struck me that I was a sailor's wife. You went to sea and left me on my own. But now it's the other way around. Now I'm the sailor."

She laughed.

I laughed too, because she was wearing her striped sweater and did a sailor's salute.

We kissed. She pressed against me, breathed in my ear, I wrestled myself free.

"Not now," I said.

"I know," she said. "Now I'm casting my moorings."

And then she was gone.

A few hours later they called from the hospital and asked if Linda was at home. I apologized, saying it had been impossible to accompany her because of the children, and I had taken a risk.

The following day I asked her what she had done. She said she had just drifted around a little. Been to a few bars, talked to people. One man she had spoken to, my age, visited her just before I arrived later that week. She said they were good friends. I had never seen or heard of him. The same applied to many others, suddenly she had a large circle of acquaintances in Malmö. That evening she was refused permission to go out, so we visited her in the park, where she was composed again, a long way from the impatient, restless teenager she had been the evening before. Ingrid came down from Stockholm; the first thing she did was visit Linda. We talked about it on her return.

"The children come first," Ingrid said. "They're the most important. They're the top priority."

"I agree," I said.

"It was like that when her father became ill. The children came first, whatever happened."

The Saturday before school started I took Vanja with me to IKEA. We bought a bed, a desk, a wardrobe, and a chest of drawers. On Sunday we bought a satchel, a pencil case, and new clothes. I assembled all the furniture, apart from the drawers, after they had gone to bed because I got so angry with do-it-yourself kits that I might have taken my annoyance out on the children if they were around.

Early on Monday morning Linda came home to be there on Vanja's first day of school. I was apprehensive about her appearance, hoping she wouldn't turn up in green eye shadow and purple tights, but she didn't, she wore a simple flowery dress and had taken care with her makeup, which, apart from the red lipstick, was neutral.

I took a photo outside the front entrance to the building, exactly as someone, presumably my mother, had done with me, outside our house, on my first day of school.

We took John and Heidi to the nursery and then we walked the last stretch to the school with Vanja. She held Linda's hand and mine. She was a little afraid, I sensed, but also full of excitement.

The atmosphere in the classroom was as I remembered from all my first days. Half formal, half uncertain. Linda talked to the teacher and other parents. Vanja stood with her best friend and stared at the other children. When the teacher called them and they had to sit on a carpet in the middle of the floor, she was undaunted, she had her friend behind her.

Linda and I sat next to each other looking at Vanja in the

middle of this group of children. After half an hour Linda leaned toward me and whispered she had to go. I nodded. We agreed to meet at the little café by Möllan. Only twenty minutes later it was over as far as the parents were concerned, and I walked to the café, where Linda talked and talked and could finally go wherever her mind led her.

Toward the end of the week I was due to go to the Louisiana Museum of Modern Art. After taking the children to the school, I rented a car and drove over the bridge to Denmark. The weather was magnificent. Sun, high blue sky, Indian summer. I sat outside the boathouse by the sea drinking coffee and smoking and chatting to the other authors, among them Tomas Espedal, who had shown such heart and defended me in *Bergens Tidende*, and Dag Solstad and Tua Forsström, the Finnish poet, who turned out to be a warm, generous person. There was a full house, two hundred people, and when it was over I drove back in the darkness and went to bed in a quiet apartment where everyone was asleep. The next day I did exactly the same. Linda was worried while I was away, even if it was only for the day, at the same time she told everyone I had to go to Denmark to appear at Louisiana.

The doctors suggested electric-shock therapy. They called it by a different name, but that is what it was. They wanted to halt the mania in its tracks. She was given an appointment, but when the time came she didn't turn up. She was frightened, I understood that, she didn't want it.

One afternoon she came with me to pick up the children. First Heidi and John, who we took with us to Vanja's school. Her classmates were in the schoolyard, but Vanja was nowhere to be seen.

"I'll go behind there and look for her," I said.

Linda nodded.

In a corner, barely visible, she stood with her friend, clapping their hands against each other's and singing.

"Come on, Vanja," I said.

Both of them came and we walked over to the others. Linda

was speaking with one of the teachers, with Heidi clinging to her leg.

"Where's John?" I said.

"I don't know," Linda said. "I'm not responsible for them now."

Again and again I misjudged her.

I looked around. No John. I ran to the back of the school. There, by the playground equipment, he was staring at the bigger children. I lifted him up and took him back with me, and we all walked home together.

Ingrid returned to Stockholm, and a few days later my mother traveled down. She also visited Linda and was shocked by the place she was in. She said it had been like that in Norway in the sixties. The nurses had white uniforms, she couldn't believe her eyes when she saw that, Mom said. The rooms were run-down and, to a great extent, institutional. Linda's enthrallment couldn't last that much longer, I suspected, because she was becoming more and more tired, and at some point she would collapse with exhaustion and plummet into what she was fleeing.

One morning the real estate agent called, she was angry, I could hear. The key had gone, she hadn't been able to get in, she had been forced to turn people away and tell them there was no viewing. We had agreed that we'd leave the key in a flowerpot, hadn't we? I said I didn't know what had happened, but I would investigate and contact her later.

I called Linda.

"You haven't been to the cabin, have you?"

"No," she said. "But I might've done something a little stupid."

"Oh?"

"Well, I told a man here about our place. I told him the cabin was empty and that the key was in a flowerpot beside the front step. He needed somewhere to live, you see. I just wanted to help him."

"What sort of a man?" I said.

"He's been here in the ward a few times. He was going to be deported, I think, and needed somewhere to hide."

"What!" I said.

"He was nice," she said.

"What sort of a person is he?"

"He's from Bosnia or Serbia or somewhere like that," she said. "He was in the war there."

"You know we're trying to sell the cabin, don't you?" I said. "There was a viewing organized and the key had disappeared. Thank God he wasn't there. But now we need to get hold of the key. You'll have to go and get it from him."

"But I can't do that," she said. "He might be a bit dangerous."

"Dangerous?"

"Yes."

"Take a nurse with you then. Tell them. Take two nurses. Can you do that?"

"Yes," she said.

Next time I went I talked to the nurse who had read *Mein Kampf*. He had gone to the cabin together with another nurse and Linda. The man had turned aggressive and refused to hand over the key, he was going to live there, she'd promised him. They managed to wrest the key from him, but his actions were so threatening afterward that the nurses called for the police. I phoned the real estate agent and tried to explain what had happened. I said there had been a kind of break-in and a man had been living there. The place was probably a mess, but I would go and clean it up, and then we could make a fresh start. The real estate agent accepted that, but not without some skepticism in her voice.

Then Linda came home.

First she phoned late at night, she was absolutely hysterical, she hadn't been given any food, she'd smashed a glass in her fury, extra staff had been called, it was humiliating, now she wanted to come home. She had gone there of her own accord, it was her right, and half an hour later she was home. She was perfectly calm, and said it was enough now, she wanted to be at home. I said that was what I wanted as well. We talked for several hours, she was as she had been before, everything was good. The next morning she was on a high and restless again, and walked back to the hospital, but nevertheless something had happened, she was closer to herself, the energy was slowly draining from her, and one evening one of the nurses there, the motherly one, knelt in front of Linda and told her she had to go back to her husband and children, this had gone on for long enough and wasn't leading anywhere. The intensity of her plea had shocked Linda, shaken her, at the same time she was on her way down, she had begun to talk at a normal speed about normal things, to tell us she longed to be with us, and then one morning she came home with her backpack, and it was over.

It was over.

She embraced her children when they came back from school and said she was staying.

"Can you sleep now?" Vanja said.

"Yes," she said. "Now I can sleep."

We stayed up chatting that evening. She was worn out, quiet, but when she looked at me, it was Linda looking at me, no one else.

"I've been on a long journey," she said.

"Yes," I said.

"Now I'm home," she said.

"Yes," I said. "But it was no big deal."

"Okay," she said. "I think I called your editor. Geir Gulliksen. I told him not to put you under any pressure. And to take care of you."

"That was nicely put," I said. "Not a problem."

"And I've called Tore. And Yngve. And all my old friends. People I haven't seen for years. I don't remember what I said."

"Not a problem. And now we know where we stand. Perhaps it will happen again. It might. But we know it's not a problem. You're just on your travels."

"Away from my family."

"No. You haven't been. It's been fine. You're a hero. You coped so well."

She cried.

I cried.

It was over.

But the cabin was a problem. I had to go and deal with it. Linda didn't want me to go, the guy was dangerous, the police had said we shouldn't confront him under any circumstances if we met him. I e-mailed Aage, one of the few friends I had in Malmö, explained the situation, and asked if he would be willing to accompany me with a baseball bat or something. He called me minutes later. He was in London. He said he could go with me when he was back and I shouldn't go on my own. I said I wouldn't. But a crazed ex-Yugoslav seemed like a minor problem after the summer I'd had, so I went to Åhléns and bought some new rugs, curtains, tablecloths, and cushion covers, and some flowers from a florist, detergents and cloths from Hemköp, took the bus to the cabins, which were deserted in the rain, the season was already long over. My heart was thudding in my chest as I approached our cabin. I carefully opened the wicket gate, stopped, listened. Nothing. I walked around the back. Nothing. And the door was in one piece. He wasn't here. I unlocked the door and entered. It was a mess. It stank of smoke, and there were cigarette butts everywhere. The floor was filthy. There were bottles all over the place. But nothing was broken. I threw out all the rugs, curtains, tablecloths, and cushion covers, all the bottles and cigarette butts and detritus. I was on my guard the whole time, expecting the door to be kicked in at any moment and the crazed guy to come in and gun me down. It didn't happen. I washed every single centimeter, from the ceiling over the cramped mezzanine to the floor. In several places there were fairly large piles of fine sawdust. I sighed. That had to be woodworm, the whole damned house must have been rotten to the core. I decided not to say a

1230

word. I laid the new rugs on the floor, hung the new curtains over the windows, put a cloth on the table, and arranged the flowerpots. The cabin looked flawless. With a garbage bag in each hand, I left, the rain was pouring down and dusk had started to fall. Not a soul in sight anywhere. I threw the bags into a trash container and caught the bus home. I had a hot bath and then watched a film with everyone – *Dumbo*, the elephant with the big ears. Linda was tired but collected and present.

The viewing was held: no offers. At the next viewing someone saw the triangular piles of fine sawdust, so new ones had appeared and people had shaken their heads, I assumed. We got Anticimex in, a pest-control company, it wasn't woodworm but some relatively harmless insect, they said, which they now had under control.

The real estate agent took the cabin off the market and put it back in spring, at the first viewing there was an offer, it was low, but we accepted it, money was no longer of any consequence in this dream. From October that autumn we spent every weekend in the new house. We celebrated Christmas there, all twelve of us, the snow was meters high outside, Vanja and Heidi saw me put on a Christmas elf outfit, but were still spellbound when I came across the snow with a lantern in my hand. After Christmas I ditched the manuscript and started anew with this one. I got up at four every morning and worked until the children had to be picked up, and I have been doing that until now, as I sit here writing this. The story of last summer that I have just told looks different now, I know, from the way it really was. Why? Because Linda is a human being and her unique essence is indescribable, her own distinctive presence, her nature and her soul, which were always there beside me, which I saw and felt regardless of whatever else was going on. It didn't reside in what she did, it didn't reside in what she said, it resided in what she was.

It resides in what she is. Leaning over Heidi, whispering something in her ear, Heidi laughing her trilled laugh. Lying on the sofa with Vanja on top, laughing at something our clever daughter has said. The tenderness in her gaze as she looks at John. And her hand at the base of my neck, warm, those totally unguarded eyes of hers.

I am so happy about Linda, and I am so happy about our children. I will never forgive myself for what I've exposed them to, but I did it, and I will have to live with it.

Now it is 7:07, and the novel is finally finished. In two hours Linda will be coming here, I will hug her and tell her I've finished, and I will never do anything like this to her and our children again. Then we'll take the train to Louisiana. I am going to be interviewed onstage, after which it will be her turn, because her own book has come out and it glitters and sparkles like a star-filled night sky. Afterward we will catch the train to Malmö, where we will get in the car and drive back to our house, and the whole way I will revel in, truly revel in, the thought that I am no longer a writer.

Malmö, Glemmingebro,
February 27, 2008–September 2, 2011

To Linda, Vanja, Heidi, and John.
I love you.

Bibliography

Giorgio Agamben, *Homo Sacer. Sovereign Power and Bare Life* (tr. Daniel Heller-Roazen), Stanford University Press, 1998.

Giorgio Agamben, *Midler uten mål. Notater om politikk,* Cappelen Damm 2008

Hannah Arendt, *Eichmann in Jersusalem,* Penguin, 1963.

Hannah Arendt, *Vita activa. Det virksomme liv,* Pax Forlag, 1996.

Ingeborg Bachmann, *Ny tenkning, nytt språk,* Pax Forlag, 1996.

Philip Ball, *Critical Mass,* Arrow Books, 2004.

Eduard Bloch, "My Patient, Hitler: A Memoir of Hitler's Jewish Physician," Collier's, 1941.

Jorge Luis Borges, "Pierre Menard, Author of the Quixote," *Labyrinths* (tr. James E. Irby), New Directions, 1962.

Hermann Broch, *The Death of Virgil* (tr. Jean Starr Untermeyer), Vintage International, 1995.

Thomas Browne, *Religio Medici,* CreateSpace, 2016.

Elias Canetti, *Masse og makt,* Solum Forlag, 1995.

Paul Celan, *Gesammelte Werke in sieben Bänden,* Suhrkamp, 2000.

Paul Celan, *Selected Poems* (tr. Michael Hamburger), Penguin Modern Classics, 1996. [Hamburger's translation of the poem "Engführung" – "The Straitening" – has been slightly modified by Martin Aitken to accord with Karl Ove Knausgaard's analysis of Øyvind Berg's Norwegian translation (itself with minor changes by Karl Ove Knausgaard).]

Jacques Derrida, *Schibboleth,* Symposium, 1999.

Olav Duun, *The Trough of the Wave* (Book One of *The People of Juvik*) (tr. Arthur G. Chater), A. A. Knopf, 1935 (some excerpts tr. from the Norwegian original by Martin Aitken).

Joachim C. Fest, *Hitler* (tr. Richard and Clara Winston), Mariner Books, 2002.

Northrop Frye, *The Great Code,* Harcourt Brace Jovanovich, 1982.

Jean Genet, *Essäer och artiklar*, Site edition/Propexus, 2006.

René Girard, *Syndabocken – en antologi*, Themis, 2007.

René Girard, *A Theatre of Envy: William Shakespeare*, Oxford University Press, 1991.

René Girard, *Violence and the Sacred* (tr. Patrick Gregory), Continuum, 2005.

Richard Glazar, *Trap with a Green Fence: Survival in Treblinka*, Northwestern University Press, 1995.

Witold Gombrowicz, *Diary* (tr. Lillian Vallee), Yale University Press, 2012.

Brigitte Hamann, *Hitler's Vienna. A Dictator's Apprenticeship* (tr. Thomas Thornton), Oxford University Press, 1999.

Peter Handke, *A Sorrow Beyond Dreams* (tr. Ralph Manheim), Pushkin Press, 2013.

Ernst Hanfstaengl, *Hitler. The Memoir of a Nazi Insider Who Turned Against the Führer* (tr. John Toland), Arcade, 2011.

Ernst Hanfstaengl, *Hitler: The Missing Years*, Arcade reprint 1994 of *Unheard Witness* (tr. unknown), Eyre & Spottiswoode, 1957.

Reinhold Hanisch, "I Was Hitler's Buddy," *New Republic*, 1939.

Olav H. Hauge, *Dikt i omsetjing*, Det norske samlaget, 1982.

Martin Heidegger, *Being and Time* (tr. John Macquarrie and Edward Robinson), Blackwell, 2001.

Carl-Göran Heidegren, *Preussiska anarkister. Ernst Jünger och hans krets under Weimar-republikens krisår*, Brutus Östlings Bokförlag Symposion, 1997.

Heraclitus, "Fragments," in J. Burnet, *Early Greek Philosophy*, Veritatis Splendor Publications, 2014 .

Adolf Hitler, *Mein Kampf* (tr. Ralph Manheim), Pimlico, 1992.

Annegret Hoberg, "Alfred Kubin. The early work up to 1909," in Hoberg (ed.), *Alfred Kubin: Drawings 1897–1909*, Prestel Verlag, 2008.

Max Horkheimer and Theodor W. Adorno, *Dialectic of Enlightenment: Philosophical Fragments* (tr. Edmund Jephcott), Stanford University Press, 2002.

James Joyce, *Dubliners*, Gyldendal, 2004.

James Joyce, *Stephen Hero*, New Directions, 1963.

James Joyce, *Ulysses*, Vintage, 1990.

Ernst Jünger, *Storm of Steel* (tr. Michael Hofmann), Penguin Modern Classics, 2004.

Franz Kafka, *The Diaries of Franz Kafka, 1910–1923* (tr. Joseph Kresh and Martin Greenberg with the cooperation of Hannah Arendt), Schocken, 1988.

Franz Kafka, *Letters to Felice* (tr. James Stern and Elisabeth Duckworth), Schocken, 1973.

Ian Kershaw, *Hubris/Nemesis*, Penguin, 2001.

Victor Klemperer, *The Language of the Third Reich* (tr. Martin Brady), Bloomsbury, 2013.

Guido Knopp, *Hitler's Women* (tr. Angus McGeoch), Sutton, 2006.

August Kubizek, *The Young Hitler I Knew* (tr. Geoffrey Brooks), Frontline Books/Greenhill, 2011.

Olof Lagercrantz, *Att finnas till. En studie i James Joyces roman "Odysseus,"* Wahlström & Widstrand, 1970.

Bruno Latour, *We Have Never Been Modern* (tr. Catherine Porter), Harvard University Press, 1993.

Gotthold E. Lessing, *Laocoon* (tr. Ellen Frothingham), Noonday Press, 1969.

Emmanuel Levinas, *Beyond the Verse* (tr. Gary D. Mole), Continuum, 2007.

Emmanuel Levinas, *In the Time of the Nations* (tr. Michael B. Smith), Continuum, 2007.

Emmanuel Levinas, "Reflections on the Philosophy of Hitlerism" (tr. Seán Hand), *Critical Inquiry*, 1990.

Bengt Liljegren, *Adolf Hitler*, Historiska Media, 2008.

Jack London, *The People of the Abyss*, Macmillan, 1903.

Kurt G. W. Ludecke, *I Knew Hitler*, Coda Books, 2011.

H. Lundborg, F. J. Linders (eds), *The Racial Characters of the Swedish Nation*, Swedish State Institute for Race Biology, University of Uppsala, 1926.

Karl Marx, *Capital. A Critique of Political Economy* (tr. Samuel Moore and Edward Aveling), marxists.org, 2015.

George L. Mosse, *The Crisis of German Ideology*, Howard Ferdig, 1999.

Thomas Nevin, *Ernst Jünger and Germany. Into the Abyss, 1914–1945*, Duke University Press, 1996.

Svante Nordin, *Filosofernas krig. Den europeiska filosofin under första världskriget*, Nye Doxa, 1998.

Rudolf Otto, *The Idea of the Holy* (tr. John W. Harvey), Oxford University Press, 1958.

Geir Angell Øygarden, *Bagdad Indigo*, Pelikanen Forlag, 2011.

Paracelsus, *Four Treatises*, Hopkins, 1996.

Ernst Pawel, *The Nightmare of Reason: A Life of Franz Kafka*, Farrar, Straus and Giroux, 1984.

Rainer Maria Rilke, *The Possibility of Being: A Selection of Poems by Rainer Maria Rilke* (tr. J. B. Leishman), New Directions, 1977.

Rainer Maria Rilke, *The Selected Poetry of Rainer Maria Rilke* (tr. Stephen Mitchell), Vintage International, 1989.

Timothy W. Ryback, *Hitler's Private Library*, Vintage Books, 2010.

Rüdiger Safranski, *Martin Heidegger: Between Good and Evil* (tr. Ewald Osers), Harvard University Press, 1999.

Gershom Scholem, *Major Trends in Jewish Mysticism*, Schocken, 1995.

Alon Segev, *Thinking and Killing: Philosophical Discourse in the Shadow of the Third Reich*, de Gruyter, 2013.

Gitta Sereny, *Into That Darkness*, Pimlico, 1995.

Michel Serres, *Statues* (tr. Randolph Burks), Bloomsbury, 2015.

Peter Sloterdijk, *Critique of Cynical Reason* (tr. Michael Eldred), University of Minnesota Press, 1988.

Albert Speer, *Inside the Third Reich* (tr. Richard and Clara Winston), Simon and Schuster, 1997.

Péter Szondi, *Celan Studies*, Stanford University Press, 2003.

John Toland, *Adolf Hitler: The Definitive Biography*, Anchor Books, 1992.

Leonardo da Vinci, *Notebooks*, Oxford University Press, 2008.

Cris Whetton, *Hitler's Fortune*, Pen and Sword, 2004.

Roger Woods, *Germany's New Right as Culture and Politics*, Palgrave Macmillan, 2007.

Stefan Zweig, *The World of Yesterday* (tr. Benjamin W. Huebsch and Helmut Ripperger), Plunkett Lake Press, 2011.